Tom Clancy
TWO COMPLETE NOVELS

ALSO BY TOM CLANCY

FICTION

The Hunt for Red October

Red Storm Rising

Patriot Games

The Cardinal of the Kremlin

Clear and Present Danger

The Sum of All Fears

Without Remorse

Debt of Honor

Executive Orders

Rainbow Six

The Bear and the Dragon

Red Rabbit

Teeth of the Tiger

NONFICTION

Submarine:
A Guided Tour Inside a Nuclear Warship

Armored Cav:
A Guided Tour of an Armored Cavalry Regiment

Fighter Wing:
A Guided Tour of an Air Force Combat Wing

Marine:
A Guided Tour of a Marine Expeditionary Unit

Airborne:
A Guided Tour of an Airborne Task Force

Carrier:
A Guided Tour of an Aircraft Carrier

Into the Storm:
A Study in Command
(With General Fred Franks, Jr. (Ret.))

Every Man a Tiger
(With General Chuck Hotner (Ret.))

Shadow Warriors
(With General Carl Stiner (Ret.))

Battle Ready
(With General Tony Zinni (Ret.))

Tom Clancy

TWO COMPLETE NOVELS

Red Storm Rising

The Cardinal of the Kremlin

G.P. PUTNAM'S SONS
New York

G. P. PUTNAM'S SONS
Publishers Since 1838
Published by the Penguin Group
Penguin Group (USA) Inc., 375 Hudson Street, New York, New York 10014, USA
Penguin Group (Canada), 90 Eglinton Avenue East, Suite 700, Toronto, Ontario M4P 2Y3,
Canada (a division of Pearson Penguin Canada Inc.)
Penguin Books Ltd, 80 Strand, London WC2R 0RL, England
Penguin Ireland, 25 St Stephen's Green, Dublin 2, Ireland (a division of Penguin Books Ltd)
Penguin Group (Australia), 250 Camberwell Road, Camberwell, Victoria 3124, Australia
(a division of Pearson Australia Group Pty Ltd)
Penguin Books India Pvt Ltd, 11 Community Centre, Panchsheel Park, New Delhi–110 017, India
Penguin Group (NZ), 67 Apollo Drive, Rosedale, North Shore 0745, Auckland, New Zealand
(a division of Pearson New Zealand Ltd.)
Penguin Books (South Africa) (Pty) Ltd, 24 Sturdee Avenue, Rosebank, Johannesburg 2196,
South Africa

Penguin Books Ltd, Registered Offices: 80 Strand, London WC2R 0RL, England

The Library of Congress has catalogued the hardcover edition as follows:
Clancy, Tom, date.
[Red storm rising]
Two complete novels / Tom Clancy.
p. cm.
Contents: red storm rising—the cardinal of the Kremlin.
ISBN 0-399-13841-2
I. Clancy, Tom, date. Cardinal of the Kremlin. 1993.   II. Title.
  PS3553.L245A6   1993   92-39237 CIP
  813'.54—dc20
Special Markets ISBN, 2007: 978-0-399-15479-9

Printed in the United States of America
1 3 5 7 9 10 8 6 4 2

Contents

Red Storm Rising

ACKNOWLEDGMENTS

It is impossible for Larry and me to thank all those who assisted us in so many ways in the preparation of this book. Were we to try, we would leave out the names of people whose contributions were more than merely important. To all those who gave freely of their time, answering endless questions, then explaining their answers at length—we know who you are and what you did. All of you are in this book. Particular thanks, however, are due to the captain, officers, and the men of FFG-26, who for one marvelous week showed an ignorant landlubber something of what it means to be a sailor.

From time immemorial, the purpose of a navy has been to influence, and sometimes decide, issues on land. This was so with the Greeks of antiquity; the Romans, who created a navy to defeat Carthage; the Spanish, whose armada tried and failed to conquer England; and, most eminently, in the Atlantic and Pacific during two world wars. The sea has always given man inexpensive transport and ease of communication over long distances. It has also provided concealment, because being over the horizon meant being out of sight and effectively beyond reach. The sea has supplied mobility, capability, and support throughout Western history, and those failing in the sea-power test—notably Alexander, Napoleon and Hitler—also failed the longevity one.

—Edward L. Beach,
in *Keepers of the Sea*

AUTHOR'S NOTE

This book began sometime ago. I got to know Larry Bond through an advertisement in the U.S. Naval Institute *Proceedings,* when I purchased his war game, "Harpoon." It turned out to be amazingly useful, and served as a primary source for *The Hunt for Red October.* I was intrigued enough about it that I drove to a wargamers' convention that summer (1982) to meet him in person, and we ended up becoming close friends.

In 1983, while *Red October* was in pre-production, Larry and I started talking about one of his projects: "Convoy-84," a macro-wargame or "campaign" game which, using the "Harpoon" system, would fight out a new Battle of the North Atlantic. I thought this was fascinating and we began talking about building a book around the idea, since, we both agreed, no one outside the Defense Department had ever examined in adequate detail what such a campaign would be like with modern weapons. The more we talked, the better the idea got. Soon we were fiddling with an outline and trying to find a way to limit the scenario to a manageable scope—but to do so without removing any essential elements from the stage. (This proved to be a problem without a really adequate solution, despite endless discussion and not a few violent disagreements!)

Although Larry's name does not appear on the title page, this book is his as much as mine. We never did figure out the division of labor, but what Larry and I accomplished was to complete a book as co-authors when our only contract was a handshake—and have a whole lot of fun doing it! It is for the reader to decide how successful we have been.

1. The Slow Fuse

NIZHNEVARTOVSK, R.S.F.S.R.

They moved swiftly, silently, with purpose, under a crystalline, star-filled night in western Siberia. They were Muslims, though one could scarcely have known it from their speech, which was Russian, though inflected with the singsong Azerbaijani accent that wrongly struck the senior members of the engineering staff as entertaining. The three of them had just completed a complex task in the truck and train yards, the opening of hundreds of loading valves. Ibrahim Tolkaze was their leader, though he was not in front. Rasul was in front, the massive former sergeant in the MVD who had already killed six men this cold night—three with a pistol hidden under his coat and three with his hands alone. No one had heard them. An oil refinery is a noisy place. The bodies were left in shadows, and the three men entered Tolkaze's car for the next part of their task.

Central Control was a modern three-story building fittingly in the center of the complex. For at least five kilometers in all directions stretched the cracking towers, storage tanks, catalytic chambers, and above all the thousands of kilometers of large-diameter pipe which made Nizhnevartovsk one of the world's largest refining complexes. The sky was lit at uneven intervals by waste-gas fires, and the air was foul with the stink of petroleum distillates: aviation kerosene, gasoline, diesel fuel, benzine, nitrogen tetroxide for intercontinental missiles, lubricating oils of various grades, and complex petrochemicals identified only by their alphanumeric prefixes.

They approached the brick-walled, windowless building in Tolkaze's personal Zhiguli, and the engineer pulled into his reserved parking place, then walked alone to the door as his comrades crouched in the back seat.

Inside the glass door, Ibrahim greeted the security guard, who smiled back, his hand outstretched for Tolkaze's security pass. The need for security here was quite real, but since it dated back over forty years, no one took it more seriously than any of the pro forma bureaucratic complexities in the Soviet Union. The guard had been drinking, the only form of solace in this harsh, cold land. His eyes were not focusing and his smile was too fixed. Tolkaze fumbled handing over his pass, and the guard lurched down to retrieve it. He never came back up. Tolkaze's pistol was the last thing the man felt, a cold circle at the base of his skull, and he died without knowing why—or even how. Ibrahim went behind the guard's desk to get the weapon the man had been only too happy to display for the engineers he'd protected. He lifted the body and moved it awkwardly to leave it slumped at the desk—just another swingshift worker asleep at his post—then waved his comrades into the building. Rasul and Mohammet raced to the door.

"It is time, my brothers." Tolkaze handed the AK-47 rifle and ammo belt to his taller friend.

Rasul hefted the weapon briefly, checking to see that a round was chambered and the safety off. Then he slung the ammunition belt over his shoulder and snapped the bayonet in place before speaking for the first time that night: "Paradise awaits."

Tolkaze composed himself, smoothed his hair, straightened his tie, and clipped the security pass to his white laboratory coat before leading his comrades up the six flights of stairs.

Ordinary procedure dictated that to enter the master control room, one first had to be recognized by one of the operations staffers. And so it happened. Nikolay Barsov seemed surprised when he saw Tolkaze through the door's tiny window.

"You're not on duty tonight, Isha."

"One of my valves went bad this afternoon and I forgot to check the repair status before I went off duty. You know the one—the auxiliary feed valve on kerosene number eight. If it's still down tomorrow we'll have to reroute, and you know what that means."

Barsov grunted agreement. "True enough, Isha." The middle-aged engineer thought Tolkaze liked the semi-Russian diminutive. He was badly mistaken. "Stand back while I open this damned hatch."

The heavy steel door swung outward. Barsov hadn't been able to see Rasul and Mohammet before, and scarcely had time now. Three 7.62mm rounds from the Kalashnikov exploded into his chest.

The master control room contained a duty watch crew of twenty, and looked much like the control center for a railroad or power plant. The high walls were crosshatched with pipeline schematics dotted with hundreds of lights to indicate which control valve was doing what. That was only the main display. Individual segments of the system were broken off onto separate status boards, mainly controlled by computer but constantly monitored by half the duty engineers. The staff could not fail to note the sound of the three shots.

But none of them were armed.

With elegant patience, Rasul began to work his way across the room, using his Kalashnikov expertly and firing one round into each watch engineer. At first they tried to run away—until they realized that Rasul was herding them into a corner like cattle, killing as he moved. Two men bravely got on their command phones to summon a fast-response team of KGB security troops. Rasul shot one of them at his post, but the other ducked around the line of command consoles to evade the gunfire and bolted for the door, where Tolkaze stood. It was Boris, Tolkaze saw, the Party favorite, head of the local *kollektiv,* the man who had "befriended" him, making him the special pet native of the Russian engineers. Ibrahim could remember every time this godless pig had patronized him, the savage foreigner imported to amuse his Russian masters. Tolkaze raised his pistol.

"Ishaaa!" the man screamed in terror and shock. Tolkaze shot him in the mouth, and hoped Boris didn't die too quickly to hear the contempt in his voice: "Infidel." He was pleased that Rasul had not killed this one. His quiet friend could have all the rest.

The other engineers screamed, threw cups, chairs, manuals. There was nowhere left to run, no way around the swarthy, towering killer. Some held up their hands in useless supplication. Some even prayed aloud—*but not to Allah, which might have saved them.* The noise diminished as Rasul strode up to the bloody corner. He smiled as he shot the very last, knowing that this sweating infidel pig would serve him in paradise. He reloaded his rifle, then went back through the control room. He prodded each body with his bayonet, and again shot the four that showed some small sign of life. His face bore a grim, content expression. At least twenty-five atheist pigs dead. Twenty-five foreign invaders who would no longer stand between his people and their God. Truly he had done Allah's work!

The third man, Mohammet, was already at his own work as Rasul took his station at the top of the staircase. Working in the back of the room, he switched the room systems-control mode from computer-automatic to emergency-manual, bypassing all of the automated safety systems.

A methodical man, Ibrahim had planned and memorized every detail of his task over a period of months, but still he had a checklist in his pocket. He unfolded it now and set it next to his hand on the master supervisory control board. Tolkaze looked around at the status displays to orient himself, then paused.

From his back pocket he took his most treasured personal possession, half of his grandfather's Koran, and opened it to a random page. It was a passage in The Chapter of the Spoils. His grandfather having been killed during the futile rebellions against Moscow, his father shamed by helpless subservience to the infidel state, Tolkaze had been seduced by Russian schoolteachers into joining their godless system. Others had trained him as an oil-field engineer to work at the State's most valuable facility in Azerbaijan. Only then had the God of his fathers saved him, through the words of an uncle, an "unregistered" imam who had remained faithful to Allah and safeguarded this tattered fragment of the Koran that had accompanied one of Allah's own warriors. Tolkaze read the passage under his hand:

And when the misbelievers plotted to keep thee prisoner, or kill thee, or drive thee forth, they plotted well; but God plotted, too. And God is the best of plotters.

Tolkaze smiled, certain that it was the final Sign in a plan being executed by hands greater than his own. Serene and confident, he began to fulfill his destiny.

First the gasoline. He closed sixteen control valves—the nearest of them three kilometers away—and opened ten, which rerouted eighty million liters of gasoline to gush out from a bank of truck-loading valves. The gasoline did not ignite at once. The three had left no pyrotechnic devices to explode this first of many disasters. Tolkaze reasoned that if he were truly doing the work of Allah, then his God would surely provide.

And so He did. A small truck driving through the loading yard took a turn too fast, skidded on the splashing fuel, and slid broadside into a utility pole. It only took one spark . . . and already more fuel was spilling out into the train yards.

With the master pipeline switches, Tolkaze had a special plan. He rapidly typed in a computer command, thanking Allah that Rasul was so skillful and had not damaged anything important with his rifle. The main pipeline from the nearby production field was two meters across, with many branch-lines running to all of the production wells. The oil traveling in those pipes had its own mass and its own momentum supplied by pumping stations in the fields. Ibrahim's commands rapidly opened and closed valves. The pipeline ruptured in a dozen places, and the computer commands left the pumps on. The escaping light crude flowed across the production field, where only one more spark was needed to spread a holocaust before the winter wind, and another break occurred where the oil and gas pipelines crossed together over the river Ob'.

"The greenskins are here!" Rasul shouted a moment before the quick-response team of KGB border guards stormed up the staircase. A short burst from the Kalashnikov killed the first two, and the rest of the squad stopped cold behind a turn in the staircase as their young sergeant wondered what the hell they had walked into.

Already, automatic alarms were erupting around him in the control room. The master status board showed four growing fires whose borders were defined by blinking red lights. Tolkaze walked to the master computer and ripped out the tape spool that contained the digital control codes. The spares were in the vault downstairs, and the only men within ten kilometers who knew its combination were in this room—dead. Mohammet was busily ripping out every telephone in the room. The whole building shook with the explosion of a gasoline storage tank two kilometers away.

The crashing sound of a hand grenade announced another move by the KGB troops. Rasul returned fire, and the screams of dying men nearly equaled the earsplitting fire-alarm klaxons. Tolkaze hurried over to the corner. The floor there was slick with blood. He opened the door to the electrical fusebox, flipped the main circuit breaker, then fired his pistol into the box. Whoever tried to set things aright would also have to work in the dark.

He was done. Ibrahim saw that his massive friend had been mortally hit in the chest by grenade fragments. He was wobbling, struggling to stay erect at the door, guarding his comrades to the last.

" 'I take refuge in the Lord of the worlds,' " Tolkaze called out defiantly to the security troops, who spoke not a word of Arabic. " 'The King of men, the God of men, from the evil of the whispering devil—' "

The KGB sergeant leaped around the lower landing and his first burst tore the rifle from Rasul's bloodless hands. Two hand grenades arched through the air as the sergeant disappeared back around the corner.

There was no place—and no reason—to run. Mohammet and Ibrahim stood immobile in the doorway as the grenades bounced and skittered across the tiled floor. Around them the whole world seemed to be catching fire, *and because of them, the whole world really would.*

"Allahu akhbar!"

SUNNYVALE, CALIFORNIA

"God almighty!" the chief master sergeant breathed. The fire which had begun in the gasoline/diesel section of the refinery had been sufficient to alert a strategic early-warning satellite in geosynchronous orbit twenty-four thousand miles above the Indian Ocean. The signal was downlinked to a top-security U.S. Air Force post.

The senior watch officer in the Satellite Control Facility was an Air Force colonel. He turned to his senior technician: "Map it."

"Yes, sir." The sergeant typed a command into his console, which told the satellite cameras to alter their sensitivity. With the flaring on the screen reduced, the satellite rapidly pinpointed the source of the thermal energy. A computer-controlled map on the screen adjacent to the visual display gave them an exact location reference. "Sir, that's an oil refinery fire. Jeez, and it looks like a real pisser! Colonel, we got a Big Bird pass in twenty minutes and the course track is within a hundred twenty kilometers."

"Uh-huh," the colonel nodded. He watched the screen closely to make sure that the heat source was not moving, his right hand lifting the Gold Phone to NORAD headquarters, Cheyenne Mountain, Colorado.

"This is Argus Control. I have Flash Traffic for CINC-NORAD."

"Wait one," said the first voice.

"This is CINC-NORAD," said the second, Commander-in-Chief of the North American Aerospace Defense Command.

"Sir, this is Colonel Burnette at Argus Control. We show a massive thermal energy reading at coordinates sixty degrees fifty minutes north, seventy-six degrees forty minutes east. The site is listed as a POL refinery. The thermal source is not, repeat not moving. We have a KH-11 pass close to the source in two-zero minutes. My preliminary evaluation, General, is that we have a major oil-field fire here."

"They're not doing a laser-flash on your bird?" CINC-NORAD asked. There was always a possibility the Soviets were trying to play games with their satellite.

"Negative. The light source covers infrared and all of the visible spectrum, not, repeat not, monochromatic. We'll know more in a few minutes, sir. So far everything is consistent with a massive ground fire."

Thirty minutes later they were sure. The KH-11 reconnaissance satellite came over the horizon close enough for all of its eight television cameras to catalog the chaos. A side-link transmitted the signal to a geosynchronous communications satellite, and Burnette was able to watch it all "in real time." Live and in color. The fire had already engulfed half of the refinery complex and more than half of the nearby production field, with more burning crude oil spreading from the ruptured pipeline onto the river Ob'. They were able to watch the fire spread, the flames carried rapidly before a forty-knot surface wind. Smoke obscured much of the area on visible light, but infrared sensors penetrated it to show many heat sources that could only be vast pools of oil products burning intensely on the ground. Burnette's sergeant was from east Texas, and had worked as a boy in the oil fields. He keyed up daylight photographs of the site and compared them with the adjacent visual display to determine what parts of the refinery had already ignited.

"Goddamn, Colonel." The sergeant shook his head reverently. He spoke with quiet expertise. "The refinery—well, it's gone, sir. That fire'll spread in front of that wind, and ain't no way in hell they'll stop it. The refinery's gone, total loss, burn maybe three, four days—maybe a week, parts of it. And unless they find a way to stop it, looks like the production field is going to go, too, sir. By next pass, sir, it'll all be burnin', all those wellheads spillin' burnin' o'l . . . Lordy, I don't even think Red Adair would want any part of this job!"

"Nothing left of the refinery? Hmph." Burnette watched a tape rerun of the Big Bird pass. "It's their newest and biggest, ought to put a dent in their POL production while they rebuild that from scratch. And once they get those field fires put out, they'll have to rearrange their gas and diesel production quite a bit. I'll say one thing for Ivan. When he has an industrial accident, he doesn't screw around. A major inconvenience for our Russian friends, Sergeant."

This analysis was confirmed the next day by the CIA, and the day after that by the British and French security services.

They were all wrong.

2. Odd Man In

DATE-TIME 01 / 31 - 06:15 COPY 01 of 01 SOVIET FIRE
   BC-Soviet Fire, Bjt, 1809•FL•
Disastrous Fire Reported in Soviet Nizhnevartovsk Oil Field•FL•
EDS: Moved in advance for WEDNESDAY PMs•FL•
By William Blake •FC•
AP Military / Intelligence Writer
   WASHINGTON (AP)—"The most serious oil field fire since the Mexico City disaster of 1984, or even the Texas City fire of 1947," sundered the darkness in the central region of the Soviet Union today, according to military and intelligence sources in Washington.

The fire was detected by American "National Technical Means," a term that generally denotes reconnaissance satellites operated by the Central Intelligence Agency. CIA sources declined comment on the incident.

Sources in the Pentagon confirmed this report, noting that the energy given off by the fire was sufficient to cause a brief stir in the North American Aerospace Defense Command, which was concerned that the fire was a possible missile launch directed at the United States, or an attempt to blind American Early-Warning satellites with a laser or other ground-based device.

At no time, the source pointed out, was there any thought of increasing American alert levels, or of bringing American nuclear forces to higher states of readiness. "It was all over in less than thirty minutes," the source said.

No confirmation was received from the Russian news agency, TASS, but the Soviets rarely publish reports of such incidents.

The fact that American officials referred to two epic industrial accidents is an indication that many fatalities might result from this major fire. Defense sources were unwilling to speculate on the possibility of civilian casualties. The city of Nizhnevartovsk is bordered by the petroleum complex.

The Nizhnevartovsk oil production field accounts for roughly 31.3 percent of total Soviet crude oil, according to the American Petroleum Institute, and the adjacent, newly built Nizhnevartovsk refinery for approximately 17.3 percent of petroleum distillate production.

"Fortunately for them," Donald Evans, a spokesman for the Institute explained, "oil underground is pretty hard to burn, and you can expect the fire to burn itself out in a few days." The refinery, however, depending on how much of it was involved, could be a major expense. "When they go, they usually go pretty big," Evans said. "But the Russians have sufficient excess refining capacity to take up the slack, especially with all the work they've been doing at their Moscow complex."

Evans was unable to speculate on the cause of the fire, saying, "The climate could have something to do with it. We had a few problems in the Alaskan fields that took some careful work to solve. Beyond that, any refinery is a potential Disneyland for fire, and there simply is no substitute for intelligent, careful, well-trained crews to run them."

This is the latest in a series of setbacks to the Soviet oil industry. It was admitted only last fall at the plenum of the Communist Party Central Committee that production goals in both the Eastern Siberian fields "had not entirely fulfilled earlier hopes."

This seemingly mild statement is being seen in Western circles as a stinging indictment of the policies of now-departed Petroleum Industry minister Zatyzhin, since replaced by Mikhail Sergetov, former chief of the Leningrad Party apparatus, regarded as a rising star in the Soviet Party. A technocrat with a background of engineering and Party work, Sergetov's task of reorganizing the Soviet oil industry is seen as a task that could last years.
AP-BA-01-31 0501EST·FL·

MOSCOW, R.S.F.S.R.

Mikhail Eduardovich Sergetov never had a chance to read the wire service report. Summoned from his official dacha in the birch forests surrounding Moscow, he'd flown at once to Nizhnevartovsk and stayed for only ten hours before being recalled to make his report in Moscow. *Three months on the job,* he thought, sitting in the empty forward cabin of the IL-86 airliner, *and this has to happen!*

His two principal deputies, a pair of skilled young engineers, had been left behind and were trying even now to make sense of the chaos, to save what could be saved, as he reviewed his notes for the Politburo meeting later in the day. Three hundred men were known to have died fighting the fire, and, miraculously, fewer than two hundred citizens in the city of Nizhnevartovsk. That was unfortunate, but not a matter of great significance except insofar as those trained men killed would eventually have to be replaced by other trained men drawn from the staffs of other large refineries.

The refinery was almost totally destroyed. Reconstruction would take a minimum of two to three years, and would account for a sizable percentage of national steel pipe production, plus all the other specialty items unique to a facility of this type: *Fifteen thousand million rubles.* And how much of the special equipment would have to be purchased from foreign sources—how much precious hard currency and gold would be wasted?

And that was the good news.

The bad news: the fire that had engulfed the production field had totally destroyed the welltops. Time to replace: at least thirty-six months!

Thirty-six months, Sergetov reflected bleakly, *if we can divert the drillrigs and crews to redrill every damned well and at the same time rebuild the EOR systems. For a minimum of eighteen months the Soviet Union will have an enormous shortfall in oil production. Probably more like thirty months.* What will happen to our economy?

He pulled a pad of lined paper from his briefcase and began to make some calculations. It was a three-hour flight, and Sergetov did not notice it was over until the pilot came back to announce they had landed.

He looked with squinted eyes at the snow-covered landscape of Vnukovo-2, the VIP-only airport outside of Moscow, and walked alone down the boarding stairs to a waiting ZIL limousine. The car sped off at once, without stopping at any of the security checkpoints. The shivering militia officers snapped to attention as the ZIL passed, then returned to the business of keeping warm in the subzero temperatures. The sun was bright, the sky clear but for some thin, high clouds. Sergetov looked vacantly out the windows, his mind mulling over figures he had already rechecked a half-dozen times. The Politburo was waiting for him, his KGB driver told him.

Sergetov had been a "candidate," or nonvoting member, of the Politburo for just six months, which meant that, along with his eight other junior colleagues, he advised the thirteen men who alone made the decisions that mattered in the Soviet Union. His portfolio was energy production and distribution. He had held that post since September, and was only beginning to establish his plan for a total reorganization of the seven regional and all-union ministries that handled energy functions—and predictably spent most of their time battling one another—into a full department that reported directly to the Politburo and Party Secretariat, instead of having to work through the Council of Ministers bureaucracy. He briefly closed his eyes to thank God—there might be one, he reasoned—that his first recommendation, delivered only a month earlier, had concerned security and political reliability in many of the fields. He had specifically recommended further Russification of the largely "foreign" workforce. For this reason, he did not fear for his own career, which up to now had been an uninterrupted success story. He shrugged. The task he was about to face would decide his future in any case. And perhaps his country's.

The ZIL proceeded down Leningradskiy Prospekt, which turned into Gor'kogo, the limousine speeding through the center lane that policemen kept clear of traffic for the exclusive use of the *vlasti.* They motored past the Intourist Hotel into Red Square, and finally approached the Kremlin gate. Here the driver did stop for the security checks, three of them, conducted by KGB troops and soldiers of the Taman Guards. Five minutes later the limousine pulled to the door of the Council of Ministers building, the sole modern structure in the fortress. The guards here knew Sergetov by sight, and saluted crisply as they held open the door so that his exposure to the freezing temperatures would last but a brief span of seconds.

The Politburo had been holding its meetings in this fourth-floor room for only a month while their usual quarters in the old Arsenal building were undergoing a belated renovation. The older men grumbled at the loss of the old Czarist comforts, but Sergetov preferred the modernity. About time, he thought, that the men of the Party surrounded themselves with the works of socialism instead of the moldy trappings of the Romanovs.

The room was deathly quiet as he entered. Had this been in the Arsenal, the fifty-four-year-old technocrat reflected, the atmosphere would have been altogether like a funeral—and there had been all too many of those. Slowly, the Party was running out of the old men who had survived Stalin's terror, and the current crop of members, all "young" men in their fifties or early sixties, was finally being heard. The guard was being changed. Too slowly—too damned slowly—for Sergetov and his generation of Party leaders, despite the new General Secretary. The man was already a grandfather. It sometimes seemed to Sergetov that by the time these old men were gone, he'd be one himself. But looking around this room now, he felt young enough.

"Good day, Comrades," Sergetov said, handing his coat to an aide, who withdrew at once, closing the doors behind him. The other men moved at once to their seats. Sergetov took his, halfway down the right side.

The Party General Secretary brought the meeting to order. His voice was controlled and businesslike. "Comrade Sergetov, you may begin your report. First, we wish to hear your explanation of exactly what happened."

"Comrades, at approximately twenty-three hundred hours yesterday, Moscow Time, three armed men entered the central control complex of the Nizhnevartovsk oil complex and committed a highly sophisticated act of sabotage."

"Who were they?" the Defense Minister asked sharply.

"We only have identification for two of them. One of the bandits was a staff electrician. The third"—Sergetov pulled the ID card from his pocket and tossed it on the table—"was Senior Engineer I.M. Tolkaze. He evidently used his expert knowledge of the control systems to initiate a massive fire which spread rapidly before high winds. A security team of ten KGB border guards responded at once to the alarm. The one traitor still unidentified killed or wounded five of these with a rifle taken from the building guard, who was also shot. I must say, having interviewed the KGB sergeant—the lieutenant was killed leading his men—that the border guards responded quickly and well. They killed the traitors within minutes, but were unable to prevent the complete destruction of the facility, both the refinery *and* production fields."

"And if the guards responded so fast, how then did they fail to prevent this act?" the Defense Minister demanded angrily. He examined the photographic pass with palpable hatred in his eyes. "What was this black-ass Muslim doing there in the first place?"

"Comrade, work in the Siberian fields is arduous, and we have had serious difficulties in filling the posts we have there. My predecessor decided to conscript experienced oil-field workers from the Baku region to Siberia. This was madness. You will recall that my first recommendation last year was to change this policy."

"We have noted it, Mikhail Eduardovich," the Chairman said. "Go on."

"The guard post records all telephone and radio traffic. The response team was moving in under two minutes. Unfortunately, the guard post is located adjacent to the original control building. The current building was constructed three kilometers away when new computerized control equipment was obtained from the West two years ago. A new guard post was also supposed to have been built, and the proper materials were allocated for this purpose. It would appear that these building materials were misappropriated by the complex director and local Party secretary, for the purpose of building dachas on the river a few kilometers away. Both of these men have been arrested by my order, for crimes against the State," Sergetov reported matter-of-factly. There was no reaction around the table. By unspoken consensus, those two men were sentenced to death; the formalities would be worked out by the proper ministries. Sergetov continued: "I have already ordered greatly increased security at all petroleum sites. Also on my orders, the families of the two known traitors have been arrested at their homes outside Baku and are being rigorously interrogated by State Security, along with all who knew and worked with them.

"Before the border guards were able to kill the traitors, they were able to sabotage the oil-field control systems in such a way as to create a massive conflagration. They were also able to wreck the control equipment so that even if the guard troops had been able to get a crew of engineers in to restore control, it is unlikely that anything would have been saved. The KGB troops were forced to evacuate the building, which was later consumed by the fire. There was nothing more they could have done." Sergetov remembered the sergeant's badly burned face, the tears flowing down over the blisters as he told his story.

"The fire brigade?" the General Secretary asked.

"More than half of them died fighting the fire," Sergetov replied. "Along with over a hundred citizens who joined the battle to save the complex. Truly there is no blame to be assessed here, Comrade. Once this bastard Tolkaze began his devil's work, it would have been as easy to control an earthquake. For the most part, the fire has been put out by now, due to the fact that most of the fuels stored in the refinery were consumed in about five hours; also because of the destruction of the wellheads in the oil field."

"But how was this catastrophe possible?" a senior member asked. Sergetov was surprised by the quiet mood in the room. Had they met and discussed this affair already?

"My report of December 20 described the dangers here. This room quite literally controlled the pumps and valves for over a hundred square kilometers. The same is true of all of our large oil complexes. From the nerve center, a man familiar with control procedures could manipulate the various systems throughout the field at will, causing the entire complex quite simply to self-destruct. Tolkaze had such skill. He was an Azerbaijani chosen for special treatment for his intelligence and supposed loyalty, an honor student educated at Moscow State University and a member in good standing of the local Party. It would also seem that he was a religious fanatic capable of astounding treachery. All the people killed in the control room were friends of his—or so they thought. After fifteen years in the Party, a good salary, the professional respect of his comrades, even his own automobile, his last words were a shrill cry to Allah," Sergetov said dryly. "The reliability of people from that region cannot be accurately predicted, Comrades."

The Defense Minister nodded again. "So, what effect will this have on oil production?" Half the men at the table leaned forward to hear Sergetov's answer:

"Comrades, we have lost thirty-four percent of our total crude oil production for a period of at least one year, possibly as many as three." Sergetov looked up from his notes to see the impassive faces cringe as though from a slap. "It will be necessary to redrill every production well and finally reconstruct the pipelines from the fields to the refinery and elsewhere. The concurrent loss of the refinery is serious, but not an immediate concern since the refinery can be rebuilt, and in any case represents less than a seventh of our total refining capacity. The major injury to our economy will come from the loss of our crude oil production.

"In real terms, due to the chemical makeup of the Nizhnevartovsk oil, the net total production loss understates the actual impact on our economy. Siberian oil is 'light, sweet' crude, which means that it contains a disproportionately large amount of the most valuable fractions—those which we use to make gasoline, kerosene, and diesel fuel, for example. The net loss in these particular areas is forty-four percent of our gasoline production, forty-eight percent of kerosene, and fifty percent of diesel. These figures are rough calculations I made on the flight back, but they should be accurate to within two percent. My staff will have more precise figures ready in a day or so."

"Half?" the General Secretary asked quietly.

"Correct, Comrade," Sergetov responded.

"And how long to restore production?"

"Comrade General Secretary, if we bring in every drilling rig and operate them around the clock, my rough estimate is that we can begin to restore production in twelve months. Clearing the site of wreckage will take at least three months, and another three will be needed to relocate our equipment and commence drilling operations. Since we have exact information for well locations and depths, the usual element of uncertainty is not part of the equation. Within a year—that is, six months after we commence the redrilling—we will begin to bring the production wells back on stream, and full restoration of the wells will be achieved within two more years. While all this is going on, we will need to replace the EOR equipment also—"

"And what might that be?" Defense asked.

"Enhanced Oil Recovery systems, Comrade Minister. Had these been relatively new wells, pressurized from underground gas, the fires might have lasted for weeks. As you know, Comrades, these are wells from which a good deal of oil has already been extracted. To enhance production we have been pumping water into the wells, which has the effect of forcing more oil out. It may also have had the effect of damaging the oil-bearing strata. This is something our geologists are even now attempting to evaluate. As it was, when power was lost, the force driving the oil from the ground was removed, and the fires in the production fields rapidly began to run out of fuel. They were for the most part dying out when my flight left for Moscow."

"So even three years from now production may not be completely restored?" the Minister of the Interior asked.

"Correct, Comrade Minister. There is simply no scientific basis for making an estimate of total production. The situation we have here has never happened before, either in the West or the East. We can drill some test wells in the next two or three months that will give us some indications. The staff engineers I left behind are making arrangements to begin the process as quickly as possible with equipment already at the site."

"Very well," the General Secretary nodded. "The next question is how long the country can operate on this basis."

Sergetov went back to his notes. "Comrades, there is no denying that this is a disaster of unprecedented scale for our economy. The winter has drawn down our heavy oil inventories more than usual. Certain energy expenditures must remain relatively intact. Electrical power generation last year, for example, accounted for thirty-eight percent of our oil products, far more than planned, due to past disappointments in coal and gas production, which we had expected to reduce oil demand. The coal industry will require at least five years to restore due to failures in modernization. And gas drilling operations are currently slowed by environmental conditions. For technical reasons it is extremely hard to operate such equipment in extreme cold weather—"

"So make those lazy bastards on the drilling crews work harder!" suggested the chief of the Moscow Party.

"It is not the workers, Comrade." Sergetov sighed. "It is the machines. Cold temperature affects metal more than men. Tools and equipment break simply because they are brittle with cold. Weather conditions make resupply of spare parts to the camps more difficult. Marxism-Leninism cannot dictate the weather."

"How difficult would it be to conceal the drilling operations?" Defense asked.

Sergetov was surprised. "Difficult? No, Comrade Minister, impossible. How can one conceal several hundred drilling rigs, each twenty to forty meters high? One might as easily attempt to conceal Plesetsk's missile launch complexes." Sergetov noticed for the first time the glances being exchanged by Defense and the General Secretary.

"Then we must reduce the consumption of oil by the electrical industry," the General Secretary pronounced.

"Comrades, allow me to give you some rough figures on the way in which we consume our oil products. Please understand that I am going from memory, since the annual departmental report is in the process of formulation at this time.

"Last year we produced 589 million tons of crude oil. This fell short of planned production by thirty-two million tons, and the amount actually produced was only possible due to the artificial measures that I have already discussed. Roughly half of that production was semirefined into *mazut*, or heavy fuel oil, for use in electrical power plants, factory boilers, and the like. Most of this oil simply cannot be used otherwise, since we have only three—excuse me, now only two—refineries with the sophisticated catalytic cracking chambers needed to refine heavy oil into light distillate products.

"The fuels we produce serve our economy in many ways. As we have already seen, thirty-eight percent goes for electrical and other forms of power generation, and fortunately much of this is *mazut*. Of the lighter fuels—diesel, gasoline, and kerosene—agricultural production and the food industries, transportation of goods and commodities, public consumption and passenger transportation, and finally military uses, these alone absorbed more than half of last year's production. In other words, Comrades, with the loss of the Nizhnevartovsk field the end users I just mentioned account for more than we are able to produce, leaving nothing at all for metallurgy, heavy machinery, chemical, and construction uses, not to mention what we customarily export to our fraternal socialist allies in Eastern Europe and throughout the world.

"To answer your specific question, Comrade General Secretary, we can make perhaps a modest reduction in the use of light oils in electrical power usage, but even now we have a serious shortfall in electric power production, resulting in occasional brownouts and complete power outages. Further cuts in power generation will adversely affect such crucial State activities as factory production and rail transport. You will recall that three years ago we experimented with altering the voltage of generated power to conserve fuels, and this resulted in damage to electric motors throughout the Donets industrial basin."

"What about coal and gas?"

"Comrade General Secretary, coal production is already sixteen percent below planned output, and getting worse, which has caused conversion of many coal-fired boilers and power plants to oil. Moreover, the conversion of such facilities from oil back to coal is costly and time-consuming. Conversion to gas is a much more attractive and cheaper alternative that we have been vigorously pursuing. Gas production is also under-plan, but it is improving. We had expected to exceed planned targets later this year. Here we must also account for the fact that much of our gas goes to Western Europe. It is from this that we gain Western currency with which to purchase foreign oil, and, of course, foreign grain."

The Politburo member in charge of agriculture winced at this reference. How many men, Sergetov wondered, had been done in by their inability to make the Soviet agricultural industry perform? Not the current General Secretary, of course, who had somehow managed to advance despite his failures there. But good Marxists weren't supposed to believe in miracles. His elevation to the titular chairmanship had had its own price, one which Sergetov was only beginning to understand.

"So, what is your solution, Mikhail Eduardovich?" the Defense Minister inquired with unsettling solicitude.

"Comrades, we must bear this burden as best we can, improving efficiency at every level of our economy." Sergetov didn't bother talking about increasing imports of oil. The shortfall he had explained would result in more than a thirtyfold increase in imports, and hard currency reserves would scarcely allow a doubling of foreign oil purchases. "We will need to increase production and quality control at the Barricade drilling rig factory in Volgograd, and to purchase more drilling equipment from the West so that we can expand exploration and exploitation of known fields. And we need to expand our construction of nuclear reactor plants. To conserve what production we do have, we can restrict supplies available to trucks and personal automobiles—there is much waste in this sector, as we all know, perhaps as much as a third of total usage. We can *temporarily* reduce the amount of fuel consumed by the military, and perhaps also divert some heavy machine production from military hardware to necessary industrial areas. We face three very hard years—but only three," Sergetov summarized on an upbeat note.

"Comrade, your experience in foreign and defense areas is slim, no?" the Defense Minister asked.

"I have never pretended otherwise, Comrade Minister," Sergetov answered warily.

"Then I will tell you why this situation is unacceptable. If we do what you suggest, the West will learn of our crisis. Increased purchases of oil production equipment and unconcealable signs of activity at Nizhnevartovsk will demonstrate to them all too clearly what is happening here. That will make us vulnerable in their eyes. Such vulnerability will be exploited. And, at the same time"—he pounded his fist on the heavy oak table—

"you propose reducing the fuel available to the forces who defend us against the West!"

"Comrade Defense Minister, I am an engineer, not a soldier. You asked me for a technical evaluation, and I gave it." Sergetov kept his voice reasonable. "This situation is very serious, but it does not, for example, affect our Strategic Rocket Forces. Cannot they alone shield us against the Imperialists during our recovery period?" *Why else had they been built?* Sergetov asked himself. All that money sunk into unproductive holes. Wasn't it enough to be able to kill the West ten times over? Why twenty times? And now *this* wasn't enough?

"And it has not occurred to you that the West will not allow us to purchase what we need?" the Party theoretician asked.

"When have the capitalists refused to sell us—"

"When have the capitalists had such a weapon to use against us?" the General Secretary observed. "For the first time, the West has the ability to strangle us in a single year. What if now they also prevent our purchase of grain?"

Sergetov hadn't considered that. With yet another disappointing grain harvest, the seventh out of the last eleven years, the Soviet Union needed to make massive purchases of wheat. And this year America and Canada were the only reliable sources. Bad weather in the Southern Hemisphere had damaged Argentina's harvest, and to a lesser extent Australia's, while the U.S. and Canada had enjoyed their customary record crops. Negotiations were even now under way in Washington and Ottawa to secure such a purchase, and the Americans were making no trouble at all, except that the high value of the dollar made their grain disproportionately expensive. But that grain would take months to ship. How easy would it be, Sergetov wondered, for "technical difficulties" in the grain ports of New Orleans and Baltimore to slow or even stop shipments entirely at a crucial moment?

He looked around the table. Twenty-two men, of whom only thirteen really decided matters—and one of those was missing—were silently contemplating the prospect of over two hundred fifty million Soviet workers and peasants, all hungry and in the dark, at the same time that the troops of the Red Army, the Ministry of the Interior, and the KGB found their own fuel supplies—and because of it, their training and mobility—restricted.

The men of the Politburo were among the most powerful in the world, far more so than any of their Western counterparts. They answered to no one, not the Central Committee of the Communist Party, not the Supreme Soviet, certainly not the people of their nation. These men had not walked on the streets of Moscow for years, but been whisked by chauffeured, handmade cars to and from their luxury apartments within Moscow, or to their ceremonial dachas outside the city. They shopped, if at all, in guarded stores restricted to the elite, were served by doctors in clinics established only for the elite. Because of all this, these men regarded themselves as masters of their destiny.

It was only now beginning to strike them that like all men, they too were subject to a fate which their immense personal power merely made all the more intractable.

Around them was a country whose citizens were poorly fed and poorly housed, whose only abundant commodities were the painted signs and slogans praising Soviet Progress and Solidarity. Some of the men at this table actually believed those slogans, Sergetov knew. Sometimes he still did, mainly in homage to his idealistic youth. But Soviet Progress had not fed their nation, and how long would Soviet Solidarity endure in the hearts of people hungry, cold, in the dark? Would they be proud of the missiles in the Siberian forests then? Of the thousands of tanks and guns produced every year? Would they then look to the sky that held a Salyut space station and feel inspired—or would they wonder what kind of food was being eaten by that elite? Less than a year before, Sergetov had been a regional Party chieftain, and in Leningrad he had been careful to listen to his own staff people's description of the jokes and grumblings in the lines which people endured for two loaves of bread, or toothpaste, or shoes. Detached even then from the harsher realities of life in the Soviet Union, he had often wondered if one day the burden of the ordinary worker would become too heavy to endure. How would he have known then? How would he know now? Would the older men here ever know?

Narod, they called it, a masculine noun that was nonetheless raped in every sense: the masses, the faceless collection of men and women who toiled every day in Moscow and throughout the nation in factories and on collective farms, their thoughts hidden behind unsmiling masks. The members of the Politburo told themselves that these workers and peasants did not grudge their leaders the luxuries that accompanied responsibility. After all, life in the country had improved in measurable terms. That was the compact. But the compact was about to be broken. What might happen then? Nicholas II had not known. These men did.

The Defense Minister broke the silence. "We must obtain more oil. It is as simple as that. The alternative is a crippled economy, hungry citizens, and reduced defense capacity. The consequences of which are not acceptable."

"We cannot purchase oil," a candidate member pointed out.

"Then we must take it."

FORT MEADE, MARYLAND

Bob Toland frowned at his spice cake. I shouldn't be eating dessert, the intelligence analyst reminded himself. But the National Security Agency commissary served this only once a week, and spice cake was his favorite, and it was only about two hundred calories. That was all. An extra five minutes on the exercise bike when he got home.

"What did you think of that article in the paper, Bob?" a co-worker asked.

"The oil-field thing?" Toland rechecked the man's security badge. He wasn't cleared for satellite intelligence. "Sounds like they had themselves quite a fire."

"You didn't see anything official on it?"

"Let's just say that the leak in the papers came from a higher security clearance than I have."

"Top Secret—Press?" Both men laughed.

"Something like that. The story had information that I haven't seen," Toland said, speaking the truth, mostly. The fire was out, and people in his department had been speculating on how Ivan had put it out so fast. "Shouldn't hurt them too bad. I mean, they don't have millions of people taking to the road on summer vacations, do they?"

"Not hardly. How's the cake?"

"Not bad." Toland smiled, already wondering if he needed the extra time on the bike.

MOSCOW, R.S.F.S.R.

The Politburo reconvened at nine-thirty the next morning. The sky outside the double-paned windows was gray and curtained with the heavy snow that was beginning to fall again, adding to the half-meter already on the ground. There would be sledding tonight on the hills of Gorkiy Park, Sergetov thought. The snow would be cleared off the two frozen lakes for skating under the lights to the music of Tschaikovskiy and Prokofiev. Moscovites would laugh and drink their vodka and savor the cold, blissfully ignorant of what was about to be said here, of the turns that all of their lives would take.

The main body of the Politburo had adjourned at four the previous afternoon, and then the five men who made up the Defense Council had met alone. Not even all of the full Politburo members were privy to that decision-making body.

Overseeing them at the far end of the room was a full-length portrait of Vladimir Ilych Ulyanov—Lenin, the revolutionary saint of Soviet Communism, his domed forehead thrown back as though in a fresh breeze, his piercing eyes looking off toward the glorious future which his stern face confidently proclaimed, which the "science" of Marxism-Leninism called a historic inevitability. A glorious future. Which future? Sergetov asked himself. What has become of our Revolution? What has become of our Party? Did Comrade Ilych really mean it to be like this?

Sergetov looked at the General Secretary, the "young" man supposed by the West to be fully in charge, the man who was even now changing things. His accession to the highest post in the Party had been a surprise to some, Sergetov among them. The West still looked to him as hopefully as we once had, Sergetov thought. His own arrival in Moscow had changed that rapidly enough. Yet another broken dream. The man who had put a happy face on years of agricultural failure now applied his superficial charm to a larger arena. He was laboring mightily—anyone at this table would admit that—but his task was an impossible one. To get here he had been forced to make too many promises, too many deals with the old guard. Even the "young" men of fifty and sixty he'd added to the Politburo had their own ties to former regimes. Nothing had really changed.

The West never seemed to absorb the idea. Not since Khrushchev had one man held sway. One-man rule held dangers vividly remembered by the older generation of the Party. The younger men had heard the tales of the great purges under Stalin often enough to take the lesson to heart, and the Army had its own institutional memory of what Khrushchev had done to its hierarchy. In the Politburo, as in the jungle, the only rule was survival, and for all collective safety lay in collective rule. Because of this the men selected for the titular post of General Secretary were not elected so much for their personal dynamism as for their experience in the Party— an organization that did not reward people for standing out too distinctly from the crowd. Like Brezhnev, and Andropov, and Chernenko, the current chief of the Party lacked the power of personality to dominate this room with his will alone. He'd had to compromise to be in his chair, and he would have to compromise to remain there. The real power blocs were amorphous things, relationships among men, loyalties that changed with circumstance and knew only expediency. The real power lay within the Party itself.

The Party ruled all, but the Party was no longer the expression of one man. It had become a collection of interests represented here by twelve other men. Defense had its interest, the KGB, and Heavy Industry, and even Agriculture. Each interest held its own brand of power, and the chief of each allied himself with others in order to secure his own place. The General Secretary would try to change this, would gradually appoint men loyal to himself to the posts that death made vacant. Would he then learn, as his predecessors had, that loyalty so easily died around this table? For now, he still carried the burden of his own compromises. With his own men not yet fully in place, the General Secretary was only the foremost member of a group that could unseat him as easily as it had unseated Khrushchev. What would the West say if it learned that the "dynamic" General Secretary mainly served as executor for the decisions of others? Even now, he did not speak first.

"Comrades," began the Defense Minister. "The Soviet Union must have oil, at least two hundred million tons more than we can produce. Such oil exists, only a few hundred kilometers from our border in the Persian Gulf—more oil than we will ever need. We have the ability to take it, of course. Inside of two weeks, we could assemble enough aircraft and airborne troops to swoop down on those oil fields and gobble them up.

"Unfortunately, there could not fail to be a violent Western response. Those same oil fields supply Western Europe, Japan, and to a lesser extent, America. The NATO countries do not have the ability to defend those fields with conventional means. The Americans have their Rapid Deployment Force, a hollow shell of headquarters and a few light troops. Even with their pre-positioned equipment at Diego Garcia, they could not hope to stop our airborne and mechanized forces. Were they to try, and they would have to try, their elite troops would be overwhelmed and exterminated in a few days—and they would be faced with a single alternative: nuclear weapons. This is a real risk that we cannot disregard. We know for a fact that American war plans call for nuclear weapons in this case. Such weapons are stored in quantity at Diego Garcia, and would almost certainly be used.

"Therefore, before we can seize the Persian Gulf, we must first do one other thing. We must eliminate NATO as a political and military force."

Sergetov sat upright in his leather chair. What was this, what was he saying? He struggled to keep his face impassive as the Defense Minister continued.

"If NATO is first removed from the board, America will be in a most curious position. The United States will be able to meet its own energy needs from Western Hemisphere sources, removing the need to defend the Arab states, who are in any case not terribly popular with the American Jewish Zionist community."

Did they really believe this, Sergetov wondered, did they actually believe the United States would sit on its hands? *What went on at the late meeting yesterday?*

At least one other person shared his concern. "So, the only thing we have to do is conquer Western Europe, Comrade?" a candidate member asked. "Are these not the countries against whose conventional forces you warn us every year? Every year you tell us of the threat the massed NATO armies present to us, and now you say casually that we must conquer them? Excuse me, Comrade Defense Minister, but do not France and England have their own nuclear arsenals? And why would America not fulfill its treaty promise to use nuclear weapons in the defense of NATO?"

Sergetov was surprised that a junior member had put the issues so quickly on the table. He was more surprised that the Foreign Minister answered. So, another piece of the puzzle. But what did the KGB think of this? Why were they not represented here? The chairman was recovering from surgery, but there should have been someone here—unless that had been taken care of last night.

"Our objectives must be limited, and obviously so. This presents us with several political tasks. First, we must engender a feeling of security in America, to put them off guard until it is too late for them to react forcefully. Second, we must attempt to unravel the NATO alliance in a political sense." The Foreign Minister ventured a rare smile. "As you know, the KGB has been working on such a plan for the past several years. It is now in its final form. I will outline it for you."

He did so, and Sergetov nodded at its audacity and also with a new understanding of the power balance in this room. So, it was the KGB. He should have known. But would the rest of the Politburo fall in line? The minister went on, "You see how it would work. One piece after another would fall into place. Given these preconditions, the waters so thoroughly muddied, and the fact that we would proclaim our unwillingness to threaten directly the two independent NATO nuclear powers, we feel that the nuclear risk, while real, is less than the risk that we already face in our economy."

Sergetov leaned back in his leather chair. So, there it was: war was less risky than a cold, hungry peace. It had been decided. Or had it? Might some combination of other Politburo members have the power or prestige to reverse that decision? Could he dare to speak out against this madness? Perhaps a judicious question first.

"Do we have the ability to defeat NATO?" He was chilled by the glib reply.

"Of course," Defense answered. "What do you think we have an army for? We have already consulted with our senior commanders."

And when you asked us last month for more steel for more new tanks, Comrade Defense Minister, was your excuse that NATO was too weak? Sergetov asked himself angrily. What machinations had taken place? Have they even spoken with their military advisers yet, or had the Defense Minister exploited his vaunted personal expertise? Had the General Secretary allowed himself to be bullied by Defense? And by the Foreign Minister? Had he even objected? Was this how the decisions were made to decide the fate of nations? What would Vladimir Ilych have thought of this?

"Comrades, this is madness!" said Pyotr Bromkovskiy. The oldest man there, frail and past eighty, his conversation occasionally rambled about the idealistic times long before, when Communist Party members really believed that they were the leading wave of history. The Yezhovshchina purges had ended that. "Yes, we have a grave economic danger. Yes, we have a grave danger to the security of the State—but do we replace this with a greater danger? Consider what can happen—how long, Comrade Defense Minister, before you can initiate your conquest of NATO?"

"I am assured that we can have our army fully ready for combat operations in four months."

"Four months. I presume that we will have fuel four months from now—enough fuel to begin a war!" Petya was old, but no one's fool.

"Comrade Sergetov." The General Secretary gestured down the table, dodging his responsibility yet again.

Which side to take? The young candidate member made a swift decision. "Inventories of light fuels—gasoline, diesel, et cetera—are high at the moment," Sergetov had to admit. "We always use the cold-weather months—the time when usage of these fuels is lowest—to build up our stocks, and added to this are our strategic defense reserves, enough for forty-five—"

"Sixty!" insisted the Defense Minister.

"Forty-five days is a more realistic figure, Comrade." Sergetov held his position. "My department has studied fuel consumption by military units as part of a program to increase the strategic fuel reserves, something neglected in past years. With savings in other consumption and certain industrial sacrifices, we might expand this to sixty days of war stocks, perhaps even seventy, plus giving you other stocks to expand training exercises. The near-term economic costs would be slight, but by midsummer this would change rapidly." Sergetov paused, greatly disturbed at how easily he had gone along with the unspoken decision. *I have sold my soul . . . Or have I acted like a patriot? Have I become like the other men around this table? Or have I merely told the truth—and what is truth?* All he could be certain of, he told himself, is that he had survived. For now. "We do have the limited ability, as I told you yesterday, to restructure our distillate production. In this case, my staff feels that a nine-percent increase in the militarily important fuels can be accomplished—based on our reduced production. I caution, however, that my staff analysts also feel that all existing estimates of fuel usage in combat conditions are grossly optimistic." A last, feeble attempt at protest.

"Give us the fuel, Mikhail Eduardovich," the Defense Minister smiled coldly, "and we'll see it is properly used. My analysts estimate that we can accomplish our goals in two weeks, perhaps less—but I will grant you the strength of the NATO armies, and double our estimates to thirty days. We will still have more than enough."

"And what if NATO discovers our intentions?" old Petya demanded.

"They will not. Already we are preparing our *maskirovka,* our trickery. NATO is not a strong alliance. It cannot be. The ministers bicker over each country's defense contribution. Their peoples are divided and soft. They cannot standardize their weapons, and because of it their supply situation is utter chaos. And their most important, most powerful member is separated from Europe by five thousand kilometers of ocean. The Soviet Union is only an overnight train ride from the German border. But, Petya, my old friend, I will answer your question. If everything fails, and our intentions are discovered, we can always stop, say that we were running an exercise, and return to peacetime conditions—and be no worse off than if we do nothing at all. We need strike only if all is ready. We can always draw back."

Everyone at the table knew that was a lie, though a clever one, because no one had the courage to denounce it as such. What army had ever been mobilized to be called back? No one else spoke up to oppose the Defense Minister. Bromkovskiy rambled on for a few minutes, quoting Lenin's stricture about endangering the home of World Socialism, but even that drew no response. The danger to the State—actually the danger to the

Party and the Politburo—was manifest. It could not become graver. The alternative was war.

Ten minutes later, the Politburo voted. Sergetov and his eight fellow candidate members were mere spectators. The vote was eleven to two for war. The process had begun.

DATE-TIME 02/03 17:15 COPY 01 OF 01 OF SOVIET-REPORT
BC-Soviet Report, Bjt, 2310•FL•
TASS Confirms Oil Field Fire•FL•
EDS: Moved in advance for SATURDAY PMs•FL•
BY: Patrick Flynn•FC•
AP Moscow Correspondent
     MOSCOW (AP)—It was confirmed today by TASS, the Soviet news agency, that "a serious fire" had taken place in the western Siberian region of the Soviet Union.
     A back-page article in *Pravda*, the official Communist Party newspaper, noted the fire, commenting that the "heroic fire brigade" had saved countless lives by its skill and devotion to duty, also preventing more serious damage to the nearby oil facilities.
     The fire was reportedly begun by a "technical malfunction" in the automatic refinery control systems and spread rapidly, but was swiftly extinguished, "not without casualties among the brave men detailed to attack the fire, and the courageous workmen who raced heroically to their comrades' side."
     Though somewhat at odds with Western reports, the fire in the area did go out more quickly than had been expected. Western officials are now speculating about a highly sophisticated firefighting system built into the Nizhnevartovsk facility that allowed the Soviets to extinguish the fire.
     AB-BA-2-3 16:01 EST•FL•
END OF STORY

3. Correlation of Forces

MOSCOW, R.S.F.S.R.

"They didn't *ask* me," explained Chief of the General Staff Marshal Shavyrin. "They didn't ask for my evaluation. The political decision was already made when they called me in Thursday night. When was the last time the Defense Minister asked me for a substantive judgmental decision?"

"And what did you say?" asked Marshal Rozhkov, Commander-in-Chief of Ground Forces. The initial response was a grim, ironic smile.

"That the armed forces of the Soviet Union were able to carry out this task, given four months of preparation."

"Four months . . ." Rozhkov stared out the window. He turned back. "We won't be ready."

"Hostilities will commence on 15 June," Shavyrin replied. "We must be ready, Yuri. And what choice did I have? Would you have had me say, 'I am sorry, Comrade General Secretary, but the Soviet Army is unable to carry out this task'? I would have been dismissed and replaced by someone more tractable—you know who my replacement will be. Would you rather answer to Marshal Bukharin—"

"That fool!" Rozhkov growled. It had been the then-Lieutenant General Bukharin whose brilliant plan had led the Soviet Army into Afghanistan. Professionally a nonentity, his political connections had not only saved him, but continued his career to near the pinnacle of uniformed power. A clever man, Bukharin. Never involved in the mountain campaigns himself, he could point to his brilliant paper plan and complain that it had been poorly executed, after he had moved on to command of the Kiev Military District, historically the shining gate to marshal's rank.

"So, would you have him in this office, dictating your plans to you?" Shavyrin asked. Rozhkov shook his head. The two men had been friends and comrades since each had commanded a tank troop in the same regiment, just in time for the final surge toward Vienna in 1945.

"How are we to go about it?" Rozhkov asked.

"Red Storm," the Marshal replied simply. Red Storm was the plan for a mechanized attack into West Germany and the Low Countries. Constantly updated for changes in the force structures of both sides, it called for a two- to three-week campaign commencing after a rapid escalation of tension between East and West. Despite this, in accordance with standard Soviet strategic doctrine, it called for strategic surprise as a precondition for success, and the use of conventional weapons only.

"At least they aren't talking about atomic arms." Rozhkov grunted. Other plans with other names applied to different scenarios, including many for the use of tactical and even strategic nuclear arms, something no one in uniform wished to contemplate. Despite all the saber-rattling of their political masters, these professional soldiers knew all too well that the use of nuclear arms made only for ghastly uncertainties. "And the *maskirovka?*"

"In two parts. The first is purely political, to work against the United States. The second part, immediately before the war begins, is from KGB. You know it, from KGB Group Nord. We reviewed it two years ago."

Rozhkov grunted. Group Nord was an ad hoc committee of KGB department chiefs, first assembled by then-chief of the KGB Yuri Andropov in the mid-1970s. Its purpose was to research means of splitting the NATO alliance, and in general to conduct political and psychological operations aimed at undermining Western will. Its specific plan to shake the NATO military and political structure in preparation for a shooting war was Nord's proudest example of legerdemain. But would it work? The two senior officers shared an ironic look. Like most professional soldiers, they distrusted spies and all their plans.

"Four months," Rozhkov repeated. "We have much to do. And if this KGB magic fails to work?"

"It is a good plan. It need only deceive the West for a week, though two weeks would be better. The key, of course, is how quickly NATO can reach full readiness. If we can delay the mobilization process seven days, victory is assured—"

"And if not?" Rozhkov asked sharply, knowing that even a seven-day delay was no guarantee.

"Then it is not assured, but the balance of forces is on our side. You know that, Yuri." The option of recalling the mobilized forces had never been discussed with the Chief of the General Staff.

"We will need to improve discipline throughout the force first of all," CINC-Ground said. "And I need to inform our senior commanders at once. We need to implement intense training operations. Just how awful is this fuel problem?"

Shavyrin handed his subordinate the notes. "It could be worse. We have enough for extended unit training. Your task is no easy one, Yuri, but four months is a long time for this task, is it not?"

It wasn't, but there was no point in saying so. "As you say, four months to instill fighting discipline. I will have a free hand?"

"Within limits."

"It is one thing to make a private soldier snap to the orders of his sergeant. It might be another for officers conditioned to pushing paper to change into combat leaders." Rozhkov skirted the issue, but his superior received the message clearly enough.

"A free hand on both, Yuri. But act carefully, for both our sakes."

Rozhkov nodded briefly. He knew whom he'd use to get this done. "With the troops we led forty years ago, Andrey, we could do this." Rozhkov sat down. "And in truth we have the same raw material now that we had then—and better weapons. The chief unknown remains the men. When we drove our tanks into Vienna, our men were tough, hard veterans—"

"And so were the SS bastards we crushed." Shavyrin smiled, remembering. "Keep in mind that the same forces are at work in the West, even more so. How well will they fight, surprised, divided? It can work. We must make it work."

"I'm meeting with our field commanders Monday. I will tell them myself."

NORFOLK, VIRGINIA

"I hope you take good care of it," the Mayor said.

It was a moment before Commander Daniel X. McCafferty reacted. USS *Chicago* had been in commission for only six weeks, her completion delayed by a yard fire and her commissioning ceremony marred by the absence of the Mayor of Chicago due to a strike of city workers. Just back from five tough weeks of workups in the Atlantic, his crew was now loading provisions for their first operational deployment. McCafferty was still entranced with his new command, and never tired of looking at her. He'd just walked the Mayor along the curved upper deck, the first part of any submarine tour, even though there was almost nothing to be seen there. "Excuse me?"

"Take good care of our ship," said the Mayor of Chicago.

"We call them boats, sir, and we'll take good care of her for you. Will you join us in the wardroom?"

"More ladders." The Mayor pretended to grimace, but McCafferty knew him to be a former fire chief. *Would have been useful a few months back,* the captain thought. "Where are you heading tomorrow?"

"To sea, sir." The captain started down the ladder. The Mayor of Chicago followed him.

"I figured that." For a man in his late fifties, he handled the steel ladder easily enough. They met again at the bottom. "What exactly do you do in these things?"

"Sir, the Navy calls it 'Oceanographic Research.' " McCafferty led him forward, turning for a smile with his answer to the awkward question. Things were starting quickly for *Chicago*. The Navy wanted to see just how effective her new quieting systems were. Everything looked good in the acoustical test range off the Bahamas. Now they wanted to see how well things worked in the Barents Sea.

The Mayor laughed at that one. "Oh, I suppose you'll be counting the whales for Greenpeace!"

"Well, I can say that there are whales where we're heading."

"What's with the tile on your deck? I never heard of rubber decks on a ship."

"It's called anechoic tile, sir. The rubber absorbs sound waves. It makes us quieter to operate, and makes it harder to detect us on sonar if somebody pings at us. Coffee?"

"You'd think that on a day like this—"

The captain chuckled. "Me, too. But it's against regulations."

The Mayor hoisted his cup and clicked against McCafferty's. "Luck."

"I'll drink to that."

MOSCOW, R.S.F.S.R.

They met at the Main Officers Club of the Moscow Military District on Ulitsa Krasnokazarmennaya, a massively impressive building dating back to Czarist times. It was the normal time of year for senior field commanders to confer in Moscow, and such events were always punctuated by elaborate ceremonial dinners. Rozhkov greeted his fellow officers at the main entrance, and when all were assembled, he led them downstairs to the ornate steam baths. Present were all Theater commanders, each accompanied by his deputy, his air force commander, and the fleet commanders: a small galaxy of stars, ribbons, and braid. Ten minutes later, naked but for a pair of towels and a handful of birch branches each, they were just another group of middle-aged men, perhaps a bit fitter than was the average in the Soviet Union.

They all knew one another. Though many were rivals, they were members of the same profession nevertheless, and with an intimacy characteristic of the Russian steam baths they exchanged small talk for several minutes. Several of them were grandfathers now, and spoke with animation about the continuation of their lines. Regardless of personal rivalries, it was expected that senior officers would look out for the careers of their comrades' sons, and so information was briefly exchanged on whose son was in which command and wanted advancement to what new posting. Finally came the classically Russian dispute over the "strength" of the steam. Rozhkov peremptorily settled the argument with a thin but steady stream of cold water onto the heated bricks in the center of the room. The resulting hiss would be sufficient to interfere with any listening devices in the room, if the foggy air hadn't already corroded them to junk. Rozhkov had not given the first hint of what was happening. Better, he thought, to shock them into the situation and get candid reactions to the situation at hand.

"Comrades, I must make an announcement."

Conversation stilled, and the men looked inquiringly in his direction.

Here we go. "Comrades, on 15 June of this year, just four months from now, we launch an offensive against NATO."

For a moment, only the hiss of the steam could be heard, then three men laughed, having imbibed a few stiff drinks in the sanctity of their staff cars on the drive over from the Kremlin. Those close enough to see CINC-Ground's face did not.

"You are serious, Comrade Marshal?" asked the Commander-in-Chief of the Western Theater. Receiving a nod in reply, he said, "Then perhaps you will be so kind as to explain the reason for this action?"

"Of course. You are all aware of the Nizhnevartovsk oil-field disaster. What you have not yet learned are its strategic and political implications." It took six brisk minutes to outline everything the Politburo had decided. "In just over four months from now, we shall launch the most crucial military operation in the history of the Soviet Union: the destruction of NATO as a political and military force. And we will succeed."

Finished, he stared at the officer in silence. The steam was having its desired effects on the assembly of flag officers. Its searing heat assaulted their breathing passages, sobering those who had been drinking. And it made them sweat. They'd be doing a lot of that in the next few months, Rozhkov thought.

Then Pavel Alekseyev, deputy commander of the Southwestern Theater, spoke. "I heard rumors," he said. "But *that* bad?"

"Yes. We have sufficient POL supplies for twelve months of normal operations, or enough for sixty days of war operations after a brief period of increased training activity." At the cost, he didn't say, of crippling the national economy by mid-August.

Alekseyev leaned forward and swatted himself with his bundle of branches. The action was strangely like a lion's swishing its tail. At fifty, he was the second-youngest officer there, a respected intellectual soldier and a fit, handsome man with the shoulders of a lumberjack. His intense, dark eyes squinted down through the rising cloud of steam.

"Mid-June?"

"Yes," Rozhkov said. "We have that long to prepare our plans and our troops." CINC-Ground looked around the room. Already the ceiling had become partially obscured by a mist.

"I presume we are here so that we may speak frankly among ourselves, no?"

"This is so, Pavel Leonidovich." Rozhkov replied, not the least surprised that Alekseyev had been the first to speak. CINC-Ground had carefully advanced the man's career over the last decade. He was the only son of a hard-charging tank general of the Great Motherland War, one of the many good men pensioned off during the bloodless purges under Nikita Khrushchev in the late 1950s.

"Comrades." Alekseyev stood, climbing slowly down the benches to the marble floor. "I accept everything Marshal Rozhkov has told us. But— four months! Four months in which we may be detected, four months in which we may lose all the element of surprise. Then what may happen? No, we have a plan already for this: Zhukov-4! Instant mobilization! We can all be back to our command posts in six hours. If we are going to conduct a surprise attack, then let us make it one no one can detect in time—seventy-two hours from now!"

Again the only sound in the room was that of the water flashing to steam on the dun-colored bricks, then the room erupted with noise. Zhukov-4 was the winter variant of a plan which hypothesized discovery of NATO's intention to launch a surprise attack of its own on the Warsaw Pact. In such a case, standard Soviet military doctrine was the same as anyone else's: the best defense is a good offense—preempt the NATO armies by attacking at once with the Category-A mechanized divisions in East Germany.

"But we are not ready!" objected CINC-West. His was the "point" command with headquarters in Berlin, the single most powerful military command in the world. An attack into West Germany was primarily his responsibility.

Alekseyev held up his hands. "Neither are they. In fact, they are less ready than we," he said reasonably. "Look, consider our intelligence data. Fourteen percent of their officers are on holidays. They are coming off a training cycle, true, but because of it much of their equipment will be down for maintenance, and many of their senior officers will be away in their respective capitals for consultations, just as we are now. Their troops are in winter quarters, on a winter routine. This is the time of year for maintenance and paperwork. Physical training is curtailed—who wants to run in the snow, eh? Their men are cold, and drinking more than usual. This is *our* time to act! We all know that historically the Soviet fighting man performs at his best in winter, and NATO is at its lowest state of readiness."

"But so are we, you young fool!" CINC-Western Theater growled back.

"We can change that in forty-eight hours," Alekseyev countered.

"Impossible," observed West's deputy, careful to back up his boss.

"To reach our maximum readiness will take some months," Alekseyev agreed. His only chance to carry his point with his seniors was to reason with them. He knew that he was almost certainly doomed to failure, but he had to try. "It will be difficult, if not impossible, for us to conceal it."

"As Marshal Rozhkov told us, Pavel Leonidovich, we are promised political and diplomatic *maskirovka*," a general pointed out.

"I have no doubt that our comrades in the KGB, and our skillful political leadership, will perform miracles." The room just might have functioning bugs, after all. "But is it not asking too much to expect that the Imperialists—as much as they fear and hate us, as active as their agents and spy satellites are—will fail to note a doubling of our training activity? We know that NATO increases its readiness when we go into major unit training, and their preparedness will automatically be increased by their own spring training cycles. If we continue our training beyond the normal pattern, they will be even more alert. Achieving full combat readiness requires that we do too many things out of the ordinary. If nothing else, East Germany is rife with Western spies. NATO will notice. NATO will react. They will meet us on the border with everything in their collective arsenals.

"If, on the other hand, we attack with what we have—*now!*—we have the advantage. Our men are not off skiing in the fucking Alps! Zhukov-4 is designed to cycle from peace to war in forty-eight hours. There is no way possible for NATO to react in so little time. They'll take forty-eight hours to get their intelligence information organized and presented to their ministers. By that time our shells will be falling on the Fulda Gap, and our tanks will be advancing behind them!"

"Too many things can go wrong!" CINC-West rose so swiftly that the towel nearly came off his waist. His left hand grabbed downward while his right fist shook at the younger man. "What about traffic control? What about training our men in their new battle equipment? What about getting my Frontal Aviation pilots ready for combat operations against the Imperialists? There—right there is an insurmountable problem! Our pilots need at least a month of intensive training. And so do my tankers, and so do my gunners, and so do my riflemen."

If you knew your job, they would be ready now, you worthless, whore-chasing son of a bitch! Alekseyev thought but did not dare to say aloud. CINC-West was a man of sixty-one who liked to demonstrate his manly prowess—boasted of it—to the detriment of his professional duties. Alekseyev had heard that story often enough, whispered jovially in this very room. But CINC-West was politically reliable. *Such is the Soviet system,* the younger general reflected. *We need fighting soldiers and what do we get with which to defend the* Rodina? *Political reliability!* He remembered bitterly what had happened to his father in 1958. But Alekseyev did not allow himself to begrudge the Party its control of the armed forces. The Party was the State, after all, and he was a sworn servant of the State. He had learned these truisms at his father's knee. One more card to play:

"Comrade General, you have good officers commanding your divisions, regiments, and battalions. Trust them to know their duties." It couldn't hurt to wave the standards of the Red Army, Alekseyev reasoned.

Rozhkov stood, and everyone in the room strained to hear his pronouncement. "What you say has merit, Pavel Leonidovich, but do we gamble with the safety of the Motherland?" He shook his head, quoting doctrine exactly, as he had been doing for too many years. "No. We rely on surprise, yes, on the first weighted blow to blast open a path for the daring thrust of our mechanized forces. And we will have our surprise. The Westerners will not wish to believe what is happening, and with the Politburo soothing them even as we prepare the first blow, we will have our strategic surprise. The West will have perhaps three days—four at most—to know what is coming, and even then they will not be mentally prepared for us."

The officers followed Rozhkov from the room to rinse the sweat from their bodies with cold-water showers. Ten minutes later, refreshed and dressed in full uniform, the officers reassembled in a second-floor banquet room. The waiters, many of them KGB informers, noted the subdued mood and quiet conversations that frustrated their efforts to listen in. The generals knew that KGB's Lefortovo prison was a bare kilometer away.

"Our plans?" CINC-Southwest asked his deputy.

"How many times have we played this war game?" Alekseyev responded. "All the maps and formulae we have examined for years. We know the troop and tank concentrations. We know the routes, the highways, the crossroads that we must use, and those that NATO will use. We know our mobilization schedules, and theirs. The only thing we don't know is whether our carefully laid plans will in fact work. We should attack at once. Then the unknowns will work against both sides equally."

"And if our attack goes too well, and NATO relies on a nuclear defense?" the senior officer asked. Alekseyev acknowledged the importance and grave unpredictability of the point.

"They might do that anyway. Comrade, all of our plans depend heavily on surprise, no? A mixture of surprise and success will force the West to consider nuclear weapons—"

"Here you are wrong, my young friend," CINC-Southwest chided. "The decision to use nuclear weapons is political. To prevent their use is also a political exercise for which time is required."

"But if we wait over four months—*how can we be assured of strategic surprise?*" Alekseyev demanded.

"Our political leadership has promised it."

"The year I entered Frunze Academy, the Party told us the date on which we would surely have 'True Communism in our lifetime.' A solemn promise. That date was six years ago."

"Such talk is safe with me, Pasha, I understand you. But if you do not learn to control your tongue—"

"Forgive me, Comrade General. We must allow for the chance that surprise will not be achieved. 'In combat, despite the most careful preparation, risks cannot be avoided,' " Alekseyev quoted from the syllabus of the Frunze Academy. " 'Attention must therefore be given, and the most detailed plans prepared, for every reasonable exigency of the overall operation. For this reason, the unsung life of a staff officer is among the most demanding of those honored to serve the State.' "

"You have the memory of a *kulak,* Pasha." CINC-Southwest laughed, filling his deputy's glass with Georgian wine. "But you are correct."

"Failure to achieve surprise means that we are forcing a campaign of attrition on a vast scale, a high-technology version of the '14 – '18 war."

"Which we will win." CINC-Ground sat down next to Alekseyev.

"Which we will win," Alekseyev agreed. All Soviet generals accepted the premise that the inability to force a rapid decision would force a bloody war of attrition that would grind each side down equally. The Soviets had far more reserves of men and material with which to fight such a war. And the political will to use them. "*If and only if* we are able to force the pace of battle, and if our friends in the Navy can prevent the resupply of NATO from America. NATO has war stocks of materiel to sustain them for roughly five weeks. Our pretty, expensive fleet must close the Atlantic."

"Maslov." Rozhkov beckoned to the Commander-in-Chief of the Soviet Navy. "We wish to hear your opinion of the correlation of forces in the North Atlantic."

"Our mission?" Maslov asked warily.

"If we fail to achieve surprise in the West, Andrey Petravich, it will be necessary for our beloved comrades in the Navy to isolate Europe from America," Rozhkov pronounced. He blinked hard at the response.

"Give me a division of airborne troops, and I can fulfill that task," Maslov responded soberly. He held a glass of mineral water, and had been careful to avoid drink on this cold February night. "The question is whether our strategic stance at sea should be offensive or defensive. The NATO navies—above all the United States Navy—is a direct threat to the *Rodina.* It alone has the aircraft and aircraft carriers with which to attack the homeland, at the Kola Peninsula. In fact, we know that they have plans to do exactly that."

"So what?" CINC-Southwest observed. "No attack on Soviet soil is to be taken lightly, of course, but we will take severe losses in this campaign no matter how brilliantly we fight it. What matters is the final outcome."

"If the Americans succeed in attacking Kola, they effectively prevent our closure of the North Atlantic. And you are wrong to shrug off these attacks. American entry into the Barents Sea will constitute a direct threat to our nuclear deterrent forces, and could have more dire consequences than you imagine." Admiral Maslov leaned forward. "On the other hand, if you persuade STAVKA to give us the resources to execute Operation Polar Glory, we can seize the combat initiative and dictate the nature of operations in the North Atlantic on our chosen terms." He held up a closed fist. "By doing this we can, first"—he raised a finger—"prevent an American naval attack against the *Rodina;* second"—another finger—"use the majority of our submarine forces in the North Atlantic basin where the trade routes are, instead of keeping them on passive defense; and, third"— a final finger—"make maximum use of our naval aviation assets. At one stroke this operation makes our fleet an offensive rather than a defensive weapon."

"And to accomplish this you need only one of our Guards Air Rifle divisions? Outline your plan for us, please, Comrade Admiral," Alekseyev said.

Maslov did so over a period of five minutes. He concluded, "With luck, we will with one blow give the NATO navies more than they can deal with, and leave us with a valuable position for postwar exploitation."

"Better to draw their carrier forces in and destroy them." CINC-West joined the discussion.

Maslov responded: "The Americans will have five or six carriers available to use against us in the Atlantic. Each one carries fifty-eight aircraft that can be used in an air superiority or nuclear strike role, aside from those used for fleet defense. I submit, Comrade, that it is in our interest to keep those ships as far from the *Rodina* as possible."

"Andrey Petravich, I am impressed," Rozhkov said thoughtfully, noting the respect in Alekseyev's eyes as well. Polar Glory was both bold and simple. "I want a full briefing on this plan tomorrow afternoon. You say that if we can allocate the resources, success in this venture is highly probable?"

"We have worked on this plan for five years, with particular emphasis on simplicity. If security can be maintained, only two things need go right for success to be achieved."

Rozhkov nodded. "Then you will have my support."

4. *Maskirovka 1*

MOSCOW, R.S.F.S.R.

The Foreign Minister entered stage left, as he always did, and walked to the lectern with a brisk step that belied his sixty years. Before him was a mob of reporters arrayed by the Soviet Guards into their respective groups, the print press grasping at their pads and backed up by their photographers, the visual media arrayed in front of their portable klieg lights. The Foreign Minister hated the damned things, hated the people in front of them. The Western press with its lack of manners, always prying, always probing, always demanding answers that he need not give to his own people. How odd, he thought, while looking up from his notes, that he often had to speak more openly to these paid foreign spies than to members of the Party Central Committee. Spies, exactly what they were . . .

They could be manipulated, of course, by a skilled man with a collection of carefully prepared disinformation—which was precisely what he was about to do. But on the whole they were a threat because they never stopped doing what it was they did. It was something the Foreign Minister never allowed himself to forget, and the reason he did not hold them in contempt. Dealing with them always held potential danger. Even while being manipulated, they could be dangerous in their quest for information. If only the rest of the Politburo understood.

"Ladies and gentlemen," he began, speaking in English. "I will be making a brief statement, and I regret that I cannot answer any questions at this time. A full handout will be given to everyone as you leave—that is, I think they are ready by now—" He gestured to a man at the back of the room, who nodded emphatically. The Foreign Minister arranged his papers one more time and began to speak with the precise diction for which he was known.

"The President of the United States has often asked for 'deeds not words' in the quest for control of strategic arms.

"As you know, and to the disappointment of the entire world, the ongoing arms negotiations in Vienna have made no significant progress for over a year, with each side blaming the other for the lack of it.

"It is well known by peace-loving people the world over that the Soviet Union has never wished for war, and that only a madman would even consider nuclear war a viable policy option in our modern world of overkill, fallout, and 'nuclear winter.' "

"Damn," muttered AP bureau chief Patrick Flynn. The Soviets scarcely acknowledged "nuclear winter" and had *never* mentioned the concept in so formal a setting. His antennae were already twitching at whatever there was in the wind.

"The time has come for substantive reductions in strategic arms. We have made numerous, serious, sincere proposals for real arms reductions, and despite this the United States has proceeded with the development and deployment of its destabilizing, openly offensive weapons: the MX first-strike missile, so cynically called the 'Peacekeeper'; the advanced Trident D-5 first-strike sea-launched ballistic missile; two separate varieties of cruise missiles whose characteristics conspire to make arms control verification almost totally impossible; and of course, the so-called Strategic Defense Initiative, which will take offensive strategic weapons into space. Such are America's deeds." He looked up from his notes and spoke with irony. "And through it all, America's pious words demand Soviet deeds.

"Starting tomorrow, we will see once and for all if America's words are to be believed or not. Starting tomorrow we will see how great a difference there is between America's words about peace and Soviet deeds for peace.

"Tomorrow, the Soviet Union will put on the table at Vienna a proposal to reduce existing arsenals of strategic and theater nuclear weapons by fifty percent, this reduction to be accomplished over a period of three years from ratification of the agreement, subject to on-site verification conducted by third-party inspection teams whose composition will be agreed upon by all signatories.

"Please note that I say 'all signatories.' The Soviet Union invites the United Kingdom, the French Republic, and"—he looked up—"the People's Republic of China to join us at the negotiating table." The explosion of flashbulbs caused him to look away for a moment.

"Ladies and gentlemen, please—" He smiled, holding his hand up to shield his face. "These old eyes are not up to such abuse as this, and I have not memorized my speech—unless you want me to continue in Russian!"

There was a wave of laughter, then a sprinkling of applause at the jibe. The old bastard was really turning on the charm, Flynn thought, furiously taking notes. This was potential dynamite. He wondered what would come next, and he especially wondered what the precise wording on the proposal was. Flynn had covered arms talks before, and knew all too well that general descriptions of proposals could grossly distort the nuts-and-bolts details of the real issues to be negotiated. The Russians couldn't be this open—they just couldn't be.

"To proceed." The Foreign Minister blinked his eyes clear. "We have been accused of never making a gesture of our good faith. The falsehood of the charge is manifest, but this evil fiction continues in the West. No longer. No longer will anyone have cause to doubt the sincerity of the Soviet people's quest for a just and lasting peace.

"Beginning today, as a sign of good faith which we challenge the United States and any other interested nation to match, the Soviet Union will remove from service an entire class of nuclear-powered missile submarine. These submarines are known to the West as the Yankee class. We call them something else, of course," he said with an ingenuous grin that drew another wave of polite laughter. "Twenty of the vessels are presently in service, each carrying twelve sea-launched ballistic missiles. All active members of the class are assigned to the Soviet Northern Fleet based on the Kola Peninsula. Beginning today, we will deactivate these vessels at a rate of one per month. As you know, complete deactivation of so complex a machine as a missile submarine requires the services of a shipyard—the missile compartment must be physically removed from the body of the vessel—and so these vessels cannot be fully disarmed overnight. However, to make the honesty of our intentions undeniable, we invite the United States to do one of two things:

"First, we will permit a selected team of six American naval officers to inspect these twenty vessels to verify that their missile tubes have been filled with concrete ballast pending removal of the entire missile rooms from all of the submarines. In return for this, we would require that a comparable inspection visit by an equal number of Soviet officers to American yards would be allowed at a later date to be agreed on.

"Second, as an alternative should the United States be unwilling to allow reciprocal verification of arms reductions, we will permit another group of six officers to perform this service, these officers to be from a country— or countries—upon which the United States and the Soviet Union can agree within the next thirty days. A team from such neutral countries as Sweden or India would be acceptable in principle to the Soviet Union.

"Ladies and gentlemen, the time has come to put an end to the arms race. I will not repeat all of the flowery rhetoric we've all heard over the past two generations. We all know the threat that these ghastly weapons represent to every nation. Let no one ever say again that the government of the Soviet Union has not done its part to reduce the danger of war. Thank you."

The room suddenly fell silent but for the sound of motor-driven still cameras. The Western press representatives assigned to their respective Moscow bureaus were among the best in their profession. Uniformly bright, uniformly ambitious, uniformly cynical about what they found in Moscow and the conditions under which they were forced to work, all were stunned to silence.

"Goddamn," muttered Flynn after a full ten seconds.

"One must admire your understatement, old boy," agreed Reuters correspondent William Calloway. "Wasn't it your Wilson who spoke of open covenants openly arrived at?"

"Yeah, my granddad covered that peace conference. Remember how well it worked out?" Flynn grimaced, watching the Foreign Minister depart, smiling at the cameras. "I want to see the handout. Want to ride back with me?"

"Yes on both."

It was a bitterly cold day in Moscow. Snow piles were heaped at the roadsides. The sky was a frigid crystal blue. And the car's heater didn't work. Flynn drove while his friend read aloud through the handout. The draft treaty proposal took up nineteen annotated pages. The Reuters correspondent was a Londoner who had begun as a police reporter, and since covered assignments all over the world. He and Flynn had met many years before at the famous Caravelle Hotel in Saigon, and shared drinks and typewriter ribbons on and off for more than two decades. In the face of a Russian winter, they remembered the oppressive heat of Saigon with something akin to nostalgia.

"It's bloody fair," Calloway said wonderingly, his breath giving ghostly substance to his words. "They propose a builddown with elimination of many existing weapons, allowing both sides to replace obsolete launchers, both sides to reach a total of five thousand deliverable warheads, that number to remain stable for five years after the three-year reduction period. There is a separate proposal to negotiate complete removal of 'heavy' missiles, replacing them with mobile missiles, but to limit missile flight tests to a fixed number per year—" He flipped that page and rapidly scanned the remainder. "Nothing in the draft treaty about your Star Wars research . . . ? Didn't he mention that in his statement? Patrick, old son, this is, as you say, dynamite. This could as easily have been written in Washington. It will take months to work out all the technical points, but this is a bloody serious, and bloody generous, proposal."

"Nothing about Star Wars?" Flynn frowned briefly as he turned right. Did that mean that the Russians had made a breakthrough of their own? Have to query Washington about that . . . "We got us a story here, Willie. What's your lead? How's 'Peace' grab you?" Calloway just laughed at that.

FORT MEADE, MARYLAND

American intelligence agencies, like their counterparts throughout the world, monitor all news wire services. Toland was examining the AP and Reuters reports before most news bureau chiefs, and comparing them with the version transmitted over Soviet microwave circuits for publication in the regional editions of *Pravda* and *Isvestia*. The way items of hard news were reported in the Soviet Union was intended to show Party members how their leaders felt.

"We've been down this road before," his section chief said. "The last time, things broke down on this issue of mobile missiles. Both sides want them, but both sides are afraid of the other side having them."

"But the tone of the report—"

"They're *always* euphoric about *their* arms-control proposals, dammit! Hell, Bob, you know that."

"True, sir, but it's the first time that I know of that the Russians have unilaterally removed a weapons platform from service."

"The 'Yankees' are obsolete."

"So what? They never throw anything away, obsolete or not. They still have World War II artillery pieces sitting in warehouses in case they need them again. This is different, and the political ramifications—"

"We're not talking politics, we're talking nuclear strategy," the section chief growled back.

As if there were a difference, Toland said to himself.

KIEV, THE UKRAINE

"Well, Pasha?"

"Comrade General, we truly have a man's work before us," Alekseyev answered, standing at attention in the Kiev headquarters of the Southwest Theater.

"Our troops need extensive unit training. Over the weekend I read through more than eighty regimental readiness reports from our tank and motor-rifle divisions." Alekseyev paused before going on. Tactical training and readiness was the bane of the Soviet military. Their troops were almost entirely conscripts, in and out in two years, half of whose uniformed service was occupied just in acquiring basic military skills. Even the noncoms, the backbone of every army since the Roman legions, were conscripts selected for special training academies, then lost as soon as their enlistment periods ended. For that reason, the Soviet military leaned heavily on its officers, who often performed what in the West was sergeants' work. The professional officer corps of the Soviet Army was its only permanent, only dependable feature. In theory. "The truth of the matter is that we *don't know* our readiness posture at the moment. Our colonels all use the same language in their reports, without the slightest deviation. Everyone reports meeting norms, with the same amount of training hours, the same amount of political indoctrination, the same number of practice shots fired—that is, a deviation of under three percent!—and the requisite number of field exercises run, all of course of the proper type."

"As prescribed in our training manuals," the Colonel General noted.

"Naturally. Exactly—too damned exactly! No deviation for adverse weather. No deviation for late fuel deliveries. No deviation for anything at all. For example, the 703rd Motor-Rifle Regiment spent all of last October on harvesting duty south of Kharkov—yet somehow they met their monthly norms for unit training at the same time. Lies are bad enough, but these are *stupid* lies!"

"It cannot be as bad as you fear, Pavel Leonidovich."

"Do we dare to assume otherwise, Comrade?"

The General stared down at his desk. "No. Very well, Pasha. You've formulated your plan. Let me hear it."

"For the moment, you will be outlining the plan for our attack into the Muslim lands. I must get into the field to whip our field commanders into shape. If we wish to accomplish our goals in time for the attack west, we must make an example of the worst offenders. I have four commanders in mind. Their conduct has been grossly and undeniably criminal. Here are the names and charges." He handed over a single sheet of paper.

"There are two good men here, Pasha," the General objected.

"They are guardians of the State. They enjoy positions of the greatest trust. They have betrayed that trust by lying, and in doing so, they have endangered the State," Alekseyev said, wondering how many men in his country could have that said of them. He dismissed the thought. There were problems enough right here.

"You understand the consequences of the charges you bring?"

"Of course. The penalty for treason is death. Did I ever falsify a readiness report? Did you?" Alekseyev looked away briefly. "It is a hard thing, and I take no pleasure in it—but unless we snap our units into shape, how many young boys will die for their officers' failings? We need combat readiness more than we need four liars. If there is a gentler way to achieve this, I don't know what that might be. An army without discipline is a worthless mob. We have the directive from STAVKA to make examples of unruly privates and restore the authority of our NCOs. It is fitting that if privates must suffer for their failings, then their colonels must suffer too. Theirs is the greater responsibility. Theirs is the greater reward. A few examples here will go a long way to restoring our army."

"The inspectorate?"

"The best choice," Alekseyev agreed. That way blame would not necessarily be traced back to the senior commanders themselves. "I can send teams from the Inspector General's service out to these regiments day after tomorrow. Our training memoranda arrived in all divisional and regimental headquarters this morning. The news of these four traitors will encourage our unit commanders to implement them with vigor. Even then, it will be two weeks before we have a clear picture of what we need to focus on, but once we can identify the areas that need buttressing, we should have ample time to accomplish what we need to accomplish."

"What will CINC-West be doing?"

"The same, one hopes." Alekseyev shook his head. "Has he asked for any of our units yet?"

"No, but he will. We will not be ordered to launch offensive operations against NATO's southern flank—part of the continuing *maskirovka*. You may assume that many of our Category-B units will be detailed to Germany, possibly some of our 'A' tank forces also. How ever many divisions that fool has, he'll want more."

"Just so we have enough troops to seize the oil fields when the time comes," Pasha observed. "Which plan are we supposed to execute?"

"The old one. We'll have to update it, of course." The old plan predated Soviet involvement in Afghanistan, and now the Red Army had a whole new perspective on sending mechanized forces into an area occupied by armed Muslims.

Alekseyev's hands bunched into fists. "Marvelous. We must formulate a plan without knowing when it will be implemented or what forces we'll have available to execute it."

"Remember what you told me about the life of a staff officer, Pasha?" CINC-Southwest chuckled.

The younger man nodded ruefully, hoist on his own petard. "Indeed, Comrade General: we will do our sleeping after the war."

5. Sailors and Spooks

THE CHESAPEAKE BAY, MARYLAND

His eyes squinted painfully at the horizon. The sun was only half a diameter above the green-brown line of Maryland's Eastern Shore, a reminder, if he needed one, that he'd worked late the day before, gone to bed later still, then arisen at four-thirty so that he could get in a day's fishing. A slowly receding sinuslike headache also let him know about the six-pack of beer he'd consumed in front of the TV.

But it was his first fishing day of the year, and the casting rod felt good in his hand as he gave it a gentle swing toward a ripple on the calm surface of the Chesapeake Bay. A blue or a rockfish? Whatever it was, it didn't nibble at his Bucktail lure. But there was no hurry.

"Coffee, Bob?"

"Thanks, Pop." Robert Toland set his rod in its holder and leaned back into the 'midships swivel chair of his Boston Whaler Outrage. His father-in-law, Edward Keegan, held out the plastic cup-cap from a large thermos jug. Bob knew the coffee would be good. Ned Keegan was a former naval officer who appreciated a good cup, preferably flavored with brandy or Irish whiskey—something to open the eyes and put a fire in the belly.

"Cold or not, damn if it ain't nice to get out here." Keegan sipped at his cup, resting one foot on the bait box. It wasn't just the fishing, both men agreed, getting out on the water was one sure cure for civilization.

"Be nice if the rock really are coming back, too," Toland observed.

"What the hell—no phones."

"What about your beeper?"

"I must have left it with my other pants." Keegan chuckled. "DIA will have to manage without me today."

"Think they can?"

"Well, the Navy did." Keegan was an academy graduate who had put in his thirty and retired to become a double-dipper. In uniform, he'd been an intelligence specialist, and now he had essentially the same job, which added civil service salary to his pension.

Toland had been a lieutenant (j.g.) serving aboard a destroyer based at Pearl Harbor when he'd first noticed Martha Keegan, a junior at the University of Hawaii, majoring in psychology and minoring in surfing. They'd been happily married for fifteen years now.

"So." Keegan stood and lifted his rod. "How are things at the Fort?"

Bob Toland was a middle-level analyst at the National Security Agency. He'd left the Navy after six years when the adventure of uniformed service had palled, but he remained an active reservist. His work at NSA dovetailed nicely with his naval reserve service. A communications expert with a degree in electronics, his current job was monitoring Soviet signals gathered by the NSA's numerous listening posts and ferret satellites. Along the way he'd also gotten a masters in the Russian language.

"Heard something real interesting last week, but I couldn't convince my boss it meant anything."

"Who's your section chief?"

"Captain Albert Redman, U.S. Navy." Toland watched a bay-built fishing boat motoring a few miles away, her captain laying out his crab pots. "He's an asshole."

Keegan laughed. "You want to be careful saying stuff like that out loud, Bob, especially seeing how you go on active duty next week. Bert worked with me, oh, must have been fifteen years ago. I had to slap him down a few times. He does tend to be slightly opinionated."

"Opinionated?" Toland snorted. "That bastard's so friggin' narrow-minded his scratch pads are only an inch wide! First there was this new arms control thing, then I came up with something really unusual last

Wednesday and he circular-filed it. Hell, I don't know why he even bothers looking at new data—he made his mind up five years ago."

"I don't suppose you could tell me what it was?"

"I shouldn't." Bob wavered for a moment. Hell, if he couldn't talk with his kids' own grandfather . . . "One of our ferret birds was over a Soviet military district headquarters last week and intercepted a microwaved telephone conversation. It was a report to Moscow about four colonels in the Carpathian Military District who were being shot for gundecking readiness reports. The story on their court-martial and execution was being set up for publication, probably in a *Red Star* this week." He had entirely forgotten about the oil-field fire.

"Oh?" Keegan's eyebrows went up. "And what did Bert say?"

"He said, 'It's Goddamned about time they cleaned their act up.' And that was that."

"And what do you say?"

"Pop, I'm not in Trends and Intentions—those idiot fortune-tellers!—but I know that even the Russians don't kill people for jollies. When Ivan kills people publicly, he does it to make a point. These were not manpower officers taking bribes to fake deferments. They weren't popped for stealing diesel fuel or building dachas with pilfered lumber. I checked our records, and it turned out we have files on two of them. They were both experienced line officers, both with combat experience in Afghanistan, both Party members in good standing. One was a graduate of Frunze Academy, and he even had a few articles published in *Military Thought,* for God's sake! But all four were court-martialed for falsifying their regimental readiness reports—and shot three days later. That story will hit the streets in *Krasnaya Zvezda* over the next few days as a two- or three-part story under 'The Observer's' by-line—and *that* makes it a political exercise with a capital P."

The Observer was the cover name for any number of high-ranking officers who contributed to *Red Star,* the daily newspaper of the Soviet armed services. Anything on the front page and under that by-line was taken quite seriously, both in the Soviet military services and by those whose job it was to watch them, because this by-line was used explicitly to make policy statements approved by both the military high command and the Politburo in Moscow.

"A multipart story?" Keegan asked.

"Yeah, that's one of the interesting things about it. The repetition means they really want this lesson to sink in. Everything about this is out of pattern, Pop. Something funny is happening. They *do* shoot officers and EMs—but not full colonels who've written for the journal of the general staff, and not for faking a few lines in a readiness statement." He let out a long breath, happy to have gotten this off his chest. The workboat was proceeding south, her wake rippling out toward them in parallel lines on the mirrored surface. The image made Toland wish for his camera.

"Makes sense," Keegan mumbled.

"Huh?"

"What you just said. That does sound out of pattern."

"Yep. I stayed in late last night, running down a hunch. In the past five years, the Red Army has published the names of exactly fourteen executed officers, none higher than a full colonel, and even then only one—a manpower officer in Soviet Georgia. The guy was taking payoffs for deferments. The others broke down into one case of spying, for us or somebody, three derelictions of duty while under the influence of alcohol, and nine conventional corruption cases, selling everything from gasoline to a whole mainframe computer *nalyevo,* 'on the left,' the shadow market. Now all of a sudden they waste four regimental commanders, all in the same military district."

"You could take that to Redman," Keegan suggested.

"Waste of time."

"Those other cases—I seem to remember the three guys who—"

"Yeah, that was part of the temperance campaign. Too many guys turn up drunk on duty, and they pick three volunteers, *pour encourager les autres.*" Bob shook his head. "Jeez, Voltaire would have loved these guys."

"You talk with people who're into civilian intelligence?"

"No, my crowd is all military telecommunications."

"At lunch last—Monday, I think, I was talking with a guy from Langley. Ex-Army, we go way back. Anyway, he was joking that there's a new shortage over there."

"Another one?" Bob was amused. Shortages were nothing new in Russia. One month toothpaste, or toilet paper, or windshield wipers—he had heard of many such things over lunch at the NSA commissary.

"Yeah, car and truck batteries."

"Really?"

"Yeah, for the last month you can't get a battery for your car or truck over there. A lot of cars are not moving, and batteries are being stolen left and right, so people are disconnecting their batteries at night and taking them home, would you believe?"

"But Togliattishtadt—" Toland said, and stopped. He referred to the massive auto factory – city in European Russia, the construction of which was a "Hero Project" for which thousands of workers had been mobilized. Among the most modern auto complexes in the world, it had been built mainly with Italian technology. "They have a hell of a battery manufacturing facility there. Hasn't blown up, has it?"

"Working three shifts. What do you think of that?"

NORFOLK, VIRGINIA

Toland examined himself in the full-sized mirror in the Norfolk BOQ complex. He'd made the drive down the evening before. The uniform still fit, he noted, maybe a little tight at the waist, but that was nature at work, wasn't it? His "salad bar" of decorations was a bleak row and a half, but he had his surface warfare officer's badge, his "water wings"—he hadn't always been a glorified radio operator. His sleeves bore the two and a half stripes of a lieutenant commander. A final swipe of a cloth across his shoes and he was out the door, ready on this bright Monday morning for his annual two weeks of duty with the fleet.

Five minutes later, he was driving down Mitcher Avenue toward headquarters of the Commander-in-Chief, Atlantic Fleet—CINCLANTFLT— a flat, thoroughly undistinguished building that had once been a hospital. An habitual early riser, Toland found the Ingersoll Street parking lot half empty, but he was still careful to take an unmarked space lest he incur the wrath of a senior officer.

"Bob? Bob Toland!" a voice called.

"Ed Morris!"

It was now Commander Edward Morris, USN, Toland noted, and a shiny gold star on his uniform jacket designated him as the commander of some ship or other. Toland saluted his friend before shaking hands.

"Still playing bridge, Bob?" Toland, Morris, and two other officers had once established the most regular bridge foursome at the Pearl Harbor officers' club.

"Some. Marty isn't much of a card player, but we got a bunch at work. that meets once a week."

"Good as we used to be?" Morris asked as they headed off in the same direction.

"Are you kidding? You know where I work now?"

"I heard you ended up at Fort Meade after you hung it up."

"Yeah, and there's bridge players at NSA who're wired into the damn computers—I'm talking assassins!"

"So how's the family?"

"Just great. How's yours?"

"Growing up too damned fast—makes you feel old."

"That's the truth," Toland chuckled. He jabbed a finger at his friend's star. "Now you can tell me about your new kid."

"Look at my car."

Toland turned around. Morris's Ford had a personalized license plate: FF-1094. To the uninitiated it was an ordinary license number, but to a sailor it advertised his command: antisubmarine frigate number one thousand ninety-four, USS *Pharris.*

"You always were nice and modest," Toland noted with a grin. "That's all right, Ed. How long you had her?"

"Two years. She's big, she's pretty, and she's *mine*! You should have stayed in, Bob. The day I took command—hell, it was like the day Jimmy was born."

"I hear you. The difference, Ed, is that I always knew you'd have your ship, and I always knew I wouldn't." In Toland's personnel jacket was a letter of admonishment for grounding a destroyer while he had the deck. It had been no more than bad luck. An ambiguity on the chart and adverse tidal conditions had caused the error, but it didn't take much to ruin a Navy career.

"So, doing your two weeks?"

"That's right."

"Celia is off visiting her parents, and I'm baching it. What're you doing for dinner tonight?"

"McDonald's?" Toland laughed.

"Like hell. Danny McCafferty's in town, too. He's got the *Chicago,* tied up at Pier 22. You know, if we can scare up a fourth, maybe we can play a little bridge, just like the old days." Morris poked his friend in the chest. "I gotta head along. Meet me in the O-Club lobby at 1730, Bob. Danny invited me over to his boat for dinner at 1830, and we'll have an hour's worth of Attitude Adjustment before we drive over. We'll have dinner in the wardroom and a few hours of cards, just like old times."

"Aye aye, Commander."

"Anyway, there I was on *Will Rogers,*" McCafferty said. "Fifty days out on patrol and I got the watch, right? Sonar says they have a goofy signal, bearing zero-five-two. We're at periscope depth,so I put the search scope up, train it out to zero-five-two, and sure enough, there's this Gulfstream-36 sailboat, moving along at four or five knots with the autosteering rig set. What the hell, it's a dull day, so I flip the scope to hi-power, and guess what? The captain and the mate—there's one gal who'll never drown!—are on top the deckhouse, horizontal and superimposed. The boat was maybe a thousand yards away—just like being there. So we turn on the scope TV camera and get the tape machine running. Had to maneuver for a better view, of course. Lasted fifteen minutes. The crew ran the tape for the next week. Great for morale to know just what you're fighting for." All three officers laughed.

"Like I always told you, Bob," Morris noted. "These sub-drivers are a nasty, sneaky bunch. Not to mention perverts."

"So how long you had the *Chicago,* Danny?" Toland asked over his second cup of after-dinner coffee. The three had the submarine's wardroom to themselves. The only officers aboard were either standing watch or asleep.

"Three busy months, not counting yard time," McCafferty said, finishing off his milk. He was the first skipper for the new attack sub, the best of all possible worlds, a captain and a "plankowner." Toland noted that Dan had not joined him and Morris for "attitude adjustment" at the base officers' club, during which they'd tossed down three stiff drinks apiece. It wasn't like the McCafferty of old. Perhaps he was unwilling to leave his sub, lest the dream of his career somehow end while he was away from her.

"Can't you tell from the pale, pasty look common to cave-dwellers and submariners?" Morris joked. "Not to mention the faint glow associated with nuclear reactor types?" McCafferty grinned, and they waited for their fourth to arrive. He was a junior engineer, just about to come off reactor watch. *Chicago*'s reactor wasn't operating. She was drawing electrical power from the dock, but regulations demanded a full reactor watch whether the teakettle was working or not.

"I tell you guys, I *was* a little pale four weeks ago." McCafferty turned serious—or about as serious as he ever got.

"How so?" Bob Toland asked.

"Well, you know the kinda shit we do with these boats, right?"

"If you mean inshore intelligence gathering, Dan, you ought to know that that electronic intelligence stuff you collect comes to my office. Hell, I probably know the people who originate a lot of the data requests that generate your op-orders. How's that for a revolting thought!" Bob laughed. He fought the urge to look around too obviously. He'd never been aboard a nuclear submarine before. It was cold—nuclear subs have nuclear-powered air conditioning—and the air was heavy with the smell of machine oil. Everything he could see sparkled both from being almost new, and from the fact that McCafferty had undoubtedly made sure that his crew had gotten things looking especially good for his friends. So, this was the billion-dollar machine that gathered all that ELINT data. . . .

"Yeah, well, we were up in the Barents Sea, you know, northeast of the Kola Fjord, trailing a Russian sub—an Oscar—about, oh, ten miles back of her—and all of a sudden we find ourselves in the middle of a friggin' live-fire exercise! Missiles were flying all over the damned place. They wasted three old hulks, and blasted hell out of a half-dozen target barges."

"Just the Oscar?" Morris asked.

"Turned out there was a Papa and a Mike out there, too. That's one problem with us being so quiet in these babies. If they don't know we're there, we can find ourselves in the middle of some really unpleasant shit! Anyway, sonar starts screaming 'Transients! Transients!' from all the missile tubes being flooded. No way we could be sure they weren't getting ready to put some real torpedoes in the water, but we stuck up the ESM and picked up their periscope radars, then I saw some of the things whipping over our heads. Damn, guys, for about three minutes there it was just a little hairy, y'know?" McCafferty shook his head. "Anyway, two hours after that, all three boats crack on twenty knots and head back to the barn. Your basic out-and-in live-fire. How's that for a lively first deployment?"

"You get the feeling that the Russians are doing anything out of the ordinary, Dan?" Toland asked, suddenly interested.

"You didn't hear?"

"Hear what?"

"They've cut back their diesel sub patrols up north, quite a bit, too. I mean, normally they're pretty hard to hear, but mostly over the past two months they just ain't there. I heard one, just one. Wasn't like that the last time I was up north. There have been some satellite photos of them, a lot of diesel boats tied up alongside for some reason or another. In fact, their patrol activity up north is down across the board, with a lot of maintenance activity going on. The current guess is that they're changing their training cycle. This isn't the usual time of year for live-firing." McCafferty laughed. "Of course, it could be that they finally got tired of chippin' and paintin' those old 'cans, and decided to use 'em up—best thing to do with a 'can anyway."

"Bubblehead," Morris snorted.

"Give me a reason you'd have a bunch of diesel boats out of service all at once," Toland said. He was wishing that he'd passed on the second and third rounds during Happy Hour. Something important was flashing lights inside his head, and the alcohol was slowing his thinking down.

"Shit," McCafferty observed. "There isn't any."

"So what are they doing with the diesel boats?"

"I haven't seen the satellite photos, Bob, just heard about them. No special activity in the drydocks, though, so it can't be too major."

The light bulb finally went off in Toland's head. "How hard is it to change batteries in a sub?"

"It's a nasty, heavy job. I mean, you don't need special machinery or anything. We do it with Tiger Teams, and it takes something like three or four weeks. Ivan's subs are designed with larger battery capacities than ours, and also for easier battery replacement—they're supposed to go through their batteries faster than Western subs, and they compensate for it by making replacement easier, hard-patches on the hull, things like that. So for them it's probably an all-hands evolution. What exactly are you getting at, Bob?"

Toland related the story about the four Soviet colonels who had been shot, and why. "Then I hear this story about how the supply of batteries in Russia has dried up. No batteries for cars and trucks. The car batteries I can understand, but the trucks—hey, every truck in Russia is government-owned. They all have mobilization uses. Same sort of batteries, right?"

"Yeah, they all use lead-acid batteries. The factory burn down?" Commander Morris asked. "I know Ivan likes One Big Factory rather than a bunch of little ones."

"It's working three shifts."

McCafferty sat back, away from the table.

"So, what uses batteries?" Morris asked rhetorically.

"Submarines," McCafferty pronounced. "Tanks, armored vehicles, command cars, starter carts for planes, lots of stuff painted green, y'know? Bob, what you're saying—shit, what you're saying is that all of a sudden Ivan has decided to increase his readiness across the board. Question: Do you know what the hell you're talking about?"

"You can bet your ass on it, Danny. The bit on the four colonels crossed my desk, I eyeballed that report myself. It was received on one of our ferret satellites. Ivan doesn't know how sensitive those Hitchhiker birds are, and he still sends a lot of stuff in the clear on surface microwave nets. We listen in to voice and telex transmissions all the time—you guys can forget you heard that, okay?" Toland got nods from the others. "The thing about the batteries I picked up by accident, but I confirmed it with a guy I know in the Pentagon. Now we have your story about increased live-fire exercises, Dan. You just filled in a blank space. Now if we can confirm that those diesel boats really are down for battery replacement, we have the beginnings of a picture. Just how important are new batteries for a diesel boat?"

"Very important," the sub skipper said. "Depends a lot on quality control and maintenance, but new ones can give you up to double the range and power of old ones, and that's obviously an important tactical factor."

"Jesus, you know what this sounds like? Ivan's always ready to go to sea, and now it looks like he wants to be *real* ready," Morris observed. "But the papers all say that they're acting like born-again angels with this arms-control stuff. Something does not compute, gentlemen."

"I have to get this to someone in the chain of command. I could drop this on a desk at Fort Meade and it might never get anywhere," Toland said, remembering his section chief.

"You will," McCafferty said after a moment's pause. "I have an appointment tomorrow morning with COMSUBLANT. I think you're coming with me, Bob."

The last member of the foursome arrived ten minutes later. He was disappointed with the quality of the game. He'd thought his skipper was better than this.

Toland spent twenty minutes reviewing his data in front of Vice Admiral Richard Pipes, Commander, Submarine Force, U.S. Atlantic Fleet. Pipes was the first black submariner to make three-star rank, a man who had paid his dues with performance as he'd climbed up the ladder in what had traditionally been a whites-only profession, and he had the reputation of a tough, demanding boss. The Admiral listened without a word as he sipped coffee from a three-starred mug. He'd been annoyed to have McCafferty's patrol report supplanted by a speech from a reservist—but that attitude had lasted only three minutes. Now the lines around his mouth deepened.

"Son, you violated a few security restrictions to give me some of that."

"I know that, sir," Toland said.

"Took balls to do that, and it's nice to see in a young officer, what with all the ones who just want to cover their ass." Pipes rose. "I don't like what you just told me, son, not one little bit. We got Ivan playing Santa Claus with all this diplomatic horseshit, and at the same time he's dialing his submarine force in. Could be a coincidence. Then again, it might not be. How about you and me go over to talk with CINCLANT and his intelligence chief?"

Toland winced. *What have I got myself into?* "Sir, I'm down here for a training rotation, not to—"

"Looks to me like you got this intelligence crap down pretty pat, Commander. You believe what you just told me is true?"

Toland stiffened. "Yes, sir."

"Then I'm giving you a chance to prove it. You afraid to stick your neck out—or do you just offer opinions to relatives and friends?" the Admiral asked harshly.

Toland had heard that Pipes was a real hard-case. The reservist rose to his feet.

"Let's do it, Admiral."

Pipes picked up his phone and dialed in a three-digit number, his direct line to CINCLANT. "Bill? Dick. I got a boy in my office I think you oughta talk to. Remember what we discussed last Thursday? We may have confirmation." A brief pause. "Yeah, that's exactly what I'm saying. . . . Aye aye, sir, on the way." Pipes set the phone down. "McCafferty, thank you for bringing this man in with you. We'll go over your patrol report this afternoon. Be here at 1530. Toland, you come along with me."

An hour later, Lieutenant Commander Robert M. Toland, USNR-R, was informed that he had been placed on extended active duty by order of the Secretary of Defense. In fact it was by order of CINCLANT, but the forms would be correctly filled out in a week or so.

At lunch that day in "flag country" of Building One of the complex, CINCLANT called in all his type commanders—the three-star admirals who controlled the aircraft, surface ships, submarines, and replenishment ships. The conversation was subdued, and ceased entirely when the stewards came in to change the courses. They were all in their fifties, experienced, serious men who both made and implemented policy, preparing for something they hoped would never come. This hope continued, but by the time each had finished his second cup of coffee, it was decided that fleet training cycles would be increased, and a few surprise inspections would be made. CINCLANT made an appointment with the Chief of Naval Operations for the following morning, and his deputy intelligence chief boarded a commercial airliner for a quick trip to Pearl Harbor, to meet with his opposite number in the Pacific.

Toland was relieved of his post and transferred to Intentions, part of CINCLANT's personal intelligence advisory staff.

6. The Watchers

NORFOLK, VIRGINIA

Intentions was a small second-floor office normally occupied by four officers. Shoehorning Toland in there was difficult, mainly because all the classified material had to be covered up while the civilian movers got the desk in place. When they finally left, Bob found he had just about enough space to get into and out of his swivel chair. The office door had a cipher lock with five rocker switches concealed in a steel container. Located in the northwest corner of CINCLANT headquarters, the office's barred windows overlooked a highway and little else. The drab curtains were closed anyway. Inside, the walls might have been painted beige once, but the plaster had whitened from underneath to give the office the sort of pallor expected in a yellow-fever ward.

The senior officer was a Marine colonel named Chuck Lowe, who had watched the moving-in process with a silent resentment that Bob only understood when the man got to his feet.

"I may never make it to the head now," Lowe grumped, sticking his cast around the corner of his desk. They shook hands.

"What happened to the leg, Colonel?"

"Mountain Warfare School out in California, day after Christmas, skiing on my own Goddamned time. The docs say you should never break the tibia close to the bottom," Lowe explained with an ironic smile. "And you never get used to the itching. Should have this thing off in another three or four weeks. Then I have to get used to running again. You know, I spent three years trying to break my ass out of intel, then I finally get my Goddamned regiment, and *this* happens. Welcome aboard, Toland. Why don't you grab us both a cup of coffee?"

There was a pot atop the farthest filing cabinet. The other three officers, Lowe explained, were giving a briefing.

"I saw the writeup you gave CINCLANT. Interesting stuff. What do you think Ivan's up to?"

"It looks like he's increasing readiness across the board, Colonel—"

"In here, you can call me Chuck."

"Fine—I'm Bob."

"You do signal intelligence at NSA, right? You're one of the satellite specialists, I heard."

Toland nodded. "Ours and theirs, mostly ours. I see photos from time to time, but mostly I do signals work. That's how we twigged to the report on the four colonels. There has also been a fair amount of operational maneuvering done, more than usual for this time of year. Ivan's been a little freer with how his tankers drive around, too, less concern about running a battalion across a plowed field, for example."

"And you're supposed to have a look at anything that's unusual, no matter how dumb it seems, right? That gives you a pretty wide brief, doesn't it? We got something interesting along those lines from DIA. Have a look at these." Lowe pulled a pair of eight-by-ten photographs from a manila envelope and handed them to Toland. They seemed to show the same parcel of land, but from slightly different angles and different times of year. In the upper left corner was a pair of *isbas,* the crude huts of Russian peasant life. Toland looked up.

"Collective farm?"

"Yeah. Number 1196, a little one about two hundred klicks northwest of Moscow. Tell me what's different between the two."

Toland looked back at the photos. In one was a straight line of fenced gardens, perhaps an acre each. In the other he could see a new fence for four of the patches, and one patch whose fenced area had been roughly doubled.

"A colonel—army-type—I used to work with sent me these. Thought I'd find it amusing. I grew up on a corn farm in Iowa, you see."

"So Ivan's increasing the private patches for the farmers to work on their own, eh?"

"Looks that way."

"Hasn't been announced, has it? I haven't read anything about it." Toland didn't read the government's secret in-house publication, *National Intelligence Digest,* but the NSA cafeteria gossip usually covered harmless stuff like this. Intelligence types talked shop as much as any others.

Lowe shook his head slightly. "Nope, and that's a little odd. It's something they should announce. The papers would call that another sure sign of the 'liberalization trend' we've been seeing."

"Just this one farm, maybe?"

"As a matter of fact, they've seen the same thing at five other places. But we don't generally use our reconsats for this sort of thing. They got this on a slow news day, I suppose. The important stuff must have been covered by clouds." Toland nodded agreement. The reconnaissance satellites were used to evaluate Soviet grain crops, but that happened later in the year. The Russians knew it also, since it had been in the open press for over a decade, explaining why there was a team of agronomists in the U.S. Department of Agriculture with Special Intelligence–Compartmented security clearance.

"Kind of late in the season to do that, isn't it? I mean, will it do any good to give 'em this land this time of year?"

"I got these a week ago. I think they're a little older than that. This is about the time most of their farms start planting. It stays cold there quite a long time, remember, but the high latitudes make up for it with longer summer days. Assume that this is a nationwide move on their part. Evaluate that for me, Bob." The colonel's eyes narrowed briefly.

"Smart move on their part, obviously. It could solve a lot of their food supply problems, particularly for—truck-farm stuff, I guess, tomatoes, onions, that sort of thing."

"Maybe. You might also note that this sort of farming is manpower-intensive but not machinery-intensive. What about the demographic aspect of the move?"

Toland blinked. There was a tendency in the U.S. Navy to assume that since they made their living by charging into machine-gun fire, Marines were dumb. "Most of the *kokolzniki* are relatively old folks. The median age is in the late forties, early fifties. So most of the private plots are managed by the older people, while the mechanized work, like driving the combines and trucks—"

"Which pays a hell of a lot better."

"—is done by the younger workers. You're telling me that this way they can increase some food production without the younger men . . . of military service age."

"One way to look at it," Lowe said. "Politically it's dynamite. You can't take away things people already have. Back in the early sixties, a rumor— wasn't even true—got started to the effect that Khrushchev was going to reduce or eliminate the private plots those poor bastards get. There was hell to pay! I was in the language school at Monterey then, and I remember the Russian papers that came through the language school. They spent weeks denying the story. Those private plots are the most productive sector of their agricultural system. Less than two percent of their arable land, it produces about half of their fruit and potatoes, more than a third of their eggs, vegetables, and meat. Hell, it's the only part of the damned agricultural system that works. The bigshots over there have known for years that by doing this they could solve their food shortage problems, and *still* they haven't done it for political reasons. They couldn't run the risk of State sponsorship for a whole new generation of *kulaks*. Until now. But it appears they've done it without making a formal announcement. And it just so happens that they're increasing their military readiness at the same time. I never believe in coincidences, even when I'm a dumb line officer running across a beach."

Lowe's uniform blouse hung in the corner. Toland sipped at his coffee and surveyed its four rows of decorations. There were three repeat pips on his Vietnam service ribbon. And a Navy Cross. Dressed in the olive-green sweater affected by Marine officers, Lowe was not a big man, and his Midwest accent gave evidence of a relaxed, almost bored outlook on life. But his brown eyes said something else entirely. Colonel Lowe was thinking along Toland's lines already, and he was not the least happy about it.

"Chuck, if they are really preparing for some action—action on a large scale, they just can't mess with a few colonels. Something else will start showing up. They'll have to do some work at the bottom, too."

"Yeah, that's the next thing we have to look for. I sent a request into DIA yesterday. From now on, when *Red Star* comes out, the attaché in Moscow will send a photo-facsimile to us via satellite. If they start doing that, it'll sure as hell turn up in *Kraznaya Zvesda*. Bob, I think you've opened a very interesting can of worms, and you're not going to be alone examining it."

Toland finished his coffee. The Soviets had taken an entire class of fleet ballistic missile submarines out of service. They were conducting arms talks in Vienna. They were buying grain from America and Canada under surprisingly favorable terms, even allowing American hulls to handle 20 percent of the cargo. How did this jibe with the signs he had seen? Logically it didn't, except in one specific case—and that wasn't possible. Was it?

SHPOLA, THE UKRAINE

The crashing sound of the 125mm tank gun was enough to strip the hair off your head, Alekseyev thought, but after five hours of running this exercise, it came through his ear protectors as a dull ringing sound. This morning the ground had been covered with grass and dotted with new saplings, but now it was a uniform wasteland of mud, marked only with the tread marks of T-80 main battle tanks and BMP armored infantry fighting vehicles. Three times the regiment had run this exercise, simulating a frontal assault of tanks and mounted infantry against an enemy of equal strength. Ninety mobile guns had supplied fire support, along with a battery of rocket launchers. Three times.

Alekseyev turned, removing his helmet and earmuffs to look at the regimental commander. "A Guards regiment, eh, Comrade Colonel? Elite soldiers of the Red Army? These tit-sucking children couldn't guard a Turkish whorehouse, *much less do anything worthwhile inside of it!* And what have *you* been doing for the past four years commanding this rolling circus, Comrade Colonel? You have learned to kill your whole command *three times!* Your artillery observers are not located properly. Your tanks and infantry carriers still can't coordinate their movements, and your tank gunners can't find targets three meters high! If that had been a NATO force holding that ridge, you and your command would be *dead!*" Alekseyev examined the colonel's face. His demeanor was changing from red-fear to white-anger. Good. "The loss of these people is no great penalty for the State, but that is valuable equipment, burning valuable fuel, shooting valuable ordnance, *and taking up my valuable time!* Comrade Colonel, I must leave you now. First I will throw up. Then I will fly to my command post. I will be back. When I come back, we will run this exercise again. Your men will perform properly, Comrade Colonel, or you will spend the rest of your miserable life counting trees!"

Alekseyev stomped off, not even acknowledging the colonel's salute. His adjutant, a full colonel of tank troops, held open the door and got in behind his boss.

"Shaping up rather well, eh?" Alekseyev asked.

"Not well enough, but there has been progress," the colonel allowed. "They have only another six weeks before they have to start moving west."

It was the wrong thing to say. Alekseyev had spent two weeks chivvying this division toward combat readiness, only to learn the day before that it had been allocated to Germany instead of toward his own as yet incomplete plan to descend into Iraq and Iran. Already four divisions—*all of his elite Guards tank units*—had been taken away, and each change in CINC-Southwest's order of battle forced him to restructure his own plan for the Gulf. An endless circle. He was being forced to select less-ready units, forcing Alekseyev to devote more time to unit training and less time to the plan that had to be completed in another two weeks.

"Those men are going to have a very busy six weeks. What about the commander?" the colonel asked.

Alekseyev shrugged. "He's been in this job too long. Forty-five is too old for this kind of command, and he reads his fucking parade manuals too much instead of going out in the field. But a good man. Too good to be sent counting trees." Alekseyev chuckled heavily. It was a Russian saying that dated back to the czars. People exiled to Siberia were said to have nothing to do but count trees. Another of the things Lenin had changed. Now people in the Gulag had plenty to do. "The last two times they did well enough to succeed, I think. This regiment will be ready, along with the whole division."

USS *PHARRIS*

"Bridge, sonar: we have a contact bearing zero-nine-four!" announced a voice on the bulkhead-mounted speaker. Commander Morris turned in his elevated swivel chair to watch his officer of the deck respond.

The OOD trained his binoculars to the direction of the contact. There was nothing there: "Bearing is clear."

Morris got up from his chair. "Set Condition 1-AS."

"Aye aye. Battle Stations," the OOD acknowledged the order. The boatswain's-mate-of-the-watch walked to the announcing system, and blew a three-note whistle on his bosun's pipe into the speaker. "General Quarters, General Quarters, all hands man your battle stations for antisubmarine warfare." The alarm gong came next, and a quiet forenoon watch ended.

Morris went aft, down the ladder to the Combat Information Center, or CIC. His executive officer would take the conn at the bridge, allowing the captain to control the ship's weapons and sensors from her tactical nerve center. All over the ship, men were running to stations. Watertight doors and hatches were dropped into place and dogged down to give the ship full watertight integrity. Damage-control arties donned emergency equipment. It took just over four minutes. Getting better, Morris noted as the "manned and ready" calls were relayed to him by the CIC talker. Since leaving Norfolk four days before, *Pharris* was averaging three GQ calls per day, as ordered by Commander, Naval Surface Forces, Atlantic. No one had confirmed it, but Morris figured that his friend's information had kicked over an anthill. His training routines had been doubled, and the orders for the increase of activity were classified as high as anything he had ever seen. More remarkably, the increased training tempos would interfere with maintenance scheduling, something not lightly set aside.

"All stations report manned and ready!" the talker finally announced. "Condition Zebra set throughout the ship."

"Very well," the tactical action officer acknowledged.

"Report, mister," Morris ordered.

"Sir, the navigation and air-search radars are in stand-by and the sonar is in passive mode," replied the TAO. "Contact looks like a snorkeling submarine. Came in clear all at once. We've got a target-motion-analysis track going. His bearing is changing fore-to-aft, and pretty fast, too. A little soon to be sure, but it's shaping up like he's on a reciprocal heading, probably no more than ten miles out."

"Contact report off to Norfolk yet?"

"Waiting for your say-so."

"Very well. Let's see how well we can run a hold-down exercise, mister."

Within fifteen minutes, *Pharris*'s helicopter was dropping sonobuoys on the submarine, and the frigate was lashing it with her powerful active sonar. They wouldn't stop until the Soviet submarine admitted defeat by coming back to schnorkeling depth—or until he evaded the frigate, which would put a large black mark in Morris's copybook. The objective of this nonlethal exercise was nasty enough: to break the submarine captain's confidence in his vessel, his crew, and himself.

USS *CHICAGO*

They were a thousand miles offshore, heading northeast at twenty-five knots. The crew was decidedly unhappy, though they'd all been through this before. What should have been a three-week layover at Norfolk had been cut short at eight days, a bitter pill after a long first cruise. Trips and vacations had been interrupted, and some minor maintenance work supposed to have been done by shoreside technicians was now being done round the clock by her own crew. McCafferty had announced his sealed orders to the crew two hours after diving: conduct two weeks of intensive tracking and torpedo drills, then proceed to the Barents Sea for further intelligence gathering. It was important, he told them. They'd heard that one before, too.

7. Initial Observations

NORFOLK, VIRGINIA

Toland hoped his uniform was properly arranged. It was 0630 on a Wednesday morning, and he'd been up since four rehearsing his presentation, and cursing CINCLANT for an early-riser who probably wanted to get in a round of golf that afternoon. He would spend the afternoon as he had for several weeks, sifting through endless intel documents and copies of Soviet publications in the Intentions cubbyhole half a building away.

The Flag Officers Briefing Room seemed a different world from the rest of the tawdry building, but that was hardly a surprise. Admirals liked their comforts. Bob made a quick trip to the nearby head to eliminate a distraction caused by too much wake-up coffee. By the time he came back, the flag officers were filing in. They exchanged greetings, but there were no jokes, none of the banter one would expect this early in the morning. The officers selected their leather seats by order of rank. Those few who smoked had ashtrays. Each had a note pad. Stewards brought in several pots of coffee, cream, and sugar on silver trays, then withdrew. The cups were already in place. Each officer poured himself a cup as part of the morning ritual. CINCLANT nodded to Toland.

"Good morning, gentlemen. Approximately a month ago, four colonels in the Soviet Army, all regimental commanders in mechanized divisions, were court-martialed and executed for falsifying data on their unit training and readiness reports," Toland began, explaining the significance of this.

"Earlier this week *Kraznaya Zvesda,* 'Red Star,' the daily newspaper of the entire Soviet military, publicized the execution of a number of privates in the Soviet Army. All but two were in the final six months of their enlistment period, and all were charged with disobeying the orders of their sergeants. Why is this significant?

"The Russian Army has long been known for its tough discipline, but as with many aspects of the Soviet Union, not everything is as it seems. A sergeant in the Soviet Army is not a professional soldier as is the case in most armies. He is a conscript, just like the privates, selected early in his enlistment term for special training due to his intelligence, political reliability, or perceived leadership ability. He is sent to a tough six-month course to make him an instant sergeant, then returned to his operational unit. In fact he has about as little practical experience as his subordinates, and his superior knowledge of tactics and weapons-use is a matter of increments rather than the more dramatic differences between sergeants and new recruits in Western forces.

"Because of this, the real pecking order in Soviet ground formations does not necessarily derive from rank, but from time in service. The Soviets induct their troops twice a year, in December and June. With the usual two-year term of service, we see that there are four 'classes' in any formation: the lowest class is in its first six-month period and the highest is in its fourth. The young men who have the actual status in a Soviet rifle company are those in their final six-month term. They typically demand and get the best—or at least the most—food, uniforms, and work details. And they typically obviate the authority of the company NCOs. In fact, orders come directly from the officers, not the platoon and squad sergeants, and are usually carried out with little regard to what we consider conventional military discipline at the sub-officer level. As you can imagine, this places an enormous strain on the junior officers, and in many ways forces the officers to live with some things that they clearly do not and cannot like."

"You're saying that their military formations operate under the principle of organized anarchy," observed the commander of Strike Fleet Atlantic. "Their Navy sure as hell doesn't."

"That is true, sir. As we know, their seamen are in for three years

instead of two, and their situation, while similar, has many differences from that of the Soviet Army. And it would seem that this situation is ending in the Soviet Army as well, that sub-unit discipline is being quickly and vigorously reestablished."

"Just how many privates got themselves popped?" asked the general commanding 2nd Marine Division.

"Eleven, sir, listed by name and unit. That information is in your handout. Most were in their 'fourth class,' meaning the last six months of their enlistment period."

"Did the article you read make general conclusions?" CINCLANT asked.

"No, Admiral. There is an unwritten rule in Soviet publications, both military and civilian, that you can criticize, but not generalize. What that means is that individual screwups can be identified and castigated at length, but for political reasons it is unacceptable to make general criticisms applying to a whole institution. You see, a critique that pointed to an all-pervasive condition would *ipso facto* critique Soviet society as a whole, and thereby the Communist Party, which oversees every aspect of Soviet life. It is a thin, but to them a philosophically important, distinction. In fact, when individual malefactors are named, the system as a whole *is* being criticized, but in a politically acceptable way. This article is a signal to every officer, NCO, and private soldier in the Soviet military: the times, they are a changin'. The question we've been asking over in Intentions is, Why?

"It would appear that this is not an isolated case of changing times." Toland flipped on an overhead projector and set a view graph in place. "Within the Soviet Navy, surface-to-surface missile live-fires are up seventy percent from last year, not quite an all-time high, but as you can see from this graph, pretty close to it. Submarine deployments, mainly those for diesel subs, are down, and intelligence reports tell us that an unusually high number of submarines are in the yards for what appears to be routine but unscheduled maintenance. We have reason to believe that this situation is connected with a nationwide shortage of lead-acid batteries. It appears likely that all Soviet submarines are undergoing battery replacement, and that regular battery production is being redirected to militarily important segments of the Soviet economy.

"We have also noted higher levels of activity by Soviet naval surface forces, naval aviation units and other long-range aircraft formations, again with increased weapons exercises. Finally, there has been an increase in the time-away-from-port days of Soviet surface combatants. Although this number represents a small increase, operational patterns are different from what we've become accustomed to. Instead of sailing from one point to another and just dropping the hook, their surface combatants appear to be running more realistic exercises. They've done this before, but never without announcing it.

"So what we are seeing in the Soviet Navy is an extensive stand-down accompanied by increasing tempos in the actual exercises that are being run. Matched with what we're seeing in the Soviet Army and Air Force, it appears that their military readiness is being increased across the board. At the same time that they are proposing reductions in strategic nuclear weapons, their conventional forces are rapidly improving their ability to engage in combat operations. We in Intentions regard this combination of factors as potentially dangerous."

"Looks kind of hazy to me," an admiral said around his pipe. "How are we supposed to persuade somebody that this means anything?"

"A good question, sir. Any of these indicators taken in isolation would appear entirely logical in and of itself. What concerns us is why they are all happening at once. The problem of manpower utilization in the Soviet military has been around for generations. The problem of training norms, and integrity in their officer corps, is not exactly new either. What caught my interest was the battery thing. We are seeing the beginnings of what could become a major disruption within the Soviet economy. The Russians plan everything centrally in their economy, and on a political basis as well. The main factory that makes batteries is operating three shifts instead of the usual two, so production is up, but supply in the civilian economy is down. In any case, Admiral, you're correct. Individually, these things mean nothing at all. It's only when taken in combination that we see anything to be concerned about."

"But you're concerned," CINCLANT said.

"Yes, sir."

"Me too, son. What else are you doing about it?"

"We have an inquiry into SACEUR to notify us of anything they think is unusual in the current activities of the Group of Soviet Forces in Germany. The Norwegians have increased their surveillance in the Barents Sea. We're starting to get more access to satellite photography of ports and fleet bases. DIA has been informed of our data, and is running its own investigation. More bits and pieces are beginning to show up."

"What about CIA?"

"DIA is handling that for us through their headquarters at Arlington Hall."

"When do their spring maneuvers begin?" CINCLANT asked.

"Sir, the annual Warsaw Pact spring exercise—they're calling it Progress this year—is scheduled to begin in three weeks. There are indications that in keeping with the spirit of détente, the Soviets will invite NATO military representatives to keep an eye on things, and Western news crews as well—"

"I'll tell you what's scary about this," Commander, Naval Surface Forces, Atlantic, grunted. "All of a sudden they've started doing what we've always asked them to do."

"Try selling that to the papers," Commander, Naval Air Forces, Atlantic, suggested.

"Recommendations?" CINCLANT asked his operations officer.

"We're already running a pretty active training schedule ourselves. I don't suppose it would hurt to beef that up. Toland, you said that what tipped you to this situation was this battery thing in the civilian economy. Are you looking for other economic disruptions?"

"Yes, sir, we are. That's DIA's brief, and my contact in Arlington Hall is also asking CIA to run some additional checks. If I might amplify on this point, gentlemen, the Soviet economy is centrally managed, as I said earlier. Those industrial plans they have are fairly rigid. They don't deviate from them lightly, since those deviations tend to have a ripple effect throughout the economy as a whole. 'Disruption' may be too strong a word at present—"

"You just have a nasty suspicion," CINCLANT said. "Fine, Toland, that's what we pay you for. Good brief."

Bob took his cue and left. The admirals stayed put to talk things over.

It was a relief to leave. Much as he liked the attention, being examined by senior officials like a tissue culture on a petrie dish could make you old rather quickly. He walked through a covered walkway back to his building, and watched the late arrivals wander about looking for parking places. The grass was greening up. A civilian crew was mowing while another was fertilizing. The shrubbery was already beginning to grow, and he hoped they'd let the bushes expand a bit before they trimmed them back again. Norfolk could be pleasant in the spring, he knew, with the fragrance of azaleas on the salt-laden air. He wondered how pleasant it would be in summer.

"How'd it go?" Chuck asked.

Toland stripped off his jacket and allowed his knees to sag theatrically in front of the Marine. "Pretty well. Nobody snapped my head off."

"Didn't want to worry you before, but there's people in there been known to do that. They say CINCLANT likes nothing better for breakfast than fried commander garnished with diced lieutenant."

"Big surprise. He's an admiral, isn't he? I've done briefs before, Chuck." All Marines thought all sailors were wimps, Toland reminded himself. No sense giving Chuck more encouragement for that view.

"Any conclusions?"

"CINCLANT ops talked about increasing training schedules. I got excused right after that."

"Good. We ought to have a packet of satellite shots later today. There are some questions coming in from Langley and Arlington. Nothing firm yet, but I think they might be stumbling onto some odd data. If it turns out you're right, Bob—well, you know how it works."

"Sure. Somebody closer to D.C. will make The Discovery. Shit, I don't care about that, Chuck, I want to be *wrong!* I want this whole friggin' thing to blow over, then I can go home and play in my garden."

"Well, maybe I got some good news for you. We got our TV tied into a new satellite receiver. I talked the communications guys into letting us tap into Russian television to catch their evening news. We won't learn anything hard, but it's a good way of catching moods. Just tried it out before you got here, and found out Ivan's running a film festival for all of Sergey Eisenstein's classics. Tonight, *The Battleship Potemkin,* followed by all the others, and ending on May 30 with *Alexander Nevsky.*"

"Oh? I have *Nevsky* on tape."

"Yeah, well, they took the original negatives, flew them to EMI in London to make digitalized masters, and rerecorded the original Prokofiev score on a Dolby format. We'll be making tapes. Your machine VHS or Beta?"

"VHS." Toland laughed. "Maybe this job has a few bennies after all. So, what new stuff do we have?"

Lowe handed him a six-inch file of documents. Time to get back to work. Toland settled in his chair and began sorting through the papers.

KIEV, THE UKRAINE

"Things are looking better, Comrade," Alekseyev reported. "Discipline in the officer corps has improved immeasurably. The exercise with 261st Guards went very well this morning."

"And 173rd Guards?" CINC-Southwest asked.

"They too need further work, but they should be ready in time," Alekseyev said confidently. "The officers are acting like officers. Now we need to get the privates to act like soldiers. We'll see when Progress begins. We must have our officers turn away from the usual set-piece choreography and seek realistic engagement scenarios. We can use Progress to identify leaders who cannot adapt to a real combat environment and replace them with younger men who can." He sat down opposite his commander's desk. Alekseyev calculated that he was exactly one month behind in his sleep.

"You look weary, Pasha," CINC-Southwest observed.

"No, Comrade General, I haven't had the time." Alekseyev chuckled. "But if I make one more helicopter trip I think I shall sprout wings."

"Pasha, I want you to go home and not return for twenty-four hours."

"I—"

"If you were a horse," the General observed, "you would have broken down by now. This is an order from your commander-in-chief: twenty-four hours of rest. I would prefer that you spend it all sleeping, but that is your affair. Think, Pavel Leonidovich. Were we now engaged in combat operations, you would be better rested—regulations require it, a harsh lesson from our last war with the Germans. I need your talents unhindered—and if you drive yourself too hard now, you won't be worth a damn when I really need you! I will see you at 1600 tomorrow to go over our plan for the Persian Gulf. You will be clear of eye and straight of back."

Alekseyev stood. His boss was a gruff old bear, so much like his own father had been. And a soldier's soldier. "Let the record show that I obey all orders from my commander-in-chief." Both men laughed. Both needed it.

Alekseyev left the office and walked downstairs to his official car. When it arrived at the apartment block a few kilometers away, the driver had to awaken his general.

USS *CHICAGO*

"Close-approach procedures," McCafferty ordered.

McCafferty had been tracking a surface ship for two hours, ever since his sonarmen had detected her at a range of forty-four miles. The approach was being made on sonar only, and under the captain's orders, sonar had not told the fire-control party what they were tracking. For the time being, every surface contact was being treated as a hostile warship.

"Range three-five hundred yards," the executive officer reported. "Bearing one-four-two, speed eighteen knots, course two-six-one."

"Up scope!" McCafferty ordered. The attack periscope slid up from its well on the starboard side of the pedestal. A quartermaster's mate got behind the instrument, dropped the handles in place, and trained it to the proper bearing. The captain sighted the crosshairs on the target's bow.

"Bearing—*mark!*"

The quartermaster squeezed the button on the "pickle," transmitting the bearing to the MK-117 fire-control computer.

"Angle on the bow, starboard twenty."

The fire-control technician punched the data into the computer. The microchips rapidly computed distances and angles.

"Solution set. Ready for tubes three and four!"

"Okay." McCafferty stepped back from the periscope and looked over at the exec. "You want to see what we killed?"

"Damn!" The executive officer laughed and lowered the periscope. "Move over, Otto Kretchmer!"

McCafferty picked up the microphone, which went to speakers throughout the submarine. "This is the captain speaking. We just completed the tracking exercise. For anyone who's interested, the ship we just 'killed' is the *Universe Ireland,* three hundred forty thousand tons' worth of ultra-large crude-carrier. That is all." He put the mike back in its cradle.

"XO, critique?"

"It was too easy, skipper," the executive officer said. "His speed and course were constant. We might have shaved four or five minutes on the target-motion analysis right after we acquired him, but we were looking for a zigzag instead of a constant course. For my money, it's better to proceed like that on a slow target. I'd say we have things going pretty well."

McCafferty nodded agreement. A high-speed target like a destroyer might well head directly for them. The slow ones would probably be altering course constantly under wartime conditions. "We're getting there." The captain looked over to his fire-control party. "That was well done. Let's keep it that way." The next time, McCafferty thought, he'd arrange for sonar not to report a target until it got really close. Then he'd see how fast his men could handle a snapshot engagement. Until then he decided on a strenuous series of computer-simulated engagement drills.

NORFOLK, VIRGINIA

"Those are batteries. Okay, it's confirmed." Lowe handed over the satellite photographs. A number of trucks were visible, and though most had their loadbeds covered by canvas, the loadbeds of three were exposed to the high-flying satellite. What he saw were the bathtub-shapes of oversized battery cells, and gangs of seamen manhandling them across a pier.

"How old are these shots?" Toland asked.

"Eighteen hours."

"Would have been useful this morning," the younger man grumped. "Looks like three Tangos nested together. These are ten-ton trucks. I count nine of them. I checked around, each individual battery cell weighs two hundred eighteen kilograms empty—"

"Ouch. How many to fill up a sub?"

"A lot!" Toland grinned. "We don't know that, exactly. I found four different estimates, with a thirty-percent spread. It probably differs from ship to ship anyway. The more you build of a design, the more you're tempted to fool around with it. That's what we do." Toland looked up. "We need more access to these."

"Already taken care of. From here on we're on the distribution list for all shots of naval sites. What do you think of the activity for the surface ships?"

Toland shrugged. The photographs showed perhaps a dozen surface combatants, ranging from cruisers to corvettes. The decks of all were littered with cables and crates; a large number of men was visible. "You can't tell much from this. No cranes, so nothing massive was being onloaded, but cranes can move, too. That's the problem with ships. Everything you need to know about is under cover. All we can tell from these photos is that they're tied alongside. Anything else is pure supposition. Even with the subs, we're inferring that they're loading batteries aboard."

"Come on, Bob," Lowe snorted.

"Think about it, Chuck," Toland replied. "They *know* what our satellites are for, right? They know what their orbital paths are, and they know when they will be at any given point in space. If they really want to fake us out, how hard is it? If *your* mission was to fake out satellites, and you knew when they came, you think you might play games with the other guy's head? We depend too much on these things. They're useful as hell, sure, but they have their limitations. It'd be nice to get some human intelligence on this."

POLYARNYY, R.S.F.S.R.

"There's just something weird about watching a guy pour cement into a ship," Flynn observed on the ride back to Murmansk. No one had ever told him about ballast.

"Ah, but it can be a beautiful thing!" exclaimed their escort, a junior captain in the Soviet Navy. "Now if only your navies can do the same!"

The small press group that had been allowed to stand on a pier and watch the neutralization of the first two Yankee-class fleet ballistic missile submarines was being carefully managed, Flynn and Calloway noted. They were being driven around in groups of two and three, each group with a naval officer and a driver. Hardly unexpected, of course. Both men were amazed that they were being allowed onto so sensitive a base at all.

"A pity that your president did not allow a team of American officers to observe this," the escort went on.

"Yeah, I have to agree with you there, Captain," Flynn nodded. It would have made a much better story. As it was, a Swede and an Indian officer, neither a submariner, had gotten a closer look at what the reporters called the "cement ceremony," and reported somberly afterward that, yes, cement had been poured into each missile launch tube on the two submarines. Flynn had timed the length of each pour, and would do some checking when he got back. What was the volume of a missile tube? How much cement to fill it? How long to pour the cement? "Even so, Captain, you must agree that the American response to your country's negotiating position has been extremely positive."

Through all this, William Calloway kept his peace and stared out the car's window. He'd covered the Falkland Islands War for his wire service, and spent a lot of time with the Royal Navy, both afloat and in naval shipyards watching preparations for sending the Queen's fleet south. They were now passing by the piers and work areas for a number of surface warships. Something was wrong here, but he couldn't quite pin it down. What Flynn did not know was that his colleague often worked informally for the British Secret Intelligence Service. Never in a sensitive capacity— the man was a correspondent, not a spy—but like most reporters he was a shrewd, observant man, careful to note things that editors would never allow to clutter up a story. He didn't even know who the station chief in Moscow was, but he could report on this to a friend in Her Majesty's embassy. The data would find its way to the right person.

"So what does our English friend think of Soviet shipyards?" the captain inquired with a broad smile.

"Far more modern than ours," Calloway replied. "And I gather you don't have dockyard unions, Captain?"

The officer laughed. "We have no need for unions in the Soviet Union. Here the workers already own everything." That was the standard Party line, both reporters noted. Of course.

"Are you a submarine officer?" the Englishman inquired.

"No!" the captain exclaimed. A hearty laugh. *Russians are big on laughs when they want to be,* Flynn thought. "I come from the steppes. I like blue sky and broad horizons. I have great respect for my comrades on submarines, but I have no wish to join them."

"My feelings exactly, Captain," Calloway agreed. "We elderly Brits like our parks and gardens. What sort of sailor are you?"

"I have shore assignment now, but my last ship was *Leonid Brezhnev,* icebreaker. We do some survey work, and also make a way for merchant ships along the Arctic Coast to the Pacific."

"That must be a demanding job," Calloway said. "And a dangerous one." *Keep talking, old boy . . .*

"It demands caution, yes, but we Russians are accustomed to cold and ice. It is a proud task to aid the economic growth of your country."

"I could never be a sailor," Calloway went on. He saw a curious look in Flynn's eyes: *The hell you couldn't . . .* "Too much work, even when you're in port. Like now. Are your shipyards always this busy?"

"Ah, this is not busy," the captain said without much thought.

The man from Reuters nodded. The ships were cluttered, but there was not that much obvious activity. Not so many people moving about. Many cranes were still. Trucks were parked. But the surface warships and auxiliaries were cluttered as if . . . He checked his watch. Three-thirty in the afternoon. The workday was hardly over. "A great day for East-West détente," he said to cover his feelings. "A great story for Pat and me to tell our readers."

"This is good." The captain smiled again. "It is time we had real peace."

The correspondents were back in Moscow four hours later, after the usual uncomfortable ride on an Aeroflot jet with its Torquemada seats. The two reporters walked to Flynn's car—Calloway's was still *hors de combat* with mechanical problems. He grumbled at having gotten a Soviet car instead of bringing his Morris over with him. Bloody impossible to get parts.

"A good story today, Patrick?"

"You bet. But I wish we'd been able to snap a picture or two." They were promised Sovfoto shots of the "cement ceremony."

"What did you think of the shipyard?"

"Big enough. I spent a day at Norfolk once. They all look alike to me."

Calloway nodded thoughtfully. Shipyards do look alike, he thought, but why did Polyarnyy seem strange? His suspicious reporter's mind? The constant question: What is he/she/it hiding? But the Soviets had never allowed him on a naval base, and this was his third tour in Moscow. He'd been to Murmansk before. Once he'd spoken with the Mayor and asked how the naval personnel affected his administration of the city. There were always uniforms visible on the street. The Mayor had tried to evade the question, and finally said, "There are no Navy in Murmansk." A typical Russian answer to an awkward question—but now they'd let a dozen Western reporters into one of their most sensitive bases. QED, they were not hiding anything. Or were they? After he filed his story, Calloway decided, he'd have a brandy with his friend at the embassy. Besides, there was a party celebrating something or other.

He arrived at the embassy, on Morisa Toreza Embankment across the river from the Kremlin walls, just after nine o'clock that night. It turned into four brandies. By the fourth, the correspondent was going over a map of the naval base and using his trained memory to indicate just what activity he'd seen where. An hour later, the data was encrypted and cabled to London.

8. Further Observations

GRASSAU, GERMAN DEMOCRATIC REPUBLIC

The TV news crew was having a great time. It had been years since they'd been allowed to film a Soviet military unit in action, and the entertainment value of the mistakes they saw gave plenty of spice for a piece on the NBC Nightly News. As they watched, a tank battalion was stalled at a crossroads on Highway 101, fifty kilometers south of Berlin. They'd taken a wrong turn somewhere, and the battalion commander was screaming at his subordinates. After two minutes of that, a captain stepped forward and made a few gestures at the map. A major was banished from the scene as the younger man apparently solved the problem. The camera followed the dejected major into a staff car, which drove north along the main road. Five minutes later, the battalion was mounted and rolling. The news crew took its time reloading its equipment into their carryall, and the chief reporter took the time to walk over to a French officer who had also observed the procedure.

The Frenchman was a member of the Joint Military Liaison Group, a convenient leftover of the Second World War which enabled both sides to spy on each other. A lean, poker-faced man, he wore paratrooper's wings and smoked Gauloises. He was an intelligence officer, of course.

"What do you make of this, Major?" the NBC reporter asked.

"They made a mistake four kilometers back. They should have turned left, but didn't." A Gallic shrug.

"Not very impressive performance for the Russians, is it?" The reporter laughed. The Frenchman was more thoughtful.

"Did you notice that they had a German officer with them?"

The reporter had noticed the different uniform, but not realized its significance. "Oh, is that what he was? Why didn't they ask him for help?"

"Yes," the French major answered. He didn't say that this was the fourth time he had seen a Soviet officer refrain from asking assistance from his East German guide . . . and all in the last two days. To have Soviet units get lost was an old story. The Russians used a different alphabet in addition to the different language. That made it easy to make navigational errors, and the Soviets always had DDR officers along to help them find their way around. Until now. He flicked his cigarette onto the road. "What else did you notice, Monsieur?"

"The colonel was pretty mad at that major. Then a captain—I think— showed him the mistake, I guess, and how to correct it."

"How long?"

"Less than five minutes after they stopped."

"Very good." The Frenchman smiled. The major was heading back to Berlin, and that battalion had a new operations officer now. The smile disappeared.

"Looks pretty dumb to get lost like that, doesn't it?"

The Frenchman got back into his car to follow the Russians. "Have you ever gotten lost in a foreign country, Monsieur?"

"Yes, who hasn't?"

"But they found their mistake quickly, no?" The major waved to his driver to pull off. And all by themselves this time, he thought. *Intéressant . . .*

The TV reporter shrugged and walked back to his own vehicle. He followed the last tank in line, annoyed that they were moving at only thirty kilometers per hour. The tanks moved northwest at that speed until they reached Highway 187, where miraculously they joined up with another Soviet unit and, dropping back to their normal speed of twenty kilometers per hour, resumed their progress west toward the exercise area.

NORFOLK, VIRGINIA

It was impressive. As they watched the Moscow television news program, a whole regiment of tanks advanced across a flat landscape. Their objective turned to a horizontal fountain of dirt as an artillery barrage pounded the simulated enemy positions. Fighter-bombers streaked across the sky and helicopters performed their own death-dance. The voice-over commentary proclaimed the readiness of the Soviet Army to meet any foreign threat. It certainly looked that way.

The next five-minute segment concerned the Vienna arms talks. There was the usual complaint about how the United States was fighting over certain aspects of the clearly generous original Soviet proposal, but the speaker went on to say that real progress was being made despite American intransigence, and that a comprehensive agreement was possible by the end of summer. Toland was puzzled by the nature of the Soviet description of the negotiations. He'd never paid much attention to this sort of rhetoric before, and found the good-guy/bad-guy descriptions curious.

"Pretty normal stuff," Lowe responded to the question. "You'll know the deal is close to being struck when the beefs start disappearing. Then they talk about how enlightened our President is for a class enemy. They can get real euphoric around signing time. Really, this stuff is pretty mild. Think about it. What sort of language do they usually use about us?"

"The exercise look normal?"

"It's normal, all right. Ever think about how much fun it is to face a hundred tanks? You did notice that they all carry five-inch guns? Then think about the artillery support they get. Then think about the aircraft. The Russians are real believers in this combined-arms stuff. When they come at you, they come with the whole inventory. They have this set-piece stuff down cold."

"How do we counter it?"

"You take the initiative. You let the other guy get all set to fight his battle his way, son, you might as well bag it."

"Same story at sea."

"Yeah."

KIEV, THE UKRAINE

Alekseyev atypically poured himself a cup of tea at the corner table before approaching his commander's desk. When he walked over, his grin was a meter wide.

"Comrade General, Progress goes well!"

"So I can see, Pavel Leonidovich."

"I would never have believed it. The improvement in our officer corps is extraordinary. The deadwood is being disposed of, and those men whom we've moved up to new posts are eager and capable."

"So, shooting those four colonels has worked?" CINC-Southwest noted sardonically. He'd run the first two days of the exercise from his command headquarters and yearned to get into the field where the real action was. But that was not a theater commander's job. Alekseyev was his best set of eyes for what was really happening.

"A hard choice, but a good one. The results speak for themselves." The edge came off the younger man's enthusiasm. His conscience still remembered that. The problem with hard decisions, he learned, was not making them, but learning to live with the consequences, however necessary. He set the thought aside yet again. "With two more weeks of intensive exercises, the Red Army will be ready. We can do it. We can defeat NATO."

"We don't have to fight NATO, Pasha."

"Then Allah help the Arabs!" Alekseyev said.

"Allah help us. West gets another of our tank divisions." The General held up a dispatch. "The one you were with today, in fact. I wonder how he has been doing?"

"My spies tell me, quite well."

"And you have joined the KGB, Pasha?"

"A classmate of mine is on CINC-West staff. They, too, have adopted a policy for eliminating incompetents. I have seen the benefits. A new man in a posting has much better incentive to do his job properly than one for whom it has become routine."

"Except at the top, of course."

"Commander-in-Chief West is one man I never expected to defend, but everything I've been told leads me to believe he's getting his forces ready in the same way as we."

"Things must indeed be improved if you are this magnanimous."

"They are, Comrade. Another tank division lost to Germany. Well, he needs it more than we. I tell you, we will sweep the Arabs aside like dirt on a smooth tile floor. In truth we always could. There are not so many of them, and if these Arabs are like the Libyans I saw three years ago—these have no mountains to hide in. This is not Afghanistan. Our mission is to conquer, not to pacify. This we can do. I estimate two weeks. The only problem I foresee is the destruction of the oil fields. They can use scorched earth as a defense just as we have, and that will be difficult for us to prevent, even with paratroops. Still and all, our objective is achievable. Our men will be ready."

9. A Final Look

NORFOLK, VIRGINIA

"There's something to be said for instant traditions, Chuck." This was their fourth Russian movie via satellite. Toland handed over the bowl of popcorn. "It'll be a pity to lose you back to the Corps."

"Bite your tongue! Sixteen-hundred hours Tuesday, Colonel Charles DeWinter Lowe goes back into the Marine business. I'll leave the paper-shuffling to you squids."

Toland laughed. "And you won't miss the evening movie?"

"Maybe a little." Half a mile away a satellite receiver was tracking a Soviet communications satellite. They'd been pirating signals off this satellite and two of her sisters for weeks now, to keep tabs on the Soviet TV news, and also to catch the evening movie. Both men admired the work of Sergey Eisenstein.

And *Alexander Nevsky* was his masterwork.

Toland popped open a can of Coke. "I wonder how Ivan would react to a John Ford Western? Somehow I get the feeling that Comrade Eisenstein might have been exposed to one or two."

"Yeah, the Duke would have fit in pretty good here. Or better yet, Errol Flynn. You heading home tonight?"

"Right after the movie. God, a four-day weekend off. Can I stand the strain?"

The titles showed a new frame, different from the one on his personal tape of the movie back home. The original soundtrack dialogue had been retained and cleaned up somewhat, but the music had been redone by the Moscow State Symphony and chorus. They did true justice to Prokofiev's evocative score.

The film began with a view of the Russian . . . steppes? Toland wondered. Or was that supposed to be the southern part of the country? Anyway, it showed rolling grassland littered with bones and weapons from an old battle against the Mongols. The Yellow Peril, still a Russian bugaboo. The Soviet Union had absorbed a lot of Mongols—but now the Chinese had nuclear weapons and the world's largest army.

"The print is terrific," Lowe observed.

"Hell of a lot better than my tape," Toland agreed. A pair of VHS machines was recording this, though the Navy wasn't supplying the tapes. Each officer had bought one himself. SACLANT's Inspector General had an evil reputation.

All this happened pretty close to the Baltic coast, Toland reminded himself. The introduction of the main character was made through a song as he was evidently out directing some men with a fishing net. A good socialist introduction, the officers agreed: the hero out doing manual labor. A brief verbal confrontation with the Mongols, then a musing about which danger to Russian integrity was greater, the German or the Mongol.

"Jesus, you know they *still* think that way?" Toland chuckled.

"The more things change . . ." Lowe popped open his own Coke.

"I kinda wonder about this guy, though. When he went back into the water after the net, he ran like a girl, what with his arms flying all over."

"You should try running in knee-deep water," the Marine growled.

And the scene shifted to the German Danger.

"A bunch of out-of-work knights, just like the crusades. Hell, just like Indian movies from the thirties. Chopping people up, throwing babies into the fire."

"You suppose they really did things like that?"

"Ever hear of a place called Auschwitz, Bob?" Lowe inquired. "You know, in the civilized twentieth century?"

"Those guys didn't bring a bishop with them."

"Try reading up on the crusaders' liberation of Jerusalem. Either they killed, or raped first and then killed, all for the Greater Glory of God, with bishops and cardinals cheering them on. Nice bunch. Yeah, it's probably true enough. Christ knows the Eastern Front in '41 – '45 saw a lot of it on both sides. Nasty campaign, that was. Want some more popcorn?"

Finally the people mobilized themselves, especially the peasants:

Vstavaitye, lyudi russkiye,
na slavny boi, na smyertny boi . . .

"Damn!" Toland sat forward. "They really punched that song up." The soundtrack was almost perfect, even accounting for the satellite transmission difficulties.

Arise, you Russian People,
in a just battle, in a fight to the death:
arise, you people free and brave,
defend our fair native land!

Toland counted more than twenty specific uses of the word "Russia" or "Russian."

"That's odd," he observed. "They're trying to get away from that. The Soviet Union is supposed to be all one happy family, not the New Russian Empire."

"I guess you'd call it a historical quirk," Lowe commented. "Stalin commissioned the film to alert his people to the Nazi threat. Ole Joe was a Georgian, but he turned out to be one hell of a Russian nationalist. Strange, but he was one strange dude."

The movie was clearly a production of the 1930s. The strident characters were right out of John Ford or Raoul Walsh: a stand-alone heroic figure in Prince Alexander Nevsky, two brave but buffoonish sidekicks, and the *de rigueur* love interest. The German enemies were arrogant and for the most part invisible behind unlikely helmets designed by Eisenstein himself. The invading Germans had already divided up Russia among themselves, one knight made "prince" of Pskov, where in a horrible example of pacification the invaders had slaughtered men, women, and children—the children were thrown into a bonfire—to show who was boss. The great battle scene took place on a frozen lake.

"What kinda lunatic is going to fight on a frozen lake when he's wearing a half ton of sheet steel?" Toland groaned. Lowe explained that it had really happened that way, more or less.

"I'm sure they played around with it some, like *They Died With Their Boots On*," the colonel observed. "But the battle really happened."

The battle was a truly epic scene. The German knights attacked with casual disregard for proper tactics, and the Russian peasants, ably led by

Alexander and his two sidekicks, encircled them with a Cannae-like envelopment maneuver. Then, of course, came single combat between Prince Alexander and the German chieftain. There was no doubt of the outcome. Their commander vanquished in single combat, the German ranks came apart, and when they tried to rally on the edge of the lake, the ice gave way, drowning nearly everyone.

"That's realistic enough," Lowe chuckled. "Think how many armies have been swallowed up by the Russian countryside!"

The remainder of the movie resolved the love interest (each buffoon got himself a pretty girl), and liberated Pskov. Curiously, while the prince hoisted a bunch of children into his saddle for the ride in, he never showed the slightest interest in female company—and ended with a sermon, Alexander standing alone and speaking about what happens to people who invaded Russia.

"Trying to make Nevsky look like Stalin, eh?"

"There is some of that," Lowe agreed. "The strong man, all alone, a fatherly benefactor—some benefactor! Anyway you cut it, this is just about the best propaganda movie ever made. The punch line is that when Russia and Germany signed their nonaggression pact a year later, Eisenstein was detailed to direct a stage production of Wagner's *The Valkyries*. Call it penance for offending the German sensibilities."

"Oof. You study these guys more than I do, Chuck."

Colonel Lowe pulled a cardboard box from under his desk and began to load up his personal effects. "Yeah, well if you have to face the possibility of fighting a man, you might as well learn all you can about him."

"You think we will?"

Lowe frowned briefly. "I saw enough of that in Nam, but that's what they pay us for, isn't it?"

Toland stood and stretched. He had a four-hour drive ahead of him. "Colonel, it has been a pleasure for this squid to work with you."

"It hasn't been half bad for this jarhead. Hey, when I get the family set up down in Lejeune, why don't you come on down sometime? There's some great fishing down there."

"Deal." They shook hands. "Good luck with your regiment, Chuck."

"Good luck here, Bob."

Toland walked out to his car. He'd already packed up, and drove quickly out Terminal Boulevard to Interstate 64. The worst part of the drive home was the traffic to the Hampton Roads tunnel, after which things settled down to the usual superhighway ratrace. All the way home, Toland's mind kept going over the scenes from Eisenstein's movie. The one that kept coming back was the most horrible of all, a German knight wearing a crusader's cross tearing a Pskov infant from his mother's breast and throwing him—her?—into a fire. Who could see that and not be enraged? No wonder the rabble-rousing song "Arise, you Russian People" had been a genuinely popular favorite for years. Some scenes cried out for bloody revenge, the theme for which was Prokofiev's fiery call to arms. Soon he found himself humming the song. *A real intelligence officer you are . . .* Toland smiled to himself, thinking just like the people you're supposed to study . . . *defend our fair native land . . . za nashu zyemlyu chestnuyu!*

"Excuse me, sir?" the toll collector asked.

Toland shook his head. Had he been singing aloud? He handed over the seventy-five cents with a sheepish grin. What would this lady think, an American naval officer singing in Russian?

MOSCOW, R.S.F.S.R.

It was just after midnight when the truck drove north across the Kemenny Bridge to Borovitskaya Square and turned right, toward the Kremlin. The driver stopped for the first group of Kremlin Guards. Their papers were fully in order, of course, and they were waved through. The truck pulled up to the second checkpoint by the Kremlin Palace, where their papers were also in order. From there it was five hundred meters to the service entrance of the Council of Ministers Building.

"What are you delivering this time of day, Comrades?" the Red Army captain asked.

"Cleaning supplies. Come, I will show you." The driver got out and walked slowly around the back of the truck. "Must be nice, working here at night when things are so peaceful."

"True enough," the captain agreed. He'd go off duty in another ninety minutes.

"Here." The driver pulled back the canvas cover. There were twelve cans of industrial-strength solvent and a crate of hardware parts.

"German supplies?" The captain was surprised. He'd been on Kremlin duty for only two weeks.

"*Da*. The Krauts make very efficient cleaning machinery, and the *vlasti* make use of it. This is carpet-cleaning fluid. This is for lavatory walls. This one here is for windows. The crate—ah, I will open it." The lid came off easily since the nails had already been loosened. "As you see, Comrade Captain, parts for some of the machines." He smirked. "Even German machines break."

"Open one of the cans," the captain ordered.

"Sure, but you won't like the smell. Which one do you want opened?" The driver picked up a small prybar.

"That one." The captain pointed to a can of bathroom cleaner.

The driver laughed. "The worst-smelling of all. Stand back, Comrade, we don't want to splash this slop on your clean uniform."

The captain was new enough on the job that he scrupulously did not step back. *Good,* the driver thought. He worked the prybar under the can's lid, twisted, and popped his free hand down on the end. The lid flew off, and the captain was splashed by some flying solvent.

"Shit!" It did smell bad.

"I *warned* you, Comrade Captain."

"What is this garbage?"

"It's used to clean mildew off bathroom tiles. It will come right out of the uniform, Comrade Captain. But be sure you have it dry-cleaned soon. An acid solution, you see, it could damage the wool."

The captain wanted to be mad, but the man had warned him, hadn't he? *Next time I'll know better,* he thought. "Very well, take it in."

"Thank you. I am sorry about the uniform. Don't forget to have it cleaned."

The captain waved to a private and walked off. The soldier unlocked the door. The driver and his assistant went inside to get a two-wheeled handtruck.

"I warned him," the driver said to the private.

"You certainly did, Comrade." The soldier was amused. He, too, was looking forward to going off duty, and it wasn't often that you saw an officer get caught.

The driver watched his assistant load the cans onto the handtruck, and followed him as he wheeled it into the building to the service elevator. Then both returned for the second load.

They took the elevator to the third floor, shut the power off, and moved their loads to a storage room directly below the large fourth-floor conference room.

"That was good with the captain," the assistant said. "Now let's get to work."

"Yes, Comrade Colonel," the driver answered at once. The four cans of carpet-cleaning fluid had false tops which the lieutenant removed and set aside. Next he took out the satchel charges. The colonel had memorized the blueprints of the building. The wall pillars were in the outside corners of the room. One charge went to each, fixed to the inboard side. The empty cans were placed next to the charges, hiding them. Next the lieutenant removed two of the false-ceiling panels, exposing the steel beams supporting the fourth floor slab. The remaining charges were attached there, and the ceiling panels replaced. The charges already had their detonators attached. The colonel took the electronic triggering device out of his pocket, he checked his watch, and waited for three minutes before pressing the button to activate the timers. The bombs would explode in exactly eight hours.

The colonel watched the lieutenant tidy up, then wheeled the handtruck back to the elevator. Two minutes later, they left the building. The captain was back.

"Comrade," he said to the driver. "You shouldn't let this old one do all the heavy work. Show some respect."

"You are kind, Comrade Captain." The colonel smiled crookedly and pulled a half-liter bottle of vodka from his pocket. "Drink?"

The captain's solicitous attitude ended abruptly. A worker drinking on duty—in the Kremlin! "Move along!"

"Good day, Comrade." The driver got into the truck and drove off. They had to pass through the same security checkpoints, but their papers were still in order.

After leaving the Kremlin, the truck turned north on Marksa Prospekt and followed it all the way to the KGB headquarters building at 2 Dzerzhinskiy Square.

CROFTON, MARYLAND

"Where are the kids?"

"Asleep." Martha Toland hugged her husband. She was wearing something filmy and attractive. "I had them out swimming all day, and they just couldn't stay awake." An impish smile. He remembered the first such smile, on Sunset Beach, Oahu, she with a surfboard and a skimpy swimsuit. She still loved the water. And the bikini still fit.

"Why do I sense a plan here?"

"Probably because you're a nasty, suspicious spook." Marty walked into the kitchen and came out with a bottle of Lancers Rosé and two chilled glasses. "Now why don't you take a nice hot shower and unwind a bit. When you're finished, we can relax."

It sounded awfully good. What followed was even better.

10. Remember, Remember

CROFTON, MARYLAND

Toland woke to hear his phone ringing in the dark. He was still dopey from the drive up from Norfolk and the wine. It took a ring or two for him to react properly. His first considered action was to check the display on the clock-radio—2:11. *Two in the fuckin' morning!* he thought, sure that the ringing was caused by a prank or a wrong number. He lifted the receiver.

"Hello," he said gruffly.

"Lieutenant Commander Toland, please."

Uh-oh. "Speaking."

"This is the CINCLANT intel watch officer," the disembodied voice said. "You are ordered to return to your duty station at once. Please acknowledge the order, Commander."

"Back to Norfolk right away. Understood." Wholly on instinct, Bob rotated himself in the bed to a sitting position, his bare feet on the floor.

"Very well, Commander." The phone clicked off.

"What is it, honey?" Marty asked.

"They need me back at Norfolk."

"When?"

"Now." That woke her up. Martha Toland bolted upright in the bed. The covers spilled off her chest, and the moonlight through the window gave her skin a pale, ethereal glow.

"But you just got here!"

"Don't I know it." Bob stood and walked awkwardly toward the bathroom. He had to shower and drink some coffee if he had any hope of reaching Norfolk alive. When he returned ten minutes later, lathering his face, he saw that his wife had clicked on the bedroom TV to Cable Network News.

"Bob, you better listen to this."

"This is Rich Suddler coming to you *live* from the Kremlin," said a reporter in a blue blazer. Behind him Toland could see the grim stone walls of the ancient citadel fortified by Ivan the Terrible—now being patrolled by armed soldiers in combat dress. Toland stopped what he was doing and walked toward the TV. Something very strange was going on. A full company of armed troops in the Kremlin could mean many things, all of them bad. "There has been an explosion in the Council of Ministers building here in Moscow. At approximately nine-thirty this morning, Moscow Time, while I was taping a report not half a mile away, we were surprised to hear a sharp sound coming from the new glass-and-steel structure, and—"

"Rich, this is Dionna McGee at the anchor desk." The image of Suddler and the Kremlin retreated to a corner of the screen as the director inserted the attractive black anchorperson who ran the night desk for CNN. "I presume that you had some Soviet security personnel with you at the time. How did they react?"

"Well, Dionna, we can show you that if you can hold a minute for my technicians to set up that tape, I—" He pressed the earphone tight into his ear. "Okay, coming up now, Dionna—"

The tape cut off the live picture, filling the entire screen. It was on a pause setting, with Suddler frozen in the middle of a gesture to something or other, probably the part of the wall where they buried important Communists, Toland thought. The tape began to roll.

Simultaneously, Suddler flinched and spun around as a thundering report echoed across the expanse of the square. By professional instinct the cameraman turned at once to the source of the sound, and after a moment's wobble, the lens settled in on a ball of dust and smoke expanding up and away from the strangely modern building in the Kremlin's otherwise Slavic Rococo complex. A second later the zoom lens darted in on the scene. Fully three floors of the building had been stripped of their glass curtain wall, and the camera followed a large conference table as it fell down off one floor slab that seemed to be dangling from a half dozen reinforcing rods. The camera went down to street level, where there was one obvious body, and perhaps another, along with a collection of automobiles crushed by debris.

In seconds, the whole square was filled with running men in uniform and the first of many official cars. A blurred figure that could only be a man in uniform suddenly blocked the camera lens. The tape stopped at that point, and Rich Suddler came back into the screen with a LIVE caption in the lower left corner.

"Now, at that point the militia captain who had been escorting us—the militia is the Soviet equivalent of, oh, like a U.S. state police force—he made us stop taping and confiscated our tape cassette. We weren't allowed to tape the fire trucks or the several hundred armed troops who arrived and are now guarding the whole area. But the tape was just returned to us and we are able to give you this live picture of the building, now that the fires have been put out. In fairness I really can't say that I blame him—things were pretty wild there for a few minutes."

"Were you threatened in any way, Rich? I mean, did they act as though they thought you—"

Suddler's head shook emphatically.

"Not at all, Dionna. In fact, more than anything they seemed concerned for our safety. In addition to the militia captain, we have a squad of Red Army infantrymen with us now, and their officer was very careful to say that he was here to protect us, not to threaten us. We were not allowed to approach the site of the incident, and of course we were not allowed to leave the area—but we wouldn't have, anyway. The tape was just returned to us a few minutes ago, and we were informed that we'd be allowed to make this live broadcast." The camera shifted to the building. "As you can see, there are roughly five hundred fire, police, and military personnel still here, sorting through the wreckage and looking for additional bodies, and just to our right is a Soviet TV news crew, doing the same thing we are." Toland examined the television picture closely. The one body he could see looked awfully small. He wrote it off to distance and perspective.

"Dionna, what we seem to have here is the first major terrorist incident in the history of the Soviet Union—"

"Since the bastards set themselves up," Toland snorted.

"We know for certain—at least we've been told—that a bomb was detonated in the Council of Ministers building. They're certain it was a bomb, not some kind of accident. And we know for sure that three, possibly more people were killed, and perhaps as many as forty or fifty wounded.

"Now the really interesting thing about this is that the Politburo had been scheduled to hold a meeting here at about that time."

"Holy shit!" Toland set the aerosol can on the night table, one hand still covered in shaving cream.

"Can you tell us if any of them were among the dead or wounded?" Dionna asked at once.

"No, Dionna. You see, we're more than a quarter of a mile away, and the senior Kremlin officials arrive by car—when they do, that is, they come in from the other side of the fortress, through another gate. So, we never even knew that they were here, but the militia captain with our team did, and he kind of blurted it out. His exact words were, 'My God, the Politburo's in there!' "

"Rich, can you tell us what the reaction in Moscow has been like?"

"It's still pretty hard for us to gauge, Dionna, since we've been right here covering the story as it unfolds. The Kremlin Guards' reaction is just what you might imagine—just like American Secret Service people would react, I suppose—a mixture of horror and rage, but I want to make it clear that that rage is not being directed against anyone, certainly not against Americans. I told the militia officer who's been with us that I was in the U.S. Capitol building when the Weathermen's bomb was set off, back in 1970, and he replied rather disgustedly that Communism was indeed catching up with capitalism, that the Soviet Union was growing a bumper crop of hooligans. It's a measure of how seriously they're taking this that a Soviet police officer would comment so openly on a subject that they're not all that willing to discuss normally. So, if I had to pick one word to describe the reaction here, that word would be 'shock.'

"So, to summarize what we know to this point, there has been a bombing incident within the Kremlin walls, possibly an attempt to eliminate the Soviet Politburo, though I must emphasize we are *not* certain of that. We have had it confirmed by police at the scene that at least three people are dead, with forty or so other wounded, those wounded being evacuated to nearby hospitals. We will be reporting throughout the day as more information becomes available. This is Rich Suddler, CNN, coming to you live from the Kremlin." The scene shifted back to the anchor desk.

"And there you have it, another exclusive report from Cable Network News." Dionna the anchorperson smiled, and the screen faded again, this time to a commercial for Lite Beer from Miller. Marty stood up and put on a robe.

"I'll get the coffee going."

"Holy shit," Toland said again. He took longer than usual to shave, nicking himself twice as he kept looking in the mirror at his own eyes rather than his jawline. He dressed quickly, then looked in on his sleeping children. He decided against waking them.

Forty minutes later, he was in his car heading south, down U.S. 301, with his windows open, allowing cool night air to wash over him, and the car radio tuned to an all-news station. It was clear enough what was happening in the U.S. military. A bomb had been set off—probably a bomb in the Kremlin. Toland reminded himself that reporters hard up against deadlines, or TV types trying to score an instant scoop, often did not have the time to check things out. Maybe it was a gas main? Did Moscow have gas mains? If it were a bomb, he was sure the Soviets would instinctively think that the West had something to do with it, regardless of what that Suddler fellow thought, and go to higher alert status. The West would automatically do the same in anticipation of possible Soviet action. Nothing too obvious, nothing to provoke them further, mainly an exercise conducted by intelligence and surveillance types. The Soviets would understand that. That's how the game was played, more from their side than from ours, Toland reflected, remembering assassination attempts against American presidents.

What if they really do *think?* Toland wondered. No, he decided, they had to know that no one was that crazy. Didn't they?

NORFOLK, VIRGINIA

He drove for another three hours, wishing that he'd drunk more coffee and less wine, and listening to his car radio to stay awake. He arrived just after seven, the normal beginning of the day's work. He was surprised to find Colonel Lowe at his desk.

"I don't report to Lejeune until Tuesday, so I decided to come in and take a look at this. How was the drive?"

"I made it alive—that's about all I can say. What's happening?"

"You'll love it." Lowe held up a telex sheet. "We pirated this off the Reuters wire half an hour ago, and CIA confirms—meaning they probably stole it, too—that the KGB has arrested one Gerhardt Falken, a West German national, and accused him of setting off a bomb in the fuckin' Kremlin!" The Marine let out a long breath. "He missed the big shots, but now they're saying that among the victims are six Young Octobrists— from Pskov, by God!—who were making a presentation to the Politburo. Kids. There's going to be hell to pay."

Toland shook his head. It couldn't get much worse than that. "And they say a German did it?"

"A *West* German," Lowe corrected. "NATO intel services are already going ape trying to run him down. The official Soviet statement gives his name and address—some suburb of Bremen—and business, a small import-export house. Nothing else yet on that subject, but the Russian Foreign Ministry did go on to say that they expect 'this despicable act of international terrorism' to have no effect on the Vienna Arms Talks, that while they do not believe at this time that Falken was acting on his own, they 'have no wish' to believe that we had anything to do with it."

"Cute. It's going to be a shame to lose you back to your regiment, Chuck. You have such a nice way of finding the important quotes."

"Commander, we just might need that regiment soon. This whole thing smells like dead fish to me. Last night: the final film in the Eisenstein film festival, *Alexander Nevsky,* a new digitalized print, a new soundtrack— and what's the message? 'Arise, ye Russian people,' the Germans are coming! This morning, we have six dead Russian kids, *from Pskov!* and a German is supposed to have planted the bomb. The only thing that doesn't fit is that it ain't exactly subtle."

"Maybe," Toland said speculatively. He spoke like a halfhearted devil's advocate. "You think we could sell this combination of factors to the papers or anybody in Washington? It's too crazy, too coincidental—what if it is subtle, but *backwards* subtle? Besides, the object of the exercise wouldn't be to convince us, it would be to convince their own citizens. You could say it works both ways. That make sense, Chuck?"

Lowe nodded. "Enough to check out. Let's do some sniffing around. First thing, I want you to call CNN in Atlanta and find out how long this Suddler guy's been trying to tape his story about the Kremlin. How much lead time did he have, when was this approved, who he worked through to get it, and if someone other than his regular press contact finally did approve it."

"Setup." Toland said it out loud. He wondered if they were being clever—or clinically paranoid. He knew what most people would think.

"You can't smuggle a *Penthouse* into Russia without using the diplomatic bag, and now we're supposed to believe a German smuggled a bomb in? Then tries to blow up the Politburo?"

"Could we do it?" Toland wondered aloud.

"If CIA was crazy enough to try it? God, that's more than just crazy." Lowe shook his head. "I don't think anybody could do it, even the Russians themselves. It's got to be a layered defense. X-ray machines. Sniffer dogs. A couple of hundred guards, all from three different commands, the Army, KGB, MVD, probably their militia, too. Hell, Bob, you know how paranoid they are against their own people. How do you suppose they feel about Germans?"

"So they can't say he was a crazy operating on his own."

"Which leaves . . ."

"Yeah." Toland reached for his phone to call CNN.

KIEV, THE UKRAINE

"Children!" Alekseyev barely said aloud. "For our *maskirovka* the Party murders children! *Our own children. What have we come to?"*

What have I come to? If I can rationalize the judicial murder of four colonels and some privates, why shouldn't the Politburo blow up a few children . . . ? Alekseyev told himself there was a difference.

His General was also pale as he switched off the television set. " 'Arise, ye Russian people.' We must set these thoughts aside, Pasha. It is hard, but we must. The State is not perfect, but it is the State we must serve."

Alekseyev eyed his commander closely. The General had almost choked on those words; he was already practicing how to use them on the crucial few who would know of this outrage, yet had to perform their duties as though it never existed. There will come a day of reckoning, Pasha told himself, a day of reckoning for all the crimes committed in the name of Socialist Progress. He wondered if he'd live to see it and decided he probably wouldn't.

MOSCOW, R.S.F.S.R.

The Revolution has come to this, he thought. Sergetov was staring into the rubble. The sun was still high, even this late in the afternoon. The firefighters and soldiers were almost finished sorting through the wreckage, heaving the loose pieces into trucks a few meters from where he stood. There was dust on his suit. *I'll have to have it cleaned,* he thought, watching the seventh small body being lifted with a gentleness all too late and obscenely out of place. One more child was still unaccounted for, and there was still some lingering hope. A uniformed Army medic stood nearby, unwrapped dressings in his quivering hands. To his left a major of infantry was weeping with rage. A man with a family, no doubt.

The television cameras were there, of course. *A lesson learned from the*

American media, Sergetov thought, the crews poking their way into the action to record every horrible scene for the evening news. He was surprised to see an American crew with their Soviet counterparts. *So, we have made mass murder an international spectator sport.*

Sergetov was far too angry for visible emotion. *That could have been me,* he thought. *I always show up early for the Thursday meetings. Everyone knows it. The guards, the clerical staff, and certainly my* Comrades *on the Politburo. So this is the penultimate segment of the* maskirovka. *To motivate, to lead our people, we must do* this. *Was there supposed to be a Politburo member in the rubble?* he wondered. *A junior member, of course.*

Surely I am wrong, Sergetov told himself. One part of his mind examined the question with chilling objectivity while another considered his personal friendships with some of the senior Politburo members. He didn't know what to think. An odd position for a leader of the Party.

NORFOLK, VIRGINIA

"I am Gerhardt Falken," the man said. "I entered the Soviet Union six days ago through the port of Odessa. I have been for ten years an agent of the *Bundesnachrichtendienst,* the intelligence apparat of the government of West Germany. My assignment was to kill the Politburo at its Thursday-morning session by means of a bomb placed in a storage room directly beneath the fourth-floor conference room in which they meet." Lowe and Toland watched their televisions in total fascination. It was perfect. "Falken" spoke perfect Russian, with the precise syntax and diction that school-teachers in the Soviet Union sought to achieve. His accent was that of Leningrad.

"I have run an import-export business in Bremen for many years, and I have specialized in trade with the Soviet Union. I have traveled into the Soviet Union many times, and on many of these occasions I have used my business identity to run agents whose mission was to weaken and spy upon the Soviet Party and military infrastructures."

The camera closed in. "Falken" was reading in a monotone from a script, his eyes seldom rising to the cameras. Behind the glasses on one side was a large bruise. His hands shook slightly when he changed pages of the script.

"Looks like they beat up on him some," Lowe observed.

"Interesting," Toland replied. "They're letting us know that they work people over."

Lowe snorted. "A guy who blows little kids up? You can burn the bastard at the stake, and who'll give a good Goddamn? Some serious thought went into this, my friend."

"I wish to make it clear," Falken went on in a firmer voice, "that I had no intention of injuring children. The Politburo was a legitimate political target, but my country does not make war on children."

A howl of disgust came from off-camera. As though on cue, the camera backed away to reveal a pair of uniformed KGB officers flanking the speaker, their faces impassive. The audience was composed of about twenty people in civilian clothes.

"Why did you come into our country?" demanded one of them.

"I have told you this."

"Why does your country wish to kill the leaders of our Soviet Party?"

"I am a spy," Falken replied. "I carry out assignments. I do not ask such questions. I follow my orders."

"How were you captured?"

"I was arrested at the Kiev Railroad Station. How I was caught they have not told me."

"Cute," Lowe commented.

"He called himself a spy," Toland objected. "You don't say that. You call yourself an 'officer.' An 'agent' is a foreigner who works for you, and a 'spy' is a bad guy. They use the same terms that we do."

The CIA/DIA report arrived on the telex printer an hour later. Gerhardt Eugen Falken. Age forty-four. Born in Bonn. Educated in public schools, good marks on his records—but his picture was missing from his high school yearbook. Military service as a draftee in a transport battalion whose records had been destroyed in a barracks fire twelve years before, honorable discharge found in his personal effects. University degree in liberal arts, good marks, but again no picture, and three professors who gave him B grades can't seem to recall him. A small import-export business. Where did the money come from to start it? Nobody could answer that one. Lived in Bremen quietly, modestly, and alone. Friendly man, after a fashion. Always nodded to his neighbors, but never socialized with them. A good— "very correct," his elderly secretary said—boss to his employees. Traveled a lot. In short, many people knew he existed, quite a few did business with his firm, but nobody really knew a thing about him.

"I can hear the papers now: this guy has 'Agency' written all over him." Toland tore off the printer paper and tucked it into a folder. He had to brief CINCLANT in half an hour—and tell him what? Toland wondered.

"Tell him the Germans are going to attack Russia. Who knows, maybe this time they'll take Moscow," Lowe mused.

"Goddamn it, Chuck!"

"Okay, maybe just an operation to cripple the Russians so that they can reunite Germany once and for all. That's what Ivan is saying, Bob." Lowe looked out the window. "What we have here is a classic intelligence op. This guy Falken is a stone spook. No way in hell we can tell who he is, where he comes from, or, of course, who he's working for, unless something big breaks, and I'll wager you that it doesn't. We know—we think—that the Germans aren't this crazy, but the only evidence there is points to them. Tell the Admiral something bad is happening."

Toland did precisely that, only to have his head nearly taken off by a senior man who wanted and needed hard information.

KIEV, THE UKRAINE

"Comrades, we will commence offensive operations against the NATO land forces in two weeks," Alekseyev began. He explained the reasons for this. The assembled corps and division commanders accepted the information impassively. "The danger to the State is as great as anything we've had to face in over forty years. We have used the past four months to whip our Army into shape. You and your subordinates have responded well to our demands, and I can only say that I am proud to have served with you.

"I will leave the usual Party harangue to your group political officers." Alekseyev ventured a single smile in his delivery. "We are the professional officers of the Soviet Army. We know what our task is. We know why we have it. The life of the *Rodina* depends on our ability to carry out our mission. Nothing else matters," he concluded. *The hell it doesn't . . .*

11. Order of Battle

SHPOLA, THE UKRAINE

"You may proceed, Comrade Colonel," Alekseyev said over his radio circuit. He didn't say, *Make a fool of me now and you will be counting trees!* The General stood on a hill five hundred meters west of the regimental command post. With him was his aide, and Politburo member Mikhail Sergetov. *As if I need that distraction,* the General thought bleakly.

First the guns. They saw the flashes long before they heard the rolling thunder of the reports. Fired from behind another hill three kilometers away, the shells arced through the sky to their left, cutting through the air with a sound like the ripping of linen. The Party man cringed at the noise, Alekseyev noted, another soft civilian—

"I never did like that sound," Sergetov said shortly.

"Heard it before, Comrade Minister?" the General asked solicitously.

"I served my four years in a motor-rifle regiment," he replied. "And I never learned to trust my comrades at the artillery plotting tables. Foolish, I know. Excuse me, General."

Next came the tank guns. They watched through binoculars as the big main battle tanks emerged from the woods like something from a nightmare, their long cannon belching flame as they glided across the rolling ground of the exercise area. Interspersed with the tanks were the infantry fighting vehicles. Then came the armed helicopters, swooping at the objective from left and right, firing their guided missiles at the mockups of bunkers and armored vehicles.

By this time the hilltop objective was nearly hidden by explosions and flying dirt as the artillery fire marched back and forth across it. Alekseyev's trained eye evaluated the exercise closely. Anyone on that hilltop would be having a very hard time. Even in a small, deep, protective hole, even in a defiladed tank, that artillery fire would be terrifying, enough to distract the guided-weapons crews, enough to rattle communications men, perhaps enough to impede the officers there. Perhaps. But what of return fire from enemy artillery? What of antitank helicopters and aircraft that could sweep over the advancing tank battalions? So many unknowns in battle. So many imponderables. So many reasons to gamble, and so many reasons not to. What if there were Germans on that hill? Did the Germans get rattled— even in 1945 at the gates of Berlin, had Germans ever been rattled?

It took twelve minutes before the tanks and infantry carriers were atop the hill. The exercise was over.

"Nicely done, Comrade General." Sergetov removed his ear protectors. It was good, to be away from Moscow, he thought, even for a few hours. Why, he wondered, did he feel more at home here than in his chosen place? Was it this man? "As I recall, the standard for this particular drill is fourteen minutes. The tanks and infantry vehicles cooperated well. I've never seen the use of armed helicopters, but that too was impressive."

"The greatest improvement was the coordination of artillery fire and infantry in the final assault phase. Before, they failed miserably. This time it was done properly—a tricky procedure."

"Well I know it." Sergetov laughed. "My company never took casualties from this, but two of my friends did, fortunately none of them fatal."

"Excuse my saying so, Comrade Minister, but it is good to see that our Politburo members have also served the State in a uniformed capacity. It makes communication easier for us poor soldiers." Alekseyev knew that it never hurt to have a friend at court, and Sergetov seemed a decent chap.

"My older son just left military service last year. My younger son will also serve the Red Army when he leaves the university."

It was not often that the General was so surprised. Alekseyev lowered his binoculars to stare briefly at the Party man.

"You need not say it, Comrade General." Sergetov smiled. "I know that too few children of high Party officials do this. I have spoken against it. Those who would rule must first serve. So I have some questions for you."

"Follow me, Comrade Minister, we shall speak sitting down." The two men walked back to Alekseyev's armored command vehicle. The General's aide dismissed the vehicle's crew and himself, leaving the two senior men alone inside the converted infantry carrier. The General pulled a thermos of hot tea from a compartment and poured two metal cups of the steaming liquid.

"Your health, Comrade Minister."

"And yours, Comrade General." Sergetov sipped briefly, then set the cup down on the map table. "How ready are we for Red Storm?"

"The improvement since January is remarkable. Our men are fit. They have been drilling in their tasks continuously. I would honestly prefer another two months, but, yes, I think we are ready."

"Well said, Pavel Leonidovich. Now shall we speak the truth?"

The Politburo member said this with a smile, but Alekseyev was instantly on guard. "I am not a fool, Comrade Minister. Lying to you would be madness."

"In our country, truth is often greater madness. Let us speak frankly. I am a candidate member of the Politburo. I have power, yes, but you and I both know what the limits of that power are. Only candidate members are out with our forces now, and we are tasked with reporting back to the full members. You might also draw some meaning from the fact that I am here with you, not in Germany."

That was not entirely true, Alekseyev noted. This unit would entrain for Germany in three days, and that was why the Party man was here.

"Are we truly ready, Comrade General? Will we win?"

"If we have strategic surprise, and if the *maskirovka* succeeds, yes, I believe we should win," Alekseyev said cautiously.

"Not 'we will surely win'?"

"You have served in uniform, Comrade Minister. On the field of battle there are no certainties. The measure of an army is not known until it has been blooded. Ours has not. We have done everything we know how to do to make our Army ready—"

"You said you wished for two more months," Sergetov noted.

"A task like this is never truly finished. There are always improvements that need to be made. Only a month ago we initiated a program of replacing some senior officers at battalion and regimental level with younger, more vigorous subordinates. It is working very well indeed, but a number of these young captains now in majors' jobs could do with some further seasoning."

"So, you still have doubts?"

"There are always doubts, Comrade Minister. Fighting a war is not an exercise in mathematics. We deal with people, not numbers. Numbers have their own special kind of perfection. People remain people no matter what we try to do with them."

"That is good, Pavel Leonidovich. That is very good. I have found an honest man." Sergetov toasted the General with his tea. "I asked to come here. A comrade on the Politburo, Pyotr Bromkovskiy, told me of your father."

"Uncle Petya?" Alekseyev nodded. "He was commissar with my father's division on the drive to Vienna. He often visited our home when I was young. He is well?"

"No, he is old and sick. He says that the attack on the West is madness. The ramblings of an old man, perhaps, but his war record is distinguished, and because of that I want your evaluation of our chances. I will not inform on you, General. Too many people are fearful of telling us—we of the Politburo—the truth. But this is a time for that truth. I need your professional opinion. If I can trust you to give it to me, you can trust me not to harm you for it." The entreaty ended as a harsh command.

Alekseyev looked his guest hard in the eyes. The charm was gone now. The blue was the color of ice. There was danger here, danger even for a general officer, but what the man had said was true.

"Comrade, we plan on a rapid campaign. The projections are that we can reach the Rhein in two weeks. Those are actually more conservative than our plans of only five years ago. NATO has improved its readiness, particularly its antitank capabilities. I would say three weeks is more realistic, depending on the degree of tactical surprise and the many imponderables present in war."

"So the key is surprise?"

"The key is always surprise," Alekseyev answered at once. He quoted Soviet doctrine exactly. "Surprise is the greatest factor in war. There are two kinds, tactical and strategic. Tactical surprise is an operational art. A skilled unit commander can generally achieve it. Strategic surprise is attained on the political level. That is your mission, not mine, and it is far more important than anything we in the Army can do. With true strategic surprise, if our *maskirovka* works, yes, we will almost certainly win on the battlefield."

"And if not?"

Then we have murdered eight children for nothing, Alekseyev thought. And what part did this charming fellow have in that? "Then we might fail. Can you answer me a question? Can we split NATO politically?"

Sergetov shrugged, annoyed at being caught in one of his own traps. "As you said, Pavel Leonidovich, there are many imponderables. If it fails, then what?"

"Then the war will become a test of will and a test of reserves. We should win. It is far easier for us to reinforce our troops. We have more trained troops, more tanks, more aircraft close to the zone of action than do the NATO powers."

"And America?"

"America is on the far side of the Atlantic Ocean. We have a plan for closing the Atlantic. They can fly troops to Europe—but only troops, not their weapons, not their fuel. Those require ships, and ships are easier to sink than it is to destroy a fighting division. If full surprise is not achieved, that operational area will become quite important."

"And what of NATO surprises?"

The General leaned back. "By definition you cannot predict surprises, Comrade. That is why we have the intelligence organs, to reduce or even eliminate them. That is why our plans allow for a number of contingencies. For example, what if surprise is totally lost and NATO attacks first?" He shrugged. "They would not go far, but they would upset things. What still concerns me are nuclear responses. Again, more of a political question."

"Yes." Sergetov's worry was for his elder son. When the reserves were mobilized, Ivan would climb back into his tank, and he didn't need to be a Politburo member to know where that tank would be sent. Alekseyev had only daughters. *Lucky man,* Sergetov thought. "So, this unit goes to Germany?"

"The end of the week."

"And you?"

"During the initial phase we are tasked to be the strategic reserve for CINC-West's operations, plus to defend the Motherland against possible incursions from the southern flank. That does not concern us greatly. To threaten us, Greece and Turkey must cooperate. They will not, unless our intelligence information is completely false. My commander and I will later execute Phase 2 of the plan, and seize the Persian Gulf. Again, this will not be a problem. The Arabs are armed to the teeth, but there are not so many of them. What is your son doing now?"

"The elder? He's ending his first year of graduate school in languages. Top of his class—Middle Eastern languages." Sergetov was surprised at himself for not thinking of this.

"I could use a few more of those. Most of our Arabic language people are Muslims themselves, and for this task I would prefer people more reliable."

"And you do not trust the followers of Allah?"

"In war I trust no one. If your son is good at these languages, I will find a use for him, be sure of that." The formal agreement was made with nods, and each wondered if the other had planned it that way.

NORFOLK, VIRGINIA

"Progress hasn't ended as scheduled," Toland said. "Satellite and other reconnaissance shows that the Soviet forces in Germany and western Poland are still together in operational formations living in the field. There are indications that rail transport is being marshaled at various points in the Soviet Union—that is, at points consistent with plans to move large numbers of troops west.

"Soviet Northern Fleet this morning sortied six submarines. The move is ostensibly a scheduled rotation to replace their operational squadron in the Med, so for the next two weeks they'll have more subs in the North Atlantic than is normally the case."

"Tell me about the group rotating out of the Med," CINCLANT ordered.

"A Victor, an Echo, three Foxtrots, and a Juliet. They all spent the last week tied alongside their tender at Tripoli—the tender stayed put, in Libyan territorial waters. They will clear the Straits of Gibraltar about 1300 Zulu tomorrow."

"They're not waiting for the new group to relieve them on station first?"

"No, Admiral. Usually they do wait for the replacement group to enter the Med, but about a third of the time they do it this way. That gives us twelve Soviet subs in transit north and south, plus a November and three more Foxtrots that have been exercising with the Cuban Navy. At the moment they are all tied alongside also—we checked up on them this morning, that data is two hours old."

"Okay, what about Europe?"

"No further information on Mr. Falken. The NATO intelligence services have run up against a blank wall, and there's been nothing new from Moscow, not even a date for the public trial. The Germans say that they have no knowledge whatever of the guy. It's just as though he appeared fully grown at age thirty-one when he started his business. His apartment was taken apart one stick at a time. No incriminating evidence was found—"

"Okay, Commander, give us your professional gut feeling."

"Admiral, Falken is a Soviet sleeper agent who was inserted into the Federal Republic thirteen years ago and used for very few missions, or more probably none at all, until this."

"So you think this whole thing's a Soviet intelligence operation. No big surprise there. What's its objective?" CINCLANT asked sharply.

"Sir, at the very least they are trying to put enormous political pressure on West Germany, perhaps to force them out of NATO. At worst—"

"I think we already figured the worst-case scenario out. Nice job, Toland. And I owe you an apology for yesterday. Not your fault that you didn't have all the information I wanted." Toland blinked. It was not often that a four-star admiral apologized to a reserve lieutenant-commander in front of other flag officers. "What's their fleet doing?"

"Admiral, we have no satellite photos of the Murmansk area. Too much cloud cover, but we expect clear weather tomorrow afternoon. The Norwegians are running increased air patrols in the Barents Sea, and they say that, aside from submarines, the Russians have relatively few ships at sea at the moment. Of course, they've had relatively few ships at sea for a month."

"And that can change in three hours," an admiral noted. "Your evaluation of their fleet readiness?"

"The best it's been since I've been studying them," Toland replied. "As close to a hundred percent as I've ever seen it. As you just said, sir, they can put to sea at any time with almost their whole inventory."

"If they sortie, we'll know it quick. I have three subs up there keeping an eye on things," Admiral Pipes said.

"I talked with the Secretary of Defense right before I came here. He's going to meet with the President today and request a DEFCON-3 alert, global. The Germans are requesting that we keep Spiral Green in operation until the Russians show signs of easing things off. What do you think the Russians will do, Commander?" CINCLANT asked.

"Sir, we'll know more later today. The Soviet Party Secretary will be speaking at an emergency meeting of the Supreme Soviet, maybe also at the funeral tomorrow."

"Sentimental bastard," Pipes growled.

In front of the office television an hour later, Toland missed having Chuck Lowe around to back up his translation. The Chairman had an annoying tendency to speak rapidly, and Toland's Russian was barely up to it. The speech took forty minutes, three-quarters of which was standard political phraseology. At the end, however, the Chairman announced mobilization of Category-B reserve units to meet the potential German threat.

12. Funeral Arrangements

NORFOLK, VIRGINIA

The House of Unions was unusually crowded, Toland saw. Ordinarily they only buried one hero at a time with such ceremony. Once there had been three dead cosmonauts, but now there were eleven heroes. Eight Young Octobrists from Pskov, three boys and five girls ranging in age from eight to ten, and three clerical employees, all men who worked directly for the Politburo, were laid out in polished birchwood coffins, surrounded by a sea of flowers. Toland examined the screen closely. The caskets were elevated so that the victims were visible, but two of the faces were covered with black silk, a framed photograph atop the coffins to show what the children had looked like in life. It was a piteous, horrible touch for the television cameras to linger on.

The Hall of Columns was draped in red and black, with even the ornate chandeliers masked for this solemn occasion. The families of the victims stood in an even line. Parents without their children, wives and children without fathers. They were dressed in the baggy, ill-cut clothes so characteristic of the Soviet Union. Their faces showed no emotion but shock, as if they were still trying to come to terms with the damage done to their lives, still hoping that they'd awake from this ghastly nightmare to find their loved ones safe in their own beds. And knowing that this would not be.

The Chairman of the Party came somberly down the line, embracing each of the bereaved, a black mourning band on his sleeve to contrast with the gaudy Order of Lenin emblem on his lapel. Toland looked closely at his face. There was real emotion there. One could almost imagine that he was burying members of his own family.

One of the mothers accepted the embrace, then the kiss, and nearly collapsed, falling to her knees and burying her face in her hands. The Chairman dropped down to her side even before her husband did, and pulled her head into his shoulder. A moment later he helped her back to her feet, moving her gently toward the protective arm of her husband, a captain in the Soviet Army whose face was a stone mask of rage.

God almighty, Toland thought. *They couldn't have staged that any better with Eisenstein himself directing.*

MOSCOW, R.S.F.S.R.

You cold-hearted bastard, Sergetov said to himself. He and the rest of the Politburo stood in another line to the left of the caskets. He kept his face pointed forward, toward the line of coffins, but he averted his eyes, only to see four television cameras recording the ceremony. The whole world was watching them, the TV people had assured them. So exquisitely organized it was. Here was the penultimate act of the *maskirovka*. The honor guard of Red Army soldiers mixed with boys and girls of the Moscow Young Pioneers to watch over the murdered children. The lilting violins. *Such a masquerade!* Sergetov told himself. *See how kind we are to the families of those we have murdered!* He had seen many lies in his thirty-five years in the Party. He had told enough of them himself—but never anything that came close to this. *Just as well,* he thought, *that I've had nothing to eat today.*

His eyes came back reluctantly to the waxen face of a child. He remembered the sleeping faces of his own children, now grown. So often after arriving home late from Party work, he had stolen a look into their bedroom at night to see their peaceful faces, always lingering to be sure that they were breathing normally, listening for the sniffles of a cold or the murmurs of a dream. How often had he told himself that he and the Party worked for their future? *No more colds, little one,* he said with his eyes to the nearest child. *No more dreams. See what the Party has done for your future.* His own eyes filled with tears—and he hated himself for it. His Comrades would think it part of the performance. He wanted to look around, to see what his Comrades of the Politburo thought of their handiwork. He wondered what the KGB team that had done the deed thought of their mission now. *If* they were still alive, he reflected. So easy to put them on an airplane and crash it into the ground so that not even executioners would know of them. All records of the bomb plot were already destroyed, he was sure, and of the thirty men who knew of it, more than half were right there, standing in line with him. Sergetov almost wished he had entered the building five minutes sooner. Better to be dead than to be a beneficiary of such infamy—but he knew better. In that case he would have played an even larger role in this brutal farce.

NORFOLK, VIRGINIA

"Comrades. We see before us the innocent children of our nation," the Chairman began, speaking with slow, quiet diction that made Toland's translation job easier. CINCLANT's intelligence chief was at his side. "Killed by the infernal engine of State terrorism. Killed by a nation that has twice defiled our Motherland with unholy dreams of conquest and murder. We see before us the dedicated, humble servants of our Party who asked nothing more than to serve the State. We see martyrs to the security of the Soviet Union. We see martyrs to the aggression of fascists.

"Comrades, to the families of these innocent children, and to the families of these three fine men, I say that a reckoning will come. I say that their deaths will not be forgotten. I say that there will be justice for this vicious crime . . ."

"Jesus." Toland stopped translating and looked over at his senior.

"Yeah. There's going to be a war. We have a linguistic team across the street doing a full translation, Bob. Let's go see the boss."

"You're sure?" CINCLANT asked.

"It's possible they will settle for something less, sir," Toland replied. "But I don't think so. Everything about this exercise has been run in such a way as to inflame the Russian population to a degree I've never seen before."

"Let's put this all the way on the table. You're saying that they deliberately murdered these people to foment a crisis." CINCLANT looked down at his desk. "It's hard to believe, even for them."

"Admiral, either we believe that or we believe that the West German government has decided to precipitate a war against the Soviet Union on their own hook. In the second case the Germans would have to be totally out of their fucking minds, sir," Toland blurted, forgetting that only admirals swear in front of admirals.

"But *why?*"

"We don't know the why. That's a problem with intelligence, sir. It's a lot easier to tell the what than the why."

CINCLANT stood and walked to the corner of his office. There was going to be a war, and he didn't know why. He wanted the why. The why might be important.

"We're starting to call up reserves. Toland, you have done one hell of a good job over the past two months. I'm going to request that you get bumped up a grade to full commander. You're outside the normal zone, but I think I just might be able to handle it. There's an open intel billet with Com Second Fleet staff. He's put in a request for you if things go sour, and it looks like they are. You would be number three on his threat team, and you'd be out on a carrier. I want you out there."

"It sure would be nice to have a day or two with the family, sir."

The Admiral nodded. "We owe you that much. *Nimitz* is in transit anyway. You can meet her off the Spanish coast. Report back here Wednesday morning with your bags packed." CINCLANT came over to shake his hand. "Well done, Commander."

Two miles away, *Pharris* was tied alongside her tender. As Ed Morris watched from the bridge, ASROC rocket-boosted torpedoes were being lowered onto his bow by crane, then fed into the magazine. Another crane was lowering supplies onto the helicopter hangar aft, and a third of his crew was hard at work moving them into proper storage spaces throughout the ship. He'd had the *Pharris* for nearly two years now, and this was the first time they'd had a full weapons loadout. The eight-cell "pepperbox" ASROC launcher was being serviced by shoreside technicians to correct a minor mechanical glitch. Another team from the tender was going over a radar problem with his own crew. This was the end of his own checklist of problems to be fixed. The ship's engineering plant was functioning perfectly, better than he would have expected for a ship nearly twenty years old. In another few hours, USS *Pharris* would be completely ready . . . for what?

"Still no sailing orders, skipper?" his executive officer asked.

"Nope. I imagine everybody's wondering what we'll be doing, but for my money even the flags"—Morris always referred to admirals as flags—"don't know yet. There's a meeting of COs tomorrow morning at CINCLANTFLT. S'pose I'll find out something then. Maybe," he said dubiously.

"What do you think of this German stuff?"

"The Krauts I've worked with at sea have been all right. Trying to blast the whole Russian command structure—nobody's that crazy." Morris shrugged, a frown spreading across his dark face. "XO, there ain't no rule that says the world has to make sense."

"Damn if that ain't the truth. I think those ASROCs are going to be needed, skipper."

"I'm afraid you're right."

CROFTON, MARYLAND

"To sea?" Martha Toland asked.

"That's where they want me, and it's where I belong, like it or not." Bob had trouble meeting his wife's eyes. Listening to the brittle edge on her voice at the moment was bad enough. It wasn't his job to bring fear into her life, but that was precisely what he'd just done.

"Bob, is it as bad as I think?"

"There's no telling, babe. It might be, but there's no telling. Look, Marty, you remember Ed Morris and Dan McCafferty, right? They both have their own commands now, and they have to go. Am I supposed to stay in a nice safe place on the beach?"

His wife's reply was devastating.

"They're professionals, you're not," she said coldly. "You play weekend warrior and serve your two weeks a year just to *pretend* that you're still in the Navy, Bob. You're a civilian spook, you don't belong out there. You can't even *swim!*" Marty Toland could give lessons to sea lions.

"The hell I can't!" Toland protested, knowing that it was an absurd thing to argue about.

"Right! I haven't seen you in a pool in five years. Oh, dammit, Bob, what if something happens to you? You go out there to play your damned games and leave me behind with the kids. What do I tell *them?*"

"You tell them I didn't run away, I didn't hide, I—" Toland looked away. He hadn't expected this. Marty came from a Navy family. She was supposed to understand. But there were tears on her cheeks now, and her mouth was quivering. He took a step forward to wrap his arms around her. "Look, I'm going to be on a carrier, okay? The biggest ship we have, the safest, best-protected ship we have, with a dozen other ships surrounding her to keep the bad guys away, and a hundred airplanes. They need me to help figure out what the bad guys are up to so they can keep them as far away as possible. Marty, what I'm doing is necessary. They need me. The Admiral asked for me by name. I'm important—at least somebody thinks so." He smiled gently to hide his lie. A carrier was the best-protected ship in the fleet because she had to be: the carrier was also the number-one target for the Russians.

"I'm sorry." She broke out of his grasp and walked to the window. "How are Danny and Ed?"

"A lot busier that I am. Danny's sub is somewhere up—well, right now he's a lot closer to the Soviets than I'll ever be. Ed's getting ready to sail. He's got a 1052—an escort ship—and he'll probably be out protecting convoys or something from submarines. They both have their own families. At least you get a chance to see me before I go."

Marty turned and smiled for the first time since he had unexpectedly walked through the door. "You will be careful."

"I'll be damned careful, babe." But would it matter?

13. The Strangers Arrive and Depart

AACHEN, FEDERAL REPUBLIC OF GERMANY

It was the traffic that did it. The envelope came as promised to the proper post office box, and the key worked as he'd been told to expect. *Minimum personnel involvement.* The major grumbled at having to expose himself in the open this way, but it wasn't the first time he'd had to work with the KGB, and he needed this up-to-date information if his mission were to have any chance of success. Besides, he smiled briefly, the Germans are *so* proud of their postal service . . .

The major folded the oversized envelope and tucked it into his jacket pocket before leaving the building. His clothing was entirely German in origin, as were the sunglasses which he donned on opening the door. He scanned the sidewalk in both directions, looking for anyone who might be trailing him. Nothing. The KGB officer had promised him that the safe house was totally secure, that no one had the least suspicion that they were here. Perhaps. The taxi was waiting for him across the street. He was in a hurry. The cars were stopped on the street, and he decided to go straight across instead of walking to the corner. The major was from Russia and not accustomed to the unruly European traffic where the pedestrians are expected to follow the rules too. He was a hundred meters from the nearest traffic cop, and the nearby German drivers could sense that the cop's back was turned. It should have been as much a surprise to the major as to American tourists that, when driving, the orderly Germans were anything but. He stepped off the curb without looking, just as the traffic started moving.

He never even saw the accelerating Peugeot. It was not moving fast, only twenty-five kilometers per hour. Fast enough. The right fender caught him on the hip, spun him around, and catapulted the major into a lamppost. He was knocked unconscious before he knew what had happened, which was just as well, since his legs remained in the street and the Peugeot's rear wheel crushed both ankles. The damage to his head was spectacular. A major artery was cut open, and blood fountained onto the sidewalk as he lay motionless on his face. The car stopped at once, its driver leaping out to see what she had done. There was a scream from a child who had never seen so much blood, and a postman raced to the corner to summon the police officer standing in the traffic circle, while another man went into a store to call an ambulance.

The stopped traffic allowed the taxi driver to leave his vehicle and come over. He tried to get close, but already a half dozen men were bending over the body.

"*Er ist tot,*" one observed, and the body was pale enough to make one think so. The major was already in shock. So was the Peugeot's driver, whose eyes were already dripping tears as her breaths came in irregular sobs. She was trying to tell everyone that the man had stepped right in front of her car, that she hadn't had a chance to stop. She spoke in French, which only made things more difficult.

Pushing through the spectators, the taxi driver was almost close enough to touch the body by now. He had to get that envelope . . . but then the policeman arrived.

"*Alles zurück!*" the cop ordered, remembering his training: first, get things under control. His training also enabled him to resist the instinct to move the body. This was a head injury, perhaps a neck injury also, and those were not to be moved except by *Experten*. A bystander called out that he had summoned an ambulance. The policeman nodded curtly and hoped it would arrive soon. Making traffic accident reports was far more routine than watching an unconscious—or dead?—man bleed untidily on the sidewalk. He looked up gratefully a moment later to see a lieutenant— a senior watch supervisor—pushing his way in.

"Ambulance?"

"On the way, Herr Leutnant. I am Dieter, Gunther—traffic detail. My post is down the street."

"Who was driving the car here?" the lieutenant asked.

The driver stood as erect as she could and started gasping out her story in French. A passerby who had seen the whole thing cut her off.

"This one just stepped off the curb without looking. The lady had no chance to stop. I am a banker, and I came out of the post office right behind this one. He tried to cross at the wrong place and stepped into the street without looking at the traffic. My card." The banker handed the lieutenant his business card.

"Thank you, Dr. Müller. You have no objection to making a statement?"

"Of course. I can come directly to your station if you wish."

"Good." The lieutenant rarely had one this clean-cut.

The taxi driver just stood at the edge of the crowd. An experienced KGB case officer, he'd seen operations go bad before, but this was . . . absurd. There was always something new that could ruin an operation, so often the most simple, most foolish thing. This proud Spetznaz commando, cut down by a middle-aged Frenchwoman driving a sedan! Why hadn't he looked at the damned traffic? *I should have gotten someone else to fetch the envelope, and screw the damned orders. Security,* he swore behind an impassive face. Orders from Moscow Center: *minimum personnel involvement.* He walked back across the street to his cab, wondering how he'd explain this to his control. Mistakes were never the Center's fault.

The ambulance arrived next. The sergeant removed the victim's wallet from his pants. The victim was one Siegfried Baum—wonderful, the lieutenant thought, a Jew—from the Altona district of Hamburg. The driver of the car was French. He decided he had to ride in to the hospital with the victim. An "international" accident: there'd be extra paperwork on this. The lieutenant wished he'd stayed in the *Gasthaus* across the street and finished his after lunch pilsener. So much for devotion to duty. Then there was his possible mobilization to worry about . . .

The ambulance crew worked quickly. A cervical collar was fitted around the victim's neck, and a backboard brought in before they rolled him over onto the stretcher. The broken lower legs were immobilized with cardboard splints. The paramedic clucked over them. Both ankles looked to be badly crushed. The whole procedure took six minutes by the lieutenant's watch, and he boarded the ambulance, leaving three police officers to manage the rest of the incident and clear the accident scene.

"How bad is he?"

"Probably fractured his skull. He has lost a lot of blood. What happened?"

"Walked out into traffic without watching."

"Idiot," the paramedic commented. "As if we don't have work enough."

"Will he live?"

"Depends on the head injury." The ambulanceman shrugged. "The surgeons will be working on him within the hour. You know his name? I have a form to fill out."

"Baum, Siegfried. Kaiserstrasse 17, Altona District, Hamburg."

"Well, he'll be in the hospital in four minutes." The paramedic took his pulse and made a notation. "Doesn't look Jewish."

"Be careful saying things like that," the lieutenant cautioned.

"My wife is Jewish. His blood pressure is dropping rapidly." The ambulanceman debated starting an IV, but decided against it. Better to let the surgeons make that decision.

"Hans, have you radioed in?"

"*Ja*, they know what to expect," the driver replied. "Isn't Ziegler on duty today?"

"I hope so."

The driver horsed the ambulance into a hard left turn, and all the while the two-tone siren cleared traffic ahead of them. One minute later he halted the Mercedes and backed it into the emergency receiving area. A doctor and two orderlies were already waiting.

German hospitals are nothing if not efficient. Within ten minutes the victim, now a patient, had been intubated to protect his airway, punctured for a unit of O-positive blood and a bottle of IV fluids, and wheeled up to neurosurgery for immediate surgery at the hands of Professor Anton Ziegler. The lieutenant had to stay in the emergency room with the registrar.

"So who was he?" the young doctor asked. The policeman gave the information over.

"A German?"

"Does that seem strange?" the lieutenant asked.

"Well, when the radio call came in, and said you were coming also, I assumed that this was, well, sensitive, as though a foreigner were injured."

"The auto was driven by a Frenchwoman."

"Ach, that explains it. I thought he was the foreigner."

"Why so?"

"His dental work. I noticed when I intubated him. He has a number of cavities, and they've been repaired with stainless steel—sloppy work."

"Perhaps he originally comes from the East Zone," the lieutenant observed. The registrar snorted.

"No German ever did that work! A carpenter could do better." The doctor filled out the admission form rapidly.

"What are you telling me?"

"He has poor dental work. Strange. He is very fit. Dressed well. Jewish. But he has miserable dental work." The doctor sat down. "We see many strange things, of course."

"Where are his personal effects?" The lieutenant was a naturally curious type, one reason he'd become a policeman after his service in the *Bundeswehr*. The doctor walked the officer to a room where the personal effects were inventoried for secure storage by a hospital employee.

They found the clothing neatly arranged, with the jacket and shirt separate so that their bloodstains would not damage anything else. Pocket change, a set of keys, and a large envelope were set aside for cataloging.

The orderly was filling out a form, looking up to list exactly what had come in with the patient.

The policeman lifted the manila envelope. It had been mailed from Stuttgart yesterday evening. A ten-mark stamp. On an impulse he pulled out a pocketknife and slit the top of the envelope open. Neither the doctor nor the orderly objected. This was a police officer, after all.

A large and two smaller envelopes were inside. He opened the large one first and extracted the contents. First he saw a diagram. It looked ordinary enough until he saw that it was a photocopy of a German Army document stamped *Geheim*. Secret. Then the name: Lammersdorf. He was holding a map of a NATO communications headquarters not thirty kilometers from where he stood. The police lieutenant was a captain in the German Army Reserves, and held an intelligence billet. Who was Siegfried Baum? He opened the other envelopes. Next he went to a phone.

ROTA, SPAIN

The transport jet arrived right on time. A fair breeze greeted them from the sea as Toland emerged from the cargo door. A pair of sailors was there to direct the arrivals. Toland was pointed to a helicopter a hundred yards away, its rotor already turning. He walked quickly toward it, along with four other men. Five minutes later he was airborne, his first visit to Spain having lasted exactly eleven minutes. No one attempted conversation. Toland looked out one of the small windows available. They were over a patch of blue water, evidently flying southwest. They were aboard a Sea King antisubmarine helicopter. The crew chief was also a sonar operator, and he was fiddling with his gear, evidently running some sort of test. The interior walls of the aircraft were bare. Aft was the sonobuoy storage, and the dipping sonar transducer was caged in its compartment in the floor. For all that, the aircraft was crowded, most of its space occupied by weapon and sensor instrumentation. They'd been in the air for half an hour when the helo started circling. Two minutes later, they landed on USS *Nimitz*.

The flight deck was hot, noisy, and stank of jet fuel. A deck crewman motioned them toward a ladder which led down to the catwalk surrounding the deck, and into a passageway beneath it. Here they encountered air conditioning and relative quiet, sheltered from the flight operations going on overhead.

"Lieutenant Commander Toland?" a yeoman called out.

"Here."

"Please come with me, sir."

Toland followed the sailor through the rabbit warren of compartments below the flight deck, and was finally pointed to an open door.

"You must be Toland," observed a somewhat frazzled officer.

"Must be—unless the time zone changes did something."

"You want the good news or the bad news?"

"Bad."

"Okay, you'll have to hot-bunk. Not enough berths for all of us intel types. Shouldn't matter much, though. I haven't slept for three days—one of the reasons you're here. The good news is that you just got another half a stripe. Welcome aboard, Commander. I'm Chip Bennett." The officer handed Toland a telex sheet. "Looks as though CINCLANT likes you. Nice to have friends in high places."

The message announced tersely that Lieutenant Commander Robert A. Toland, III, USNR, had been "frocked" as a commander, USNR, which gave him the right to wear the three gold stripes of a commander, but not to collect a commander's pay just yet. It was like a kiss from one's sister. Well, he reflected, maybe a cousin.

"I guess it's a step in the right direction. What am I going to be doing here?"

"Theoretically you're supposed to assist me, but we're so friggin' overwhelmed with information at the moment that we're divvying the territory up some. I'm going to let you handle the morning and evening briefs to the battle group commander. We do that at 0700 and 2000. Rear Admiral Samuel B. Baker, Jr. Son of a B. He's an ex-nuc. Likes it quick and clean, with footnotes and sources on the writeup to read afterward. He almost never sleeps. Your battle station will be in the CIC with the group tactical warfare officer." Walker rubbed his eyes. "So what the hell is happening in this crazy world?"

"What's it look like?" Toland answered.

"Yeah. Something new just came in. The space shuttle *Atlantis* was pulled off the pad at Kennedy today, supposedly for a computer glitch, right? Three newspapers just broke a story that she was taken down for payload replacement. They were supposed to loft three or four commercial communications birds. Instead, the payload is reconnaissance satellites."

"I guess people are starting to take this seriously."

AACHEN, FEDERAL REPUBLIC OF GERMANY

"Siegfried Baum" awoke six hours later to see three men wearing surgical garb. The effect of the anesthesia still heavy on him, his eyes could not focus properly.

"How are you feeling?" one asked. In Russian.

"What happened to me?" The major answered in Russian.

Ach so. "You were struck by a car and you are now in a military hospital," the man lied. They were still in Aachen, near the German-Belgian frontier.

"What . . . I was just coming out to—" The major's voice was that of a drunken man, but it stopped abruptly. His eyes tried to focus properly.

"It is all finished for you, my friend." Now the speaker switched to German. "We know you are a Soviet officer, and you were found in possession of classified government documents. Tell me, what is your interest in Lammersdorf?"

"I have nothing to say," replied "Baum" in German.

"A little late for that," the interrogator chided, switching back to Russian. "But we'll make it easy for you. The surgeon tells us that it is now safe to try a new, ah, medication for you, and you will tell us everything you know. Be serious. No one can resist this form of questioning. You might also wish to consider your position," the man said more harshly. "You are an officer in the army of a foreign government, here in the Federal Republic illegally, traveling with false papers, and in possession of secret documents. At the least, we can imprison you for life. But, given what your government is doing at the moment, we are not concerned with 'least' measures. If you cooperate you will live, and probably be exchanged back to the Soviet Union at a later date for a German agent. We will even say that we got all our information due to the use of drugs; no harm could possibly come to you from this. If you do not cooperate, you will die of injuries received in a motor accident."

"I have a family," Major Andre Chernyavin said quietly, trying to remember his duty. The combination of fear and drug-induced haze made a hash of his emotions. He couldn't tell there was a vial of sodium pentothol dripping into his IV line, and already impairing his higher brain functions. Soon he would be unable to consider the long-term consequences of his action. Only the here and now would matter.

"They will come to no harm," Colonel Weber promised. An Army officer assigned to the *Bundesnachrichtendienst,* he had interrogated many Soviet agents. "Do you think they punish the family of every spy we catch? Soon no one would ever come here to spy on us at all." Weber allowed his voice to soften. The drugs were beginning to take effect, and as the stranger's mind became hazy he would be gentle, cajoling the information from him. The funny part, he mused, was that he'd been instructed on how to do this by a psychiatrist. Despite the many movies about brutal German interrogators, he hadn't had the least training in forceful extraction of information. *Too bad,* he thought. *If there was ever a time I need it, it is now.* Most of the colonel's family lived outside Kulmbach, only a few kilometers from the border.

KIEV, THE UKRAINE

"Captain Ivan Mikhailovich Sergetov reporting as ordered, Comrade General."

"Be seated, Comrade Captain." The resemblance to his father was remarkable, Alekseyev thought. Short and stocky. The same proud eyes, the same intelligence. Another young man on his way up. "Your father tells me that you are an honor student in Middle East languages."

"This is correct, Comrade General."

"Have you also studied the people who speak them?"

"That is an integral part of the curriculum, Comrade." The younger Sergetov smiled. "We've even had to read through the Koran. It is the only book most of them have ever read, and therefore an important factor in understanding the savages."

"You do not like the Arabs, then?"

"Not particularly. But our country must do business with them. I get along with them well enough. My class will occasionally meet with diplomats from politically acceptable countries to practice our language skills. Mainly Libya, and occasionally people from Yemen and Syria."

"You have three years in tanks. Can we defeat the Arabs in battle?"

"The Israelis have done so with ease, and they don't have a fraction of our resources. The Arab soldier is an illiterate peasant, poorly trained and led by incompetent officers."

A young man with all the answers. And perhaps you will explain Afghanistan to me? Alekseyev thought. "Comrade Captain, you will be attached to my personal staff for the forthcoming operation against the Persian Gulf states. I will lean on you for linguistic work, and to support our intelligence estimates. I understand that you are training to be a diplomat. That is useful to me. I always like to have a second opinion of the intelligence data that KGB and GRU send us. Not that I distrust our comrades in the intelligence arms, you understand. I simply like to have someone who thinks 'Army' to review the data. The fact that you've served in tanks is doubly valuable to me. One more question. How are the reservists reacting to the mobilization?"

"With enthusiasm, of course," the captain replied.

"Ivan Mikhailovich, I presume your father told you about me. I listen attentively to the words of our Party, but soldiers preparing for battle need to know the unvarnished truth so that we can bring about the Party's wishes."

Captain Sergetov noted how carefully that had been phrased. "Our people are angry, Comrade General. They are enraged over the incident in the Kremlin, the murder of the children. I think 'enthusiasm' is not a great exaggeration."

"And you, Ivan Mikhailovich?"

"Comrade General, my father told me that you would ask this question. He told me to assure you that he had no prior knowledge of it, and that the important thing is to safeguard our country so that similar tragedies will never again be necessary."

Alekseyev did not reply at once. He was chilled by the knowledge that Sergetov had read his mind three days before, and dumbfounded that he had confided so enormous a secret to his son. But it was good to know that he had not misread the Politburo man. He was a man to be trusted. Perhaps his son also? Mikhail Eduardovich evidently thought so.

"Comrade Captain, these are things to be forgotten. We have enough to occupy us already. You will work down the hall in room twenty-two. There is work waiting for you. Dismissed."

BONN, FEDERAL REPUBLIC OF GERMANY

"It's all a sham," Weber reported to the Chancellor four hours later. The helicopter he'd flown to Bonn hadn't even left the ground yet. "The whole bomb-plot business is all a cruel and deliberate sham."

"We know that, Colonel," the Chancellor replied testily. He'd been awake for two days straight now, trying to come to grips with the sudden German-Russian crisis.

"Herr Kanzler, the man we now have in the hospital is Major Andre Ilych Chernyavin. He entered the country over the Czech border two weeks ago with a separate set of false papers. He is an officer in the Soviet Spetznaz forces, their elite *Sturmtruppen*. He was badly injured in an auto accident—the fool stepped right in front of an automobile without looking—and was carrying a complete diagram for the NATO communications base at Lammersdorf. The station's security posts were just relocated a month ago. This document is only two weeks old. He also has the watch schedule and a roster of watch officers—and that is only three *days* old! He and a team of ten men came over the Czech border, and only just got their operational orders. His current orders are to attack the base exactly at midnight, the day after receipt of his alert signal. There is also a cancellation signal should plans change. We have them both."

"He came into Germany long before—" The Chancellor was surprised in spite of himself. The entire affair was so unreal.

"Exactly. It all fits, Herr Kanzler. For whatever reason, Ivan is coming to attack Germany. Everything to this point was a sham, all designed to put us to sleep. Here is a full transcript of our interview with Chernyavin. He has knowledge of four other Spetznaz operations, all of them consistent with a full-scale assault across our borders. He is now at our military hospital in Koblenz under heavy guard. We also have a videotape of his admission."

"What of the chance that this is all some sort of Russian provocation? Why weren't these documents brought over when they crossed the border?"

"The reconstruction of the Lammersdorf installation meant that they needed correct information. As you know, we've been upgrading the security measures at our NATO communications stations since last summer, and our Russian friends must have been updating their assault plans as well. The fact that they have these documents at all—just days old, some of them—is most frightening. As for how we happened to get hold of this man—" Weber explained the circumstances of the accident. "We have every reason to believe that it was a genuine accident, not a provocation. The driver, a Madame Anne-Marie LeCourte, is a fashion agent—she sells dresses for some Paris designer or other; not a likely cover for a Soviet spy. And why do such a thing? Do they expect us to launch an attack into the DDR based on this? First they accuse of us of bombing the Kremlin, then try to provoke us? It's not logical. What we have here is a man whose mission is to prepare the way for a Soviet invasion of Germany by paralyzing NATO communication links immediately before hostilities commence."

"But to do such a thing—even if such an attack is planned. . . ."

"The Soviets are intoxicated with 'special operations' groups, a lesson from Afghanistan. These men are highly trained, very dangerous. And it's a cunning plan. The Jewish identification, for example. The bastards play on our sensitivity with the Jews, no? If he is stopped by a police officer, he can make a casual remark about how Germans treat Jews, and what would a young policeman do, eh? Probably apologize and send him on his way." Weber smiled grimly. That had been a carefully thought-out touch. He had to admire it. "What they could not allow for was the unexpected. We've been lucky. We should now make use of this luck. Herr Kanzler, this data must go to NATO high command immediately. For the moment we have their safe house under observation. We may wish to assault it. GSG-9 is ready for the mission, but perhaps it should be a NATO operation."

"I must meet with my cabinet first. Then I will speak with the President of the United States on the telephone and the other NATO chiefs of government."

"Forgive me, Chancellor, but there is no time for that. With your permission, within the hour I will give a copy of the videotape to the CIA liaison officer, and also to the British and French. The Russians are going to attack us. Better to alert the intelligence services first, which will lay the groundwork for your talk with the President and others. We must move at once, Herr Kanzler. This is a life-and-death situation."

The Chancellor stared down at his desk. "Agreed, Colonel. What do you propose to do with this Chernyavin?"

Weber had already moved on that score. "He died of injuries sustained in the auto accident. It will appear on the television news this evening, and in the newspapers. Of course he will be made available to our allies for further interrogation. I am certain the CIA and others will wish to see him before midnight."

The Chancellor of the German Federal Republic stared out the windows of his Bonn office. He remembered his armed service forty years before: a frightened teenager with a helmet that nearly covered his eyes. "It's happening again." *How many will die this time?*

"*Ja.*" *Dear God, what will it be like?*

LENINGRAD, R.S.F.S.R.

The captain looked out over the port side of his ship from the bridge wing. Tugs pushed the last barge onto the aft elevator, then backed away. The elevator rose a few meters, and the barge settled into place on the trolleys already set on the fore-and-aft tracks. *Julius Fucik*'s first officer supervised the loading process from the winch-control station aft, communicating by portable radio to other men scattered about the afterpart of the ship. The elevator matched levels with that of the third cargo deck, and the access door opened to expose the vast cargo deck. Crewmen strung cables onto the trolleys and bolted them rapidly into place.

Winches pulled the barge forward into the third, lowermost, cargo deck of the Seabee—for Seagoing Barge Carrier—ship. As soon as the trolleys were over their painted marks, the watertight door closed and lights came on to allow the crew to secure the barge firmly in place. *Neatly done,* the first officer thought. The whole loading process had been completed in only eleven hours, almost a record. He supervised the process of securing the after-portion of the ship for sea.

"The last barge will be fully secured in thirty minutes," the bosun reported to the first officer, who forwarded the information to the bridge.

Captain Kherov switched buttons on his phone to talk to the engineering spaces. "You will be ready to answer bells in thirty minutes."

"Very well. Thirty minutes." The engineer hung up.

On the bridge, the captain turned to his most senior passenger, a general of paratroops wearing the blue jacket of a ship's officer. "How are your men?"

"Some are seasick already." General Andreyev laughed. They had been brought aboard inside the sealed barges—except for the General, of course—along with tons of military cargo. "Thank you for allowing my men to walk around the lower decks."

"I run a ship, not a prison. Just so they don't tamper with anything."

"They've been told," Andreyev assured him.

"Good. We will have plenty of work for them to do in a few days."

"You know, this is my first trip aboard ship."

"Really? Fear not, Comrade General. It is much safer, and much more comfortable, than flying in an aircraft—and then jumping out of it!" The captain laughed. "He is a big ship and he rides very well even with so light a load."

"Light load?" the General asked. "This is more than half of my division's equipment you have aboard."

"We can carry well over thirty-five thousand metric tons of cargo. Your equipment is bulky, but not that heavy." This was a new thought for the General, who usually had to calculate in terms of moving equipment by air.

Below, over a thousand men of the 234th Guards Air Assault Regiment were milling about under the control of their officers and NCOs. Except for brief periods at night, they'd be stuck down there until the *Fucik* cleared the English Channel. They tolerated it surprisingly well. Even when crammed with barges and equipment, the cavernous cargo spaces were far larger than the military transport aircraft they were accustomed to. The ship's crew was rigging planks from one barge top to another so that there would be more room for them to use for sleeping, and to get the soldiers off the oily workspaces that the crew needed to patrol. Soon, the regimental officers were to be briefed on shipboard systems, with special attention to the firefighting systems. A strict no-smoking rule was being enforced, but the professional seamen took no chances. The crewmen were surprised at the humble demeanor of the swaggering paratroopers. Even elite troops, they learned, could be cowed by exposure to a new environment. It was a pleasant observation for the merchant seamen.

Three tugs pulled on lines hanging from the ship's side, drawing her slowly away from her dock. Two others joined as soon as she was clear, pushing the bow around to face out to sea from the Leningrad terminal. The General watched the ship's captain control the procedure, as he raced from one bridge wing to another with a junior officer in tow, often giving rudder orders as he passed. Captain Kherov was nearly sixty, and more than two-thirds of his life had been spent at sea.

"Rudder amidships!" he called. "Ahead slow."

The helmsman accomplished both commands in under a second, the General saw. *Not bad,* he thought, remembering the surly comments he'd heard from time to time about merchant seamen. The captain rejoined him.

"Ah, that's the hardest part behind us."

"But you had help for that," the General observed.

"Some help! Damned tugboats are run by drunks. They damage ships all the time here." The captain walked over to the chart. *Good: a deep straight channel all the way to the Baltic.* He could relax a bit. The captain walked over to his bridge chair and settled in. "Tea!"

A steward appeared at once with a tray of cups.

"There is no liquor aboard?" Andreyev was surprised.

"Not unless your men brought it, Comrade General. I do not tolerate alcohol on my ship."

"That is true enough." The first officer joined them. "All secure aft. The special sea detail is set. Lookouts posted. The deck inspection is under way."

"Deck inspection?"

"We normally check at the turn of every watch for open hatches, Comrade General," the first officer explained. "With your men aboard, we will check every hour."

"You do not trust my men?" The General was mildly offended.

"Would you trust one of us aboard one of your airplanes?" the captain replied.

"You are right, of course. Please excuse me." Andreyev knew a professional when he saw one. "Can you spare a few men to teach my junior officers and sergeants what they need to know?"

The first officer pulled a set of papers from his pocket. "The classes begin in three hours. In two weeks, your men will be proper seamen."

"We are particularly worried about damage control," the captain said. "That concerns you?"

"Of course. We stand into danger, Comrade General. I would also like to see what your men can do for ship defense."

The General hadn't thought of that. The operation had been thrown together too quickly for his liking, without the chance to train his men in their shipboard duties. Security considerations. Well, no operation was ever fully planned, was it? "I'll have my antiair commander meet with you as soon as you are ready." He paused. "What sort of damage can this ship absorb and still survive?"

"He is not a warship, Comrade General." Kherov smiled cryptically. "However, you will note that nearly all of our cargo is on steel barges. Those barges have double steel walls, with a meter of space between them, which may even be better than the compartmentalization on a warship. With luck, we will not have to learn. Fire is what concerns me most. The majority of ships lost in battle die from fire. If we can set up an effective firefighting drill, we may well be able to survive at least one, perhaps as many as three missile hits."

The General nodded thoughtfully. "My men will be available to you whenever you wish."

"As soon as we clear the Channel." The captain got up and checked the chart again. "Sorry that we cannot offer you a pleasure cruise. Perhaps the return trip."

The General lifted his tea. "I will toast that, Comrades. My men are at your disposal until the time comes. Success!"

"Yes. Success!" Captain Kherov lifted his cup also, almost wishing for a glass of vodka to toast their enterprise properly. He was ready. Not since his youth in Navy minesweepers had he had the chance to serve the State directly, and he was determined to see this mission through.

KOBLENZ, FEDERAL REPUBLIC OF GERMANY

"Good evening, Major." In a guarded wing of the military hospital, the chief of CIA's Bonn Station sat down with his British and French counterparts and a pair of translators. "Shall we talk about Lammersdorf?" Unbeknownst to the Germans, the British had a file on Major Chernyavin's activities in Afghanistan, including a poor but recognizable photograph of the man remembered by the Mudjahaddin as the Devil of the Kandahar. General Jean-Pierre de Ville of the French DGSE handled the questioning, since he spoke the best Russian. By this time Chernyavin was a broken man. His only attempt at resistance was killed by listening to a tape of his drug-induced confession. A dead man to his own countrymen, the major repeated what these men already knew but had to hear for themselves. Three hours later, Flash-priority dispatches went to three Western capitals, and representatives of the three security services prepared briefing papers for their counterparts in the other NATO countries.

14. Gas

WANDLITZ, GERMAN DEMOCRATIC REPUBLIC

SCENARIO 6

Spring-summer weather patterns (moderate humidity and temperatures; rain probability 35% per day); westerly and southwesterly winds of 10 to 30 km/ hr at ground level, indexed for altitude; use of highly persistent agents against communications nexi, POMCUS sites, airfields, supply, and nuclear weapon storage facilities (normal computed delivery error rate, see Appendix F of Annex 1). The chief of the Communist Party of the German Democratic Republic read on to the bottom of the abstract, despite the acid churning in his stomach:

As with Scenarios 1, 3, 4, and 5, any warning of over 15 minutes will ensure virtually complete MOPP-4 protection of alerted combat and support personnel. The problem of civilian casualties remains, since over a hundred targets of the categories cited above are near major population centers. Biodegradation of persistent agents such as GD (the expected Soviet agent of choice; for an analysis of Soviet literature on this topic, see Appendix C of Annex 2) will be slowed by generally mild temperatures and weather-reduced sunlight photochemical action. This will allow the agents in aerosol form to drift on wind currents. Given minimum source concentrations of 2 milligrams per cubic meter, predicted vertical temperature gradients, and cloudwidth inputs, we see that the downwind toxic vapor hazard to large areas of the FRG and DDR will be approximately 0.3 (plus or minus 50% in our calculations, allowing for expected impurities and chemical break-down in the chemical munitions) as great as that at the targets themselves.

Since open Soviet literature calls for source (that is, target) concentrations well beyond median lethal dose (LCT-50), we see that the entire German civilian population is at the gravest risk. Expected allied retaliation to such chemical strikes would be largely psychological in nature—the use of Soviet munitions alone will effectively contaminate most of Greater Germany; it is expected that no part of Germany east of the Rhein can be considered safe to unprotected personnel, beginning 12 hours after the first munitions are expended. Similar effects may be expected in parts of Czechoslovakia, and even western Poland, depending on wind direction and speed. Such con-tamination must be expected, moreover, to continue at least 1.5 times the mean persistence level of the agents used.

This is the last (and statistically most likely) of the scenarios outlined by the contract specifications.

SECTION VIII: EXECUTIVE SUMMARY

As the reader will appreciate, although given tactical warning of only a few minutes, alerted military formations can confidently be expected to suffer few casualties (albeit with 30 – 50% degradation of combat effectiveness; this degradation likely, however, to equate to both sides), expected casualties to civilians will actually be greater than those anticipated from a Level-2 exchange of tactical nuclear weapons (200 warheads @<100kt yield; see Appendix A of Annex 1) at a mix of military and civilian/industrial targets. Thus, despite the fact that chemical munitions are not of themselves directly damaging to fixed industrial assets, serious near- and long-term economic effects must be expected. Even the use of nonpersistent agents at the FEBA (Forward Edge of the Battle Area) cannot but have major impact on the civilian population due to the heavily urbanized character of the German countryside and the patent inability of any government to provide adequate protection for its civilian population.

In terms of immediate effects, the 10,000,000 + civilian fatality floor figure in Scenario 2 represents a public health problem worse by an order of magnitude than that following the Bangladesh Cyclone disaster of 1970, and is likely to include synergistic effects well beyond the scope of this study. (Contract specifications specifically excluded investigation into bioecological effects from a major chemical exchange. While the difficulty associated with an in-depth examination of this subject is impossible at this writing to esti-mate, the reader is cautioned that such far-reaching effects are less easily dealt with than studied. It might be necessary, for example, to import tons of insect larvae before the simplest food crops can again flourish in Western Europe.) *For the moment the ability even of organized armies to dispose of millions of civilian bodies in advanced stages of decomposition is not something to be taken for granted. And the civilians needed for the reestablishment of industrial production (under what are almost certainly optimistic estimates) will have been at the least decimated in the literal, classical sense.*

An Analysis of the Effects of Chemical
Warfare in the European Theater Utilizing
Atmospheric Release Advisory Capability (ARAC)
Prediction
Lawrence-Livermore National Laboratories
LLNL 88 - 2504 * CR 8305 / 89 / 178
SIGMA 2

Specified External Distribution Only
>>*SECRET*<<

Johannes Bitner did not throw the report into his trash basket—he felt like washing his hands. *Yet another similarity between East and West,* he thought coldly. *Their government reports are written by computers to be read by calculators. Just like ours. Just like ours.*

"Herr Generaloberst." The Chief of the Communist Party of the DDR looked up at his Commander-in-Chief. He and another officer had come early in the morning—and in civilian clothes—to visit him at his plush private residence in Wandlitz, the enclave of the Party elite outside Berlin. They had delivered the document obtained only two days earlier through a highly placed DDR agent in West Germany's Ministry of Defense. "Just how accurate is this document?"

"Comrade Secretary, we cannot check their computer models, of course, but their formulae, their estimates for the persistence of Soviet chemical weapons, their predicted weather patterns—that is, all of the data which supposedly underlies this study—has been examined by members of my intelligence staff and rechecked by some chosen faculty members at the University of Leipzig. There is no reason to believe that it is anything but genuine."

"In fact," said Colonel Mellethin, director of Foreign Operations Analysis—he was a spare, austere man with eyes that clearly had not known sleep for some days—"the Americans understate the total quantities of munitions employed, because they consistently overstate the accuracy of Russian delivery systems." The other two men in the room noted at once that *Russian* had been substituted for *Soviet.*

"There is something else you wish to say, Mellethin?" Bitner asked sharply.

"Comrade Secretary, from the Russian point of view, what is the objective of this war?"

"The neutralization of NATO, and access to greater economic assets. Say what you have to say, Comrade Colonel," Bitner ordered.

"Comrade, success for the Warsaw Pact would leave a united Germany. I point out that a united Germany, even a united *socialist* Germany, would be viewed as a strategic threat by the Soviet Union—after all, we are better socialists than they, *nicht wahr?*" Mellethin took a deep breath before going on. Was he risking his life? Did it matter? The family name had once been *von* Mellethin, and unwavering loyalty to the State was not something that Communism had taught his line of professional soldiers. "Comrade Party Secretary, Soviet success in this operation will leave Germany, socialist and capitalist, as barren as the surface of the moon, a minimum of ten to thirty percent of our people dead, our land poisoned, even without Western chemical retaliation. Comrade, we learned today that the Americans have begun airlifting 'Bigeye' chemical aircraft bombs into their base at Ramstein. If our 'allies' use their chemical weapons, and then NATO retaliates in kind, it is entirely possible that our country— that German culture itself—will completely cease to exist. Such an objective is not militarily defensible, but I suggest, Comrade, that this could be an additional, *political* objective of the Russian plan."

Bitner's expression didn't change a whit, and his visitors couldn't see the chill that was enveloping their national leader. The meeting he'd had the previous week in Warsaw had been unsettling enough, but now the reason behind the greasy reassurances offered him by the Soviet leadership seemed all too clear.

"There is no way to protect our civilian population?" Bitner asked.

"Comrade." The General sighed. "These persistent agents need not be breathed. They also work through the skin. If one touches a contaminated surface, one is poisoned. Even if we order our people to remain in their homes with windows and door closed, houses and apartment blocks are not airtight. And people still must eat. Factory workers in certain essential industries still must work. Medical personnel, police, and internal security personnel—some of our most valuable citizens will be the most gravely exposed. These aerosols will travel invisibly across our country, virtually undetectable. They will leave a toxic film on lawns, trees, fences, walls, trucks—nearly anything. The rain will wash much off, but tests made years ago show that some of these poisons—those on the undersides of fences, for example—will persist for weeks, even months. We would need thousands of decontamination teams even to begin the task of making our country safe enough for our citizens to walk to their markets. Colonel Mellethin is correct: if the Russians use their gas weapons, and then the Americans reply in kind, we would be fortunate if half our citizens were alive six months from today. It is actually easier to protect our citizens from nuclear weapons than against gasses, and nuclear effects are shorter-lived."

"*Du lieber Gott.*"

MOSCOW, R.S.F.S.R.

"They said *what?*" The Defense Minister almost screamed.

"Our fraternal socialist comrades of the German Democratic Republic have informed us that they can only view the use of chemical munitions inside their territory as a matter of the gravest national concern." The Foreign Minister spoke dryly. "Moreover, they have forwarded to us intelligence reports which show clearly that the use of such weapons would only serve to harden NATO resolve—and possibly open the door to other weapons of mass destruction."

"But they are part of the plan!" Defense objected.

"Comrades," Sergetov observed. "We all know that the use of chemical munitions will have calamitous effects on civilians—wouldn't this compromise our political *maskirovka*? Aren't we saying that our quarrel is with the West German *government?* How might it look then if on the first day of the war we coldly exterminate many thousands of civilians?" *How many more innocents shall we slaughter?* he thought.

"And there is another question," said Bromkovskiy. Old and frail though he was, he was still an experienced man from the last war against the Germans, and his views on defense affairs still commanded respect. "If we use these weapons against all the NATO armies—and how can we restrict them to German formations?—America and France have made it clear that they consider gas as a weapon of mass destruction, to which they would respond in kind."

"The American chemical arsenal is a joke," replied Defense.

"I have seen studies from your ministry that suggest otherwise," Bromkovskiy shot back. "And perhaps you will laugh at their nuclear weapons! If we kill many thousands of German civilians, their government will demand the use of atomic weapons against targets in our territory. If our gas weapons kill some thousands of American soldiers, do you think the American President will refrain from using his own weapons of mass destruction? Comrades, we have discussed this before. This war against NATO is a political operation, no? Do we cast away our political camouflage by using a weapon like this? We have the assurance now that at least one NATO country will not join in a Russian-German war. This is a great victory for our political policy. The use of chemical weapons will cast away that advantage and open political dangers from more than one direction.

"I feel that we should retain control of these weapons in the Politburo. Comrade Defense Minister, are you telling us that we can win only if weapons of mass destruction are used?" The old man leaned forward and spoke with harsh determination. "Has the situation changed? You will remember telling us that if strategic surprise were lost, our armies could be recalled. Has surprise been lost?"

The Defense Minister's face went rigid for a moment. "The Soviet Army is ready and able to carry out its mission. It is now too late to retreat. This is also a political question, Petya."

"NATO is mobilizing," Sergetov said.

"Too late, and too halfheartedly," replied the Director of the KGB. "We have split one country from the NATO alliance. We are working on others, and are hard at work throughout Europe and America spreading disinformation about the bomb attack. The will of the people in the NATO countries is low. They will not want to fight a war for German murderers, and their political leaders will find a way to disassociate themselves from the conflict."

"But not if we slaughter civilians with gas." The Foreign Minister nodded. "Petya and young Sergetov are correct: the political cost of these weapons is simply too high."

WASHINGTON, D.C.

"But why? Why are they doing this?" the President demanded.

"We simply do not know, sir." The Director of Central Intelligence was clearly uncomfortable with the question. "We know that this Kremlin Bomb Plot was a complete fabrication—"

"Did you see what the *Post* said this morning? The press says that this guy Falken has 'agency' or its German equivalent written all over him."

"Mr. President, the truth of the matter is that Herr Falken was almost certainly a Soviet sleeper agent under KGB control. The Germans have been unable to uncover very much about him. It's as though he just sprang into being thirteen years ago, and he's been quietly running his import-export business for the last twelve years. Sir, every indication we have is that the Soviets are prepared for an attack against NATO. There is no indication, for example, that they are demobilizing their conscripts who are at the end of their enlistment periods, nor any evidence of preparations for the new 'class' of conscripts that should have begun to arrive several days ago. Finally, there's the case of this Spetznaz major the Germans picked up. He was infiltrated into the Federal Republic before the bomb plot, with orders to attack a NATO communications base. As to why— Mr. President, we simply do not know. We can describe what the Russians are doing but not the reason for it."

"I told the country last night that we would be able to control this situation through diplomatic means . . . ."

"We still might. We need to communicate directly with the Soviets," the President's national security adviser said. "Until they respond positively, however, we have to show that we mean business, too. Mr. President, a further call-up of reservists is necessary."

NORTH ATLANTIC

The *Julius Fucik* was rolling ten degrees with a beam sea. It made life hard on the soldiers, Captain Kherov noted, but they were doing well for landsmen. His own crewmen were dangling over the sides with sprayguns, painting over the ship's Interlighter markings, preparatory to replacing them with the Lykes Lines emblem. The soldiers were cutting away parts of the superstructure to conform with the silhouette of the *Doctor Lykes,* a U.S.-flag Seabee carrier remarkably similar to the *Fucik.* The Soviet ship had been built years before in Finland's Valmet yard from plans purchased in America. Already the elevator winch area aft had been painted completely black to match the American line's house colors, and a black diamond had been painted on both sides of the superstructure. Gangs of men were changing the shape and colors of the two funnels with prefabricated parts. The hardest job remaining was the paintwork on the hull. The Interlighter markings were made of twenty-foot letters. Replacing them called for the use of canvas templates, and the lettering had to be neat and exact. Worst of all, there was no way to check the workmanship short of launching a ship's boat, something he had neither the time nor the inclination to do.

"How long, Comrade Captain?"

"Four hours at least. The work goes well." Kherov couldn't hide his concern. Here they were, mid-Atlantic, far from the usual sea lanes, but there was no telling—

"And if we are spotted by an American aircraft or ship?" General Andreyev asked.

"Then we will find out how effective our damage-control drills have been—and our mission will be a failure." Kherov ran his hand along the polished teak rail. He'd commanded this ship for six years, taken her into nearly every port on the North and South Atlantic. "We'll get some way on. The ship will ride more easily on a bow sea."

MOSCOW, R.S.F.S.R.

"When are you planning to leave?" Flynn asked Calloway.

"Soon, Patrick. I hope you'll be coming with me?" The unmarried children of both men were in college, and both had sent their wives west the day before.

"I don't know. I've never run away before." Flynn scowled at the empty stage at the end of the room. He had the scars to prove it. "They pay me to report the news."

"You'll be reporting no bloody news from inside Lefortovo Prison, my friend," Calloway observed. "Isn't one Pulitzer Prize enough?"

Flynn laughed. "I thought nobody but me remembered. What do you know that I don't, Willie?"

"I know I wouldn't be leaving without a damned good reason. And if it's good enough for me to leave, Patrick, it's bloody good enough for you." He'd been told only the night before that a peaceful resolution of this crisis was now less than a 50-percent probability. For the hundredth time, the Reuters correspondent blessed his decision to cooperate with the SIS.

"Here we go." Flynn took out his notepad.

The Foreign Minister entered from the usual door and moved to the lectern. He looked uncharacteristically frazzled, his suit rumpled, his shirt collar dingy, as though he'd been up all the previous night laboring to resolve the German crisis through diplomatic means. When he looked up, his eyes squinted through his reading glasses.

"Ladies and gentlemen, a year that has gone so well for East-West relations has turned to ashes in the mouths of us all. The United States, the Soviet Union, and the other nations that accepted our invitation to Vienna are within weeks of a comprehensive agreement on the control of strategic nuclear arms. America and the Soviet Union have agreed upon and implemented a grain sales agreement with unprecedented speed and cooperation, and even as we speak, deliveries are being made in Odessa on the Black Sea. Western tourism within the Soviet Union is at an all-time high, and this is perhaps the truest reflection of the spirit of détente—now our peoples are finally beginning to trust one another. All this effort, the efforts of East and West to bring about a just and lasting peace, have been brought to ruin by a handful of revanchist men who have not taken the lessons of the Second World War to heart.

"Ladies and gentlemen, the Soviet Union has received irrefutable evidence that the government of the Federal Republic of Germany exploded its bomb in the Kremlin as part of a plot to bring about the reunification of Germany by force. We have in our possession classified German documents which prove that the West German government planned to bring down the Soviet government and use the resulting period of internal confusion to achieve their aim of remaking Germany into the principal continental power in Europe yet again. All Europeans know what that would mean to world peace.

"In this century, Germany has invaded my country twice. Over forty million Soviet citizens died repelling those two invasions, and we do not forget the deaths of so many millions of our fellow Europeans who were also the victims of German nationalism—Polish, Belgian, Dutch, French, English, and American men and women labored as our allies to safeguard the peace of Europe. After the Second World War, we all thought that this problem was completely at an end. Such was the reasoning behind the treaties which divided Germany and Europe into spheres of influence—remember that these spheres were ratified further by the Helsinki Accords in 1975—whose balance would serve to make a European war impossible.

"We know that the rearming of Germany by the West, supposedly a defensive measure against the imagined threat from the East—despite the fact that the Warsaw Pact was not even formed until well *after* the NATO alliance was formed—was the first step in the West's own plan to unify Germany as a pawn to counterbalance the Soviet Union. That this was a foolish and unnecessary policy is now manifestly clear. I ask you if there is anyone in Europe who truly wants a unified Germany. The NATO countries themselves stopped agitating for this years ago. Except, of course, for some Germans who remember the days of German power in rather a different light from those of us who were its victims.

"The Federal Republic of Germany has evidently turned the tables on her Western allies, and plans to use the NATO alliance as a shield behind which to launch her own offensive operations, the objective of which can only upset the power balance that has safeguarded the peace in Europe for two generations. Although we can fault the West for creating this situation, the government of the Soviet Union does not—I repeat, does *not*—hold America or her NATO allies responsible for this. My country, too, has learned the bitter lesson that allies can turn on their supposed friends, much as a dog can turn on his master.

"The Soviet Union has no wish to cast away the dramatic progress made this year in foreign relations with the West." The Foreign Minister paused before going on. "But the Soviet Union cannot ignore, cannot set aside the fact, that a deliberate act of aggression has been made against the Soviet Union, on Soviet soil.

"The government of the Soviet Union will today deliver a note to the Bonn government. As a price of our forbearance, as a price of keeping the peace, we demand that the Bonn government immediately demobilize its army to a level consistent with maintenance of the civil peace. We further call upon the Bonn government to admit its aggressive action, to dissolve and call for new elections, so that the German people themselves may judge how well they have been served. Finally, we demand and expect that full reparations be paid to the government of the Soviet Union, and to the families of those so callously murdered by the revanchist German nationalists who hide in their city on the west bank of the Rhein. Failure to meet with these demands will have the gravest possible consequences.

"As I have already said, we have no reason whatever to believe that any other Western nation had the slightest complicity in this act of international terrorism. This crisis is, therefore, a matter between the government of the Soviet Union and the government in Bonn. It is our hope that this crisis can be resolved through diplomatic means. We call on the Bonn government to consider the consequences of its actions with the greatest care and to act to preserve the peace.

"That is all I have to say." The Foreign Minister gathered his papers and left. The gathered reporters did not even attempt to shout questions at the receding form.

Flynn tucked his notepad back into his pocket, and screwed his pen closed. The AP correspondent had stayed behind at Phnom Penh to see the arrival of the Khmer Rouge, almost at the cost of his life. He'd covered wars, revolutions, riots, and been wounded twice as a result of his devotion to his business. But covering wars was a young man's game.

"When are you planning to leave?"

"Wednesday at the latest. I already have two tickets reserved, SAS to Stockholm," Calloway answered.

"I'm going to cable New York to shut down the Moscow office tomorrow. I'll stick around until you leave, but, Willie, it's time to go. If I cover any more of this story, it'll be from a safer place."

"How many wars have you covered, Patrick?"

"Korea was my first. Haven't missed many since then. Damned near bled to death at a place called Con Thien. Caught two mortar fragments in the Sinai in '73."

USS *PHARRIS*

DEFCON-2. RULES OF ENGAGEMENT OPTION BRAVO NOW IN EFFECT. THIS MESSAGE IS TO BE UNDERSTOOD AS A WAR-WARNING, Morris read in the privacy of his stateroom. HOSTILITIES BETWEEN NATO AND THE WARSAW PACT ARE NOW TO BE CONSIDERED AS LIKELY BUT NOT CERTAIN. TAKE ALL MEASURES CONSISTENT WITH THE SAFETY OF YOUR COMMAND. HOSTILITIES COULD INITIATE WITHOUT RPT WITHOUT WARNING.

Ed Morris lifted his phone. "Call the XO to my stateroom."

He was there in under a minute.

"I hear you got a hot message, skipper."

"DEFCON-2, ROE Option Bravo." He handed over the terse message form. "We start maintaining round-the-clock Condition-Three steaming at once. The ASROC and torpedo tube directors are to be manned at all times."

"What do we tell the men?"

"I want to go over this with the wardroom first. Then I'll speak to the crew. We haven't got specific operations orders yet. I figure we head either to Norfolk or New York for convoy duty."

USS *NIMITZ*

"Okay, Toland, let's hear it." Baker sat back in his chair.

"Admiral, NATO has increased its alert level. The President has authorized DEFCON-2. The Naval Defense Reserve Fleet is being mobilized. Reforger will begin at 0100 Zulu. The commercial jets are already being taken into military service. The Brits have enacted Queen's Order Two. A lot of airports in Germany are going to be busy as hell."

"How long to complete Reforger?"

"Eight to twelve days, sir."

"We may not have that long."

"Yes, sir."

"Tell me about their satellite reconnaissance," Baker ordered.

"Admiral, they currently have one radar ocean reconnaissance satellite up—Kosmos 1801. It's paired with Kosmos 1813, an electronic intelligence bird. 1801 is the nuclear-powered radar bird, and we think it may have a photographic capability to back up the radar system."

"I never heard that before."

"NSA detected indications of a video signal several months ago, but that information was never released to the Navy because it was unconfirmed." Toland didn't say that it had been decided at the time the Navy didn't need-to-know this. They needed to know now, Toland judged. *I'm here now.* "I'd expect that Ivan has another of his radar satellites ready for immediate launch, probably a few more in the barn. They've been launching an unusual number of their low-altitude communications birds, plus a lot of electronic intelligence satellites—ordinarily they have six or seven of them up, but now the total is ten. That gives them awfully good ELINT coverage. If we make electronic noise, they'll hear it."

"And not a Goddamned thing we can do about them."

"Not for a while, sir," Toland agreed. "The Air Force has its antisatellite missiles, six or seven as I recall, but they've only been tested once against a real satellite, and there's been a moratorium on the ASAT tests since last year. The Air Force can probably dust them off and try to reactivate the program, but that'll take a few weeks. Their first priority is the radar satellites," Toland concluded hopefully.

"Okay, our orders are to rendezvous with *Saratoga* at the Azores and escort our Marine Amphibious Unit to Iceland. I suppose the Russians will watch us all the way up! Hopefully by the time we get there, the Icelandic government will allow us to land them. I just learned that their government can't decide if this crisis is real or not. God, I wonder if NATO will hold together?"

"Supposedly we have proof that it's all a put-up job, but we don't need to know what that evidence is. The problem is that a lot of countries are buying this charade, at least publicly."

"Yeah, I love that. I want you to refine your estimate of the threat from Soviet subs and aircraft on a continuous basis. I want information about the smallest change in what they have at sea the moment you get it."

15. The Bastion Gambit

USS *CHICAGO*

"What's the sounding?" McCafferty asked quietly.

"Fifty feet under the keel," the navigator answered at once. "We're still well outside Russian territorial waters, but we start approaching real shoals in twenty miles, skipper." It was the eighth time in half an hour that he had commented on what lay ahead.

McCafferty nodded, not wanting to speak, not wanting to make any unnecessary sound at all. The tension hung in the attack center of the *Chicago* like the cigarette smoke that the ventilators would not entirely remove. Looking around, he caught his crewmen furtively disclosing their states of mind with a raised eyebrow or a slightly shaken head.

The navigator was the most nervous of all. There were all sorts of good reasons not to be here. *Chicago* might or might not have been in Soviet territorial water, itself a legal question of no small complexity. To the northeast was Cape Kanin; to the northwest, Cape Svyatoy. The Soviets claimed the entire region as a "historic bay," while the United States chose to recognize the international twenty-four-mile closure rule. Everyone aboard knew that the Russians were more likely to shoot today than request a decision under the International Law of the Sea Convention. Would the Russians find them?

They were in a bare thirty fathoms of water—and, like the great pelagic sharks, nuclear attack submarines are creatures of the deep, not the shallows. The tactical plot showed bearings to three Soviet patrol craft, two Grisha-class frigates and a Poti-class corvette, all specialized antisubmarine ships. All were miles away, but they were still a very real threat.

The only good news was a storm overhead. The twenty-knot surface wind and sheets of falling rain made noise that interfered with sonar performance—but that included their own sonar, and sonar was their only safe means for getting information.

Then there were the imponderables. What sensing devices did the Soviets have in these waters? Might the water be clear enough that a circling helicopter or ASW aircraft could *see* them? Might there be a Tango-class diesel boat out there, moving slowly on her quiet, battery-powered electric motors? The only way they'd learn the answer to any of those questions was the metallic whine of a torpedo's high-speed propellers or the simple explosion of a falling depth-bomb. McCafferty considered all these things, and weighed the dangers against the priority of his Flash directive from COMSUBLANT:

Determine at once the operating areas of REDFLT SSBNs.

That sort of language gave him little leeway.

"How tight is the inertial fix?" McCafferty asked as casually as he could.

"Plus or minus two hundred yards." The navigator didn't even look up.

The captain grunted, knowing what the navigator was thinking. They should have gotten a NAVSTAR satellite fix a few hours ago, but the risk of detection was too high in an area crawling with Soviet surface craft. Two hundred yards, plus or minus, was fine accuracy by any rational standard—but not while submerged in shallow water off a hostile coast. How accurate were his charts? Were there unmarked wrecks out there? Even if his navigational data were completely accurate, quarters would be so tight in another few miles that a goof of two hundred yards could ground them, damaging the submarine . . . and making noise. The captain shrugged to himself. The *Chicago* was the best platform in the world for this mission. He'd done this sort of thing before, and he couldn't worry about everything at the same time. McCafferty took a few steps forward and leaned into the sonar compartment.

"How's our friend doing?"

"Continuing as before, skipper. No changes at all in the target's radiated noise level. Just toolin' right along at fifteen knots, dead ahead, no more than two thousand yards off. Pleasure cruise, like," the sonar chief concluded with no small irony.

Pleasure cruise. The Soviets were sortieing their ballistic missile submarines at intervals of one sub every four hours. Already a majority of them were at sea. They had *never* done that before. And all seemed to be heading east—not north and northeast as they usually did to cruise in the Barents or Kara seas, or most recently under the arctic ice cap itself. SACLANT had learned that piece of information from Norwegian P-3 aircraft patrolling Checkpoint Charlie, the spot fifty miles offshore where Soviet submarines always submerged. *Chicago,* the nearest sub to the area, had been sent to investigate.

They'd soon detected and gotten into trail position behind a Delta-III, a modern Soviet "boomer," as missile subs were known. Trailing her, they'd stayed within the hundred-fathom curve the whole way . . . until the target had turned southeast into shallow water toward Mys Svyatoy Nos, which led to the entrance to the White Sea—all of which was Soviet territorial water.

How far did they dare follow? *And what was going on?* McCafferty returned to control and went to the periscope pedestal.

"Look around," he said. "Up scope." A petty officer turned the hydraulic ring control and the portside search periscope slid upward from its well. "Hold!" McCafferty stooped at the conning station, catching the instrument as the quartermaster stopped it below the surface. From a position that was murderously uncomfortable, the skipper duck-walked the scope in a full circle. On the forward bulkhead was a television monitor which worked off a camera built into the scope. It was watched by the executive officer and a senior petty officer.

"No shadows," McCafferty said. Nothing to make him suspect that something was there.

"Concur, skipper," the XO agreed.

"Check with sonar."

Forward, the sonar watch listened carefully. Circling aircraft made noise, and there was about an even chance that they'd heard it. But now they heard nothing—which *didn't* mean that nothing was there, like maybe a high-flying chopper or another Grisha laying to, her diesels shut down as she drifted, listening for someone like *Chicago.*

"Sonar says they don't have anything, skipper," the XO reported.

"Two more feet," McCafferty ordered.

The quartermaster worked the lever again, bringing the periscope up by twenty-three inches, just barely out of the water in the troughs of the waves.

"Skipper!" It was the senior ESM technician. The highest item on *Chicago*'s periscope was a miniature antenna array which fed signals to a broadband receiver. The instant it projected above the surface, three lights flickered on the ESM tactical warning board. "I read three—five, maybe six India-band search radars. Signature characteristics say ship and land-based search radars, sir, not, repeat not, aircraft sets. Nothing in the Juliet-band." The technician started reading off the bearings.

McCafferty allowed himself to relax. There was no way a radar could detect so small a target as his periscope in these waves. He turned the periscope in a complete circle. "I see no surface ships. No aircraft. Seas about five feet. Estimate the surface wind from the northwest at, oh, about twenty, twenty-five knots." He snapped up the handles and stepped back. "Down scope." The oiled steel tube was heading down before he'd spoken the second word. The captain nodded approval at his quartermaster, who held out a stopwatch. The scope had been up above the surface for a total of 5.9 seconds. After fifteen years in submarines, it still amazed him how so many people could do so much in six seconds. When he'd gone through submarine school, the criterion had been a seven-second exposure.

The navigator examined his chart quickly, a quartermaster assisting him to plot the bearings to the signal sources.

"Captain." The navigator looked up. "Bearings are consistent with two known shore radar transmitters, and three Don-2 sets match the bearings of Sierra-2, -3, and -4." He referred to the plotted positions of the three Soviet surface ships. "We got one unknown, bearing zero-four-seven. What's that one look like, Harkins?"

"A land-based India-band surface search, one of those new 'Shore Cans,' " the technician responded, reading off frequency and pulse-width numbers. "Weak signal and kinda fuzzy, sir. Lots of activity, though, and all the transmitters are dialed into different frequencies." The technician meant that the radar searches were well coordinated, so that the radar transmitters would not interfere with one another.

An electrician rewound the videotape, allowing McCafferty to reexamine what he'd seen through the periscope. The only difference was that the periscope TV camera was black and white. The tape had to be run at slow speed to avoid blurring, so rapidly had the captain made his visual search.

"Amazing how good nothing can look, eh, Joe?" he asked his executive officer. The cloud ceiling was well below a thousand feet, and the wave action had rapidly coated the periscope lens with water droplets. No one had ever invented an efficient gadget for keeping that lens clear, McCafferty reflected, you'd think that after eighty-some years . . .

"Water looks a little murky, too," Joe answered hopefully. A visual sighting by antisubmarine warfare aircraft is one of the nightmares all submariners share.

"Doesn't look like a nice day to fly, does it? I don't think we have to worry about somebody getting an eyeball sight on us." The captain spoke loudly enough for the control room crew to hear.

"The water deepens out some for the next two miles," the navigator reported.

"How much?"

"Five fathoms, skipper."

McCafferty looked over at the XO, who was conning the boat at the moment. "Use it." On the other hand, some helicopter jockey might get lucky . . .

"Aye. Diving officer, take her down another twenty feet. Gently."

"Aye." The chief gave the necessary orders to the planesmen and you could feel the sighs through the attack center.

McCafferty shook his head. *When was the last time you saw your men look relieved over a twenty-foot change in depth?* he asked himself. He went forward to sonar. He did not remember being there only four minutes earlier.

"How are our friends doing, chief?"

"The patrol boats are still faint, sir. They seem to be circling—the bearings are changing back and forth like they been doin'. The boomer's blade count is also constant, sir, he's just toolin' right along at fifteen knots. Not especially quiet, either. I mean, we still got plenty of mechanical transients, y'know? There's maintenance work—lot of it—going on in there, by the sound he's making. Want to listen in, skipper?" The chief held up a pair of earphones. Most sonar scanning was done visually—the on-board computers converted acoustical signals into a display on TV-type tubes that looked most of all like some sort of arcade game. But there was still no real substitute for listening in. McCafferty took the phones.

First he heard the Delta's whirring reactor pumps. They were running at medium speed, driving water out of the reactor vessel into the steam generator. Next he concentrated on the screw sounds. The Russian boomer had a pair of five-bladed screws, and he tried to make his own count of the *chuga-chuga* noise made as each blade made its circuit. No good, he'd have to take the chief's word, as he usually did . . . *klang!*

"What was that?"

The chief turned to another senior operator. "Hatch slammin'?"

The first-class sonarman shook his head judiciously. "More like somebody dropped a wrench. Close, though, pretty close."

The captain had to smile. Everybody aboard was trying to affect a casual manner that had to be outrageously faked. Certainly everyone was as tense as he was, and McCafferty wanted nothing more than to get the hell out of this miserable lake. Of course he couldn't act in such a way as to allow his crew to become overly concerned; the captain must be in total control at all times—what fucking games we play! he told himself. *What* are *we doing here? What is going on in this crazy world? I don't* want *to fight a fucking war!*

He leaned against the doorframe, just forward of the control room, only a few feet from his own stateroom, wanting to go in, just to lie down for a minute or two, to take a few deep breaths, maybe go to his sink and splash a little cold water . . . but then he might accidentally look in the mirror. None of that, he knew. Command of a submarine was one of the last truly godlike jobs left in the world, and at times it required a truly godlike demeanor. Like now. *Play the game, Danny,* he told himself. The captain withdrew a handkerchief from his back pocket and rubbed his nose with it, his face locked into a neutral, almost bored expression as his eyes traced over the sonar displays. The cool captain . . .

McCafferty returned to the attack center a moment later, telling himself that he'd spent just enough time to inspire his sonar crewmen without pressuring them with too much attention from the CO. A fine balance. He looked around casually. The room was as crowded as an Irish bar on St. Patrick's Day. His men's outwardly cool faces were sweating, despite the nuclear-powered air conditioning. The planesmen especially were concentrating on their instruments, guiding the submarine down an electronically defined display, with the diving officer—*Chicago*'s most senior chief—right behind them.

In the center of the control room, the two side-by-side attack periscopes were fully retracted, with a quartermaster's mate poised to raise them. The XO paced as much as he could, looking at the chart every twenty seconds or so as he turned at the rear of the compartment. Not much here to complain about. Everybody was tense, but all the work was getting done.

"All things considered," McCafferty said for all to hear, "things are going pretty good. Surface conditions are working against them detecting us."

"Conn, sonar."

"Conn, aye." The captain took the phone.

"Hull-popping noises. He seems to be surfacing. Yeah, target is now blowing tanks, skipper."

"Understood. Keep us posted, chief." McCafferty put the phone back. He took three steps back to the chart table. "Why surface now?"

The navigator stole a cigarette from an enlisted man and lit it. McCafferty knew he didn't smoke. The lieutenant nearly gagged on it, drawing a brief smirk from a second-class quartermaster and a rueful grin from the navigator. He looked over at the captain.

"Sir, something is wrong about this," the lieutenant said quietly.

"Just one thing," the captain asked. "Why did he surface here?"

"Conn, sonar." McCafferty went forward and took the phone again. "Skipper, the boomer's doing a long blow, really blowing his tanks out like, sir."

"Anything else unusual?"

"No, sir, but he must've just used a lot of his reserve air, sir."

"Okay, chief, thank you." McCafferty hung up and wondered if *that* meant anything.

"Sir, you ever done this before?" the navigator asked.

"I've trailed a lot of Russian boats, but no, never in here."

"The target has to surface eventually, only sixty feet of water down here along Terskiy Bereg." The navigator traced his finger along the chart.

"And we have to break off the trail," McCafferty agreed. "But that's another forty miles."

"Yeah." The navigator nodded agreement. "But starting five miles back, this gulf starts to narrow down like a funnel, and for a submerged sub, it eventually closes down to two, then only one safe passage. Jeez, I don't know." McCafferty came aft again to examine the chart.

"He was content to run fifteen knots at periscope depth all this way down from Kola. The usable depth has been about the same for the past five hours—just bottomed out some—and figures to be the same for another hour or two . . . but he surfaces anyway. So," McCafferty said, "the only change in environmental conditions is the width of the channel, and that's still over twenty miles . . ." The captain mulled this over, staring down at the chart. The sonar room called yet again.

"Conn, aye. What is it, chief?"

"New contact, sir, bearing one-nine-two. Designate target Sierra-5. Twin-screw surface ship, diesel engines. They just came on all at once, sir. Sounds like a Natya-class. Bearing changing right to left slowly, seems to be converging with the boomer. Blade count puts her speed at about twelve knots."

"What's the boomer doing?"

"Speed and bearing are unchanged, skipper. The blow has ended. She's on the surface, sir, we're starting to get pounding and some racing on her screws—wait a minute . . . an active sonar just started up, we're getting reverbs, bearing seems to be about one-nine-zero, probably from the Natya. It's a very high frequency sonar, above aural range . . . I make it twenty-two-thousand hertz."

An icy ball suddenly materialized in McCafferty's stomach.

"XO, I'm taking the conn."

"Aye, Captain, you have the conn."

"Diving officer: get her up to sixty feet, high as you can without broaching her. Observation! Up scope!" The search scope came up and McCafferty met it as he had before and quickly checked the surface of the sea for shadows. "Three more feet. Okay, still nothing. What's the ESM reading?"

"Now seven active radar sources, skipper. Plot out about the same as before, plus the new one at one-nine-one, another India-band, looks like another Don-2."

McCafferty turned the periscope handle to twelve-power, its highest setting. The Soviet missile submarine was sitting extremely high in the water.

"Joe, tell me what you see," McCafferty asked, wanting a quick second opinion.

"That's a Delta-III, all right. Looks like she's blown dry, Cap'n, they come out pretty far, and that looks like about three or four feet higher than they usually do. He just used up a lot of his air . . . That might be the Natya's mast ahead of her, hard to be sure."

McCafferty could feel that his own *Chicago* was rolling. His hands tingled with the transmitted wave-slaps against the periscope. The seas were crashing against the Delta, too, and he could see water splashing in and out of the limber holes that lined the boomer's flanks.

"ESM board says that signal strengths are approaching detection values," the technician warned.

"His periscopes are both up," McCafferty said, knowing that his scope had already been up too long. He squeezed the trigger to double the magnification. It cost optical detail, but the picture zoomed in on the Delta's conning tower. "The control station atop his sail is fully manned. Everyone has glasses . . . not looking aft, though. Down scope. Diving officer, take her down ten feet. Nice work, planesmen. Let's see that tape, Joe." The picture returned to the TV monitor in a few seconds.

They were two thousand yards behind the Delta. Beyond her by about half a mile was a spherical radar dome, probably the Natya, rolling noticeably with the beam seas. To house her sixteen SS-18 missiles, the Russian sub had a sloped turtleback, and from directly aft it looked like a highway ramp. An ungainly design, the Delta, but she had to survive only long enough to launch her missiles, and the Americans had no doubt that her missiles worked just fine.

"Look at that, they blew her so high half her screws are clear," the XO pointed.

"Navigator, how far to shallow water?"

"Along this channel, a minimum of twenty-four fathoms for ten miles."

Why did the Delta surface this far out?

McCafferty lifted the phone. "Sonar, tell me about the Natya."

"Skipper, he's pinging away like mad. Not toward us, but we're getting lots of reflections and reverberations off the bottom."

The Natya was a specialized mine-hunter . . . also used, to be sure, as an escort for submarines in and out of safe areas. But her mine-hunting VHF sonar was operating . . . *dear God!*

"Left full rudder!" McCafferty shouted.

"Left full rudder, aye!" The helmsman would have hit the overhead but for the seatbelt. He instantly snapped his wheel to port. "Sir, my rudder is left full!"

"Minefield," the navigator breathed. Heads all over the room turned around.

"That's a good bet." McCafferty nodded grimly. "How far are we from the point where the boomer rendezvoused with the Natya?"

The navigator examined the plot closely. "Stopped about four hundred yards short of it, sir."

"All stop."

"All stop, aye." The helmsman dialed the annunciator handle. "Engine room answers all stop, sir. Passing left through one-eight-zero, sir."

"Very well. We ought to be safe enough here. You have to figure the Delta'd rendezvous with the sweeper a few miles clear of the field, right? Anybody here think Ivan would gamble with a boomer?" It was a rhetorical question. Nobody ever gambled with boomers.

Everyone in the control room took a deep breath at the same moment. The *Chicago* slowed rapidly, her turn taking her broadside to her previous course.

"Rudder amidships." McCafferty ordered one-third speed and lifted the phone for sonar. "The boomer doing anything different?"

"No, sir. Bearing is still constant at one-nine-zero. Speed still fifteen knots. We can still hear the Natya pinging, nearing one-eight-six, and her blade count is now about fifteen knots, too."

"Navigator, start figuring a way for us to get out of here. We want to keep well clear of all those patrol boats and report this news in as quick as we can."

"Aye. Three-five-eight looks pretty good for the moment, sir." The navigator had been updating that course continuously for two hours.

"Sir, if Ivan really has laid out a minefield, part of it's in international waters," the exec noted. "Cute."

"Yeah. Of course, to them it's territorial waters, so anybody bumps into a mine, it's just too damned bad—"

"And maybe an international incident?" Joe observed.

"But why did they ping at all?" the communications officer asked. "If they got a clear channel they can navigate visually."

"What if there's no channel at all?" the exec answered. "What if they set ground mines, and moored mines strung, say, at a uniform depth of fifty feet. You have to figure they'd be a little nervous that a mine or two might have too long a mooring cable. So they're playing it safe, just like we'd do. What's all that tell you?"

"Nobody can trail their boomers without surfacing . . ." the lieutenant understood.

"And we sure as hell aren't going to do that. Nobody ever said that Ivan was dumb. They got a perfect system here. They're putting all their missile boats where we can't get at them," McCafferty went on. "Even SUBROC can't make it from where we are into the White Sea. Final point, if they have to scatter the boats, they don't have to screw around in a single channel, they can all surface, spread out, and run for daylight.

"What this means, gentlemen, is that instead of detailing an attack boat to guard every boomer against somebody like us, they can put all the missile boats into one nice, safe basket and release their attack boats to other missions. Let's get the hell out of here."

NORTH ATLANTIC

"Ship in view, this is U.S. Navy aircraft on your port beam. Please identify, over." Captain Kherov handed the bridge-to-bridge phone to a Red Army major.

"Navy, this is the *Doctor Lykes*. How are y'all?" Kherov spoke halting English. The major's Mississippi accent might as well have been Kurdish for all he understood of it. They could barely make out the haze-gray patrol aircraft that was now circling their ship—circling, they noted, at a five-mile distance and certainly inspecting them through binoculars.

"Amplify, *Doctor Lykes*," the voice ordered tersely.

"We're out of New Orleans, bound for Oslo with general cargo, Navy. What's the big deal?"

"You're well north of a course to Norway. Please explain, over."

"Y'all read the damned papers, Navy? It's liable to get dangerous out here, and this big ole ship costs money. We got orders from the home office to keep close to some friendly folks. Hell, we're glad to see ya', boy. Y'all want to escort us a ways?"

"Roger, copy. *Doctor Lykes,* be advised no submarines known to be in this area."

"Y'all guarantee that?"

This drew a laugh. "Not hardly, *Doc.*"

"That's about what I thought, Navy. Well, if it's all right with you, we'll keep heading north a ways and try to stay under your air cover, over."

"We can't detail an aircraft to escort you."

"Understood, but you will come if we call you—right?"

"That's a roger," agreed Penguin 8.

"Okay, we'll continue north, then turn east for the Faroes. Will you warn us if any bad guys show up, over."

"If we find any, *Doc,* the idea is we'll try an' sink 'em first," the pilot exaggerated.

"Fair enough. Good huntin', boy. Out."

PENGUIN 8

"God, do people really talk like that?" the pilot of the Orion wondered aloud.

"Never heard about Lykes Lines?" his copilot chuckled. "They used to say they wouldn't hire a guy 'less he had a Southern accent. I never believed it until now. Nothing like tradition. He is kinda off the beaten track, though."

"Yeah, but until the convoys form up, hell, I'd try to bounce from one protected area to another. Anyway, let's finish the visual." The pilot increased power and headed in closer while his copilot lifted the recognition book.

"Okay, we have an all-black hull with 'Lykes Lines' on the side, midships. White superstructure with black diamond, a block L inside the diamond." He lifted his binoculars. "Lookout mast forward of the superstructure. Check. Superstructure is nicely raked. Electronics mast is not. Proper ensign and house flag. Black funnels. Winches aft by the barge elevator— doesn't say how many winches. Damn, she's carrying a full load of barges, isn't she? Paintwork looks a little shabby. Anyway, it all checks with the book; that's a friendly."

"Okay, let's give her a wave." The pilot turned the yoke to the left, taking the Orion directly over the barge-carrier. He waggled his wings slightly as he passed overhead, and two men on the bridge waved back at them. The flyers couldn't pick out the two men tracking them with hand-held SAMs. "Good luck, fella. You might need it."

MV *JULIUS FUCIK*

"The new paint scheme will make visual spotting difficult, Comrade General," the air-defense officer said quietly. "I saw no air-to-surface missiles attached."

"That will change quickly enough. As soon as our fleet puts to sea, they will load them. Besides, if they identify us as enemy, how far can we run while they call up other aircraft, or simply fly to their base to rearm?" The General watched the aircraft depart. His heart had been in his throat for the whole episode, but now he could walk out to where Kherov stood on the open bridge wing. Only the ship's officers had been issued American-style khaki uniforms.

"My compliments to your language officer. I presume he was speaking English?"

Andreyev laughed jovially, now that the danger was past. "So I am told. The Navy requested a man with his particular skills. He's an intelligence officer, served in America."

"In any case, he succeeded. Now we may approach our objective safely," Kherov said, using the last word relatively.

"It will be good to be on land again, Comrade Captain." The General didn't like being on such a large, unprotected target and would not feel safe until he had solid ground under his feet. At least as an infantryman you had a rifle with which to defend yourself, usually a hole to hide in, and always two legs to run away. Not so on a ship, he had learned. A ship was one large target, and this one was virtually unprotected. Amazing, he thought, that anything would feel worse than being on a transport aircraft. But there he had a parachute. He had no illusions about his ability to swim to land.

SUNNYVALE, CALIFORNIA

"There goes another one," the chief master sergeant said.

It was almost boring now. Never in the colonel's memory had the Soviets had more than six photographic reconnaissance satellites in orbit. There were now ten, plus ten electronic-intelligence gatherers, some launched from the Baikonor Cosmodrome outside Leninsk in the Kazakh S.S.R., the other half from Plesetsk in northern Russia.

"That's an F-type booster, Colonel. Burn time is wrong for the A-type," the sergeant said, looking up from his watch.

This Russian booster was a derivation of the old SS-9 ICBM, and it had only two functions—to launch radar ocean reconnaissance satellites, called RORSATS, that monitored ships at sea and to loft the Soviet antisatellite system. The Americans were watching the launch from a newly launched KH-11 reconnaissance satellite of their own, sweeping over the central region of the USSR. The colonel lifted the phone to Cheyenne Mountain.

USS *PHARRIS*

I should be sleeping, Morris told himself. *I should stockpile sleep, bank it away against the time when I can't have any.* But he was too keyed up to sleep.

USS *Pharris* was steaming figure eights off the mouth of the Delaware River. Thirty miles north, at the piers of Philadelphia, Chester, and Camden, ships of the National Reserve Defense Fleet that had been held in readiness for years were getting ready to sail. Cargo holds were loading with tanks, guns, and crates of explosive ordnance. His air-search radar showed the tracks of numerous troop transports lifting out of Dover Air Force Base. The Military Airlift Command's huge aircraft could ferry the troops across to Germany where they would be mated with their pre-positioned equipment, but when their unit loads of munitions ran out, the resupply would have to be ferried across the way it had always been, in ugly, fat, slow merchant ships—targets. Maybe the merchies weren't so slow anymore, and were larger than before, but there were fewer of them.

During his naval career, the American merchant fleet had fallen sharply, even supplemented by these federally funded vessels. Now a submarine could sink one ship and get the benefit it would have achieved in World War II by sinking four or five.

The merchant crews were another problem. Traditionally held in contempt by Navy sailors—a truism in the U.S. Navy was to steer well clear of any merchantman, lest he decide to liven up his day by ramming you—the average age of the crews running the ships was about fifty, more than double that in any American naval vessel. How would those grandfathers take the stress of combat operations? Morris wondered. They were quite well paid—some of the senior seamen made as much as he did—but would their comfortable, union-negotiated salaries devalue in the face of missiles and torpedoes? He had to erase the thought from his mind. These old men with kids in high school and college were his flock. He was the shepherd, and there were wolves hiding under the gray surface of the Atlantic.

Not a large flock. He had seen the figures only a year ago: the total number of privately owned cargo ships in operation under the American flag was 170 and averaged about eighteen thousand tons apiece. Of those, a mere 103 were routinely engaged in overseas trade. The supplemental National Defense Reserve Fleet consisted of only 172 cargo ships. To call the situation a disgrace was to describe gang rape as a mild social deviation.

They couldn't allow even one to be lost.

Morris wandered over to the bridge radarscope and looked down into the rubber eyeshield to watch the aircraft lifting out of Dover. Each blip contained three to five hundred men. What would happen when they ran out of shells?

"Another merchie, skipper." The officer of the deck pointed to a dot on the horizon. "She's a Dutch container boat. I expect she's inbound for military cargo."

Morris grunted. "We need all the help we can get."

SUNNYVALE, CALIFORNIA

"It's definite, sir," the colonel said. "That's a Soviet ASAT-bird, seventy-three nautical miles behind one of ours."

The colonel had ordered his satellite to turn in space and point its cameras at its new companion. The light wasn't all that good, but the shape of the Soviet killer satellite was unmistakable: a cylinder nearly a hundred feet long, with a rocket motor at one end and a radar seeker antenna at the other.

"What's your recommendation, Colonel?"

"Sir, I am requesting unlimited authority to maneuver my birds at will. As soon as anything with a red star on it gets within fifty miles, I'm going to do a series of delta-V maneuvers to screw up their intercept solution."

"That will cost you a lot of fuel, son," CINC-NORAD warned.

"What we have here, General, is a binary solution set." The colonel responded like a true mathematician. "Choice one, we maneuver the birds and risk the fuel loss. Choice two, we don't maneuver the birds and risk having them taken out. Once they close to fifty miles, they can achieve intercept and negate our bird in as little as five minutes. Maybe faster. Five minutes is only the best we've observed them to do. Sir, you have my recommendation." The colonel had a Ph.D. in mathematics from the

University of Illinois, but that was not where he'd learned to back generals into corners.

"Okay. This one goes to Washington, but I'll forward your recommendation with my endorsement."

USS *NIMITZ*

"Admiral, we've just had a disturbing report from the Barents Sea." Toland read the dispatch from CINCLANTFLT.

"How many more subs can they throw at us now?"

"Perhaps as many as thirty additional boats, Admiral."

"Thirty?" Baker hadn't liked anything he'd been told for a week now. He especially didn't like this.

The *Nimitz* battle group, in company with *Sarotoga* and the French carrier *Foch*, was escorting a marine amphibious unit, called a MAU, to reinforce the ground defenses on Iceland. A three-day run. If the war started soon after they made their delivery, their next mission would be to support the GIUK barrier defense plan, the critically important link that covered the ocean between Greenland, Iceland, and the United Kingdom. Carrier Task Force 21 was a powerful force. But would it be powerful enough? Doctrine required a four-carrier group to fight and survive up here, but the fleet had not yet been fully assembled. Toland was getting reports on frantic diplomatic activity aimed at averting the war that appeared about to start, much as everyone hoped it wouldn't. How would the Soviets react to four or more carriers in the Norwegian Sea? It seemed that no one in Washington wanted to find out, but Toland was wondering if it would matter at all. As it was, Iceland had approved the reinforcements they were escorting only twelve hours before, and this NATO outpost needed immediate reinforcement.

USS *CHICAGO*

McCafferty was thirty miles north of the entrance to the Kola Fjord. The crew was relatively happy to be here after a tense sixteen-hour run from Cape Svyatoy. Though the Barents Sea was alive with antisubmarine ships, immediately after making their report they had been withdrawn from the entrance to the White Sea for fear of fomenting a major incident. Here there was a hundred thirty fathoms of water and room to maneuver, and they were confident in their ability to keep out of trouble. There was supposed to be a pair of American subs within fifty miles of *Chicago,* plus a Brit and two Norwegian diesel boats. His sonarmen couldn't hear any of them, though they could hear a quartet of Grisha-class frigates pinging away at something to the southeast. The allied submarines here were assigned to watch and listen. It was a nearly ideal mission for them, since they only had to creep along, avoiding contact with surface ships, which they could detect from a good, long distance.

There was no hiding it now. McCafferty didn't even consider not telling his men the significance of what they had learned about the Russian boomers. Submarines have no long-lived secrets. It looked like they were about to fight a war. The politicians in Washington and the strategists in Norfolk and elsewhere might still have their doubts, but there, at the sharp end of the lance, the officers and men aboard *Chicago* discussed the way the Soviets were using their ships and came up with a single answer. The submarine's torpedo tubes were loaded with MK-48 torpedoes and Harpoon missiles. Her vertical missile tubes forward of the pressure hull held twelve Tomahawks, three nuclear-tipped land-attack missiles, and nine conventional antiship models. When a shipboard machine showed the first suggestion of a fault, a technician immediately tore it down to fix it. McCafferty was pleased and not a little surprised by his crew. So young they were—the average age on his submarine was twenty-one—to have to adapt to this.

He stood in the sonar room, forward and to starboard of the attack center. A few feet from him, a massive computer system sifted through an avalanche of waterborne sound, analyzing individual frequency bands known from experience to mark the acoustical signature of a Soviet vessel. The signals were displayed on a visual screen called a waterfall display, a monocolor curtain of yellow whose brighter lines indicated the bearing to a sound that might be a source of interest. Four lines indicated the Grishas, and offset dots marked the pings from their active sonars. McCafferty wondered what they were after. His interest was mainly academic. They weren't pinging his ship, but there was always something to learn from how the enemy did his job. A team of officers in the attack center was plotting the movement of the Soviet patrol ships, carefully noting their formation patterns and hunting technique for later comparison with intelligence estimates.

A new series of dots appeared at the bottom of the screen. A sonarman punched a button for a more selective frequency setting, altering the display slightly, then plugged in a pair of microphones. The display was on fast-speed image generation, and McCafferty saw the dots grow to lines around bearing one-nine-eight, the direction to the Kola channel.

"Lots of confused noise, skipper," the sonarman reported. "I read Alfas and Charlies coming out, with other stuff behind them. Blade count on one Alfa is something like thirty knots. Lots of noise behind them, sir."

The visual display confirmed it a minute later. The frequency- or tone-lines were in the areas known to depict specific classes of submarines, all moving at high speed to clear the harbor. The bearing-to-contact lines spread apart as the boats fanned out. The boats had already dived, he noted. Usually Soviet submarines didn't dive until they were well offshore.

"Ship count is over twenty, sir," the chief sonarman said quietly. "We have a major sortie here."

"Sure looks like it." McCafferty moved back to the attack center. His men were already entering the contact positions into the fire-control computer, and sketching paper tracks on the chart table. The war hadn't started yet, and though it appeared it could come at any time, McCafferty's orders were to keep clear of any Soviet formation until the Word came. He didn't like it—better to get his blows in quick—but Washington had made it clear they wanted no one to cause an incident that might prevent some kind of diplomatic settlement. That made sense, the captain admitted to himself. Maybe the lace-panty folks could still get things under control. A faint hope, but a real one. Real enough to overcome his tactical desire to hold an attack position.

He ordered his submarine moved farther offshore. In half an hour, things were clearer still, and the captain had a SLOT-buoy launched. The buoy was programmed to allow *Chicago* thirty minutes to clear the area, then it started sending a series of burst transmissions on a UHF satellite band. From ten miles away, he listened to Soviet ships going berserk around the radio buoy, doubtlessly thinking it was the location of the submarine. The game was becoming all too real.

The buoy operated for over an hour, continuously sending its data to a NATO communications satellite. By nightfall the data was being broadcast to all NATO units at sea. *The Russians are coming.*

16. Last Moves / First Moves

USS *NIMITZ*

The speaker had announced sunset two hours before, but Bob had to finish his work. Sunsets at sea far away from the polluted city air, with a sharp horizon for the sun to slide under, were always something he enjoyed watching. What he saw now was almost as good. He stood with his hands on the rail, first looking down at the foam alongside the carrier's sleek hull, then after a brief moment of preparation, up. Born and raised in Boston, Toland hadn't known what the Milky Way was until joining the Navy, and the discovery of the wide, bright belt of stars overhead was always a source of wonder to him. There were the stars he'd learned to navigate by, with sextant and trigonometric tables—largely replaced now by electronic aids like Omega and Loran—but they were still beautiful to behold. Arcturus, and Vega, and Altair, all blinking at him with their own colors, their own unique characteristics that made them benchmarks in the night sky.

A door opened, and a sailor dressed in what looked like a purple plane-fueler's shirt joined him on the flight deck catwalk.

"Darkened ship, sailor. I'd dump that cigarette," Toland said sharply, more annoyed to have his precious solitude destroyed.

"Sorry, sir." The butt sailed over the side. The man was silent for a few minutes, then looked at Toland. "You know about the stars, sir?"

"What do you mean?"

"This is my first cruise, sir, an' I grew up in New York. Never saw the stars like this, but I don't even know what they are—the names, I mean. You officers know all that stuff, right?"

Toland laughed quietly. "I know what you mean. Same with my first time out. Pretty, isn't it?"

"Yes, sir. What's that one?" The boy's voice sounded tired. *Small wonder,* Toland thought, *with all the flight operations they've been through today.* The youngster pointed to the brightest dot in the eastern sky, and Bob had to think for a few seconds.

"That's Jupiter. A planet, not a star. With the quartermaster's spyglass, you can pick out her moons—some of them anyway." He went on to point out some of the stars used for navigation.

"How do you use 'em, sir?" the sailor asked.

"You take a sextant and plot their height above the horizon—sounds harder than it is, just takes some practice—and you check that against a book of star positions."

"Who does that, sir?"

"The book? Standard stuff. I imagine the book we use comes from the Naval Observatory in D.C., but people have been measuring the tracks of the stars and planets for three or four thousand years, long before tele-scopes were invented. Anyway, if you know the exact time, and you know where a particular star is, you can plot out where you are on the globe pretty accurately, within a few hundred yards if you really know your stuff. Same thing with the sun and the moon. That knowledge has been around for hundreds of years. The tricky part was inventing a clock that kept good time. That happened about two hundred and some years ago."

"I thought they used satellites and stuff like that."

"We do now, but the stars are just as pretty."

"Yeah." The sailor sat down, his head leaning way back to watch the curtain of white points. Beneath them the ship's hull churned the water to foam with the whispering sound of a continuously breaking wave. Somehow the sound and the sky matched each other perfectly. "Well, at least I learned something about the stars. When's it gonna start, sir?"

Toland looked up at the constellation of Sagittarius. The center of the galaxy was behind it. Some astrophysicists said there was a black hole in there. The most destructive force known to physics, it made the forces under man's control appear puny by comparison. But men were a lot easier to destroy.

"Soon."

USS *CHICAGO*

The submarine was far offshore now, west of the surging Soviet submarine and surface forces. They'd heard no explosions yet, but it couldn't be far off. The nearest Soviet ship was about thirty miles off to the east, and a dozen more were plotted. All were blasting the sea with their active sonars.

McCafferty was surprised by his Flash operational order. *Chicago* was being pulled out of the Barents Sea and shifted to a patrol area in the Norwegian Sea. Mission: to interdict Soviet submarines expected to head south toward the North Atlantic. A political decision had been made: It must not appear that NATO was forcing the Soviets into a war. In a stroke, the pre-war strategy of engaging the Soviet Fleet in its own backyard had been tossed away. Like every pre-war battle plan in this century, the sub skipper reflected, this one too was being torn up because the enemy wasn't going to cooperate and do what we thought he'd do. Of course. He was putting many more submarines in the Atlantic than had been expected—even worse, we were making it easier for him! McCafferty wondered what other surprises were in store. The submarine's torpedoes and missiles were now fully armed, her fire-control systems continuously manned, her crew standing Condition-3 wartime watch routine. But their orders at present were to run away. The captain swore to himself, angry with whoever had made this decision, yet still hoping in a quiet corner of his mind that somehow the war could be stopped.

BRUSSELS, BELGIUM

"It's gotta happen soon," COMAIRCENT observed. "Shit, they got their troops as ready as I've ever seen. They can't wait until all our Reforger units are fully in place. They *have* to hit us soon."

"I know what you're saying, Charlie, but we can't move first."

"Any word on our visitors?" The Air Force general referred to Major Chernyavin's team of Spetznaz commandos.

"Still sitting tight." A unit of the elite GSG-9 German border guards had the safe house under continuous surveillance, with a second English ambush team between them and their supposed target in Lammersdorf. Intelligence officers from most of the NATO countries were part of the surveillance team, each with a direct line to his government. "What if they're bait, trying to get us to strike first?"

"I know we can't do that, General. What I want is a green light to initiate Dreamland when we know it's all for-real. We have to get our licks in fast, boss."

SACEUR leaned back. Trapped by his duties in his underground command post, he hadn't been to his official residence in ten days. He wondered if any general officer in the whole world had gotten any sleep in the past two weeks.

"If you put the orders up, how fast can you react?"

"I have all the birds loaded and ready now. My crews are briefed. If I order them to stand to, I can have Dreamland running thirty minutes from your signal."

"Okay, Charlie. The President has given me authority to react to any attack. Tell your people to stand to."

"Right."

SACEUR's phone rang. He lifted it, listened briefly, and looked up. "Our visitors are moving," he told COMAIRCENT. To his operations officer, "The code word is Firelight." NATO forces would now go to maximum alert.

AACHEN, FEDERAL REPUBLIC OF GERMANY

The Spetznaz team left the safe house in two small vans and drove south on the road to Lammersdorf. With their leader killed in a traffic accident, the second in command, a captain, had been delivered copies of the papers his boss had died to get, and fully briefed his men. They were quiet and tense. The officer had taken pains to explain to his men that their escape had been carefully planned, that once clear of the target they'd get to another safe house and wait for their Red Army comrades to arrive in five days. They were the cream of the Red Army, he'd told them, thoroughly trained to carry out dangerous missions behind enemy lines, hence valuable to the State. Every man had combat experience fighting in the mountains of Afghanistan, he reminded them. They were trained. They were ready.

The men accepted this speech as elite troopers usually did, in total silence. Chosen most of all for their intelligence, each of them knew that the speech was merely that. The mission depended largely on luck, and their luck had already gone bad. Every one of them wished that Major Chernyavin were there, and wondered if somehow the mission might have been blown. One by one, they set these thoughts aside. Soon every man was reviewing his part in the mission to destroy Lammersdorf.

The drivers were KGB agents well experienced at working in foreign lands, and wondering exactly the same thing. Both vehicles stayed together, driving conservatively, wary of vehicles that followed them. Each had a scanner radio tuned to the local police frequencies, and another for communicating with each other. The KGB officers had discussed the mission an hour before. Moscow Center had told them that NATO was not yet fully alerted. The lead driver, whose regular cover job was driving a taxi, wondered if a "full" NATO alert meant a parade through Red Square.

"Turning right now. Car three, close in. Car one, turn left at the next intersection and get ahead of them." Colonel Weber spoke over a tactical radio of the sort used by FIST—fire-support team—units. The ambush had been ready for several days now, and as soon as their targets had emerged from their safe house, the word had been flashed all over the Federal Republic. NATO establishments already on alert were brought to full battle-readiness. This could only be the opening move in a shooting war . . . unless, Weber admitted to himself, they were simply moving from one secure place to wait further in another one. He didn't know which way things would turn, though surely it had to begin soon. Didn't it?

The two trucks were now in a rural part of Western Germany, driving southeast through the German – Belgian Nature Park, a scenic route often traveled by tourists and sightseers. They had chosen this side road to avoid the military traffic on the major highways, but as they passed through Mulartshutte, the lead driver frowned as he saw a military convoy of tanks on low-hauler trailers. Strangely, the tanks were loaded backwards, with their massive guns facing aft. British tanks, he saw, new Challengers. Well, he hadn't expected to see any German Leopard tanks on the Belgian border. There had never been any possibility of preventing a German mobilization, and he tried to convince himself that the rest of the NATO countries had not moved as quickly as they could have. Ah, if this mission were successful, then NATO's communications would be seriously damaged, and maybe the armored spearheads would indeed come to rescue them. The convoy slowed. The driver considered pulling around them, but his orders were to be inconspicuous.

"Everyone ready?" Weber asked from his chase car.

"Ready." *Bloody complex op, this,* Colonel Armstrong thought. *Tankers, SAS, and the Germans all working together. But worth it to bag a bunch of Spetznaz.* The convoy slowed and stopped at a picnicking area. Weber halted his car a hundred meters away. It was now in the hands of the English ambush team.

Flares erupted around the two small vans.

The KGB driver cringed at being in the center of so much light. Then he looked forward to see the barrel of the tank just fifty meters ahead of him rise from its travel-rest and center on his windshield.

"Attention," a voice called in Russian over a megaphone. "Spetznaz soldiers, attention. You are surrounded by a company of mechanized troops. Come out of your vehicles singly and unarmed. If you open fire, you will be killed within seconds." A second voice began speaking.

"Come out, Comrades, this is Major Chernyavin. There is no chance."

The commandos exchanged looks of horror. In the lead vehicle the captain started to pull the pin on a grenade. A sergeant leaped on him and wrapped his hand around the captain's.

"We cannot be taken alive! Those are our orders!" the captain shouted.

"The devil's mother we can't!" the sergeant screamed. "One at a time, Comrades—out with hands high. And be careful!"

A private emerged from the back door of the van, one slow foot at a time.

"Come to the sound of my voice, Ivanov," Chernyavin said from a wheelchair. The major had told much to earn the chance to save his detachment. He had worked with these men for two years, and he could not let them be slaughtered to no purpose. It was one thing to be loyal to the State, another to be loyal to the men he'd led in combat operations. "You will not be hurt. If you have any weapons, drop them now. I know about the knife you carry, Private Ivanov . . . Very good. Next man."

It went quickly. A joint team of Special Air Service and GSG-9 commandos collected their Soviet counterparts, handcuffed them, and led them off to be blindfolded. Soon only two were left. The grenade made it tricky. By this time the captain had seen the futility of his action, but it proved impossible to locate the pin for the grenade. The sergeant shouted a warning to Chernyavin, who wanted to come forward himself, but couldn't. The captain came out last. He wanted to throw the grenade at the officer who, he thought, had betrayed his country, only to see a man whose legs were swathed in plaster.

Chernyavin could see the look on the man's face.

"Andrey Ilych, would you prefer that your life should end for nothing?" the major asked. "The bastards drugged me and learned enough to kill you all. I could not let them do this."

"I have a live grenade!" the captain said loudly. "I will throw it into the truck." This he did before anyone could shout to stop him. A moment later the truck exploded, destroying the group's maps and plans for escape. For the first time in a week, Chernyavin's face broke into a wide grin. "Well done, Andrushka!"

Two other Spetznaz groups were less lucky, and were intercepted within sight of their targets by German units privy to Chernyavin's capture. But twenty additional groups were in the Federal Republic, and not every NATO site had gotten the word in time. A score of vicious firefights erupted on both sides of the Rhein. A war to involve millions began with squad- and platoon-sized units fighting desperate actions in the dark.

17. The Frisbees of Dreamland

GERMANY, FORWARD EDGE OF THE BATTLE AREA

The view would have been frightening to most men. There were solid clouds overhead at four thousand feet. He flew through showers that he more heard than saw on this black night, and the dark outlines of trees appeared to reach up and snatch at his speeding fighter. Only a madman would be so low on such a night—so much the better, he smiled inside his oxygen mask.

Colonel Douglas Ellington's fingertips caressed the control stick of his F-19A Ghostrider attack fighter, while his other hand rested on the side-by-side throttle controls on the left-side cockpit wall. The head-up display projected on the windshield in front of him reported 625 knots Indicated Air Speed, a hundred six feet of altitude, a heading of 013, and around the numbers was a monocolor holographic image of the terrain before him. The image came from a forward-looking infrared camera in the fighter's nose, augmented by an invisible laser that interrogated the ground eight times per second. For peripheral vision, his oversized helmet was fitted with low-light goggles.

"Raisin' hell over our heads," his back-seater reported. Major Don Eisly monitored the radio and radar signals, as well as their own instruments: "All systems continue nominal, range to target now ninety miles."

"Right," the Duke responded. It had been an automatic nickname for Ellington, who even looked vaguely like the jazz musician.

Ellington relished the mission. They were skimming north at perilously low level over the angular terrain of East Germany, and their Frisbee, never more than two hundred feet off the ground, jerked up and down to the pilot's constant course adjustments.

Lockheed called her the Ghostrider. The pilots called her the Frisbee, the F-19A, the secretly developed Stealth attack fighter. She had no corners, no box shapes to allow radar signals to bounce cleanly off her. Her high-bypass turbofans were designed to emit a blurry infrared signature at most. From above, her wings appeared to mimic the shape of a cathedral bell. From in front, they curved oddly toward the ground, earning her the affectionate nickname of Frisbee. Though she was a masterpiece of electronic technology inside, she usually didn't use her active systems. Radars and radios made electronic noise that an enemy might detect, and the whole idea of the Frisbee was that she didn't seem to exist at all.

Far over their heads on both sides of the border, hundreds of fighter aircraft played a deadly game of bluff, racing toward the border and then turning away, both sides trying to goad the other into committing to battle. Each side had airborne radar aircraft with which to control such a battle and so gain the advantage in a war which, though few yet knew it, had already begun.

And we're getting a quick one in, Ellington thought. *We're finally doing something smart!* He'd had a hundred missions over Vietnam in the first production F-111A fighters. The Duke was the Air Force's leading expert on covert low-level missions, and it was said that he could "bull's-eye a chuckhole in a Kansas tornado at midnight." That wasn't quite true. The Frisbee could never handle a tornado. The sad truth was that the F-19 handled like a pig—a consequence of her ungainly design. But Ellington didn't care. Being invisible was better than being agile, he judged, knowing that he was about to prove or disprove that proposition.

The Frisbee squadron was now penetrating the most concentrated SAM belt the world had ever known.

"Range to primary target is now sixty miles," Eisly advised. "All onboard systems continue nominal. No radars are locked onto us. Lookin' good, Duke."

"Roger." Ellington pushed the stick forward and dived as they passed over the crest of a small hill, then bottomed out at eighty feet over a wheatfield. The Duke was playing his game to the limit, drawing on years of experience in low-level attacks. Their primary target was a Soviet IL-76 Mainstay, an AWACS-type aircraft that was circling near Magdeburg, agreeably within ten miles of their secondary target, the E-8 highway bridges over the Elbe at Hohenroarthe. The mission was getting a lot hairier. The closer they got to the Mainstay the more radar signal hit their aircraft, its intensity growing at a square function. Sooner or later, enough signal would be reflected back to the Mainstay to be detectable, even by curved wings made of radar-transparent composites. All the Stealth technology did was to make radar detection harder, not impossible. Would they be seen by the Mainstay? If so, when, and how quickly would the Russians react?

Keep her on the deck, he told himself. *Play the game by the rules you've practiced out.* They had rehearsed this mission for nine days in "Dreamland," the top-secret exercise area in the sprawl of Nellis Air Force Base, Nevada. Even the E-3A Sentry could barely make them out at forty miles, and the Sentry was a far better radar platform that the Mainstay, wasn't it?

That's what you're here to find out, boy . . .

There were five Mainstays on duty, all a hundred klicks east of the inter-German border. A nice safe distance, what with over three hundred fighters between them and the border.

"Twenty miles, Duke."

"Right. Call it off, Don."

"Roge. Still no fire-control emanations on us, and no search stuff is lingering our way. Lots of radio chatter, but mostly west of us. Very little VOX coming from the target."

Ellington reached his left hand down to arm the four AIM-9M Sidewinder missiles hanging under his wings. The weapon-indicator light blinked a lethal, friendly green.

"Eighteen miles. Target appears to be circling normally, not taking evasive action."

Ten miles to the minute, Ellington computed in his mind, *one minute forty seconds.*

"Sixteen miles." Eisly read the numbers off a computer readout keyed to the NAVSTAR satellite navigation system.

The Mainstay would not have a chance. The Frisbee would not begin to climb until she was directly underneath the target. Fourteen miles. Twelve. Ten. Eight. Six miles to the converted air transport.

"The Mainstay just reversed her turn—yeah, she's jinking. A Foxfire just swept over us," Eisly said evenly. A MiG-25 interceptor, presumably acting on instructions from the IL-76, was now searching for them. With its high power and small arc, the Foxfire stood a good chance of acquiring them, Stealth technology or not. "The Mainstay might have us."

"Anything locked on us?"

"Not yet." Eisly's eyes were glued to the threat-receiver instruments. No missile-control radars had centered on the Frisbee yet. "Coming under the target."

"Right. Climbing now." Ellington eased back on his stick and punched up full afterburners. The Frisbee's engines could only give him Mach 1.3, but this was the place to use all the power he had. According to the weather people, these clouds topped out at twenty thousand feet, and the IL-76 would be about five thousand above that. Now the Frisbee was vulnerable. No longer lost in the ground clutter, her engines radiating their maximum signature, the Stealth aircraft was broadcasting her presence. *Climb faster, baby . . .*

"*Tallyho!*" Ellington said too loudly over the intercom as he burst through the clouds, and the night-vision systems instantly showed him the

Mainstay, five miles away and diving for cover in front of him. Too late. The head-on closing speed was nearly a thousand miles per hour. The colonel centered his gunsight pipper on the target. A warbling tone came into his headset: the Sidewinders' seekers had locked onto the target. His right thumb toggled the launch-enable switch, and his forefinger squeezed the trigger twice. The Sidewinders left the aircraft half a second apart. Their brilliant exhaust flames dazzled him, but he did not take his eyes off the missiles as they raced for the target. It took eight seconds. He looked them all the way in. Both missiles angled for the Mainstay's starboard wing. Thirty feet away, laser proximity fuses detonated, filling the air with lethal fragments. It happened too fast. Both of the Mainstay's right-side engines exploded, the wing came off, and the Soviet aircraft began cartwheeling violently downward, lost seconds later in the clouds.

Jesus! Ellington thought as he rolled and dived back to the ground and safety. *Nothing like the movies. The target was hit and gone between blinks. Well, okay, that was easy enough. Primary target gone. Now for the hard part . . .*

Aboard an E-3A Sentry circling over Strasbourg. the radar technicians noted with satisfaction that all five Soviet radar craft had been killed within two minutes: it all worked, the F-19 really did surprise them.

The brigadier general in command of Operation Dreamland leaned forward in his command chair and toggled his microphone.

"Trumpeter, Trumpeter, Trumpeter," he said, then switched off. "Okay, boys," he breathed. "Make it count."

Amid the clouds of NATO tactical fighters hovering near the border, a hundred low-level attack fighters broke clear and dove for the ground. Half were F-111F Aardvarks, the other half "GR.1" Tornados, their wings heavy with fuel tanks and smart bombs. They followed the second wave of Frisbees, already sixty miles into East Germany, fanning out to their ground targets. Behind the strike aircraft, all-weather Eagle and Phantom interceptors, directed by the Sentries circling over the Rhein, began to launch their radar-guided missiles at Soviet fighters that had just lost their airborne controllers. Finally, a third team of NATO aircraft swooped in low, seeking out the ground radar sites that were coming on to replace the radar coverage of the dead Mainstays.

HOHENROARTHE, GERMAN DEMOCRATIC REPUBLIC

Ellington circled his target at a thousand feet, several miles away. It was a double bridge, a pair of concrete arches, each about five hundred yards across, and with two traffic lanes, that crossed the River Elbe in the middle of a gentle S-curve. Pretty bridges. Ellington guessed that they dated back to the thirties, since this main road from Berlin to Braunschweig had been one of the first autobahns. *Ole Adolf himself might have driven across these bridges,* Ellington reflected. So much the better.

At the moment, a low-light television in his targeting systems showed them to be covered with Russian T-80 tanks, all heading west. Ellington evaluated the picture on his television screen. This could only be the second echelon of the army deployed to attack NATO. There was an SA-6 battery atop Hill 76 south of the bridges on the east bank, sited there to defend them. It had to be fully alert now. His earphones chirped constantly with noise from his threat receiver as the search radars from a score of air-defense batteries swept continuously over his aircraft. If only one of them got a good return . . . *Pucker factor*, Ellington reflected grimly.

"How's the Pave Tack?"

"Nominal," Eisly responded curtly. Pilot and back-seater were both under enormous stress.

"Illuminate," Ellington ordered. In the back seat, Eisly activated the Pave Tack target-illumination laser.

The elaborate Pave Tack gear was built into the Frisbee's drooping nose-cone. Its lowermost part was a rotating turret containing a carbon-dioxide laser and television camera. The major used his joystick controls to center the TV picture on the bridge, then unmasked the infrared laser. An invisible dot appeared in the center of the north span's bridge deck. A computer system would keep it there until told to do otherwise, and a videotape recorder would make a visual record of the raid's success or failure.

"The target is lit," Eisly said. "Still no fire-control radars on us."

"Nemo, this is Shade 4. The target is lit."

"Roge."

Fifteen seconds later the first Aardvark screamed south a bare thirty feet over the water, popped up, and loosed a single GBU-15 Paveway laser-guided bomb before it turned hard to the east over Hohenroarthe. An optical-computer system in the bomb's nose noted the reflected infrared beam, centered it, and adjusted the fins accordingly.

South of the bridge, the SAM battery commander was trying to decide what the noise was. His search radar did not show the Frisbee. He had been told not to expect the presence of "friendly" aircraft—the safe travel lane was fifteen miles to the north, over the Frontal Aviation base at Mahlminkel. *Maybe that's where the noise was coming from*, he thought. *No special alarm has been sent out—*

The northern horizon went bright yellow. Though he did not know it, four Luftwaffe Tornados had just made a single pass over Mahlminkel, leaving hundreds of explosive cluster munitions in their wake. A half-dozen Soviet Sukhoi attack fighters went up in flames, sending a fireball of jet fuel that rose up into the rain-filled sky.

The battery commander hesitated not at all—he shouted an order for his men to switch their fire-control radars from stand-by to active, and trace them around "their" bridges. A moment later, one detected an F-111 coming upriver.

"Oh, shit!" The Aardvark's systems operator instantly loosed a Shrike antiradar missile at the SAM battery, another for good measure at the search radar, a second Paveway at the bridge, then the F-111 turned violently left.

A missile-launch officer blanched as he realized what had just appeared from nowhere onto his scopes, and salvoed his three missiles in return. The incoming aircraft had to be hostile, and had just separated three smaller objects . . .

His first SAM struck and exploded on the high-tension power lines that spanned the river just south of the bridges. The entire valley was strobe-lighted as the power lines fell sparking into the river. The other two SAMs raced past the surreal explosion and locked onto the second F-111.

The first Paveway impacted precisely in the center of the northern span. It was a delayed-action bomb, and penetrated into the thick concrete before exploding a few yards from a battalion commander's tank. The north span was strong—it had been in use for over fifty years—but the 945 pounds of high explosive ripped it apart. In an instant the graceful concrete arch was cut in two, a ragged twenty-foot gap appearing between the two unsecured flying buttresses. They were not designed to stand alone, particularly with armored vehicles rumbling over them. The bomb released by the second Aardvark struck closer to shore, and the eastern side of the span failed entirely, taking eight tanks into the Elbe with it.

The second F-111 did not live to see this, however. One of the racing SA-6 missiles struck it broadside and blew it to pieces three seconds after the aircraft-launched Shrikes obliterated the pair of Soviet radar vehicles. Neither side had time for grief. Another F-111 screamed upriver as the surviving SAM crews frantically searched for targets.

Thirty seconds later, the north span was totally destroyed, brick-sized chunks of ferroconcrete scattered on the river bottom from three smart-bomb impacts.

Eisly switched his laser-designator to the south span. It was clogged with tanks, logjammed by a BMP-1 personnel carrier blown whole from one bridge span to the other by the first bomb, torn asunder and blazing on the west end of the bridge. The fourth Aardvark lofted a pair of bombs which homed in remorselessly on the laser-spot now stuck on the turret of a stopped tank. The sky was alight with blazing diesel fuel and streaked with hand-launched SAMs that had been blind-fired by panicked riflemen.

Both Paveways exploded a scant ten feet apart, and the entire bridge span failed at once, dropping a company of armored vehicles into the Elbe.

One more thing to do, Ellington told himself, *there!* The Soviets had stockpiled bridging equipment on the secondary road paralleling the river. The engineers were probably nearby. The Frisbee screeched over the rows of trucks, each of which carried a section of ribbon bridge, and deployed a row of flares before skimming back west toward the Federal Republic of Germany, and safety. The three surviving Aardvarks came in one at a time, each dropping a pair of Rockeye canisters into the truck park, ripping the bridging equipment to bits, and, their pilots fervently hoped, killing some of the skilled bridging engineers as well. Then the Aardvarks turned west to follow the F-19 home.

By this time, a second team of F-15 Eagle fighters had darted into East Germany to clear four lanes for the returning NATO strike aircraft. They fired their radar- and infrared-guided missiles at the MiGs trying to vector toward the returning fighter-bombers—but the American fighters still had their aerial radars to direct them, and the Soviets did not. The results reflected it. The Soviet fighters had not had time to reorganize after the loss of the Mainstays, and their formations were savaged. Even worse, the SAM batteries that were supposed to support the MiGs were ordered to engage the invading aircraft, and the surface-to-air missiles began to pluck targets out of the sky entirely without discrimination as the NATO aircraft clung to the nap of the earth.

By the time the last aircraft recrossed the border into West Germany, Operation Dreamland had lasted a total of twenty-seven minutes. It had been a costly mission. Two of the priceless Frisbees and eleven strike aircraft had been lost. Yet it had been a success. Over two hundred Soviet all-weather fighters had been destroyed by the NATO fighters, and perhaps a hundred more by "friendly" SAMs. The most elite squadrons of the Soviet air-defense force had been brutalized, and because of it, for the time being NATO would own the night skies over Europe. Thirty-six major bridges had been targeted: thirty had been destroyed and all of the rest damaged. The initial Soviet ground attack scheduled to begin in two hours would not be supported by the second echelon, nor by specialty units of mobile SAMs, engineers, and other crucial late-arrivals fresh from special training in the Soviet homeland. Finally, the attacks against airfields would give NATO air parity, at least for the moment. The NATO air forces had fulfilled their most crucial mission: the much-feared Soviet ground superiority was decisively reduced. The land battle for Western Europe would now be fought on nearly even terms.

USS *PHARRIS*

It was still the previous day on the American East Coast. USS *Pharris* led the way out of the Delaware at 2200 hours. Behind her was a convoy of thirty ships, with a dozen escorting vessels. In both cases it was all that could be assembled on the short notice. Dozens of American and foreign-flag vessels were racing to American ports, many taking southerly routings to keep as far away as possible from the Soviet submarines reported surging south from the Norwegian Sea. The first few days would be tough, Morris knew.

"Captain, please come to communications," the announcing system squawked. Morris immediately went aft to the always-locked radio room.

"It's for real." The communications officer handed him the yellow message form. Morris read it in the dim lights.

```
Z0357Z15JUNE
FR: SACLANT
TO: ALL SACLANT SHIPS
TOP SECRET
1. EXECUTE UNRESTRICTED AIR AND SEA WARFARE
AGAINST WARSAW PACT FORCES.
2. WARPLAN GOLF TAC 7.
3. STOUT HEARTS. SACLANT SENDS.
```

Rules of Engagement War Option Seven. That meant no nukes, he was perfectly happy to see—*Pharris* didn't have any at the moment. He was now free to engage without warning any East Bloc warship or merchant vessel. *Well* . . . Morris nodded. He tucked the message form into his pocket, returned to the bridge, and went without a word to the microphone.

"This is the captain speaking. Listen up: It's official. We are now in a shooting war. No more drills, gentlemen. If you hear an alarm from now on, it means there's a Bad Guy out there, and they have live weapons, too. That is all." He hung up and looked over to the officer of the deck. "Mr. Johnson, I want the Prairie / Masker systems operating continuously. If they go down, I want to know about it at once. That goes in the order book."

"Aye, Captain."

Prairie / Masker was a system for defeating submarine sonars. Two metallic bands surrounded the frigate's hull, fore and aft of the engine spaces. This was Masker. It took compressed air and bled it into the water around the ship in the form of millions of tiny bubbles. The Prairie part of the system did the same with the propeller blades. The air bubbles created a semipermeable barrier that tended to trap sounds made by the ship, letting only a fraction of her propulsion noises escape—which made the ship extremely difficult for a submarine to detect.

"How long till we clear the channel?" Morris asked.

"We'll be at the sea buoy in ninety minutes."

"Okay, tell the bosun's mate of the watch to be ready to stream the tail and the Nixie"—the towed-array sonar and the Nixie torpedo decoy—"at twenty-three forty-five. I'm going to take a nap. Wake me at twenty-three thirty. Anything happens, call me."

"Aye aye, sir."

A trio of P-3C Orion antisubmarine aircraft swept the area ahead of them. The only hazard was that of normal navigation, and suddenly the prospect of grazing the bottom or smashing an errant buoy looked like a minor affair. He'd need his sleep now, Morris knew, and he would not be at all surprised to find a submarine waiting right on the continental shelf in three hours. He'd want to be rested for that eventuality.

SUNNYVALE, CALIFORNIA

What was holding Washington up? the colonel asked himself. All he needed was a simple yes or no. He checked his boards. Three KH-type photo-reconnaissance satellites were currently in orbit, plus nine electronic surveillance birds. That was his low-level "constellation." He didn't fear for his higher-flying navigation and communications satellites, but the twelve in low earth orbit, especially the KHs, were valuable and vulnerable. Two of them had Russian killersats in close proximity, and one of his birds was now approaching Soviet territory, with another only forty minutes behind. The third Key-Hole bird didn't have a satellite assigned yet, but the last pass over Leninsk showed another F-type booster being fueled on the pad.

"Take another look at the trailer," he ordered.

A technician made the requisite commands, and half a world away, the satellite fired its altitude control thrusters and pivoted in space to allow its cameras to search for the Russian killer satellite. It had held position fifty miles behind, and nine miles below the American satellite, but now was . . . gone.

"They moved it. They moved it in the last half hour." He lifted the phone to tell CINC-NORAD that he was moving the satellite on his own authority. Too late. As the satellite turned again to point its cameras at the ground, a cylindrical mass covered a sizable percentage of the earth's face—there was a flash and the TV screen went blank. Just like that.

"Chris, you have those maneuver commands set up?"

"Yes, sir," the captain answered, still staring at the screen.

"Execute them right now!"

The captain called up the command sequence on his computer console and punched Enter. The colonel's phone rang as the satellites' onboard rocket motors made subtle changes in their orbital paths.

"Argus Control," the colonel answered.

"This is CINC-NORAD. What the hell happened?"

"That Russian killersat closed and detonated. We have no signal from the KH-11, sir. I must assume they have successfully negated the bird. I've just ordered the other two Key-Holes to make a hundred-foot-per-second delta-V. Tell Washington they waited too long, sir."

18. Polar Glory

KIEV, THE UKRAINE

It had been decided that all Soviet theater and front commanders would be briefed on developments in Germany. Alekseyev and his superior knew why: if anyone were to be relieved from his command, the new man would have to know the situation. They listened to the intelligence report with fascination. Neither of them had expected many of the Spetznaz attacks to fare well, but it seemed that some had been successful, especially those in the German ports. Then the operational intelligence brief got to the bridges on the Elbe.

"Why weren't we warned about this?" CINC-Southwest demanded.

"Comrade General," the Air Force officer responded. "Our information was that this Stealth aircraft was a prototype, not yet in regular service. Somehow the Americans have managed to construct a number of them, at least part of a squadron. They used it to eliminate our airborne radar coverage, thus paving the way for a massive penetration raid against our airfields and lines of supply, plus a well-planned air battle against our all-weather fighter aircraft. Their mission was successful, but not decisively so."

"Oh, and the commander of Air Forces West was arrested for successfully repelling it, eh?" Alekseyev snarled. "How many aircraft did we lose?"

"I am not authorized to reveal that, Comrade General."

"Can you tell us of the bridges, then!"

"Most of the bridges on the Elbe have been damaged to some extent or another, plus attacks on the bridging units stationed near them for tactical replacement."

"The fucking maniac—he had his bridging units right next to the primary targets!" Southwest looked up at the ceiling as though expecting an air attack right there in Kiev.

"That is where the roads are, Comrade General," the intelligence officer said quietly. Alekseyev waved him out of the room.

"Not a good start, Pasha." Already a general had been arrested. His replacement had not yet been named.

Alekseyev nodded agreement, then checked his watch. "The tanks will cross the border in thirty minutes, and we have a few surprises in store for them. Only half of their reinforcements are in place. They still have not achieved the psychological degree of preparedness that our men have. Our first blow will hurt them. If our friend in Berlin has made his deployments properly."

KEFLAVIK, ICELAND

"Perfect weather," First Lieutenant Mike Edwards pronounced, looking up from the chart just off the facsimile machine. "We have this strong cold front due in from Canada in twenty to twenty-four hours. That'll bring a lot of rain with it, maybe an inch worth, but for all of today we have clear skies—less than two-tenths high clouds—and no precip. Surface winds west to southwest at fifteen to twenty knots. And lots of 'shine," he concluded with a grin. The sun had risen for the last time nearly five weeks before, and wouldn't truly set for another five. They were so close to the North Pole here in Iceland that in summer the sun wandered in a lazy circle around the azure sky, dipping fractionally below the northwestern horizon but never truly setting. It was something that took getting used to.

"Fighter weather," agreed Lieutenant Colonel Bill Jeffers, commander of the 57th Fighter Interceptor Squadron, the "Black Knights," most of whose F-15 Eagle interceptors were sitting in the open a bare hundred yards away. The pilots were in those fighters, waiting. They'd been waiting for ninety minutes now. Two hours before, they'd been warned of a large number of Soviet aircraft taking off from their tactical air bases on the Kola Peninsula, destination unknown.

Keflavik was always a busy place, but for the last week it had been a madhouse. The airport was a combination Navy and Air Force base *and* a busy international airport at which many airliners stopped to refuel.

The past week had seen this traffic supplemented by grim tactical fighters transiting from the United States and Canada to Europe, cargo aircraft transporting overloads of critical equipment, and airliners returning to America crowded with pale tourists and dependents of the military men who were now on the battle line. The same had happened to Keflavik. Three thousand wives and children had been evacuated. The base facility was cleared for action. If the Soviets kicked off the war that seemed to be springing from the ground like a new volcano, Keflavik was as ready as it could be.

"With your permission, Colonel, I want to check a few things at the tower. This forecast is pretty solid, for the next twelve hours anyway."

"Jet stream?" Colonel Jeffers looked up from the yard-square chart of isobars and wind-trees.

"Same place it's been all week, sir, no sign at all of a change."

"Okay, go ahead."

Edwards put on his cap and walked out the door. He wore a thin blue officer's jacket over his Marine-style fatigues, pleased that the Air Force was still pretty casual about dress codes. His jeep held the rest of his "battle gear," a .38 revolver and pistol belt, and the field jacket that went with the camouflage gear everybody had been issued three days before. They'd thought of everything, Edwards reflected as he started up the jeep for the quarter-mile drive to the tower. Even the flak jacket.

Keflavik had to get hit, Edwards reminded himself. Everybody knew it, prepared for it, and then tried not to think about it. This most isolated of all NATO outposts on the western coast of Iceland was the barred gate to the North Atlantic. If Ivan wanted to fight a naval war, Iceland had to be neutralized. From Keflavik's four runways flew eighteen Eagle interceptors, nine sub-hunting P-3C Orions, and deadliest of all, three E-3A AWACS birds, the eyes of the fighters. Two were operating now; one was circling twenty miles northeast of Cape Fontur, the other directly over Ritstain, 150 miles north of Keflavik. This was most unusual. With only three AWACS birds available, keeping one constantly in the air was difficult enough. The commander of the Iceland defense forces was taking all of this very seriously. Edwards shrugged. If there really were Backfires bearing down on them, there was nothing else for him to do. He was the brand-new squadron meteorological officer, and he'd just given his weather report.

Edwards parked his jeep in an officer's slot next to the tower and decided to take his .38 with him. The lot was not fenced, and there was no telling if someone might want to "borrow" his handgun. The base was crawling with a company of Marines and another of Air Force police, all looking very nasty with their M-16 rifles and web belts festooned with grenades. He hoped they'd be careful with those. Late the next day, a whole Marine Amphibious Unit was due to arrive to beef up base security, something that should have been done a week earlier but had been delayed, partly because of the Icelandic sensitivity regarding large numbers of armed foreigners, but mainly due to the unreal speed with which this crisis had developed. He trotted up the outside stairs and found the tower's control room crowded with eight people rather than the usual five.

"Hi, Jerry," he said to the boss, Navy lieutenant Jerry Simon. The Icelandic civilian controllers who usually worked here were nowhere to be seen. *Well,* Edwards thought, *there's no civilian traffic for them to control.*

"Morning, Mike," was the response. The ongoing joke at Keflavik. It was 0315 hours local time. Morning. The sun was already up, glaring in at them from the northeast through roll-down shades inside of the tilted glass windows.

"Let's have an attitude check!" Edwards said as he walked over to his meteorological instruments.

"I *hate* this fucking place!" the tower crew answered at once.

"Let's have a positive attitude check."

"I *positively* hate this fucking place!"

"Let's have a negative attitude check."

"I *don't like* this fucking place!"

"Let's have a short attitude check."

"Fuckit!" Everyone had a good laugh. They needed it.

"Nice to see that we're all maintaining our equilibrium," Edwards observed. The short, scrawny officer had become instantly popular on his arrival two months earlier. A native of Eastpoint, Maine, and a graduate of the Air Force Academy, his glasses prevented him from flying. His diminutive size—five-six and a hundred twenty pounds—was not designed to command respect, but his infectious grin, ready supply of jokes, and recognized expertise at making sense of the confused North Atlantic weather patterns had combined to make him an acceptable companion for anyone at Keflavik. Everyone thought he would make one hell of a TV weatherman one day.

"MAC Flight Five-Two-Zero, roger. Roll her out, Big Guy, we need the room," said a tired controller. A few hundred yards away, a C-5A Galaxy cargo plane began to accelerate down runway one-eight. Edwards took a pair of binoculars to watch. It was hard to get used to the fact that something so monstrous could actually fly.

"Any word from anywhere?" Simon asked Edwards.

"Nope, nothing since the Norwegian report. Lots of activity at Kola. You know, I picked a hell of a time to come here to work," Mike replied. He went back to checking the calibration of his digital barometer.

It had started six weeks before. The Soviet Naval and Long-Range Aviation groups based at a half-dozen airfields around Severomorsk had exercised almost continuously, flying attack-profile missions that could have been directed at nearly anyone or anything. Then two weeks before, the activity had been cut way back. That was the ominous part: first they drilled all their flight crews to perfection and then they went to a stand-down maintenance period to make sure that every bird and every instrument was also fully operational . . . What were they doing now? An attack against Bodø in Norway? Or Iceland maybe? Another exercise? There was no telling.

Edwards lifted a clipboard to sign off for having checked his tower instruments that day. He could have left it to his enlisted technicians, but they were backstopping the aircraft techs with the fighter squadron, and he could handle it for them. Besides, it gave him an excuse to visit the tower and—

"Mr. Simon," the senior enlisted controller said rapidly. "I just copied a Flash from Sentry One: Warning Red. Many bandits inbound, sir. Approaching from due north to northeast—Sentry Two is checking in . . . they got 'em, too. Jesus. Sounds like forty to fifty bandits, sir." Edwards noted that the inbounds were being called Bandits instead of the usual Zombies.

"Anything friendly coming in?"

"Sir, we got a MAC C-141 twenty minutes out, eight more behind it at five-minute intervals, all inbound from Dover."

"Tell them to turn back, *and get an acknowledgment!* Keflavik is closed to all inbounds until further notice." Simon turned to his telecommunications man. "Tell Air-Ops to radio SACLANT that we're under attack, and to get the word out. I—"

Klaxons erupted all around them. Below, in the early-morning shadows, ground crewmen pulled red-flagged safety pins off the waiting interceptors. Edwards saw a pilot drain a styrofoam cup and begin to strap himself in tight. The starter carts next to each fighter belched black smoke as they generated power to turn the engines.

"Tower, this is Hunter Leader. We're scrambling. Clear those runways, boy!"

Simon took the microphone. "Roger, Hunter Leader, the runways are yours. Scatter Plan Alpha. Go for it! Out."

Below, canopies were coming down, chocks were pulled away from wheels, and each crew chief gave his pilot a smart salute. The shriek of jet engines changed to a roar as the aircraft started to roll awkwardly off the flight line.

"Where's your battle station, Mike?" Simon asked.

"The met building." Edwards nodded and headed for the door. " 'Luck, guys."

Aboard Sentry Two, the radar operators watched a broad semicircle of blips converging on them. Each blip had "BGR" painted next to it, plus data on course, altitude, and speed. Each blip was a Tu-16 Badger bomber of Soviet Naval Aviation. There were twenty-four of them, inbound for Keflavik at a speed of six hundred knots. They had approached at low altitude to stay below the E-3A's radar horizon, and, once detected, were now climbing rapidly, two hundred miles away. This mission profile enabled the radar operators to classify them instantly as hostile. There were four Eagles on Combat Air Patrol, two of them with operating AWACS, but it was close to changeover point and the fighters were too low on fuel to race after the Badgers on afterburner. They were directed to head for the incoming Russian bombers at six hundred knots, and could not yet detect the Badgers on their own missile-targeting radars.

Sentry One off Cape Fontur reported something worse. Her blips were supersonic Tu-22M Backfires, coming in slowly enough to indicate that they were heavily loaded with external ordnance. The Eagles here also moved off to intercept. A hundred miles behind them, the two F-15s kept on point defense over Reykjavik had just been topped off from an orbiting tanker and were charging northeast at a thousand knots while the remainder of the squadron was even now leaving the ground. The radar picture from both AWACS aircraft was being transmitted by digital link to Keflavik's fighter-ops center so that ground personnel could monitor the action. Now that the fighters were rotating off the ground, the crews for every other aircraft at the air station worked frantically to ready their birds for flight.

They had practiced this task eight times in the past month. Some flight crews had been sleeping with their aircraft. Others were summoned from their quarters, no more than four hundred yards away. Those aircraft just back from patrol had their fuel tanks topped off, and were pre-flighted by the ground crews. Marine and Air Force guards not already at their posts rushed to them. It was just as well that the attack had come at this hour. There was only a handful of civilians about, and civilian air traffic was at its lowest. On the other hand, the men at Keflavik had been on double duty for a week now, and they were tired. Things which might have been done in five minutes now took seven or eight.

Edwards was back in his meteorological office, wearing his field jacket, flak jacket, and "fritz" style helmet. His emergency duty station—he could not think of his office as a "battle" station—was his assigned post. As if someone might need an especially deadly weather chart with which to attack an incoming bomber! The service had to have a plan for everything, Edwards knew. There had to be a plan. It *didn't* have to make sense. He went downstairs to Air-Ops.

"I got breakaway on Bandit Eight, one—two birds launched. The machine says they're AS-4s," a Sentry controller reported. The senior officer got on the radio for Keflavik.

MV *JULIUS FUCIK*

Twenty miles southwest of Keflavik, the *"Doctor Lykes"* was also a beehive of activity. As each Soviet bomber squadron launched its air-to-ground missiles, its commander transmitted a predetermined codeword that the *Fucik* copied. Her time had come.

"Rudder left," Captain Kherov ordered. "Bring his bow into the wind."

A full regiment of airborne infantry, many of them seasick from two weeks aboard the huge barge-carrier, was at work testing and loading weapons. The *Fucik*'s augmented crew was stripping the falsework from the aftermost four "barges," revealing each in fact to be a Lebed-type assault hovercraft. The six-man crew of each removed the covers over the air intakes that led to the engines they had tended with loving care for a month. Satisfied, they waved to the craft commanders, who lit off the three engines in each of the aftermost pair.

The ship's first officer stood at his elevator control station aft. On a hand signal, an eighty-five-man infantry company plus a reinforced mortar team were loaded into each craft. Power was increased, the hovercraft lifted up on their air cushions and were winched aft. In another four minutes, the vehicles were resting on the barge-loading elevator that formed the stern of the Seabee vessel.

"Lower away," the first officer ordered. The winch operators lowered the elevator to the surface. The sea was choppy, and four-foot waves lapped at the *Fucik*'s bifurcated stern. When the elevator was level with the sea, first one, then the other Lebed commander increased power and moved off. At once, the elevator returned to the topmost deck while the first pair of hovercraft circled their mothership. In five more minutes, the four assault craft moved off in box formation toward the Keflavik Peninsula.

The *Fucik* continued her turn, returning to a northerly course to make the next hovercraft trip a shorter one. Her weather deck was ringed with armed troops carrying surface-to-air missiles and machine guns. Andreyev remained on the bridge, knowing this was where he belonged, but wishing he were leading his assault troops.

KEFLAVIK, ICELAND

"Kef-Ops, the bandits are all turning right back after launching their ASMs. So far it's been two birds per aircraft. We got fifty—make that fifty-six inbound missiles, and more are being launched. Nobody behind them, though. I repeat, nothing behind the bomber force. At least we don't have any paratroopers headed in. Hunker down, guys, we now have sixty inbound missiles," Edwards heard as he came through the door.

"At least they won't be nukes," said a captain.

"They're shooting a hundred missiles at us—they don't fuckin' *need* nukes!" replied another.

Edwards watched the radar picture over the shoulder of one of the officers. It was eerily like an arcade game. Big, slow-moving blips denoted the aircraft. Smaller, quicker blips were the Mach-2 missiles.

"Gotcha!" hooted the enlisted radar operator. The leading Eagle had gotten within missile range of the Badgers and exploded one with a Sparrow missile—ten seconds *after* it had launched its own missiles. A second Sparrow missed its separate target, but a third appeared locked on it. The first fighter's wingman was just launching at yet another Russian. The Soviets had thought this one out, Edwards saw. They were attacking from all around the northern littoral, with lots of space between the bombers so that no single fighter could engage more than one or two. It was almost like—

"Anybody check the geometry of this?" he asked.

"What do you mean?" The captain looked around. "How come you aren't where you belong?"

Edwards ignored the irrelevancy. "What's the chance they're trying to draw our fighters out, like?"

"Expensive bait." The captain dismissed the idea. "You're saying they might have launched their ASMs from farther out. Maybe they don't fly as far as we thought. Point is, those missiles are ten minutes out now, the first of them, with about a five- or seven-minute delay to the last. And not a Goddamned thing we can do about it."

"Yeah." Edwards nodded. The Air-Ops/Met building was a two-story frame structure that vibrated every time the wind hit fifty knots. The lieutenant took out a stick of gum and started chewing on it. In ten minutes a hundred missiles, each carrying about a ton of high explosives—*or a nuclear warhead*—would start falling. The men outside would get the worst of it; the enlisted men and the flight crews trying to get the airplanes ready to race off. His assigned job was merely to keep out of the way. It made him a little ashamed. The fear he could now taste along with the peppermint made him more ashamed.

The Eagles were now all airborne, racing north. The last of the Backfires had just launched their missiles and were turning back northeast at full power as the Eagles raced at twelve hundred knots to catch up. Three of the interceptors launched missiles, and they succeeded in killing a pair of Backfires and damaging a third. The "Zulu" fighters which had scrambled off the deck could not catch the Backfires, the commanding controller on Sentry One noted, cursing himself for not having sent them after the older, less valuable Badgers, some of which they might have caught. Instead, he ordered them to slow down, and had his controllers vector them toward the supersonic missiles.

Penguin 8, the first of the P-3C Orion antisubmarine warfare aircraft, was rolling now, down runway two-two. It had been on patrol only five hours before, and its flight crew was still trying to shake off the sleep as they rotated the propjet aircraft off the concrete.

"Tipping over now," the radar operator said. The first Russian missile was almost overhead, beginning its terminal dive. The Eagles had hit two of the incoming missiles, but courses and altitudes had been against them, and most of their Sparrows had missed, unable to catch the Mach-2 missiles. The F-15s orbited over central Iceland, well away from their base, as each pilot wondered if he'd have an airfield to return to.

Edwards cringed as the first landed—or didn't land. The air-to-surface missile had a radar-proximity fuse. It detonated twenty meters off the ground, and the effects were horrific. It exploded directly over International Highway, two hundred yards from Air-Ops, its fragments ripping into a number of buildings, the worst hit being the base fire station. Edwards fell to the floor as fragments lashed through the wooden wall. The door was torn off its hinges by the blast and the air filled with dust. A moment later, at the Esso facility a hundred yards away, a fuel truck exploded, sending a fireball towering into the sky, and dropping burning jet fuel for blocks around. Electrical power was immediately lost. Radars, radios, and room lights went out at once, and battery-powered emergency lights didn't come on as they were supposed to. For a terrified moment, Edwards wondered if the first missile really might have been a nuke. The blast had rippled through his chest, and he felt sudden nausea as his body tried to adjust to the sensations that assaulted it. He looked around and saw a man knocked unconscious by a falling light fixture. He didn't know if he was supposed to buckle his helmet strap or not, and somehow this question seemed enormously important at the moment, though he didn't remember why.

Another missile landed farther away, and then for a minute or so the sounds blended into a series of immense thunderclaps. Edwards was choking from the dust. It felt as though his chest would burst, and impulsively he bolted for the door to get fresh air.

He was greeted by a solid wall of heat. The Esso facility was a roaring mass of flames which had already engulfed the nearby photo lab and base thrift shop. More smoke rose from the enlisted housing area to the east. A half-dozen aircraft still on the flightline would never leave it, their wings snapped like toys from the blast of a missile that had exploded directly over the runway crossroads. A smashed E-3A Sentry burst into flames before his eyes. He turned to see that the control tower had been damaged, too, all its windows gone. Edwards ran that way, not thinking to take his jeep.

Two minutes later, he entered the tower breathlessly to find the crew all dead, torn apart by flying glass, the tiled floor covered with blood. Radio receivers were still making noise over desk-mounted speakers, but he couldn't seem to find a working transmitter.

PENGUIN 8

"What the hell is that?" the Orion pilot said. He turned his aircraft violently to the left and increased power. They had been orbiting ten miles out from Keflavik, watching the smoke and flames rising from their home field, when four massive objects passed under them.

"It's a—" the copilot breathed. *"Where—"*

The four Lebeds were moving at over forty knots, bouncing roughly over the four- to five-foot waves. About eighty feet long and thirty-five wide, each had a pair of ducted propellers atop, immediately forward of a tall, aircraft-type rudder painted with the Soviet naval ensign, a red hammer and sickle over a blue stripe. They were already too close to shore for the Orion to use any of her weapons.

The pilot watched incredulously as he approached, and any doubts he had ended as a 30mm cannon fired at them. It missed wide, but the pilot jerked the Orion around to the west.

"Tacco, tell Keflavik ASW Ops they got company coming. Four armed hovercraft, type unknown, but Russian—and they gotta be carrying troops."

"Flight," the tactical coordinator reported back thirty seconds later. "Keflavik is off the air. ASW Ops Center is gone; the tower is gone, too. I'm trying to raise the Sentries. Maybe we can get a fighter or two."

"Okay, but keep trying Keflavik. Get our radar lit off. We'll see if we can find where they came from. Get our Harpoons lit off, too."

KEFLAVIK, ICELAND

Edwards was surveying the damage through binoculars when he heard the message come in—and could not answer it. *Now what do I do?* He looked around and saw one useful thing, a Hammer Ace radio. He took the oversized backpack and ran down the steps. He had to find the Marine officers and warn them.

The hovercraft raced up Djupivogur Cove and came to land a minute later less than a mile from the airbase. The troopers gratefully noted the smoother ride as their craft spread out to line abreast, three hundred yards between them as they tore across the flat, rocky gorse toward the NATO air base.

"What in the hell—" a Marine corporal said. Like a dinosaur coming to the picnic, a massive object appeared on the horizon, apparently coming overland at high speed.

"You! Marine, get over here!" Edwards screamed. A jeep with three enlisted men stopped, then raced toward him. "Get me to your CO fast!"

"CO's dead, sir," the sergeant said. "CP took a hit, Lieutenant—fuckin' gone!"

"Where's the alternate?"

"Elementary school."

"Go, I gotta let them know, we got bad guys coming in from the sea— shit! You got a radio."

"Tried calling, sir, but no answer." The sergeant turned south down International Highway. At least three missiles had landed here, judging by the smoke. All around, the small city that had been the Keflavik air base was a loose collection of smoking fires. A number of people in uniforms were running around, doing things that Edwards didn't have time to guess at. Was anybody in charge?

The elementary school had also been hit. The third of the building still standing was a mass of flame.

"Sergeant, that radio work?"

"Yes, sir, but it ain't tuned into the perimeter guards."

"Well, fix it!"

"Right." The sergeant dialed into a different frequency.

The Lebeds halted in two pairs, each a quarter mile from the perimeter. The bow door on each opened, and out rolled a pair of BMD infantry assault vehicles, followed by mortar crews who began at once to set up their weapons. The 73mm guns and missile launchers on the mini-tanks began to engage the Marine defensive positions as the reinforced company in each vehicle advanced slowly and skillfully, using their cover and taking advantage of their fire support. The assault force had been handpicked from units that had fought in Afghanistan. Every man had been under fire before. The Lebeds immediately turned crablike and sped back to sea to pick up yet more infantrymen. Already, elements of two elite airborne battalions were engaging a single company of Marines.

The frantic words on the platoon radio nets were all too clear. The base electrical supply was cut, and along with it the main radios. The Marine officers were dead, and there was no one to coordinate the defense. Edwards wondered if anyone really knew what the hell was going on. He decided that it probably didn't matter.

"Sergeant, we gotta get the hell outa here!"

"You mean run away!"

"I mean get away and report what's happened here. Looks like we lost this one, Sarge. Somebody's gotta report in so they don't send any more planes to land here. What's the fastest way to Reykjavik?"

"Dammit, sir, there's Marines out there—"

"You wanna be a Russian prisoner? We lost! I say we gotta report in and you'll do what I Goddamned tell you, Sergeant, you got that!"

"Aye aye, sir."

"How we fixed for weapons?"

On his own, a private ran to what was left of the school. A Marine was lying there facedown, a pool of red spreading from some invisible, fatal wound. The private came back with the man's M-16, field pack, and ammo belt, handing the collection to Edwards.

"We all got one now, sir."

"Let's get the hell outa here."

The sergeant threw the jeep into gear. "How we gonna report in?"

"Let me worry about that, okay?"

"You say so." The sergeant turned the jeep completely around, back up International, toward the wrecked satellite antennae.

MV *JULIUS FUCIK*

"Aircraft sighted, port bow!" a lookout screamed. Kherov raised his binoculars to his eyes and swore softly. He saw what could only be missiles dangling from each wing of the multiengined aircraft.

PENGUIN 8

"Well, lookie what we got here," the Orion's pilot said quietly. "Our old friend, the *Doctor Lykes*. Combat, Flight, what else is around?"

"Nothin', Flight, not another surface ship for over a hundred miles." They had just completed a complete circuit of the horizon, scanning with their surface-search radar.

"And it's for Goddamned sure those hovercraft didn't come in off no submarine." The pilot adjusted course to pass within two miles of the ship, with the sun behind the four-engine patrol aircraft. His copilot examined the ship through binoculars. Onboard TV cameras operated by the weapons crew would provide even better close-up pictures. They saw a pair of helicopters warming up. Someone aboard the *Fucik* panicked and fired a hand-held SA-7 missile. It failed to lock onto the Orion and blazed off directly into the low sun.

MV *JULIUS FUCIK*

"Idiot!" Kherov growled. The smoke from the rocket motor didn't even come close to the aircraft. "He'll shoot at us now. All ahead flank! Helmsman, be alert!"

PENGUIN 8

"Okay," the pilot said, turning away from the merchantman. "Tacco, we got a target for your Harpoons. Any luck with Keflavik?"

"Negative, but Sentry One is relaying the data into Scotland. They say a bunch of missiles hit Keflavik, looks like the place is closed whether we keep it or not."

The pilot cursed briefly. "Okay. We'll blow this pirate right out of the water."

"Roge, Flight," the tactical coordinator replied. "Two minutes before we can launch the—damn! I got a red light on the portside Harpoon. The sucker won't arm."

"Well, play with the bastard!" the pilot growled. It didn't work. In the haste to get off the ground, the missile's control cables had not been fully attached by the weary ground crew.

"Okay, I got one working. Ready!"

"Shoot!"

The missile dropped clear of the wing and fell thirty feet before its engine ignited. *Fucik*'s weather deck was lined with paratroopers, many holding hand-launched SAMs and hoping to intercept the incoming ASM.

"Tacco, see if you can raise an F-15. Maybe they can rip this baby up with twenty-millimeters."

"Doing that already. We got a pair of Eagles coming in, but they're skosh fuel. One or two passes'll be all they can manage."

Forward, the pilot had binoculars to his eyes, watching the white-painted missile skimming the wavetops. "Go, baby, go . . ."

MV JULIUS FUCIK

"Rocket coming in, low on the horizon, portside." *At least we have good lookouts,* Kherov thought. He estimated the distance to the horizon, and gave the missile a speed of a thousand kilometers per hour . . .

"Right hard rudder!" he screamed. The helmsman threw the wheel over as far as it would go and held it down.

"You cannot run from a missile, Kherov," the General said quietly.

"I know this. Watch, my friend."

The black-hulled vessel was turning radically to starboard. As she did so, the ship heeled in the opposite direction, the same way a car rolls away from a turn on a flat road, which artificially raised the waterline on the vulnerable portside.

Some enterprising officers aboard fired signal flares, hoping to decoy the missile away, but all the missile's microchip brain cared about was the enormous blip that occupied the center of its radar seeker head. It noted that the ship's heading was changing slightly, and altered its own course accordingly. Half a mile from the target, the Harpoon lurched upward from its ten-foot altitude in its programmed "pop-up" terminal maneuver. The troopers aboard the *Fucik* instantly fired an even dozen SAMs. Three locked onto the Harpoon's engine exhaust plume, but were unable to turn rapidly enough to hit the incoming missile, and continued past it. The Harpoon tipped over and dove.

PENGUIN 8

"All right . . ." the pilot whispered. There was no stopping it now.

The missile struck the *Fucik*'s hull six feet above the waterline, slightly abaft the bridge. The warhead exploded at once, but the missile body kept moving forward, spreading two hundred pounds of jet fuel that fireballed into the lowest cargo deck. In an instant, the ship disappeared behind a wall of smoke. Three paratroopers, thrown off their feet by the impact, accidentally triggered their SAMs straight up.

"Tacco, your bird hit just fine. We got warhead detonation. Looks like . . ." The pilot's eyes strained at his binoculars to assess the damage.

MV JULIUS FUCIK

"Rudder amidships!" Kherov had expected to be knocked from his feet, but the missile was a small one, and *Julius Fucik* still had thirty-five thousand tons of mass. He ran out to the bridge wing to survey the damage. As the ship returned to an even keel, the ragged hole in her side rose ten feet from the lapping waves. Smoke poured from the hole. There was fire aboard, but the ship should not flood from the blow, the captain judged. There was only one danger. Kherov rapidly gave orders to his damage-control teams, and the General sent one of his own officers to assist. A hundred of the paratroopers had been trained over the last ten days in shipboard firefighting. They would now put what they had learned to use.

PENGUIN 8

The *Fucik* emerged at twenty knots from the smoke, a fifteen-foot hole in the ship's side. Smoke poured from the opening, but the pilot knew at once that the damage would not be fatal. He could see hundreds of men on the upper deck, some of them already running toward ladders to fight the fire below.

"Where are those fighters?" the pilot asked. The tactical coordinator didn't answer. He switched his radio circuits.

"Penguin Eight, this is Cobra One. I got two birds. Our missiles are all gone, but we both got a full load of twenty-mike-mike. I can give you two passes, then we gotta bingo to Scotland."

"That's a roge, Cobra Lead. The target has some helos spooling up. Watch out for hand-held SAMs. I seen 'em fire about twenty of the bastards."

"Roger that, Penguin. Any further word of Keflavik?"

"We're gonna have to find a new home for a while."

"Roger, copy. Okay, keep clear, we're coming in from up-sun, on the deck."

The Orion continued to orbit three miles out. Her pilot didn't see the fighters until they started firing. The two Eagles were a few feet apart, perhaps twenty feet over the water as their noses sparkled with the flash from their 20mm rotary cannon.

MV *JULIUS FUCIK*

Nobody aboard saw them come in. A moment later, the water around the *Fucik*'s side turned to froth from short-falling rounds, then her main deck was hidden with dust. A sudden orange fireball announced the explosion of one of the Russian helicopters, and burning jet fuel splattered over the bridge, narrowly missing the General and captain.

"What was that?" Kherov gasped.

"American fighters. They came in very low. They must only have their cannon, else they'd have bombed us already. It is not over yet, my captain."

The fighters split, passing left and right of the ship, which continued to move at twenty knots in a wide circle. No SAMs followed the Eagles away, and both turned, re-formed, and closed on the *Fucik*'s bow. The next target was the superstructure. A moment later, the freighter's bridge was peppered with several hundred rounds. Every window was blown away, and most of the bridge crew killed, but the ship's watertight integrity hadn't been damaged a whit.

Kherov surveyed the carnage. His helmsman had been blown apart by a half-dozen exploding bullets and every man present on the bridge was dead. It took a second for him to overcome the shock and notice a crippling pain in his own abdomen, his dark jacket darkening further with blood.

"You are hit, Captain." Only the General had had the instinct to duck behind something solid. He looked at the eight mutilated bodies in the pilothouse and wondered once again why he was so lucky.

"I must get the ship to port. Go aft. Tell the first officer to continue landing operations. You, Comrade General, supervise the fires topside. We must get my ship to port."

"I will send you help." The General ran out the door as Kherov went to the wheel.

KEFLAVIK, ICELAND

"Stop, hold it right here!" Edwards screamed.

"What now, Lieutenant?" the sergeant demanded. He stopped the jeep by the BOQ parking lot.

"Let's get my car. This jeep's too friggin' conspicuous." The lieutenant jumped out of the jeep, pulling his car keys from his pants pocket. The Marines just looked at each other for a moment before running after him.

His car was a ten-year-old Volvo that he'd purchased from a departing officer a few months before. It had seen rugged service on Iceland's mainly unpaved roads, and it showed. "Well, get in!"

"Sir, what the hell are we doing, exactly?"

"Look, Sarge, we gotta clear the area. What if Ivan's got helicopters? What do you suppose a jeep looks like from the air?"

"Oh, okay." The sergeant nodded. "But what are we doing, sir?"

"We'll drive at least as far as Hafnarfjördur, ditch the car, and start walking back into the boonies. Soon as we get to a safe place, we'll radio in. That's a satellite radio I got. We have to let Washington know what's happening here. That means we gotta be able to see what Ivan's got coming in. Our people are gonna at least try to take this rock back. Our mission, Sergeant, is to stay alive, report in, and maybe make that easier." Edwards hadn't thought this out until a few moments before he said it. Would they try to take Iceland back? Would they be able to try? What else was going wrong all over the friggin' world? Did any of this make sense? He decided it didn't have to make sense. *One thing at a time,* he told himself. He for damned sure didn't want to be a prisoner of the Russians, and maybe if they could radio some information in they could get even for what had happened to Keflavik.

Edwards started up the car and drove east up Highway 41. Where to ditch the car? There was a shopping center at Hafnarfjördur . . . and Iceland's only Kentucky Fried Chicken outlet. What better place to ditch a car than that? The young lieutenant smiled in spite of himself. They were alive, and they had the most dangerous weapon known to man—a radio. He'd work out the problems as they arose. His mission, he decided, was to stay alive and report in. After they did that, someone else could tell them what to do. *One thing at a time,* he repeated to himself, and pray to God somebody knows what the hell is going on . . .

PENGUIN 8

"Looks like the fire's under control," the copilot commented sourly.

"Yeah, how do you think they managed that? Shit, that boat should've gone up like—but it didn't." As they watched, a second load of troops was dispatched on the four hovercraft. The pilot hadn't thought of having the two available Eagle fighters—now heading for England—shoot them up instead of this huge black ship. *Some fucking officer you are,* he told himself. Penguin 8 carried eighty sonobuoys, four Mk-46 ASW torpedoes, and some other high-technology weapons—none of which were of the least use against a simple large target like this merchie. Unless he wanted to play kamikaze . . . the pilot shook his head.

"If you want to head for Scotland, we got another thirty minutes of fuel," the flight engineer advised.

"Okay, let's take a last look at Keflavík. I'm going up to six thousand. Oughta keep us out of SAM range."

They were over the coast in two minutes. A Lebed was approaching the SOSUS and SIGINT station opposite Hafnir. They could just make out some movement on the ground, and a wisp of smoke coming from the building. The pilot didn't know much about the SIGINT activities, but SOSUS, the oceanic Sonar Surveillance System, was the principal means of detecting targets for the P-3C Orion crews to pounce on. This station covered the gaps from Greenland to Iceland, and from Iceland to the Faroe Islands. The main picketline needed to keep Russian subs out of the trade routes was about to go permanently off the air. Great.

They were over Keflavik a minute after that. Seven or eight aircraft had not gotten off the ground. All were burning. The pilot examined the runways through binoculars and was horrified to see that it was uncratered.

"Tacco, you got a Sentry on the line?"

"You can talk to one right now, Flight. Go right ahead, you got Sentry Two."

"Sentry Two, this is Penguin 8, do you read, over?"

"Roger, Penguin 8, this is the senior controller. We show you over Keflavik. What's it look like?"

"I count eight birds on the ground, all broke and burning. The missiles did not, repeat not, crater the airfield."

"You sure about that, Eight?"

"Affirmative. A whole lot of blast damage, but I don't see any holes in the ground. The in-close fuel tanks appear undamaged, and nothing at all seems to have hit the tank farm at Hakotstangar. We left our friends a whole shitload of jet fuel and an airfield. The base—let's see. Tower's still standing. Lots of smoke and fire around Air/Ops . . . base looks pretty badly beat-up, but those runways are sure as hell usable. Over."

"How about the ship you shot at?"

"One solid hit, I eyeballed the missile in, and two of your '15s strafed his ass, but it ain't enough. She'll probably make port. I'd guess she'll try to come into Reykjavik, maybe Hafnarfjördur, to unload. She's gotta be carrying a lot of stuff. It's a forty-thousand-ton ship. She can make port in two or three hours unless we can whistle up something to take her out."

"Don't count on it. What's your fuel state?"

"We gotta head for Stornoway right now. My camera guys have shot pictures of the area, and that ship. About all we can do."

"Okay, Penguin 8. Go find yourself a place to land. We're leaving in a few minutes, too. 'Luck. Out."

HAFNARFJÖRDUR, ICELAND

Edwards parked the car in the shopping center. There had been some people outside along the drive in, mainly looking west toward Keflavik.

Awakened by the noise a few miles away and wondering what was happening. *Just like us,* Edwards thought. Fortunately, there seemed to be no one about right here yet. He locked the car and pocketed the keys without thinking about it.

"Where to, Lieutenant?" Sergeant Smith asked.

"Sergeant, let's straighten a few things out. You're the ground-pounder. You got any ideas, I want to know about 'em, okay?"

"Well, sir, I'd say we oughta head straight east for a while, to get away from the roads, like, and find you a place to play with that radio. An' do it quick."

Edwards looked around. There was no one on the streets here yet, but they'd want to get into the back country before being noticed by anybody who might tell someone about it afterward. He nodded, and the sergeant directed a private to lead off. They took off their helmets and slung their rifles to appear as harmless as possible, each sure that a hundred pairs of eyes were locked on them from behind the curtained windows. *What a way to start a war,* he thought.

MV *JULIUS FUCIK*

"The fires are out, by God!" General Andreyev proclaimed. "There is much damage to our equipment, mainly from water, but the fires are out!" His expression changed when he saw Kherov.

The captain was ghostly pale. An Army medic had bandaged his wound, but there had to be internal bleeding. He struggled to hold himself erect over the chart table.

"Come right to zero-zero-three."

A junior officer was on the wheel. "Right to zero-zero-three, Comrade Captain."

"You must lie down, my captain," Andreyev said softly.

"I must get my ship to safe harbor first!"

The *Fucik* ran almost due north, the westerly wind and sea on her beam, and water was lapping at the missile wound. His earlier optimism was fading. Some seams in the lower hull had sprung from the missile impact, and water was entering the lower cargo deck, though so far the pumps were keeping up with it. There was twenty thousand tons of cargo to deliver.

"Captain, you must have medical attention," Andreyev persisted.

"After we round the point. When we have the damaged port side alee, then I shall be tended to. Tell your men to stay alert. One more successful attack could finish us. And tell them they have done well. I would be happy to sail with them again."

USS *PHARRIS*

"Sonar contact, possible submarine bearing three-five-three," the sonar-man announced.

And so it begins, Morris said to himself. *Pharris* was at general quarters for the first leg of the trip away from the U.S. coast. The frigate's tactical towed-array sonar was trailed out in her wake. They were twenty miles north of the convoy, a hundred ten miles east of the coast, just crossing the continental shelf line into truly deep water at the Lindenkohl Canyon. A perfect place for a submarine to hide.

"Show me what you have," the ASW officer ordered. Morris kept his peace and just watched his men at work.

The sonarman pointed to the waterfall display. It showed as a series of small digital blocks, numerous shades of green on a black background. Six blocks in a row were different from the random background pattern. Then a seventh. The fact that they were in a vertical row meant that the noise was being generated at a constant bearing from the ship, just west of north. Up to now, all they had was a direction to a possible noise source. They had no way of knowing the distance nor any of determining if it were really a submarine, a fishing boat with an overly loud motor, or simply a disturbance in the water. The signal source did not repeat for a minute, then came back. Then it disappeared again.

Morris and his ASW officer looked at the bathythermograph reading. Every two hours they dropped an instrument that measured water temperature as it fell through the water, reporting back by wire until it was cut loose to fall free to the bottom. The trace showed an uneven line. The water temperature decreased with depth, but not in a uniform way.

"Could be anything," the ASW officer said quietly.

"Sure could," the captain agreed. He went back to the sonar scope. It was still there. The trace had remained fairly constant for nine minutes now.

But what was the range to it? Water was a fine medium for carrying sound energy, far more efficient at it than air, but it had its own rules. One hundred feet below the *Pharris* was "the layer," a fairly abrupt change in water temperature. Like an angled pane of glass, it allowed some sound to pass through, but reflected most of it. Some of the energy would be ducted between layers, retaining its intensity for an enormous distance. The signal source they were listening to could be as close as five miles or as distant as fifty. As they watched, the scope trace started leaning a bit to the left, which meant that they were pulling east of it . . . or it was pulling west of them, as a submarine might slide aft of her target as part of her own hunting maneuver. Morris went forward to the plotting table.

"If it's a target, it's pretty far off, I think," the quartermaster said quietly. It was surprising how quiet people were during antisubmarine warfare exercises, Morris thought, as though a submarine might hear their voices.

"Sir," the ASW officer said after a moment. "With no perceptible change in bearing, the contact has to be a good fifteen miles off. That means it has to be a fairly noisy source, probably too far to be an immediate threat. If it's a nuclear sub, we can get a cross-bearing after a short sprint."

Morris looked to the CIC's after bulkhead. His frigate was steaming at four knots. He lifted a "growler" phone.

"Bridge, Combat."

"Bridge aye. XO speaking."

"Joe, let's bend on twenty knots for five minutes. See if we can get a cross-bearing on the target we're working."

"Aye, skipper."

A minute later, Morris could feel the change in his ship's motion as her steam plant drove the frigate hard through the six-foot seas. He waited thoughtfully, wishing his ship had one of the more sensitive 2X arrays being fitted to the Perry-class fast-frigates. It was a predictably long five minutes, but ASW was a game that demanded patience.

Power was reduced, and as the ship slowed, the pattern on the sonar screen changed from random flow noise to random ambient noise, something more easily perceived than described. The captain, his ASW officer, and the sonar operator watched the screen intently for ten minutes. The anomalous sound tracing did not reappear. In a peacetime exercise they would have decided that it was a pure anomaly, water-generated noise that had stopped as unpredictably as it had started, perhaps a minor eddy that subsided on the surface. But now everything they detected had a potential red star and a periscope attached.

My first dilemma, Morris thought. If he investigated by sending his own helicopter or one of the Orion patrol aircraft, he might be sending them after nothing at all, and away from a path that could end with a real contact. If he did nothing, he might not be prosecuting a real contact. Morris sometimes wondered if captains should be issued coins with YES and NO stamped on either side, perhaps called a "digital decision generator" in keeping with the Navy's love for electronic-sounding titles.

"Any reason to think it's real?" he asked the ASW officer.

"No, sir." The officer wondered by this time if he had been right to call it to his captain's attention. "Not now."

"Fair enough. It won't be the last one."

19. Journeys End / Journeys Begin

HAFNARFJÖRDUR, ICELAND

Sergeant James Smith was a company clerk, which meant that he carried his commander's maps, Edwards was grateful to learn. He would have been less happy to learn what Smith thought about what they were doing, and who was leading this party. A company clerk was also supposed to pack an ax with him, but since Iceland was almost entirely devoid of trees, his was still in the company headquarters, probably burned down to a charred axhead by now. They walked east in silence, their eyes punished by the low sun, past two kilometers of lava field that gave mute testimony to Iceland's volcanic birth.

They moved fast, without pausing for rest. The sea was at their back, and as long as they could see it, men on the coast might see them. Each puff of dust raised by their boots made them feel increasingly vulnerable, and Private Garcia, who brought up the rear of their small unit, periodically turned and walked backward for a few yards to be sure that no one was following them. The others looked ahead, to the sides, and up. They were sure that Ivan had thought to bring a helicopter or two along. Few things can make a man feel as naked as an aircraft filled with eyes.

The ground was almost totally barren. Here and there a few sprigs of grass fought their way through the rocks to sunlight, but for the most part the terrain was as barren as the surface of the moon—the Apollo astronauts had trained somewhere in Iceland for that very reason, Edwards remembered. The mild surface winds scoured up the slopes they were climbing, raising small quantities of dust that made the lieutenant sneeze periodically. He was already wondering what they would do when their rations ran out. This was no place to try living off the land. He'd been in Iceland only for a few months, and hadn't had a single chance to tour the countryside. *Cross one bridge at a time,* Edwards told himself. *People grow their own food everywhere. There have to be farms around, and you'll be able to find them on the maps.*

"Chopper!" Garcia called out.

The private had a great set of eyes, Edwards noted. They couldn't hear it yet, but there it was on the horizon, coming in from the sea.

"Everybody down. Let me see those glasses, Sergeant." Edwards held out his hand as he sat. Smith came down next to him, the binoculars already at his eyes.

"It's a Hip, sir. Troop carrier." He handed the glasses over.

"I'll take your word for it," Edwards replied. He could see the ungainly shape, perhaps three miles away, heading southeast toward Hafnarfjördur. "Looks like it's heading for the piers. Oh. They came in on a ship. They want to dock it, and they'll want to secure the waterfront first."

"Makes sense," Sergeant Smith agreed.

Edwards followed the helicopter until it dropped behind some buildings. Less than a minute later, it was up again, heading back northwest. He gave the horizon a close look.

"Looks like a ship out there."

MV *JULIUS FUCIK*

Kherov moved slowly back to the chart table with an Army medic at his side. His pumps were almost keeping up with the inflow of water. The *Fucik* was down half a meter at the bow. Portable fire pumps were being set near the bilges to draw more seawater out and eject it over the side—through the hole the American missile had made. He smiled wanly to himself. An Army medic followed him around. The General had practically pulled a gun on the captain, forcing him to allow the medic to give him a bottle of blood plasma and some morphine. He was grateful for the latter—his pain was still there, but not nearly so bad as it had been. The plasma container was a damned nuisance, with the medic holding it aloft as he moved around the pilothouse. But he knew he needed it. Kherov wanted to stay alive a few hours longer—*and who knows,* he thought, *if the regimental surgeon has skill, I might even live . . .*

There were more important things at hand. He had studied the charts of this port, but he had never been here before. He had no pilot. There would be no harbor tugs, and the tiny barge-tugs carried in his ship's split stern would be useless for docking.

The helicopter circled his ship after making its first trip. A miracle that it flew at all, the captain thought, after having the one next to it shattered by that strafing run. The mechanics had managed to extinguish that fire rapidly and place a curtain of water fog around the other aircraft. Some minor repairs had been needed, there were an even dozen holes in the sheet metal, but there it was, hovering just aft of the superstructure, landing slowly and awkwardly in the roiled air.

"How are you feeling, my captain?" the General inquired.

"How do I look?" A brave smile that failed to draw one in return. The

General knew that he should physically carry the man to his surgeon's emergency medical post, but who then would dock the ship? Captain Kherov was dying before his eyes. The medic had made that clear enough. There was internal bleeding. The plasma and bandages couldn't hope to keep up with it. "Have your men secured their objectives?"

"They report some fighting still at the air base, but it will soon be under control. The first team at the main quay reports no one there. That will be secure, my captain. You should rest a bit."

Kherov shook his head like a drunken man. "That will come soon enough. Fifteen more kilometers. We race in too fast as it is. The Americans may yet have some aircraft heading for us. We must get to the dock and unload your equipment before noon. I have lost too many of my crewmen to fail."

HAFNARFJÖRDUR, ICELAND

"We gotta report this," Edwards said quietly. He shrugged out of his pack and opened it. He'd watched a man test the radio before, and saw that instructions were printed on the side of the radio set. The six pieces of the antenna fitted easily into the pistol grip. Next he plugged in his headset and switched the radio on.

He was supposed to point the flowerlike antenna at a satellite on the 30° meridian, but he didn't have a compass to tell him where that was. Smith unfolded a map and selected a landmark in that general direction. Edwards pointed the antenna at it and waved it slowly across the sky until he heard the warbling carrier wave of the communications bird.

"Okay." Edwards turned the frequency knob to a preselected channel and toggled the Transmit switch.

"Anyone on this net, this is Mike Edwards, first lieutenant, United States Air Force, transmitting from Iceland. Please acknowledge, over." Nothing happened. Edwards reread the instructions to make sure he was doing the right thing, and rebroadcast the same message three more times.

"Sender on this net, please identify. Over." A voice finally answered.

"Edwards, Michael D., first lieutenant, U.S. Air Force, serial number 328-61-4030. I'm the meteorological officer attached to the 57th Fighter Interceptor Squadron at Keflavik. Who is this? Over."

"If you don't know that, pal, you don't belong on this net. Clear off, we need this for official traffic," the voice answered coldly. Edwards stared at the radio in mute rage for several seconds before exploding.

"Listen up, asshole! The guy who knows how to work this damned radio is dead, and I'm all you got. The base at Keflavik was hit seven hours ago by a Russian air and ground attack. The place is crawling with bad guys, there's a Russian ship coming into Hafnarfjördur harbor right now, and you're playing fucking word games! Let's get it together, mister. Over!"

"Copy that. Stand by. We have to verify who you are." Not a trace of remorse.

"Dammit, this thing works on batteries. You want me to run them down while you open a file cabinet?"

A new voice came on the circuit. "Edwards, this is the senior communications watch officer. Get off the air. They might be able to monitor you. We'll check you out and be back in three-zero minutes from now. You got that? Over."

That was more like it. The lieutenant checked his watch. "Roger, understand. We'll be back in three-zero minutes. Out." Edwards flipped the power switch off. "Let's get moving. I didn't know they could track in on this." The good news was that the radio broke down in under two minutes, and they were moving again.

"Sarge, let's head for this Hill 152. We should be able to see pretty good from up there, and there's water on the way."

"It's hot water, sir, full of sulfur. Just as soon not drink that shit, if you know what I mean."

"Suit yourself." Edwards moved off at a slow trot. Once as a boy he'd had to call in to report a fire. They'd believed him then. Why not now?

MV *JULIUS FUCIK*

Kherov knew that he was finishing the work that the Americans had begun. Driving his ship into the harbor at eighteen knots was worse than reckless. The sea bottom here was rock, not mud, and a grounding could easily rip his bottom out. But he feared another air attack even more, and he was sure that a flight of American fighters was heading this way, laden with missiles and bombs that would rob him of success in the most important mission of his life.

"Midships!" he called.

"Rudder amidships," the helmsman acknowledged.

He'd learned minutes before that his first officer was dead, from wounds sustained in the first strafing attack. His best helmsman had died screaming before his eyes, along with many of his skilled deck crewmen. He had only one man qualified to take the shore sightings necessary for a positive position fix. But the quay was in sight, and he'd depend on a seaman's eye.

"Slow to half speed," he ordered. The helmsman relayed the order on the engine room telegraph.

"Rudder right full." He watched his ship's head come slowly right. He stood on the centerline of the bridge, carefully lining his jackstaff up with the quay. There was no one trained to handle the mooring lines. He wondered if the soldiers could manage it.

The ship touched bottom. Kherov was thrown from his feet and cursed loudly with pain and rage. He'd misjudged his approach. The *Fucik* shuddered as she slid across the rocky bottom. There was no time to check his chart. When the tide turned, the harbor's strong eddy currents would make his landing an impossible nightmare.

"Reverse your rudder." A minute later the ship was fully afloat again. The captain ignored the flooding alarms that hooted behind him. The hull was penetrated, or maybe the damaged seams had sprung further. No matter. The dock was a mere thousand meters away. It was a massive quay made of rough stone. "Midships. All stop."

The ship was moving far too fast to stop. The soldiers on the dock could already see that, and were slowly backing up, away from the edge, fearing that it would crumble when the ship struck. Kherov grunted with dark amusement. So much for the line handlers. Eight hundred meters.

"All back full."

Six hundred meters. The ship's whole mass shuddered as the engines fought to slow her. She headed into the berth at a thirty-degree angle, her speed now eight knots. Kherov walked to the engine room voice tube.

"On my order, shut down the engines, pull the manual sprinkler handle, and evacuate the engine spaces."

"What are you doing?" the General asked.

"We cannot moor to the quay," Kherov answered simply. "Your soldiers don't know how to handle the lines, and many of my seamen are dead." The berth Kherov had selected was precisely half a meter shallower than his ship's draft. He went back to the voice tube.

"Now, Comrades!"

Below, the chief engineer gave the orders. His chief machinist cut off the diesel engines and ran to the escape ladder. The engineer yanked the emergency handle for the fire-suppression system and followed, after counting heads to make sure that all his men had gotten out.

"Rudder hard right!"

A minute later the bow of *Julius Fucik* rammed the quay at a speed of five knots. Her bow crumpled as though constructed of paper, and the whole ship pivoted to the right, her side slamming against the rocks in a shower of orange sparks. The impact ripped the ship's bottom open at the turn of her starboard bilges. Instantly her lower decks flooded, and the ship settled rapidly to the bottom, only a few feet below her flat keel. The *Julius Fucik* would never sail again. But she had reached her objective.

Kherov waved to the General. "My men will deploy the two baby tug-boats we have in the stern. Tell them to remove two barges and set them between the stern and the end of the quay. My men will show you how to secure the barges properly so they don't drift off. Then use your bridging equipment to take your vehicles off the elevator onto the barges, then from the barges to the quay."

"We can do this easily. Now, Comrade Captain, you will see my surgeon. I will brook no further argument." The General waved to his orderly and both men assisted the captain below. There might still be time.

HILL 152, ICELAND

"You decide who I am yet?" Edwards asked testily. Another really annoying thing was the quarter-second delay caused by the signal's travel time to and from the satellite.

"That's affirmative. The problem is, how do we know it's really you?" The officer had a telex in his hand confirming that one First Lieutenant Michael D. Edwards, USAF, had indeed been the met officer for the 57th FIS, information that could easily have been in Russian hands before the attack.

"Look, turkey, I'm sitting here on Hill 152, east of Hafnarfjördur, okay? There is a Russian helicopter flying around, and some godawful big ship just docked in the harbor. It's too far to see a flag, but I don't figure the son of a bitch came from New York, y'know? The Russians have invaded this rock. They pounded hell out of Keflavik, and they got troops all over the place."

"Tell me about the ship."

Edwards locked the binoculars to his eyes. "Black hull, white superstructure. Big block letters on the side. Can't quite make it out. Something-Lines. The first word begins with an L. Some kind of barge-carrying ship. There's a tugboat moving a barge around right now."

"Have you seen any Russian troops?"

Edwards paused before answering. "No. I've just heard radio reports of the Marines at Keflavik. They were being overrun. They've been off the air ever since. I can see some people on the dock, but I can't tell what they are."

"Okay, we'll be checking that out. For the moment I'd suggest that you find a good, safe place to belly-up, and stay off the air. If we have to contact you, we'll broadcast on the hour, every even hour. If you want to talk to us, we'll be here. Understood?"

"Roger, copy. Out." Edwards switched off. "I don't believe this."

"Nobody knows what the hell's going on, Lieutenant," Smith observed. "Why should they? We sure as hell don't."

"Ain't that the truth!" Edwards repacked his radio. "If those idiots would listen to me, we could have some fighter-bombers here to blast that ship inside two hours. God, but she's a big one. How much equipment can you Marines load in something that big?"

"A lot," Smith said quietly.

"You think they'll be trying to land more troops?"

"It figures, sir. They couldn't have hit Keflavik with all that many—figure a battalion, tops. This here's a pretty big rock. I'd sure as hell want more troops to hold it than that. Course, I'm just a buck sergeant."

HAFNARFJÖRDUR, ICELAND

The General could finally get to work. The first order of business was to board the single working helicopter, now operating off the dock, its pilots delighted to see the ship sunk alongside the quay. He left a rifle company to secure the harbor area, sent another to Reykjavik airport to reinforce that, and detailed his last to get the division's equipment moving off the ship. Then he flew to Keflavik to survey the situation.

Most of the fires were still burning, he saw. The aircraft fuel dump nearest the base was ablaze, but the main storage tanks five kilometers away seemed intact, and, he could see, were already guarded by a BMD assault vehicle and some men. The assault regiment commander met him on one of the undamaged runways.

"Keflavik air base is secure, Comrade General!" he proclaimed.

"How did it go?"

"Hard. The Americans were uncoordinated—one of the missiles hit their command post—but they did not give up easily. We have nineteen dead and forty-three wounded. We have accounted for most of the Marines and other security troops, and we are still counting the other prisoners."

"How many armed troops escaped?"

"None that we know of. Too early to tell, of course, but some undoubtedly died in the fires." The colonel waved at the smashed base area to the east. "How is the ship? I heard he took a missile hit."

"And we were strafed by American fighters. He's tied to the dock, and the equipment is being unloaded now. Can we use this airfield? I—"

"Getting that report now." The colonel's radio operator handed his radiophone over. The colonel spoke for a minute or so. A five-man party of Air Force personnel had accompanied the second wave and was evaluating the base facilities.

"Comrade General, the base radar and radio systems are destroyed. The runways are littered with debris, and they tell me that they need some hours to sweep them clear. Also the fuel pipeline is broken in two places. Fortunately it did not burn. For the moment we'll have to use the airport's trucks to transfer fuel. All of them seem to be intact . . . they recommend that the airlift come into Reykjavik. Have we secured that?"

"Yes, and it is intact. Any hope of getting information from the American aircraft?"

"Unfortunately not, Comrade. The aircraft were badly damaged from incoming missiles. Those that did not burn of their own accord were burned by their crews. As I said, they fought hard."

"Very well. I'll send the remainder of your two battalions with your equipment as soon as we can get things organized. I'll need the third at the dock for the moment. Set up your perimeter. Start the cleanup, we need this airfield operational as soon as possible. Get the prisoners together and ready to move. We'll be flying them out tonight. They are to be treated correctly." His orders on that score were very precise. Prisoners are assets.

"As you say, Comrade General. And please get me some engineers so that we can repair that fuel pipe."

"Well done, Nikolay Gennadyevich!"

The General ran back to his helicopter. Only nineteen dead. He'd expected a higher number than that. Taking out the Marine command center had been a real stroke of luck. By the time his Hip returned to the dock, the equipment was already rolling off. The ship's barges had been fitted with loading doors in their hulls, like miniature landing craft, which allowed vehicles to roll straight out. The units already were being organized on the dock and nearby lots. His staff officers were fully in charge of things, the General saw. To this point, Operation Polar Glory was a total success.

When the Hip landed, it refueled from a line draped down from the ship's side. The General went to his operations officer.

"Reykjavik airport is secure also, Comrade General, and there we have complete fueling facilities. Is that where you want the airlift to come in?"

The General thought about that one. Reykjavik's airport was a small one, but he didn't want to wait until the larger Keflavik was clear to bring in his reinforcements. "Yes. Send the code word to headquarters: I want the airlift to begin at once."

HILL 152, ICELAND

"Tanks." Garcia had the binoculars. "A bunch of 'em and they all got red stars. Heading west on Route 41. This oughta convince 'em, sir."

Edwards took the field glasses. He could see the tanks, but not the stars. "What kind are they? They don't look like real tanks."

It was now Smith's turn. "That's BMPs—maybe BMDs. It's an infantry assault vehicle, like an amtrak. Holds a squad of men and a 73-millimeter gun. They're Russian, that's for sure, Lieutenant. I count eleven of the bastards, and maybe twenty trucks with men in 'em."

Edwards broke out his radio again. Garcia was right. This did get their attention.

"Okay, Edwards, who do you have with you?"

Edwards rattled off the names of his Marines. "We bugged out before the Russians got into the base."

"Where are you now?"

"Hill 152, four kilometers due east of Hafnarfjördur. We can see all the way into the harbor. There are Russian vehicles heading west toward Keflavik, and some trucks—we can't tell what kind—heading northeast toward Reykjavik on Highway 41. Look, guys, if you can whistle up a couple of Aardvarks, maybe we can kill that ship before she unloads," the lieutenant said urgently.

"I'm afraid the Varks are a little busy right now, fella. In case nobody told you, there's a shooting war in Germany. World War III kicked off ten hours ago. We're trying to get a recon bird up your way, but it might take awhile. Nobody's decided what to do about you either. For right now, you're on your own."

"No shit," Edwards replied, looking at his men.

"Okay, Edwards. Use your head, avoid contact with the enemy. If I read this right, you're the only friendly we have there right now. It figures they'll want you to keep the reports coming in. Observe and report. Conserve the battery power you have. Play it nice and cool, guy. Help will be coming, but it might take awhile. Just hang in there. You can listen for us on the hour, on even hours. You got a good watch?" *In the meantime,* the communications officer thought, *we'll try to figure a way to find out if you're really who you say, and that you haven't got a Russian pistol at your head.*

"Roger, it's set to Zulu time. We'll be listening. Out."

"More tanks," Smith said. "Jeez, that ship sure is a busy place!"

HAFNARFJÖRDUR, ICELAND

The General would not have believed how well things were going. When he had seen the Harpoon coming, he was sure that his mission would be a failure. Already a third of his vehicles had rolled off the ship and were en route to their destinations. Next, he wanted the rest of his division flown in. After that came more helicopters. For the present, all around him were a hundred thousand Icelanders whose friendship he did not expect. A few hardy souls were watching him from the opposite side of the harbor, and he'd already sent a squad of men to get rid of them. How many people were making telephone calls? Was the telephone-satellite relay base still intact? Might they be calling the United States to tell what was happening in Iceland? So many things to worry about.

"General, the airlift is under way. The first aircraft took off ten minutes ago with a fighter escort. They should begin to arrive in four hours," his communications officer reported.

"Four hours." The General looked up from the ship's bridge into a clear blue sky. How long before the Americans reacted and threw a squadron of fighter-bombers at him? He pointed to his operations officer.

"We have too many vehicles sitting on the quay. As soon as a platoon-sized grouping is together, move them off to their objectives. There is no time to wait for company groups. What about Reykjavik airport?"

"We have one company of infantrymen in place, with another twenty minutes away. No opposition. The civilian air controllers and the airport maintenance people are all under guard. A patrol going through Reykjavik reports little activity on the streets. Our embassy personnel report that a government radio broadcast told people to remain in their homes, and for the most part they seem to be doing this."

"Tell the patrol to seize the main telephone exchange. Leave the radio and television stations alone, but get the telephone exchange!" He turned as a squad of paratroopers arrived at the crowd on the far side of the harbor. He estimated perhaps thirty people there. The eight soldiers approached quickly after dismounting from their truck, rifles at the ready. One man walked up to the soldiers, waving his arms wildly. He was shot down. The rest of the crowd ran.

The General shouted a curse. "Find out who did that!"

USS *CHICAGO*

McCafferty returned to the attack center after a brief visit to his private head. Coffee would always keep you awake, he thought, either through the caffeine or the discomfort of an always-full bladder. Things were already not going well. Whatever genius had decided to order the American submarines out of the Barents Sea in the hope of avoiding an "incident" had neatly gotten them out of the way. *Just in time for the war to start,* the captain grumbled, forgetting that the idea hadn't seemed all that bad at the time.

Had they stuck to the plan, he might already have put a dent in the Soviet Navy. Instead, someone had panicked over the new Soviet missile sub dispositions, and so far as he could tell, the result was that no one had accomplished much of anything. The Soviet subs that had come storming out of the Kola Fjord had not come south into the Norwegian Sea as expected. His long-range sonar reported possible submarine noises far to his north, heading west before fading out. *So,* he thought, *Ivan's sending his boats down the Denmark Strait? The SOSUS line between Iceland and Greenland could make that idea a costly one.*

USS *Chicago* was steaming at five hundred feet just north of the 69° parallel, about a hundred miles west of Norway's rocky coastline. The Norwegians' collection of diesel boats was inside of him, guarding their own coast. McCafferty understood that, but didn't like it.

So far nothing had gone right, and McCafferty was worried. That was expected, and he could suppress it. He could fall back on his training. He knew what his submarine could do, and had a pretty good idea of what the Russian subs were capable of. He had the superior capabilities, but some Russian could always get lucky. This was war. A different sort of environment, not one judged by umpires and rule books. Mistakes now were not a matter of a written critique from his squadron commander. And so far luck seemed to be on the other side.

He looked around at his men. They had to be thinking the same thoughts, he was sure, but they all depended on him. The crewmen of his submarine were essentially the physical extensions of his own mind. He was the central control for the entire corporate entity known as USS *Chicago,* and for the first time the awesome responsibility struck him. If he messed up, all these men would die. And he, too, would die—with the knowledge that he had failed them.

You can't think like this, the captain told himself. *It will eat you up. Better to have a combat situation where I can limit my thinking to the immediate.* He checked the clock. Good.

"Take her up to periscope depth," he ordered. "It's time to check for orders, and we'll try an ESM sweep to see what's happening."

Not a simple procedure, that. The submarine came up slowly, cautiously, turning to allow her sonar to make certain that there was not a ship around.

"Raise the ESM."

An electronics technician pressed the button to raise the mast for his broad-band receiver. The board lit up instantly.

"Numerous electronic sources, sir. Three J-band search sets, lots of other stuff. Lots of VHF and UHF chatter. The recorders are going."

That figures, McCafferty thought. *The odds against having anyone here after us are pretty low, though.* "Up scope."

The captain angled the search-scope lens upward to scan the sky for a nearby aircraft and made a quick turn around the horizon. He noticed something odd, and had to angle down the lens to see what it was.

There was a green smoke marker not two hundred yards away. McCafferty cringed and spun the instrument back around. A multiengine aircraft was coming out of the haze—directly in at them.

The captain reached up and spun the periscope wheel, lowering the instrument. *"Take her down!* All ahead flank! Make your depth eight hundred feet!" *Where the hell did he come from?*

The submarine's engines fairly exploded into action. A flurry of orders had the helmsmen push their controls to the stops.

"Torpedo in the water, starboard side!" a sonarman screamed.

McCafferty reacted at once. "Left full rudder!"

"Left full rudder, aye!" The speed log was at ten knots and rising quickly. They passed below one hundred feet.

"Torpedo bearing one-seven-five relative. It's pinging. Doesn't have us yet."

"Fire off a noisemaker."

Seventy feet aft of the control room, a five-inch canister was ejected from a launcher. It immediately started making all kinds of noise for the torpedo to home in on.

"Noisemaker away!"

"Right fifteen degrees rudder." McCafferty was calmer now. He'd played this game before. "Come to new course one-one-zero. Sonar, I want true bearings on that torpedo."

"Aye. Torpedo bearing two-zero-six, coming port-to-starboard."

Chicago passed through two hundred feet. The boat had a twenty-degree down angle. The planesmen and most of the technicians had seatbelts to hold them in place. The officers and a few others who had to circulate around grasped at rails and stanchions to keep from falling.

"Conn, Sonar. The torpedo seems to be following a circular path. Now traveling starboard-to-port, bearing one-seven-five. Still pinging, but I don't think it has us."

"Very well. Keep those reports coming." McCafferty climbed aft to the plot. "Looks like he made a bad drop."

"Could be," the navigator agreed. "But how in hell—"

"Had to be a MAD pass. The magnetic anomaly detector. Was the tape running? I didn't have him long enough for an ID." He checked the plot. They were now a mile and a half from where they'd been when the torpedo was dropped. "Sonar, tell me about the fish."

"Bearing one-nine-zero, dead aft. Still circling, seems to be going down a little. I think maybe the noisemaker drew him in and he's trying to hit it."

"All ahead two-thirds." *Time to slow down,* McCafferty thought. They'd cleared the initial datum point, and the aircraft's crew would need a few minutes to evaluate their attack before beginning a new search. In that time they'd be two or three miles away, below the layer, and making little noise.

"All ahead two-thirds, aye. Leveling off at eight hundred feet."

"We can start breathing again, people," McCafferty said. His own voice was not as even as he would have preferred. For the first time, he noted a few shaky hands. *Just like a car wreck,* he thought. *You only shake after you're safe.* "Left fifteen degrees rudder. Come left to two-eight-zero." If the aircraft dropped again, no sense in traveling in a straight path. But they should be fairly safe now. The whole episode, he noted, had lasted less than ten minutes.

The captain walked to the forward bulkhead and rewound the videotape, then set it up to run. It showed the periscope breaking the surface, the first quick search . . . then the smoke marker. Next came the aircraft. McCafferty froze the frame.

The plane looked like a Lockheed P-3 Orion.

"That's one of ours!" the duty electrician noted. The captain stepped forward into sonar.

"The fish is fading aft, Cap'n. Probably still trying to kill the noisemaker. I think when it hit the water it circled in the wrong direction, away from us, I mean."

"What's it sound like?"

"A lot like one of our Mark-46s"—the leading sonarman shuddered— "it really did sound like a forty-six!" He rewound his own tape and set it on speaker. The *screee*ing sound of the twin-screw fish was enough to raise the hairs on your neck. McCafferty nodded and went back aft.

"Okay, that might have been a Norwegian P-3. Then again it might have been a Russian May. They look pretty much alike, and they have exactly the same job. Well done, people. We're going to clear the area." The captain congratulated himself on his performance. He'd just evaded his first war shot—dropped by a friendly aircraft! But he had evaded it. Not all the luck was with the other side. Or was it?

USS *PHARRIS*

Morris was catnapping in his bridge chair, wondering what was missing from his life. It took a few seconds to realize that he wasn't doing any paperwork, his normal afternoon pastime. He had to transmit position reports every four hours, contact reports when he had any—he hadn't yet—but the routine paper-shuffling that ate up so much of his time was a thing of the past. A pity, he thought, that it took a war to relieve one of that! He could almost imagine himself starting to enjoy it.

The convoy was still twenty miles to his southeast. *Pharris* was the outlying sonar picket. Her mission was to detect, localize, and engage any submarine trying to close the convoy. To do that, the frigate was alternately dashing—"sprinting"—forward at maximum speed, then drifting briefly at slower speed to allow her sonar to work with maximum efficiency. Had the convoy proceeded at twenty knots on a straight course, it would have been nearly impossible. The three columns of merchantmen were zigzagging, however, making life a little easier on all concerned. Except on the merchant sailors, for whom stationkeeping was as foreign as marching.

Morris sipped at a Coke. It was a warm afternoon and he preferred his caffeine cold.

"Signal coming in from *Talbot,* sir," the junior officer of the deck reported.

Morris rose and walked to the starboard bridge wing with his binoculars. He prided himself on being able to read Morse almost as quickly as his signalmen: REPORT ICELAND ATTACKED AND NEUTRALIZED BY SOVIET FORCES X EXPECT MORE SERIOUS AIR AND SUB THREAT X.

"More good news, skipper," the OOD commented.

"Yeah."

USS *NIMITZ*

"How did they do it?" Chip wondered aloud.

"How don't matter a damn," Toland replied. "We gotta get this to the boss." He made a quick phone call and left for flag country.

He almost got lost. *Nimitz* had over two *thousand* compartments. The Admiral lived in only one of them, and Toland had only been there once. He found a Marine sentry at the door. The carrier's commander, Captain Svenson, was already there.

"Sir, we have a Flash message that the Soviets have attacked and neutralized Iceland. They may have troops there."

"Do they have aircraft there?" Svenson asked at once.

"We don't know. They're trying to get a recon bird to take a look, probably the Brits, but we won't have any hard information for at least six hours. The last friendly satellite pass was two hours ago, and we won't have another one of those for nine hours."

"Okay, tell me what you have," the Admiral ordered.

Toland went over the sketchy data that had come in the dispatch from Norfolk. "From what we know, it was a pretty off-the-wall plan, but it seems to have worked."

"Nobody ever said Ivan was dumb," Svenson commented sourly. "What about our orders?"

"Nothing yet."

"How many troops on Iceland?" the Admiral asked.

"No word on that, sir. The P-3 crew watched two relays of four hovercraft. At a hundred men per load, that's eight hundred men, at least a battalion, probably more like a regiment. The ship is large enough to carry the equipment load for a full brigade and then some. It's in one of Gorshkov's books that this sort of ship is uniquely useful for landing operations."

"That's too much for a MAU to take on, sir," Svenson said. A Marine Amphibious Unit consisted of a reinforced battalion of troops.

"With three carriers backing them up?" Admiral Baker snorted, then adopted a more thoughtful pose. "You could be right at that. What does this do to the air threat to us?"

"Iceland had a squadron of F-15s and a couple AWACS birds. That's a lot of protection for us—gone. We've lost raid warning, attrition, and raid-tracking capabilities." Svenson didn't like this at all. "We should be able to handle their Backfires ourselves, but it would have been a lot easier with those Eagles running interference."

Baker sipped at his coffee. "Our orders haven't changed."

"What else is going on in the world?" Svenson asked.

"Norway is being hit hard, but no details yet. Same story in Germany. The Air Force is supposed to have gotten a heavy hit in on the Soviets, again no details. It's still too early for any substantive intel assessments of what's happening."

"If Ivan was able to suppress the Norwegians and fully neutralize Iceland, the air threat against this battle group has at least doubled," Svenson said. "I have to get talking with my air group."

The captain left. Admiral Baker was silent for several minutes. Toland had to stay put. He hadn't been dismissed yet. "They just hit Keflavik?"

"Yes, sir."

"Find out what else is there and get back to me."

"Yes, sir." As Toland walked back to the intelligence shack, he pondered what he'd told his wife: *The carrier is the best-protected ship in the fleet.* But the captain was worried . . .

HILL 152, ICELAND

They were almost thinking of it as home. The position was at least easily defensible. No one could approach Hill 152 without being seen, and that meant crossing a lava field, then climbing up a steep, bare slope. Garcia found a small lake a kilometer away, evidently filled with water from the winter snows that had only lately melted. Sergeant Smith observed that it would have made a good mixer for bourbon, if they had any bourbon.

They were hungry, but all had four days of rations along, and they feasted on such delicacies as canned lima beans and ham. Edwards learned a new and indelicate name for this item.

"Anybody here know how to cook a sheep?" Rodgers asked. Several miles south of them was a large herd of the animals.

"Cook with what?" Edwards asked.

"Oh." Rodgers looked around. There wasn't a tree in sight. "How come there ain't no trees?"

"Rodgers only been here a month," Smith explained. "Prive, you ain't never seen a windy day till you been here in the winter. The only way a tree can grow here is if you set her in concrete. I seen wind strong enough to blow a deuce-and-a-half right off the road."

"Airplanes." Garcia had the binoculars. He pointed northeast. "Lots."

Edwards took the field glasses. They were just dots, but they grew rapidly into shapes. "I count six, big ones, look like C-141s . . . that makes them IL-76s, I think. Maybe some fighters, too. Sergeant, get a pad and a pencil—we have to do a count."

It lasted for hours. The fighters landed first, rolling off to the refueling area at once, then taxiing to one of the shorter runways. One aircraft came in every three minutes, and Edwards couldn't help be impressed. The IL-76, code-named the Candid by the NATO countries, was an awkward, ungainly design, like its American counterpart. The pilots landed, stopped, and rolled their aircraft onto the taxiway off the main north-south runway as though they had practiced for months—as Edwards rather suspected they had. They unloaded at the airport terminal building, then rolled to the refueling area and took off, coordinating neatly with the landing aircraft. Those lifting off came very close to their hill, close enough that Edwards was able to copy down a few tail numbers. When the count reached fifty, he set up his radio.

"This is Edwards transmitting from Hill 152. Do you copy, over."

"Roger, copy," the voice came back at once. "From now on, your code name is Beagle. We are Doghouse. Continue your report."

"Roger, Doghouse. We have a Soviet airlift in progress. We have counted fifty—five-zero—Soviet transport aircraft, India-Lima-Seven-Six type. They are coming into Reykjavik, unloading, and rolling back out to the northeast."

"Beagle, are you sure, repeat are you sure of your count?"

"That is affirmative, Doghouse. The takeoff run brings them right over our heads, and we got a paper record. No shit, mister, five-zero aircraft"—Smith held up his pad—"make that five-three aircraft, and the operation is continuing. We also have six single-seat aircraft sitting at the end of runway four. I can't make out the type, but they sure as hell look like fighters. You copy that, Doghouse?"

"I copy five-three transports and six possible fighters. Okay, Beagle, we gotta get this information upstairs fast. Sit tight and we'll keep to the regular transmission schedule. Is your position safe?"

That's a good question, Edwards thought. "I hear you, Doghouse. We're staying put. Out." He took off the headset. "We safe, Sergeant?"

"Sure, Lieutenant, I haven't felt this safe since Beirut."

HAFNARFJÖRDUR, ICELAND

"A beautiful operation, Comrade General." The Ambassador beamed.

"Your support was most valuable," the General lied through his teeth. The Soviet embassy to Iceland had over sixty members, almost all intelligence types of one sort or another. Instead of doing something useful, like seizing the telephone exchange, on donning their uniforms they had been rounding up local political figures. Most of the members of Iceland's ancient Parliament, the Althing, had been arrested. Necessary, the General agreed, but too roughly done, with one of them killed in the process and two more shot. *Better to be gentle with them,* he thought. This was not Afghanistan. The Icelanders had no warrior tradition, and a gentler approach might have shown better returns. But that aspect of the operation was under KGB control, its control team already in place with the embassy personnel. "With your permission, there is much yet to be done."

The General went back up the jacob's ladder onto the *Fucik*. Problems had developed in off-loading the division's missile battalion. The barges that contained that equipment had been damaged by the missile strike. The newly installed landing doors had jammed solid and had to be torched free. He shrugged. Up to now, Polar Glory had been a near textbook operation. Not bad for a scratch crew. Most of his rolling equipment—two hundred armored vehicles and many trucks—had already been mated with their troops and dispersed. The SA-11 battalion was all that remained.

"Bad news, Comrade General," the SAM commander reported.

"Must I wait for it?" the General asked testily. It had been a very long day.

"We have three usable rockets."

"Three?"

"Both these barges were ruptured when the American missile hit us. The shock damage accounted for several. The main damage came from the water used to fight the fire."

"Those are mobile missiles," the General objected. "Surely the designers anticipated that they might get wet!"

"Not with saltwater, Comrade. This is the army version, not the naval, and it is not protected against saltwater corrosion. The men who fought the fire did so with great gusto, and most of the rockets were soaked. The exposed control wiring and the radar seeker heads on the missile noses were badly damaged. My men have run electronic tests of all the rockets. Three are fully functional. Four more we can probably clean off and repair. The rest are ruined. We have to fly more in."

The General controlled his temper. So, a small thing that no one had thought of. Aboard ship, fires are fought with saltwater. They should have asked for the naval variant of this rocket. It was always the small things.

"Divide your launchers as planned. Place all the usable missiles at the Reykjavik airport, and the ones you think you can fix at Keflavik. I'll order the replacement rockets to be flown in. Is there other damage?"

"Apparently not. The radar antennae were covered with plastic, and the instruments inside the vehicles were safe because the vehicles themselves were sealed. If we get new rockets, my battalion is fully ready. We'll be ready to travel in twenty minutes. Sorry, Comrade."

"Not your fault. You know where you are to go?"

"Two of my battery commanders have already checked the routes."

"Excellent. Carry on, Comrade Colonel." The General climbed back up the ladder to the bridge to look for his communications officer. Within two hours a plane loaded with forty SA-11 surface-to-air missiles was rolling off Murmansk's Kilpyavr airfield bound for Iceland.

20. The Dance of the Vampires

USS *NIMITZ*

Toland had been a busy fellow for the past twelve hours. The data on Iceland came in slowly, one confusing piece at a time, and even now he didn't have enough to call a clear picture. The group's orders had been changed, though only after too many hours of indecision. The mission to reinforce Iceland was a washout. For the past ten hours the battle group had been heading due east toward friendly air cover from England and France. Someone had decided that if the Marines could not go to Iceland, then they might find useful employment in Germany. Bob had expected them to be diverted to Norway, where a Marine Amphibious Brigade was already in place, but getting them there could prove difficult. A furious air battle had been raging over northern Norway for almost twenty hours, with losses heavy on both sides. The Norwegians had started the war with scarcely a hundred modern fighters. They were screaming for help, but there was no help for anyone as yet.

"They're not just chewing the Norwegians up," Toland observed. "They're driving them south. Most of the attacks are on the northern bases, and they're not giving them any breather at all."

Chip nodded. "That figures. Gives their Backfires a straighter shot at us. Briefing time."

"Yeah." Toland packed up his notes and walked again toward flag country. It was easier this time.

"Okay, Commander," Admiral Baker said. "Start with the peripheries."

"Nothing much seems to be happening in the Pacific as yet. The Soviets are evidently putting a lot of diplomatic pressure on Japan. The same story they've given the rest of the world—it's all a German plot."

"Horseshit," Baker observed.

"True enough, Admiral, but it's a plausible enough story that Greece is refusing to honor its treaty commitments, and a lot of neutral and third-world countries are buying it. Anyway, the Russians are making noises about giving the Sakhalin Islands back if they play ball—or pounding hell out of them if they don't. Bottom line: Japan is not allowing any bases on its soil to be used for offensive strikes against the Soviet Union. What we have in Korea is needed there. The only carrier group we have in the Western Pacific is centered on *Midway*. They're well out to sea at present, and they don't have the moxie to go after Kamchatka alone. There's some air activity in the South China Sea west of the Philippines, but nothing major yet. Cam Ranh Bay appears to be empty of Soviet shipping. So the Pacific is quiet, but that won't last long.

"In the Indian Ocean, somebody launched a missile attack against Diego Garcia, probably a submarine. Not much damage—just about everything there was sent out to sea five days ago—but it got their attention. At last report, their IO squadron was at fifteen-north, ninety-east, a long way from our guys, and heading south.

"No activity at all on NATO's southern flank. The Turks aren't about to attack Russia on their own hook, and Greece is staying out of what they call 'this German-Russian dispute.' So Ivan has a secure southern flank, too, and so far it looks like he's happy enough to keep it that way. So far the Russians are only fighting in Western Europe and against selected American installations elsewhere. They are telling anyone who'll listen that they don't even want to fight us. They've even guaranteed the safety of American tourists and businessmen in the Soviet Union. Supposedly, they're flying them all out through India. We've underestimated the political dimension here, sir. So far it's working for them.

"Okay. In Europe their operations began with from twenty to thirty Spetznaz commando attacks throughout Germany. For the most part they were defeated, but they scored big in two places. The port of Hamburg has been blocked. A pair of merchantmen was scuttled in the main channel, and the team that pulled it off got away clean. The same thing was attempted in Bremen—they blocked one channel partially and burned three ships at one of the container terminals. This team didn't get away. The other attacks were against nuclear weapons storage sites, communications posts, and one big one against a tank site. Our guys were ready for it. We took losses, but those Spetznaz troops got chewed up in most cases.

"The Soviet Army attacked west just before dawn yesterday. The good news here is that the Air Force pulled something really wild. That new Stealth fighter we've been hearing rumblings about is in squadron service, and it was used to raise a lot of hell behind Russian lines. The Air Force says they've got air superiority, or something close to it, so Ivan must have taken a big hit. Whatever they did, the initial Russian attack was not as powerful as expected. They're moving forward, but as of midnight nothing more than fifteen kilometers, and in two places they got stopped cold. So far no word on nukes or chemical weapons. Losses are reported heavy on both sides, especially up in northern Germany, where they moved the farthest. Hamburg is threatened. The Kiel Canal may have been hit with an airborne or airmobile attack, we're not sure, but part is under Russian control. That situation is a little confused. A lot of activity on the Baltic, too. The fast attack boats of the German and Danish navies claim to have beaten up hard on a combined Soviet and East German attack, but again things are pretty confused."

Toland went on to describe the situation in Norway.

"The direct threats against us are from submarines and aircraft. Ivan's subs have been pretty busy. We have reports of twenty-two merchant ships sunk. The worst was *Ocean Star,* a Panamanian-flag passenger liner coming back from a Med cruise. Eight hundred miles northwest of Gibraltar she took a missile hit, type unknown, but probably from a Juliet. She burned, lots of casualties. Two Spanish frigates are moving in for the search-and-rescue.

"We have three submarines reported close to our course track, an Echo, a Tango, and a Foxtrot. There could be more, but intelligence reports have most of them south and west of us. When Iceland got neutralized, we lost the G-I-UK SOSUS line, and that will allow Ivan's subs an easier access to the North Atlantic. SACLANT is dispatching subs to block the gaps. They'll have to hustle; we have reports of numerous Soviet submarines heading for the Denmark Strait."

"How many subs have we taken out?" Svenson asked.

"Lajes and Brunswick claim four kills. The P-3s got off to a good start. The bad news here is that one Orion is missing, and another reported being shot at by a sub-launched missile. This is being evaluated now, and we expect something firm by noon. In any case, the main threat to us now appears to be from aircraft, not subs. That could change by tomorrow, though."

"One day at a time. Get to Iceland," Baker ordered.

"The reports we had yesterday were correct. Evidently a regimental-sized unit came in by sea, and the rest of its division was airlifted in, starting around 1400 hours. We have to assume they're all in by now."

"Fighters?" Svenson asked.

"None reported, but it's possible. Iceland has four usable airfields—"

"Wrong, Toland, it's three," Baker said harshly.

"Beg pardon, sir, four. The big base is Keflavik. Five runways, two of them over ten thousand feet long. We built the place to stage B-52s out of, and it's quite a facility. Ivan got it virtually intact. His attack was planned deliberately not to crater the runways. Second, they have the civilian airfield at Reykjavik. The longest runway there is about two thousand meters, plenty big enough for fighters, and it's got a city wrapped around it. Hitting that place means running the risk of civilian casualties. On the north side of the island is Akureyri, one hard-surface strip. The fourth one, Admiral, is old Keflavik, about two miles southeast of the current NATO air base. It shows on the maps as unusable, but I ran into a guy who put in two years on Iceland. That strip is usable, certainly for rough-surface-capable aircraft like our C-130. The base personnel use it for racing their go-carts and sports cars. He thinks you could use fighters out of there, too. Finally, every city on that island has a gravel strip for their domestic airline. The MiG-23 and several other Russian fighters have a rough-field capability, and could use any one of those."

"You're full of good news," observed *Nimitz*'s commander, air group, known as the CAG. "What about the other base facilities, like fuel?"

"The fuel depot right on the base was destroyed in the attack, but the base tank-farm was not, and neither was the new terminal at Hakotstanger. Unless somebody takes it out, we've left the Russians enough jet fuel to operate for months.''

"How solid is all this?" Baker wanted to know.

"We have an eyeball report from a Navy P-3 crew who surveyed the damage immediately after the attack. The RAF sent two recce birds for a look-see. The first one got good shots of Keflavik and the surrounding area. The second didn't make it back, reason unknown.''

"SAMs." The CAG really looked unhappy now.

Toland nodded. "A good bet. The photos show vehicles consistent with the presence of a reinforced Soviet Air Rifle division. Icelandic radio and TV are off the air. The Brits report contact with ham radio operators on the Icelandic coast, but nothing at all is coming out of the southwest corner of the island. That's where most of the people are, and it looks to be completely under Soviet control. We're getting some intel information, but it can't last.''

"What you're telling us is that we can't expect raid warning from the Norwegians, and we've lost our picket fence at Iceland. What other assets do we have?" Svenson asked.

"Evidently something. I've been told to expect possible raid warning from an asset code-named Realtime. If a large force of Soviet aircraft leaves Kola, we ought to know about it.''

"What's Realtime?" the CAG asked.

"They didn't tell me that.''

"Submarine." Baker smiled thinly. "Jesus protect him when he transmits. Well, Ivan sent his bombers against Iceland yesterday. Anybody wonder where they'll be coming today?''

"In case anyone wants it, my official intelligence estimate is, right here," Toland said.

"Always nice to have a professional opinion," the CAG observed acidly. "We ought to head north and pound on those Russians"—by training and experience the CAG was an attack pilot—"but we can't do that until we deal with the Backfires. What is the strength of the threat to us?''

"I'm assuming no assistance from the Air Force units. With Soviet Naval Aviation alone we have six regiments of strike aircraft, three each of Backfires and Badgers. One regiment of Badger jammers. One regiment of Bear reconnaissance birds. Add some tanker assets to that. Twenty-seven aircraft to the regiment. That's about a hundred sixty strike aircraft, each of which can carry two or three air-to-surface missiles.''

"Those Badgers will have to stretch to get here. The round trip must be a good four thousand miles, even if they cut across Norway. Those are tired old birds," CAG said. "What about their satellites?''

Toland checked his watch. "There will be a RORSAT pass over us in fifty-two minutes. They got us twelve hours ago, too.''

"I hope the Air Force gets its act together with their ASAT pretty soon," Svenson said quietly. "If Ivan can real-time that satellite intelligence, they don't need those damned Bears. They can figure our course easily enough, and it's only a four-hour cruise down here for them.''

"Try a course change as it passes overhead?" CAG wondered.

"Not much point in it," Baker replied. "We've been heading east for ten hours. They can't miss that, and we can only do twenty knots. We can give them a plus-minus of eighty miles. How long does it take to fly that?''

Toland noted that Svenson and the CAG didn't like that decision, but neither disputed the point. He'd been told that Baker wasn't a man to argue with, and wondered if that was a good trait in a combat commander.

HILL 152, ICELAND

Edwards took some solace in having predicted the cold front's arrival properly. The rain had come exactly on time, just after midnight. If there was anything to make the worst situation worse still, it was a steady cold rain. The showers were intermittent now, a ceiling of gray clouds two thousand feet over their heads, blown along by thirty-knot winds toward Iceland's mountainous center.

"Where are the fighters?" Edwards asked. He swept Reykjavik airport with his binoculars, but couldn't find the six fighters he'd reported on the previous evening. All the transports were gone also. He saw one Soviet helicopter and some tanks. There was very little traffic on the streets and roads he could see. Certainly not much for a Monday morning. Surely the commercial fishermen would be driving to their boats? "Anybody see them lift out?"

"No, sir. Weather we had last night, the whole Russian Air Force could have come in and left." Sergeant Smith was annoyed too, mainly with the weather. "Could be in those hangars, maybe."

About 2300 the previous night, they'd observed a streak of light like that of a rocket taking off, but whatever it had been aimed at had been lost in a rain shower. Edwards had not reported that, halfway wondering if it might have been lightning.

"What's that? That's no tank. Garcia, check it out—five hundred yards west of the terminal." The lieutenant handed the glasses over.

"Okay. That's some kinda tracked vehicle. Looks like it has some sort of—not a gun, there's three of them. Rocket launcher, maybe."

"SAMs," the sergeant commented. "How much you wanna bet that's what we saw shot off last night?"

"E.T., phone home." Edwards started putting his radio together.

"How many launchers and what type?" Doghouse asked.

"We see one launcher, possibly three missiles on it. We can't tell the type. I wouldn't know the difference anyway. They might have fired off a missile last night about 2300 local."

"Why the hell didn't you tell us?" Doghouse demanded.

" 'Cause I didn't know what it was!" Edwards nearly yelled. "Goddammit! We're reporting on everything we see, and you don't even believe half of what we tell you!"

"Settle down, Beagle. We believe you. I know it's hard. Anything else happening?"

"He knows it's hard," Edwards told his men. "Can't see much activity at all, Doghouse. Still early, but we'd expect civilian traffic on the streets."

"Copy that. Okay now, Edwards, real fast, what's your father's middle name?"

"Doesn't have one," Edwards said. "What—"

"The name of his boat?"

"The *Annie Jay*. What the hell is this?"

"What happened to your girlfriend Sandy?"

It was like a knife in the guts. The tone of his voice answered for him. "You go and fuck yourself!"

"Copy that," the voice replied. "Sorry, Lieutenant, but you had to pass that test. We have no further orders for you yet. Tell you the truth, nobody's decided what to do about you. Stay cool and avoid contact. Same transmission schedule. If you get tagged and they try to make you play radio games, start off every transmission with our call sign and say that everything is going great. Got that? Going great."

"Roger. If you hear me say that, you know something's wrong. Out."

KEFLAVIK, ICELAND

The major commanding the Air Force detachment was enjoying himself despite having been up for over thirty hours. Keflavik was a magnificent base, and the paratroopers had captured it nearly intact. Most importantly, the Americans had thoughtfully stored their maintenance equipment in protective shelters dispersed throughout the base, and all of it had survived. As he watched from the smashed control tower, a half-dozen sweeper trucks were brushing the last fragments from runway nine. In thirty minutes it would be safe to use. Eight fuel bowsers sat filled and ready on the field, and by the end of the day the pipeline should be repaired. Then this would be a fully functional Soviet air base.

"How long before our fighters arrive?"

"Thirty minutes, Comrade Major."

"Get the radar operating."

The Soviets had packed most of the equipment for a forward air base in one of the *Fucik*'s barges. A mobile long-range radar was now operating just west of the main runway intersection, plus a van from which ground controllers could direct radar intercepts of incoming targets. Three truck-vans of spare parts and air-to-air missiles were on the base, and three hundred maintenance personnel had been flown in the previous day. A full battery of SA-11 missiles guarded the runways, plus eight mobile antiaircraft guns and a platoon of infantrymen armed with hand-held SAMs for low-flying raiders. The only hangup had been with the SAMs, and the replacements flown in a few hours ago had already been loaded on the launcher vehicles. Any NATO aircraft that came waltzing into Iceland was in for a rude surprise, as a Royal Air Force Jaguar had discovered the night before, shot out of the sky over Reykjavik before its pilot could react.

"Runway nine is cleared for operation," the radio operator reported.

"Excellent! Now get them working on one-eight. I want every strip operational by this afternoon."

HILL 152, ICELAND

"What's that?" Edwards saw it first for a change. The wide silver wings of a Badger bomber skirted in and out of the lower cloud layer. Then something else. It was smaller, and it disappeared back into the clouds.

"Was that a fighter?"

"I didn't see anything, sir." Garcia had been looking in the wrong direction. The sound passed overhead, the distinctive whine of turbojets on a low throttle setting.

The lieutenant was becoming a master at getting his radio in operation. "Doghouse, this is Beagle, and things are rotten. Do you copy?"

"Roger, Beagle. What do you have for us?"

"We have aircraft flying overhead, westbound, probably for Keflavik. Stand by."

"I can hear 'em, but I don't see nothin'." Garcia handed the glasses over.

"I saw one twin-engine aircraft, probably a bomber, and one other aircraft, a lot smaller, like a fighter. We have aircraft sounds overhead, but we got solid clouds at about two thousand feet. No more visual sightings."

"You say heading toward Keflavik?"

"That's affirm. The bomber appeared to be westbound and descending."

"Any chance you can walk back to Keflavik to see what's happening there?"

Edwards didn't speak for a second. Couldn't the bastard read a map? That meant walking thirty miles over bare ground.

"Negative. Say again, negative, no chance. Over."

"Understood, Beagle. Sorry about that. I had orders to ask. Get back to us when you have a better count. You're doing good, guys. Hang in there. Out."

"They asked if we wanted to walk over to Keflavik," Edwards announced as he took off his headset. "I said no."

"Real good, sir," Smith observed. At least Air Force officers weren't total idiots.

KEFLAVIK, ICELAND

The first MiG-29 Fulcrum landed at Keflavik a minute later. It taxied behind a base jeep and stopped close to the tower. The major in command of the base was there to meet it.

"Welcome to Keflavik!"

"Excellent. Find me a lavatory," the colonel replied.

The major motioned him to his own jeep—the Americans had left seventy jeeps behind, plus over three hundred private automobiles—and drove toward the tower. The American radios had been destroyed, but the plumbing was made of sterner stuff.

"How many?"

"Six," the colonel answered. "A Goddamned Norwegian F-16 jumped us off Hammerfest and got one before we knew he was there. Another aborted with engine trouble, and a third had to land at Akureyri. Do we have men there?"

"Not yet. We have only one helicopter. More should be coming in today." They pulled to the door. "Inside, second door on the right."

"Thank you, Comrade Major!" The colonel was back in three minutes. "The unglamorous side of flying fighter aircraft. Somehow we never warn our cadets about this."

"Here, coffee. The previous occupants were most kind to us." The major unscrewed an American thermos. The colonel took the cup, savoring the flavor as though it were fine brandy while he watched his fighters land. "We have your missiles all ready for you, and we can refuel every aircraft from our trucks. How soon can you fly again?"

"I'd prefer that my men get at least two hours to rest and eat. And I want those aircraft dispersed after they're fueled. Have you been hit yet?"

"Only two reconnaissance aircraft, and we killed one. If we're lucky—"

"Luck is for fools. The Americans will hit us today. I would."

USS *NIMITZ*

"We have a new intel source on Iceland, code name Beagle," Toland reported. They were in the carrier's Combat Information Center now. "He counted over eighty transport flights into Reykjavik last night, at least six fighters with them. That's enough airlift capacity for a whole airborne division and then some. Doghouse in Scotland says that they have an unconfirmed report of Soviet fighters landing now."

"Have to be a long-range one. Foxhound, maybe a Fulcrum," CAG said. "If they have them to spare. Well, we weren't planning to visit the place just yet. We might have a problem with them trying raid-escort, though."

"Any word on E-3 support from the U.K.?" Baker asked Svenson.

"Looks like none."

"Toland, when do you expect our friends to arrive?"

"The RORSAT passes overhead in twenty minutes. They'll probably want that data before they take off. They could take off at any time after that, Admiral. If the Backfires tank up partway down and proceed at max power, two hours. That's worst case. More likely four to five hours."

"CAG?"

The air group commander looked tense. "Each carrier has a Hummer radar bird up, a pair of F-14 Tomcats with each. Two more Tomcats on the catapults, ready to go at five minutes' notice, another Hummer and a tanker. The rest of the fighters are at plus-fifteen on the roof, loaded and fueled. The flight crews are briefed. One Prowler over the formation, the rest ready to go at fifteen. The A-7s have buddy stores rigged. We're ready. *Foch* has her Crusaders at plus-fifteen. Good birds, but short legs. When the time comes we'll use them for overhead coverage."

KIROVSK, R.S.F.S.R.

The Radar Ocean Reconnaissance Satellite, called a RORSAT, passed over the formation at 0310. Its radar transmitter noted the formation and its cameras tracked in on their wakes. Five minutes later, the data was in Moscow. Fifteen minutes after that, flight crews were given their final brief at four military air bases grouped around the city of Kirovsk on the Kola Peninsula. The crews were quiet, no less tense than their American targets. Both sides mulled over the same thoughts. This was the exercise both sides had practiced for over fifteen years. Millions of hours of planning, studies and simulations were about to be put to the test.

The Badgers lifted off first, pushed by their twin Mikulin engines. Each takeoff was an effort. The bombers were so heavily loaded that the tower controllers reached out with their minds to wish every aircraft into the still morning air. Once off the ground they headed north, forming up into loose regimental formations just north of Murmansk before heading west and skirting past the North Cape, before their slow left turns took them toward the North Atlantic.

Twenty miles off the North Russian coast, USS *Narwhal* hovered beneath the surface of a slate-gray sea. The quietest submarine in the U.S. fleet, she was a specialized intelligence-gathering platform that spent more time on the Soviet coast than did some ships in the Russian Navy. Her three thin ESM antennae were raised, as was a million-dollar search periscope.

Technicians aboard listened in on low-power radio conversations between aircraft as they formed up. Three uniformed intelligence specialists and a civilian from the National Security Agency evaluated the strength of the raid and decided that it was large enough to risk a warning broadcast. An additional mast was raised and aimed at a communications satellite twenty-four thousand miles away. The burst transmission lasted less than a fifteenth of a second.

USS *NIMITZ*

The message was automatically relayed to four separate communications stations, and within thirty seconds was at SACLANT headquarters. Five minutes after that, Toland had the yellow message form in his hand. He walked immediately to Admiral Baker, and handed the message over: 0418Z REALTIME SENDS WARNING AIR RAID TAKE OFF 0400 HEADING WEST FROM KOLA ESTIMATE FIVE REGIMENT PLUS

Baker checked his watch. "Fast work. CAG?"

The air group commander looked at the form and walked to a phone. "Shoot off the plus-fives, recall the patrol aircraft when they get to station, and set up two more Tomcats and a Hummer on plus-five. I want the returning aircraft turned around immediately. Reserve one catapult for tankers." He came back. "With your permission, sir, I propose to put another pair of F-14s and another Hummer up in an hour, and put all the fighters on plus-five. At 0600, the rest of the fighters go up, with tankers in support. We'll meet them with everything we have about two hundred miles out and kick their ass."

"Very well. Comments?"

Svenson looked pensively at the master plot. Circles were already being drawn for the farthest possible advance of the Soviet bombers.

"The Brits get the same warning?"

"Yes, sir," Toland answered. "Norwegians, too. With luck, one or the other might make contact with the raid and nibble at it some, maybe put a trailer with them."

"Nice idea, but don't count on it. If I was running the attack, I'd come way west and turn south right over Iceland." Svenson looked back at the plot. "You think Realtime would have broadcast a warning for Bear-Ds?"

"My information, sir, is that they are allowed to broadcast only for three regiments or more. Ten or twenty Bears wouldn't be enough. They might not even notice."

"So right now we probably have a herd of Bears out there, not emitting anything, just flying around listening for our radar signals."

Toland nodded agreement. The battle group was a circle of ships with a radius of thirty miles, the carriers and troop ships in the center surrounded by nine missile-armed escorts and six more specialized antisubmarine ships. None of the ships had a radar transmitter working. Instead, they got all their electronic information from the two circling E-2C air-surveillance aircraft, known colloquially as Hummers, whose radars swept a circle over four hundred miles across.

The drama being played out was more complex than the most intricate game. More than a dozen variable factors could interact, with their permutations running into the thousands. Radar detection range depended on altitude and consequent distance to the horizon that neither eyes nor radar can see past. An aircraft could avoid, or at least delay, detection by skimming the waves. But this carried severe penalties in fuel consumption and range.

They had to locate the battle group without being detected by it first. The Russians knew where the carrier group was, but it would move in the four hours required for the bombers to get there. Their missiles needed precise information if they were to home in on the raid's primary target, the two American and one French carrier, or the mission was a wasted effort.

Putting the group's fighters on station to intercept the incoming raid depended on expert prognostication of its direction and speed. Their job: to locate and engage the bombers before they could find the carriers.

For both sides, the fundamental choice was whether or not to radiate, to use their radar transmitters. Either choice carried benefits and dangers, and there was no "best" solution to the problem. Nearly every American ship carried powerful air-search radars that could locate the raid two hundred or more miles away. But those radar signals could be detected at an even greater range, generating a return signal, that would potentially allow the Soviets to circle the formation, pinpoint it, then converge in from all points of the compass.

The game was hide and seek, played over a million square miles of ocean. The losers died.

NORTH ATLANTIC

The Soviet Bear-D reconnaissance bombers were passing south of Iceland. There were ten of them, covering a front of a thousand miles. The monstrous propeller-driven aircraft were packed full of electronics gear and crewed by men with years of training and experience in locating the American carrier groups. At the nose, tail, and wingtips, sensitive antennae were already reaching out, searching for the signals from American radar transmitters. They would close on those signals, chart them with great care, but remain forever outside the estimated detection radius. Their greatest fear was that the Americans would use no radar at all, or that they would switch their sets on and off at random intervals and locations, which posed the danger of the Bears' blundering directly into armed ships and aircraft. The Bear had twenty hours of endurance, but the penalty for it was virtually no combat capability. It was too slow to run from an interceptor, and had no ability to fight one. "We have located the enemy battle force," the crews' bitter joke ran: *"Dosvidania, Rodina!"* But they were a proud group of professionals. The attack bombers depended on them—as did their country.

Eight hundred miles north of Iceland, the Badgers altered their course to one-eight-zero, due south at five hundred knots. They had avoided the still-dangerous Norwegians, and it was not thought that the British would reach this far out. These air crews kept a nervous watch out their windows nevertheless, their own electronic sensors fully operative and under constant scrutiny. An attack by tactical fighters against Iceland was expected at any time, and the bomber crews knew that any NATO fighter pilot worthy of his name would instantly jettison his bombload for a chance at air-to-air combat with so helpless a target as a twenty-year-old Badger. They had reached the end of their useful lives. Cracks were developing in the wings. The turbine blades in their jet engines were worn, reducing performance and fuel efficiency.

Two hundred miles behind them, the Backfire bombers were finishing their refueling operations. The Tu-22Ms had been accompanied by tankers, and, after topping off their tanks, they headed south, slightly west of the Badgers' course track. With an AS-6 Kingfish missile hanging under each wing, the Backfires, too, were potentially vulnerable, but the Backfire had the ability to run at high Mach numbers and stood a fair chance at survival, even in the face of determined fighter opposition. Their crews were the elite of Soviet Naval Aviation, well-paid and pampered by Soviet society, their commanders had reminded them at the regimental briefings. Now it was time to deliver.

All three groups of aircraft came south at optimum cruise speed, their flight crews monitoring fuel consumption, engine heat, and many other gauges for the long over-water flight.

USS *NIMITZ*

Toland stepped outside for a breath of air. It was a fine morning, the cotton-ball clouds overhead turning briefly pink from the sunrise. *Saratoga* and *Foch* were visible on the horizon, perhaps eight miles away, their size impressive even at this distance. Closer in, *Ticonderoga* was cutting through the five-foot seas, white-painted missiles visible on her twin launchers. A few blinker lights traded signals. Otherwise the ships in view were gray shapes without noise, waiting. *Nimitz*'s deck was covered with aircraft. F-14 Tomcat interceptors sat everywhere. Two were hooked up on the midships catapults, only a hundred feet from him, their two-man flight crews dozing. The fighters carried Phoenix long-range missiles. The attack bombers carried buddy-store tanks instead of weapons. They'd be used to refuel the fighters in flight, enabling them to remain aloft an extra two hours. Deck crewmen in multicolored shirts scurried about, checking and rechecking the aircraft. The carrier began turning to port, coming around into the westerly wind in preparation for launching aircraft. He checked his watch. 0558. Time to get back to CIC. The carrier would go to general quarters in two minutes. The intelligence watch officer took one more breath of fresh sea air and wondered if it would be his last.

NORTH ATLANTIC

"Contact!" the technician said over the Bear's interphone. "Signals indicate an American airborne radar transmitter, carrier type."

"Give me a bearing!" the pilot commanded.

"Patience, Comrade Major." The technician made an adjustment on his board. His radio-interferometers timed the signals as they arrived at antennae arrayed all over the aircraft. "Southeast. Bearing to signal is one-three-one. Signal strength one. He is quite distant. Bearing is not changing as yet. I recommend we maintain a constant course for the present."

The pilot and copilot exchanged a look, but no words. Somewhere off to their left was an American E-2C Hawkeye radar aircraft. A flight crew of two—a radar intercept officer and two radar operators. It could manage the air battle for over a hundred enemy aircraft, could vector a missile-armed interceptor in at them within seconds of detection. The pilot wondered just how accurate his information was on the Hawkeye's radar. What if they had already detected his Bear? He knew the answer to that. His first warning would come when he detected the fire-control radar of an American F-14 Tomcat heading right at him. The Bear held course one-eight-zero while the plotting officer tracked the change in bearing to the radar signal. In ten minutes they might just have an accurate fix. If they lived that long. They would not break radio silence until they had a fix.

"I have it," the plotting officer reported. "Estimate distance to contact is six hundred fifty kilometers, position forty-seven degrees, nine minutes north, thirty-four degrees, fifty minutes west."

"Get it out," the pilot ordered. A directional HF antenna in the aircraft's tail fin turned within its housing and radioed the information to the raid commander, whose Bear command aircraft was a hundred miles behind the snoopers.

The raid commander compared this datum with that from the reconnaissance satellite. Now he had two pieces of information. The Americans' position three hours ago was sixty miles south of the estimated plot for the Hawkeye. The Americans probably had two of them up, northeast and northwest of the formation. That was normal fleet doctrine. So, the carrier group was right about . . . here. The Badgers were heading right for it. They would encounter the American radar coverage in . . . two hours. Good, he said to himself. Everything is going according to plan.

USS *NIMITZ*

Toland watched the aircraft plot in silence. The radar picture from the Hawkeyes was being transmitted to the carrier by digital radio link, enabling the battle group commander to follow everything. The same data went to the group air defense boss on *Ticonderoga* and every other ship fitted with the Naval Tactical Data System. That included the French ships, which had long since been equipped to operate closely with the U.S. Navy. So far there was nothing to be seen except the tracks of American military and commercial aircraft ferrying men and supplies across the ocean, and dependents back to the States. These were beginning to swing south. Warned that an air battle was possible, the pilots of DC-10s and C-5As were prudently keeping out of the way, even if it meant having to land and refuel on the way to their destinations.

The group's forty-eight Tomcat interceptors were now mostly on station, spread in a line three hundred miles across. Each pair of Tomcats had a tanker aircraft in attendance. The attack birds, Corsairs and Intruders, carried oversized fuel tanks with refueling drogues attached, and one by one the Tomcats were already beginning to top off their fuel tanks from them. Soon the Corsairs began returning to their carriers for refills. They could keep this up for hours. The aircraft remaining on the carriers were spotted on the decks for immediate takeoff. If a raid came in, they would be shot off the catapults at once to eliminate the fire hazard inherent in any type of aircraft.

Toland had seen all this before, but could not fail to be amazed by it. Everything was going as smoothly as a ballet. The aircraft loitered at their patrol stations, tracing lazy, fuel-efficient circles in the sky. The carriers were racing east now at thirty knots to make up the distance lost during launch operations. The Marines' landing ships *Saipan, Ponce,* and *Newport* could make only about twenty knots, and were essentially defenseless. East of the group, carrier S-3A Viking and land-based P-3C Orion antisubmarine aircraft were patrolling for Soviet submarines. They reported to the group ASW commander on the destroyer *Caron.* There was as yet nothing for anyone to direct his frustration against. The old story known to all fighting men. You wait.

NORTH ATLANTIC

The raid commander was rapidly accumulating data. He now had positions on four American Hawkeyes. The first two had barely been plotted when the second pair had showed up, outside and south of the first. The Americans had unwittingly given him a very accurate picture of where the battle group was, and the steady eastward drift of the Hawkeyes gave him course and speed. His Bears were now in a wide semicircle around the Americans, and the Badgers were thirty minutes north of American radar cover, four hundred miles north of the estimated location of the ships.

"Send to Group A: 'Enemy formation at grid coordinates 456 / 810, speed twenty, course one-zero-zero. Execute Attack Plan A at 0615 Zulu time.' Send the same to Group B. Tactical control of Group B switches to Team East Coordinator." The battle had begun.

The Badger crews exchanged looks of relief. They had detected the American radar signals fifteen minutes before, and knew that each kilometer south meant a greater chance that they would run into a cloud of enemy fighters. Aboard each aircraft the navigator and bombardier worked quickly to feed strike information into the Kelt missiles slung under each wing.

Eight hundred miles to their southwest, the Backfire crews advanced their throttles slightly, plotting a course to the datum point supplied by the raid commander. Having circled far around the American formation, they would now be controlled by the strike officer aboard the first Bear to make electronic contact with the Hawkeyes. They had a solid fix on the NATO formation, but they needed better if they were to locate and engage the carriers. These crews were not relieved, but excited. Now came the challenging part. The battle plan had been formulated a year before and practiced—over land exclusively—five times. Four times it had worked.

Aboard eighty Badger bombers, pilots checked their watches, counting off the seconds to 0615 Zulu.

"Launch!"

The lead Badger launched eight seconds early. First one, then the second, aircraft-shaped Kelt dropped free of its pylon, falling several hundred feet before their turbojet engines ran up to full power. Running on autopilot, the Kelts climbed back to thirty thousand feet and cruised on south at six hundred knots indicated air speed. The bomber crews watched their birds proceed for a minute or two, then each of the bombers turned slowly and gracefully for home, their mission done. Six Badger-J stand-off jamming aircraft continued south. They would stay sixty kilometers behind the Kelts. Their crews were nervous but confident. It would not be easy for American radar to burn through their powerful jammers, and in any case, the Americans would soon have many targets to concern them.

The Kelts continued on, straight and level. They carried their own electronic equipment, which would be triggered automatically by sensors in their tail fins. When they entered the theoretical arc of the Hawkeyes' radar range, transponders in their noses clicked on.

USS *NIMITZ*

"Radar contacts! Designate Raid-1, bearing three-four-niner, range four-six-zero miles. Numerous contacts, count one-four-zero contacts, course one-seven-five, speed six hundred knots."

The master tactical scope plotted the contacts electronically, and a pair of plexiglass plates showed another visual display.

"So, here they come," Baker said quietly. "Right on time. Comments?"

"I—" Toland didn't get a chance.

The computer display went white.

"Clipper Base, this is Hawk-Three. We're getting some jamming," reported the senior airborne control officer. "We plot six, possibly seven jammers, bearing three-four-zero to zero-three-zero. Pretty powerful stuff. Estimate we have stand-off jammers, but no escort jammers. Contacts are lost for the present. Estimate burn-through in ten minutes. Request weapons free, and release to vector intercepts."

Baker looked over to his air operations officer. "Let's get things started."

Air / Ops nodded and picked up a microphone. "Hawk-Three, this is Clipper Base. Weapons free. I say again, weapons are free. Release authority is granted. Splash me some bombers. Out."

Svenson frowned at the display. "Admiral, we're coming about to clear decks. Recommend the formation stays together now." He got a nod. "Clipper Fleet, this is Clipper Base, come left to two-seven-zero. Launch all remaining aircraft. Execute."

On the single command, the formation made a hundred-eighty-degree left turn. Those ships that did not as yet have missiles on their launchers rectified this. Fire-control radars were trained north, but kept in standby mode. Thirty different captains waited for the word to activate.

NORTH ATLANTIC

She was pissed off. *Sure,* she thought, *I'm good enough to fly. I'm good enough to be an* instructor *pilot for the Eagle. Engineering test pilot, assistant project officer for the ASAT program—I'm good enough to get an invite to Houston, even—but will they let me fly* combat? *No, there's a war going on and I'm nothing but a Goddamned ferry pilot!*

"Shit." Her name was Amy Nakamura. She was a major, United States Air Force, with three thousand hours of jet time, two-thirds of it in F-15s. Short and stocky like many fighter pilots, only her father had ever called her beautiful. He also called her Bunny. When her fellow pilots found that one out, they shortened it to Buns. She and three men were ferrying four brand-new Eagle fighters to Germany where others—men!—would get to use them properly. They each carried fast-pack conformal fuel tanks to make the trip in one long hop, and for self-defense a single Sidewinder missile, plus their usual load of 20mm cannon shells. *The* Russians *let women fly combat in World War II!* she thought. *A couple even made ace!*

"Hey, Buns, check your three o'clock!" called her wing*man*.

Nakamura had phenomenal eyesight, but she could scarcely believe it. "Tell me what you see, Butch."

"Badgers . . . ?"

"Fuckin' Tu-16 Badgers—*tallyho!* Where's the Navy supposed to be?"

"Close. Try and raise 'em, Buns!"

"Navy task force, Navy task force, this is Air Force ferry flight Golf-Four-Niner. We are eastbound with four Foxtrot-One-Fives. We have a visual on a Russian bomber formation position—shit, do you read, over?"

"Who the hell is that?" a Hawkeye crewman asked aloud.

The communications technician answered, "Golf-Four-Niner, we need authentication. November Four Whiskey." This could be a Russian playing radio games.

Major Nakamura swore to herself as she ran her finger down the list of communication codes. There! "Alpha Six Hotel."

"Golf-Four-Niner, this is Navy Hawk-One, say your position. Warning, we are calling in the clans on those Badgers. You'd better get clear, acknowledge."

"Like hell, Navy, I got visual on three-plus Badgers northbound, position forty-nine north, thirty-three east."

"*North*bound?" the intercept officer said. "Golf, this is Hawk-One. Confirm your visual. Say again your visual."

"Hawk-One, this is Golf, I now have a dozen Badger, say again Tango-Uniform-One-Six bombers visual, south of my position, heading toward me and closing fast. We are engaging.Out."

"Nothing on radar, boss," the radar operator said. "That's way the hell north of here."

"Then what the *hell* is he talking about?"

Major Amelia "Buns" Nakamura reached down without looking to toggle up her missile and head-up display to tactical. Then she flipped the switch for her air-intercept radar. Her IFF system interrogated the target as a possible friendly and came up blank. That was enough.

"Frank, take your element east. Butch, follow me. Everybody watch your fuel states. Charge!"

The Badger pilots were a little too relaxed, now that the most dangerous part of their mission was behind them. They didn't spot the four American fighters until they were less than a mile away, their robin's-egg-blue paint blending them in perfectly with the clear morning sky.

Buns selected her cannon for the first pass and triggered two hundred rounds into the cockpit of a Badger. The twin-engine bomber went instantly out of control and rolled over like a dead whale. One. The major howled with delight, pulled the Eagle up into a five-g loop, then over to dive on the next target. The Soviets were alerted now, and the second Badger attempted to dive away. It had not the slightest chance. Nakamura fired her Sidewinder from a range of less than a mile and watched the missile trace all the way into the Badger's left-side engine, and blast the wing right off the airplane. Two. Another Badger was three miles ahead. *Patience,* she told herself. *You have a big speed advantage.* She nearly forgot that the Russian bomber had tail guns. A Soviet sergeant reminded her of it, missing, but scaring the hell out of her. The Eagle jerked in a six-g turn to the left and closed on a parallel course before turning in. The next burst from her cannon exploded the Badger in midair, and she had to dive to avoid the wreckage. The engagement lasted all of ninety seconds, and she was wringing wet with perspiration.

"Butch, where are you?"

"I got one! Buns, I got one!" The Eagle pulled up alongside.

Nakamura looked around. Suddenly the sky was clear. Where had they all gone?

"Navy Hawk-One, this is Golf, do you read, over?"

"Roger, Golf."

"Okay, Navy. We just smoked four, repeat four, Badgers for you."

"Make that five, Buns!" the other element leader called in.

"Something's wrong, sir." The radar operator on Hawk-One motioned to his scope. "We have these buggers just popped through, and they say they bagged some, gotta be three, four hundred miles away."

"Clipper Base, this is Hawk-One, we just had contact with an Air Force ferry flight eastbound. They claim they just splashed five Badgers north-bound several hundred miles north of us. Say again *north*bound."

Toland's eyebrows went up.

"Probably some had to abort," Baker observed. "This is close to their fuel limit, isn't it?"

"Yes, sir," replied Air / Ops. He didn't look happy with his own answer.

"Burn-through," announced the radar operator. "We have reacquired the targets."

The Kelts had flown on, oblivious to the furor around them. Their radar transponders made them look like hundred-ten-foot Badgers. Their own white-noise jammers came on, somewhat obscuring them yet again on the radar scopes, and autopilot controls began to jerk them up, down, left, right, in hundred-meter leaps as an aircraft might do when trying to avoid a missile. The Kelts had been real missiles once, but on retirement from front-line service six years earlier, their warheads had been replaced with additional fuel tankage, and they had been relegated to a role as target drones, a purpose they were serving admirably now.

"Tallyho!" The first squadron of twelve Tomcats was now a hundred fifty miles away. The Kelts showed up perfectly on radar, and the intercept officers in the back seat of each fighter quickly established target tracks. The Kelts were approaching what would have been nominal missile-launch distance—if they were the bombers everyone thought they were.

The Tomcats launched a volley of million-dollar AIM-54C Phoenix missiles at a range of a hundred forty miles. The missiles blazed in on their targets at Mach-5, directed by the fighters' targeting radars. In under a minute the forty-eight missiles had killed thirty-nine targets. The first squadron broke clear as the second came into launch position.

USS *NIMITZ*

"Admiral, something is wrong here," Toland said quietly.

"What might that be?" Baker liked the way things were going. Enemy bomber tracks were being wiped off his screen just as the war games had predicted they would.

"The Russians are coming in dumb, sir."

"So?"

"So this far the Soviets have not been very dumb! Admiral, why aren't the Backfires going supersonic? Why one attack group? Why one direction?"

"Fuel constraints," Baker answered. "The Badgers are at the limit of their fuel, they have to come in direct."

"But not the Backfires!"

"The course is right, the raid count is right." Baker shook his head and concentrated on the tactical plot.

The second squadron of fighters had just launched. Unable to get a head-on shot, their missile accuracy suffered somewhat. They killed thirty-four targets with forty-eight missiles. There had been a hundred fifty-seven targets plotted.

The third and fourth Tomcat squadrons arrived together and launched as a group. When their Phoenixes had been fully expended, nineteen targets were left. The two fighter squadrons moved in to engage the remaining targets with their cannon.

"Clipper Base, this is SAM Boss. We're going to have some leakers. Recommend we start lighting up SAM radars."

"Roger, SAM Boss. Permission granted," answered the group tactical warfare coordinator.

NORTH ATLANTIC

"I have air-search radars, bearing zero-three-seven," the Bear ESM officer noted. "They have detected us. Recommend we illuminate also." The Bear lit off its Big Bulge look-down radar.

USS *NIMITZ*

"New radar contact. Designate Raid-2—"

"What?" snapped Baker. Next came a call from the fighters.

"Clipper Base, this is Slugger Lead. I have a visual on my target." The squadron commander was trying to examine the target on his long-range TV camera. When he spoke, the anguish in his voice was manifest. "Warning, warning, this is not a Badger. We've been shooting at Kelt missiles!"

"Raid-2 is seventy-three aircraft, bearing two-one-seven, range one-three-zero miles. We have a Big Bulge radar tracking the formation," said the CIC talker.

Toland cringed as the new contacts were plotted. "Admiral, we've been had."

The group tactical warfare officer was pale as he toggled his microphone. "Air Warning Red. Weapons free! Threat axis is two-one-seven. All ships turn as necessary to unmask batteries."

The Tomcats had all been drawn off, leaving the formation practically naked. The only armed fighters over the formation were *Foch*'s eight Crusaders, long since retired from the American inventory. On a terse command from their carrier, they went to afterburner and rocketed southwest toward the Backfires. Too late.

* * *

The Bear already had a clear picture of the American formations. The Russians could not determine ship type, but they could tell large from small, and identify the missile cruiser *Ticonderoga* by her distinctive radar emissions. The carriers would be close to her. The Bear relayed the information to her consorts. A minute later, the seventy Backfire bombers launched their hundred forty AS-6 Kingfish missiles and turned north at full military power. The Kingfish was nothing like the Kelt. Powered by a liquid-fuel rocket engine, it accelerated to nine hundred knots and began its descent, its radar-homing head tracking on a pre-programmed target area ten miles wide. Every ship in the center of the formation had several missiles assigned.

"Vampire, Vampire!" the CIC talker said aboard *Ticonderoga.* "We have numerous incoming missiles. Weapons free."

The group antiair warfare officer ordered the cruiser's Aegis weapons system into full automatic mode. *Tico* had been built with this exact situation in mind. Her powerful radar / computer system immediately identified the incoming missiles as hostile and assigned each a priority of destruction. The computer was completely on its own, free to fire on its electronic will at anything diagnosed as a threat. Numbers, symbols, and vectors paraded across the master tactical display. The fore and aft twin missile launchers trained out at the first targets and awaited the orders to fire. Aegis was state-of-the-art, the best SAM system yet devised, but it had one major weakness: *Tico* carried only ninety-six SM2 surface-to-air missiles; there were one hundred forty incoming Kingfish. The computer had not been programmed to think about that.

Aboard *Nimitz,* Toland could feel the carrier heeling into a radical turn, her engines advanced to flank speed, driving the massive warship at over thirty-five knots. Her nuclear-powered escorts, *Virginia* and *California,* were also tracking the Kingfish, their own missiles trained out on their launchers.

The Kingfish were at eight thousand feet, one hundred miles out, covering a mile every four seconds. Each had now selected a target, choosing the largest within their fields of view. *Nimitz* was the nearest large ship, with her missile-ship escorts to her north.

Tico launched her first quartet of missiles as the targets reached a range of ninety-nine miles. The rockets exploded into the air, leaving a trail of pale gray smoke. They had barely cleared the launch rails when the mounts went vertical and swiveled to receive their reloads. The load-and-fire time was under eight seconds. The cruiser would average one missile fired every two seconds. Just over three minutes later, her missile magazines were empty. The cruiser emerged from the base of an enormous gray arch of smoke. Her only remaining defenses were her gun systems.

The SAMs raced in at their targets with a closing speed of over two thousand miles per hour, directed in by the reflected waves of the ship's own fire-control radars. At a range of a hundred fifty yards from their targets, the warheads detonated. The Aegis system did quite well. Just over 60 percent of the targets were destroyed. There were now eighty-two incoming missiles targeted on a total of eight ships.

Other missile-equipped ships joined the fray. In several cases two or three missiles were sent for the same target, usually killing it. The number of incoming "vampires" dropped to seventy, then sixty, but the number was not dropping quickly enough. The identity of the targets was now known to everyone. Powerful active jamming equipment came on. Ships began a radical series of maneuvers like some stylized dance, with scant attention paid to station-keeping. Collision at sea was now the least of anyone's worries. When the Kingfish got to within twenty miles, every ship in the formation began to fire off chaff rockets, which filled the air with millions of aluminized Mylar fragments that fluttered on the air, creating dozens of new targets for the missiles to select from. Some of the Kingfish lost lock with their targets and started chasing Mylar ghosts. Two of them got lost, and selected new targets on the far side of the formation.

The radar picture on *Nimitz* suddenly was obscured. What had been discrete pips designating the positions of ships in the formation became shapeless clouds. Only the missiles stayed constant: inverted V-shapes, with line vectors to designate direction and speed. The last wave of SAMs killed three more. The vampire count was down to forty-one. Toland counted five heading for *Nimitz*.

Topside, the final defensive weapons were now tracking the targets. These were the CIWS, 20mm Gatling guns, radar-equipped to explode incoming missiles at a range of under two thousand yards. Designed to operate in a fully automatic mode, the two after gun mounts on the carrier angled up and began to track the first pair of incoming Kingfish. The portside mount fired first, the six-barrel cannon making a sound like that of an enormous zipper. Its radar system tracked the target, and tracked the outgoing slugs, adjusting fire to make the two meet.

The leading Kingfish exploded eight hundred yards from *Nimitz*'s port quarter. The thousand kilograms of high explosive rocked the ship. Toland felt it, wondering if the ship had been hit. Around him, the CIC crewmen were concentrating frantically on their jobs. One target track vanished from the screen. Four left.

The next Kingfish approached the carrier's bow and was blasted out of the sky by the forward CIWS, too close aboard. Fragments ripped across the carrier's deck, killing a dozen exposed crewmen.

Number three was decoyed by a chaff cloud and ran straight into the sea half a mile behind the carrier. The warhead caused the carrier to vibrate and raised a column of water a thousand feet into the air.

The fourth and fifth missiles came in from aft, not a hundred yards apart. The after gun mount tracked on both, but couldn't decide which to engage first. It went into Reset mode and petulantly didn't engage any. The missiles hit within a second of one another, one on the after port corner of the flight deck, the other on the number two arrestor wire.

Toland was thrown fifteen feet, and slammed against a radar console. Next he saw a wall of pink flame that washed briefly over him. Then came the noises. First the thunder of the explosion. Then the screams. The after CIC bulkhead was no longer there; instead there was a mass of flame. Men twenty feet away were ablaze, staggering and screaming before his eyes. Toland's only thought was escape. He bolted for the watertight door. It opened miraculously under his hand and he ran to starboard. The ship's fire-suppression systems were already on, showering everything with a curtain of saltwater. His skin burned from it as he emerged, hair and uniform singed, to the flight deck catwalk. A sailor directed a water hose on him, nearly knocking him over the side.

"Fire in CIC!" Toland gasped.

"What the hell ain't!" the sailor screamed.

Toland fell to his knees and looked outboard. *Foch* had been to their north, he remembered. Now there was a pillar of smoke. As he watched, the last Kingfish was detonated a hundred feet over *Saratoga*'s flight deck. The carrier seemed undamaged. Three miles away, *Ticonderoga*'s after superstructure was shredded and ablaze from a rocket that had blown up within yards of her. On the horizon a ball of flame announced the destruction of yet another—*my God,* Toland thought, *might that be* Saipan? She had two thousand Marines aboard . . .

"Get forward, you dumbass!" a firefighter yelled at him. Another man emerged to the catwalk.

"Toland, you all right?" It was Captain Svenson, his shirt torn away and his chest bleeding from a half-dozen cuts.

"Yes, sir," Bob answered.

"Get to the bridge. Tell 'em to put the wind on the starboard beam. Move!" Svenson jumped up onto the flight deck.

Toland did likewise, racing forward. The deck was awash in firefighting foam, slippery as oil. Toland ran recklessly, falling hard on the deck before he reached the carrier's island. He was in the pilothouse in under a minute.

"Captain says put the wind on the starboard beam!" Toland said.

"It *is* on the fucking beam!" the executive officer snapped back. The bridge deck was covered with broken glass. "How's the skipper?"

"Alive. He's aft with the fire."

"And who the hell are you?" the XO demanded.

"Toland, group intel. I was in CIC."

"Then you're one lucky bastard. That second bird hit fifty yards from you. Captain got out? Anyone else?"

"I don't know. Burning like hell."

"Looks like you caught part of it, Commander."

Bob's face felt as if he'd shaved with a piece of glass. His eyebrows crumpled to his touch. "Flashburns, I guess. I'll be okay. What do you want me to do?"

The XO pointed to Toland's water wings. "Can you conn the ship? Okay, do it. Nothing left to run into anyway. I'm going aft to take charge of the fire. Communications are out, radar's out, but the engines are okay and the hull's in good shape. Mr. Bice has the deck. Mr. Toland has the conn," XO announced as he left.

Toland hadn't conned anything bigger than a Boston Whaler in over ten years, and now he had a damaged carrier. He took a pair of binoculars and looked around to see what ships were nearby. What he saw chilled him.

Saratoga was the only ship that looked intact, but on second glance her radar mast was askew. *Foch* was lower in the water than she ought to have been, and ablaze from bow to stern.

"Where's *Saipan?*"

"Blew up like a fucking firework," Commander Bice replied. "Holy Jesus, there were twenty-five hundred men aboard! *Tico* took one close aboard. *Foch* took three hits, looks like she's gone. Two frigates and a destroyer gone, too—just fucking gone, man! Who fucked up? You were in CIC, right? Who fucked up?"

The eight French Crusaders were just making contact with the Backfires. The Russian bombers were on afterburner and were nearly as fast as the fighters. The carrier pilots had all heard their ship go off the air and were consumed with rage at what had happened, no longer the cool professionals who drove fighters off ships. Only ten Backfires were within their reach.

They got six of them with their missiles and damaged two more before they had to break off.

USS *Caron,* the senior undamaged ship, tracked the Russians on her radar, calling Britain for fighters to intercept them on the trip home. But the Russians had anticipated this, and detoured far west of the British Isles, meeting their tankers four hundred miles west of Norway.

Already the Russians were evaluating the results of their mission. The first major battle of modern carriers and missile-armed bombers had been won and lost. Both sides knew which was which.

The fire on *Nimitz* was out within an hour. With no aircraft aboard, there were few combustibles about, and the ship's firefighting abilities equaled that of a large city. Toland brought her back to an easterly course. *Saratoga* was recovering aircraft, refueling them, and sending all but the fighters to the beach. Three frigates and a destroyer lingered to recover survivors, as the large ships turned back toward Europe.

"All ahead full," Svenson ordered from his seat on the bridge. "Toland, you all right?"

"No complaints." No point in it, the ship's hospital was more than full with hundreds of major injury cases. There was no count of the dead yet, and Toland didn't want to think about that.

"You were right," the captain said, his voice angry and subdued. "You were right. They made it too easy and we fell for it."

"There'll be another day, Captain."

"You're Goddamned right there will! We're heading for Southampton. See if the Brits can fix anything this big. My regulars are still busy aft. Think you can handle the conn a little longer?"

"Yes, sir."

Nimitz and her nuclear escorts bent on full speed, nearly forty knots, and rapidly left the formation behind. A reckless move, racing too fast for antisubmarine patrols, but a submarine would have to move quickly indeed to catch them.

21. Nordic Hammer

HILL 152, ICELAND

"I know that was a fighter, and there had to be more than one," Edwards said. It was raining again, probably for the last time. The clouds to the southwest were breaking up, and there was a hint of clear sky on the horizon. Edwards just sat there in his helmet and poncho, staring into the distance.

"I suppose you're right, sir," Smith replied. The sergeant was nervous. They'd been on this hilltop for almost twenty-four hours, a long time to be stationary in hostile country. The best time to move out would have been during the rain showers, when visibility was cut to a few hundred yards. Soon the sky might be clear again, and it wouldn't get dark again for quite a while. As it was, they sat on their hilltop in camouflage ponchos that kept them partly dry and wholly miserable.

There was a heavy shower north of them that prevented their seeing Reykjavik, and they could barely make out Hafnarfjördur to the west, which worried the sergeant, who wanted to know what Ivan was up to. What if they detected Edwards's satellite radio and began to triangulate on it? What if there were patrols out?

"Lieutenant?"

"Yeah, Sarge?"

"We got those phone lines on one side of us, and those power lines on the other—"

"You want to blow some up?" Edwards smiled.

"No, sir, but Ivan is going to start patrolling them soon, and this ain't a very good place for us to make contact."

"We're supposed to observe and report, Sarge," Edwards said without conviction.

"Yes, sir."

Edwards checked his watch. It was 1955Z. Doghouse might want to talk with them, though they hadn't called in to him yet. Edwards broke the radio out of the pack again, assembled the pistol-grip antenna, and donned his headset. At 1959 he switched on and tracked in on the satellite carrier wave.

"Doghouse calling Beagle. Doghouse calling Beagle. Do you copy? Over."

"Well, how about that." He toggled the Transmit switch. "Roger, we're here, Doghouse."

"Anything new to report?"

"Negative, unless you want to know about the rain. Visibility is down. We can't see very much."

The communications watch officer at Doghouse looked at a weather map. So it really was raining there. He hadn't been able to convince his boss that Beagle could be trusted. Edwards had answered the questions that the counterintelligence guys had come up with. They'd even had a voice-stress analyzer handy to check the tapes of his answers. The needle had pegged on the last answer about his girlfriend. That hadn't been faked. Copies of the relevant parts of his personnel package had been faxed to them. Upper fifth of his class at Colorado Springs. Good in math and engineering studies, did extremely well in his postgraduation studies in meteorology. His eyesight had worsened slightly during his tenure at Colorado Springs, becoming just bad enough to keep him from flying. Regarded as quiet and shy, but evidently well liked by his classmates. Not a warrior type, the psychological profile said. How long would the kid last?

KEFLAVIK, ICELAND

One MiG-29 was flying. The others were in the hardened shelters the Americans had only just finished at the end of runway eleven. The fighter's mission was twofold. It was a standing combat air patrol aircraft should an incoming raid be detected, but more importantly, it was being tracked carefully by the ground radar controllers: their radar needed to be calibrated. Iceland's irregular terrain made for troublesome radar performance, and as with the surface-to-air missiles, the instruments themselves had been badly jostled by the trip aboard the *Fucik*. The fighter flew circles around the airport while the radar operators determined that what their instruments told them was correct.

The fighters were fully fueled and armed, their pilots resting on cots near them. At the moment, the bowsers were fueling the Badger bomber that had given the fighters navigational and electronic support. Soon it would be leaving to bring in nine more. The Air Force detachment was rapidly finishing their job of clearing the airfield. All but one of the runways was swept clear of fragments now. The remains of the American aircraft had been bulldozed off the pavement. The fuel pipeline would be repaired in an hour, the engineers said.

"Quite a busy day," the major said to the fighter commander.

"It's not over yet. I'll feel better when we get the rest of the regiment in," the colonel observed quietly. "They should have hit us already."

"How do you expect them to attack?"

The colonel shrugged. "Hard to say. If they're really serious about closing this field, they'll use a nuclear warhead."

"Are you always so optimistic, Comrade Colonel?"

The raid was an hour away. The eighteen B-52H bombers had left Louisiana ten hours before and landed to refuel at Sondrestrom Air Force Base on Greenland's west coast. Fifty miles ahead of them were a single Raven EF-111 jamming aircraft and four F-4 Phantoms configured for defense-suppression.

The radar was about halfway calibrated, though what had been done was the easy part. The fighter that had just landed had flown racetrack ovals from due north around the western horizon to due south of Keflavik. The area to the west of the air base, though not exactly flat, was nearly so, with low rocky hills. Next came the hard part, plotting radar coverage of the eastern arc over Iceland's mountainous center, a solid collection of hills that worked up to the island's tall central peak. Another Fulcrum rolled off the runway to begin this task, its pilot wondering how long it might take to map all the nulls—areas blanked to radar coverage by the steep valleys—areas that an attacking aircraft could use to mask its approach to Keflavik.

The radar officers were plotting probable troublesome spots on their topographical maps when an operator shouted a warning. Their clear radar screens had just turned to hash from powerful electronic jammers. That could mean only one thing.

The klaxons sounded in the fighter shelters at the end of runway eleven. Fighter pilots who had been dozing or playing dominos jumped to their feet and raced to their aircraft.

The tower officer lifted the field phone to give more exact warning to the fighters, then called up the missile battery commander: "Incoming air raid!"

Men leaped into action all across the air base. The fighter ground crews hit the built-in self-starters, turning the jet engines even as the pilots climbed into the cockpits. The SAM battery turned on its search and fire-control systems while the launch vehicles slewed their missiles into firing position.

Just under the radar horizon, eighteen B-52 bombers had just lit off their ECM jamming systems. They were deployed in six groups of three each. The first skimmed over the top of Mt. Snaefells, sixty miles north of Keflavik, and the rest came from all around the west side of the compass, converging on the target behind a wall of electronic noise provided by their own systems and the supporting EF-111 Raven jammer.

The Russian fighter just lifting off climbed to altitude, the pilot keeping his radar off as he scanned the sky visually, waiting for intercept information from the ground-based radar. His comrades were even now taxiing into the open, racing straight down the runway and into the sky. The aircraft that had just landed taxied to a fuel bowser, its pilot gesturing and cursing at the ground crewmen who were struggling to fuel his fighter. In their haste, they spilled ten gallons of fuel over the wing. Amazingly, it did not ignite, and a dozen men ran in with CO_2 extinguishers to prevent an explosion as the fighter drank in a full load of fuel.

HILL 152, ICELAND

Edwards's head jerked up at the noise, the distinctive roar of jet fighters. He saw a dark trail of smoke approaching in from the east, and the silhouettes passed within a mile. The shapes were heavy with ordnance, the up-angled wingtips making identification easy.

"F-4s!" he hooted. "They're our guys!"

They were Phantom jets of the New York Air National Guard, configured as Wild Weasel SAM-killers. While Russian attention was on the converging bomber raid, they skimmed over hilltops and down valleys, using the crenellated landscape to mask their low-level approach. The backseat crewman in each aircraft counted the missile radars, selecting the most dangerous targets. When they got to within ten miles of Keflavik, they popped up high and fired a salvo of Standard-ARM antiradar missiles.

The Russians were caught by surprise. Laboring to direct missile fire at the bombers, they didn't expect a two-part raid. The incoming missiles were not detected. Three of the ARMs found targets, killing two search radars and a missile-launch vehicle. One launch commander turned his vehicle around and trained manually on the new threat. The Phantoms jammed his fire-control radar, leaving behind a series of chaff clouds as they came in at thirty-foot height. As each pilot raced to the target area assigned to him, he conducted a hasty visual search. One saw an undamaged SAM launcher and streaked toward it, dropping Rockeye cluster-bomb canisters that fell short but spread over a hundred bomblets all over the area. The SA-11 launcher exploded in his wake; its crew never knew what had happened. A thousand yards beyond it was a mobile antiaircraft gun vehicle. The Phantom engaged it with his own cannon, badly damaging it as he swept across the rest of the peninsula and escaped back over the sea, a cloud of chaff and flares in his wake. It was a letter-perfect Weasel mission. All four aircraft were gone before the Soviet missile crews were able to react. The two SAMs that were launched exploded harmlessly in chaff clouds. The battery had lost two-thirds of its launcher vehicles and all of its search radars. Three of the mobile guns were also destroyed or damaged. The bombers were now a mere twenty miles out, their powerful ECM jamming systems drowning the Soviet radar with electronic noise.

They could not defeat the radar on the mobile guns, however. The new system had a radar for which they were not equipped, but it didn't matter. The guns had been designed to deal with small fighters, and when their radars tried to lock on the huge bombers, they found a target so large that their radar signals traced from one part to another. The computers could not decide what the target range was, and kept recycling automatically, rendering the electronics package useless. The gun crews cursed as one man and switched over to manual fire-control, using their eyes to sight in on the massive incoming targets.

The bombers popped up to nine hundred feet now, hoping to avoid the worst of the gunfire and escape without loss. They had not been warned of a possible fighter presence. Their mission was to wreck Keflavik before fighters could get there.

Now surprise was on the Soviet side. The Fulcrums dived out of the sun at the bombers. Their own fire-control radars were nearly useless as they approached, but half their missiles were infrared-guided, and the American bombers gave off enough heat to attract the attention of a blind man in a fur coat.

The southbound flight of three never saw them coming in. Two took missile hits and exploded in midair. The third radioed for fighter cover, jinking his aircraft hard—too hard. His second dive bottomed out too late, and the aircraft disintegrated on the ground north of Keflavik in a fireball visible to Edwards thirty miles away.

The Russian fighters were experiencing an airman's dream. All eight aircraft had individual targets, and they split to hunt them singly before Keflavik absorbed too many bomb hits. The bomber crews pressed in on their targets. It was too late to run away, and all that they could do was scream for the fighters to come back and support them.

The ground-based gunners joined in. Firing over open sights, a young sergeant hit a bomber just dropping its load. The bomb bay took a dozen rounds, and the aircraft vanished in a deafening explosion that shook the sky and damaged yet another B-52. One missile-launch crew successfully switched their missile-control systems to the backup infrared mode and fired a single rocket at a bomber. It hit just after the bombs were released. The bomber's wing erupted in flame and the aircraft swooped east trailing a black river of smoke.

They watched it approach their hill, a wounded monster whose right wing trailed burning fuel. The pilot was trying to maintain altitude so that his crew could eject, but all four of his right engines were gone and the burning wing collapsed. The bomber staggered in the air and dropped, rolling into the west face of Hill 152. None of the crew escaped. Edwards didn't have to give an order. In five seconds, his men had packed their gear and were running northeast.

The remaining bombers were now over the target and screaming for help from their escorting fighters. Eight successfully dropped their bomb-loads before turning clear of the area. The Soviet fighters had claimed five by now, and the surviving crews were desperate to escape the unexpected hazard. The Russians were now out of missiles, and attempting to engage with their cannon. That was dangerous. The B-52s retained their tail guns, and one Fulcrum was damaged by machine-gun fire from his target and had to break off.

The final element of confusion was the return of the American Phantoms. They carried only three Sparrow missiles each, and when they lit off their missile-intercept radars, the Soviet fighters all received warning tones from their defense systems. The Fulcrums scattered before the twelve incoming missiles and dove for the ground. Four dropped down right on top of Edwards's group, swooping low over a crashed B-52 east of Hafnarfjördur. When they came back up, the sky was clear again. The Phantoms were short on fuel. They could not press their attack and turned away without a single kill. The surviving bombers were now safely hidden in the cloud of jamming. The Soviets re-formed and moved back to Keflavik.

Their first impression was a bad one. Fully two hundred bombs had fallen within the airport perimeter, and nine of them had found runway targets. But runway eleven was unscarred. As they watched, the single Fulcrum left on the ground roared off into the sky, its pilot frantic with rage, demanding a vector to a target. He was ordered to patrol as the rest of the squadron landed to refuel.

The first battle had mixed results. The Americans lost half their bomber force in return for damaging three of Keflavik's five runways. The Soviets had most of a SAM battery smashed to little gain, but Keflavik was still usable. Already the ground personnel were running to the runway-repair equipment left behind by the Americans. At the end of each runway was a pile of gravel, and a half-dozen bunkers contained steel mats. Heavy equipment would bulldoze the debris back into the holes, even it out, then cover it over with gravel and steel. Keflavik was damaged, but its runways would be fully operational again before midnight.

USS *PHARRIS*

"I think this one's for-real, Captain," the ASW officer said quietly. The line of colored blocks on the passive sonar display had lasted for seven minutes. Bearing was changing slowly aft, as though the contact were heading for the convoy, but not *Pharris*.

The frigate was steaming at twelve knots, and her Prairie / Masker systems were operating. Sonar conditions were better today. A hard thermocline layer at two hundred feet severely impeded the utility of a surface sonar. *Pharris* was able to deploy her towed-array sonar below it, however, and the lower water temperature there made for an excellent sound channel. Better still, the layer worked in both directions. A submarine's sonar had as much trouble penetrating the thermocline as a surface sonar. *Pharris* would be virtually undetectable to a submarine below the layer.

"How's the plot look?" the tactical action officer asked.

"Firming up," ASW answered. "Still the distance question. Given the water conditions and our known sonar performance, our sonar figure of merit gives us a contact distance of anything from five to fourteen miles on direct path, or into the first convergence zone. That predicts out from nineteen to twenty-three miles . . ." A convergence zone is a trick of physics. Sound traveling in water radiates in all directions. Noise that traveled down was gradually turned by water temperature and pressure into a series of curves, rising to the surface, then bending again downward. While the frigate could hear noise out from herself for a distance of about fourteen nautical miles, the convergence zone was in the shape of an annulus—the area between two concentric circles—a donut-shaped piece of water that began nineteen miles and ended twenty-three miles away. The distance to the submarine was unknown, but was probably less than twenty-three miles. That was already too close. The submarine could attack them or the convoy they guarded with torpedoes, or with surface-to-surface missiles, a technology pioneered by the Soviets.

"Recommendation, gentlemen?" Morris asked. The TAO spoke first.

"Let's put the helicopter up for the near solution, and get an Orion working the far one."

"Sounds good," ASW agreed.

Within five minutes, the frigate's helo was five miles out, dropping Lofar-type sonobuoys. On striking the water, these miniature passive sonar sets deployed a nondirectional sonar transducer at a preselected depth. In this case all dipped above the thermocline layer to determine if the target was close. The data was relayed back to *Pharris*'s combat information center: nothing. The passive sonar track, however, still showed a submarine or something that *sounded* like a submarine. The helo began moving outward, dropping sonobuoys as it went.

Then the Orion arrived. The four-engine aircraft swooped low along the frigate's reported bearing-to-target. The Orion carried over fifty sono-buoys, and was soon dropping them in sets both above and below the layer.

"I got a weak signal on number six and a medium on number five," a sonar operator reported. Excitement crept into his voice.

"Roger, confirm that," the tactical coordinator on Bluebird-Three agreed. He'd been in the ASW game for six years, but he was getting excited, too. "We're going to start making MAD runs."

"You want our helo to back you up?"

"Roger that, yes, but tell him to keep low."

Seconds later the frigate's SH-2F Sea Sprite helicopter sped off north, her magnetic anomaly detector trailing out by cable from a shroud on the right side of the aircraft. Essentially a highly sensitive magnetometer, it could detect the disturbance in the earth's magnetic field made by a large chunk of ferrous metal—like the steel hull of a submarine.

"Signal on number six is now medium-strength. Signal on seven remains medium." The plotting team took this to mean that the submarine was heading south.

"I can give you a working range figure," ASW said to the TAO. "Forty-two to forty-five thousand yards, bearing three-four-zero to three-three-six." The frigate relayed this at once to the Orion.

As they watched on radar, the P-3C quartered the area, flying very precise tracks across the box of ocean defined by *Pharris*'s sonar data as the probable location of the submarine. A computer system plotted the lines as they extended to the south.

"*Pharris,* this is Bluebird. Our data indicates no friendly subs in the area. Please confirm, over."

"Roger that, Bluebird. We confirm no reports of friendlies in the area." Morris had checked that himself half an hour before.

"Signal strength increasing on number six. We now have a weak signal on number five. Number seven is fading out." The technician was really struggling to be professionally impassive now.

"Range is firming up. Estimate target speed roughly eight knots, distance forty-three thousand yards."

"Transient! Transient!" called the ship sonar operator. A metallic noise had come from the target bearing. A closing hatch, a dropped tool, an opening torpedo tube door—something had made a uniquely man-made sound.

"Confirm mechanical transient, copied on buoys five and six," the air-craft called immediately.

"Confirmed," *Pharris*'s TAO answered. "We got that on the towed-array, too. We evaluate the contact as positive submarine at this time."

"Concur," the Orion replied. "Positive Redboat classification—mad-man! Madman, madman, smoke away! We have a MAD contact." A big spike appeared on the MAD readout. Instantly, a crewman flipped a switch to deploy a smoke marker and the aircraft turned hard right to circle back on the contact point.

"Plotted!" The tactical action officer marked the position on his tactical display scope with a large V symbol.

The helo raced in on the contact as the Orion circled back.

"Madman!" its systems operator called out, and the helo dropped its own smoke bomb, slightly south and west of the Orion's.

The data was now being relayed to the frigate's torpedo-tube and ASROC attack directors. Neither had anything like the range to engage the target, but that could change quickly.

"Patience," Morris breathed from his chair in the CIC, then louder: "Take your time, people. Let's lock this guy in before we fire."

The Orion's tactical coordinator agreed, forcing himself to relax and take the time needed. The P-3 and the helicopter made another MAD run north to south. This time the Orion got a reading and the helo did not. Another run, and both had the contact's course line. Next came an east-to-west run. At first, both missed, but on the second run both had him. The contact was no longer an *it*. Now it was a *he*, a submarine being driven by a man. Control of the operation now passed exclusively to the tactical coordinator on the Orion. The big patrol aircraft orbited two miles away as the helicopter lined up for the final pass. The pilot made a very careful check of his tactical display, then locked his eyes on the gyrocompass.

The helo began the last MAD run, with the Orion two miles behind it.

"Madman, madman, smoke away!" The final smoke marker dropped, a green flare floating on the surface. The Sea Sprite banked hard to the right to clear the area as the Orion came in low. The pilot watched the smoke's movement to figure wind drift as he lined up on the target. The P-3C's bomb bay doors opened. A single Mk-46 ASW torpedo was armed for launch.

"Torp away!"

The torpedo dropped cleanly, its braking parachute trailed out of the tail to make sure the weapon entered the water nose down. The Orion also dropped an additional sonobuoy, this time a directional DIFAR.

"Strong signal, bearing one-seven-niner."

The torpedo dove to two hundred feet before beginning its circular search. Its high-frequency sonar came on as it reached search depth. Things started happening quickly.

The submarine had been oblivious to the activity over her head. She was an old Foxtrot. Too old and too noisy for front-line operations, she was there nonetheless, hoping to catch up with the convoy reported to her south. Her sonar operator had noted and reported a possible overhead splash, but the captain was busy plotting the position of the convoy he had been ordered to approach. The torpedo's homing sonar changed that. Instantly, the Foxtrot went to flank speed, turning hard to the left in a pre-planned evasion maneuver. The suddenly increased noise of her cavitating screws was discernible to several sonobuoys and *Pharris*'s tactical sonar.

The torpedo was in ping-and-listen mode, using both active and passive sonar to find its target. As it completed its first circle, the passive receptors in the nose heard the cavitation noises of the submarine and homed in on them. Soon the active sonar pings were reflecting off the submarine's stern as it dodged left and right trying to get away. The torpedo automatically went to continuous pinging, increasing to maximum speed as it homed in on its target like the remorseless robot it was.

The sonar operators on the aircraft and the frigate had the best picture of what was happening. As they watched, the bearing lines of the submarine and torpedo began to converge. At fifteen knots, the Foxtrot was too slow to run away from the forty-knot torpedo. The submarine began a radical series of turns with the torpedo in pursuit. The Mk-46 missed its first attempt for a kill by twenty feet, and immediately turned for another try. Then the submarine's captain made a mistake. Instead of continuing his left turn, he reversed it, hoping to confuse the oncoming torpedo. He ran directly into its path . . .

Immediately overhead, the helicopter crew saw the water appear to leap, then froth, as the shock wave of the explosion reached the surface.

"We have warhead detonation," the pilot reported. A moment later his systems operator dropped a passive buoy. The sound came into them in less than a minute.

The Foxtrot was dying. They heard the sounds of air blowing into her ballast tanks and continued flank power from her electric motors, her propellers struggling to overcome the weight of water entering the hull and drive the wounded submarine to the surface. Suddenly the engine sounds stopped. Two minutes later, they heard the metallic scream of internal bulkheads being torn asunder by water pressure as the submarine fell below crush depth.

"This is Bluebird. We score that one as a kill. Can you confirm, over?"

"Roger, Bluebird," the ASW officer answered. "We copied blowing air and breakup noises. We confirm your kill." The crewmen cheered, forgetting the decorum that went with duty in CIC.

"All right! That's one less to worry about. We'll give you a big assist on that one, *Pharris*. Nice job from your sonar folks and the helo. Out." The Orion increased power and returned to her patrol station forward of the convoy.

"Assist, hell!" snorted the ASW officer. "That was our contact. We could have dropped the torp on him just as easy as he did." Morris punched him in the shoulder and went up the ladder to the pilothouse.

The bridge crew was all grins. Soon the bosun's mate would paint half of a red submarine silhouette next to the pilothouse door. It had not struck them yet that they had just helped in the killing of a hundred young men not at all unlike themselves, their lives cut short by the hammering pressure of the North Atlantic.

"What's that?" called a lookout. "Possible explosion on the starboard beam!"

Morris grabbed his binoculars and raced out the open door. The lookout pointed.

A column of black smoke was reaching into the sky from the direction of the convoy. Someone else had just gotten his first kill.

USS *NIMITZ*

Toland had never seen so many welding torches operating. Under the supervision of the executive officer and three damage-control experts, crewmen were using acetylene torches to cut away the damaged portions of *Nimitz*'s flight deck and its supporting steel beams. What had been bad enough became worse on more thorough examination. Six of the enormous frames under the flight deck had been wrecked, and the damage extended two decks below that. A third of the hangar deck was burned out. Most of the plane-fueling network and all of the ordnance elevators had to be repaired. CIC was gone, and with it all of the computers and communications needed to fight the ship. The arrester wire systems would have to be fully replaced. The main search radar was gone. The list went on.

Tugs were pushing the wounded carrier into Southampton's Ocean Dock, a task made doubly hard because of the ship's induced ten-degree list. Water cascaded from the carrier's clifflike hull into the harbor while more entered the bilges below. Already a senior Royal Navy repair expert and the chief of the Vosper Ship Repair Yard were aboard, reviewing the damage below and cataloging the material needed to enable the ship to operate again. Captain Svenson watched the messenger lines being shot off to handlers who would secure the ship. He was an angry man, Toland noted. Five hundred of his men known dead, another three hundred wounded, and the count was nowhere near complete. The most grievous losses were in the flight deck crews, many of whose shelters had been immolated by the two Soviet missiles. They would also have to be replaced before *Nimitz* could sail and fight again.

"Toland, you'll be heading to Scotland."

"Excuse me, sir?"

"The air wing is being split. The fighters and Hawkeyes are going north. Ivan's been pounding on the Brits' northern radar line, and their fighters have taken a beating trying to help the Norwegians out. The Tomcats are already on the way, and we'll be loading their missiles onto the dock so the Brits can fly them north. I want you to operate with the fighter teams to evaluate what Ivan's up to with his Badgers, and maybe help our guys to cull off some of the bastards. The attack birds are joining the NATO tactical air reserve for the present."

"When do I leave?" Toland reflected that he had nothing to pack. The Kingfish had taken care of that, too. His first order of business was to cable his family that he was all right.

ICELAND

"Doghouse, this is Beagle, and what the hell just happened, over?"

"Beagle, I am authorized to tell you that an attack was just made against Keflavik."

"No kidding, guy. A B-52 just crashed right on our Goddamned hill. Didn't you tell anybody that I reported fighters?"

"Your information was evaluated as unconfirmed and was not passed on, Beagle. I did not concur in that. Continue your report."

"I saw four, repeat four, Soviet single-seat aircraft with a twin-rudder configuration. I can't be sure of the type, but they had double tails, you copy that?"

"Twin rudders, copy that. Confirm you saw four."

"One-two-three-four, Doghouse. I can't arrange them to parade overhead. But if you send bombers in here unescorted again, mister, don't blame me."

"Any survivors from the crash you saw?"

"Negative. No 'chutes, and no way anyone would have survived the crash. Saw one fireball on the horizon, but I'm not sure what that was. How did the Weasels do?"

"Can't say, Beagle, but thanks for the word on the SAMs."

"You have instructions for me?"

"Your status is being reevaluated now. We'll be back on the hour."

"Make it two, fella. We have to move some before the bad guys send a patrol this way. Out." The Marines were around him, weapons ready, alert for the patrol or helicopter, or both, that had to be heading their way. Edwards tore off the headset and repacked the radio. "Great, just great," he muttered. "Let's move it, people."

They had already jogged a full kilometer from their former home, heading due east into the uninhabited wasteland that formed this part of the island. Smith kept them on slopes, off the crests and hilltops that could silhouette them against the clearing sky. There was a lake off to their left, with many houses on its western side. They had to be careful here. There was no telling who might note their passing and inform someone of it. They passed under the main power transmission lines at a run, angling south to keep a crest line between them and most of the houses. An hour later, they were in the Holmshraun lava field, an incredible collection of rocks overlooking Highway 1, one of Iceland's two major thoroughfares. There were vehicles on the road heading in both directions. Many of them carried soldiers.

"What are we figuring to do now, sir?" Smith asked pointedly.

"Well, Sarge, we got good concealment here. Hell, a guy fifty yards away would have trouble spotting us in this crap. I say we wait for it to get a little dark tonight and get north of the road. Once we get past that, the population thins out—at least that's what the map says. It ought to be fairly safe once we get away from the population centers."

"What will our friends on the other side of that radio say about that?"

"I guess we better find out." Edwards checked his watch. He was nearly two hours overdue. Doghouse was annoyed with him.

"What kept you off the air?"

"We just moved about eight klicks. Maybe you'd prefer we waited around and counted the Russians picking over the wreckage. Listen up, we're all alone here and that's a little scary, you know?"

"Understood, Beagle. Okay, we got orders for you. You have a map of the area you're in?"

"That's affirm, a one-to-fifty-thousand one."

"Okay, they want you to move to Grafarholt. There's a hill there. You're supposed to find a safe place near there and belly-up for further instructions."

"Hey, Doghouse, before we get any farther, what if Ivan starts playing DF games and tries to track us down from our radio transmissions?"

"Okay, about time you asked that. The radio you got is encrypted UHF, single-sideband. That means it's got thousands of channels, and having him lock into one is not real likely. Second, you have a directional antenna. When you transmit, make sure there's a hill between you and them. UHF is line-of-sight only. So you ought to be safe on that score, too. Happy?"

"It helps."

"How soon can you get to that hill for us?"

Edwards looked at the map. About seven kilometers. A comfortable two-hour walk in peacetime, maybe three or four not so comfortable hours, given the terrain here. They'd have to wait for darkness, detour around a few villages . . . and there was that one other little thing to be concerned about . . . "Twelve hours, minimum."

"Roger, understood, Beagle. Copy twelve hours. That's fine. We'll be calling for you then. Anything else to report?"

"Some activity on the road below us. Several trucks, Army-type, painted green. A lot of personal vehicles, four-by-fours. No armored stuff, though."

"Okay. Take your time and play it safe. Your mission is to avoid contact and report. We'll be here if you need us. Out."

At Doghouse in northern Scotland, the communications officer leaned back in his swivel chair.

"The lad sounds somewhat rattled," an intelligence officer commented over his tea.

"Not quite SAS material, is he?" another asked.

"Let's not be too hasty," said a third. "He's bright, something of an athlete, and he had the presence of mind to escape when events called for it. Seems a bit high-strung, but given his position that's understandable, I think."

The first pointed on the map. "Twelve hours to go this little distance?"

"Across hilly, open terrain, with a whole bloody division of paras running about in lorries and BMPs, *and* with a sun that never sets, what the hell do you expect of four men?" demanded the fourth, a man dressed in civilian clothes who had been gravely wounded while in the 22nd SAS Regiment. "If that lad had any sense, he'd have packed it in yesterday. Interesting psychological profile here. If he manages to get to this hill on time for us, I think he'll do all right."

USS *PHARRIS*

The convoy had scattered. Toland looked at the radar display, an expanding ring of ships, now beginning to turn back east to reassemble. One merchantman had been sunk, another badly damaged and limping west. Three frigates were trying to locate the submarine that had done the damage. *Gallery* had gotten a possible contact and fired a torpedo at it, without result. Four helicopters were dropping sonobuoys in hope of reacquiring it, and a half-dozen sonars were pinging away, but so far it looked as though the submarine had evaded the angry escorts.

"That was a beautiful approach," the tactical action officer observed grudgingly. "His only goof was hitting the back end of the convoy."

"His fire control wasn't all that great," Morris said. "They say they had sonar readings on five fish. Figure three targets. Two hits for a kill on one, and a scratch hit on another for damage. The other was a clean miss. Not a bad afternoon's work. What's he doing now, people?"

"How much you want to bet it's an old nuc boat?" TAO asked. "Their fire-control systems aren't up to current standards, and they can't run very fast and still stay covert. He just barely made the intercept, and bit off two ships. When they scattered he didn't have the speed to pursue without advertising his position, and he's too smart for that."

"Then what did he do?" ASW asked.

"He was in close when he launched. Ducked inside the convoy and went deep. Used the noise from the thundering herd to mask himself, then motored off clear . . ."

"North." Morris bent over the display. "Most of the merchies went northeast when the scatter order went out. He probably went north to trail, and maybe hope to get another shot in later. What do you think we're up against?"

"Intel says this area had three Foxtrots and a November, plus maybe another nuc. The one we killed was probably a Fox. Doesn't have the speed to trail the convoy." The ASW officer looked up. "But a November would. We're not up against a new nuc. He'd still be shooting. Call it a November."

"Okay, say he came north at six or seven knots, then turned east hoping to pick us up again tomorrow, say. Where would he be?"

"Right now . . . here, sir," ASW said. He pointed to a spot fifteen miles aft of the frigate. "We can't go back after him."

"No, but we can listen for him if he tries to play catchup." Morris thought hard. The convoy would be altering base course to one-two-zero on the hour to head farther south, away from the suddenly increased threat of Soviet long-range bombers. More time would be needed for them to re-form and establish proper stations. That would allow the submarine to cut the corner and close the target. With all the zigzagging the merchies were doing, their effective speed of advance was only about sixteen knots, and a November might try to catch up with that. "I want the operators to pay particular attention to this sector. Our friend just might be back."

"Call in a P-3?" TAO wondered.

Morris shook his head. "They want to keep station forward. The main threat is still ahead of us. Us 'cans have to worry about the trailers, until we get a hot contact, anyway. I think this guy will trail, and he might try and get off a contact report."

KIEV, THE UKRAINE

"Good news," the naval officer said. "Our bombers report sinking three aviation ships, two cruisers, and two destroyers."

Alekseyev and his boss exchanged a look: their colleagues in blue would be insufferable now.

"How firm is that evaluation?" CINC-Southwest asked.

"There were four carrier-type ships photographed before the attack. The next satellite pass eight hours after the attack showed only one. Two cruisers and two destroyers were also missing. Finally we have intelligence reports of numerous carrier-type aircraft landing at French naval air bases in Brittany. Our submarines were unable to make contact with the formation—it would seem that one was sunk, unfortunately, but our first naval air battle was a smashing success. We will close the Atlantic for you, Comrades," the captain predicted.

"We may need it closed," Alekseyev said after the captain left.

His boss grunted agreement. Things in Germany were not going well. The Soviet Air Force had been hurt even worse than they had feared, and as a result the land campaign was already far behind schedule. On the second day of the war, the first day's objectives had been met in only one army's zone, and that one was being heavily counterattacked twenty kilometers east of Hamburg. Tank losses had been 50 percent higher than predicted, and control of the air was in jeopardy, with many units reporting heavier-than-expected air attacks. Only half of the Elbe bridges had been replaced as yet, and the floating ribbon bridges could not carry all the load of the highway bridges they replaced. The NATO armies had not yet reached their peak strength. American reinforcements were still arriving by air, mating up with their pre-positioned equipment. The Soviet first echelon was being bled, and the second echelon was still largely trapped behind the Elbe.

ICELAND

"About as dark as it's gonna get," Edwards said. The light level was what meteorologists and sailors called nautical twilight. Visibility was down to five hundred yards with the sun just below the northwest horizon. The lieutenant put on his pack and rose. His Marines did the same, with as much enthusiasm as a child on his way to school.

They headed down the shallow slope toward the Sudura River, more a fair-sized creek, Edwards thought. The lava field provided good cover. The ground was littered with rocks, some as much as three feet high, a landscape that broke up shapes and disguised movement to the casual observer. He hoped there was nothing more than that out there. They had observed a number of Soviet patrols, mainly on military trucks that passed through the area at intervals of about thirty minutes. They saw no fixed positions. Certainly they had garrisoned the hydroelectric power station at Burfell, farther east on Route 1. No one had bombed that yet: the lights were still bright in some of the homes below them.

The rocks got smaller as the land changed to a grassy meadow. There had been sheep here recently—the smell was unmistakable and the grass was short. Instinctively the men walked in a crouch toward a gravel road. The houses and barns here were spread irregularly. They picked a spot where the space between buildings was about five hundred yards, hoping that the dim light and their camouflage uniforms would make them invisible to any observer. No one was about in the open. Edwards halted his group and looked carefully through his binoculars at the nearest houses. Lights burned in some, but no people were visible outside. Perhaps the Russians had imposed a curfew . . . meaning that anyone seen moving might be shot on sight. Happy thought.

The riverbanks sloped downward sharply about twenty feet to the water, and were covered with rocks smoothed by years of erosion at high-water time. Smith went down first as the others lay with weapons ready at the lip of the south bank. The sergeant moved slowly at first, checking the water depth before hurrying across, rifle held high in the air. Edwards was surprised how quickly he went through it, then up the far bank. The sergeant waved, and the rest of the men followed. Edwards soon found out why the sergeant had crossed the stream quickly. The waist-deep water was icy cold, like most of the streams on Iceland, fed by melting glaciers. He gasped and went across as fast as he could, his rifle and radio held above his head. A minute later he was atop the far bank.

Smith chuckled in the dark. "I guess that woke everybody up."

"Like to froze my balls off, Sarge," Rodgers groused.

"Looks clear ahead," Edwards said. "Beyond this meadow is another creek, then the main road, a secondary road, then up a hill into a lava field. Let's keep moving."

"Right, Lieutenant." Smith got to his feet and moved off. The others trailed behind him at five-yard intervals. *The little bastard's in a hurry, isn't he?*

The ground here was agreeably flat, the grass as high as their boot tops. They moved rapidly, keeping low, weapons held ready across their chests as they angled slightly east to avoid the village of Holmur. The next stream was shallower than the Sudura, though no less cold. They stopped on crossing it, now only two hundred yards from the highway. Again Smith moved off first, this time with his back bent double, moving in rushes followed by pauses while he knelt to examine the terrain repeatedly. The men behind him matched his movements exactly, and the team got together again in tall grass fifty feet from the road.   .

"Okay," Smith said. "We cross one at a time, a minute apart. I go first. I'll stop fifty feet on the other side by those rocks. When you cross, don't screw around—run and keep low, and come to me. If you see something coming, get as far from the road as you can and drop. They can't see you if you lay still, people. Take things real easy. Okay?" Everyone, Edwards included, nodded agreement.

The sergeant was as good as his word. After a final look to be sure that nothing was moving in their direction, he raced off across the road, his personal gear flopping and slapping against his body as he did so. They waited a minute, then Garcia followed. After another minute, Rodgers went. Edwards counted to sixty and darted forward. The lieutenant was amazed—and appalled—at how stressful this was. His heart pounded with terror as he reached the roadway, and he froze dead in the center. Automobile lights were approaching them from the north. Edwards just stood there, watching them come closer—

"Move your ass, Lieutenant!" the sergeant's voice rasped at him.

The lieutenant shook his head clear and ran to the sound of the sergeant's voice, one hand holding his helmet in place on his head.

"Lights coming down!" he gasped.

"No shit. Be cool, sir. People, let's get spread out. Find some good cover and freeze. And make Goddamned sure those weapons are on *safe!* You stay with me, sir."

The two privates moved left and right into tall weeds, disappearing from view as soon as they stopped moving. Edwards lay next to Sergeant Smith.

"You think they saw me?"

The darkness prevented him from seeing the angry expression accompanying Smith's reply: "Prob'ly not. Don't freeze in the road like that again, sir."

"I won't. Sorry, Sarge, this isn't exactly my thing."

"Just listen and learn what we tell ya', okay?" Smith whispered. "We're Marines. We'll take good care of you."

The lights approached slowly, proceeding down the steep grade to their north. The driver didn't trust the loose gravel surface. The north-south road split here, forking left and right to Route 1. It had to be a military truck, they saw. The lights were rectangular, taped slips over headlights installed at the Soviets' massive Kama River factory, built largely with Western aid. The truck stopped.

Edwards did not allow himself to react, except that his grip tightened on the plastic stock of his rifle. What if someone had seen them cross the road and telephoned the Russians? Smith's hand reached out and pushed the lieutenant's rifle down.

"Let's be careful with that, Lieutenant," Smith whispered.

The ten men in the truck dismounted and spread into the grass off the road, perhaps fifty yards away. Edwards couldn't tell if they carried weapons or not. Each man stopped, and almost in unison they unbuttoned their flies to urinate. Edwards gawked and nearly laughed. Finished, they moved back to the truck, which started up and proceeded west on the fork to the main road, motoring off with the sound on a poorly muffled diesel engine. The Marines re-formed as the truck's taillights dipped under the horizon.

"Too bad." Rodgers smiled in the semidarkness. "I coulda blow'd one guy's pecker right off!"

"You done good, people," Smith said. "Ready to move out, Lieutenant?"

"Yeah." Shamed by his performance, the lieutenant let Smith lead them off. They crossed the gravel road and a hundred yards later were in yet another lava field, climbing over rocks into the wasteland. Their wet fatigue pants clung to their legs, drying slowly in the cool westerly breeze.

USS *PHARRIS*

"Our friend the November doesn't have an anechoic coating," ASW said quietly, pointing to the display. "I think that's him, running to catch up with the convoy."

"We have this trace plotted at about forty-six thousand yards," the tactical action officer said.

"Get the helo up," Morris ordered.

Five minutes later, *Pharris*'s helicopter was running southwest at full speed, and Bluebird-Seven, another P-3C Orion, was closing on the datum point from the east. Both aircraft flew low, hoping to surprise the submarine that had killed one of their flock and gravely damaged another. The Russian had probably made a mistake by increasing his speed. Maybe he had orders to trail the convoy and radio data for other submarines to use. Maybe he wanted to catch up to make another attack. Whatever the reason, his reactor pumps were running and making noise that his hull could not contain. His periscope was up, and that gave the aircraft a chance to spot him with their look-down radars. The helo was closer, and its pilot was communicating with the tactical coordinator of the Orion. This could be a textbook attack if things worked out right.

"Okay, Bluebird, we are now three miles from datum center. Say your position."

"We're two miles behind you, Papa-One-Six. Illuminate!"

The systems operator flipped the cover off the radar switch and moved it from Standby to Active. Instantly, energy began to radiate from the radar transmitter slung under the helicopter's nose.

"Contact, we have a radar contact bearing one-six-five, range eleven hundred yards!"

"Stream the MAD gear!" The pilot advanced his throttles to race toward the contact.

"We got him, too," the Tacco called swiftly. The petty officer beside him armed a torpedo, setting its initial search depth for a hundred feet.

The helicopter's anticollision lights came on, the red lights flashing in the darkness. No sense in hiding their approach now. The sub must have detected their radar signals and would now be attempting a crash dive. But that took more time than he had.

"Madman, madman, smoke away!" the systems operator screamed.

The smoke was invisible in the darkness, but the short green flame was an unmissable beacon in the darkness. The helo banked left, clearing the way for the Orion now only five hundred yards behind him.

The P-3C's powerful searchlights came on, spotting the telltale wake left by the now-invisible periscope. The MAD contact had been right on, the pilot saw at once. The Orion's bomb doors swung open and the torpedo dropped toward the black waters along with a sonobuoy.

"Positive sonar contact, evaluate as submarine!" a sonar-board operator said over the intercom. The tone lines displayed on his screen were exactly what a November at high speed looked like, and the torpedo chasing her was already on continuous pinging. "Torpedo is closing the target rapidly . . . Looks good, Tacco, closing . . . closing—*impact!*" The torpedo's sound tracing merged with that of the submarine, and a brilliant splotch appeared in the waterfall display. The Orion's operator switched the sonobuoy from active to passive, recording the recurring rumbles of the torpedo warhead explosion. The submarine's screw sounds stopped, and again he heard the sound of blowing air that quickly stopped as the submarine began her last dive.

"That's a kill, that's a kill!" exulted the Tacco.

"Confirm the kill," Morris said over the radio. "Nice job, Bluebird. That was a real quick-draw!"

"Roger, copy, *Pharris*. Thank you, sir! Beautiful job with the helo and the detection, guy. You just got another assist. Hell, we might just orbit you for a while, Captain, looks like you got all the action. Out."

Morris walked to the corner and poured himself a cup of coffee. So, they had just helped to kill a pair of Soviet submarines.

The TAO was less enthusiastic. "We got a noisy old Foxtrot and a November who did something dumb. You suppose he had orders to trail and report, and that's why we got him?"

"Maybe," Morris nodded. "If Ivan's making his skippers do things like that—well, they like central control, but that can change if they find out it's costing them boats. We learned that lesson ourselves once."

USS *CHICAGO*

McCafferty had his own contact. They had been tracking it for over an hour now, the sonar operators struggling to discern random noise from discrete signal on their visual displays. Their data was passed to the fire-control tracking party, four men hovering over the chart table in the after corner of the attack center.

Already the crew was whispering, McCafferty knew. First the yard fire before they were commissioned. Then being pulled out of the Barents Sea at the wrong time. Then being attacked by a friendly aircraft . . . was *Chicago* an unlucky boat? they wondered. The chiefs and officers would work to dispel that thought, but the chiefs and officers held it, too, since all sailors believed in luck, an institutional faith among submariners. *If you're not lucky, we can't use you*, a famous submarine admiral once said. McCafferty had heard that story often enough. He had so far been devoid of luck.

The captain moved back to the chart table. "What's happening?"

"Not much in the way of a bearing change. He has to be way out there, skipper, like the third convergence zone. Maybe eighty miles. He can't be closing us. We would have lost the signal as he passed out of the zone." The executive officer was showing the strain of the past week's operations, too. "Captain, if I had to guess, I'd say we're tracking a nuclear sub. Probably a noisy one. Acoustical conditions are pretty good, so we have three CZs to play with. And I'd bet he is doing the same thing we are, patrolling a set position. Hell, he could be running back and forth on a racetrack pattern, same as us. That would account for the minimal bearing changes."

The captain frowned. This was the only real contact he'd had since the war started. He was close to the northern border of his patrol area, and the target was probably just on the other side of it. Going after it meant leaving the bulk of his assigned sector unprotected . . .

"Let's go after him," McCafferty ordered. "Left ten degrees rudder, come left to new course three-five-one. All ahead two thirds."

Chicago rapidly turned to a northerly heading, accelerating to fifteen knots, her maximum "silent" speed. At fifteen knots the submarine radiated only a small amount of noise. The risk of counterdetection was slight, since even at this speed her sonars could detect a target five to ten miles off. Her four tubes were loaded with a pair of Mk-48 torpedoes and two Harpoon antiship missiles. If the target was a submarine or a surface ship, *Chicago* could handle it.

GRAFARHOLT, ICELAND

"You're early, Beagle," Doghouse replied.

Edwards was sitting between two rocks and leaning back against a third, the antenna resting on his knee. He hoped it was pointing in a safe direction. The Russians, he figured, were strung mostly along the coast from Keflavik to Reykjavik, well to the west of the direction to the satellite. But there were houses and factories below him, and if they had a listening post down there . . .

"We had to get here before it got too light," the lieutenant explained. They had run the last kilometer with the rising sun behind them. Edwards took some small comfort in the fact that the Marines were puffing harder than he was.

"How secure are you?"

"There is some movement on the road below us, but that's a good ways off, maybe a mile."

"Okay, you see the electrical switching station southwest of you?"

Edwards got out his binoculars with one hand to check. The map called the place Artun. It held the main electrical transformers for the power grid on this part of the island. The high-voltage lines came in from the east, and the feeder cables radiated out from this point.

"Yeah, I see it."

"How are things going, Beagle?"

Edwards almost said they were going great, but stopped himself. "Lousy. Things are going lousy."

"Roger that, Beagle. You keep an eye on that power station. Anything around it?"

"Stand by." Edwards set down the antenna and gave the place a closer look. Aha! "Okay, I got one armored vehicle, just visible around the corner on the west side. Three—no, four armed men are in the open. Nothing else that I can see."

"Very good, Beagle. Now you keep watch on that place. Let us know if any SAMs show up. We also want data if you see any more fighters. Start keeping records of how many trucks and troops you see, where they're heading. Be sure to write things down. Got that?"

"Okay. We write it all down and report in."

"Good. You're doing all right, Beagle. Your orders are to observe and report," Doghouse reminded them. "Avoid contact. If you see enemy troops heading in your direction, bug out. Don't worry about calling in, just bug the hell out and report when you can. Now get off the air for a while."

"Roger that. Out." Edwards repacked the radio. It was getting so that he could do it with his eyes closed.

"What gives, Lieutenant?" Smith asked.

The lieutenant grunted. "We sit tight and watch that electrical place off that way."

"You s'pose they want us to turn some lights off?"

"There's too many troops down there, Sarge," Edwards replied. He stretched and opened his canteen. Garcia was on guard atop the knoll to his right, and Rodgers was asleep. "What's for breakfast?"

"Well, if you got peanut butter and crackers, I'll trade you my peaches for it."

Edwards ripped open the C-Ration container and inspected the contents. "Deal."

22. Ripostes

USS *CHICAGO*

The submarine slowed to reacquire the target. She'd run deep at fifteen knots for over an hour, and now reduced speed and came up to five hundred feet, right in the middle of the deep sound channel. McCafferty ordered an easterly course, which allowed the towed-array sonar—his "tail"—to bear on the supposed target to the north. It took several minutes before the array was straight and aligned in the proper direction so that the sonar operators could begin their work in earnest. Slowly the data came up on their displays, and a senior petty officer plugged in a set of headphones, hoping for an aural detection. There was nothing to detect. For twenty minutes the screen showed only random noise patterns.

McCafferty examined the paper plot. Their erstwhile contact would now be exactly two convergence zones away and should have been easily detected, given known water conditions. But their screens showed nothing.

"We never did have a classification." The executive officer shrugged. "He's gone."

"Take her up to antenna depth. Let's see what's cooking topside." McCafferty moved back to the periscope pedestal. He could not fail to note the instant tension in the compartment. The last time they'd done this, they'd nearly been sunk. The submarine leveled off at a depth of sixty feet. Sonar did another check and found nothing. The ESM mast went up, and the electronics technician reported only weak signals. The search periscope went up next. McCafferty made a very quick check of the horizon—nothing in the air, nothing on the surface.

"There's a storm to the north, line squall," he said. "Down scope."

The executive officer grumbled an inaudible curse. The noise from the storm would make the normally difficult task of finding a conventional sub motoring along on battery power nearly impossible. It was one thing for them to dart a short distance out of their patrol area with a good chance for a kill. It was another to leave for a whole day looking for something that they might never find. He looked at the captain, waiting for the decision to be made.

"Secure from general quarters," McCafferty said. "XO, take us back to station at ten knots. Keep her deep. I'm going to take a nap. Wake me in two hours."

The captain walked a few steps forward to his stateroom. The bunk was already folded down, unmade, from the portside bulkhead. Instrument repeaters would show him course and speed, and a TV set could show him whatever the periscope might be looking at, or a taped movie. McCafferty had been awake for about twenty hours now, and the added stress that comes from a combat environment made it feel like a week. He took off his shoes and lay down, but sleep would not come.

KEFLAVIK, ICELAND

The colonel ran his hand along the bomber silhouette painted on the side of his fighter. His first combat victory, recorded on his gun cameras. Not since a handful of his comrades had fought in the skies of North Vietnam had a Soviet Air Force pilot won a real air-to-air victory, and this one had been over a nuclear-capable bomber that might otherwise have threatened the homeland.

There were now twenty-five MiG-29 fighters on Iceland, and four of them were aloft at all times to protect the bases as the ground troops tightened their control of the island.

The B-52 raid had hurt them. Their main search radar was slightly damaged, but another was being flown out today, a more modern, mobile unit whose position would be changed twice a day. He wished they had an airborne radar, but learned that losses over Germany had severely limited their availability. The news of the air war there was not good, though the two regiments of MiG-29s were doing well. The colonel checked his watch. In two hours he would be leading a squadron escorting a small force of Backfires that was searching for a convoy.

GRAFARHOLT, ICELAND

"Okay, Doghouse, I can see six fighter aircraft sitting on the runways at Reykjavik. They all got red stars on them. They have twin-rudder configuration and appear to be armed with air-to-air missiles. Two SAM launchers, and some kind of gun—looks like a Gatling gun—mounted on a tracked vehicle."

"That's a Zulu-Sierra-Uniform Three-Zero, Beagle. They're very bad news. We want to know all about those bastards. How many of them?"

"Only one, located on the grassy triangle a few hundred yards west of the terminal building."

"Are the fighters together or dispersed?"

"Dispersed, two on each runway. There's a small van with each pair, plus five or six soldiers. I estimate a hundred troops here, with two armored vehicles and nine trucks. They're patrolling the airport perimeter, and there are several machine-gun emplacements. The Russians also seem to be using the local short-haul airliners for moving troops around. We've seen soldiers boarding the little twin-prop birds. I've counted four flights today. We have not seen a Russian chopper since yesterday."

"How's Reykjavik city look?" Doghouse asked.

"It's hard to see into the streets. We can look down a valley toward the airport, but we can only see down a few streets. One armored vehicle is visible in there parked, like, at an intersection. Troops are just hanging around, like cops or something at every intersection we can see. If I had to guess, I'd say most of their troops are around Reykjavik and Keflavik. Not many civilians around, and almost no civilian traffic. There's a lot of movement on the main roads, both along the coast to our west, and also east on Route 1. It's all back-and-forth traffic, like they're patrolling. We've counted a total of fifty-some trips, split about even on the two highways. One other thing. We saw some Russians using a civilian vehicle. We haven't seen a jeep yet, except a few of ours on the airport grounds. The Russians have jeeps—their kind, I mean—right? I think they've commandeered the people's four-by-fours. That's practically the national vehicle here, and a lot of them are moving around on the roads."

"Any more incoming transport flights?"

"Five. We have clear skies, and we can watch them going in toward Keflavik. Four were IL-76s, and the other one looked kind of like a C-130. I don't know the designation for that one."

"Are the fighters flying?"

"We saw one take off two hours ago. I'd say they have a patrol up, and have fighters here and Keflavik both. That's a guess, but I'll bet money on it. I'd also say the fighters we're looking at can roll off in less than five minutes. Looks a lot like a hot-pad alert status."

"Okay, copy that, Beagle. How is your situation?"

"We're pretty well concealed, and the sarge has two escape routes scouted. We haven't seen the Russians beat any bushes yet. Mostly they seem to be hanging in populated areas and on the roads. If they start heading this way, we'll be bugging out."

"Exactly right, Beagle. We will probably be ordering you off that hill soon anyway. You're doing good, boy. Hang in there. Out."

SCOTLAND

"The kid's doing all right," the major said. He was in an awkward position—an American officer in a NATO communications post run by Brit intelligence types who were evenly split on Edwards's reliability.

"I'd say he's doing bloody marvelously," nodded the senior Brit. He'd lost an eye, quite some time ago by the look of it, but was still one tough-looking bastard, the major thought. "Notice how he discriminates between what his observations and opinions are."

"Weather forecaster," snorted another. "We must get some professionals in there. How quickly can we whistle some up?"

"Perhaps by tomorrow. The Navy wants to put them in by submarine, though, and I agree. A bit dicey for a parachute infiltration, you know. Iceland's covered with rocks, the place is made to break ankles and legs. Then there's the Soviet fighters. No hurry on putting troops there, is it? We've got to reduce their air assets first and generally make life as difficult for them as we can."

"That starts tonight," the major said. "Nordic Hammer Phase Two will hit around the local sunset time."

"Hope it works better than Phase One did, old boy."

STORNOWAY, SCOTLAND

"So how are things going up here?" Toland asked his Royal Air Force counterpart. Right before boarding the flight he'd sent the telegram to Marty: I'M ALL RIGHT ON THE BEACH FOR A WHILE. LOVE. He hoped that would reassure her. Probably the news of the carrier battle was already in the papers.

"Could be better. We've lost eight Tornados trying to assist the Norwegians. We're about down to a bare minimum for local defense, and Ivan's begun to attack our northern radar installations. Sorry about what happened to your aircraft carrier, but I must say we're very happy indeed to have you chaps with us for a bit."

Nimitz's interceptors and radar birds were split among three RAF bases. The maintenance crews were still arriving by transport aircraft, and some hitch had developed with the missiles, but the F-14s each carried a full load for one engagement, and they could use RAF Sparrows to reload. Operating off a land base, the fighter could carry a larger load of fuel and ordnance, packing a heavier punch than off a ship. The fighter crews were in a foul humor. Having used their aircraft and precious missiles to kill drones, they had returned to the formation to see the fearful results of the mistake. The total loss of life was still uncertain, but scarcely two hundred men had escaped from *Saipan,* and only a thousand from *Foch.* In terms of casualties this had been the bloodiest defeat in the history of the United States Navy, with thousands of men gone and not a single kill to offset the losses. Only the French had scored against the Backfires, succeeding with twenty-year-old Crusaders where the vaunted Tomcats had failed.

Toland sat in on their first briefing, conducted by the RAF. The fighter pilots were absolutely silent. He had trouble gauging their mood. No jokes. No whispered remarks. No smiles. They knew that the error had not been theirs, that it was not their fault at all, but that didn't seem to matter. They were shaken by what had happened to their ship.

As was he. Toland's mind kept coming back to the image of the four-inch-thick flight deck steel bent into the sky like cellophane, a blackened cavern below it where the hangar deck used to be. The rows of bags— crewmen who had died aboard the world's most powerful warship . . .

"Commander Toland?" An airman tapped him on the shoulder. "Would you come with me, please?" The two men walked to the operations room. Bob noted instantly that a new raid was being plotted. The operations officer, a flight lieutenant, motioned for Toland to join him.

"One regiment, perhaps less. One of your EP-3s is snooping up there and caught their radio chatter while they were refueling north of Iceland. They'll be going for one of these convoys, we think."

"You want the Tomcats to ambush them on the way home? The timing's going to be tricky."

"Extremely. Another complication. They will use Iceland as a navigational check and a secure assembly point. We know Ivan has fighters there, and now it's reported that he has fighters operating from these two airfields on Iceland."

"Is the source for this something called Beagle?"

"Ah, you've heard about that one. Yes."

"What kind of fighters?"

"Twin tails, is what your chap reported. Could be MiG-25s, -29s, or -31s."

"Fulcrums," Toland said. "The others are interceptors. Didn't the B-52s get a look at them?" The briefing he'd just left had gone over the Air Force mission against Keflavik. More good news to cheer the troops up.

"Evidently not a good one, and superficially they are quite similar. I agree they're probably Fulcrums, and the sensible thing for Ivan to do is have the fighters establish a safe corridor for his bombers."

"They might have to tank coming back . . . go for the tankers?"

"We've thought of that. But they have a million square miles of ocean to use." The area on the chart was obvious. "The timing for that will be damned near impossible, but we think it would be worth the effort some time in the future. For the moment our primary concern is air defense. After that, we think Ivan may be planning an amphibious operation for Norway. If his surface fleet sorties, it's our job to hammer it."

USS *PHARRIS*

"Raid warning, skipper," the executive officer said. "There's about twenty-five Backfires downbound, target unknown."

"Well, they won't be going after the carrier group, not with twenty-five aircraft now that they're under NATO fighter cover. Where are they now?"

"Probably over Iceland. Three to five hours off. We're not the biggest convoy in range, but we are the most exposed."

"On the other hand, if they go for all those independents out there, they can hunt undefended ships in open ocean. But I wouldn't. Our ships are carrying war materiel . . ." The convoy had only five SAM-equipped ships. A ripe target.

GRAFARHOLT, ICELAND

"Contrails, Doghouse, we have contrails overhead, looks like twenty or so. Passing overhead right now."

"Can you get an ID?"

"Negative. Large aircraft with no engines visible on the wings, but I can't be sure of the type. They're pretty high, heading south. Can't gauge the speed, either—no sonic booms, though if they were busting Mach 1, we should have heard it by now."

"Repeat your count," Doghouse ordered.

"I count twenty-one sets of contrails, two-one sets, heading about one-eight-zero. All the fighters at Reykjavik lifted off and went north about thirty minutes before they passed overhead. They still haven't landed back here yet, but we do not know where they are. The bombers do not appear to be escorted. Nothing else new to report."

"Roger, Beagle. Let us know when the fighters land. Might be nice to get a feel for their cycle time. Out." The major turned to his sergeant. "Get that one out on the printer right now. Confirm the one-regiment Backfire raid downbound, over Reykjavik right now, estimated course one-eight-zero. Possibly with fighter escort . . . yeah, better put that in, too."

The NATO communications center was about the only thing working as planned. The communications satellites in their as-yet unreachable orbits over the equator were supplying information to units all over the world, and here in Scotland was one of the main "nodes," military parlance for a high-tech telephone exchange.

USS *PHARRIS*

A good day for contrails, Morris saw. Just the right mixture of temperature and humidity at high altitude, it would cause condensation in the hot exhaust from aircraft engines. They could see the tracks of air traffic crossing the Atlantic. The big twenty-power binoculars usually kept on the bridge wings for surface lookout work had been moved to the flying bridge atop the forward superstructure, and his lookouts were using them to identify the aircraft. They were mainly looking for Bears, the Soviet search aircraft that scouted targets for the Backfires.

Everyone was tense, and no relief was in sight. The submarine threat was bad enough, but with the carrier group savaged the day before, the convoy was virtually naked to air attack. They were too far at sea for any hope of land-based fighter protection. *Pharris* had only the most rudimentary air defenses. She could barely protect herself and was of no use whatever to anyone else. The ships equipped with surface-to-air missiles were now assembling in line on the north side of the convoy, twenty miles south of the frigate, while *Pharris* continued her antisubmarine search. All the frigate could do was keep watch on her threat-warning instruments and radio any data developed. They were sure that Ivan would be using his own Big Bulge search radars aboard the Bears to locate and classify the target. The convoy commander's plan was to use the SAM-ships as an additional row of targets, formed up just like the merchantmen. With luck, an especially curious Bear might mistake them for unarmed ships and be lured in for a visual search. A long shot, it was the only card they had to play . . .

"Contact! We have a Big Bulge radar bearing zero-zero-nine. Signal strength is low."

"Miss us, you bastard," the tactical action officer breathed.

"Not much chance of that," Morris said. "Get the data to the escort commander."

The Bear was on a southerly heading, using its radar only two minutes out of every ten as it approached the convoy. Soon another was detected slightly to the west. Plotting teams estimated their positions, and a report was sent via satellite to CINCLANTFLT in Norfolk with an urgent request for assistance. Norfolk receipted their message; ten minutes later they learned that no help was available.

Pharris manned her gun mount. The point-defense missile system and Gatling gun radar aft were switched to standby. Other radar was kept off. The radar operators in the combat information center sat nervously at their posts, fingering their switches while listening to the ESM reports and stealing an occasional look at the plot.

"Both of them probably have us now."

Morris nodded. "Next come the Backfires."

The captain thought of the battles he had studied at the naval academy—early in World War II, when the Japanese fleet had had air superiority, or when the Germans had used long-range Condors to circle convoys, radioing their positions to any interested party, and not a thing the Allies back then could do about. He'd never expected to be in the same fix. The same tactical situation repeating itself after forty years? It was absurd, Morris told himself. Absurd and terrifying.

"We have a visual sight on a Bear, just over the horizon at two-eight-zero," the talker said.

"Director, use your optics to track the target aft," the tactical action officer said at once. He looked over to Morris. "Maybe he'll fly close enough for a shot."

"Don't light off any radars just yet. He might just wander into somebody's missile envelope if he's not careful."

"No way he'll be that dumb."

"He will try to evaluate the convoy defenses," Morris said quietly. "He can't have them visually yet, not quite yet. Then for a while all he'll be able to see is bumps with wakes behind them. Not easy to identify a ship from an airplane, mister. Let's see just how curious this guy is . . ."

"Aircraft just changed course," the talker reported. "Turning east toward us."

"Air action starboard! Right standard rudder. All ahead full! Come to new course one-eight-zero," Morris ordered immediately. He turned south to lure the Bear closer to the SAM ships. "Illuminate the target. Weapons free! Engage when he gets within range."

Pharris heeled hard to the left as she changed course. Forward, the five-inch gun mount rotated clockwise as the ship brought her stern across the target bearing. As soon as the gun mount was unmasked, fire-control radars gave it a target solution, and the long-barrel gun elevated to thirty degrees and locked on the target. The point-defense missile mount on the fantail did the same.

"Target is at thirty thousand feet, range fifteen miles and closing."

The escort commander still had not authorized a missile launch. Better to have Ivan shoot his missiles first, before he knew what lay in his path. Data from the carrier battle was already out to the fleet. The big Russian air-to-surface missiles were not especially hard targets to hit, since they ran straight for their targets, though you did have to react in a hurry: they were mighty fast. He figured that the Bear was still doing a target evaluation and did not yet know the strength of the escort force. The longer he was kept in the dark, the better, because the Backfires would not have much time to loiter this far from their bases. And if the Bear came in just a little closer . . .

"Commence firing!" the TAO shouted.

Pharris's gun mount went to full-automatic mode, firing a round every two seconds. The Bear was barely within range of her gun, and there was scant chance of a kill, but it was time to give him something to worry about.

The first five rounds fell short, exploding harmlessly a mile from the Bear, but the next three came closer, one exploding only two hundred yards from his left wing. The Soviet pilot instinctively turned right to evade. That was a mistake. He didn't know that the nearest row of "merchantmen" carried missiles.

Seconds later, two missiles launched and the Bear immediately dove to evade, a shower of chaff in her wake as she headed right for *Pharris*, which gave the frigate's gun crew another chance to score a kill. They fired off twenty new rounds as the plane approached. Perhaps two were close enough to damage the bomber, but there was no visible result. The missiles came in next, tiny white darts trailing columns of gray smoke. One missed and detonated in the chaff cloud, but the second detonated a hundred yards away from the bomber. The warhead expanded explosively like a watchspring, breaking into thousands of fragments, and several ripped into the Bear's port wing. The massive propjet lost power in one engine and suffered major wing damage before the pilot regained control just outside *Pharris*'s gun range. She headed off north, trailing smoke.

The other Bear remained discreetly out of everyone's range. The raid commander had just learned a lesson that he'd pass on to his regimental intelligence officer.

"More radars coming on. Down Beats!" warned the ESM technician. "I count ten—count is increasing. Fourteen—eighteen!" the air-search radar operator sang out next.

"Radar contacts, bearing zero-three-four, range one-eight-zero miles. I count four targets, now five—six targets. Course two-one-zero, speed six hundred knots."

"Here come the Backfires," TAO said.

"Radar contact!" came the next call. "Vampire! Vampire! We have inbound missiles."

Morris cringed inwardly. The escorts all switched on their radar transmitters. Missiles trained out on the incoming targets. But *Pharris* was not part of that game. Morris ordered his ship to flank speed, turning north to race away from the missiles' probable target area.

"The Backfires are turning back. The Bear is holding position. We have some radio chatter. Now twenty-three inbound missiles. Bearing changing on all contacts," TAO said. "They're all headed for the convoy. Looks like we're in the clear."

Morris could hear the crew in the Combat Information Center take one deep collective breath. He watched the radar display with marginal relief. The missiles were streaking in from the northeast, and the SAMs were coming up to meet them. The convoy was again ordered to scatter, the merchantmen racing away from the center of the target. What followed had an eerie resemblance to an arcade game. Of the twenty-three Soviet-launched missiles, nine broke through the SAMs and dove into the convoy. They hit seven merchantmen.

All seven were lost. Some disintegrated at once under the hammering impact of the thousand-kilogram warheads. The others lingered long enough for their crews to escape with their lives. The convoy had left the Delaware with thirty ships. Only twenty were left, and there was almost fifteen hundred miles of open ocean between them and Europe.

GRAFARHOLT, ICELAND

Two Backfires ran short of fuel and decided to land at Keflavik. Behind them was the damaged Bear. It circled Reykjavik waiting for the Backfires to clear the runway. Edwards reported it in as a propeller aircraft with a damaged engine. The sun was low over the northwestern horizon, and the Bear gleamed yellow against the cobalt-blue sky.

"Stay on the air, Beagle," Doghouse ordered. Three minutes later, Edwards saw why.

This time there was no standoff jamming to warn the Soviets. Eight FB-111s swept in over the rocks, southwest from the island's rocky center. They skimmed down the bottom of Selja Valley in elements of two, their green and gray camouflage making them almost invisible to the fighters circling overhead. The lead pair turned due west, with another pair half a mile behind it. The remaining four went south around Mt. Hus.

"Holy shit." Smith saw them first, two fast-moving tail fins to the south. Just as Edwards found them, the lead aircraft popped up and launched a pair of TV-guided bombs. The wingman did the same, and both attackers turned north. The four bombs homed in on the transformer station below them, and all landed within the fence perimeter. As though a single switch had been thrown, every light in view went out. The second pair of Aardvarks roared low over Highway 1, blazing over the rooftops of Reykjavik to line up on their target. The leader lofted his own smart-bombs, and his wingman broke left for the airport tank farm on the waterfront. Moments later, the control tower exploded, along with a hangar, and Rockeye cluster-bombs blew the fuel tanks apart. Caught by surprise, the Russian gun and missile crews fired too late.

The defense troops at Keflavik were surprised, too, first by the sudden loss of electrical power, then by the bombers, which arrived only a minute later. Here, too, the control tower and hangars were the primary targets, and most came apart under the impact of two-thousand-pound bombs. The second team found two parked Backfires and a missile-launch vehicle for their Rockeyes to hit, and sprinkled more softball-sized bomblets over the runways and taxiways. Meanwhile, the FB-111s continued west on afterburner, with gunfire and missiles chasing them—and fighters. Six Fulcrums dove for the retreating Varks, whose protective jammers filled the sky with electronic noise.

Free of their ordnance loads, the American bombers blazed away at seven hundred knots, a scant hundred feet over the wavetops, but the Soviet fighter commander would not turn away from this one. He'd seen what they had done to Keflavik, and he was furious at having been caught unaware despite having his fighters aloft. The Fulcrums had a slight speed advantage and closed the gap slowly. They were over a hundred miles offshore when their missile radars burned through the Americans' jamming. Two fighters immediately launched missiles, and the American aircraft jinked up, then down to lose them. One FB-111 took a hit and cartwheeled into the sea, and the Soviets were preparing a second volley when their threat receivers came on.

Four American Phantoms were waiting in ambush for them. In a moment eight Sparrow missiles were diving toward the Fulcrums. Now it was time for the Soviets to run. The MiG-29s wheeled and ran back for Iceland on afterburner. One was felled by a missile, and another damaged. The battle had lasted all of five minutes.

"Doghouse, this is Beagle. The electrical station is *gone!* The Varks knocked it flat, guy. One hell of a fire at the southwest edge of the airport, and looks like the tower got chopped in half. Two hangars look shot up. I see two, maybe three burning aircraft, civilian types. The fighters got off half an hour ago. Damn, that tank farm is burning like a sonuvagun! Lots of people running around on the ground below us." As Edwards watched, a dozen vehicles with headlights blazing ran back and forth over the roads below him. Two stopped a kilometer away and dismounted troops. "Doghouse, I think it's time for us to leave this hill."

"That's a roger, Beagle. Head northeast toward Hill 482. We'll expect to hear from you in ten hours. Get moving, boy! Out."

"Time to leave, sir." Smith tossed the lieutenant his pack and motioned for the privates to move. "Looks like we can score one for the good guys."

KEFLAVIK, ICELAND

The MiGs landed on the still undamaged runway one-eight, the base's longest. They had barely stopped rolling when ground crews began the process of turning them around for further combat operations. The colonel was surprised to see the base commander still alive.

"How many did you get, Comrade Colonel?"

"Only one, and they got one of mine. Didn't you get anything on radar?" the colonel demanded.

"Not a thing. They hit Rejkyavik first. Two groups of aircraft, they came in from the north. The bastards must have flown between the rocks," the major snarled. He pointed to the big mobile radar that sat in the open between two runways. "They missed it completely. Amazing."

"We must move it. Someplace high, very high. We'll never get an airborne radar, and unless we improve radar warning, this low-level business will eat us up. Find a good hilltop. How badly are our facilities damaged?"

"Many small holes in the runways from these bomblets. We'll have them all patched in two hours. The loss of the tower will hinder our ability to operate large numbers of aircraft. When we lost electrical power, we lost the ability to move fuel through our pipeline, probably lost the local telephone service." He shrugged. "We can make adjustments, but it's a major inconvenience. Too much work, too few men. We must disperse the fighters, and we must make alternate arrangements for fueling. The next target will be the fuel dumps."

"Did you expect this to be easy, Comrade?" The colonel looked over at the blazing pyres that only thirty minutes before had been a pair of Tu-22M Backfires. The damaged Bear was just touching down. "Their timing was too good. They caught us when half my fighters were escorting a bomber force off the north coast. Luck, perhaps, but I do not believe in luck. I want ground troops to check for enemy infiltrators around all the airports. And I want better security arrangements. I—what the hell is that?"

A Rockeye bomblet lay on the concrete not twenty feet from them. The major took a plastic flag from his jeep and set it near the bomb.

"The Americans set some for delayed detonation. My men are already searching for them. Be at ease, Comrade, all your fighters have landed safely. Your dispersal areas are clear."

The colonel drew back a few feet. "What do you do with them?"

"We've already practiced this. We'll use a specially fitted bulldozer to push them off the concrete. Some will explode, some won't. Those that do not go off of their own accord will be detonated by a marksman with a rifle."

"The tower?"

"Three men were on duty. Good men." The major shrugged again. "You must excuse me. I have work to do."

The colonel took a last look at the bomblet before walking toward his fighters. He'd underestimated the major.

ICELAND

"There's a light on our hill," Garcia said. Everyone dropped to the ground. Edwards got next to the sergeant.

"Some bastard just lit a cigarette," Smith observed sourly. He'd finished his last one several hours before and was going through withdrawal symptoms. "Now you see why we're carrying our trash with us?"

"They're looking for us?" Edwards asked.

"Figures. That attack was pretty cute. They'll wonder if the airedales had any help. I'm surprised they didn't do it sooner. Guess they were pretty busy with other stuff."

"Think they can see us?" Edwards didn't like that idea.

"From two miles? Pretty dark for that, and if they're smoking, they're being pretty casual. Relax, Lieutenant. It isn't all that easy to find four guys. Lots of hills to check out on this rock. We want to be careful where we walk. Keep off the ridges, like. Even if they got low-light gear, we won't be easy to see if we keep to the valleys. Let's move it out, troops, and keep low."

USS *PHARRIS*

One last merchant was burning. Her crew had abandoned ship two hours before, but still she burned on the western horizon. *More deaths,* Morris thought. Only about half of the crews had been saved, and there wasn't time for a more careful search. The convoy had sailed without a designated rescue ship. The helicopters had pulled many out of the water, but most of them were still needed to hunt submarines. He held a dispatch saying that Orions out of Lajes had prosecuted and probably killed an Echo-class missile submarine in their path. Some good news, but intelligence reported indications of two more.

The loss of Iceland was a disaster whose dimensions were only now becoming apparent. The Soviet bombers had a clear lane to reach into the trade route. Their submarines were racing through the Denmark Strait even as the NATO navies were trying to position their submarines to re-form the barrier they had lost—the barrier upon which the convoys depended. The Air Force and Navy would soon try to rearrange fighter coverage to harass the Backfires, but those measures were all stopgaps. Until Iceland was fully neutralized, or better yet retaken, the Third Battle of the North Atlantic hung in an uneven balance.

At the Pacific fleet bases of San Diego and Pearl Harbor, darkened ships stood out to sea. Once in open ocean they all headed south toward Panama.

23. Returns

USS *PHARRIS*

Things had settled down again. A very relative term: the Backfires were still coming down the gap over Iceland, but they'd hit another convoy this afternoon, killing eleven merchantmen in the process. All the eastbound convoys were angling south, trading a longer voyage to Europe for reduction of the air threat. As bad as losses were to this point—nearly sixty ships had already been sunk—a routing south at least meant the Soviet bombers could carry only one missile instead of two.

The strain was beginning to tell on everyone. Morris's crew had been "port and starboard" for almost a week now, four hours on duty, four hours off. Sleep patterns had been broken up. People didn't eat proper meals. Crucial maintenance requirements cut into what sleep allocations his men had. On top of that was the knowledge that a submarine or aircraft attack could come at any time. The work was still getting done, but Morris noted that his men were becoming terse and ill-tempered. People were beginning to trip over doorsills, a sure sign of fatigue. More serious mistakes would soon follow. The relationship between fatigue and errors was as certain as gravity. In another day or so he hoped a solid routine would establish itself, something for his men to adjust to. There were signs of this, and his chiefs were telling him not to worry. Morris worried.

"Bridge, Combat. Sonar contact, possible submarine, bearing zero-zero-nine."

"Here we go again," the conning officer said. For the twenty-fourth time on this voyage, *Pharris*'s crew raced to battle stations.

It took three hours this time. No Orions were available for them, and the escorts pooled their helicopters to track down the submarine, all directed by Morris and his CIC crew. This submarine driver really knew his business. At the first suspicion that he had been detected—perhaps his sonar had detected a helicopter overhead or heard the splash of a falling sonobuoy—he went deep and began a confusing series of sprints and drifts, porpoising over and under the layer, working hard to break contact—*toward* the convoy. This one wasn't interested in running away. The submarine disappeared and reappeared on their tactical plot, always closing but never revealing his position clearly enough for a shot.

"Gone again," the antisubmarine-warfare officer said pensively. A sonobuoy dropped ten minutes earlier had detected a weak signal, held it for two minutes, then lost it. "This guy's beautiful."

"And too close," Morris said. If the submarine was continuing south, he was now at the edge of the frigate's active sonar range. Up to now, *Pharris* had not revealed herself. The sub's captain would know surface ships were about from the presence of the helicopters, but it wasn't likely that he suspected a frigate only ten miles south of his position.

Morris looked up at the ASW officer. "Let's update our temperature profile."

Thirty seconds later they dropped a bathythermograph probe. The instrument measured water temperature and reported it to a display in the sonar compartment. Water temperature was the most important environmental condition affecting sonar performance. Surface ships checked it periodically, but a submarine could do it continuously—yet another edge that went with a submarine.

"There!" Morris pointed. "The gradient's a lot stronger now and this guy's exploiting it. He's staying out of the deep channel, probably doing his sprints on top of the layer instead of under it where we expect. Okay . . ."

The helicopters continued to drop buoys, and the brief glimpses they got were of a target heading south, toward *Pharris*. Morris waited ten minutes.

"Bridge, Combat, left standard rudder, come to new course zero-one-one," Morris ordered, pointing his ship at the submarine's estimated position. The frigate was doing five knots, moving quietly on the calm seas. The CIC crew watched the heading readout on the aft bulkhead change slowly from the easterly heading.

The tactical display was useless. Confused by many brief reports from sonobuoys, most of which were probably false signals to begin with, the computer-generated estimate for the submarine's position covered over a hundred square miles. Morris walked over to the paper display in the after corner of the room.

"I think he's right about here." Morris tapped the chart. "Comments?"

"Running shallow? That's contrary to doctrine," ASW pointed out. Soviet submariners were supposed to stick with established doctrine, the fleet intelligence reports said.

"Let's find out. Yankee-search."

The ASW officer gave the order at once. Yankee-search meant turning on the frigate's active sonar and hammering the water to find the sub. Morris was taking a chance. If the submarine was as close as he thought, then he was advertising his own ship's location and inviting a missile attack that his point-defense systems were ill-equipped to stop. The sonar operator watched his screen intently. The first five pings came up blank as the sonar beam swept west-to-east. The next one painted a bright dot on the screen.

"Contact—positive sonar contact, direct path, bearing zero-one-four, range eleven thousand six hundred yards. Evaluate as probable submarine."

"Nail him," Morris ordered.

The solid-fuel ASROC booster ignited, blasting clear of the ship and curving across the sky with a trail of pale gray smoke. The rocket burned out in three seconds, coasting through the sky like a bullet. A thousand feet over the water, the torpedo separated from the booster, retarded by a parachute in its fall toward the water.

"He's changed course, sir," the sonar operator warned. "Target is turning and increasing speed. I—there's the fish, we have the torp in the water and pinging. Dropped in pretty close."

The tactical action officer was ignoring this. Three helicopters were converging on the target datum point now. There was a good chance the torpedo would miss, and the task now was to pin the contact down. He ordered a right turn, allowing the frigate's passive sonar array to track in on the submarine, which was moving swiftly now to evade the torpedo, and making a lot of noise. The first helicopter arrived and dropped a buoy.

"Twin screws and cavitation noise. Sounds like a Charlie at full speed, sir," a petty officer announced. "I think the torp may have him."

The torpedo switched from ping-and-listen to continuous pinging, chasing after the racing submarine, arcing downward. The weapon momentarily lost the sub as she passed through the thermocline layer, then reacquired when it too entered the colder deep water, rapidly closing the distance. The submarine loosed a noisemaker, but it malfunctioned. Another was loaded into the launcher. Too late. The torpedo struck the submarine on her port screw and exploded.

"All right!" hooted a petty officer on the sonar crew. "We have warhead detonation. We got the sucker!"

"We have impact. We have detonation," confirmed a helo crew. "Stand by. Target engines have not stopped completely . . . additional propulsion noises—clanking. Air blowing, he's blowing tanks. Coming up, target is coming up. We have bubbles on the surface. Hot damn, there he is!"

The Charlie's bow broke the surface six miles from the frigate. Three helicopters circled the wounded vessel like wolves, and *Pharris* turned north to close the target, her five-inch gun tracking it. It wasn't necessary. The forward hatch opened and men began scrambling out. More appeared on the sail, jumping overboard as the submarine's engine room filled with water. A total of ten got off before the submarine slid backward below the waves. Another appeared on the surface a few seconds later, but no more.

The helicopters dropped life jackets to the men in the water. The helo with the rescue hoist aboard managed to lift two men before the frigate arrived on the scene. Morris supervised the operation from the bridge. The motor whaleboat was swiftly launched, and the rescue was an easy one. The Russian crewmen were stunned and did not resist. The helicopters guided the boat to each man, carefully searching the area for more. All eleven were recovered and the whaleboat returned to the drop lines. *Pharris*'s chief boatswain supervised the operation, an ensign standing quietly at his side.

No one had seriously considered this possibility. A torpedo hit on a submarine was supposed to kill her entirely. *Prisoners,* Morris thought to himself. *What the hell am I supposed to do with* prisoners? He had to decide where to keep them, how to treat them. How to interrogate them—did he have anyone aboard who spoke Russian? The captain turned the conn over to his executive officer and hurried aft.

Armed crewmen were already there, holding their M-14 rifles awkwardly as they looked down with great curiosity at the whaleboat. The boat crew secured the hoist lines to the lift points, and the seaman on the winch lifted the boat up into the davits.

The Soviets were not an impressive lot, many of them clearly in shock from their near escape from death. Morris counted three officers, one of them probably the captain. He whispered a quick command to Bosun Clarke.

The chief had his armed party step back, and took the whistle from his pocket. As the whaleboat settled into place, he blew a three-tone note on his whistle and saluted the Soviet captain like an arriving dignitary.

The Russian's reaction was one of astonishment. Morris stepped forward to help him off the boat.

"Welcome aboard, Captain. I'm Captain Morris, United States Navy." Ed looked around briefly to see the incredulous expressions on his crew's faces. But his ploy failed. The Russian said something in Russian, and either spoke no English or had the presence of mind to pretend he didn't.

Someone else would have to handle the interrogation. Morris told his bosun to carry on. The Russians were taken below for a medical check. For the moment, they'd be kept under guard in sickbay. The bosun hurried back for a moment.

"Skipper, what the hell was that all about?" Chief Boatswain's Mate Clarke inquired.

"They've probably been told that we'd shoot them in the head. I read a book once that said the most effective technique—look, there was this German, the guy specialized in getting information out of our guys in World War Two, okay? He was good at it, and what he did was treat our guys decently. Hell, they sponsored him to come over after the war, and now he's an American citizen. Separate the officers from the enlisted, and the senior EMs from the juniors. Keep 'em separate. Then make sure they're kept comfortable. Feed 'em, give 'em cigarettes, make 'em feel safe. If you happen to know anyone aboard who has a bottle, get it, and give our guests a couple of stiff drinks. Everybody gets new clothes. We keep theirs. Send all of it to the wardroom. We'll see if they have anything valuable. Make sure they're treated nice, and just maybe we can get one or two to spill his guts."

"You got it, skipper." The chief went away shaking his head. At least he'd get to paint a whole submarine on the pilothouse this time.

Morris went back to the pilothouse. He ordered his men to secure from general quarters, and the frigate to return to her patrol station. Next he called up the escort commander and reported on the prisoners.

"*Pharris*," the Commodore replied. "You are directed to paint a gold 'A' on your ASROC launcher. Well done to all aboard, Ed. You're the champs for this crossing. I'll get back to you on the prisoners. Out."

The captain turned around to see that the bridge watch had not left. They'd all heard the Commodore on the radio. Their fatigue was gone, and the grins directed at Morris meant more to him than the words of his boss.

KIEV, THE UKRAINE

Alekseyev looked over the intelligence material on his desk. His boss was in Moscow for a high-level briefing, but this data was—should be, he corrected himself—little different from what his commander was hearing.

"Things are not going well in Germany?" Captain Sergetov asked.

"No. We were supposed to have reached the outskirts of Hamburg by H + 36. A day and a half, the plan called for. Instead we're not quite there yet, and Third Shock Army has taken murderous losses from NATO aircraft." He paused, staring at the map. "If I were the NATO commander, I'd counterattack again, right there."

"Perhaps they are unable to do so. Their first counterattack was repulsed."

"At the cost of a broken tank division and sixty aircraft. Victories like that we can do without. The picture in the south is scarcely better. The NATO forces are trading space for time, and doing it very well. Their ground forces and tactical aircraft are operating over the same ground they've practiced on for thirty years. Our losses are nearly double the estimates, and we can't sustain that." Alekseyev leaned back. He chided himself for being defeatist. It was mainly a manifestation of his desire to join the action. He was certain, as any general would be certain, that he could do things better.

"What about NATO losses?"

"Heavy, we think. They have been remarkably profligate in their weapons expenditures. The Germans have staked too much on defending Hamburg, and it has to be costing them dearly. If I could not counterattack in their place, I would withdraw. A city is not worth breaking the balance of your army. We learned that lesson at Kiev—"

"Excuse me, Comrade General, what about Stalingrad?"

"A somewhat different situation, Captain. Remarkable, nonetheless, how history can repeat itself," Alekseyev muttered, studying the map on the wall. He shook his head. West Germany had too much in the way of road communications for that to work. "The KGB reports that NATO has two, at most three weeks' supply of munitions left. That will be the decisive factor."

"What of our supplies and fuel?" the young captain asked. His answer was a scowl.

ICELAND

At least there was water. The streams were fed by glaciers that lay in the center of the island—water that had fallen as snow over a thousand years before, long before atmospheric pollution, and been compressed to ice. When finally it melted to fill the rocky streams, it turned back into water of crystalline purity and marvelous taste, but absolutely no nutritional value. It was also ice cold, and fords were not easily found.

"Down to one day's rations, Lieutenant," Smith observed as they finished off their meal.

"Yeah, we'll have to think that one over." Edwards assembled his trash. Garcia collected it all for burial. If there had been a way to cover their footprints in the dirt, Smith would have had them doing that too.

It wasn't easy. As Edwards assembled his radio, he listened to muttered Spanish curses and the sound of a folding shovel slamming against the loose rocks that passed for soil atop Hill 482.

"Doghouse, this is Beagle, and we're running out of food, over."

"Sorry to hear that, Beagle. Maybe we'll have some pizzas sent out."

"You funny bastard," Edwards said without toggling the Transmit key. "What do you want us to do this time?"

"Have you been spotted by anyone?"

"We're alive, ain't we? Negative."

"Tell me what you can see."

"Okay, there's a gravel road downhill to the north, maybe two miles away. Looks like a farm—plowed fields, like, but can't tell what's growing there. Another sheep farm to the west of us, we passed it coming here. Lots of sheep. Ten minutes ago we saw a truck on the road heading west. Haven't seen anything flying yet today, but I suppose that'll change. The only civilians we've seen have been right by their houses, we haven't even seen farmers with their sheep, and the farm to the north has no visible activity. No—say again zero—civilian road traffic. Ivan's got this island shut down, Doghouse, really shut down. That's about all I can say. Tell those Vark drivers they really did the job on that powerhouse. Nothing left but a hole in the ground. We haven't seen an electric light lit since."

"Copy that, Beagle. Okay, your orders are to head north toward Hva-mmsfjördur. You need to take a wide detour east to avoid all these bays I see. We want you there in ten days. Say again ten days, twelve at the most. You can make it easy. Stay out in the boonies and avoid contact with anyone. Continue the normal contact schedule and report on anything you see that may be of interest. Acknowledge."

"Roger, Doghouse, you want us in sight of Hvammsfjördur at the end of next week, and keep up the usual radio routine. Anything else?"

"Be careful. Out."

"Hvammsfjördur?" Smith asked. "That's a hundred miles on a straight line."

"They want us to detour east to avoid contact."

"Two hundred miles—walking over this shit." Smith's frown was enough to split a rock. "End of next week? Ten or eleven days?"

Edwards nodded dumbly. He hadn't known it would be that far.

"Gonna be a little tough, Mr. Edwards." The sergeant pulled a large-scale map from his case. "I don't even have cards for the whole coastline. Damn. Look here, Lieutenant. The ridges and rivers on this rock come out from the center like the spokes on a wheel, y'see? That means we climb a lot, and these here ain't little hills. All the low places got roads, and sure as hell we can't follow no roads, right?" He shook his head.

Edwards forced a grin. "Can't hack it? I thought you Marines were in good shape."

Smith was a man who ran five miles every morning. He could not recall ever seeing this little Air Force wimp out doing roadwork. "Okay, Mr. Edwards. They say nobody ever drowned in sweat. On your feet, Marines, we got orders for a little hike." Rodgers and Garcia exchanged a look. "Mister" was not exactly a term of endearment for an officer, but Smith figured that insubordination only counted if the officer *knew* he was being insulted.

KEFLAVIK, ICELAND

The helicopters took time to assemble. The big AN-22 transport had de-livered two Mi-24 attack choppers, quite a load even for that four-engine monster. Another IL-76 flight had delivered the technicians and flight crews to assemble, service, and fly them. There had been a major oversight in the plan, the General thought. The one helicopter that had survived the strafing attack on the first day was now broken down—and of course the broken part was not one which had been included in their pre-packaged equipment. There should have been more helicopters. He shrugged elo-quently. No plan was ever perfect. More helicopters would be flown in, plus a few more mobile radar sets and some additional SAM launchers. The Americans looked to have every intention of making his tenure on Iceland difficult, and he needed more equipment to counter that . . .

Then there were those KGB bastards. *We have to pacify the island,* they said. As if Iceland wasn't already passive enough. There had been not a single incident of active resistance yet—*not one,* the General thought, remembering his year's service in Afghanistan. Compared with that moun-tainous hell, this was paradise itself. But that wasn't good enough for the KGB! *Nekulturny* barbarians. A thousand hostages had been taken, only to learn that there was no jail space to keep them. *So my paratroopers must guard the poor, harmless wretches, using up a whole company of troops.* His orders were to cooperate with the local KGB contingent. One did not cooperate with the KGB, of course, one was dominated by them. There were KGB officers with his mobile patrols, to *advise,* they put it.

General Andreyev was beginning to worry. Crack paratroopers were not the sort to be good jailers. Had they been ordered to go easily on the Icelanders, that would be one thing. Instead, their orders forced them to be harsh, which generated hostility. Some people had actually been heard to cheer when the last American bombers had come through. Absurd, the General thought. They had lost electricity but we had lost nothing—and they cheered. Because of the KGB's orders. What stupidity. An opportunity lost. He considered protesting his orders to his central command in Moscow, but to what point? An officer who disliked the KGB was an officer who disliked the Party itself.

He was aroused from his reveries by the whining sound of turboshaft engines. The first of the Mi-24 Hinds was turning its rotor, testing its engines. An officer ran toward him.

"Comrade General, with your permission, we are ready for a test flight. We're doing it light, unarmed. We'll load weapons when we get back."

"Very well. Captain, just check out the hilltops around Keflavik and Rejkyavik. How long on the second one?" Andreyev asked.

"Two hours."

"Excellent. Good work, Comrade Captain."

A minute later the heavy attack chopper lifted into the air.

"Down and freeze!" Garcia screamed. It didn't come close to them, but seeing it was enough.

"What kind is it?"

"Hind. It's an attack bird, like the Cobra. Bad news, Lieutenant. It carries eight troops and a whole shitload of rockets and guns. An' don't even think about shooting at it. Sucker's armored like a damned tank."

The Mi-24 circled the hill they'd just been on, then disappeared, heading south to loop over another hill.

"Didn't see us, I guess," Edwards said.

"Let's keep it that way. Keep the radio stowed awhile, Lieutenant. We can call this one in after we move out a ways, okay?"

Edwards nodded agreement. He remembered a brief on Soviet helicopters in the Air Force Academy. "We are not afraid of the Russians," an Afghan had been quoted, "but we are afraid of their helicopters."

BITBURG, FEDERAL REPUBLIC OF GERMANY

Colonel Ellington awoke at six that evening. He shaved and walked outside, the sun still high in the evening sky. He wondered what mission they'd have tonight. He was not a bitter man, but to have nearly a quarter of his crews—men with whom he had worked for two straight years—lost in a week was a difficult thing to accept. It had been too long since his experience in Vietnam. He'd forgotten how terrible losses could be. His men could not stand down a day to mourn their dead and ease the pain, much as they needed to. They were being carefully rested. Standing orders gave them eight hours of sleep a day—like night-hunters, they slept only by day.

They were making a difference, however. He was sure of that. Every night the black and green Frisbees lifted off for some special target or other, and the Russians still had not figured a counter. The strike cameras mounted in each aircraft were bringing back pictures that the wing intelligence officers could scarcely believe. But at such a cost.

Well. The colonel reminded himself that one sortie a day was a lighter load than the other air crews were bearing, and that the close-support crews were taking losses equal to his own. Tonight held another mission. He ordered his brain to occupy itself with that task alone.

The briefings took an hour. Ten aircraft would fly tonight: two planes each at five targets. As commander he drew the toughest. Surveillance indicated that Ivan had a previously unsuspected forward fuel dump at a position west of Wittenburg that was supporting the drive on Hamburg, and the Germans wanted it taken out. His wingman would go in with Durandals, and he'd follow with Rockeyes. There would be no supporting aircraft on this one, and the colonel didn't want jammer aircraft to go in with him. Two of his lost birds had had such support, and the jamming had merely alerted the defenses.

He examined the topographical maps closely. The land was flat. Not much in the way of mountains and hills to hide behind, but then he could skim at treetop level, and that was almost as good. He'd approach from the east, behind the target. There was a twenty-knot west wind, and if he came in from leeward, the defenders would be unable to hear his approach until bomb release . . . probably. They'd egress the area by heading southwest. Total mission time seventy-five minutes. He computed his necessary fuel load, careful as always to allow for the drag of his bombs. To the bare-bones fuel requirements he added five minutes on afterburner in case of air-to-air combat and ten minutes to orbit Bitburg for landing. Satisfied, he went off for breakfast. With each bite of toast his mind ran through the mission like a movie, visualizing every event, every obstacle, every SAM site to be avoided. He randomly inserted the unexpected. A flight of low-level fighters at the target, what effect would this have on the mission? What would the target look like on this approach? If he had to make a second bombing pass, from what direction? Major Eisly ate with his commander in silence, recognizing the blank look on his face and running through his own mental checklist.

They headed straight into East Germany for fifty miles before turning north at Rathenow. Two Soviet Mainstay aircraft were up, a good distance back from the border and surrounded by agile Flanker interceptors. Staying well outside the effective range of their radar, the two aircraft flew low and in tight formation. When they screeched over main roads, it was always in a direction away from a course to their target. They avoided cities, towns, and known enemy depots where there might be SAMs.

The inertial navigation systems kept track of their progress on a map display on the pilot's instrument panel. The distance to the target shrank rapidly as the aircraft curved west.

They flashed over Wittenberg at five hundred knots. The infrared cameras showed fueling vehicles on the roads heading right for the target area . . . there! At least twenty tank trucks were visible in the trees, fueling from underground tanks.

"Target in sight. Execute according to plan."

"Roge," acknowledged Shade-Two. "I have them visual."

The Duke broke left, clearing the way for his wingman to make the first run. Shade-Two's aircraft was the only one left with the proper ejector racks for the bulky hard-target munitions.

"Gawd!" The Duke's display showed an SA-11 launcher right in his flight path, its missiles aimed northwest. One of his aircraft had learned the hard way that the SA-11 had an infrared homing capacity that no one had suspected. The colonel reefed his aircraft into a hard right turn away from the launcher, wondering where the rest of the missile battery's vehicles were.

Shade-Two skimmed over the target. The pilot toggled off his four bombs and kept heading west. Gunfire rippled across the sky in his wake. Too late.

The French-made Durandal weapons fell off the ejector racks and scattered. Once free, they pointed down, and rockets fired to accelerate the munitions straight at the ground. They were designed to break up concrete runways and were ideal for underground fuel tanks. The bombs did not explode on impact. Instead, the hard-steel weapons lanced into the ground, penetrating several feet before detonating. Three found underground fuel tanks. The Durandals exploded upward, breaking open a path for burning fuel to leap into the air.

It was the next thing to a nuclear detonation. Three white columns of flame rocketed into the air, spreading like fountains and dropping fuel for hundreds of yards. Every vehicle in the compound was engulfed in flame, and only those men near the perimeter escaped with their lives. Rubber fuel bladders brought to the site exploded a few seconds later, and a river of burning diesel and gasoline spread through the trees. In a matter of seconds, twenty acres of woods were transformed into a fireball that raced skyward, punctuated by secondary explosions. Ellington's fighter rocked violently as the shock wave passed.

"Damn," he said quietly. The plan called for him to use his cluster munitions to ignite what the Durandals had burst open.

"Don't think the Rockeyes are necessary, Duke," Eisly observed.

Ellington tried to blink away the dots as he turned away, keeping as low as he could. He found himself flying right down a road.

The Soviet Commander-in-Chief of the Western Theater was already angry, and what he saw to the east didn't help. He'd just conferred with the commander of the Third Shock Army at Zarrentin to learn that the attack had again bogged down within sight of Hamburg. Furious that his most powerful tank force had failed to achieve its objective, he'd relieved its commander on the spot and was returning to his own command post. Now he saw what could only be one of his three major fuel depots rising into the clear sky. The General cursed and stood, pushing aside the roof panel on his armored command vehicle. As he blinked his dazzled eyes, a black mass seemed to appear at the lower edge of the fireball.

What's that? Ellington wondered. His TV display showed four armored vehicles in a tight column—one of them a SAM launcher! He flicked his bomb-release controls to Armed and dropped his four Rockeye canisters, then turned south. His tail-mounted strike cameras recorded what followed.

The Rockeyes split open, distributing their bomblets at a shallow angle across the road. They exploded on impact.

* * *

CINC-West died a soldier's death. His last act was to seize a machine gun and fire at the aircraft. Four bomblets fell within a few meters of his vehicle. Their fragments sliced through the light armor, killing everyone inside even before its fuel tank exploded, adding another fireball to a sky that had still not returned to darkness.

USS *CHICAGO*

The submarine came slowly to the surface, spiraling up to allow her sonar to check the entire area as she rose to antenna depth. His luck had been bad so far, McCafferty considered, which was not a situation that encouraged risk taking. As the submarine leveled off beneath the waves, the ESM mast went up first, sniffing for hostile electronic signals, then the search periscope. The captain made a quick sweep around the sky, then the surface, his executive officer closely watching the television readout to back up the skipper's observations. Everything looked clear. There was a moderate sea running, with five-foot swells, and the clear blue sky was decorated with fair-weather cumulus clouds. On the whole, a beautiful day. Except for the war.

"Okay, transmit," McCafferty ordered. His eyes never left the periscope, which he turned continuously, angling the lens up and down to look for trouble. A petty officer raised the UHF antenna, and the "okay to transmit" light blinked on in the radio room aft of the attack center.

They had been summoned to the surface by an extremely low-frequency radio message with their call sign, QZB. The senior radioman powered up his transmitter, keyed out QZB on the UHF satellite broadcast band, and waited for a reply. There was none. He gave his neighbor a look and repeated the procedure. Again the satellite missed the signal. The petty officer took a deep breath and transmitted QZB yet a third time. Two seconds later the hot printer in the after corner of the room began to print up a coded reply. The communications officer keyed a command into the cipher machine, and the clear text came up on another printer.

TOP SECRET
FR: COMSUBLANT
TO: USS CHICAGO
1. REPORT LARGE REDFLT AMPHIBIOUS GRP DEPARTING KOLA 1150Z19JUNE. FORCE COMPOSITION 10-PLUS PHIBS WITH 15-PLUS COMBATANT ESCORT INCL KIROV, KIEV. HEAVY RPT HEAVY AIR ASW SUPPORT THIS GRP. EXPECT ALSO REDFLT SS / SSN SUPPORT THIS GRP. WESTERLY COURSE, HIGH SPEED.
2. EVALUATE OBJECTIVE THIS GRP BOD0.
3. PROCEED AT BEST SPEED TO 70N 16W.
4. ENGAGE AND DESTROY. REPORT CONTACT IF POSSIBLE BEFORE ATTACK. OTHER NATO SS / SSN TRAFFIC THIS AREA. AIR SUPPORT POSSIBLE BUT NOT RPT NOT LIKELY AT PRESENT.
5. WILL AMPLIFY LOCATION THIS GRP AS POSSIBLE.

McCafferty read the dispatch without comment, then handed it to the navigator. "How long to get there at fifteen knots?"

"About eleven hours." The navigator took a pair of dividers and walked them across the chart. "Unless they're flying, we'll be there long before they are."

"Joe?" The captain looked at his executive officer.

"I like it. Right on the hundred-fathom curve, and water conditions are a little squirrelly there, what with the Gulf Stream coming in so close and fresh water coming out of the fjords. They won't want to be too close inshore because of the Norwegian diesel boats, and they won't stray too far out because of the NATO nucs. If I had to bet, I'd say they'll come right to us."

"Okay, take her down to nine hundred feet and head east. Secure from general quarters. Let's get everybody fed and rested."

Ten minutes later, *Chicago* was on a heading of zero-eight-one, steaming at fifteen knots. Deep, but in relatively warm water from the ocean current that begins in the Gulf of Mexico and runs all the way to the Barents Sea, she enjoyed sonar conditions that made detection by a surface ship nearly impossible. The water pressure prevented cavitation noises. Her engines could drive the submarine at this speed with only a fraction of her total rated power, obviating the need for the reactor pumps. The reactor's cooling water circulated on natural convection currents, which eliminated the major source of radiated noise. *Chicago* was completely in her element, a noiseless shadow moving through black water.

The crew's mood changed slightly, McCafferty noticed. Now they had a mission. A dangerous mission, but one they had trained for. Orders were carried out with calm precision. In the wardroom his tactical officers reviewed tracking and attack procedures long since memorized, and a pair of exercises were run on a computer. Charts were examined to predict likely places for especially bad water conditions in which they might hide. In the torpedo room two decks below the attack center, sailors ran electronic tests on green-painted Mk-48 "fish" and the Harpoon missiles in their white canisters. One weapon showed an electronic fault, and a pair of torpedomen immediately stripped off an inspection plate to replace a component. Similar checks were made of the Tomahawk missiles in their vertical launch tubes nested in the bow. Finally the weapons-control team ran a computer simulation through the Mk-117 attack director to ensure that it was fully operational. Within two hours they were sure that every system aboard was operating within expected limits. The crewmen exchanged hopeful smiles. After all, they reasoned, it wasn't their fault that no Russian had been dumb enough to come their way, was it? Just a few days before, hadn't they practically landed on the beach—in Russia!—without being detected? The Old Man was a real pro, wasn't he?

USS *PHARRIS*

Dinner was awkward to say the least. The three Russian officers sat at the end of the table, mindful of the two armed guards ten feet away, and the cook in the wardroom pantry who kept a large knife conspicuously in view. The officers were served by a young seaman, a beardless boy of seventeen who scowled mightily at the Russians as he served the salad.

"So," Morris said cordially, "do any of you speak English?"

"I do," answered one. "I am instructed my captain to thank you for rescue our men."

"Tell your captain that war has rules, and so does the sea. Please tell him also that he showed great skill in his approach." Morris poured some Thousand Island dressing on his lettuce as the message was translated. His officers were keeping a close eye on their guests. Morris was careful to avert his gaze. His remark had the desired effect. A rapid exchange took place at the other end of the table.

"My captain ask how you find us. We—how you say—get away from your helicopters, no?"

"Yes, you did," Morris answered. "We did not understand your operating pattern."

"Then how you find us?"

"I knew you were attacked earlier by the Orion, and that you ran at high speed to catch up with us. The angle for your attack was predictable."

The Russian shook his head. "What attack is this? Who attack us?" He turned to his commander and spoke for thirty seconds.

There's another Charlie out there, Morris thought, *if he's not lying to us. We ought to get someone who speaks Russian to talk to the crewmen below. Damn, why don't I have one of those?*

"My captain says you are mistake in this. Our first contact with you was from helicopters. We did not expect your ship to be here. Is this new tactic?"

"No, we've practiced this for some years."

"How you find us, then?"

"You know what a towed-array sonar is? We first detected you on that, about three hours before we shot at you."

The Russian's eyes went wide. "Your sonar so good as that?"

"Sometimes." After this was translated the Russian captain spoke what seemed a terse order, and the conversation stopped. Morris wondered if his radio technicians had wired the microphone into the Russians' quarters yet. Perhaps what they said among themselves would be useful to fleet intelligence. Until then he'd continue to make them comfortable. "How is the food aboard a Soviet submarine?"

"Not same as this," the navigator answered after conferring with his boss. "Good, but not same. We eat different foods. More fish, less meat. We have tea, not coffee."

Ed Morris saw that his prisoners were going after their plates with scarcely concealed gusto. *Even our sub guys don't get enough fresh vegetables,* he reminded himself. An enlisted man entered the wardroom and stood by the door. It was his leading radioman. Morris waved him over.

The sailor handed the captain a message form. THE SPECIAL JOB IS DONE, it read, and Morris noted that the man had taken the time to print it up on a standard message format so that no one would suspect what it meant. The Russians' accommodations were all bugged now. Morris dismissed his man with a nod and pocketed the form. His bosun had miraculously discovered two bottles of hard liquor—probably from the chiefs' quarters, but Morris knew better than to inquire—and these would find their way to the Russians tonight. He hoped the liquor would loosen tongues.

24. Rape

USS *PHARRIS*

Morris didn't wave at the low-flying aircraft, but wanted to. The French Navy's patrol plane signaled that they were within range of land-based air cover. It would take a very brave Russian sub skipper to want to play games here, with a screen of French diesel subs a few miles north of the convoy lane and several ASW patrol aircraft forming a tricolored umbrella over the convoy.

The French had also sent out a helicopter to collect the Russian submariners. They were being flown to Brest for a full interrogation by NATO intelligence types. Morris didn't envy them the trip. They'd be held by the French, and he had no doubt that the French Navy was in an evil mood after the loss of one of its carriers. The tapes his crew had made of their conversations were also being sent. The Russians had talked among themselves, aided by the chiefs' liquor, and perhaps their whispered conversations had some value.

They were about to turn the convoy over to a mixed British-French escort force and take over a group of forty merchantmen bound for America. Morris stood on the bridge wing, turning every five minutes or so to look at the two half and one full silhouettes that the bosun had painted on *both* sides of the pilothouse—"No sense having some jerk on the wrong side of the ship missing them," the bosun had pointed out seriously. Their ASW tactics had worked fairly well. With *Pharris* as outlying sonar picket, and heavy support from the Orions, they had intercepted all but one of the inbound Russian subs. There had been a lot of skepticism on this point, but the tactic had worked, by God. But it had to work better still.

Morris knew that things would be getting harder. For the first trip the Soviets had been able to put no more than a fraction of their submarines into action against them. Those submarines were now forcing their way down the Denmark Strait. The NATO sub force trying to block the passage no longer had the SOSUS line to give them intercept vectors, nor Orions to pounce on the contacts that submarines could not reach. They would score kills, but would they score enough? How much larger would the threat be this week? Morris could see from their return route to the States that they were adding nearly five hundred miles to the passage by looping far to the south—partially because of the Backfires, but more now to dilute the submarine threat. Two threats to worry about. His ship was equipped to deal with only one.

They'd lost a third of the convoy, mainly to aircraft. Could they sustain that? He wondered how the merchant crews were holding up.

They had closed in on the convoy, and he could see the northernmost line of merchies. On the horizon a big container ship was blinking a light at them. Morris raised his glasses to read the signal.

THANKS FOR NOTHING NAVY. One question answered.

USS *CHICAGO*

"So, there they are," McCafferty said.

The trace showed almost white on the screen, a thick spoke of broadband noise bearing three-two-nine. It could only be the Soviet task force heading for Bodø.

"How far out?" McCafferty asked.

"At least two CZs, skipper, maybe three. The signal just increased in intensity four minutes ago."

"Can you get a blade count on anything?"

"No, sir." The sonarman shook his head. "Just a lot of undifferentiated noise for the moment. We've tried to isolate a few discrete frequencies, but even that's all screwed up. Maybe later, but all we got now is a thundering herd."

McCafferty nodded. The third convergence zone was a good hundred miles off. At such ranges acoustical signals lost definition, to the point that their bearing to target was only a rough estimate. The Russian formation could be several degrees left or right of where they thought, and at this range that was a difference measured in miles. He went aft to Control.

"Take her west five miles at twenty knots," McCafferty ordered. It was a gamble, but a small one. On reaching station, they'd found unusually good water conditions, and the small move risked losing the contact temporarily. On the other hand, getting precise range information would give him a much better tactical picture and enable them to make a solid contact report—and make it by line-of-sight UHF radio before the Soviet formation got close enough that they could intercept the submarine's transmission. As the boat raced west, McCafferty watched the bathythermograph trace. As long as the temperature didn't change, he'd keep that good sound channel. It didn't. The submarine slowed rapidly and McCafferty went back to sonar.

"Okay, where are they now?"

"Got 'em! Right there, bearing three-three-two."

"XO, plot it and get a contact report made up."

Ten minutes later the report was sent via satellite. The reply ordered *Chicago* in: GO FOR THE HEAVIES

ICELAND

The farm was three miles away, thankfully downhill through tall, rough grass. On first sighting it through binoculars, Edwards called it the Gingerbread House. A typical Icelandic farmhouse, it had white stucco walls buttressed by heavy wooden beams, a contrasting red-painted trim, and a steeply pitched roof right out of the Brothers Grimm. The outlying barns were large, but low-slung with sod-covered roofs. The lower meadows by the stream were dotted with hundreds of large, odd-looking sheep with massively thick coats of wool, asleep in the grass half a mile beyond the house.

"Dead-end road," Edwards said, folding up the map. "And we could use some food. Gentlemen, it's worth the chance, but we approach *carefully*. We'll follow this dip to the right and keep that ridgeline between us and the farm till we're within half a mile or so."

"Okay, sir," Sergeant Smith agreed. The four men struggled into a sitting position to don their gear yet again. They'd been moving almost continuously for two and a half days, and were now about thirty-five miles northeast of Reykjavik. A modest pace on flat roads, it was a man-killing effort cross country, particularly while staying watchful for the helicopters that were now patrolling the countryside. They had consumed their last rations six hours before. The cool temperatures and hard physical effort conspired to drain the energy from their bodies as they picked their way around and over the two-thousand-foot hills that dotted the Icelandic coast like so many fence pickets.

Several things kept them moving. One was the fear that the Soviet division they had watched airlifted in would expand its perimeter and snap them up. No one relished the thought of captivity under the Russians. But worse than this was fear of failure. They had a mission, and no taskmaster is harsher than one's own self-expectations. Then there was pride. Edwards had to set an example for his men, a principle remembered from Colorado Springs. The Marines, of course, could hardly let a "wing-wiper" outperform them. Thus, without thinking consciously about it, four men contrived to walk themselves into the ground, all in the name of pride.

"Gonna rain," Smith said.

"Yeah, the cover will be nice," Edwards said, still sitting back. "We'll wait for it. Jesus, I never thought working in daylight would be so Goddamned tough. There's just something weird about not having the friggin' sun go down."

"Tell me about it. And I ain't even got a cigarette," Smith growled.

"Rain *again?*" Private Garcia asked.

"Get used to it," Edwards said. "It rains seventeen days in June, on average, and so far this's been a wet year. How d'you think the grass got so tall?"

"You like this place?" Garcia asked, dumbfounded enough to forget the "sir." Iceland had little in common with Puerto Rico.

"My dad's a lobsterman working out of Eastpoint, Maine. When I was a kid I went out on the boat every time I could, and it was always like this."

"What we gonna do when we get down to that house, sir?" Smith brought them back to things that mattered.

"Ask for food—"

"Ask?" Garcia was surprised.

"Ask. And pay for it, with cash. And smile. And say, 'Thank you, sir,' " Edwards said. "Remember your manners, guys, unless you want him to phone Ivan ten minutes after we leave." He looked around at his men. The thought sobered them all.

The rain started with a few sprinkles. Two minutes later it was falling heavily, cutting visibility down to a few hundred yards. Edwards wearily got to his feet, forcing his Marines to do likewise, and they all moved downhill as the sun above the clouds dipped in the northwestern sky and slid down behind a hill. The hill—since they'd probably have to climb it the next day, they thought of it as a mountain—had a name, but none of them could pronounce it. By the time they were a quarter mile from the farmhouse, it was as dark as it would get, and the rain had the visibility down to about eighty yards.

"Car coming." Smith saw the glare of the lights first. All four men dropped and instinctively aimed their rifles at the dots on the horizon.

"Relax, guys. This road here breaks off the main road, and those lights could just be—*shit!*" Edwards cursed. The lights hadn't taken the sweeping turn on the coastal highway. They were coming down the road to the farm. Was it a car or a track with its driving lights on? "Spread out and stay awake." Smith stayed with Edwards, and the two privates moved downhill about fifty yards.

Edwards lay prone, his elbows propped up on the wet grass and binoculars to his eyes. He didn't think they could be spotted. The Marine pattern camouflage made them nearly invisible in daylight as long as they didn't move rapidly. In the dark they were transparent shadows.

"Looks like a pickup, four-by-four, something like that. Lights are pretty far off the ground, bouncing around too much to be a track," Edwards thought aloud.

The lights came directly—but slowly—to the farmhouse and stopped. Its doors opened, men got out, and one stepped in front of the headlights before they were extinguished.

"Damn!" Smith snarled.

"Yep, looks like four or five Ivans. Get Garcia and Rodgers over here, Sergeant."

"Right."

Edwards kept his binoculars on the house. There were no electric lights lit. He guessed that this area got its power from Artun, and he'd watched the bombs wipe that plant off the map. There was some internal illumination, though, maybe from candles or a hurricane lamp. It really was a lot like home, Edwards told himself; our electricity went off often enough, from nor'eastern storms or ice on the wires. The people in that house had to be asleep. *Working farmers, early to bed, early to rise—wears you out and dulls the brain,* Edwards thought. Through the lenses he watched the Russians—he counted five—circle the house. *Like burglars,* he thought. They looking for . . . us? No. If they were looking for us, there'd be more than five guys in a four-by-four. *That's interesting. They must be looting—but what if somebody . . . Jesus, we know that* somebody *lives there. Somebody lit that lamp. What are they up to?*

"What gives, sir?" Smith asked.

"Looks like we got five Russkies. They're playing peeper, looking in the windows and—one just kicked the door in! I don't like the way this is going, troops, I—"

A scream confirmed his evaluation. A woman's scream, it cut right through the falling rain and made them feel someone's terror, chilling men already cold.

"People, let's move in a little. We stay together and we damned well stay alert."

"Why we movin' in now, sir?" Smith asked sharply.

" 'Cuz I say so." Edwards stowed his field glasses. "Follow me."

Another light was lit in the building, and it seemed to be moving around. Edwards walked quickly, keeping low in a way that punished his back. In two minutes he was a few yards from the truck that had driven in, no more than twenty yards from the home's front door.

"Sir, you're getting a little careless," Smith warned.

"Yeah, well, if I guess right, so are they. I bet—"

There was a sound of breaking glass. A shot rang out through the semi-darkness. It was followed by a blood-chilling shriek—and a second shot, and a third. Then there was another scream.

"What the hell's going on in there?" Garcia asked in a rasp.

A hoarse male voice shouted something in Russian. The front door opened and four men came out. They conferred for a moment, then split into pairs, going left and right to side windows, where all four men stood to look inside. Then there came another scream, and it was perfectly clear what was going on.

"Those son of a bitches," Smith observed.

"Yeah," Lieutenant Edwards agreed. "Let's back off and think about this for a minute." The four men retreated about fifty yards and bunched together.

"I think it's time we do something. Anybody disagree?" Edwards asked. Smith just nodded, interested in Edwards's change of demeanor. "Okay, we take our time and do it right. Smith, you come with me and we go around the left. Garcia and Rodgers go around the right. Go wide and come in slow. Ten minutes. If you can take 'em alive, that's okay. If not, stick 'em. We try not to make noise. But if you gotta shoot, make God-damned sure the first burst does it. Okay?" Edwards looked around for additional Russians. None. The four men slipped out of their packs, checked their watches, and moved out, crawling through the wet grass.

There was another scream, but none after that. Edwards was glad there weren't—he didn't need the distraction. The crawling was a slow, tiring effort that sapped the strength from his arms. Edwards and Smith took a long route, around a tractor and some other implements. When they came into the clear there was only one man on their side of the house. *Where's the other one?* the lieutenant asked himself. *Now what do we do? You gotta stick to the plan. Everyone's depending on you.*

"Back me up."

Smith was amazed. "Let me, sir, I—"

"Back me up," Edwards whispered. He set his M-16 down and drew his combat knife.

The Russian soldier made it easy, as he stood on tiptoe, entranced with the goings-on within the farmhouse. Ten feet behind him, Edwards got to his feet and approached one slow step at a time. It took him a moment to realize that his target was a full head taller than he was—how was he supposed to take this monster alive?

He didn't have to. There must have been an intermission inside. The Soviet private slumped down and reached in his pocket for a pack of cigarettes, then turned slightly to light one from a cupped match. He caught Edwards out of the corner of his eye, and the American lieutenant lunged forward with his knife, stabbing the larger man in the throat. The Russian started to cry out, but Edwards wrestled him down and slapped his left hand over the man's mouth as he struck again with the knife. Edwards twisted the man's head one way, and the knife the other. The blade grated against something hard, and his victim went slack.

Edwards felt nothing, his emotions submerged in a flood of adrenaline. He wiped the knife on his trousers and stood on the man's body to look in the window. What he saw caught the breath in his throat.

"Hi, guys!" Garcia whispered. Two Russian privates turned to face a pair of M-16s. They had left their rifles in the truck. Garcia gestured at the ground with his rifle, and both men went facedown, spread-eagled. Rodgers frisked them both for weapons, then went around the front to report in.

"Took 'em both alive, sir." He was surprised to see their "wing-wiper" lieutenant with blood on his hands.

"I'm going in," Edwards told Smith. The sergeant nodded quickly.

"I'll cover you from here. Rodgers, you back him up."

The lieutenant moved through the half-open door. The living room was empty and unlit. The noise of heavy breathing came from around the corner, and a steady pale light. Edwards approached the corner—and found himself faced with a Russian in the process of unbuttoning his pants. There was no time for much of anything.

Edwards rammed his knife under the man's ribs, turning his right hand within the brass-knuckled grip as he pushed the blade all the way in. The man screamed and lifted himself up on his toes before falling backward, trying to get himself off the knife. Edwards withdrew and stabbed again, falling atop the man in a grotesquely sexual position. The paratrooper's hands tried to force him off, but the lieutenant felt the strength drain from his victim as he moved farther forward to stab him again in the chest. A shadow moved and he looked up to see a man stumbling forward with a pistol—and the room exploded with noise.

"*Freeze, motherfucker!*" Rodgers screamed, his M-16 aimed at the man's chest, and everyone's ears ringing from the thunder of the three-round burst. "You okay, skipper?" It was the first time they had called him that.

"Yeah." Edwards got to his feet, letting Rodgers precede him as he backed the Russian up. The man was exposed below the waist, his pants hobbling his ankles. The lieutenant picked up the pistol the Soviet had dropped and looked down at the man he'd knifed. There was no doubt that he was dead. His handsome Slavic face was contorted with surprise and pain, and his uniform blouse was soaked black with blood. The eyes might have been marbles for all the life they contained.

"You okay, ma'am?" Rodgers asked, briefly turning his head around.

Edwards saw her for the second time, sprawled out on the wooden floor. A pretty girl, her woolen nightdress torn apart, barely covering one breast, and the rest of her pale body, already red and bruised in several places, exposed for all to see. Beyond her in the kitchen Edwards saw the unmoving legs of another woman. He went into the room and saw a dog and a man, also dead. Each body displayed a single red circle in the chest.

Smith came in. He looked around the room, then at Edwards. The wimp had fangs. "I'll check the upstairs. Heads up, skipper."

Rodgers kicked the Russian down to the floor and placed his bayonet point in the small of his back. "You move and I'll fuckin' cut you in half," the private snarled.

Edwards stooped down to the blond girl. Her face was puffing up from blows to the jaw and cheek, her breath coming in shudders. He guessed her age at twenty or so. Her nightdress was destroyed. Edwards looked around and, pulling the cloth off the dining room table, draped it over her.

"You okay? Come on, you're alive, honey. You're safe. You're okay now."

Her eyes seemed pointed in different directions at first, then they focused and came over to the young lieutenant. Edwards cringed to see the look in them. His hand touched her cheek as gently as he could.

"Come on, let's get you up off the floor. Nobody's going to hurt you, not now." She started shaking so violently that it seemed the whole house would join her. He helped her up, careful to wrap the tablecloth all around her. "Come on."

"Upstairs is clear, sir." Smith returned, holding a robe. "You wanna put this on the lady? They do anything else to her?"

"Killed her mom and dad. And a dog. I imagine they were going to do her, too, when they got finished. Sarge, get things organized. Search the Russians, get some food, anything else that looks useful. Move quick, Jim. Lots of things we gotta do. You have a first-aid pack?"

"Right, skipper. Here." Smith tossed him a small package of bandages and antiseptics, then went back out the door to check on Garcia.

"Let's get you upstairs and cleaned off." Edwards wrapped his left arm around her shoulders and helped her up the steep old wooden steps. His heart went out to the girl. She had china-blue eyes, obscenely empty of life though even now they caught the light in a way certain to attract any man's attention. *As they just had,* Edwards thought. She was only an inch shorter than he, with pale, almost transparent skin. Her figure was marred by a slight bulge at the abdomen, and Mike had a good idea what that was, the rest of her figure was so perfect. And she'd just been raped by one Russian, paving the way for a long night of it, Mike Edwards thought, enraged that once more this foul crime had touched his life. There was a small room at the top of the twisting stairs. She entered it and sat on the single bed.

"Wh-wh-who—" she stammered in accented English.

"We're Americans. We escaped from Keflavik when the Russians attacked. What's your name?"

"Vigdis Agustdottir." The slightest sign of life in her voice. Vigdis, the daughter of Agust, dead in the kitchen. He wondered what Vigdis meant, sure that it wasn't pretty enough.

He set the hurricane lamp on the night table and broke open the pack. Her skin was broken along the jawline, and he swabbed disinfectant there. It had to hurt, but the girl didn't wince at all. The rest of her, he'd seen, was just bruised, maybe some scrapes on her back from the hardwood floor. She'd fought hard to defend herself, and taken a dozen punches. And certainly she was no virgin. Just a bloodied face. It could have been far worse, but Edwards's rage continued to grow. Such a pretty face desecrated—well, he'd already reached that decision. "You can't stay here. We have to leave soon. You'll have to leave, too."

"But—"

"I'm sorry. I understand—I mean, when the Russians attacked, I lost some friends, too. Not the same as your mom and dad, but—Jesus!" Edwards's hands shook in frustration as he stumbled through the meaningless words. "I'm sorry we didn't get here sooner." *What is it that some of the feminists say? That rape is the crime that all men use to subjugate all women? Then why do you want to go downstairs and—* Edwards knew that something almost as satisfying was in the works. He took her hand and she didn't resist. "We're going to have to leave. We'll take you anywhere we can. You must have family around here, or friends. We'll take you to them and they can take care of you. But you can't stay here. If you stay here, you're sure to get killed. Do you understand?" He saw her head nod jerkily in the shadows.

"Yes. Please—please leave me alone. I must be alone for a little."

"Okay." He touched her cheek again. "If you need anything, call us." Edwards went back downstairs. Smith had taken charge. There were three men on their knees, blindfolded, gagged, and hands tied behind their backs. Garcia was standing over them. Rodgers was in the kitchen. Smith was sorting through a pile of stuff on the table.

"Okay, what d'we got here?"

Smith regarded his officer with something akin to affection. "Well, sir, we got us a Russian lieutenant with a wet dick. A dead sergeant. A dead private, and two live ones. The lieutenant had this, sir."

Edwards took the map and unfolded it. "Damn, ain't that nice!" The map was covered with scribbled markings.

"We got another set of binoculars, a radio—shame we can't use that! Some rations. Looks like shit, but better'n nothin'. We done good, skipper. Bag five Russians with three rounds expended."

"What do we need to take, Jim?"

"Just food, sir. I mean, we could take a couple of their rifles, and that'd double up our ammo load, y'know? But we're already loaded pretty heavy—"

"And we aren't here to fight a war, just to play scout. Right."

"I think we oughta take some clothes, sweaters and like that. We taking the lady with us?"

"Have to."

Smith nodded. "Yeah, makes sense. Hope she likes walkin', sir. Looks like she's in decent shape, 'cept for being pregnant. Four months, I'd say."

"Pregnant?" Garcia turned. "Rapin' a pregnant girl?" He muttered something in Spanish.

"Any of them say anything?" Mike asked.

"Not a word, sir." Garcia answered.

"Jim, take a look at the girl, and get her down here. Her name's Vigdis. Easy on her."

"Don't worry, sir." Smith went upstairs.

"The lieutenant's the one with it hanging out, right?" Garcia nodded and Edwards went around to face him. He had to remove the gag and blindfold. The man was his own age. He was sweating. "You speak English?"

The man shook his head. *"Spreche deutsch."*

Edwards had taken two years of German in high school, but suddenly found himself unwilling to talk with this man. He had already decided to kill him, and he didn't wish to speak with someone he was about to kill— it might bother his conscience. Edwards didn't want his conscience to remember this. But he watched the man for a minute or two, examining what sort of person would do what he had done. He expected to discover something monstrous, but didn't. He looked up. Smith was leading Vigdis down the stairs.

"She's got good gear, skipper. Nice warm clothes, her boots are all broke in. I expect we can get her a canteen, a parka, and a field pack. I'd let her bring a brush an' girl stuff, sir. I'll get us some soap, too, and maybe a razor."

"Way to go, Sergeant. Vigdis," Edwards said, getting her attention. "We will be leaving soon." He turned to look back down at the Russian:

"Leutnant. Wofür? Warum?" What for—why did you do all this? Not for me. For her.

The man knew what was coming. He shrugged. "Afghanistan."

"Skipper, they're prisoners," Rodgers blurted. "I mean, sir, you can't—"

"Gentlemen, you are charged under Uniform Code of Military Justice with one specification of rape and two specifications of murder. These are capital crimes," Edwards said, mainly so that he could assuage his conscience for the other two. "Do you have anything to say in your defense?

No? You are found guilty. Your sentence is death." With his left hand, Edwards pushed the lieutenant's head back. His right hand flipped the knife into the air, reversing it; then he swung it viciously, striking the man's larynx with the pommel. The sound was surprisingly loud in the room, and Edwards kicked him backward.

A terrible thing to watch, it lasted several minutes. The lieutenant's larynx was instantly fractured, and its swelling blocked his trachea. Unable to breathe, his torso bucked from side to side as his face darkened. Everyone in the room who could see watched. If any felt pity for the man, none showed it. Finally he stopped moving.

"I'm sorry we weren't faster, Vigdis, but this *thing* won't be hurting anyone else." Edwards hoped that his amateur psychiatry would work. The girl went back upstairs, probably to wash, he thought. He'd read that after being raped one thing women wanted to do was bathe, as though there were a visible stigma from being the victim of an animal's lust. He turned toward the remaining two. There was no way they could manage prisoners, and what they had been up to merely provided him with a good excuse. But these two hadn't hurt the girl yet, and—

"I'll take care of it, sir," Garcia said quietly. The private was standing behind the kneeling prisoners. One of them was making some noise, but even if he hadn't been gagged, none of the Americans knew a word of Russian. They had no chance at all. Garcia stabbed from the side, sticking his knife completely through one neck, then the other. Both men fell. It was over quickly. The private and the lieutenant went into the kitchen to wash their hands.

"Okay, we load them back into the four-by-four and drive it back to the main road. We'll see if we can fake an accident and torch the vehicle. Get some liquor bottles. We'll make it look like they were drinking."

"They were, sir." Rodgers held up a bottle of clear liquor.

Edwards gave the bottle a brief look, but shook off the thought. "Figures. If I guess right, these guys were the crossroads guards from the main highway—or maybe just a patrol. I don't think they can guard every crossroads on this island. If we're just a little lucky, maybe their bosses'll never figure out we were involved in this." *A long shot,* he thought, *but what the hell?*

"Skipper," Smith said. "If you want to do that, we gotta—"

"I know. You and Rodgers stay here and get ready. If you see anything else we can use, pack it up. When we get back, we'll have to haul ass."

Edwards and Garcia loaded all the bodies into the back of the truck, careful to sort through the battle gear. They unloaded waterproof parkas whose camouflage pattern was almost identical with their own and a few other items that wouldn't be missed, then drove off quickly down the road.

Luck was with them. There was no permanent guard post at the crossroads, perhaps because the farm road led nowhere. The Russians had probably been a patrol team, and had chosen the farm for a little informal R&R. Two hundred yards down the coastal highway the road paralleled a steep cliff. They halted the vehicle there and manhandled the bodies into the seats. Garcia emptied a jerrican of gasoline into the back and the two men pushed it toward the edge with the rear hatch open. Garcia tossed a Russian grenade into the back as it went over the edge. Neither man wanted to admire their handiwork. They ran back the half mile to the farmhouse. Everything was ready.

"We have to burn the house, Miss Vigdis," Smith was explaining. "If we don't, the Russians'll know for sure what happened here. Your mom and dad are dead, ma'am, but I'm sure they'd want you to stay alive, okay?''

She was still too much in shock to offer more than token resistance. Rodgers and Smith had cleaned off the bodies, and moved them upstairs to their own bedroom. It would have been better to bury them, but there just wasn't time.

"Let's get moving, people," Edwards ordered. They should have been moving already. Somebody had to be coming to investigate the burning truck, and if they used a chopper . . . "Garcia, you watch the lady. Smith has the rear. Rodgers, take the point. We have to put six miles between us and this place in the next three hours."

Smith waited ten minutes before tossing his grenade into the house. The kerosene he'd spread on the first floor went up at once.

USS *CHICAGO*

The contact was a lot better now. They had classified one ship as a Kashin-class missile destroyer, and her propeller-blade count indicated a speed of twenty-one knots. The leading elements of the Soviet formation were now thirty-seven miles away. There seemed to be two groups, the leading formation fanned out and screening the second. McCafferty ordered the ESM mast raised. It showed lots of activity, but he expected that.

"Up scope." The quartermaster worked the operating ring, then snapped the handles into place and stepped back. McCafferty swept the horizon quickly. After ten seconds, he flipped the handles up, and the periscope was instantly lowered back into its well.

"It's going to be a busy day, troops," the captain said; he always let the attack center crew know as much of what was going on as possible. The more they knew, the better they could do their jobs. "I saw a pair of Bear-Fs, one due north, the other west. Both a good way off, but you can bet they're dropping sonobuoys. XO, take her back down to five hundred feet, speed five knots. We'll let them come to us."

"Conn, sonar."

"Conn, aye," McCafferty answered.

"We got some pingers, active sonobuoys to the northwest. We count six of them, all very faint." The sonar chief read off the bearings to the signal sources. "Still no active sonar signals coming from the target formation, sir."

"Very well." McCafferty returned the mike to its holder. *Chicago*'s depth was changing quickly, as they dove at a fifteen-degree angle. He watched the bathythermograph readout. At two hundred twenty feet the water temperature began to drop rapidly, changing twelve degrees inside of seventy feet. Good, a strong layer to hide under, and cold water deep to allow good sonar performance for his own sensors.

Two hours before he had removed a torpedo from one of his tubes and replaced it with a Harpoon missile. It gave him only one torpedo ready for instant use if he found a submarine target, but a salvo of three missiles available to fling at surface ships, plus his Tomahawks. He could fire either now, and expect hits, but McCafferty didn't want to fire at just anything. There was no sense wasting a missile on a small patrol craft when there was a cruiser and a carrier out there waiting for him. He wanted to identify specific targets first. It wouldn't be easy, but he knew that easy things didn't have to be done by the 688-class subs. He went forward into sonar.

The chief caught him out the corner of his eye. "Skipper, I may have a bearing to *Kirov*. I just copied six pings from a low-frequency sonar. I think that's him, bearing zero-three-nine. Trying to isolate his engine signature now. And if—okay, some more sonobuoys are dropping to the right." The display showed new points of light well to the right of the first string, and a sizable gap between the two.

"Think he's dropping them in chevrons, Chief?" McCafferty asked. He got a smile and a nod for an answer. If the Soviets were deploying their sonobuoys in angled lines left and right of the formation, that could mean that their ships were heading right for *Chicago*. The submarine would not have to maneuver at all to intercept them. She could stay as quiet as an open grave.

"They seem to be alternating them above and below the layer, sir. A pretty fair gap between them, too." The chief lit a cigarette without averting his eyes from the screen. The ashtray next to him was crammed with butts.

"We'll plot that one out. Good work, Barney." The captain patted his sonar chief on the shoulder and went back to the attack center. The fire-control tracking party was already plotting the new contacts. It looked like an interval of just over two miles between the sonobuoys. If the Soviets were alternating them above and below the layer, there was a good chance he could sneak between a pair. The other question was the presence of passive buoys, whose presence he could not detect.

McCafferty stood at the periscope pedestal, watching his men at work as they entered data into the fire-control computers, backed up by other men with paper plots and hand-held calculators. The weapons-control panel was lit up by indicators showing ready. The submarine was at battle stations.

"Take her up to two hundred feet, we'll listen above the layer for a few minutes." The maneuver paid off at once.

"I got direct-path to the targets," the sonar chief announced. They could now detect and track sound energy radiating directly from the Soviet ships, without depending on the on-again, off-again convergence zones.

McCafferty commanded himself to relax. He'd soon have work enough.

"Captain, we're about due for another sonobuoy drop. They've been averaging about every fifteen minutes, and this one might be close."

"Getting that Horse-Jaw sonar again, sir," sonar warned. "Bearing three-two-zero at this time. Signal weak. Classify this contact as the cruiser *Kirov*. Stand by—another one. We have a medium-frequency active sonar bearing three-three-one, maneuvering left-to-right. We classify this contact as a Kresta-II ASW cruiser."

"I think he's right," the plotting officer said. "Bearing three-two-zero is close to our bearings for a pair of screen ships, but far enough off that it's probably a different contact. Three-three-one is consistent with the center screen ship. It figures. The Kresta will be the screen commander, with the flagship a ways behind him. Need some time to work out the ranges, though."

The captain ordered his submarine to stay above the layer, able to duck beneath it in seconds. The tactical display was evolving now. He had a workable bearing on *Kirov*. Almost good enough to shoot on, though he still needed range data. There seemed to be a pair of escorts between him and the cruiser, and unless he had a proper range estimate, any missile he launched at the Soviet flagship might attack a destroyer or frigate by mistake. In the interim, the solution on the attack director set the Harpoons to fly straight for what he believed to be the battle cruiser *Kirov*.

Chicago began to zigzag left and right of her course track. As the submarine changed her position, the bearing to her sonar contacts changed also. The tracking party could use the submarine's own course deviation as a baseline to compute ranges to the various contacts. A straightforward process—essentially an exercise in high-school trigonometry—it nevertheless took time because they had to estimate the speed and course of the moving targets. Even computer support couldn't make the process go much faster, and one of his quartermasters took great pride in his ability to use a circular slide rule and race the computer to a hard solution.

The tension seemed to grow by degrees, then it plateaued. The years of training were paying off. Data was handled, plotted, and acted upon in seconds. The crew suddenly seemed a physical part of the gear they were operating, their feelings shut off, their emotions submerged, only the sweat on their foreheads betraying that they were men after all, and not machines. They depended absolutely on their sonar operators. Sound energy was their only indication of what was happening, and each new bearing report triggered furious activity. It was clear that their targets were zigzagging, which made the range computations even more difficult.

"Conn, sonar! Active sonobuoy close aboard to port! Below the layer, I think."

"Right full rudder, all ahead two-thirds," the executive officer ordered instantly.

McCafferty went to sonar and plugged in a set of headphones. The pings were loud but . . . distorted, he thought. If the buoy was below the temperature gradient, the signals radiating upward would be unable to detect his submarine—probably. "Signal strength?" he asked.

"Strong," the chief replied. "Even money they might have picked us up. Five hundred yards farther out and they lose us for sure."

"Okay, they can't monitor them all at once."

The XO moved *Chicago* a thousand yards before returning to base course. Overhead, they knew, was a Bear-F ASW aircraft armed with homing torpedoes and a crew whose job it was to listen to the sonobuoy signals. How good were the buoys and the men? That was one thing that they didn't know. Three tense minutes passed and nothing happened.

"All ahead one-third, come left to three-two-one," the executive officer ordered. They were now through the line of buoys. Three more such lines were between them and their target. They'd nearly determined range for three of the escorts, but not to the *Kirov* yet.

"Okay, people, the Bears are behind us. That's one less thing to worry about. Range to the nearest ship?" he asked the approach officer.

"Twenty-six thousand yards. We think he's a Sovremenny. The Kresta is about five thousand yards east of him. He's pinging away with hull and VDS sonars." McCafferty nodded. The variable-depth sonar would be below the layer and had scant chance of detecting them. The hull sonar they'd have to pay attention to, but it wouldn't be a problem for a while yet. Okay, the captain thought, things are going pretty much according to plan—

"Conn, sonar, torpedoes in the water, bearing three-two-zero! Signal faint. Say again torpedoes in the water, three-two-zero, bearing changing—additional, lots of active sonars just lit up. We're getting increased screw noises for all contacts." McCafferty was in the sonar room before the report ended.

"Torpedo bearing change?"

"Yes! Moving left-to-right—Jesus, I think somebody's attacking the Russians. Impact!" The chief jabbed his finger at the display. A series of three bright spokes appeared right on the bearing to *Kirov.* The display suddenly went berserk. The high- and medium-frequency segment lit up with active sonar lines. The lines indicating ships became brighter as the ships increased engine speeds and changed direction as they began to maneuver.

"Secondary explosion on this contact—holy shit! Lots of explosions in the water now. Depth charges, maybe, something's really ripping the water up. There's another torpedo—way off, bearing changing right to left."

The display was now too complex for McCafferty to follow. The chief expanded the time scale to allow easier interpretation, but only he and his experienced operators could understand it.

"Skipper, it looks like somebody just got inside on them and launched an attack. He got three solid hits on *Kirov,* and now they're trying to beat on him. These two ships appear to be converging on something. I—another torpedo in the water, don't know whose. Gawd, look at all these explosions!"

McCafferty went aft.

"Periscope depth, now!" *Chicago* angled upward, taking a minute to reach her position.

He saw what might have been a mast on the horizon, and a column of black smoke, bearing three-two-zero. Over twenty radars were operating along with a number of voice radios.

"Down scope. We have any target solutions?"

"No, sir," the XO answered. "When they started maneuvering, all our data went to hell."

"How far to the next sonobuoy line?"

"Two miles. We're positioned to run right through a gap."

"Make your depth eight hundred feet. Ahead full, move us in."

Chicago's engines sprang into life, accelerating the submarine to thirty knots. The executive officer dived the boat to eight hundred feet, ducking deep below a sonobuoy set for shallow search. McCafferty stood over the chart table, took a pen from his pocket, and unconsciously began chewing on the plastic end as he watched his sub's course take him closer and closer to the enemy formation. Sonar performance dropped virtually to nil with the high speed, but soon the low-frequency sounds of the exploding ordnance echoed through the steel hull. *Chicago* ran for twenty minutes, zigzagging slightly to avoid the Russian sonobuoys, as the fire-control men kept updating their solutions.

"Okay, all ahead one-third and take her back up to periscope depth," McCafferty said. "Tracking party, stand by for a firing run."

The sonar picture cleared up rapidly. The Soviets were continuing to hunt frantically for whoever had fired at their flagship. One ship's trace was entirely gone—at least one Russian ship had been sunk or crippled. Explosions rippled through the water, punctuated by the *scree*ing sound of homing torpedoes. All were close enough to be a matter of real concern.

"Shooting observation. Up scope!"

The search periscope slid upward. McCafferty caught it low and swept the horizon. "I—Jesus!" The TV monitor showed a Bear only half a mile to their right, heading north for the formation. He could see seven ships, mainly mast tops, but one Sovremenny-class destroyer was hull-down, perhaps four miles away. The smoke he'd seen before was gone. The water resounded with the noise of Russian sonars.

"Raise the radar, power-up, and stand by."

A petty officer pushed the button to raise the submarine's surface-search radar, activated the system, but kept it in standby mode.

"Energize and give me two sweeps," the captain ordered. There was a real danger here. The Soviets would almost certainly detect the submarine's radar and try to attack it.

The radar was on for a total of twelve seconds. It "painted" a total of twenty-six targets on the screen, two of them close together about where he would have expected *Kirov* to be. The radar operator read off ranges and bearing, which were entered into the Mk-117 fire-control director and relayed to the Harpoon missiles in the torpedo tubes, giving them bearing to target and the range at which to switch on their seeker-heads. The weapons officer checked his status lights, then selected the two most promising targets for the missiles.

"Set!"

"Flood tubes." McCafferty watched the weapons-panel operator go through the launch sequence. "Opening outer doors."

"Solution checked and valid," the weapons officer said calmly. "Firing sequence: two, one, three."

"Shoot!" McCafferty ordered.

"Fire two." The submarine shuddered as the powerful impulse of high-pressure air ejected the weapon from the tube, followed by the whoosh of water entering the void. "Fire one . . . fire three. Two, one, and three fired, sir. Torpedo tube doors are shut, pumping out to reload."

"Reload with Mark-48s. Prepare to fire Tomahawks!" McCafferty said. The fire-control men switched the attack director over to activate the bow-mounted missiles.

"Up scope!" The quartermaster spun the control wheel. McCafferty let it come all the way up. He could see the smoke trail of the last Harpoon, and right behind it . . . McCafferty slapped the periscope handles up and stepped back. "Helix heading in! Take her down, all ahead flank!" The submarine raced downward. A Soviet antisub helicopter had seen the missile launch and was racing in at them. "Left full rudder."

"Left full rudder, aye!"

"Passing through one hundred feet. Speed fifteen knots," the XO reported.

"There he is," McCafferty said. The pings from the helicopter's active sonar reverberated through the hull. "Reverse your rudder. Shoot off a noisemaker." The captain ordered his submarine back to an easterly course and reduced speed as they dropped through the layer. With luck the Soviets would mistake the noisemaker for the cavitation noises of the submarine and attack it as *Chicago* drew clear.

"Conn, sonar, we have a destroyer heading in, bearing three-three-nine. Sounds like a Sovremenny—torpedo in the water aft. We have one torpedo in the water bearing two-six-five."

"Right twenty degrees rudder. All ahead two-thirds. Come to new course one-seven-five."

"Conn, sonar, new contact, twin screws, just started with a low-frequency sonar, probably a Udaloy, blade count says twenty-five knots, bearing three-five-one and constant. Torpedo bearing changing, heading aft and fading."

"Very well." McCafferty nodded. "The helicopter dropped on the noisemaker. We don't have to sweat that one. All ahead one-third, make your depth one thousand feet."

The Sovremenny he didn't worry too greatly about, but the Udaloy was another thing entirely. The new Soviet destroyer carried a low-frequency sonar that could penetrate the layer under certain conditions, plus two helicopters and a long-range rocket-boosted torpedo weapon that was better than the American ASROC.

Ba-wah! The sound of a low-frequency sonar. It had hit them on the first shot. Would it report *Chicago*'s position to the Udaloy? Or would the submarine's rubber coating prevent it?

"Target bearing three-five-one. Blade count is down, indicates speed of ten knots," sonar reported.

"Okay, he's slowed to search for us. Sonar, how strong was that ping?"

"Low edge of detection range, sir. Probably did not get a return off us. Contact is maneuvering, bearing now three-five-three. Continuing to ping, but his sonar is searchlighting west-to-east away from us. Another helo is pinging, sir, bearing zero-nine-eight. This one's below the layer, but fairly weak."

"XO, take us west. We'll try to loop around them to seaward and approach their amphibs from the west." McCafferty returned to the sonar room. He was tempted to engage the Udaloy, but could not launch a torpedo this deep without using a dangerously high amount of his reserve high-pressure air. Besides, his job was to kill the command ships, not the escorts. His fire-control team set up a solution anyway in case killing the Russian destroyer became a necessity.

"God, what a mess," the chief breathed. "The depth-charging up north has tapered off some. Bearing is steadying down on these contacts here. Either they've resumed their base course or they're heading away. Can't tell which. Uh-oh, more sonobuoys are dropping down." The chief's finger traced the new dots, in a steady line—heading toward *Chicago*. "Next one's going to be real close, sir."

McCafferty stuck his head into the attack center. "Bring her around south, and go to two-thirds."

The next sonobuoy splashed into the water directly overhead. Its cable deployed the transducer below the layer and began automatic pinging.

"They got us for sure, skipper!"

McCafferty ordered a course change to the west and again increased to full speed to clear the area. Three minutes later a torpedo dropped into the water, either dropped by the Bear or fired from the Udaloy, they couldn't tell. The torpedo started searching for them from a mile off and turned away. Again their rubber anechoic coating had saved them. A helo's dipping sonar was detected ahead of them. McCafferty went south to avoid it, knowing that he was being driven away from the Soviet fleet, but unable to do much about it at the moment. A pair of helicopters was now after him, and for a submarine to defeat two dipping sonars was no simple exercise. It was clear that their mission was not so much to find him as to drive him off, and he could not maneuver fast enough to get past them. After two hours of trying, he broke off for the last time. The Soviet force had moved beyond sonar range, their last reported course being southeast toward Andøya.

McCafferty swore to himself. He'd done everything right, gotten through the outer Soviet defenses, and had had a clear idea of how to duck under the destroyer screen. But someone had gotten there first, probably attacked *Kirov*—his target!—and messed everything up for his approach. His three

Harpoons had probably found targets unless Ivan had shot them down—but he'd been unable even to monitor their impacts. If they had made impacts. The captain of USS *Chicago* wrote up his contact report for transmission to COMSUBLANT and wondered why things were going the way they were.

STORNOWAY, SCOTLAND

"A long way to go," the fighter pilot said.

"Yeah," Toland agreed. "Our last report had the group heading southeast to evade a submarine attack. We figure they're back to a southerly course now, but we don't know where they are. The Norwegians sent their last RF-5 in to look, and it disappeared. We have to hit them before they get to Bodø. To hit them, we need to know where they are."

"No satellite intel?"

"Nope."

"Okay. I go in with the reconnaissance pod, out and back . . . four hours. I'll need a tanker to top me off about three hundred miles out."

"No problem," the RAF group captain agreed. "Do be careful, we need all your Tomcats to escort the strike tomorrow."

"I'll be ready in an hour." The pilot left.

"Wish you luck, old boy," the group captain said quietly. This was the third attempt to locate the Soviet invasion force by air. After the Norwegian reconnaissance aircraft had disappeared, the Brits had tried with a Jaguar. That, too, had vanished. The most obvious solution was to send a Hawkeye with the strike to conduct a radar search, but the Brits weren't letting the E-2s stray too far from their shore. The U.K. radar stations had taken a fearful pounding, and the Hawkeyes were needed for local defense.

"It's not supposed to be this hard," Toland observed. Here was a golden opportunity to pound the Soviet fleet. Once located, they could strike the force at dawn tomorrow. The NATO aircraft would swoop in with their own air-to-surface missiles. But the extreme range of the mission gave no time for the strike force to loiter around looking. They had to have a target location before they took off. The Norwegians were supposed to have handled this, but NATO plans had not anticipated the virtual annihilation of the Royal Norwegian Air Force in a week's time. The Soviets had enjoyed their only major tactical successes at sea, and they were successes indeed, Toland thought. While the land war in Germany was heading toward a high-technology stalemate, up to now the vaunted NATO navies had been outmaneuvered and outthought by their supposed dullard Soviet adversaries. Taking Iceland had been a masterpiece of an operation. NATO was still scrambling to reestablish the Greenland-Iceland-United Kingdom barrier with submarines that were supposed to have other missions. The Russian Backfires were ranging far into the North Atlantic, hitting one convoy a day, and the main Russian submarine force hadn't even gotten there yet. The combination of the two might just close the Atlantic, Toland thought. Then the NATO armies would surely lose, for all their brilliant performance to date.

They had to stop the Soviets from taking Bodø in Norway. Once emplaced there, Russian aircraft could attack Scotland, draining resources from the German front and hampering efforts to interdict the bomber forces heading into the Atlantic. Toland shook his head. Once the Russian force was located, they'd pound hell out of it. They had the right weapons, the right doctrine. They could launch their missiles outside the Russian SAM envelopes, just as Ivan was doing to the convoys. It was about time things changed.

The tanker lifted off first, followed half an hour later by the fighter. Toland and his British counterpart sat in the intelligence center napping, oblivious to the teletype printer that chattered in the corner. If anything important came in, the junior watch officers would alert them, and senior officers needed their sleep, too.

"Huh?" Toland started when the man tapped his shoulder.

"Coming in, sir—your Tomcat is arriving, Commander." The RAF sergeant handed Bob a cup of tea. "Fifteen minutes out. Thought you might wish to freshen up."

"Thanks, Sergeant." Toland ran a hand over his unshaven face and decided not to shave. The group captain did, mainly to preserve the look that went with an RAF mustache.

The F-14 came in gracefully, its engines idling and wings outstretched as though grateful for the chance for a landing on something larger than a carrier. The pilot taxied into a hard shelter and quickly dismounted. Technicians were already removing the film cartridge from the camera pod.

"Nothing on their fleet, guys," he said at once. The radar-intercept officer came down behind him.

"God, there's fighters up there!" the RIO said. "Haven't seen so much activity since the last time we went through aggressor school."

"And I got one of the bastards, too. But no joy on the fleet. We covered the coast from Orland to Skagen before we turned back, not one surface ship visible."

"You're certain?" the group captain asked.

"You can check my film, Captain. No visual sightings, nothing on infrared, no radar emissions but airborne stuff—nothing, but lots of fighters. We started finding those just south of Stokke and counted—what was it, Bill?"

"Seven flights, mainly MiG-23s, I think. We never got a visual, but we picked up a lot of High Lark radars. One guy got a little close and I had to pop him with a Sparrow. We saw the flash. That was a hard kill. In any case, guys, our friends ain't coming to Bodø unless it's by submarine."

"You turned back at Skagen?"

"Ran out of film, and we were low on fuel. The fighter opposition really started picking up north of Bodø. If you want a guess, we need to check out Andøya, but we need something else to do it, SR-71 maybe. I don't think I can get in and out of there except on burner. I'd have to tank right close to there even to try that, and—like I said, lots of fighters were operating there."

"Hardly matters," the group captain said. "Our aircraft haven't the legs for a strike that far without massive tanker support, and most of our tankers are committed elsewhere."

25. Treks

ICELAND

Once clear of the meadow, they were back in what the map called wasteland. It was level for the first kilometer, then the uphill effort began in earnest on the Glymsbrekkur, a seven-hundred-foot climb. *So soon your legs forget,* Edwards thought. The rain hadn't let up, and the deep twilight they had to guide them forced a slow pace. Many of the rocks they tried to walk on were loose. The footing was treacherous, and a misstep could easily be fatal. Their ankles were sore from the constant twists on the uneven ground, and their tightly laced boots didn't seem to help anymore.

After six days in the back country, Edwards and his Marines were beginning to understand what fatigue was. At each step their knees gave just an inch or so too much, making the next step that much more of an effort. Their pack straps cut cruelly into their shoulders. Their arms were tired from carrying their weapons and from constantly adjusting their gear. Necks sagged. It was an effort to look up and around, always having to be alert for a possible ambush.

Behind them the glow of the house fire disappeared behind a ridgeline, the first good thing that had happened. No helicopters yet, no vehicles investigating the fire. Good, but how long would that last? How soon would the patrol be missed? they all wondered.

All but Vigdis. Edwards walked a few yards in front of her, listening to her breathing, listening for sobs, wanting to say something to her, but not knowing what. Had he done the right thing? Was it murder? Was it expediency? Or was it justice? Did that matter? So many questions. He set them aside. They had to survive. That mattered.

"Take a break," he said. "Ten minutes."

Sergeant Smith checked to see where the others were, then sat down beside his officer.

"We done good, Lieutenant. I figure four, maybe five miles in the past two hours. I think we can ease up a little."

Edwards smiled wanly. "Why not just stop and build a house here?"

Smith chuckled in the darkness. "I hear you, skipper."

The lieutenant studied the map briefly, looking up to see how well it matched with what he could see. "What say we go left around this marsh? The map shows a waterfall here, the Skulafoss. Looks like a nice deep canyon. Maybe we'll get lucky and find a cave or something. If not, it's deep. No choppers'll come in there, and we'll have shadows to hide in. Five hours?"

" 'Bout that," Smith agreed. "Roads to cross?"

"Nothing shows but foot trails."

"I like it." Smith turned to the girl, who watched them without a word as she sat with her back against a rock. "How do you feel, ma'am?" he inquired gently.

"Tired." Her voice said more than that, Edwards thought. There was no emotion there, none at all. He wondered if this was good or bad. What was the right thing to do for the victims of serious crime? Her parents murdered before her eyes, her own body brutally violated, what kind of thoughts were going through that head? Get her mind off it, he decided.

"How well do you know this area?" the lieutenant asked.

"My father fish here. I come with him many times." Her head leaned back into a shadow. Her voice cracked and dropped into quiet sobs.

Edwards wanted to wrap an arm around her, to tell her things were all right now, but he was afraid it might only make things worse. Besides, who would believe that things were all right now?

"How we fixed for food, Sarge?"

"I figure we got maybe four days' worth of canned stuff. I went through the house pretty good, sir," Smith whispered. "Got a pair of fishing rods and some lures. If we take our time, we ought to be able to feed ourselves. Lots of good fishin' creeks around here, maybe at this place we're goin'. Salmon and trout. Never could afford to do it myself, but I heard tell that the fishing's really something. You said your daddy's a fisherman, right?"

"Lobsterman—close enough. You said you couldn't afford—"

"Lieutenant, they charge you like two hundred bucks a day to fish up here," Smith explained. "Hard to afford on a sergeant's pay, you know? But if they charge that much, there must be a shitload of fish in the water, right?"

"Sounds reasonable," Edwards agreed. "Time to move. When we get to that mountain, we'll belly-up for a while and get everybody rested."

"I'll drink to that, skipper. Might make us late getting to—"

"Screw it! Then we're late. The rules just changed some. Ivan's liable to be looking for us. We take it slow from now on. If our friends on the other end of this radio don't like it, too damned bad. We'll get there late, but we'll get there."

"You got it, skipper. Garcia! Take the point. Rodgers, cover the back door. Five more hours, Marines, then we sleep."

USS *PHARRIS*

The spray stung his face, and Morris loved it. The convoy of ballasted ships was steaming into the teeth of a forty-knot gale. The sea was an ugly, foam-whipped shade of green, droplets of seawater tearing off the white-caps to fly horizontally through the air. His frigate climbed up the steep face of endless twenty-foot swells, then crashed down again in a succession that had lasted six hours. The ship's motion was brutal. Each time the bow nosed down it was as though the brakes had been slammed on a car. Men held on to stanchions and stood with their feet wide apart to compensate for the continuous motion. Those in the open like Morris wore life pre-servers and hooded jackets. A number of his young crewmen would be suffering from this, ordinarily—even professional sailormen wanted to avoid this sort of weather—but now mainly they slept. *Pharris* was back to normal Condition-3 steaming, and that allowed the men to catch up on their rest.

Weather like this made combat nearly impossible. Submarines were mainly a one-sensor platform. For the most part, they detected targets on sonar and the crashing sea noise tended to blanket the ship sounds sub-marines listened for. A really militant sub skipper could try running at periscope depth to operate his search radar, but that meant running the risk of broaching and momentarily losing control of his boat, not something a nuclear submarine officer looked kindly upon. A submarine would prac-tically have to ram a ship to detect it, and the odds against that were slim. Nor did they have to worry about air attacks for the present. The sea's crenellated surface would surely confuse the seeker head of a Russian missile.

For their own part, their bow-mounted sonar was useless, as it heaved up and down in a twenty-foot arc, sometimes rising completely clear of the water. Their towed-array sonar trailed in the placid waters a few hundred feet below the surface, and so could theoretically function fairly well, but in practice, a submarine had to be moving at high speed to stand out from the violent surface noise, and even then engaging a target under these conditions was no simple matter. His helicopter was grounded. Taking off might have been possible, but landing was a flat impossibility under these conditions. A submarine would have to be within ASROC torpedo range—five miles—to be in danger from the frigate, but even that was a slim possibility. They could always call in a P-3 Orion—two were operating with the convoy at present—but Morris did not envy their crews a bit, as they buffeted through the clouds at under a thousand feet.

For everyone a storm meant time off from battle, for both sides to rest up for the next round. The Russians would have it easier. Their long-range aircraft would be down for needed maintenance, and their submarines, cruising four hundred feet down, could keep their sonar watches in comfort.

"Coffee, skipper?" Chief Clarke came out of the pilothouse, a cup in his hand with a saucer on top to keep the saltwater out.

"Thanks." Morris took the cup and drained half of it. "How's the crew doing?"

"Too tired to barf, sir." Clarke laughed. "Sleeping like babies. How much longer this slop gonna last, Cap'n?"

"Twelve more hours, then it's supposed to clear off. High-pressure system right behind this." The long-range weather report had just come in from Norfolk. The storm track was moving farther north. Mostly clear weather for the next two weeks. Wonderful.

The chief leaned outboard to see how the forward deck fittings were taking the abuse. Every third or fourth wave, *Pharris* dug her nose in hard, occasionally taking green water over the bow. This water slammed into things, and the chief's job was to get them fixed. Like most of the 1052s assigned to the stormy Atlantic, *Pharris* had been given spray strakes and higher bow plating on her last overhaul, which reduced but did not entirely eliminate the problem known to sailors since men first went to sea: the ocean will try very hard to kill you if you lack the respect she demands. Clarke's trained eye took in a hundred details before he turned back.

"Looks like she's riding this one out okay."

"Hell, I'd settle for this all the way back," Morris said after finishing off his coffee. "After it's over, we'll have to round up a lot of merchies, though."

Clarke nodded agreement. Station-keeping was not especially easy in this kind of weather.

"So far, so good, Captain. Nothing big has come loose yet."

"How 'bout the tail?"

"No sweat, sir. I got a man keeping an eye on that. Should hold up nice, 'less we have to speed up." Both men knew they wouldn't speed up. They were making ten knots, and the frigate couldn't run much faster than that in these seas no matter what the cause. "Heading aft, sir."

"Okay. Heads up." Morris looked aloft to check that his lookouts were still alert. Probabilities or not, there was danger out there. All kinds.

STORNOWAY, SCOTLAND

"Andøya. They weren't heading for Bodø after all," Toland said as he pored over the satellite photographs of Norway.

"How many troops on the ground do you think?"

"At least a brigade, Group Captain. Maybe a short division. Lots of tracked vehicles here, lots of SAMs, too. They're already basing fighters at the airfield. Be bombers next—maybe there by now. These shots are three hours old." The Russian naval force was already headed back to the Kola Fjord. They could reinforce by air now. He wondered what had happened to the regiment of Norwegians supposed to be based there.

"Their Blinder light bombers can reach us from there. Bastards can dash in and out at high-mach numbers, be bloody difficult to intercept." The Soviets had launched a systematic attack on the RAF radar stations arrayed on the Scottish coast. Some attacks were by air-to-surface missiles, others by submarine-launched cruise missiles. One had even been by fighter-bombers with massive jamming support—but that one had been costly. RAF Tornados had killed half of the raiders, mainly on the return leg. Twin-engine Blinder bombers could deliver their heavy bombloads after running in low and fast. Probably why Ivan wanted Andøya, Toland thought. Perfectly located for them. Easy to support from their own northern bases, and just a little too far for fighter-bombers in Scotland to counterattack without heavy tanker support.

"We can get there," the American said, "but it means getting half our attack birds loaded up with buddy stores."

"No chance. They'll never release them from the reserve force." The group captain shook his head.

"Then we have to start running a heavy patrol over the Faroes, and that keeps us from bothering Iceland too much." Toland looked around the table. "Don't you just love it when a plan comes together? How do we take the initiative away from these bastards? We're playing their game. We're reacting to their actions, not doing what we want to do. That's how you lose, people. Ivan's got his Backfires standing down because of this front moving across the central Atlantic. They'll be flying again tomorrow after a good day's rest, gunning for our convoys. If we can't hit Andøya, and we can't do much about Iceland, what the hell are we going to do, just sit here and worry about defending Scotland?"

"If we allow Ivan to establish air superiority over us—"

"If Ivan can kill the convoys, Group Captain, we lose the fucking war!" Toland pointed out.

"True. You're quite correct, Bob. The problem is, how do we hit the Backfires? They appear to be flying directly down over Iceland. Fine, we have a known area of transit, but it's protected by MiGs, laddy. We'd end up sending fighters to battle fighters."

"So we try something indirect. We gun for the tankers they're using."

The fighter pilots present, two squadron operations officers had silently been watching the intelligence types talk.

"How the hell are we going to find their tankers?" one asked now.

"You think they can refuel thirty or more bombers without *some* radio chatter?" Toland asked. "I've listened in on Russian tanker ops by satellite, and I *know* there's chatter. Let's say we can get a snooper up there, and he finds out where they're tanking. Why not then put some Toms astride their flightpath home?"

"Hit them *after* they tank the strike . . . ." the fighter jock mused.

"It won't do diddly for the strike today, say, but it'll hurt the bastards tomorrow. If we succeed even once, then Ivan has to change his operational pattern, maybe send fighters out with them. If nothing else, we'll have them reacting to us for a change."

"And perhaps take the heat off us," the group captain went on. "Right, let's look at this."

ICELAND

The map didn't begin to show how hard it would be. The Skula River had carved a series of gorges over the centuries. The river was high, and the falls generated a cloud of spray from which a rainbow arched in the morning sun. It made Edwards angry. He'd always liked rainbows before, but this one meant the rocks they had to climb down were slick and wet. He figured it to be two hundred feet down to a floor of granite boulders. It looked a lot farther than that.

"You ever do any rock climbin', Lieutenant?" Smith asked.

"Nope, nothing like this. You?"

"Yeah, 'cept we mostly practice goin' up. This here oughta be easier. Don't worry too much about slipping. These boots hold pretty good. Just make sure you set your feet on something solid, okay? And you take it nice and slow. Let Garcia lead off. I already like this place, skipper. See that pool below the falls? There's fish in there, and I don't think anybody'll ever spot us down this hole."

"Okay, you watch the lady."

"Right. Garcia, lead off. Rodgers, cover the rear." Smith slung his rifle across his back as he walked to Vigdis.

"Ma'am, you think you can handle this?" Smith held out his hand.

"I have been here before." She almost smiled until she remembered who had brought her here, and how many times. She didn't take his hand.

"That's good, Miss Vigdis. Maybe you can teach us a thing or two. You be careful, now."

It would have been fairly easy except for their heavy packs. Each man carried a fifty-pound load. The added weight and their fatigue affected their balance, with the result that someone watching from a distance might have taken the Marines for old women crossing an icy street. It was a fifty-degree slope down, in some places almost vertical, with some paths worn into the slopes, perhaps by the wild deer that throve here. For the first time fatigue worked in their favor. Fresher, they might have tried to move more quickly; as it was, each man was near the end of his string, and feared his own weakness more than the rocks. It took over an hour, but they made it down with nothing worse than cuts on their hands and bruises somewhere else.

Garcia crossed the river to the east side, where the canyon wall was steeper, and they camped out on a rocky shelf ten feet above the water. Edwards checked his watch. They had been on the move continuously for more than two days. Fifty-six hours. Each found himself a place in the deep shadows.

First they ate. Edwards downed a can of something without troubling to see what it was. His burps tasted like fish. Smith let the two privates sleep first, and gave his own sleeping bag to Vigdis. The girl fell mercifully asleep almost as quickly as the Marines. The sergeant made a quick tour of the area while Edwards watched, amazed that he had any energy left at all.

"This is a good spot, skipper," the sergeant pronounced finally, collapsing down next to his officer. "Smoke?"

"I don't smoke. Thought you were out."

"I was. The lady's dad did, though, and I got a few packs." Smith lit an unfiltered cigarette with a Zippo lighter bearing the globe and anchor of the Marine Corps. He took a long pull. "Jesus, ain't this wonderful!"

"I figure we can spend a day here to rest up."

"Sounds good to me." Smith leaned back. "You held up pretty good, Lieutenant."

"I ran track at the Air Force Academy. Ten-thousand-meter stuff, some marathons, that sort of thing."

Smith gave him a baleful look. "You mean I've been trying to walk a damned runner into the ground?"

"You *have* walked a marathoner into the friggin' ground." Edwards massaged his shoulders. He wondered if the pain from his pack straps would ever go away. His legs felt as though someone had hammered on them with a baseball bat. He leaned back and commanded every muscle in his body to relax. The rocky ground didn't help, but he could not raise the energy even to look for a better spot. He remembered something. "Shouldn't somebody stand guard?"

"I thought about that," Smith said. He was lying back also, his helmet down over his eyes. "I think just this once we can forget it. Only way anybody'll spot us is if a chopper hovers right overhead. Nearest road's ten miles from here. Screw it. What d'you think, skipper?"

Edwards didn't hear the question.

KIEV, THE UKRAINE

"Ivan Mikhailovich, are your bags packed?" Alekseyev asked.

"Yes, Comrade General."

"Commander-in-Chief West is missing. He was en route from Third Shock Army to his forward headquarters and disappeared. It is thought he might have been killed by an air attack. We're taking over."

"Just like that?"

"Not at all," Alekseyev said angrily. "They took thirty-six hours to decide that he was probably dead! The maniac had just relieved Third Shock's commander, then disappeared, and his deputy couldn't decide what to do. A scheduled attack never began, and the fucking Germans counterattacked while our men were waiting for orders!" Alekseyev shook his head to clear it and went on more calmly. "Well, now we will have soldiers running the campaign, not some politically reliable whoremonger."

Sergetov again noted his superior's puritanical streak. It was one of the few traits that agreed exactly with Party policy.

"Our mission?" the captain asked.

"While the General takes charge at the command post, you and I will tour the forward divisions to ascertain the situation at the front. Sorry, Ivan Mikhailovich, I'm afraid this is not the safe posting I promised your father."

"I speak good English in addition to Arabic," the younger man sniffed. Alekseyev had checked that out before writing up the transfer orders. Captain Sergetov had been a good company officer before being lured out of uniform by the promise of a comfortable life of Party work. "When do we leave?"

"We fly out in two hours."

"In daylight?" The captain was surprised at that.

"It would appear that air travel by day is safer. NATO claims to dominate the night sky. Our people say otherwise, but they are flying us out in daylight. Draw your own conclusions, Comrade Captain."

DOVER AIR FORCE BASE, DELAWARE

A C-5A transport aircraft sat outside its hangar, waiting. Within the cavernous structure a team of forty—half officers in naval dress, half civilians wearing General Dynamics coveralls—worked on Tomahawk missiles. While one group removed the massive antiship warheads and replaced them with something else, the other group's task was more difficult. They were replacing the missile guidance systems, the usual ship-hunting packages being removed in favor of terrain-matching systems that the men knew were used only for nuclear-tipped missiles intended for land targets. The guidance boxes were new, fresh from the factory. They had to be checked and calibrated. A delicate job. Though the systems had already been certified by the manufacturer, the usual peacetime routines were gone, replaced with an urgency that all of them felt but none of them knew the reason for. The mission was a complete secret.

Delicate electronic instruments fed pre-programmed information into the guidance packages, and other monitors examined the commands generated by the on-board computers. There were only enough men to check out three missiles at a time, and each check took just over an hour. Occasionally one would look up to see the massive Galaxy transport, still waiting, its crew pacing about between trips to the weather office. When each missile was certified, a grease pencil mark was made next to the "F" code letter on the warhead, and the torpedo-shaped weapon was carefully loaded into its launch canister. Nearly a third of the guidance packages were discarded and replaced. Several had failed completely, but the problems with most were quite minor, though serious enough to warrant replacement instead of adjustment. The technicians and engineers from General Dynamics wondered about that. What sort of target demanded this sort of precision? All in all, the job took twenty-seven hours, six more than expected. About half of the men boarded the aircraft, which lifted off the concrete twenty minutes later, bound for Europe. They slept in the rear-facing seats, too tired to care about the dangers that might await them at their destination, wherever that was.

THE SKULAFOSS, ICELAND

Edwards was sitting up almost before he knew why. Smith and his Marines were even faster, already on their feet, weapons in their hands and racing to cover. Their eyes scanned the rocky rim of their small canyon as Vigdis continued to scream. Edwards left his rifle and went to her.

The automatic reaction of the Marines was to assume that she had seen some danger upon them. Instinctively, Edwards knew different. Her eyes looked blankly toward the bare rocks a few yards away, her hands gripped at the bedroll. By the time he reached her, she had stopped screaming. This time Edwards did not stop to think. He grabbed her around the shoulders and pulled her head toward his own.

"You're safe. Vigdis, you are safe."

"My family," she said, her chest heaving as she caught her breath. "They kill my family. Then—"

"Yes, but you are alive."

"The soldiers, they—" The girl had evidently loosened her clothes to sleep more comfortably. Now she drew back from Edwards, pulling them tight around her. The lieutenant kept his hands away from her clothes and wrapped the sleeping bag around her.

"They will not hurt you again. Remember all of what happened. They will not hurt you again."

She looked into his face. He didn't know what to make of her expression. The pain and grief were evident, but there were other things there, and Edwards didn't know this girl well enough to read what she was thinking.

"The one who kill my family. You kill—killed him."

Edwards nodded. "They are all dead. They cannot hurt you."

"Yes." Vigdis looked down at the ground.

"You all right?" Smith asked.

"Yeah," Edwards answered. "The lady had a—a bad dream."

"They come back," she said. "They come back again."

"Ma'am, they ain't never coming back to hurt you." Smith grasped her arm through the sleeping bag. "We'll protect you. Nobody will hurt you while we are here. Okay?"

The girl nodded jerkily.

"Okay, Miss Vigdis, now why don't you try to get some sleep? Ain't nobody gonna hurt you while we're around. You need us, you can call us."

Smith walked away. Edwards started to rise, but the girl's hand came out of the bag and took his arm.

"Please, do not go away. I—fear, fear to be alone."

"Okay. I'll stay with you. You lie back and get some sleep."

Five minutes later her eyes were closed and her breathing was regular. Edwards tried not to look at her. Should she suddenly awake and see his eyes on her—what might she think? And she could be right, Edwards admitted to himself. Two weeks ago, had he encountered her at the Keflavik Officers Club . . . he was a young, unattached man, and she was evidently a young, unattached woman. His main thought after the second drink would have been to get her back to his quarters. A little soft music. How beautiful she would have looked there, slipping demurely from her fashionable clothes in the soft light coming through the shades. Instead he had met her stark naked, cuts and bruises on her exposed flesh. So strange it was now. Edwards knew without thinking that if another man tried to put hands on her, he'd kill him without hesitation, and he couldn't bring himself to think of what taking the girl himself might be like—his only likely thought if he had encountered her on the street. What if I hadn't decided to come to her house? he wondered. She'd be dead by now, along with her parents. Probably someone would have found them in a few days . . . like they'd discovered Sandy. And that, Edwards knew all along, was the reason he'd killed the Russian lieutenant and enjoyed the man's slow trip to hell. A pity no one had seen fit to do that—

Smith waved to him. Edwards rose quietly and walked over.

"I got Garcia on guard. I think we better go back to being Marines after all. If that'd been for real, we'd all be cold meat by now, Lieutenant."

"We're all too tired to move out just yet."

"Yes, sir. The lady okay?"

"She's had a tough time. When she wakes up—hell, I don't know. I'm afraid she might just come apart on us."

"Maybe." Smith lit a cigarette. "She's young. She might bounce back if we give her a chance."

"Get her something to do?"

"Same as us, skipper. You're better off doin' than thinkin'."

Edwards checked his watch. He'd actually gotten six hours of sleep before all this had happened. Though his legs were stiff, otherwise he felt better than he would have imagined. It was an illusion, he knew. He needed at least another four hours, and a good meal, before he'd be ready to move.

"We won't move out until about eleven. I want everybody to get some more sleep and one decent meal before we head out of here."

"Makes sense. When you gonna radio in?"

"I should have done that a long time ago, I just don't want to climb those damned rocks."

"Lieutenant, I'm just a dumbass grunt, but insteada doing that, why don't you just walk downstream about half a mile? You oughta be able to track in on your satellite that way, right?"

Edwards turned to look north. Walking about that far would lower the angle to the satellite as well as climbing . . . why didn't *I* think of that? *Because like any good Air Force Academy graduate, you thought in terms of up-and-down instead of sideways.* The lieutenant shook his head angrily, noting the sergeant's sly grin before he lifted the radio pack and heading down the canyon's rocky floor.

"You're very late, Beagle," Doghouse said at once. "Repeat your status."

"Doghouse, things are just terrible. We had a run-in with a Russian patrol." Edwards explained for another two minutes.

"Beagle, are you out of your Goddamned mind? Your orders are to avoid, repeat avoid, contact with the enemy. How do you know that somebody doesn't know you're there? Over!"

"They're all dead. We rolled their vehicle over a cliff and set fire to it. We made it look like an accident, just like on TV. It's all over, Doghouse. No sense worrying about it now. We are now ten klicks from where it happened. I'm resting my men for the rest of the day. We will continue our march north tonight. This may take longer than you expect. The terrain is rugged as hell, but we'll do our best. Nothing more to report. We can't see much from where we are."

"Very well. Your orders are unchanged, and please don't play white knight again—acknowledge."

"Roger that. Out." Edwards smiled to himself as he repacked the radio. When he got back to the others, he saw that Vigdis was stirring in her sleep. He lay down beside her, careful to stay a few feet away.

SCOTLAND

"Bloody cowboy—John Wayne rescuing the settlers from the bloody red Indians!"

"We weren't there," said the man with the eye patch. He fingered it briefly. "It is a mistake to judge a man from a thousand miles away. He was there, he saw what was happening. The next thing is, what does this tell us about Ivan's troops?"

"The Sovs do not exactly have an exemplary record for dealing with civilians," the first man pointed out.

"The Soviet airborne troops are known for their stern discipline," the second replied. Formerly a major in the SAS, and invalided out, he was now a senior man with the Special Operations Executive, the SOE. "Conduct like this is not indicative of well-disciplined troops. That may be important later on. For the moment, as I told you earlier, this lad is turning out very nicely indeed." He said it without a trace of smugness.

26. Impressions

STENDAL, GERMAN DEMOCRATIC REPUBLIC

The flight in was bad enough. They'd come in aboard a light bomber, racing in at low level to a military airport east of Berlin, no more than four staff members to an aircraft. All had arrived safely, but Alekseyev wondered how much of it was skill and how much luck. This airfield had clearly been visited by NATO aircraft recently and the General already had his doubts about what his colleagues in the Air Force had told him about their ability to control the sky even in daylight. From Berlin a helicopter took his party to CINC-West's forward command post outside Stendal. Alekseyev was the first senior officer to arrive at the underground bunker complex, and he did not like what he found. The staff officers present were too concerned with what the NATO forces were doing and not concerned enough with what the Red Army was supposed to be doing to them. The initiative had not been lost, but his first impression was that the danger was real. Alekseyev located the command operations officer and started assembling information on how the campaign was going. His commander arrived half an hour later, and immediately took Alekseyev into his office.

"Well, Pasha?"

"I have to see the front at once. We have three attacks under way. I need to see how they are going. The German counterattack at Hamburg was repulsed, again, but this time we lack the forces to exploit it. The northern area is currently in stalemate. Our deepest penetration to date is just over one hundred kilometers. The timetable has gone completely to hell, losses are far higher than expected—on both sides, but worse for us. We have gravely underestimated the lethality of NATO antitank weapons. Our artillery has been unable to suppress them enough for our forces to achieve a major breakthrough. NATO air power is hurting us badly, especially at night. Reinforcements are not getting forward as well as we expected. We still have the initiative in most areas, but unless we achieve a breakthrough, that may not last more than another few days. We must find a weakness in NATO lines and launch a major coordinated attack soon."

"The NATO situation?"

Alekseyev shrugged. "Their forces are fully in the field. Further reinforcements are coming in from America, but from what our prisoners have told us, not so well as they expected. My impression is that they are stretched very thin in some areas, but we have not as yet identified a major area of weakness. If we can find one, and exploit it, I think we can rupture the front and stage a multidivisional breakout. They can't be strong everywhere. The German demand for forward defense compels the NATO forces to try and stop us everywhere. We made the same mistake in 1941. It cost us heavily. It must be doing the same to them."

"How soon do you wish to visit the front?"

"Within the hour. I'll take Captain Sergetov with me—"

"The Party man's son? If he's hurt, Pasha . . ."

"He's an officer in the Soviet Army, whatever his father might be. I need him."

"Very well. Keep me posted on where you are. Send the operations people in. We have to get control of this whorehouse."

Alekseyev commandeered a new Mi-24 attack helicopter for his reconnaissance. Overhead, a flight of agile MiG-21 fighters guarded the General as the helicopter skimmed low over the treetops. He eschewed the seat, instead crouching by the windows to see what he could. A lifetime of military service had not prepared him for the destruction that lay on the landscape below him. It seemed that every road held a burned-out tank or truck. The major crossroads had gotten particularly severe attention from NATO air power. Here a bridge had been knocked out, and immediately behind it a company of tanks waiting its repair had been savaged. The charred remains of aircraft, vehicles, and men had transformed the neat, picturesque German countryside into a junkyard of high-technology weapons. As they crossed the border into West Germany, things only got worse. Each road had been fought for, each tiny village. He counted eleven smashed tanks outside one such village, and wondered how many others had been pulled off the battlefield for repair. The town itself was almost totally destroyed by artillery and resulting fires. He saw only one building that looked like it might be habitable. Five kilometers west, the same story was repeated, and Alekseyev realized that a whole regiment of tanks had been lost in a ten-kilometer advance down a single road. He began to see NATO equipment, a German attack helicopter identifiable only from the tail rotor that stuck out from the circle of ashes, a few tanks and infantry carriers. For both sides the proud vehicles manufactured at the greatest expense and skill were scattered on the landscape like trash thrown from a car window. The Soviets had more to expend, the General knew, but how many more?

The helicopter landed at the edge of a forest. Just within the treeline, Alekseyev saw, antiaircraft guns tracked them all the way to the ground. He and Sergetov jumped out, ducking under the still-turning main rotor as they ran into the trees. There they found a cluster of command vehicles.

"Welcome, Comrade General," said a dirty-faced Red Army colonel.

"Where is the divisional commander?"

"I'm in command. The General was killed day before yesterday by enemy artillery fire. We have to move the CP twice a day. They are becoming very skilled at locating us."

"Your situation?" Alekseyev asked curtly.

"The men are tired, but they can still fight. We are not getting sufficient air support, and the NATO fighters give us no rest at night. We have about half our nominal combat strength, except in artillery. That's down to a third. The Americans have just changed tactics on us. Now, instead of attacking the leading tank formations, they are sending their aircraft after our guns first. We were badly hurt last night. Just as we were launching a regimental attack, four of their ground-attack fighters nearly wiped out a battalion of mobile guns. The attack failed."

"What about concealment!" Alekseyev demanded.

"Ask the devil's mother why it doesn't work," the colonel shot back. "Their radar aircraft can evidently track vehicles on the ground—we've tried jamming, we've tried lures. Sometimes it works, but sometimes not. The division command post has been attacked twice. My regiments are commanded by majors, my battalions by captains. NATO tactics are to go for the unit commanders, and the bastards are good at it. Every time we approach a village, my tanks have to fight through a swarm of missiles. We've tried rockets and artillery to suppress them, but you can't take the time to blast every building in sight—we'd never get anywhere."

"What do you need?"

"Air support and lots of it. Get me the support to smash through what's opposing me, and I'll give you your damned breakout!" Ten kilometers behind the front, a tank division was waiting for this very unit to rupture the front—but how could it exploit a breakthrough that was never made?

"Your supply situation?"

"Could be better, but we're getting enough forward to supply what we have left—not enough to support an intact division."

"What are you doing now?"

"We launch a two-regiment attack just over an hour from now. Another village, named Bieben. We estimate enemy strength as two understrength battalions of infantry, supported by tanks and artillery. The village commands a crossroads we need. Same one we tried to get last night. This assault should work. Do you wish to observe?"

"Yes."

"Then we'd better get you forward. Forget the helicopter unless you want to die. Besides"—the colonel smiled—"I can use it to support the attack. I'll give you an infantry carrier to get you forward. It will be dangerous up there, Comrade General," the colonel warned.

"Fine. You can protect us. When do we leave?"

USS *PHARRIS*

The calm sea meant that *Pharris* was back on port-and-starboard steaming. Half the crew was always on duty as the frigate held her station north of the convoy. The towed sonar was streamed aft, and the helicopter sat ready on the flight deck, its crew dozing in the hangar. Morris slept also, snoring away in his leather bridge chair, to the amusement of his crewmen. So, officers did it, too. The crew accommodations often sounded like a convention of chainsaws.

"Captain, message from CINCLANTFLT."

Morris looked up at the yeoman and signed for the message form. An eastbound convoy one hundred fifty miles north of them was under attack. He walked back to the chart table to check distances. The submarines there were not a threat to him. That was that. He had his own concerns, and his world had shrunk to include them only. Another forty hours to Norfolk, where they would refuel, replace expended ordnance, and sail again within twenty-four hours.

"What the hell's that?" a sailor said loudly. He pointed to a low-lying trail of white smoke.

"That's a missile," answered the officer of the deck. "General quarters! Captain, that was a cruise missile southbound a mile ahead of us."

Morris snapped upright in his seat and blinked his eyes clear. "Signal the convoy. Energize the radar. Fire the chaff." Morris ran to the ladder to CIC. The ship's alarm was sounding its strident note before he got there. Aft, two Super-RBOC chaff rockets leaped into the sky and exploded, surrounding the frigate with a cloud of aluminum foil.

"I count five inbounds," a radar operator was saying. "One's heading toward us. Bearing zero-zero-eight, range seven miles, speed five hundred knots."

"Bridge, come right full rudder to zero-zero-eight," the tactical action officer ordered. "Stand by to fire off more chaff. Air action forward, weapons free."

The five-inch gun swiveled slightly and loosed several rounds, none of which came near the incoming missile.

"Range two miles and closing," reported the radarman.

"Fire four more Super-RBOCs."

Morris heard the rockets launch. The radar showed their chaff as an opaque cloud that enveloped the ship.

"CIC," called a lookout. "I see it. Starboard bow, inbound—it's gonna miss, I got a bearing change. There—there it goes, passing aft. Missed us by a couple hundred yards."

The missile was confused by the chaff. Had its brain had the capacity to think, it would have been surprised that it struck nothing. Instead, on coming back to a clear sky, the radar seeker merely looked for another target. It found one, fifteen miles ahead, and altered course toward it.

"Sonar," Morris ordered, "check bearing zero-zero-eight. There's a missile-armed sub out there."

"Looking now, sir. Nothing shows on that bearing."

"A five-hundred-knot sea-skimmer. That's a Charlie-class sub, maybe thirty miles out," Morris said. "Get the helo out there. I'm going topside."

The captain reached the bridge just in time to see the explosion on the horizon. That was no freighter. The fireball could only mean a warship had had her magazines exploded by a missile, perhaps the one that had just missed them. Why hadn't they been able to stop it? Three more explosions followed. Slowly the noise traveled across the sea toward them, reaching *Pharris* as the deep sound of an enormous bass drum. The frigate's Sea Sprite helicopter was just lifting off, racing north in the hope of catching the Soviet sub near the surface. Morris ordered his ship to slow to five knots in the hope that the lower speed would allow his sonar to perform just a little better. Still nothing. He returned to CIC.

The helicopter's crew dropped a dozen sonobuoys. Two showed something, but the contact faded, and was not reestablished. Soon an Orion showed up and carried on the search, but the submarine had escaped cleanly, her missiles having killed a destroyer and two merchantmen. *Just like that,* Morris thought. *No warning at all.*

STORNOWAY, SCOTLAND

"Raid warning again," the Group Captain said.

"Realtime?" Toland asked.

"No, an asset we have in Norway. Contrails overhead heading southwest.

He counts twenty or so, aircraft type unknown. We have a Nimrod patrolling north of Iceland now. If they're Backfires, and if they rendezvous with a tanker group, we might just get something. See if your idea works, Bob."

Four Tomcat interceptors were sitting ready on the flight line. Two were armed with missiles. The other pair carried buddy-stores, fuel tanks designed to transfer fuel to other aircraft. The distance they expected for a successful intercept meant a round trip of two thousand miles, which meant that only two aircraft could reach far enough, and they were stretching to the limit.

The Nimrod circled two hundred miles east of Jan Mayen Land. The Norwegian island had been subjected to several air attacks, destroying the radar there, though so far the Russians had not launched a ground attack as expected. The British patrol aircraft bristled with antennae but carried no armament of her own. If the Russians sent escorting fighters out with the bomber / tanker force, she could only evade. One team listened in on the bands used by the Russians to communicate between aircraft, another on radar frequencies.

It was a long, tense wait. Two hours after the raid warning, a garbled transmission was heard, interpreted as a warning to a Backfire pilot approaching a tanker. The bearing was plotted, and the Nimrod turned east hoping for a cross bearing on the next such signal. None was detected. Without a firm fix, the fighters had only the slimmest hope of an intercept. They were kept on the ground. Next time, they decided, there'd be a pair of snoopers up.

USS *CHICAGO*

The QZB bell-ringer call arrived just after lunch. McCafferty brought his submarine to antenna depth and received orders to proceed to Faslane, the Royal Navy submarine base in Scotland. Since losing contact with the Russian surface force, they had not tracked a single positive contact. It was crazy. All the pre-war assessments told McCafferty to expect a "target-rich environment." So far he was rich only in frustration. The executive officer took them back down to a deep cruising depth while McCafferty began to write up his patrol report.

BIEBEN, FEDERAL REPUBLIC OF GERMANY

"You're pretty exposed here," the captain observed, crouching just behind the turret.

"True enough," Sergeant Mackall agreed. His M-1 Abrams tank was dug into the reverse slope of a hill, its gun barely clear of the ground behind a row of shrubs. Mackall looked down a shallow valley to a treeline fifteen hundred meters away. The Russians were in there, surveying the ridges with powerful field glasses, and he hoped that they could not make out the squat, ominous profile of the main battle tank. He was in one of three prepared firing positions, a sloped hole in the ground dug by the engineers' bulldozers, helped over the last few days by local German farmers who had taken to the task with a will. The bad news was that the next line of such positions required traversing five hundred meters of open fields.

They'd been planted with something a bare six weeks before. Those crops would never amount to much, the sergeant knew.

"Ivan must love this weather," Mackall observed. There was an overcast at about thirteen hundred feet. Whatever air support he could expect would have a bare five seconds to acquire and engage their targets before having to break clear of the battlefield. "What can you give us, sir?"

"I can call four A-10s, maybe some German birds," the Air Force captain replied. He surveyed the terrain himself from a slightly different perspective. What was the best way to get the ground-attack fighters in and out? The first Russian attack on this position had been repulsed, but he could see the remains of two NATO aircraft that had died in the effort. "There should be three choppers, too."

That surprised Mackall—and worried him. Just what sort of attack were they expecting here?

"Okay." The captain stood and turned back to his armored command vehicle. "When you hear 'Zulu, Zulu, Zulu,' that means the air is less than five minutes out. If you see any SAM vehicles or antiair guns, for Christ's sake take them out. The Warthogs have been hit real hard, Sarge."

"You got it, Cap'n. You better get your ass outa here, it's gonna be showtime soon." One thing Mackall had learned was just how important a good forward air-control officer was, and this one had dug the sergeant's troop out of a really bad scrape three days before. He watched the officer sprint fifty yards to the waiting vehicle, its engine already turning. The rear door hadn't yet closed when the driver pulled out fast, zigzagging down the slope and across the plowed field toward the command post.

B Troop, 1st Squadron, 11th Armored Cavalry Regiment had once been fourteen tanks. Five of the originals were gone, and there had been only two replacements. Of the rest, all had been damaged to one degree or another. His platoon leader had been killed on the second day of the war, leaving Mackall in command of the three-tank platoon, covering nearly a kilometer of front. Dug in between his tanks was a company of German infantry—men of the *Landwehr,* the local equivalent of the National Guard, farmers and shopowners for the most part, men fighting to defend not just their country, but their own homes. They, too, had taken serious losses. The "company" was no more than two platoons of effectives. *Surely the Russians know just how thin we're spread,* Mackall thought. Everyone was dug in—deep. The power of Russian artillery had come as a shock despite all the pre-war warnings they'd had.

"The Americans must love this." The colonel gestured at the low clouds. "Their damned airplanes come swooping in too low for our radar, and this way we have practically no chance to see them before they fire."

"How badly have they hurt you?"

"See for yourself." The colonel gestured at the battlefield. Fifteen tanks lay in view—the burned-out remains. "That American low-level fighter did this—the Thunderbolt. Our men call it the Devil's Cross."

"But you killed two aircraft yesterday," Sergetov objected.

"Yes, and only one of four gun vehicles survived the effort. The same vehicle got both—Senior Sergeant Lupenko. I recommended him for the Red Banner. It will be posthumous—the second aircraft crashed right on his vehicle. My best gunner," the colonel said bitterly. Two kilometers away, the wreckage of a German Alphajet was a charred garnish atop the remains of a ZSU-30 gun vehicle. No doubt it had been deliberate, the colonel thought, that German had wanted to kill just a few more Soviets before he died. A sergeant handed his colonel a radio headset. The officer listened for half a minute before speaking a few words that he punctuated with a quick nod.

"Five minutes, Comrades. My men are fully in place. Would you follow me, please?"

The command bunker had been hastily built of logs and earth, with a full meter of overhead cover. Twenty men were crammed into it, communications men for the two regiments in the assault. The division's third regiment waited to exploit the breakthrough and pave the way for the reserve armored division to break into the enemy's rear. If, Alekseyev reminded himself, everything went as planned.

No enemy troops or vehicles could be seen, of course. They would be in the woods atop the ridge less than two kilometers away, dug in deep. He watched the divisional commander nod to his artillery chief, who lifted a field phone and spoke two words:

"Commence firing."

It took several seconds for the sound to reach them. Every gun the division owned, with an additional battery from the tank division, spoke as one dreadful voice, and the thunder echoed across the countryside. The shells arched overhead, at first striking short of the opposite ridgeline, then closing on it. What had once been a gentle hill covered with lush grass turned into a brown obscenity of bare earth and smoke.

"I think they're serious, Sarge," the loader said, pulling his hatch down tight.

Mackall adjusted his helmet and microphone as he peered out the view ports built into his commander's cupola. The thick armor plate kept most of the noise out, but when the ground shook beneath them, the shock came through the treads and suspension to rock the vehicle, and each crewman reflected to himself on the force needed to budge a sixty-ton tank. This was how the lieutenant had bought it—a one-in-a-thousand shot from a heavy gun had landed a round right on his turret, and it had burrowed through the thin overhead armor to explode the vehicle.

Left and right of Mackall's tank, the largely middle-aged German territorials cowered in their deep, narrow holes, their emotions oscillating between terror and rage at what was happening to them and their country— *and their homes!*

"Good fire plan, Comrade Colonel," Alekseyev said quietly. A screaming sound passed overhead. "There is your air support."

Four Russian ground-attack fighters wheeled overhead to trace parallel to the ridgeline and dropped their loads of napalm. As they turned back toward Russian lines, one exploded in midair.

"What was that?"

"Probably a Roland," the colonel answered. "Their version of our SA-8 rocket. Here we go. One minute."

Five kilometers behind the command bunker, two batteries of mobile rocket launchers ripple-fired their weapons in a continuous sheet of flame. Half were high-explosive warheads, the other half smoke.

Thirty rockets landed in Mackall's sector and thirty in the valley before him. The impact of the explosives shook his tank violently, and he could hear the *pings* of fragments bouncing off his armor. But it was the smoke that frightened him. That meant Ivan was coming. From thirty separate points, gray-white smoke billowed into the air, forming an instant man-made cloud that enveloped all the ground in view. Mackall and his gunner activated their thermal-imaging sights.

"Buffalo, this is Six," the troop commander called in over the command circuit. "Check in."

Mackall listened in closely. All eleven vehicles were intact, protected by their deep holes. Again he blessed the engineers—and the German farmers—who had dug the shelters. No further orders were passed. None were needed.

"Enemy in view," the gunner reported.

The thermal sight measured differences in temperature and could penetrate most of the mile of smoke cover. And the wind was on their side. A ten-mile-per-hour breeze was driving the cloud back east. Sergeant First Class Terry Mackall took a deep breath and went to work.

"Target tank, ten o'clock. Sabot! Shoot!"

The gunner trained left and centered the sight reticle on the nearest Soviet battle tank. His thumbs depressed the laser button, and a thin beam of light bounced off the target. The range display came up in his sight: 1310 meters. The fire-control computer plotted target distance and speed, elevating the main gun. The computer measured wind speed and direction, air density and humidity, the temperature of the air, and the tank's own shells, and all the gunner had to do was place the target in the center of his sights. The whole operation took less than two seconds, and the gunner's fingers jammed home on the triggers.

A forty-foot muzzle blast annihilated the shrubs planted two years earlier by some German Boy Scouts. The tank's 105mm gun jerked back in recoil, ejecting the spent aluminum case. The shell came apart in the air, the sabot falling free of the projectile, a 40mm dart made of tungsten and uranium that lanced through the air at almost a mile a second.

The projectile struck the target one second later at the base of the gun turret. Inside, a Russian gunner was just picking up a round for his own cannon when the uranium core of the shot burned through the protective steel. The Russian tank exploded, its turret flying thirty feet into the air.

"Hit!" Mackall said. "Target tank, twelve o'clock. Sabot! Shoot!"

The Russian and American tanks fired at the same instant, but the Russian shot went high, missing the defiladed M-1 by nearly a meter. The Russian was less lucky.

"Time to leave," Mackall announced. "Straight back! Heading for alternate one."

The driver already had reverse engaged, and twisted hard on his throttle control. The tank surged backward, then spun right and headed fifty yards to another prepared position.

"Damned smoke!" Sergetov swore. The wind blew it back in their faces, and they couldn't tell what was going on. The battle was now in the hands of captains, lieutenants, and sergeants. All they could see was the orange fireballs of exploding vehicles, and there was no way to know whose they were. The colonel in command had his radio headset on and was barking orders to his subunit commanders.

*　　　*　　　*

Mackall was in his first alternate position in less than a minute. This one had been dug parallel to the ridgeline, and his massive turret trained to the left. He could see the infantry now, dismounted and running ahead of their assault carriers. Allied artillery, both German and American, ripped through their ranks, but not quickly enough . . .

"Target—tank with an antenna, just coming out of the treeline."

"Got 'em!" the gunner answered. He saw a Russian T-80 main battle tank with a large radio antenna projecting from the turret. That would be a company commander—maybe a battalion commander. He fired.

The Russian tank wheeled just as the shot left the muzzle. Mackall watched the tracer barely miss his engine compartment.

"Gimme a HEAT round!" the gunner shouted over the intercom.

"Ready!"

"Turn back, you mother—"

The Russian tank was driven by an experienced sergeant who zigzagged his way across the valley floor. He jinked every five seconds, and now brought his tank left again—

The gunner squeezed off his round. The tank jumped at the recoil and the spent round *clang*ed off the turret's rear wall. Already the closed tank hull stank of the ammonia-based propellant.

"Hit! Nice shot, Woody!"

The shell hit the Russian between the last pair of road wheels and wrecked the tank's diesel engine. In a moment the crew began to bail out, "escaping" into an environment alive with shell fragments.

Mackall ordered his driver to move again. By the time they were in their next firing position, the Russians were less than five hundred meters away. They fired two more shots, killing an infantry carrier and knocking the tread off a tank.

"Buffalo, this is Six, begin moving to Bravo Line—execute."

As platoon leader, Mackall was the last to leave. He saw both of his companion tanks rolling down the open reverse slope of the hill. The infantry was moving also, into their armored carriers, or just running. "Friendly" artillery blanketed the ridgeline with high explosives and smoke to mask their withdrawal. On command, the tank leaped forward, accelerating to thirty miles per hour and racing to the next defense line before the Russians could occupy the ridge they were leaving behind. Artillery fire was all over them, exploding a pair of German personnel carriers.

"Zulu, Zulu, Zulu!"

"Get me a vehicle!" Alekseyev ordered.

"I cannot permit this. I cannot let a general—"

"Get me a damned vehicle! I must observe this," Alekseyev repeated.

A minute later, he and Sergetov joined the colonel in a BMP armored command vehicle that raced to the position the NATO troops had just vacated. They found a hole that had sheltered two men—until a rocket had landed a meter away.

"My God, we've lost twenty tanks here!" Sergetov said, looking back.

"Down!" The colonel pushed both men into the bloody hole. A storm of NATO shells landed on the ridge.

"There's a Gatling gun!" the gunner said. A Russian antiaircraft gun carrier came over the ridge. A moment later a HEAT round exploded it like a plastic toy. His next target was a Russian tank coming down the hill they'd just left.

"Heads up, friendly air coming in!" Mackall cringed, hoping the pilot could tell the sheep from the goats.

Alekseyev watched the twin-engine fighter swoop straight down the valley. Its nose disappeared in a mass of flame as the pilot fired his antitank cannon. Four tanks exploded before his eyes as the Thunderbolt appeared to stagger in midair, then turned west, a missile chasing after him. The SA-7 fell short.

"The Devil's Cross?" he asked. The colonel nodded in reply, and Alekseyev realized where the name had come from. From an angle, the American fighter did look like the stylized Russian Orthodox crucifix.

"I just called up the reserve regiment. We may have them on the run," the colonel said.

This, Sergetov thought incredulously to himself, *is a successful attack?*

Mackall watched a pair of antitank missiles reach out into the Russian lines. One miss, one kill. More smoke came in from both sides as the NATO troops fell back another five hundred meters. The village they were defending was now in sight. The sergeant had counted a total of five kills to his tank. He hadn't been hit yet, but that wouldn't last. The friendly artillery was really in the fight now. The Russian infantry was down to half the strength he'd first seen, and their tracked vehicles were laying back, trying to engage the NATO positions with their own missiles. Things looked to be going reasonably well when the third regiment appeared.

Fifty tanks came over the hill in front of him. An A-10 swept across the line and killed a pair, then was blotted out of the sky by a SAM. The burning wreckage fell three hundred yards in front of him.

"Target tank, one o'clock. Shoot!" The Abrams rocked backward with yet another shot. "Hit."

"Warning, warning," called the troop commander. "Enemy choppers approaching from the north."

Ten Mi-24 Hinds arrived late, but they made up for it by killing a pair of tanks in less than a minute. German Phantom jets then appeared, engaging them with air-to-air missiles and cannon in a wild melee that suddenly included surface-to-air missiles also. The sky was crisscrossed with smoke trails, and suddenly there were no aircraft in view.

"It's bogging down," Alekseyev said. He'd just learned one important lesson: attack helicopters cannot hope to survive in the face of enemy fighters. Just when he thought the Mi-24s would make a decisive difference, they'd been forced away by the appearance of the German fighters. Artillery support was slacking off. The NATO gunners were counterbatterying the Soviet guns expertly, helped by ground-attack fighters. He had to get more front-line air support.

"The hell it is!" the colonel answered. He radioed new orders to the battalions on his left flank.

"Looks like a command vehicle at ten o'clock, on the ridgeline, can you reach it?"

"Long shot, I—"

Whang! A shot glanced off the turret's face.

"Tank, three o'clock, close in—"

The gunner turned his yoke controls and nothing happened. Immediately he reached for the manual traverse. Mackall engaged the target with his machine gun, bouncing bullets off the advancing T-80 that had come out of nowhere. The gunner cranked frantically at the handle as another round crashed into their armor. The driver aided him, turning the vehicle and praying that they could return the fire.

The computer was out, damaged by the shock of the first hit. The T-80 was less than a thousand meters away when the gunner settled on it. He fired a HEAT round, and it missed. The loader slammed another home in the breech. The gunner worked his controls and fired again. Hit.

"There's more behind that one," the gunner warned.

"Buffalo Six, this is three-one, bad guys coming in from our flank. We need help here," Mackall called; then to the driver: "Left track and back up fast!"

The driver needed no encouragement. He cringed, looking out his tiny viewing prisms, and rocked the throttle handle all the way back. The tank raced backward and left as the gunner tried to lock onto another target— but the automatic stabilization was also out. They had to sit still to fire accurately, and it was death to sit still.

Another Thunderbolt came in low, dropping cluster munitions on the Russian formation. Two more Soviet tanks were stopped, but the fighter went away trailing smoke. Artillery fire joined in to stop the Soviet maneuver.

"For Christ's sake, stop so I can shoot one of the fuckers!" the gunner screamed. The tank stopped at once. He fired, hitting a T-72 on the tread. "Reload!"

A second tank joined Mackall's, a hundred meters to his left. It was intact and fired off three quick rounds for two hits. Then a Soviet helicopter reappeared and exploded the troop commander's tank with a missile. A shoulder-fired Stinger missile then killed the chopper as the German infantry redeployed. Mackall watched a pair of HOT antitank missiles go left and right of his turret, reaching for the advancing Soviets. Both hit.

"Antenna tank, dead ahead."

"I see him. Sabot!" The gunner cranked the turret back to the right. He elevated his gun to battle sights and fired.

"Captain Alexandrov!" the division commander shouted into his microphone. The battalion commander's transmission had stopped in midword. The colonel was using his radio too much. Ten miles away, a German battery of 155mm mobile guns tracked in on the radio signals and fired twenty quick rounds.

Alekseyev heard the incoming and jumped into a German-dug foxhole, dragging Sergetov with him. Five seconds later the area was blanketed by smoke and noise.

The General stuck his head up to see the colonel still standing, still giving radio orders. Behind him the command vehicle was burning, the radios with it. Five men were dead, another half-dozen screaming with the pain of their injuries. Alekseyev looked with annoyance at a bloody streak on the back of his hand.

Mackall killed one more tank, but it was the Germans who stopped the attack, using the last of their HOT missiles to do so. The remaining Russian commander lost his nerve when half the tanks in the battalion were hit. The survivors turned on their smoke generators and retreated back around the hill to the south. Artillery chased after them. The land battle was over for the moment.

"Mackall, what's happening down your way?" the troop executive officer inquired.

"Where's Six?"

"To your left." Mackall looked and saw the troop commander's burning tank. So that's who it was . . .

"Just us, sir. What's left?"

"I count four."

My God, the sergeant thought.

"Get me a Regiment from the tank division and I can do it. They have nothing left!" the colonel insisted. His face was bloody from a superficial wound.

"I will do this. How soon can you continue the attack?" Alekseyev asked.

"Two hours. I need that long to regroup my forces."

"Very well. I must return to headquarters. The enemy opposition was tougher than you expected, Comrade Colonel. Otherwise your forces performed well. Tell your intelligence section to work harder. Gather up your prisoners and interrogate them rigorously!" Alekseyev moved off with Sergetov in his wake.

"Worse than I expected," the captain observed once they were inside their vehicle.

"They must have had nearly a Regiment facing us." Alekseyev shrugged. "We can't make that kind of mistake very often and expect to succeed. We advanced four kilometers in two hours, but the cost was murderous. And those bastards in the Air Force! I'll have something to say to our Frontal Aviation generals when we get back!"

"That makes you troop XO," the lieutenant said. It turned out there were five surviving tanks. One had both radios broken. "You did good, real good."

"How'd the Germans make out?" Mackall asked his new boss.

"Fifty-percent losses, and Ivan kicked us back four klicks. We can't expect to survive much more of this. We may have some reinforcements in an hour. I think I convinced Regiment that Ivan really wants this place. We'll be getting help. Same for the Germans. They promised another battalion by nightfall, maybe a second one by dawn. Take your track down for refuel and reload. Our friends may be back soon."

"That's one little and two big attacks for this village. They ain't got it yet, sir."

"One other thing. I talked to Regiment about you. The colonel says you're an officer now."

Mackall's tank spent ten minutes getting to the rearm point. Fueling took ten minutes while the exhausted crewmen loaded a new collection of shells. The sergeant was surprised that he had to head back to the front five rounds short.

"You've been hit, Pasha." The younger man shook his head.

"I scratched my hand getting out of the helicopter. I'll let it bleed awhile to punish myself for clumsiness." Alekseyev sat opposite his commander and downed a full liter canteen of water. He was embarrassed by his slight wound and decided to lie about it.

"The attack?"

"Opposition was ferocious. We'd been told to expect two infantry battalions, plus tanks. I estimate the actual enemy strength as a damaged regiment, and they had well-prepared positions. Even so, we almost broke through. The colonel in command had a good plan, and his men pushed as hard as anyone could expect. We forced them back to within sight of the objective. I want to release a regiment of tanks from the OMG to the next attack."

"We are not permitted to do this."

"What?" Alekseyev was stunned.

"The Operational Maneuver Groups are to remain intact until the breakthrough is achieved. Orders from Moscow."

"One more regiment will do it. The objective is in sight! We've chewed up one motor rifle division to get this far, and lost half the strength of another. We can win this battle and get the first major rupture in NATO lines—but we have to act now!"

"You're certain?"

"Yes, but we must move fast. The Germans must realize how close this battle has become. They'll try to reinforce also. The lead regiment from 30th Guards Tank Division is one hour from the front. If we can get them moving within thirty minutes, they'll be part of the next attack. In fact, we should move the whole division up. This opportunity will not last long."

"Very well. I'll call STAVKA for permission."

Alekseyev leaned back and closed his eyes. The Soviet command structure: to deviate from the Plan, even a Theater commander had to get *permission!* It took over an hour while the staff geniuses in Moscow examined the maps. The lead regiment of 30th Guards was released and ordered to join the motor-rifle division in the next attack. But they were late, and the attack was delayed ninety minutes.

Second Lieutenant Terry Mackall—he still wore his stripes and was too tired to care about his change in rank—wondered how seriously Command was taking this little tank battle. Two battalions of German regulars arrived in tracked vehicles, relieving the exhausted *Landwehr* men, who moved back to prepare defensive positions in and around the village to their rear. A company of Leopard tanks and two platoons of M-1s reinforced the position, with a German colonel in overall command. He arrived by helicopter and surveyed all the defensive positions. A tough-looking little bastard, Mackall thought, with some bandages on his face and a tight unsmiling mouth. Mackall remembered that if Ivan broke through here, he just might be able to flank the German and British forces that had stopped the Russians' deepest penetration at the suburbs of Hannover. That made the battle important to the Germans.

The German Leopards took the frontal positions, relieving the Americans. It was a full troop now, back to fourteen vehicles. The troop commander split the force into two parts, with Mackall commanding the southern group. They found the last line of dug shelters, just southeast of the village. Mackall arrayed his newly assigned command with care, checking each position on foot and conferring with each tank commander. The Germans were thorough enough. Any position that did not already have natural shrubbery in place had had it transplanted in. Nearly all of the civilians who lived here had been evacuated, but a handful of people were unwilling to desert the homes they'd built. One of them brought some of the tankers hot food. Mackall's crew didn't have time to eat it. The gunner repaired two loose connectors and reset the balky fire-control computer. The loader and driver worked on a loose tread. Artillery was falling around them before they finished.

Alekseyev wanted to be there. He had a telephone link with the division, and listened in on the division command circuit. The colonel—Alekseyev wanted to make him a general if the attack succeeded—complained that they had been forced to wait too long. He'd asked for and gotten a reconnaissance mission over enemy lines. One of the aircraft had vanished. The other's pilot reported movement, but could not provide a strength estimate, so busy had he been dodging surface-to-air missiles. The colonel feared there had been an increase in enemy strength, but without hard evidence could not justify either a further delay or further reinforcements.

Mackall also watched from a distance. The last row of hills was a mile away, across what had been a farm but was now covered mostly with small trees, as though the soil had been exhausted. His forces were organized in two three-tank platoons. As commander, his job was to lie back and direct them by radio.

Twenty minutes after the radio reported a strong Russian advance, he began to see movement. German personnel carriers began streaming down the hill, toward the village. Some Soviet helicopters appeared to the north, but this time a Roland battery hidden in the village engaged them, exploding three before they retreated out of sight. Next came the German Leopard tanks. Mackall counted and came up three short. NATO artillery pounded the hilltops, and Soviet guns dropped shells in the fields around the American tanks. Then the Russians appeared.

"Buffalo, all units hold fire. Repeat, everyone hold fire," the troop commander said over the radio.

Mackall saw that the retreating Germans were passing through the village. *So, that's what that little Kraut bastard has planned*, he thought. *Beautiful . . .*

"We have them on the run!" the colonel told Alekseyev over the command circuit. On the map table in front of the General, counters were moved and plotting officers made marks with grease pencils. They penciled in a red gap in the German lines.

The leading Soviet tanks were now five hundred meters from the village, racing down the two-kilometer gap between B-Troop's tanks. The German colonel gave his order to the American troop commander.

"Buffalo, this is Six—take 'em!" Twelve tanks fired at once and hit nine targets.

"Woody, look for antennas," Mackall ordered his gunner. He used his viewing prisms to keep an eye on his subordinates as the gunner traversed right and searched the rear Soviet ranks.

"There's one! Load a HEAT round! Target tank. Range twenty-six hundred—" The tank lurched sideways. The gunner watched the tracer on the shell arc through the air on its two-mile path . . . "Hit!"

The second volley from the M-1s killed eight tanks, then others began to explode from antitank missiles launched out of the village. The Russians had defiladed tanks on their flanks, and in front of them was a village bristling with antitank missiles: the German colonel had set a moving ambush, and the pursuing Russians had fallen into it. Already the Leopards were sweeping around left and right from behind the village to catch the Russians in the open. The air-control officer brought his fighter-bombers in on the Soviet artillery positions yet again. Soviet fighters engaged them, but while doing that they could not interfere with the land battle, and now a squadron of German Gazelle missile-armed choppers added their fire into the killing ground. The Soviet tanks fired off smoke and desperately tried to engage their enemies, but the Americans were dug in deep, and the German missileers in the village skillfully changed firing points after every shot.

Mackall shifted one platoon right and the other left. His own gunner located and killed a second command tank, then the Germans enveloped the Russian formation from north and south. Still outnumbered, the Germans nevertheless caught the Russians off balance, raking the tank column with their big 120mm gun tubes. The Soviet commander ordered his helicopters back in to blast open an escape route. They surprised and killed three German tanks before missiles began to drop them from the sky yet again. Suddenly it became too much. As Mackall watched, the Soviet force wheeled and retreated toward the hills, with the Germans in pursuit. The counterattack was pressed to the limit, and Mackall knew that *nobody* did that as well as the Krauts. By the time he had orders to move, the initial defense position was back in friendly hands. The battle had lasted barely over an hour. Two Soviet motor-rifle divisions had now been decimated on the road to Bieben.

The crewmen opened their hatches to let fresh air into the stifling turret. Fifteen empty cases rattled about on the floor. The fire-control computer was out again, but Woody had killed another four tanks, two of them belonging to Soviet officers. The troop commander came over to him in a jeep.

"Three tanks damaged," Mackall reported. "Have to drag them clear for repairs." His face split into a wide grin: "They ain't never gonna take this town away from us!"

"Those *Bundeswehr* regulars made the difference." The lieutenant nodded. "Okay, start getting your people reloaded."

"Oh, yeah. Last time I came back five rounds short."

"They're thinning out the ammo issue. It's not getting across to us as quick as we thought."

Mackall thought that one over and didn't like what he came up with. "Have somebody tell those Navy pukes that we can stop these bastards if they get their shit together!"

USS *PHARRIS*

Morris had never seen Hampton Roads so crowded. At least sixty merchantmen were swinging at anchor, with a beefed-up escort force preparing to take them to sea. *Saratoga* was in also, her mainmast gone and a replacement being fabricated on the quay while repairs were under way for less visible damage from her near-miss. Numerous aircraft circled overhead, and several ships had their search radars on lest a Soviet submarine sneak close inshore and launch cruise missiles into the mass of shipping.

Pharris was tied to the fueling pier, taking on fuel oil for her boilers and jet fuel for her helicopter. The single ASROC she'd expended had already been replaced, as had the six chaff rockets. Aside from that, the only thing that needed to be taken aboard was food. Ed Morris handed his patrol report to a messenger who would deliver it to his squadron commander. He would have gone himself, but there was no time. They were scheduled to sail in another twelve hours. This was another twenty-knot convoy, bound for the French ports of LeHavre and Brest with heavy equipment and munitions.

Morris had been given the fleet intelligence report. If anything, matters had gotten worse. Twenty NATO submarines were now staked out in the G-I-UK gap, trying to make up for the loss of the SOSUS line. They reported killing a sizable number of Soviet submarines, but they also reported that some had gotten through, and for each known leaker, Morris was sure that there were four or five unknowns. The first convoy had gotten virtually a free ride. Those few Soviet submarines in the Atlantic at the time had been spread thin, and were forced to race noisily to their convoy targets. No longer. About sixty were thought to be in the Atlantic now, at least half of them nuclear-powered. Morris thought over the numbers, what the Soviet inventory was, how many kills NATO claimed, and wondered if sixty was an optimistic assessment.

Then there were the Backfires. The convoy would be taking a southerly routing, adding two full days to the crossing time but forcing the Soviet bombers to stretch to the limit of their fuel. Also, thirty minutes before each satellite pass, the convoy would reverse course to a westerly heading in the hope that the Soviets would then vector their bombers and submarines to the wrong point. A pair of carrier battle groups was at sea and would offer support if possible. Clearly they wanted to spring a trap on the Backfires. The carrier groups would be steaming an evasive path, trying to avoid satellite detection entirely. Morris knew this was possible, an exercise in geometry, but it placed serious limits on the carriers' freedom of action—and having the carrier groups at sea would take up some of the antisubmarine patrol aircraft that the convoys depended on. A compromise, but then all life, and certainly any war operation, was a collection of compromises. Morris lit an unfiltered cigarette. He'd broken the habit years before, but halfway through the outbound leg of his first war cruise he'd found himself at the ship's store purchasing a carton of tax-free "at sea" smokes. The added hazard to his health, he judged, was no more than incidental. Already nine destroyers and frigates had been sunk, two with all hands.

ICELAND

Edwards had learned to hate the rust-colored contour lines on his maps. Each one announced a change of twenty meters. He tried to work it out in his head, but got no further than sixty-five-point-six feet for every one of the Goddamned red-brown lines. Sometimes the lines were spread apart by as much as an eighth of an inch. Other times they were packed together tightly enough that the lieutenant half expected to find a sheer wall. He remembered the one visit he'd had to Washington, D.C., and the time he and his father had scornfully walked past the tourists lined up to wait for an elevator ride to the top of the Washington Monument, preferring to walk the five hundred feet up the square-spiral staircase to the observation deck. They'd arrived at the top tired but proud. He was now making that same climb about every ninety minutes, except this time there were no smooth, even steps, and no elevator awaited them at the top for a more relaxing trip down . . . and no taxi to the hotel.

They climbed ten contour lines—two hundred meters, or six hundred fifty-six feet—three hours after breaking camp; crossing, the map said, from the Skorradalshreppur second-order administrative division to the Lundarreykjadashreppur second-order administrative division. There was no green highway sign to announce this, the Icelanders being bright enough to know that anyone who traveled out here lived here and needed no directions. They were rewarded with two kilometers of fairly level terrain as they walked between a pair of marshes. It was littered with rock and ash from what seemed to be an extinct volcano about four miles away.

"Take a break," Edwards said. He sat down next to a three-foot rock so that he'd have something to lean against, and was surprised when Vigdis came over. She sat down three feet away, facing him.

"How are you today?" he asked. There was life in her eyes now, Mike saw. Perhaps the demons that had awakened her the previous day were now gone? No, he thought, they'd never be completely gone—but you had to be alive to have nightmares, and they would probably fade in time. With time you could recover from anything, except murder.

"I have not thank you for my life."

"We could not stand by and let them kill you," he said, wondering if it was a lie. If the Russians had simply killed all three people in the house, would he have attacked them or would he have waited and simply looted the house after they'd left? It was a time for the truth.

"I didn't do it for you, not only for you."

"I do not understand."

Edwards took his wallet from a back pocket and opened it to a five-year-old photograph. "That's Sandy, Sandra Miller. We grew up on the same block, all the way through school. Maybe we would have gotten married someday," he said quietly. *And maybe not,* he admitted to himself. *People change.* "I went to the Air Force Academy, she went to the University of Connecticut in Hartford. October of her second year, she disappeared. She was raped and murdered. They found her a week later in a ditch. The guy who did it—they never proved he killed Sandy, but he raped two other girls at the school—well, he's in a mental hospital now. They said he was crazy, wasn't really responsible. So someday the docs'll say he's cured, and they'll let him out, and Sandy'll still be dead." Edwards looked down at the rocks.

"I couldn't do anything about that. I'm not a cop, I was two thousand miles away. But not this time." His voice showed no emotion at all. "This time was different."

"You love Sandy?" Vigdis asked.

How to answer that one? Mike wondered. It sure did seem like that, five years ago, didn't it? But would it have worked out? *You haven't exactly been celibate these last few years, have you? But it hasn't been the same, either, has it?* He looked at the photograph taken three days before Sandy had been killed. It had arrived in his box at Colorado Springs after her death, though he hadn't known it at the time. Her dark, shoulder-length hair, the tilt of the head, the impish smile that went with an infectious laugh . . . all gone.

"Yes." There was emotion in his voice now.

"You do for her then, yes?"

"Yes," Edwards lied. *I did it for me.*

"I do not know your name."

"Mike, Michael Edwards."

"You do this for me, Michael. Thank you for my life." There were the first beginnings of a smile. She placed her hand on his. It was soft and warm.

27. Casualties

KEFLAVIK, ICELAND

"At first we thought that they simply drove off the cliff road. We found this in the vehicle." The major of field police held up the top of a broken bottle of vodka. "But the medical corpsman who collected their personal effects found this."

The major pulled the rubberized sheet off the one body that had been thrown clear when the vehicle hit the rocks. The stab wound in the chest was unmistakable.

"And you said that the Icelanders were as peaceful as sheep, Comrade General," the KGB colonel observed sardonically.

The major continued, "It is difficult to reconstruct exactly what happened. There was a farm a short distance away whose house was burned to the ground. We found two bodies in the wreckage. Both had been shot."

"Who were they?" General Andreyev asked.

"Impossible to identify the bodies. The only way we knew they were shot was the bullet hole in the sternum, so that was likely done at very close range. I had one of our surgeons look at them. A man and a woman, probably in their middle years. According to a local government official, the farm was occupied by a married couple with one daughter, age"—the major checked his notes—"twenty. The daughter has not been found."

"What of the patrol?"

"They were southbound on the coast road when they disappeared—"

"No one spotted the fires?" the KGB colonel asked sharply.

"There was heavy rain that night. Both the burning vehicle and the farmhouse were below the horizon for the neighboring observation patrols. As you know, the road conditions here have upset our patrol schedules, and the mountains interfere with radio performance. So when the patrol was late getting in, no particular note was made of it. You can't see the vehicle from the road, and as a result they were not spotted until the helicopter flew over it."

"The other bodies, how did they die?" the General wanted to know.

"When the vehicle burned, the soldiers' hand grenades cooked off, with the obvious results. Except for the sergeant here, there is no telling how they died. So far as we can tell, no weapons were taken. All the rifles were there, but some items are unaccounted for: a map case and some other minor things. Possibly they were blown clear of the vehicle by the explosions and fell into the sea, but I doubt this."

"Conclusions?"

"Comrade General, there is not a great deal to go on, but I surmise that the patrol visited the farmhouse, 'liberated' this bottle of vodka, probably shot and killed the two people who lived there, and burned the house. The daughter is missing. We are searching the area for her body. At some time after this happened, the patrol was surprised and killed by an armed party which then tried to make their deaths look like a vehicle accident. We should assume that there is at least one band of resistance fighters at large."

"I disagree," the KGB colonel announced. "Not all the enemy troops have been accounted for. I think that your 'resistance fighters' are probably NATO personnel who escaped when we took Keflavik. They ambushed our troops, then murdered the farm people in the hope of stirring the local population against us."

General Andreyev shared a furtive look with his major of field police. It had been a KGB lieutenant commanding the patrol. The *chekisti* had insisted that some of their people accompany the roving patrols. Just what he needed, the General thought. Bad enough that his crack paratroopers were consigned to garrison duty—always destructive to unit morale and discipline—but now they were jailers, too, and in some cases commanded by jailers. So the arrogant young KGB officer—he'd never met a humble one—had thought to have himself some fun. Where was the daughter? The answer to this mystery certainly lay with her. But the mystery wasn't the important thing, was it?

"I think we should interrogate the local inhabitants to see what they know," the KGB officer announced.

"There are no 'local inhabitants,' Comrade," the major answered. "Look at your map. This is an isolated farm. The nearest neighbor is seven kilometers away."

"But—"

"Who killed these unfortunates, and why, is unimportant. We have armed enemies out there," Andreyev said. "This is a military matter, not something for our colleagues in the KGB. I'll have a helicopter search the area around the farm. If we find this resistance group, or whatever it is, we will deal with it as with any band of armed enemies. You may interrogate any prisoners we manage to capture, Comrade Colonel. Also, for the moment any KGB officer who accompanies our security patrols will be an observer, not a commander. We cannot risk your men in combat situations for which they have not been fully trained. So. Let me talk to my operations officer to see how we will handle the search. Comrades, you did well to bring this to our attention. Dismissed." The *chekist* wanted to stay, but KGB or not, he was only a colonel, and the General was exercising his legitimate prerogatives as commander on the scene.

An hour later, a Mi-24 attack helicopter lifted off to check the area around the burned farm.

STORNOWAY, SCOTLAND

"Again?" Toland asked.

"Not a bank holiday, Commander," the group captain replied. "Two regiments of Backfires departed their bases twenty minutes ago. If we want to catch their tankers, we must move smartly."

Within minutes, two EA-6B Prowlers, designed to find and jam enemy radar and radio signals, were climbing to altitude on a northwest heading. Known with backhanded affection as the Queer, the EA-6B's most striking characteristic was its canopies, inlaid with real gold to protect sensitive on-board instruments against electromagnetic radiation. As the planes climbed, their pilots and electronics officers were already working in their gilt cages.

Two hours later they spotted their prey, radioed back the signal bearings—and four Tomcats rolled down the runway of Stornoway.

NORWEGIAN SEA

Cruising at an altitude of thirty-six thousand feet the Tomcats flew race-track-shaped patterns north and south of the predicted course for the Soviet tankers. Their powerful search / missile-guidance radars were shut down. Instead, they swept the skies with a built-in TV camera that could identify aircraft as far as forty miles away. Conditions were ideal, a clear sky with only a few high cirrus clouds; the fighters left no contrails that might warn another aircraft of their presence. The pilots curved their fighters around the sky, their eyes shifting out to check the horizon, then in to check engine instruments, a cycle repeated every ten seconds.

"Well, lookie here . . ." the squadron commander said to his weapons operator. The flight officer in the Tomcat's back seat centered the TV camera on the aircraft.

"Looks like a Badger to me."

"I don't suppose he's alone. Let's wait."

"Roge."

The bomber was over forty miles off. Soon two more appeared, along with something smaller.

"That's a fighter. So, they have fighter escorts this far out, eh? I count a total of . . . six targets." The weapons operator tightened up his shoulder straps, then activated his missile controls. "All weapons armed and ready. Fighters first?"

"Fighters first, light 'em up," the pilot agreed. He toggled up his radio. "Two, this is Lead, we have four tankers and a pair of fighters on a course of about zero-eight-five, forty miles west of my position. We are engaging now. Come on in. Over."

"Roger that. On the way, Lead. Out." Two brought his interceptor into a tight turn and advanced his throttles to the stops.

The leader's radar activated. They now had two fighters and four tankers identified. The first two Phoenixes would be targeted on the fighters.

"Shoot!"

The two missiles dropped clear of their shackle points and ignited, leading the Tomcat to the targets.

The Russian tankers had detected the fighter's AWG-9 radar and were already trying to evade. Their escorting fighters went to full power and activated their own missile-guidance radars, only to find that they were still outside missile range to the attacking fighters. Both switched on their jamming pods and began to jink their aircraft up and down as they closed in hope of launching their own missiles. They couldn't run away, there wasn't enough fuel for that, and their mission was to keep the fighters off the tankers.

The Phoenix missiles burned through the air at Mach 5, closing the distance to their targets in just under a minute. One Soviet pilot never saw the missile, and was blotted from the sky in a ball of red and black. The other did, and threw his stick over, a second before the missile exploded. It nearly missed, but fragments tore into the fighter's port wing. The pilot struggled to regain control as he fell from the sky.

Behind the fighters, the tankers split up, two heading north, the other pair south. The lead Tomcat took the northern pair and killed both with his remaining two Phoenixes. His wingman racing up from the north fired two missiles, hitting with one, and missing with the other, as the missile was confused by the Badger's jamming gear. The Tomcat continued to close, and fired another missile. By this time he was close enough to track the bird visually. The AIM-54 missile ran straight and true, exploding only ten feet from the Badger's tail. Hot fragments ripped into the converted bomber and detonated the remaining fumes in its refueling tanks. The Soviet bomber disappeared in a thundering orange flash.

The fighters swept their radars around the sky, hoping to find targets for their remaining missiles. Six more Badgers were a hundred miles off, but they had already been warned by the leading tankers and were heading north. The Tomcats didn't have enough fuel to pursue. They turned for home and landed at Stornoway an hour later with nearly dry tanks.

"Five confirmed kills and a damage," the squadron commander told Toland. "It worked."

"This time." Toland was pleased nevertheless. The U.S. Navy had just completed its first offensive mission. Now for the next one. Information was just in on the Backfire raid. They'd hit a convoy off the Azores, and a pair of Tomcats was waiting two hundred miles south of Iceland to meet them on the return leg.

STENDAL, GERMAN DEMOCRATIC REPUBLIC

"Our losses have been murderous," said the General of Soviet Frontal Aviation.

"I will tell our motor-rifle troops just how serious your losses have been," Alekseyev replied coldly.

"We have lost nearly double our projections."

"So have we! At least our ground troops are fighting. I watched an attack. You sent in *four* attack fighters. *Four!*"

"I know of this attack. There was a full regiment assigned, more than twenty, plus your own attack helicopters. The NATO fighters are engaging us ten kilometers behind the front. My pilots must fight for their lives simply to get where your tanks are—and then all too often they are engaged by our own surface-to-air missiles!"

"Explain," ordered Alekseyev's superior.

"Comrade General, the NATO radar surveillance aircraft are not easy targets—they are too well protected. With their airborne radar, they can vector their fighters against ours to launch their missile attacks from beyond visual range. When our pilots learn that they are being attacked, they must evade, no? Do your tankers sit still to give their enemies an easy shot? This often means that they must drop their bombs to maneuver. Finally, when they do manage to reach the battle zone they are frequently shot at by friendly missile units who don't take the time to distinguish between friend and foe." It was an old story, and not merely a Soviet problem.

"You are telling us that NATO has command of the air," Alekseyev said.

"No, they do not. Neither side does. Our surface-to-air missiles deny them the ability to control the air over the battle line, and their fighters—helped by their surface-to-air missiles, and ours!—deny it to us. The sky over the battlefield belongs to no one." *Except the dead,* the Air Force General thought to himself.

Alekseyev thought of what he had seen at Bieben, and wondered how correct he was.

"We must do better," the Theater Commander said. "The next massed attack we launch will have proper air support if it means stripping fighters from every unit on the front."

"We are trying to get more aircraft forward by using deceptive maneuvering. Yesterday we tried to feint NATO's fighters to the wrong place. It nearly worked, but we made a mistake. That mistake has been identified."

"We attack south of Hannover at 0600 tomorrow. I want two hundred aircraft at the front line supporting my divisions."

"You'll have them," the Air Force General agreed. Alekseyev watched the flyer leave.

"So, Pasha?"

"That's a start—if the two hundred fighters show up."

"We have our helicopters, too."

"I watched what happens to helicopters in a missile environment. Just when I thought they'd blast a hole through the German lines, a combination of SAMs and fighters nearly annihilated them. They have to expose themselves too greatly when they fire their missiles. The courage of the pilots is remarkable, but courage alone is not enough. We have underestimated NATO firepower—no, more properly we have overestimated our ability to neutralize it."

"We've been attacking prepared positions since this war began. Once we break into the open—"

"Yes. A mobile campaign will reduce our losses and give us a much more even contest. We have to break through." Alekseyev looked down at the map. Just after dawn tomorrow, an army—four motor-rifle divisions, supported by a division of tanks—would hurl itself into the NATO lines. "And here seems to be the place. I want to be forward again."

"As you wish, Pasha. But be careful. By the way, the doctor tells me the cut on your hand was from a shell fragment. You are entitled to a decoration."

"For this?" Alekseyev looked at his bandaged hand. "I've cut myself worse than this shaving. No medal for this, it would be an insult to our troops."

ICELAND

They were climbing down a rocky slope when the helicopter appeared two miles west of them. It was low, about three hundred feet over the ridge line, and moving slowly toward them. The Marines immediately fell to the ground and crawled to places where they might hide in shadows. Edwards took a few steps to Vigdis and pulled her down also. She was wearing a white patterned sweater that was all too easy to spot. The lieutenant stripped off his field jacket and draped it around her, holding her head down as he wrapped the hood over her blond hair.

"Don't move at all. They're looking for us." Edwards kept his own head up briefly to see where his men were. Smith waved for him to get down. Edwards did so, keeping his eyes open so that he could look sideways at the chopper. It was another Hind. He could see rocket pods hanging from stubby wings on either side of the airframe. Both the doors to the passenger compartment were open, revealing a squad of infantrymen, weapons at the ready, looking down. "Oh, shit."

The noise from its turboshaft engines increased as the Hind came closer, and the massive five-bladed main rotor beat at the air, stirring up the volcanic dust that coated everything on the plateau they had just left. Edwards's hand tightened on the M-16's pistol grip, and he thumbed off the safety. The helicopter was coming almost sideways, its rocket pods pointed at the flatlands behind the Marines. Edwards could make out the machine guns in the Hind's nose, some kind of rotary gun like the American minigun that spat out four thousand rounds per minute. They wouldn't have a chance in hell against that.

"Turn, you son of a bitch," Mike said under his breath.

"What is it doing?" Vigdis asked.

"Just relax. Don't move at all." Oh, God, don't let them see us now . . .

"There! Look there at one o'clock," the gunner said from the front seat of the helicopter.

"So this mission isn't a waste after all," the pilot replied. "Go ahead."

The gunner centered his sights and armed the machine gun, setting his selector for a five-shot burst. His target was agreeably still as he depressed the trigger.

"Got him!"

Edwards jumped at the sound. Vigdis didn't move at all. The lieutenant moved his rifle slightly, bringing it to bear on the chopper—which moved south, dropping below the ridgeline. He saw three heads come up. What had they shot at? The engine sounds changed as the helicopter landed, not far away.

The gunner had hit the buck with three bullets, with little damage to the edible tissue. There was just enough in the eighty-pound animal to feed the squad and the helicopter crew. The paratroop sergeant slit the deer's throat with his combat knife, then set to remove the viscera. The local deer were nothing like the animals his father hunted in Siberia, but for the first time in three weeks he'd have some fresh meat. That was sufficient to make this boring mission worthwhile. The carcass was loaded into the Hind. Two minutes later it circled up to cruise altitude and flew back to Keflavik.

They watched it depart, the stuttering rotor sound diminishing on the breeze.

"What was that all about?" Edwards asked his sergeant.

"Beats the hell out of me, skipper. I think we better boogie on outa here. They were sure as hell looking for something, and I'll betcha it's us. Let's keep to places with some kind of cover."

"You got it, Jim. Lead off." Edwards walked back to Vigdis.

"Is safe now?"

"They've gone. Why don't you keep that jacket on. It makes you harder to spot."

It was two sizes too large for Edwards, and looked like a tent on Vigdis's diminutive frame. She held her arms out straight in an effort to get her hands out of the sleeves, and for the first time since he met her, Vigdis Agustdottir smiled.

USS *PHARRIS*

"All ahead one-third," the executive officer ordered.

"All ahead one-third, aye," the quartermaster of the watch responded, moving the annunciator handle up from the Ahead Full setting. A moment later the inside pointer changed also. "Engine room answers all ahead one-third."

"Very well."

Pharris slowed, coming off a twenty-five-knot sprint to commence another drift maneuver, and allowing her towed-array sonar to listen for hostile submarines. Morris was in his bridge chair, going over messages from shore. He rubbed his eyes and lit up another Pall Mall.

"Bridge," called the urgent voice of a lookout. "Periscope feather on the port bow! Halfway to the horizon, port bow!" Morris snatched his binoculars from the holder and had them to his eyes in an instant. He didn't see anything.

"Battle stations!" ordered the XO. The alarm gong went off a second later and weary men ran again to their posts. Morris looped his binoculars around his neck and ran down the ladder to his battle station in CIC.

The sonar loosed a dozen ranging pings to port as Morris took his position in CIC. Nothing. The helo lifted off as the frigate maneuvered north, allowing her towed-array sonar to track on the possible contact.

"Passive sonar contact, evaluate as possible submarine bearing zero-one-three," announced the towed-array operator. "Steam noises, sounds like a possible nuke."

"I got nothing there," said the active-sonar operator.

Morris and his ASW officer examined the water-conditions board. There was a layer at two hundred feet. The passive sonar was below it, and could well be hearing a submarine that the active pings could not reach. The lookout might have seen anything from a spouting whale—this was the mating season for humpbacks—to a streak of foam . . . or the feathery wake left by a periscope. If it was a submarine, he had plenty of time to duck under the layer. The target was too close to be bottom-bounced and too far for the sonar to blast directly through the layer.

"Less than five miles," ASW said. "More than two. If this is a sub, we're up against a good one."

"Great. Get the helo on him right now!" Morris examined the plot. The submarine could have heard his frigate as it sprinted at twenty-five knots. Now, at reduced speed, and with Prairie / Masker operating, *Pharris* would be very hard to detect . . . so the sub's fire-control solution had probably just gone out the window. But Morris didn't have one either, and the submarine was perilously close. An urgent contact report was radioed to the screen commander twenty miles away.

The Sea Sprite dropped a pattern of sonobuoys. Minutes passed.

"I got a weak signal on number six and a medium on number four," the sonobuoy petty officer said. Morris watched the plot. That made the contact less than three miles off.

"Drop some pingers," he ordered. Behind him the ship's weapons officer ordered the arming of the ASROC and torpedo launchers. Three miles off, the helicopter turned and swept across the target area, dropping three CASS buoys this time, which sent out active, nondirectional pings.

"Contact, a strong contact on buoy nine. Classify as possible submarine."

"I got him, bearing zero-one-five—this one's a sub, classify as positive submarine contact," said the towed-array man. "He just increased power. Some cavitation sounds. Single-screw submarine, maybe a Victor-class, bearing changing rapidly left-to-right."

The active sonar still didn't have him despite continuous maximum-power pings down the correct line of bearing. The submarine was definitely under the layer.

Morris wanted to maneuver but decided against it. A radical turn would cause his towed-array sonar to curve, rendering it useless for several minutes. Then he would have to depend on sonobuoys alone, and Morris trusted his towed sonar more than the buoys.

"Bearing to contact is now zero-one-five and steady . . . noise level is down somewhat." The operator pointed at his screen. Morris was surprised. The contact bearing had been changing rapidly and was now steadied down?

The helicopter made yet another pass. A new sonobuoy registered the contact, but the MAD gear didn't confirm the presence of a submarine and the contact was fading. The noise level continued to drop. Morris watched the relative position of the contact pass aft. What the hell was this character doing?

"Periscope, starboard bow!" the talker reported.

"Wrong place, sir . . . unless we're looking at a noisemaker," the operator said.

The ASW officer had the active sonar change bearing and the results were immediate.

"Contact bearing three-four-five, range fifteen hundred yards!" A bright pip glowed on the sonar scope.

"All ahead flank!" Morris yelled. Somehow the submarine had evaded the towed sonar, then popped up atop the layer and run up his periscope. That could only mean one thing. "Right full rudder."

"Hydrophone effects—torpedoes inbound, bearing three-five-one!"

Instantly the weapons officer ordered the launch of an antisubmarine torpedo down the same bearing in the hope that it would disturb the attacking submarine. If the Russian's torpedoes were wire-guided, he'd have to cut the wires free to maneuver the sub clear of the American return shot.

Morris raced up the ladder to the bridge. Somehow the submarine had broken contact and maneuvered into firing position. The frigate changed course and speed in an attempt to ruin the submarine's fire-control solution.

"I see one!" the XO said, pointing over the bow. The Soviet torpedo left a visible white trail on the surface. Morris noted it, something he had not expected. The frigate turned rapidly.

"Bridge, I show two torpedoes, bearing constant three-five-zero and decreasing range," the tactical action officer said rapidly. "Both are pinging at us. The Nixie is operating."

Morris lifted a phone. "Report the situation to the escort commander."

"Done, skipper. Two more helos are heading this way."

Pharris was now doing twenty knots and accelerating, turning her stern to the torpedoes. Her helicopter was now aft of the beam, frantically making runs with its magnetic anomaly detector, trying to locate the Soviet sub.

The torpedo's wake crossed past the frigate's bow as Morris's ship kept her helm over. There was an explosion aft. White water leaped a hundred feet into the air as the first Russian "fish" collided with the nixie torpedo decoy. But they had only one nixie deployed. There was another torpedo out there.

"Left full rudder!" Morris told the quartermaster. "Combat, what about the contact?" The frigate was now doing twenty-five knots.

"Not sure, sir. The sonobuoys have our torp but nothing else."

"We're gonna take a hit," the XO said. He pointed to a white trail on the water, less than two hundred yards away. It must have missed the frigate on its first try, then turned for another. Homing torpedoes kept looking until they ran out of fuel.

There was nothing Morris could do. The torpedo was approaching on his port bow. If he turned right, it would only give the fish a larger target. Below him the ASROC launcher swung left toward the probable location of the submarine, but without an order to fire, all the operator could do was train it out. The white wake kept getting closer. Morris leaned over the rail, staring at it with mute rage as it extended like a finger toward his bow. It couldn't possibly miss now.

"That's not real smart, Cap'n." Bosun Clarke's hand grabbed Morris's shoulder and yanked him down to the deck. He was just grabbing for the executive officer when it hit.

The impact lifted Morris a foot off the steel deck. He didn't hear the explosion, but an instant after he had bounced off the steel a second time, he was deluged with a sheet of white water that washed him against a stanchion. His first thought was that he'd been thrown overboard. He rose to see his executive officer—headless, slumped against the pilothouse door. The bridge wing was torn apart, the stout metal shielding ripped by fragments. The pilothouse windows were gone. What he saw next was worse.

The torpedo had struck the frigate just aft of the bow-mounted sonar. Already the bow had collapsed, the keel sundered by the explosion. The foc's'l was awash, and the horrible groaning of metal told him that the bow was being ripped off his ship. Morris staggered into the bridge and yanked the annunciator handle to All Stop, failing to notice that the engineers had already stopped engines. The ship's momentum pushed her forward. As Morris watched, the bow twisted to starboard, ten degrees off true, and the forward gunmount became awash, its crew trying to head aft. Below the mount were other men. Morris knew that they were dead, hoped that they had died instantly, and were not drowning, trapped in a sinking steel cage. His men. How many had their battle stations forward of the ASROC launcher?

Then the bow tore away. A hundred feet of the ship left the remainder to the accompaniment of screeching metal. It turned as he watched, colliding with the afterpart of the ship as it rotated in the water like a small berg. There was movement at an exposed watertight door. He saw a man try to get free, and succeed, the figure jumping into the water and swimming away from the wallowing bow.

The bridge crew was alive, all cut by flying glass but at their posts. Chief Clarke took a quick look at the pilothouse, then ran below to assist with damage control. The damage-control parties were already racing forward with fire hoses and welding gear, and at damage-control central the men examined the trouble board to see how severe the flooding was. Morris lifted a sound-powered phone and twisted the dial to this compartment.

"Damage-control report!"

"Flooding aft to frame thirty-six, but I think she'll float—for a little while anyway. No fires. Waiting for reports now."

Morris switched settings on the phone. "Combat, radio the screen commander that we've taken a hit and need assistance."

"Done, sir. *Gallery*'s heading out this way. Looks like the sub got away. They're still searching for her. We have some shock damage here. All the radars are down. Bow sonar is out. ASROC is out. The tail is still working, though, and the Mark-32 mounts still work. Wait—screen commander's sending us a tug, sir."

"Okay, you have the conn. I'm going below to look at the damage." *You have the conn,* Morris thought. How do you conn a ship that ain't moving? A minute later he was at a bulkhead, watching men trying to shore it up with lumber.

"This one's fairly solid, sir, the next one forward's leaking like a damn sieve, no way we'll patch it all. When the bow let go, it must have twisted everything loose." The officer grabbed a seaman by the shoulder. "Go to the after D / C locker and get more four-by-fours!"

"Will this one hold?"

"I don't know. Clarke is checking the bottom out now. We'll have to weld in some patches and stiffeners. Give me about ten minutes and I'll tell you if she'll float or not."

Clarke appeared. He was breathing heavily. "The bulkhead's sprung at the tank tops, and there's a small crack, too. Leaking pretty good. The pumps are on, and just about keeping even. I think we can shore it up, but we have to hustle."

The damage-control officer led the welders below at once. Two men appeared with a portable pump. Morris ordered them below.

"How many men missing?" Morris asked Chief Clarke. He was holding his arm strangely.

"All the guys made it out of the five-inch mount, but I haven't seen anybody from belowdecks. Shit, I think I broke something myself." Clarke looked at his right arm and shook his head angrily. "I don't think many guys made it outa the bow, sir. The watertight doors are twisted some, they gotta be jammed tight."

"Get that arm looked at," Morris ordered.

"Oh, fuck the arm, skipper! You need me." The man was right. Morris went back topside with Clarke behind him.

On reaching the bridge, Morris dialed up engineering. The noise on the phone answered his first question.

The engineer spoke over the hiss of escaping steam. "Shock damage, Captain. We got some ruptured steam pipes on the number one boiler. I think number two will still work, but I've popped the safeties on both just in case. The diesel generators are on line. I got some hurt men here. I'm sending them out. I—okay, okay. We just did a check of number two boiler. A few minor leaks, but we can fix 'em quick. Otherwise everything looks pretty tight. I can have it back on line in fifteen minutes."

"We need it." Morris hung up.

Pharris lay dead in the water. With the safety valves opened, steam vented onto the massive stack structure, giving off a dreadful rasping sound that seemed like the ship's own cry of pain. The frigate's sleek clipper bow had been replaced by a flat face of torn metal and hanging wires. The water around the ship was foul with oil from ruptured fuel tanks. For the first time Morris noticed that the ship was down by the stern; when he stood straight, the ship was misaligned. He knew he had to wait for another damage-control report. As with an accident victim, the prognosis depended on the work of surgeons, and they could not be rushed or disturbed. He lifted the phone to CIC.

"Combat, Bridge. What's the status of that submarine contact?"

"*Gallery*'s helo dropped on it, but the torp ran dry without hitting anything. Looks like he ran northeast, but we haven't had anything for about five minutes. There's an Orion in the area now."

"Tell them to check inside of us. This character isn't going to run away unless he has to. He might be running in, not out. Tell the screen commander."

"Aye, Cap'n."

He hadn't hung the phone up when it buzzed.

"Captain speaking."

"She'll float, sir," the damage-control officer said at once. "We're patching the bulkhead now. It won't be tight, but the pumps can handle the leakage. Unless something else goes bad on us, we'll get her home. They sending the tug out to us?"

"Yes."

"If we get a tow, sir, it better be sternfirst. I don't want to think about trying to run this one into a seaway."

"Right." Morris looked at Clarke. "Get a gang of men aft. We'll be taking the tow at the stern, rig it up. Have them launch the whaleboat to look for survivors. I saw at least one man in the water. And get a sling on that arm."

"You got it, Cap'n." Clarke moved aft.

Morris went to CIC and found a working radio.

"X-Ray Alfa, this is *Pharris*," Morris called to the screen commander. "State your condition."

"We took one hit forward, the bow is gone all the way to the ASROC launcher. We cannot maneuver. I can keep her afloat unless we hit some bad weather. Both boilers currently down, but we should have power back in less than ten minutes. We have casualties, but I don't know how many or how bad yet.

"Commodore, we got hit by a nuke boat, probably a Victor. Unless I miss my guess, he's headed your way."

"We lost him, but he was heading out," the Commodore said.

"Start looking inside, sir," Morris urged. "This fellow got to knife-fighting range and pulled a beautiful number on us. This one isn't going to run away for long, he's too damned good for that."

The Commodore thought that one over briefly. "Okay, I'll keep that in mind. *Gallery*'s en route to you. What other assistance do you need?"

"You need *Gallery* more than we do. Just send us the tug," Morris answered. He knew that the submarine wouldn't be coming back to finish the kill. He'd accomplished that part of his mission. Next, he'd try to kill some merchants.

"Roger that. Let me know if you need anything else. Good luck, Ed."

"Thank you, sir. Out."

Morris ordered his helo to drop a double ring of sonobuoys around his ship just in case. Then the Sea Sprite found three men in the water, one of them dead. The whaleboat recovered them, allowing the helo to rejoin the convoy. It was assigned to *Gallery*, which took *Pharris*'s station as the convoy angled south.

Below, welders worked their gear in waist-deep saltwater as they struggled to seal off the breaks in the frigate's watertight bulkheads. The task lasted nine hours, then the pumps drained the water from the flooded compartments.

Before they had finished, the fleet tug *Papago* pulled alongside the frigate's square stern. Chief Clarke supervised as a stout towing wire was passed across and secured. An hour later, the tug was pulling the frigate on an easterly course at four knots, backwards to protect the damaged bow. Morris ordered his towed-array sonar to be strung over the bow, trailing it out behind to give them some small defense capability. Several extra lookouts were posted to watch for periscopes. It would be a slow, dangerous trip back home.

28. Breakthroughs

STENDAL, GERMAN DEMOCRATIC REPUBLIC

"Be careful, Pasha."

"As always, Comrade General." Alekseyev smiled. "Come, Captain."

Sergetov fell in behind his superior. Unlike during their previous front-line outing, both men wore protective body armor. The General carried only a sidearm to go along with his map case, but the captain was now officially a bodyguard in addition to a staff officer and had a small Czech submachine gun slung over his shoulder. He was a different man today, the captain saw. On Alekseyev's first trip to the front, he'd been tentative, almost hesitant in manner—it hadn't occurred to the younger man that, as senior as Alekseyev was, he had never seen combat before and had approached this gravest of contests with the same sort of apprehension as a new private. No longer. He had smelled the smoke. Now he knew how things worked or didn't work. The change was remarkable. His father was right, Sergetov thought, he was a man to be reckoned with. They were joined in their helicopter by an Air Force colonel. The Mi-24 lifted off in darkness, its fighter escort overhead.

LAMMERSDORF, FEDERAL REPUBLIC OF GERMANY

Not many people appreciated the importance of the videocassette recorder. A useful convenience for the home, to be sure, but not until a captain in the Royal Dutch Air Force had demonstrated a bright idea two years before had its battlefield utility been proven in secret exercises first in Germany, then in the Western United States.

NATO radar surveillance aircraft kept their customary positions high over the Rhein. The E-3A Sentry aircraft, better known as AWACS, and the smaller, lesser-known TR-1, flew their missions in boring circles or straight lines far behind the fighting front. They had similar but different functions. The AWACS was mainly concerned with air traffic. The TR-1, an upgraded version of the venerable U-2, looked for vehicles on the ground. Initially the TR-1 had been something of a failure. Because it tracked too many targets, many of them immobile radar reflectors set everywhere by the Soviets, the NATO commanders had been deluged with information that was too disordered to use. Then came the VCR. All the data relayed from the aircraft was recorded on videotape anyway since it was a convenient medium for data storage, but the VCRs built into the NATO system possessed only a few operating features. The Dutch captain thought to bring his personal machine into his office, and demonstrated how by using fast forward and fast reverse, the radar data could be used to show not only where things were going, but also where they had come *from.* Computer support made the task easier by eliminating items that moved no more than once every two hours—thus erasing the Russian radar lures—and there it was, a brand-new intelligence tool.

With several copies made of each tape, a staff of over a hundred intelligence and traffic-control experts examined the data round the clock. Some engaged in straight tactical intelligence. Others looked for patterns. A large number of trucks moving at night to and from front-line units could only mean shuttle runs to fuel and ammunition dumps. A number of vehicles breaking away from a divisional convoy and deploying in line parallel to the front meant artillery preparing for an attack. The real trick, they had learned, was to get the data to the forward commanders quickly enough so they could make use of it.

At Lammersdorf, a Belgian lieutenant was just finishing up a tape that was six hours old, and his report was sent by land line to the forward NATO commanders. At least three divisions had been moved north and south on Autobahn-7, he reported. The Soviets would attack at Bad Salzdetfurth in strength, sooner than expected. Immediately, reserve units from the Belgian, German, and American armies were rushed forward, and allied air units alerted for a major land action. Fighting in this sector had been vicious enough already. The German forces covering the area south of Hannover were at less than 50-percent strength, and the battle that had not yet begun was already a race, as both sides tried to get reserves to the point of attack before the other.

HOLLE, FEDERAL REPUBLIC OF GERMANY

"Thirty minutes," Alekseyev told Sergetov. Four motor-rifle divisions were on line, covering a front of less than twenty kilometers. Behind them a tank division waited to exploit the first breach in German lines. The objective was the town of Alfeld on the Leine River. The town commanded two roads being used by NATO to shuttle units and supplies north and south, and its capture would open a breach in the NATO lines, allowing the Soviet operational / maneuver groups to burst into NATO's rear.

"Comrade General, how are things progressing in your opinion?" the captain asked quietly.

"Ask me in a few hours," the General answered. The river valley to his rear was yet another wasteland of men and arms. They were only thirty kilometers from the border—and the Red Army's tanks had been expected to reach Holle in only two days. Alekseyev frowned, wondering what staff genius had come up with that timetable. Again the human factor had been overlooked. The morale and fighting spirit of the Germans was like nothing he had ever seen. He remembered his father's stories of the battles across the Ukraine and Poland, but he had never quite believed them. He believed them now. The Germans contested every lump of dirt in their country like wolves defending their cubs, retreating only when they were forced to, counterattacking at every opportunity, draining the blood from the advancing Russian units as they brought every weapon they had to bear.

Soviet doctrine had predicted heavy losses. The battle of movement could be achieved only by costly frontal assault which first had to blast a hole in the front lines—but the NATO armies were denying that hole to the Soviets. Their sophisticated weapons, firing from safe, prepared positions, were ripping through each attack wave. Their aircraft attacks in the Soviet rear sapped the strength of units before they could be committed to decisive battle and played hob with artillery support despite the most careful deceptive measures.

The Red Army was moving forward, Alekseyev reminded himself, and NATO was paying its own price. Their reserves were also being thinned out. The German forces were not using their mobility as Alekseyev would have, too often tying themselves to geographic locations instead of fighting the Soviet forces on the move. Of course, the General thought, they didn't have very much terrain to trade for time. He checked his watch.

A sheet of flame rose from the forests below him as Russian artillery began its preparatory bombardment. Next came the multiple-rocket launchers, and the morning sky was alight with streaks of fire. Alekseyev turned his binoculars downrange. In a few seconds he saw the orange-white explosions of the rounds as they impacted on NATO lines. He was too far from the fighting front to see any detail, but an area that had to be many kilometers across, lit up like the neon signs so popular in the West. There was a roar overhead, and the General saw the leading elements of the ground-attack fighters racing to the front.

"Thank you, Comrade General," Alekseyev breathed. He counted at least thirty Sukhoi and MiG fighter-bombers, all hugging the ground as they headed toward the battle line. His face crinkled into a determined smile as he walked into the command bunker.

"The lead elements are moving now," a colonel announced. On a table made of rough planks laid across sawhorses, grease pencil marks were made on the tactical maps. Red arrows began their march toward a series of blue lines. The plotters were all lieutenants, and each wore a telephone headset linked to a specific regimental headquarters. The officers connected to reserve units stood away from the table, puffing on their cigarettes as they watched the march of the arrows. Behind them the commander of 8th Guards Army stood quietly, watching his plan of attack unfold.

"Meeting moderate resistance. Enemy artillery and tank fire is being encountered," a lieutenant said.

Explosions rocked the command bunker. Two kilometers away, a flight of German Phantoms had just torn into a battalion of mobile guns.

"Enemy fighters overhead," the air defense officer said belatedly. A few eyes looked apprehensively up at the log ceiling of the bunker. Alekseyev's didn't join them. A NATO smart-bomb would kill them all in a blink. Much as he enjoyed his post as deputy commander of the theater, he wished himself back to the days when he had commanded a fighting division. Here he was only an observer, and he felt the need to have the reins in his own two hands.

"Artillery reports heavy counterbattery fire and air attacks. Our missiles are engaging enemy aircraft in the 57th Motor-Rifle Division's rear area," the air defense officer went on. "Heavy air activity over the front."

"Our fighters are engaging NATO aircraft," the Frontal Aviation officer reported. He looked up angrily. "Friendly SAMs are shooting down our fighters!"

"Air Defense Officer!" Alekseyev shouted. "Tell your units to identify their targets!"

"We have fifty aircraft over the front. We can handle the NATO fighters alone!" the aviator insisted.

"Tell all SAM batteries to hold fire on all targets above one thousand meters," Alekseyev ordered. He had *discussed* this with his Frontal Aviation commander the night before. The MiG pilots were to stay high after making their own attack runs, leaving the missile and gun batteries free to engage only those NATO aircraft that were an immediate threat to ground units. Why were his own planes getting hit?

Thirty thousand feet over the Rhein, two NATO E-3A radar aircraft fought for their lives. A determined Soviet attack was under way, two regiments of MiG-23 interceptors rocketing through the sky toward them. The onboard controllers were calling for help. This both distracted them from countering the attack, and stripped fighters from other missions. Heedless of their own safety, the Russians came west at over a thousand miles per hour with heavy jamming support. American F-15 Eagles and French Mirage jets converged on the threat, filling the sky with missiles. It was not enough. When the MiGs got to within sixty miles, the AWACS aircraft shut down their radars and dove for the ground to evade the attack. The NATO fighters over Bad Salzdetfurth were on their own. For the first time the Soviets had achieved air superiority over a major battlefield.

"Hundred-forty-third Guards Rifle Regiment reports they have broken through German lines," a lieutenant said. He didn't look up, but extended the arrow for which he was responsible. "Enemy units retreating in disarray."

"Hundred-forty-fifth Guards checking in," reported the plotting officer next to him. "The first line of German resistance has collapsed. Proceeding south along the axis of the rail line . . . enemy units are on the run. They are not regrouping, not attempting to turn."

The general commanding 8th Guards Army gave Alekseyev a triumphant look. "Get that tank division moving!"

The two understrength German brigades covering this sector had suffered too much, been called upon to stop too many attacks. Their men spent, their weapons depleted, they had no choice but to run from the enemy, hoping to form a new line in the woods behind Highway 243. At Hackenstedt, four kilometers away, 20th Guards Tank Division started moving down the road. Its three hundred T-80 main battle tanks, supported by several hundred more infantry assault carriers, spread left and right of the secondary road and formed its attack formation in columns of regiments. The 20th Tanks was the operation / maneuver group for 8th Guards Army. Since the war had begun, the Soviet Army had been trying to break one of these powerful units into the NATO rear. It was now possible.

"Well done, Comrade General," Alekseyev said. The plotting table showed a general breakthrough. Three of the four attacking motor-rifle divisions had broken through the German lines.

The MiGs succeeded in killing one of the AWACS aircraft and three Eagle fighters, at the price of nineteen of their own, in a furious air battle that lasted fifteen minutes. The surviving AWACS was back at altitude now, eighty miles *behind* the Rhein, and its radar operators were working to reestablish control of the air battle over central Germany as the MiGs ran for home through a cloud of NATO surface-to-air missiles. At murderous cost they had accomplished a mission for which they had not even been briefed.

But this was only the beginning. Now that the initial attack had succeeded, the most difficult part of the battle was under way. The generals and colonels commanding the attack had to move their units forward rapidly, careful to keep the formations intact as they leapfrogged their artillery southwest to provide continuous support for the advancing regiments. The tank division had the highest priority. It had to hit the next set of German lines only minutes behind the motor-rifle troops, in order to reach Alfeld before nightfall. Units of the field police established pre-planned traffic-control points, and directed units down roads whose marker signs had been removed by the Germans—of course. The process was not as easy as might have been expected. Units were not intact. Some commanders were dead, vehicles had broken down, and damaged roads slowed traffic well below normal rates of advance.

For their part the German troops were trying to reorganize. Rear-guard units lingered behind every turn in the road, pausing to loose their antitank missiles at the hard-charging Soviet advance guard, which took a particularly heavy toll of unit commanders. Allied aircraft were reorganizing also, and low-level attack fighters began to engage the Soviet units in the open.

Behind the sundered battle line a German tank brigade rolled into Alfeld, with a Belgian motorized regiment ten minutes behind. The Germans proceeded northeast on the main road, watched by citizens who had just been ordered to evacuate their homes.

FASLANE, SCOTLAND

"No luck, eh?" asked Todd Simms, commander of USS *Boston.*

"None," McCafferty confirmed. Even the trip into Faslane had been unlucky. The guard ship for the safe-transit corridor, HMS *Osiris,* had gotten into attack position without their having detected her. Had that Brit diesel sub been a Russian, McCafferty could very well be dead now. "We had our big chance against that amphibious group. Things were going perfect, y'know? The Russians had their sonobuoy lines out, and we beat them clean, just about had our targets lined up for the missile attack—I figured we'd hit with our missiles first, then go in with torpedoes—"

"Sounds good to me," Simms agreed.

"And somebody else launches his own torpedo attack. Screwed everything up. We lofted three Harpoons, but a helo saw us do it, and, bingo! we had the bastards all over us." McCafferty pulled open the door to the Officers Club. "I need a drink!"

"Hell, yes!" Simms laughed. "Everything looks better after a few beers. Hey, that sort of thing happens. Luck changes, Danny." Simms leaned over the bar. "Two strong ones."

"As you say, Commander." A white-coated steward drew two mugs of warm, dark beer. Simms picked up the bill and led his friend to a corner booth. There was some sort of small party going on at the far end of the room.

"Danny, for crying out loud, let up on yourself. Not your fault that Ivan didn't send you any targets, is it?"

McCafferty took a long pull on his mug. Two miles away *Chicago* was reprovisioning. They'd be in port for two days. *Boston* and another 688-class sub were tied to the same quay, with another pair due in later today. They were to be outfitted for a special mission, but they didn't yet know what it was. In the meantime, the officers and crewmen were using their modicum of free time to breathe fresh air and unwind. "You're right, Todd, right as ever."

"Good. Have some pretzels. Looks like quite a shindig over there. How about we wander over?" Simms lifted his beer and walked to the end of the room.

They found a gathering of submarine officers, which was not a surprise, but the center of attention was. He was a Norwegian captain, a blond man of about thirty who clearly hadn't been sober for several hours. As soon as he drained one jar of beer, a Royal Navy commander handed him another.

"I *must* find the man who save us!" the Norwegian insisted loudly and drunkenly.

"What gives?" Simms asked. Introductions were exchanged. The Royal Navy officer was captain of HMS *Oberon*.

"This is the chappie who blasted *Kirov* all the way back to Murmansk," he said. "He tells the story about every ten minutes. About time for him to begin again."

"Son of a bitch," McCafferty said. This was the guy who had sunk *his* target! Sure enough, the Norwegian began speaking again.

"We make our approach slowly. They come right"—he belched—"to us, and we creep very slow. I put periscope up, and there he is! Four thousand meters, twenty knots, he will pass within five hundred meters starboard." The beer mug swept toward the floor. "Down periscope! Arne—where are you, Arne? Oh, is drunk at table. Arne is weapons officer. He set to fire four torpedoes. Type thirty-seven, American torpedoes." He gestured at the two American officers who had just joined the crowd.

Four Mark-37s! McCafferty winced at the thought. That could ruin your whole day.

"*Kirov* is very close now. Up periscope! Course same, speed same, distance now two thousand meters—I shoot! One! Two! Three! Four! Reload and dive deep."

"You're the guy who ruined my approach!" McCafferty shouted.

The Norwegian almost appeared sober for a moment. "Who are you?"

"Dan McCafferty, USS *Chicago*."

"You were there?"

"Yes."

"You shoot missiles?"

"Yes."

"Hero!" The Norwegian submarine commander ran to McCafferty, almost knocking him down as he wrapped the American in a crushing bear hug. "You save my men! You save my ship!"

"What the hell is this?" Simms asked.

"Oh, introductions," said a Royal Navy captain. "Captain Bjorn Johannsen of His Norwegian Majesty's submarine *Kobben*. Captain Daniel McCafferty of USS *Chicago*."

"After we shoot *Kirov*, they come around us like wolves. *Kirov* blow up—"

"Four fish? I believe it," Simms agreed.

"Russians come to us with cruiser, two destroyers," Johannsen continued, now quite sober. "We, ah, evade, go deep, but they find us and fire their RBU rockets—many, many rockets. Most far, some close. We reload and I shoot at cruiser."

"You hit her?"

"One hit, hurt but not sink. This take, I am not sure, ten minutes, fifteen. It was very busy time, yes?"

"Me, too. We came in fast, flipped on the radar. There were three ships where we thought *Kirov* was."

"*Kirov* was sunk—blow up! What you see was cruiser and two destroyers. Then you shoot missiles, yes?" Johannsen's eyes sparkled.

"Three Harpoons. A Helix saw the launch and came after us. We evaded, never did know if the missiles hit anything."

"Hit? Hah! Let me tell you." Johannsen gestured. "We dead, battery down. We have damage now, cannot run. We already evade four torpedoes, but they have us now. Sonar have us. Destroyer fire RBU at us. First three miss, but they have us. Then—Boom! Boom! Boom! Many more. Destroyer blow up. Other hit, but not sink, I think."

"We escape." Johannsen hugged McCafferty again, and both spilled their beer on the floor. The American had never seen a Norwegian display this much emotion, even around his wife. "My crew alive because of you, *Chicago!* I buy you drink. I buy all your men drink."

"You are sure we killed that tin can?"

"You not kill," Johannsen said. "My ship dead, my men dead, I dead. You kill." A destroyer wasn't exactly as good as sinking a nuclear-powered battle cruiser, McCafferty told himself, but it was a whole lot better than nothing, too. And a piece of another, he reminded himself. And who knows, maybe that one sank on the way home.

"Not too shabby, Dan," Simms observed.

"Some people," said the skipper of HMS *Oberon*, "have all the bloody luck!"

"You know, Todd," said the commanding officer of USS *Chicago*, "this is pretty good beer."

USS *PHARRIS*

There were only two bodies to bury. Another fourteen men were missing and presumed dead, but for all that, Morris counted himself fortunate. Twenty sailors were injured to one extent or another. Clarke's broken forearm, a number of broken ankles from the shock of the torpedo impact, and a half-dozen bad scaldings from ruptured steam pipes. That didn't count minor cuts from flying glass.

Morris read through the ceremony in the manual, his voice emotionless as he went through the words about the sure and certain hope of how the sea will one day give up her dead . . . On command the seamen tilted up the mess tables. The bodies wrapped in plastic bags and weighted with steel slid out from under the flags, dropping straight into the water. It was ten thousand feet deep here, a long last trip for his executive officer and a third-class gunner's mate from Detroit. The rifle salute followed, but not taps. There was no one aboard who could play a trumpet, and the tape recorder was broken. Morris closed the book.

"Secure and carry on."

The flags were folded properly and taken to the sail locker. The mess tables were carried below and the stanchions were replaced to support the lifelines. And USS *Pharris* was still only half a ship, fit only to be broken up for scrap, Morris knew.

The tug *Papago* was pulling her backwards at just more than four knots. Three days to shore. They were heading toward Boston, the closest port, rather than a naval base. The reason was clear enough. Repairs would take over a year and the Navy didn't want to clutter up one of its own repair facilities with something that would take that long. Only those ships that could be repaired for useful war service would get rapid attention.

Even his continued command of *Pharris* was a joke. The tug had a reserve crew, many of them salvage experts in civilian life. Three of them were aboard to keep an eye on the towing cable and "advise" Morris on the things he had to do. Their pieces of advice were really orders, but polite ones.

There were plenty of things to keep his crew busy. The forward bulkheads required constant watching and attention. Repairs were under way to the engine plant. Only one boiler was working, providing steam to turn the turbogenerators and provide electrical power. The second boiler needed at least another day of work. His main air-search radar, they said, would be working in four hours. The satellite antenna was just back on line also. By the time they reached port—if they reached port—everything aboard that his crew could fix would be fixed. That didn't really matter, but a busy crew, the Navy has always said, is a happy crew. In practical terms it meant that the crewmen, unlike their captain, did not have time to brood on what mistakes had been made, the lives that had been lost because of them, and who had made them.

Morris went to the Combat Information Center. The tactical crew was rerunning the tape and paper record of the encounter with the Victor, trying to find what had happened.

"I don't know." The sonar operator shrugged. "Maybe it was two subs, not just one. I mean, here he is, right? This bright trail here—then a couple minutes later the active sonar picked him up over here."

"Only one sub," Morris said. "Getting from here to there is about a four-minute run at twenty-five knots."

"But we didn't hear him, sir, an' it don't show on the screen. Besides, he was heading the other way when we lost him." The sonarman rewound the tape to run it all again.

"Yeah." Morris went back to the bridge, playing it over again in his mind. He had the entire sequence memorized now. He walked out on the bridge wing. The spray shields were still perforated, and there was a faint bloodstain where the XO had died. Someone would be painting over that today. Chief Clarke had all kinds of work gangs going. Morris lit a cigarette and stared at the horizon.

REYDARVATH, ICELAND

The helicopter was the last warning they needed. Edwards and his party were heading northeast. They passed through an area of many small lakes, crossed a gravel road after waiting an hour to see what the traffic there was like—none—and began to traverse a series of marshes. By this time Edwards was thoroughly confused by the terrain. The mixture of bare rock, grassy meadows, lava fields, and now a freshwater marsh made him wonder if Iceland might not be the place where God had put everything that had been left over after the world was built. Evidently He'd made just the right amount of trees, though, because there were none here, and their best cover was the knee-high grass that sprouted from the water. It must be hardy grass, Edwards thought, since this marsh had been frozen not too long ago. It was still cold, and within minutes of entering the marshes everyone's legs ached with it. They endured the misery. The alternative was to travel on bare and slightly elevated ground, not something to be contemplated with enemy helicopters about.

Vigdis surprised them with her endurance. She kept up with the Marines without faltering or complaining. A true country girl, Edwards thought, she was still benefiting from a childhood of chasing the family sheep around—or whatever it was you did with sheep—and climbing these God-damned hills.

"Okay, people, take ten," Edwards called. Immediately everyone looked for a dry spot to collapse. Mainly they found rocks. *Rocks in a marsh!* Edwards thought. Garcia kept watch with the purloined Russian binoculars. Smith lit up a cigarette. Edwards turned around to see Vigdis sitting down next to him.

"How do you feel?"

"Very tired," she said with a slight smile. "But not so tired as you."

"Is that so!" Edwards laughed. "Maybe we should step up the pace."

"Where we go?"

"We're going to Hvammsfjördur. They didn't say why. I figure another four or five days. We want to stay clear of all the roads we can."

"To protect me, yes?" Edwards shook his head.

"To protect all of us. We don't want to fight anybody. There's too many Russians around to play soldier games."

"So, I don't hurt—ah, stop you from important things?" Vigdis asked.

"Not at all. We're all happy to have you with us. Who wouldn't like a walk in the country with a beautiful girl?" Edwards asked gallantly. *Was that a smart thing to say?*

She gave him a strange look. "You think I pretty, after—after—"

"Vigdis, if you were hit by a truck—yes, you are very beautiful. No man could change that. What happened to you was not your fault. Whatever changes it made are inside, not outside. And I know somebody must like you."

"My baby, you mean? Mistake. He find another girl. This is not important, all my friends have babies." She shrugged it off.

That stupid son of a bitch, Edwards thought. He remembered that bastardy carried no stigma on Iceland. Since no one had a surname—most of the Icelanders had given names followed by patronymics—you couldn't even tell the difference between the legitimate and illegitimate. Besides which, the Icelanders didn't seem to give a damn one way or the other. Young unmarried girls had babies, took proper care of them, and that was that. But who would walk away from this girl?

"Well, speaking for myself: Vigdis, I've never met a girl prettier than you."

"Truly?"

Her hair looked like hell, tangled and filthy, Edwards admitted to himself. Her face and clothing were covered with dust and mud. A hot shower could change that in a few minutes, revealing the lovely thing that she was. But beauty comes from within, and he was only beginning to appreciate the person inside. He ran his hand along her cheek.

"Any man who says different is an idiot." He turned to see Sergeant Smith coming over.

"Time to move, 'less you want our legs to stiffen up, Lieutenant."

"Okay. I want to make another eight or ten miles. There's farms and roads on the far side of this mountain we're walking around. We'll want to eyeball that area before we try to cross it. I'll call in from there, too."

"You got it, skipper. Rodgers! Take the point and bend it a little west."

BODENBURG, FEDERAL REPUBLIC OF GERMANY

The ride forward had not been an easy one. Eighth Guards Army moved its forward command post as close behind the leading troops as possible. Its commander, like Alekseyev, believed in having his eyes and ears as close to the front as possible. The trip took forty minutes in armored troop carriers—it was far too dangerous to use helicopters—during which Alekseyev had observed a pair of savage air attacks on Russian columns.

German and Belgian reinforcements had joined the action, and intercepts of radio messages indicated that American and British units were also en route. Alekseyev had called up more Russian units as well. What had begun as a relatively simple push by one mechanized army was now growing into a major engagement. He took this to be a good sign. NATO would not be reinforcing if they did not regard the situation as dangerous. The Soviet task was to achieve the desired result before reinforcements came into play.

The General commanding 20th Guards Tank Division was in the command post. They'd set it up in a secondary school. A new building, it had lots of space, and until an underground bunker could be prepared, it would have to do. The pace of the advance had slowed, as much because of traffic control difficulties as from the Germans.

"Straight down this road to Sack," 8th Guards Army told the tanker. "My motor-rifle troops should have it clear by the time you get there."

"Four more kilometers to Alfeld. Yes, just make sure you can support us when we jump across the river." The General set his helmet atop his head and moved out the door. It was going to work, Alekseyev thought. This general had done a magnificent job of delivering his unit to the front in nearly perfect order.

The next thing he heard was an explosion. Windows shattered, pieces of ceiling dropped around him. The Devil's Cross had returned yet again.

Alekseyev raced outside to see a dozen burning armored vehicles. As he watched, the crew bailed out of a brand-new T-80 tank. An instant later the vehicle brewed up: a fire swept through the ammunition racks inside and a pillar of flame rose toward the sky as from a small volcano.

"The General is dead—the General is dead!" a sergeant shouted. He pointed to a BMD infantry carrier from which no one had escaped alive.

Alekseyev found the commander of the 8th Guards Army cursing beside him. "The assistant commander of that tank division is a new colonel."

Pavel Leonidovich reached a quick and convenient decision. "No, Comrade General. What about me?"

Startled, the commander stared at him, then remembered Alekseyev's reputation as a tank commander, and his father's. He made a quick decision of his own. "Twentieth Tanks is yours. You know the mission."

Another infantry assault carrier rolled up. Alekseyev and Sergetov boarded it, and the driver sped off toward the divisional command post. It took half an hour before they stopped. Alekseyev saw rows of tanks parked inside the treeline. Allied artillery was falling close by, but he ignored it. His regimental commanders were grouped together. The General quickly gave orders for objective and timing. It spoke well of the General not dead an hour that everyone here knew his mission. The division was finely organized, with every part of the assault plan already firmed up. Alekseyev saw at once that he had a good battle staff. He set them to work as his unit commanders rejoined their regiments.

His first battle headquarters was fittingly in the shade of a tall tree. His father could have wished for no better. Alekseyev smiled. He found his divisional intelligence officer. "What's the situation?"

"A battalion of German tanks is counterattacking on this road leading east from Sack. They should be contained, and in any case our vehicles are moving southwest behind them. The lead motor-rifle troops are just inside the town, and report only minor resistance. Our leading elements are now moving and should be there within the hour."

"Air Defense Officer?"

"SAMs and mobile antiaircraft guns are just behind the leading echelons. We also have friendly air cover. Two regiments of MiG-21s are on call for air defense, but we haven't had any ground-attack fighters assigned yet. They took a beating this morning—but so did the other side. We killed twelve NATO aircraft before noon."

Alekseyev nodded, dividing that number by three, as he had learned.

"Excuse me, Comrade General. I am Colonel Popov, your divisional political officer."

"Fine, Comrade Colonel. My Party dues are paid to the end of the year, and with luck I will live to pay them again. If you have something important to say, be quick!" If there was anything Alekseyev didn't need now, it was a *zampolit!*

"After we capture Alfeld—"

"*If* we capture Alfeld I will let you have the keys to the city. For the present, let me do my job. Dismissed!" *Probably wanted permission to shoot suspected fascists.* As a four-star general, Alekseyev could not ignore political officers, but at least he could ignore those under the rank of general. He walked over to the tactical maps. On one side as before, lieutenants showed the advance of his—*his!*—units. On the other, intelligence officers were assembling what data they had on enemy opposition. He grabbed the shoulder of his operations officer.

"I want that lead regiment right behind the motor-rifle troops. If they need some help, give it to them. I want this breakthrough and I want it today. What artillery do we have set up?"

"Two battalions of heavy guns are ready now."

"Good. If those infantry have targets for them, find out, and let's start hitting them now. This is not a time for finesse. NATO knows we're here, and our worst enemy is time. Time works for them, not for us." The operations officer and artillery commander got together, and two minutes later his 152mm guns were delivering fire to the front. He'd have to have a medal awarded to the dead commander of 20th Tanks, Alekseyev decided; the man deserved a reward of some kind for the training he saw evident in this staff.

"Enemy air attack in progress," a plotting officer said.

"Enemy tanks emerging from woods east of Sack, estimate battalion strength. Heavy artillery fire supporting the Germans."

He had to trust his colonels now, Alekseyev knew. The time at which a general could observe the entire battle and control it was long past. His staff officers made their little marks on the map. The Germans should have waited, the General thought, they should have let the division spearhead go through, then attack the division supply column. That was foolish, the first time he had seen a German commander make a tactical error. Probably a junior officer who had relieved a dead or wounded superior, or perhaps a man whose home was nearby. Whatever the reason, it was a mistake and Alekseyev was profiting by it. His leading two tank regiments took losses, but they smashed the German counterattack in ten furious minutes.

"Two kilometers—leading elements now two kilometers from Sack. Opposition from artillery only. Friendly units are in sight. Infantry troops in Sack report minor resistance only. The town is nearly clear. Forward scouts report the road to Alfeld is open!"

"Bypass Sack," Alekseyev ordered. "The objective is Alfeld on the Leine."

ALFELD, FEDERAL REPUBLIC OF GERMANY

It was a scratch team. American mechanized infantrymen and the lead tank squadron of an advancing British brigade reinforced the remains of Germans and Belgians who had been crushed by five Soviet divisions that day. There was little time. Combat engineers worked furiously with their armored bulldozers to scrape shelters for the tanks while infantrymen dug holes for their antitank weapons. A cloud of dust on the horizon was all the warning they needed. A division of tanks was reported heading their way, and the civilians had not entirely evacuated the town behind them. Twenty miles behind them, a squadron of ground-attack aircraft circled, waiting for the call-down signal.

"Enemy in sight!" a lookout on a church steeple radioed. In seconds, artillery fire lashed at the leading Soviet columns. Antitank-missile crews popped the covers off their targeting scopes and loaded the first weapons of what promised to be a long afternoon. The Challenger tanks of 3rd Royal Tank Regiment settled into their holes, hatches shut tight as the gunners zeroed their sights on distant targets. Things were too confused, and there had not been enough time to establish a firm chain of command here. An American was first to fire. The TOW-2 missile sped downrange, its control wires trailing out behind like a spider's web as it reached four kilometers to a T-80 tank . . .

"Advanced elements are now under fire from enemy missile teams," reported a plotting officer.

"Flatten them!" Alekseyev ordered his artillery commander. Within a minute the division's multiple-rocket launchers were filling the sky with trails of fire. Tube artillery fire added to the carnage at the battle line. Then NATO artillery joined the fray in earnest.

"Lead regiment is taking losses."

Alekseyev watched the map in silence. There was no room for deceptive maneuver here, nor was there time. His men had to race through the enemy lines as quickly as possible in order to seize the bridges on the Leine. That meant that his leading tank crews would suffer heavily. The breakthrough would have its own heavy price, but the price had to be paid.

Twelve Belgian F-16 fighters swept in low over the front at five hundred knots, dropping tons of cluster munitions on the lead Soviet regiment, killing nearly thirty tanks and a score of infantry carriers less than a kilometer from the allied lines. A swarm of missiles rose into the sky after them, and the single-engine fighters turned west, skimming over the ground in their attempt to evade. Three were smashed to the ground, and fell among the NATO troops, adding to the carnage already created by Soviet fire. The commander of the British tanks saw that he lacked the firepower to stop the Soviet attack. There just wasn't enough. It was time to leave while his battalion was still able to fight. He alerted his companies to be ready to pull out and tried to get the word to neighboring units. But the troops around Alfeld came from four different armies, with separate languages and radio settings. There hadn't been time to establish exactly who was in overall command. The Germans didn't want to leave. The town had not yet been fully evacuated, and the German troops would not desert their positions until their countrymen were safely across the river. The Americans and Belgians began to move when the British colonel told them to, but not the Germans, and the result was chaos within the NATO lines.

"Forward observers report enemy units moving back on the right, repeat, enemy units appear to be disengaging on the northern side of the town."

"Move the second regiment north, loop around and head for the bridges, fast as they can. Disregard losses and charge for those damned bridges! Operations Officer, keep pressure on all enemy units. We want to trap them on this side and finish them if we can," Alekseyev ordered. "Sergetov, come with me. I have to go forward."

The attack had ripped the heart out of his lead regiment, Alekseyev knew, but it had been worth the cost. The NATO forces would have to move their units through a smashed town to get to the bridges, and having the allied units on the north side disengage first was a godsend. Now with a fresh regiment he'd be able to run over them and, if he were very lucky, get the bridges intact. This he'd have to supervise himself. Alekseyev and Sergetov boarded a tracked vehicle, which motored southeast to catch the maneuvering regiment. Behind them his operations officer began to give new orders over the divisional radio net.

Five kilometers on the far side of the river, a battery of German 155mm guns was waiting for this opportunity. They had remained silent, waiting for their radio-intercept experts to pin down the divisional headquarters. Quickly the gunners punched the target data into their fire-control computers while others loaded high-explosive shells. Every gun in the battery trained out on an identical azimuth. The ground shook when they began rapid fire.

A hundred shells fell in and around the divisional headquarters in less than two minutes. Half the battle staff was killed outright, most of the others wounded.

Alekseyev looked at his radio headset. His third close brush with death. *That was my fault. I should have checked the siting of the radio transmitters. I must not make that mistake again . . . Damn! Damn! Damn!*

Alfeld's streets were clogged with civilian vehicles. The Americans in their Bradley tracked vehicles avoided the town entirely, hurrying down the right bank of the Leine and crossing to the other side in good order. There, they took positions on the hills overlooking Leine, and set up to cover the crossing of the other allied troops. The Belgians were next. Only a third of their tanks had survived, and these covered the southern flank on the far side of the river, hoping to stop the Russians before they were able to cross. German *Staatspolizei* had held back civilian traffic and allowed the armored units to pass, but this changed when Soviet artillery began bursting in the air close to the river. The Russians had hoped it would impede traffic, and it did. Civilians who had been late to follow orders to leave their homes now paid for their error. The artillery did scant damage to fighting vehicles but thoroughly wrecked civilian cars and trucks. In minutes, the streets of Alfeld were jammed with disabled and burning cars. People left them, braving the fire to run for the bridges, and the tanks trying to make their way to the river found their way blocked. Their only escape was over the bodies of innocent civilians, and even when ordered to proceed, the drivers shrank from it. Gunners rotated their turrets to face over the rear and began to engage the Russian tanks now entering the town. Smoke from burning buildings wafted across everyone's field of view. Cannon fired at targets glimpsed for a moment, rounds went wild, and the streets of Alfeld turned into a slaughterhouse of soldiers and noncombatants.

"There they are!" Sergetov pointed. Three highway bridges spanned the Leine. Alekseyev started to give orders, but they weren't necessary. The regimental commander already had his radio microphone keyed, and directed a battalion of tanks with infantry support to proceed up the west bank, following the same route, still relatively open, that the Americans had used.

The American fighting vehicles on the far side of the river opened fire with missiles and their light cannon, killing a half-dozen tanks, and the remainder of the regiment engaged them with direct fire while Alekseyev personally called down artillery on the hilltops.

In Alfeld the battle had come to a bloody standstill. The German and British tanks took up positions at intersections largely hidden from view by wrecked cars and trucks, and backed toward the river slowly as they fought to give the civilians time. The Russian infantry tried to engage them with missiles, but too often debris lying in the streets tore the flight-control wires, causing the missiles to fall out of control and explode harmlessly. Russian and allied artillery fire churned the town to rubble.

Alekseyev watched his troops advancing toward the first bridge.

South of him, the commander of the lead regiment swore at his losses. More than half his tanks and assault vehicles had been destroyed. Victory was within his grasp, and now his troops had been stopped again by impassable streets and murderous fire. He saw the NATO tanks pulling slowly back, and, enraged that they were escaping, called in for artillery.

Alekseyev was surprised when the artillery fire shifted from the center of the town to the riverfront. He was shocked when he realized that it was not tube artillery fire, but rockets. As he watched, explosions appeared at random over the riverfront. Then rounds began exploding in the river in rapid succession. The rate of fire increased as more and more launchers were trained on the target, and it was already too late for him to stop them. The farthest bridge went first. Three rockets landed at once, and it came apart. Alekseyev watched in horror as over a hundred civilians fell into the churning water. His horror was not for the loss of life—he needed that bridge! Two more rockets landed on the center bridge. It did not collapse, but the damage it took was serious enough to prevent tanks from using it. The fools! Who was responsible for this? He turned to Sergetov.

"Call up the engineers. Get bridging units and assault boats to the front. They have absolute priority. Next, I want every surface-to-air missile and antiair gun battery you can find. Anyone who gets in their way will be shot. Make sure the traffic-control officers know this. Go!"

The Soviet tanks and infantry had reached the only surviving bridge. Three infantry vehicles raced to the far side and were taken under fire by the Belgians and Americans as they raced to cover. A tank followed. The T-80 rumbled across, got to the far side and exploded from an impacting missile. Another followed, then a third. Both reached the west bank. Then a British Chieftain emerged from behind a building and followed the Soviet tanks across. Alekseyev watched in amazement as it ran right between the two Soviet vehicles, neither of which saw it. An American missile ran just behind it and plowed into the ground, raising a cloud of dirt and dust. Two more Chieftains emerged at the bridgehead. One exploded from a point-blank shot by a T-80, the other fired back, killing the Russian tank a second later. Alekseyev remembered a tale from his boyhood of a brave peasant on a bridge as the British tank engaged and killed two more Soviet tanks before succumbing to a barrage of direct fire. Five more Soviet vehicles raced across the bridge.

The General lifted his headset and dialed up 8th Guards Army Headquarters. "This is Alekseyev. I have a company of troops across the Leine. I need support. We have broken through. Repeat: we have broken through the German front! I want air support and helicopters to engage NATO units north and south of Bridge 439. I need two regiments of infantry to assist with the river crossing. Get me support and I might have my division across by midnight."

"You'll get everything I have. My bridging units are on the way."

Alekseyev leaned against the side of his BMP. He unbuckled his canteen and took a long drink as he watched his infantry climb the hills under fire. Two complete companies were across now. Allied fire was now attempting to destroy the remaining bridge. He had to get at least a full battalion across if he wanted to hold this bridgehead for more than a few hours. "I'll get the bastard," he promised himself, "who fired on my bridges."

"Boats and bridges are en route, Comrade General," Sergetov reported. "They have first priority, and the sector traffic-control officers have been informed. Two SAM batteries are starting this way, and I found three mobile AA guns three kilometers off. They said they can be here in fifteen minutes."

"Good." Alekseyev trained his binoculars on the far bank.

"Comrade General, our infantry carriers are amphibious. Why don't we swim them across?"

"Look at the riverbank, Vanya." The General handed his glasses over. As far as he could see, the far side was all set with stone and concrete to prevent erosion. It would be difficult if not impossible for the tracked vehicles to climb that. Damn the Germans for that! "Besides, I wouldn't want to try that in anything less than regimental strength. That bridge is all we have, and it can't last very long. With the best of luck we won't have any assault bridges in place for several hours. The troops on the far side are on their own for at least that long. We'll run as many troops and vehicles across the bridge as we can, then reinforce with infantry assault boats as soon as they arrive. The book calls for this sort of crossing to be made in assault boats, under cover of darkness or smoke. I don't want to wait for night, and I need the guns to fire live shells, not harmless ones. We must break the rules, Vanya. Fortunately the book allows for that also. You have performed well, Ivan Mikhailovich. You are now a major. Don't thank me—you've earned it."

STORNOWAY, SCOTLAND

"We didn't miss 'em by much. If we'd seen them five minutes sooner, we could have taken a few out. As it was—" The Tomcat pilot shrugged.

Toland nodded. The fighters had orders to remain outside Soviet radar coverage.

"You know, it's a funny thing. There were three of them flying a nice tight formation. I had them on my TV system from fifty miles away. No way in hell they could tell we were there. If we had better range, we could follow them all the way home. Like that game the Germans played on us once upon a time—send a bird right behind a returning raid and drop a few bombs right after they landed."

"We'd never get anything through their IFF," Toland replied.

"True, but we'd know their arrival time at their bases to within, oh, ten minutes. That's gotta be useful to somebody."

Commander Toland set his cup down. "Yeah, you're right." He decided he'd put that idea on the printer to Commander, Eastern Atlantic.

LAMMERSDORF, FEDERAL REPUBLIC OF GERMANY

There was no mistaking it. NATO lines had been decisively broken south of Hannover. Two brigades were taken from the perilously thin NATO ground reserve and sent toward Alfeld. Unless this hole was plugged, Hannover would be lost, and with it all of Germany east of the Weser.

29. Remedies

ALFELD, FEDERAL REPUBLIC OF GERMANY

As predicted, the bridge lasted less than an hour. In that time Alekseyev had gotten a full battalion of mechanized infantry across, and though the NATO troops launched a pair of vicious counterattacks on his bridgehead, the tanks he'd placed on the east bank had been able to break them up with direct fire. Now NATO had caught its breath, and was assembling artillery. Heavy guns pounded his bridgehead and the tanks on the Soviet side of the river, and to make matters worse, the assault boats had been held up by incredible traffic snarls on the road between Sack and Alfeld. German heavy guns were littering the road and surrounding land with artillery-deployed mines, each powerful enough to knock the tread off a tank or the wheel off a truck. Sappers swept the roads continuously, using heavy machine guns to detonate the mines, but every one took time, and not all were seen before they exploded under a heavily loaded vehicle. The loss of the individual trucks and tanks was bad enough; worse still were the traffic tieups that resulted from each disabled vehicle.

Alekseyev's headquarters were in a camera shop overlooking the river. The plate-glass window had long since been blown away, and his boots crackled with every step. He surveyed the far bank through his binoculars and anguished for his men as they tried to fight back at the men and tanks on the hills above them. A few kilometers away, every mobile gun in 8th Guards Army was racing forward to provide fire support for his tank division, and he and Sergetov set them to counterbattery the NATO guns.

"Enemy aircraft!" a lieutenant shouted.

Alekseyev craned his neck and saw a dot to the south, which grew rapidly into a German F-104 fighter. Yellow tracer lines reached out from his AA guns and blotted it from the sky before it could release, but instantly another appeared, this one firing its own cannon at the gun vehicle and exploding it. Alekseyev swore as the single-engine fighter bored in, dropped two bombs on the far side of the river, and streaked away. The bombs fell slowly, retarded by small parachutes, then, twenty meters over the ground, appeared to fill the air with fog—Alekseyev dove to the floor of the shop as the cloud of explosive vapor detonated from the fuel-air-explosive bombs. The shock wave was fearful, and above his head a display case shattered, dropping broken glass all over him.

"What the hell was that?" Sergetov yelled, deafened by the blast, then, looking up, "You're hit, Comrade General!"

Alekseyev ran his hand over his face. It came away red. His eyes stung, and he poured the contents of his canteen over his face to clear them of the blood. Major Sergetov slapped a bandage on his general's forehead with only one hand, Alekseyev noticed.

"What happened to you?"

"I fell on some of this damned glass! Stay still, Comrade General, you're

bleeding like a slaughtered cow." A lieutenant general showed up. Alekseyev recognized him as Viktor Beregovoy, 8th Guards Army's second in
command.

"Comrade General, you have orders to return to headquarters. I am
here to relieve you."

"The hell you say!" Alekseyev bellowed.

"The orders come from Commander-in-Chief West, Comrade. I am a
general of tank troops. I can carry on here. If you will permit me to say
so, you have performed brilliantly. But you are needed elsewhere."

"Not until I'm finished!"

"Comrade General, if you want this crossing to succeed, we need more
support here. Who can better arrange that support, you or I?" Beregovoy
asked reasonably.

Alekseyev let out a long angry breath. The man was right—but for the
first time Pavel Leonidovich Alekseyev had led—really led!—men in combat, and he had done well. Alekseyev knew it—he had done well!

"There is no time to argue. You have your task and I have mine," the
man said.

"You know the situation?"

"Fully. There is a vehicle in the back to return you to headquarters."

Alekseyev held the bandage to his head—Sergetov hadn't tied it properly—and walked out the back of the shop. Where the door had once
been, he found a gaping hole. A BMD infantry carrier was there, its motor
running. Alekseyev got in and found a medical orderly who clucked over
the General and went immediately to work. As the carrier pulled off,
Alekseyev listened to the noise of combat diminish. It was the saddest
sound he had ever heard.

LANGLEY AIR FORCE BASE, VIRGINIA

There was nothing like a Distinguished Flying Cross to make a person
happy about flying, and she wondered if she might be the first female Air
Force pilot to have one. If not, Major Nakamura decided, what the hell?
She had a gun-camera videotape of all three of her Badgers, and a Navy
pilot she'd met in Brittany before catching a flight Stateside had called her
one damned fine pilot, for an Air Force puke. After which she had reminded him that if the dumbass Navy pilots had listened to her, maybe
their air base wouldn't be in a body and fender shop. Game, set, and
match, she grinned, to Major Amelia Nakamura, USAF.

All the F-15s that could be ferried across the Atlantic had been ferried,
and now she had another job. Only four of the 48th Fighter Interceptor
Squadron's Eagles were still at Langley. The rest were scattered up and
down the East Coast, including the two pilots who were qualified for the
ASAT antisatellite missiles. As soon as she'd heard that, she had made a
phone call and informed Space Command that she was the Eagle driver
who had worked out the ASAT flight profile, and why take a combat pilot
off the line when she could handle the mission very well, thank you.

She checked to make sure the ugly missile was properly attached to the
airframe. It had been taken out of secure storage and reexamined by a
team of experts. Buns shook her head. There had only been one real test
of the system before a moratorium had been slapped on the project. A
successful test, to be sure, but only one. She hoped it would work. The

Navy really needed help from the Air Force pukes. Besides, that A-6 driver was cute.

The major finished her walkaround, taking her time—her target wasn't over the Indian Ocean yet—then strapped herself into her Eagle, ran her eyes and hands over the gauges and handles, adjusted the seat, and finally input the numbers painted on the wall of the aircraft shelter into the aircraft's inertial navigation system so that the fighter would know where it was. Finished, she began to fire up her engines. Her flight helmet protected her from the shriek of the two Pratt and Whitney engines. The needles on her engine gauges rotated into proper position. Below her, the crew chief gave the aircraft a careful examination, then waved to her to taxi the aircraft into the open. Six people were out there, standing behind the red warning line to protect their ears from the noise. *Always nice to have an audience,* she thought, ignoring them.

"Eagle One-Zero-Four ready to taxi," she told the tower.

"One-Zero-Four, roger. You are cleared to taxi," the tower controller replied. "Wind is two-five-three at twelve knots."

"Roger that, One-Zero-Four is rolling."

Buns brought her canopy down. The crew chief snapped to attention and gave the major a perfect salute. Nakamura answered it with panache, advanced her throttles slightly, and the Eagle fighter moved off to the runway like a crippled stork. A minute later, she was in the air, a silky smooth feeling of pure power enveloping her as she pointed her Eagle at the sky.

Kosmos 1801 was just completing its southbound leg, bending around the Straits of Magellan to head north over the Atlantic. The orbital pass would take it two hundred miles off the American coast. At the ground-control station, technicians prepared to switch on the powerful sea-surveillance radar. They were sure an American carrier battle group was at sea, but had been unable to locate it. Three regiments of Backfires were waiting for information that would allow them to repeat the feat accomplished on the second day of the war.

Nakamura eased her fighter under the tanker's tail, and the boom operator expertly shoved the refueling probe into the back of her fighter. Ten thousand pounds of fuel transferred into her tanks in only a few minutes, and as she disengaged, a small cloud of kerosene vapor escaped into the sky.

"Gulliver, this is One-Zero-Four, over," she called over the radio.

"One-Zero-Four, this is Gulliver," replied a colonel in the passenger compartment of a LearJet cruising at forty thousand feet.

"All tanked and ready to go. All on-board systems show green. Orbiting at Point Sierra. Ready to initiate intercept climb. Standing by."

"Roger that, One-Zero-Four."

Major Nakamura kept her Eagle in a small turning circle. She didn't want to waste a drop of fuel when she started her climb. She shifted ever so slightly in her seat, which for her was a violent show of emotion when flying, and concentrated on her aircraft. As her eyes traced over her cockpit instruments, she told herself to control her breathing.

Space Command's radars picked up the Soviet satellite as it passed the bulge of South America. Computers compared its course and speed with known data, matched them with the position of Nakamura's fighter, and a computer spat out its commands, which were relayed to the LearJet.

"One-Zero-Four, come to heading two-four-five."

"Turning now." The major brought her fighter into a tight turn. "Holding on two-four-five."

"Stand by . . . stand by—initiate!"

"Roger." Buns pushed her throttles to the stops and punched up the afterburners. The Eagle leaped forward like a spurred horse, accelerating through Mach 1 in seconds. Next she eased back on the stick, bringing her Eagle into a forty-five-degree climb, still accelerating into a darkening sky. She didn't look out. Her eyes were locked on her cockpit gauges: the fighter had to maintain a specific flight profile for the next two minutes. As the Eagle rocketed into the sky, the altimeter needle whirled around its clockface. Fifty thousand feet, sixty thousand feet, seventy, eighty, ninety thousand feet. Stars were visible now in the nearly black sky, but Nakamura didn't notice.

"Come on, baby, find the son of a bitch . . ." she thought aloud.

Beneath the aircraft the ASAT missile's tracking head came on, searching the sky for the infrared heat signature of the Soviet satellite. A light blinked on Buns's instrument panel.

"My weapon is tracking! Repeat, my weapon is tracking. Auto launch sequence equipment is activated. Altitude ninety-four thousand feet seven hundred—breakaway, breakaway!" She felt her aircraft lurch as the heavy missile dropped free and immediately brought her throttles back to low power and brought the stick back to loop the fighter. She checked her fuel state. The afterburning climb had nearly emptied her tanks, but she had enough to make Langley without tanking again. She had already turned for home when she realized that she hadn't seen the missile. It didn't matter anyway. Nakamura turned west, letting the Eagle settle into a shallow dive that would terminate on the Virginia Coast.

Aboard the LearJet, a tracker camera followed the missile upward. The solid-fuel rocket motor burned for thirty seconds, then the warhead separated. The Miniature Homing Vehicle, an infrared heat sensor embedded in its flat face, had long since acquired its target. The Soviet satellite's onboard nuclear reactor radiated waste heat out into space, and the resulting infrared signature rivaled the sun. As its microchip brain computed the intercept course, the MHV made a tiny course alteration and the distance between warhead and satellite dropped at a precipitous rate. The satellite was northbound at eighteen thousand miles per hour, the MHV southbound at over ten thousand, yet another hi-tech kamikaze. Then—

"Jesus!" said the senior officer on the LearJet as he blinked his eyes and turned away from the TV screen. Several hundred pounds of steel and ceramic had just turned to vapor. "That's a kill, say again that's a *kill!*"

The TV picture was downlinked to Space Command, where a radar picture backed it up. The massive satellite was now an expanding cloud of orbiting rubble. "Target is negated," said a calmer voice.

LENINSK, KAZAKH S.S.R.

The loss of signal from the Kosmos 1801 satellite was recorded scant seconds after it was obliterated from the sky. It was no surprise to the Russian space experts, since 1801 had used up its maneuvering thrusters several days before, and had been an easy target. Another F-1M rocket booster was sitting on a launch pad of the Baikonur Kosmodrome Complex. An abbreviated launch sequence countdown would be under way inside of two hours—but from now on the ability of the Soviet Navy to locate convoys and fighting fleets would be in jeopardy.

LANGLEY AIR FORCE BASE, VIRGINIA

"Well?" Buns asked as she jumped down from her fighter.

"Kill. We have it on tape," another major said. "It worked."

"How soon do you think they'll launch a replacement?" *One more kill and I'll be an ace!*

"We think they have one on the pad now. Twelve to twenty-four hours. No telling how many spares they have ready."

Nakamura nodded. The Air Force had a total of six remaining ASAT rockets. Maybe enough, maybe not—one successful mission did not make it a reliable weapon. She walked over to the squadron headquarters for coffee and donuts.

STENDAL, GERMAN DEMOCRATIC REPUBLIC

"Goddammit, Pasha!" CINC-West swore. "I don't have a four-star deputy so that he can run around playing divisional commander. Look at you! You might have got your head cut off!"

"We needed a breakthrough. The tank commander was killed and his deputy was too young. I have given us the breakthrough."

"Where is Captain Sergetov?"

"Major Sergetov," Alekseyev corrected. "He performed well as my aide. His hand got carved up and he's having it attended to. So. What reinforcements do we have moving to the 8th Guards Army?"

Both generals moved over to a large map. "These two tank divisions are already en route—ten to twelve hours. How firm is your bridgehead?"

"Could be better," Alekseyev admitted. "There were three bridges there, but some madman started dropping rockets into the town and wrecked two of them. That left one. We managed to get a mechanized battalion across, along with some tanks, before the Germans were able to destroy it. They have plenty of artillery support, and when I left, we had boats and bridging equipment coming in. The man who relieved me will be trying to reinforce as soon as he can arrange a crossing in force."

"Opposition?"

"Thin, but the terrain is on their side. I'd estimate one regiment or so, the remains of other NATO units. Some tanks, but mainly mechanized infantry. They also have plenty of artillery support. When I left it was a very even match. We have more firepower, but most of it's trapped on our side of the Leine. It's a race to see who can reinforce quickest."

"After you left, NATO threw aircraft in. Our people are trying to hold them back, but NATO seems to be ahead in the air."

"We can't wait for night. Those bastards own the night sky."

"Go now?"

Alekseyev nodded, thinking of what casualties he was bringing down on "his" division. "As soon as we can assemble the boats. Expand the bridgehead to two kilometers, then get the bridges across. What's NATO bringing in?"

"Radio intercepts have identified two brigades en route. One British and one Belgian."

"They'll send more than that. They must know what we can do if we exploit this. We have 1st Guards Tank Army in reserve . . ."

"Commit half of our reserves here?"

"I can't think of a better place." Alekseyev gestured at the map. The drive toward Hannover had been stopped within sight of the city. The northern army groups had gotten into the outskirts of Hamburg, at the cost of gutting 3rd Shock Army's tank formations. "With luck, we can break all of the 1st into the enemy rear. That will get us to the Weser at least—maybe the Rhein."

"A large gamble, Pasha," CINC-West breathed. But the odds here were better than anything else on the map. If the NATO forces were stretched as thinly as his intelligence staff said, they had to crumble someplace. Perhaps this was it? "Very well. Start posting the orders."

FASLANE, SCOTLAND

"What about their ASW forces?" asked the captain of USS *Pittsburgh*.

"Considerable. We estimate that Ivan has two major antisubmarine-warfare groups, one centered on *Kiev*, the other on a Kresta cruiser. There are also four smaller groups, each composed of a Krivak-class frigate and four to six patrol frigates of the Grisha and Mirka type. Add to that a large collection of ASW aircraft and finally twenty or so submarines, half nuclear, half conventional," answered the briefing officer.

"Why don't we let them keep the Barents Sea?" muttered Todd Simms of USS *Boston*.

There's an idea, Dan McCafferty agreed silently.

"Seven days to get there?" *Pittsburgh* asked.

"Yes, that gives us a good deal of freedom on how to enter the area. Captain Little?"

The captain of HMS *Torbay* took the podium. McCafferty wondered if the Brits had any need for NFL-style noseguards in their team sports. Under six feet, but very broad across the shoulders, his head topped by a shock of sandy, unruly hair, James Little certainly looked like one. When he spoke, it was with toughly won assurance.

"We've been running a campaign we call Keypunch. The objective of Keypunch is to evaluate what ASW defenses Ivan has operating in the Barents Sea—and also, of course, to lop off the odd Sov who gets in our way." He smiled. *Torbay* had four kills. "Ivan's set a barrier from Bear Island to the coast of Norway. The immediate area around Bear Island is a solid minefield. Ivan's been laying the things since he took the island by parachute assault two weeks ago. South of this area, so far as we can determine, the barrier is composed of some small minefields and Tango-class diesel subs as a front line, backed by the mobile ASW groups and Victor-III-class nuclear submarines. Their aim appears to be not so much prosecute-to-kill as prosecute-to-drive-off. Every time one of our subma-rines has made an attack on this barrier line, there has been a vigorous response.

"Inside the Barents, things are pretty much the same. These small hunter-killer groups can be bloody dangerous. I personally had an en-counter with a Krivak and four Grishas. Inshore, they have helicopters and fixed-wing aircraft in direct support, and it was a most unpleasant experience. We also found several new minefields. The Soviets appear to be sowing them almost at random in water as deep as one hundred fathoms. Finally they seem to have set a number of traps. One of them cost us *Trafalgar*. They set a small minefield and placed a noisemaker within it that sounds exactly like a Tango snorkeling her diesels. As near as we can make out, *Trafalgar* moved in to collect the Tango and ran right into a mine. Something to keep in mind, gentlemen." Little paused to let that bit of hard-won intelligence sink in.

"Right. What we intend you chaps to do is head north-northwest toward the edge of the Greenland Icepack, then east along the edge of the pack to the Svyatana Anna Trough. Five days from today three of our submarines will raise pure bloody hell on the barrier, supported by our own ASW aircraft and some fighters if that can be arranged. That ought to get Ivan's attention and draw his mobile forces west. You should then be able to proceed south to your objective. It's a roundabout route, of course, but it enables you to use your towed sonars for the maximum period of time, and you should be able to run at relatively high speed at the edge of the icepack without being detected."

McCafferty thought that one over. The edge of the icepack was a noisy place, with billions of tons of ice in constant movement.

"The route has been scouted, by HMS *Sceptre* and *Superb*. They encountered minor patrolling only. Two Tangos were found in that area. Our chaps had orders not to engage." That told the Americans how important this mission was. "They will be waiting for you, so do be careful about engaging something in your path."

"How do we get out?" Todd Simms wondered.

"As quickly as you can. By that time we should have at least one more submarine to assist you. They'll stay roughly twelve hours ahead of your estimate speed of advance, eliminating any opposition they find. Once you reach the icepack, you're on your own. Our chaps will be there only as long as it takes to reach the pack. After that they have other duties to perform. We expect that Ivan's ASW groups will come after you—no surprise there, is it? We'll try to maintain pressure south of Bear Island to tie down as many as we can, but speed will be your best defense in this case."

The skipper of USS *Boston* nodded. He could run faster than the Russians could hunt.

"Further questions?" asked Commander, Submarines, Eastern Atlantic. "Good luck, then. We'll give you all the support we can."

McCafferty leafed through his briefing papers to check for the firing orders, then tucked the ops orders into his back pocket. Operation Doolittle. He and Simms left together. Their submarines were at the same quay. It was a short, quiet drive. They arrived to see Tomahawk missiles being loaded, in *Chicago*'s case into the twelve vertical tubes installed forward of the pressure hull in the submarine's bow. *Boston* was an older boat and had had to offload some of her torpedoes to make room for them. No submarine captain is ever happy offloading torpedoes.

"Don't worry, I'll back you up," McCafferty said.

"You do that. Looks like they're almost finished. Be nice to have one more beer, wouldn't it?" Simms chuckled.

"See you when we get back." Simms and McCafferty shook hands. A minute later both were below, seeing to the final arrangements for going back to sea.

USS *PHARRIS*

The Sikorsky Sea King helicopter was a tight fit on the frigate's helo deck, but for casualties the rules were always bent. The ten worst cases, all scald / burns and broken limbs, were loaded aboard after the helo was refueled, and Morris watched it lift off for the beach. The captain of what was left of USS *Pharris* put his cap back on and lit another cigarette. He still didn't know what had gone wrong with that Victor-class. Somehow the Russian skipper had teleported himself from one place to another.

"We killed three o' the bastards, sir." Chief Clarke appeared at Morris's side. "Maybe this one just got lucky."

"Reading minds, Chief?"

"Beg pardon, sir. You wanted me to report on some things. The pumps have just about dried things out. I'd say we're leaking ten gallons an hour at the crack on the lower starboard corner, hardly worth talking about. The bulkhead's holding, and we got people keeping an eye on it. Same story with the tow cable. Those tugboat guys know their stuff. The engineer reports both boilers are fully repaired, number two still on line. The Prairie Masker is operating. The Sea Sparrow is working again in case we need that, but the radars're still down."

Morris nodded. "Thank you, Chief. How are the men?"

"Busy. Kinda quiet. Mad."

That's one advantage they have over me, Morris thought. *They're busy.*

"If you'll pardon me saying so, skipper, you look awful tired," Clarke said. The bosun was worried about his captain, but had already said more than he was supposed to.

"We'll all get a good rest soon enough."

SUNNYVALE, CALIFORNIA

"We show one bird lifting off," the watch officer told North American Aerospace Defense Command. "Coming out of Baikonur Kosmodrome on a heading of one-five-five, indicating a probable orbital inclination of sixty-five degrees. Signature characteristics say it's either an SS-11 ICBM or an F-1-type space booster."

"Only one?"

"Correct, one bird only."

A lot of U.S. Air Force officers had suddenly become very tense. The missile was on a heading that would take it directly over the central United States in forty to fifty minutes. The rocket in question could be many things. The Russian SS-9 missile, like many American counterparts, was obsolete and had been adapted as a satellite booster rocket. Unlike its American counterparts, it had been originally designed as a fractional-orbital-bombardment system: FOBS, *a missile that could put a 25-megaton nuclear warhead into a flight path mimicking that of a harmless satellite.*

"Booster-engine cutoff—okay, we show separation and second-stage ignition," the colonel said on the phone. *The Russians would freak if they knew how good our cameras are,* he thought. "Flight path continues as before."

Already NORAD had flashed a warning to Washington. If this was a nuclear strike, National Command Authority was ready to react. So many current scenarios began with a large warhead exploded at orbital height over the target country, causing massive electromagnetic damage to communications systems. The SS-9 FOBS system was tailor-made for that sort of thing.

"Second-stage cutoff . . . and there's third-stage ignition. Do you copy our position fix, NORAD?"

"That's a roger," acknowledged the general under Cheyenne Mountain. The signal from the early-warning satellite was linked into NORAD headquarters, and a watch crew of thirty was holding its breath, watching the image of the space booster move across the map projection. *Dear God, don't let it be a nuke . . .*

Ground-based radar in Australia now tracked the vehicle, showing the climbing third stage and the spent second stage falling into the Indian Ocean. Their information also was linked by satellite to Sunnyvale and Cheyenne Mountain.

"That looks like shroud release," the man in Sunnyvale said. The radar picture showed four new objects fluttering away from the third stage. Probably the protective aluminum shroud needed for atmospheric flight, but unnecessary weight for a space vehicle. People began to breathe more regularly. A reentry vehicle needed such a shroud, but a satellite did not. After five tense minutes, this was the first piece of good news. The FOBS didn't do that.

An Air Force RC-135 aircraft was already lifting off the ground at Tinker Air Force Base, Oklahoma, its engines firewalled as the flight crew raced the converted 707 airliner to altitude. The roof of what otherwise would be a passenger compartment held a large telescope / camera assembly used to inspect Soviet space vehicles. In the back, technicians activated the sophisticated tracking systems used to lock the camera in on its distant target.

"Burnout," they announced at Sunnyvale. "The vehicle has achieved orbital velocity. Initial numbers look like an apogee of one hundred fifty-six miles and a perigee of one hundred forty-eight." They'd have to refine those numbers, but NORAD and Washington needed something right now.

"Your evaluation?" NORAD asked Sunnyvale.

"Everything is consistent with a radar-ocean-reconnaissance-satellite launch. The only change is the orbital insertion path was southerly instead of northerly." Which made perfectly good sense, as everyone knew. Any kind of rocket launched over the pole entailed dangers that no one wanted to contemplate.

Thirty minutes later they were sure. The crewmen on the RC-135 got good pictures of the new Soviet satellite. Before it had completed its first revolution, it was classified as a RORSAT. The new radar-ocean-surveillance satellite would be a problem for the Navy, but not something to end the world. The people in Sunnyvale and Cheyenne Mountain maintained their vigil.

ICELAND

They followed a footpath around the mountain. Vigdis told them it was a favorite place for tourists to visit. A small glacier on the northern side of the mountain fed a half-dozen streams, which led in turn to a sizable valley full of small farms. They had a fine vantage point. Almost everything in sight was below them, including several roads that were kept under constant scrutiny. Edwards debated the advantages of cutting straight across the valley toward their objective or staying on the rough ground to the east.

"I wonder what kinda radio station that is," Smith said. There was a tower of some sort eight miles west of them.

Mike looked at Vigdis and got a shrug. She didn't listen to the radio.

"Not easy to tell from this far," Edwards observed. "But probably they have some Russians." He unfolded his big map. This part of the island showed lots of roads, but the information had to be taken with a grain of salt. Only two of the roads had decent surfaces. The rest were called "seasonal" on the map—meaning exactly what? Edwards wondered. Of these, some were well maintained, others were not. The map didn't say which was which. All of the Soviet troops they'd seen on the ground were driving jeep-type vehicles, not the tracked infantry-carriers they'd observed on the invasion day. A good driver in a four-by-four could go almost anywhere, however. How good were the Soviets at driving jeeps over broken ground . . . so *many* things to worry about, Edwards thought.

Edwards tracked his field glasses over the area to his west. He saw a twin-prop airliner lift off from a small airfield. *You forgot about that, didn't you? The Russians are using those puddle-jumpers to ferry troops around . . .*

"Sarge, what do you think?" *Might as well get a professional decision.*

Smith grimaced. The choice was between physical danger and physical exhaustion. *Some choice,* he thought. *That's supposed to be why we have officers.*

"I'd at least have some patrols down there, Lieutenant. Lots of roads, figure some checkpoints so they can keep an eye on the local folks. Let's say that radio's a navigation beacon. It'll be guarded. Regular radio station'll be guarded, too. All these farms—what kinda farms, Miss Vigdis?"

"Sheep, some milk cows, potatoes," she answered.

"So when the Russkies are off duty, there'll be some wandering around to get some fresh food instead of their canned crap. We would, too. I don't much like it, Lieutenant."

Edwards nodded agreement. "Okay, we head east. Just about out of food."

"There's always fish."

FASLANE, SCOTLAND

Chicago led the procession. A Royal Navy fleet tug had helped her away from the quay, and the American sub was heading out the channel at six knots. They were taking advantage of a "window" in Soviet satellite coverage. It would be at least six hours before another Russian reconnaissance satellite came overhead. Behind McCafferty came *Boston, Pittsburgh, Providence, Key West,* and *Groton,* at two-mile intervals.

"What's the sounding?" McCafferty asked over the intercom.

"Five hundred seventy feet."

Time. McCafferty ordered the lookouts below. The only ships in sight were aft. *Boston* was clearly visible, her black sail and twin diving planes gliding over the water like the angel of death. *That was apt enough,* he thought. The captain of USS *Chicago* made a final check of the control station atop the sail, then dropped down the ladder, pulling the hatch closed behind him. Another twenty-five feet and he was in the attack center, where he closed another hatch, turning the locking wheel as far as it would go.

"Straight board shut," the executive officer reported, going through the official litany that signified that the submarine was rigged for dive. Submariners evolved check lists long before aviators discovered them. McCafferty checked the status boards himself—and so, furtively, did several others of the attack center crew. Everything was as it should be.

"Dive. Make your depth two hundred feet," McCafferty ordered.

The submarine filled with the sound of rushing air and water, and the sleek black hull began her descent.

McCafferty reviewed the chart in his head. Seventy-four hours to the icepack, and turn east. Forty-three hours to Svyatana and turn south. Then came the really hard part.

STENDAL, GERMAN DEMOCRATIC REPUBLIC

The Battle of Alfeld was turning into a living thing that ate men and tanks like a wolf eats rabbits. Alekseyev chafed at being two hundred kilometers distant from the tank division he now regarded as his own. He could not complain about his relief—which only made things worse. The new commander had staged a successful forced river crossing, putting another two regiments of mechanized infantry on the far bank, and now three ribbon bridges were being built across the Leine—or at least a spirited attempt was under way to build them, despite murderous artillery fire from NATO units.

"We have created a 'meeting engagement,' Pasha," CINC-West said, staring down at the map.

Alekseyev nodded agreement. What had begun as a limited attack was fast becoming the focal point of the whole fighting front. Two more Soviet tank divisions were now near the battle area, racing to the Leine. Three NATO brigades were known to be heading the same way, along with artillery. Both sides were pulling tactical fighters from other sectors, one to smash the bridgehead, the other to support it. The terrain at the front didn't give the SAM crews enough time to discriminate friend from foe. The Russians had many more surface-to-air missiles, and so a free-fire zone had been established at Alfeld. Anything that flew was automatically a target for the Russian missiles, while Soviet aircraft kept clear, working instead to locate and kill NATO artillery and reinforcements. That ran contrary to pre-war doctrine—another gamble, but a favorable one, Alekseyev judged, given his experiences at the front. That was an important lesson not stressed enough in pre-war training: senior commanders had to see what was happening with their own eyes. *How did we ever forget that?* Pasha wondered.

He fingered the bandage on his forehead. Alekseyev was suffering from a murderous headache, and a doctor had used twelve stitches to close the wound. Crude stitches, the doctor had told him—they would leave a scar. His father had had several such scars, all worn with pride. He'd accept the decoration for this one.

"We have the ridge north of the town!" 20th Tanks' commander called in. "We've pushed the Americans off."

Alekseyev took the phone. "How soon on the bridges?"

"We ought to have one ready in another half hour. Their artillery support is slackening off. They blew one bridging unit to hell, but this one will be completed. I have a battalion of tanks lined up already. The SAMs are doing well. I can see the wreckage of five aircraft from where I'm standing. I see—" The General was interrupted by man-made thunder.

Alekseyev could do nothing but stare at the telephone receiver. His fist tightened in anger around the handset.

"Excuse me. That was close. The final section of bridge is rolling out now. Those engineers have taken terrible losses, Comrade General. They deserve particular attention. The major in command of the unit has been exposed for three hours now. I want the gold star for him."

"Then he'll get it."

"Good, good—the bridge section is off the truck and in the water. If they give us ten minutes to anchor the far end, I'll get those damned tanks across for you. How long on my reinforcements?"

"The lead elements will arrive just after sunset."

"Excellent! I must leave now. I'll be back when we start rolling tanks."

Alekseyev handed the phone back to a junior officer. It was like listening to a hockey game on the radio!

"The next objective, Pasha?"

"Northwest to Hameln and beyond. We might be able to cut off NATO's northern army groups. If they start to disengage their forces around Hamburg, we go to a general attack and chase them all the way to the English Channel! I think we have the situation we've been hoping for."

BRUSSELS, BELGIUM

At NATO headquarters, staff officers looked at the same maps and reached the same conclusions with less enthusiasm. Reserves were dangerously low—yet there was no choice. Men and guns converged on Alfeld in ever increasing numbers.

PANAMA

It was the biggest transit of U.S. Navy ships in years. The gray hulls used both sides of each lock system, preventing westbound traffic from moving. They were in a hurry. Helicopters moved the Canal pilots to and from ships; speed restrictions were broken, regardless of the erosion problems at the Gaillard Cut. Those ships needing refueling had it done as soon as they exited the Canal at the Gatun Locks, then formed an antisubmarine barrier outside Limón Bay. The formation's transit from Pacific to Atlantic lasted twelve hours under ruthless security. Finished, they departed north at a fleet speed of twenty-two knots. They had to go through the Windward Passage at night.

30. Approaches

BOSTON, MASSACHUSETTS

They call it the smell of the sea, Morris thought, *but really it's not. It's the smell of land.* It came from the tidal marshes—all the things that lived and died and rotted at the water's edge, all the smells that fermented in the marginal wetlands and when released blew out to sea. Sailors considered it a friendly odor because it meant that land, port, home, family were near. Otherwise it was something to be neutralized with Lysol.

As Morris watched, the tug *Papago* shortened her towline for better control in the restricted waters. Three harbor tugs came alongside, their crews throwing messenger lines to the frigate's sailors. When they were secured, *Papago* cast off and proceeded up the river to refuel.

"Good afternoon, Captain." The harbor pilot had come out on one of the tugs. He looked to have been bringing ships in and out of Boston for fifty years.

"And to you, Captain," Morris acknowledged.

"I see you killed three Russian subs?"

"Only one by ourselves. The others are assists."

"How much water are you drawing forward?"

"Just under twenty-five feet—no," Morris had to correct himself. The sonar dome was at the bottom of the Atlantic now.

"You did well to bring her back, Captain," the pilot said, looking forward. "My 'can didn't survive. Before you were born, I guess. *Callaghan,* seven ninety-two. Assistant gunnery officer, I'd just made j.g. We got twelve Jap planes, but just after midnight the thirteenth kamikaze got through on us. Forty-seven men—well." The pilot took the walkie-talkie from his pocket and started giving directions to the tugs. *Pharris* began to move sideways toward a pier. A medium-sized drydock was straight ahead, but they were not moving that way.

"Not the drydock?" Morris asked, surprised and angry that his ship was being moved to an ordinary pier.

"Mechanical problems in the dock. They're not ready for you yet. Tomorrow, day after for sure. I know how you feel, Captain. Like your kid's hurt and they won't let her in the hospital. Cheer up, I watched mine sink."

It made no sense to grumble, Morris knew. The man was right. If *Pharris* hadn't sunk during the tow, she was safe enough alongside the pier for a day or two. The pilot was an expert. His trained eye measured the wind and the tide, and he gave the proper orders to the tug captains. Within thirty minutes the frigate was secured to the cargo pier. Three TV news crews were waiting for them behind a screen of sailors in shore patrol livery. As soon as the brow was rigged, an officer hurried aboard and came right to the bridge.

"Captain, I'm Lieutenant Commander Anders. I have this for you, sir." He handed over an official-looking envelope.

Morris tore it open and found a standard Navy dispatch form. The message ordered him in terse Navy prose to Norfolk by the quickest available transport.

"I have a car waiting. You can catch the shuttle to D.C., then hop a short-hauler to Norfolk."

"What about my ship?"

"That's my job, Captain. I'll take good care of her for you."

Just like that, Morris thought. He nodded and went below to pack his gear. Ten minutes later he walked without speaking past the TV cameras and was taken to Logan International Airport.

STORNOWAY, SCOTLAND

Toland went over the satellite photographs of Iceland's four airfields. Strangely, the Russians were not making any use of the old Keflavik field, preferring instead to base their fighters at Reykjavik and the new NATO base. Occasionally, a Backfire or two were landing at Keflavik, bombers with mechanical problems or running short of fuel, but that was it. The northerly fighter sweeps had had their effect, too—the Russians were doing their tanking farther north and east now, which had produced a marginal but nevertheless negative effect on the Backfires' range. The experts estimated that it cut twenty minutes off the time they had to search for convoys. Despite the searching done by the Bears and satellite reconnaissance, only two-thirds of the raids actually launched attacks. Toland didn't know why. Was there a problem with Soviet communications? If so, could they find a way to exploit it?

The Backfires were still hurting the convoys, and badly. After considerable Navy prodding, the Air Force was starting to base fighters in Newfoundland, Bermuda, and the Azores. Supported by tankers borrowed from the Strategic Air Command, they were trying to maintain a combat air patrol over those convoys they could reach. There was no hope of actually breaking up a Backfire raid, but they could start thinning the Bears out. The Soviets had only about thirty of the wide-ranging Bear-D reconnaissance aircraft. Roughly ten flew every day with their powerful Big Bulge radars turned on to guide the bombers and submarines in on the convoys, which made them relatively easy to find, if a fighter could be put out there to find them. After much experimentation, the Russians had fallen into a predictable pattern of air operations. They would be made to pay for that. Tomorrow the Air Force would have a two-plane patrol over six different convoys.

The Russians would be made to pay a toll for basing aircraft on Iceland, too.

"I make it a regiment, say twenty-four to twenty-seven aircraft. All MiG-29 Fulcrums," Toland said. "We never seem to see more than twenty-one on the ground. I figure they're running a fairly steady combat air patrol, say four birds aloft almost around the clock. They also appear to have three ground-based radars, and they're moving them around a lot. That probably means that they're set up for ground-controlled intercepts. Any problem jamming the search radars?"

A fighter pilot shook his head. "With the right support, no."

"So we'll just have to flush the MiGs off the ground and kill some." The commanders of both Tomcat squadrons were with Toland, examining the maps. "Want to keep clear of those SAMs, though. From what the guys in Germany say, the SA-11 is very bad news."

The first Air Force effort to flatten Keflavik with B-52s had been a disaster. Follow-up efforts with smaller, faster FB-111s had harassed the Russians but could not put Keflavik totally out of business. SAC was unwilling to part with enough of its fastest strategic bombers to do this. There still had not been a successful mission against the main fuel-storage site. It was too close to a populated area, and satellite photos revealed that the civilians were still there. Of course.

"Let's get the Air Force to try another B-52 mission," one fighter jock suggested. "They come in like before, except . . ." He outlined some changes in the attack profile. "Now that we have our Queers with us, it might work out all right."

"If you want my help, Commander, you might at least be a little polite about it." The Prowler pilot in the room clearly didn't like to have his forty-million-dollar aircraft referred to by that nickname. "I can knock those SAM radars back some, just keep in mind that SA-11 has a backup infrared tracker system. You get within ten miles of the launchers, they have an even-money chance of smoking your Tomcat right out of the sky." The really nasty thing about the SA-11, pilots had learned, was that it left almost no exhaust trail, which made it very hard to spot, and it was even harder to evade a SAM you couldn't see.

"We'll stay clear of Mr. SAM. First time, gentlemen, we got the odds on our side." The fighter pilots started putting a plan together. They now had solid intelligence of how Russian fighters operated in combat. The Soviets had good tactics, but they were also predictable. If the American aircraft could contrive to present a situation for which the Russians were trained, they knew how Ivan would react to it.

STENDAL, GERMAN DEMOCRATIC REPUBLIC

He had never expected it to be easy, but neither had Alekseyev expected NATO air forces to have control of the night skies. Four minutes after midnight, an aircraft that had never registered on their radar had obliterated the radio transmitter station for CINC-West's headquarters. They'd only had three alternate stations, each more than ten kilometers from the underground bunker complex. Now they had one, plus a mobile transmitter that had already been bombed once. The underground telephone cables were still being used, of course, but advances into enemy territory had made telephone communications unreliable. Too often, the cables strung by Signal Corps troops were being destroyed by air attack and badly driven vehicles. They needed the radio links, and NATO was systematically eliminating them. They'd even attempted an attack on the bunker complex itself—the decoy site set exactly between two transmitter stations had been hit by eight fighter-bombers and liberally sprinkled with napalm, cluster munitions, and delay-fused high explosives. If the attack had been on the real complex, the ordnance experts said, there might have been casualties. *So much for the skill of our engineers.* The bunkers were supposed to withstand a near-miss from a nuclear warhead.

He now had a full fighting division across the Leine—the remains of one, he corrected himself. The two reinforcing tank divisions were trying to cross now, but the ribbon bridges had been bombed overnight along with the advancing divisions. The NATO reinforcements were beginning to arrive—their road advances had also suffered from air attacks, though at ghastly cost to the Soviet fighter-bombers. *The tactics . . . no, amateurs discuss tactics,* Alekseyev thought wryly. *Professional soldiers study logistics.* The key to his success would pivot on his ability to maintain bridges on the river Leine and to run traffic efficiently down the roads to Alfeld. The traffic-control system had already broken down twice before Alekseyev had dispatched a team of colonels to handle things.

"We should have picked a better place," Alekseyev muttered.

"Excuse me, Comrade General?" Sergetov asked.

"There's only one good road into Alfeld." The General smiled ironically. "We should have made our breakthrough at a town with at least three."

They watched wooden counters march—creep—down the line on the map. Each counter was a battalion. Missile and antiaircraft-gun units lined the corridor north and south of this road, and the road itself constantly swept to rid it of the remotely deployed mines that NATO was using in large numbers for the first time.

"Twentieth Tanks has taken a serious mauling," the General breathed. *His* troops. It might have been a quick breakthrough—should have been but for NATO aircraft.

"The two reinforcing divisions will complete the maneuver," Sergetov predicted confidently.

Alekseyev thought him right. Unless something else went wrong.

NORFOLK, VIRGINIA

Morris sat across the deck from COMNAVSURFLANT: Commander, Naval Surface Forces, U.S. Atlantic Fleet. A three-star admiral, he'd spent his whole career in what he liked to call "the real Navy," frigates, destroyers, and cruisers. The small gray ships lacked the glamour of aviation and the mystery of the submarines, but right now they were the key to getting the convoys across the Atlantic.

"Ivan's changed tactics on us—a hell of a lot faster than we thought he was able to. They're going for the escorts. The attack on your frigate was deliberate, you didn't just stumble across him. He was probably laying for you."

"They're trying to roll back the escorts?"

"Yes, but with particular attention to the ships with tails. We've hurt their submarine force—not enough, but we have hurt them. The towed-array pickets have worked out very well. Ivan picked up on that and he's trying to take them out. He's looking for the SURTASS ships, too, but that's a harder proposition. We've killed three submarines that tried to move in on them."

Morris nodded. The Surface Towed-Array Sonar Ships were modified tuna clippers that trailed enormous passive sonar cables. There weren't enough of them to provide coverage for more than half the convoy routes, but they fed good information into ASW headquarters in Norfolk. "Why don't they send Backfires after the ships?"

"We've wondered about that, too. Evidently the Russians don't think they're worth the diversion of that much effort. Besides, we've got a lot more electronic capability built into them than anyone thought. They're not easy to locate on radar." The Admiral went no further than that, but Morris wondered if stealth technology—which the Navy had been working on for years—had been applied to the SURTASS force. If the Russians were limiting their effort to locate and kill the tuna boats with submarines, he thought, so much the better.

"I'm putting you in for a decoration, Ed. You did very well. I've only got three skippers who've done better, and one of them was killed yesterday. So how bad was your damage?"

"She may be a total loss, sir. It was a Victor. We took one hit in the bow. The keel let go, and—the bow tore off, sir. We lost everything forward of the ASROC launcher. Lots of shock damage, but most of it's already fixed. Before she'll sail again, we have to build her a new bow." The Admiral nodded. He'd already seen the casualty reports.

"You did well to save her, Ed. Damned well. *Pharris* doesn't need you for the moment. I want you here with my operations people. We have to change tactics, too. I want you to look over what intelligence and operational information we have and feed me some ideas."

"For starters, we might stop those damned Backfires."

"That's being worked on." The reply held both confidence and skepticism.

THE WINDWARD PASSAGE

To the east was Haiti on the island of Hispaniola. To the west was Cuba. Blacked out, radar systems fully energized but placed on standby, the ships sailed in battle formation, escorted by destroyers and frigates. Missiles were hung on launchers and trained out to port, while the launch controllers sweated in their air-conditioned battle stations.

They didn't expect trouble. Castro had gotten word to the American government that he had had no part in this, and was angered that the Soviets had not informed him of their plans. It was diplomatically important, however, that the American fleet traverse the passage in darkness so that the Cubans could say truthfully that they had seen nothing. As a sign of good faith, Castro had also alerted the Americans to the presence of a Soviet submarine in the Florida Straits. To be used as a vassal was one thing, to have his country used as a base for a war without being informed was too much.

The sailors didn't know all of this, just that no serious opposition was expected. They took it with a grain of salt, as they did all intelligence reports. Their helicopters had laid a string of sonobuoys, and their ESM radar receivers listened for the pulsing signal of a Soviet-made radar. Aloft, lookouts trained clumsy starlight scopes around the sky, searching for aircraft that might be hunting them visually—which would not be hard. At twenty-five knots, every ship left a foaming wake that seemed to fluoresce like neon in the darkness.

Maalox didn't work anymore, one frigate captain grumbled to himself. He sat in the command chair in his ship's Combat Information Center. To his left was the chart table, in front of him (he faced aft) the young tactical action officer stood over his plotting scope. The Cubans were known to have surface-to-surface missile batteries arrayed on their coastline like the fortresses of old. At any moment the ships might detect a swarm of incoming vampires. Forward, his single-arm missile launcher was loaded and trained out, as were his three-inch gun and CIWS topside. The coffee was a mistake, but he had to stay alert. The price was a stabbing pain in his upper abdomen. *Maybe I should talk to the corpsman*, he thought, and shrugged it off. There wasn't time for that. He'd been working around the clock for three months to get his ship ready for action, racing through the acceptance trials and conducting continuous workups, working his men and ship hard, but working himself hardest of all. He was too proud to admit that he'd pushed too hard, even to himself.

It came just as he finished his third cup of coffee. For all the warnings, it was a pain as severe and surprising as a thrown knife. The captain doubled over and vomited on the tiled deck of CIC. A sailor mopped it up at once, and it was too dark to see that there'd been blood on the tile. He couldn't leave his post, despite the pains, despite the sudden chill from the blood loss. The captain made a mental note to keep off the coffee for a few hours. Maybe he'd see the corpsman when he got the chance. *If* he got the chance. There'd be a three-day layover in Norfolk. He could rest a little then. He knew he needed rest. The fatigue that had been building for days hammered at him. The captain shook his head. Throwing up was supposed to make you feel better.

VIRGINIA BEACH, VIRGINIA

Morris found his home empty. At his suggestion, his wife had gone home to Kansas to stay with her family. No sense having you and the kids home worrying about me, he'd told her. He regretted it now. Morris needed the company, needed a hug, needed to see his kids. Within a minute of opening the door, he was on the phone. His wife already knew what had happened to his ship, but had withheld it from the kids. It took two minutes to assure her that he was indeed all right, at home, and uninjured. Then came the kids, and finally the knowledge that they couldn't arrange a flight home. All the airliners were either ferrying men and supplies overseas or booked solid until mid-August. Ed saw no sense in having his family drive all the way from Salina to Kansas City to wait on standby. Good-byes were hard.

What came next was harder. Commander Edward Morris donned his whites and from his wallet took a list of family calls he had to make. They'd all been officially notified, but another of the duties that came with command was to make the trips himself. The widow of his executive officer lived only half a mile away. A good man with a barbecue, the XO, Morris remembered. How many weekends had he spent in their backyard watching steaks sizzle over charcoal? What would he tell her now? What would he tell the rest of the widows? What would he tell the *kids?*

Morris walked to his car and was mocked by the license plate, FF-1094. Not every man got to carry his failure around with him. Most were fortunate enough to leave it behind. As he started the engine, Morris wondered if he'd ever be able to sleep without the fear of reliving again that moment on the bridge of his ship.

ICELAND

For the first time Edwards had beaten his sergeant at his own game. For all his alleged expertise with a fishing rod, Smith had come away with nothing after an hour's effort, and handed the rod to Mike in disgust. Ten minutes later, Edwards landed a four-pound trout.

"Ain't that some shit," Smith growled.

The last ten kilometers they'd covered had taken eleven hours. The one road they'd had to cross, they learned, was a busy one. Every few minutes a vehicle headed north or south. The Russians were using this gravel strip as their principal means of overland travel to Iceland's northern coast. Edwards and his party had spent six hours hiding in the rocks of yet another lava field, watching and waiting for a safe time to cross. Twice they'd seen Mi-24 helicopters patrolling the area, but neither had come close. They'd seen no foot patrols either, and Edwards had concluded that Iceland was too big for the Soviet force to control. At that point he'd taken out his Russian map and set to analyzing the symbols. The Soviet troops were concentrated in an arc extending north and south of the Reykjavik peninsula. He'd radioed that into Scotland, spending ten minutes describing the Russian symbology.

Road traffic had dropped off at dusk, allowing them to cross the road on the run. They'd found themselves without food in another area of lakes and streams. Enough was enough, Edwards had decided. They had to rest again and began fishing to get themselves some food. The next leg of their journey would keep them well clear of inhabited areas.

His rifle and other gear lay next to a rock, covered with his camouflage jacket. Vigdis was with him. She'd hardly left his side all day. Smith and the Marines had found places to relax while their lieutenant did most of the work.

The local bug population was out in force today. His sweater kept most of them off his skin, but his face attracted their share. He tried to ignore them. Quite a few bugs had found their way to the surface of the stream, and the trout were going after them. Every time he saw a ripple, he cast the feathery lure toward it. The rod bent again.

"Got another one!" he hooted. Smith's head came up, shook angrily, and went back down in the bushes fifty yards away.

Edwards had never done this sort of fishing. All his experience was in his father's boat, but the principles were pretty much the same. He let the trout pull against the line, but not too much, just enough to wear him out as Edwards worked the rod up and down, drawing the fish upstream and into the rocks. Suddenly he tripped over a rock and fell into the shallow water, managing, however, to keep his rod-tip high. Struggling to his feet, he stepped back, his fatigue pants black and wet against his legs.

"This is a big one." He turned to see Vigdis laughing. She watched him work the fish in and began moving toward it. A minute later she grabbed the leader and pulled the trout clear of the water.

"Three kilos, this one." She held it up.

At age ten Mike had caught a hundred-pound albacore, but this brown trout looked a lot bigger. He reeled in the line as Vigdis walked toward him. *Ten pounds of fish in twenty minutes*, he thought. *We might just be able to live off the land yet.*

The helicopter appeared without warning. There was a westerly wind—it had probably been patrolling the road to the east—and the aircraft was less than a mile away before they heard the stuttering sound of its five-bladed rotor headed right toward them. "Everyone freeze!" Smith yelled. The Marines were in good cover, but Mike and Vigdis were in the open.

"Oh, God," Edwards breathed. He finished reeling his line in. "Take the fish off the hook. Relax."

She looked at him as the helicopter approached, afraid to turn around toward the incoming chopper. Her hands shook as she worked the hook free of the wriggling trout.

"It's going to be all right, Vigdis." He wrapped his arm about her waist and walked slowly away from the stream. Her arm pulled his body close against hers. It came as a greater shock than the Russian chopper. She was stronger than he'd expected, and her arm was a heated path around his back and chest.

The chopper was less than five hundred yards off, bearing directly at them, nose down, the multibarreled gun trained directly at them.

He'd never make it, Edwards saw. His rifle was fifty feet away under his camouflage jacket. If he moved fast enough to get there, they'd know why. His legs were weak beneath him as he watched death approach.

Slowly, carefully, Vigdis moved the hand in which she held the fish. She used two fingers to grab Mike's hand at her waist, moving it up and around until it rested on her left breast. Then she held the fish high above her head. Mike dropped his rod and stooped to get the other trout. Vigdis followed his movements and managed to keep his left hand in place. Mike held up his fish as the Mi-24 attack helicopter hovered fifty yards away. Its rotor tossed up a circle of spray from the surrounding marsh.

"Go away," Mike rasped through his grinning teeth.

"My father loves to fish," the senior lieutenant said, manipulating the flight controls to Hover.

"Shit on the fish," the gunner snapped back. "I want to catch one of those. Look where that young bastard has his hand!"

They probably don't even know what's going on, he thought. *Or if they know, they have sense enough not to do anything about it. Nice to see that some people are untouched by the madness that's sweeping the world . . .* The pilot looked down at his fuel gauges.

"They look harmless enough. We're down to thirty minutes' fuel. Time to return."

The chopper settled at the tail, and for a terrible moment Edwards thought it might be landing. Then it pivoted in midair and moved to the southwest. One of the soldiers riding in the back waved at them. Vigdis waved back. They stood there as it flew off. Their hands came down, and her left arm held his tight against her. Edwards had not realized that Vigdis didn't wear a bra. He was afraid to move his hand, afraid to appear to make an advance. Why had she done that? To help fool the Russians—to reassure him, or herself? That it had in fact worked seemed unimportant. The Marines were still concealed. They stood there quite alone, and his left hand seemed to burn as his mind stumbled over what he ought to do.

Vigdis acted for him. His hand slid away as she turned to him and buried her head against his shoulder. *Here I am holding the prettiest girl I ever met in one hand,* Edwards thought, *and a Goddamned fish in the other.* That was easily solved. Edwards dropped the fish, wrapped both arms around her, and held on tight.

"Are you all right?"

She looked up at his face. "I think yes."

There was only one word for what he felt toward the girl in his arms. Edwards knew this wasn't the time, and wasn't the place, but the look and the word remained. He kissed her gently on the cheek. The smile that answered him counted more than all the passionate encounters of his life.

"Excuse me, folks," Sergeant Smith said from a few feet away.

"Yeah." Edwards disengaged himself. "Let's get moving before they decide to come back."

USS *CHICAGO*

Things were going well. American P-3C Orions and British Nimrods were scouting the route to the icepack. The submarines had been forced to detour east around one suspected Russian submarine, but that was all. Ivan was sending most of his boats south, it seemed, confident that the Norwegian Sea was under his control. Another six hours to the pack.

Chicago was drifting now, finished with her turn at the head of the "freight train" procession of submarines. Her sonar gear searched the black water for the telltale noise of a Russian submarine. They heard nothing but the distant growling of the icepack.

The tracking team plotted the position of the other American submarines. McCafferty was glad to see they had trouble doing so, even with America's best sonar equipment. If they had trouble, so would the Russians. His crew looked to be in good shape. Three days on the beach had counted for a lot. The beer supplied by the Norwegian skipper, plus word on what their Harpoon had done in *Chicago*'s one real engagement, had counted for even more. He'd already briefed the crew on their current mission. The information was accepted quietly, with a couple of jokes about going back home—to the Barents Sea.

"That was *Boston,* skipper," the XO said. "Now we're the caboose."

McCafferty walked back to examine the chart. Everything looked okay, but he checked everything carefully. With so many submarines running the same course track, the risk of collision was real. A quartermaster ran down the list of the sister subs that had passed *Chicago*. The skipper was satisfied.

"All ahead two-thirds," he ordered. The helmsman acknowledged the order and twisted the annunciator dial.

"Engine room answers all ahead two-thirds."

"Very well. Left ten degrees rudder. Come to new course three-four-eight."

Chicago accelerated to fifteen knots, taking her station at the end of the column as the freight train raced to the Arctic.

31. Demons

VIRGINIA BEACH, VIRGINIA

"Left full rudder!" Morris screamed, pointing at the torpedo's wake.

"Right full rudder, aye!" the helmsman replied, spinning the wheel right, then left, then centering it.

Morris stood on the port bridge wing. The sea was flat calm, and the torpedo's wake was clearly visible, following every turn and maneuver the frigate made. He even tried reversing, and that didn't work—the torpedo appeared to go sideways. It stopped dead in the water and rose to the surface where he could see it. It was white, with what seemed to be a red star on the nose . . . and it had eyes, like all homing torpedoes. He ordered flank speed, but the torpedo stayed with him on the surface now, skimming along like a flying fish, clearly visible to all who could see—but only Morris saw it.

It closed ever so slowly as the frigate maneuvered. Fifty feet, thirty, ten . . .

"Where did my daddy go?" the little girl asked. "I want my daddy!"

"What's the problem, skipper?" the exec asked. This was very strange, because he didn't have a head—

Sweat poured from Morris's face as he bolted upright in his bed, his heart racing. The digital clock on the headboard said 4:54. Ed got up and walked shakily into the bathroom to splash cold water on his face. *The second time tonight,* he thought. Twice more during the tow back to Boston the nightmare had come, robbing him of the few hours of rest he allowed himself. Morris wondered if he had screamed in his sleep.

You did everything you could have done. It's not your fault, he told the face in the mirror.

But you were the captain, it replied.

Morris had gotten through five homes when he'd had to stop. It was one thing to talk to wives and parents. They understood. Their sons and husbands were sailors, and had taken a sailor's risk. But the four-year-old daughter of Gunner's Mate Second Class Jeff Evans had not understood why her daddy would never come home again. A second-class petty officer didn't make much, Morris knew. Evans must have worked like a madman on that little house to make it as neat as it was. A good man with his hands, he remembered, a good gunner's mate. Every wall was newly painted. Much of the interior woodwork had been replaced. They'd been in the house only seven months, and Morris wondered how the petty officer had found the time to get all that work done. He had to have done it himself. No way he could have afforded contractors. Ginny's room had been a testimony to her father's love. Dolls from all over the world had stood on hand-made shelves. As soon as he'd seen Ginny's room, Morris had had to leave. He'd felt himself on the verge of breaking down, and some absurd code of conduct wouldn't allow him to do that in front of strangers. So he'd left and driven home, with the rest of the list tucked back in his wallet. Certainly the fatigue that had enveloped him would allow him a night's sleep . . .

But now he stood in front of the mirror, looking at a man with hollow eyes who wished his wife were there.

Morris went out to the kitchen of his one-story house and went mindlessly through the process of making coffee. The morning paper was on the doorstep, and he found himself reading stories about the war that he knew to be inaccurate or out of date. Things were happening much too fast for reporters to keep up. There was an eyewitness account from an unnamed destroyer about a missile that had leaked through her missile defenses. An "analysis" piece explained how surface warships were obsolete in the face of determined missile attacks and asked where the fleet's vaunted carriers were. That, he thought, was a pretty good question.

Morris finished his coffee and returned to the bathroom for a shower. If he had to be awake, he thought, he might as well be at work. He had one set of undress whites in the closet. He donned them a few minutes later and walked out to his car. It was already first light when he drove to the Norfolk Navy Base.

Forty minutes later he was in one of several operations rooms, where the positions of convoys and suspected submarine locations were plotted. On the far wall the threat board listed estimated Russian assets and the numbers and types of kills accumulated to date. Another wall showed losses. If the intel guys were right, he thought, the war at sea had the look of a draw—but for the Russians a draw was the same as a win.

"Good morning, Commander," COMNAVSURFLANT said. Another man who had not slept very much. "You look a little better."

Better than what? Morris wondered.

"We have some good news for a change."

NORTH ATLANTIC

The B-52 crews were nervous despite the heavy fighter escort. Five thousand feet above them, a full squadron of F-14 Tomcats flew top cover, having just refueled from KC-135 tankers. The other squadron was tanking now for their part in the mission. The sun was just peeping above the horizon, and the ocean below them was still dark. It was 0300 local time, when human reaction times are at their worst.

KEFLAVIK, ICELAND

The alarm klaxon jolted the sleeping Russian pilots off their cots. Their ground crews took fewer than ten seconds to begin preflight procedures as the airmen climbed the steel ladders into their cockpits and plugged in their helmet radios to learn what the emergency was.

"Heavy enemy jamming activity to the west," the regimental commander announced. "Plan Three. Repeat: Plan Three."

In the control trailer, radar operators had just seen their radar screens turn to a cluttered nightmare of white-noise jamming. An American raid was coming in—probably B-52s, probably in force. Soon the American aircraft would be so close that the ground-based radars could burn through the jamming. Until then, the fighters would try to engage as far out as they could to reduce the number of bombers before they could strike their target.

The Soviet pilots had been well drilled in their time on Iceland. Within two minutes the first pair of MiG-29s was rolling; in seven all were in the air. The Soviet plan left a third of the fighters over Keflavik while the others charged west toward the jamming, their own missile-targeting radars on, seeking targets. They were ten minutes out when the jamming stopped. A single MiG got a radar contact off a retreating jamming aircraft and radioed Keflavik, only to learn from his ground controllers that nothing was on the scopes out to a range of three hundred kilometers.

A minute later, the jamming began again, this time from the south and east. More cautiously this time, the MiGs flew south. On orders, they kept their radar systems shut down until they were a hundred miles offshore, but when they switched on they found nothing. Whoever was jamming was doing it from a great distance. The ground controllers reported that three jammers had been involved in the first incident and four in the second. *Quite a lot of jammers,* the regimental commander thought. *They're trying to run us around, trying to make us use up our fuel.*

"Come east," he ordered his flight leaders.

The B-52 crews were really nervous now. One of the escorting Prowlers had picked up the voice radio orders from the MiGs, and another had caught a flash of their air-intercept radars to the southwest. The fighters eased south also. They were now one hundred fifty miles from Keflavik, crossing the Icelandic coast. The mission commander evaluated the situation and ordered the bombers to turn slightly north.

The B-52s carried no bombs, just the powerful radar jammers designed to allow other bombers to reach targets within the Soviet Union. Below them, the second squadron of Tomcats was heading for the deck, the eastern slopes of the Vatna glacier. With them were four Navy Prowlers for additional protection against air-to-air missiles in case the MiGs got too close.

"Starting to get some airborne radars, bearing two-five-eight. Seems to be closing," one Prowler reported. Another copied the same signal and they triangulated the range to fifty miles. Close enough. The mission commander was flying a Prowler.

"Amber Moon. Say again, Amber Moon."

The B-52s turned back east and dove, opening their bomb bays to disgorge tons of aluminum chaff that no radar signal could penetrate. As soon as they saw that, the American fighters all dropped their external fuel tanks, and the Prowlers broke off from the bombers to orbit just west of the chaff. Now came the tricky part. The fighters of both sides were closing at a combined speed of over one thousand miles per hour.

"Queer check," the mission commander radioed.

"Blackie check," acknowledged the skipper of VF-41.

"Jolly check," replied the commander of VF-84. Everyone was in position.

"Execute." The four Prowlers flipped on their antimissile jamming gear.

The twelve Tomcats of the Jolly Rogers were strung on a line at thirty thousand feet. On command they activated their missile-guidance radars.

"American fighters!" shouted a number of Russian pilots. Their threat receivers instantly told the pilots that fighter-type radars were locked on their aircraft.

The Soviet fighter commander was not surprised. Surely the Americans would not risk their heavy bombers again without a proper escort. He'd ignore these and bore in for the B-52s, as his training dictated. The MiG radars were heavily jammed, their ranges cut in half and as yet unable to track any targets at all. He ordered his pilots to be alert for incoming missiles, confident that they could avoid those that they saw, and had all his aircraft increase power. Next, he ordered all but two of his reserve force to leave Keflavik and come east to support him.

The Americans needed only seconds to lock onto targets. Each Tomcat carried four Sparrows and four Sidewinders. The Sparrows went first. There were sixteen MiGs in the air. Most had at least two missiles targeted, but the Sparrows were radar-guided. Each American fighter had to remain pointed at its target until the missile hit. This ran the risk of closing within range of Soviet missiles, and the Tomcats were not equipped with protective jammers.

The Americans had taken position up-sun from the Russians. Just as their radars began to burn through the American jamming, the Sparrows arrived, the first directly from the sun, exploding its MiG in midair and warning everyone in its flight. The Soviet aircraft began radical jinks up and down, some pilots breaking into hard turns as they saw the seven-inch wide missiles racing in, but four more found their targets, and in moments there were three hard kills and one severely damaged aircraft that turned to limp for home.

The Jolly Rogers turned as soon as their missiles were spent and ran northeast with the Soviets in pursuit. The Russian commander was relieved that the American missiles had performed so poorly, yet still enraged at the loss of five aircraft. His remaining aircraft bore in on afterburner as their targeting radars began to defeat the American jamming. The American fighter escort had had its turn, he knew. Now it was his turn. They ran northeast, their visored eyes alternating between squints into the sun and quick looks at their radarscopes to pick out targets. They never looked down. The lead MiG finally had a target and launched two missiles.

Twenty thousand feet below them, shielded from ground radar by a pair of mountains, twelve Tomcats of the Black Aces went to afterburner, their radars shut off as the twin-engined fighters rocketed skyward. Within ninety seconds the pilots began to hear the growling signal that indicated their Sidewinder heat-seeking missiles were tracking targets. Seconds later, sixteen missiles were fired from a range of two miles.

Six Russian pilots never knew what hit them. Of the eleven MiGs, eight were hit in a matter of seconds. The commander's luck remained briefly as he jerked his fighter around, causing a Sidewinder to break lock and fly into the sun, but now what could he do? He saw two Tomcats running south, away from his remaining fighters. It was too late to organize an attack—his wingman was gone, and the only friendly aircraft he could see was to his north—so the colonel reefed his MiG into an eight-g turn and dove at the American, oblivious to the warning buzz of his threat receiver. Both Sparrows launched from the second group of Black Aces struck his wing. The MiG came apart around him.

The Americans had no time to gloat. The mission commander reported a second group of MiGs heading their way and the American squadrons regrouped to meet them, forming a solid wall of twenty-four aircraft, their radars shut down for two minutes as the MiGs raced into the cloud of jamming. The Russian second-in-command was making a serious error. His fellow pilots were in danger. He had to go to their rescue. One group of Tomcat volleyed off its remaining Sparrows; the other fired Sidewinders. A total of thirty-eight missiles closed in on eight Soviet aircraft who had no clear picture of what they were running into. Half of them never did, blotted out of the sky by American air-to-air missiles; three more were damaged.

The Tomcat pilots all wanted to close, but the commander ordered them off. They were all short of fuel, and Stornoway was seven hundred miles off. They turned east, ducking through the cloud of aluminum chaff left by the B-52s. The Americans would claim thirty-seven kills, quite a score since they had expected a total of only twenty-seven Russian aircraft. In fact, of twenty-six MiGs, only five undamaged aircraft remained. A stunned air base commander immediately began rescue operations. Soon the parachute division's attack helicopters were flying northeast, searching for downed pilots.

STENDAL, GERMAN DEMOCRATIC REPUBLIC

Thirty kilometers from Alfeld to Hameln, Alekseyev thought. An hour's drive in a tank. Elements of three divisions were making that drive now, and since the crossing had been achieved, they'd advanced a total of only eighteen kilometers. This time it was the English: the tanks of the Royal

Tank Regiment and 21st Lancers had stopped his leading elements cold halfway to Hameln and hadn't budged in eighteen hours.

There was real danger here. For a mechanized formation, safety lay in movement. The Soviets were feeding units into the gap, but NATO was using its air power to the utmost. The bridges on the Leine were being destroyed almost as fast as they could be repaired. Engineers had prepared crossing points on the riverbanks, and the Russians were able to swim their infantry carriers across now, but the tanks couldn't swim, and every attempt to run them across underwater—as they were supposedly equipped to do—had been a failure. Too many units had had to be deployed to protect the breach in NATO's lines, and too few were able to exploit it. Alekseyev had achieved a perfect textbook breakthrough—only to see that the other side had its own textbook for containing and smashing it. Western Theater had a total of six reserve class-A divisions to send into the fighting. After that they would have to start using class-B units composed of reservists, with older men and equipment. There were many of them, but they would not—could not—perform as well as the younger soldiers. The General bridled at the necessity of committing units to battle that would certainly take higher casualties than normal. But he had no choice. His political masters wanted it, and he was only the executor of political policy.

"I have to go back forward," Alekseyev told his boss.

"Yes, but no closer than five kilometers to the front line, Pasha. I cannot afford to lose you now."

BRUSSELS, BELGIUM

The Supreme Allied Commander, Europe, looked at his own tally sheet. Nearly all of his reserves were committed to the fighting now, and the Russians seemed to have an endless supply of men and vehicles moving forward. His units had no time to reorganize and redeploy. NATO faced the nightmare of all armies: they could only react to the moves of their opponent, with almost no chance to launch their own initiatives. So far things were holding together—but only barely. Southeast of Hameln his map showed a British brigade. In fact it was nothing more than a reinforced regiment composed of exhausted men and damaged equipment. Artillery and aircraft were all that allowed him to prevent a collapse, and even that would not be enough if his units didn't get much more replacement equipment. More ominously, NATO was now down to two weeks of ordnance, and the resupply coming from America had been seriously impeded by attacks on the convoys. What could he tell his men? Reduce munitions expenditures—when the only thing stopping the Russians was the profligate use of every weapon at hand?

His morning intelligence brief was starting. The chief NATO intelligence officer was a German general who was accompanied by a Dutch major carrying a videotape cassette. For something this important, the intel officer knew, SACEUR wanted to see the raw data, not just the analysis. The Dutch officer set up the machine.

A computer-generated map appeared, then units showed up. The tape took under two minutes to display five hours of data, repeating it several times so that the officers could discern patterns.

"General, we estimate that the Soviets are sending six full divisions toward Alfeld. The movement you see here on the main road from Braunschweig is the first of them. The others come from their theater reserve, and these two coming south are reserve formations from their northern army group."

"So you think that they are making this their main point of attack?" SACEUR asked.

"*Ja.*" The German General nodded. "The *Schwerpunkt* is here."

SACEUR frowned. The rational thing to do would be to withdraw behind the river Weser to shorten his defensive line and reorganize his forces. But that would mean abandoning Hannover. The Germans would never accept that. Their own national strategy of defending each home and field had cost the Russians dear—and stretched NATO forces to the breaking point. Politically they would never accept such a strategic withdrawal. West German units would fight on alone if they had to: he could see it clearly enough in the eyes of his own intelligence chief. *And if somebody invaded New Hampshire,* he admitted to himself, *would I withdraw into Pennsylvania?*

An hour later, half of the existing NATO reserves were heading east from Osnabrück to Hameln. The battle for Germany would be won or lost on the right bank of the Weser.

STORNOWAY, SCOTLAND

The returning Tomcats got little rest. As soon as they landed, the British and American ground crewmen refueled and rearmed the fighters. The Russians were raiding the British northern airfields more carefully now. The American airborne radar aircraft supporting the British Nimrods and Shackletons were making life hard on the twin-engine Blinder bombers flying out of Andøya in Norway. Royal Air Force Tornados flew combat air-patrol missions two hundred miles offshore while the American pilots rested, a few enterprising crew chiefs painted red stars underneath the cockpits, and intelligence officers evaluated gunsight videotapes and recordings of Soviet missile radars.

"Looks like we hurt them," Toland judged. The kill claims were too high, but with fighter pilots they always were.

"Bet your ass!" replied the commander of the Jolly Rogers. The Navy commander chewed on a cigar. He claimed personal credit for a pair of MiGs. "Question is, will they reinforce? It worked once, but they won't fall for that gag again. You tell me, Toland: can they replace what we culled out?"

"I don't think so. The MiG-29 is about the only fighter they can stage out that far. The rest of those are in Germany, and they've taken a beating there, too. If the Russians decide to cut loose some MiG-31s, I think they can reach that far, but I don't see them releasing their prime bomber-interceptor for this kind of mission."

The Jolly Rogers's skipper nodded agreement. "Okay. Next step then is we put a combat air patrol close to Iceland and start beating on those Backfire raids for-real."

"They might just come looking for us, too," Toland warned. "They have to know now what we did, and where we did it from." The commander of VF-41 looked out the window. One of his Tomcats sat half a mile away between two piles of sandbags. Four missiles were visible on the airframe. He fingered the Ace of Spades emblem on his chest and turned back.

"Good. If they want to fight us on our turf, in our radar cover, fine."

ALFELD, FEDERAL REPUBLIC OF GERMANY

Alekseyev left his helicopter on the outskirts of the town and climbed into yet another BMP infantry carrier. Two ribbon bridges were operating. Fragments of at least five others littered the riverbanks, along with countless burned-out tanks and trucks. The commander of 20th Tanks rode with them.

"NATO air attacks are murderous," General Beregovoy said. "I've never seen anything like it. Even with our SAMs they close in. We get our share, but it's not enough, and things only get worse as we approach the front."

"What progress have you made today?"

"The main opposition at the moment is English. At least a brigade of tanks. We've pushed them back two kilometers since dawn."

"There's supposed to be a Belgian force out there also," Sergetov pointed out.

"They've disappeared. We don't know where they are—and, yes, that worries me also. I've placed one of the new divisions on our left flank to guard against counterattack. The other will join 20th Tanks when we resume the attack this afternoon."

"Strength?" Alekseyev asked.

"The Twentieth is down to ninety working tanks. Maybe less," the General said. "That number is four hours old. Our infantry has done better, but the division is now under fifty-percent nominal strength."

Their vehicle angled down onto the floating ribbon bridge. Each boxlike segment was bolted to two others, and the vehicle bobbed up and down like a small boat in the surf as they drove across the Leine. All three officers controlled their feelings, but none liked being locked inside a steel box over the water. The BMP infantry assault vehicle was technically amphibious, but many had sunk without warning and it was rare for anyone to escape when that happened. They could hear distant artillery fire. Air attacks at Alfeld happened without warning. It took just over a minute to complete the crossing.

"In case you're curious, that bridge we just crossed holds the record for the longest survival." He checked his watch. "Seven hours."

"What of that major you requested the gold star for?" Alekseyev asked.

"He was wounded in an air attack. He'll live."

"Give him this. Perhaps it will speed his recovery." Alekseyev reached into a pocket and came out with a five-pointed gold star attached to a blood-red ribbon. He handed it to the General. That major of engineers was now a Hero of the Soviet Union.

USS *CHICAGO*

All the boats slowed on reaching the icepack. McCafferty inspected it through his periscope, a thin white line less than two miles away. There was nothing else visible. Few ships lingered so near the ice, and no aircraft were visible.

Sonar reported a gratifying amount of noise. The serrated fringe of the pack was composed of thousands of individual floes, slabs of ice a few feet thick, ranging in size from a few square feet to several acres. Every year they came loose with the spring thaw and drifted at random until the freeze began again. While loose in the brief arctic summer, they drifted at random, grinding against one another in a process that destroyed some of the smaller floes, which added to the never-ending groans and pops of the solid ice that went across the top of the pole all the way to the North Slope of Alaska.

"What's that?" McCafferty adjusted the scope slightly, turning the handle to the twelve-power setting. He'd glimpsed what might have been a periscope for the merest instant. It was gone now and—reappeared: the swordlike dorsal fin of a male killer whale. A puff of spray marked its breath, condensing to vapor in the polar air, then a few more whales appeared. What was it they called a family of orcas? A school—no, a pod. Up here hunting seals, probably. He wondered if the omen was good or bad. *Orcinus orca* was the scientific name: Bringer of Death.

"Sonar, do you have anything at one-three-nine?"

"Conn, we have eleven killer whales on that bearing. I make it three males, six females, and two adolescents. Pretty close in, I think. Bearing is changing slowly." The sonar chief responded as if insulted. There were standing orders not to report "biologicals" unless specifically ordered otherwise.

"Very well." McCafferty had to grin in spite of himself.

The other submarines of Operation Doolittle were strung out on a line more than ten miles across. One by one they went deep and headed under the pack. An hour later the freight train headed east, five miles inside the nominal edge of the pack. Twelve thousand feet below them was the floor of the Barents Abyssal Plain.

ICELAND

"Haven't seen a chopper all day," Sergeant Smith observed.

Conversation, Edwards noted, made a nice distraction from the fact that they were eating raw fish. He checked his watch. It was time to call in again. It had gotten so that he could assemble the radio antenna in his sleep.

"Doghouse, this is Beagle, and things could be a lot better, over."

"Beagle, we read you. Where are you now?"

"About forty-six kilometers from our objective," Edwards replied. He gave them map coordinates. There was one road yet to cross, and only one more row of hills, according to the map. "Nothing much to report except we have not seen any choppers today. In fact we haven't seen any aircraft at all." Edwards looked up. The sky was pretty clear, too. Usually they spotted fighters once or twice a day as they patrolled overhead.

"Roger that, Beagle. Be advised that the Navy sent some fighters over and beat them up pretty good around dawn."

"All right! We haven't seen any Russians since the chopper looked us over." In Scotland his controller shuddered at that. Edwards went on, "We're down to eating fish we catch, but the fishing's pretty good."

"How's your lady friend?"

Mike had to smile at that one. "She's not holding us back, if that's what you mean. Anything else?"

"Negative."

"Okay, we'll be back if we see anything. Out." Edwards flipped the power switch on the radio pack. "Our friends say the Navy chewed up some Russian fighters today."

" 'Bout time," Smith said. He was down to his last five cigarettes and stared at one now, deciding whether or not to reduce his supply to four. As Edwards watched, he opened his lighter to poison himself again.

"We go to Hvammsfjördur?" Vigdis asked. "Why?"

"Somebody wants to know what's there," Edwards said. He unfolded the tactical map. It showed the entrance to the bay to be crammed with rocks. It took him a moment to realize that while the land elevations were in meters, the depth curves on the map were in fathoms . . .

KEFLAVIK

"How many?"

The fighter regiment commander was lowered gently from the helicopter, his arm tied across his chest. Ejecting from his disintegrating aircraft, the colonel had dislocated his shoulder, and then his parachute had landed him on a mountainside, giving him a sprained ankle plus several facial cuts. It had taken eleven hours to find him. On the whole, the colonel considered himself lucky—for a fool who had allowed his command to be ambushed by a superior force.

"Five aircraft are mission capable," he was told. "Of the damaged ones, we can repair two."

The colonel swore, angered in spite of the morphine that coursed through his veins. "My men?"

"We've found six, including you. Two are uninjured and can still fly. The rest are in the hospital."

Another helicopter landed close by. The paratroop general got out and came over.

"Good to see you alive."

"Thank you, Comrade General. You are continuing the search?"

"Yes. I have detailed two helicopters to the task. What happened?"

"The Americans staged a raid with heavy bombers. We never saw them, but we could tell from the jamming. They had fighters mixed in with them. The bombers fled when we approached." The Air Force colonel tried to put the best face on it, and the General did not press him. This was an exposed post, and such things were expected. The MiGs could hardly have ignored the American raid. There was no point in punishing this man.

The General had already radioed for more fighters, though he didn't expect any. The plan said they would not be necessary, but the plan had also said his division had to hold the island unsupported for only two weeks. By that time Germany was supposed to be fully defeated, and the land war in Europe mainly over. He received reports from the front that were mere embellishments of the news on Radio Moscow. The Red Army was driving on the Rhein—and they'd been driving on the Rhein since the first day of the damned war! The names of the cities under daily attack were strangely left out. His intelligence chief was risking his life by listening in on Western radio broadcasts—the KGB regarded it as a disloyal act—in order to get an idea of how the fighting was going. If Western reports were true—he didn't really believe them either—the campaign in Germany was a bloody mess. Until that was over, he was vulnerable.

Would NATO try to invade? His operations officer said it was impossible unless the Americans were able to destroy the long-range bombers flying out of Kirovsk first, and the whole point of seizing Iceland had been to prevent the American carriers from moving to a position from which they could do just that. On paper, then, the General expected only increased air attacks, and he had surface-to-air missiles to defend against those. But he hadn't become a divisional commander by merely shuffling papers.

NORTH ATLANTIC

"What the hell happened?" The captain looked up to see a tube stuck in his arm. The last thing he remembered was being on the bridge halfway through the afternoon watch. Now the porthole on the starboard side of his stateroom was covered. Darkened ship: it was night outside.

"You passed out, Captain," the chief hospital corpsman said. "Don't—"

The captain tried to rise. His head made it about eighteen inches off the pillow when his strength gave way.

"You have to rest. You got internal bleeding, skipper. You threw up blood last night. I think it's a perforated ulcer. You scared the hell outa me last night. Why didn't you come see me?" The chief held up a bottle of Maalox tablets. *People gotta be so damned smart about everything.* "Your blood pressure's down twenty points and you durned near went into shock on me. This ain't no bellyache you got, Captain. You might have to have surgery. There's a helo on the way out now to medevac you to the beach."

"I can't leave the ship, I—"

"Doc's orders, Captain. If you die on me I lose my perfect record. I'm sorry, sir, but unless you get real medical attention real quick, you could be in real trouble. You're heading for the beach."

32. New Names, New Faces

NORFOLK, VIRGINIA

"Good morning, Ed." Commander, Naval Surface Forces, U.S. Atlantic Fleet was seated behind a desk covered with dispatches that seemed to be organized into piles. Morning—half an hour after midnight. Morris hadn't left Norfolk since arriving at dawn on the previous day. If he went home, he'd have to sleep again . . .

"Morning, sir. What can I do for you?" Morris didn't want to sit down.

"You want to go back out?" COMNAVSURFLANT asked bluntly.

"Who with?"

"*Reuben James*'s skipper came down with a bleeding ulcer. They flew him in this morning. She arrives in another hour with the 'phibs from PACFLT. I'm assigning her to convoy duty. We have a big one assembling in New York harbor. Eighty ships, all big, all fast, loaded with heavy equipment for Germany. It sails in four days with a heavy U.S. / U.K. escort, plus carrier support. *Reuben James* will be in port long enough to refuel and reprovision. She sails for New York this evening in company with HMS *Battleaxe*. If you're up to it, I want you to take her." The Vice Admiral eyed Morris closely. "She's yours if you want her. You up to it?"

"My personal gear's still aboard *Pharris*." Morris temporized. Did he really want to go back out?

"Packed up and on the way down, Ed."

There were plenty of men who could do it, Morris thought. The operations staff he'd been working with since he arrived in Norfolk was full of people who'd leap at this. *Go back to sea and put it on the line again—or drive back every night to an empty home and nightmares?*

"If you want me, I'll take her."

FÖLZIEHAUSEN, FEDERAL REPUBLIC OF GERMANY

The northern horizon flashed with artillery fire that backlit the trees. The sky was never free of the thunder. The drive to the divisional command post was a mere fifteen kilometers from Alfeld. Three vicious air attacks and twenty separate artillery barrages had converted the morning drive into a nightmare lasting into dusk and beyond.

The forward headquarters of 20th Tanks was now the command post for the entire drive toward Hameln. Lieutenant General Beregovoy, who had relieved Alekseyev, now wore the hats of commander 20th Tanks and operational-maneuver group commander. The OMG concept had been one of the most precious Soviet pre-war ideas. The "daring thrust" would open a corridor into the enemy's rear, and the operational-maneuver group would exploit it, racing into the corridor to seize important economic or political targets. Alekseyev stood with his back against an armored vehicle, looking north at the flashing outline of a forest. *Another thing that hasn't gone according to plan,* he thought. *As if we expected NATO to cooperate with our plans!*

There was a yellow flash overhead. Alekseyev blinked his eyes clear and watched the fireball turn to a comet that fell to the earth, landing several kilometers away. Ours or theirs? he wondered. Another promising young life snuffed out by a missile. Now we kill our young men with robots. *Who said mankind was not using his technology to worthwhile ends?*

He had prepared his whole life for this. Four years in officer school. The difficult initiation as a junior officer, promotion to command a company. Three more years at Frunze Military Academy in Moscow after he'd been recognized as a rising star. Then command of a battalion. Back to Moscow to the Voroshilov Academy of the General Staff. Top man in his class. Command of a regiment, then a division. *All for this?*

A field hospital was in the trees five hundred meters away, and the wind carried the shrieks of the wounded to the command post. Not like that in the movies he'd watched as a child—and still watched. The wounded were supposed to suffer in quiet, determined dignity, puffing on cigarettes proffered by the kindly, hardworking medics, waiting their turn for the courageous, hard-working surgeons and the pretty, dedicated nurses. *A fucking lie, all of it a monstrous fucking lie,* he told himself. The profession for which he had prepared his life was organized murder. He sent boys with pimples on their faces into a landscape rained on with steel and watered with blood. The burns were the worst. The tank crews who escaped from their brewed-up vehicles with their clothes alight—they never stopped screaming. Those killed by shock or the pistol of a merciful officer were only replaced by more. The lucky ones who reached the casualty-clearing stations found medics too busy to offer cigarettes, and doctors who were dropping from fatigue.

His brilliant tactical success at Alfeld had led nowhere yet, and he wondered in his soul if it ever would, if he had cast young lives away for nothing more than words in books written by men who did their best to forget the horrors they had inflicted and endured.

Second thoughts now, *Pasha?* he asked himself. *And what of those four colonels you had shot? Rather late to discover a conscience, isn't it?* But now it wasn't a map-table game or an exercise at Shpola, nor a handful of routine training accidents. It was one thing for a company commander to see all this after following orders from above. It was another for the man who gave the orders to view his handiwork.

"There is nothing so terrible as a battle won—except a battle lost." Alekseyev remembered the quote from Wellington's commentary on Waterloo, one of the two million books in the Frunze library. Certainly not something written by a Russian general. Why had he ever been allowed to read that? If soldiers read more of those remarks and less of glory, then what would they do when their political masters ordered them to march? *Now there,* the General told himself, *there is a radical idea . . .* He urinated against a tree and walked back toward the command post.

He found Beregovoy leaning over the map. A good man, and an effective soldier, Alekseyev knew, what did he think of all this?

"Comrade, that Belgian brigade just reappeared. It's attacking our left flank. They caught two regiments moving into new positions. We have a problem here."

Alekseyev strode to Beregovoy's side and surveyed the available units. NATO still was not cooperating. The attack had come at the junction of two divisions, one worn out, the other fresh but unblooded. A lieutenant moved some counters. The Soviet regiments were pulling back.

"Keep the reserve regiment in place," Alekseyev ordered. "Have this one move northwest. We'll try to catch the Belgians' flank as they approach this road junction." Professionalism dies hard in the soldier.

ICELAND

"Well, there it is." Edwards handed his binoculars to Sergeant Smith. Hvammsfjördur was still miles away. Their first sight of it came from the top of a two-thousand-foot hill. A sparkling river below them fed into the fjord, more than ten miles away. Everyone kept low, afraid to be skylined with the low sun behind them. Edwards broke out his radio.

"Doghouse, this is Beagle. The objective is in sight." This was a particularly dumb thing to say, Edwards knew. Hvammsfjördur was almost thirty miles long, about ten miles across at its widest point.

The man in Scotland was impressed. Edwards's party had covered fifteen kilometers in the past ten hours.

"What kind of shape are you in?"

"If you want us to go any farther, fella, this radio might malfunction."

"Roger, copy that." The major tried not to laugh. "Where exactly are you?"

"About five miles east of Hill 578. Now that we're here, maybe you might tell us why," Edwards suggested.

"If you see any, repeat any Russian activity, we want to know about it immediately. One guy taking a leak against a rock, we want to know about it. Do you copy that?"

"Roger. You want the size in inches. No Russkies in view yet. Some ruins to our left, and a farm a ways downriver from us. Nothing moving at either place. Any particular location you want us?"

"We're working on that. Sit tight for the moment. Find a nice place to hide and stay put. What's your food situation?"

"We have enough fish to last out the day, and I can see a lake where we might get some more. Remember when you said you'd have some pizzas sent out, Doghouse? Right now I'd kill for one. Pepperoni and onions."

"Fish is good for you. Beagle, your signal strength is down. You want to start thinking about conserving your batteries. Anything else to report?"

"Negative. We'll be back if we see anything. Out." Edwards slapped his hand down on the power switch. "People, we are home!"

"That's nice, skipper." Smith laughed. "Where's home?"

"Budhardalur is other side that mountain," Vigdis offered. "My Uncle Helgi live there."

We could probably get a decent meal there, Edwards told himself. *Maybe some lamb, a few beers or something stronger, and a bed . . . a real, soft bed with sheets and the down quilts they use here. A bath, hot water to shave. Toothpaste.* Edwards could smell every part of himself. They tried to wash in the streams when they could, but mostly they couldn't. *I smell like a goat,* Edwards thought. *Whatever a goat smells like. But we didn't walk this far to do something as stupid as that.*

"Sarge, let's secure this place."

"You got it, skipper. Rodgers, sack out. Garcia, you and me have the first watch. Four hours. You take that little knoll over there. I'll head over to the right." Smith stood and looked down at Edwards. "Good idea that we all get some rest while we can, skipper."

"Sounds great to me. You see anything important, give me a kick." Smith nodded and moved about a hundred yards.

Rodgers was already half asleep, his head resting on his folded jacket. The private's rifle was cradled on his chest.

"We stay here?" Vigdis asked.

"I'd sure like to go see your uncle, but there might be Russians in that town. How do you feel?"

"Tired."

"Tired as us?" he asked with a grin.

"Yes, tired as you," she admitted. Vigdis lay back next to Edwards. She was filthy. Her woolen sweater was torn in several places, and her boots scuffed beyond repair. "What will happen to us now?"

"I don't know. They wanted us here for a reason, though."

"But they don't tell you reason!" she objected.

Now there's an intelligent observation, Edwards thought.

"They tell you and you not tell us?" Vigdis asked.

"No, you know as much as I do."

"Michael, why all this happen? Why do the Russians come here?"

"I don't know."

"But you are officer. You must know." Vigdis propped herself up on her elbows. She seemed genuinely astonished. Edwards smiled. He couldn't blame her for being confused. Iceland's only armed force was its police. A real-to-life Peaceable Kingdom, the country had no military to speak of. A few small armed ships for fishery protection and the police were all the country had ever needed to maintain security. This war had ruined their perfect record. For a thousand years, without an army or a navy, Iceland had never been attacked. It had only happened now because they were in the way. He wondered if that would have happened if NATO hadn't built its base at Keflavik. Of course not! You idiot, you've seen what wonderful folks the Russians are! NATO base or not, Iceland was in their way. But why the hell *had* all this happened?

"Vigdis, I'm a meteorologist—a weatherman, I predict the weather for the Air Force." That only made her more confused.

"Not soldier? Not, ah, Marine soldier?"

Mike shook his head. "I'm an officer in the U.S. Air Force, yes, but I am not really a soldier like the sergeant. I have a different job."

"But you save my life. You are soldier."

"Yeah, I suppose I am—by accident."

"When this all over, what will you do?" Her eyes held a great deal of interest now.

"One thing at a time." He was thinking in terms of hours, not days or weeks. *If we do survive, then what? Put that one aside. First comes survival. You think about "after the war," and there won't* be *any.* "I'm too tired to think about that. Let's get some sleep."

She fought it. He knew that she wanted to know things he hadn't consciously considered, but she was more fatigued than she'd admitted, and ten minutes later she was asleep. She snored. Mike hadn't noticed before. This was no china doll. She had strengths and weaknesses, good points and bad. She had the face of an angel, but she'd gotten herself pregnant— *so what!* Edwards thought. *She's braver than she's beautiful. She saved* my *life when that chopper came in on us. A man could do far worse.*

Edwards commanded himself to lie down and sleep. He couldn't think about this. First he had to survive.

SCOTLAND

"If the area checks out?" the major asked. He had never really expected Edwards and his party to make it this far, not with eight thousand Russian troops on the island. Every time he thought about those five people trekking over bare, rocky ground and Soviet helicopters circling overhead, his skin crawled.

"Around midnight, I think," the man from Special Operations Executive said. You could see the smile crinkling the skin around his eyepatch. "You chaps had better decorate this young man. I've been in his boots myself. You cannot imagine how difficult it is to do what these people have done. And having a bloody Hind helicopter sit right on top of them! I've always said it's the quiet little bastards that you have to watch out for."

"In any case, it's time we got some professionals in to back them up," pronounced the captain of Royal Marines.

"Make sure they take in some food," suggested the USAF major.

LANGLEY AIR FORCE BASE, VIRGINIA

"So, what's the problem?" Nakamura asked.

"There are irregularities in some of the rocket motor casings," the engineer explained.

" 'Irregularities' meaning they go boom?"

"Possibly," the engineer admitted.

"Super," said Major Nakamura. "I'm supposed to carry that monster seventeen miles straight the hell up and then find out who goes into orbit, me or it!"

"When this sort of rocket explodes, it doesn't do much. It just breaks into a couple of pieces that burn out by themselves."

"I imagine from seventeen miles off it doesn't look like much—what about when the sucker ignites twenty feet from my F-15?" *A long way to skydive,* Buns thought.

"I'm sorry, Major. This rocket motor is nearly ten years old. Nobody checked our spec sheet on proper storage after it was mated with the ASAT warhead. We've checked it out with X rays and ultrasound. I think it's okay, but I might be wrong," the man from Lockheed said. Of the six remaining ASAT missiles, three had been decertified by the man for cracks in the solid-fuel propellant. The other three were question marks. "You want the truth or you want a song and dance?"

"You gotta fly it, Major," the deputy commander of Tactical Air Command said. "It's your decision."

"Can we rig it so the bird doesn't ignite until I'm clear?"

"How long will you need?" the engineer asked. Buns thought about her speed and maneuverability at that altitude.

"Say ten or fifteen seconds."

"I'll have to make a small change in the programming software, but that shouldn't be much of a problem. We'll have to make sure that the missile will retain enough forward velocity to keep its launch attitude, though. You sure that's enough time?"

"No. We'll have to check that out on the simulator, too. How long we got?"

"Minimum two days, maximum six days. Depends on the Navy," replied the General.

"Great."

STORNOWAY, SCOTLAND

"Here's some good news," Toland announced. "An Air Force F-15 Eagle fighter was flying over a fast convoy north of the Azores. Two Bears came looking for the ships and the Eagle got 'em both. That makes three in the past four days. The Backfire raid appears to have aborted."

"What's their position?" the group captain asked.

Toland ran his hand along the chart, checking latitude and longitude against the numbers on the dispatch form. "Looks like right about here, and that datum is twenty minutes old."

"That puts them over Iceland in just under two hours."

"What about tankers?" the Navy fighter commander asked.

"Not on such short notice."

"We can stretch that far with two fighters, using another two for buddy stores, but it only gives them about twenty minutes on station, under five on burner, and a ten-minute reserve when they get back here." The fighter boss whistled. "Close. Too close. We have to wave off on this."

A phone rang. The British base commander grabbed.

"Group Captain Mallory. Yes . . . very well, scramble." He hung up. Klaxons went off at the ready shack half a mile away. Fighter pilots raced to their aircraft. "Ivan's settled the argument in any case, Commander. Your radar aircraft report heavy jamming activity inbound from the north."

The commander raced out the door and jumped into a jeep.

NORFOLK, VIRGINIA

The drive from SACLANT headquarters took ten minutes. The Marines at the main gate were checking everyone and everything carefully, even a Chevy with a three-star flag. They drove to the waterfront amid an unending flurry of activity. Trains rolled down the tracks set in the streets, repair shops and testing facilities worked around the clock. Even the McDonald's on the road immediately outside was working a twenty-four-hour day, feeding hamburgers and fries to the men who took a few minutes for nourishment. For sailors spending a day or so on land it was an important, if seemingly trivial, touchstone. The car turned right as it reached the docks, past the submarine piers to the ones that held destroyers.

"She's brand new, only a month in commission, just about long enough to calibrate the electronics, and they must have shaved some time on that," the Admiral said. "Captain Wilkens did continuous workups on the transit from San Diego, but nothing with helicopters yet. PACFLT kept hers, and I can't give you a regular helo complement either. All we have left is one Seahawk-F variant, a prototype helo they were evaluating down at Jacksonville."

"The one with the dipping sonar?" Ed Morris asked. "I can live with that. How about a driver who knows how to use it?"

"It's covered. Lieutenant Commander O'Malley. We pulled him out of a training billet at Jax."

"I've heard the name. He was doing systems qualifications on *Moosbrugger* when I was tactical action officer on *John Rodgers*. Yeah, he knows the job."

"Have to drop you off here. I'll be back in an hour, after I have a look at what's left of the *Kidd*."

Reuben James. Her raked clipper bow marked with hull number 57 hung over the dock like a guillotine blade. His weariness momentarily forgotten, Morris stepped out of the Chevy to examine his new command with all the quiet enthusiasm of a man with his newborn child.

He'd seen FFG-7-class frigates, but never been aboard one. Her severe hull lines reminded him of a Cigarette racing yacht. Six five-inch mooring lines secured her to the pier, but the sleek form already seemed to be straining at them. At only 3900 tons full load, not a large ship but manifestly a fast one to go in harm's way.

Her superstructure was an aesthetic embarrassment, with all the grace of a brick garage, topped with antenna whips and radar masts that looked like they had been built by a child's erector set, but Morris saw the functional simplicity of the design. The frigate's forty missiles were tucked away in circular racks forward. Her boxy after deckhouse contained enough room for a pair of deadly ASW helicopters. Her hull was sleek because speed required it. Her superstructure was boxy because it had to be. This was a warship, and whatever beauty *Reuben James* might have had was accidental.

Sailors wearing blue shirts and jeans moved rapidly across three gangways, bringing supplies aboard for an immediate sailing. Morris walked briskly to the after gangway. A Marine guard saluted him at the foot of the brow and an officer on the frigate's deck frantically ordered preparations to receive his new CO. The ship's bell was struck four times, and Commander Ed Morris assumed his new identity.

"*Reuben James*, arriving."

Morris saluted the colors, then the officer of the deck.

"Sir, we didn't expect you for another—" the lieutenant blurted.

"How's the work going?" Morris cut him off.

"Two more hours, tops, sir."

"Fine." Morris smiled. "We can worry about the Mickey Mouse later. Get back to work, Mister—"

"Lyles, sir. Ship control officer."

And what the hell is that? Morris wondered. "Okay, Mr. Lyles. Where's the XO?"

"Right here, skipper." The executive officer had grease on his shirt and a smudge on his cheek. "I was in the generator room. Pardon the way I look."

"What kind of shape are we in?"

"It'll do. Full load of fuel and weapons. The tail's fully calibrated—"

"How'd you do that so fast?"

"It wasn't easy, sir, but we got it done. How's Captain Wilkens?"

"The docs say he'll be all right, but—well, he's out of the business for a while. I'm Ed Morris." Captain and executive officer shook hands.

"Frank Ernst. First time I've operated in the Atlantic Fleet." The lieutenant commander smiled crookedly. "Picked a great time for it. Anyway, we're in good shape, skipper. Everything works. Our helo pilot's up in the Combat Information Center with the tactical guys. We got Jerry the Hammer. I played ball with him at Annapolis, he's good people. We got three real good chiefs. One's a qualified officer of the deck. The crew's on the young side, but I'd say we're about as ready as you could ask. Ready to sail in two, three hours, tops. Where's your personal gear, sir?"

"It ought to be here in half an hour. What was the problem below?"

"No sweat. An oil line let go on number-three diesel generator. Yard goof, wasn't welded right. It's fixed. You'll love the engine room, skipper. On builder's trials in five-foot seas we topped out at thirty-one-and-a-half knots." Ernst raised his eyebrows. "Fast enough?"

"And the stabilizers?" Morris asked.

"They work just fine, skipper."

"What about the ASW troops?"

"Let's meet 'em."

Morris followed his XO into the superstructure. They proceeded forward between the two helicopter hangars, then to the left past officers' country and up a ladder. The Combat Information Center was located one level below and just aft of the bridge, adjoining the commanding officer's stateroom. Dark as a cave, it was newer than *Pharris*'s and larger, but no less crammed. Twenty or more people were at work running a simulation.

"No, Goddammit!" howled a loud voice. "You have to react *faster*. This here's a Victor, and he ain't gonna wait for you to make up your damn mind!"

"Attention on deck! Captain in Combat," called Ernst.

"As you were," called Morris. "Who's that loud sunuvabitch?"

A barrel-chested man emerged from the shadows. His eyes were surrounded by crinkles from looking into too many low suns. So this was Jerry the Hammer O'Malley. He knew him only by a crackling voice on a UHF radio, and by his reputation as a sub-hunter who cared more for his trade than promotion boards.

"I guess you mean me, Captain. O'Malley. I'm supposed to drive your Seahawk-Foxtrot."

"You're right about the Victor. One of those bastards blew my first ship near in half."

"Sorry to hear that, but you oughta know that Ivan's putting his best skippers in the Victors. She handles better than anything else they got, and that rewards a smart driver. So you were up against the varsity. Did you have him outside?"

Morris shook his head. "We were late picking him up, just coming off a sprint, and acoustical conditions weren't all that great, but we detected him, he couldn't have been more than five miles out. We had the helo after him, just about had him localized, then he broke contact neat as you please and got inside on us."

"Yeah, the Victor's good at that. Pump-fake, I call it. He starts going one way, then turns hard the other, leaves a knuckle in the water, and probably a noisemaker, too, right in the middle of it. Then he dives down under the layer and makes a quick sprint in. They've been refining that tactic for the past few years, and we've had trouble programming a reliable counter for it. You need a sharp crew in the helo, and you need good teamwork with these guys here."

"Unless you read my report, my friend, you must be a mind reader."

"Right, Captain. But all the minds I read think in Russian. The pump-fake's what the Victor is best at, and you have to pay attention, what with his ability to accelerate and turn so quick. What I've been trying to teach people is when he shows turn to port, you start thinkin' he's really going to starboard, and you slide over maybe two thousand yards and wait a minute or two, then you hammer the bastard hard and pickle off the fish before he can react."

"And if you're wrong?"

"Then you're wrong, skipper. Mostly, though, Ivan's predictable *if* you think like a submariner and you look at his tactical situation instead of your own. You can't keep him from running away, but his mission is to close on the target, and you can make life real hard for him if he does."

Morris looked O'Malley hard in the eyes. He didn't like having the loss of his first command analyzed so glibly. But there was no time for these thoughts. O'Malley was a pro, and if there was a man to handle another Victor, this might be the one. "You all ready?"

"The bird is at the air station. We'll join up after you clear the capes. I wanted to talk things over with the ASW team while we had the time. We're gonna play outside ASW picket?"

"Probably. With a towed-array, it doesn't figure that we're going to be in close. And we might be teamed with a Brit for the convoy mission."

"Fair enough. If you want my opinion, we have a pretty solid ASW team here. We might just give the bad guys a hard time. Weren't you on *Rodgers* a few years back?"

"When you were working with the *Moose*. We worked together twice, but never met. I was 'X-Ray Mike' when we exercised against *Skate*."

"I thought I remembered you." O'Malley came closer and dropped his voice. "How bad is it out there?"

"Bad enough. We lost the G-I-UK line. We're getting some pretty good SURTASS info, but you can bet Ivan's going to be gunning for those tuna boats pretty soon. Between the air threat and the sub threat—I don't know." His face showed more than his voice did. Close friends dead or missing. His own first command blown in half. Morris was tired in a way that sleep alone would not cure.

O'Malley nodded. "Skipper, we got us a shiny new frigate, a great new helo, and a tail. We can hold our end up."

"Well, we'll have a shot soon enough. We sail for New York in two hours and take a convoy out on Wednesday."

"Alone?" O'Malley asked.

"No, we'll have Brit company for the New York run, HMS *Battleaxe*. The orders haven't been confirmed yet, but it looks like we'll be working together all the way across."

"That'll be useful," Ernst agreed. "Come on aft, skipper, I'll show you what we're up to." The sonar room was aft of CIC, closed off by a curtain. Here real lighting was on, as opposed to the darkened, red-light world of Combat.

"Jeez, nobody ever tells me anything!" growled a young lieutenant commander. "Good morning, Captain. I'm Lenner, combat systems officer."

"How come you're not at your scope?"

"We froze the game, skipper, and I wanted to check out the display on playback."

"I brought the game tape myself," O'Malley explained. "This is the track of a Victor-III that faked out one of our carriers in the eastern Med last year. See here? That's the pump-fake. You'll notice that the contact fades out, then brightens up. That's the noisemaker inside the knuckle. At this point he ducked under the layer and sprinted inside the screen. Would've hit the carrier, too, because they didn't get him for another ten minutes. That"—he jammed his finger at the display—"is what you look for. This tells you you're up against a driver who knows his stuff, and he's out for your ass." Morris examined the screen closely enough to recognize the pattern. He'd seen it once before.

"What if they use the maneuver to break clear?" Lenner asked.

"Because if they can break contact, why not break contact *toward* the target?" Morris asked quietly, noting that he had a very young combat systems officer.

"That's right, skipper." O'Malley nodded ruefully. "Like I said, this is a standard tactic for them, and it rewards a sharp driver. The aggressive ones will always bore in. The ones who break off—that's effectively a kill. We have to reacquire, but so do they. With a twenty-knot speed of advance, once we get past them, they have to play catch-up. That means making noise. The guy who runs away probably won't run the risk, or if he does, he'll do it badly and we'll get him. No, this tactic is for the guy who really wants to get in close. Question is, how many of their skippers are that aggressive?"

"Enough." Morris looked away for a moment. "How's the helicopter complement?"

"Only one flight crew for the bird. My copilot's pretty green, but our on-board systems operator's a first-class petty officer who's been around the block a few times. The maintenance guys are a pickup bunch, mostly from the readiness group at Jax. I've talked to them, they should do just fine."

"We got berths for them all?" Morris asked.

Ernst shook his head. "Not hardly. We're packed pretty tight."

"O'Malley, is your copilot deck-qualified?"

"Not on a frigate. I am—hell, I did some of the first systems trials back in '78. We'll have to do workups on the way to New York, both day and night to get my ensign in the groove. Scratch team, skipper. The bird doesn't even belong to an operational squadron."

"You sounded confident a minute ago," Morris objected.

"I *am* fairly confident," O'Malley said. "My people know how to use the tools they got. They're sharp kids. They'll learn fast. And we even get to make up our own call signs." A wide grin. Certain things are important to aviators. There was one other unspoken message: when O'Malley referred to the aviation department as "my people," he meant that he didn't want any interference in how he ran his shop. Morris ignored it. He didn't want an argument, not now.

"Okay, XO, let's look around. O'Malley, I expect we'll rendezvous off the capes."

"The helo's ready to launch right now, Captain. We'll be there when you want us."

Morris nodded and went forward. The captain's personal ladder to the bridge was a bare three feet from the CIC door, and his own. He trotted up—or tried to, his legs rubbery with exhaustion.

"Captain on the bridge!" a petty officer announced.

Morris was not impressed. He was appalled to see that the ship's "wheel" was only a brass dial about the size of a telephone's. The helmsman actually had a *seat,* offset from the centerline, and to his right was a clear plastic box containing the direct-control throttle to the ship's jet-turbine engines. A metal rod suspended from the overhead ran completely from one side of the pilothouse to the other at a height that allowed it to be grabbed easily in heavy seas, an eloquent comment on this ship's stability.

"Have you served on a 'fig' before, sir?" the XO asked.

"Never been aboard one," Morris answered. The heads of the four men on bridge watch each turned a hair at that. "I know the weapons systems; I was part of the design team at NAVSEA back a few years ago, and I know more or less how she handles."

"She handles, sir. Like a sports car," Ernst assured him. "You'll especially like the way we can turn the engines off, drift as quiet as a log, then be up to thirty knots in two minutes flat."

"How quickly can we get under way?"

"Ten minutes from your say-so, Captain. The engine lube oil is already warmed up. There's a harbor tug standing by to assist us away from the dock."

"NAVSURFLANT, arriving," boomed the announcing system. Two minutes later, the Admiral appeared in the pilothouse.

"I have a man bringing your gear up. What do you think?"

"XO, will you see to the provisioning?" Morris said to Ernst, then, "Shall we discover my stateroom together, Admiral?"

A steward was waiting for them below with a tray of coffee and sandwiches. Morris poured himself a cup, another for the Admiral, and ignored the food.

"Sir, I've never handled one of these before. I don't know the engines—"

"You've got a great chief engineer and she's a dream to handle. Besides, you have your conning officers. You're a weapons and tactics man, Ed. All your work is done in CIC. We need you out there."

"Fair enough, sir."

"XO, take her out," Morris ordered two hours later. He watched Ernst's every move, embarrassed that he had to depend on another to do it.

But it was amazingly easy. The wind was off the pier, and the frigate had a huge sail area that invited help. As the mooring lines were slackened off, the wind and the auxiliary power units located on the hull directly under the bridge pushed *James*'s bow into the clear, then the gas-turbine engines moved her forward into the channel. Ernst took his time, though he was clearly capable of doing it faster. Morris took careful note of this, too. The man didn't want to make his captain look bad.

From there on it was easy, and Ed Morris watched his new crew at work. He'd heard stories about the California Navy—*like, okay, man*—but the quartermasters at the chart table updated the position with crisp assurance, despite the unfamiliar harbor. They glided noiselessly past the piers of the navy yard. He saw empty berths that would not soon be filled, and not a few ships whose sleek gray hulls were marred with scorched holes and twisted steel. *Kidd* was there, her forward superstructure wrecked by a Russian missile that had gotten past her multilayered defenses. One of his sailors was looking that way, too, a boy still in his teens, puffing on a cigarette which he flicked over the side. Morris wanted to ask what he was thinking, but could scarcely describe his own thoughts.

It went quickly after that. They turned east at the empty carrier berthings, over the Hampton bridge-tunnel, then past the crowded amphibious basin at Little Creek. Now the sea beckoned them, forbiddingly gray under the cloudy sky.

HMS *Battleaxe* was already out there, three miles ahead, a subtly different shade on her hull, and the White Ensign fluttering at her mast. A signal light started blinking at them.

WHAT THE DEVIL IS A REUBEN JAMES *Battleaxe* wanted to know.

"How do you want to answer that, sir?" a signalman asked.

Morris laughed, the ominous spell broken. "Signal, 'At least we don't name warships for our mother-in-law.' "

"All right!" The petty officer loved it.

STORNOWAY, SCOTLAND

"The Blinder isn't supposed to be able to carry missiles," Toland said, but what he saw gave the lie to that intelligence assessment. Six missiles had gotten through the defending fighters and landed inside the perimeter of the RAF base. Two aircraft were burning, half a mile away, and one of the base's radars was wrecked.

"Well, now we know why their activity has been light the past few days. They were refitting their bombers to deal with our new fighter force," Group Captain Mallory said, surveying the damage to his base. "Action, reaction. We learn, they learn."

The fighters were returning. Toland counted them off in his head. He came up short by two Tornados and one Tomcat. As soon as the landing rolls were completed, each fighter taxied to its shelter. The RAF did not have enough permanent ones. Three of the American fighters ended up in sandbag revetments where ground crews immediately refueled and rearmed their aircraft. The crews climbed down their ladders to waiting jeeps and were driven off for debriefing.

"Bastards used our own trick on us!" one Tomcat pilot exclaimed.

"Okay, what did you run into?"

"There were two groups, about ten miles apart. Lead group was MiG-23 Floggers with the Blinders behind them. The MiGs launched before we did. They really knocked our radars back with white noise, and some of their fighters were using something brand new, a deceptive jammer we haven't run across yet. They must have been at the edge of their fuel, 'cause they didn't try to mix it up with us. I guess they just wanted to keep us off the bombers until they launched. Damn near worked. A flight of Tornados came around them on the left and bagged four of the Blinders, I think. We got a pair of MiGs—no Blinders—and the boss vectored the rest of the Toms onto the missiles. I splashed two. Anyway, Ivan's changed tactics on us. We lost one Tomcat, I don't know what got him."

"Next time," another pilot said. "We go up with some of our missiles pre-set to go after the jammers. We didn't have enough time to set that up. If we can get the jammers first, it'll be easier to handle the fighters."

And then the Russians will change their tactics again, Toland thought. *Well, at least we have them reacting to us for a change.*

FÖLZIEHAUSEN, FEDERAL REPUBLIC OF GERMANY

After eight hours of vicious fighting that saw artillery fire dropping on the forward command post, Beregovoy and Alekseyev stopped the Belgian counterattack. But stopping them wasn't enough. They'd advanced six kilometers before running into a solid wall of tanks and missiles, and the Belgian artillery was laying heavy intermittent fire on the main road supporting the Russian advance toward Hameln. Certainly they were preparing for another attack, Alekseyev thought. *We have to hit them first—but with what?* He needed his three divisions to advance on the British formations standing before Hameln.

"Every time we break through," Major Sergetov observed quietly, "they slow us down and counterattack. This was not supposed to happen."

"A splendid observation!" Alekseyev snarled, then regained his temper. "We expected that a breakthrough would have the same effect as in the last war against the Germans. The problem is these new light antitank missiles. Three men and a jeep"—he even used the American title for it—"can race along the road, set up, fire one or two missiles, be gone before we can react, then repeat the process a few hundred meters away. Defensive firepower was never so strong before, and we failed to appreciate how effectively a handful of rear-guard troops can slow down an advancing column. Our security is based on movement"—Alekseyev explained the basic lesson from tank school—"a mobile force under these conditions cannot afford to be slowed down. A simple breakthrough is not enough! We must blast a massive hole in their front and race at least twenty kilometers to be free of these roving missile-crews. Only then can we switch over to true mobile doctrine."

"You say we cannot win?" Sergetov had begun to have his own doubts, but did not expect to hear them from his commander.

"I say what I did four months ago, and I was correct: this campaign of ours has become a war of attrition. For the moment, technology has defeated the military art, ours and theirs. What we're doing now is seeing who runs out of men and arms first."

"We have more of both," Sergetov said.

"That is true, Ivan Mikhailovich. I have many more young men to throw away." More casualties were arriving at the field hospital. The line of trucks running in and out never stopped.

"Comrade General, I received a message from my father. He wishes to know how things progress at the front. What should I tell him?"

Alekseyev walked away from his aide for a minute to ponder that.

"Ivan Mikhailovich, tell the Minister that NATO opposition is far more serious than we expected. The key now is supplies. We need the best information we can get on NATO's supply situation and a determined effort to worsen that situation. We have received little information on how well the naval operations to kill NATO convoys are going. I need that in order to evaluate NATO's endurance. I don't want analyses out of Moscow. I want the raw data."

"You are unhappy with what we get from Moscow?"

"We were told that NATO was politically divided and militarily uncoordinated. How would you evaluate that report, Comrade Major?" Alekseyev asked sharply. "I can't go through military channels with that sort of request, can I? Write up your travel orders. I want you back here in thirty-six hours. I'm sure we'll still be here."

ICELAND

"They should be there in half an hour."

"Roger that, Doghouse," Edwards replied. "Like I said, no Russians visible. We haven't seen any aircraft all day. There was some movement on the road west of us six hours ago. Four jeep-type vehicles. Too far off to tell what was in them, and they were southbound. The coast is clear. Over."

"Okay, let us know when they get there."

"Will do. Out." Edwards killed the radio. "People, we got some friends coming in."

"Who and when, skipper?" Smith asked at once.

"Didn't say, but they'll be here in half an hour. Must be an air drop."

"They come take us out?" Vigdis asked.

"No, they can't land a plane here. Sarge, you got any opinions?"

"Same as yours, I 'spect."

*   *   *

The plane was early, and for once Edwards saw it first. The C-130 Hercules four-engine transport skimmed down from the northwest, only a few hundred feet over the eastern slope of the ridge they were on. A stiff breeze blew from the west as four small shapes emerged from the aft cargo door and the Hercules turned abruptly north to leave the area. Edwards concentrated on the descending parachutes. Instead of drifting down into the valley below them, the parachutists were coming straight down to a rock-filled slope.

"Oh, shit, he misjudged the wind! Come on!"

The parachutes dropped below them as they ran downhill. One by one they stopped, losing their shape in the semidarkness as the men landed. Edwards and his party moved rapidly, trying to remember where the men had landed. Their camouflage 'chutes turned invisible as soon as they touched the ground.

"Halt!"

"Okay, okay. We're here to meet you," Edwards said.

"Identify yourself!" The voice had an English accent.

"Code name Beagle."

"Proper name?"

"Edwards, first lieutenant, U.S. Air Force."

"Approach slowly, mate."

Mike went forward alone. At length he saw a vague shape half-hidden by a rock. The shape held a submachine gun.

"Who are you?"

"Sergeant Nichols, Royal Marines. You picked a bloody poor place to receive us, Lieutenant."

"I didn't do it!" Edwards answered. "We didn't know you were coming until an hour ago."

"Balls-up, another bloody balls-up." The man stood and walked forward with a pronounced limp. "Parachuting's dangerous enough without coming into a fucking rock garden!" Another figure came up.

"We found the lieutenant—I think he's dead!"

"Need help?" Mike asked.

"I need to wake up and find myself home in bed."

Edwards soon found that the party sent to rescue him—or whatever their mission was—had gotten off to a disastrous start. The lieutenant in command of the group had landed on one boulder and fallen backward on another. His head hung from the rest of his body as if on a string. Nichols had sprained his ankle badly, and the other two were uninjured but shaken. It took over an hour to locate all their gear. There was no time for sentiment. The lieutenant was wrapped in his parachute and covered with loose rocks. Edwards led the rest back to his perch on the hilltop. At least they'd brought a new battery pack for his radio.

"Doghouse, this is Beagle, and things suck, over."

"What took so long?"

"Tell that Herky-Bird driver to get a new eye doctor. The Marines you sent here got their boss killed, and their sergeant ripped his ankle up."

"Have you been spotted?"

"Negative. They landed in rocks. It's a miracle they weren't all killed. We're back on the hilltop. We covered our tracks."

Sergeant Nichols was a smoker. He and Smith found a sheltered spot to light up.

"Sounds rather excitable, your lieutenant."

"He's only a wing-wiper, but he's doin' all right. How's the ankle?"

"I'll have to walk on it whether it's fit or not. Does he know what he's about?"

"The skipper? I watched him kill three Russians with a knife. That good enough?"

"Bloody hell."

33. Contact

USS *REUBEN JAMES*

"Captain?"

Morris started at the hand on his shoulder. He'd just wanted to lie down in his stateroom for a few minutes after conducting helicopter night landing practice, and—he checked his watch. After midnight. His face was sweaty. The dream had just started again. He looked up at his executive officer.

"What is it, XO?"

"We got a request to check something out. Probably a snowbird, but— well, see for yourself."

Morris took the dispatch with him to his private bathroom, tucked it in his pocket, then washed his face quickly.

" 'Unusual contact repeated several times, have attempted localization without success'? What the hell is this supposed to be?" he asked, toweling off.

"Beats the hell out of me, skipper. Forty degrees, thirty minutes north, sixty-nine, fifty west. They got a location but no ID. I'm having the chart pulled now."

Morris ran his hand through his hair. Two hours' sleep was better than none. Wasn't it? "Okay, let's see how it looks from CIC."

The tactical action officer had the chart out on the table next to the captain's chair. Morris checked the main tactical-display scope. They were still far offshore in accordance with their orders to check out the hundred-fathom curve.

"That's way the hell away from here," Morris observed immediately. There was something familiar about the location. The captain bent over the chart.

"Yes, sir, about a sixty-mile run," Ernst agreed. "Shallow water, too. Can't use the towed array there."

"Oh, I know what this place is! That's where the *Andrea Doria* sank. Probably somebody's got a MAD contact and didn't bother checking his chart."

"Don't think so." O'Malley emerged from the shadows. "A frigate heard something first. The winch on their tail was busted. They didn't want to lose it, so they were heading into Newport instead of New York because the harbor's deeper. They say they copied a strange passive-sonar contact that faded out. They did a target-motion analysis and generated this position. Their helicopter made a few passes, and its magnetic anomaly detector registered right over the *Doria,* and that was that."

"How'd you find that out?"

O'Malley handed over a message form. "Came in right after the XO went to get you. They sent an Orion to check it. Same story. They heard something odd, and it faded out."

Morris frowned. They were chasing after a wild goose, but the orders came from Norfolk. That made it an *official* wild-goose chase.

"What's the helo status?"

"I can be up in ten minutes. One torpedo and an auxiliary fuel tank. All the gear's on line."

"Tell the bridge to take us there at twenty-five knots. *Battleaxe* know about this?" He got a nod. "Okay. Signal them what we're up to. Winch in the tail. Won't do us any good where we're going. O'Malley, we'll close to within fifteen miles of the contact and have you search for it. That puts you in the air about 0230. If you need me, I'll be in the wardroom." Morris decided to sample his new ship's "mid-rats." O'Malley was headed the same way.

"These ships are a little weird," the flyer said.

Morris grunted agreement. The main fore-and-aft passageway was on the port side instead of the centerline, for one thing. The "figs" broke a number of long-standing traditions in ship design.

O'Malley went down the ladder first and opened the wardroom door for the captain. They found two junior officers in front of the TV set, watching a taped movie that had mainly to do with fast cars and naked women. The tape machine, Morris had already learned, was run from the chiefs' quarters. One result of this was that a particularly attractive chest was instant-replayed for all hands.

Midwatch rations, or "mid-rats," was an open loaf of bread and a plate of cold cuts. Morris got himself a cup of coffee and built a sandwich. O'Malley opted for a fruit drink from the cooler on the after bulkhead. The official Navy term for it was bug juice.

"No coffee?" Morris asked. O'Malley shook his head.

"Too much makes me jumpy. You don't want shaky hands when you're landing a helo in the dark." He smiled. "I really am getting too old for this crap."

"Kids?"

"Three boys, and ain't none of them gonna be a sailor if I have anything to say about it. You?"

"Boy and a girl. They're back in Kansas with their mother." Morris went after his sandwich. The bread was a little stale and the cold cuts weren't cold, but he needed to eat. This was the first meal in three days he hadn't eaten alone. O'Malley pushed the potato chips over.

"Get all your carbohydrates, Captain."

"That bug juice'll kill you." Morris nodded at the fruit drink.

"It's been tried before. I flew two years over 'Nam. Mostly search-and-rescue stuff. Got shot down twice. Never got scratched, though. Just scared to death."

Was he that old? Morris wondered. He had to have been passed over for promotion a few times. The captain made a mental note to check O'Malley's date of rank.

"How come you were in CIC?" the captain asked.

"I wasn't very sleepy and I wanted to see how the towed array was working."

Morris was surprised. Aviators didn't generally show this much interest in the ship's equipment.

"The word is you did pretty well with *Pharris*."

"Not good enough."

"That happens, too." O'Malley watched his skipper very closely. The only man aboard with extended combat experience, O'Malley recognized something in Morris that he hadn't seen since Vietnam. The flyer shrugged. It wasn't his problem. He fished in his flight suit and came out with a pack of cigarettes. "Mind if I smoke?"

"I just restarted myself."

"Thank God!" O'Malley raised his voice. "With all these virtuous children in the wardroom, I thought I was the only dirty old man here!" The two young lieutenants smiled at that, without taking their eyes from the television screen.

"How much experience you have on figs?"

"Most of my time is on carriers, skipper. Last fourteen months I've been an instructor down at Jax. I've done a lot of odd jobs, most of them with the Seahawk. I think you'll like my bird. The dipping sonar is the best I've ever worked with."

"What do you think about this contact report?"

O'Malley leaned back and puffed on his cigarette with a faraway look. "It's interesting. I remember seeing something on TV about the *Doria*. She sank on her starboard side. A lot of people have dived to look at the wreck. It's about two hundred feet of water, just shallow enough for amateurs to try. And there's a million cables draped over her."

"Cables?" Morris asked.

"Trawls. Lot of commercial fishing goes on there. They tangle their nets on the wreck. It looks like Gulliver on the beach at Lilliput."

"You're right! I remember that," Morris said. "That explains the noise. It's the tide, or currents whistling through all those cables."

O'Malley nodded. "Yep, that could explain it. I still want to give it a look."

"Why?"

"All the traffic coming out of New York has to pass right overtop the place for one thing. Ivan knows we got a big convoy forming up in New York—he has to know unless the KGB has gone out of business. That's one hell of a good place to park a submarine if they want to put a trailer on the convoy. Think about it. If you get a MAD contact there, you write it off. The noise from a reactor plant at low power probably won't be louder than the flow noise over the wreck if they get in close enough. If I was a real nervy sub-driver, I'd think hard about using a place like that to belly-up."

"You really do think like them," Morris observed. "Okay, let's see how we should handle this . . ."

0230 hours. Morris watched the takeoff procedures from the control tower, then walked forward to CIC. The frigate was at battle stations, doing eight knots, her Prairie/Masker systems operating. If there were a Russian sub out there, fifteen or so miles away, there was no way she'd suspect a frigate was nearby. In CIC the radar plot showed the helo moving into position.

"Romeo, this is Hammer. Radio check, over," O'Malley said. The helicopter's on-board data link also transmitted a test message to the frigate. The petty officer on the helicopter communications panel checked it out, and grunted with satisfaction. What was that expression he'd heard? Yeah, right—they had a "sweet lock on momma's gadget." He grinned.

The helo began its search two miles from the grave of *Andrea Doria*. O'Malley halted his aircraft and hovered fifty feet above the rolling surface.

"Down dome, Willy."

In the back, the petty officer unlocked the hoist controls and lowered the dipping sonar transducer down a hole in the belly of the helicopter. The Seahawk carried over a thousand feet of cable, enough to reach below the deepest of thermocline layers. It was only two hundred feet to the bottom here, and they had to be careful not to let the transducer come near the bottom for risk of damage. The petty officer paid close attention to the cable and halted the winch when the transducer was a hundred feet down. As with surface ships, the sonar readout was both visual and aural. A TV-type tube began to show frequency lines while the sailor listened in on his headphones.

This was the hard part, O'Malley reminded himself. Hovering a helicopter in these wind conditions required constant attention—there was no autopilot—and hunting for a submarine was always an exercise in patience. It would take several minutes for the passive sonar to tell them anything, and they could not use their active sonar systems. The pinging would only serve to alert a target.

After five minutes they had detected nothing but random noise. They recovered the sonar and moved east. Again there was nothing. *Patience,* the pilot told himself. He hated being patient. Another move east and another wait.

"I got something at zero-four-eight. Not sure what it is, a whistle or something in the high-frequency range." They waited another two minutes to make sure it wasn't a spurious signal.

"Up dome." O'Malley brought the helicopter up and moved off northeast for three thousand yards. Three minutes later the sonar went down again. Nothing this time. O'Malley changed positions again. *If I ever write a song about hunting submarines,* he thought, *I'll call it "Again, and Again, and AGAIN!"* This time a signal came back—two signals, in fact.

"That's interesting," the ASW officer aboard *Reuben James* observed. "How close is this to the wreck?"

"Very close," Morris answered. "Just about the same bearing, too."

"Could be flow noise," Willy told O'Malley. "Very faint, just like the last time."

The pilot reached up to flip a switch to feed the sonar signal into his headset. *We're looking for a very faint signal,* O'Malley reminded himself. "Could be steam noise, too. Prepare to raise dome, I'm gonna go east to triangulate."

Two minutes later, the sonar transducer went into the water for a sixth time. The contact was now plotted on the helicopter's on-board tactical display that sat on the control panel between pilot and copilot.

"We got two signals here," Ralston said. "About six hundred yards apart."

"Looks that way to me. Let's go see the near one. Willy—"

"Cable within limits, ready to raise, skipper."

"Up dome. Romeo, Hammer. You got what we got?"

"Affirmative, Hammer," Morris answered. "Check out the southern one."

"Doing that right now. Stand by." O'Malley paid close attention to his instruments as he flew toward the nearer of the two contacts. Again he halted the aircraft. "Down dome."

"Contact!" the petty officer said a minute later. He examined the tone lines on his display and mentally compared them with data he had on Soviet submarines. "Evaluate this contact as steam and plant noises from a nuclear submarine, bearing two-six-two."

O'Malley listened for thirty seconds. His face broke into a slight smile. "That's a nuc boat all right! Romeo, Hammer, we have a probable submarine contact bearing two-six-two our position. Moving to firm that fix up right now."

Ten minutes later they had the contact locked in. O'Malley made directly for it and lowered his sonar right on top of the contact.

"It's a Victor-class," the sonarman aboard the frigate said. "See this frequency line? A Victor with his reactor plant turned down to minimum power output."

"Hammer," Morris called. "Romeo. Any suggestions?"

O'Malley was flying away from the contact, having left a smoke float to mark it. The submarine probably hadn't heard them because of the surface conditions, or if he had, he knew his safest bet was to sit on the bottom. The Americans carried only homing torpedoes, which couldn't detect a submarine on the bottom. Once launched, they'd either motor along in a circle until running out of fuel or drive straight into the bottom. He could go active and try to flush the submarine off the bottom, he thought, but active sonar wasn't all that effective in shallow water, and what if Ivan didn't move? The Seahawk was down to one hour's fuel. The pilot made his decision.

"*Battleaxe*, this is Hammer. Do you read, over?"

"Took your time to call us, Hammer," Captain Perrin replied at once. The British frigate was monitoring the search closely.

"You have any Mark-11s aboard?"

"We can load them in ten minutes."

"We'll be waiting. Romeo, do you approve a VECTAC?"

"Affirmative," Morris answered. The vectored attack approach was perfect, and he was too excited at what they had here to be annoyed at O'Malley for bypassing him. "Weapons free."

O'Malley circled his aircraft at one thousand feet while he waited. This was really crazy. Was Ivan just sitting there? Was he waiting for a convoy to pass by? It was about an even-money chance that he'd heard the helicopter. If he'd heard the helo, did he want the frigate to come in so he could attack her? His systems operator watched the sonar display intently for any change in the signal from the contact. So far there'd been none. No increase in engine power, no mechanical transients. Nothing at all but the hissing of a reactor plant at fractional power, a sound undetectable from more than two miles off. No wonder several people had looked and found nothing. He found himself admiring the nerve of the Soviet submarine commander.

"Hammer, this is Hatchet."

O'Malley smiled to himself. Unlike American procedures, the Brits assigned helicopter names associated with that of their mother ships. HMS *Brazen*'s helo was "Hussy." *Battleaxe*'s was "Hatchet."

"Roger, Hatchet. Where are you?"

"Ten miles south of you. We've two depth charges aboard."

O'Malley switched his flying lights back on. "Very well, stand by. Romeo, the way I want to work this, you give Hatchet a radar steer to our sonobuoy and we'll use our sonar for the cross-bearing to drop. Do you concur, over?"

"Roger, concur," Morris answered.

"Arm the fish," O'Malley told his copilot.

"Why?"

"If the charges miss, you can bet he'll come off the bottom like a salmon at spawning time." O'Malley brought his helo around and spotted the blinking anticollision lights of the British Lynx helicopter. "Hatchet, tallyho, I have you now at my nine o'clock. Please hold your current position while we get set. Willy, any change in the contact?"

"No, sir. This dude's playing it awful cool, sir."

You poor brave bastard, O'Malley thought to himself. The smoke float atop the contact was about burned out. He dropped another. After rechecking his tactical display he moved to a position one thousand yards east of the contact, hovered fifty feet above the surface and deployed the dipping sonar.

"There he is," the petty officer reported. "Bearing two-six-eight."

"Hatchet, Hammer. We're ready for your VECTAC. Take your steer from Romeo."

Control of the British helicopter's course came now from *Reuben James*'s radar, which steered it onto a precise northerly course. O'Malley watched the Lynx approach, checking to make sure the wind wasn't driving him off his own position.

"You will drop your charges one at a time, on my mark. Stand by, Hatchet."

"Standing by." The British pilot armed his depth charges and came forward at ninety knots. O'Malley lined up the blinking lights with the smoke float.

"Charge one—Mark-mark! Charge two—Mark-mark! Get clear!"

The Lynx pilot needed no encouragement. Scarcely had the second depth charge fallen free when the helo leaped upward and raced northeast. Simultaneously, O'Malley yanked up on his collective control to bring his delicate sonar transducer out of the water.

There was an odd flash of light from the bottom, then another. The surface of the sea turned to foam that leaped into the starry sky. O'Malley closed in and switched on his landing lights. The surface was churned with mud, and . . . oil? *Just like in the movies,* he thought, and dropped another sonobuoy into the water.

The bottom reverberated with the rumbles from the depth charges, but the system filtered them out and locked in on the higher frequency sounds. They heard escaping air and rushing water. Someone aboard the submarine might have hit the ballast controls in a vain attempt to blow the submarine to the surface. Then there was something else, like water dropped on a hot plate. It was a moment before O'Malley had it figured out.

"What's that, skipper?" Willy asked over the intercom. "I never heard that before."

"The reactor vessel's ruptured. You're hearing a runaway nuclear reactor." *God, what a mess that'll be this close into shore!* he thought. No more diving on the *Doria* for a few years . . . O'Malley switched to the radio circuit. "Hatchet, this is Hammer. I copy collapse noises. We score that one as a kill. Do you claim the kill, over?"

"Our fox, Hammer. Thanks for the steer in."

O'Malley laughed. "Roger that, Hatchet. If you want the kill, you also get to file the environmental-impact statement. Out."

Aboard the Lynx, pilot and copilot exchanged a look. "What the devil is that?"

The two helicopters returned in loose formation and made a pass over both the British and American frigates to celebrate their kill. It was the second for *Battleaxe,* and *Reuben James* would now paint half a submarine on the side of her pilothouse. The ships recovered their helicopters and turned west for New York.

MOSCOW, R.S.F.S.R.

Mikhail Sergetov embraced his son in the Russian way, with passion and kisses to welcome him back from the front. The Politburo member took his son's arm and led him to his chauffeured Zil for the drive into Moscow.

"You've been hurt, Vanya."

"I cut my hand on some glass." Ivan shrugged it off. His father offered him a small glass of vodka, which he took. "I haven't had a drink in two weeks."

"Oh?"

"The General does not permit it in his command post," Ivan explained.

"Is he as good an officer as I thought?"

"Perhaps a better one. I've seen him in command at the front. He is a truly gifted leader."

"Then why haven't we conquered Germany?"

Ivan Mikhailovich Sergetov had grown up while his father had climbed the Party ladder nearly to the top, and he had often seen him switch in a moment from affable host to abrasive Party apparatchik. This was the first time it had ever happened to him, however.

"NATO was far readier than we had been led to expect, father. They were waiting for us to come, and their first mission of the war—before we had even crossed the border in force—came as a rude shock." Ivan explained the effects of Operation Dreamland.

"We were not told it was that bad. Are you sure?"

"I've seen some of the bridges. Those same aircraft raided a dummy command post outside Stendal. The bombs were falling before we knew they were there. If their intelligence had been better, I might not be here."

"So it's their air power?"

"That's a major part of it. I've seen their ground-attack fighters cut through a tank column like a harvester through a wheatfield. It's horrible."

"But our missiles?"

"Our missile troops practice once or twice a year, firing at target drones that plod along in a straight line up where everyone can see them. The NATO fighters fly between the trees. If the antiaircraft missiles on either side worked as well as their makers said, every airplane in the world would have been shot down twice over by now. But the worst thing of all are their antitank missiles—you know, just like ours, and these missiles work all too well." The younger man gestured with his hands. "Three men in a wheeled vehicle. One driver, one loader, one gunner. They hide behind a tree at a turn in the road and wait. Our column comes into view and they fire from a range of—say two kilometers. They're trained to go for the command tank—the one with the radio antenna up. As often as not the first warning we have is when the first weapon hits. They fire one more and kill another tank, then race away before we can call down artillery fire. Five minutes later, from another spot, it happens again.

"It's eating us up," the young man said, echoing the words of his commander.

"You say we are losing?"

"No. I say that we are not winning," Ivan said. "But for us that is the same thing." He continued with the message from his commander and saw his father settle into the leather seat of the car.

"I knew it. I warned them, Vanya. The fools!" Ivan gestured with his head to the driver. His father smiled and made a dismissive gesture. Vitaly had served Sergetov for years. His daughter was now a doctor because of the Minister's patronage, his son safe in the university while most of the young men in the country were under arms. "Oil expenditures are twenty-five percent above predictions. That is, twenty-five percent above my ministerial predictions. They are *forty* percent above the Defense Ministry's predictions. It never occurred to anyone that NATO aircraft would be able to find our hidden petroleum storage facilities. My people are reevaluating national reserves even now. I am to receive the interim report this afternoon if it's ready on time. Look around, Vanya. See for yourself."

There were hardly any vehicles in view, not even trucks. Never a lively city, now Moscow was grim even to Russian eyes. People hurried along half-empty streets, not looking around, not looking up. So many men were gone, Ivan realized. So many of them would never return. As usual his father read his thoughts.

"How bad are casualties?"

"Dreadful. Far over estimates. I do not have exact numbers—my posting is intelligence, not administration—but losses are very bad."

"This is all a mistake, Vanya," the Minister said quietly. *But the Party is always right. How many years did you believe that?*

"Nothing can be done about that now, father. We also need information on NATO's supplies. The data that gets to us at the front is—overprocessed, shall we say. We need better data to make our own estimates."

At the front, Mikhail thought. His anger at those words could not entirely suppress the pride he felt at what his son had become. He'd worried often that he'd turn into another young "nobleman" of a Party family. Alekseyev was not the sort to promote lightly, and from his own sources he'd learned that Ivan had accompanied the General to the battle line many times. The boy had become a man. Pity it had taken a war to make that happen.

"I'll see what I can do."

USS *CHICAGO*

The Svyatana Anna Trough was their last bit of deep water. The freight train of fast-attack submarines slowed almost to a halt as it approached the edge of the icepack. They expected to find two friendly submarines here, but "friendly" was not a word that went well with combat operations. All the American submarines were at battle stations. McCafferty checked the time and the location. So far everything had gone according to plan. *Amazing,* he thought.

He didn't like being the lead boat. If there were a Russian patrolling the edge of the pack . . . he'd get first shot, McCafferty knew. Wondering if the "he" would be a speaker of English or Russian.

"Conn, sonar, I got faint machinery noises bearing one-nine-one."

"Bearing change?"

"Just picked it up, sir. Bearing is not changing at the moment."

McCafferty reached past the duty electrician's mate and switched on the gertrude, a sonar telephone as archaic as it was effective. The only noise was the hissing and groaning of the icepack. Behind him the exec got the fire-control tracking party working on a torpedo solution for the new target.

A garbled group of syllables came over the speaker.

McCafferty took the gertrude phone off the receiver and depressed the Transmit trigger.

"Zulu X-ray." There came a pause of several seconds, then a scratchy reply.

"Hotel Bravo," replied HMS *Sceptre.* McCafferty let out a long breath that went unnoticed by the rest of the attack center crew, all of whom were doing exactly the same thing.

"All ahead one-third," the captain said. Ten minutes later they were within easy range of the gertrude. *Chicago* halted to communicate.

"Welcome to the Soviet back garden, old boy. Slight change in plans. Keyboard"—the code name for HMS *Superb*—"is two-zero miles south to check further on your route. We've encountered no hostile activity for the past thirty hours. The coast is clear. Good hunting."

"Thank you, Keylock. The gang's all here. Out." McCafferty hung the phone set back in its place. "Gentlemen, the mission is a *go!* All ahead two-thirds!"

The nuclear attack submarine increased speed to twelve knots on a heading of one-nine-seven degrees. HMS *Sceptre* counted the American boats as they passed, then resumed her station, circling slowly at the edge of the icepack.

"Good luck, chaps," her captain breathed.

"They should get in all right."

"It's not getting in that I'm worried about, Jimmy," the captain replied, using the traditional name for a British sub's first officer. "The ticklish part's getting back out."

STORNOWAY, SCOTLAND

"Telex for you, Commander." An RAF sergeant handed the message form over to Toland.

"Thank you." He scanned the form.

"Leaving us?" Group Captain Mallory asked.

"They want me to fly down to Northwood. That's right outside London, isn't it?"

Mallory nodded. "No problem getting you there."

"That's nice. It says 'immediate.' "

NORTHWOOD, ENGLAND

He'd been to England many times, all on business with his opposite numbers at Government Communications Headquarters outside Cheltenham. His flights always seemed to arrive at night. He was flying at night now, and something was wrong. Something obvious . . .

Blackout. There were few lights below. Did that really matter now that aircraft had sophisticated navigation aids, or was it mainly a psychological move to remind the people of what was going on? If the continuous television coverage, some of it "live" from the battlefront, didn't do that already. Toland had been spared most of that. Like most men in uniform, he had no time for the big picture while he concentrated on his little corner of it. He imagined it was the same for Ed Morris and Danny McCafferty, then realized this was the first time he'd thought of them in over a week. How were they doing? They were certainly more exposed to danger than he was at the moment, though his experience on *Nimitz* the second day of the war had given him enough terror to last the remainder of his life. Toland did not yet know that with a routine telex message sent a week before, he would directly affect their lives for the second time this year.

The Boeing 737 airliner touched down ten minutes later. Only twenty people were aboard, almost all of them in uniform. Toland was met by a car and a driver which sped him off to Northwood.

"You're Commander Toland?" a Royal Navy lieutenant asked. "Please come with me, sir. COMEASTLANT wants to see you."

He found Admiral Sir Charles Beattie chewing on an unlit pipe in front of a huge map of the eastern and northern Atlantic.

"Commander Toland, sir."

"Thank you," the Admiral said without turning. "Tea and coffee in the corner, Commander."

Toland availed himself of the tea. He drank it only in the U.K., and after several weeks he found himself wondering why he didn't have it at home.

"Your Tomcats have done well up in Scotland," Beattie said.

"It was the aerial radar that made the real difference, sir. More than half the kills were made by the RAF."

"Last week you sent a message to our air operations chaps to the effect that your Tomcats were able to track Backfires visually at very long range."

It took Toland a few seconds to remember it. "Oh, yes. It's the video-camera system they have, Admiral. It's designed to identify fighter-size aircraft at thirty miles or so. Tracking something as big as a Backfire they can do at fifty or so if the weather's good."

"And the Backfires would not know they were there?"

"Not likely, sir."

"How far could they follow a Backfire?"

"That's a question for a driver, sir. With tanker support, we can keep a Tomcat aloft for almost four hours. Two hours each way, that would take them almost all the way home."

Beattie turned to face Toland for the first time. Sir Charles was a former aviator himself, last commander of the old *Ark Royal,* Britain's last real carrier. "How sure are you of Ivan's operating airfields?"

"For the Backfires, sir? They operate from the four airfields around Kirovsk. I would presume you have satellite photos of the places, sir."

"Here." Beattie handed him a folder.

There was a degree of unreality to this, Toland thought. Four-star admirals didn't chew the fat with newly frocked commanders unless they had nothing better to do, and Beattie had lots of things to do. Bob opened the folder.

"Oh." He looked at a photo set for Umbozero, the field east of Kirovsk. There'd been lit smokepots during the satellite pass, and the resulting black smoke had completely hidden the runways to visual light, with flares messing up the infrared imaging systems as well. "Well, there are the hardened shelters, and maybe three aircraft. Was this taken during a raid?"

"Correct. Very good, Commander. The Backfire force left the airfield three hours before the satellite pass."

"Trucks, too—fuel bowsers?" He got a nod. "They refuel them right after they land?"

"We think yes, before they get into the shelters. Evidently they don't like the idea of fueling inside a building. Seems reasonable enough. Ivan's had problems with accidental explosions the last few years."

Toland nodded, remembering the explosion at the main ordnance storage facility for the Russian Northern Fleet in 1984. "Be a hell of a nice time to catch them on the ground—but we don't have any tactical aircraft that'll reach nearly that far. B-52s could do it, but they'd be murdered. We learned that over Iceland."

"But a Tomcat could trail the Backfires nearly to the Russian doorstep, and that *could* allow you to predict exactly when they'll land?" Sir Charles persisted.

Toland looked at the map. The Backfires reentered Russian fighter cover about thirty minutes' flying time from their home bases.

"Plus or minus fifteen minutes . . . yes, Admiral, I think we can do that. I wonder how long it takes to refuel a Backfire." There was a lot of thinking going on behind those blue eyes, Toland saw.

"Commander, my operations officer will brief you on something called Operation Doolittle. We named it after one of your chaps as a clever bit of subterfuge to weasel the assets from your navy. For the moment, this information is eyes-only to you. Be back here in an hour. I want your evaluation of how we can improve the basic operational concept."

"Yes, sir."

USS *REUBEN JAMES*

They were in New York harbor. O'Malley was in the wardroom finishing up the written account of the destruction of the Soviet submarine when the growler phone on the port bulkhead started making noise. He looked up and discovered he was the only officer in the room. That meant he had to answer it.

"Wardroom. Lieutenant Commander O'Malley."

"*Battleaxe* here. May I please speak to your CO?"

"He's taking a nap. Can I help you, or is it important?"

"If he's not too busy, the captain wishes to invite him to dinner. Half an hour from now. Your XO and helicopter pilot also if he's available."

The pilot laughed. "The XO's on the beach, but the helo driver's available if the Queen's ships are still wet."

"Indeed we are, Commander."

"Okay. I'll go wake him up. Be back to you in a few minutes." O'Malley hung up and went out the door. He bumped into Willy.

"Excuse me, sir. The torpedo-loading practice?"

"Okay, I'm going to see the skipper anyway." Willy had complained that the last practice had gone a little slow. He handed the petty officer his report. "Take this down to the ship's office and tell 'em to type it up."

O'Malley went forward and found the door to the captain's stateroom closed, but the do-not-disturb light was switched off. He knocked and went in. The noise surprised him.

"Don't you see it!" The words came out as a gasp. Morris was lying on his back, his hands balled into fists on the blanket. His face was covered in sweat and he breathed like a man finishing a marathon.

"Jesus." O'Malley hesitated. He didn't really know the man.

"*Look out!*" This was louder, and the pilot wondered if anyone in the passageway outside might hear it and wonder if the captain were—he had to do something.

"Wake up, Captain!" Jerry grabbed Morris by the shoulders and lifted him up into a sitting position.

"Don't you see it!" Morris shouted, still not really awake.

"Settle down, pal. You're tied to the pier in New York harbor. You're safe. The ship is safe. Come around, Captain. It's okay." Morris blinked his eyes about ten times. He saw O'Malley's face about six inches away.

"What the hell are you doing here?"

"Glad I came. You all right?" The pilot lit a cigarette and handed it to the captain.

Morris refused it and stood. He walked to his basin and got a glass of water. "Just a dumb dream. What do you want?"

"We've been invited out to dinner next door in half an hour—I guess a reward for giving them the Victor. Also, I'd like your deck crew to practice loading torps on my bird. Last time was a little slow, my petty says."

"When do you want 'em to do it?"

"Soon as it gets dark, Captain. Better they should learn it the hard way."

"Okay. Half an hour on dinner?"

"Yes, sir. Be nice to have a drink."

Morris smiled without much enthusiasm. "Guess it would. I'll wash up. Meet you in the wardroom. This thing formal?"

"They didn't say so. I wasn't planning to change, if that's all right with you, skipper." O'Malley was wearing his flight suit. He got lonely without all the pockets.

"Twenty minutes."

O'Malley went to his stateroom and ran a cloth over his flight boots. The flight suit was new, and he figured that was dressy enough. Morris worried him. The man might come apart, not something that should happen to a commanding officer. That made it partly his problem. *Besides,* O'Malley told himself, *he's a pretty good man.*

He looked better when they met again. Amazing what a shower could do. His hair was brushed back and his service khakis pressed. The two officers went aft to the helicopter pad, then down the brow to the dock.

HMS *Battleaxe* gave the appearance of a larger ship than the American frigate. In fact she was about twelve feet shorter, but seven hundred tons heavier, various differences in her design reflecting the philosophies of her builders. She was undeniably prettier than her American counterpart, her unexciting hull lines more than balanced by a superstructure that looked as though it had been sculpted to sit atop a ship instead of a parking lot.

Morris was glad to see that things were informal. A youthful midshipman met them at the foot of the brow and escorted them aboard, explaining that the captain was on the radio at the moment. After the customary salutes of flag and duty officer, the midshipman led them into the ship's air-conditioned citadel, then forward to the wardroom.

"Hot damn, a piano!" O'Malley exclaimed. A battered upright was secured to the port bulkhead with two-inch line. Several officers rose and introduced themselves.

"Drinks, gentlemen?" a steward asked. O'Malley got himself a can of beer and moved toward the piano. A minute later he was battering his way through some Scott Joplin. The wardroom's forward door opened.

"Jerr-O!" a man with four stripes on his shoulder boards exclaimed.

"Doug!" O'Malley jumped up from the stool and ran to shake his hand. "How the hell are you!"

"I knew it was your voice on the radio. 'Hammer,' indeed. The American Navy's run out of competent pilots and scraped you up, eh?" Both men laughed out loud. O'Malley waved his captain over.

"Captain Ed Morris, meet Captain Doug Perrin, MBE, RN, and a shit-load of other acronyms. Watch this turkey, skipper, he used to drive submarines before he went straight."

"I see you guys know each other."

"Some bloody fool decided to send him to lecture at HMS *Dryad,* our ASW school, when I was taking the advanced course. Set back our relations by at least a hundred years."

"Is the Fox and Fence put back together yet?" O'Malley asked. "Skipper, there was this pub about half a mile from the place, and one night Doug and me—"

"I am trying to forget that night, Jerr-O. Susan gave me hell about it for weeks." He led them aft and got himself a drink. "Marvelous job with that Victor last night! Captain Morris, I understand you did very well with your previous command."

"Killed a Charlie and picked up two assists."

"We stumbled across an Echo on our last convoy. Old boat, but she had a good driver. Took us six hours. But a pair of diesel submarines, probably Tangos, got inside and killed five ships and an escort. *Diomede* may have gotten one of them. We're not sure."

"Was the Echo coming after you?" Morris asked.

"Possibly," Perrin answered. "It does appear that Ivan's going after the escorts quite deliberately. We had two missiles shot at us by the last Back-fire raid. One ran into our chaff cloud, and fortunately our Sea Wolf intercepted the other. Unfortunately, the one that exploded behind us amputated our towed array and we're down to just our 2016 sonar."

"So you've been assigned to ride shotgun on us then?"

"It would seem so."

The captains lapsed into shoptalk, which was the whole point of the dinner in any case. O'Malley found the English helicopter pilot while the tables were set, and they started the same thing while the American played the piano. Somewhere in the Royal Navy was a directive: when dealing with American naval officers, get them over early, get a drink in them first, then talk business.

Dinner was excellent, though the Americans' judgment was somewhat affected by the liquid refreshments. O'Malley listened closely as his captain described the loss of *Pharris,* the tactics employed by the Russians, and how he had failed to counter them properly. It was like listening to a man relate the death of his child.

"Under the circumstances, hard to see what you could have done differently," Doug Perrin sympathized. "Victor is a capable opponent, and he must have timed your coming off the sprint very carefully."

Morris shook his head. "No, we came off sprint well away from him, and that blew his solution right out the window. If I'd done things better, those men wouldn't be dead. I was the captain. It was my fault."

Perrin said, "I've been there in the submarine, you know. He has the advantage because he's already been tracking you." He flashed O'Malley a look.

Dinner ended at eight. The escort commanders would meet the following afternoon, and the convoy would sail at sundown. O'Malley and Morris left together, but the pilot stopped at the brow.

"Forgot my hat. I'll be back in a minute." He hurried back to the wardroom. Captain Perrin was still there.

"Doug, I need an opinion."

"He shouldn't go back out in his current state. Sorry, Jerry, but that's how I see things."

"You're right. There's one thing I can try." O'Malley made a small purchase and rejoined Morris two minutes later.

"Captain, any particular reason you have to head right back to the ship?" he asked quietly. "Something I need to talk about and I don't want to do it aboard. It's a personal thing. Okay?" The pilot looked very embarrassed.

"How about we take a little walk?" Morris agreed. The two officers walked east. O'Malley looked up and down the street, and found a waterfront bar with sailors going in and out. He steered Morris into it and they found a booth in the back.

"Two glasses," O'Malley told the barmaid. He unzipped the leg pocket of his flight suit and withdrew a bottle of Black Bush Irish whiskey.

"You want to drink here, you buy it here." O'Malley handed her two twenty-dollar bills.

"Two glasses and ice." His voice did not brook argument. "And leave us alone." Service was quick.

"I checked my logbook this afternoon," O'Malley said after tossing off half his first drink. "Four thousand three hundred sixty hours of stick time. Counting last night, three hundred eleven hours of combat time."

"Vietnam. You said you were there." Morris sipped at his own.

"Last day, last tour. Search-and-rescue mission for an A-7 pilot shot down twenty miles south of Haiphong." He had never even told his wife this story. "Saw a flash, made the mistake of ignoring it. Thought it was a reflection off a window or a stream or something. Kept going. Turned out it was probably a reflection of a gunsight, maybe a pair of binoculars. One minute later some hundred-millimeter flak goes off around us. Helo just comes apart. I get her down, we're on fire. Look left—copilot's torn apart, his brains are in my lap. My crew chief, a third-class named Ricky, he's in the back. I look. Both his legs are torn off. I think he was still alive then, but there wasn't a damned thing I could do about it—couldn't even get to him the way things were—and there's three people heading toward us. I just ran away. Maybe they didn't see me. Maybe they didn't care— hell, I don't know. Another helo found me twelve hours later." He poured himself another drink and topped off the one for Morris. "Don't make me drink alone."

"I've had enough."

"No, you haven't. And neither have I. It took me a year to get over that. You don't have a year. All you got's tonight. You gotta talk about it, Captain. I know. Think it's bad now? It gets worse."

He took another pull on the drink. At least it was good stuff, O'Malley told himself. He watched Morris sit there for five minutes, sipping at his drink and wondering if he should just go back to the ship. The proud captain. Like all captains, condemned to live alone, and this one was lonelier than most. *He's afraid I'm right,* O'Malley thought. *He's afraid it will get worse. You poor bastard. If you only knew.*

"Run through it," the pilot said quietly. "Analyze it one step at a time."

"You already did that for me."

"I have a big mouth. Has to be for my feet to fit in it. You do it in your sleep, Ed. Might as well do it when you're awake."

And, slowly, he did. O'Malley coached him through the sequence. Weather conditions, ship's course and speed. What sensors were operating. In an hour they were three quarters of the way down the bottle. Finally they got to the torpedoes. Morris's voice started to crack.

"There just wasn't anything else I could *do!* The Goddamned thing just came in. We only had one nixie out, and the first fish blew that the hell away. I tried to maneuver the ship, but—"

"But you were up against a homing torpedo. You can't outrun 'em and you can't outturn 'em."

"I'm not supposed to let—"

"Oh, horseshit!" The pilot refilled the glasses. "You think you're the first guy ever lost a 'can? Didn't you ever play ball, Ed? Hell, there's two sides, and both of 'em play to win. You expect those Russian sub skippers are just gonna sit there and say, 'Kill me, kill me'? You must be dumber 'n I thought."

"My men—"

"Some of them are dead, most of them aren't. I'm sorry some're dead. I'm sorry Ricky died. Kid wasn't even nineteen yet. But I didn't kill him, and you didn't kill your men. You saved your ship. You brought her back with most of the crew."

Morris drained his glass with one long pull. Jerry refilled it, not bothering with ice.

"It's my *responsibility.* Look, when I got back to Norfolk, I visited—I mean, I *had* to visit their families. I'm the captain. I gotta—there was this little girl, and . . . Jesus, O'Malley, what the hell do you say?" Morris demanded. He was sobbing, near tears, Jerry saw. Good.

"They don't put that in the book," O'Malley agreed. *You think they would have learned by now.*

"Pretty little girl. What do you tell the kids?" The tears started. It had taken nearly two hours.

"You tell the little girl that her daddy was a good man and he did his best, and you did your best, 'cause that's all we can do, Ed. You did everything right, but sometimes it just doesn't matter." It wasn't the first time O'Malley had had men cry on his shoulder. He remembered doing it himself. *What a miserable life this can be,* he thought, *that it can bring good men to this.*

Morris recovered a few minutes later, and by the time they finished the bottle both men were as drunk as either ever got. O'Malley helped his captain up and walked him to the door.

"What's the matter, Navy, can't take it?" He was a merchant seaman standing alone at the bar. It was the wrong thing to say.

It was hard to tell from the baggy flight suit that O'Malley was a man of considerable strength. His left arm was wrapped around Morris. His right hand grabbed the other man by the throat and dragged him away from the bar.

"You got anything else to say about my friend, Dickweed?" O'Malley tightened his grip.

The reply came in a whisper. "All I meant was he has trouble with his liquor."

The pilot released him. "Good night."

Maneuvering the captain back to the ship was difficult, partly because O'Malley was also drunk but mainly because Morris was on the point of passing out. That had been part of the plan, too, but the Hammer had cut his timing a little close. The brow looked awfully steep from the pier.

"What seems to be the problem?"

"Good evening, Master Chief."

"Good evening, Commander. You got the captain with you?"

"Sure could use a hand, too."

"You're not kidding." The chief came down the gangway. Together they got the captain aboard. The really hard part was the ladder up to his stateroom. For this another sailor was summoned.

"Damn," the youngster observed. "The old man really knows how to tie one on!"

"Takes a real sailorman to know how to get blasted," the master chief agreed. The three of them got him up the ladder. O'Malley took it from there and landed Morris on his bunk. The captain was sleeping soundly, and the flyer hoped the nightmare wouldn't come back. His still did.

NORTHWOOD, ENGLAND

"Well, Commander?"

"Yes, sir. I think it'll work. I see most of the assets are nearly in place."

"The original plan had a lesser chance of success. I'm sure it would have got their attention, of course, but this way we just might be able to damage the force severely."

Toland looked up at the map. "The timing is still tricky, but not very different from that attack we made on the tankers. I like it, sir. Sure would solve a few problems. What's the convoy situation?"

"There are eighty ships assembled in New York harbor. They sail in twenty-four hours. Heavy escort, carriers in support, even a new Aegis cruiser with the merchants. And the next step after that, of course—" Beattie went on.

"Yes, sir. And Doolittle is the key."

"Exactly. I want you back at Stornoway. I'll also be sending one of my air operations types to work with your chaps. We'll keep you informed of all developments. Remember that distribution for this is to be strictly limited to the personnel involved."

"Understood, sir."

"Off with you, then."

34. Feelers

USS *REUBEN JAMES*

0700 hours came rather early for Jerry O'Malley. He had the lower bunk in a two-man stateroom—his copilot had the upper—and his first considered move was to take three aspirins and sit back down. It was almost funny, he thought. "The Hammer." He felt it inside his head. No, he corrected himself, he had his dipping sonar in there, on automatic ping. Still and all, he had performed something remembered from his youth as a corporal work of mercy, and that helped give purpose to his suffering. He gave the aspirins ten minutes to get into his bloodstream, then went forward to the shower. First cold, then hot water cleared his head.

The wardroom was full but quiet, the officers assembled according to age into little knots of whispered conversation. These young officers hadn't faced combat before, and the bravado they might have felt on leaving San Diego some weeks before had been replaced with the sober reality of the task at hand. Ships had been sunk. Men they knew were dead. For these kids, fear was a more terrible unknown than the technical aspects of combat for which they had been trained. He could see the question in their faces; only time would answer it. They would learn to endure it, or they would not. Combat held no mysteries for O'Malley. He knew that he would be afraid, and that he would put the fear aside as best he could. There was no sense dwelling on it. It would come soon enough.

"Good morning, XO!"

"Morning, Jerry. I was just going to call the skipper."

"He needs his sleep, Frank." The pilot had disconnected Morris's alarm clock before leaving the stateroom. Ernst read O'Malley's face.

"Well, nothing we really need him for till eleven."

"I knew you were a good XO, Frank." O'Malley debated between bug juice and coffee. The fruit drink this morning was the orange kind—the flavors didn't relate to any particular fruit. O'Malley liked the red kind, but not the orange. He poured some coffee.

"I supervised the torpedo loading last night. We cut a minute off our best time—in the dark."

"Sounds good to me. When's the pre-sail brief?"

"Fourteen hundred, in a theater two blocks from here. COs, XOs, and selected others. I expect you'll want to come, too?"

"Yeah."

Ernst's voice dropped. "You sure the skipper's all right?" There are no secrets aboard a ship.

"He's been on straight combat ops since Day One of this fracas. He needed to get a little unwrapped, an ancient and honored naval tradition"— he raised his voice—"damned shame that all these little boys are too young to partake in it! Didn't anybody think to get a newspaper? NFL summer camps are opened all over the country, and there ain't no paper! What the hell kind of wardroom is this!"

"I've never met a dinosaur before," a junior engineering officer observed *sotto voce.*

"You get used to him," Ensign Ralston explained.

ICELAND

Two days' rest was just what the doctor ordered for everyone. Sergeant Nichols could almost walk normally on his ankle, and the Americans, who were beginning to regard fish with distinct distaste, filled up on the extra rations the Royal Marines had packed in.

Edwards's eyes traced around the horizon again. The human eye automatically locks onto movement, and she was moving. It was hard not to look. It was almost impossible. In *fact,* Edwards told himself, it *was* impossible to stand guard and not look around. The hell of it was, she thought it was funny. Their rescuers—Edwards knew better, but why upset her?— had also brought soap. A tiny lake half a mile from their hilltop perch was the designated bathing area. In hostile country no one went that far alone, and the lieutenant had naturally been detailed to look after her—and she after him. Guarding her as she bathed with a loaded rifle seemed absurd, even with Russians around. Her bruises were nearly healed, he noted as she dressed.

"Finished, Michael." They didn't have towels, but that was a small price to pay for smelling human. She came up to him with her hair still wet and an impish expression on her face. "I embarrass you. Sorry."

"It's not your fault." It was also impossible to be angry with her.

"The baby makes me fat," she said. Mike could scarcely tell, but then it wasn't his figure being changed.

"You look fine. I'm sorry if I looked when I shouldn't have."

"What is wrong?"

Edwards found himself struggling with his words again. "Well, after— after what happened to you, I mean, you probably don't need a bunch of strange men standing around looking at you when you're, well, naked."

"Michael, you are not like that one. I know you would never hurt me. Even after what he do to me, you say I am pretty—when I grow fat."

"Vigdis, baby or no baby, you are the prettiest girl I have ever known. You're strong, and you're brave." *And I think I love you, but I'm afraid to say so.* "We just picked a bad time to meet, that's all."

"For me was a very good time, Michael." She took his hand. She smiled a lot now. She had a gentle, friendly smile.

"As long as you know me, every time you think about me, you'll remember that—Russian."

"Yes, Michael, I will remember that. I remember that you save my life. I ask Sergeant Smith. He say you have orders not to come near Russians because it so dangerous for you. He say you come because of me. You do not even know me then, but you come."

"I did the right thing." He held both of her hands now. *What do I say now? Darling, if we ever get out of this alive . . . that sounds like a bad movie.* Edwards hadn't been sixteen in a long time, but now all the awkwardness that had poisoned his adolescence came back to him. Mike hadn't exactly been the makeout king of Eastpoint High School. "Vigdis, I'm not any good at this. It was different with Sandy. She understood me. I don't know how to talk to girls—hell, I'm not that good talking to *people.* I do weather maps, and play with computers, but I usually have to have a few beers in me before I get the nerve to say—"

"I know you love me, Michael." Her eyes sparkled when she revealed the secret.

"Well, yes."

She handed him the soap. "Your time to wash. I will not look too much."

FÖLZIEHAUSEN, FEDERAL REPUBLIC OF GERMANY

Major Sergetov handed over his notes. The Leine had been forced at a second place—Gronau, fifteen kilometers north of Alfeld—and now six divisions were involved in the drive on Hameln and others were attempting to widen the breach. Still they were handicapped. There were relatively few roads in this part of Germany, and those routes they controlled were still suffering from air and artillery attacks that bled reinforcement columns long before they could be committed to battle.

What had begun with three motor-rifle divisions attempting to forge an opening for one tank division had now become the focus of two complete Soviet armies. Where they had attacked into a pair of depleted German brigades, now they faced a hodgepodge of units from nearly all NATO members. Alekseyev anguished over lost chances. What if divisional artillery hadn't dropped multiple rocket fire on the bridges? Could he have reached the Weser in a day as he had thought? *That is in the past,* Pasha told himself. He looked over the information on fuel availability.

"One month?"

"At current operational tempos, yes," Sergetov said grimly. "And to do this we have crippled the whole national economy. My father asks if we can reduce expenditures at the front—"

"Certainly," the General exploded. "We can lose the war! That ought to save his precious fuel!"

"Comrade General, you requested that I provide you with accurate information. I have done this. My father was also able to give me this." The younger man took a document from his coat pocket. Ten pages thick, it was a KGB intelligence assessment marked POLITBURO EYES ONLY. "It makes very interesting reading. My father asks me to point out the risk he has taken in giving you this document."

The General was a fast reader and ordinarily not a man given to displays of emotion. The West German government had established direct contact with the Soviets through the embassies both maintained in India. The preliminary discussion had been an inquiry into the possibility of a negotiated settlement. The KGB's assessment was that the inquiry reflected the fragmentation of NATO politically, and possibly a grave supply situation on the other side of the battle line. There followed two pages of graphs and claims of damage to NATO shipping, plus analysis of NATO's munitions expenditures to date. The KGB calculated that NATO supplies were down to the two-week mark now, despite all the shipping that had arrived to date. Neither side had produced enough consumable ordnance and fuel to sustain its forces.

"My father feels that this data on the Germans is particularly significant."

"Potentially so," Alekseyev said cautiously. "They will not slacken their fighting while their political leadership works to achieve an acceptable settlement, but if we can make them an acceptable offer and remove the Germans from NATO, then our objective is achieved, and we can seize the Persian Gulf at leisure. What offer are we making to the Germans?"

"That has not yet been decided. They have asked for our withdrawal to pre-war lines, with final terms to be negotiated on a more formal basis

under international supervision. Their withdrawal from NATO is to be
contingent upon the terms of the final treaty."

"Not acceptable. It gives us nothing. Why are they negotiating at all, I
wonder?"

"Evidently there has been considerable turmoil in their government over
the dislocation of civilians, and destruction of economic assets."

"Ah." The economic damage to Germany was not something in which
Alekseyev had the slightest interest, but the German government was
watching the work of two generations being dismantled by Soviet explosives. "But why haven't they told us this?"

"The Politburo feels that news of a possible negotiated settlement would
discourage further pressure on the Germans."

"Idiots. This sort of thing tells us what to attack!"

"That is what my father said. He wants your opinion on all this."

"Tell the Minister that I see no indication at all of weakening NATO
resolve on the battle line. German morale in particular is still high. They
resist everywhere."

"Their government could be doing this without the knowledge of their
own army. If they are deceiving their NATO allies, why not their high
command also?" Sergetov suggested. After all, it worked that way in his
country . . .

"A possibility, Ivan Mikhailovich. There is another one, as well." Alekseyev turned back to the papers. "That this is all a sham."

NEW YORK

The briefing was conducted by a captain. As he spoke, the escort commanders and their senior officers leafed through the briefing documents
like high school students at a Shakespeare play.

"Outlying sonar pickets will be positioned along the threat axis here."
The captain moved his pointer across the viewgraph. The frigates *Reuben
James* and *Battleaxe* were to be almost thirty miles from the rest of the
formation. That put them outside SAM coverage from the other ships.
They had their own surface-to-air missiles, but they would be completely
on their own. "We will have SURTASS support for most of the trip. The
ships are repositioning themselves now. We can expect Soviet submarine
and air attacks.

"To deal with the air threat, the carriers *Independence* and *America* will
be supporting the convoy. The new Aegis cruiser *Bunker Hill,* as you may
have noticed, will be traveling in the convoy. Also, the Air Force will be
taking out the Russian radar-ocean-reconnaissance satellite on its next pass,
about twelve hundred hours zulu tomorrow."

"All right!" a destroyer captain observed.

"Gentlemen, we are delivering a total load of over two million tons of
equipment, plus a complete armored division made up of reserve and
National Guard formations. Not counting the materiel reinforcements, this
is enough supplies to keep NATO in action for three weeks. This one goes
through.

"Any questions? No? Then, good luck."

The theater emptied, the officers filing past the armed guards onto the
sunny street.

"Jerry?" Morris said quietly.

"Yes, Captain?" The pilot donned his aviator's sunglasses.

"About last night—"

"Captain, last night we both had too much to drink, and to tell you the truth, I don't remember all that much. Maybe six months from now we can decide what happened. You sleep well?"

"Almost twelve hours. My alarm clock didn't go off."

"Maybe you should get a new one." They walked past the bar both had visited the night before. The captain and the pilot gave it a look, then laughed.

"Once more into the breach, dear friends!" Doug Perrin joined them.

"Just don't give us any of this laying your ship alongside the enemy crap," O'Malley suggested. "That 'away boarders' shit is dangerous."

"Your job to keep the bastards away from us, Jerr-O. Up to it?"

"He'd better be," Morris observed lightly. "I'd hate to think he's *all* talk!"

"We got a real nice bunch here," the pilot observed angrily. "Jeez, I fly up all on my own, find a damned submarine, *give* it to Doug here, and do I get any respect?"

"That's the problem with aviators. You don't tell them how great they are every five minutes, they go and get depressed on you," Morris said with a smile. He was a different person from the one who had mumbled through dinner last night. "Anything you need that we might have, Doug?"

"Perhaps we might exchange some foodstuffs?"

"No problem. Send your supply officer over. I'm sure we can negotiate something." Morris checked his watch. "We don't sail for another three hours. Let's have a sandwich and talk over a few things. I got an idea for spoofing those Backfires that I want to try out on you . . ."

Three hours later, a pair of Moran harbor tugs eased the frigates away from the pier. *Reuben James* moved slowly, her turbine engines pushing her through the polluted water at a gentle six knots. O'Malley watched from the right seat of his helicopter, on alert for a possible Russian sub near the entrance to the harbor, though four Orion patrol aircraft were vigorously sanitizing the area. Probably the Victor they had killed two days before had been detailed to trail and report on the convoy, first to direct a Backfire raid, then to close and launch her own attack. The trailer was dead, but that did not mean that the sailing was a secret. New York was a city of eight million, and surely one of them was standing at his window with a pair of binoculars, cataloging the ship types and numbers. He or she would make an innocent telephone call, and the data would be in Moscow in a few hours. Other submarines would close on their expected track. As soon as they were outside of shore-based air cover, Soviet search aircraft would come looking, with missile-armed Backfires behind them.

So many ships, O'Malley thought. They passed a series of Ro/Ros, roll-on/roll-off container ships loaded with tanks, fighting vehicles, and the men of a whole armored division. Others were piled high with containers that could be loaded right onto trucks for dispatch to the front, their contents recorded on computer for rapid delivery to the proper destination. He thought about the news reports, the taped scenes of land combat in Germany. That was what this was all about. The Navy's mission: keep the sea-lanes open to deliver the tools those men in Germany needed. Get the ships across.

*   *   *

"How does she ride?" Calloway asked.

"Not too bad," Morris answered the reporter. "We have fin stabilizers. She doesn't roll very much. If you have any problem, our corpsman can probably come up with something. Don't be bashful about asking."

"I will try to keep out of your way."

Morris gave the man from Reuters a friendly nod. He'd arrived with only an hour's warning, but he seemed to be a pro, or at least experienced enough to have all his gear packed in one bag. He took the last available bunk in officers' country.

"Your admiral said that you're one of his best commanders."

"I guess we'll find that out," Morris said.

35. Time on Target

USS *REUBEN JAMES*

The first two days went well. The escort force sailed first, blasting with their sonars at the shallow coastal water for possible submarines and finding none. The merchant ships followed, forming slowly into eight columns of ten each. The twenty-knot convoy was in a hurry to deliver its goods. Covered by a massive umbrella of land-based aircraft, it pressed on through the first forty-eight hours with only minor zigzagging as it sailed past the coast of New England and Eastern Canada, Sable Island, and the Grand Banks. The easy part was behind them now. As they left coastal waters for the Atlantic Ocean proper, they entered the unknown territory.

"About filing my dispatches . . . ." Calloway said to Morris.

"Twice a day you can use my satellite transmitter as long as it doesn't interfere with official traffic. You understand that your reports will be run through Norfolk for sensitive information?"

"Quite so. Captain, you may believe me when I say that as long as I'm here with you, I will reveal nothing that would endanger your ship! I had quite enough excitement this year in Moscow."

"What?" Morris turned and lowered his binoculars. Calloway explained what his spring had been like.

"Patrick Flynn, my opposite number from Associated Press, is aboard *Battleaxe*. Doubtless drinking beer," he concluded.

"So you were there when all this boiled up. Do *you* know why all this started?"

Calloway shook his head. "If I did, Captain, I'd have filed the story long ago."

A messenger appeared on the bridge wing with a clipboard. Morris took it, read through three messages, and signed for them.

"Something dramatic?" Calloway asked hopefully.

"Fleet weather-update and something about that Russian reconnaissance satellite. It comes overhead in another three hours. The Air Force is going to try and shoot it down before it gets to us, though. Nothing major. You're comfortable, I presume. Any problems?"

"None, Captain. Nothing like a nice sea voyage."

"True enough." Morris stuck his head into the pilothouse. "General Quarters, Air Action."

Morris led the reporter into the Combat Information Center, explaining that the drill he was about to see was to make sure his men could do everything properly even in the dark.

"One of those dispatches give you a warning?"

"No, but in six hours we'll be outside of land-based fighter cover. That means Ivan is going to come looking for us." *And it's going to get awfully lonely out here by ourselves,* Morris thought. He gave his men an hour's worth of drill. The CIC crew ran a pair of computer simulations. On the second one an enemy missile got through their defenses.

LANGLEY AIR FORCE BASE, VIRGINIA

The F-15 fighter rolled to a halt just outside the shelter building. The crew chief set the ladder next to the aircraft, and Major Nakamura climbed down, already looking aft at her scorched airplane. She walked over to examine the damage.

"Don't look bad, Major," the sergeant assured her. A fragment from the exploding rocket motor had drilled a hole the size of a beer can right through her left wing, missing a fuel tank by three inches. "I can fix that in a couple of hours."

"You all right?" the Lockheed engineer asked.

"It blew, fifty feet away, and it just blew the hell up. You were wrong, by the way. When they blow, it's pretty spectacular. Pieces all over the damned place. I was lucky I only caught one of them." It had scared hell out of the pilot, but she'd then had an hour to recover. Now she was just mad.

"Sorry, Major. Wish I could say more than that."

"Just have to try again," Buns said, looking up at the sky through the hole. "When's the next window?"

"Eleven hours, sixteen minutes."

"That's it, then." She walked into the building, then upstairs to the pilots' lounge. There was carpeting on the walls of the building for noise absorption. It also prevented serious injury to the pilots' fists.

KIROVSK, R.S.F.S.R.

Unhampered, the Radar Ocean Reconnaissance Satellite continued its orbit, and on its next pass over the North Atlantic found itself looking down on a collection of nearly a hundred ships in even columns. This must be the convoy their intelligence reports had told them about, the Russian analysts decided—and, they noted with satisfaction, it was out in the open, right where they could get at it.

Ninety minutes later, two regiments of missile-armed Backfire bombers, preceded by Bear-D search aircraft, lifted off the four airfields around Kirovsk, topped off their fuel tanks, and headed for the radar gap over Iceland.

USS *REUBEN JAMES*

"So this is the surprise you have in store for them?" Calloway asked. He tapped some symbols on the main tactical-display scope.

Morris nodded thoughtfully. "So far we've sent most of the convoys across under EMCON—that's emission control—with their radars blacked out to make them hard to find. This time we're doing something a little different. This is the display from the SPS-49 radar—"

"That black monster atop the pilothouse?"

"Right. These symbols are Tomcats from the carrier *America*. This is a KC-135 tanker, and this baby here is an E-2C Hawkeye radar bird. The Hawkeye's radar is shut down. When Ivan shows up, he'll have to close to see what's here."

"But he already knows," Calloway objected.

"No, he knows there's a convoy around here *somewhere*. That's not good enough to launch missiles. All he knows for sure is that there is one operating SPS-49 radar. He'll have to light off his own radar to see what's on the water. If Mr. Bear does that, we see him, and we'll have fighters on his ass so fast he'll never know what hit him."

"And if the Backfires don't come today?"

"Then we'll see them some other time. The Bears talk to submarines, too, Mr. Calloway. They are still worth killing."

ICELAND

It was the first time they'd been bored. Edwards and his party had been terrified often enough, but never bored. Now they had been in the same place for four complete days, and still they had no orders to move. They observed, and reported minor Russian activity, but without anything substantive to do, time was heavy on them.

"Lieutenant." Garcia pointed up. "I got airplanes heading south."

Edwards got out his binoculars. The sky was dotted with white, fleecy clouds. There were no contrails to be seen today, but—there! he saw a flash, a reflection off something. He strained his eyes to identify it.

"Nichols, what do you think?" He handed the glasses over.

"That's a Russian Backfire," Nichols said simply.

"You sure?"

"Quite sure, *Left*enant. I've seen them before often enough."

"Get a count." Edwards unpacked his radio.

"I only see four. All heading south, sir."

"You're sure they're Backfires?" Edwards persisted.

"I am bloody sure, *Left*enant Edwards!" Nichols answered testily. He watched the officer turn on the radio.

"Beagle calling Doghouse, over." The communications station was a little slow today. It took three calls before they acknowledged.

"Doghouse, this is Beagle, and I have some information for you. We see Backfire-type bombers southbound over our position."

"How do you know they're Backfires?" Doghouse wanted to know.

"Because Sergeant Nichols of the Royal Marines says he's bloody sure they're Backfires. Four of them"—Nichols held up five fingers now—"correction five aircraft southbound."

"Roger, thank you, Beagle. Anything else happening?"

"Negative. How long do you expect us to sit on this hill, over?"
"We'll let you know. Patience, Beagle. We haven't forgotten you. Out."

NORTH ATLANTIC

Bears advanced in an oblique line, their crews scanning the air with their eyes and probing the radar and radio frequencies. Presently the leading Bear detected the emissions of a single American radar, and it took only a minute to identify it as an SPS-49 air-search model of the type used by Perry-class missile frigates. The technicians on board measured the signal's intensity and, plotting its position, judged that they were far outside the radar's detection range.

The raid commander riding in the third Bear received the information and compared it with his intelligence data for the convoy. The position was exactly in the middle of the circle he had drawn on his map. He was suspicious of things that were so exact. The convoy was taking a direct route to Europe? Why? Most convoys to date had taken a more evasive course, detouring far south to the Azores in order to force his aircraft to reach farther than they wanted—and thereby forcing the Backfires trailing the scouts to carry only one missile instead of two. Something was strange here. On his order, the patrol line reoriented itself to a north-south disposition and began reducing altitude to keep below the horizon of the American radar.

USS *REUBEN JAMES*

"How far can you see?" Calloway asked.

"Depends on the altitude and size of the target, and atmospheric conditions," Morris answered, staring down from his chair to the electronic displays. Two Navy Tomcats were ready for combat. "For the Bear, at thirty thousand feet or so, we can probably spot it about two hundred fifty miles away. But the lower he flies, the closer he can get. Radar can't see through the horizon."

"But flying low will cost him fuel."

Morris looked down at the reporter. "Those damned things carry enough fuel to stay up all week," he exaggerated.

"Message from LANTFLT, Captain." The communications officer handed the form over: REPORT POSSIBLE BACKFIRE RAID SOUTHBOUND OVER ICELAND 1017Z. Morris handed the message to his tactical action officer, who immediately looked at the chart.

"Good news?" Calloway asked. He had better sense than to ask to see the dispatch.

"We may be seeing Backfire bombers in a little over two hours."

"Shooting for the convoy?"

"No, probably they'll want to shoot at us first. They have a good four days to blast the convoy, and getting the escorts out of the way makes that job a lot easier."

"Are you concerned?"

Morris smiled thinly. "Mr. Calloway, I'm always concerned."

The captain reflexively checked the various status boards. All his weapons and sensor systems were fully operational—so nice to have a brand-new ship! The threat board showed no known submarine activity in the immediate area, a datum to be taken with a considerable bit of skepticism. He could call General Quarters now, but much of his crew was at lunch. Better to have everyone fed and alert.

The damned waiting, Morris thought. He watched the displays in silence. The blips indicating friendly aircraft orbited slowly as their pilots waited too.

"More CAP coming up," an officer reported. Another pair of Tomcats, part of the combat air patrol, appeared on the scope. *America* had gotten the same raid warning. The carrier was two hundred miles away, westbound for Norfolk. The same was true of *Independence,* returning from the Azores. The carriers had been at sea since the war began, cruising back and forth to avoid the orbiting Soviet ocean-reconnaissance satellites. They had been able to provide antisubmarine protection for a number of convoys, though only at great hazard to the carriers themselves. Up to now, the American flattops had not been able to act as they were supposed to act. They were not yet offensive weapons. The fate of the *Nimitz* group had come as a bitter lesson. Morris lit another cigarette. Now he remembered why he'd quit in the first place. Too many of them burned his throat, destroyed his sense of taste, and made his eyes water. On the other hand, they did give him something to do while he waited.

NORTH ATLANTIC

The Bears were on a precise north-south line now centered on the position of the frigate's radar signals. The raid commander ordered them to turn west and reduce altitude. Two aircraft failed to acknowledge the order, and he had to repeat it.

Two hundred miles west of them, aboard the circling E-2C Hawkeye surveillance aircraft, a technician's head went up. He'd just heard someone speaking Russian; in code, but definitely Russian.

Within minutes, every ship in the escort force had the information, and they all came up with the same answer: the Backfires couldn't be here yet. These were Bears. Everyone wanted to kill the Bears. The carrier *America* started launching her fighters and additional radar aircraft. After all, the Russians could be looking for her.

USS *REUBEN JAMES*

"He's gotta be heading right for us," the tactical action officer said.

"That's the general idea," Morris agreed.

"How far?" Calloway asked.

"No way to know that. The Hawkeye copied a voice radio transmission. Probably it's fairly close, but freak atmospheric conditions can let you hear that sort of thing from half a world away. Mr. Lenner, let's go to battle stations for air action."

Five minutes later the frigate was ready.

NORTH ATLANTIC

"Good morning, Mr. Bear." The Tomcat pilot stared at his TV display tube. The Russian aircraft was about forty miles away, the sun glinting off its massive propellers. Deciding to close without using his radar for the moment, the fighter pilot advanced his throttles to 80-percent power and activated his missile controls. The head-on closure rate was over a thousand miles per hour, seventeen miles per minute.

Then: "Energize!" the pilot ordered, and instantly the radar intercept officer in the rear seat powered up the fighter's AWG-9 radar.

"We've got him," the RIO reported a moment later.

"Shoot!" Two missiles dropped free and accelerated to over three thousand miles per hour.

The Soviet electronics-warfare technician was trying to isolate the signature characteristics of the frigate's search radar when a *beep* sounded on a separate warning receiver. He turned to see what the noise was and went pale.

"Air-attack warning!" he shouted over the intercom.

Reacting at once, the pilot rolled the Bear left and dove for the surface of the ocean, while aft the EW technician activated his protective jamming systems. However, the turn had masked the jammer pods from the incoming missiles.

"What's happening?" the raid commander demanded over the intercom.

"We have an interceptor radar on us," the technician replied, scared but cool. "Jamming pods are activated."

The raid commander turned to his communications man. "Get a warning out: enemy fighter activity this position."

But there wasn't time. The Phoenixes covered the distance in less than twenty seconds. The first went wild and missed, but the second locked on the diving bomber and blew its tail off. The Bear fell to the sea with as little grace as a dropped sheet of paper.

USS *REUBEN JAMES*

The radar showed the Tomcat, and they watched as it launched two missiles that immediately disappeared from sight, and then, silently, as the Tomcat continued east for thirty seconds. Then it turned around and headed back west.

"That, gentlemen, is a kill," Morris said. "Splash one Bear."

"How do you know?" Calloway asked.

"You think he would have turned back if he missed? And if it was anything but a Bear, he'd have broken radio silence. ESM, we copy any radio traffic from zero-eight-zero?"

The petty officer in the forward starboard corner of the compartment didn't look up. "No, Captain, not a peep."

"Damn," Morris said. "It works."

"And if the bugger didn't get a message out—" Calloway understood.

"We're the only ones who know. Maybe we can bushwhack the whole attack force." Morris stepped over to the display screen. The *America*'s fighters were now all in the air, seventy miles south of the convoy. He looked at the bulkhead clock: the Backfires were about forty minutes away. He lifted a phone. "Bridge, Combat. Signal *Battleaxe* to close in."

Within seconds, *Battleaxe* turned hard a'port and headed west toward *Reuben James*. One new thing had already worked today, Morris thought. Why not another?

"Stand by to launch helo," he ordered.

O'Malley was sitting in his cockpit reading a magazine, or at least letting his eyes scan the pictures while his mind struggled to detach itself from what was going on around him. The announcement over the loudspeaker tore him away from Miss July. Immediately, Ensign Ralston began the engine start sequence while O'Malley scanned the trouble board for any mechanical problems, then looked out the door to be sure that the deck crewmen were clear.

"What are we supposed to be doing, Commander?" the systems operator inquired.

"We're supposed to be missile bait, Willy," O'Malley replied amiably, and lifted off.

NORTH ATLANTIC

The southernmost Bear was within sixty miles of the convoy, but didn't yet know it, nor did the Americans, since he was below the horizon from *Reuben James*'s radar. The Bear's pilot did know that it was about time for the aircraft to climb and switch on their own search radars. But word hadn't come yet from the raid commander. Though there was no indication of trouble, the pilot was worried. His instinct told him something strange was happening. One of the Bears that had disappeared last week reported tracking a single American frigate radar—nothing more. *Just like now* . . . The raid commander then had aborted the Backfire mission for fear of enemy fighter activity, only to be dressed down for supposed cowardice. As was so often the case in combat, the only data available were negative. They knew that four Bears had *not* returned. He knew that his raid commander had *not* yet given the expected order. He knew there had *not* been any positive sign of trouble. He also knew that he was *not* happy.

"Estimated distance to that American frigate?" he asked over his intercom.

"One hundred thirty kilometers," the navigator answered.

Maintain radio silence, the pilot told himself. *Those are the orders* . . .

"Screw the orders!" he said aloud. The pilot reached down and flipped on his radio. "Gull Two to Gull One, over." Nothing. He repeated the call twice more.

Lots of radio receivers heard that, and in less than a minute the Bear's position was plotted, forty miles southeast of the convoy. A Tomcat dove after the contact.

The raid commander didn't answer . . . he would have answered, the pilot told himself. He would have answered. The Backfires should now be less than two hundred kilometers away. *What are we leading them into?*

"Activate the radar!" he ordered.

Every screen ship detected the distinctive emissions from the Big Bulge radar. The nearest SAM-equipped ship, the frigate *Groves*, immediately energized her missile radars and fired a surface-to-air missile at the oncoming Bear—but the Tomcat fighter that was also racing toward the Bear was too close. The frigate shut down her tracking radar, and the SM1 missile lost radar lock and self-destructed automatically.

Aboard the Bear the warnings came back to back, first surface-to-air missile alarm, then an air-intercept radar—and then the radar operator acquired the convoy.

"Many ships to the northwest." The radar operator passed the information to the navigator, who worked out a position report for the Backfires. The Bear shut down her radar and dove while the communications officer broadcast his sighting report. And then everyone's radars lit up.

USS *REUBEN JAMES*

"There are the Backfires," the tactical action officer said as the symbols appeared on the scope. "Bearing zero-four-one, range one hundred eighty miles."

On the bridge the executive officer was as nervous as he would ever get. In addition to the inbound bomber raid, he was now conning his ship exactly fifty feet from the side of HMS *Battleaxe*. The ships were so close together that on a radarscope they'd appear as a single target. Five miles away, O'Malley and the helicopter from *Battleaxe* were also flying close formation over the ocean at twenty knots. Each had its blip-enhance transponder turned on. Ordinarily too small to register on this sort of radar, the helicopters would now appear to be a ship, something worthy of a missile attack.

NORTH ATLANTIC

The air action now had all the elegance of a saloon fight. The Tomcats on combat air patrol near the convoy flew toward the three Bears, the first of which already had a missile streaking toward it. The other two had not yet detected the convoy, and never would, as they ran due east to get away. It was a vain attempt. Propeller-driven patrol bombers cannot run from supersonic fighters.

Gull Two died first. The pilot managed to get his contact report out and acknowledged before a pair of Sparrow missiles exploded close aboard, setting his wing afire. He ordered his men to bail out, kept the aircraft level so they could, and a minute later struggled out of his seat and jumped through the escape hatch in the floor. The Bear exploded five seconds after he opened his parachute. As the pilot watched his aircraft fireball into the sea, he wondered if he'd drown.

Above him a squadron of Tomcats headed toward the Backfires, and the race was to see who got into missile-firing position first. The Soviet bombers climbed steeply on afterburner, activating their own look-down radars to find targets for their missiles. Their orders were to locate and kill escorts, and they found what they were looking for thirty miles from the body of the convoy: two blips. The large blip in the rear drew six shots. The smaller one five miles away drew four.

STORNOWAY, SCOTLAND

"We have a multiregiment Backfire raid in progress now at forty-five degrees north, forty-nine west." Toland held the Red Rocket telex in his hand.

"What does COMEASTLANT have to say about it?"

"He's probably going over this one now. You ready?" he asked the fighter pilot.

"Damned right I'm ready!"

The teleprinter in the corner of the room started chattering: INITIATE OPERATION DOOLITTLE

USS *REUBEN JAMES*

"Vampire, vampire! We have incoming missiles."

Here we go again, Morris thought. The tactical display was more modern than what he'd had on *Pharris*—each of the incoming missiles was marked with a velocity vector that indicated speed and direction. They were coming in low.

Morris lifted his phone. "Bridge, Combat. Execute separation maneuver."

"Bridge, aye. *Separating now,*" Ernst said. "Crash stop! All back emergency!"

The helmsman pulled the throttle control back, then abruptly reversed the pitch of the propeller blades, throwing the ship from ahead to full astern. *Reuben James* slowed so rapidly that men had to brace themselves, and *Battleaxe* forged ahead, accelerating to twenty-five knots. As soon as it was safe, the British frigate turned hard to port, and *Reuben James* went to ahead full and turned sharply to starboard.

Any Soviet radar operator who had lingered behind would have been impressed by the deception. The oncoming AS-4 missiles had been targeted on a single blip. Now there were two, and they were separating. The missiles divided their attention evenly, with three opting for either target.

Morris watched his display intently. The distance between his ship and his companion was widening rapidly.

"Missiles are tracking us!" the ESM operator said loudly. "We have multiple missile seeker heads tracking us."

"Right full rudder, reverse course. Fire off chaff rockets!"

Everyone in the Combat Information Center jumped as four canisters exploded directly overhead, filling the air with aluminum foil and creating a radar target for the missiles to track while the frigate heeled violently to port as she turned. Her forward missile launcher turned around with her, a SAM already assigned to the first incoming Russian missile. The frigate righted herself on a northerly course, three miles behind *Battleaxe*.

"Here we go," the weapons officer said. The solution light blinked on the fire-control console.

The first of the white-painted SM1 missiles shot into the sky. It had scarcely cleared the launch rail when the launcher twisted in two dimensions and accepted another missile from the circular magazine, then turned and elevated again, firing seven seconds after the first missile was launched, then repeated the cycle twice more.

"That's it!" O'Malley said when he saw the first smoke trail. He punched his finger on the blip-enhance button. "Hatchet, shut down your emitter and break left!" Both helicopters went to full power and ran away. Four missiles suddenly had no targets. They kept heading west to look for more, but there were none to be found.

"More chaff," Morris ordered, watching the electronic traces of friendly and unfriendly missiles converge. The CIC shook again as another cloud of aluminum blasted into the air, and the wind carried it toward the incoming missiles.

"We still have missiles tracking us!"

"Hit!" the weapons officer exclaimed. The first missile disappeared from the scope, intercepted sixteen miles out, but the second Soviet missile kept coming. The first SAM sent after it missed, exploding harmlessly behind it, and then the second one missed, too. Another SAM was fired. Range was down to six miles. Five. Four. Three.

"Hit! One missile left—veering off. Going after the chaff! Passing aft!"

The missile struck the water two thousand yards from *Reuben James*. Even at that distance the noise was impressive. It was followed by total silence in the CIC. Men kept staring at their instruments, looking for additional missiles, and it took several seconds before they were satisfied that there were no more. One by one the sailors looked at their comrades and began to breathe again.

"What modern combat lacks in humanity," Calloway observed, "it more than makes up for in intensity."

Morris leaned back in his chair. "Or something like that. What's the story on *Battleaxe*?"

"Still on radar, sir," the tactical action officer replied. Morris lifted the radiotelephone.

"Bravo, this is Romeo. Do you read, over."

"I do believe we're still alive." Perrin was examining his tactical display and shaking his head in amazement.

"Any damage?"

"None. Hatchet is checking in. He's all right, too. Remarkable," Captain Perrin said. "Any further inbound traffic? We show none."

"Negative. The Tomcats chased the Backfires off the scope. Let's get reformed."

"Roger, Romeo."

Morris hung up and looked around the CIC. "Well done, people."

The sailors in the room looked at each other, and presently some grins started showing. But they didn't last long.

The TAO looked up. "For your information, Captain, Ivan fired a quarter of his missiles at us. So far as I can tell, the Tomcats got about six, and *Bunker Hill* got most of the rest . . . but we show one frigate hit, and three merchies. The fighters are returning." He kept his voice neutral. "They report zero kills on the Backfire force."

"Damn!" Morris said. The trap had failed—and he didn't know why.

He had no idea that Stornoway considered it a success.

STORNOWAY, SCOTLAND

The key to the operation, as with all military operations, was communications, and not enough time had been spent setting the lines up on this one to suit Toland. The *America*'s radar aircraft tracked the Backfires all the way off the scope. The data from the aircraft was linked to the carrier, thence by satellite to Norfolk, and by satellite again to Northwood. His data came by land line from Royal Navy headquarters. The most important NATO mission of the war depended on transistors and telephone wire more than the weapons that were to be employed.

"Okay, their last course was zero-two-nine, speed six hundred ten knots."

"That puts them over Iceland's north coast in two hours, seventeen minutes. How much time did they have on burner?" Commander Winters asked.

"About five, according to *America*." Toland frowned. This was pretty thin intelligence information.

"Any way you cut it, their fuel reserves are thinned down some . . . Okay. Three aircraft, eighty miles apart." He looked over at the newest satellite weather photo. "Good visibility. We'll spot 'em. Whoever does, follows—the other planes come right back home."

"Good luck, Commander."

NORTH ATLANTIC

The three Tomcats climbed slowly to altitude on a course northwest from Stornoway, and at thirty-five thousand feet linked up with their tankers. Several hundred miles away the Backfire crews did much the same thing. The presence of American fighters over the convoy in large numbers had come as a rude shock, but time and distance had been in their favor, and they'd managed to escape without loss this time. The crew of each aircraft talked among themselves, their emotions released by the climax of yet another dangerous mission. They discussed the claims they'd make on returning to Kirovsk, based on a straightforward mathematical formula. One missile in three was judged to have hit a target, even accounting for enemy SAM fire. Today SAM opposition had been light—though none had lingered to evaluate it properly. By consensus they would claim sixteen ship kills, and claim both the outside sonar pickets that their comrades in submarines were having such a bad time with. The flight crews relaxed and sipped tea from thermos jugs as they contemplated their next visit to the eighty-ship convoy.

The Tomcats separated as they spotted the mountains of Iceland. No radio signals were passed; the flyers exchanged hand signals before breaking off on their patrol stations. They knew the radars couldn't reach them there. Commander Winters checked his watch. The Backfires should be here in about thirty minutes.

"Such a beautiful island," the Backfire pilot observed to his copilot.

"Pretty to look at, living there I am not so certain about. I wonder if the women are as pretty as I have heard? One day we must have 'mechanical difficulties.' Then we could land there and find out."

"We must get you married, Volodya."

The copilot laughed. "So many tears would be shed! How can I deny myself to the women of the world?"

The pilot punched up his radio. "Keflavik, this is Sea Eagle Two-Six, status check."

"Sea Eagle, we show no contacts except for your group. Count is correct. IFF transponders show normal."

"Acknowledged. Out." The pilot switched off. "So, Volodya, our friends are still there. Lonely place."

"If there are women about, and you are *kulturny,* you need never be lonely." Another voice came over the intercom.

"Will somebody shut that horny bastard up!" the navigator suggested.

"Studying to be a political officer?" the copilot inquired. "How long to home?"

"Two hours twenty-five minutes."

The Backfire continued northeast at six hundred knots as it passed over the desolate center of the island.

"Tallyho!" the pilot said quietly. "One o'clock and low." The Tomcat's on-board television system showed the distinctive shape of the Russian bomber. *Say what you want about the Russians,* Winters thought, *they do build 'em pretty.*

He turned the aircraft, which took his nose-mounted camera off the target, but his back-seat officer put his binoculars on the Backfire and soon spotted two more flying in a loose formation. As expected, their course was northeast, and they were cruising at about thirty thousand feet. Winters looked for a big cloud to hide in and found one. Visibility dropped to a few yards. *There could be another Backfire out there,* Winters thought, *and maybe he likes flying in clouds, too. That could really ruin this mission.*

He ran out of cloud a moment later, banked his fighter hard, and ducked back inside, his mind computing time and distance. *The Backfires should all be past now.* He pulled back on his stick and popped out of the cloud top.

"There they be," the back-seater said first. "Heads up! I see more of 'em at three o'clock."

The pilot vanished back into the cloud for another ten minutes. Finally: "Nothing to the south of us. They should all be past by now, don't you think?"

"Yeah, let's go looking."

One terrifying minute later, Winters was wondering if he hadn't let them get too far ahead, as his TV system swept across the sky and found nothing. *Patience,* he told himself, and increased his speed to six hundred ninety knots. Five minutes later, a dot appeared on his screen. It grew to three dots. He estimated he was forty miles behind the Backfires, and with the sun at his back, there was no way they could spot him. His back-seater made a check of the radar warning receiver and the air behind them for additional aircraft, a procedure repeated three times a minute. If an American fighter could be out here, why not a Russian?

The pilot watched the numbers click off on his inertial navigation system, kept an eye on fuel, and watched forward for any change in the Russian bomber formation. It was both exciting and boring. He knew the significance of what he was doing, but the actual *doing* was no more thrilling than driving a 747 from New York to L.A. For over an hour they flew, covering the seven hundred miles between Iceland and the Norwegian coast.

"Here's where it gets cute," the back-seater said. "Air-search radar ahead, looks like Andøya. Still over a hundred miles away, they'll probably have us in two or three minutes."

"That's nice." Where there was air-search radar, there would be fighters. "Got their position worked out?"

"Yep."

"Start transmitting." Winters turned the aircraft and headed back out to sea.

Two hundred miles away, a circling British Nimrod receipted the signal and retransmitted to a communications satellite.

NORTHWOOD, ENGLAND

Admiral Beattie was trying to remain calm, but it didn't come easily to a man whose nerves had been stretched and abused by crisis after crisis since the war began. Doolittle was his baby. For the past two hours, he'd waited for word from the Tomcat. Two had returned without sighting the Russians. One had not. Was it tracking them as planned or had it merely fallen into the sea?

The printer in the corner of the communications room began to make the screeing sound that the Admiral had learned to hate: EYEBALLS REPORTS HARES AT 6920N 1545E AT 1543Z COURSE 021 SPEED 580 KTS ALT 30

Beattie tore the page off and handed it to his air-operations officer. "That puts them on the ground in thirty-seven minutes. Assuming it's the last group, and a fifteen-minute spread, the first bombers will be landing in twenty-two minutes."

"Fifteen minutes from now, then?"

"Yes, Admiral."

"Get the order out!"

In thirty seconds half a dozen separate satellite channels began transmitting the same message.

USS *CHICAGO*

The three American submarines had lain on the bottom of the Barents Sea near the Russian coastline—so near, it was only one hundred seventy-four feet of water—for what seemed like half a lifetime, before finally receiving the signal to move south. McCafferty smiled with relief. The three British submarines, including HMS *Torbay,* had already done their job. They had sneaked up on a Russian frigate and four patrol boats patrolling the Russian/Norwegian coastline and attacked with torpedoes. The Russians could only assume a major effort was under way to penetrate their patrol barrier, and had sent their antisub patrol force west to meet it.

Leaving the way clear for *Chicago* and her mates. He hoped.

As they closed in, his electronics technicians plotted and replotted their bearings. They had to be in exactly the right place when they fired their missiles.

"How long before we shoot?" the XO asked.

"They'll let us know," McCafferty said.

And then, with the chatter of the message from Northwood, they did know.

They would launch at 1602 Zulu Time.

"Up scope." McCafferty spun the instrument around. A rainstorm overhead drove four-foot waves.

"Looks clear to me," the XO said, watching the TV display.

The captain slapped the handles up on the scope. It headed down into its well. "ESM?"

"Lots of radar stuff, Cap'n," the technician replied. "I show ten different transmitters in operation."

McCafferty inspected the Tomahawk weapons status board on the starboard side of the attack center. His torpedo tubes were loaded with two Mark-48s and two Harpoon missiles. The clock ticked away toward 1602.

"Commence launch sequence."

Toggle switches were thrown, and the weapons status lights blinked red; the captain and the weapons officer inserted their keys in the panel, and turned them; the petty officer on the weapons board turned the firing handle to the left—and the arming process was complete. Forward, in the bow of the submarine, the guidance systems of twelve Tomahawk cruise missiles were fully activated. On-board computers were told where their flight would begin. They already knew where it was supposed to end.

"Initiate launch," McCafferty ordered.

Ametist was not part of the regular Soviet Navy. Principally concerned with security operations, this Grisha-class patrol frigate was manned by a KGB crew, and her captain had spent the last twelve hours sprinting and drifting, dipping his helicopter-type sonar and listening in the American fashion rather than the Russian. With her diesel engines shut down, she made no noise at all, and her short profile was hard to spot from more than a mile away. She had not heard the American submarines approach.

The first Tomahawk broke the surface of the Barents Sea at 16:01:58, two thousand yards from the Russian frigate. The lookout took a second or two to react. As he saw the cylindrical shape rise on its solid-rocket booster and arc southwest, an icy lead ball materialized in his stomach.

"Captain! Missile launch to starboard!"

The captain raced out onto the bridge wing and looked on in amazement as a second missile broke the surface, then he leaped back into the pilothouse.

"Battle stations! Radio room, call Fleet HQ, tell them enemy missiles launching from grid square 451 / 679 - now! All ahead full! Rudder right!"

The frigate's diesel engines roared into life.

"What in hell is that?" the sonar chief asked. His submarine shuddered every four seconds with the missile launches, but— "Conn, sonar, we have a contact bearing zero-nine-eight. Diesel—surface ship, sounds like a Grisha, and he's close, sir!"

"Up scope!" McCafferty whirled the periscope around and snapped the handle to full power. He saw the Russian frigate turning hard. "Snap shot! Set it up! Surface target bearing zero-nine-seven, range"—he worked the stademeter control—"one six hundred, course, shit! he's turning away. Call it zero-nine-zero, speed twenty." Too close for a missile shot, they had to engage with torpedoes. "Down scope!"

The fire-control man tapped the numbers into the computer. The computer needed eleven seconds to digest the information. *"Set!* Ready for tubes one and three."

"Flooding tubes, outer doors open—ready!" the XO said.

"Match generated bearings and *shoot!"*

"Fire one, fire three." The executive officer struggled with his emotions and won. Where had that Grisha come from? "Reload with 48s!"

"Last bird away!" the missile technician announced. "Securing from launch."

"Left full rudder!"

Ametist never saw the missiles launching behind her. The men were too busy racing to stations, while her captain rang up full power and the ship's weapons officer ran up in his shorts to work the rocket launchers. They didn't need sonar for this; they could see all too well where the submarine was—firing missiles at the *Motherland!*

"Fire when ready!" the captain yelled.

The lieutenant's thumb came down on the firing key. Twelve antisubmarine rockets arched through the air.

"Ametist," the radio squawked. "Repeat your message—what missiles? What *kind* of missiles!"

USS *Providence* discharged her last missile just as the frigate fired at her. The captain ordered flank speed and a radical turn even as the rockets tipped over and began to fall toward his submarine. They fell in a wide circular pattern designed to cover the maximum possible area, two exploding within one hundred yards, close enough to startle but not to damage. The last one hit the water directly over the submarine's sail. A second later, the forty-six-pound warhead exploded.

Ametist's captain ignored the radio while he tried to decide if his first salvo had hit the target or not. The last rocket had exploded faster than the others. He was about to give the order to fire again when the sonar officer reported two objects approaching from aft, and he shouted rudder orders. The ship was already at full speed as the radio speaker continued to scream at him.

"Both fish have acquired the target!"

"Up scope!" McCafferty let it go all the way up before pulling the handles down. At full magnification the Grisha nearly filled the lens, and then both fish hit her port side and the thousand-ton patrol frigate disintegrated before his eyes. He turned completely around, sweeping the horizon to check for additional enemy ships. "Okay, it's clear."

"That won't last very long. He was shooting at *Providence,* sir."

"Sonar, what do you have on zero-nine-zero?" McCafferty asked.

"Lotsa noise from the fish, sir, but I think we have blowing air at zero-nine-eight."

"Get us over there." McCafferty kept the periscope up as the XO conned the sub toward *Providence.* The Grisha was well and truly destroyed. Together the torpedoes carried nearly fifteen hundred pounds of high explosives. He saw two life rafts that had inflated automatically on hitting the water, but no men.

"*Boston* is calling on the gertrude, skipper. They want to know what the hell happened."

"Tell 'em." The captain adjusted the periscope slightly. "Okay, there she is, she's surfacing—holy shit!"

The submarine's sail was wrecked, the after third of it completely gone, and the rest shredded. One diving plane hung down like the wing of a crippled bird, and the periscopes and masts housed in the structure were bent into the shape of a modernistic sculpture.

"Try to raise *Providence* on the gertrude."

Sixty Tomahawk missiles were now in the air. On leaving the water, solid-fuel rockets had boosted them to an altitude of one thousand feet, where their wings and jet-engine air inlets had deployed. As soon as their jet engines had begun to function, the Tomahawks began a shallow descent that ended thirty feet above the ground. On-board radar systems scanned ahead to keep the missiles close to the ground, and to match the terrain with map coordinates stored in their computer memories. Six separate Soviet radars detected the missiles' boost phase, then lost them as they went low.

The Russian technicians whose job it was to watch for a possible nuclear attack against their homeland were every bit as tense as their Western counterparts, and the weeks of sustained conventional conflict, coupled with continuous maximum-alert status, had frayed nerves to the breaking point. As soon as the Tomahawks had been detected rising from the sea, a ballistic-missile attack warning had flashed to Moscow. *Ametist*'s visual missile warning arrived at naval headquarters in Severomorsk almost as fast, and a THUNDERBOLT alert sent immediately, the code-word prefix guaranteeing instant passage to the Ministry of Defense. Launch authority for the antiballistic missiles deployed around Moscow was automatically released to the battery commanders, and though it was several minutes before radar officers were able to confirm to Moscow's satisfaction that the missiles had dropped off their scopes and were not on ballistic trajectories, defense units stayed on alert, and all over northern Russia air-defense interceptors scrambled.

The missiles could not have cared about the furor they had caused. At this point, the Russian coast was composed of rocky bluffs and cliffs that gave way to tundra, the flat marsh of northern climes. It was ideal terrain for the cruise missiles, which settled down to a flight path scant feet over the grassy swamps at a speed of five hundred knots. Each flew over Lake Babozero, their first navigational reference point, and there their flight paths diverged.

The Soviet fighters now lifting off the ground had little idea what they were after. Radar information gave the course and speed of the targets, but if they were cruise missiles, they could reach as far as the Black Sea coast. They could even be targeted on Moscow and be flying a deceptive course far off the direct path to the Soviet capital. On orders from their ground controllers, the interceptors arrayed themselves south of the White Sea, and switched on their look-down radars to see if they could spot the missiles crossing the flat surface.

But they weren't going to Moscow. Dodging between the occasional hills, the missiles flew on a bearing of two-one-three until they reached the scrub pine forest. One by one they banked hard to the right and changed course to two-nine-zero. One missile went out of control and fell to the earth, another failed to make the turn and went south. The rest continued to their targets.

SEA EAGLE TWO-SIX

The last Backfire bomber circled Umbozero-South, waiting to land. The pilot checked his fuel. About thirty minutes left, there was not that much of a hurry. For security reasons the three regiments were divided among four airfields clustered south of the mining city of Kirovsk. The tall hills around the town held powerful radars and mobile SAM batteries to stave off a NATO air attack. Most of the smelters were still operating, the pilot saw, the smoke rising from the many tall chimneys.

"Sea Eagle Two-Six, you are cleared to land," the tower said finally.

"Who will it be tonight, Volodya?"

"Twenty degrees of flaps. Air speed two hundred. Landing gear is down and locked. Irina Petrovna, I think. The tall, skinny one at the telephone exchange."

"What's that?" the pilot asked. A small white object suddenly appeared over the runway in front of him.

The first of twelve Tomahawk missiles assigned to Umbozero-South cut across the runway at a shallow angle, then the blunt nose cover sprang off the airframe, and several hundred small bomblets began to sprinkle over the area. Seventeen Backfires were already on the ground. Ten were being refueled from trucks in the open, the others were armed and ready for another mission, dispersed in concrete revetments. Each bomblet was the equivalent of a mortar shell. The Tomahawk dropped its complete load, then climbed straight up, stalled, and crashed back to earth, adding its own fuel load to the destruction. A ready-force Backfire went first. Two bomblets fell on its wing and the bomber fireballed into the sky.

The pilot of Two-Six advanced his throttles and climbed out of the landing pattern, watching in horror as ten bombers exploded before his eyes and telltale puffs of smoke told him of less serious damage to many others. In two minutes, it was over. Crash trucks raced like toys along the concrete as men played fire hoses on the burning trucks and aircraft. The pilot headed north for his alternate field and saw smoke rising there also.

"Fifteen minutes' fuel. You'd better find us a place fast," Volodya warned. They turned left for Kirovsk-South and the same story was repeated. The attack had been timed for the missiles to hit all four targets simultaneously.

"Afrikanda, this is Sea Eagle Two-Six. We are low on fuel and need to land immediately. Can you take us?"

"Affirmative, Two-Six. Runway is clear. Wind is two-six-five at twenty."

"Very well, we're coming in. Out." The pilot turned. "What the hell was that?" he asked Volodya.

USS CHICAGO

"Communications is gone, fire-control is gone, fairwater planes gone. We stopped the leaks. Engines are okay, we can steam," the skipper of USS Providence said over the gertrude.

"Very well. Stand by." *Boston* was also alongside. "Todd, this is Danny. What do you think?"

"She won't make it out alone. I suggest we send the rest back out. You and me escort her."

"Agreed. You follow 'em out. We'll try to clear datum as quick as we can."

"Good luck, Danny." *Boston* raised her radio whip and made a quick transmission. A minute later *Chicago*'s sonar showed the noise of the other submarines racing north.

"*Providence*, recommend you come to course zero-one-five and go as fast as you can. We'll cover your tail. *Boston* will rendezvous later and we'll both escort you to the pack."

"You can't risk it, we can—"

"Move your fucking boat!" McCafferty shouted into the microphone. He was exactly three months senior in rank to his counterpart on *Providence*. Presently the wounded submarine dived and headed northeast at fifteen knots. Her damaged sail structure sounded like a junk wagon in the waterflow, but there was nothing they could do about it. If the submarines were to have any chance of survival, they had to put as much distance between themselves and the firing point as they could.

MOSCOW, R.S.F.S.R.

Mikhail Sergetov looked around at a group of men still pale at what might have been.

"Comrade Defense Minister," the General Secretary said. "Can you tell us what has happened?"

"It would seem that submarines launched a number of cruise missiles at some of our northern airfields. Their aim was evidently to destroy a number of our Backfire bombers. How successful they were I do not yet know."

"Where did they launch their missiles from?" Pyotr Bromkovskiy asked.

"East of Murmansk, less than thirty kilometers from our coast. A frigate saw and reported the launch, then went off the air. We have aircraft searching for him now."

"*How the hell did he get there!* If that submarine had launched ballistic missiles at us," Bromkovskiy demanded, "how much warning would we have had?"

"Six to seven minutes."

"Wonderful! We cannot react that fast. How can you let them get so close!"

"They won't get out, Petya, I promise you that!" the Defense Minister replied heatedly.

The General Secretary leaned forward. "You will see to it that this can never happen again!"

"While we are all here, Comrades," Sergetov spoke up. "Can the Comrade Defense Minister review overnight developments on the German Front?"

"NATO forces are strained to the breaking point. As the KGB has told us, their supplies are critically low, and with the diplomatic developments of the past few days, I think we may safely assume that NATO is on the verge of political disintegration. All we have to do is keep the pressure on, and they must collapse!"

"But we are running out of fuel also!" Bromkovskiy said. "The offer the Germans have given us is a reasonable one."

"No." The Foreign Minister shook his head emphatically. "This gives us nothing."

"It gives us peace, Comrade," Bromkovskiy said quietly. "If we continue—consider, my friends, consider what we were all thinking a few hours ago when the rocket warning came in."

For the first time, Sergetov realized, the old man had made a point they all agreed with. After weeks and months of promises and plans and assurances on how things could be kept under control, that one false alarm had forced them to look at what lay over the edge of the abyss. For ten minutes they feared that control had been lost, and all the Defense Minister's bluster could not make them forget that.

After a moment of consideration, the General Secretary spoke. "Our representatives are meeting with the Germans in a few hours. The Foreign Minister will report to us tomorrow on the substance of their new offer."

On that note the session ended. Sergetov tucked his notes in his leather briefcase, left the room alone, and walked downstairs to his official car. A junior aide held the door open when a voice called.

"Mikhail Eduardovich, may I ride with you? My car has broken down." It was Boris Kosov, chairman of the Committee for State Security, the KGB.

36. Shoot-out at 31 West!

MOSCOW, R.S.F.S.R.

"Shall we take a drive today, Mikhail Eduardovich? Perhaps we can talk?" Sergetov's blood chilled, though he did not let it show. Was it possible for the Chief of the KGB *not* to look sinister? he wondered. From Leningrad, like Sergetov, Kosov was a short, rotund man who had taken over the KGB after running the Central Committee's shadowy "General Department." He had a jolly laugh when he wanted to, and in another guise could be the personification of Grandfather Frost, the State's acceptable version of Santa Claus. But he was not in another guise now.

"Certainly, Boris Georgiyevich," Sergetov said, and pointed at his driver. "You may speak freely. Vitaly is a good man."

"I know it," Kosov replied. "He's worked for us the last ten years." Sergetov only had to watch the back of his driver's neck to know that Kosov spoke the truth.

"So what shall we talk about?"

The Director of the KGB reached into his briefcase and came out with a device about the size of a paperback book. He flipped a switch and it gave off an unpleasant buzz.

"A clever new device made in the Netherlands," he explained. "It gives off a noise that renders most microphones useless. Something to do with harmonics, my people tell me." Then his manner changed abruptly.

"Mikhail Eduardovich, do you know the significance of the American attack on our airfields?"

"A troublesome development to be sure, but—"

"I thought not. Several NATO convoys are at sea. A major one left New York several days ago. It carries two million tons of essential war materiel, plus a complete American division, to Europe. In destroying a number of our bombers, NATO has significantly reduced our ability to deal with the convoys. They have also cleared the way for direct attacks against Soviet soil."

"But Iceland—"

"Has been neutralized." Kosov explained what had happened to the Soviet fighters at Keflavik.

"You're telling me the war goes badly? Then why is Germany making overtures for peace?"

"Yes, that is a very good question."

"If you have suspicions, Comrade Director, you should not bring them to me!"

"I will tell you a story. Back in January when I had my bypass surgery, day-to-day control of KGB passed to the First Deputy Chairman, Josef Larionov. Have you met little Josef?" Kosov asked.

"No, he never took your place at Politburo meetings—what about the Defense Council?" Sergetov's head snapped around. "They did not consult you? You were recovering then."

"An exaggeration. I was quite ill for two weeks, but naturally this information was kept quiet. It took another month before I was back working full time. The members of the Defense Council had no wish to impede my recovery, and so young, ambitious Josef was called in to give KGB's official intelligence assessment. As you might imagine, we have many schools of thought in the intelligence services—it is not like your precious engineering where all things are broken into neat little numbers and graphs. We have to look inside the heads of men who often as not do not themselves know what they think on an issue. Sometimes I wonder why we do not employ gypsy fortune-tellers . . . but I digress.

"KGB maintains what we call the Strategic Intelligence Estimate. This is a document updated on a daily basis which gives our assessment of the political and military strength of our adversaries. Because of the nature of our work, and because of serious mistakes made in the past, we have three assessment teams who make the estimate: Best Case, Worst Case, and Middle Case. The terms are self-explanatory, are they not? When we make a presentation to the Politburo, we generally use the Middle Case estimate, and for the obvious reasons we annotate our estimates with data from the other two."

"So when he was called in to give his assessment to the Politburo—"

"Yes. Young Josef, the ambitious little bastard who wants my job as a wolf wants a sheep, was clever enough to bring all three with him. When he saw what they wanted, he gave them what they wanted."

"But when you returned, why didn't you correct the mistake?"

Kosov gave his companion an ironic smile. "Misha, Misha, sometimes you can be most engagingly naive. I *should* have killed the son of a bitch, but this was not possible. Josef suffers from poor health, though he is not aware of it. The time is not yet right," Kosov said, as though discussing a vacation. "KGB is split into several factions at the moment. Josef controls one. I control another. Mine is larger, but not decisively so. He has the ear of the General Secretary and the Defense Minister. I am a sick old man—they have told me this. Except for the war I would have been replaced already."

"But he lied to the Politburo!" Sergetov nearly shouted.

"Not at all. You think Josef is foolish? He handed over an official KGB intelligence estimate drawn up under my chairmanship, by my department heads."

Why is he telling me all this? He fears losing his post, and he wants support with other Politburo members. Is that all?

"You're telling me that this is all a mistake."

"Exactly," Kosov answered. "Bad luck and poor judgment in our oil industry—not *your* fault, of course. Add some fear in the hearts of our Party hierarchy, some ambition in one of my subordinates, the Defense Minister's sense of importance, and outright stupidity on the part of the West; and here we are today."

"So, what do you think we should do?" Sergetov asked warily.

"Nothing. I ask that you keep in mind, however, that the next week will probably decide the outcome of our war. Ah!" he exclaimed. "Look, my car has been repaired. You may pull over here, Vitaly. Thank you for the ride, Misha. Good day." Kosov retrieved his jamming device and stepped out of the car.

Mikhail Eduardovich Sergetov watched the KGB limousine pull away and disappear around the corner. He had played many power games in his life. Sergetov's climb up the Party ladder had been more than an exercise in efficiency. Men had stood in his way, and needed brushing aside. Promising careers had been broken so that he could sit in this Zil automobile and aspire to real power in his country. But never had the game been this dangerous. He didn't know the rules, was not sure what Kosov was really up to. Was his story even true? Might he be trying to cover his own flanks for errors he had made and blame it all on Josef Larionov? Sergetov could not recall ever meeting the First Deputy Chairman.

"Straight to the office, Vitaly," Sergetov ordered. He was too deep in thought to worry about his driver's other activities.

NORTHWOOD, ENGLAND

Toland scanned the satellite photographs with great interest. The KH-11 satellite had passed over Kirovsk four hours after the missile attack and the signals sent by real-time link to the NATO command center. There were three frames for each of the Backfire bases. The intelligence officer took out a pad and started his tally, commanding himself to be conservative. The only aircraft he counted as destroyed were those with large pieces broken or burned off.

"We figured a total force of about eighty-five aircraft. Looks to me like twenty-one totally destroyed, and another thirty or so damaged. The base facilities took a real beating. The only other thing I'd like to know is how hard their personnel were hit. If we killed a lot of crews, too—the Backfires are out of business for at least a week. They still have the Badgers, but those birds have shorter legs, they're a lot easier to kill. Admiral, it's a new ball game."

Admiral Sir Charles Beattie smiled. His intelligence chief had said almost exactly the same thing.

LANGLEY AIR FORCE BASE, VIRGINIA

The F-15 interceptor streaked over the runway at a height of one hundred feet. As she passed the tower, Major Nakamura threw her fighter into a slow roll, then turned around for a more sedate landing. She was an Ace! Three Badger bombers and two satellites! The first female Ace in the history of the U.S. Air Force. The first Space Ace.

She rolled to a stop at the ready shelter, jumped off the ladder, and ran to the reception committee. The deputy commander of Tactical Air Command was red-faced with anger.

"Major, if you ever pull something like that again I'll bust your ass back to doolie!"

"Yes, sir. Sorry, sir." She grinned. Nothing was going to spoil today. "Won't ever happen again, sir. You only make Ace once, sir."

"Intelligence says Ivan has one more RORSAT ready to use. Probably they'll think it over some before launching," the General said, calming down somewhat.

"Have they put any more birds together?" Buns asked.

"They're working on two, and we might have them by the end of the week. If we get them, your next target will be their real-time photo reconnaissance satellite. Until then the RORSATs have highest priority." The General smiled briefly. "Don't forget to paint that fifth star on the bird, Major."

NORFOLK, VIRGINIA

They would have sailed anyway. The destruction of the Soviet RORSAT merely made it safer. First came the destroyers and frigates, fanning out, looking for submarines under an umbrella of patrol aircraft. Then the cruisers and carriers. Last of all came the ships from Little Creek, *Tarawa, Guam, Nassau, Inchon,* and twenty more. Over sixty ships in all, they formed into three groups and steamed northeast at twenty knots. It would be a six-day trip.

USNS *PREVAIL*

Even at three knots she didn't ride well. The ship was just over two hundred feet long, and she responded to every wave like a horse to a fence. She had a mixed crew, not really Navy, not really civilian. The civilians ran the ship. The naval personnel ran the electronics gear. The really amazing thing, everyone agreed, was that they were still alive.

Prevail was an adaptation of a blue-water fishing boat. Instead of a trawl, she pulled a sonar array at the end of a six-thousand-foot cable filled with sonar sensors. The signals received were pre-processed by on-board computers, then sent via satellite to Norfolk at a rate of thirty-two thousand bits of data per second. The ship was driven by quiet electric motors, and her hull had been installed with the Prairie/Masker system to eliminate even her tiny amount of machinery noise. Her topsides were made of fiberglass to reduce her radar signature. In a very real sense she was one of the first Stealth ships, and despite the fact that she carried no weapon other than a rifle for dealing with sharks, she was also the most dangerous antisubmarine platform ever made. *Prevail* and three sister ships were cruising the North Atlantic on the great circle route between Newfoundland and Ireland, listening for the telltale noise of a submarine in transit. Two already had kills painted up on their bridges since each had an Orion patrol aircraft in constant attendance, and Soviet submarines had twice had the misfortune to approach one of them. But their job was not to kill submarines. It was to warn others of them, far away.

In the midships operations center of *Prevail,* a team of oceanographic technicians watched a bank of TV-type display tubes, while others worked up tracks of anything that might be close enough to be a direct threat.

A petty officer ran his finger down a fuzzy line on the display. "That must be the convoy from New York."

"Yeah," said the technician next to him. "And there're the folks who want to meet them."

USS *REUBEN JAMES*

"At least we're not going to be lonely," O'Malley observed.

"You always have such a positive attitude?" Frank Ernst inquired.

"Our Russian friends must have excellent intelligence. I mean, your Air Force chaps did kill their satellite." Captain Perrin set his coffee down on the table. The five officers conferred in Morris's stateroom. Perrin had flown over by helicopter from *Battleaxe.*

"Yeah, so they know our composition," Morris said. "And they'll want to cut this bunch down to size."

The message from Norfolk stated in clipped navalese that at least six Soviet submarines were believed to be heading for the convoy. Four would be on the north. That was their area of responsibility.

"We should be getting some data off the tail any time now," Morris said. "Jerry, you up to three days of continuous ops?"

O'Malley laughed. "If I say no, will it matter?"

"I think we should remain close together," Perrin said. "Five miles' separation at most. The real trick will be timing our sprints. The convoy wants to make as straight a run as possible, right?"

"Yeah." Morris nodded. "Hard to blame the Commodore for that. Zigzagging all those ships could create almost as much confusion as a real attack."

"Hey, the good news is no more Backfires for a while," O'Malley pointed out. "We're back to a one-dimension threat."

The ship's motion changed as power was reduced. The frigate was ending a twenty-eight-knot sprint and would now drift for several minutes at five knots to allow her passive sonar to function.

USS *CHICAGO*

"Sonar contact, bearing three-four-six."

Seven hundred miles to the icepack, McCafferty thought as he went forward. *At five knots.*

They were in deep water. It was a gamble, but a good one, to run away from the coast at fifteen knots despite the noise *Providence* made. It had taken four hours to reach the hundred-fathom curve, a period of constant tension as he had worried about the Russian reaction to their missile attack. The Russians had sent antisubmarine patrol aircraft first of all, the ubiquitous Bears dropping sonobuoys, but they'd been able to avoid them. *Providence* still had most of her sonar systems in operation, and though she could not defend herself, she could at least hear the danger coming.

Throughout the four-hour run the wounded submarine had sounded like a wagonload of pipes, and McCafferty didn't want to think about how she had handled, with her fairwater planes hanging like laundry in a breeze. But that was behind them. Now they were in seven hundred feet of water. With their towed-array sonars deployed, they'd have an extra measure of warning for approaching danger. *Boston* and *Chicago* cruised three miles on either side of their wounded sister. *Seven hundred miles at five knots,* McCafferty thought. *Almost six days . . .*

"Okay, what do we have here, Chief?"

"Came in slowly, sir, so it's probably direct path. We have a slow bearing-change rate. My first guess would be a diesel boat on batteries, and close." The sonar chief showed no emotion.

The captain leaned back into the attack center. "Come right to zero-two-five."

The helmsman applied five degrees of right rudder, gently bringing the submarine to a northeasterly course. At five knots *Chicago* was "a hole in the ocean" that made almost no noise at all, but her contact was almost as quiet. McCafferty watched the line on the screen change shape ever so slightly over a period of several minutes.

"Okay, we have a bearing change to the contact. Bearing is now three-four-one."

"Joe?" McCafferty asked his executive officer.

"I make the range eight thousand yards, plus or minus. He's on a reciprocal heading, speed about four knots."

Too close, the captain thought. *He probably doesn't hear us yet, though.* "Let's get him."

The Mark-48 torpedo fired at its slowest speed setting, turned forty degrees to the left on leaving the tube, then settled down to head for the contact, its guidance wires trailing back to the submarine. The sonarmen directed the fish toward its target while *Chicago* moved slowly away from the launch point. Suddenly the sonar chief's head jerked up.

"He's heard it! He just kicked his engines. I got a blade count—it's a Foxtrot-class, doing turns for fifteen. Transient, transient, he just flooded tubes."

The torpedo accelerated and switched on its homing sonar. The Foxtrot knew it had been found, and her captain reacted automatically, increasing speed and ordering a radical turn to starboard, then firing a homing torpedo back down the line of bearing at its attacker. Finally he dove deep, hoping to shake off the closing fish.

The hard turn left a knuckle in the water, an area of turbulence which confused the Mark-48 briefly, but then the torpedo charged right through it, and on coming back to undisturbed water, found its target again. The green-painted weapon dove after the Foxtrot and caught it at a depth of four hundred feet.

"Bearing is changing rapidly on the inbound," the sonar chief said. "It's going to pass well aft of us—hit, we got a hit on the target." The sound echoed through the steel hull like distant thunder. McCafferty plugged in a set of phones in time to hear the Foxtrot's frantic attempt to blow to the surface, and the screech of metal as the internal bulkheads gave way. He did not hear the captain's last act. It was to deploy the rescue buoy located on the aft corner of the sail. The buoy floated to the surface and began transmitting a continuous message. All the men aboard the Foxtrot were already dead, but the rescue buoy told their fleet headquarters where they had died—and several submarines and surface ships immediately set off to that point.

USS *REUBEN JAMES*

O'Malley pulled up on the collective control and climbed to five hundred feet. From this height he could see the northern edge of the convoy off to the southwest. Several helicopters were in the air—a good idea of someone's. Many of the merchant ships were carrying Army helicopters as deck cargo, and most of them were flyable. Their crews were taking them up to patrol the convoy perimeter, looking for periscopes. The one thing any submariner would admit to being afraid of was a helicopter. This procedure was called "black-sky" ASW. Throughout the convoy, soldiers were being told to watch the ocean and report *anything* they saw, which made for many false sighting reports, but it gave the men something to do, and sooner or later they might just spot a real periscope. The Seahawk moved twenty miles east before circling. They were looking for a possible submarine detected on the frigate's passive sonar array during the last drift.

"Okay, Willy, drop a LOFAR—now-now-now!"

The petty officer punched a button to eject a sonobuoy out the side panel. The helicopter continued forward, dropping four additional buoys at intervals of two miles to create a ten-mile barrier, then O'Malley held his aircraft in a wide circle, watching the sea himself as the petty officer examined the sonar display on his screen.

"Commander, what's this I hear about the skipper? You know, the night before we sailed."

"I felt like getting drunk, and he was kind enough not to make me drink alone. Didn't you ever get drunk before?"

"No, sir. I don't drink."

"What's this Navy coming to! You take her for a minute." O'Malley took his hand off the stick and adjusted his helmet. It was a new one and he hadn't quite gotten used to it yet. "You got anything, Willy?"

"Not sure yet, sir. Give me another minute or two."

"Fair enough." The pilot contemplated his instruments briefly, then resumed his outside scanning. "I ever tell you about this thirty-five-footer in the Bermuda-to-Newport race? Storm beat hell out of it. Anyway, it had an all-girl crew and when the boat swamped they lost all their—"

"Skipper, I got a weak signal on number four."

"Grateful as hell for being rescued, too." O'Malley took the stick and brought the helicopter around to the northwest. "You don't do any of that either, Mr. Ralston?"

"Strong drink giveth the desire, sir, but taketh away the ability," the copilot said. "Two more miles, sir."

"He even knows Shakespeare. There may be hope for you yet. Talk to me, Willy."

"Still a 'weak' on number four. Nothing else."

"One mile," Ralston said, watching the tactical display.

O'Malley's eyes scanned the surface, looking for a straight vertical line or a wisp of foam.

"Number four's signal strength is now medium, sir. Getting a twitch on five."

"Romeo, Hammer, I think we may have something here. I'm going to drop another LOFAR between four and five. Designate this one number six. Dropping—now!" Another sonobuoy was ejected clear of the aircraft.

"Hammer, this is Romeo," called the controller. "Looks to us like the contact is north of the line, say again north."

"Roger, concur on that. We ought to know something in a minute."

"Skipper," Willy called. "I have a 'medium' on six."

"Romeo, Hammer, we're going to dip on this character right now."

Aboard *Reuben James* they marked the helicopter's position, along with the line of sonobuoys.

O'Malley eased back on the stick to kill forward velocity, while his other hand eased the collective control down very gently until the helicopter was in hover fifty feet over the water. Willy unlocked the dipping sonar and lowered it to a depth of two hundred feet.

"Sonar contact, sir. Classify as possible submarine, bearing three-five-six."

"Up dome!" O'Malley commanded.

The Seahawk lifted high and raced north for one mile. Hovering once more, O'Malley dipped his sonar a second time.

"Contact! Bearing one-seven-five. Sounds like a twin screw doing turns for maybe ten knots."

"We've bracketed him," the pilot said. "Let's set this one up." Ralston entered the numbers into the tactical computer.

"Bearing change, looks like he's turning to port—yeah," Willy confirmed. "Turning to port."

"He hear us?" Ralston asked.

"He might hear the convoy and be turning to get a fix on them. Willy, up dome," O'Malley ordered. "Romeo, Hammer, we have a maneuvering target, classify as probable submarine. Request weapons free."

"Roger, Hammer, weapons free, repeat weapons are free."

The pilot flew one thousand yards southeast. The sonar dome went down again and the helicopter hovered head into the wind.

"Got him again, sir," Willy said excitedly. "Bearing three-five-five. Bearing is changing right to left, sir."

"Going right past us," Ralston said, looking at the TACNAV.

"Romeo, this is Hammer. We're calling this a positive submarine and we are making a deliberate attack on this contact." O'Malley held the aircraft in hover as his petty officer called off the bearing change. "Attack sequence."

"Master Arm." Ralston ran his hands across the buttons. "Torpedo Select, position one."

"Set initial search depth two-fifty; course-select, Snake." Ralston made the proper settings.

"Set."

"Okay, Willy, get ready for Yankee-search," O'Malley ordered, meaning a search using active sonar.

"Ready, sir. Bearing to contact now two-zero-zero, changing right-to-left rapidly."

"Hammer his ass!" O'Malley switched the sonar signals into his headset.

Willy thumbed the button and the sonar transducer fired off a series of pings. The wave fronts of sound energy reflected off the submarine's hull and came back to the transducer. The contact suddenly increased engine power.

"Positive contact, bearing one-eight-eight, range eight hundred yards."

Ralston fed the last numbers into the fire-control system: "Set!"

The pilot brought his thumb across the stick to a button on the right side and pressed it home. The Mark-46 torpedo dropped free of its shackles and plunged into the sea. "Torp away."

"Willy, secure pinging." O'Malley keyed his radio. "Romeo, we just dropped on a diving two-screw submarine, approximately eight hundred yards from us on a bearing of one-eight-eight. Torpedo is in the water now. Stand by."

The Mark-46 torpedo was set on a "snake" pursuit pattern, a series of undulating curves that carried it in a southerly direction. Alerted by the helicopter's sonar, the Soviet submarine was running at flank speed and diving to evade the torpedo.

"Hammer, Romeo, be advised that Hatchet is en route to you in case your torp misses, over."

"Roger that," O'Malley acknowledged.

"It's got him!" Willy said excitedly. The torpedo was on automatic pinging as it closed with the submarine. The captain made a hard right turn, but the fish was too close to be fooled.

"Hit! That's a hit!" Willy said almost as loudly as the noise of the explosion. Directly ahead of them the surface seemed to jump, but no gout of foam leaped up. The torpedo had gone off too deep for that.

"Well," O'Malley said. In all his years of practice he'd never fired a live fish at a live sub. The sounds of the dying sub seemed the saddest thing he'd ever heard. Some oil bubbled to the surface. "Romeo, we're calling that one a kill. Tell the bosun to get out his paintbrush. We are now orbiting to look for wreckage and possible survivors." Another frigate had rescued the entire crew from a downed Russian Bear the previous day. They were already on the mainland for interrogation. But there would be none from this incident. O'Malley circled for ten minutes, then turned for home.

ICELAND

"Beagle, you all fed and rested?" Doghouse asked.

"I guess you could say that." Edwards had been waiting for this, but now that it had come it sounded ominous enough.

"We want you to patrol the southern shore of the Hvammsfjördur and let us know of any Russian activity you see. We are particularly interested in the town of Stykkisholmur. That's a small port about forty miles west of you. As before, your orders are to evade, observe, and report. You got that?"

"Roger. How long we got?"

"I can't say that, Beagle. I don't know. You want to move right along, though."

"Okay, we'll be moving in ten minutes. Out." Edwards dismantled the antenna, then stowed the complete radio assembly in the backpack. "People, it's time to leave this mountain retreat. Sergeant Nichols?"

"Yes, sir?" Nichols and Smith came over together.

"Were you briefed on what we're supposed to be up to?"

"No, sir. Our orders were to relieve your party and await further in-structions." Edwards had already seen the sergeant's map case. He had cards for the whole western Icelandic coast, all but their drop zone in a pristine condition. Of course, the purpose of their coastal reconnaissance was clear enough, wasn't it? The lieutenant took out a tactical map and plotted their course west.

"Okay, we'll pair off. Sergeant Smith, you take the point along with one of our new friends. Nichols, you take Rodgers with you and cover the back door. You both have a radio, and I'll take the third and keep the rest of the party with me. The groups stay within sight of each other. We keep to the high ground as much as possible. The first hard-surface road we hit is ten miles west of here. If you see anything, you drop and report in to me. We are supposed to avoid contact. No hero crap, okay? Good, we'll move out in ten minutes." Edwards assembled his gear.

"Where we go, Michael?" Vigdis asked.

"Stykkisholmur," he answered. "You feel okay?"

"I can walk with you, yes." She sat down beside him. "And when we get to Stykkisholmur?"

Mike smiled. "They didn't tell me that."

"Why they never tell you anything?"

"It's called security. That means the less we know, the better it is for us."

"Stupid," she replied. Edwards didn't know how to explain that she was both right and wrong.

"I think when we get there, we can start thinking about a normal life again."

Her face changed. "What is normal life, Michael?"

Another good question, Edwards thought. *But I have too much on my mind to chew that one over.* "We'll see."

STENDAL, GERMAN DEMOCRATIC REPUBLIC

The battle for Hameln and the battle for Hannover were now essentially the same action. Two hours before, the NATO forces had withdrawn to the west, south of the industrial city, allowing them to shorten lines and consolidate. Soviet units were probing forward cautiously, suspicious of another German trap. Alekseyev and Commander-in-Chief West pored over their maps in an attempt to analyze the consequences of the NATO withdrawal.

"It allows them to put at least one, probably two brigades in reserve," Alekseyev thought. "They can use this Highway 217 to move troops rapidly from one sector to another."

"How often have the Germans given ground voluntarily?" his superior asked. "They didn't do this because they wanted to. Their lines were overextended. Their units are depleted."

"So are ours. The Category-B units we're committing to battle are taking losses almost a third greater than the 'A' units they replace. We are paying dearly for our advances now."

"We have paid dearly already! If we fail now it will all have been for nothing. Pasha, we must attack in force. This entire sector is ready to collapse."

"Comrade General, that is not my impression. Resistance is spirited. German morale remains high despite their losses. They have hurt us badly and they know it." Alekseyev had returned from the forward command post at Fölziehausen only three hours before.

"Viewing the action from the front lines is very useful, Pasha, but it hinders your ability to perceive the larger picture."

Alekseyev frowned at that. "The larger picture" was frequently an illusion. His commander had told him that very thing many times.

"I want you to organize an attack along this entire front. NATO formations are gravely depleted. Their supplies are low, they have taken massive casualties. A vigorous attack now will sunder their lines on a fifty-kilometer front."

"We don't have enough A units to attack on this scale," Alekseyev objected.

"Keep them in reserve to exploit the breakthrough. We'll launch the attack with our best reserve divisions from Hannover in the north to Bodenwerder in the south."

"We don't have the strength for that, and it will use up too much fuel," Alekseyev warned. "If we have to attack, I suggest an assault on a two-division front here, south of Hameln. The units are in place. What you propose is too ambitious."

"This is not a time for half measures, Pasha!" CINC-West shouted. He'd never raised his voice to Alekseyev before. The younger man found himself wondering what pressure was being applied to his commander, who calmed down now. "An attack along a single axis allows a counterattack along a single axis," he continued. "This way we can greatly complicate the enemy's task. He can't be strong everywhere. We will find a weakness, break out, and drive our remaining A units through to the Rhein."

USS *REUBEN JAMES*

"Drop now-now-now!" O'Malley yelled. The eighth sonobuoy ejected from the side of the Seahawk, and the pilot brought the helicopter around and headed back east.

O'Malley had already been up for three long, grueling hours this time, with precious little to show for it. Stop, dip, listen; stop, dip, listen. He knew there was a sub down there, but every time he thought he was beginning to get a line on it, the damn thing slipped away! What was it doing different?

Hatchet was having the same problem, except *its* sub had turned around on it and nearly scored a hit on *Battleaxe*. The frigate's violent wake turbulence had detonated the Russian torpedo astern, but it had been close, too close by half. He brought the helicopter into hover.

"Down dome!" They hovered for a minute. Nothing. It began again. "Romeo, this is Hammer. You got anything, over?"

"Hammer, he just faded out a moment ago. Our last bearing was three-four-one."

"Cute. This character's listening for you to stop your sprint, and he cuts his power back."

"That's a fair guess, Hammer," Morris said.

"Okay, I got a barrier to the west if he heads that way. I think he's going due south, and we're dipping for him now. Out." O'Malley switched to intercom. "You got anything, Willy?"

"Nothing, sir."

"Prepare to raise dome." A minute later the helicopter was moving again. They dipped their sonar six more times in the next twenty minutes and came up blank.

"Again, Willy. Prepare to lower. Set it down to, uh, eight hundred feet this time."

"Ready, sir."

"Down dome." O'Malley squirmed in his seat. The outside temperature was moderate, but the sun made a greenhouse of the cockpit. He'd need a shower when he got back to the frigate.

"Searching at eight hundred feet, sir," the petty officer said. He was hot, too, though he'd brought a pair of cold drinks along for the flight. "Sir, I have something . . . possible contact bearing one-eight-five."

"Up dome! Romeo, Hammer, we got a possible contact south of us. Going after it now."

"Hammer, we have nothing anywhere near you. Be advised Bravo and Hatchet are working a contact. Two torps have been launched with no hits."

Nobody ever said it was easy, the pilot thought. He moved three thousand yards and dipped the sonar again.

"Contact, this one's for real. Type-two engine plant bearing one-eight-three."

O'Malley checked his fuel. Forty minutes. He had to get this one in a hurry. He ordered the dome up again and went another three thousand yards south. His shoulders flexed against the seat straps. It seemed to take forever for the sonar dome to get down to search depth.

"There it is again, sir, north of us, bearing zero-one-three. Bearing is changing. Zero-one-five now."

"Set it up!" Thirty minutes' fuel. Time was their enemy now. Ralston punched up the Master Arm and Select buttons.

"Willy: hammer!" The sonar sent out five ranging pings.

"Zero-one-nine, range nine hundred!"

Ralston set search depth and pattern. O'Malley brought his thumb across the stick and dropped the torpedo.

The submarine went to full power and turned left away from the helicopter while the torpedo plunged to eight hundred feet before beginning its search. O'Malley growled to himself that he'd launched from a bad angle, but it would have taken too long to reel in and reacquire. He held the aircraft in hover and listened over his headset as the whine of the torpedo screws chased after the deeper *thrum* of the Charlie's powerful twin screws. The nuclear sub maneuvered frantically, trying to turn inside the pursuing torpedo.

"They're on the same bearing now," Willy reported. "I think the fish has him—hit!"

But the Charlie didn't die. They heard the sound of blowing air, then it stopped. A wild cacophony of mechanical noise followed as the contact moved off to the north, then faded as the submarine slowed. O'Malley didn't have enough fuel to pursue. He came around west and headed for *Reuben James.*

"Hammer, Romeo, what happened?"

"We hit him, but he's still alive. Stand by, Romeo, we're coming in skosh fuel. Five minutes out."

"Roger that, we'll be ready for you. We're vectoring another helo onto the Charlie. I want you to join Hatchet."

"How come we didn't kill him?" Ralston asked.

"Almost all Russian subs have double hulls, and that dinky hundred-pound warhead on the Mark-46 isn't gutsy enough to give you a kill every time. You try to attack from the stern if you can, but this time we couldn't. If you get a stern hit, you pop the shaft seals and flood his engine room. That'll kill anybody. They didn't tell you to go for a stern shot in school, did they?"

"Not especially."

"Figures," O'Malley growled.

It was good to see the *Reuben James* after four hours. It would have been even better to visit the officers' head, O'Malley thought bleakly. He brought the Seahawk over the port corner of the frigate's stern and paced the ship. Aft, Willy opened the sliding door and tossed down a messenger line. The frigate's deck crew attached a refueling hose to the line and Willy hauled it in, plugging the hose into the fuel tank. The procedure was called HIFR, for helicopter in-flight refueling. While O'Malley fought his helo through the roiled air behind the ship, fuel was pumped into his tanks, giving him another four hours' endurance. Ralston kept his eyes on the fuel indicators while O'Malley flew the aircraft.

"We're full up, Willy. Secure."

The petty officer lowered the fuel hose and retrieved his line. He was glad to close the door and strap himself back into his chair. Officers, he told himself, were too smart to do what he just did.

"Bravo, this is Hammer, where do you want us, over?"

"Hammer, Bravo, come right to one-three-zero and rendezvous with Hatchet eight miles from Bravo."

"On the way." O'Malley curved around *Reuben James* and headed southeast.

"Hammer, Romeo, be advised Sea Sprite from *Sims* just finished off that Charlie for you. We got a 'well done' from the screen commander for that prosecution, over."

"Tell the Commodore 'you're welcome.' Bravo, Hammer, what is it we're after, over?"

"We thought it was a twin-screw submarine. We're not quite so sure now, Hammer," Perrin replied. "We've fired three torpedoes at this target now for zero hits. He got one off at us, but it prematured in our wake."

"How close was it?"

"Fifty yards."

Ouch! the pilot thought.

"Okay, I have Hatchet in sight. Bravo, it's your ball game. Where do you want me now?"

Morris had allowed himself to fall far behind in the hunt for the now-dead Charlie. On his command the frigate went to full speed, closing on *Battleaxe* at twenty-five knots. In response to the multiple submarine contacts, the convoy was turning slightly south.

O'Malley's Seahawk hovered seven miles from *Battleaxe* while Hatchet ran back home for fuel and sonobuoys. Again the process of dipping and moving began.

"Nothing," Willy reported.

"Bravo, Hammer, can you give me a rundown of what this target's been doing?"

"We've nearly gotten him twice atop the layer. His course is generally south."

"Sounds like a missile boat."

"Agreed," Perrin answered. "Our last datum point was within one thousand yards of your position. We have nothing at this time."

O'Malley examined the data transmitted from *Battleaxe*'s plot. As was usually true of submarine course tracks, it was a collection of vague opinions, shaky judgments, and not a few wild guesses.

"Bravo, you're a sub-driver. Talk to me, over." This was lousy radio procedure, but what the hell?

"Hammer, the only thing that makes the least bit of sense is that he's extremely fast." O'Malley examined the tactical display more closely.

"You're right, Bravo." O'Malley pondered this. A Papa, maybe? he wondered. Twin screws, cruise missiles, fast as a thief.

"Hammer, Bravo, if we proceed on the assumption that he's very fast, I recommend you go east until Romeo comes off sprint and can give us a bearing."

"Concur, Bravo. Give me a vector." On command from *Battleaxe*, the Seahawk ran twenty miles east and began dipping his sonar. It took fifteen minutes to load another pair of Stingray torpedoes on Hatchet, along with fuel and sonobuoys.

"What do you think we're after, skipper?" Ralston asked.

"How's a Papa grab you?" O'Malley asked.

"But the Russians only have one of those," the copilot objected.

"Doesn't mean they're saving it for a museum, mister."

"Nothing, sir," Willy reported.

Reuben James came off sprint, turning to a southerly heading to bring her sonar to bear on the remaining contact. *If only* Battleaxe *still had her tail*, Morris thought, *we could triangulate on every contact, and with two helos . . .*

"Contact, evaluate as possible submarine, bearing zero-eight-one, bearing—changing slowly, looks like. Yeah, bearing changing north to south." The data went at once to *Battleaxe* and the screen commander. Another helicopter joined the hunt.

"Down dome!" This was the thirty-seventh time today, O'Malley thought. "My ass is asleep."

"Wish mine was." Ralston laughed without much humor. Again they detected nothing.

"How can something be exciting and boring at the same time?" the ensign asked, unconsciously echoing the Tomcat pilot days ago.

"Up dome! You know, I've wondered that a few times myself." O'Malley keyed his radio. "Bravo, Hammer, I got an idea for you."

"We're listening, Hammer."

"You have Hatchet dropping a line of buoys south of us. Deploy another line west. Then I start pinging. Maybe we can flush the guy into doing something. You ever get herded by a dipping helo when you were driving subs?"

"Not herded, Hammer, but I have gone far out of my way to avoid one. Stand by while I get things organized."

"You know, this one's a nervy bastard. He's gotta know we're onto him, but he isn't breaking off. He really thinks he can beat us."

"He has for the last four hours, boss," Willy observed.

"You know what the most important part of gambling is? You have to know when it's time to quit." O'Malley circled up high and turned his search radar on for the first time that day. It was not very useful for detecting a periscope, but it might just scare a sub running near the surface into heading back under the layer. The sun was sinking, and O'Malley could pick out the two other helicopters working this contact from their flying lights. They dropped two lines of passive sonobuoys, each eight miles long, at right angles to each other.

"The picket lines are in place, Hammer," Captain Perrin called. "Begin."

"Willy: hammer!" Six hundred feet below the helicopter, the sonar transducer pounded the water with high-frequency sonar pulses. He did this for one minute, then reeled in and flew southeast. The process lasted half an hour. By this time his legs were knotting up, making his control movements awkward.

"Take over for a few minutes." O'Malley took his feet off the pedals and worked his legs around to restore circulation.

"Hammer, Bravo, we have a contact. Buoy six, line Echo." This was the east-west line. Buoy number six was third from the west end, where the north-south "November" line began. "Weak signal at this time."

O'Malley took the controls back and headed west while the other two helicopters circled behind their respective lines.

"Gently, gently," he murmured over the intercom. "Let's not spook him too much." He picked his course carefully, never heading directly for the contact, never heading far away from it. Another half hour passed, one miserable second at a time. Finally they had the contact running east at about ten knots, far below the layer.

"We now have him on three buoys," Perrin reported. "Hatchet is moving into position."

O'Malley watched the blinking red lights about three miles away. Hatchet dropped a pair of directional DIFAR buoys and waited. The display came up on O'Malley's scope. The contact passed right between the DIFARS.

"Torpedo away!" Hatchet called. The black-painted Stingray dropped invisibly into the water, half a mile in front of the oncoming submarine. O'Malley closed and dropped his own buoy to listen as he brought the Seahawk into hover.

Like the American Mark-48 torpedo, the Stingray didn't use conventional propellers, which made it hard to locate on sonar both for O'Malley and the submarine. Suddenly they heard the sound of propeller cavitation as the submarine went to full power and turned. Then came hull-popping noises as she changed depth abruptly to throw the fish off. It didn't work. Next came the metallic crash of the exploding warhead.

"Hit!" Hatchet called.

"Down dome!"

Willy lowered the sonar transducer one last time. The submarine was coming up.

"Again!" Ralston wondered. "That's two in a row."

"Set it up! Willy, hammer him."

"Range four hundred, bearing one-six-three, I have an up-doppler."

"Circular search, initial search depth one hundred."

"Set," Ralston replied.

O'Malley dropped his torpedo at once. "Up dome! Bravo, the hit did not kill the target, we just dropped another one on him."

"He might be trying to surface to get his crew off," Ralston said.

"He might want to fire his missiles, too. He should have run when he had the chance. I would have."

The second hit finished the submarine. O'Malley flew straight back to *Reuben James*. He let Ralston land the Seahawk. As soon as its wheels were chocked and chained down, he got out and walked forward. Morris met him in the passageway between the helo hangars.

"Great job, Jerry."

"Thanks, skipper." O'Malley had left his helmet in the aircraft. His hair was matted to his head with perspiration and his eyes stung from hours of it.

"I want to talk over a few things."

"Can we do it while I shower and change, Cap'n?" O'Malley went through the wardroom and into his stateroom. He stripped out of his clothing in under a minute and headed for the officers' shower.

"How many pounds you sweat off on a day like this?" Morris said.

"A lot." The pilot pushed the shower button, closing his eyes as the cold water sprayed over him. "You know, I've been saying for ten years that the -46 needed a bigger warhead. I hope to hell those bastards in ordnance will listen to me now!"

"The second one. What was it?"

"If I had to bet, I'd say it was Papa. Great job from the sonar guys. Those steers you gave us were beautiful." He pushed the button again for more cold water. O'Malley emerged a minute later, looking and feeling human again.

"The Commodore is writing you up for something. Your third DFC, I guess."

O'Malley thought about that briefly. His first two were for rescues, not for killing other men.

"How soon will you be ready to go up again?"

"How does next week grab you?"

"Get dressed. We'll talk in the wardroom."

The pilot raked his hair into place and changed into fresh clothing. He remembered the last time his wife had told him to use baby powder to protect his skin from the abuse of sweaty, tight clothes, and how stupid he'd been to reject the suggestion as not in keeping with aviator machismo. Despite the shower, there were a few patches of skin that would continue to itch and chafe. When he went to the wardroom, he found Morris waiting for him with a pitcher of iced bug juice.

"You got a diesel boat and two missile boats. How were they operating? Anything unusual?"

"Awfully aggressive. That Papa should have backed off. The Charlie took a smart route, but he was boring in pretty hard, too." O'Malley thought it over as he drained his first glass. "You're right. They are pushing awful hard."

"Harder than I expected. They're taking chances they ordinarily wouldn't take. What's that tell us?"

"It tells us we got two more busy days ahead, I guess. Sorry, Captain, I'm a little too wasted for deep thinking at the moment."

"Get some rest."

37. The Race of the Cripples

STENDAL, GERMAN DEMOCRATIC REPUBLIC

Two o'clock in the morning. The attack would begin in four hours despite all his efforts to change it. Alekseyev stared at the map with its symbols of friendly units and intelligence estimates of enemies.

"Cheer up, Pasha!" Commander-in-Chief West said. "I know that you think we use up too much fuel. It will also destroy their remaining stocks of war supplies."

"They can resupply, too."

"Nonsense. Their convoys have suffered heavily, as our own intelligence reports have told us. They are sending one massive shipment across now, but the Navy tells me they are sending everything they have against it. And in any case it will arrive too late."

Alekseyev told himself that his boss was probably right. After all, he had made his rank on the basis of a distinguished career. But still . . .

"Where do you want me?"

"With the OMG command post. No closer to the front than that."

The OMG command post, Pavel thought ironically. First 20th Guards Tank Division was supposed to be the operational-maneuver group, then a two-division formation, then three divisions. Every time the breakthrough maneuver had been frustrated, until the very term "operational-maneuver group" sounded like some kind of absurd joke. His pessimism returned. The reserve formations held for exploitation of the attack were far behind the front, so as to be able to move to wherever the best penetration of NATO lines happened. It might take hours for them to reach the proper point. NATO had demonstrated a remarkable ability to compensate for sudden breakthroughs, he reminded himself. Alekseyev set this thought aside as he had with so many others and left the command center, collected Sergetov, and once again found a helicopter to take him on the trip west. His aircraft waited on the ground for its usual fighter escort.

The use of fighters to escort a single helicopter lifting off from Stendal was a pattern NATO air-control officers had noted before, but they'd never had the available units to do anything about it. This time it was different. An AWACS control aircraft over the Rhein watched the chopper lift off with three MiGs in attendance. The sector controller had a pair of F-4 Phantoms returning from a counter-air mission south of Berlin, and he vectored them north. The fighters skimmed the trees, their own radars off as they followed a safe-transit lane used by Russian aircraft.

Alekseyev and Sergetov sat alone in the back of the Mi-24 attack helicopter. There was room for eight combat-loaded infantrymen, so both had room to stretch and Sergetov took the chance for a nap. Their escorting MiGs were a thousand meters overhead, circling continuously as they watched for low-flying NATO fighters.

"Six miles," came the call from the AWACS.

One Phantom popped up, illuminated two MiGs with its radar, and loosed a pair of Sparrow missiles. The other fired two Sidewinders at the helicopter.

The MiGs were caught looking the wrong way when their threat receivers went off. One dashed to the ground and evaded. The other exploded in midair as the surviving wingman radioed a warning. Alekseyev blinked in surprise at the sudden gout of light overhead, then grabbed for his seatbelt as the helicopter turned hard left and dropped like a stone. It was almost in the trees when the Sidewinder chopped off the tail rotor. Sergetov awoke and shouted in surprise and alarm. The Mi-24 spun in the air as it crashed into the trees and bounced the last fifty feet to the ground. The main rotor came apart, sending pieces in all directions, and the sliding door on the left side of the aircraft popped off as though made of plastic. Alekseyev went out right behind it, dragging Sergetov with him. Once again his instincts had saved him. The two officers were twenty meters away when the fuel tanks exploded. They never heard or saw the Phantoms that continued west to safety.

"Are you hurt, Vanya?" the General asked.

"I didn't even piss my pants. That must mean I'm a seasoned veteran." The joke didn't work. The young man's voice shook along with his hands. "Where the hell are we?"

"An excellent question." Alekseyev looked around. He hoped to see lights, but the entire country had a blackout in force, and Soviet units had learned the hard way about using lights on the highways. "We have to find a road. We'll head south until we hit one."

"Where is south?"

"Opposite from north. That is north." The General pointed to a star, then turned to select another. "That one will lead us south."

SEVEROMORSK, R.S.F.S.R.

Admiral Yuri Novikov monitored the progress of the battle from his underground headquarters a few kilometers from his main fleet base. He was stung by the loss of his principal long-range weapon—the Backfire bombers—but the way the Politburo had reacted to the missile attack was a greater shock. Somehow the politicians thought that it meant a ballistic-missile attack from the same area was possible, and no amount of argument to the contrary would change their minds. *As if the Americans would risk their precious ballistic-missile subs in such restricted waters!* the Admiral growled to himself. He was up against fast-attack boats—he was certain of it—and he was being forced to go after them with half his assets to prevent their escape. He didn't have that many assets to go around.

The Commander-in-Chief of Soviet Northern Fleet had had a good war to this point. The operation to seize Iceland had gone almost perfectly—the boldest Soviet attack ever staged! The very next day he had smashed a carrier battle group, an epic victory for his forces. His plan to use his missile-armed bombers and submarines in combination against the convoys had worked well, particularly after he'd decided to use the bombers to eliminate the escort ships first. Submarine losses to date had been heavy, but he'd expected that. The NATO navies had practiced antisubmarine warfare for generations. There had to be losses. He'd made mistakes, Novikov admitted to himself. He should have gone after the escorts in a systematic way sooner—but Moscow wanted the merchants killed most of all, and he'd acceded to the "suggestion."

Things were changing now. The sudden loss of his Backfire force—it would be out of action for another five days—forced him to take his dedicated anticarrier submarine teams and send them against the convoys, which meant crossing NATO's picket line of submarines, and losses there were heavy, too. His force of Bear reconnaissance bombers was hard hit. *The damned war was supposed to be over by now,* Novikov thought angrily. He had a powerful surface force waiting to escort additional troops to Iceland, but he couldn't move that group until the campaign in Germany was within sight of its conclusion. No battle plan survives the first contact with the enemy, he reminded himself.

"Comrade Admiral, satellite photographs have arrived." His aide handed over a leather dispatch case. The fleet intelligence chief arrived a few minutes later with his senior photo-interpretation expert. The photos were spread out across a table.

"Ah, we have a problem here," the photo expert said.

Novikov didn't need the expert to tell him that. The piers at Little Creek, Virginia, were empty. The American amphibious assault force had sailed with a full Marine division. Novikov had watched the progress of Pacific Fleet units to Norfolk with great interest, but then his ocean-reconnaissance satellites had both been killed, and launch authority on the last of them had been withheld. The next photo showed the carrier berths, also empty.

"*Nimitz* is still at Southampton," his intelligence chief pointed out. "He came into port with a severe list, and there is no drydock large enough to accommodate him. He's tied to the Ocean Dock; he's not going anywhere. That gives the Americans three carriers: *Coral Sea, America,* and *Independence. Saratoga* is being used for convoy escorting duties. The rest of their Atlantic Fleet carriers are in the Indian Ocean."

Novikov grunted. That was bad news for the Indian Ocean squadron, but they were part of the Soviet Pacific Fleet. Not his problem. He had enough of his own. For the first time he faced a dilemma that he'd inflicted on the NATO navies. He had more tasks than he had ships, and sending half of his dedicated ASW forces after submarines that were already retreating didn't help matters!

NORTHWOOD, ENGLAND

"Hello again, Admiral," Toland said.

Beattie looked much better. The blue eyes had the gleam of crystal now and the Admiral's back was ramrod-straight as he stood in front of his wall-sized map with his arms folded.

"How are things in Scotland, Commander?"

"Good, sir. The last two raids got chewed up. May I ask how the Doolittle force made out? One of the boats is commanded by a friend of mine."

Beattie turned. "Which?"

"*Chicago,* sir. Dan McCafferty."

"Oh. It would seem that one of the boats was damaged. *Chicago* and one other are escorting her out. In fact, they are raising quite a rumpus in the eastern Barents. We have indications that the Soviets are sending a sizable force after them. In any case, you're going back to your carrier fleet, and you're to meet with my intelligence staff so that you can bring your chaps up to date when you get there. I wanted to see you personally to thank you for that telex you sent about trailing the Backfires to their doorstep. That idea was very useful to us. You're a reservist, I understand. How on earth did they ever let you go?"

"I put my destroyer on a sandbar once."

"I see. You have atoned for that error, Commander." Beattie offered his hand.

WACHERSLEBEN, GERMAN DEMOCRATIC REPUBLIC

"Stop that Goddamned truck!" Alekseyev screamed. He stood in the middle of the road, daring the vehicle to run over him. It stopped and he ran around to the cab.

"Who the hell are you?" the corporal asked.

"I am General Colonel Alekseyev," he answered agreeably. "Who might you be, Comrade?"

"I am Corporal Vladimir Ivan'ch Maryakhin." He managed to say this despite a mouth that hung open on seeing the General's shoulder boards.

"Since I appear to outrank you, Corporal, you will take me and my aide to the next traffic-control point as quickly as this truck will go. Move!"

Alekseyev and Sergetov got in the back. They found a solid mass of crates, but had enough room to sit on top of them.

The General swore. "Three wasted hours."

"It could have been worse."

BRUSSELS, BELGIUM

"It's a major attack, sir. They just started moving on what looks like an eighty-kilometer front."

SACEUR looked at the map impassively. It wasn't as though they hadn't expected this. Intelligence had predicted it twelve hours earlier from Soviet traffic patterns. He had exactly four reserve brigades that he could use in this sector. *Thank God,* he thought, *that I managed to persuade the Germans to shorten the line at Hannover.* Half his reserves had come from that, and not a day too soon.

"Main axis of the attack?" the General asked his operations officer.

"None is apparent at the moment. It looks like a general attack—"

"Pushing hard to find a weak point," SACEUR finished the statement. "Where's their reserve force?"

"Sir, we've identified elements of three divisions here south of Fölzie-hausen. They appear to be A units. The attack now under way appears to be mainly B formations."

"Have we hurt them that bad?" SACEUR asked rhetorically. His intelligence officers were working hard to establish just what enemy casualties were, and he got a report every evening. B-class reserve units had started appearing at the front five days before, which was puzzling. He knew the Soviets had at least six Category-A units in reserve in the southern Ukraine, but there were no indications they were moving. Why wasn't this force being committed to the German front? Why were they sending reservists instead? He'd been asking that question for several days, only to get shrugs from his intelligence chief. *Not that I'm complaining,* he thought. Those two field armies might have been enough to rupture his front entirely.

"Where's a good place to hit back?"

"Sir, we have these two German tank brigades at Springe. The Russian attack appears to have two reserve motor-rifle divisions, with a divisional border right here, ten kilometers from them. They've been off the line for two days now. I wouldn't call them well rested, but—"

"Yeah." SACEUR was given to cutting his officers off. "Get 'em moving."

USS *REUBEN JAMES*

O'Malley circled the frigate after a long morning's search for what turned out to be nothing. Three merchant ships had died in the past three hours, two to missiles that had leaked through the convoy's SAM defenses and one to a torpedo. Both submarines had been prosecuted, one sunk by *Gallery*'s helo inside the convoy itself. They were about to come within ground-based air coverage from the European mainland, and it seemed to the pilot that they'd won this battle. The convoy was getting across with acceptable losses. Thirty-six more hours to landfall.

The landing was routine, and after a trip to the head, O'Malley went into the wardroom for a drink and a sandwich. He found Calloway waiting for him. The pilot had met the reporter briefly but not really spoken with him.

"Is landing your helicopter on this little toy ship as dangerous as it looks?"

"A carrier has a slightly larger deck. You're not doing a story about me, are you?"

"Why not? You killed three submarines yesterday."

O'Malley shook his head. "Two ships, two helos, plus some help from the rest of the screening force. I just go where they send me. There's a lot to sub-hunting. All the parts have to work or the other guy wins."

"Is that what happened last night?"

"Sometimes the other guy does something right, too. I just spent four hours looking and came away empty. Maybe that was a sub, maybe not. Yesterday was pretty lucky all the way around."

"Does it bother you, sinking them?" Calloway asked.

"I've been in the Navy for seventeen years and I've never met anybody who likes killing people. We don't even call it that, except maybe when we're drunk. We sink ships and try to pretend that they're just ships— things without people in them. It's dishonest, but we do it anyway. Hell, this is the first time I've actually done what my main job is supposed to be. Until now all my combat experience has been search-and-rescue stuff. I never even dropped a war-shot on a real sub until yesterday. I haven't thought about it enough to know if I like it or not." He paused. "It's an awful sound. You hear rushing air. If you penetrate the hull at deep depth, the sudden pressure change inside the hull supposedly causes the air to ignite and everyone inside the boat incinerates. I don't know if it's true, but somebody told me that once. Anyway, you hear the rushing air, then you hear the screech—like a car throwing its brakes on hard. That's the bulkheads letting go. Then comes the noise of the hull collapsing, hollow boom, sort of. And that's it: a hundred people just died. No, I don't much like it.

"The hell of it is, it's exciting," O'Malley went on. "You're doing something extremely difficult. It requires concentration and practice and a lot of abstract thought. You have to get inside the other guy's head, but at the same time you think of your mission as destroying an inanimate object. Doesn't make much sense, does it? So, what you do is, you don't think about that aspect of the job. Otherwise the job wouldn't get done."

"Are we going to win?"

"That's up to the guys on land. All we do is support them. This convoy's going to make it."

FÖLZIEHAUSEN, FEDERAL REPUBLIC OF GERMANY

"They told me you were dead," Beregovoy said.

"Not even scratched this time. It startled Vanya here out of a sound sleep, however. How does the attack go?"

"Initial signs are promising. We have an advance of six kilometers here, and almost as much here at Springe. We might have Hannover surrounded by tomorrow."

Alekseyev found himself wondering if his superior had been right. Perhaps NATO lines had been thinned so much they'd been forced to give ground.

"Comrade General." It was the Army intelligence officer. "I have a report of German tanks at Eldagsen. He—he just went off the air."

"Where the hell is Eldagsen?" Beregovoy peered down at the map. "That's ten kilometers behind the line! Confirm that report!"

The ground shook under them, followed by the roar of jet engines and launching missiles.

"They just hit our radio transmitters," the communications officer reported.

"Switch to the alternate!" Alekseyev shouted.

"That *was* the alternate. They took out the primary last night," Beregovoy answered. "Another is being assembled now. So we use what we have here."

"No," Alekseyev said. "If we do that, we do it on the move."

"I can't coordinate well that way!"

"You can't coordinate at all if you're dead."

USS *CHICAGO*

All hell was breaking loose. It was like a nightmare, except you woke up from those, McCafferty reminded himself. At least three Bear-F patrol aircraft were overhead, dropping sonobuoys all over the place, two Krivak-type frigates and six Grisha patrol boats had shown up on the sonar, and a Victor-III submarine had decided to come to the party.

Chicago had nibbled the odds down some. For the past few hours, fancy footwork had killed the Victor and a Grisha and damaged a Krivak, but the situation was deteriorating. The Russians were mobbing him, and he would not be able to keep them at arm's length much longer. In the time it had taken him to localize and kill the Victor, the surface groups had closed five miles on him. Like a boxer against a puncher, he had the advantage only as long as he kept them away.

What McCafferty wanted and needed to do was talk with Todd Simms on *Boston* to coordinate their activities. He couldn't, because the underwater telephone couldn't reach that far and made too much noise. Even if he tried to make a radio broadcast, *Boston* would have to be near the surface, with her antenna up to hear him. He was sure Todd had his boat as deep as he could drive her. American submarine doctrine was for each boat to operate alone. The Soviets practiced cooperative tactics, but the Americans never felt the need. McCafferty needed some ideas now. The "book" solution to the tactical problem at hand was to maneuver and look for openings, but *Chicago* was essentially tied to a fixed position and could not stray too far from her sisters. As soon as the Russians understood that there was a cripple out there, they'd close in like a pack of dogs to finish *Providence* off, and he would not be able to stop them. Ivan would gladly exchange some of his small craft for a 688.

"Ideas, XO?" McCafferty asked.

"How about, 'Scotty, beam us up!' " The executive officer tried to brighten things a bit. It didn't work. So, okay, maybe the skipper wasn't a *Star Trek* fan. "The only way I see to keep them off our friends is to get them to chase us awhile."

"Go east and attack this group from the beam?"

"It's a gamble," the exec admitted. "But what isn't?"

"You conn her. Two-thirds, and hug the bottom."

Chicago turned southeast and increased speed to eighteen knots. This was a fine time to find out how accurate our charts are, McCafferty thought. Did Ivan have any minefields set here? He had to shut that thought out. If they hit one, he'd never know it. The executive officer kept the submarine within fifty feet of where the chart said the bottom was—actually he hedged, keeping fifty feet above the highest bottom marker within a mile. Even that would do no good if there was an uncharted wreck. McCafferty remembered his first trip into the Barents Sea. Somewhere close to here were those destroyers sunk as targets. If he hit one of those at eighteen knots . . . The run lasted forty minutes.

"All ahead one-third!" McCafferty ordered when he couldn't stand it anymore. *Chicago* slowed to five knots. To the diving officer: "Take her up to periscope depth."

The planesmen pulled back on their controls. There was some minor groaning from the hull as the outside water pressure relented, allowing the hull to expand an inch or so. On McCafferty's order the ESM mast went up first. As before there were several radar sources. The search periscope went up next.

A weather front was moving in, with a rain squall to the west. *Fabulous,* McCafferty thought. *There goes ten percent of our sonar performance.*

"I got a mast at two-six-four—what is it?"

"No radar signals on that bearing," a technician said.

"It's broken—it's the Krivak. We got a piece of her, let's finish her off. I—" A shadow went across the lens. McCafferty angled the instrument up and saw the swept wings and propellers of a Bear.

"Conn, sonar, multiple sonobuoys aft!"

McCafferty slapped the scope handles up and lowered the scope. "Take her down! Make your depth four hundred feet, left full rudder, all ahead full."

A sonobuoy deployed within two hundred yards of the submarine. The brassy sound of its pings reverberated through the hull.

How long for the Bear to turn and drop on us? On McCafferty's order a noisemaker was ejected into the water. It didn't work, and he fired off another. One minute passed. *He'll try to get a magnetic fix on us first.*

"Rewind the tape." The duty electrician was grateful to have something to do. The video record of his five-second periscope exposure showed what looked like the remains of a Krivak's topsides.

"Passing three hundred feet. Speed twenty and increasing."

"Scrape the bottom, Joe," McCafferty said. He watched the tape rerun, but that was only to have something for his eyes to do.

"Torpedo in the water port quarter! Torpedo bearing zero-one-five."

"Right fifteen degrees rudder! All ahead flank! Come to new course one-seven-five." McCafferty put the torpedo on his stern. His mind went through the tactical situation automatically. *Russian ASW torpedo: sixteen-inch diameter, speed about thirty-six knots, range four miles, runs about nine minutes. We're doing*—he looked—*twenty-five knots. It's behind us. So if he's a mile behind us . . . seven minutes to cover the distance. It can get us. But we're accelerating at ten knots per minute . . . No, it can't.*

"High-frequency pinging aft! Sounds like a torpedo sonar."

"Settle down, people, I don't think it can catch us." *Any Russian ship in the neighborhood can hear us, though.*

"Passing through four hundred feet, starting level out."

"Torpedo is closing, sir," the sonar chief reported. "The pings sound a little funny, like—" The sub shook with a powerful explosion aft.

"All ahead one-third, right ten degrees rudder, come to new course two-six-five. What you just heard was their fish hitting the bottom. Sonar, start feeding me data."

The Russians had a new line of sonobuoys north of *Chicago,* probably too far off to hear them. Bearings to the nearest Soviet ships were steadying down: they were heading right for *Chicago.*

"Well, that'll keep them off our friends for a while, XO."

"Super."

"Let's go south some more and see if we can get them to pass us. Then we'll remind 'em what they're up against."

ICELAND

If I ever get off this rock alive, Edwards thought, *I'll move to Nebraska.* He remembered flying over the state many times. It was so agreeably flat. Even the counties were nice neat squares. Not so in Iceland. For all that, it was easier going than they had enjoyed since leaving Keflavik. Edwards and his party kept to the five-hundred-foot elevation line, which kept them at least two miles from the gravel coast road, with mountains at their backs and a good long field of view. Up to now they had seen nothing more than routine activity. They assumed that every vehicle on the move had Russians aboard. That probably was not true, but since the Soviet troops had appropriated so many civilian vehicles there was no way to tell the sheep from the goats. That made them all goats.

"Enjoying your rest, Sarge?" Edwards and his group caught up with Smith. There was a road half a mile farther ahead, the first they'd seen in two days.

"See that mountaintop?" Smith pointed. "A chopper landed on it twenty minutes ago."

"Great." Edwards unfolded his map and sat down. "Hill 1063—that's thirty-five hundred feet."

"Makes a nice lookout point, don't it? You suppose they can see us from there?"

"Ten or eleven miles. Depends, skipper. I figure they're using it to watch the water on both sides. If they have any brains, they'll keep an eye on the rocks, too."

"Any idea how many people they have there?" Edwards asked.

"No way. Maybe nobody—hell, they might have been making a pickup, but I wouldn't bet on it. Maybe a squad, maybe a platoon. You gotta figure they have a good pair of spotting glasses and a radio."

"And how do we get past them?" Edwards asked. The ground was mostly open, with only a few bushes in sight.

"That's a real good question, skipper. Pick our routes carefully, keep low, use dead ground—all the usual stuff. But the map shows a little bay that comes within four miles of them. We can't detour around the far side without running into the main road—can't hardly do that."

"What's the problem?" Sergeant Nichols arrived. Smith explained matters. Edwards got on the radio.

"You just know they're on the hilltop, not strength or weapons, right?" Doghouse asked.

"Correct."

"Damn. We wanted you on that hill." *Now there's a surprise,* Edwards thought. "No chance you can go up that hill?"

"None. Say again no chance at all. I can think of easier ways to commit suicide, mister. Let me think this one over and get back to you. Okay?"

"Very well, we'll be waiting. Out."

Edwards got his sergeants together and they started exploring the maps.

"Really a question of how many men they have there, and how alert they are," Nichols thought. "If they have a platoon there, we can expect some patrol activity. Next question is how much? I wouldn't be very keen on doing that hill twice a day myself."

"How many men would you put there?" Edwards asked.

"Ivan has a whole paratroop division here, plus other attachments. Call it ten thousand men total. He can't garrison the entire island, can he? So, would he have a rifle platoon on this or any other hilltop, or just a spotting team—artillery observers, that sort of mob. They're looking for your invasion force, and from up there a man with a decent spyglass can cover all of this bay to our north, and probably see all the way to bloody Keflavik the other way. They'll also be looking for aircraft."

"You're trying to make it sound easy?" Smith wondered.

"I think we can approach the hill safely enough, then wait for nightfall—what of it we have—and try to pass under them then. They will have the sun in their eyes, you know."

"You've done this before?" Edwards asked.

Nichols nodded. "Falklands. We were there a week before the invasion to scout various things. Same thing we're doing now."

"They haven't said anything on the radio about an invasion."

"*Left*enant, this is where your Marines are going to land. No one's told me as much, but they didn't send us here to find a football pitch, did they?" Nichols was in his mid-thirties, approaching twenty years of service. He was by far the oldest member of the party, and the past few days of serving under a rank amateur had chafed on him. The one nice thing about this young weatherman, however, was his willingness to listen.

"Okay, they wanted us on this hill to eyeball things, too. How about this smaller peak to the west of the main summit?"

"We'll have to go far out of our way to be able to climb without being seen, but yes, we can establish ourselves there, I think. So long as they are not terribly alert, that is."

"Okay, once we cross this road, we keep together in one group. You got the point, Sergeant Nichols. I'd suggest we rest up a bit. Looks like we'll have to be on the move for quite a while once we get moving."

"Eight miles to the foot of the hill. We will want to be there about sunset."

Edwards checked his watch. "Okay, we start moving in an hour." He walked over to Vigdis.

"So, Michael, what do we do now?" He explained the situation to her at length.

"We're going to be close to some Russians. It might be dangerous."

"You ask if I want to not go with you?"

Say yes and hurt her feelings. Say no and . . . shit!

"I don't want to see you hurt any more."

"I stay with you, Michael. I am safe with you."

SOUTHAMPTON, ENGLAND

It took several hours to pump out the water that had given her the false list, an impression that had been reinforced by the ostentatious activities of divers. The powerful tugs *Catcombe* and *Vecta* moved her slowly aft into the Solent. Her flight deck had been fully repaired by the Vosper shipwrights though so much of the gray steel showed the slapdash bandage work of a job done more in haste than in consideration for the ship's proud name. Two thousand men had done the job. New arresting gear had been flown in from America, along with electronic equipment that came nowhere near replacing what the Russian missiles had destroyed. The tugs escorted her to Calshot Castle, then she moved alone south to Thorn Channel, east by the yachts docked at Cowes. Escorts were waiting at Portsmouth, then the small formation turned south and west into the English Channel.

Flight operations began at once. The first aircraft to arrive were the Corsair attack bombers, then the heavier Intruders and the sub-hunting Vikings. USS *Nimitz* was back in business.

USS *CHICAGO*

"—and shoot!" Three hours of excruciating work distilled down to half a second. The now-familiar shudder of compressed air ejected a pair of torpedoes into the black water of the Barents Sea.

The Soviet commander had been just a little too eager to verify *Chicago*'s death and allowed his frigate to run in close behind his two remaining

Grishas. All three ships were pinging at the bottom, looking for a dead submarine. *You didn't expect us to run south, did you*? North or east, maybe, but not south. McCafferty had maneuvered his submarine wide around the Russian frigate, staying at the fringe of her sonar range, then closed up two thousand yards behind her. One fish for the Krivak and one running for the nearest patrol boat.

"No change in target course and speed, sir." The torpedo raced after the Soviet frigate. "He's still pinging the other way, sir."

The waterfall display lit up, a bright dot on the contact's tone line. Simultaneously the thundering explosion echoed through the hull.

"Up scope!" McCafferty met the eyepiece at deck level and worked it up slowly. "That's a kill. We broke her back. Okay . . ." He turned to the bearing of the near Grisha. "Okay, target number two is turning— wow, there go his engines. Increasing speed and going left."

"Skipper, the wire's cut on the fish."

"How long on the run?"

"Another four minutes, sir." In four minutes at full speed the Grisha would be outside the torpedo's acquisition radius.

"Damn, it's going to miss. Down scope. Let's get out of here. We'll go east this time. Make your depth four hundred, all ahead two-thirds. Come right to zero-five-five."

"Must have been the shock of the explosion, sir. Half a second later, the control wires let go on the number-two fish." McCafferty and his weapons officer reexamined the plot.

"You're right. I cut that one too close. Okay." The captain stepped over to the chart table. "Where do you figure our friends are?"

"Right about here, sir. Twenty- to twenty-five miles."

"I think we've taken enough heat off them. Let's see if we can get back up there while Ivan tries to figure out what's going on."

"We've been lucky, skipper," the exec observed.

"That's true enough. I want to know where their submarines are. That Victor we got just walked across our sights. Where are the rest of 'em? They can't just be chasing after us with these." Of course not, McCafferty realized. The Russians set up hunting preserves, sectors limited to specific types of ships. Their surface ships and aircraft would be in one sector, and next to it their submarines would have exclusive hunting rights . . .

He told himself that he'd done well to date. Three patrol boats, a full-sized frigate, and a sub, quite a week in anybody's book. But it wasn't over. Not until they got *Providence* to the ice.

38. Stealth on the Rocks

ICELAND

The first leg of the trip was only eight miles in a straight line, but the line they traveled was straight in no dimension. The terrain here was volcanic also, littered with rocks large and small. The large ones made shadows, and whenever possible they stayed in them, but with every step they had also to detour, uphill and down, left and right, until every yard of forward travel was accompanied by a yard in another direction, and eight miles became sixteen.

For the first time, Edwards knew that he was under possible observation. Even when the hilltop they skirted was hidden by a ridge, who could say that the Russians did not have another scouting party out? Who could be sure that they were not being watched, that some Russian sergeant with binoculars had noticed their rifles and packs, then picked up his portable radio and sent out a call for an armed helicopter? The effort of the walk made their hearts beat fast. Fear made their hearts beat faster still, compounding their fatigue like interest on a usurer's loan.

Sergeant Nichols proved an efficient leader, and a hard one. The oldest member of the party, his stamina—sore ankle and all—amazed Edwards. They all kept quiet, no one wanted to make noise, and Nichols was unable to growl at those too slow to keep up. His contemptuous look was enough. *He's ten years older than me,* Edwards told himself, *and I'm a track man. I can keep up with this bastard. Can't I?*

Nichols managed to keep them clear of the coast road for most of their journey, but there was one point where the road looped around a small cove to within a mile of their path. Here they faced a cruel choice: risk observation from the road, where the traffic was probably Russian, or from the mountaintop. They risked the road, slowly and gingerly as they watched traffic motor along every fifteen minutes or so. The sun was low in the northwestern sky as they crept up a ravine with steep walls. They found a rockpile to rest in before their dash below the observation post.

"Well, that was a nice day's walk, wasn't it?" the sergeant of Royal Marines asked. He wasn't even sweating.

"You trying to prove something, Sergeant?" Edwards asked. He was.

"Sorry, *Lef*tenant. Your friends told me you were in proper shape."

"I don't think I'll have a heart attack just yet, if that's what you mean. Now what?"

"I'd suggest that we wait an hour, until the sun sinks lower, then press on. Nine more miles. We'll want to move as quick as we can."

Sweet Jesus! Edwards thought. He kept his face impassive. "You sure they won't see us?"

"Sure? No, I am not sure, *Lef*tenant. Twilight is the hardest time to see, however. The eye cannot adjust from the bright sky to the dark ground."

"Okay, you got us this far. I'm going to go and check on the lady."

Nichols watched him walk off. "I would not mind seeing 'the lady' myself."

"That wasn't a good thing to say, Nick," Smith observed quietly.

"Come on, you know what he's—"

"Nick, talk nice about the lady," Smith warned. He was tired, but not that tired. "She's had a bad time, man. And the skipper's a gentleman, y'dig? Hey, I thought he was a wimp, too. I was wrong. Anyway, Miss Vigdis, man, that's one hell of a lady."

Mike found her curled in a fetal position next to a rock. Rodgers was keeping an eye on her, and moved off when the lieutenant arrived.

"How are you?" Mike asked. She turned her head fractionally.

"Dead. Michael, I am so tired."

"Me, too, babe." Mike sat down beside her and stretched his legs out, wondering if the muscle tissue would just fall off the bones. He was strong enough to stroke her hair. It was matted with sweat, but Mike was past noticing such things. "Just a little while longer. Hey, you're the one who wanted to stay with us, remember?"

"I am fool!" There was a note of humor in her voice. *As long as you can laugh,* Mike remembered his father saying, *you are not defeated.*

"Come on, you better stretch those legs out or they're gonna knot up. Come on, roll over." Edwards straightened her legs and massaged her calves briefly. "What we need is some bananas."

"What?" Her head came up.

"Bananas have lots of potassium. Helps to prevent cramps." Or was it calcium for pregnant women? he wondered.

"What do we do when we get to our new hill?"

"We wait for the good guys."

"They come?" Her voice changed slightly.

"I think so."

"And you leave then?" Mike was quiet for a moment, measuring his boldness against his shyness. *What if she says—*

"Not without you, I don't." He hesitated again. "I mean, if that's—"

"Yes, Michael."

He lay down beside her. Edwards was startled by the fact that he desired her now. She was no longer the victim of rape, or a girl pregnant by another man, or a strange person from another culture. He was awed by her inner strength and other things for which he had no names, and needed none.

"You're right. I do love you." *Son of a bitch.* He held her hand as both rested for the task ahead.

USS *CHICAGO*

"That's one of 'em, sir. *Providence,* I think. I got some funny transients, like metal pieces beating against each other."

They'd been tracking the target—every contact was a target—for two hours, closing very carefully as the possible noise source changed into a probable one. The overhead storm degraded their sonar performance measurably, and the target's stealth prevented their developing a signature identification for an agonizing period. Might she be a Russian sub creeping in search of her own target? Finally the faint rattles from the damaged sail betrayed her. McCafferty ordered his boat to close the target at eight knots.

Had *Providence* repaired her sonar systems? Certainly they'd try, McCafferty thought, and if they then detected a submarine approaching very cautiously from the rear, would they think this was their old friend *Chicago,* or another Victor-III? For that matter, how sure were they that their target was *Providence*? That was why American subs were trained to operate alone. Too many uncertainties attached to cooperative operations.

They'd left the Soviet surface forces behind. McCafferty's hit-and-run maneuver had fooled them, and before the noise faded out, they listened to a spirited hunt involving aircraft and surface forces, now thirty miles astern. That was a positive development, but the absence of any surface ships in this area made McCafferty uneasy. He might now be in a submarine-dedicated sector, and submarines were by far the more dangerous opponents. His earlier success against the Victor had been pure luck. That Soviet skipper had been too interested in starting his own hunt to check his flanks. It was a mistake he did not expect to be repeated.

"Range?" McCafferty asked his tracking party.

"About two miles, sir."

That was the fringe of gertrude range, but McCafferty wanted to get a lot closer than that. *Patience,* he told himself. Submarining was a continuous exercise in patience. You spent hours in preparation for a few seconds of activity. *It's a wonder we don't all have ulcers.* Twenty minutes later, they had closed to within a thousand yards of *Providence.* McCafferty lifted the gertrude phone.

"*Chicago* calling *Providence,* over."

"You took your time about it, Danny."

"Where's Todd?"

"He went off west after something two hours ago. We lost him. No noise at all from that direction."

"What's your condition?"

"The tail works. Rest of our sonar's shot. We can shoot fish from the torpedo-room control systems. Still raining in the control room, but we can live with it as long as we stay above three hundred feet."

"Can you go any faster?"

"We tried going to eight knots. Found out we couldn't keep it up. The sail's coming apart. The noise just gets worse. I can give you six, that's it."

"Very well. If you got a working tail, we'll try to take station a few miles ahead. Call it five miles."

"Thanks, Danny."

McCafferty hung up the phone. "Sonar, you got anything that even looks like it might be something?"

"No, sir, it's clear right now."

"All ahead two-thirds." *So, where the hell is* Boston? the captain asked himself.

"Funny how quiet things have got," the exec pointed out.

"Tell me about it. I know I'm acting paranoid, but am I acting paranoid enough!" McCafferty needed the laugh. "Okay. We sprint and drift north, fifteen minutes sprint, ten drift, until we're five miles ahead of *Providence.* Then we settle down to six knots and continue the mission. I'm going to catch a nap. Wake me in two hours. Talk to the division officers and chiefs, make sure the troops are getting some rest. We've been pushing pretty hard. I don't want anybody to fold up." McCafferty grabbed half a sandwich as he walked forward. It was only eight steps to his stateroom. The food was swallowed by then.

"Captain to control!" It seemed he had only just closed his eyes when the speaker over his head went off. McCafferty checked his watch on the way out the door. He'd been asleep for ninety minutes. It would have to do.

"What do we got?" he asked the exec.

"Possible submarine contact on the port quarter. Just picked it up. We got a bearing change already—it's close. No signature yet."

"*Boston?*"

"Could be."

I wish Todd hadn't gone off like that, McCafferty told himself. He found himself wondering if they shouldn't just tell *Providence* to go to her best speed and screw the noise. That was fatigue talking, he knew. Tired people make mistakes, especially judgmental errors. *Captains can't afford those, Danny.*

Chicago was making six knots. *No noise at all*, the captain thought. *Nobody can hear us . . . maybe, probably. You don't really know anymore, do you?* He went into the sonar room.

"How you feeling, Chief?"

"Hangin' in there, skipper. This contact's a beaut. See how he fades in and out. He's there, all right, but it's a cast-iron bitch to hold him."

"*Boston* headed off west a few hours ago."

"Could be him coming back, sir. Lord knows he's quiet enough. Or it could be a Tango on batteries, sir. I don't have enough signal to tell the difference. Sorry, sir. I just don't know." The chief rubbed raw eyes and let out a long breath.

"How long since you had any rest?"

"I don't know that either, sir."

"When we finish up this one, you hit the sack, Chief." The tracking party officer called forward next.

"I have a working range for you, sir. Five thousand yards. I think he's on an easterly course. Trying to firm that up." McCafferty ordered a fire-control solution to be run on the contact.

"What's this?" the chief asked. "Another sonar contact behind the first one, bearing two-five-three. He's following the other guy!"

"I need an ID, Chief."

"I don't have enough data, Captain. Both these guys are creeping."

Is Boston *one of them? If so, which? If the one in front, do we warn him and reveal our position? Or shoot and risk shooting at the wrong one? Or just do nothing at all?*

McCafferty went aft to the plotting board. "How close is this one to *Providence?*"

"Just over four thousand yards, coming in on her port bow."

"He probably has her then," the captain thought aloud.

"But who the hell is he?" the tracking officer asked quietly. "And what's this Sierra-2 contact behind him?"

"Transient! Transient!" the sonar chief called. "Mechanical transient on Sierra-2!"

"Left fifteen degrees rudder," McCafferty ordered quietly.

"Torpedo in the water, bearing two-four-nine!"

"All ahead two-thirds!" This order was loud.

"Conn, sonar, we got increased machinery noises on Sierra-1. Okay, the front contact is a two-screw boat, blade count indicates speed of ten knots and increasing, getting some cavitation. Target Sierra-1 is maneuvering. Classify this target as a Tango-class."

"*Boston*'s the one in back. All ahead one-third." McCafferty ordered his submarine to slow back down. "Get him, Todd!"

His wish was rewarded with an explosion fifteen seconds later. Simms had come up with the same tactic as his friend on *Chicago*. Close to a few thousand yards of the target, and give him no chance to maneuver clear. Fifteen minutes later, *Boston* joined her healthy sister.

"Talk about a tough four hours. That Tango was good!" Simms called over on the gertrude. "You in good shape?"

"Yes. We have the front guard position. You want to take the rear for a while?"

"You got it, Danny. See ya'."

ICELAND

"Lead off, Sergeant Nichols."

The Russian outpost was three miles south and three thousand feet up. They climbed up the walls of the ravine and into relatively open ground. They were between the sun and the outpost. Edwards found that intellectually he believed what Nichols said about light conditions, and how the eye reacted to them—and how easy was it to spot something three miles away?—but walking like this felt like being naked on the street at rush hour. They had darkened their faces with camouflage makeup, and their uniforms blended in well with the color and texture of the land. *But the human eye looks for movement,* Edwards told himself, *and we're moving. What am I doing here?*

One step at a time. Walk softly. Don't raise any dust. Slow, easy pace. No sudden moves. Heads down. All the things Nichols had said echoed through his mind. *Look at me, I'm invisible.*

He commanded himself not to look up, but Edwards would have been less than human not to sneak an occasional look. The hill—*mountain*— towered above them. It really got steep near the top. *A volcano?* he wondered. There was no sign of activity at the summit. *Maybe nobody is there? Right. Do us all a favor and be blind, or asleep, or eating, or looking for airplanes.* He had to pull his eyes away from it.

The rocks he stepped over and around blended together after a while. Each member of the party walked alone. No one said anything. Every face was couched in a neutral expression that might have meant quiet determination or concealed exhaustion. Just walking the rocks safely required concentration.

This is the end of it. The last hike. The last hill to climb. The end, Edwards promised himself. *After this I drive a car to get the morning paper. If I can't have a one-story house I'll damned well have an elevator installed. I'll get kids to cut the grass for me and sit on the porch watching them.*

Finally the hilltop was behind him. He had to sneak his looks over his shoulder now. For some reason the helicopter full of Russian paratroopers didn't come. They were somewhat safer now. So Nichols stepped up the pace.

Four hours later the mountaintop was behind a knife-edge ridge of volcanic rock. Nichols called a halt. They'd been moving for seven hours.

"Well," the sergeant said. "That was easy enough, wasn't it?"

"Sarge, next time you jump out of an airplane, please break your ankle," Mike suggested.

"Hard part's behind us. Now all we have left is to climb this wee hill," Nichols pointed out.

"Might want to get some water first," Smith said. He pointed to a stream a hundred yards away.

"Good idea. *Lef*tenant, I do think we should be atop the hill as quick as we can."

"Agreed. This is absolutely the last Goddamned hill I ever climb!"

Nichols chuckled. "I have said that myself once or twice, sir."

"I don't believe it."

USS *INDEPENDENCE*

"Welcome aboard, Toland!" Commander, Strike Fleet Atlantic was a three-star billet, but Rear Admiral Scott Jacobsen would have to settle for the job instead of the rank for the moment. The life-long aviator was the most senior carrier-division commander in the Navy, and was the replacement for the late Admiral Baker. "You have one hell of a letter of introduction here from Admiral Beattie."

"He made too big a deal of it. All I did was pass along an idea somebody else came up with."

"Okay. You were on *Nimitz* when the task force got hit, right?"

"Yes, sir, I was in CIC."

"The only other guy who got out was Sonny Svenson?"

"Captain Svenson, yes, sir."

Jacobsen picked up his phone and punched three digits. "Ask Captain Spaulding to join me. Thank you. Toland, you, me, and my operations officer are going to relive that experience. I want to see if there might be something our briefing left out. They're not going to punch any holes in my carriers, son."

"Admiral, don't underestimate them," Toland warned.

"I won't underestimate them, Toland. That's why I have you here. Your group got caught too far north for the circumstances. Taking Iceland was a beautiful move on their part. It screwed our plans pretty well. We are going to fix that, Commander."

"So I gather, sir."

USS *REUBEN JAMES*

"Ain't she pretty!" O'Malley said. He flipped his cigarette over the side and crossed his arms, staring at the massive carrier on the horizon. She was just a dim gray shape, with aircraft landing on the flat deck.

"My story is supposed to be about the convoy," Calloway sniffed.

"Well, they're making port right about now. End of story." The pilot turned with a wide grin. "Hell, you made me famous, didn't you?"

"You bloody aviators are all the same!" the Reuters correspondent snapped angrily. "The captain won't even tell me where we're going."

"You don't know?" O'Malley asked in surprise.

"Well, where are we going?"

"North."

LE HAVRE, FRANCE

The port had been cleared in expectation of the convoy. The merchantmen were brought past several wrecks of ships that had died from Soviet mines, some laid before the war, others dropped from aircraft. The port had also been bombed six times by long-range fighter-bombers, each time at a murderous price from French air defense forces.

The first ships in were the big Ro/Ros, the roll-on/roll-off container ships. Eight of them together carried a full armored division, and these were taken quickly to the Bassin Théophile Ducrocq. One by one, the ships lowered their curved stern ramps to the dock and the tanks began to roll off. They met a continuous taxi-rank of low-loader tractor-trailers, each of which would carry a tank or other armored fighting vehicle to the front lines. Loaded, they rolled off one by one to the assembly point at the Renault facility adjacent to the port. It would take hours to unload the division, but it had been decided nevertheless to move everything in a body to the fighting front, less than five hundred kilometers away.

After what had seemed an endless, tense voyage, arrival was a culture shock for the American troops, many of them National Guardsmen who rarely went overseas. The dock workers and traffic police were too exhausted from weeks of frantic work to show any human emotion, but ordinary people who had learned, despite heavy security, that reinforcing troops were landing came out, first in small groups, soon in small mobs, to watch the new arrivals. The American troops were not allowed to leave their company areas. After some informal negotiations, it was decided small delegations would be allowed to meet briefly with some of the troops. The security risk was minor—the telephone lines in and out of all NATO ports were under tight control—and there was an unexpected result to this exercise in simple courtesy. Like their fathers and grandfathers, the arriving troops saw that Europe was worth fighting for. The people who were often seen merely as threats to American jobs had faces and hopes and dreams, all of which were in danger. They were not fighting for a principle, or a political decision, or a treaty made of paper. They were here for these people and others not the least different from those they'd left at home.

It took two hours longer than they'd hoped. Some vehicles were broken down, but the port and police officials had organized the assembly points with skill. The division moved off in the early afternoon at a steady fifty kilometers per hour, driving down a multilane highway cleared for its path. Every few yards, someone stood to wave while the troops made final checks on their gear. The easy part of their journey was about to end.

ICELAND

It was four in the morning when they reached the top, only to find that this mountain had a number of "tops." The Russians had the highest one, three miles away. Edwards's group had a choice of two subsidiary peaks, each a few hundred feet lower than the adjacent thousand-meter summit. They picked the higher of the two, overlooking the small fishing port of Stykkisholmur, almost due north, and the large rock-filled bay that the map called Hvammsfjördur.

"Looks like a fine observation point, *Left*enant Edwards," Nichols judged.

"That's good, Sarge, 'cause I am not going another foot." Edwards already had his binoculars on the eastern peak. "I don't see any movement."

"They're there," Nichols said.

"Yeah," Smith agreed. "Sure as hell."

Edwards slid down from the crestline and unpacked his radio.

"Doghouse, this is Beagle, and we are where you want us, over."

"Give me your exact position."

Edwards opened his map and read off the coordinates. "We believe there's a Russian observation post on the next peak over. They're about five klicks away, according to this map. We're well concealed here and we have food and water for two days. We can see the roads leading into Stykkisholmur. Matter of fact, it's nice and clear now, and we can see all the way to Keflavik. We can't pick anything out, but we can see the peninsula."

"Very well. I want you to look north and tell us what you see in detail."

Edwards handed the radio antenna to Smith, then turned and put his field glasses on the town.

"Okay. The land is pretty flat, but higher than the water, on a shelf, like. The town is fairly small, maybe eight square blocks. There are some little fishing boats tied up to the docks . . . I count nine of them. The harbor north and east of the port is wall-to-wall rocks that go on for miles. I do not see any armored vehicles, no obvious signs of Russian troops—wait. I do see two four-by-fours parked in the middle of the street, like, but nobody around 'em. The sun's still low, and there's lots of shadows. Nothing moving on the roads. I guess that's about it."

"Very well, Beagle. Good report. Let us know if you see any Soviet personnel at all. Even one, we want to know about him. Stay put."

"Somebody coming to get us?"

"Beagle, I don't know what you're talking about."

USS *INDEPENDENCE*

Toland stood in the Combat Information Center, watching the displays. Submarines concerned him the most. Eight allied subs were in the Denmark Strait, west of Iceland, forming a barrier that few submarines would be able to pass. They were supported by Navy Orions operating out of Sondrestrom, Greenland, something impossible until the Russian fighters at Keflavik had been whittled down. That closed off one possible avenue of access to Strike Fleet Atlantic. More submarines formed a line parallel to the fleet's line of advance, and those were supported by the carrier-borne S-3A Vikings that operated continuously off the flight decks.

The Pentagon had leaked to the press that this Marine division was en route to Germany, where the battle hung in the balance. In fact, the tight formation of amphibs was twenty miles from his carrier on a course of zero-three-nine, four hundred miles from its real objective.

USS *REUBEN JAMES*

"We're not heading north any longer," Calloway said. Dinner was being served in the wardroom. The officers were plowing through the last fresh lettuce aboard.

"I believe you're right," O'Malley agreed. "I think we're heading west now."

"You might as well tell me what the devil we're up to. I've been shut off from your satellite transmitters."

"We're screening the *Nimitz* battle group, except that when you're motoring along at twenty-five knots, it's not all that easy." O'Malley didn't like this. They were running a risk. It was part of war, but the pilot didn't like any part of war. Especially risks. *They pay me to do it, not to like it.*

"The escort is mostly British, isn't it?"

"Yeah, so?"

"That's a story I can use to tell the people at home how important—"

"Look, Mr. Calloway, let's say you file your story, and it got published in the local papers. Then let's say a Soviet agent reads the story and passes it along to—"

"How would he do that? The government has undoubtedly put severe restrictions on all forms of communication."

"Ivan has lots of communications satellites, same as us. We have two satellite transmitters on this dinky little frigate. You've seen 'em. How expensive do they look? Think maybe you could have one in your backyard, inside a bush maybe? Besides, the whole group is blacked out. Total EMCON. Nobody is transmitting anything at the moment."

Morris arrived and took his seat at the head of the table.

"Captain, where are we going?" Calloway asked.

"I just found out. Sorry I can't tell you. *Battleaxe* and we will continue to work together for a while as stern guard for the *Nimitz* group. We are now designated 'Mike Force.' "

"We getting any more help?" O'Malley asked.

"*Bunker Hill* is heading this way. She had to reload her magazines and join up with HMS *Illustrious*. They'll operate in close when they catch up. We're going to outside picket again. We start doing real ASW work in another four hours. Still going to be a bastard trying to keep up with the carrier, though."

USS *CHICAGO*

There were three contacts. All arrived within ten minutes. Two were ahead of *Chicago*, left and right of her bow. The third was on her port beam. Somehow, McCafferty realized, the Russians knew of the submarines they had killed. Probably some sort of radio buoy, he was sure. That meant all that his tactical successes had really accomplished was to draw more dangers in on the trio of American submarines.

"Conn, sonar. We have some sonobuoy signals at two-six-six. Count three buoys—four, make it four."

More Bears? McCafferty wondered. *A cooperative hunt?*

"Skipper, you better come forward," the sonar chief called.

"What's happening?" The waterfall display screen was suddenly crowded.

"Sir, we have three lines on sonobuoys forming up right now. Gotta be at least three aircraft up there. This one's fairly close, looks like it'll extend aft of us, maybe right on our friends."

McCafferty watched the new signal lines appear at the rate of one per minute. Each was a Russian sonobuoy, and the line marched east as two others grew on different azimuths.

"They're trying to box us in, Chief."

"Looks that way, sir."

Every time we destroyed a Russian ship we gave them a location reference. They've confirmed our course and speed of advance many times over. McCafferty had gotten his submarine back to the Svyataya Anna Trough. His path to the icepack was a hundred miles wide and three hundred fathoms deep. But how many Russian subs were there? The sonar crew continued to call off bearings to the submarine contacts while the captain watched the buoy lines extend.

"I think this is *Providence,* sir. She just increased speed—yeah, look at the noise now, she's really increased speed. This buoy must be right near her. Still can't find *Boston,* though."

Bearing was constant to the two forward submarine contacts. He couldn't develop a range figure unless he or they maneuvered. If he turned left, he'd then close on a third contact, which might not be a good idea. If he turned right, he'd run away from the submarine that might then close on *Providence.* If he did nothing, he'd accomplish nothing, but McCafferty didn't know what to do.

"There's another buoy, sir." The new one was between the bearings of two existing contacts. They were trying to localize *Providence.*

"There's *Boston.* She's—yeah, she's running past a buoy." A new contact line appeared suddenly bright where nothing had been before. *Todd just increased power and he's going to allow himself to be picked up,* McCafferty thought. *Then he'll dive deep to evade.*

Look at it from the Russian side, the captain told himself. *They don't really know what they're up against, do they? They probably figure they're up against more than one, but how many more? They can't know that. So they'll want to flush the game before they shoot, just to see what's here.*

"Torpedo in the water, bearing one-nine-three!"

A Russian Bear had dropped on *Boston.* McCafferty watched the sonar display as Simms took his boat deep with the torpedo in pursuit. He'd change depth and make a few radical changes in course and speed, trying to evade the fish. The bright line of a noisemaker appeared, holding a constant bearing as *Boston* maneuvered further. The torpedo chased the noisemaker, running another three minutes before it ran out of fuel.

The screen was relatively clear again. The sonobuoy signals remained. *Boston* and *Providence* had reduced power and disappeared—but so had the Russian sub signals.

What are they doing? What is their plan? the captain asked himself. *What submarines are out there?*

Tangos, has to be Tangos. They cut their electric motors back, slowed to steerageway, and that's why they disappeared off the scopes. Okay, they're not coming in after us anymore. They stopped moving when the aircraft detected Providence *and* Boston. *They're coordinating with the Bears! That means they have to be at shallow depth, and their sonar performance is down because they're close to the surface.*

"Chief, assume that these two contacts you had were Tangos doing about ten knots. The figure of merit gives us a detection range of what?"

"These water conditions . . . ten to twelve miles. I'd be real careful using that number, sir."

Three more sonobuoy lines began to appear north of *Chicago.* McCafferty went aft to see how they were plotted out. They assumed about a two-mile spacing on the sonobuoy lines, and that gave them range figures.

"Not being very subtle, are they?" the exec observed.

"Why bother when you don't have to? Let's see if we can pick our way through the buoys."

"What are our friends doing?"

"They'd better be coming north, too. I don't want to think about what other assets they have moving in on us. Let's head right through here."

The executive officer gave the orders. *Chicago* began to move forward again. Now they'd really find out if the rubber tiles on the hull absorbed sonar waves or not. The last bearings to the Russian submarines were plotted also. McCafferty knew that they too could be moving behind that wall of noise. When he detected them again it would be at perilously close range. They went deep. The submarine dove to a thousand feet and cruised toward the precise midpoint between a pair of pinging buoys.

Another torpedo appeared in the water aft, and McCafferty maneuvered quickly to evade, only to realize that it was aimed at someone else, or nothing at all. They listened to it run for several minutes, then fade out. *A perfect way to break a man's concentration,* McCafferty thought, bringing his sub back to a northerly course.

Bearings to the sonobuoys changed as they got closer. They were almost exactly two miles apart, a mile on either beam, as *Chicago* went through the first line, crawling just above the bottom. They were set on a frequency that could be heard clearly through the hull. *Just like the movies,* the captain thought, as the crewmen not directly involved in navigating the boat looked up and outward at the hull as though it were being caressed by the noise. Some caress. The second line was three miles beyond the first. *Chicago* turned slightly left to head for another gap.

Speed was down to four knots now. Sonar called out a possible contact to the north that immediately faded away. Maybe a Tango, maybe nothing. It was plotted anyway, as the submarine took nearly an hour to reach the second line of pinging buoys.

"Torpedo in the water, port side!" sonar screamed out.

"Right full rudder, all ahead flank!"

Chicago's propeller thrashed at the water, creating a bonanza of noise for the Russian aircraft who'd dropped a fish on a possible contact. They ran for three minutes while waiting for additional data on the torpedo.

"Where's the torpedo?"

"It's pinging, sir—but it's pinging the other way, bearing changing south, left to right, and weakening."

"All ahead one-third, rudder amidships," McCafferty ordered.

"Another one—torpedo in the water bearing zero-four-six."

"Right full rudder, all ahead flank," McCafferty ordered yet again. He turned to the exec. "You know what they just did? They dropped a fish to spook us into moving! *Damn!*" *Beautiful tactic, whoever you are. You know we can't afford to ignore a torpedo.*

"But how'd they know we were here?"

"Maybe they just guessed well, maybe they got a twitch. Then we gave 'em the contact."

"Torpedo bearing zero-four-one. The torpedo is pinging at us, don't know if it has us, sir. Captain, I got a new contact bearing zero-nine-five. Sounds like machinery noises—possible submarine."

"Now what?" McCafferty whispered. He put the Russian torpedo on his stern and hugged the bottom. Sonar performance dropped to zero as *Chicago* accelerated past twenty knots. Their instruments could still hear the ultrasonic pings of the torpedo, however, and McCafferty maneuvered to keep the weapon behind him as it dove down after the American sub.

"Bring her up! Make your depth one hundred feet. Shoot off a noisemaker."

"Full rise on the planes!" The diving officer ordered a short blow on the forward trim tanks to effect the maneuver. Along with the noisemaker, it created an enormous disturbance in the water. The torpedo raced in after it, missing below *Chicago*. A good maneuver, it was also a desperate one. The submarine rose quickly, her elastic hull popping as the pressure on the steel diminished. There was an enemy sub out there, and he now had all sorts of noise from *Chicago*. All McCafferty could do was run. He was confident that the other sub would chase after him with a homing torpedo circling below, but didn't understand why the other sub was there at all. He slowed *Chicago* to five knots and turned as the torpedo ran out of fuel below him. Next problem: there was a Soviet submarine close by.

"He's gotta know about where we are, skipper."

"You got that one right, XO. Sonar, Conn, Yankee-search!" Both sides could use unusual tactics. "Fire-control party, stand by, this one's going to be a snapshot."

The powerful but seldom-used active sonar installed in *Chicago*'s bow blasted the water with low-frequency energy.

"Contact, bearing zero-eight-six, range four six hundred!"

"Set it up!"

Chicago's steel hull reverberated three seconds later with Soviet sonar waves.

"Set! Ready for tubes three and two."

"Match bearings and shoot!" The torpedoes were fired within seconds of one another. "Cut the wires. Take her down! Make your depth one thousand feet, all ahead flank, left full rudder, come to new course two-six-five!" The submarine wheeled and sped west as her torpedoes raced toward their target.

"Transients—torpedoes in the water aft, bearing zero-eight-five."

"Patience," McCafferty said. *You didn't expect us to do that, did you?* "Nice job, fire-control! We got our shots off a minute faster than the other guy. Speed?"

"Twenty-four knots and increasing, sir," the helmsman answered. "Passing four hundred feet, sir."

"Sonar, how many fish we got chasing us?"

"At least three, sir. Sir, our units are pinging. I believe they have the target."

"XO, in a few seconds we're going to turn and change depth. When we do, I want you to fire off four noisemakers at fifteen-second intervals."

"Aye, Cap'n."

McCafferty went over to stand behind the helmsman. He'd just turned twenty the day before. The rudder indicator was amidships, with ten degrees of down angle on the planes, and the submarine was just passing through five hundred feet and hurtling down. The speed log now showed thirty knots. The rate of acceleration slowed as *Chicago* neared her maximum speed. He patted the boy on the shoulder.

"Now. Ten degrees rise on the planes and come right twenty degrees rudder."

"Yes, sir!"

The hull thundered with the news that their fish had found their target. Everyone jumped or cringed—they had their own problems chasing after them. *Chicago*'s maneuver left a massive knuckle in the water that the executive officer punctuated with four noisemakers. The small gas canisters filled the disturbance with bubbles that made excellent sonar targets while *Chicago* sped north. She raced right under a sonobuoy, but the Russians could not put another torpedo down for fear of interfering with those already running.

"Bearing is changing on all contacts, sir," sonar reported.

McCafferty started to breathe again. "Ahead one-third."

The helmsman dialed the annunciator handle. The engineers responded at once, and again *Chicago* slowed.

"We'll try to disappear again. They probably aren't sure yet who killed who. We'll use that time to get back down to the bottom and crawl northeast. Well done, people, that was sorta hairy."

The helmsman looked up. "Skipper, the south side of Chicago ain't the baddest part of town anymore!"

Sure as hell is the tiredest, though, the captain thought. *They can't keep coming at us this way. They* have to *back off and rethink, don't they?* He had the chart memorized. Another hundred fifty miles to the icepack.

39. The Shores of Stykkisholmur

HUNZEN, FEDERAL REPUBLIC OF GERMANY

They'd finally defeated the counterattack. *No,* Alekseyev told himself, *we didn't defeat it, we drove it off.* The Germans had withdrawn of their own accord after blunting half of the Russian attack. There was more to victory than being in possession of the battlefield.

It only got harder. Beregovoy had been right when he'd said that coordinating a large battle on the move was much harder than doing it from a fixed command post. Just the effort of getting the right map opened inside a cramped command vehicle was a battle against time and space, and eighty kilometers of front made for too many tactical maps. The counterattack had forced the generals to move one of their precious A reserve formations north, just in time to watch the Germans withdraw after savaging the rear areas of three B motor-rifle divisions, and spreading panic throughout the thousands of reservists who were trying to cope with old equipment and barely remembered training.

"Why did they pull back?" Sergetov asked his general.

Alekseyev did not respond. There was a fine question that he had already asked half a dozen times. *There were probably two reasons,* he told himself. *First, they'd lacked the strength to pursue the effort and had had to settle for a spoiling attack to unbalance our operation. Second, the central axis of our attack was on the verge of reaching the Weser, and they might have been called back to deal with this possible crisis.* The Army group intelligence officer approached.

"Comrade General, we have a disturbing report from one of our reconnaissance aircraft." The officer related the sketchy radio message from a low-flying recce aircraft. NATO's control of the air had brought particularly grim losses to those all-important units. The pilot of this MiG-21 had seen and reported a massive column of allied armor on the E8 highway south of Osnabrück before disappearing. The General immediately lifted the radiophone to Stendal.

"Why were we not informed of this as soon as you received it?" Alekseyev demanded of his superior.

"It is an unconfirmed report," CINC-West replied.

"Dammit, we *know* the Americans landed reinforcements at Le Havre!"

"And they can't be at the front for at least another day. How soon will you have a bridgehead on the Weser?"

"We have units on the river now at Rühle—"

"Then move your bridging units there and *get them across!*"

"Comrade, my right flank is still in disarray, and now we have this report of a possible enemy division forming up there!"

"You worry about crossing the Weser and let me worry about this phantom division! That's an order, Pavel Leonidovich!"

Alekseyev set the phone back in its place. *He has a better overall picture of what's going on,* Pasha told himself. *After we bridge the Weser, we have no really serious obstacle in front of us for over a hundred kilometers. After the river Weser, we can race into the Ruhr, Germany's industrial heart. If we destroy that, or even threaten it, then perhaps the Germans will seek their political solution and the war is won. That is what he is telling me.*

The General looked at his maps. Soon the lead regiment would try to force men across the river at Rühle. A bridging regiment was already en route. And he had his orders.

"Start moving the OMG troops."

"But our right flank!" Beregovoy protested.

"Will have to look after itself."

BRUSSELS, BELGIUM

SACEUR was still worried about his supplies. He'd also been forced to gamble in giving highest transport priority to the armored division now approaching Springe. The container ships loaded with munitions, spare parts, and the millions of other specialty items were just now sending their cargoes to the front. His largest reserve formation, the tank force, was about to team up with two German brigades, and what was left of the 11th Armored Cavalry Regiment, once a brigade in all but name, now only two battalions of weary men.

His supply situation was still tenuous. Many of his line units were down to four days of consumable stores, and the resupply effort would take two days, even if things went perfectly: a thin margin that in a pre-war exercise might have seemed equitable enough, but not now, when men and nations were at stake. Yet what choice did he have?

"General, we have a report here of a regiment-sized attack on the Weser. It looks like Ivan's trying to put troops on the left bank."

"What do we have there?"

"One battalion of *Landwehr,* and they're pretty beat up. There are two companies of tanks on the way, ought to be there in a little over an hour. There are preliminary indications that Soviet reinforcements are heading that way. This might be the main axis of their attack, at least it seems that they're orienting in that direction."

SACEUR rocked back in his chair, looking up at the map display. He had one reserve regiment within three hours of Rühle. The General was a man who loved to gamble. He was never happier than when sitting at a table with a deck of cards and a few hundred dollars' worth of chips. He usually won. If he attacked south from Springe and failed . . . the Russians would put two or three divisions across the Weser, and he had precisely one regiment in reserve to stand in their way. If he moved his new tank division there, and by some miracle they got there in time, he would have frittered away his best chance for a counterattack by *reacting* to a Soviet move again. No, he couldn't just react anymore. He pointed to Springe.

"How long before they're ready to move?"

"The whole division—six hours at best. We can divert the units still on the road south to—"

"No."

"Then we go south from Springe with what's ready now?"

"No." SACEUR shook his head and outlined his plan . . .

ICELAND

"I see one," Garcia called. Edwards and Nichols were beside him in a moment.

"Hello, Ivan," Nichols said quietly.

Even with binoculars, the distance was still a little over three miles. Edwards saw a tiny figure walking along the crest of the mountaintop. He carried a rifle and appeared to be wearing a soft hat—perhaps a beret—instead of a helmet. The figure stopped and brought his hands up to his face. He had binoculars, too, Edwards saw. He looked north, slightly downward, training his field glasses left to right and back again. Then he turned and looked off in the direction of Keflavik.

Another man appeared, approaching the first. Perhaps they were talking, but it was impossible to tell at this distance. The one with binoculars pointed at something to the south.

"What do you suppose this is all about?" Edwards asked.

"Talking about the weather, girls, sports, food—who knows?" Nichols replied. "Another one!"

The third figure appeared, and the trio of Russian paratroopers stood together doing whatever it was that they were doing. One had to be an officer, Edwards decided. He said something, and the others moved off quickly, dropping out of sight below the crest. *What order did you just give?*

Presently a group of men appeared. The light was bad, and they shuffled around too much to get an accurate count, but there had to be at least ten. About half of them were carrying their personal weapons, and these started moving downhill. To the west.

"Right, he's a smart soldier," Nichols announced. "He's sending out a patrol to make certain the area's secure."

"What do we do about it?" Edwards asked.

"What do you think, *Lef*tenant?"

"Our orders are to sit tight. So we sit tight and hope they don't see us."

"Not likely they will, you know. I shouldn't think they'd climb down—must be eight hundred feet—then cross that rock yard, then climb up here just to see if any Yanks are about. Remember, the only reason we know they're there is that we saw their helicopter."

Otherwise we might have walked right into them, and that would have been that, Edwards reminded himself. *I won't be safe until I'm back home in Maine.* "Is that more of them?"

"Must be at least a platoon over there. That is rather clever of our friends, isn't it?"

Edwards got on the radio to report this development to Doghouse while the Marines kept track of the Russians.

"A platoon?"

"That's Sergeant Nichols's estimate. Kinda hard to count heads from three miles away, fella."

"Okay, we'll pass that one along. Any air activity?"

"Haven't seen any aircraft at all since yesterday."

"How about Stykkisholmur?"

"Too far to make anything out. We still can see those four-by-fours sitting in the street, but no armored vehicles. I'd say they had a small garrison force there to keep an eye on the port. The fishing boats aren't going anywhere."

"Very well. Good report, Beagle. Hang in there." The major switched off and turned to his neighbor at the communications console. "It's a shame to keep them in the dark like this, isn't it?"

The SOE man sipped at his tea. "It would be a greater shame to blow the operation."

Edwards didn't take the radio apart, but left it leaning against a rock. Vigdis was still asleep on a flat ledge twenty feet below the top. Sleep was about the most attractive thing Edwards could think of at the moment.

"They're heading in this direction," Garcia said. He handed the glasses to Edwards. Smith and Nichols were conferring a few yards away.

Mike trained the binoculars on the Russians. He told himself that to have them come right to his position was a very low order of probability. *Keep telling yourself that.* He shifted his glasses to the Russian observation post.

"There it is again," the sergeant told his lieutenant.

"What's that?"

"I saw a flash from that hilltop, sun reflected off something."

"A shiny rock," the lieutenant snorted, not taking the time to look. "Comrade Lieutenant!" The officer turned at the sharp tone to see a rock flying through the air at his face. He caught it, and was too surprised to be angry. "How shiny does that rock look?"

"An old can, then! We've found enough trash here from tourists and mountain climbers, haven't we?"

"Then why does it come and go and come back?"

The lieutenant got visibly angry at last. "Sergeant, I know you have a year's combat experience in Afghanistan. I know I am a new officer. *But I am a Goddamned officer and you are a Goddamned sergeant!*"

The wonders of our classless society, the sergeant thought, continuing to look at his officer. Few officers could bear his look.

"Very well, Sergeant. You tell them." The lieutenant pointed at the radio.

"Markhovskiy, before you come back, check out the hilltop to your right."

"But it's two hundred meters high!" the squad leader shot back.

"Correct. It shouldn't take long at all," the platoon sergeant said comfortingly.

USS *INDEPENDENCE*

Toland switched viewgraphs in the projector. "Okay, these satellite shots are less than three hours old. Ivan has three mobile radars, here, here, and here. He moves them about daily—meaning that one's probably been moved already—and usually has two operating around the clock. At Keflavik we have five SA-11 launch vehicles, four birds per vehicle. This SAM is very bad news. You've all been briefed on its known capabilities, and you'd better figure on a few hundred hand-held SAMs, too. The photo shows six mobile antiaircraft guns. We don't see any fixed ones. They're there, gentlemen, they're just camouflaged. At least five, perhaps as many as ten MiG-29 fighter interceptors. This used to be a regiment until the guys from *Nimitz* cut them down to size. Remember that the ones who're left are the ones who survived two squadrons of Tomcats. That is the opposition at Keflavik."

Toland stepped aside while the wing operations officer went over the mission profile. It sounded impressive to Toland. He hoped it would be so for the Russians.

The curtain went up fifty minutes later. The first aircraft launched for the strike were the E-2C Hawkeyes. Accompanied by fighters, they flew to within eighty miles of the Icelandic coast and radiated their own radar coverage all over the formation. More Hawkeyes reached farther out to cover the formation from possible air- and submarine-launched missile attack.

KEFLAVIK, ICELAND

Ground-based Soviet radar detected the Hawkeyes even before their powerful systems went active. They could see two of the slow propeller-driven aircraft hovering beyond SAM range, each accompanied by two other aircraft whose extended figure-eight-course tracks denoted them as Tomcat interceptors guarding the Hawkeyes. The alarm was sounded. Fighter pilots boarded their aircraft while missile and gun crews raced to their stations.

The fighter-force commander was a major with three kills to his credit—but who had learned the virtue of caution the hard way. He'd been shot down once already. The Americans had sprung one trap on his regiment and he had no wish to participate in a second. If this was an attack and not a feint to draw out what fighters remained on Iceland—how would he know? He reached his decision. On the major's command, the fighters lifted off, climbed to twenty thousand feet, and orbited over the peninsula, conserving their fuel and remaining over land, where they could be supported by friendly SAMs. They had exercised carefully the previous few days with these tactics, and were as confident as they could be that the missile crews could distinguish between friendly and unfriendly aircraft. When they got to altitude, their radar threat receivers told them of more American Hawkeyes to the east and west. The information was relayed home with a request for a strike by the Backfires. What they got back was a request to identify the American fleet's location and composition. The air-base commander didn't bother forwarding that. The Soviet fighter commander swore under his breath. The American radar aircraft were prime targets, and tantalizingly within reach. With a full regiment, he'd streak after them and risk losses from their fighter escorts, but he was sure that that was precisely what the Americans were hoping he'd do.

The Intruders went in first, skimming above the wavetops from the south at five hundred knots, Standard-ARM missiles hanging from their wings. More Tomcat fighters were behind them at high altitude. When the fighters passed the radar aircraft, they illuminated the circling MiGs with their radars and began to fire off Phoenix missiles.

The MiGs couldn't ignore them. The Soviet fighters separated into two-plane elements and scattered, coached from their ground-based radar controllers.

The Intruders popped up at a range of thirty miles, just outside range of the SAMs, and loosed four Standard-ARM missiles each, which homed in on the Russian search radars. The Russian radar operators faced a cruel choice. They could leave their search radars on and almost certainly have them destroyed or turn them off and lessen the chance—and completely lose track of the overhead air battle. They chose a middle ground. The Soviet SAM commander ordered his men to flip their systems on and off at random intervals, hoping to confuse the incoming missiles while keeping tenuous coverage of the incoming strike. The missile flight time was just over a minute, and most of the radar crews took the time to switch their systems off and leave them off—each misunderstanding the order in the most advantageous manner.

The Phoenixes arrived first. The MiG pilots suddenly lost their ground-control guidance, but kept maneuvering. One aircraft had four missiles targeted, and evaded two missiles only to blunder into another one. The major in command swore at his inability to hit back as he tried to think of something that would work.

Next came the Standard-ARMs. The Russians had three air-search radars and three more for missile-acquisition. All had been turned on when the first alarm sounded, then all had gone black after the missiles had been detected in the air. The Standards were only partially confused. Their guidance systems had been designed to record the position of a radar in case it did go off the air, and they homed in on those positions now. The missiles killed two transmitters entirely and damaged two others.

The American mission commander was annoyed. The Russian fighters were not cooperating. They hadn't come out even when the Intruders had popped up—he'd had more fighters waiting low for that eventuality. But the Soviet radars were down. He gave the next order. Three squadrons of F/A-18 Hornets streaked in low from the north.

The Russian air-defense commander ordered his radars back on, saw that no more missiles were in the air, and soon picked up the low-flying Hornets. The MiG commander saw the American attack aircraft next, and with them, his chance. The MiG-29 was a virtual twin to the new American aircraft.

The Hornets sought out the Russian SAM launchers and began to launch their guided weapons at them. Missiles crisscrossed the sky. Two Hornets fell to missiles, two more to guns, as the American fighter-bombers scoured the ground with bombs and gunfire. Then the MiGs arrived.

The American pilots were warned, but were too close to their bombing targets to react at once. Once free of their heavy ordnance, they were fighters again, and climbed into the sky—they feared MiGs more than missiles. The resulting air battle was a masterpiece of confusion. The two aircraft would have been hard to distinguish sitting side by side on the ground. At six hundred knots, in the middle of battle, the task was almost impossible, and the Americans, with their greater numbers, had to hold fire until they were sure of their targets. The Russians knew what they were attacking, but they too shrank from shooting with abandon at a target that looked too much like a comrade's aircraft. The result was a swarming mix of fighters closing to a range too short for missiles, as pilots sought positive target identification, an anachronistic gun duel punctuated by surface-to-air missiles from the two surviving Russian launchers. Controllers on the American aircraft and the Russian ground station never had a chance to direct matters. It was entirely in the hands of the pilots. The fighters went to afterburner and swept into punishing high-g turns while heads swiveled and eyes squinted at familiar shapes while trying to decide if the paint scheme was friendly or not. That part of the task was fairly even. The American planes were haze-gray and harder to spot, allowing easier target identification at long range than at short. Two Hornets died first, followed by a MiG. Then another MiG fell to cannon fire, and a Hornet to a snap-shot missile. An errant SAM exploded a MiG and a Hornet together.

The Soviet major saw that and screamed for the SAMs to hold fire; then he fired his cannon at a Hornet blazing across his nose, missed, and turned to follow him. He watched the American close for a high-deflection shot on a MiG-29 and damage its engine. The major didn't know how many of his aircraft were left. It was beyond that. He was engaged in a struggle for personal survival—which he expected to lose. Caution faded to nothing as he closed on afterburner and ignored his low-fuel-state light. His target turned north and led him over the water. The major fired his last missile and then watched it track right into the Hornet's right engine as his own engines flamed out. The Hornet's tail fragmented and the major screamed with delight as he and the American pilot ejected a few hundred meters apart. *Four kills,* the major thought. *At least I have done my duty.* He was in the water thirty seconds later.

Commander Davies crawled into his raft despite a broken wrist, cursing and blessing his luck at the same time. His first considered action was to activate his rescue radio. He looked around and saw another yellow raft a short distance away. It wasn't easy paddling with one arm, but the other guy was paddling toward him. What came next was quite a surprise.

"You are prisoner!" The man was pointing a gun at him. Davies's revolver was at the bottom of the sea.

"Who the hell are you?"

"I am Major Alexandr Georgiyevich Chapayev—Soviet Air Force."

"Howdy. I'm Commander Gus Davies, U.S. Navy. Who got you?"

"No one get me! I run out of fuel!" He waved the gun. "And you are my prisoner."

"Oh, horseshit!"

Major Chapayev shook his head. Like Davies, he was in a near-state of shock from the stress of combat and his close escape from death.

"Hold on to that gun, though, Major. I don't know if there're sharks around here or not."

"Sharks?"

Davies had to think for a moment. The code name for that new Russian sub. "*Akula. Akula* in the water."

Chapayev went pale. *"Akula?"*

Davies unzipped his flight suit and tucked in his injured arm. "Yeah, Major. This is the third time I've had to go swimming. Last time I was on the raft for twelve hours, and I saw a couple of the Goddamned things. You got any repellant on your raft?"

"What?" Chapayev was really confused now.

"This stuff." Davies dipped the plastic envelope in the water. "Let's rope your raft to mine. Safer that way. This repellant stuff's supposed to keep the *akula* away."

Davies tried to secure the rafts one-handed and failed. Chapayev set the gun down to help. After being shot down once, then surviving an air battle, the major was suddenly obsessed with the idea of being alive. The idea of being eaten by a carnivorous fish horrified him. He looked over the side of the raft into the water.

"Christ, what a morning," Davies groaned. His wrist was really hurting now.

Chapayev grunted agreement. He looked around for the first time and realized he couldn't see land. Next he reached for his rescue radio and found that his leg was lacerated, the radio pocket on his flight suit ripped away in the ejection.

"Aren't we two sorry sons of bitches," he said in Russian.

"What's that?"

"Where is land?" The sea had never looked so vast.

"About twenty-five miles that way, I think. That leg doesn't look too good, Major." Davies laughed coldly. "We must have the same kind of ejector seats. Oh, shit! This arm hurts."

"Damn, what do you suppose that's all about?" Edwards wondered aloud. They were too far away to hear anything, but they could not miss the smoke rising from Keflavik.

A more immediate concern was the squad of Russians now at the base of their hill. Nichols, Smith, and the four privates were spread out across a front of a hundred yards centered on Edwards, faces darkened, mainly squatting behind rocks and watching the Russians half a mile away.

"Doghouse, this is Beagle, and we got trouble here, over." He had to call twice more to get an answer.

"What's the problem, Beagle?"

"We got five or six Russians climbing our hill. They're about six hundred feet below us, half a mile away. Also, what's going on at Keflavik?"

"We have an air attack under way there, that's all I know at the moment. Keep us posted, Beagle. I'll see if I can send you some help."

"Thank you. Out."

"Michael?"

"Good morning. Glad one of us got a decent night's sleep." She sat down beside him, resting her hand on his leg, and the fear subsided for a moment.

"I'd swear I just saw some movement on the top there," the platoon sergeant said.

"Let me see." The lieutenant moved his powerful spotting glasses on the peak. "Nothing. Nothing at all. Maybe you saw a bird. Those little puffin things are all over the place."

"Possibly," the sergeant allowed. He was starting to feel guilty for sending Markhovskiy up there. *If this lieutenant had half a brain*, he thought, *he'd have sent a larger force, maybe led it himself, like an officer should.*

"The air base is being heavily attacked."

"Have you radioed in?"

"Tried to. They're off the air at the moment." There was concern in his voice. Sixty miles was too far for the small tactical radios. Their heavy VHF set reported into the air base. As much as he wanted to be with the patrol, the lieutenant knew his proper place was here. "Warn Markhovskiy."

Edwards saw one of the Russians stop and fiddle with his walkie-talkie. *Tell him he's climbing the wrong hill—tell him to come home to Mama.*

"Keep your head down, babe."

"What is it, Michael?"

"We got some people climbing this hill."

"Who?" There was concern in her voice.

"Guess."

"Skipper, they're coming up for sure," Smith warned over the radio.

"Yeah, I see that. Everybody got a good place?"

"*Lef*tenant, I strongly recommend that we let them get in very close before opening fire," Nichols called.

"Makes sense, skipper," Smith agreed on the same circuit.

"Okay. You got ideas, gentlemen, I want to hear them right away. Oh, yeah, I've called in for some help. Maybe we can get some air support."

Mike pulled back on the charging handle of his rifle to make sure a round was chambered, set it on safe, then put the M-16 down. The Marines had all the hand grenades. Edwards had never been taught how to use them, and they frightened him.

Come on, fellows, just go the hell away and we'll be glad to leave you alone. They kept coming. Each paratrooper climbed slowly, rifle in one hand and the other hand grabbing or fending off rocks. They spent their time evenly looking up toward Edwards and down at their footing. Mike was truly frightened. These Russians were elite soldiers. So were his Marines—but he was not. He didn't belong here. The other times he'd faced Russians, in Vigdis's house, the terrifying incident with the helicopter, all those were behind him and for the moment forgotten. He wanted to run away—but what if he did? He'd earned the respect of his Marines, and could he throw that away and still live with himself? What of Vigdis—could he run away in front of her? *What are you most afraid of, Mike?*

"Stay cool," he muttered to himself.

"What?" Vigdis asked. She too was afraid, just from seeing his face.

"Nothing." He tried to smile and half succeeded. *You can't let her down, can you?*

The Russians were now five hundred yards away and still well below them. Their approach became more cautious. There were six of them, and they moved two at a time, fanning out and no longer taking what looked to be the easy route to the top.

"Skipper, we got a problem," Smith called. "I think they know we're here."

"Nichols, I want to hear you."

"We wait until they get within one hundred yards, and for Christ's good sake, keep heads down! If you can get some support, I would suggest you do so."

Edwards switched radios. "Doghouse, this is Beagle, and we need some help here."

"We're working on that. We're trying to get—to get some friends to listen in on this frequency. It takes time, Lieutenant."

"I got about another five minutes—tops—before the shooting starts."

"Keep this channel open."

Where are they? Edwards asked himself. He couldn't see anyone now. The rocks and cover that had so often worked for them were now working against them. He stopped bobbing his head up and down. He was the officer, he was in command, he had the best vantage point, and he had to see what was happening. Edwards moved slightly to get a decent view of the events below him.

"There *is* somebody there!" the platoon sergeant said, grabbing for the radio. "Markhovskiy, you're heading into a trap! I see a man with a helmet atop the hill."

"You're right," the lieutenant said. He turned. "Get the mortar set up!" The officer ran over to the big VHF radio and tried to raise Keflavik. Armed troops on this hill could only mean one thing—but Keflavik was still off the air.

Edwards saw one Russian rise up, then drop back down on a shout from someone else. When the shape reappeared, it was behind a rifle. He heard a whistling sound, then there was an explosion fifty yards away.

"Oh, shit!" Edwards fell to his face and cowered next to his rock. Bits of other rocks fell around him. He looked at Vigdis, who seemed all right, then over at the far peak, where men were racing downhill. Another mortar round fell to his right, and was followed by automatic-rifle fire. He grabbed his satellite radio.

"Doghouse, this is Beagle. We are under attack."

"Beagle, we are now in contact with a Navy carrier. Stand by." The ground shook again. The round fell less than thirty feet in front of his position, but he was well shielded. "Beagle, the Navy carrier is now on your frequency. Go ahead and transmit. Their call sign is Starbase, and they know where you are."

"Starbase, this is Beagle, over!"

"Roger, Beagle, we show your position five klicks west of hill 1064. Tell me what's happening."

"Starbase, we are under attack by a squad of Russian infantrymen, with reinforcements on the way. Their observation post on 1064 has a mortar and we're getting fire from that. We need help fast."

"Roger, copy, Beagle. Stand by . . . Beagle, be advised we're diverting some help your way, ETA two-five minutes. Can you mark your position?"

"Negative, we don't have anything to do it with."

"Roger, understand. Hang in there, Beagle. We'll be back. Out."

Edwards heard a scream to his left. He stuck his head up and saw mortar rounds falling near Nichols's position—and Russians less than a hundred yards to his front. Mike grabbed his rifle and sighted it on a moving shape, only to have it drop out of sight again. He picked his walkie-talkie up with his free hand.

"Nichols, Smith, this is Edwards, report in."

"Nichols here. Whoever has that mortar knows what he's about. I have two wounded men here."

"We're okay, skipper. We seen two Russians go down hard. I sent Garcia to cover you."

"Okay, guys, we have air cover on the way in. I—" The shape came up again. Edwards dropped the radio, aimed his rifle, and fired three rounds, missing the shape that dodged out of sight. Back to the radio. "Nichols, you need help?"

"Two of us can still shoot. I'm afraid your Rodgers is dead. There—" The radio went dead for a moment. "All right, all right. We killed one, and the other is backing away. Look out, *Left*enant, there are two fifty yards to your left front."

Mike looked around his rock and got shot at for his trouble. He shot back without hitting anything.

"Hi, skipper!" Garcia crashed down next to him.

"Two bad guys, that way." Edwards pointed. The private nodded and moved left behind cover of the hill crest. He got thirty feet when another mortar round exploded four strides behind him. The private fell hard and didn't move.

It's not fair, it's not fair. I got them this far, and it's not fair!

"Smith, Garcia's down. Get back up here. Nichols, if you can get to my position, move!" He switched radios. "Starbase, this is Beagle. Tell your birds to hurry."

"Two-zero minutes out, Beagle. Four A-7s. We have some other help coming, but they'll get to you first."

Edwards took his rifle and moved over to Garcia. The private was still breathing, but his back and legs were peppered with fragments. The lieutenant crawled to the crest and saw a Russian crouched thirty feet away. He aimed his rifle and fired two bursts. The Russian went down, firing his own weapon in a wide arc that missed Edwards by a scant yard. Where was the other one? Mike stuck his head up and saw something the size of a baseball flying through the air. He scrambled backwards as the grenade went off ten feet from where he'd been. Mike rolled to his right and went back uphill.

The Russian had disappeared again, but Edwards saw the others had reached the foot of his hill on a dead run and were starting up to his position. He strained to look and keep his head down at the same time. The other one—there! He was clambering down the hill, apparently dragging a wounded man with him. Mortar fire started to drop behind him, covering the man's retreat.

"You okay, Lieutenant?" It was Smith. He was wounded in the arm. "Whoever's working that Goddamned mortar must be the Russian Davy Crockett!"

Nichols arrived three minutes later. He was unhurt, but the Royal Marine private with him was bleeding from the abdomen. Edwards looked at his watch.

"We got air support coming in about ten minutes. If we stay here at the top in one place, they can drop all around us."

The men took position within fifty feet of Edwards. Mike grabbed Vigdis by the arm and set her between two boulders.

"Michael, I'm—"

"I'm scared, too. Stay here no matter what happens, stay here! You can—" The whistling sound came again, and this one was close. Mike stumbled and fell right on top of her. A hot needle seemed to penetrate his lower leg.

"Shit!" The wound was just above his boot. He tried to rise, but the leg wouldn't take any weight. He looked around for the radio and hopped over to it, cursing all the way. "Starbase, this is Beagle, over."

"Nine minutes out, Beagle," the voice said patiently.

"Starbase, we're all on top of this hilltop, okay? We're all within fifty feet of the summit." He stuck his head up. "We have about fifteen bad guys coming toward us, maybe seven hundred yards away. We beat off the first attack, but we're down to—four, I guess, and three of us are wounded. For God's sake, get that mortar first, it's murdering us."

"Roger that. Hold it together, son. Help is coming."

"You're wounded, *Lef*tenant," Nichols said.

"I noticed. The planes are eight or nine minutes out. I told them to take the mortar position out first."

"Very good. Ivan's in love with the bloody things." Nichols cut the pants away from the wound and tied a bandage on. "You won't be doing much dancing for a while."

"What can we do to slow them down?"

"We'll open fire at five hundred. That will make them more cautious, I think. Come on." Nichols grabbed his arm and pulled him to a position on the crest.

The Russians were moving forward with great skill. Men alternated brief rushes with dives behind whatever cover was available. The mortar was quiet at the moment, but that would change as soon as the paratroopers got close enough for their final assault. Nichols had discarded his submachine gun, and was aiming a semiautomatic rifle. When he figured the range at five hundred yards, the sergeant took careful aim and squeezed the trigger. He missed, but every Russian on the hill dropped.

"You know what you just did?" Edwards asked.

"Yes, I just invited more mortar fire on us." Nichols turned to look at his lieutenant. "Bloody poor choice we have, isn't it?"

"Michael, you need this." Vigdis came down beside him.

"I told you to stay—"

"Here is your radio. I go—"

"Down!" Mike yanked her beside him as a mortar round dropped thirty feet away. A series of five dropped across their position.

"Here they come!" Smith yelled.

The Marines opened fire, and the Russians returned it, dashing from one piece of cover to another in a two-pronged advance that threatened to envelop the hilltop. Mike got back on the radio.

"Starbase, this is Beagle, over."

"Roger, Beagle."

"They're coming in on us now."

"Beagle, our A-7s have you in sight. I want to know exactly where you and your people are—say again *exactly*."

"Starbase, there are two secondary summits on this hill, about three miles west of hill 1064. We are on the northern one, repeat northern one. My group is all within five-zero feet of the top of that hill. Anything that moves is the enemy, we are all sitting tight. The mortar is on hill 1064, and we need that taken out quick."

There was a long pause. "Okay, Beagle, they've been told where you are. Get your head down, they're one minute away, approaching from the south. Good luck. Out."

"Two hundred yards," Nichols said. Edwards joined him and leveled his M-16. Three men rose at once, both men fired, but Edwards couldn't tell if he'd hit anyone or not. Bullets kicked up dirt and stone chips a few feet away, and the whistle of more mortar rounds came down again. The group of five landed right on the crest as Edwards caught the shape of a haze-gray fighter-bomber diving from his right.

The stubby A-7E Corsair pulled out a thousand feet above the mountaintop three miles away. Four canisters of cluster bombs fell, splitting open in the air. A small cloud of bomblets cascaded on the Russian observation post. From three miles, it sounded like a loud string of firecrackers as the hilltop disappeared in a cloud of dust and sparks. A second aircraft repeated the maneuver twenty seconds later. There could be nothing left alive on the hilltop.

The attacking Russians stopped cold in their tracks and turned to see what had happened to their base camp. Then they saw that more aircraft were circling only two thousand yards away. It was clear to everyone that their best chance to stay alive another five minutes was to get as close to the Americans as they could. As one man, the Russian squads rose firing their weapons and ran up the hill. Two more Corsairs wheeled in the sky and darted in, their pilots drawn by the movement. They swept in level only a hundred feet above the slopes and loosed pairs of cluster bombs. Edwards heard the screams over the thunder of the explosives, but could see nothing through the cloud of dust that rose before his eyes.

"Christ, they can't drop much closer than that."

"They can't drop *any* closer than that," Nichols said, wiping blood from his face.

They could still hear rifle fire from within the dust. The wind blew it away, and at least five Russians were still up and moving toward them. The Navy Corsairs made another run in but broke off, unable to drop so close to friendly troops. They curved back in seconds, firing their cannon. The shells scattered wildly, with some exploding ten yards from Edwards's face.

"Where'd they go?"

"The left, I think," Nichols answered. "You can't talk directly to the fighters?"

Edwards shook his head. "Not that kind of radio, Sarge."

The A-7s circled overhead while their pilots watched the ground for movement. Edwards tried to wave at them, but couldn't tell if they recognized the gesture or not. One of them dove to his left and fired a cannon burst into the rocks. Edwards heard a scream, but saw nothing.

"Stalemate." Edwards turned to look at his satellite radio. The last set of mortar rounds had sent a fragment through the backpack.

"Down!" Nichols grabbed the lieutenant as a grenade arced through the air. It exploded a few feet away. "Here they come again."

Edwards turned and put a fresh magazine in his rifle. He saw two Russians fifty feet away and fired a long burst. One went down on his face. The other returned fire and dodged left. He felt a weight on his legs and saw Nichols down on his back with a trio of red holes in his shoulder. Edwards put the last magazine in his rifle and moved awkwardly across the hill to the left, unable to put much weight on his right leg.

"Michael . . ."

"Go the other way," Edwards replied. "Look out!"

He saw a face and a rifle—and a flash. Edwards dove right, too late to keep from being hit in the chest. Only shock kept the pain from becoming unbearable. He fired a few rounds into the air to keep the man's head down as he backpedaled his feet to get away. Where was everyone? There was rifle fire to his right. Why wasn't anybody helping him? He heard the roar of jet engines as the A-7s continued to circle, unable to do anything but watch in frustration. He cursed them as he bled. His wounded leg revolted at being used this way, and his left arm was useless. Edwards held the rifle like an oversized handgun as he waited for the Russian to appear. He felt hands under his arms dragging him backwards.

"Drop me, Vigdis, for Christ's sake, drop me and run."

She said nothing. Her breathing was heavy as she struggled, stumbling, to pull him over the rocks. He was losing consciousness from the blood loss, and looked up to see the A-7s drawing off. There was another sound that didn't seem to make much sense. Dust rose around him with a sudden wind and there was another long burst of machine-gun fire as a huge green-black shape appeared overhead. Men jumped out, and it was all over. He closed his eyes. The Russian commander had gotten through to Keflavik. Here was the Mi-24 to reinforce the outpost . . . Edwards was too drained to react. He'd run a good race and lost. There was more chattering rifle fire, then silence as the helicopter moved off. How did the Russians treat prisoners who'd killed helpless men?

"Your name Beagle?"

It required the greatest effort of his life to open his eyes. He saw a black man standing over him.

"Who're you?"

"Sam Potter. I'm a lieutenant with Second Force Recon. You're Beagle, right?" He turned. "We need a corpsman over here!"

"My people are all hurt."

"We're working on it. We'll have you outa here in five minutes. Hang in there, Beagle. I gotta go do some work. Okay, people," he called loudly. "Let's get those Russians checked out. If we got any live ones, we wanna move them the hell off this rock right now!"

"Michael?" Edwards was still confused. Her face was right above his when he lost consciousness.

"Just who the hell is this guy?" Lieutenant Potter asked five minutes later.

"Wing-wiper. He done good," Smith said, wincing with his own injuries.

"How'd you get here?" Potter waved for his radio operator.

"We fucking walked all the way from Keflavik, sir."

"Quite a trip, Sarge." Potter was impressed. He gave a short radio order. "Chopper's on the way in now. I guess the lady goes out too."

"Yes, sir. Welcome to Iceland, sir. We been waiting for you."

"Take a look, Sarge." Potter's arm swept to the west. A series of gray bumps on the horizon headed east toward Stykkisholmur.

USS *CHICAGO*

They were still out there, McCafferty was sure—but where? After killing the last Tango, contact had never been reestablished with the other two Russian submarines. Eight hours of relative peace rewarded his evasive maneuvering. The Russian ASW aircraft were still overhead, still dropping sonobuoys, but something had gone wrong for them. They weren't coming very close now. He'd had to maneuver clear only four times. That would have been a lot in peacetime, but after the past few days it seemed like a vacation.

The captain had taken the chance to rest himself and his crew. Though they would all have gratefully accepted a month in bed, the four or six hours of sleep they'd all had were like a cup of water for a man in the desert, enough to get them a little farther. And there was only a little farther to go: exactly one hundred miles to the jagged edge of the arctic ice. Sixteen hours or so.

Chicago was about five miles ahead of her sisters. Every hour, Mc-Cafferty would maneuver his sub to an easterly course and allow his towed-array sonar to get a precise fix on them. That was hard enough: *Boston* and *Providence* were difficult to pick up even at this distance.

He wondered what the Russians were thinking. The mobbing tactics of the Krivak-Grisha teams had failed. They'd learned that it was one thing to use those ships for barrier operations against the Keypunch team, but something very different to rush after a submarine with long-range weapons and computerized fire-control. Their dependence on active sonobuoys had reduced the effectiveness of their ASW patrol aircraft, and the one thing that had nearly worked—placing a diesel sub between two sonobuoy lines, then spooking their target into moving with a randomly dropped torpedo— had failed also. *Thank God they didn't know how close they came with that,* McCafferty thought to himself. Their Tango-class subs were formidable opponents, quiet and hard to locate, but the Russians were still paying for their unsophisticated sonars. All in all, McCafferty was more confident now than he'd been in weeks.

"Well?" he asked his plotting officer.

"Looks like they're steaming as before, sir, about ten thousand yards behind us. I think this one's *Boston.* She's maneuvering a lot more. *Providence* here is plodding along pretty straight. We got a good fix on her."

"Left ten degrees rudder, come to new course three-five-five," Mc-Cafferty ordered.

"Left ten degrees rudder, aye, coming to new course three-five-five. Sir, my rudder is left ten degrees."

"Very well." The captain sipped at a cup of hot cocoa. It made a nice change of pace from coffee. *Chicago* turned slowly north. In the engine spaces aft, the submarine's engineer crew kept watch on their instruments as the reactor plant turned out an even 10-percent power.

About the only bad news was the storm on the surface. For some reason a series of squalls was parading around the top of the world, and this one was a real growler. The sonar crew estimated fifteen-foot waves and forty-knot winds, unusual for the arctic summer. It knocked 10 to 20 percent off their sonar performance, but would make for ideal conditions as they approached the icepack. The sea conditions would be grinding acre-sized ice floes into ice chips, and that much noise would make the American subs very hard to detect in the ice. *Sixteen hours,* McCafferty told himself. *Sixteen hours and we're out of here.*

"Conn, sonar, we have a contact bearing three-four-zero. Not enough data to classify at this time."

McCafferty went forward to sonar.

"Show me."

"Right here, skipper." The chief tapped the display. "I can't give you a blade-count yet, too sketchy for anything. Well, it smells like a nuclear boat," the chief allowed.

"Put up your model."

The chief pushed a button and a secondary screen displayed the predicted sonar range, generated by computer from known local water conditions. Their direct-path sonar range was just over thirty thousand yards. The water was not deep enough yet for convergence zones, and they were beginning to get low-frequency background noise from the icepack. It would impede their ability to discriminate sonar contacts in the same way bright sunlight lessens the apparent intensity of an electric light.

"Getting a slow bearing change here. Going left-to-right, bearing to target is now three-four-two . . . fading out a little bit. What's this?" The chief looked at a new fuzzy line on the bottom of the display. "Possible new contact bearing zero-zero-four." The line faded out and stayed out for two minutes, then came back on bearing zero-zero-six.

McCafferty debated whether to go to battle stations. On one hand he might need to engage a target very soon . . . but probably not. Wouldn't it be better to give his crew a few more minutes' rest? He decided to wait.

"Firming up. We now have two possible submarine contacts, bearing three-four-zero and zero-zero-four."

McCafferty went back to control and ordered a turn east, which would track his towed array on the new targets, plus give a cross bearing on each from which to compute range. It gave him more than he bargained for.

"*Boston* is maneuvering west, sir. I can't detect anything out that way, but she's definitely heading west."

"Sound general quarters," McCafferty ordered.

It was no way to wake up from needed sleep, the captain knew. In berthing spaces all over the boat, men snapped instantly awake and rolled out of their bunks, some dropping to the deck, others climbing upright in the crowded spaces. They ran to stations, relieving the routine watchstanders to head for their own battle stations.

"All stations report manned and ready, sir."

Back to work. The captain stood over the plotting table and considered the tactical situation. Two possible enemy submarines were astride his course to the ice. If *Boston* was moving, Simms probably had something also, maybe to the west, maybe aft. In twenty short minutes, McCafferty had gone from coolly confident to paranoid again. What were they doing? Why were two subs almost directly in his path?

"Take her up to periscope depth." *Chicago* rose slowly from her cruising depth of seven hundred feet. It took five minutes. "Raise the ESM."

The slender mast went up on hydraulic power, feeding information to the electronic-warfare technician.

"Skipper, I got three J-band aircraft search sets." He read off the bearings. *Bears or Mays,* McCafferty thought.

"Look around. Up scope." He had to let the periscope go all the way up to see over the wave tops. "Okay, I got a May bearing one-seven-one, low on the horizon, heading west—she's dropping buoys! Down scope. Sonar, you have anything to the south?"

"Nothing but the two friendly contacts. *Boston* is fading out on us, sir."

"Take her back down to six hundred." *The Russians are supposed to depend almost exclusively on active sonobuoys, dammit.* He ordered a turn back to the north once they reached the ordered depth, and slowed to five knots. *So they're trying to track us passively now. They must have gotten a twitch somewhere . . . or maybe nowhere.* Passive sonar tracking was technically very demanding, and even the sophisticated signal-processing equipment in Western navies made for many false contacts . . . *On the other hand, we've pretty well telegraphed our course. They could flood the area. Why didn't we try something different? But what?* The only other passage north was even narrower than this. The western route between Bear Island and the North Cape of Norway was wider, but half of the Soviet Northern Fleet had a barrier there. He wondered if *Pittsburgh* and the rest had escaped safely. Probably. They should have been able to run faster than Ivan was able to hunt. *As opposed to us.*

This is how we hunt the Russians, McCafferty thought. *They can't hear our passive buoys, and they never know when they're being tracked or not.* The captain leaned against the rail surrounding the periscope pedestal. *The good news*, he told himself, *is that we're damned hard to hear. Maybe Ivan got a twitch, maybe not. Probably not. If they heard us for sure, we'd have a torpedo in the water after us right now. But we don't, so they don't.*

"Bearings are firming up on both forward contacts."

In open ocean water, they'd have a layer to fool with, but there was none here. The combination of fairly shallow water and the overhead storm eliminated any chance of that. *Good news and bad news*, McCafferty thought.

"Conn, sonar, new contact, bearing two-eight-six, probable submarine. Trying to get a blade count now."

"Come left to three-four-eight. Belay that!" McCafferty changed his mind. Better to be cautious than bold here. "Come right to zero-one-five." Then he ordered *Chicago* down to one thousand feet. The farther he got from the surface, the better the sonar conditions he would have. If the Russians were near the surface to communicate with their aircraft, their sonar performance would suffer accordingly. He'd play every card he had before committing to battle. But what if—

He faced the possibility that one or more of the contacts were friendly. What if *Sceptre* and *Superb* had received new orders because of the damage to *Providence?* The new contact at two-eight-six could be friendly, too, for that matter.

Damn! No provision had been made for that. The Brits said they'd leave as soon as the boats reached the pack, that they had other things to do— but how often had *his* orders been changed since May? McCafferty asked himself.

Come on, Danny! You're the captain, you're supposed to know what to do . . . even when you don't.

The only thing he could do was try to establish the range to and identity of his three contacts. It took another ten minutes for sonar to work on the contacts.

"They're all three single-screw boats," the chief said finally.

McCafferty grimaced. That told him more about what they weren't than what they were. The British submarines were all of a single-propeller design. So were the Russian Victor and Alfa classes.

"Machinery signatures?"

"They're all running at very low power settings, skipper. Not enough for a classification. I got steam noises on all three, that makes 'em nucs, but if you look here you can see that we're just not getting enough signal for anything else. Sorry, sir, that's the best I got."

The farther we go east, McCafferty knew, the less signal his sonar would have to work on. He ordered a turn to reverse course, coming to a southwesterly heading.

At least he had range. The northerly targets were eleven and thirteen miles away respectively. The western one was nine miles off. All were within range of his torpedoes.

"Conn, sonar, we have an explosion bearing one-nine-eight . . . something else, a possible torpedo at two-zero-five, very faint, comes in and out. Nothing else in that area, sir. Maybe some breaking-up noises at one-nine-eight. Sorry, sir, these signals are very weak. Only thing I'm really sure of is the explosion." The captain was back in sonar yet again.

"Okay, Chief. If it was easy, I wouldn't need you." McCafferty watched the screen. The torpedo was still running, with a slowly changing bearing. It was no danger to *Chicago*. "Concentrate on the three submarine contacts."

"Aye, Cap'n."

You'd think with all the practice I've had that I would have learned patience by now.

Chicago continued southwest. McCafferty was stalking his western target now. He thought it the least likely to be friendly. The range closed to eight miles, then seven.

"Captain, classify the target at two-eight-zero as an Alfa-class!"

"You sure?"

"Yes, sir. That is an Alfa-type engine plant. I have it clearly now."

"Set it up! We'll run one fish in deep, dogleg it at low speed, then pop it up right underneath him."

His fire-control crew was getting better by the day. It almost seemed that they were working faster than the computer support.

"Skipper, if we shoot from this deep, it'll take a lot of our reserve high-pressure air," the exec warned.

"You're right. Take her to one hundred feet." McCafferty winced. *How the hell did you let yourself forget that?*

"Fifteen-degree rise on the planes!"

"Set—solution set, sir."

"Stand by." The captain watched the depth-gauge needle turn counterclockwise.

"One hundred feet, sir."

"Fire-control?"

"Set!"

"Match generated bearings and shoot!"

"Two fired, sir."

The Alfa might hear the air blast or he might not, McCafferty knew. The torpedo moved off at forty knots on a heading of three-five-zero, well off the bearing to the target. Three thousand yards out, a command sent down the control wires told the torpedo to turn and go deep. McCafferty was being very cagey with this shot, more than he would have preferred. When the Alfa detected the incoming fish, it would be from a bearing that *Chicago* wasn't at—if he fired a return shot, it would not come toward them. The disadvantage of this was the increased chance of losing the control wires and getting a clean miss. The torpedo was running deep to take advantage of the water pressure that reduced cavitation noise, hence reducing the range at which the Alfa could detect it. They had to play some extra angles on this because the Soviet sub had a top speed of more than forty knots and was almost as fast as the torpedo itself. *Chicago* continued to move southwest, putting as much distance as possible between herself and the torpedo.

"Torpedo continues to run normal, sir," sonar reported.

"Range to target?" McCafferty asked.

"About six thousand yards, sir. Recommend that we bring her up at four thousand and go to high-speed," the weapons officer suggested.

"Very well."

The tracking party plotted the course of the torpedo and its target—

"Conn, sonar, the Alfa just increased engine power."

"He hears it. Bring the fish up now, full speed, switch on the sonar."

"Hull-popping noises, sir. The Alfa is changing depth," the sonar chief called, excitement in his voice. "I have the torpedo sonar on my scope. Our unit is pinging. The target seems to be pinging also."

"Sir, we lost the wires, the fish has lost the wires."

"Shouldn't matter now. Sonar, give me a blade count on the Alfa."

"Doing turns for forty-two knots, sir, lots of cavitation noise. Seems to be turning. He may have just deployed a noisemaker."

"Anybody ever shoot at an Alfa before?" the executive officer asked.

"Not that I know about."

"Miss! Conn, sonar, the fish has passed aft of the target. Target appears to be heading east. The fish is still—no, it's turning now. The torpedo is still pinging, sir. Torpedo also heading east—turning again, I have a bearing change on the fish. Skipper, I think it's chasing after the noisemaker. I show an opening bearing between the fish and target."

"Damn, I thought we had that one locked in," the weapons officer growled.

"How far are we from launch point?"

"About seven thousand yards, sir."

"Bearing to the Alfa?"

"Three-four-eight, target bearing is moving east, machinery noises are down, blade count shows about twenty knots."

"He'll keep putting distance between himself and the torpedo," McCafferty said. As long as it was running and pinging, nobody wanted to get near it. The fish would circle until it ran out of fuel, but anything that came within its four-thousand-yard sonar radius risked detection. "What about the other two contacts?"

"No change, sir." The plotting officer said, "They seem to be pretty much holding their positions."

"That means they're Russians." McCafferty looked down at the plot. If they were Brits, they would have maneuvered and fired their own fish as soon as they'd heard the Alfa, and probably everyone in twenty miles had heard the Alfa.

Three to one, and they're alerted now. McCafferty shrugged. *At least I know what I'm up against.* Sonar reported another contact to the south. *It should be* Boston, Danny thought. If it wasn't, *Providence* would have done something. He ordered *Chicago* south. If he had to blast a hole through three submarines, he wanted help. He rendezvoused with *Boston* an hour later.

"I heard an Alfa."

"We missed. What did you get?"

"It had twin screws, and it's dead," Simms answered. Their gertrude phones were on a very low power setting.

"Three boats ahead about fourteen miles. One's the Alfa. I don't know about the others." McCafferty outlined his plan quickly. The submarines would proceed north, ten miles apart, and would try to engage the targets from their flanks. Even if they missed, *Providence* should be able to go straight through when the Russians split to pursue. Simms agreed, and the boats split up yet again.

McCafferty noted that he was still about sixteen hours from the ice. There were probably still Soviet patrol aircraft overhead. He'd wasted a torpedo—*no,* he told himself, *that was a well-planned attack.* It just hadn't worked, as sometimes happened.

A line of sonobuoys appeared—active ones this time—to his northeast. He wished angrily that the Russians would select one set of tactics and stick to it. Hell, all he wanted to do was leave! Of course he had launched missiles at the Soviet homeland and they were probably still angry about that. Nobody had ever told him whether the mission was successful or not. McCafferty commanded himself to stop this random thinking. He had trouble enough right here.

Chicago moved northwest. As she did so, the bearing to all of her sonar contacts changed to the right. The Alfa was still there, her machinery noise fading in and out. Technically speaking, he could shoot at her, but he'd just seen that her speed and maneuverability were enough to beat a Mark-48 torpedo. He wondered what the Alfa's skipper had done. Surprisingly, he hadn't fired a torpedo of his own down the bearing of the incoming fish. What did that mean? It was an American tactic, and was supposed to be a Soviet tactic also. Was it because he knew that "friendly" boats were in the area? McCafferty filed it away, yet another case where the Russians were not acting the way they were expected to act.

The northwest course closed the distance markedly to one of the contacts. The Alfa and the other unknown maneuvered east themselves, maintaining the ten-plus mile range—unknowingly, the captain thought. He stood over the plot. A fire-control solution was already set on the nearest contact. Range was down to eight miles. McCafferty went to the sonar room again.

"What can you tell me about this one?"

"Starting to look like a Type-2 reactor plant, the new version. He may be a Victor-III. Give me five more minutes and I'll know for sure, sir. The closer we get, the clearer he looks."

"Power output?"

"Pretty low, sir. I thought I might have a blade count a few minutes ago, but it didn't work out. He's probably just making steerage."

McCafferty leaned back against the bulkhead separating the room from the monstrous computer used to process signals. The line on the waterfall display that would show the unique frequency pattern of the machinery on the Victor-III was fuzzy but narrowing. Three minutes later it was a fairly sharp vertical stroke of light.

"Captain, I can now call target Sierra-2 a Victor-III-class Russian sub."

McCafferty went aft to control. "Range to target Sierra-2?"

"Fourteen thousand five hundred yards, sir."

"Solution is set, sir," the weapons officer reported. "Ready for tube one. Tube one is flooded, outer door is closed."

"Right ten degrees rudder," McCafferty said. *Chicago* turned to unmask her ready torpedo. He checked depth: two hundred feet. On firing, he'd run east rapidly and dive to a thousand feet. The submarine turned slowly at six knots; bearing to the target was three-five-one, and *Chicago*'s midship torpedo tubes were angled slightly outward from her center line. "Solution?"

"Set!"

"Open outer door." The petty officer on the torpedo board pushed the proper button and waited for the status light to change.

"Outer door is open, sir."

"Match bearings and shoot!" The seven thousand tons of USS *Chicago* shuddered again with the torpedo launch.

"One fired, sir."

McCafferty gave orders to change course and depth, increasing speed to ten knots.

Another exercise in patience. How soon will he hear the fish coming in? This one ran in at shallow depth. McCafferty hoped that its propulsion sounds might be lost in the surface noise. *How good is Victor's sonar?* he wondered.

"One minute." The weapons officer held a stopwatch. The Mark-48 ran thirteen hundred yards per minute at this speed setting. About ten minutes to go. It was like watching some perverse sports event, McCafferty thought, a two-minute drill in a football game, two minutes of playing time that could stretch to half an hour if the quarterback knew his stuff. Except that they weren't trying to score points. "Three minutes. Seven minutes to go."

Chicago leveled out at one thousand feet and the captain ordered speed cut back to six knots again. Already he had fire-control solutions set on the other two targets. But they'd have to wait.

"Five minutes. Five to go."

"Conn, sonar, target Sierra-2 has just increased power. Cavitation sounds, blade count shows twenty knots and increasing."

"Kick the fish to full speed," McCafferty ordered. The Mark-48 accelerated to a speed of forty-eight knots: sixteen hundred yards per minute.

"Target is turning east, her blade count shows thirty-one knots. Sir, I'm getting a funny signal slightly aft of the target. Target bearing is now three-five-eight. The new signal is three-five-six."

"Noisemaker?"

"Doesn't sound like that. Sounds like something different . . . not a nixie, but something like that, sir. Target is continuing to turn, sir, bearing now three-five-seven. I believe she may be reversing course."

"Take her up to two hundred feet," the captain said.

"What the hell's he doing?" the exec wondered as the submarine rose again.

"Sir, that new signal has masked the target," sonar announced.

"The fish is now pinging, sir."

"If he has a decoy deployed—he put it between himself and the fish," the captain said quietly. "Fire-control, I want another fish on target Sierra-2, and update the solution for Sierra-1."

Range and bearing figures were re-input into the computer.

"Set for tube three on target Sierra-2 and tube two for target Sierra-1." The submarine passed through three hundred feet.

"Match bearings and shoot." McCafferty gave the order quietly, then took his submarine down again. "That pod on the Victor-III that we thought was a towed-array housing, what if it's a decoy like our nixie?" *We don't use them on submarines,* McCafferty thought, *but Ivan does things his own way.*

"The fish might still ignore it."

"He doesn't think so. He thinks it'll work—then he can turn behind the noise of the explosion and get one off at us." McCafferty walked over to the plot. The other new fish was running toward what was probably another Victor-class. The second target was maneuvering east now. The Alfa was also. The obvious tactical move: clear the danger area, turn, and begin your own stalk. While both were turned away, their sonar would be ineffective along the route of the advancing torpedo. Sonar called out.

"Captain, I have an explosion bearing three-five-four. We have lost contact with target Sierra-2. I don't know if the fish hit her or not. The other two fish seem to be running normally."

"Patience," the captain breathed.

"Conn, sonar, we show some sonobuoys dropping aft." The bearings were plotted. They were in a north-south line two miles aft of *Chicago*.

"One of the other boats got a message out to his friends," the exec suggested.

"Good bet. These cooperative tactics'll be a cast-iron bitch if they ever figure out how to do it right."

"Sierra-2 is back, sir. I have a Type-2 machinery signature at three-four-nine. Some possible hull-popping noises. Sierra-2 is changing depth."

The weapons officer commanded one of the running torpedoes to turn left a few degrees. McCafferty picked up a pen and started chewing on it.

"Okay, probably his sonar is a little messed up. I'll bet he's trying to get an antenna up to tell his friends where we fired from. All ahead two-thirds."

"Torpedoes in the water bearing zero-three-one!"

"Do we have anything else on that bearing?"

"No, sir, I show nothing else."

McCafferty checked his plot. It was working, by God. He'd spooked the Russians into moving east toward Todd Simms in the *Boston!*

"Conn, sonar, torpedo in the water aft, bearing two-eight-six!"

"Make your depth twelve hundred feet," the captain said instantly. "Right full rudder, come to new course one-six-five. Our friend the Victor got word out to his airedale friends."

"Sir, we lost the wires to both fish," Weapons reported.

"Estimated range to Sierra-2?"

"The fish should be about six thousand yards out; it's programmed to start pinging in another minute."

"Mr. Victor made a mistake this time. He should have covered his ass before he went topside to radio the airplanes. Sonar, what's the position of the torpedo on our stern?"

"Bearing changing—sir, I'm losing sonar performance due to flow noise. Last bearing on the Russian fish is two-seven-eight."

"All ahead one-third!" McCafferty brought his submarine back to slow, quiet speed. In two minutes they realized that the air-dropped torpedo was well clear of them, and that their second shot at the Victor was close to its target.

By this time the sonar display was totally confused. Target Sierra-2 had picked up the incoming fish late, but was racing directly away from it at full speed now. Their shot at the other Victor was still running, but that target was maneuvering to avoid another fish from *Boston*. The Alfa was at full power heading due north, another Mark-48 in pursuit. Two more Russian torpedoes were in the water to the east, probably heading after

Boston, but *Chicago* didn't have her sister ship on sonar. Five submarines were racing around, four of them chased by smart-weapons.

"Sir, I have another decoy deployed on Sierra-2. Sierra-1 has one deployed also. Our fish is pinging on -2. Somebody's fish is pinging on -1, and one of the Russian fish is pinging at zero-three-five—sir, I have an explosion at bearing three-three-nine."

Dad wanted me to be an accountant, McCafferty thought. *Maybe then I could keep all these damned numbers straight.* He walked over to the plot.

The paper plot wasn't much clearer. The pencil lines that designated sonar contacts and running torpedoes looked like electrical wire dropped at random on the chart.

"Captain, I have very loud machinery noises at bearing three-three-nine. Sounds like something's broke, sir, lots of metallic noise. Getting some air noise now, he's blowing tanks. No breakup noises yet."

"Left full rudder, come to new course zero-one-zero."

"We didn't kill the Victor?"

"I'll settle for a small piece of him, if it sends him home. We'll score that one as a damage. What's going on with the other two?"

"The fish after Sierra-1 is pinging, and so's *Boston*'s—I guess it's from *Boston.*"

The slight abatement of the confusion lasted ten minutes. The second target put her stern on both torpedoes and ran northwest. More sonobuoy lines appeared across *Chicago*'s path. Another air-dropped torpedo was detected to the west, but they didn't know what it had been dropped on—just that it wasn't close enough to worry about. The torpedo they'd put in pursuit of the second Victor-class sub was struggling to catch a target running directly away as fast as it could go, and another fish was angling in from the opposite direction. Possibly *Boston* had fired at the Alfa too, but the Alfa was racing away at a speed almost as great as the torpedo's. McCafferty reestablished sonar contact with *Providence* and continued north. Chaos worked in his favor, and he took maximum advantage of it. He hoped *Boston* could evade the torpedoes that had been launched in her direction, but that was out of his hands.

"Two explosions bearing zero-zero-three, sir." That was the last bearing to the second Victor, but sonar detected nothing more. Had the fish killed the sub, the decoy, or had they homed in on each other?

Chicago continued north, increasing speed to ten knots as she zig-zagged through the sonobuoy lines to increase her distance from the injured *Providence*. The attack-center crew was emotionally exhausted, as drained as their captain from the frantic tracking and shooting exercise. The technical aspects of the work had been handled well in pre-war workups, but nothing could simulate the tension of firing live weapons. The captain sent them in pairs to the galley for food and a half-hour's rest. The cooks brought up a platter of sandwiches for the ones who couldn't leave. McCafferty sat behind the periscope, eyes closed, head back against something metallic while he munched on a ham sandwich. He remembered seeing the cans loaded aboard. The Navy had gotten a good price earlier in the year on canned Polish hams. *Polish hams,* he thought. *Crazy.*

He allowed his crew to go off battle stations an hour later. Half his men were allowed to go off duty. They didn't head for the galley and a meal. They all preferred sleep. The captain knew that he needed it at least as badly as they. *After we get to the ice,* he promised himself. *I'll sleep for a month.*

They picked up *Boston* on sonar, a ghostly trace on the sonar screens due east of them. *Providence* was still aft, still cruising along at six knots, and still making too much noise from her battered sail. Time passed more rapidly now. The captain remained seated, forgetting his dignity and listening to reports of . . . nothing.

McCafferty's head came up. He checked his watch and realized he'd been dozing for half an hour. Five more hours to the ice. It came up clearly on sonar now, a low-frequency growl of noise that covered thirty degrees on either side of the bow.

Where did the Alfa go? McCafferty was in sonar ten seconds after asking himself that question.

"What was your last bearing on the Alfa?"

"Sir, we lost him three hours ago. Last we had him, he was at flank speed on a steady northeasterly bearing. Faded out and he hasn't come back, sir."

"What's the chance he's hiding in the ice, waiting for us?"

"If he does, we'll pick him up before he picks us up, sir. If he's moving, his engine plant turns out a lot of medium- and high-frequency noise," the sonar chief explained. McCafferty knew all that, but wanted to hear it again anyway. "All the low-frequency ice noise'll ruin his chance to detect us at long range, but we should be able to hear him a good ways off if he's moving." The captain nodded and went aft.

"XO, if you were driving that Alfa, where would you be?"

"Home!" The exec smiled. "He has to know there are at least two boats out here. Those are awful short odds. We crippled that one Victor, and *Boston* probably killed the other one. What's he going to think? Ivan's brave, but he's not crazy. If he has any sense at all, he'll report a lost contact and leave it at that."

"I don't buy it. He beat our fish, and he probably beat one from *Boston,*" the captain said quietly.

"You could be right, skipper, but he ain't on sonar."

McCafferty had to concede that point. "We'll be very careful approaching the ice."

"Agreed, sir. We're being paranoid enough."

McCafferty didn't think so, but he didn't know why. *What am I missing?*

Their fix on the edge of the icepack was old. Currents and wind would have moved the ice a few miles south as increasing summer temperatures weakened the thick white roof on the ocean. *Maybe an hour's worth?* the captain wondered hopefully.

The plot showed *Boston* fifteen miles to the east, and *Providence* eight miles southeast. Three more hours to the ice. Eighteen nautical miles, maybe less, and they'd be safe. *Why should there be anything else out here? They can't send their whole fleet after us. They have plenty of other problems to worry about.* McCafferty dozed off again.

"Conn, sonar!" McCafferty's head came up.

"Conn, aye," the exec answered.

"*Providence* has speeded up somewhat, sir. Estimate she's doing ten knots."

"Very well."

"How long was I out?" the captain asked.

"About an hour and a half. You've been awake quite a while, sir, and you weren't snoring loud enough to bother anybody. Sonar is still blank except for our friends."

McCafferty got up and stretched. *That wasn't enough. It's catching up with me. Much more of this and I'm more dangerous to my own crew than I am to the Russians.*

"Distance to the ice?"

"About twelve thousand yards, near as we can make out."

McCafferty went to look at the chart. *Providence* had caught up and was even with him now. He didn't like that.

"Go to twelve knots and come right to zero-four-five. He's getting too eager."

"You're right," the exec said after giving the proper orders, "but who can blame him?"

"I can. What the hell does another few minutes matter after all the time it's taken to get this far?"

"Conn, sonar, we have a possible contact bearing zero-six-three. Sounds like machinery noise, very faint. Fading out now. We're getting flow noise that's blanking it out."

"Slow down?" the executive officer asked. The captain shook his head.

"All ahead two-thirds." *Chicago* accelerated to eighteen knots. McCafferty stared down at the chart. There was something important here that he wasn't seeing. The submarine was still deep, at one thousand feet. *Providence* still had her tail working, but she was running close to the surface, and that made trouble for her sonar performance. Was *Boston* running shallow, too? The quartermasters on the fire-control tracking party kept advancing the positions of the two American subs in keeping with the known course and speed of each. *Chicago* rapidly closed the distance. After half an hour she was broad on *Providence*'s port bow, and McCafferty ordered speed reduced to six knots again. As the submarine slowed, the exterior flow noise abated and her sonars returned to full performance.

"Sonar contact bearing zero-nine-five!"

The plotting team ran a line across the chart. It intersected the previous bearing line . . . almost exactly between *Boston* and *Providence!* McCafferty bent down to check the depth there—nineteen hundred feet. Deeper than a 688-class sub could dive . . .

. . . but not too deep for an Alfa . . .

"Holy shit!"

He couldn't fire at the contact. The bearing to the target was too close to *Providence*. If the control wires broke, the fish would go into automatic mode and not care a whit that *Providence* was a friendly.

"Sonar, go active, Yankee-search on bearing zero-nine-five!"

It took a moment to power-up the system. Then the deep *ba-wah* sound shook the ocean. McCafferty had meant to alert his comrades. He'd also alerted the Alfa.

"Conn, sonar, I have hull-popping noises and increased machinery noise at bearing zero-nine-five. No target on the scope yet."

"Come on, Todd!" the captain urged.

"Transients, transients! *Boston* just increased power, sir—there goes *Providence*. Torpedoes in the water, bearing zero-nine-five! Multiple torpedoes in the water at zero-nine-five!"

"All ahead full!" McCafferty looked at the plot. The Alfa was perilously close to both subs, behind both, and *Providence* couldn't run, couldn't dive, couldn't do a Goddamned thing! He could only watch as his fire-control team readied two torpedoes. The Alfa had fired four fish, two at each American boat. *Boston* changed course west, as did *Providence.* McCafferty and the exec went to the sonar room.

He watched the contact lines swing left and right across the screen. The thick ones denoted the submarines; the thinner, brighter lines each of the four torpedoes. The two aimed at *Providence* closed rapidly. The wounded sub was up to twenty knots, and made noise like a gravel truck trying to run. It was clear that she'd never make it. Three noisemakers appeared on the screen, but the torpedoes ignored them. The lines converged to a single point that blossomed bright on the screen.

"They got her, sir," the chief said quietly.

Boston had a better chance. Simms was at full speed now, with the torpedoes less than a thousand yards behind. He, too, deployed noise-makers and made radical changes in course and depth. One torpedo went wild, diving after a decoy and exploding on the bottom. The other locked on *Boston* and slowly ate up the distance. Another bright dot appeared, and that was that.

"Yankee-search the Alfa," McCafferty said, his voice low with rage. The submarine vibrated with the powerful sonar pulses.

"Bearing one-zero-nine, range thirteen thousand."

"Set!"

"Match and *shoot!*"

The Alfa didn't wait to hear the incoming torpedoes. Her skipper knew that there was a third sub out there, knew that he'd been pinged. The Soviet sub went to maximum speed and turned east. *Chicago*'s weapons officer tried to move the torpedoes on a closing course, but they had a scant five-knot advantage on the Alfa, and the math was clear: they'd come up two thousand yards short at the end of their fuel. McCafferty was past caring. He too went to flank speed and chased after her for half an hour, coming down to five knots three minutes before the torpedoes ran out of fuel. The flow noise cleared off his sonars just in time to hear the Alfa decelerate safely.

"Okay, now we'll try again." They were three miles from the ice now, and *Chicago* was quiet. The Alfa turned west, and McCafferty's tracking party gathered data to compute her range. The turn west was a mistake. He evidently expected *Chicago* to run for the pack and safety.

"Conn, sonar. New contact, bearing zero-zero-three."

Now what? Another Russian trap?

"I need information!"

"Very faint, but I got a bearing change, just moved to zero-zero-four."

A quartermaster looked up from his slide rule. "Range has to be under ten thousand yards, sir!"

"Transients, transients!—*torpedo in the water bearing zero-zero-five!*"

"Left full rudder, all ahead flank!"

"Bearing change! Torpedo bearing now zero-zero-eight!"

"Belay that order!" McCafferty shouted. The new contact was shooting at the Alfa.

"Jesus, what is this thing?" the sonar chief asked.

The Alfa heard the new fish and reversed course. Again they heard and saw the thunder of the Alfa's engines . . . but the torpedo closed the distance rapidly.

"It's a Brit. That's one of their new Spearfish. I didn't know they had any in the fleet yet."

"How fast?" the sonar chief asked.

"Sixty or seventy knots."

"Gawd! Let's buy some."

The Alfa ran straight for three miles, then turned north to head for the ice. She didn't make it. The Spearfish cut the corner. The lines on the display merged again, and a final bright dot appeared.

"Bring her around north," McCafferty told the exec. "Go to eighteen knots. I want to be sure he knows who we are."

"We are HMS *Torbay*. Who are you?"

"*Chicago.*"

"We heard the commotion earlier. Are you alone?" Captain James Little asked.

"Yes. The Alfa ambushed us—we're alone."

"We will escort you."

"Understood. Do you know if the mission was successful?"

"Yes, it was."

40. The Killing Ground

STYKKISHOLMUR, ICELAND

There was much to do, and time was short.

Lieutenant Potter and his team of Force Recon commandos found eight Russian troops in the town. They were trying to escape down the only road south when they ran into an ambush which killed or wounded five of their number. Those were the last who could have warned Keflavik of the ships on the horizon.

The first regular troops came by helicopter. Platoon- or company-sized units were placed on every hilltop overlooking the bay. Particular care was taken to keep the aircraft below the radar horizon from Keflavik, where a single Russian transmitter remained in operation despite all efforts to the contrary. A CH-53 Super Stallion helicopter airlifted the components of a mobile radar transmitter to a hill on the island's northwest coast, and a team of Army technicians went to work at once to get it operational. By the time the ships entered the rock-filled nightmare called Stykkisholmur harbor, five thousand troops were already in position over the handful of roads leading into the town.

The captain of one big LST—Landing Ship, Tank—had tried to count the rocks and shoals on the trip up from Norfolk. He'd stopped on reaching five hundred and concentrated on memorizing his particular area of responsibility, known as Green-Two-Charlie. The daylight and low tide helped. Many of the rocks were exposed by low water, and helicopter crews relieved of their immediate duties of landing troops dropped radar-reflectors and lighted beacons on most of them, which improved matters greatly. The remaining task was marginally safer than crossing a highway blindfolded. The LSTs went first, winding through the rocks at the recklessly high speed of ten knots, relying on their auxiliary bow thrusters to assist rudder movements to steer the ships through the lethal maze.

Again, Lieutenant Potter's team of commandos helped matters. They went from house to house, locating the captains and mates of local fishing boats. The skilled seamen were flown to the lead ships to help pilot the big gray amphibs through the tightest of the passages. By noon the first LST had her ramp on land, and the first Marine tanks rolled onto the island. Right behind them were trucks loaded with steel, pierced-plank runway material, which was dispatched east to a flat piece of ground pre-selected as a base for Marine helicopters and Harrier jump-jet fighters.

Once the fleet helicopters had completed their task of marking the rocks and shoals, they returned to moving troops. The troop carriers were escorted by SeaCobra gunships and Harriers as they extended the Marine perimeter to the hills overlooking the Hvita River. There contact was made with outlying Russian observation posts and the first real fighting began.

KEFLAVIK, ICELAND

"So much for our intelligence reports," General Andreyev muttered. From his headquarters he could see the massive shapes steaming slowly into view. They were the battleships *Iowa* and *New Jersey,* accompanied by missile cruisers for air defense.

"We can engage them now," the artillery chief said.

"Then do so." *While you can.* He turned to his communications officer. "Has word gotten out to Severomorsk?"

"Yes, Northern Fleet will sortie its aircraft today and submarines are being sent as well."

"Tell them their primary targets are the American amphibious ships at Stykkisholmur."

"But we are not sure they are there. The harbor is too dangerous for—"

"Where the hell else would they be?" Andreyev demanded. "Our observation posts there do not answer us, and we have reports of enemy helicopters moving south and east from that direction. Think, man!"

"Comrade General, the Navy's primary objective will be the enemy carrier force."

"Then explain to our comrades in blue that carrier aircraft cannot take Iceland away from us, but their fucking Marines *can!*"

Andreyev saw smoke rise from one of his heavy gun batteries. The sound followed a few seconds later. The first Russian salvo landed several thousand yards short.

"Fire mission!"

Iowa had not fired her guns in anger since Korea, but now the massive sixteen-inch rifles turned slowly to starboard. In the central gunnery control station, a technician worked the joystick controls for a Mastiff remotely piloted vehicle. The miniature airplane purchased a few years earlier from Israel circled eight thousand feet above the Russian gun battery, its television camera shifting from one emplacement to another.

"I count six guns, look like one-fifty-five or so. Call 'em six-inch."

The precise location of the Russian battery was plotted. Next the computer analyzed data on air density, barometric pressure, relative humidity, wind direction and speed, and a dozen other factors. The gunnery officer watched his status board for the solution light to come up.

"Commence firing."

The center gun of the number two turret loosed a single round. A millimeter-band radar atop the after director-tower tracked the shell, comparing its flight path with the one predicted by the fire-control computer. Not surprisingly, there were some errors in predicted wind velocity. The radar's own computer forwarded the new empirical readings to the master system, and the remaining eight main-battery guns altered position slightly. They fired even before the first round landed.

"Mother of God!" Andreyev whispered. The orange flash obscured the ship momentarily. Someone to his left shouted, perhaps thinking that one of the Russian artillery rounds had struck home. Andreyev had no such illusions. His artillerymen were out of practice and had not yet bracketed their target. He turned his field glasses to his gun battery, four kilometers away.

The first round landed fifteen hundred meters southeast of the nearest gun. The next eight landed two hundred meters behind them.

"Get that battery moved right now!"

"Drop two hundred and fire for effect!"

Already the guns were going through their thirty-second reload cycle. Inert gas ejected scraps of the silk propellant-bags out the muzzles to clear the bores, then the breeches opened and loading ramps unfolded into place. The bores were checked for dangerous residue, then elevators from the handling rooms rose to the back edge of the ramps and the shells were rammed into the waiting gun barrels. The heavy power bags were dropped onto the ramps and rammed behind the shells. The ramp came up, the breeches closed hydraulically, and the guns elevated. The turret crews moved out of the loading compartments and held their hands over their muff-style ear-protectors. In fire-control fingers depressed the keys and the breeches surged backwards once more. The cycle began again, the teenage seamen performing the same tasks that their grandfathers had done forty years before.

Andreyev stepped outside to watch in ghastly fascination. He could hear the sound of ripping linen that announced the passage of the monstrous projectiles, and turned to look at the battery. Trucks were pulling up to the guns as the crews fired off their last rounds and began frantic preparations for relocating their guns. The battery had six 152mm pieces and many trucks for the crews and ammunition. A curtain of dirt and rock appeared, followed by three secondary explosions, then four more salvos as *New Jersey* joined her older sister in the bombardment.

"What's that?" A lieutenant pointed to a dot in the sky.

The artillery commander tore his eyes away from what had been a third of his heavy guns and identified the remotely piloted vehicle. "I can have it shot down."

"No!" Andreyev shouted. "You want to tell them where our last SAM launchers are?" The General had faced mortar and rocket fire in Afghanistan. This was his first experience on the receiving end of heavy guns.

"My other batteries are all camouflaged."

"I want at least three new alternate positions prepared for every gun you have, fully camouflaged, all of them." The General went back inside the building. He felt confident that the Americans would not shell the city of Keflavik, at least not soon. The map room contained wall-sized charts of the western Icelandic coast. Already his intelligence staff was placing flags to denote the position of suspected American units.

"What do we have on the Hvita?" he asked his operations chief.

"One battalion. Ten BMD infantry carriers; the rest of the transport is trucks and commandeered vehicles. They have mortars, antitank missiles, and hand-held SAMs. They are deployed to cover the highway bridge above Bogarnes."

"The Americans are already looking down at them from this hill. What sort of aircraft have we seen?"

"The Americans have several carriers within striking distance of us. Twenty-four fighters and thirty-four attack aircraft per carrier. If they also landed a full division of Marines, we are facing a significant number of helicopters, plus fixed-wing Harriers. These can operate off their amphibious aviation ships or from land bases set up for the purpose—with the right materials it can be done in four to six hours. A Marine division is about double our strength in men, one heavy battalion of tanks, stronger in artillery, but not so many mortars. It's their mobility that worries me. They can dance all around us, using helicopters and landing craft to place troops anywhere they choose—"

"Just as we did when we landed. Yes," the General agreed soberly. "How good are they?"

"The American Marines regard themselves as elite troops, just as we do. Some of their senior officers and NCOs doubtless have combat experience, but few company officers and squad sergeants will have seen any real action."

"How bad is it?" A new man came into the room. It was the KGB station chief.

"You *chekista* bastard! You told me the Marine division was going to Europe! They're killing my men while we speak." The distant thunder of heavy guns punctuated Andreyev's words. The battleships were shifting fire to a supply dump. Fortunately not much was left there.

"Comrade General, I—"

"Get out of here! I have work to do." Andreyev was already wondering if his mission might be hopeless, but he was a general of paratroops and not accustomed to failure. He had ten attack helicopters, all dispersed and hidden after the attack on the Keflavik airfield. "What's our chance of getting someone in to look at this harbor?"

"We are under continuous surveillance from the American radar aircraft. Our helicopter would have to fly over enemy positions to get there. The Americans have their own armed helicopters and jet fighters—it's a suicide mission, and it would take a miracle for our man to get close enough to see anything, much less live long enough to tell us something useful."

"Then see if you can get us a reconnaissance aircraft from the mainland or satellite support. I must know what we're pitted against. If we can smash their invasion beach, we stand a good chance of defeating the troops they have on the ground, and to hell with their naval aircraft!"

It was complicated to do, but a Flash information request from the Commander Northern Fleet cut through most of the bureaucracy. One of the two real-time-capable Soviet reconnaissance satellites burned a quarter of its maneuvering fuel to alter its orbit and came low over Iceland two hours later. Minutes later, the last Soviet RORSAT was launched south from the Baikonor Kosmodrome, and its first revolution took it within radar range of Iceland. Four hours after Andreyev's message, the Russians had a clear picture of what was arrayed at Iceland.

BRUSSELS, BELGIUM

"Are they ready?" SACEUR asked.

"Another twelve hours would be better, but they're ready." The operations officer checked his watch. "They go off on the hour. Ten minutes." The hours spent getting the new division in place had been used profitably. Several additional brigades had been assembled into a pair of new polyglot divisions. The front had been almost entirely stripped of reserves to do it, while a hastily thought-out cover and deception plan had radio units all over the front, broadcasting radio messages to simulate the presence of the relocated formations. NATO had deliberately limited its own "maskirovka" until now, allowing SACEUR to bet all of Western Europe on a pair of fives.

HUNZEN, FEDERAL REPUBLIC OF GERMANY

It was a stimulating exercise. Alekseyev had to move his A exploitation forces forward while a battered B motor-rifle division bled to force a crossing of the Weser. All the while the General waited nervously for news from his shaky right flank. There was none. CINC-West was as good as his word, and launched a covering attack against Hamburg to draw off NATO forces from the latest Soviet breakthrough.

That was no easy maneuver. Antiaircraft missile and gun units had been drawn from other sectors. When NATO appreciated what was in the offing, they would break every effort to prevent a Soviet advance on the Ruhr. Resistance so far had been light. Perhaps they didn't understand what was happening, or perhaps, Alekseyev thought, they really were at the end of their personnel and logistical string.

The first A unit was 120th Motor-Rifle, the famous Rogachev Guards, whose leading elements were just now crossing at Rühle, and right behind was 8th Guards Tank. Two more tank divisions were bunched on the roads to Rühle, while an engineer regiment labored to erect seven bridges. Intelligence estimated two, perhaps three, NATO regiments coming to meet them. *Not enough*, Alekseyev thought. *Not this time.* Even their air power was depleted. His frontal aviation groups reported minor opposition only around Rühle. *Perhaps my superior was right after all.*

"Heavy enemy air activity at Salzhemmendorf," an Air Force communications officer reported.

That's where 40th Tanks is, Alekseyev thought. The B unit had been badly chewed up by the German spoiling attack—

"Fortieth Tanks reports a major enemy attack under way on its front."

"What do they mean by 'major'?"

"The report comes from the alternate command post. I can't reach the divisional HQ. The assistant commander reports American and German tanks advancing in brigade force."

Brigade force? Another spoiling attack?

"Enemy attack in progress at Dunsen."

"Dunsen? That's close to Gronau. How the hell did they get there?"

Alekseyev snapped. "Confirm that report! Is it an air or ground attack?"

"Hundred twentieth Motor-Rifle has a full regiment across the Weser. They are advancing on Brökeln. Eighth Tanks' leading elements have the Weser in sight. SAM units are setting up to cover the crossing point."

It was like having people read different parts of the paper to him simultaneously, Alekseyev thought. General Beregovoy was at the front, coordinating traffic control and setting final assignments for the post-crossing maneuver. Pasha knew that was his proper place, but, as before, he was annoyed to be far from the real action, giving orders like a Party boss instead of a fighting commander. The artillery from all the advancing divisions was well forward to protect the crossing against counterattack.

My rear areas are awfully weak . . .

"Comrade General, the attack at Dunsen is composed of enemy tank and motorized troops with heavy tactical air support. The regimental commander at Dunsen estimates brigade strength."

A brigade at Dunsen, and a brigade at Salzhemmendorf?

Those are B unit commanders. Out of practice, inexperienced. If they were really effective officers, they'd be in A units, not shepherding out-of-shape reservists.

"Enemy ground units at Bremke, strength unknown."

That's only fifteen kilometers from here! Alekseyev reached for some maps. It was cramped in the command vehicle, so he went outside and spread them on the ground with his intelligence officer beside him.

"What the hell's going on here?" His hand moved across the map. "That's an attack on a twenty-kilometer front."

"The new enemy division is not supposed to be in place yet, and Theater Intelligence says it will be broken up for spot-reinforcement use all over the northern front area."

"Headquarters at Fölziehausen reported a heavy air attack and went off the air!"

As if to emphasize this latest report, there was a massive explosion to the north in the direction of Bremke, where 24th Tanks had its main fuel and ordnance dump. Suddenly aircraft began to appear low on the horizon. The mobile command post was in woods overlooking the small town of Hunzen. The town was largely deserted, and the unit's radio transmitters were there. NATO aircraft had so far shown a reluctance to damage civilian buildings unless they had to—

Not today. Four tactical fighters leveled the center of the town, where the transmitters were, with high-explosive bombs.

"Get Alternate One going immediately," Alekseyev ordered.

More aircraft swept overhead, heading southwest toward Highway 240, where Alekseyev's A units were moving toward Rühle. The General found a working radio and called CINC-West at Stendal.

"We have a major enemy attack coming southeast from Springe. I would estimate at least two-division strength."

"Impossible, Pasha—they don't have two reserve divisions!"

"I have reports of enemy ground units at Bremke, Salzhemmendorf, and Dunsen. It is my opinion that my right flank is in jeopardy, and I must reorient my forces to meet it. I request permission to suspend the attack at Rühle to meet this threat."

"Request denied."

"Comrade General, I am the commander at the scene. The situation can be managed if I have authority to handle it properly."

"General Alekseyev, your objective is the Ruhr. If you are not able to achieve that objective, I will find a commander who is."

Alekseyev looked at the radiotelephone receiver in disbelief. He had worked for this man—two years. They were friends. *He's always trusted my judgment.*

"You order me to continue the attack regardless of enemy action?"

"Pasha, they make another spoiling attack—nothing more serious than that. Get those four divisions across the Weser," the man said more gently. "Out."

"Major Sergetov!" Alekseyev called. The young officer appeared a moment later. "Get yourself a vehicle and head for Dunsen. I want your personal observations on what you find. Be careful, Ivan Mikhailovich. I want you back here in less than two hours. Move."

"You will do nothing else?" the intelligence officer asked.

Pasha watched Sergetov board a light truck. He could not face his officer. "I have my orders. The operation to cross the Weser continues. We have an antitank battalion at Holle. Tell them to move north and be alert for enemy forces on the road from Bremke. General Beregovoy knows what he's supposed to do."

If I warn him, he'll change his dispositions. Then Beregovoy will be blamed for violating orders. That's a safe move. I prudently pass on a warning, and—no! If I can't violate orders, I cannot co-opt someone else into doing so.

What if they're right? This could be another spoiling attack. The Ruhr is a strategic objective of vast importance.

Alekseyev looked up. "The battle orders stand."

"Yes, Comrade General."

"The report of enemy tanks at Bremke was incorrect." A junior officer came over. "The observer saw our tanks coming south and misidentified them!"

"And this is good news?" Alekseyev demanded.

"Of course, Comrade General," the captain answered lamely.

"Did it occur to you to inquire why our tanks were heading *south?* Goddamn it, *must I do all the thinking here?*" He couldn't scream at the right person. He had to scream at somebody. The captain wilted before his eyes. Part of Alekseyev was ashamed, but another part needed the release.

They had the job because they had more battle experience than anyone else. It had never occurred to anyone that they had no experience at all in this sort of operation. They were *advancing.* Except for local counterattacks, no NATO unit had done very much of that, but Lieutenant—he still thought like a sergeant—Mackall knew that they were best suited to it. The M-1 tank had an engine governor that limited its speed to about forty-three miles per hour. It was always the first thing the crews removed.

His M-1 was going south at fifty-seven miles per hour.

The ride was enough to rattle the brain loose inside his skull, but he'd never known such exhilaration. His life was balanced on the knife-edge of boldness and lunacy. Armed helicopters flew ahead of his company, scouting the route, and pronounced it clear all the way to Alfeld. The Russians weren't using this route for anything. It wasn't a road at all, but the right-of-way for an underground pipeline, a grassy strip one hundred feet wide that took a straight line through the forests. The tank's wide treads threw off dirt like the roostertail from a speedboat as the vehicle raced south.

The driver slowed for a sweeping turn while Mackall squinted ahead, trying to see whatever enemy vehicle the helicopters missed. It didn't have to be a vehicle. It just could be three guys with a missile launcher, and Mrs. Mackall would get The Telegram, regretting to inform her that her son . . .

Thirty kilometers, he thought. Damn! Only a half-hour since the German grenadiers had punched a hole in the Russian lines, and *zoom!* goes the Black Horse Cav! It was crazy, but hell, it was crazy to have stayed alive ever since his first engagement—an hour after the war started. Ten klicks to go.

"Look at that! More of our tanks southbound. What the hell is going on?" Sergetov snarled to his driver, even talking like his general now.

"Are they our tanks?" the driver asked.

The new major shook his head. Another one passed through the gap in the trees—the turret had a flat top, not the usual dome shape of Soviet tanks!

A helicopter appeared over the gap and pivoted in the sky. Sergetov didn't mistake this for a Russian, and the stubby wings on either side of the fuselage marked it as an armed attack-chopper. The driver lurched to the right just before the nose-mounted machine gun flashed at them. Sergetov jumped clear as the tracers reached out. He landed on his back and rolled toward the treeline. His head was down, but he could feel the heat blast when the machine-gun tracers ignited the spare gas tank on the back of the truck. The young officer scampered into the trees and looked around the edge of a tall pine. The American helicopter flew to within a hundred meters of his vehicle to ensure its destruction, then spun off to the south. His radio was in the overturned, burning truck.

"Buffalo Three-One, this is Comanche, over."

"Comanche, this is Three-One. Report, over."

"We just popped a Russian truck. Everything else looks clear. Roll 'em, cowboy!" the helicopter pilot urged.

Mackall laughed at that. He had to remind himself that this wasn't really fun. Quite a few tank drivers had gotten into trouble by getting just a little too unwound on the German countryside, and now they were being *ordered* to! Two more minutes and three kilometers passed.

Here's where it gets tricky.

"Buffalo Three-One, we show three Russian vehicles standing guard on the hilltop. Look like Bravo-Tango-Romeos. All the bridge traffic seems to be trucks. The repair shop is on the east bank north of the town."

The tank slowed as they came to the last turn. Mackall ordered his "track" off the road, onto the meadow grass, as it edged ponderously around a stand of trees.

"Target BTR, eleven o'clock, twenty-seven hundred! Fire when ready, Woody!"

The first of the eight-wheel vehicles exploded before any of their crews knew a tank was near. They were looking for aircraft, not enemy tanks forty kilometers in the rear. The next two died within a minute, and Mackall's platoon of four tanks dashed forward.

They all reached the ridge three minutes later. One by one, the huge Abrams tanks crested the hill overlooking what had once been a small city.

Many days of continuous air attacks and artillery fire had ended that. Four ribbon bridges were in operation, with numerous trucks crossing or waiting to cross.

First the tanks located and engaged anything that looked even vaguely dangerous. Machine-gun fire began working on the trucks, while the main guns reached into the tank-repair yard established in the fields north of the town. By this time, two full troops were in place, and infantry vehicles took on the trucks with their light 25mm cannon. Within fifteen minutes, over a hundred trucks were burning, along with enough supplies to keep a whole Russian division in business for a hard day of combat. But the supplies were incidental. The rest of the squadron was catching up with the advance party, and their job was to hold this Russian communications nexus until relieved. The Germans already had Gronau, and the Russian forces east of the Leine were now cut off from their supplies. Two of the Russian bridges were clear, and a company of M-2 Bradley infantry carriers darted across to take up position on the eastern edge of the town.

Ivan Sergetov crawled to the edge of the grassy road—he didn't know what it was—and watched the units pass while his stomach contracted into an icy ball. They were Americans, at least a battalion in strength, he estimated, traveling light. No trucks, just their tracked vehicles. He kept his wits enough to begin a count of the tanks and personnel carriers that raced before him at a speed that he'd never really appreciated before. It was the noise that was most impressive. The turbine-driven M-1 tanks did not make the roar of diesel-powered tanks. Until they were a few hundred meters away, you couldn't even know they were there—the combination of low noise and high speed . . . *They're heading toward Alfeld!*

I have to report this. But how? His radio was gone, and Sergetov had to think for a minute to determine where he was . . . *two kilometers from the Leine, right across that wooded ridge.* His choice was a difficult one. If he returned to the command post, it was a walk of twenty kilometers. If he ran to the rear, he might find friendly units in half the time and get the alarm out. But running that way was cowardice, wasn't it?

Cowardice or not, he had to go east. Sergetov had the sickening feeling that the alarm had not been sounded. He moved to the edge of the trees and waited for a gap in the American column. It was only thirty meters to the far side. *Five seconds to cross the gap,* he told himself. *Less.*

Another M-1 blazed past him. He looked left and saw that the next was nearly three hundred meters away. Sergetov took a deep breath and ran into the open.

The tank commander saw him, but couldn't get to his machine gun fast enough. Besides, one man on foot without even a rifle wasn't worth stopping for. He reported the sighting on his radio and returned to the mission at hand.

Sergetov didn't stop running until he was a hundred meters into the trees. Such a short distance, but he felt as if his heart would spring from his chest. He sat down with his back against a tree to catch his breath and continued to watch the vehicles pass. It took several minutes before he could move again, then it was up the steep hill, and soon he was once more looking down at the Leine.

The shock of seeing the American tanks was bad enough. What he saw here was far worse. The Army tank-repair yard was a smoking ruin. Everywhere there were burning trucks. At least it was downhill. He ran down the east side of the ridge right up to the river. Quickly stripping off his pistol belt, Sergetov leaped into the swift current.

"What's that? Hey, I see a Russian swimming!" A machine gunner swiveled his .50 caliber around. The vehicle commander stopped him.

"Save it for the MiGs, soldier!"

He climbed up the east bank and turned to look back. The American vehicles were digging into defensive positions. He ran to cover and stopped again to make a count before proceeding. There was a traffic-control point at Sack. Sergetov ran all the way.

After the first hour, things settled down. Lieutenant Mackall got out of his tank to inspect his platoon's positions. One of the few ammunition carriers to accompany the troop stopped briefly at each tank, its crew tossing out fifteen rounds each. Not enough to replace what they'd fired, but not bad. The air attacks would be next. Crews were out chopping down trees and shrubs to camouflage their vehicles. The accompanying infantry set out their Stinger crews, and Air Force fighters were already circling overhead. Intelligence said that eight Russian divisions were on the west side of this river. Mackall was sitting on their supply route. That made it a very important plot of real estate.

USS *INDEPENDENCE*

Quite a change from the last time, Toland thought. The Air Force had an E-3 Sentry operating out of Sondrestrom to protect the fleet, and four of their own E-2C Hawkeyes were also up. There was even an Army-manned ground radar just coming up on Iceland. Two Aegis cruisers were with the carriers, and a third with the amphibious force.

"You think they'll hit us first, or the 'phibs?" Admiral Jacobsen asked.

"That's a coin-toss, Admiral," Toland replied. "Depends on who gives the orders. Their navy will want to kill us first. Their army will want to kill the 'phibs."

Jacobsen crossed his arms and stared at the map display. "This close, they can come in from any direction they want."

They expected no more than fifty Backfires, but there were still plenty of the older Badgers, and the fleet was only fifteen hundred miles from the Soviet bomber bases: they could come out with nearly their maximum ordnance loads. To stop the Russians, the Navy had six squadrons of Tomcats, and six more of Hornets, nearly a hundred forty fighters in all. Twenty-four were aloft now, supported by tankers while the ground-attack aircraft pounded Russian positions continuously. The battleships had ended their first visit to the Keflavik area and were now in Hvalfjördur—Whale Bay—providing fire support to the Marines north of Bogarnes. The entire operation had been planned with the likelihood of a Russian air-to-surface missile attack in mind. There would be more vampires.

The loss of northern Norway had eliminated the utility of Realtime. The submarine was still on station gathering signal intelligence, but the task of spotting the outbound Russian bomber streams passed on to British and Norwegian patrol aircraft operating out of Scotland. One of the latter spotted a three-plane Vic of Badgers heading southwest and radioed a warning. The Russian aircraft were roughly seventy minutes from the fleet.

Toland's station in CIC was immediately below the flight deck, and he listened to the roar of jet engines overhead as the fighters catapulted off. He was nervous. Toland knew that the tactical situation was very different now from that on the second day of the war, but he also remembered that he was one of the two men who'd escaped alive from a compartment just like this. A flood of information came into the room. The land-based radar, the Air Force E-3, and the Navy E-2s all linked their data to the carriers. There was enough electromagnetic energy in the sky to cook the birds in flight. The display showed the fighters proceeding to their stations. The Tomcats reached out to the northern Icelandic shore, curving into loitering circles as they awaited the Russian bombers.

"Ideas, Toland. I want ideas!" the Admiral said quietly.

"If they're after us, they'll approach from the east. If they're going for the 'phibs, they'll come straight in. There's just no percentage in deceptive tactics if they're heading for Stykkisholmur."

Jacobsen nodded. "That's how I see it."

The pounding on the flight deck continued overhead as strike aircraft landed to rearm for new bombing strikes. Aside from the expected material effect, they hoped to wreck the morale of the Soviet paratroopers by violent and continuous air attacks. Marine Harriers were also in action, along with attack helicopters. Initial progress was somewhat better than expected. The Russians did not have their troops as widely dispersed as they'd thought, and the known concentrations were being subjected to a hurricane of bombs and rockets.

"Starbase, this is Hawk-Blue-Three. I'm getting some jamming, bearing zero-two-four . . . more jamming now." The data was linked directly to the carrier, and the thick yellow strobes came up on the electronic display. The other Hawkeyes quickly reported the same information.

The fleet air-ops officer smiled thinly as he lifted his microphone. His units were fully in place, and this gave him several options.

"Plan Delta."

Hawk-Green-One carried *Independence*'s air-wing commander. A fighter pilot who would have much preferred riding his Tomcat for the mission, he directed two fighters from each Tomcat squadron to seek out the Russian jamming aircraft. The converted Badgers were spread on a wide front to cover the approach of the missile-armed bombers and advanced at five hundred knots, three hundred miles now from the line of radar-picket aircraft. The Tomcats homed in on them at five hundred knots as well.

Each jammer created a "strobe," an opaque wedge shape on the U.S. radar screens, so that they looked like the spokes of a wagon wheel. Since every such spoke was particular to each of the radar transmitters, the controllers were able to compare data, triangulate, and plot the position of the jammers. The Tomcats closed in quickly while the radar-intercept officers in the back seat of each fighter flipped the Phoenix missile seekers to home-on-jam guidance mode. Instead of depending on the aircraft's own radar for guidance, the missiles would seek out the noise transmitted from the Badgers.

Twenty jamming aircraft were plotted. Eighteen fighters headed for them, targeting at least two missiles at each.

"Delta—execute!"

The Tomcats launched on orders forty miles from their targets. Once more, Phoenix missiles streaked through the air. Flight time was a mere fifty-six seconds. Sixteen of the Badger jammers went off the air. The surviving four all switched off when they saw the smoke trails of missiles and dove for the deck with Tomcats in pursuit.

"Numerous radar contacts. Raid One is fifty aircraft, bearing zero-zero-nine, range three-six-zero, speed six hundred knots, altitude three-zero thousand. Raid Two—" the talker went on as the enemy aircraft were plotted.

"We have the main raid, probably Badgers going for the 'phibs. This one will be Backfires. They'll try to launch on us, probably far out to draw our fighters off," Toland said.

Jacobsen spoke briefly to his operations officer. Hawk-Green-One would control the defense of the amphibious force. Hawk-Blue-Four from *Nimitz* would defend the carrier groups. The fighters divided according to plan and went to work. Toland noted that Jacobsen was leaving control of the air action to the officers in the control aircraft. The fleet air-defense officer on USS *Yorktown* controlled the SAM ships, all of which went to full alert but left their radar transmitters on standby.

"The only thing that worries me is they might try that drone crap again," Jacobsen murmured.

"It worked once," Toland agreed. "But we didn't have them this far out before."

The Tomcats divided into four-plane divisions, each controlled by radar. They, too, had been briefed about the drones that had fooled *Nimitz*. The fighters kept their radars off until they were within fifty miles of their targets, then used the radars to locate targets for their on-board TV systems.

"Hawk-Blue-Four," one called. "Tallyho, I got eyeballs on a Backfire. Engaging now. Out."

The Russian plan of attack had anticipated that the American fighters would try to burn through the jamming aircraft to the north, then be caught off balance by the appearance of the Backfires to the east. But the jammers were gone, and the Backfires did not yet have the American carrier fleet on radar and could not launch their missiles on the basis of hours-old satellite photographs. Neither could they run away. The supersonic Russian bombers went to afterburner and activated their radars in a contest with time, distance, and American interceptors.

Again it was like watching a video game. The symbols designating the Backfires changed as the planes switched on their own protective jammers. The jamming reduced the effectiveness of the Phoenix missiles, but Russian losses were already serious. The Backfires were three hundred miles away. Their radars had an effective range of only half that, and already fighters swarmed over their formations. "Tallyho" calls cluttered the radio circuits as the Tomcats converged to engage the Russian bombers, and the *symbols started dropping off the radar screens. The Backfires closed at seventeen miles per minute, their radars searching desperately for the American fleet.

"Going to get some leakers," Toland said.

"Six or eight," Jacobsen agreed.

"Figure three missiles each."

By now the Tomcats had fired all of their missiles, and drew off for the

Hornets to join the action with Sparrows and Sidewinders. It wasn't easy for the fighters to keep up with their targets. The Backfires' speed made for difficult pursuit curves, and the fighters were notoriously short on fuel. Their missiles continued to score, however, and no amount of jinking and jamming could defeat all of them. Finally one aircraft got a surface radar contact and radioed a position. The seven remaining Backfires fired their missiles and turned north at Mach 2. Three more fell to missiles before the fighters had to turn away.

Again the Vampire call came in, and again Toland cringed. Twenty incoming missiles were plotted. The formation activated jammers and SAM systems, with a pair of Aegis cruisers on the threat axis. In seconds they were launching missiles, and the other SM2-equipped SAM ships added their own missiles to the "basket," allowing their birds to be guided by the Aegis computer systems. The twenty incoming missiles had ninety SM2s targeted on them. Only three got through the SAM cloud, and only one of them headed for a carrier. *America*'s three-point-defense guns tracked the AS-6 and destroyed it a thousand feet from the ship. The other two missiles both found the cruiser *Wainwright* and exploded her four miles from *Independence*.

"Damn." Jacobsen's face took a hard set. "I thought we had that one beat. Let's start recovering aircraft. We got some dry fighters up there."

Everyone's attention turned to the Badgers. The northern Tomcat groups were just coming within range of the older bombers. The Badger crews had expected to follow their jammers in, reversing earlier tactics. Some were slow to realize that they had no electronic wall to hide behind, but none had a choice. They detected incoming fighters while still five minutes from their launch points. The Badgers held course and increased to full speed to lessen their time of vulnerability while their crews looked anxiously for missiles.

The Tomcat pilots were surprised that their incoming targets were not altering course, which made the possibility of drones seem even more likely. They closed to get visual identification of their targets for fear of being tricked again into shooting at drones.

"Tallyho! Badger at twelve o'clock and level." The first Tomcat loosed a pair of missiles from forty miles out.

Unlike the Backfires, the Badgers had a location fix for their targets, which enabled them to launch their AS-4s from maximum range. One by one, the twenty-year-old bombers launched and turned as tight as their pilots dared to escape. Their escape maneuvers allowed half to survive, since the Navy fighters were unable to pursue. Aboard the radar aircraft, kills were being tallied even as the missiles flew toward Stykkisholmur. Soviet Naval Aviation had just taken fearful losses.

USS *NASSAU*

Edwards was still in the twilight of anesthesia when he heard the electronic gonging of the General Quarters alarm. He was only vaguely aware of where he was. He seemed to remember the helicopter ride, but his next impression was that of lying in a bunk with needles and tubes stuck in various parts of his body. He knew what the alarm meant, and knew intellectually that he should be afraid. But he couldn't quite work his emotions up through the drug-induced haze. He succeeded in raising his head. Vigdis was sitting on a chair next to his bed, holding his right hand. He squeezed back, not knowing that she was asleep. A moment later he was, too.

Five levels up, *Nassau*'s captain was standing on the bridge wing. His normal battle station was in CIC, but the ship was not moving, and he figured that this was as good a place as any to watch. Over a hundred missiles were inbound from the northeast. As soon as raid warning had been received an hour earlier, all of his boat crews had set to lighting off the smoke pots set on the rocks in this so-called anchorage. That was his best defense, he knew, hardly believing it himself. The point-defense guns at the corners of the flight deck were in automatic mode. Called R2D2s for their shape, the Close-In-Weapons-System Gatling guns were elevated twenty degrees, pointing off to the threat axis. That was all he could do. It had been decided by the air-defense experts that even firing off their chaff rockets would do more harm than good. The captain shrugged. One way or another, he'd know in five minutes.

He watched the cruiser *Vincennes* to the east, steaming in slow circles. Suddenly four smoke-trails erupted from her missile launchers, and the missile-firing cycle began. Soon the northeastern sky was a solid mass of gray smoke. Through his binoculars he began to pick out the sudden black puffs of successful intercepts. They seemed to be coming closer, and he noticed that the missiles were, too. And the Aegis cruiser could not get them all. *Vincennes* emptied her magazines in four minutes, then bent on full speed to race between a pair of rocky islands. The captain was amazed to see it. Someone was taking a billion-dollar cruiser into a rock garden at twenty-five knots! Even off Guadalcanal—

An explosion rocked the island of Hrappsey, four miles away. Then another on Seley. It was working!

Ten miles up, the Russian missiles switched on their radar seeker heads and found their target windows crammed with blips. Overloaded, they automatically scanned the largest for infrared signatures. Many of the blips gave off heat, and the missiles automatically selected the largest for their attention as they made their final Mach 3 dives. They had no way of knowing that they were attacking volcanic rocks. Thirty missiles got through the SAM defenses. Only five of them actually aimed themselves at ships.

Two of *Nassau*'s R2D2s swiveled together and fired at a missile traveling too fast to see. The captain looked in the direction of the barrels just in time to see a white flash a thousand feet overhead. The sound that followed nearly deafened him, and he realized how foolish it was to be exposed when fragments *ding*ed off the pilothouse next to him. Two more missiles fell into the town to his west. Then the sky cleared. A fireball to the west told him that at least one ship had been hit. *But not mine!*

"Son of a bitch." He lifted the phone to the Combat Information Center. "Combat, Bridge, two missiles fell into Stykkisholmur. Let's get a helo over there, there's gonna be some casualties."

As Toland watched, the tapes of the air engagement were replayed at fast speed. A computer tallied the kills. Everything was automated now.

"Wow," the intelligence officer said to himself.

"Not like before, was it, son?" Jacobsen observed. "Spaulding, I want word on the 'phibs!"

"Just coming in now, sir. *Charleston* took a hit and broke in half. We have minor damage to *Guam* and *Ponce*—and that's it, Admiral!"

"Plus *Wainwright*." Jacobsen took a deep breath. Two valuable ships and fifteen hundred men were gone, yet he had to call it a success.

KEFLAVIK, ICELAND

"The attack should be over by now."

Andreyev didn't expect rapid information. The Americans had finally succeeded in damaging his last radar, and he had no way of tracking the air battle. His radio-intercept crews had copied numerous voice transmissions, but they'd been too faint and too fast for any conclusion other than that a battle had in fact been fought.

"The last time we caught a NATO carrier force, we smashed it," the operations officer said hopefully.

"Our troops above Bogarnes are still under heavy fire," another reported. The American battleships had been hitting them for over an hour. "They are taking serious losses."

"Comrade General, I have a—you'd better listen to this, it's on our command circuit."

The message repeated four times, in Russian: "Commander Soviet Forces Iceland, this is Commander Strike Fleet Atlantic. If you don't get this, somebody will get it to you. Tell your bombers better luck next time. We'll be seeing you soon. Out."

SACK, FEDERAL REPUBLIC OF GERMANY

Sergetov staggered up to the traffic-control point in time to see a battalion of tanks move down the road toward Alfeld. He stood slumped over, hands on his knees, as he watched the tanks roll off.

"Identify yourself!" It was a KGB lieutenant. The KGB had taken over traffic management. The authority to shoot violators came easy to the KGB.

"Major Sergetov. I must see the area commander at once."

"Attached to what unit, Sergetov?"

Ivan stood up straight. Not *Comrade Major*, not *Comrade*, just *Sergetov*.

"I am personal aide to General Alekseyev, Deputy Commander West. Now get me the hell to your commander!"

"Papers." The lieutenant held out his hand, a coldly arrogant look on his face.

Sergetov smiled thinly. His identification documents were in a waterproof plastic envelope. He handed the top card over to the KGB officer. It was something his father had managed to get for him before mobilization.

"And what might you be doing with a Class-1-Priority pass?" The lieutenant was wary now.

"And who the fuck are you to ask?" The son of a Politburo member brought his face to within a centimeter of the other man's. "Get me to your commander *now* or we'll see who gets shot here today!"

The *chekist* deflated abruptly and led him to a farm cottage. The commander of the traffic-control station was a major. Good.

"I need a radio on the Army command circuit," Sergetov snapped.

"All I have is regimental and division," the major answered.

"Nearest division headquarters?"

"Fortieth Tanks at—"

"It's destroyed. Damn, I need a vehicle. Now! There is an American force at Alfeld."

"We just sent off a battalion—"

"I know. Call them back."

"I have no such authority."

"You damned fool, they're heading into a trap! Call them *now!*"

"I don't have the auth—"

"Are you a German agent? Haven't you seen what's going on there?"

"It was an air attack, wasn't it?"

"There are American tanks in Alfeld, you idiot. We must launch a counterattack, but one battalion isn't enough. We—" The first explosions started, six kilometers away. "Major, I want one of two things. Either you give me transport right now or you give me your name and service number so that I can denounce you properly."

The two KGB officers shared a look of incredulity. *Nobody* talked that way to them, but anyone who did . . . Sergetov got his vehicle and raced off. Half an hour later he was in the supply base at Holle. There he found a radio.

"Where are you, Major?" Alekseyev demanded.

"Holle. The Americans got through our lines. They have at least one battalion of tanks at Alfeld."

"*What?*" The radio was silent for a moment. "Are you certain?"

"Comrade General, I had to swim the damned river to get here. I counted a column of twenty-five armored vehicles a few kilometers north of the town. They shot up the tank-repair station and massacred a column of trucks. I repeat, General, there is an American force at Alfeld in at least battalion strength."

"Get transport to Stendal and report personally to Commander-in-Chief West."

USS *INDEPENDENCE*

"Good evening, Major Chapayev. How's the leg?" Toland asked, sitting down beside the hospital bunk. "Are you being treated properly?"

"I have no complaints. Your Russian is—fair."

"I do not often get to practice with a Soviet citizen. Perhaps you can help me somewhat." *Major Alexandr Georgiveyich Chapayev,* the computer printout read. *Age 30. Second son of General Georgiy Konstantinovich Chapayev, commander of the Moscow Air Defense District. Married to the youngest daughter of a Central Committee member, Ilya Nikolayevich Govorov.* And therefore probably a young man with access to lots of under-the-counter information . . .

"With your grammar?" Chapayev snorted.

"You were the commander of the MiGs? Be at ease, Major, they're all finished now. You know that."

"I was the senior flying officer, yes."

"I've been told to compliment you. I am not a flyer myself, but they tell me your tactics over Keflavik were excellent. I believe you had five MiGs. We lost a total of seven aircraft yesterday, three to MiGs, two to missiles, and two to ground fire. Considering the odds, we were disagreeably surprised."

"I had my duty."

"*Da*. We all have our duty," Toland agreed. "If you are concerned at how we will treat you, you should not be. You will be treated properly in all respects. I don't know what you have been told to expect, but probably you have noticed once or twice that not everything the Party says is completely true. I see from your identification papers that you have a wife and two children. I have a family, too. We'll both live to see them again, Major. Well, probably."

"And when our bombers attack you?"

"That happened three hours ago. Didn't anyone tell you?"

"Ha! The first time—"

"I was on *Nimitz*. We took two hits." Toland described the attack briefly. "This time things worked out differently. We're conducting rescue operations now. You'll know for sure when we bring some survivors in. Your air force is no longer a threat to us. Submarines are another matter, but there is no sense asking a fighter pilot about that. In fact, this isn't really an interrogation."

"So why are you here?"

"I will be asking you some questions later. I just wanted to come down and say hello. Is there anything I can get you, anything you need?"

Chapayev did not know what to make of this. Aside from the possibility the Americans would shoot him outright, he didn't know what to expect. He'd had the usual lectures about trying to escape, but clearly these did not apply to being aboard a ship in the middle of the ocean.

"I do not believe you," he said finally.

"Comrade Major, there is no point in asking you about the MiG-29, because none are left on Iceland. All the others in the Soviet Air Force are in Central Europe, but we're not going there. There is no point in asking you about ground-defense positions on Iceland; you're a pilot and you don't know anything about that. The same is true of the remaining threat against us: submarines. What do you know about submarines, eh? Think, Major, you are an educated man. Do you think you have information that we need? I doubt it. You will be exchanged in due course for our prisoners—a political question, for our political masters. Until then we will treat you properly." Toland paused. *Talk to me, Major . . .*

"I'm hungry," Chapayev said after a moment.

"Dinner should be in about thirty minutes."

"You will just send me home, after—"

"We don't have labor camps and we don't kill prisoners. If we were going to mistreat you, why did the surgeon sew up your leg and prescribe pain medications?"

"The pictures I had with me?"

"Almost forgot." Toland handed the Russian's wallet over. "Isn't it against the rules to take this up with you?"

"I carry it for luck," he said. Chapayev pulled out the black-and-white shot of his wife and twin daughters. *I will see you again. It may be some months, but I will see you again.*

Bob chuckled. "It worked, Comrade Major. Here are mine."

"Your wife is too skinny, but you are a lucky man also." Chapayev paused as his eyes teared up for a moment. He blinked them away. "I would like a drink," he said hopefully.

"Me, too. Not allowed on our ships." He looked at the photos. "Your daughters are beautiful, Major. You know, we have to be crazy to leave them."

"We have our duty," Chapayev said. Toland gestured angrily.

"It's the damned politicians. They just tell us to go—and we go, like idiots! Hell, we don't even know why the Goddamned war started!"

"You mean you do not know?"

Bingo. Codeine and sympathy . . . The tape recorder he had in his pocket was already turned on.

HUNZEN, FEDERAL REPUBLIC OF GERMANY

"If I continue the attack, we'll be destroyed here!" Alekseyev protested. "I have two full divisions on my flank, and I have a report that American tanks are at Alfeld."

"Impossible!" CINC-West replied angrily.

"The report came from Major Sergetov. He saw them arrive. I have ordered him to Stendal to make his report to you personally."

"I have 26th Motor-Rifle approaching Alfeld now. If any Americans are present, they'll handle matters."

That's a Category-C unit, Alekseyev thought. *Reservists, short on equipment, out-of-date training.*

"What progress have you made on the crossing?"

"Two regiments across, a third moving now. Enemy air activity has picked up—dammit! I have enemy units in my rear!"

"Get back to Stendal, Pasha. Beregovoy is in command at Hunzen. I need you here."

I'm being relieved. I'm being relieved of my command!

"Understood, Comrade General," Alekseyev replied. He switched off the radio. *Can I leave my troops this vulnerable to counterattack? Can I forgo warning my commanders?* Alekseyev slammed his fist on the worktable. "Get me General Beregovoy!"

ALFELD, FEDERAL REPUBLIC OF GERMANY

It was too far for artillery support from the NATO lines, and they'd been forced to leave their own guns behind. Mackall trained his gunsights through the haze and saw the advancing Russian formations. He estimated two regiments. That made it a division-sized attack in the classic two-up, one-back fashion. *Hmm. I don't see any SAM launchers up front.* The colonel in overall command started giving his orders over the command circuit. Friendly air was coming in.

Apache attack choppers popped up right behind the Cav's positions. They moved south to flank the advancing Russian vehicles, jinking and skidding as they launched their Hellfire missiles into the leading echelon of tanks. Their pilots sought out missile-launch vehicles but found none. Next came the A-10s. The ugly twin-engine aircraft swooped low, free for once of the SAM threat. Their rotary cannon and cluster bombs continued the job of the Apaches.

"They're coming in dumb, boss," the gunner commented.

"Maybe they're green, Woody."

"Okay by me."

The Bradleys on the eastern edge of the town engaged next with their missiles. The leading Soviet ranks were savaged even before they came into range of the tanks over the river. The attack began to falter. The Russian tanks stopped to shoot. They popped smoke and shot wildly from inside it. A few wild rounds landed close to Mackall's position, but they were not aimed shots. The attack was stopped two kilometers short of the town.

"Head north," Alekseyev said over the headset.

"Comrade General, if we head north—" the pilot started to say.

"I said head north! Keep low," he added.

The heavily armed Mi-24 swooped low abruptly. Alekseyev's gorge rose in his throat as the pilot tried to get even with him for giving the stupid, dangerous order. He sat in the back, hanging on to the seatbelt and leaning out the left-side door to see what he could. The helicopter jinked violently left and right, up and down—the pilot knew the dangers here.

"There!" Alekseyev called. "Ten o'clock. I see—American or German? Tanks at ten o'clock."

"I see some missile vehicles, too, Comrade General. Do you wish to see them more closely?" the pilot inquired acidly. He brought the chopper down a wooded road, barely two meters above the pavement as he dipped out of sight.

"That was at least a battalion," the General said.

"I'd say more," the pilot commented. He was at full power, his nose low for maximum speed, and his eyes scanned ahead for enemy aircraft.

The General fumbled with his map. He had to sit down and strap in to use both hands on it. "My God, this far south?"

"As I told you," the pilot answered over the intercom, "they have staged a breakthrough."

"How close can you go to Alfeld?"

"That depends on how much the General wishes to be alive tonight." Alekseyev noted the fear and anger in the words, and reminded himself that the captain flying this helicopter was already twice a Hero of the Soviet Union for his daring over the battlefield.

"As close as you think safe, Comrade Captain. I must see for myself what the enemy is doing."

"Understood. Hang on, it will be a very rough ride." The Mi-24 jumped up to avoid some power lines, then dropped again like a stone. Alekseyev winced at how close to the ground they stopped. "Enemy aircraft overhead. Look like the Devil's Cross . . . four of them heading west."

They passed over a—not a road, Alekseyev thought, a grassy strip with tracked vehicles on it. The grass had been churned to bare dirt. He checked his map. This route led to Alfeld.

"I will cross over the Leine and approach Alfeld from the east. That way we'll be over friendly troops if anything happens," the pilot advised. Immediately thereafter the aircraft jumped up and down again. Alekseyev caught a glimpse of tanks on the ridge as they raced past. Many of them.

A few strings of tracer bullets reached out at the chopper, but fell behind. "Quite a few tanks there, Comrade General. I'd say a regimental force. The tank-repair yard is to the south—what's left of it—shit! Enemy helicopters to the south!"

The aircraft stopped and pivoted in the air. There was a roar as an air-to-air missile leaped off the wingtip, then the Mi-24 started moving again. It jinked up, then down hard, and the General saw a smoke trail go overhead.

"That was close."

"Did you get him?"

"Does the General wish me to stop and see? What's that? That wasn't here before."

The chopper stopped briefly. Alekseyev saw burning vehicles and running men. The tanks were old T-55s . . . this was the counterattack he'd been told about! Smashed. A minute later he saw vehicles assembling for another effort.

"I've seen enough. Straight to Stendal as fast as you can." The General leaned back with his maps and tried to formulate a clear picture of what he'd seen. Half an hour later the helicopter flared and landed.

"You were right, Pasha," CINC-West said as soon as he walked into the operations room. He held three reconnaissance photographs.

"Twenty-Sixth Motor-Rifle's initial attack was crushed two kilometers in front of enemy lines. When I flew over, they were re-forming for another. This is a mistake," Alekseyev said with quiet urgency. "If we want that position back, we have to attack with full preparation."

"We must have that bridgehead back in our hands as quickly as possible."

"Fine. Tell Beregovoy to detach two of his units and drive back east."

"We can't abandon the Weser crossing!"

"Comrade General, either we pull those units back or we let NATO destroy them in place. That is the only choice we have at the moment."

"No. Once we get Alfeld back, we can reinforce. That will defeat the counterattack on their flank and allow us to continue the advance."

"What do we have to strike Alfeld with?"

"Three divisions are en route now—"

Alekseyev scanned the unit designations on the map. "They're all C formations!"

"Yes. I had to divert most of my B units north. NATO counterattacked at Hamburg as well. Cheer up, Pasha, we have many C units coming onto the front."

Wonderful. All these old, fat, out-of-practice reservists are marching to a front held by battle-seasoned troops.

"Wait until all three divisions are in place. Get their artillery up front first so that we can pound the NATO positions. What about Gronau?"

"The Germans crossed the Leine there, but we have them contained. Two divisions are moving to attack there also."

Alekseyev walked over to the main map display and looked for changes in the tactical situation since he'd last been here. The battle lines in the north had not changed appreciably, and the NATO counterattack on the Alfeld-Rühle salient was only now being posted. Blue flags were at Gronau, and Alfeld. There was the counterattack at Hamburg.

We've lost the initiative. How do we get it back?

The Soviet Army had started the war with twenty A divisions based in Germany, with another ten moved in at the start, and more since. All of them had now been committed to battle, many pulled off the line due to losses. The last reserve of the full-strength formations was at Rühle, and they were about to be trapped. Beregovoy was too good a soldier to violate orders, even though he knew his forces had to be pulled back before they were irretrievably cut off.

"We must abandon the attack. If we press on, those divisions will be trapped behind two rivers, not just one."

"The attack is a political and military necessity," CINC-West answered. "If they push forward, NATO will have to draw forces off this attack to defend the Ruhr. Then we'll have them."

Alekseyev didn't argue further. The thought that came to him felt like a blast of cold air on exposed skin. *Have we failed?*

USS *INDEPENDENCE*

"Admiral, I need to see somebody in the MAF."

"Who?"

"Chuck Lowe—he's a regimental commander. Before he took it over, we worked together on CINCLANT's intelligence staff."

"Why not—"

"He's good, Admiral, very good at this stuff."

"You think the information is that hot?" Jacobsen asked.

"I sure do, sir, but I need a second opinion. Chuck's the best guy who's handy."

Jacobsen lifted his phone. "Get me General Emerson, quick . . . Billy? Scott. You have a Colonel Chuck Lowe serving with you? Where? Okay, one of my intel people needs to see him right now . . . important enough, Billy. Very well, he'll be on his way in ten minutes." The Admiral set the phone down. "Have you copied that tape?"

"Yes, sir. This is one of the copies. The original's in the safe."

"There'll be a helo waiting for you."

It was a one-hour flight to Stykkisholmur. From there a Marine chopper took him southeast. He found Chuck Lowe in a tent looking over some maps.

"You get around pretty good. I heard about *Nimitz,* Bob. Glad to see you made it. What's up?"

"I want you to listen to this tape. It'll take you about twenty minutes." Toland explained who the Russian was. He handed over a small Japanese personal tape player with earphones. The two officers walked out of the tent to a relatively quiet place. Twice Lowe rewound the tape to repeat a section.

"Son of a bitch," he said quietly when it was finished.

"He thought we already knew."

Colonel Lowe stooped down and picked up a rock. He hefted it in his hand for a moment, then hurled it as hard as he could. "Why not? We assume the KGB is competent, why should they assume that we're not! We had the information all along . . . and we *blew it!*" His voice was full of wonder and disgust. "You sure this isn't a cock-and-bull story?"

"When we pulled him out of the water, he had a nasty cut on the leg. The docs sewed that up and gave him pain pills. I caught him weak from blood loss, and pretty well juiced on codeine. Kinda hard to lie well when you're drunk, isn't it? Chuck, I really need your opinion."

"Trying to land me back in the intel business?" Lowe smiled briefly. "Bob, it makes a hell of a lot of sense. This should go up the ladder fast."

"I think SACEUR should get it."

"You can't just call up for an appointment, Bob."

"I can go through COMEASTLANT. The original goes to Washington. CIA will want to use a voice-stress-analysis machine on it. But I saw the man's eyes, Chuck."

"I agree. It should go to the top as fast as you can get it there—and SACEUR can make the fastest use of it."

"Thanks, Colonel. How do I call the chopper back?"

"I'll handle that. Welcome to Iceland, by the way."

"How's it going?" Toland followed the colonel back to the tent.

"We're up against good troops, but they have a tough defensive problem here, and we have all the firepower we need. We got 'em by the ass!" The colonel paused. "Nice work, Squid!"

Two hours later, Toland was aboard a plane bound for Heathrow.

MOSCOW, R.S.F.S.R.

The briefing was given by Marshal Fyodr Borissovich Bukharin. The KGB had arrested Marshals Shavyrin and Rozhkov the day before, a move that told Minister Sergetov more than this briefing ever would.

"The attack west from Alfeld has bogged down due to poor planning and execution by Commander-in-Chief West. We need to regain the initiative. Fortunately we have the troops available, and nothing changes the fact that NATO has suffered grievous losses.

"I propose replacement of the Western Theater command staff and—"

"Wait. I wish to say something," Sergetov interrupted.

"Make your point, Mikhail Eduardovich," the Defense Minister said, his annoyance clear.

"Marshal Bukharin, you propose complete staff replacement?" *The practical consequences to the replacees was unspoken,* Sergetov thought, *but plain enough.*

"My son is on the staff of the Deputy Commander West, General Alekseyev. This general is the one who led the breakthrough at Alfeld, *and* the one at Rühle! He's been wounded twice and had his helicopter shot down by enemy fighters—after which he commandeered a truck and raced to the front to lead yet another successful attack. He's the only effective general we have that I know of, and you want to replace him with someone unfamiliar with the situation—what madness is this?" he asked angrily. The Minister of the Interior leaned forward.

"Just because your son is on his staff—"

Sergetov's face went beet-red. " '*Just because my son,*' you say? *My* son is at the front, serving the State. He's been wounded, and barely escaped death when he was shot down at his general's side. Who else at this table can say that, Comrades? *Where are your sons?*" He pounded on the table in rage. Sergetov concluded in a softer voice, wounding his colleagues in a way that mattered, really mattered: "Where are the Communists here?"

There was a brief but deadly silence. Sergetov knew that he had either ended his political career or boosted it beyond measure. His fate would be decided by whoever spoke next.

"In the Great Patriotic War," Pyotr Bromkovskiy said with an old man's dignity, "Politburo members lived at the front. Many lost sons. Even Comrade Stalin gave his sons to the State, serving alongside the sons of ordinary workers and peasants. Mikhail Eduardovich speaks well. Comrade Marshal, your evaluation of General Alekseyev, if you please? Is Comrade Sergetov correct in his assessment?"

Bukharin looked uneasy. "Alekseyev is a young, bright officer, and, yes, he has done fairly well at his present post."

"But you wish to replace him with one of your own people?" Bromkovskiy didn't wait for an answer. "It is amazing, the things we learn and the things we forget. We forget that it is necessary for all Soviet citizens to share the burden together—but we *remember* the mistakes made in 1941, arresting good officers because their superiors erred, and replacing them all with political cronies who could lead us to disaster! If Alekseyev is a bright young officer who knows how to fight, why do you replace him?"

"Perhaps we were hasty," the Defense Minister admitted, watching the mood around the table shift dramatically. *I'll get you for this, Mikhail Eduardovich. If you wish to ally yourself with our oldest member, it is fine with me. He won't live forever. Neither will you.*

"That is decided then," the Party Chairman said. "Next, Bukharin, what of the situation on Iceland?"

"There are reports that some enemy troops have landed, but we immediately attacked the NATO fleet. We are waiting now for an assessment of the losses we inflicted. We have to wait for satellite reconnaissance before we can be sure of that." Bukharin knew only what Soviet losses were, and he would not reveal those until he could report favorable strike results.

STENDAL, GERMAN DEMOCRATIC REPUBLIC

They arrived just after dark, the KGB officers in battle dress. Alekseyev was working on deployments of newly arrived C divisions and didn't see them enter CINC-West's office. Five minutes later he was summoned.

"Comrade General Alekseyev, you are now Commander-in-Chief of the Western Theater of Military Operations," his superior said simply. "I wish you luck."

Alekseyev felt the hair rise up on his neck at the General's tone. The man was flanked by a pair of KGB colonels wearing the standard KGB battle dress, camouflage cloth tailored in the pattern of a class-A uniform, the "State Security" GB emblem shoulder boards. It was an institutional form of arrogance that suited the KGB as perfectly as the look on the colonels' faces.

What do I say? What can I do? This is my friend.

The former Commander-in-Chief of the Western Theater of Military Operations said it for him: "Good-bye, Pasha."

They took the General out. Alekseyev watched him go, then stop at the door. He turned with a look of hopeless fatalism before proceeding. Alekseyev's last sight was of the General's pistol belt, the leather flap loose over an empty holster. He turned away and saw on the desk a telex confirming his command status. It told him that he had the complete confidence of the Party, the Politburo, and the People. He crumpled it and threw it against the wall. He had seen the same words on the same form a few brief weeks before. The recipient of that message of confidence was now in a car heading east.

How long do I have? Alekseyev summoned his communications officer. "Get me General Beregovoy!"

BRUSSELS, BELGIUM

SACEUR allowed himself a meal. He'd lost ten pounds since the war had begun by subsisting on coffee and sandwiches and stomach acid. Alexander had commanded armies in his teens and twenties—maybe that's why he did so well, the General thought. He was young enough to stand it.

It was working. The Cav was at Alfeld. The Germans were firmly in control of Gronau and Brüggen, and unless Ivan reacted quickly, his divisions on the Weser were in for a very nasty surprise. The door to his office opened. It was his German intelligence officer.

"Excuse me, Herr General, I have a naval intelligence officer here."

"Is it important, Joachim?"

"Ja."

SACEUR looked down at his plate. "Show him in."

The General was not impressed. The man was dressed in his shipboard khakis. Only a very sharp eye could see where the creases used to be.

"General, I'm Commander Bob Toland. Until a few hours ago, I was on the threat team with Strike Fleet Atlantic—"

"How's it going on Iceland?"

"The air attack on the fleet was chewed up, sir. There's still the submarine problem to deal with, but the Marines are moving. I think we'll win this one, General."

"Well, the more subs they send after the carriers, the fewer go after my convoys."

That's one way to look at it, Toland thought. "Admiral, we captured a Russian fighter pilot. He comes from an important family. I interrogated him; here's the tape. I think we know why the war started."

"Joachim, did you check his data?"

"No, sir. He has already briefed COMEASTLANT, and Admiral Beattie wanted the data to come directly to you."

SACEUR's eyes narrowed. "Let's hear it, son."

"Oil."

41. Targets of Opportunity

BRUSSELS, BELGIUM

Three copies were made of the tape. One went to one of SACEUR's intelligence staff for a separate translation to be checked against Toland's. Another was taken to French intelligence for electronic analysis. The third was analyzed by a Belgian psychiatrist who was fluent in Russian. While that was going on, half of the intelligence officers at NATO headquarters updated all their information about Soviet fuel consumption to date. CIA and other national intelligence services began a frantic investigation into Soviet oil production and utilization. Toland predicted the outcome hours before it came in: *insufficient data.* The range of possible conclusions predicted that the Russians had enough fuel for several months—or had already run out!

SACEUR took his time before accepting the data at face value. Prisoner interrogations had given his intelligence people a wealth of information—most of it patently false or contradictory. Since supply officers naturally lagged behind the fighting troops, few of them had been captured. It was the Air Force that bought the story first. They knew that enemy fuel-supply dumps were smaller than expected. Instead of the One Big Facility so prevalent throughout Russian society (and after the big dump at Wittenburg had been blown up), the Russians had gone to small ones, accepting the price of increased air-defense and security requirements. NATO's deep-strike air missions had been concentrating on airfields, munitions dumps, transport junctions, and the tank columns approaching the front . . . more lucrative targets than the smaller-than-expected fuel depots, which were also harder to spot. The traffic signatures associated with the large fuel-posts usually showed hundreds of trucks cycling in and out. The small ones, with fewer trucks involved, were harder for the look-down radar aircraft to locate. All these factors militated to a different targeting priority.

After fifteen minutes' discussion with his Air Chief, SACEUR changed all that.

STENDAL, GERMAN DEMOCRATIC REPUBLIC

"I can't do both things," Alekseyev whispered to himself. He'd spent the last twelve hours trying to find a way, but it wasn't there. It was a marvel what it meant finally to be in command himself, no longer the aggressive subordinate. He was now *responsible* for success or failure. A mistake was *his* mistake. A failure was *his* failure. It had been much more comfortable the other way. Like his predecessor, Alekseyev had to mark his orders, even though his orders were impossible. He had to maintain the salient and continue the advance. He had the resources to do one or the other, but not both. *You will advance northwest from the Weser, cutting off the forces on the right flank of the advancing troops and preparing the way for a decisive attack into the Ruhr Valley.* Whoever issued the orders either didn't know or didn't care that this was impossible.

But NATO knew. Their air power had smashed convoys on every road between Rühle and Alfeld. The two B tank divisions guarding Beregovoy's northern flank had been caught off-balance and routed. Battalion-sized blocking forces occupied the major crossroads while the NATO commanders reinforced the regiment at Alfeld. Probably two full tank divisions lurked in the forests north of Rühle, but for the present they had not attacked Beregovoy. Instead their inaction both *dared* him to cross and invited him to counterattack north.

Alekseyev remembered an important lesson from the Frunze Academy: the Kharkov Offensive of 1942. The Germans had allowed the advancing Red Army forces to penetrate deep—then cut them off and chewed them up. *High Command* [meaning Stalin] *ignored the objective realities of the situation (hence violating the Second Law of Armed Combat), concentrating instead on subjective perceptions of apparent progress that unfortunately proved false,* the lesson concluded. The General wondered if this battle would be an object lesson for some future class of captains and majors who would then write their test answers and essays in bluebooks, pointing out what an ass General Colonel Pavel Leonidovich Alekseyev was!

Or he could pull them back . . . and admit defeat, and perhaps be shot, and then be remembered, if at all, as a traitor to the Motherland. It was so fitting. After sending so many thousands of boys into fire, now he faced death as well, though from an unexpected direction.

"Major Sergetov, I want you to go back to Moscow to tell them in person what I am up to. I am going to detach one division from Beregovoy and drive it east to open the way at Alfeld again. The attack on Alfeld will be from two directions, and after it succeeds, we will be able to continue the Weser crossing without fear of having our spearhead cut off."

"A skillful compromise," the major said hopefully.

That's just the thing I need to hear!

BITBURG, FEDERAL REPUBLIC OF GERMANY

Twelve Frisbees were left. Twice they'd been pulled out of action briefly to determine what new tactics would lessen the hazards—with some success, Colonel Ellington told himself. A few of the Soviet systems had proved to have unsuspected capabilities, but half of his losses were unexplained. Were they the kind of accidents that accompanied flying heavily loaded aircraft at minimum altitude or simply the laws of probability catching up with everyone? A pilot might think a 1-percent chance of being shot down on a given mission acceptable, then realize that fifty such missions made it a 40-percent chance.

His flight crews were unnaturally quiet. The elite Frisbee squadron was a tight family of men, a third of whom were gone. The professionalism that allowed them to shut this out and do their weeping in private had its limits. That limit had been passed. Mission performance was down. But combat requirements were not, and Ellington knew that sentiment's place in the great military scheme of things fell below the need to hit targets.

He rotated the aircraft off the pavement and headed east alone. Tonight he carried no weapons save Sidewinders and antiradar missiles for self-defense. His F-19A was burdened with fuel tanks instead of bombs. He settled to an initial flight altitude of three thousand feet and checked his instruments, making a slight adjustment in the aircraft's trim before starting a slow descent to five hundred feet. That was his altitude on crossing the Weser.

"Got some activity on the ground, Duke," Eisly reported. "Looks like a column of tanks and troop carriers heading northeast on Highway 64."

"Report it in." In this sector, everything that moved was a target. A minute later, they crossed the Leine north of Alfeld. They could see the distant flashes of artillery, and Ellington banked left to keep clear. A six-inch shell in its ballistic arc didn't care if the Frisbee was invisible or not.

This ought to be safer than a strike mission, Ellington told himself. They flew east, two miles from a secondary road that Eisly kept under surveillance with their nose-mounted television camera. The threat-warning receiver was lit up from SAM radars sweeping the sky for intruders.

"Tanks," he said quietly. "Lots of 'em."

RED STORM RISING • 473

"Moving?"

"Don't think so. Looks like they're sitting alongside the road near the treeline. Wait—missile-launch warning! SAM three o'clock!"

Ellington pushed the stick down and to the left. In a matter of seconds he had to dive his aircraft one way, turn his head the other to see the incoming missile, then turn back to make sure he didn't plow a furrow in the dirt with his fifty-million-dollar aircraft. All he saw of the SAM was a yellow-white gout of flame, and it was heading for him. As soon as he leveled out, he wrenched the Frisbee into a hard right turn. In the back Eisly had his eyes on the missile.

"Veering off, Duke—yeah!" The missile leveled out at the treetops behind the F-19, then dipped and exploded in the woods. "The instruments say that was an SA-6. The search radar is one o'clock and very close."

"Okay," Ellington said. He activated a single Sidearm antiradar missile and fired it at the transmitter from a range of four miles. The Russians were slow to detect it. Ellington saw the detonation. *Take that, Darth Vader!*

"I think you're right on how they're getting us, Duke."

"Yeah." The Frisbee was designed to defeat overhead radars. Something looking up had a much better chance of detecting them. They could defeat that by flying very low, but then they couldn't see as well as they wanted to see. He turned for another look at the tanks. "How many you think, Don?"

"Lots, over a hundred."

"Tell 'em." Ellington turned back north while Major Eisly made his report. In minutes some German Phantom jets would visit the tank assembly point. That many tanks sitting still probably meant a fueling point, he thought. Either the fuel trucks were already there or they were en route. Fuel trucks were now his primary targets, a surprising change after weeks of going for supply dumps and moving columns . . . *What's that?*

"Trucks dead ahead!" The Duke watched the enhanced view on his Head-Up Display. A long line of . . . fuel trucks, traveling in a tight column, blacked out and moving fast. The curved metal tops made the identification easy. He turned the fighter again to circle two miles from the road. Eisly's infrared picture showed the glow of engines and exhaust piping, hotter than the cool night air. It was like a procession of ghosts down the tree-lined road.

"I count fifty or so, Duke, and they're heading for that tank park."

Five thousand gallons per truck, Ellington thought. *Two hundred fifty thousand gallons of diesel fuel . . . enough to fill every tank in two Soviet divisions.* Eisly called that one in also.

"Shade Three," the AWACS controller radioed back. "We have eight birds en route, ETA four minutes. Orbit and evaluate."

Ellington did not acknowledge. He put his aircraft right down on the treetops for several minutes, wondering how many trees had Russian soldiers standing nearby with their SA-7 hand-held missiles.

A long time since he'd flown over Vietnam, a long time since he'd first realized that random chance could reach up into the sky and end his life despite all his skill. His years of peacetime flying had allowed him to forget that—Ellington never thought an accident could kill him. But one man with an SA-7 could, and there was no way to know when he was flying over one . . . *Stop thinking about that, Duke.*

The Royal Air Force Tornados swept in from the east. The lead aircraft dropped its cluster bombs in front of the column. The rest swept over the road at a shallow angle, raining the bomblets on the convoy. Trucks exploded, sending burning fuel high into the air. Ellington saw the silhouettes of two fighter-bombers against the orange flames as they headed west for home. The fuel spread out on both sides of the road, and he watched the undamaged trucks stop and turn, desperately trying to escape the conflagration. Some were abandoned by their drivers. Others steered clear of the fire and tried to continue south. A few succeeded. Most bogged down, too heavily loaded to move on the soft earth.

"Tell 'em they got about half. Not bad at all."

A minute later, the Frisbee was ordered northeast again.

In Brussels the radar signals downlinked from the ground-search radar aircraft plotted the fuel convoy's path. A computer was now programmed to perform the function of the videotape recorder, and it traced the convoy's movements back to its point of origin. Eight more attack aircraft headed toward this patch of woods. The Frisbee got there first.

"I show SAM radars, Duke," Eisly said. "I'll call it one battery of SA-6 and another of SA-11. They must think this place is important."

"And a hundred little bastards with hand-held SAMs," Ellington added. "ETA on the strike?"

"Four minutes."

Two batteries of SAMs would be very bad news for the strike aircraft. "Let's cut those odds down some."

Eisly singled out the SA-11 search/acquisition radar. Ellington headed toward it at four hundred knots, using a road to travel *below* the trees until he was two miles away. Another Sidearm dropped off the airframe and rocketed toward the radar transmitter. At the same moment, two missiles came their way. The Duke applied maximum power and turned hard to the east, dropping chaff and flares as he did so. One missile went for the chaff and exploded harmlessly. The other locked onto the fuzzy radar signal reflected from the Frisbee and wouldn't let go. Ellington jinked up hard, then pulled the aircraft into a maximum-g turn in hope of outmaneuvering the missile. But the SA-11 was too fast. It exploded a hundred feet behind the Frisbee. The two crewmen ejected from the distintegrating aircraft a moment later, their parachutes opening a scarce four hundred feet off the ground.

Ellington landed at the edge of a small clearing. He quickly detached himself from the chute and activated his rescue radio before drawing his revolver. He caught a glimpse of Eisly's chute dropping into the trees and ran in that direction.

"Fuckin' trees!" Eisly said. His feet were dangling off the ground. Ellington climbed up and cut him down. The major's face was bleeding.

Explosions thundered to the north.

"They got it!" Ellington said.

"Yeah, but who's got us?" Eisly said. "I hurt my back."

"Can you move, Don?"

"Hell, yes!"

STENDAL, GERMAN DEMOCRATIC REPUBLIC

The dispersal of fuel reserves into small depots had reduced NATO attacks on them nearly to zero. The resulting sense of security had lasted nearly a month. The attacks on tank columns and munitions stores were serious, but there were plenty of replacements for both. Fuel was a different story.

"Comrade General, NATO has changed its pattern of air attacks."

Alekseyev turned from the map display to listen to his air-intelligence officer. Five minutes later, his supply chief came in.

"How bad is it?"

"Overall, perhaps as much as ten percent of our forward supplies. In the Alfeld sector, over thirty percent."

The phone rang next. It was the general whose divisions were to attack Alfeld in five hours.

"My fuel is gone! The convoy was attacked and destroyed twenty kilometers from here."

"Can you attack with what you have?" Alekseyev asked.

"I can, but I won't be able to maneuver my units worth a damn!"

"You must attack with what you have."

"But—"

"There are four divisions of Soviet soldiers who will die if you do not relieve them. The attack will go as scheduled!" Alekseyev set the phone down. Beregovoy was also short on fuel. A tank could have enough fuel to drive three hundred kilometers in a straight line, but they almost never traveled in a straight line, and despite orders, the crews invariably left the engines running when sitting still. The time needed to start their diesels could mean death if a sudden air attack fell on them. Beregovoy had been forced to give all of his reserve fuel to his eastbound tanks so that they could hit Alfeld in conjunction with the westbound C divisions. The two divisions on the left bank of the Weser were essentially immobilized. Alekseyev was gambling the offensive on his ability to reestablish his supply routes. He told his supply chief to get more fuel. If his attack succeeded he'd need more still.

MOSCOW, R.S.F.S.R.

The transition was ridiculous—less than two hours from Stendal to Moscow by jet, from war to peace, from danger to safety. His father's chauffeur, Vitaly, met him at the military airport and drove at once to the Minister's official dacha in the birch forests outside the capital. He entered the front room to see a stranger with his father.

"So this is the famous Ivan Mikhailovich Sergetov, Major of the Soviet Army."

"Excuse me, Comrade, but I do not think we have met before."

"Vanya, this is Boris Kosov."

The young officer's face betrayed just a fraction of his emotions on being introduced to the Director of the KGB. He leaned back into the easy chair and observed the man who had ordered the bombing of the Kremlin—after arranging for children to be there. It was two in the morning. KGB troops loyal—*thought to be loyal,* Minister Sergetov corrected himself—to Kosov patrolled outside to keep this meeting a secret.

"Ivan Mikhailovich," Kosov said genially, "what is your assessment of the situation at the front?"

The young officer suppressed a desire to look to his father for guidance. "The success or failure of the operation hangs in the balance—remember that I am a junior officer and I lack the expertise for a reliable evaluation. But as I see things, the campaign could now go either way. NATO is short on manpower but they've had a sudden infusion of supplies."

"About two weeks' worth."

"Probably less," Sergetov said. "One thing we've learned at the front is that supplies get used up much faster than expected. Fuel, ordnance, everything seems almost to evaporate. So our friends in the Navy must keep hitting the convoys."

"Our ability to do this is seriously reduced," Kosov said. "I would not expect— The truth is that the Navy has been defeated. Iceland will soon be back in NATO hands."

"But Bukharin didn't say that!" the elder Sergetov objected.

"He didn't tell us that Northern Fleet's long-range aircraft were nearly exterminated either, but they were. The fool thinks he can keep *me* from learning this! The Americans have a full division on Iceland now, with massive support from their fleet. Unless our submarines can defeat this collection of ships—and remember that while they are there, they cannot strike at the convoys—Iceland will be lost within a week. That will obviate the Navy's strategy for isolating Europe. If NATO can resupply at will, then what?"

Ivan Sergetov shifted nervously in his chair. He could see where the conversation was leading. "Then possibly we have lost."

"Possibly?" Kosov snorted. "Then we are doomed. We will have lost our war against NATO, we still have only a fraction of our energy needs, and our armed forces are a shadow of their former selves. And what will the Politburo do then?"

"But if the Alfeld offensive succeeds . . ." Both Politburo men ignored this statement.

"What of the secret German negotiations in India?" Minister Sergetov asked.

"Ah, you noted that the Foreign Minister glossed over that?" Kosov smiled wickedly. He was a man born to conspiracy. "They have not changed their bargaining position a dot. At most it was a hedge against the collapse of NATO forces. It might also have been a trick from the beginning. We're not sure." The KGB Chief poured himself a glass of mineral water. "The Politburo meets in eight hours. I will not be there. I feel an angina attack coming on from my damaged heart."

"So Larionov will deliver your report?"

"Yes." Kosov grinned. "Poor Josef. He is trapped by his own intelligence estimates. He will report that things are not going according to plan, but still going. He will say that NATO's current attack is a desperate attempt to forestall the Alfeld offensive, and that the German negotiations still hold promise. I should warn you, Major, that one of his men is on your staff. I know his name, but I have not seen his reports. It was probably he who provided the information that got the former commander arrested and put your general in his place."

"What will happen to him?" the officer asked.

"That is not your concern," Kosov answered coldly. A total of seven senior officers had been arrested in the past thirty-six hours. All were now in Lefortovo Prison, and Kosov could not have altered their fates even if he'd had the mind to.

"Father, I need to know the fuel situation."

"We are down to minimum national reserves—you have a week's fuel delivered or being shipped now, and roughly one week's supply is available for the forces deployed in Germany, plus a week for the armies detailed to go into the Persian Gulf."

"So tell your commander that he has two weeks to win the war. If he fails, it will mean his head. Larionov will blame the Army for his own intelligence mistakes. Your life will be in danger too, young man."

"Who is the KGB spy on our staff?"

"The Theater Operations Officer. He was co-opted years ago, but his control officer is in the Larionov faction. I don't know exactly what he is reporting."

"General Alekseyev is—technically he's violating orders by taking a unit on the Weser and sending it east to relieve Alfeld."

"Then he is already in danger, and I cannot help him." *Not without tipping my hand.*

"Vanya, you should return now. Comrade Kosov and I have other things to discuss." Sergetov embraced his son and walked him to the door. He watched the red taillights disappear behind the birch trees.

"I don't like using my own son in this!"

"Whom else can you trust, Mikhail Eduardovich? The *Rodina* faces possible destruction, the Party leadership has gone mad, and I don't even have full control of the KGB. Don't you see: we have *lost!* We must now save what we can."

"But we still hold enemy territory—"

"Yesterday does not matter. Today does not matter. What matters is one week from today. What will our Defense Minister do when it becomes obvious even to him that we have failed? Have you considered that? When desperate men realize they have failed—and those desperate men have control of atomic weapons, then what?"

Then what, indeed? Sergetov wondered. He pondered two more questions. *What do I—we?—do about it?* Then he looked at Kosov and asked himself the second.

ALFELD, FEDERAL REPUBLIC OF GERMANY

The Russians were not responding very fast, Mackall was surprised to see. There had been air attacks and several vicious artillery bombardments during the night, but the expected ground assault hadn't materialized. For the Russians this was a crucial mistake. More ammunition had arrived, bringing them to full loads for the first time in weeks. Better still, a full brigade of German Panzer Grenadiers had reinforced the depleted troopers of the 11th Cav, and Mackall had learned to trust these men as he trusted his tank's composite armor. Their defensive positions were arrayed in depth to the east and west. The armored forces pushing down from the north could now support Alfeld with their long-range guns. Engineers had repaired the Russian bridges on the Leine, and Mackall was about to move his tanks east to support the mechanized troops guarding the rubble that was Alfeld.

It was strange crossing the Soviet ribbon bridge—it was strange to be moving east at all! Mackall thought—and his driver was nervous, crossing the narrow, flimsy-looking structure at five miles per hour. Once across, they moved north along the river, swinging around the town. It was raining lightly, with fog and low-hanging clouds, typical European summer weather that cut visibility to under a thousand yards. He was met by troops who guided the arriving tanks to selected defensive positions. The Soviets had helped for once. In their constant efforts to clear the roads of rubble, they'd given the Americans neat piles of brick and stone about two meters high, almost exactly the right size for tanks to hide behind. The lieutenant dismounted from his vehicle to check the placement of his four tanks, then conferred with the commander of the infantry company he was detailed to support. There were two battalions of infantry dug in deep and hard on the outskirts of Alfeld, supported by a squadron of tanks. He heard the overhead whistling of artillery shells, the new kind that dropped mines on the fog-shrouded battlefield ahead of him. The whistling changed as he mounted his tank. Incoming.

STENDAL, GERMAN DEMOCRATIC REPUBLIC

"It's taken too long to get them moving," Alekseyev growled to his operations officer.

"It's still three divisions, and they are moving now."

"But how many reinforcements have arrived?"

The operations man had warned Alekseyev against trying to coordinate a two-pronged attack, but the General had stuck to the plan. Beregovoy's A tank division was now in place to strike from the west, while the three C reserve divisions hit from the east. The regular tank force had no artillery—they'd had to move too fast to bring it—but three hundred tanks and six hundred personnel carriers were a formidable force all by themselves, the General thought . . . but what were they up against, and how many vehicles had been destroyed or damaged by air attack on the approach march?

Sergetov arrived. His class-A uniform was rumpled from his traveling.

"And how was Moscow?" Alekseyev asked.

"Dark, Comrade General. The attack, how did it go?"

"Just starting now."

"Oh?" The major was surprised at the delay. He looked rather closely at the Theater Operations Officer, who hovered over the map table, frowning at the dispositions while the plotting officers prepared to mark the progress of the attack.

"I have a message from high command for you, Comrade General." Sergetov handed over an official-looking form. Alekseyev scanned it—and stopped reading. His fingers went taut on the paper briefly before he regained self-control.

"Come to my office." The General said nothing more until the door was closed. "Are you sure of this?"

"I was told by Director Kosov himself."

Alekseyev sat on the edge of his desk. He lit a match and burned the message form, watching the flame march across the paper almost to his fingertips as he twisted it in his hand.

"That fucking weasel. *Stukach!*" *An informer on my own staff!* "What else?"

Sergetov related the other information he'd learned. The General was silent for a minute, computing his fuel requirements against fuel reserves.

"If today's attack fails . . . we've—" He turned away, unwilling, unable, to make himself say it aloud. *I have not trained my whole life to fail!* He remembered the first notice he'd had of the campaign against NATO. *I told them to attack at once. I told them that we needed strategic surprise, and that we'd have difficulty achieving it if we waited so long. I told them that we'd have to close the North Atlantic to prevent resupply of the NATO forces. So. Now that we've accomplished none of these, my friend is in a KGB prison and my own life is in jeopardy because I may fail to do what I told them we could not do—because I was right all along!*

Come now, Pasha. Why should the Politburo listen to its soldiers when it can just as easily shoot them?

The Theater Operations Officer stuck his head through the door. "The troops are moving."

"Thank you, Yevgeny Ilych," Alekseyev answered amiably. He rose from the desk. "Come, Major, let's see how quickly we can smash through the NATO lines!"

ALFELD, FEDERAL REPUBLIC OF GERMANY

"Bar fight," Woody said from his gunner's position.

"Looks like it," Mackall agreed.

They'd been told to expect two or three Soviet reserve divisions. Together they had perhaps the artillery strength of two regular units, and they were firing at both sides of the river. The miserable visibility hurt both sides. The Russians could not direct their artillery fire well, and the NATO troops would have minimal air support. As usual, the worst part of the preliminary bombardment was the rockets, which lasted two minutes, the unguided missiles falling like hail. Though men died and vehicles exploded, the defending force was well prepared and casualties were light.

Woody switched on his thermal-imaging sights. It allowed him to see roughly a thousand yards, double the visual range. On the left side of the turret, the loader sat nervously, his foot resting lightly on the pedal that controlled the doors to the ammo compartment. The driver in his coffin-sized box under the main gun drummed his fingers on the control bar.

"Heads up. Friendlies coming in," Mackall told his crew. "Movement reported to the east."

"I see 'em," Woody acknowledged. Just a few infantrymen were returning from their forward listening posts. Not as many as there should have been, Mackall thought. *So many casualties over the past—*

"Target tank, twelve o'clock," Woody said. He squeezed the triggers on his yoke, and the tank seemed to leap from its first shot.

The spent round ejected from the breech. The loader stomped his foot on the pedal. The door slid clear of the ammo compartment and he pulled out another sabot round, turning it in a narrow circle to slam it in the breech.

"Ready!"

Woody already had another target. He was largely on his own while Mackall watched out for the whole platoon's front. The troop commander was calling in artillery fire. Immediately behind the first row of tanks, they saw dismounted infantrymen running to keep up with the tanks. Eight-wheeled infantry carriers were mixed in as well. The Bradleys engaged them with their 25mm guns as proximity-fused artillery rounds began to detonate twenty feet off the ground, showering the infantrymen with fragments.

They couldn't miss. The Russian tanks advanced at half the normal hundred-yard interval, concentrating on a narrow front. They were old T-55s, Woody saw, with obsolete 100mm guns. He killed three before they could even see the NATO positions. One shell landed in the stone pile ahead of their tank, sending a mix of steel fragments and stone chips over the vehicle. Woody dispatched that tank with a HEAT round. Smoke rounds began falling—they didn't help the Russians at all. The electronic sights on the NATO vehicles saw right through it. More artillery fire landed on the Cav now that the Russians could see well enough to direct fire in on their positions, and that began an artillery duel as NATO guns searched for the Russian batteries.

"Antenna tank! Sabot!" The gunner locked his sights on the T-55 and fired. The round missed this time and they reloaded another round. The second shot blew the turret into the sky. The thermal sight showed the bright dots of antitank missiles running downrange, and the fountaining explosions of the vehicles they hit. Suddenly the Russians stopped. Most of the vehicles died in place, but some turned and ran off.

"Cease fire, cease fire!" Mackall told his platoon. "Report in."

"Three-two has a track blown off," one replied. The others were intact, protected by their stone revetments.

"Nine rounds fired, boss," Woody said. Mackall and the loader opened their hatches to vent the acrid propellant smell out of the turret. The gunner pulled off his leather helmet and shook his head. His sandy hair was filthy. "You know, there's one thing I miss from the M-60."

"What's that, Woody?"

"We ain't got no hatch in the bottom. Nice to be able to take a piss without climbing outside."

"Did you have to say that!" the driver moaned.

Mackall laughed. It was a moment before he realized why. For the first time they'd stopped Ivan cold, without having to pull back at all—a good thing since their current position didn't allow for that possibility! And how did the crew react? They were making *jokes*.

USS *REUBEN JAMES*

O'Malley lifted off again. He was averaging ten flight hours per day. Three ships had been torpedoed, two more hit by submarine-launched missiles in the past four days, but the Russians had paid dearly for that. They'd sent perhaps as many as twenty submarines into Icelandic waters. Eight had died trying to get through the picket line of submarines that was the fleet's outer defense. More had fallen to the line of towed-array ships whose helicopters were now backed up by those of HMS *Illustrious*. A bold Tango skipper had actually penetrated one of the carrier groups and put a fish into *America*'s tough hide, only to be pounced on and sunk by the destroyer *Caron*. The carrier could now make only twenty-five knots, barely enough to conduct flight operations, but she was still there.

Mike Force—*Reuben James*, *Battleaxe*, and *Illustrious*—was escorting a group of amphibs south for another landing. There were still bears in the woods, and Ivan would go for the amphibious-warfare ships as soon as he had the chance. From a thousand feet, O'Malley could see *Nassau* and three others to the north. Smoke rose from Keflavik. The Russian troops were getting no rest at all.

"Won't be easy for them to track in on us," Ralston thought aloud.

"You suppose those Russian troops have radios?" O'Malley asked.

"Sure."

"You suppose maybe they can see us from those hills—and maybe radio a submarine what they see?"

"I didn't think of that," the ensign admitted.

"That's all right. I'm sure Ivan did." O'Malley looked north again. There were three thousand Marines on those ships. The Marines had saved his ass in Vietnam more than once.

Reuben James and O'Malley had the inshore side of the small convoy while the British ships and helos guarded to seaward. It was relatively shallow water. Their towed-array sonars were reeled in.

"Willy, drop—now, now, now!" The first active sonobuoy was ejected into the water. Five more were deployed in the next few minutes. The passive buoys used for open-ocean search were the wrong choice here. Stealth was not in the cards if the Russian subs were being informed where to go. Better to scare them off than to try finesse.

Three hours, O'Malley thought.

"Hammer, this is Romeo," Morris called. "Bravo and India are working a possible contact to seaward, two-nine miles bearing two-four-seven."

"Roger that, Romeo." O'Malley acknowledged. To Ralston: "Bastard's within missile range. That oughta make the Marines happy."

"Contact! Possible contact on buoy four," Willy said, watching the sonar display. "Signal is weak."

O'Malley turned his helo and moved back up the line.

KEFLAVIK, ICELAND

"Where do you suppose they are?" Andreyev asked his naval liaison officer. The position of the formation had been plotted on the map from the reports of several mountaintop lookout stations.

The man shook his head. "Trying to get to the targets."

The General remembered his own time aboard ship, how vulnerable he'd felt, how dangerous it had been. A distant part of his consciousness felt sympathy for the American Marines. But gallantry was a luxury the General could not afford. His paratroopers were heavily engaged, and he didn't need more enemy troops and heavy equipment—of course!

His division was deployed to keep the Americans away from the Reykjavik-Keflavik area as long as possible. His original orders remained operative: deny the Keflavik Air Base to NATO. That he could do, though it would mean the probable annihilation of his elite troopers. His problem was that Reykjavik airport would be equally useful to the enemy, and one light division wasn't enough to cover both places.

So now the Americans trailed their coats in plain view of his observers— a full regiment of troops plus heavy weapons and helicopters that they could land anywhere they wished. If he redeployed to meet this threat, he risked disaster when he disengaged his forward units. If he moved his reserves, they would be in the open where naval guns and aircraft could massacre them. This unit was being moved, not to join the others deployed against his airborne infantrymen, but to exploit a weakness within minutes instead of hours. Once in place, the landing ships could wait for relative darkness or a storm and race unseen across the water to landbound troops. How could he deploy his own forces to deal with that? His radars were finished, he had a single remaining SAM launcher, and the battleships had systematically exterminated most of his artillery.

"How many submarines out there?"

"I don't know, Comrade General."

USS *REUBEN JAMES*

Morris watched the sonar plot. The sonobuoy contact had faded off after a few minutes. A school of herring, perhaps. The ocean waters abounded with fish, and enough of them on active sonar looked like a sub. His own sonar was virtually useless as his ship struggled just to keep up with the 'phibs. A possible submarine to seaward—every sub contact was a possible cruise-missile sub—was all the Commodore needed to go to full speed.

O'Malley was dipping his sonar now, trying to reacquire the lost contact. He was the only one who could keep up with things.

"Romeo, this is Bravo. Be advised we are prosecuting a possible missile-carrying submarine." Doug Perrin had to assume the worst case.

"Roger that, Bravo." According to the data-link picture, three helicopters were backing *Battleaxe* up, and the British frigate had interposed herself on the line from the contact to the amphibious ships. *Be careful, Doug.*

"Contact!" Willy said. "I have an active sonar contact bearing three-zero-three, range two three hundred."

O'Malley didn't have to look at his tactical display. The submarine was between him and the 'phibs.

"Up dome!" The pilot hovered while the sonar transducer was winched in. The contact was alerted now. That made it harder. "Romeo, Hammer, we have a possible contact here."

"Roger, understood." Morris was looking at the display. He ordered the frigate to close at flank speed. Not a smart tactic, he had no choice but to pounce on the contact before it got within range of the 'phibs. "Signal *Nassau* we're working a possible contact."

"Down dome!" O'Malley ordered. "Drop it to four hundred and hammer!"

Willy activated the sonar as soon as the proper depth was reached. He got a screenful of echoes. The transducer was so close to the rocky bottom that nearly twenty rocky spires showed up. A swiftly running tide didn't help matters. Flow noise around the rocks gave numerous false readings on the passive plot also.

"Sir, I got a whole lot of nothing here."

"I can feel him, Willy. The last time we pinged, I bet we had him at periscope depth and he ducked down deep while we came over."

"That fast?" Ralston asked.

"That fast."

"Skipper, one of these things might be moving a little."

O'Malley keyed his radio and got permission to launch from Morris.

Ralston set the torpedo for circular search, and the pilot dropped it into the sea. The pilot keyed the sonar into his headphones. He heard the whine of the torpedo's propellers, then the high-frequency ping of its homing sonar. It continued to circle for five minutes, then switched over to continuous pinging—and exploded.

"Explosion sounded funny, sir," Willy said.

"Hammer, Romeo—report."

"Romeo, Hammer, I think we just killed a rock." O'Malley paused. "Romeo, there's a sub here, but I can't prove it just yet."

"What makes you think that, Hammer?"

"Because it's one damned fine place to hide, Romeo."

"Concur." Morris had learned to trust O'Malley's hunches. He called up the amphibious commander on *Nassau*. "November, this is Romeo, we have a possible contact. Recommend you maneuver north while we prosecute."

"Negative, Romeo," the Commodore replied at once. "India is working a probable, repeat probable contact that's acting like a missile boat. We're heading for our objective at max speed. Get him for us, Romeo."

"Roger. Out." Morris set the phone back in place. He looked at his tactical action officer. "Continue to close the datum point."

"Isn't this dangerous, rushing after a submarine contact?" Calloway asked. "Don't you have your helicopter to keep them at arm's length?"

"You're learning, Mr. Calloway. It's dangerous, all right. I think they mentioned that the job could get that way when I was at Annapolis . . ."

Both her jet turbines were running flat-out, and the frigate's knife-edge bow sliced through the water at over thirty knots. The torque from her single screw gave the ship a four-degree list to port as she raced to close the submarine.

"This is getting nasty." O'Malley could see the frigate's mast clearly now, the distinctive crosstrees well above the horizon as he covered fifty feet over the water. "Talk to me, Willy!"

"Lots of bottom echoes, sir. The bottom must look like a city, all these damned things sticking up. We got eddies—we got too many things here, sir. Sonar conditions suck!"

"Go passive." The pilot reached up and flipped the switch to listen in. Willy was right. Too much flow noise. *Think!* he told himself. The pilot looked at his tactical display. The amphibs were a scant ten miles away. He couldn't hear them on his sonar, but there was about a 30-percent chance that a submarine could. *If we had him at antenna depth before, he probably has a fair idea where they are . . . but not good enough to shoot.*

"Romeo, Hammer, can you warn the 'phibs off? Over."

"Negative, Hammer. They are running away from a probable contact to seaward."

"Great!" O'Malley growled over the intercom. "Prepare to raise dome, Willy." A minute later they were heading west.

"This sub-driver's got real balls," the pilot said. "He's got brains, too . . ." O'Malley keyed his radio.

"Romeo, Hammer, put November's course track on your tactical display and transmit to my gadget."

It took a minute. O'Malley blessed the unknown engineer who'd built this feature into the Seahawk's tactical computer. The pilot drew an imaginary line from their only contact on the sub and *Nassau*'s projected course. *Figure the sub is going at twenty- to twenty-five knots . . .* The pilot reached down and stabbed his finger on the glass tube.

"That's where the bastard is!"

"How do you know?" Ralston asked. O'Malley already had the Seahawk heading that way.

" 'Cause if I was him, that's where *I'd* be! Willy, next time we dip, keep the dome at exactly one hundred feet. Tell you one other thing, Mr. Ralston—this guy thinks he's beat us." *Nobody beats the Hammer!* O'Malley circled over the spot he'd selected and brought the Seahawk into hover.

"Down dome, Willy. Passive search only."

"One hundred feet, listening, skipper." Seconds stretched out into minutes while the pilot worked his controls to keep the helicopter stationary. "Possible contact bearing one-six-two."

"Go active?" Ralston asked.

"Not yet."

"Bearing is changing slowly, now one-five-nine."

"Romeo, Hammer, we have a possible submarine contact." The helicopter's on-board computer transmitted the data to *Reuben James*. Morris altered course to bear down on the contact. O'Malley raised his sonar dome and deployed a sonobuoy to mark the position and hold the contact while he moved to another position. The frigate was now four miles from the helicopter.

"Down dome!" Another minute's wait.

"Contact, bearing one-nine-seven. Buoy six shows contact bearing one-four-two."

"Gotcha, sucker! Up dome, let's go get him!"

Ralston worked the attack system as O'Malley moved south to get right behind the target. He set their last torpedo for a search depth of two hundred feet, and a snake course.

"Down dome!"

"Contact, bearing two-nine-eight."

"Hammer!"

Willy punched the active sonar button. "Positive contact, bearing two-nine-eight, range six hundred."

"Set!" Ralston said immediately, and the pilot jammed his thumb on the red release button. The burnished green torpedo dropped into the water.

And nothing happened.

"Skipper, the torp didn't activate—dead torp, sir."

There wasn't time to curse. "Romeo, Hammer, we just dropped on a positive contact—bad torpedo, negative function on the torp."

Morris clenched his fist on the radiotelephone receiver. He gave course and rudder orders. "Hammer, Romeo, can you continue to track the target?"

"Affirmative, he's running hard on course two-two-zero—wait, turning north . . . seems to be slowing down now."

Reuben James was now six thousand yards from the submarine. The ships were on converging courses, with each in firing range of the other.

"Crash stop!" Morris ordered. In seconds the entire ship was vibrating from the reverse power. The frigate slowed to five knots inside a minute, and Morris ordered a speed of three knots, bare steerageway. "Prairie / Masker?"

"Operating, sir," the ship control officer confirmed.

Calloway had kept out of the way with his mouth shut—but this was too much. "Captain Morris, aren't we a sitting duck?"

"Yep." Morris nodded. "But we can stop faster than he can. His sonar should just be coming back on line—and we're not making enough noise to hear. Sonar conditions are bad for everybody. It's a gamble," the captain admitted. He radioed for another helicopter. *Illustrious* would have one to him in fifteen minutes.

Morris watched O'Malley's helicopter on radar. The Russian sub had slowed and gone deep again.

"Vampire, vampire!" the radar technician called. "Two missiles in the air—"

"Bravo reports her helo just dropped on an SSGN, sir!" the ASW officer sang out.

"This is getting complicated," Morris observed coolly. "Weapons free."

"Bravo has splashed one missile, sir! The other one's heading for the India!"

Morris's eyes focused on the main display. A * symbol was marching toward HMS *Illustrious*—moving very fast.

"Evaluate vampire as SS-N-19—Bravo evaluates her contact as Oscar-class. She reports a hit, sir." Four helicopters were swarming around the § submarine-contact symbol now.

"Romeo, Hammer, the bastard's right underneath us—bearing just reversed on us."

"Sonar, Yankee-search on bearing one-one-three!" Morris lifted the radiotelephone. "November, turn north now!" he ordered the *Nassau*.

"India is hit, sir. The vampire scored on India . . . wait, India helo reports he dropped another torp on the contact!"

Illustrious would have to look out after herself, Morris thought.

"Sonar contact, sir, bearing one-one-eight, range fifteen hundred." The data went into the fire-control director. The solution light blinked on.

"Set!"

"Shoot!" Morris paused for a moment. "Bridge, combat: all ahead flank! Come right to zero-one-zero."

"Bloody hell," observed Mr. Calloway.

On the frigate's starboard side, the triple torpedo tube mount swung out and loosed a single fish. Below, the engineers listened to their engines go from idle to maximum power. The frigate settled at the stern as the propeller churned the water to foam. The powerful jet turbines accelerated the ship almost like an automobile.

"Romeo, Hammer: warning, warning, the target just fired a fish at you!"

"Nixie?" Morris asked. The ship was moving too fast for her own sonar to work.

"One in the water and another ready to stream, sir," a petty officer responded.

"That's it, then," Morris said. He reached into his pocket for a cigarette, looked at it, then tossed the whole pack into a waste can.

"Romeo, Hammer, this contact is a Type-Two engine plant. I evaluate this contact as a Victor-class. Now at full speed, turning north. Your torp is pinging the target. We've lost the fish he sent your way."

"Roger, stick with the sub, Hammer."

*   *   *

"Aren't you one cool bastard!" O'Malley said into the intercom. He could see smoke rising from HMS *Illustrious*. *Idiot,* the pilot said to himself. *You shouldn't have dropped the first torp!* All he could do now was ping.

"Skipper, the torp just went to continuous ping. It seems to be closing the target, ping interval is shortening. Hull-popping noise, the sub is changing depth again, coming up, I think."

O'Malley saw a disturbance in the water. Suddenly the spherical bow of the Victor came through the surface—the submarine had lost depth control trying to evade the fish. What followed a moment later was the first warhead explosion O'Malley had ever really seen. The submarine was sliding back down when a plume of water appeared a hundred feet from where the bow had poked up.

"Romeo, Hammer, that was a hit—I *saw* the sunuvabitch! Say again, that's a hit!"

Morris checked with his sonar officer. They hadn't picked up the Russian torpedo's homing sonar. It had missed.

Captain Perrin scarcely believed it. The Oscar had taken three torpedo hits so far and still there were no breaking-up noises. But the machinery noise had stopped, and he had the submarine on his active sonar. *Battleaxe* closed at fifteen knots when the black shape appeared amid a mass of bubbles on the surface. The captain ran to the bridge and put his binoculars on the Russian ship. The sub was a bare mile away. A man appeared atop the submarine's sail, waving wildly.

"Check fire! Check fire!" he screamed. "Ship Control, bring us alongside quick as you can!"

He didn't believe it. The Oscar showed a pair of jagged rents on her upper hull and floated with a 30-degree list from the ruptured ballast tanks. Men were scrambling out of the sail and the forward deck hatch.

"Bravo, Romeo. We just killed a Victor-class inshore. Please advise your situation, over."

Perrin lifted the phone. "Romeo, we have a wounded Oscar on the surface, the crew is abandoning ship. He fired two missiles. Our Sea Wolves splashed one. The other hit India in the bows. We are preparing to conduct rescue operations. Tell November that he may continue his promenade. Over."

"Way to go, Bravo! Out." He switched channels. "November, this is Romeo, did you copy Bravo's last transmission, over?"

"Affirmative, Romeo. Let's get this parade to the beach."

General Andreyev took the report from the observation post himself before handing the radiophone to his operations officer. The American landing ships were now five kilometers from Akranes lighthouse. They'd proceed probably to the old whaling station in Hvalfjördur to wait their chance.

"We will resist to the end," the KGB colonel said. "We'll show them how Soviet soldiers can fight!"

"I admire your spirit, Comrade Colonel." He walked over to the corner and picked up a rifle. "Here, you may take this to the front yourself."

"But—"

"Lieutenant Gasporenko, get the colonel a driver. He's going to the front to show the Americans how Soviet soldiers fight." Andreyev watched with dark amusement. The *chekist* could not back down. After he was gone, the General summoned his divisional communications officer. All long-range radio transmitters except for two would be destroyed. Andreyev knew he could not surrender yet. His troopers would have to pay a bill in blood first, and the General would suffer for every drop. But he knew it would soon reach a point at which further resistance was futile, and he would not sacrifice his men for nothing.

ALFELD, FEDERAL REPUBLIC OF GERMANY

It was over for a while. The second attack had nearly done it, Mackall thought. The Russians had run their tanks flat-out and gotten to within fifty yards of the American positions, close enough that their old, obsolete cannon had destroyed half of the troop's tanks. But that attack had faltered on the brink of success, and the third attack at dusk was a halfhearted affair executed by men too tired to advance into the kill zone. He could hear the noise behind him of another action under way. The Germans west of the town were under heavy attack.

STENDAL, GERMAN DEMOCRATIC REPUBLIC

"General Beregovoy reports a heavy counterattack from the north—toward Alfeld."

Alekseyev accepted the news impassively. His gamble had failed. *That's why it's called gambling, Pasha.*

Now what?

It was very quiet in the map room. The junior officers who plotted the movements of friendly and enemy forces had never talked much, and now were not even looking over to the other map sectors. It was no longer a race to see whose forces got to their objectives first.

The word you're looking for is gloom, *Pasha.* The General stood next to his operations officer.

"Yevgeny Ilych, I am open to suggestions."

He shrugged. "We must continue. Our troops are tired. So are theirs."

"We're throwing inexperienced troops against veterans. We have to change that. We will take officers and NCOs from the A units that are off the line and use them to beef up the C units now arriving. These reservists must have experienced combat soldiers to leaven their ranks, else we send them like cattle to the slaughter. Next, we will temporarily suspend offensive operations—"

"Comrade General, if we do that—"

"We have enough strength for one last hard push. That push will be at the time and place of my choosing, and it will be a fully prepared attack. I will order Beregovoy to escape the best way he can—I cannot trust that order to the radio. Yevgeny Ilych, I want you to fly to Beregovoy's headquarters tonight. He'll need a good operational brain to assist him. That will be your assignment." *I'll give you a chance to redeem yourself, you traitorous bastard. Use it well.* More importantly, it got the KGB informer out of the way. The operations officer walked off to arrange transport. Alekseyev took Sergetov back into his office.

"You're going back to Moscow."

42. The Resolution of Conflict

BRUSSELS, BELGIUM

"Amazing what a pair of fives can do . . ."

"What's that, General?" his intelligence chief inquired. SACEUR shook his head, looking at the map with confidence for once. Alfeld held—a couplet, the General thought. The Germans to the west had taken a murderous pounding, but while their lines had bent, they hadn't broken. More help was on the way. A tank brigade was en route to reinforce them. The newly arrived armored division was pressing south now to isolate this Russian division from those on the Weser. The farthest-advanced Russian divisions had shot out their supply of surface-to-air missiles, and NATO air power was blasting their positions with grim regularity.

Aerial reconnaissance showed the open ground east of Alfeld to be a charnel house of burned-out tanks. Reinforcements were heading there also. Ivan would be back, but skies were clearing again. The full weight of NATO aircraft was coming into play.

"Joachim, I think we've stopped them."

"Ja, Herr General! Now we'll begin to drive them back."

MOSCOW, R.S.F.S.R.

"Father, General Alekseyev has ordered me to tell you that he does not think it possible to defeat NATO."

"You are certain?"

"Yes, father." The young man sat down in the Minister's office. "We failed to achieve strategic surprise. We underestimated NATO's air power—too many things. We failed to prevent NATO's resupply. Except for that last counterattack it might have worked, but . . . There is one more chance. The General is suspending offensive operations in preparation for a final attack. To do this—"

"If all is lost, what is this you're talking about?"

"If we can damage the NATO forces sufficiently to forestall a major counteroffensive, we will hold on to our gains, enabling you—enabling the Politburo to negotiate from a position of strength. Even this is uncertain, but it is the best option the General sees. He asks that you put it to the Politburo that a diplomatic settlement is necessary, and quickly, before NATO recovers its strength sufficiently for their own offensive."

The Minister nodded. He turned in his chair to look out the window for a few minutes while his son waited for a response.

"Before that is possible," the Minister said finally, "they will order Alekseyev's arrest. You know what's happened to the others they arrested, don't you?" It took his son a moment to grasp the father's words.

"They couldn't have!"

"Last night, all seven of them, including your former Commander-in-Chief."

"But he was an effective commander—"

"He failed, Vanya," the elder Sergetov said quietly. "The State does not suffer failure gladly, and I have allied myself, for your sake, with Alekseyev . . ." His voice trailed off. *I have no choice now. I must cooperate with Kosov, bastard or not, consequences or not. And I must risk your life also, Vanya.* "Vitaly will take you to the dacha. You will change into civilian clothes and wait for me. You will not go outside, you will not allow yourself to be seen by anyone."

"But surely you are being watched!"

"Of course." His father smiled briefly. "I am being watched by officers of the Committee for State Security, officers of Kosov's personal staff."

"And if he plays you for a fool?"

"Then I am a dead man, Vanya, and so are you. Forgive me, I never dreamed that something like this would—you have made me very proud these last few weeks." He rose and embraced his son. "Go now, you must trust me."

After his son left, Sergetov lifted his phone and dialed KGB headquarters. Director Kosov was out, and the Petroleum Minister left a message that the figures Kosov had requested on oil production in the Gulf States were ready.

The meeting requested by the Minister's use of the code phrase took place soon after sunset. By midnight, Ivan Mikhailovich was again on a plane bound for Germany.

STENDAL, GERMAN DEMOCRATIC REPUBLIC

"Director Kosov applauds your method for dealing with the traitor. He said that killing him, even accidentally, would have aroused suspicion, but now that he is safely behind enemy lines and doing his duty, they will be certain that he is not under suspicion."

"The next time you see the bastard, tell him thank you."

"Your friend was shot thirty-six hours ago," Sergetov said next. The General snapped to rigid attention.

"What?"

"The former Commander-in-Chief West was shot, along with Marshal Shavyrin, Rozhkov, four others."

"And that fucking Kosov congratulates me for—"

"He said there was nothing he could do about it and offers his condolences."

Condolences from the Committee for State Security, Alekseyev thought. *There will come a time, Comrade Kosov . . .*

"I am next, of course."

"You were right to have me float your rationale for future operations with my father. He and Kosov both feel that for you to propose this to STAVKA would mean your instant arrest. The Politburo still feels that victory is possible. When they lose that belief, anything can happen."

Alekseyev knew exactly what *anything* meant.

"Go on."

"Your idea to put experienced troops in the arriving C divisions has merit—anyone will see that. A number of such divisions are cycling through Moscow every day." Sergetov halted to allow his general to draw his own conclusions.

The General's whole body appeared to shudder. "Vanya, you are talking treason."

"We are talking about the survival of the Motherland—"

"Do not confuse the importance of your own skin with the importance of our country! You are a soldier, Ivan Mikhailovich, as am I. Our lives are expendable pawns—"

"For our political leadership?" Sergetov scoffed. "Your respect for the Party comes late, Comrade General."

"I hoped that your father could persuade the Politburo to a more moderate course of action. I did not intend to incite a rebellion."

"The time for moderation is long past," Sergetov replied, speaking like a young Party chieftain. "My father spoke against the war, as did others, to no avail. If you propose a diplomatic solution, you will be arrested and shot, first for failing to achieve your assigned objective, second for daring to propose political policy to the Party hierarchy. With whom would you be replaced, and what would be the result? My father fears that the Politburo will lean toward a nuclear resolution of the conflict." *My father was right,* Sergetov thought, *for all his anger at the Party, Alekseyev has served the State too long and too well to allow himself to think realistically of treason.*

"The Party and the Revolution have been betrayed, Comrade General. If we do not save them, both are lost. My father says that you must decide whom and what you serve."

"And if I decide wrongly?"

"Then I will die, and my father, and others. And you will not have saved yourself."

He's right. He's right on all things. The Revolution has been betrayed. The idea of the Party has been betrayed—but—

"You try to manipulate me like a child! Your father told you that I would not cooperate unless you convinced me of the idealistic"—the General sputtered for a moment, seeking the right word—"rightness, rightness of your action."

"My father told me that you have been conditioned, just as the *science* of Communism says men can be conditioned. You have been told all your life that the Army serves the Party, that you are the guardian of the State. He told me to remind you that you are a man of the Party, that it is time for the people to reclaim the Party for themselves."

"Ah, this is why he conspires with the Director of the KGB!"

"Perhaps you would prefer that we have some bearded priests from the Orthodox Church, or some dissident Jews from the Gulag to make the revolution a pure one? We must fight with what we have." It was heady wine indeed for Sergetov to talk this way to a man with whom he had served under fire, but he knew that his father was right. Twice in fifty years, the Party had broken the Army to its will. For all their pride and power, the generals of the Soviet Army had as much instinct for rebellion as a lapdog. *But once the decision is made,* his father had told him . . . "The *Rodina* cries out for rescue, Comrade General."

"Don't tell me about the Motherland!" *The Party is the soul of the people.* Alekseyev remembered the slogan for a thousand repetitions.

"Then what of the children of Pskov?"

"The KGB did that!"

"Do you blame the sword for the hand that wields it? If so, what does that make you?"

Alekseyev wavered. "It is not an easy thing to overturn the State, Ivan Mikhailovich."

"Comrade General, is it your duty to carry out orders that will only bring about its destruction? We do not seek to overturn the State," Sergetov said gently. "We seek to restore the State."

"We will probably fail." Alekseyev took a perverse comfort in the statement. He sat down at his desk. "But if I must die, better that it should be as a man than a dog." The General took out a pad of paper and a pencil. He began to formulate a plan to ensure that they would not fail, and that he would not die until he had accomplished at least one thing.

HILL 914, ICELAND

They were good troops up there, Colonel Lowe knew. Nearly all of the division's artillery was lashing the hill, plus continuous air attacks, plus the battleships' five-inch guns. He watched his troops advancing up the steep slopes under fire from the remaining Russians. The battlewagons were close inshore, delivering VT proximity rounds from their secondary batteries. The shells exploded twenty feet or so from the ground in ugly black puffs that sprayed the hill with fragments, while the Marines' own heavy guns plowed up the hilltop. Every few minutes the artillery would stop for a moment to allow the aircraft to swoop in with napalm and cluster bombs— and still the Russians fought back.

"Now—move the choppers now!" Lowe ordered.

Ten minutes later, he heard the stuttering sound of rotors as fifteen helicopters passed his command post to the east, curving around the back side of the hill. His artillery coordinator called to halt the fire briefly as the two companies of men landed on the hill's southern rim. They were supported by SeaCobra attack choppers and advanced at a run toward the Russian positions on the northern crests.

The Russian commander was wounded, and his second in command was slow to realize that he had enemy troops in his rear. When he did, a hopeless situation became one of despair. The word got out slowly. Many of the Russian radios were destroyed. Some of the troopers never got the word and had to be killed in their holes. But they were the exceptions. Most heard the diminishing fire and saw the raised hands. With a mixture of shame and relief, they disabled their weapons and waited for capture. The battle for the hill had lasted four hours.

"Hill 914 does not answer, Comrade General," the communications officer said.

"It's hopeless," Andreyev muttered to himself. His artillery was destroyed, his SAMs were gone. He'd been ordered to hold the island for only a few weeks, been promised seaborne reinforcement, been told that the war in Europe would last two weeks, four at the most. He'd held longer than that. One of his regiments had been destroyed north of Reykjavik, and now that the Americans had Hill 914, they could see into the island's capital. Two thousand of his men were dead or missing, another thousand wounded. It was enough.

"See if you can raise the American commander on the radio. Say that I request a cease-fire and desire to meet with him at a place of his choosing."

USS *NASSAU*

"So, you're Beagle?"

"Yes, General." Edwards tried to sit up a little straighter in the bed. The tubes in his arm and the cast on his leg didn't help. The landing ship's hospital was full of wounded men.

"And this must be Miss Vigdis. They told me you were pretty. I have a daughter about your age."

The Navy corpsmen had gotten her clothes that nearly fit. A doctor had examined her and pronounced her pregnancy normal and healthy. She was rested and bathed; to Mike and everyone else who had seen her she was a reminder of better times and better things.

"Except for Michael, I would be dead."

"So I've heard. Is there anything you need, miss?"

She looked down at Edwards, and that answered the question.

"You've done pretty well for a weatherman, Lieutenant."

"Sir, all we did was keep out of the way."

"No. You told us what Ivan had on this rock, and where they were— well, at least where they weren't. You and your people did a lot more than just keep out of the way, son." The General pulled a small box out of his pocket. "Well done, Marine!"

"Sir, I'm Air Force."

"Oh, yeah? Well, this here says you're a Marine." The General pinned a Navy Cross to his pillow. A major approached the General and handed him a message form. The General pocketed it and looked down the rows of hospital beds.

"About time," he breathed. "Miss Vigdis, would you please look after this man for us?"

SVERDLOVSK, R.S.F.S.R.

Two more days and they'd be leaving for the front. The 77th Motor-Rifle Division was a Category-C unit, and like all such units was composed of reservists in their thirties and possessed a little over a third of its normal outlay of equipment. Since mobilization they had been training incessantly, the older men with military experience passing along their knowledge to the newly inducted conscripts. It was a strange match. The young arrivals were physically fit but ignorant of military life. The older men remembered much of their own military service, but had softened with age. The young men had the ardor of youth, and as much as they naturally feared exposure to danger on the battlefield, they would not hesitate to defend their country. The older men with families had much more to lose. Lectures to their officers from a veteran combat officer had filtered down to the ranks. Germany would not be pleasant. A sergeant from communications re- ceipted the message, and the word got out quickly: experienced combat officers and NCOs would join them at Moscow. The experienced reservists knew that they'd need such men to teach them the lessons hard-won at the front.

They knew something else it meant: the 77th Motor-Rifle Division would be committed to action within a week. It was quiet that night in the en- campment. Men stood outside the unheated barracks, looking at the pine forests on the eastern slopes of the Ural Mountains.

MOSCOW, R.S.F.S.R.

"Why are we not attacking?" the General Secretary demanded.

"General Alekseyev has informed me that he is preparing for a major attack now. He says he needs time to organize his forces for a weighted blow," Bukharin answered.

"You tell Comrade General Alekseyev," the Defense Minister said, "that we want action, not words!"

"Comrades," Sergetov said, "I seem to recall from my own military service that one should not attack until one has a decisive advantage in men and weapons. If we order Alekseyev to attack before he is ready, we condemn our army to failure. We must give him time to do his job properly."

"And now you are an expert on defense matters?" the Defense Minister inquired. "A pity you are not so expert in your own field, or we should not be in this predicament!"

"Comrade Minister, I told you that your projections for oil use at the front were overly optimistic, and I was correct. You said 'Give us the fuel, and we'll see it is properly used,' did you not? You said a two-week campaign, four at the worst, did you not?" Sergetov looked around the table. "Such expertise as this has brought us to disaster!"

"We will not fail! We will defeat the West."

"Comrades," Kosov walked into the room. "Forgive me for being late. I just received notification that our forces on Iceland are surrendering. The general in command cites thirty-percent casualties and a hopeless tactical situation."

"Have him arrested at once!" Defense roared. "And arrest the family of the traitor."

"Our Comrade Defense Minister seems far more efficient in arresting our own people than in defeating our enemies," Sergetov observed dryly.

"You young whelp!" The Defense Minister went white with rage.

"I do not say that we have been defeated, but it is clear that we have not yet been victorious. It is time that we seek a political conclusion to this war."

"We could accept the German terms," the Foreign Minister said hopefully.

"I regret to inform you that this is no longer a possibility," Kosov replied. "I have reason to believe that this was a sham—a German *maskirovka*."

"But your deputy said only the day before yesterday—"

"I warned him and you that I had my doubts. A story appeared today in the French newspaper *Le Monde* that the Germans have rejected a *Soviet* offer for a political settlement to the war. They give the correct times and location that the meetings took place—the story could only have come from official German channels, and the clear implication is that this was all along a NATO effort to affect our strategic thinking. They are sending us a message, Comrades. They say that they are prepared to fight the war to the finish."

"Marshal Bukharin, what is the strength of the NATO forces?" the General Secretary asked.

"They have taken massive losses in men and materiel. Their armies are exhausted. They must be, else they would have counterattacked in strength already."

"One more push, then," Defense said. He looked to the head of the table for support. "One more very very hard push. Perhaps Alekseyev is right—we need to coordinate a single massive attack to smash their lines."

Now you are grasping at other men's straws, Sergetov thought.

"The Defense Council will consider this in private," the General Secretary said.

"No!" Sergetov objected. "This is now a political question for the entire Politburo. The fate of the country will not be decided by five men only!"

"You have no place to object, Mikhail Eduardovich. You have no vote at this table." Sergetov was stunned to hear these words from Kosov.

"Perhaps he should," Bromkovskiy said.

"That is not a question to be decided now," the General Secretary announced.

Sergetov watched the faces arrayed around the oak table. No one had the courage to speak up now. He had almost altered the power balance of the Politburo, but until it was clear which faction was stronger, the old rules would prevail. The meeting adjourned. The members filed out except for the five Defense Council members, who kept Bukharin with them.

The candidate member lingered outside looking for allies. His fellow chieftains filed past. Several met his eyes, then looked away.

"Mikhail Eduardovich?" It was the Minister for Agriculture. "How much fuel will be available for food distribution?"

"How much food will there be?" Sergetov asked. *How much food can there be?*

"More than you think. We have tripled the size of private plots throughout the Russian Republic—"

"What?"

"Yes, the old people on the farms are growing plenty of food now—at least enough to feed us for the time being. The problem is now one of distribution."

"No one told me." *Some* good *news?* Sergetov wondered.

"Do you know how many times I have proposed this? No, you weren't here last July, were you? I've said for years that by doing this we could solve many problems, and finally they listened to me! We have food, Mikhail Eduardovich—I just hope we will have people to eat it! I need fuel to transport it to the cities. Will I have the fuel?"

"I will see what I can do, Filip Moiseyevich."

"You have spoken well, Comrade. I hope some will listen."

"Thank you."

"Your son is well?"

"The last I heard from him, yes."

"I am ashamed that my son is not there, too." The Minister for Agriculture paused. "We must—well, we have no time for that now. Get me the fuel figures as quickly as you can."

A convert? Or an agent provocateur?

STENDAL, GERMAN DEMOCRATIC REPUBLIC

Alekseyev held the message in his hand: FLY AT ONCE TO MOSCOW FOR CONSULTATIONS. Was it his death sentence? The General summoned his deputy.

"Nothing new. We have some probes around Hamburg, and what looks like preparations for an attack north of Hannover, but nothing we should not be able to handle."

"I have to go to Moscow." Alekseyev saw the concern on the man's face. "Don't worry, Anatoliy, I haven't been in command long enough to be shot. We will have to arrange our personnel transfers in a systematic way if we have any hope of transforming these C divisions into a fighting force. I should be back in twenty-four hours or less. Tell Major Sergetov to get my map case and meet me outside in ten minutes."

Alekseyev handed his aide the message form in the back of the staff car, along with an ironic look.

"What does this mean?"

"We'll find out in a few hours, Vanya."

MOSCOW, R.S.F.S.R.

"They are truly mad."

"You should choose your words with greater care, Boris Georgiyevich," Sergetov said. "What has NATO done now?"

The KGB Chief shook his head in surprise. "I mean the Defense Council, you young fool!"

"This young fool has no vote on the Politburo. You pointed that out yourself." Sergetov had held the fleeting hope that the Politburo might be brought to its senses.

"Mikhail Eduardovich, I have worked very hard to protect you to this point. Please do not make me regret this. If you had managed to force a Politburo decision in the open, you would have lost and possibly destroyed yourself. As it is"—Kosov paused for another of his grins—"as it is, they have asked me to discuss their decision with you in hope of getting your support.

"They are doubly mad," Kosov went on. "First, the Defense Minister wishes to initiate the use of a few small tactical nuclear warheads. Second, he hopes for your support. They propose the *maskirovka* all over again. They will explode a small tactical device in the DDR, forcing us to retaliate while proclaiming that NATO has violated the no-first-use agreement. But it could be worse. They've summoned Alekseyev to Moscow to seek his assessment of the plan and how best to implement it. He should be on his way here now."

"The Politburo will never agree to this. We're not all crazy, are we? Have you told them how NATO will react?"

"Of course. I've told them that NATO will not react at all at first, they will be too confused."

"You encouraged them?"

"I wish you would keep in mind that they prefer Larionov's opinions to my own."

Comrade Kosov, Sergetov thought to himself, *you care less about the danger to the* Rodina *than you do for your own future. You'd be quite satisfied to bring the whole country down if you bring them down first, wouldn't you?*

"The votes on the Politburo . . ."

"Will support the Defense Council. Think. Bromkovskiy will vote no, perhaps Agriculture also, though I doubt it. They want you to speak in favor of the plan. This will reduce the opposition to old Petya. Petya is a good old man, but no one really listens to him anymore."

"I will never do this!"

"But you must. And Alekseyev must agree." Kosov got up and looked out the window. "There is nothing to fear—no nuclear bombs will be used. I have already seen to that."

"What do you mean?"

"Surely you know who controls the nuclear weapons in this country?"

"Certainly, the strategic rocket forces, the Army's artillerymen—"

"Excuse me, I phrased my question poorly. Yes, they control the rockets. It is *my* people who control the *warheads,* and Josef Larionov's faction does not include that segment of the KGB! This is why you must play along."

"Very well. Then we must warn Alekseyev."

"With caution now. No one seems to have noticed that your son has made several trips to Moscow, but if you are seen with General Alekseyev before he meets with them . . ."

"Yes, I can understand that." Sergetov thought for a moment. "Perhaps Vitaly can meet them at the airport and pass a message?"

"Very good! I will make a *chekist* of you yet!"

The Minister's driver was summoned and handed a written note. He departed at once, taking the Minister's Zil out toward the airport. A military convoy of wheeled armored personnel carriers held him up. Forty minutes later, he noticed that his gas gauge was down. Odd, he'd just filled the car up the day before—the Politburo members were never short of anything. But it kept dropping. Then the engine stopped. Vitaly pulled the car over, seven kilometers from the airport, got out, and opened the hood. The chauffeur checked belts and electrical connections. Everything seemed as it should. He got back in and tried to start the car, and nothing happened. He figured out a moment later that the alternator had gone bad, and the car had been running off battery power. He tried the car phone. The battery was completely flat.

Alekseyev's transport was just arriving. A staff car provided by the commander of the Moscow Military District motored up to the plane, and the General and his aide got in at once for the ride to the Kremlin. For Alekseyev the most frightening part of the flight was getting out of the aircraft—he halfway expected to see KGB troops waiting for him instead of the staff car. It would almost have been a relief to be arrested.

The General and his aide rode in silence—all their talking had been done on the noisy aircraft where listening devices could not possibly have worked. Alekseyev noted the empty streets, the absence of trucks—most of them now at the front—even the shorter-than-usual lines outside the food stores. *A country at war,* he thought.

Alekseyev had expected the ride to the Kremlin to seem slow. The reverse was true. Seemingly in the blink of an eye the car pulled through the Kremlin gates. A sergeant outside the Council of Ministers building pulled open the door, saluting smartly. Alekseyev returned it and walked up the steps to the door, where another sergeant waited. Alekseyev walked like a soldier, back straight, his face set in a stern mien. His newly polished boots glistened, and his eyes caught the flashing reflection of the ceiling lights as he walked into the lobby. The General disdained the elevator, preferring the stairs for the trip to the conference room. He noted that the building had been repaired since the bombing incident.

A captain of the Taman Guards, the ceremonial unit stationed at Alabino outside Moscow, met the General at the top of the stairs and escorted him to the double doors of the conference room. Alekseyev ordered his aide to wait as he entered, his visored cap tucked tightly under his arm.

"Comrades: General Colonel P. L. Alekseyev reports as ordered!"

"Welcome to Moscow, Comrade General," the Defense Minister said. "What is the situation in Germany?"

"Both sides are exhausted but still fighting. The current tactical situation is one of stalemate. We have more troops and weapons available, but we are critically short of fuel."

"Can you win?" the General Secretary asked.

"Yes, Comrade Secretary! Given several days to organize my forces, and if I can do some crucial work with the arriving reserve formations, I think it likely that we can sunder the NATO front."

"Likely? Not certain?" the Defense Minister asked.

"In war there is no certainty," Alekseyev answered simply.

"We have learned that," the Foreign Minister answered dryly. "Why have we not won yet?"

"Comrades, we failed initially to achieve strategic and tactical surprise. Surprise is the most important variable factor in war. With it we would probably—almost certainly—have succeeded in two or three weeks."

"To achieve certain success now, what else will you need?"

"Comrade Defense Minister, I need the support of the people and the Party, and I need a little time."

"You evade the question!" Marshal Bukharin said.

"We were never allowed to use our chemical weapons in the initial assault. That could have been a decisive advantage—"

"The political cost of those weapons was deemed too great," the Foreign Minister said defensively.

"Could you make profitable use of them now?" the General Secretary asked.

"I think not. Those weapons should have been used from the first on equipment-storage depots. The depots are now mainly empty, and hitting them would have only a limited effect. Use of chemicals at the front is no longer a viable option. The newly arriving C formations lack the modern equipment necessary to operate efficiently in a chemical environment."

"Again I ask the question," the Defense Minister repeated. "What do you need to make victory certain?"

"To achieve a decisive breakthrough, we need to be able to blast a hole in NATO lines at least thirty kilometers wide and twenty kilometers in depth. To do that, I need ten full-strength divisions on line, ready to advance. I need several days to prepare that force."

"How about tactical nuclear weapons?" Alekseyev's face did not change. *Are you mad, Comrade General Secretary?*

"The risks are high." *There's a prize understatement.*

"And if we can prevent, politically, NATO retaliation?" Defense asked.

"I do not know how that is possible." *And neither do you.*

"But if we can make it possible?"

"Then it would increase our chances measurably." Alekesyev paused, inwardly chilled at what he saw in those faces. *They want to use nuclear weapons at the front—and when NATO responds in kind and vaporizes my troops, then what? Will it stop with a single exchange or will more and more be used, the explosions advancing west and east? If I tell them they are crazy, they will find a general who will not.* "The problem is one of control, Comrades."

"Explain."

If he were to stay alive and prevent this . . . Alekseyev spoke carefully, mixing truth and lies and guesses. Dissimulation did not come easily to the General, but at least this was an issue he had discussed with his peers for over a decade. "Comrade General Secretary, nuclear weapons are, foremost, political weapons for both sides, controlled by political leaders. This limits their battlefield utility. A decision to use an atomic warhead in a tactical environment must be passed on by those leaders. By the time approval is granted, the tactical situation will almost certainly have changed, and the weapon is no longer useful. NATO never has seemed to grasp this. The weapons they have are mainly designed to be used by battlefield commanders, yet I have never thought myself that NATO's political leadership would lightly give use authority to those battlefield commanders. Because of this, the weapons they would more probably use against us are actually strategic weapons aimed at strategic targets, not the tactical weapons in the field."

"That is not what they say," Defense objected.

"You will note that when we made our breakthroughs at Alfeld and Rühle, nuclear weapons were not used on the bridgeheads even though some pre-war NATO writings would seem to suggest they should have been. I conclude that there are more variable factors in the equation than were fully appreciated. We have learned ourselves that the reality of war can be different from the theory of war."

"So you support our decision to use tactical nuclear weapons?" the Foreign Minister asked.

No! The lie rolled off his lips. "If you are certain that you can prevent retaliation, of course I support it. I caution you, however, that my reading of NATO's response might be very different from what we might otherwise expect. I would expect retaliation to fall some hours later than we think, and against strategic rather than tactical targets. They are more likely to hit road and rail junctions, airfields, and supply facilities. These do not move. Our tanks do." *Think on what I just said, Comrades: things will quickly go out of control. Make peace, you fools!*

"So you think we could use tactical weapons with impunity if we simultaneously threaten strategic targets of our own?" the General Secretary asked hopefully.

"That is essentially the NATO pre-war doctrine. It overlooks the fact that the use of nuclear weapons over friendly territory is not something undertaken lightly. Comrades, I warn you that the prevention of a NATO response will not be an easy exercise."

"You worry about the battlefield, Comrade General," the Defense Minister suggested lightly. "We will worry about the political questions."

There was only one more thing he could say to discourage them. "Very well. In that case I will need direct control of the weapons."

"Why?" the General Secretary demanded.

So they won't be fired, you fucking idiot! "We have here a question of practicality. Targets will appear and disappear on a minute-to-minute basis. If you want me to blast a hole in NATO lines with atomic arms, I will not have the time to get your approval."

Alekseyev was horrified to see that even this did not dissuade them.

"How many would you need?" the Defense Minister wanted to know.

"That is a question contingent upon the time and place of the breakthrough operation, and we would use small weapons against discrete point targets—not population centers. I would say a maximum of thirty weapons in the five- to ten-kiloton range. We would launch them with free-flight artillery rockets."

"How soon will you be ready for your attack?" Marshal Bukharin asked.

"That depends on how quickly I can get veteran troops into the new divisions. If these reservists are to survive on the battlefield, we must get experienced men to firm up their ranks."

"A good idea, Comrade General," the Defense Minister approved. "We will not detain you further. In two days, I want to see detailed plans for your breakthrough."

The five members of the Defense Council watched Alekseyev salute, pivot on his heels, and depart. Kosov looked up at Marshal Bukharin.

"And you wanted to replace this man?"

The General Secretary agreed. "That's the first real fighting soldier I've seen in years."

Alekseyev waved for Major Sergetov to follow him. Only he felt the cold lead weight in his belly. Only he knew how weak his knees were as they trod down the marble steps. Alekseyev didn't believe in God, but he knew that he had just seen the door to hell cracked open.

"Major," he said casually as they entered the staff car, "since we're in Moscow, perhaps you would like to visit your father the Minister before we return to the front?"

"That is very kind of you, Comrade General."

"You have earned it, Comrade Major. Besides, I want figures on our oil supply."

The driver would report what he'd heard, of course.

"They want me to use nuclear weapons at the front!" Alekseyev whispered as soon as the Minister's door was closed.

"Yes, I was afraid of that."

"They must be stopped! There is no predicting what catastrophe this could bring about."

"The Defense Minister says that a tactical nuclear environment could easily be controlled."

"He's talking like one of those NATO idiots! There is no wall between a tactical and a strategic nuclear exchange, just a fuzzy line in the imagination of the amateurs and academics who advise their political leaders. The only thing that would then stand between us and a nuclear holocaust— our survival would be at the mercy of whichever NATO leader is the *least* stable."

"What did you tell them?" the Minister asked. Had Alekseyev retained his wits enough to say the right thing?

"I must be alive to stop them—I told them it's a wonderful idea!" The General sat down. "I also told them that I must have tactical control of the weapons. I think they will agree to that. I'll make sure those weapons are never used. I have just the man on my staff to do that, too."

"You agree then that the Defense Council must be stopped?"

"Yes." The General looked down at the floor, then back up. "Otherwise—I don't know. It is possible that their plan might start something that no one could stop. If we die, we die in a good cause."

"How do we stop them?"

"When does the Politburo meet?"

"Every day now. We usually meet at nine-thirty."

"Whom can we trust?"

"Kosov is with us. There will be a few others, Politburo members, but I do not know whom I can approach."

Wonderful—our only certain ally is the KGB!

"I need some time."

"Perhaps this will help." Sergetov handed over a file he'd gotten from Kosov. "Here is a list of officers in your command who are suspected of political unreliability."

Alekseyev scanned the list. He recognized the names of three men who had served with distinction in battalion and regimental commands . . . one good staff officer and one terrible one. *Even when my men fight a war for the Motherland, they are under suspicion!*

"I'm supposed to formulate my attack plan before I return to the front. I will be at Army Headquarters."

"Good luck, Pavel Leonidovich."

"And to you, Mikhail Eduardovich." The General watched father and son embrace. He wondered what his own father would think of this. *To whom do I turn for guidance?*

KEFLAVIK, ICELAND

"Good afternoon, I am Major General William Emerson. This is Colonel Lowe. He will act as interpreter."

"General Major Andreyev. I speak English."

"Do you propose a surrender?" Emerson asked.

"I propose that we negotiate," Andreyev answered.

"I require that your forces cease hostilities at once and surrender their weapons."

"And what will become of my troops?"

"They will be interned as prisoners of war. Your wounded will receive proper medical attention and your men will be treated in accordance with the usual international conventions."

"How do I know you speak truly?"

"You do not."

Andreyev noted the blunt, honest answer. *But what choice do I have?*

"I propose a cease-fire"—he checked his watch—"at fifteen hours."

"Agreed."

BRUSSELS, BELGIUM

"How long?" SACEUR asked.

"Three days. We'll be able to attack with four divisions."

What's left of four divisions, SACEUR thought. *We've stopped them, all right, but what do we have to drive them back with?*

They did have confidence. NATO had begun the war with an advantage only in its technology, which was even more pronounced now. The Russian stocks of new tanks and guns had been ravaged, and the divisions coming into the line now had twenty-year-old castoffs. They still had numbers, though, and any offensive SACEUR planned would have to be carefully planned and executed. Only in the air did he have an important advantage, and air power had never won a war. The Germans were pushing hard for a counterstrike. Too much of their land, and too many of their citizens, were on the wrong side of the line. Already the *Bundeswehr* was probing aggressively on several fronts, but they'd have to wait. The German Army was not strong enough to push forward alone. They'd taken too many losses in their prime role of stopping the Soviet advance.

KAZAN, R.S.F.S.R.

The youngsters were too excited to sleep. The older men were too worried to sleep. Conditions didn't help. The men of the 77th Motor-Rifle Division were crammed into passenger cars, and while all had seats, it was at the cost of rubbing against their comrades even as they breathed. The troop trains moved along at a speed of a hundred kilometers per hour. The tracks were set in the Russian way, with the rail segments ending together instead of offset; so, instead of the clickity-click familiar to Western riders, the men of this C division heard only a series of thuds. It tested nerves already raw.

The interval between the jarring sounds slowed. A few soldiers looked out to see that their train was stopping at Kazan. The officers were surprised. They weren't supposed to stop until they got to Moscow. The mystery was soon solved. No sooner had the twenty-car train stopped than new men filed into the carriages.

"Attention," called one loud voice. "Combat soldiers arriving!"

Though they had been issued new uniforms, their boots showed the weeks of abuse. Their swagger marked them as veterans. About twenty got onto each passenger car, and rapidly secured comfortable seating for themselves. Those displaced would have to stand. There were officers, too, and they found their counterparts. The officers of the 77th began to get firsthand information of NATO doctrine and tactics, what worked and what didn't work, all the lessons paid for in blood by the soldiers who did not join the division at Kazan. The enlisted men got no such lessons. They watched men who were able to sleep even as they rode to the fighting front.

FASLANE, SCOTLAND

Chicago was alongside the pier, loading torpedoes and missiles for her next mission. Half her crew was ashore stretching their legs and buying drinks for the crew of *Torbay*.

Their boat had acquired quite a reputation for her work in the Barents Sea, enough so that they'd be heading back as soon as she was ready, to escort the carrier battle groups now in the Norwegian Sea, heading for the Soviet bases on the Kola Peninsula.

McCafferty sat alone in his stateroom, wondering why a mission that had ended in disaster was considered successful, hoping that he wouldn't be sent out again—but knowing that he would . . .

MOSCOW, R.S.F.S.R.

"Good news, Comrade General!" A colonel stuck his head in the office Alekseyev had taken for himself. "Your people were able to join up with the 77th at Kazan."

"Thank you." Alekseyev's head went back to his maps when the colonel withdrew.

"It's amazing."

"What's that, Vanya?"

"The men you selected for the 77th, the paperwork, the orders—they went through just like that!"

"A routine transfer of personnel—why shouldn't it go through?" the General asked. "The Politburo approved the procedure."

"But this is the only group of men flown out."

"They had the farthest to go." Alekseyev held up a message form he'd just filled out. Captain—no, now he was Major Arkady Semyonovich Sorokin of the 76th Guards Airborne Division was ordered to report to Moscow immediately. He would fly also. A pity he could not have the captain bring some of his men along, but they were where no Soviet general could reach.

"So, Mikhail Eduardovich, what does General Alekseyev plan?"

Sergetov handed over some notes. Kosov leafed through the pages in a few minutes.

"If he succeeds, at least an Order of Lenin from us, yes?" *That general is overly smart. Too bad for him.*

"We are far from that point. What about the timing? We depend on you to set the stage."

"I have a colonel who specializes in this sort of thing."

"I'm sure."

"One other thing we should do," Kosov said. He explained for several minutes before taking his leave. Sergetov shredded the notes he had from Alekseyev and had Vitaly burn them.

The trouble light and buzzer caught the dispatcher's attention at once. Something was wrong with the trackage on the Elektrozavodskaya Bridge, three kilometers east of Kazan Station.

"Get an inspector out there."

"There's a train half a kilometer away," his assistant warned.

"Tell it to stop at once!" The dispatcher flipped the switch controlling the tower signal.

The deputy dispatcher lifted his radiotelephone. "Train eleven ninety-one, this is Kazan Central Dispatch. Trouble on the bridge ahead, stop immediately!"

"I see the signal! Stopping now," the engineer replied. "We won't make it!"

And he couldn't. Eleven ninety-one was a hundred-car unit, flatcars loaded with armored vehicles and boxcars loaded with munitions. Sparks flew in the pre-dawn light as the engineer applied the brakes on every car, but he needed more than a few hundred meters to halt the train. He peered ahead looking for the problem—a bad signal, he hoped.

No! A track was loose just at the west side of the bridge. The engineer shouted a warning to his crew and cringed. The locomotive jumped the track and ground sideways to a halt. This could not prevent the three engines behind it and eight flatcars from surging forward. They too jumped off the track, and only the bridge's steel framework prevented them from spilling into the Yauza River. The track inspector arrived a minute later. He cursed all the way to the telephone box.

"We need two big wreckers here!"

"How bad?" the dispatcher asked.

"Not as bad as the one last August. Twelve hours, perhaps sixteen."

"What went wrong?"

"All the traffic on this bridge—what do you think?"

"Anyone hurt?"

"Don't think so—they weren't going very fast."

"I'll have a crew out there in ten minutes." The dispatcher looked up at the blackboard list of arriving trains.

"Damn! What are we going to do with these?"

"We can't split them up, it's a whole Army division traveling as a unit. They were supposed to go around the north side. We can't send them around to the south either. Novodanilovskiy Bridge is packed solid for hours."

"Reroute them into Kursk Station. I'll call the Rzhevskaya dispatcher and see if he can get us a routing on his track."

The trains arrived at seven-thirty. One by one they were shunted onto the sidings at Kursk Station and stopped. Many of the troops aboard had never been to Moscow before, but except for those on the outermost sidings, all they could see were the trains of their fellow soldiers.

"A deliberate attempt to sabotage the State railroads!" the KGB colonel said.

"More probably it was worn trackage, Comrade," the Kazan dispatcher said. "But you are correct to be prudent."

"Worn trackage?" the colonel snarled. He knew for certain that it had been a different cause. "I think perhaps you do not take this seriously enough."

The dispatcher's blood chilled at that statement. "I have my responsibilities, too. For the moment that means clearing the wreckage off that damned bridge and getting my trains rolling again. Now, I have a seven-train unit sitting at Kursk, and unless I can get them moving north—"

"From what I see of your map, moving all the traffic around the city's northern perimeter depends on a single switch."

"Well, yes, but that's the responsibility of the Rzhevskaya dispatcher."

"Has it ever occurred to you that saboteurs are not assigned in the same way as dispatchers? Perhaps the same man could operate in a different district! Has anyone checked that switch?"

"I don't know."

"Well, find out! No, no, I will send my own people to check before you railroad fools wreck anything else."

"But, my scheduling . . ." The dispatcher was a proud man, but he knew that he had pressed his luck too far already.

"Welcome to Moscow," Alekseyev said genially.

Major Arkady Semyonovich Sorokin was short, like most paratroop officers. A handsome young man with light brown hair, his blue eyes burned for a reason that Alekseyev understood better than the major did. He limped slightly from two bullets he'd taken in the leg during the initial assault on the Keflavik air base on Iceland. On his breast was the ribbon of the Order of the Red Banner, earned for leading his company into enemy fire. Sorokin and most of the early casualties had been flown out for medical treatment. He and they were now awaiting new assignment since their division had been captured on Iceland.

"How may I serve the General?" Sorokin asked.

"I need a new aide, and I prefer officers with combat experience. More than that, Arkady Semyonovich, I will need you to perform a delicate task. But before we discuss that, there is something I need to explain to you. Please sit down. Your leg?"

"The doctors advised me not to run on it for another week. They were right. I tried to do my ten kilometers yesterday and pulled up lame after only two." He didn't smile. Alekseyev imagined that the boy hadn't smiled at all since May. The General explained to him for the first time why this was true. Five minutes later, Sorokin's hand was opening and closing beside the arm of the leather chair, about where his pistol holster would be if he'd been standing.

"Major, the essence of a soldier is discipline," Alekseyev concluded. "I have brought you here for a reason, but I must know that you will carry out your orders exactly. I will understand if you cannot."

There was no emotion on his face at all, but the hand relaxed. "Yes, Comrade General, and I thank you from my soul for bringing me here. It will be exactly as you say."

"Come, then. We have work to do."

The General's car was already waiting. Alekseyev and Sorokin drove to the inner ring road around central Moscow that changes its name every few kilometers. It is called Chkalova where it passes the Star Theater toward the Kursk Railroad Station.

The commander of the 77th Motor-Rifle Division was dozing. He had a new deputy commander, a brigadier from the front to replace the overaged colonel who had held the post. They had talked for ten hours on NATO tactics, and now the Generals were taking advantage of their unexpectedly extended stop in Moscow to get some sleep.

"What the hell is this!"

The 77th's commander opened his eyes to see a four-star general staring down at him. He jumped to attention like a cadet.

"Good morning, Comrade General!"

"And good morning to you! *What the hell is a division of the Soviet Army doing asleep on a Goddamned railroad siding while men are dying in Germany!*" Alekseyev nearly screamed at the man.

"We—we can't make the trains move, there is some problem with the tracks."

"There is a problem with the tracks? You have your vehicles, don't you?"

"The train goes to Kiev Station, where we switch locomotives for the trip to Poland."

"I'll arrange transport for you. We don't have time," Alekseyev explained as though to a wayward child, "to have a fighting division sit on its ass. If the train can't move, you can! Roll your vehicles off the flatcars, we'll take you through Moscow, and you can get to Kiev Station yourself. Now rub the sleep out of your eyes and get this division rolling before I find someone else who can!"

It never failed to amaze the General what a little screaming could do. Alekseyev watched the division commander scream at his regimental commanders, who went off to scream at their battalion commanders. In ten minutes the screaming was done at the squad level. Ten minutes after that, the tie-down chains were being stripped off the BTR-60 infantry carriers and the first of them rolled off the back of the train for assembly in Korskogo Square in front of the station. The infantrymen mounted their vehicles, looking very dangerous in battle dress, their weapons in their hands.

"You got your new communications officers?" Alekseyev asked.

"Yes, they have completely replaced my own people," the division commander nodded.

"Good. We've learned the hard way about communications security at the front. Your new men will serve you well. And the new riflemen?"

"One company of veterans in each regiment, plus others spread individually throughout the rifle companies." The commander was also pleased to have some new combat officers to replace a few of his less-well-regarded subordinates. Alekseyev had clearly sent him good ones.

"Good, get your division formed up in columns of regiments. Let's show the people something, Comrade. Show them what a Soviet Army division is supposed to look like. They need it."

"How do we proceed through the city?"

"I have gotten some KGB border guards for traffic control. Keep your people in proper order, I don't want anyone to get lost!"

A major came running up. "Ready to move in twenty minutes."

"Fifteen!" the commander insisted.

"Very good," Alekseyev observed. "General, I will accompany you. I want to see how familiar your men are with their equipment."

Mikhail Sergetov arrived early for the Politburo meeting, as was his habit. The usual complement of Kremlin guards was about, one company of infantry with light arms. They were from the Taman Guards division, ceremonial troops with minimal weapons training—a praetorial guard without teeth, like many ceremonial units they practiced parading and boot-shining and looking like soldiers, though at Alabino they did have a full divisional set of tanks and guns. The real Kremlin guardians were the KGB border guards and the division of MVD troops garrisoned outside Moscow. It was typical of the Soviet system that there would be three armed formations loyal to three separate ministries. The Taman division had the best weapons but the least training. The KGB had the best training but only light weapons. The MVD, which answered to the Ministry of the Interior, was also short on weapons and trained mainly as a paramilitary police force, but they were composed of Tartars, troops of known ferocity and antipathy toward the ethnic Russian people. The relationship among the three was more than merely complex.

"Mikhail Eduardovich?"

"Ah." It was the Agriculture Minister. "Good morning, Filip Moiseyevich."

"I am worried," the man said quietly.

"About what?"

"I fear they—the Defense Council—may be thinking about atomic weapons."

"They cannot be so desperate." *If you are an agent provocateur, Comrade, you know that I've been told this. Better that I should know now what you are.*

The man's open Slavic face did not change. "I hope you are right. I have not managed to feed this country for once to see someone blow it up!"

An ally! Sergetov told himself. "If they put it to a vote, what then?"

"I don't know, Misha, I wish I did. Too many of us are being swept away by events."

"Will you speak out against this madness?"

"Yes! I will soon have a grandchild, and he will have a country to grow up in even if it means my life!"

Forgive me, Comrade, forgive me for all the things I have thought of you before.

"Always the early bird, Mikhail Eduardovich?" Kosov and the Defense Minister arrived together.

"Filip and I had to discuss fuel allocations for food transport."

"You worry about my tanks! Food can wait." Defense walked past them into the conference room. Sergetov and his compatriot shared a look.

The meeting came to order ten minutes later. The General Secretary began it, immediately turning over discussions to Defense.

"We must make a decisive move in Germany."

"You have been promising us one of those for weeks!" Bromkovskiy said.

"This time it will work. General Alekseyev will be here in an hour to present his plan. For the moment, we will discuss the use of tactical nuclear weapons at the front and how to prevent a NATO nuclear response."

Sergetov's was one of the impassive faces at the table. He counted four who displayed obvious horror. The discussion that followed was spirited.

Alekseyev rode with the division commander for the first few kilometers, past the Indian Embassy and the Justice Ministry. The latter drew an ironic look from the General. *How fitting that I should pass that building today!* The command vehicle was essentially a radio with eight wheels. Six communications officers rode in the back to allow the commander to run his division right from here. The communications officers were from the front, and loyal to the combat officers who'd brought them back.

Progress was slow. The combat vehicles were designed for speed, but speed also made for breakdowns, and at anything over twenty kilometers per hour the tanks would tear the pavement apart. As it was, they motored along placidly, attracting small knots of people who watched and waved and cheered as the soldiers passed. The procession was not as precise as one of the parades for which the Taman Guards practiced every day. If anything this made the people more enthusiastic. Here were real soldiers going to the front. KGB officers stood along the route, "advising" the officers of the Moscow Militia to let the division pass—they'd explained the reason, the foulup in the eastern rail network, and the traffic policemen were only too happy to make way for the soldiers of the Motherland.

Alekseyev stood up in the gunner's hatch as the column reached Nogina Square.

"You've done well to get your men to this level of training," he told the divisional commander. "I want to dismount and see how the rest of your troops are doing. I will see you again at Stendal." Alekseyev told the driver not to stop. He jumped off the command vehicle carrier with the agility of a young corporal and stood in the street, waving the vehicles past, saluting the officers who rode proudly in their vehicles. It was five minutes until the second regiment reached him, and he waited for its second battalion. Major Sorokin was in the battalion command vehicle, and leaned over to grasp the General's hand and pull him up off the street.

"An old man like you could get hurt that way, Comrade General," Sorokin warned.

"You young buck!" Alekseyev was proud of his physical condition. He looked at the battalion commander, a man newly arrived from the front. "Ready?"

"I am ready, Comrade General."

"Remember your orders and keep control of your men." Alekseyev pulled the flap loose on his holster. Sorokin had himself an AK-47 rifle.

He could see St. Basil's now, the collection of towers and onion domes at the end of Razina Street. One by one the procession of vehicles turned right past the old cathedral. Behind him the soldiers in the infantry carriers all had their heads up, looking at the sights. This was the oldest model of the BTR, and lacked overhead cover.

There! Alekseyev said to himself. The gate built by Ivan the Terrible that led right to the Council of Ministers building. Just through the gate under the clock tower. The time was ten-twenty. He was ten minutes early for his appointment with the Politburo.

"Are we all crazy?" the Agriculture Minister asked. "Do we think we can gamble with atomic arms like so many firecrackers?"

A good man, Sergetov thought, *but he has never been an eloquent one.* The Petroleum Minister rubbed sweaty hands over his trouser legs.

"Comrade Defense Minister, you have led us to the brink of destruction," Bromkovskiy said. "Now you wish us to leap in after you!"

"It is too late to stop," the General Secretary said. "The decision has been made."

An explosion gave the lie to that statement.

"Now!" Alekseyev said. In the back of the command vehicle the communications officers activated the divisional radio net and announced an explosion in the Kremlin. A battalion of riflemen under General Alekseyev's personal command was going in to investigate.

Alekseyev was already moving. Three BTRs ran through the smashed gate, stopping at the front steps of the Council of Ministers building.

"What the hell's going on here?" Alekseyev screamed at the captain of the Taman Guards.

"I don't know—you can't be here, you are not allowed, you must—"

Sorokin cut him down with a three-round burst. He jumped down off the vehicle, nearly collapsing on his bad leg, and raced for the building, with the General in pursuit. Alekseyev turned at the door.

"Secure the area, there is a plot to kill the Politburo!" The order was relayed to the arriving troops. Taman Guard troops were running across the open spaces from the old Arsenal Building. A few warning shots were fired. The Guards wavered, then a lieutenant fired a full magazine from his rifle, and a firefight began within the Kremlin walls. Two bodies of Soviet soldiers, only ten of whom really knew what was happening, began exchanging fire while members of the Politburo watched from the windows.

Alekseyev hated Sorokin for taking the lead, but the major knew whose life was more profitably risked. He encountered a Guards captain on the second-floor landing and killed him. He kept going up, with Alekseyev and the battalion commander behind, remembering the diagram of the building's fourth floor. Another soldier—this one a major—was there with a rifle. He managed to get one burst off, missing high as his target dove, but the major of paratroops rolled clear and killed him. The conference room was only twenty meters away. They found a colonel of the KGB who held his hands out in the clear.

"Where is Alekseyev?"

"Here!" The General had his pistol in his hand.

"No more Guards alive on this floor," the *chekist* said. He'd just killed four with a silenced automatic hidden under his tunic.

"Door." Alekseyev motioned Sorokin. He didn't kick it down, it was unlocked, and led into an anteroom. The double oak doors beyond led to the Politburo.

Sorokin went through first.

They found twenty-one old and middle-aged men, mainly standing at the windows watching a small infantry engagement that had about run its course. The Taman Guards stationed throughout the Kremlin grounds were not organized for this sort of assault, and had not the smallest chance of overwhelming a company of experienced riflemen.

Alekseyev came in next, holstering his pistol.

"Comrades, please go back to your seats. Evidently there is a plot to seize the Kremlin. Fortunately, I was just arriving for my appointment when this column of troops passed by. Sit down, Comrades!" the General ordered.

"What the hell is going on here?" the Defense Minister asked.

"When I entered military school thirty-four years ago I swore an oath to defend the State and the Party from all enemies," Alekseyev said coldly. "Including those who would kill my country because they don't know what the hell else to do! Comrade Sergetov?" The Petroleum Minister pointed to two men. "You Comrades and Comrade Kosov will stay. The others will be leaving with me in a few minutes."

"Alekseyev, you have signed your own death warrant," the Minister of the Interior said. He reached for a telephone. Major Sorokin lifted his rifle and destroyed the phone with a single round.

"Do not make that mistake again. We can very easily kill you all. That would be much more convenient than what we have in mind." Alekseyev waited for a moment. Another officer ran into the room and nodded. "We will now leave, Comrades. If one of you attempts to speak to anyone, you will all be killed immediately. Two-by-two—start moving!" The KGB colonel who had just set off his second Kremlin bomb took out the first group.

After they left, Sergetov and Kosov came up to the General.

"Well done," said the Director of the KGB. "Things are ready at Lefortovo. The men on duty are all mine."

"We're not going to Lefortovo. A change in plans," Alekseyev said. "They go to the old airport, and after that I helicopter them to a military camp commanded by someone *I* trust."

"But I have it all arranged!"

"I'm sure you do. This is my new aide, Major Sorokin. Major Sergetov is at that camp right now, making final arrangements. Tell me, Comrade Director, does Sorokin look familiar to you?"

He *did* look vaguely familiar, but Kosov couldn't place him.

"He was a captain—since promoted for bravery—in the 76th Guards Airborne Division."

"Yes?" Kosov sensed the danger but not the reason.

"Major Sorokin had a daughter in the Young Octobrists. Seventy-sixth Airborne is home-based at Pskov," Alekseyev explained.

"For my little Svetlana," Sorokin said, "who died without a face." All Kosov had time to see was a rifle and a white flash.

Sergetov leaped out of the way and looked to Alekseyev in shock.

"Even if you were right to trust the *chekist*, I will not take orders from one. I leave you with a company of loyal troops. I must get control of the Army. Your job is to get control of the Party apparatus."

"How can we trust you now?" Agriculture asked.

"By now we should be on our way to control of the communications lines. All will be done in accordance with our plan. They will announce an attempt to topple the government, prevented by loyal troops. Later today one of you will appear on television. I must go. Good luck."

Directed by their KGB guides, the motorized battalions headed for the television and radio stations, and the main telephone exchanges. They moved rapidly now, responding to emergency calls to secure the city against an unknown number of counterrevolutionaries. In fact they had not the least idea what they were doing, only that they had orders from a four-star general. That was enough for the officers of the 77th Motor-Rifle. The communications teams had done well. The division political officer appeared at the Council of Ministers building to find four Politburo members on the telephones giving orders. All was not as it should be, but the Party men seemed to have things under control. The other members, he learned, had all been killed or wounded in a vicious attack by the Kremlin Guards themselves! The director of the KGB had detected the plot barely in time to summon loyal troops, but died heroically resisting the attackers. None of this made much sense to the divisional *zampolit*, but it didn't have to. His orders made perfectly good sense, and he radioed instructions to the divisional commander.

Sergetov was surprised at how easy it was. The number of people who actually knew what had happened was under two hundred. The fighting had all taken place within the Kremlin walls, and while many had heard the noise, the cover story explained it well enough for the moment. He had several friends in the Central Committee, and they did what they were told in the emergency. By the end of the day, the reins of power were shared among three Party men. The other Politburo members were under armed guard outside the city, with Major Sorokin in charge of their care. Without instructions from the Minister of the Interior, the MVD troops took their orders from the Politburo, while the KGB wavered leaderless. It was the final irony of the Soviet system that, headless, it could not save itself. The Politburo's pervasive control of all aspects of Soviet life prevented people now from asking the questions that had to be asked before any organized resistance could begin, and every hour gave Sergetov and his clique more time to consolidate their rule. He had the aged but distinguished Pyotr Bromkovskiy to head the Party apparatus and act as Defense Minister. Remembered in the Army as a commissar who cared about the men he served with, Petya was able to anoint Alekseyev as Deputy Defense Minister and Chief of the General Staff. Filip Moiseyevich Krylov retained Agriculture and acquired Internal Affairs. Sergetov would be acting General Secretary. The three men formed a troika, which would appeal to their countrymen until more of their people could be brought in. One paramount task remained.

43. A Walk in the Woods

BRUSSELS, BELGIUM

There is no more natural fear than of the unknown, and the greater the unknown, the greater had to be the fear. SACEUR had four intelligence reports side by side on his desk. The only thing they agreed on was that they did not know what was happening, but that it might be bad.

For that I need an expert? SACEUR thought.

A snippet of information from a ferret satellite had given him the word that there was some fighting in Moscow, and told him of the movement of troops to communications centers, but State television and radio had kept to a normal schedule for twelve hours until a news broadcast at five in the morning, Moscow time, had broken the official word.

An attempted coup d'état by the Defense Minister? That would not be good news, and the fact that it had been put down was only marginally better. The monitoring stations had just heard a brief speech by Pyotr Bromkovskiy, known as the last of the Stalinist hard-liners: maintain calm and keep your faith in the Party.

What the hell did that mean? SACEUR wondered.

"I need information," he told his intelligence chief. "What do we know about the Russian command structure?"

"Alekseyev, the new Commander-West, is evidently not at his command post. Good news for us, since we have our attack scheduled in ten hours."

SACEUR's phone buzzed. "I told you no calls—go ahead, Franz . . . Four hours? Potsdam. No reply yet. I'll be back to you in a little while." He hung up. "We just received an open radio message that the Soviet Chief of Staff urgently wishes to meet with me in Potsdam."

" 'Urgently' wishes, Herr General?"

"That's what the message said. I can come by helicopter and they'll provide a helicopter escort to a meeting place." SACEUR leaned back. "You suppose they want to shoot me down because I've done such a great job?" The Supreme Allied Commander Europe allowed himself an ironic smile.

"We have their troops massing northeast of Hannover," the Chief of Intelligence pointed out.

"I know, Joachim."

"Don't go," the intel Chief said. "Send a representative."

"Why didn't he ask for that?" SACEUR wondered. "That's the way it's normally done."

"He's in a hurry," Joachim said. "They haven't won. They haven't really lost anything yet, but their advance has been stopped and they still have their fuel problems. What if a wholly new power bloc has taken over in Moscow? They shut down the news media while they try to consolidate power, and they will want to terminate hostilities. They don't need the distraction. A good time to push hard," he concluded.

"When they're desperate?" SACEUR asked. "They still have plenty of nukes. Any unusual patterns of Soviet activity, anything that even looks unusual?"

"Aside from the newly arriving reserve divisions, no."

What if I can stop this damned war?

"I'm going." SACEUR lifted his phone and informed the Secretary General of the North Atlantic Council of his decision.

It was easy to be nervous with a pair of Russian attack choppers flying in close formation. SACEUR resisted the temptation to look out the windows at them, and concentrated instead on the intelligence folders. He had the official NATO intel dossiers for five senior Soviet commanders. He didn't know who it might be that he was meeting. His aide sat across from the General. He was looking out the windows.

POTSDAM, GERMAN DEMOCRATIC REPUBLIC

Alekseyev paced the ground, nervous to have to be away from Moscow, where the new Party bosses—but Party bosses nonetheless, he reminded himself—were trying to pull things together. *That idiot asked how they could trust* me! he thought. He reviewed the briefing information on his NATO counterpart. Age fifty-nine. Son and grandson of a soldier. Father a paratroop officer killed by the Germans west of St. Vith during the Battle of the Bulge. West Point, fifteenth in his class. Vietnam, four tours of duty, last as commander of the 101st Airborne; regarded by the North Vietnamese as an unusually dangerous and innovative tactician—he'd proved that, Alekseyev grunted to himself. University masters degree in international relations, supposed to be gifted in languages. Married, two sons and a daughter, none of them in uniform—someone decided that three generations was enough, Alekseyev thought—four grandchildren. *Four grandchildren . . . when a man has grandchildren . . .* Enjoys gambling with cards, only known vice. Moderate drinker. No known sexual deviations, the report said. Alekseyev smiled at that. We're both too old for that nonsense! And who has the time?

The sound of helicopter rotors filtered through the trees. Alekseyev stood in a small clearing next to a command vehicle. The crew was in the trees, along with a platoon of riflemen. It was unlikely, but NATO could seize this opportunity to attack and kill—no, we're not that crazy and neither are they, the General told himself.

It was one of their new Blackhawks. The helicopter flared and settled gracefully to the grassy meadow, with the pair of Mi-24s circling overhead. The door didn't open at once. The pilot killed his engines, and the rotor took two minutes to slow to a complete stop. Then the door slid open and the General stepped out hatless.

Tall for a paratrooper, Alekseyev thought.

SACEUR could have brought the bone-handled .45 Colt that he'd been given in Vietnam, but he judged it better to impress the Russian by coming unarmed in ordinary fatigues. Four black stars adorned his collar, and the badges of a master parachutist and combat infantrymen were sewn on his left breast. On the right side was a simple nametag: ROBINSON. *I don't have to show off, Ivan. I've won.*

"Tell the men in the woods to stand down and withdraw."

"But, Comrade General!" It was a new aide and he didn't know his general yet.

"Quickly. If I need an interpreter I will wave." Alekseyev walked toward the NATO commander. The aides gravitated together.

Salutes were exchanged, but neither wanted to offer a hand first.

"You are Alekseyev," General Robinson said. "I expected someone else."

"Marshal Bukharin is in retirement—your Russian is excellent, General Robinson."

"Thank you, General Alekseyev. Some years ago I got interested in the plays of Chekhov. You can really understand a play only in its original language. Since then I have read a good deal of Russian literature."

Alekseyev nodded. "The better to understand your enemy." He went on in English. "Very sensible of you. Shall we take a walk?"

"How many men do you have in the trees?"

"A platoon of motor-riflemen." Alekseyev switched back to his native language. Robinson's mastery of Russian was better than his of English, and Pasha had made his point. "How were we to know what would come out of the helicopter?"

"True," SACEUR conceded. *Yet you were standing out in the open— to show me that you are fearless.* "What shall we talk about?"

"A termination of hostilities, perhaps."

"I am listening."

"You know of course that I had no part in starting this madness."

Robinson's head turned. "What soldier ever does, General? We merely shed the blood and get the blame. Your father was a soldier, was he not?"

"A tanker. He was luckier than your father."

"That's often what it is, isn't it? Luck."

"We should not tell our political leaders that." Alekseyev almost ventured a smile until he saw that he'd given Robinson an opening.

"Who are your political leaders? If we are to reach a workable agreement, I must be able to tell mine who is in charge."

"The General Secretary of the Communist Party of the Soviet Union is Mikhail Eduardovich Sergetov."

Who? SACEUR wondered. He did not remember the name. He'd refreshed his memory on all the full Politburo members, but that name wasn't on the list. He temporized. "What the hell happened?"

Alekseyev saw the puzzlement on Robinson's face, and this time he did venture a smile. *You do not know who he is, do you, Comrade General? There is an unknown for you to ponder.* "As you Americans are fond of saying, it was time for a change."

Who taught you to play poker, son? SACEUR wondered. *But I'm holding aces over kings. What are you holding?*

"What is your proposal?"

"I do not know how to be a diplomat, only how to be a soldier," Alekseyev said. "We propose a cease-fire in place, followed by a phased withdrawal to pre-war positions over a period of two weeks."

"In two weeks I can achieve that without a cease-fire," Robinson said coldly.

"At great cost—and greater risk," the Russian pointed out.

"We know that you are short of fuel. Your entire national economy could come apart."

"Yes, General Robinson, and if our army comes apart, as you say, we have only one defense option to safeguard the State."

"Your country has launched a war of aggression against the NATO alliance. Do you suppose that we can let you return to *status quo ante,* nothing else?" SACEUR asked quietly. He was keeping close rein on his emotions. He'd already made one slip, and that was two too many. "And don't tell me about the Kremlin Bomb Plot—you know sure as hell we had no part of that."

"I have told you that I had no part in this. I follow orders—but did you expect the Politburo to sit still while our national economy ground to a halt? What political pressure would you have put on us, eh? If you knew about our oil shortage—"

"We didn't until a few days ago."

The maskirovka *worked?*

"Why didn't you tell us you needed oil?" Robinson asked.

"And you would have given it to us? Robinson, I do not have your degree in international relations, but I am not so much of a fool as that."

"We would have demanded and gotten concessions of some kind—but don't you think we would have tried to prevent all this?"

Alekseyev tore a leaf off a tree. He stared at it for a moment, the marvelous networking of veins, everything interconnected with everything else. *You have just killed another living thing, Pasha.*

"I suppose the Politburo never thought about that."

"They launched a war of aggression," Robinson repeated. "How many are dead because of them?"

"The men who made that decision are under arrest. They will be tried in a People's Court for crimes against the State. Comrade Sergetov spoke against the war, and has risked his life, as have I, to bring it to a just end."

"We want them. We will reconvene the Nürnberg Tribunal and try them for crimes against humanity."

"You may have them only after we are finished with them—it will be a dull trial, General Robinson," Alekseyev added. Both men were now talking like soldiers, not diplomats. "You think your countries have suffered? Someday I will tell about the suffering we have endured from these corrupt men!"

"And your junta will change that?"

"How should I know? But we will try. In any case, that is not your concern!"

The hell it isn't! "You talk with great confidence for the representative of a new and very shaky government."

"And you, Comrade General, talk very confidently for a man who less than two weeks ago was on the brink of defeat! Remember what you said of luck? Push us hard if you wish. The Soviet Union can no longer win, but both sides can still lose. You know how close it was. We nearly defeated you. If those damned invisible bombers of yours hadn't hit our bridges on the first day, or if we had managed to smash three or four more of your convoys, you would be offering me terms."

Make that one or two more convoys, Robinson reminded himself. *It was that close.*

"I offer you a cease-fire in place," Alekseyev repeated. "It could begin as early as midnight. After that, in two weeks, we return to our pre-war lines, and the killing will stop."

"Exchange of prisoners?"

"We can work that out later. For the moment, I think Berlin is the obvious place." Berlin, as expected, had remained largely untouched by the war.

"What about the German civilians behind your lines?"

Alekseyev thought that one over. "They may leave freely after the cease-fire—better than that, I will allow supplies of food to pass through our lines to them, under our supervision."

"And mistreatment of German civilians?"

"That is my affair. Anyone who has violated field service regulations will be court-martialed."

"How do I know that you will not use your two weeks to prepare a new offensive?"

"How do I know that you will not launch the counterattack you have scheduled for tomorrow?" Alekseyev countered.

"Actually a few hours from now." Robinson wanted to accept. "Will your political leaders abide by your terms?"

"Yes. Will yours?"

"I must present it to them, but I do have the authority to honor a cease-fire."

"Then the decision is yours, General Robinson."

The Generals' aides were standing uneasily together at the edge of the trees. Also watching was the platoon of Soviet infantrymen and the crew of the helicopter. General Robinson extended his hand.

"Thank God," said the Soviet aide.

"Da," agreed his American counterpart.

Alekseyev pulled a half-liter bottle of vodka from his back pocket. "I have not had a drink in several months, but we Russians cannot have an agreement without one."

Robinson took a swig and handed it back. Alekseyev did the same, and threw the bottle against a tree. It didn't break. Both men laughed out loud as the relief of what they had just agreed to swept over each like a wave.

"You know, Alekseyev, if we were diplomats instead of soldiers—"

"Yes, that is why I am here. It is easier for men who understand war to stop one."

"You have that right."

"Tell me, Robinson." Alekseyev paused, remembering SACEUR's first name, Eugene; father's name Stephen. "Tell me, Yevgeni Stepanovich, when we made the breakthrough at Alfeld, how close—"

"Very close. Close enough that even I don't know for sure. We were down to five days of supplies at one point, but a couple of convoys got through nearly intact, and that kept us going." Robinson stopped walking. "What will you do with your country?"

"I cannot say; I do not know; Comrade Sergetov does not know. But the Party must answer to the people. The leaders must be responsible to someone, we have learned that."

"I must go. Pavel Leonidovich, I wish you luck. Perhaps later . . ."

"Yes, perhaps later." They shook hands again.

Alekseyev watched SACEUR summon his aide, who shook hands with his Russian counterpart. Together they boarded the helicopter. The turbine engines whined into life, the four-bladed main rotor turned, and it lifted off from the grass. The Blackhawk circled the field once to give the escorting choppers a chance to form up, then headed west.

You will never know, Robinson. Alekseyev smiled to himself, standing alone in the field. *You will never know that when Kosov died we were unable to find his personal codes for control of our nuclear weapons. It would have been at least another day until we could have made use of them.* The General and his aide walked to their command vehicle, where Alekseyev made a terse radio broadcast that would be relayed to Moscow.

SACK, FEDERAL REPUBLIC OF GERMANY

Colonel Ellington helped Eisly through the trees. Both men had been through escape and evasion training, a course so tough that Ellington once swore that if he had to go through it again, he'd turn in his wings. Which was why he remembered the lessons, he knew. Fourteen hours they'd waited to cross just one damned road. He figured fifteen miles from where they'd crashed to friendly lines. A walk in the country that had turned into a week of hiding, drinking water from streams like animals and moving from tree to tree.

Now they were on the edge of some open ground. It was dark and surprisingly quiet. Had the Russians pulled back here?

"Let's give it a try, Duke," Eisly said. His back had gotten worse, and he could walk only with assistance.

"Okay." They moved forward as quickly as they could. They'd gotten a hundred yards when shadows moved around them.

"Shit!" Eisly whispered. "Sorry, Duke."

"Me, too," the colonel agreed. He didn't even think about reaching for his revolver. He counted at least eight men, and they all seemed to be carrying rifles. They converged quickly on the two Americans.

"Wer sind Sie?" a voice asked.

"Ich bin Amerikaner," Ellington answered. *Thank God—they're Germans.* They weren't. The shape of the helmets told him that a moment later.

Shit! We've come so *close!*

The Russian lieutenant examined his face with a flashlight. Strangely, he didn't take Ellington's revolver. Then something even stranger happened. The lieutenant flung his arms around both men and kissed them. He pointed west.

"That way, two kilometer."

"Don't argue with the man, Duke," Eisly whispered. As they walked off, the Russian eyes were a physical weight on their backs. The two flyers reached friendly lines an hour later, where they learned of the cease-fire.

USS *INDEPENDENCE*

The battle group was heading southwest. In another day they would have been in position to hit the Russian bases around Murmansk, and Toland was going over estimates of Russian fighter and SAM strengths when the recall order came. He closed the folder and tucked it back in the security cabinet, then went below to tell Major Chapayev that they would indeed live to see their families again.

NORTH ATLANTIC

The C-9 Nightingale hospital plane cruised southwest also, heading for Andrews Air Force Base outside Washington, D.C. It was filled with Marine casualties from the last fighting on Iceland, one Air Force lieutenant, and a civilian. The plane's crew had objected to the civilian until a two-star general of Marines explained to them over the radio that the Corps would take it as a personal matter if *anyone* took the lady away from the lieutenant's side. Mike was awake most of the time now. His leg needed further surgery—the Achilles tendon was torn—but none of that mattered. In another four and a half months he'd be a father. After that they could plan a child of his, too.

NORFOLK, VIRGINIA

O'Malley had already flown to the beach, taking the reporter with him. Morris hoped the Reuters correspondent would be able to file his last story on the war before he moved on to something else—an after-the-war story, no doubt. *Reuben James* had escorted the damaged *America* to Norfolk for repairs. He looked down from the bridge wing at the harbor he knew so well, mindful of the tide and the wind as he docked his frigate. One part of his mind pondered by itself What It All Meant.

A ship lost, friends gone, the deaths he had caused, and those he had seen himself . . .

"Rudder amidships," Morris ordered. A puff of southerly wind helped *Reuben James* up to the pier.

Aft, a seaman tossed a messenger line to the men on the pier. The officer in charge of the special sea-detail waved to a petty officer, who keyed the announcing system.

What It All Means, Morris decided, is that it's over.

A crackle of static emerged, and then the petty officer's voice. "Mooring."

The Cardinal of the Kremlin

ACKNOWLEDGMENTS

If there was ever a case of casting pearls before swine, it is to be found in the efforts of numerous members of the scientific community who endeavored to explain the theoretical and engineering aspects of strategic defense to this writer. To George, and Barry, and Bruce, and Russ, and Tom, and Danny, and Bob, and Jim I owe a great deal of thanks. But so does a country, and on one day to come, a world.

Special thanks, moreoever, are due to Chris Larsson and Space Media Network, whose commercially generated "overhead imagery" was good enough to make a few people nervous—and this is only the beginning . . .

For Colonel and Mrs. F. Carter Cobb

> . . . Love is not love
> Which alters when it alteration finds,
> Or bends with the remover to remove.
> O, no! it is an ever-fixèd mark
> That looks on tempests and is never shaken; . . .

Sonnet 116
William Shakespeare

[T]he operations of spies, saboteurs and secret agents are generally regarded as outside the scope of national and international law. They are therefore anathema to all accepted standards of conduct. Nevertheless history shows that no nation will shrink from such activities if they further its vital interests.

—Field Marshal Viscount
Montgomery of Alamein

The difference between a good man and a bad one is the choice of cause.

—William James

Prologue: Threats—Old, New, and Timeless

They called him the Archer. It was an honorable title, though his countrymen had cast aside their reflex bows over a century before, as soon as they had learned about firearms. In part, the name reflected the timeless nature of the struggle. The first of the Western invaders—for that was how they thought of them—had been Alexander the Great, and more had followed since. Ultimately, all had failed. The Afghan tribesmen held their Islamic faith as the reason for their resistance, but the obstinate courage of these men was as much a part of their racial heritage as their dark pitiless eyes.

The Archer was a young man, and an old one. On those occasions that he had both the desire and opportunity to bathe in a mountain stream, anyone could see the youthful muscles on his thirty-year-old body. They were the smooth muscles of one for whom a thousand-foot climb over bare rock was as unremarkable a part of life as a stroll to the mailbox.

It was his eyes that were old. The Afghans are a handsome people whose forthright features and fair skin suffer quickly from wind and sun and dust, too often making them older than their years. For the Archer, the damage had not been done by wind. A teacher of mathematics until three years before, a college graduate in a country where most deemed it enough to be able to read the holy Koran, he'd married young, as was the custom in his land, and fathered two children. But his wife and daughter were dead, killed by rockets fired from a Sukhoi-24 attack-fighter. His son was gone. Kidnapped. After the Soviets had flattened the village of his wife's family with air power, their ground troops had come, killing the remaining adults and sweeping up all the orphans for shipment to the Soviet Union, where they would be educated and trained in other modern ways. All because his wife had wanted her mother to see the grandchildren before she died, the Archer remembered, all because a Soviet patrol had been fired upon a few kilometers from the village. On the day he'd learned this—a week after it had actually happened—the teacher of algebra and geometry had neatly stacked the books on his desk and walked out of the small town of Ghazni into the hills. A week later he'd returned to the town after dark with three other men and proved that he was worthy of his heritage by killing three Soviet soldiers and taking their arms. He still carried that first Kalashnikov.

But that was not why he was known as the Archer. The chief of his little band of *mudjaheddin*—the name means "Freedom Fighter"—was a perceptive leader who did not look down upon the new arrival who'd spent his youth in classrooms, learning foreign ways. Nor did he hold the young man's initial lack of faith against him. When the teacher joined the group, he'd had only the most cursory knowledge of Islam, and the headman remembered the bitter tears falling like rain from the young man's eyes as their imam had counseled him in Allah's will. Within a month he'd become the most ruthless—and most effective—man in the band, clearly an expression of God's own plan. And it was he whom the leader had chosen to travel to Pakistan, where he could use his knowledge of science and numbers to learn the use of surface-to-air missiles. The first SAMs with which the quiet, serious man from *Amerikastan* had equipped the *mudjaheddin* had been the Soviets' own SA-7, known by the Russians as *strela*, "arrow." The first "man-portable" SAM, it was not overly effective unless used with great skill. Only a few had such skill. Among them the arithmetic teacher was the best, and for his successes with the Russian "arrows," the men in the group took to calling him the Archer.

He waited with a new missile at the moment, the American one called Stinger, but all of the surface-to-air missiles in this group—indeed, throughout the whole area—were merely called arrows now: tools for the Archer. He lay on the knife-edge of a ridge, a hundred meters below the summit of the hill, from which he could survey the length of a glacial valley. Beside him was his spotter, Abdul. The name appropriately meant "servant," since the teenager carried two additional missiles for his launcher and, more importantly, had the eyes of a falcon. They were burning eyes. He was an orphan.

The Archer's eyes searched the mountainous terrain, especially the ridgelines, with an expression that reflected a millennium of combat. A serious man, the Archer. Though friendly enough, he was rarely seen to smile; he showed no interest in a new bride, not even to join his lonely grief to that of a newly made widow. His life had room for but a single passion.

"There," Abdul said quietly, pointing.

"I see it."

The battle on the valley floor—one of several that day—had been under way for thirty minutes, about the proper time for the Soviet soldiers to get support from their helicopter base twenty kilometers over the next line of mountains. The sun glinted briefly off the Mi-24's glass-covered nose, enough for them to see it, ten miles off, skirting over the ridgeline. Farther overhead, and well beyond his reach, circled a single Antonov-26 twin-engine transport. It was filled with observation equipment and radios to coordinate the ground and air action. But the Archer's eyes followed only the Mi-24, a Hind attack helicopter loaded with rockets and cannon shells that even now was getting information from the circling command aircraft.

The Stinger had come as a rude surprise to the Russians, and their air tactics were changing on a daily basis as they struggled to come to terms with the new threat. The valley was deep, but more narrow than the rule. For the pilot to hit the Archer's fellow guerrillas, he had to come straight down the rocky avenue. He'd stay high, at least a thousand meters over the rocky floor for fear that a Stinger team might be down there with the riflemen. The Archer watched the helicopter zigzag in flight as the pilot surveyed the land and chose his path. As expected, the pilot approached from leeward so that the wind would delay the sound of his rotor for the few extra seconds that might be crucial. The radio in the circling transport would be tuned to the frequencies known to be used by the *mudjaheddin* so that the Russians could detect a warning of its approach, and also an indication where the missile team might be. Abdul did indeed carry a radio, switched off and tucked in the folds of his clothing.

Slowly, the Archer raised the launcher and trained its two-element sight on the approaching helicopter. His thumb went sideways and down on the activation switch, and he nestled his cheekbone on the conductance bar. He was instantly rewarded with the warbling screech of the launcher's seeker unit. The pilot had made his assessment, and his decision. He came down the far side of the valley, just beyond missile range, for his first firing run. The Hind's nose was down, and the gunner, sitting in his seat in front of and slightly below the pilot, was training his sights on the area where the fighters were. Smoke appeared on the valley floor. The Soviets used mortar shells to indicate where their tormentors were, and the helicopter altered course slightly. It was almost time. Flames shot out of the helicopter's rocket pods, and the first salvo of ordnance streaked downward.

Then another smoke trail came *up*. The helicopter lurched left as the smoke raced into the sky, well clear of the Hind, but still a positive indication of danger ahead; or so the pilot thought. The Archer's hands tightened on the launcher. The helicopter was sideslipping right at him now, expanding around the inner ring of the sight. It was now in range. The Archer punched the forward button with his left thumb, "uncaging" the missile and giving the infrared seeker-head on the Stinger its first look at the heat radiating from the Mi-24's turboshaft engines. The sound carried through his cheekbone into his ear changed. The missile was now tracking the target. The Hind's pilot decided to hit the area from which the "missile" had been launched at him, bringing the aircraft farther left, and turning slightly. Unwittingly, he turned his jet exhaust almost right at the Archer as he warily surveyed the rocks from which the rocket had come.

The missile screamed its readiness at the Archer now, but still he was patient. He put his mind into that of his target, and judged that the pilot would come closer still before his helicopter had the shot he wanted at the hated Afghans. And so he did. When the Hind was only a thousand meters off, the Archer took a deep breath, superelevated his sight, and whispered a brief prayer of vengeance. The trigger was pulled almost of its own accord.

The launcher bucked in his hands as the Stinger looped slightly upward before dropping down to home on its target. The Archer's eyes were sharp enough to see it despite the almost invisible smoke trail it left behind. The missile deployed its maneuvering fins, and these moved a few fractions of a millimeter in obedience to the orders generated by its computer brain— a microchip the size of a postage stamp. Aloft in the circling An-26, an observer saw a tiny puff of dust and began to reach for a microphone to relay a warning, but his hand had barely touched the plastic instrument before the missile struck.

The missile ran directly into one of the helicopter's engines and exploded.

The helicopter was crippled instantly. The driveshaft for the tail rotor was cut, and the Hind began spinning violently to the left while the pilot tried to autorotate the aircraft down, frantically looking for a flat place while his gunner radioed a shrill call for rescue. The pilot brought the engine to idle, unloading his collective to control torque, locked his eyes on a flat space the size of a tennis court, then cut his switches and activated the onboard extinguishing system. Like most fliers he feared fire above all things, though he would learn the error soon enough.

The Archer watched the Mi-24 hit nose-down on a rocky ledge five hundred feet below his perch. Surprisingly, it didn't burn as the aircraft came apart. The helicopter cartwheeled viciously, the tail whipping forward and over the nose before it came to rest on its side. The Archer raced down the hill with Abdul right behind. It took five minutes.

The pilot fought with his straps as he hung upside down. He was in pain, but he knew that only the living felt pain. The new model helicopter had had improved safety systems built in. Between those and his own skill he'd survived the crash. Not his gunner, he noticed briefly. The man in front hung motionless, his neck broken, his hands limply reaching for the ground. The pilot had no time for that. His seat was bent, and the chopper's canopy had shattered, its metal frame now a prison for the flyer. The emergency release latch was jammed, the explosive release bolts unwilling to fire. He took his pistol from the shoulder holster and started blasting at the metal framework, one piece at a time. He wondered if the An-26 had gotten the emergency call. Wondered if the rescue helicopter at his base was on the way. His rescue radio was in a pants pocket, and he'd activate it as soon as he got away from his broken bird. The pilot cut his hands to ribbons as he prised the metal away, giving himself a clear path out. He thanked his luck again that he was not ending his life in a pillar of greasy smoke as he released his straps and climbed out of the aircraft to the rocky ground.

His left leg was broken. The jagged end of a white bone stuck clear of his flight suit; though he was too deeply in shock to feel it, the sight of the injury horrified him. He holstered his empty pistol and grabbed a loose piece of metal to serve as a cane. He had to get away. He hobbled to the far end of the ledge and saw a path. It was three kilometers to friendly forces. He was about to start down when he heard something and turned. Hope changed to horror in an instant, and the pilot realized that a fiery death would have been a blessing.

The Archer blessed Allah's name as he withdrew his knife from its sheath.

There couldn't be much left of her, Ryan thought. The hull was mainly intact—at least superficially—but you could see the rough surgery made by the welders as clearly as the stitches made on Frankenstein's monster. An apt-enough comparison, he thought silently. Man had made these things, but they could one day destroy their makers in the space of an hour.

"God, it's amazing how big they look on the outside . . ."

"And so small on the inside?" Marko asked. There was a wistful sadness in his voice. Not so long before, Captain Marko Ramius of the Voyenno Morskoi Flot had conned his ship into this very drydock. He hadn't been there to watch U.S. Navy technicians dissect her like pathologists over a cadaver, removing the missiles, the reactor plant, the sonars, the onboard computers and communications gear, the periscopes, and even the galley stoves for analysis at bases spread all over the United States. His absence had been at his own request. Ramius' hatred for the Soviet system did not extend to the ships that system built. He'd sailed this one well—and *Red October* had saved his life.

And Ryan's. Jack fingered the hairline scar on his forehead and wondered if they'd ever cleaned his blood off the helmsman's console. "I'm surprised you didn't want to take her out," he observed to Ramius.

"No." Marko shook his head. "I only want to say goodbye. He was good ship."

"Good enough," Jack agreed quietly. He looked at the half-repaired hole that the Alfa's torpedo had made in the port side and shook his head in silence. *Good enough to save my ass when that torpedo hit.* The two men watched in silence, separated from the sailors and Marines who'd secured the area since the previous December.

The drydock was flooding now, the filthy water from the Elizabeth River rushing into the concrete box. They'd take her out tonight. Six American fast-attack submarines were even now "sanitizing" the ocean east of the Norfolk Navy Base, ostensibly part of an exercise that would also involve a few surface ships. It was nine o'clock on a moonless night. It would take an hour to flood the drydock. A crew of thirty was already aboard. They'd fire up the ship's diesel engines and sail her out for her second and final voyage, to the deep ocean trench north of Puerto Rico, where she would be scuttled in twenty-five thousand feet of water.

Ryan and Ramius watched as the water covered the wooden blocks that supported the hull, wetting the submarine's keel for the first time in nearly a year. The water came in more quickly now, creeping up the plimsoll marks painted fore and aft. On the submarine's deck, a handful of seamen wearing bright orange lifejackets for safety paced around, making ready to slip the fourteen stout mooring lines that held her steady.

The ship herself remained quiet. *Red October* gave no sign of welcome for the water. Perhaps she knew the fate that awaited her, Ryan said to himself. It was a foolish thought—but he also knew that for millennia sailors had imputed personalities to the ships they served.

Finally she started to move. The water buoyed the hull off the wooden blocks. There was a muted series of thuds, more felt than heard as she rose off them ever so slowly, rocking back and forth a few inches at a time.

A few minutes later the ship's diesel engine rumbled to life, and the line handlers on the ship and the drydock began to take in the lines. At the same time, the canvas that covered the seaward end of the drydock was taken down, and all could see the fog that hung on the water outside. Conditions were perfect for the operation. Conditions had to be perfect; the Navy had waited six weeks for them, a moonless night and the thick seasonal fog that plagued the Chesapeake Bay region this time of year. When the last line was slipped, an officer atop the submarine's sail raised a hand-held air horn and blew a single blast.

"Under way!" his voice called, and the sailors at the bow struck the jack and put down the staff. For the first time, Ryan noticed that it was the Soviet jack. He smiled. It was a nice touch. On the sail's aft end, another seaman ran up the Soviet naval ensign, its bright red star emblazoned with the shield of the Red Banner Northern Fleet. The Navy, ever mindful of traditions, was saluting the man who stood at his side.

Ryan and Ramius watched the submarine start to move under her own power, her twin bronze propellers turning gently in reverse as she backed out into the river. One of the tugs helped her turn to face north. Within another minute she was gone from sight. Only the lingering rumble of her diesel came across the oily water of the navy yard.

Marko blew his nose once and blinked a half-dozen times. When he turned away from the water, his voice was firm.

"So, Ryan, they fly you home from England for this?"

"No, I came back a few weeks ago. New job."

"Can you say what job is?" Marko asked.

"Arms control. They want me to coordinate the intelligence side for the negotiations team. We have to fly over in January."

"Moscow?"

"Yes, it's a preliminary session—setting the agenda and doing some technical stuff, that sort of thing. How about you?"

"I work at AUTEC in Bahamas. Much sun and sand. You see my tan?" Ramius grinned. "I come to Washington every two-three months. I fly back in five hours. We work on new quieting project." Another smile. "Is classified."

"Great! I want you to come over to my house then. I still owe you a dinner." Jack handed over a card. "Here's my number. Call me a few days before you fly in, and I'll set things up with the Agency." Ramius and his officers were under a very strict protection regime from CIA security officers. The really amazing thing, Jack thought, was that the story hadn't leaked. None of the news media had gotten word, and if security really was that tight, probably the Russians also didn't know the fate of their missile submarine *Krazny Oktyabr*. She'd be turning east about now, Jack thought, to pass over the Hampton Roads tunnel. Roughly an hour after that she'd dive and head southeast. He shook his head.

Ryan's sadness at the submarine's fate was tempered by the thought of what she'd been built for. He remembered his own reaction, in the sub's missile room a year before, the first time he'd been so close to the ghastly things. Jack accepted the fact that nuclear weapons kept the peace—if you could really call the world's condition *peace*—but like most of the people who thought about the subject, he wished for a better way. Well, this was one less submarine, twenty-six less missiles, and one hundred eighty-two less warheads. Statistically, Ryan told himself, it didn't count for much.

But it was something.

Ten thousand miles away and eight thousand feet above sea level the problem was unseasonable weather. The place was in the Tadzhik Soviet Socialist Republic, and the wind came from the south, still bearing moisture from the Indian Ocean that fell as miserably cold drizzle. Soon it would be the real winter that always came early here, usually on the heels of the blazing, airless summer, and all that fell would be cold and white.

The workers were mostly young, eager members of the Komsomol. They had been brought in to help finish a construction project that had been begun in 1983. One of them, a masters candidate at Moscow State University's school of physics, rubbed the rain from his eyes and straightened to ease a crick in his back. This was no way to utilize a promising young engineer, Morozov thought. Instead of playing with this surveyor's instrument, he could be building lasers in his laboratory, but he wanted full membership in the Communist Party of the Soviet Union, and wanted even more to avoid military service. The combination of his school deferment and his Komsomol work had helped mightily to this end.

"Well?" Morozov turned to see one of the site engineers. A civil engineer, he was, who described himself as a man who knew concrete.

"I read the position as correct, Comrade Engineer."

The older man stooped down to look through the sighting scope. "I agree," the man said. "And that's the last one, the gods be praised." Both men jumped with the sound of a distant explosion. Engineers from the Red Army obliterating yet another rocky outcropping outside of the fenced perimeter. You didn't need to be a soldier to understand what that was all about, Morozov thought to himself.

"You have a fine touch with optical instruments. Perhaps you will become a civil engineer, too, eh? Build useful things for the State?"

"No, Comrade. I study high-energy physics—mainly lasers." *These, too, are useful things.*

The man grunted and shook his head. "Then you might come back here, God help you."

"Is this—"

"You didn't hear anything from me," the engineer said, just a touch of firmness in his voice.

"I understand," Morozov replied quietly. "I suspected as much."

"I would be careful voicing that suspicion," the other said conversationally as he turned to look at something.

"This must be a fine place to watch the stars," Morozov observed, hoping for the right response.

"I wouldn't know," the civil engineer replied with an insider's smile. "I've never met an astronomer."

Morozov smiled to himself. He'd guessed right after all. They had just plotted the position of the six points on which mirrors would be set. These were equidistant from a central point located in a building guarded by men with rifles. Such precision, he knew, had only two applications. One was astronomy, which collected light coming down. The other application involved light going up. The young engineer told himself that here was where he wanted to come. This place would change the world.

1. The Reception of the Party

Business was being conducted. All kinds of business. Everyone there knew it. Everyone there was part of it. Everyone there needed it. And yet everyone there was in one way or another dedicated to stopping it. For every person there in the St. George Hall of the Great Kremlin Palace, the dualism was a normal part of life.

The participants were mainly Russian and American, and were divided into four groups.

First, the diplomats and politicians. One could discern these easily enough from their better-than-average clothing and erect posture, the ready, robotic smiles, and careful diction that endured even after the many alcoholic toasts. They were the masters, knew it, and their demeanor proclaimed it.

Second, the soldiers. One could not have arms negotiations without the men who controlled the arms, maintained them, tested them, pampered them, all the while telling themselves that the politicians who controlled the *men* would never give the order to launch. The soldiers in their uniforms stood mainly in little knots of homogeneous nationality and service branch, each clutching a half-full glass and napkin while blank, emotionless eyes swept the room as though searching for a threat on an unfamiliar battlefield. For that was precisely what it was to them, a bloodless battlefield that would define the real ones if their political masters ever lost control, lost temper, lost perspective, lost whatever it is in man that tries to avoid the profligate waste of young life. To a man the soldiers trusted none but one another, and in some cases trusted their enemies in different-colored uniforms more than their own soft-clothed masters. At least you knew where another soldier stood. You couldn't always say the same of politicians, even your own. They talked with one another quietly, always watching to see who listened, stopping occasionally for a quick gulp from the glass, accompanied by another look about the room. They were the victims, but also the predators—the dogs, perhaps, kept on leashes by those who deemed themselves the masters of events.

The soldiers had trouble believing that, too.

Third, the reporters. These could also be picked out by their clothing, which was always wrinkled by too many packings and unpackings in airline suitcases too small for all they carried. They lacked the polish of the politicians, and the fixed smiles, substituting for it the inquisitive looks of children, mixed with the cynicism of the dissolute. Mainly they held their glasses in their left hands, sometimes with a small pad instead of the paper napkin, while a pen was half-hidden in the right. They circulated like birds of prey. One would find someone who would talk. Others would notice and come over to drink in the information. The casual observer could tell how interesting the information was by how quickly the reporters moved off to another source. In this sense the American and other Western reporters were different from their Soviet counterparts, who for the most part hung close to their masters like favored earls of another time, both to show their loyalty to the Party and to act as buffers against their colleagues from elsewhere. But together, they were the audience in this performance of theater in the round.

Fourth came the final group, the invisible one, those whom no one could identify in any easy way. These were the spies, and the counterespionage agents who hunted them. They could be distinguished from the security officers, who watched everyone with suspicion, but from the room's perimeter, as invisible as the waiters who circulated about with heavy silver trays of champagne and vodka in crystal glasses that had been commissioned by the House of Romanov. Some of the waiters were counterespionage agents, of course. Those had to circulate through the room, their ears perked for a snippet of conversation, perhaps a voice too low or a word that didn't fit the mood of the evening. It was no easy task. A quartet of strings in a corner played chamber music to which no one appeared to listen, but this too is a feature of diplomatic receptions and doing without it would be noticed. Then there was the volume of human noise. There were well over a hundred people here, and every one of them was talking at least half the time. Those close to the quartet had to speak loudly to be heard over the music. All the resulting noise was contained in a ballroom two hundred feet long and sixty-five wide, with a parquet floor and hard stucco walls that reflected and reverberated the sound until it reached an ambient level that would have hurt the ears of a small child. The spies used their invisibility and the noise to make themselves the ghosts of the feast.

But the spies were here. Everyone knew it. Anyone in Moscow could tell you about spies. If you met with a Westerner on anything approaching a regular basis, it was the prudent thing to report it. If you did so only once, and a passing police officer of the Moscow Militia—or an Army officer strolling around with his briefcase—passed by, a head would turn, and note would be taken. Perhaps cursory, perhaps not. Times had changed since Stalin, of course, but Russia was still Russia, and distrust of foreigners and their ideas was far older than any ideology.

Most of the people in the room thought about it without really thinking about it—except those who actually played this particular game. The diplomats and politicians had practice guarding their words, and were not overly concerned at the moment. To the reporters it was merely amusing, a fabulous game that didn't really concern them—though each Western reporter knew that he or she was *ipso facto* thought an agent of espionage by the Soviet government. The soldiers thought about it most of all. They knew the importance of intelligence, craved it, valued it—and despised those who gathered it for the slinking things they were.

Which ones are the spies?

Of course there was a handful of people who fitted into no easily identified category—or fitted into more than one.

"And how did you find Moscow, Dr. Ryan?" a Russian asked. Jack turned from his inspection of the beautiful St. George clock.

"Cold and dark, I'm afraid," Ryan answered after a sip of his champagne. "It's not as though we have had much chance to see anything." Nor would they. The American team had been in the Soviet Union only for a little over four days, and would fly home the next day after concluding the technical session that preceded the plenary one.

"That is too bad," Sergey Golovko observed.

"Yes," Jack agreed. "If all of your architecture is this good, I'd love to take a few days to admire it. Whoever built this house had style." He nodded approvingly at the gleaming white walls, the domed ceiling, and the gold leaf. In fact he thought it overdone, but he knew that the Russians had a national tendency to overdo a lot of things. To Russians, who rarely had enough of anything, "having enough" meant having more than anyone else—preferably more than *everyone* else. Ryan thought it evidence of a national inferiority complex, and reminded himself that people who feel themselves inferior have a pathological desire to disprove their own perceptions. That one factor dominated all aspects of the arms-control process, displacing mere logic as the basis for reaching an agreement.

"The decadent Romanovs," Golovko noted. "All this came from the sweat of the peasants." Ryan turned and laughed.

"Well, at least some of their tax money went for something beautiful, harmless—and immortal. If you ask me, it beats buying ugly weapons that are obsolete ten years later. There's an idea, Sergey Nikolay'ch. We will redirect our political-military competition to beauty instead of nuclear weapons."

"You are satisfied with the progress, then?"

Business. Ryan shrugged and continued to inspect the room. "I suppose we've settled on the agenda. Next, those characters over by the fireplace have to work out the details." He stared at one of the enormous crystal chandeliers. He wondered how many man-years of effort had gone into making it, and how much fun it must have been to hang something that weighed as much as a small car.

"And you are satisfied on the issue of verifiability?"

That confirms it, Ryan thought with a thin smile. *Golovko is GRU.* "National Technical Means," a term that denoted spy satellites and other methods of keeping an eye on foreign countries, were mainly the province of CIA in America, but in the Soviet Union they belonged to the GRU, the Soviet military intelligence agency. Despite the tentative agreement in principle for on-site inspection, the main effort of verifying compliance on an agreement would lie with the spy satellites. That would be Golovko's turf.

It was no particular secret that Jack worked for CIA. It didn't have to be; he wasn't a field officer. His attachment to the arms-negotiation team was a logical matter. His current assignment had to do with monitoring certain strategic weapons systems within the Soviet Union. For any arms treaty to be signed, both sides first had to satisfy their own institutional paranoia that no serious tricks could be played on them by the other. Jack advised the chief negotiator along these lines; when, Jack reminded himself, the negotiator troubled himself to listen.

"Verifiability," he replied after another moment, "is a very technical and difficult question. I'm afraid I'm not really that conversant on it. What do your people think about our proposal to limit land-based systems?"

"We depend on our land-based missiles more than you," Golovko said. His voice became more guarded as they discussed the meat of the Soviet position.

"I don't understand why you don't place as much emphasis on submarines as we do."

"Reliability, as you well know."

"Aw, hell. Submarines are reliable," Jack baited him as he reexamined the clock. It was magnificent. Some peasant-looking fellow was handing a sword to another chap, and waving him off to battle. *Not exactly a new idea,* Jack thought. *Some old fart tells a young kid to go off and get killed.*

"We have had some incidents, I regret to say."

"Yeah, that Yankee that went down off Bermuda."

"And the other."

"Hmph?" Ryan turned back. It took a serious effort not to smile.

"Please, Dr. Ryan, do not insult my intelligence. You know the story of *Krazny Oktyabr* as well as I."

"What was that name? Oh, yeah, the Typhoon you guys lost off the Carolinas. I was in London then. I never did get briefed on it."

"I think the two incidents illustrate the problem we Soviets face. We cannot trust our missile submarines as completely as you trust yours."

"Hmm." *Not to mention the drivers,* Ryan thought, careful not to let his face show a thing.

Golovko persisted. "But may I ask a substantive question?"

"Sure, so long as you don't expect a substantive answer." Ryan chuckled.

"Will your intelligence community object to the draft treaty proposal?"

"Now, how am I supposed to know the answer to that?" Jack paused. "What about yours?"

"Our organs of State security do what they are told," Golovko assured him.

Right, Ryan told himself. "In our country, if the President decides that he likes an arms treaty, and he thinks he can get it through the Senate, it doesn't matter what the CIA and Pentagon think—"

"But your military-industrial complex—" Golovko cut Jack off.

"God, you guys really love to beat on that horse, don't you? Sergey Nikolayevich, you should know better."

But Golovko was a *military* intelligence officer, and might not, Ryan remembered too late. The degree to which America and the Soviet Union misunderstood each other was at one and the same time amusing and supremely dangerous. Jack wondered if the intelligence community over here tried to get the truth out, as CIA usually did now, or merely told its masters what they wanted to hear, as CIA had done all too often in the past. Probably the latter, he thought. The Russian intel agencies were undoubtedly politicized, just as CIA used to be. One good thing about Judge Moore was that he'd worked damned hard to put an end to that. But the Judge had no particular wish to be President; that made him different from his Soviet counterparts. One director of the KGB had made it to the top over here, and at least one other tried to. That made KGB a political creature, and that affected its objectivity. Jack sighed into his drink. The problems between the two countries wouldn't end if all the false perceptions were laid to rest, but at least things could be more manageable.

Maybe. Ryan admitted to himself that this might be as false a panacea as all the others; it had never been tried, after all.

"May I make a suggestion to you?"

"Certainly," Golovko answered.

"Let's drop the shop talk, and you tell me about this room while I enjoy the champagne." *It'll save us both a lot of time when we write up our contact reports tomorrow.*

"Perhaps I could get you some vodka?"

"No, thanks, this bubbly stuff is great. Local?"

"Yes, from Georgia," Golovko said proudly. "I think it is better than the French."

"I wouldn't mind taking a few bottles home," Ryan allowed.

Golovko laughed, a short bark of amusement and power. "I will see to it. So. The palace was finished in 1849, at the cost of eleven million rubles, quite a sum at the time. It's the last grand palace ever built, and, I think, the best . . ."

Ryan wasn't the only one touring the room, of course. Most of the American delegation had never seen it. Russians bored with the reception led them around, explaining as they went. Several people from the embassy tagged along, keeping a casual eye on things.

"So, Misha, what do you think of American women?" Defense Minister Yazov asked his aide.

"Those coming this way are not unattractive, Comrade Minister," the Colonel observed.

"But so skinny—ah, yes, I keep forgetting, your beautiful Elena was also thin. A fine woman she was, Misha."

"Thank you for remembering, Dmitri Timofeyevich."

"Hello, Colonel!" one of the American ladies said in Russian.

"Ah, yes, Mrs. . . ."

"Foley. We met at the hockey game last November."

"You know this lady?" the Minister asked his aide.

"My nephew—no, my grand-nephew Mikhail, Elena's sister's grand-son—plays junior-league hockey, and I was invited to a game. It turned out that they allowed an imperialist on the team," he replied with a raised eyebrow.

"Your son plays well?" Marshal Yazov asked.

"He is the third-leading scorer in the league," Mrs. Foley replied.

"Splendid! Then you must stay in our country, and your son can play for Central Army when he grows up." Yazov grinned. He was a grandfather four times over. "What do you do here?"

"My husband works for the embassy. He's over there, shepherding the reporters around—but the important thing is, I got to come here tonight. I've never seen anything like this in my whole life!" she gushed. Her glistening eyes spoke of several glasses of something. Probably champagne, the Minister thought. She looked like the champagne type, but she was attractive enough, and she had bothered to learn the language reasonably well, unusual for Americans. "These floors are so pretty, it seems a crime to walk on them. We don't have anything like this at home."

"You never had the czars, which was your good fortune," Yazov replied like a good Marxist. "But as a Russian I must admit that I am proud of their artistic sense."

"I haven't seen you at any other games, Colonel," she said, turning back to Misha.

"I don't have the time."

"But you're good luck! The team won that night, and Eddie got a goal and an assist."

The Colonel smiled. "All our little Misha got was two penalties for high-sticking."

"Named for you?" the Minister asked.

"Yes."

"You didn't have those on when I saw you." Mrs. Foley pointed to the three gold stars on his chest.

"Perhaps I didn't take off my topcoat—"

"He always wears them," the Marshal assured her. "One *always* wears his Hero of the Soviet Union medals."

"Is that the same as our Medal of Honor?"

"The two are roughly equivalent," Yazov said for his aide. Misha was unaccountably shy about them. "Colonel Filitov is the only man living who has ever won three in battle."

"Really? How does someone win *three*?"

"Fighting Germans," the Colonel said tersely.

"Killing Germans," Yazov said even more bluntly. When Filitov had been one of the Red Army's brightest stars, he'd been a mere lieutenant. "Misha is one of the best tank officers who ever lived."

Colonel Filitov actually blushed at that. "I did my duty, as did many soldiers in that war."

"My father was decorated in the war, too. He led two missions to rescue people from prison camps in the Philippines. He didn't talk about it very much, but they gave him a bunch of medals. Do you tell your children about those bright stars of yours?"

Filitov went rigid for a moment. Yazov answered for him.

"Colonel Filitov's sons died some years ago."

"Oh! Oh, Colonel, I am so sorry," Mrs. Foley said, and she really was.

"It was long ago." He smiled. "I remember your son well from the game, a fine young man. Love your children, dear lady, for you will not always have them. If you will excuse me for a moment." Misha moved off in the direction of the rest rooms. Mrs. Foley looked to the Minister, anguish on her pretty face.

"Sir, I didn't mean—"

"You could not have known. Misha lost his sons a few years apart, then his wife. I met her when I was a very young man—lovely girl, a dancer with the Kirov Ballet. So sad, but we Russians are accustomed to great sadnesses. Enough of that. What team does your son play for?" Marshal Yazov's interest in hockey was amplified by the pretty young face.

Misha found the rest room after a minute. Americans and Russians were sent to different ones, of course, and Colonel Filitov was alone in what had been the private water closet of a prince, or perhaps a czar's mistress. He washed his hands and looked in the gilt-edged mirror. He had but one thought: *Again. Another mission.* Colonel Filitov sighed and tidied himself up. A minute later he was back out in the arena.

"Excuse me," Ryan said. Turning around, he'd bumped into an elderly gentleman in uniform. Golovko said something in Russian that Ryan didn't catch. The officer said something to Jack that sounded polite, and walked over, Ryan saw, to the Defense Minister.

"Who's that?" Jack asked his Russian companion.

"The Colonel is personal aide to the Minister," Golovko replied.

"Little old for a colonel, isn't he?"

"He is a war hero. We do not force all such men to retire."

"I guess that's fair enough," Jack commented, and turned back to hear about this part of the room. After they had exhausted the St. George Hall, Golovko led Jack into the adjacent St. Vladimir Hall. He expressed the hope that he and Ryan would next meet here. St. Vladimir Hall, he explained, was set aside for the signing of treaties. The two intelligence officers toasted one another on that.

The party broke up after midnight. Ryan got into the seventh limousine. Nobody talked on the ride back to the embassy. Everyone was feeling the alcohol, and you didn't talk in cars, not in Moscow. Cars were too easy to bug. Two men fell asleep, and Ryan came close enough himself. What kept him awake was the knowledge that they'd fly out in another five hours, and if he was going to have to do that, he might as well keep tired enough to sleep on the plane, a skill he had only recently acquired. He changed his clothes and went down to the embassy's canteen for coffee. It would be enough to keep himself going for a few hours while he made his own notes.

Things had gone amazingly well these past four days. Almost too well. Jack told himself that averages are made up of times when things went well and times they went poorly. A draft treaty was on the table. Like all draft treaties of late, it was intended by the Soviets to be more a negotiating tool than a negotiating document. Its details were already in the press, and already certain members of Congress were saying on the floor how fair a deal it was—and why don't we just agree to it?

Why not, indeed? Jack wondered with an ironic smile. Verifiability. That was one reason. The other . . . was there another? Good question. Why had they changed their stance so much? There was evidence that General Secretary Narmonov wanted to reduce his military expenditures, but despite all the public perceptions to the contrary, nuclear arms were not the place you did that. Nukes were cheap for what they did; they were a very cost-effective way of killing people. While a nuclear warhead and its missile were expensive gadgets, they were far cheaper than the equivalent destructive power in tanks and artillery. Did Narmonov genuinely want to reduce the threat of nuclear war? But that threat didn't come from the weapons; as always it came from the politicians and their mistakes. Was it all a symbol? Symbols, Jack reminded himself, were far easier for Narmonov to produce than substance. If a symbol, at whom was it aimed?

Narmonov had charm, and power—the sort of visceral presence that came with his post, but even more from his personality. What sort of man was this? What was he after? Ryan snorted. That wasn't his department. Another CIA team was examining Narmonov's political vulnerability right here in Moscow. His far easier job was to figure out the technical side. Far easier, perhaps, but he didn't yet know the answer to his own questions.

Golovko was already back at his office, making his own notes in a painful longhand. Ryan, he wrote, would uneasily support the draft proposal. Since Ryan had the ear of the Director, that probably meant that CIA would, too. The intelligence officer set down his pen and rubbed his eyes for a moment. Waking up with a hangover was bad enough, but having to stay awake long enough to welcome it with the sunrise was above and beyond the duty of a Soviet officer. He wondered why his government had made the offer in the first place, and why the Americans seemed so eager. Even Ryan, who should have known better. What did the Americans have in mind? Who was outmaneuvering whom?

Now there was a question.

He turned back to Ryan, his assignment of the previous evening. Well along for a man of his years, the equivalent of a colonel in the KGB or GRU and only thirty-five. What had he done to rise so quickly? Golovko shrugged. Probably connected, a fact of life as important in Washington as in Moscow. He had courage—the business with the terrorists almost five years before. He was also a family man, something Russians respected more than their American counterparts would have believed—it implied stability, and that in turn implied predictability. Most of all, Golovko thought, Ryan was a thinker. Why, then, was he not opposed to a pact that would benefit the Soviet Union more than it benefited America? *Is our evaluation incorrect?* he wrote. Do the Americans know something we do not? That was a question, or better still: Did Ryan know something that Golovko did not? The Colonel frowned, then reminded himself what *he* knew that Ryan did not. That drew a half-smile. It was all part of the grand game. The grandest game there was.

"You must have walked all night."

The Archer nodded gravely and set down the sack that had bowed his shoulders for five days. It was almost as heavy as the one Abdul had packed. The younger man was near collapse, the CIA officer saw. Both men found pillows to sit on.

"Have something to drink." The officer's name was Emilio Ortiz. His ancestry was sufficiently muddled that he could have passed for a native of any Caucasian nation. Also thirty years of age, he was of medium height and build, with a swimmer's muscles, which was how he'd won a scholarship to USC, where he'd won a degree in languages. Ortiz had a rare gift in this area. With two weeks' exposure to a language, a dialect, an accent, he could pass for a native anywhere in the world. He was also a man of compassion, respectful of the ways of the people with whom he worked. This meant that the drink he offered was not—could not be—alcoholic. It was apple juice. Ortiz watched him drink it with all the delicacy of a wine connoisseur sampling new bordeaux.

"Allah's blessings upon this house," the Archer said when he finished the first glass. That he had waited until drinking the apple juice was as close as the man ever came to making a joke. Ortiz saw the fatigue written on the man's face, though he displayed it no other way. Unlike his young porter, the Archer seemed invulnerable to such normal human concerns. It wasn't true, but Ortiz understood how the force that drove him could suppress his humanity.

The two men were dressed almost identically. Ortiz considered the Archer's clothing and wondered at the ironic similarity with the Apache Indians of America and Mexico. One of his ancestors had been an officer under Terrazas when the Mexican Army had finally crushed Victorio in the Tres Castillos Mountains. The Afghans, too, wore rough trousers under their loincloths. They, too, tended to be small, agile fighters. And they, too, treated captives as noisy amusements for their knives. He looked at the

Archer's knife and wondered how it was used. Ortiz decided he didn't want to know.

"Do you wish something to eat?" he asked.

"It can wait," the Archer replied, reaching for his pack. He and Abdul had brought out two loaded camels, but for the important material, only his backpack would do. "I fired eight rockets. I hit six aircraft, but one had two engines and managed to escape. Of the five I destroyed, two were helicopters, and three were bombing-fighters. The first helicopter we killed was the new kind of twenty-four you told us about. You were correct. It did have some new equipment. Here is some of it."

It was ironic, Ortiz thought, that the most sensitive equipment in military aircraft would survive treatment guaranteed to kill its crew. As he watched, the Archer revealed six green circuit boards for the laser-designator that was now standard equipment on the Mi-24. The U.S. Army Captain who'd stayed in the shadows and kept his mouth shut to this point now came forward to examine them. His hands fairly trembled as he reached for the items.

"You have the laser, too?" the Captain asked in accented Pashtu.

"It was badly damaged, but, yes." The Archer turned. Abdul was snoring. He nearly smiled until he remembered that he had a son also.

For his part, Ortiz was saddened. To have a partisan with the Archer's education under his control was rare enough. He'd probably been a skilled teacher but he could never teach again. He could never go back to what he'd been. War had changed the Archer's life as fully and certainly as death. Such a goddamned waste.

"The new rockets?" the Archer asked.

"I can give you ten. A slightly improved model, with an additional five-hundred-meter range. And some more smoke rockets, too."

The Archer nodded gravely, and the corners of his mouth moved in what, in different times, might have been the beginnings of a smile.

"Perhaps now I can go after their transports. The smoke rockets work very well, my friend. Every time, they push the invaders close to me. They have not yet learned about that tactic."

Not a *trick*, Ortiz noted. He called it a *tactic. He wants to go after transports now, he wants to kill a hundred Russians at a time. Jesus, what have we made of this man?* The CIA officer shook his head. That wasn't his concern.

"You are weary, my friend. Rest. We can eat later. Please honor my house by sleeping here."

"It is true," the Archer acknowledged. He was asleep within two minutes.

Ortiz and the Captain sorted through the equipment brought to them. Included was the maintenance manual for the Mi-24's laser equipment, and radio code sheets, in addition to other things they'd seen before. By noon he had it all fully catalogued and began making arrangements to ship it all to the embassy; from there it would be flown immediately to California for a complete evaluation.

The Air Force VC-137 lifted off right on time. It was a customized version of the venerable Boeing 707. The "V" prefix on its designation denoted that it was designed to carry VIP passengers, and the aircraft's interior reflected this. Jack lay back on the couch and abandoned himself to the fatigue that enveloped him. Ten minutes later a hand shook his shoulder.

"The boss wants you," another member of the team said.

"Doesn't he ever sleep?" Jack growled.

"Tell me about it."

Ernest Allen was in the VIP-est accommodations on the aircraft, a cabin set exactly atop the wing spar with six plush swivel chairs. A coffeepot sat on the table. If he didn't have some coffee he'd soon be incoherent. If he did, he'd be unable to go back to sleep. Well, the government wasn't paying him to sleep. Ryan poured himself some coffee.

"Yes, sir?"

"Can we verify it?" Allen skipped the preliminaries.

"I don't know yet," Jack replied. "It's not just a question of National Technical Means. Verifying the elimination of so many launchers—"

"They're giving us limited on-site inspection," noted a junior member of the team.

"I'm aware of that," Jack replied. "The question is, does that really mean anything?" *The other question is, why did they suddenly agree to something we've wanted for over thirty years . . . ?*

"What?" the junior member asked.

"The Soviets have put a lot of work into their new mobile launchers. What if they have more of them than we know about? Do you think we can find a few hundred mobile missiles?"

"But we have surface-scanning radar on the new birds, and—"

"And they know it, and they can avoid it if they want to—wait a minute. We know that our carriers can and do evade Russian radar-ocean-recon satellites. If you can do it with a ship, you can damned sure do it with a train," Jack pointed out. Allen looked on without comment, allowing his underling to pursue the line in his stead. A clever old fox, Ernie Allen.

"So, CIA is going to recommend against—damn it, this is the biggest concession they've ever made!"

"Fine. It's a big concession. Everyone here knows that. Before we accept it, maybe we ought to make sure that they haven't conceded something that they've made irrelevant to the process. There are other things, too."

"So you're going to oppose—"

"I'm not opposing anything. I'm saying we take our time and use our heads instead of being carried away by euphoria."

"But their draft treaty is—it's almost too good to be true." The man had just proved Ryan's point, though he didn't see it quite that way.

"Dr. Ryan," Allen said, "if the technical details can be worked out to your satisfaction, how do you view the treaty?"

"Sir, speaking from a technical point of view, a fifty-percent reduction in deliverable warheads has no effect at all on the strategic balance. It's—"

"That's crazy!" objected the junior member.

Jack extended his hand toward the man, pointing his index finger like the barrel of a gun. "Let's say I have a pistol pointed at your chest right now. Call it a nine-millimeter Browning. That has a thirteen-round clip. I agree to remove seven rounds from the clip, but I still have a loaded gun, with six rounds, pointed at your chest—do you feel any safer now?" Ryan smiled, keeping his "gun" out.

"Personally, I wouldn't. That's what we're talking about here. If both sides reduce their inventories by half, that still leaves five *thousand* warheads that can hit our country. Think about how big that number is. All this agreement does is to reduce the overkill. The difference between five thousand and ten thousand only affects how far the rubble flies. If we start talking about reducing the number to one thousand warheads on either side, then *maybe* I'll start thinking we're on to something."

"Do you think the thousand-warhead limit is achievable?" Allen asked.

"No, sir. Sometimes I just wish it were, though I've been told that a thousand-warhead limit could have the effect of making nuclear war 'winnable,' whatever the hell that means." Jack shrugged and concluded: "Sir, if this current agreement goes through, it'll look better than it is. Maybe the symbolic value of the agreement has value in and of itself; that's a factor to be considered, but it's not one within my purview. The monetary savings to both sides will be real, but fairly minor in terms of gross military expenditures. Both sides retain half of their current arsenals—and that means keeping the newest and most effective half, of course. The bottom line remains constant: in a nuclear war, both sides would be equally dead. I do not see that this draft treaty reduces the 'threat of war,' whatever that is. To do that, we either have to eliminate the damned things entirely or figure something to keep them from working. If you ask me, we have to do the latter before we can attempt the former. Then the world becomes a safer place—maybe."

"That's the start of a whole new arms race."

"Sir, that race started so long ago that it isn't exactly new."

2. Tea Clipper

"More photos of Dushanbe coming in," the phone told Ryan.

"Okay, I'll be over in a few minutes." Jack rose and crossed the hall to Admiral Greer's office. His boss had his back to the blazing white blanket that covered the hilly ground outside the CIA headquarters building. They were still clearing it off the parking lot, and even the railed walkway outside the seventh-floor windows had about ten inches' worth.

"What is it, Jack?" the Admiral asked.

"Dushanbe. The weather cleared unexpectedly. You said you wanted to be notified."

Greer looked at the TV monitor in the corner of his office. It was next to the computer terminal that he refused to use—at least when anyone might watch his attempts to type with his index fingers and, on good days, one thumb. He could have the real-time satellite photos sent to his office "live," but of late he'd avoided that. Jack didn't know why. "Okay, let's trot over."

Ryan held open the door for the Deputy Director for Intelligence, and they turned left to the end of the executive corridor on the building's top floor. Here was the executive elevator. One nice thing about it was that you didn't have to wait very long.

"How's the jet lag?" Greer asked. Ryan had been back for nearly a day now.

"Fully recovered, sir. Westbound doesn't bother me very much. It's the eastbound kind that still kills me." *God, it's nice to be on the ground.*

The door opened and both men walked across the building to the new annex that housed the Office of Imagery Analysis. This was the Intelligence

Directorate's own private department, separate from the National Photographic Intelligence Center, a joint CIA-DIA effort which served the whole intelligence community.

The screening room would have done Hollywood proud. There were about thirty seats in the mini-theater, and a twenty-foot-square projection screen on the wall. Art Graham, the chief of the unit, was waiting for them.

"You timed that pretty well. We'll have the shots in another minute." He lifted a phone to the projection room and spoke a few words. The screen lit up at once. It was called "Overhead Imagery" now, Jack reminded himself.

"Talk about luck. That Siberian high-pressure system took a sharp swing south and stopped the warm front like a brick wall. Perfect viewing conditions. Ground temp is about zero, and relative humidity can't be much higher than that!" Graham chuckled. "We maneuvered the bird in specially to take advantage of this. It's within three degrees of being right overhead, and I don't think Ivan has had time to figure out that this pass is under way."

"There's Dushanbe," Jack breathed as part of the Tadzhik SSR came into view. Their first look was from one of the wide-angle cameras. The orbiting KH-14 reconnaissance satellite had a total of eleven. The bird had been in orbit for only three weeks, and this was the first of the newest generation of spy satellites. Dushanbe, briefly known as Stalinabad a few decades earlier—*that* must have made the local people happy! Ryan thought—was probably one of the ancient caravan cities. Afghanistan was less than a hundred miles away. Tamurlane's legendary Samarkand was not far to the northwest . . . and perhaps Scheherazade had traveled through a thousand years earlier. He wondered why was it that history worked this way. The same places and the same names always seemed to show up from one century to the next.

But CIA's current interest in Dushanbe did not center on the silk trade.

The view changed to one of the high-resolution cameras. It peered first into a deep, mountainous valley where a river was held back by the concrete and stone mass of a hydroelectric dam. Though only fifty kilometers southeast of Dushanbe, its power lines did not serve that city of 500,000. Instead they led to a collection of mountaintops almost within sight of the facility.

"That looks like footings for another set of towers," Ryan observed.

"Parallel to the first set," Graham agreed. "They're putting some new generators into the facility. Well, we knew all along that they were only getting about half the usable power out of the dam."

"How long to bring the rest on-stream?" Greer asked.

"I'd have to check with one of our consultants. It won't take more than a few weeks to run the power lines out, and the top half of the powerhouse is already built. Figure the foundations for the new generators are already done. All they have to do is rig the new equipment. Six months, maybe eight if the weather goes bad."

"That fast?" Jack wondered.

"They diverted people from two other hydro jobs. Both of them were 'Hero' projects. This one has never been talked about, but they pulled construction troops off two high-profile sites to do this one. Ivan does know how to focus his effort when he wants to. Six or eight months is conservative, Dr. Ryan. It may be done quicker," Graham said.

"How much power'll be available when they finish?"

"It's not all that big a structure. Total peak output, with the new generators? Figure eleven hundred megawatts."

"That's a lot of power, and all going to those hilltops," Ryan said almost to himself as the camera shifted again.

The one the Agency called "Mozart" was quite a hill, but this area was the westernmost extension of the Himalayan Range, and by those standards it was puny. A road had been blasted to the very top—there wasn't a Sierra Club in the USSR—along with a helicopter pad for bringing VIPs out from Dushanbe's two airports. There were sixteen buildings. One was for apartments, the view from which must have been fantastic, though it was a prototypical Russian apartment building, as stylish and attractive as a cinderblock, finished six months before. A lot of engineers and their families lived in it. It seemed strange to see such a building there, but the message of the building was: The people who lived here were privileged. Engineers and academicians, people with enough skill that the State wanted to look after them and their needs. Food was trucked up the new mountain road—or, in bad weather, flown in. Another of the buildings was a theater. A third was a hospital. Television programming came in via satellite earth-station next to a building that contained a few shops. That sort of solicitude was not exactly common in the Soviet Union. It was limited to high Party officials and people who worked in essential defense projects. This was not a ski resort.

That was also obvious from the perimeter fence and guard towers, both of which were recent. One of the identifiable things about Russian military complexes was the guard towers; Ivan had a real fixation for the things. Three fences, with two ten-meter spaces enclosed. The outer space was usually mined, and the inner one patrolled by dogs. The towers were on the inner perimeter, spaced two hundred meters apart. The soldiers who manned the towers were housed in a better-than-average new concrete barracks—

"Can you isolate one of the guards?" Jack asked.

Graham spoke into his phone, and the picture changed. One of his technicians was already doing this, as much to test camera calibration and ambient air conditions as for the purpose Ryan intended.

As the camera zoomed in, a moving dot became a man-shape in greatcoat and probably a fur hat. He was walking a big dog of uncertain breed and had a Kalashnikov rifle slung over his right shoulder. Man and dog left puffs of vapor in the air as they breathed. Ryan leaned forward unconsciously, as though this would give him a better view.

"That guy's shoulder boards look green to you?" he asked Graham.

The reconnaissance expert grunted. "Yep. He's KGB, all right."

"That close to Afghanistan?" the Admiral mused. "They know we have people operating there. You bet they'll take their security provisions seriously."

"They must have really wanted those hilltops," Ryan observed. "Seventy miles overland are a few million people who think killing Russians is God's will. This place is more important than we thought. It isn't just a new facility, not with that kind of security. If that's all it was, they wouldn't have had to put it here, and they for damned sure wouldn't have picked a place where they had to build a new power supply and risk exposure to hostiles. This may be an R and D facility now, but they must have bigger plans for it."

"Like what?"

"Going after my satellites, maybe." Art Graham thought of them as his.

"Have they tickled any of 'em recently?" Jack asked.

"No, not since we rattled their cage last April. Common sense broke out for once."

That was an old story. Several times in the past few years, American reconnaissance and early-warning satellites had been "tickled"—laser beams or microwave energy had been focused on the satellites, enough to dazzle their receptors but not enough to do serious harm. Why had the Russians done it? That was the question. Was it merely an exercise to see how we'd react, to see if it caused a ruckus at the North American Aerospace Defense Command—NORAD—at Cheyenne Mountain, Colorado? An attempt to determine for themselves how sensitive the satellites were? Was it a demonstration, a warning of their ability to destroy the satellites? Or was it simply what Jack's British friends called bloody-mindedness? It was so hard to tell what the Soviets were thinking.

They invariably protested their innocence, of course. When one American satellite had been temporarily blinded over Sary Shagan, they said that a natural-gas pipeline had caught fire. The fact that the nearby Chimkent-Pavlodar pipeline carried mostly oil had escaped the Western press.

The satellite pass was complete now. In a nearby room a score of videotape recorders were rewound, and now the complete camera coverage would be reviewed at leisure.

"Let's have a look at Mozart again, and Bach also, please," Greer commanded.

"Hell of a commute," Jack noted. The residential and industrial site on Mozart was only one kilometer or so from the emplacement on Bach, the next mountaintop over, but the road looked frightful. The picture froze on Bach. The formula of fences and guard towers was repeated, but this time the distance between the outermost perimeter fence and the next was at least two hundred meters. Here the ground surface appeared to be bare rock. Jack wondered how you planted mines in that—or maybe they didn't, he thought. It was obvious that the ground had been leveled with bulldozers and explosives to the unobstructed flatness of a pool table. From the guard towers, it must have looked like a shooting gallery.

"Not kidding, are they?" Graham observed quietly.

"So that's what they're guarding . . ." Ryan said.

There were thirteen buildings inside the fence. In an area perhaps the size of two football fields—which had also been leveled—were ten holes, in two groups. One was a group of six arranged hexagonally, each hole about thirty feet across. The second group of four was arrayed in a diamond pattern, and the holes were slightly smaller, perhaps twenty-five feet. In each hole was a concrete pillar about fifteen feet across, planted in bedrock, and every hole was at least forty feet deep—you couldn't tell from the picture on the screen. Atop each pillar was a metal dome. They appeared to be made of crescent-shaped segments.

"They unfold. I wonder what's in them?" Graham asked rhetorically. There were two hundred people at Langley who knew of Dushanbe, and every one wanted to know what was under those metal domes. They'd been in place for only a few months.

"Admiral," Jack said, "I need to kick open a new compartment."

"Which one?"

"Tea Clipper."

"You're not asking much!" Greer snorted. "*I'm* not cleared for that."

Ryan leaned back in his chair. "Admiral, if what they're doing in Dushanbe is the same thing we're doing with Tea Clipper, we sure as hell ought to know. Goddammit, how are we supposed to know what to look for if we're not told what one of these places looks like!"

"I've been saying that for quite a while." The DDI chuckled. "SDIO won't like it. The Judge will have to go to the President for that."

"So he goes to the President. What if the activity here is connected with the arms proposal they just made?"

"Do you think it is?"

"Who can say?" Jack asked. "It's a coincidence. They worry me."

"Okay, I'll talk to the Director."

Ryan drove home two hours later. He drove his Jaguar XJS out onto the George Washington Parkway. It was one of the many happy memories from his tour of duty in England. He loved the silky-smooth feeling of the twelve-cylinder engine enough that he'd put his venerable old Rabbit into semiretirement. As he always tried to do, Ryan set his Washington business aside. He worked the car up through its five gears and concentrated on his driving.

"Well, James?" the Director of Central Intelligence asked.

"Ryan thinks the new activity at Bach and Mozart may be related to the arms situation. I think he might be correct. He wants into Tea Clipper. I said you'd have to go to the President." Admiral Greer smiled.

"Okay, I'll get him a written note. It'll make General Parks happier, anyway. They have a full-up test scheduled for the end of the week. I'll set it up for Jack to see it." Judge Moore smiled sleepily. "What do you think?"

"I think he's right: Dushanbe and Tea Clipper are essentially the same project. There are a lot of coarse similarities, too many to be a pure coincidence. We ought to upgrade our assessment."

"Okay." Moore turned away to look out the windows. *The world is going to change again. It may take ten or more years, but it's going to change. Ten years from now it won't be my problem,* Moore told himself. *But it sure as hell will be Ryan's problem.* "I'll have him flown out there tomorrow. And maybe we'll get lucky on Dushanbe. Foley got word to CARDINAL that we're very interested in the place."

"CARDINAL? Good."

"But if something happens . . ."

Greer nodded. "Christ, I hope he's careful," the DDI said.

Ever since the death of Dmitri Fedorovich, it has not been the same at the Defense Ministry, Colonel Mikhail Semyonovich Filitov wrote into his diary left-handed. An early riser, he sat at a hundred-year-old oak desk that his wife had bought for him shortly before she'd died, almost—what was it? Thirty years, Misha told himself. Thirty years this coming February. His eyes closed for a moment. *Thirty years.*

Never a single day passed that he did not remember his Elena. Her photograph was on the desk, the sepia print faded with age, its silver frame tarnished. He never seemed to have time to polish it, and didn't wish to be bothered with a maid. The photo showed a young woman with legs like spindles, arms high over her head, which was cocked to one side. The round, Slavic face displayed a wide, inviting smile that perfectly conveyed the joy she'd felt when dancing with the Kirov Company.

Misha smiled also as he remembered the first impression of a young armor officer given tickets to the performance as a reward for having the best-maintained tanks in the division: *How can they do that?* Perched up on the tips of their toes as though on needle-point stilts. He'd remembered playing on stilts as a child, *but to be so graceful!* And then she'd smiled at the handsome young officer in the front row. For the briefest moment. Their eyes had met for almost as little time as it takes to blink, he thought. Her smile had changed ever so slightly. Not for the audience any longer, for that timeless instant the smile had been for him alone. A bullet through the heart could not have had a more devastating effect. Misha didn't remember the rest of the performance—to this day he couldn't even remember which ballet it had been. He remembered sitting and squirming through the rest of it while his mind churned over what he'd do next. Already Lieutenant Filitov had been marked as a man on the move, a brilliant young tank officer for whom Stalin's brutal purge of the officer corps had meant opportunity and rapid promotion. He wrote articles on tank tactics, practiced innovative battle drills in the field, argued vociferously against the false "lessons" of Spain with the certainty of a man born to his profession.

But what do I do now? he'd asked himself. The Red Army hadn't taught him how to approach an artist. This wasn't some farm girl who was bored enough by work on the *kolkhoz* to offer herself to anyone—especially a young Army officer who might take her away from it all. Misha still remembered the shame of his youth—not that he'd thought it shameful at the time—when he'd used his officer's shoulder boards to bed any girl who'd caught his eye.

But I don't even know her name, he'd told himself. *What do I do?* What he'd done, of course, was to treat the matter as a military exercise. As soon as the performance had ended, he'd fought his way into the rest room and washed hands and face. Some grease that still remained under his fingernails was removed with a pocketknife. His short hair was wetted down into place, and he inspected his uniform as strictly as a general officer might, brushing off dust and picking off lint, stepping back from the mirror to make sure his boots gleamed as a soldier's should. He hadn't noticed at the time that other men in the men's room were watching him with barely suppressed grins, having guessed what the drill was for, and wishing him luck, touched with a bit of envy. Satisfied with his appearance, Misha had left the theater and asked the doorman where the artists' door was. That had cost him a ruble, and with the knowledge, he'd walked around the block to the stage entrance, where he found another doorman, this one a bearded old man whose greatcoat bore ribbons for service in the revolution. Misha had expected special courtesy from the doorman, one soldier to another, only to learn that he regarded all the female dancers as his own daughters—not wenches to be thrown at the feet of soldiers, certainly! Misha had considered offering money, but had the good sense not to imply the man was a pimp. Instead, he'd spoken quietly and reasonably—and truthfully—that he was smitten with a single dancer whose name he didn't know, and merely wanted to meet her.

"Why?" the old doorman had asked coldly.

"Grandfather, she smiled at me," Misha had answered in the awed voice of a little boy.

"And you are in love." The reply was harsh, but in a moment the doorman's face turned wistful. "But you don't know which?"

"She was in—the line, not one of the important ones, I mean. What do they call that?—I will remember her face until the day I die." Already he'd known that.

The doorman looked him over and saw that his uniform was properly turned out, and his back straight. This was not a swaggering pig of an NKVD officer whose arrogant breath stank of vodka. This was a soldier, and a handsome young one at that. "Comrade Lieutenant, you are a lucky man. Do you know why? You are lucky because I was once young, and old as I am, I still remember. They will start to come out in ten minutes or so. Stand over there, and make not a sound."

It had taken thirty minutes. They came out in twos and threes. Misha had seen the male members of the troupe and thought them—what any soldier would think of a man in a ballet company. His manhood had been offended that they held hands with such pretty girls, but he'd set that aside. When the door opened, his vision was damaged by the sudden glare of yellow-white light against the near blackness of the unlit alley, and he'd almost missed her, so different she looked without the makeup.

He saw the face, and tried to decide if she were the right one, approaching his objective more carefully than he would ever do under the fire of German guns.

"You were in seat number twelve," she'd said before he could summon the courage to speak. *She had a voice!*

"Yes, Comrade Artist," his reply had stammered out.

"Did you enjoy the performance, Comrade Lieutenant?" A shy, but somehow beckoning smile.

"It was wonderful!" Of course.

"It is not often that we see handsome young officers in the front row," she observed.

"I was given the ticket as a reward for performance in my unit. I am a tanker," he said proudly. *She called me handsome!*

"Does the Comrade Tanker Lieutenant have a name?"

"I am Lieutenant Mikhail Semyonovich Filitov."

"I am Elena Ivanova Makarova."

"It is too cold tonight for one so thin, Comrade Artist. Is there a restaurant nearby?"

"Restaurant?" She'd laughed. "How often do you come to Moscow?"

"My division is based thirty kilometers from here, but I do not often come to the city," he'd admitted.

"Comrade Lieutenant, there are few restaurants even in Moscow. Can you come to my apartment?"

"Why—yes," his reply had stuttered out as the stage door opened again.

"Marta," Elena said to the girl who was just coming out. "We have a military escort home!"

"Tania and Resa are coming," Marta said.

Misha had actually been relieved by that. The walk to the apartment had taken thirty minutes—the Moscow subway hadn't yet been completed, and it was better to walk than to wait for a tram this late at night.

She was far prettier without her makeup, Misha remembered. The cold winter air gave her cheeks all the color they ever needed. Her walk was as graceful as ten years of intensive training could make it. She'd glided along the street like an apparition, while he gallumped along in his heavy boots. He felt himself a tank, rolling next to a thoroughbred horse, and was careful not to go too close, lest he trample her. He hadn't yet learned of the strength that was so well hidden by her grace.

The night had never before seemed so fine, though for—what was it?—twenty years there had been many such nights, then none for the past thirty. *My God,* he thought, *we would have been married fifty years this . . . July 14th.* My God. Unconsciously he dabbed at his eyes with a handkerchief.

Thirty years, however, was the number that occupied his mind.

The thought boiled within his breast, and his fingers were pale around the pen. It still surprised him that love and hate were emotions so finely matched. Misha returned to his diary . . .

An hour later he rose from the desk and walked to the bedroom closet. He donned the uniform of a colonel of tank troops. Technically he was on the retired list, and had been so before people on the current colonel's list had been born. But work in the Ministry of Defense carried its own perks, and Misha was on the personal staff of the Minister. That was one reason. The other three reasons were on his uniform blouse, three gold stars that depended from claret-colored ribbons. Filitov was the only soldier in the history of the Soviet Army who'd won the decoration of Hero of the Soviet Union three times on the field of battle, for personal bravery in the face of the enemy. There were others with such medals, but so often these were political awards, the Colonel knew. He was aesthetically offended by that. This was not a medal to be granted for staff work, and certainly not for one Party member to give to another as a gaudy lapel decoration. Hero of the Soviet Union was an award that ought to be limited to men like himself, who had risked death, who'd bled—and all too often, died—for the *Rodina.* He was reminded of this every time he put his uniform on. Beneath his undershirt were the plastic-looking scars from his last gold star, when a German 88 round had lanced through the armor of his tank, setting the ammo racks afire while he'd brought his 76mm gun around for one last shot and extinguished that Kraut gun crew while his clothing burned. The injury had left him with only fifty percent use of his right arm, but despite it, he'd led what was left of his regiment nearly two more days in the Kursk Bulge. If he'd bailed out with the rest of his crew—or been evacuated from the area at once as his regimental surgeon had recommended—perhaps he would have recovered fully, but, no, he knew that he could not have *not* fired back, could not have abandoned his men in the face of battle. And so he'd shot, and burned. But for that Misha might have made General, perhaps even Marshal, he thought. *Would it have made a difference?* Filitov was too much a man of the real, practical world to dwell on that thought for long. Had he fought in many more campaigns, he might have been killed. As it was, he'd been given more time with Elena than could otherwise have been the case. She'd come nearly every day to the burn institute in Moscow; at first horrified by the extent of his wounds, she'd later become as proud of them as Misha was. No one could question that her man had done his duty for the *Rodina.*

But now, he did his duty for his Elena.

Filitov walked out of the apartment to the elevator, a leather briefcase dangling from his right hand. It was about all that side of his body was good for. The *babushka* who operated the elevator greeted him as always. They were of an age, she the widow of a sergeant who'd been in Misha's regiment, who also had the gold star, pinned on his breast by this very man.

"Your new granddaughter?" the Colonel asked.

"An angel," was her reply.

Filitov smiled, partly in agreement—was there any such thing as an ugly infant?—and partly because terms like "angel" had survived seventy years of "scientific socialism."

The car was waiting for him. The driver was a new draftee, fresh from sergeant school and driving school. He saluted his Colonel severely, the door held open in his other hand.

"Good morning, Comrade Colonel."

"So it is, Sergeant Zhdanov," Filitov replied. Most officers would have done little more than grunt, but Filitov was a combat soldier whose success on the battlefield had resulted from his devotion to the welfare of his men. A lesson that few officers ever understood, he reminded himself. Too bad.

The car was comfortably warm, the heater had been turned all the way up fifteen minutes ago. Filitov was becoming ever more sensitive to cold, a sure sign of age. He'd just been hospitalized again for pneumonia, the third time in the past five years. One of these times, he knew, would be the last. Filitov dismissed the thought. He'd cheated death too many times to fear it. Life came and went at a constant rate. One brief second at a time. When the last second came, he wondered, would he notice? Would he care?

The driver pulled the car up to the Defense Ministry before the Colonel could answer that question.

Ryan was sure that he'd been in government service too long. He had come to—well, not actually to *like* flying, but at least to appreciate the convenience of it. He was only four hours from Washington, flown by an Air Force C-21 Learjet whose female pilot, a captain, had looked like a high-school sophomore.

Getting old, Jack, he told himself. The flight from the airfield to the mountaintop had been by helicopter, no easy feat at this altitude. Ryan had never been to New Mexico before. The high mountains were bare of trees, the air thin enough that he was breathing abnormally, but the sky was so clear that for a moment he imagined himself an astronaut looking at the unblinking stars on this cloudless, frigid night.

"Coffee, sir?" a sergeant asked. He handed Ryan a thermos cup, and the hot liquid steamed into the night, barely illuminated by a sliver of new moon.

"Thanks." Ryan sipped at it and looked around. There were few lights to be seen. There might have been a housing development behind the next set of ridges; he could see the halolike glow of Santa Fe, but there was no way to guess how far off it might be. He knew that the rock he stood on was eleven thousand feet above sea level (the nearest level sea was hundreds of miles away), and there is no way to judge distance at night. It was altogether beautiful, except for the cold. His fingers were stiff around the plastic cup. He'd mistakenly left his gloves at home.

"Seventeen minutes," somebody announced. "All systems are nominal. Trackers on automatic. AOS in eight minutes."

"AOS?" Ryan asked. He realized that he sounded a little funny. It was so cold that his cheeks were stiff.

"Acquisition of Signal," the Major explained.

"You live around here?"

"Forty miles that way." He pointed vaguely. "Practically next door by local standards." The officer's Brooklyn accent explained the comment.

He's the one with the doctorate from State University of New York at Stony Brook, Ryan reminded himself. At only twenty-nine years old, the Major didn't look like a soldier, even less like a field-grade officer. In Switzerland he'd be called a gnome, barely over five-seven, and cadaverously thin, acne on his angular face. Right now, his deep-set eyes were locked on the sector of horizon where the space shuttle *Discovery* would appear. Ryan thought back to the documents he'd read on the way out and knew that this major probably couldn't tell him the color of the paint on his living-room wall. He really lived at Los Alamos National Laboratory, known locally as the Hill. Number one in his class at West Point, and a doctorate in high-energy physics only two years after that. His doctor's dissertation was classified Top Secret. Jack had read it, and didn't understand why they had bothered—despite a doctorate of his own, the two-hundred-page document might as well have been written in Kurdish. Alan Gregory was already being talked of in the same breath as Cambridge's Stephen Hawking, or Princeton's Freeman Dyson. Except that few people knew his name. Jack wondered if anyone had thought of classifying *that*.

"Major Gregory, all ready?" an Air Force lieutenant general asked. Jack noted his respectful tone. Gregory was no ordinary major.

A nervous smile. "Yes, sir." The Major wiped sweaty hands—despite a temperature of fifteen below zero—on the pants of his uniform. It was good to see that the kid had emotions.

"You married?" Ryan asked. The file hadn't covered that.

"Engaged, sir. She's a doctor in laser optics, on the Hill. We get married June the third." The kid's voice had become as brittle as glass.

"Congratulations. Keeping it in the family, eh?" Jack chuckled.

"Yes, sir." Major Gregory was still staring at the southwest horizon.

"AOS!" someone announced behind them. "We have signal."

"Goggles!" The call came over the metal speakers. "Everyone put on their eye-protection."

Jack blew on his hands before taking the plastic goggles from his pocket. He'd been told to stash them there to keep them warm. They were still cold enough on his face that he noticed the difference. Once in place, however, Ryan was effectively blinded. The stars and moon were gone.

"Tracking! We have lock. *Discovery* has established the downlink. All systems are nominal."

"Target acquisition!" another voice announced. "Initiate interrogation sequencing . . . first target is locked . . . auto firing circuits enabled."

There was no sound to indicate what had happened. Ryan didn't see anything—*or did I?* he asked himself. There had been the fleeting impression of . . . what? *Did I imagine it?* Next to him he felt the Major's breath come out slowly.

"Exercise concluded," the speaker said. Jack tore off his goggles.

"*That's all?*" What had he just seen? What had they just done? Was he so far out of date that even after being briefed he didn't understand what was happening before his eyes?

"The laser light is almost impossible to see," Major Gregory explained. "This high up, there isn't much dust or humidity in the air to reflect it."

"Then why the goggles?"

The young officer smiled as he took his off. "Well, if a bird flies over at the wrong time, the impact might be, well, kind of spectacular. That could hurt your eyes some."

Two hundred miles over their heads, *Discovery* continued toward the horizon. The shuttle would stay in orbit another three days, conducting its "routine scientific mission," mainly oceanographical studies this time, the press was told, something secret for the Navy. The papers had been speculating on the mission for weeks. It had something to do, they said, with tracking missile submarines from orbit. There was no better way to keep a secret than to use another "secret" to conceal it. Every time someone asked about the mission, a Navy public-affairs officer would do the "no comments."

"Did it work?" Jack asked. He looked up, but he couldn't pick out the dot of light that denoted the billion-dollar space plane.

"We have to see." The Major turned and walked to the camouflage-painted truck van parked a few yards away. The three-star General followed him, with Ryan trailing behind.

Inside the van, where the temperature might have been merely at freezing, a chief warrant officer was rewinding a videotape.

"Where were the targets?" Jack asked. "That wasn't in the briefing papers."

"About forty-five south, thirty west," the General replied. Major Gregory was perched in front of the TV screen.

"That's around the Falklands, isn't it? Why there?"

"Closer to South Georgia, actually," the General replied. "It's a nice, quiet, out-of-the-way sort of place, and the distance is about right."

And the Soviets had no known intelligence-gathering assets within three thousand miles, Ryan knew. The Tea Clipper test had been timed precisely for a moment when all Soviet spy satellites were under the visible horizon. Finally, the shooting distance was exactly the same as the distance to the Soviet ballistic missile fields arrayed along the country's main east-west railway.

"Ready!" the warrant officer said.

The video picture wasn't all that great, taken from sea level, specifically the deck of the *Observation Island*, a range-instrumentation ship returning from Trident missile tests in the Indian Ocean. Next to the first TV screen was another. This one showed the picture from the ship's "Cobra Judy" missile-tracking radar. Both screens showed four objects, spaced in a slightly uneven line. A timer box in the lower right-hand corner was changing numbers as though in an Alpine ski race, with three digits to the right of the decimal point.

"Hit!" One of the dots disappeared in a puff of green light.

"Miss!" Another one didn't.

"Miss!" Jack frowned. He'd half-expected to see the beams of light streaking through the sky, but that happened only in movies. There wasn't enough dust in space to denote the energy's path.

"Hit!" A second dot vanished.

"Hit!" Only one was left.

"Miss."

"Miss." The last one didn't want to die, Ryan thought.

"Hit!" But it did. "Total elapsed time, one point eight-zero-six seconds."

"Fifty percent," Major Gregory said quietly. "And it corrected itself." The young officer nodded slowly. He managed to keep from smiling, except around the eyes. "It works."

"How big were the targets?" Ryan asked.

"Three meters. Spherical balloons, of course." Gregory was rapidly losing control. He looked like a kid whom Christmas had taken by surprise.

"Same diameter as an SS-18."

"Something like that." The General answered that one.

"Where's the other mirror?"

"Ten thousand kilometers up, currently over Ascension Island. Officially it's a weather satellite that never made its proper orbit." The General smiled.

"I didn't know you could send it that far."

Major Gregory actually giggled. "Neither did we."

"So you sent the beam from over there to the shuttle's mirror, from *Discovery* to this other one over the equator, and from there to the targets?"

"Correct," the General said.

"Your targeting system is on the other satellite, then?"

"Yes," the General answered more grudgingly.

Jack did some numbers in his head. "Okay, that means you can discriminate a three-meter target at . . . ten thousand kilometers. I didn't know we could do that. How do we?"

"You don't need to know," the General replied coldly.

"You had four hits and four misses—eight shots in under two seconds, and the Major said the targeting system corrected for misses. Okay, if those had been SS-18s launched off of South Georgia, would the shots have killed them?"

"Probably not," Gregory admitted. "The laser assembly only puts out five megajoules. Do you know what a joule is?"

"I checked my college phyzzies book before I flew down. A joule is one newton-meter per second, or zero-point-seven foot-pounds of energy, plus change, right? Okay, a megajoule is a million of them . . . seven hundred thousand foot-pounds. In terms I can understand—"

"A megajoule is the rough equivalent of a stick of dynamite. So we just delivered five sticks. The actual energy transferred is like a kilogram of explosives, but the physical effects are not exactly comparable."

"What you're telling me is that the laser beam doesn't actually burn through the target—it's more of a shock effect." Ryan was stretching his technical knowledge to the limit.

"We call it an 'impact kill,' " the General answered. "But, yeah, that's about it. All the energy arrives in a few millionths of a second, a lot faster than any bullet does."

"So all that stuff I've heard about how polishing the missile body, or rotating it, will prevent a burn-through—"

Major Gregory giggled again. "Yeah, I like that one. A ballet dancer can pirouette in front of a shotgun and it'll do her about as much good. What happens is that the energy has to go somewhere, and that can only be into the missile body. The missile body is full of storable liquids—nearly all of their birds are liquid fueled, right? The hydrostatic effect alone will be to rupture the pressure tanks—*ka-boom!* no more missile." The Major smiled as though describing a trick played on his high-school teacher.

"Okay, now, I want to know how it all works."

"Look, Dr. Ryan—" the General started to say. Jack cut him off.

"General, I am cleared for Tea Clipper. You know that, so let's stop screwing around."

Major Gregory got a nod from the General. "Sir, we have five one-megajoule lasers—"

"Where?"

"You're standing right on top of one of them, sir. The other four are buried around this hilltop. The power rating is per pulse, of course. Each one puts out a pulse-chain of a million joules in a few microseconds—a few millionths of a second."

"And they recharge in . . . ?"

"Point zero-four-six seconds. We can deliver twenty shots per second, in other words."

"But you didn't shoot that fast."

"We didn't have to, sir," Gregory replied. "The limiting factor at present is the targeting software. That's being worked on. The purpose of this test was to evaluate part of the software package. We know that these lasers work. We've had them here for the past three years. The laser beams are converged on a mirror about fifty meters that way"—he pointed—"and converted into a single beam."

"They have to be—I mean, the beams all have to be exactly in tune, right?"

"Technically it's called a Phased-Array Laser. All the beams have to be perfectly in phase," Gregory answered.

"How the hell do you do that?" Ryan paused. "Don't bother, I probably wouldn't understand it anyway. Okay, we have the beam hitting the down-side mirror . . ."

"The mirror is the special part. It's composed of thousands of segments, and every segment is controlled by a piezoelectric chip. That's called 'adaptive optics.' We send an interrogation beam to the mirror—this one was on the shuttle—and get a reading on atmospheric distortion. The way the atmosphere bends the beam is analyzed by computer. Then the mirror corrects for the distortion, and we fire the real shot. The mirror on the shuttle also has adaptive optics. It collects and focuses the beam, and sends it off to the 'Flying Cloud' satellite mirror. That mirror refocuses the beam on the targets. Zap!"

"That simple?" Ryan shook his head. It was simple enough that over the previous nineteen years, forty billion dollars had gone into basic research, in twenty separate fields, just to run this one test.

"We did have to iron out a few little details," Gregory acknowledged. These little details would take another five or more years, and he neither knew nor cared how many additional billions. What mattered to him was that the goal was now actually in sight. Tea Clipper wasn't a blue-sky project anymore, not after this system test.

"And you're the guy who made the breakthrough on the targeting system. You figured a way for the beam to provide its own targeting information."

"Something like that," the General answered for the kid. "Dr. Ryan, that part of the system is classified highly enough that we will not discuss it further without written authorization."

"General, the purpose in my being here is to evaluate this program relative to Soviet efforts along similar lines. If you want my people to tell you what the Russians are up to, I have to know what the hell we're supposed to look for!"

This did not elicit a reply. Jack shrugged and reached inside his coat.

He handed the General an envelope. Major Gregory looked on in puzzlement.

"You still don't like it," Ryan observed after the officer folded the letter away.

"No, sir, I don't."

Ryan spoke with a voice colder than the New Mexico night. "General, when I was in the Marine Corps, they never told me that I was supposed to like my orders, just that I was supposed to obey them." That almost set the General off, and Jack added: "I really am on your side, sir."

"You may continue, Major Gregory," General Parks said after a moment.

"I call the algorithm 'Fan Dance,' " Gregory began. The General almost smiled in spite of himself. Gregory could not have known anything about Sally Rand.

"That's all?" Ryan said again when the youngster finished, and he knew that every computer expert in Project Tea Clipper must have asked himself the same thing: Why didn't I think of that! No wonder they all say that Gregory is a genius. He'd made a crucial breakthrough in laser technology at Stony Brook, *then* one in software design. "But that's simple!"

"Yes, sir, but it took over two years to make it work, and a Cray-2 computer to make it work fast enough to matter. We still need a little more work, but after we analyze what went wrong tonight, another four or five months, maybe, and we got it knocked."

"Next step, then?"

"Building a five-megajoule laser. Another team is close to that already. Then we gang up twenty of them, and we can send out a hundred-megajoule pulse, twenty times per second, and hit any target we want. The impact energy then will be on the order of, say, twenty to thirty kilograms of explosives."

"And that'll kill any missile anybody can make . . ."

"Yes, sir." Major Gregory smiled.

"What you're telling me is, the thing—Tea Clipper works."

"We've validated the system architecture," the General corrected Ryan. "It's been a long haul since we started looking at this system. Five years ago there were eleven hurdles. There are three technical hurdles left. Five years from now there won't be any. Then we can start building it."

"The strategic implications . . ." Ryan said, and stopped. "Jesus."

"It's going to change the world," the General agreed.

"You know that they're playing with the same thing at Dushanbe."

"Yes, sir," Major Gregory answered. "And they might know something that we don't."

Ryan nodded. Gregory was even smart enough to know that someone else might be smarter. This was some kid.

"Gentlemen, out in my helicopter is a briefcase. Could you have somebody bring it in? There are some satellite photos that you might find interesting."

"How old are these shots?" the General asked five minutes later as he leafed through the photos.

"A couple of days," Jack replied.

Major Gregory peered at them for a minute or so. "Okay, we have two slightly different installations here. It's called a 'sparse array.' The hexagonal array—the six-pillar one—is a transmitter. The building in the middle here is probably designed to house six lasers. These pillars are optically stable mounts for mirrors. The laser beams come out of the building, reflect off the mirrors, and the mirrors are computer-controlled to concentrate the beam on a target."

"What do you mean by optically stable?"

"The mirrors have to be controlled with a high degree of accuracy, sir," Gregory told Ryan. "By isolating them from the surrounding ground you eliminate vibration that might come from having a man walk nearby, or driving a car around. If you jiggle the mirrors by a small multiple of the laser-light frequency, you mess up the effect you're trying to get. Here we use shock mountings to enhance the isolation factor. It's a technique originally developed for submarines. Okay? This other diamond-shaped array is . . . oh, of course. That's the receiver."

"What?" Jack's brain had just met another stone wall.

"Let's say you want to make a really good picture of something. I mean, *really* good. You use a laser as your strobe light."

"But why four mirrors?"

"It's easier and cheaper to make four small mirrors than one big one," Gregory explained. "Hmph. I wonder if they're trying to do a holographic image. If they can really lock their illuminating beams in phase . . . theoretically it's possible. There are a couple of things that make it tricky, but the Russians like the brute-force approach . . . Damn!" His eyes lit up. "That's one hell of an interesting idea! I'll have to think about that one."

"You're telling me that they build this place just to take pictures of our satellites?" Ryan demanded.

"No, sir. They can use it for that, no sweat. It makes a perfect cover. And a system that can image a satellite at geosynchronous altitude might be able to clobber one in low earth orbit. If you think of these four mirrors here as a telescope, remember that a telescope can be a lens for a camera, or part of a gunsight. It could also make a damned efficient aiming system. How much power runs into this lab?"

Ryan set down a photo. "The current power output from this dam is something like five hundred megawatts. But—"

"They're stringing new power lines," Gregory observed. "How come?"

"The powerhouse is two stories—you can't tell from this angle. It looks like they're activating the top half. That'll bring their peak power output to something like eleven hundred megawatts."

"How much comes into this place?"

"We call it 'Bach.' Maybe a hundred. The rest goes to 'Mozart,' the town that grew up on the next hill over. So they're doubling their available power."

"More than that, sir," Gregory noted. "Unless they're going to double the size of that town, why don't you assume that the increased power is just going to the lasers?"

Jack nearly choked. *Why the hell didn't you think of that!* he growled at himself.

"I mean," Gregory continued, "I mean . . . that's like five hundred megawatts of new power. Jesus, what if they just made a breakthrough? How hard is it to find out what's happening there?"

"Take a look at the photos and tell me how easy you think it would be to infiltrate the place," Ryan suggested.

"Oh." Gregory looked up. "It would be nice to know how much power they push out the front end of their instruments. How long has this place been there, sir?"

"About four years, and it's not finished yet. Mozart is new. Until recently the workers were housed in this barracks and support facility. We took notice when the apartment building went up, same time as the perimeter fence. When the Russians start pampering the workers, you know that the project has a really high priority. If it has a fence and guard towers, we know it's military."

"How did you find it?" Gregory asked.

"By accident. The Agency was redrawing its meteorological data on the Soviet Union, and one of the technicians decided to do a computer analysis of the best places over there for astronomical observation. This is one of them. The weather over the last few months has been unusually cloudy, but on average the skies are about as clear there as they are here. The same is true of Sary Shagan, Semipalatinsk, and another new one, Storozhevaya." Ryan set out some more photographs. Gregory looked at them.

"They sure are busy."

"Good morning, Misha," Marshal of the Soviet Union Dmitri Timofeyevich Yazov said.

"And to you, Comrade Defense Minister," Colonel Filitov replied.

A sergeant helped the Minister off with his coat while another brought in a tray with a tea setting. Both withdrew when Misha opened his briefcase.

"So, Misha, what does my day look like?" Yazov poured two cups of tea. It was still dark outside the Council of Ministers building. The inside perimeter of the Kremlin walls was lit with harsh blue-white floods, and sentries appeared and disappeared in the splashes of light.

"A full one, Dmitri Timofeyevich," Misha replied. Yazov wasn't the man that Dmitri Ustinov was, but Filitov had to admit to himself that he did put in a full day's work as a uniformed officer should. Like Filitov, Marshal Yazov was by background a tank officer. Though they had never met during the war, they did know one another by reputation. Misha's was better as a combat officer—purists claimed that he was an old-fashioned cavalryman at heart, though Filitov cordially hated horses—while Dmitri Yazov had won a reputation early on as a brilliant staff officer and organizer—and a Party man, of course. Before everything else, Yazov was a Party man, else he would never have made the rank of Marshal. "We have that delegation coming in from the experimental station in the Tadzhik SSR."

"Ah, 'Bright Star.' Yes, that report is due today, isn't it?"

"Academicians," Misha snorted. "They wouldn't know what a real weapon was if I shoved it up their asses."

"The time for lances and sabers is past, Mikhail Semyonovich," Yazov said with a grin. Not the brilliant intellect that Ustinov had been, neither was Yazov a fool like his predecessor, Sergey Sokolov. His lack of engineering expertise was balanced by an uncanny instinct for the merits of new weapons systems, and rare insights into the people of the Soviet Army. "These inventions show extraordinary promise."

"Of course. I only wish that we had a real soldier running the project instead of these starry-eyed professors."

"But General Pokryshkin—"

"He was a fighter pilot. I said a *soldier*, Comrade Minister. Pilots will support anything that has enough buttons and dials. Besides, Pokryshkin has spent more time in universities of late than in an aircraft. They don't even let him fly himself anymore. Pokryshkin stopped being a soldier ten years ago. Now he is the procurer for the wizards." *And he is building his own little empire down there, but that's an issue we'll save for another day.*

"You wish a new job assignment, Misha?" Yazov inquired slyly.

"Not that one!" Filitov laughed, then turned serious. "What I am trying to say, Dmitri Timofeyevich, is that the progress assessment we get from Bright Star is—how do I say this?—warped by the fact that we don't have a real military man on the scene. Someone who understands the vagaries of combat, someone who knows what a weapon is supposed to be."

The Defense Minister nodded thoughtfully. "Yes, I see your point. They think in terms of 'instruments' rather than 'weapons,' that is true. The complexity of the project concerns me."

"Just how many moving parts does this new assembly have?"

"I have no idea—thousands, I should think."

"An instrument does not become a weapon until it can be handled reliably by a private soldier—well, at least a senior lieutenant. Has anyone outside the project ever done a reliability assessment?" Filitov asked.

"No, not that I can recall."

Filitov picked up his tea. "There you are, Dmitri Timofeyevich. Don't you think that the Politburo will be interested in that? Until now, they have been willing to fund the experimental project, of course, but"—Filitov took a sip—"they are coming here to request funding to upgrade the site to operational status, and we have no independent assessment of the project."

"How would you suggest we get that assessment?"

"Obviously I cannot do it. I am too old, and too uneducated, but we have some bright new colonels in the Ministry, especially in the signals section. They are not combat officers, strictly speaking, but they are soldiers, and they are competent to look at these electronic marvels. It is only a suggestion." Filitov didn't press. He had planted the seed of an idea. Yazov was far easier to manipulate than Ustinov had ever been.

"And what of the problems at the Chelyabinsk tank works?" Yazov asked next.

Ortiz watched the Archer climbing the hill half a mile away. Two men and two camels. They probably wouldn't be mistaken for a guerrilla force the way that twenty or so would have. Not that this had to matter, Ortiz knew, but the Soviets were to the point now that they attacked almost anything that moved. *Vaya con Dios.*

"I sure could use a beer," the Captain observed.

Ortiz turned. "Captain, the thing that allowed me to deal with these people effectively is that I live the way they do. I observe their laws and respect their ways. That means no booze, no pork; that means I don't fool with their women."

"Shit." The officer snorted. "These ignorant savages—" Ortiz cut him off.

"Captain, the next time I hear you say that, or even think it real loud, will be your last day here. These people are working for us. They're bringing us stuff that we can't get any place else. You will, repeat *will* treat them with the respect they deserve. *Is that clear!*"

"Yes, sir." *Christ, this guy's turned into a sand nigger himself.*

3. The Weary Red Fox

"It's impressive—if you can figure out what they're doing." Jack yawned. He'd taken the same Air Force transport back to Andrews from Los Alamos, and was behind in his sleep again. For all the times this had happened to him, he'd never quite learned to deal with it. "That Gregory kid is smart as hell. He took about two seconds to identify the Bach installation, practically word for word with the NPIC assessment." The difference was that the photointerpreters at the National Photographic Intelligence Center had taken four months and three written reports to get it right.

"You think he belongs in the assessment team?"

"Sir, that's like asking if you want to have surgeons in the operating room. Oh, by the way, he wants us to infiltrate somebody into Bach." Ryan rolled his eyes.

Admiral Greer nearly dropped his cup. "That kid must watch ninja movies."

"It is nice to know that somebody believes in us." Jack chuckled, then turned serious. "Anyway, Gregory wants to know if they've made a breakthrough in laser power output—excuse me, I think the new term is 'throughput.' He suspects that most of the new power from the hydroelectric dam will go to Bach."

Greer's eyes narrowed. "That's an evil thought. Do you think he's right?"

"They've got a lot of good people in lasers, sir. Nikolay Bosov, remember, won the Nobel Prize, and he's been in laser-weapons research ever since, along with Yevgeniy Velikhov, noted peace activist, and the head of the Laser Institute is Dmitri Ustinov's son, for God's sake. Site Bach is almost certainly a sparse array laser. We need to know what kind of lasers, though—could be gas-dynamic, free-electron, chemical. He thinks it'll be the free-electron kind, but that's just a guess. He gave me figures to establish the advantage of putting the laser assembly on this hilltop, where it's above about half of the atmosphere, and we know how much energy it takes to do some of the things they want to do. He said he'd try to do some backwards computations to estimate the total power of the system. The figures will be on the conservative side. Between what Gregory said, and the establishment of the residential facilities at Mozart, we have to assume that this site is intended to go into formal test and evaluation in the near future, maybe operational in two or three years. If so, Ivan may soon have a laser that can snuff one of our satellites right out of business. Probably a soft kill, the Major says—it'll smoke the camera receptors and the photovoltaic cells. But the next step—"

"Yeah. We're in a race, all right."

"What are the chances that Ritter and the Operations people can find out something inside one of those Bach-site buildings?"

"I suppose we can discuss the possibility," Greer said diffidently, and changed the subject. "You look a little ragged."

Ryan got the message: he didn't need to know what Operations had in mind. He could talk like a normal person now. "All this traveling around has been pretty tiring. If you don't mind, sir, I'd just as soon take the rest of the day off."

"Fair enough. See you tomorrow. But first—Jack? I got a call about you from the Securities and Exchange Commission."

"Oh." Jack bowed his head. "I forgot all about that. They called me right before I flew to Moscow."

"What gives?"

"One of the companies I own stock in, the officers are being investigated for insider trading. I bought some of it right when they did, and SEC wants to know how I decided to buy it just then."

"And?" Greer asked. CIA had had enough scandals, and the Admiral didn't want one in his office.

"I got a tip that it might be an interesting company, and when I checked it out I saw that the company was buying itself back. So what got me to buy in was that I saw they were buying in. That's legal, boss. I have all the records at home. I do all this by computer—well, I *don't* since I came to work here—and I have hard copies of everything. I didn't break any rules, sir, and I can prove it."

"Let's try to settle that in the next few days," Greer suggested.

"Yes, sir."

Jack was in his car five minutes later. The drive home to Peregrine Cliff was easier than usual, taking only fifty minutes instead of the usual seventy-five. Cathy was at work, as usual, and the kids were at school—Sally at St. Mary's and Jack at kindergarten. Ryan poured himself a glass of milk in the kitchen. Finished, he wandered upstairs, kicked off his shoes, and collapsed into bed without even bothering to take off his pants.

Colonel of Signal Troops Gennady Iosifovich Bondarenko sat across from Misha, straight of back and proud, as so young a field-grade officer should be. He did not show himself to be the least intimidated by Colonel Filitov, who was old enough to be his father, and whose background was a minor legend in the Defense Ministry. *So this was the old war-horse who fought in nearly every tank battle in the first two years of the Great Patriotic War.* He saw the toughness around the eyes that age and fatigue could never erase, noted the impairment to the Colonel's arm, and remembered how that had happened. It was said that Old Misha still went out to the tank factories with some of the men from his old regiment, to see for himself if quality control was up to standards, to make certain that his hard blue eyes could still hit a target from the gunner's seat. Bondarenko was somewhat in awe of this soldier's soldier. More than anything else, he was proud to wear the same uniform.

"How may I serve the Colonel?" he asked Misha.

"Your file says that you are very clever with electronic gadgets, Gennady Iosifovich." Filitov waved at the file folder on his desk.

"That is my job, Comrade Colonel." Bondarenko was more than just "clever," and both knew it. He had helped develop laser range-finders for battlefield use, and until recently had been engaged in a project to use lasers in place of radios for secure front-line communications.

"What we are about to discuss is classified Most Secret." The young Colonel nodded gravely and Filitov went on. "For the past several years the Ministry has been financing a very special laser project called Bright Star—the name itself is also classified, of course. Its primary mission is to make high-quality photographs of Western satellites, though when fully developed, it may be able to blind them—at a time when such action is politically necessary. The project is run by academicians and a former fighter pilot from Voyska PVO—this sort of installation comes under the authority of the air-defense forces, unfortunately. I would have preferred myself that a real soldier was running it, but—'' Misha stopped and gestured at the ceiling. Bondarenko smiled in agreement. *Politics*, they both communicated silently. *No wonder we never get anything done.*

"The Minister wants you to fly down there and evaluate the weapons potential of the site, particularly from a reliability standpoint. If we are to bring this site to operational status, it would be well to know if the damned-fool thing will work when we want it to."

The young officer nodded thoughtfully while his mind raced. This was a choice assignment—much more than that. He would report to the Minister through his most trusted aide. If he did well, he would have the personal stamp of the Minister in his personnel jacket. That would guarantee him general's stars, a bigger apartment for his family, a good education for his children, so many of the things he'd worked all these years for.

"Comrade Colonel, I presume that they know of my coming?"

Misha laughed derisively. "Is that the way the Red Army does it now? We *tell* them when they are to be inspected! No, Gennady Iosifovich, if we are to evaluate reliability, we do it by surprise. I have a letter for you here from Marshal Yazov himself. It will be sufficient to get you past security—site security comes under our KGB colleagues," Misha said coolly. "It will give you free access to the entire facility. If you have any difficulty at all, call me at once. I can always be reached through this number. Even if I am in the *banya,* my driver will come and fetch me."

"How detailed an evaluation is required, Comrade Colonel?"

"Enough that a weary old tanker like me can understand what their witchcraft is all about," Misha said humorlessly. "Do you think you can understand it all?"

"If not, I will so inform you, Comrade Colonel." It was a very good answer, Misha noted. Bondarenko would go far.

"Excellent, Gennady Iosifovich. I would much rather have an officer tell me what he does not know than try to impress me with a truckload of *mudnya.*" Bondarenko got that message loud and clear. It was said that the carpet in this office was rust-red from the blood of officers who'd tried to bullshit their way past this man. "How soon can you leave?"

"This is an extensive installation?"

"Yes. It houses four hundred academicians and engineers, and perhaps six hundred other support personnel. You can take up to a week doing your evaluation. Speed here is less important than thoroughness."

"Then I'll have to pack another uniform. I can be on my way in two hours."

"Excellent. Off with you." Misha opened a new file.

As was generally the case, Misha worked a few minutes later than his Minister. He locked his personal documents in secure files and had the rest picked up by a messenger whose cart wheeled them to Central Files a few meters down the main corridor from his office. The same messenger handed over a note saying that Colonel Bondarenko had taken the 1730 Aeroflot flight to Dushanbe, and that ground transport from the civil airport to Bright Star had been arranged. Filitov made a mental note to congratulate Bondarenko for his cleverness. As a member of the Ministry's in-house General Inspectorate, he could have requisitioned special transport and flown directly to the city's military airfield, but the security office at Bright Star undoubtedly had some of its people there to report the arrival of such a flight. This way, however, a colonel from Moscow could just as easily be mistaken for what colonels in Moscow usually were—messenger boys. That fact offended Filitov. A man who had worked hard enough to attain the rank of a regimental commander—which really was the best job in any army—should not be a staff slave who fetched drinks for his general. But he was sure that this was a fact in any military headquarters. At least Bondarenko would have a chance to try out his teeth on the feather merchants down in Tadzhikistan.

Filitov rose and reached for his coat. A moment later, briefcase dangling from his right hand, he walked out of the office. His secretary—a warrant officer—automatically called downstairs for his car to be ready. It was waiting when Misha walked out the front door.

Forty minutes later, Filitov was in soft clothes. The television was on, broadcasting something mindless enough to have been imported from the West. Misha sat alone at his kitchen table. There was an open half-liter bottle of vodka beside his evening meal. Misha ate sausage, black bread, and pickled vegetables, not very different from what he'd eaten in the field with his men, two generations before. He'd found that his stomach dealt more easily with rough foods than the fancy ones, a fact that had thoroughly confused the hospital staff during his last bout of pneumonia. After every other bite, he'd take a brief sip of vodka, staring out the windows, whose blinds were adjusted just so. The city lights of Moscow burned brightly, along with the numberless yellow rectangles of apartment windows.

He could remember the smells at will. The verdant odor of good Russian earth, the fine, green smell of meadow grass, along with the stink of diesel fuel and above all the acidic reek of propellant from the tank's guns that stayed in the cloth of your coveralls no matter how many times you tried to wash it out. For a tanker, that was the smell of combat, that and the uglier smell of burning vehicles, and burning crews. Without looking, he lifted the sausage and cut off a piece, bringing it to his mouth atop the knife. He was staring out the window, but as though it were a television screen, what he saw was the vast, distant horizon at sunset, and columns of smoke rising along the perimeter of green and blue, orange and brown. Next, a bite of the rich, thickly textured black bread. And as always on the nights before he committed treason, the ghosts came back to visit.

We showed them, didn't we, Comrade Captain? a weary voice asked.

We still had to retreat, Corporal, he heard his own voice answer. *But, yes, we showed the bastards not to trifle with our T-34s. This is good bread you stole.*

Stole? But, Comrade Captain, it is heavy work defending these farmers, is it not?

And thirsty work? was the Captain's next question.

Indeed, Comrade. The corporal chuckled. From behind, a bottle was handed down. Not State-produced vodka, this was Samogan, the Russian bootleg liquor that Misha himself knew well. Every true Russian claimed to love the taste, though not one would touch it if vodka was handy. Nevertheless, for this moment Samogan was the drink he craved, out here on Russian soil, with the remains of his tank troop standing between a State farm and the leading elements of Guderian's panzers.

They'll be coming again tomorrow morning, the driver thought soberly.

And we'll kill some more slug-gray tanks, the loader said.

After which, Misha did not say aloud, *we'll withdraw another ten kilometers. Ten kilometers only—if we're lucky again, and if regimental headquarters manages to control things better than they did this afternoon. In either case, this farm will be behind German lines when tomorrow's sun sets. More ground lost.*

It was not a thought on which to dwell. Misha wiped his hands carefully before unbuttoning the pocket on his tunic. It was time to restore his soul.

A delicate one, the corporal observed as he looked over his Captain's shoulder at the photograph for the hundredth time, and as always, with envy. *Delicate like crystal glass. And such a fine son you have. Lucky for you, Comrade Captain, that he has his mother's looks. She is so tiny, your wife, how can she have had such a big boy as that and not be hurt by it?*

God knows, was his unconscious reply. So strange that after a few days of war even the most adamant atheist invoked the name of God. Even a few of the commissars, to the quiet amusement of the troops.

I will come home to you, he'd promised the photograph. *I* will *come home to you. Through all the German Army, through all the fires of hell, I will come home to you, Elena.*

Just then mail had come, a rare-enough occurrence at the front. Only one letter for Captain Filitov, but the texture of the paper and the delicate handwriting told him of its importance. He slit the envelope open with the bright edge of his combat knife and extracted the letter as carefully as his haste allowed so as not to soil the words of his love with grease from his battle tank. Seconds later he leaped to his feet and screamed at the stars in the twilight sky.

I will be a father again in the spring! It must have been that last night on leave, three weeks before this brutal madness began . . .

I am not surprised, the corporal observed lightly, *after the fucking we gave the Germans today. Such a man leads this troop! Perhaps our Captain should stand at stud.*

You are nekulturny, *Corporal Romanov. I am a married man.*

Then perhaps I can stand in the Comrade Captain's stead? he asked hopefully, then handed the bottle down again. *To another fine son, my Captain, and to the health of your beautiful wife.* There were tears of joy in the young man's eyes, along with the grief that came with the knowledge that only the greatest good fortune would ever allow him to be a father. But he would never say such a thing. A fine soldier Romanov was, and a fine comrade, ready for command of his own tank.

And Romanov had gotten his own tank, Misha remembered, staring at the Moscow skyline. At Vyasma, he'd defiantly placed it between his Captain's disabled T-34 and an onrushing German Mark-IV, saving his Captain's life as his own ended in red-orange flames. Aleksey Il'ych Romanov, Corporal of the Red Army, won an Order of the Red Banner that day. Misha wondered if it was fair compensation to his mother for her blue-eyed, freckled son.

The vodka bottle was three-quarters empty now, and as he had so many times, Misha was sobbing, alone at his table.

So many deaths.

Those fools at High Command! Romanov killed at Vyasma. Ivanenko lost outside Moscow. Lieutenant Abashin at Kharkov—Mirka, the handsome young poet, the slight, sensitive young officer who had the heart and balls of a lion, killed leading the fifth counterattack, but clearing the way for Misha to extract what was left of his regiment across the Donets before the hammer fell.

And his Elena, the last victim of all . . . All of them killed not by an external enemy, but by the misguided, indifferent brutality of their own Motherland—

Misha took a long last swallow from the bottle. No, not the Motherland. Not the *Rodina*, never the *Rodina*. By the inhuman bastards who . . .

He rose and staggered toward the bedroom, leaving on the lights in his sitting room. The clock on the nightstand said quarter of ten, and some distant part of Misha's brain took comfort in the fact that he'd get nine hours' sleep to recover from the abuse that he inflicted on what had once been a lean, hard body, one that had endured—even thrived on—the ghastly strain of prolonged combat operations. But the stress Misha endured now made combat seem a vacation, and his subconscious rejoiced in the knowledge that this would soon end, and rest would finally come.

About a half hour later, a car drove down the street. In the passenger's seat, a woman was driving her son home from a hockey game. She looked up and noted that the lights in certain windows were on, and the shades adjusted just so.

The air was thin. Bondarenko arose at 0500, as he always did, put on his sweatsuit, and took the elevator downstairs from his guest quarters on the tenth floor. It took him a moment to be surprised—the elevators were operating. So the technicians travel back and forth to the facility round the clock. *Good*, the Colonel thought.

He walked outside, a towel wrapped around his neck, and checked his watch. He frowned as he began. He had a regular morning routine in Moscow, a measured path around the city blocks. Here he couldn't be sure of the distance, when his five kilometers ended. Well—he shrugged—that was to be expected. He started off heading east. The view, he saw, was breathtaking. The sun would soon rise, earlier than Moscow because of the lower latitude, and the jagged spires of mountains were outlined in red, like dragons' teeth, he smiled to himself. His youngest son liked to draw pictures of dragons.

The flight in had ended spectacularly. The full moon had illuminated the Kara Kum desert flatlands under the aircraft—and then these sandy wastes had ended as though at a wall built by the gods. Within three degrees of longitude, the land had changed from three-hundred-meter lowlands to five-thousand-meter peaks. From his vantage point he could see the glow of Dushanbe, about seventy kilometers to the northwest. Two rivers, Kafirnigan and Surkhandarya, bordered the city of half a million, and like a man halfway around the world, Colonel Bondarenko wondered why it had grown here, what ancient history had caused it to grow between the two mountain-fed rivers. Certainly it seemed an inhospitable place, but perhaps the long caravans of Bactrian camels had rested here, or perhaps it had been a crossroads, or— He stopped his reverie. Bondarenko knew that he was merely putting off his morning exercise. He tied the surgical mask over his mouth and nose as a protection against the frigid air. The Colonel began his deep knee-bends to loosen up, then stretched his legs against the building wall before he started off at an easy, double-time pace.

Immediately he noticed that he was breathing more heavily than usual through the cloth mask over his face. The altitude, of course. Well, that would shorten his run somewhat. The apartment building was already behind him, and he looked to his right, passing what his map of the facility indicated to be machine and optical shops.

"Halt!" a voice called urgently.

Bondarenko growled to himself. He didn't like having his exercise interrupted. Especially, he saw, by someone with the green shoulder boards of the KGB. Spies—thugs—playing at soldiers. "Well, what is it, Sergeant!"

"Your papers, if you please, Comrade. I do not recognize you."

Fortunately, Bondarenko's wife had sewn several pockets onto the Nike jogging suit that she'd managed to get on the gray market in Moscow, a present for his last birthday. He kept his legs pumping as he handed over his identification.

"When did the Comrade Colonel arrive?" the sergeant asked. "And what do you think you are doing so early in the morning?"

"Where is your officer?" Bondarenko replied.

"At the main guard post, four hundred meters that way." The sergeant pointed.

"Then come along with me, Sergeant, and we will speak with him. A colonel of the Soviet Army does not explain himself to sergeants. Come on, you need exercise, too!" he challenged and moved off.

The sergeant was only twenty or so, but wore a heavy greatcoat and carried a rifle and ammo belt. Within two hundred meters, Gennady heard him puffing.

"Here, Comrade Colonel," the young man gasped a minute later.

"You should not smoke so much, Sergeant," Bondarenko observed.

"What the hell is going on here?" a KGB lieutenant asked from behind his desk.

"Your sergeant challenged me. I am Colonel G. I. Bondarenko, and I am doing my morning run."

"In Western clothing?"

"What the hell do you care what clothes I wear when I exercise?" *Idiot, do you think spies jog?*

"Colonel, I am the security watch officer. I do not recognize you, and my superiors have not made me aware of your presence."

Gennady reached into another pocket and handed over his special visitors pass, along with his personal identification papers. "I am a special representative of the Ministry of Defense. The purpose of my visit is not your concern. I am here on the personal authority of Marshal of the Soviet Union D. T. Yazov. If you have any further questions, you may call him directly at that number!"

The KGB Lieutenant scrupulously read the identification documents to make sure they said what he'd been told.

"Please excuse me, Comrade Colonel, but we have orders to take our security provisions seriously. Also, it is out of the ordinary to see a man in Western clothes running at dawn."

"I gather that it is out of the ordinary for your troops to run at all," Bondarenko noted dryly.

"There is hardly room on this mountaintop for a proper regime of physical training, Comrade Colonel."

"Is that so?" Bondarenko smiled as he took out a notebook and pencil. "You claim to take your security duties seriously, but you do not meet norms for physical training of your troops. Thank you for that piece of information, Comrade Lieutenant. I will discuss that matter with your commanding officer. May I go?"

"Technically, I have orders to provide escort for all official visitors."

"Excellent. I like to have company when I run. Will you be so kind as to join me, Comrade Lieutenant?"

The KGB officer was trapped, and knew it. Five minutes later, he was puffing like a landed fish.

"What is your main security threat?" Bondarenko asked him—maliciously, since he did not slow down.

"The Afghan border is one hundred eleven kilometers that way," the Lieutenant said between wheezes. "They have occasionally sent some of their bandit raiders into Soviet territory, as you may have heard."

"Do they make contact with local citizens?"

"Not that we have established, but that is a concern. The local population is largely Muslim." The Lieutenant started coughing. Gennady stopped.

"In air this cold, I have found that wearing a mask helps," he said. "It warms the air somewhat before you breathe it. Straighten up and breathe deeply, Comrade Lieutenant. If you take your security provisions so seriously, you and your men should be in proper physical shape. I promise you that the Afghans are. Two winters ago I spent time with a *Spetznaz* team that chased them over a half dozen miserable mountains. We never did catch them." *But they caught us*, he didn't say. Bondarenko would never forget that ambush . . .

"Helicopters?"

"They cannot always fly in bad weather, my young Comrade, and in my case we were trying to establish that we, too, could fight in the mountains."

"Well, we have patrols out every day, of course."

It was the way he said it that bothered Bondarenko, and the Colonel made a mental note to check that out. "How far have we run?"

"Two kilometers."

"The altitude does make things difficult. Come, we will walk back."

The sunrise was spectacular. The blazing sphere edged above a nameless mountain to the east, and its light marched down the nearer slopes, chasing the shadows into the deep, glacial valleys. This installation was no easy objective, even for the inhuman barbarians of the *mudjaheddin*. The guard towers were well sited, with clear fields of fire that extended for several kilometers. They didn't use searchlights out of consideration for the civilians who lived here, but night-vision devices were a better choice in any case, and he was sure that the KGB troops used those. And—he shrugged—site security wasn't the reason he'd been sent down, though it was a fine excuse to needle the KGB security detail.

"May I ask how you obtained your exercise clothing?" the KGB officer asked when he was able to breathe properly.

"Are you a married man, Comrade Lieutenant?"

"Yes, I am, Comrade Colonel."

"Personally, I do not question my wife on where she buys her birthday presents for me. Of course, I am not a *chekist*." Bondarenko did a few deep knee-bends to show that he was, however, a better man.

"Colonel, while our duties are not quite the same, we both serve the Soviet Union. I am a young, inexperienced officer, as you have already made quite clear. One of the things that disturbs me is the unnecessary rivalry between the Army and the KGB."

Bondarenko turned to look at the Lieutenant. "That was well said, my young Comrade. Perhaps when you wear general's stars, you will remember the sentiment."

He dropped the KGB Lieutenant back at the guard post and walked briskly back to the apartment block, the morning breeze threatening to freeze the sweat on his neck. He went inside and took the elevator up. Not surprisingly, there was no hot water for his shower this early in the morning. The Colonel endured it cold, chasing away the last vestiges of sleep, shaved and dressed before walking over to the canteen for breakfast.

He didn't have to be at the Ministry until nine, and on the way was a steam bath. One of the things Filitov had learned over the years was that nothing could chase away a hangover and clear your head like steam. He'd had enough practice. His sergeant drove him to the Sandunovski Baths on Kuznetskiy Most, six blocks from the Kremlin. It was his usual Wednesday morning stop in any case. He was not alone, even this early. A handful of other probably important people trudged up the wide marble steps to the second floor's first-class (not called that now, of course) facilities, since thousands of Moscovites shared with the Colonel both his disease and its cure. Some of them were women, and Misha wondered if the female facilities were very different from those he was about to use. It was strange. He'd been coming here since he joined the Ministry in 1943, and yet he'd never gotten a peek into the women's section. *Well, I am too old for that now.*

His eyes were bloodshot and heavy as he undressed. Naked, he took a heavy bath towel from the pile at the end of the room, and a handful of birch branches. Filitov breathed the cool, dry air of the dressing room before opening the door that led to the steam rooms. The once-marble floor was largely replaced now with orange tiles. He could remember when the original floor had been nearly intact.

Two men in their fifties were arguing about something, probably politics. He could hear their rasping voices above the hiss of steam coming off the hotbox that occupied the center of the room. Misha counted five other men, their heads stooped over, each of them enduring a hangover in grumpy solitude. He selected a seat in the front row, and sat.

"Good morning, Comrade Colonel," a voice said from five meters away.

"And to you, Comrade Academician," Misha greeted his fellow regular. His hands were wrapped tightly around his bundle of branches while he waited for the sweat to begin. It didn't take long—the room temperature was nearly one hundred forty degrees Fahrenheit. He breathed carefully, as the experienced ones did. The aspirins he'd taken with his morning tea were beginning to work, though his head was still heavy and the sinuses around his eyes swollen. He swatted the branches across his back, as though to exorcize the poisons from his body.

"And how is the Hero of Stalingrad this morning?" the academic persisted.

"About as well as the genius of the Ministry of Education." This drew a painful laugh. Misha never could remember his name . . . Ilya Vladimirovich Somethingorother. What sort of fool could laugh during a hangover? The man drank because of his wife, he said. *You drink to be free of her, do you? You boast of the times you've fucked your secretary, when I would trade my soul for one more look at Elena's face.* And my sons' faces, he told himself. My two handsome sons. It was well to remember these things on such mornings.

"Yesterday's *Pravda* spoke of the arms negotiations," the man persisted. "Is there hope for progress?"

"I have no idea," Misha replied.

An attendant came in. A young man, perhaps twenty-five or so and short. He counted heads in the room.

"Does anyone wish a drink?" he asked. Drinking was absolutely forbidden in the baths, but as any true Russian would say, that merely made the vodka taste better.

"No!" came the reply in chorus. No one was the least interested in the hair of the dog this morning, Misha noted with mild surprise. Well, it was the middle of the week. On a Saturday morning it would be very different.

"Very well," the attendant said on the way out the door. "There will be fresh towels outside, and the pool heater has been repaired. Swimming is also fine exercise, Comrades. Remember to use the muscles that you are now baking, and you will be refreshed all day."

Misha looked up. *So this is the new one.*

"Why do they have to be so damned cheerful?" asked a man in the corner.

"He is cheerful because he is *not* a foolish old drunk!" another answered. That drew a few chuckles.

"Five years ago vodka didn't do this to me. I tell you, quality control is not what it used to be," the first went on.

"Neither is your liver, Comrade!"

"A terrible thing to get old." Misha turned around to see who said that. It was a man barely fifty, whose swollen belly was the color of dead fish and who smoked a cigarette, also in violation of the rules.

"A more terrible thing not to, but you young men have forgotten that!" he said automatically, and wondered why. Heads came up and saw the burn scars on his back and chest. Even those who did not know who Mikhail Semyonovich Filitov was knew that this was not a man to be trifled with. He sat quietly for another ten minutes before leaving.

The attendant was outside the door when he emerged. The Colonel handed over his branches and towel, then walked off to the cold-water showers. Ten minutes later he was a new man, the pain and depression of the vodka gone, and the strain behind him. He dressed quickly and walked downstairs to where his car was waiting. His sergeant noted the change in his stride and wondered what was so curative about roasting yourself like a piece of meat.

The attendant had his own task. On asking again a few minutes later, it turned out that two people in the steam room had changed their minds. He trotted out the building's back door to a small shop whose manager made more money selling drink "on the left" than he did by dry-cleaning. The attendant returned with a half-liter bottle of "Vodka"—it had no brand name as such; the premium Stolichnaya was made for export and the elite—at a little over double the market price. The imposition of sales restrictions on alcohol had begun a whole new—and extremely profitable— part of the city's black market. The attendant had also passed along a small film cassette that his contact had handed over with the birch branches. For his part, the bath attendant was also relieved. This was his only contact. He didn't know the man's name, and had spoken the code phrase with the natural fear that this part of the CIA's Moscow network had long since been compromised by the KGB's counterintelligence department, the dreaded Second Chief Directorate. His life was already forfeit and he knew it. But he had to do something. Ever since his year in Afghanistan, the things he'd seen, and the things he'd been forced to do. He wondered briefly who that scarred old man was, but reminded himself that the man's nature and identity were not his concern.

The dry-cleaning shop catered mainly to foreigners, providing service to reporters, businessmen, and a few diplomats, along with the odd Russian who wished to protect clothing purchased abroad. One of these picked up an English overcoat, paid the three rubles, and left. She walked two blocks to the nearest Metro station, taking the escalator down to catch her train on the Zhdanovsko-Krasnopresnenskaya line, the one marked in purple on the city maps. The train was crowded, and no one could have seen her pass the cassette. In fact, she herself didn't see the face of the man. He in turn made his way off the train at the next station, Pushkinskaya, and crossed over to Gor'kovskaya Station. One more transfer was made ten minutes later, this one to an American who was on his way to the embassy a little late this morning, having stayed long at a diplomatic reception the previous night.

His name was Ed Foley; he was the press attaché at the embassy on Ulitsa Chaykovskogo. He and his wife, Mary Pat, another CIA agent, had been in Moscow for nearly four years, and both were looking forward to putting this grim, gray town behind them once and for all. They had two children, both of whom had been denied hot dogs and ball games long enough.

It wasn't that their tour of duty hadn't been successful. The Russians knew that CIA had a number of husband-wife teams in the field, but the idea that spies would take their children abroad wasn't something that the Soviets could accept easily. There was also the matter of their cover. Ed Foley had been a reporter with the *New York Times* before joining the State Department—because, as he explained it, the money wasn't much different and a police reporter never traveled farther than Attica. His wife stayed home with the children for the most part—though she did substitute-teach when needed at the Anglo-American School at 78 Leninsky Prospekt—often taking them out in the snow. Their older son played on a junior hockey team, and the KGB officers who trailed them around had it written up in their file that Edward Foley II was a pretty good wingman for a seven-year-old. The Soviet government's one real annoyance with the family was the elder Foley's inordinate curiosity about street crime in their capital, which was at its worst a far cry from what he had written about in New York City. But that proved that he was relatively harmless. He was far too obviously inquisitive to be any kind of intelligence officer. They, after all, did everything possible to be inconspicuous.

Foley walked the last few blocks from the Metro station. He nodded politely to the militiaman who guarded the door to the grimly decorous building, then to the Marine sergeant inside before going to his office. It wasn't much. The embassy was officially described in the State Department's USSR Post Report as "cramped and difficult to maintain." The same writer might call the burned-out shell of a South Bronx tenement a "fixer-upper," Foley thought. In the building's last renovation, his office had been remade from a storage room and broom closet into a marginally serviceable cubicle about ten feet square. The broom closet, however, was his private darkroom, and that was why the CIA station had had one of its people in this particular room for over twenty years, though Foley was the first station chief to be housed there.

Only thirty-three, tall but very thin, Foley was an Irishman from Queens whose intellect was mated to an impossibly slow heart rate and a pokerface that had helped him earn his way through Holy Cross. Recruited by CIA in his senior year, he'd spent four years with the *Times* to establish his own personal "legend." He was remembered in the city room as an adequate, if rather lazy reporter who turned out workmanlike copy but never would really go anywhere. His editor hadn't minded losing him to government service, since his departure made room for a youngster from Columbia's School of Journalism with hustle and a real nose for what was happening. The current *Times* correspondent in Moscow had described him to his own colleagues and contacts as a nebbish, and rather a dull one at that, and in doing so gave Foley the most sought-after compliment in the business of espionage: *Him? He's not smart enough to be a spy.* For this and several other reasons, Foley was entrusted with running the Agency's longest-lived, most productive agent-in-place, Colonel Mikhail Semyonovich Filitov, code name CARDINAL. The name itself, of course, was sufficiently secret that only five people within the Agency knew that it meant more than a red-caped churchman with princely diplomatic rank.

Raw CARDINAL information was classified Special Intelligence/Eyes Only-Δ, and there were only six Δ-cleared officials in the entire American government. Every month the code word for the data itself was changed. This month's name was SATIN, for which less than twenty others were cleared. Even under that title, the data was invariably paraphrased and subtly altered before going outside the Δ fraternity.

Foley took the film cassette from his pocket and locked himself in the darkroom. He could go through the developing process drunk and half-asleep. In fact, a few times, he had. Within six minutes, the job was done, and Foley cleaned up after himself. His former editor in New York would have found his neatness in Moscow surprising.

Foley followed procedures that had been unchanged for nearly thirty years. He reviewed the six exposed frames through a magnifying glass of the type used to inspect 35mm slides. He memorized each frame in a few seconds, and began typing a translation on his personal portable typewriter. It was a manual whose well-worn cloth ribbon was too frayed to be of use to anyone, particularly the KGB. Like many reporters, Foley was not a good typist. His pages bore strikeovers and X-outs. The paper was chemically treated, and you couldn't use an eraser on it. It took nearly two hours for him to finish the transcription. When done, he made a final check of the film to guarantee that he hadn't left anything out, nor made any serious grammatical mistakes. Satisfied, but with a tremor that he never quite got over, he crumpled the film into a ball and set it in a metal ashtray, where a wooden kitchen match reduced the only direct evidence of CARDINAL's existence to ashes. He then smoked a cigar to disguise the distinctive smell of burning celluloid. The folded typescript pages went into his pocket, and Foley walked upstairs to the embassy's communications room. Here he drafted an innocuous dispatch to Box 4108, State Department, Washington: "Reference your 29 December. Expense report en route via pouch. Foley. Ends." As press attaché, Foley had to pick up a lot of bar bills for former colleagues who held him in contempt that he didn't bother returning; he had to do quite a few expense reports for the cookie-pushers at Foggy Bottom, and it amused him greatly that his press brethren worked so hard at maintaining his cover for him.

Next he checked with the embassy's courier-in-residence. Though little known, this was one aspect of life at the Moscow post that hadn't changed since the 1930s. There was always a courier to take the bag out, though nowadays he had other duties, too. The courier was also one of four people in the embassy who knew which government agency Foley really worked for. A retired Army warrant officer, he had a DSC and four Purple Hearts for flying casualties out of Vietnam battlefields. When he smiled at people, he did so in the Russian way, with the mouth but almost never the eyes.

"Feel like flying home tonight?"

The man's eyes lit up. "With the Super Bowl this Sunday? You're kidding. Stop by your office around four?"

"Right." Foley closed the door and returned to his office. The courier booked himself on the British Airways 5:40 P.M. flight to Heathrow.

The difference in time zones between Washington and Moscow virtually guaranteed that Foley's messages reached D.C. early in the morning. At six, a CIA employee walked into the State Department mail room and extracted the message forms from a dozen or so boxes, then resumed his drive to Langley. A senior field officer in the Operations Directorate, he was barred from any further overseas duty due to an injury sustained in Budapest—where a street hoodlum had fractured his skull, and been locked up for five years by the irate local police. *If only they'd known,* the agent thought, *they'd have given him a medal.* He delivered the messages to the appropriate offices, and went to his own office.

The message form was lying on Bob Ritter's desk when he got to work at 7:25. Ritter was the Agency's Deputy Director for Operations. His turf, technically known as the Directorate of Operations, included all of the CIA's field officers and all of the foreign citizens they recruited and employed as agents. The message from Moscow—as usual there was more than one, but this one counted the most—was immediately tucked into his personal file cabinet, and he prepared himself for the 8:00 brief, delivered every day by the night-watch officers.

"It's open." Back in Moscow, Foley looked up when the knock came at the door. The courier stepped in.

"The plane leaves in an hour. I have to hustle."

Foley reached into his desk and pulled out what looked like an expensive silver cigarette case. He handed it over, and the courier handled it carefully before tucking it into his breast pocket. The typed pages were folded inside, along with a tiny pyrotechnic charge. If the case were improperly opened, or subjected to a sudden acceleration—like being dropped to a hard floor—the charge would go off and destroy the flash paper inside. It might also set fire to the courier's suit, which explained his care in handling it.

"I should be back Tuesday morning. Anything I can get you, Mr. Foley?"

"I hear there's a new *Far Side* book out . . ." That got a laugh.

"Okay, I'll check. You can pay me when I get back."

"Safe trip, Augie."

One of the embassy's drivers took Augie Giannini to Sheremetyevo Airport, nineteen miles outside of Moscow, where the courier's diplomatic passport enabled him to walk past the security checkpoints and right onto the British Airways plane bound for Heathrow Airport. He rode in the coach section, on the right side of the aircraft. The diplomatic pouch had the window seat, with Giannini in the middle. Flights out of Moscow were rarely crowded, and the seat on his left was also vacant. The Boeing started

rolling on schedule. The Captain announced the time of flight and destination, and the airliner started moving down the runway. The moment it
lifted off Soviet soil, as often happened, the hundred and fifty passengers
applauded. It was something that always amused the courier. Giannini
pulled a paperback from his pocket and started reading. He couldn't drink
on the flight, of course, nor sleep, and he decided to wait for dinner until
his next flight. The stewardess did manage to get a cup of coffee into him,
however.

Three hours later, the 747 thumped down at Heathrow. Again he was
able to clear customs perfunctorily. A man who spent more time in the air
than most commercial pilots, he had access to the first-class waiting rooms
still allowed in most of the world's airports. Here he waited an hour for a
747 bound for Washington's Dulles International.

Over the Atlantic, the courier enjoyed a Pan Am dinner, and a movie
that he hadn't seen before, which happened rarely enough. By the time
he'd finished his book, the plane was swooping into Dulles. The courier
ran his hand over his face and tried to remember what time it was supposed
to be in Washington. Fifteen minutes later he climbed into a nondescript
government Ford that headed southeast. He got into the front seat because
he wanted the extra leg room.

"How was the flight?" the driver asked.

"Same as always: borrr-inggg." On the other hand, it beat flying medevac
missions in the Central Highlands. The government was paying him twenty
grand a year to sit on airplanes and read books, which, combined with his
retirement pay from the Army, gave him a fairly comfortable life. He never
bothered himself wondering what he carried in the diplomatic bag, or in
this metal case in his coat. He figured it was all a waste of time anyway.
The world didn't change very much.

"Got the case?" the man in the back asked.

"Yeah." Giannini took it from his inside pocket and handed it back,
with both hands. The CIA officer in the back took it, using both hands,
and tucked it inside a foam-lined box. The officer was an instructor in the
CIA's Office of Technical Services, part of the Directorate of Science and
Technology. It was an office that covered a lot of bureaucratic ground.
This particular officer was an expert on booby traps and explosive devices
in general. At Langley, he took the elevator to Ritter's office and opened
the cigarette case on the latter's desk, then returned to his own office
without looking at the contents.

Ritter walked to his personal Xerox machine and made several copies
of the flash-paper pages, which were then burned. It was not so much a
security measure as a simple safety precaution. Ritter didn't want a sheaf
of highly flammable material in his personal office. He started reading the
pages even before all the copies were done. As usual, his head started
moving left and right by the end of the first paragraph. The Deputy Director
for Operations walked to his desk and punched the line to the Director's
office.

"You busy? The bird landed."

"Come on over," Judge Arthur Moore replied at once. Nothing was
more important than data from CARDINAL.

Ritter collected Admiral Greer on the way, and the two of them joined
the Director of Central Intelligence in his spacious office.

"You gotta love this guy," Ritter said as he handed the papers out.
"He's conned Yazov into sending a colonel into Bach to do a 'reliability

assessment' of the whole system. This Colonel Bondarenko is supposed to report back on how everything works, in layman's terms, so that the Minister can understand it all and report to the Politburo. Naturally, he detailed Misha to play gofer, so the report goes across his desk first."

"That kid Ryan met—Gregory, I think—wanted us to get a man into Dushanbe," Greer noted with a chuckle. "Ryan told him it was impossible."

"Good," Ritter observed. "Everybody knows what screw-ups the Operations Directorate is." The entire CIA took perverse pride in the fact that only its failure made the news. The Directorate of Operations in particular craved the public assessment that the press constantly awarded them. The foul-ups of the KGB never got the attention that CIA's did, and the public image, so often reinforced, was widely believed even in the Russian intelligence community. It rarely occurred to anyone that the leaks were purposeful.

"I wish," Judge Moore observed soberly, "that somebody would explain to Misha that there are old spies and bold spies, but very few old *and* bold ones."

"He's a very careful man, boss," Ritter pointed out.

"Yeah, I know." The DCI looked down at the pages.

Since the death of Dmitri Fedorovich, it is not the same at the Defense Ministry, the DCI read. *Sometimes I wonder if Marshal Yazov takes these new technological developments seriously enough, but to whom can I report my misgivings? Would KGB believe me? I must order my thoughts. Yes, I must organize my thoughts before I make any accusations. But can I break security rules . . .*

But what choice do I have? If I cannot document my misgivings, who will take me seriously? It is a hard thing to have to break an important rule of security, but the safety of the State supersedes such rules. It must.

As the epic poems of Homer began with the invocation of the Muse, so CARDINAL's messages invariably began like this. The idea had developed in the late 1960s. CARDINAL's messages began as photographs of his personal diary. Russians are inveterate diarists. Each time he began one, it would be as a Slavic *cri de coeur*, his personal worries about the policy decisions made in the Defense Ministry. Sometimes he would express concern with the security on a specific project or the performance of a new tank or aircraft. In each case, the technical merits of a piece of hardware or a policy decision would be examined at length, but always the focus of the document would be a supposed bureaucratic problem within the Ministry. If Filitov's apartment were ever searched, his diary would be easily found, certainly not hidden away as a spy was expected to do, and while he was definitely breaking rules of security, and would certainly be admonished for it, there would at least be a chance that Misha could successfully defend himself. Or, that was the idea.

When I have Bondarenko's report, in another week or two, perhaps I can persuade the Minister that this project is one of truly vital importance to the Motherland, it ended.

"So, it looks like they made a breakthrough on laser power output," Ritter said.

" 'Throughput' is the current term," Greer corrected. "At least that's what Jack tells me. This is not very good news, gentlemen."

"Your usual keen eye for detail, James," Ritter said. "God, what if they get there first?"

"It's not the end of the world. Remember that it'll take ten years to deploy the system even after the concept is validated, and they haven't come close to doing that yet," the DCI pointed out. "The sky is not falling. This could even work to our benefit, couldn't it, James?"

"If Misha can get us a usable description of their breakthrough, yes. In most areas we're further along than they are," the DDI replied. "Ryan will need this for his report."

"He's not cleared for this!" Ritter objected.

"He had a look at Delta information before," Greer noted.

"Once. Only once, and there was a good reason for it—and, yes, he did damned well for an amateur. James, there's nothing here he can use except that we have reason to suspect Ivan has made a power—through-put?—breakthrough, and that Gregory kid already suspects it. Tell Ryan we've confirmed the suspicion through other assets. Judge, you can tell the President yourself that something's up, but it'll have to wait a few weeks. It shouldn't go any farther than that for a while."

"Makes sense to me." The Judge nodded. Greer conceded the point without argument.

There was the temptation to voice the opinion that this was CARDI-NAL's most important mission, but that would have been too dramatic for any of the three senior executives, and besides, CARDINAL had provided CIA with a good deal of important data over the years. Judge Moore reread the report after the others had left. Foley had tagged onto the end that Ryan had literally bumped into CARDINAL after Mary Pat had given him the new assignment—and right in front of Marshal Yazov. Judge Moore shook his head. *What a pair, the Foleys.* And how remarkable that Ryan had, after a fashion, made contact with Colonel Filitov. Moore shook his head. It was a crazy world.

4. Bright Stars and Fast Ships

Jack didn't bother asking which "asset" had confirmed Major Gregory's suspicions. Field operations were something that he struggled—success-fully for the most part—to keep at arm's length. What mattered was that the information was graded as Class-1 for reliability—CIA's newly adopted grading system used numbers 1–5 instead of letters A–E, surely the result of six months' hard work by some deputy-assistant-to educated at Harvard Business School.

"What about specific technical information?"

"I'll let you know when it comes in," Greer replied.

"I got two weeks to deliver, boss," Ryan pointed out. Deadlines were never fun. This was especially true when the document being prepared was for the President's eyes.

"I do seem to recall reading that somewhere or other, Jack," the Admiral noted dryly. "The people at ACDA are calling me every day for the damned thing, too. I think what we'll do is have you run over to brief them in person."

Ryan winced. The whole point of his Special National Intelligence Estimate was to help set the stage for the next session of arms negotiations. The Arms Control and Disarmament Agency needed it also, of course, so that they'd know what to demand and how much they could safely concede. That was quite a bit of additional weight on his shoulders, but as Greer liked to tell him, Ryan did his best work under pressure. Jack wondered if maybe he should screw one up sometime, just to disprove that idea.

"When will I have to go over?"

"I haven't decided yet."

"Can I have a couple of days' warning?"

"We'll see."

Major Gregory was actually at home. This was fairly unusual; even more so, he was taking the day off. But that wasn't his doing. His General had decided that all work and no play were beginning to take their toll on the young man. It hadn't occurred to him that Gregory could work at home as well.

"Don't you ever stop?" Candi asked.

"Well, what are we supposed to do in between?" He smiled up from the keyboard.

The housing development was called Mountain View. It wasn't a rousing bit of originality. In that part of the country the only way not to see mountains was to close your eyes. Gregory had his own personal computer—a very powerful Hewlett-Packard provided by the Project—and occasionally wrote some of his "code" there. He had to be careful about the security classification of his work, of course, though he often joked that he himself wasn't cleared for what he was doing. That was not an unknown situation inside government.

Dr. Candace Long was taller than her fiancé at nearly five-ten, willowy, with short, dark hair. Her teeth were a little crooked because she'd never wanted to suffer through braces, and her glasses were even thicker than Alan's.

She was thin because like many academics she was so enthralled with her work that she often forgot to eat. They'd first met at a seminar for doctoral candidates at Columbia University. She was an expert in optical physics, specifically in adaptive-optics mirrors, a field she'd selected to complement her life-long hobby, astronomy. Living in the New Mexico highlands, she was able to do her own observations on a $5,000 Meade telescope, and, on occasion, to use the instruments at the Project to probe the heavens—because, she pointed out, it was the only effective way to calibrate them. She had little real interest in Alan's obsession with ballistic-missile defense, but she was certain that the instruments they were developing had all kinds of "real" applications in her field of interest.

Neither of them was wearing very much at the moment. Both young people cheerfully characterized themselves as nerds, and as is often the case, they had awakened feelings in one another—feelings that their more attractive college fellows would have not thought possible.

"What are you doing?" she asked.

"It's the misses we had. I think the problem's in the mirror-control code."

"Oh?" It was *her* mirror. "You're sure it's software?"

"Yeah." Alan nodded. "I have the readouts from the Flying Cloud at the office. It was focusing just fine, but it was focusing on the wrong place."

"How long to find it?"

"Couple of weeks." He frowned at the screen, then shut it down. "The hell with it. If the General finds out that I'm doing this, he might never let me back in the door."

"I keep telling you." She wrapped her hands around the back of his neck. He leaned back, resting his head between her breasts. They were rather nice ones, he thought. For Alan Gregory it had been a remarkable discovery, how nice girls were. He'd dated occasionally in high school, but for the most part his life at West Point, then at Stony Brook, had been a monastic existence, devoted to studies and models and laboratories. When he'd met Candi, his initial interest had been in her ideas for configuring mirrors, but over coffee at the Student Union, he'd noticed in a rather clinical way that she was, well, attractive—in addition to being pretty swift with optical physics. The fact that the things they frequently discussed in bed could be understood by less than one percent of the country's population was irrelevant. *They* found it as interesting as the things that they did in bed—or almost so. There was a lot of experimentation to do there, too, and like good scientists, they'd purchased textbooks—that's how they thought of them—to explore all the possibilities. Like any new field of study, they found it exciting.

Gregory reached up to grasp Dr. Long's head, and pulled her face down to his.

"I don't feel like working anymore for a while."

"Isn't it nice to have a day off?"

"Maybe I can arrange one for next week . . ."

Boris Filipovich Morozov got off the bus an hour after sunset. He and fourteen other young engineers and technicians recently assigned to Bright Star—though he didn't even know the project name yet—had been met at the Dushanbe airport by KGB personnel who'd scrupulously checked their identity papers and photographs, and on the bus ride a KGB captain had given them a security lecture serious enough to get anyone's attention. They could not discuss their work with anyone outside their station; they could not write about what they did, and could not tell anyone where they were. Their mailing address was a post-office box in Novosibiirsk—over a thousand miles away. The Captain didn't have to say that their mail would be read by the base security officers. Morozov made a mental note not to seal his envelopes. His family might be worried if they saw that his letters were being opened and resealed. Besides, he had nothing to hide. His security clearance for this posting had taken a mere four months. The KGB officers in Moscow who'd done the background check had found his background beyond reproach, and even the six interviews that he'd gone through had ended on a friendly note.

The KGB Captain finished his lecture on a lighter note as well, describing the social and sport activities at the base, and the time and place for the biweekly Party meetings, which Morozov had every intention of attending as regularly as his work allowed. Housing, the Captain went on, was still a problem. Morozov and the other new arrivals would be placed in the dormitory—the original barracks put up by the construction gangs who'd blasted the installation into the living rock. They would not be crowded, he said, and the barracks had a game room, library, and even a telescope on the roof for astronomical observation; a small astronomy club had just formed. There was hourly bus service to the main residential facility, where there was a cinema, coffee shop, and a beer bar. There were exactly thirty-one unmarried females on the base, the Captain concluded, but one of them was engaged to him, "and any one of you who trifles with her *will be shot!*" That drew laughter. It wasn't very often that you met a KGB officer with a sense of humor.

It was dark when the bus pulled through the gate into the facility, and everyone aboard was tired. Morozov was not terribly disappointed at the housing. All the beds were two-level bunks. He was assigned the top berth in a corner. Signs on the wall demanded silence in the sleeping area, since the workers here worked three shifts around the clock. The young engineer was perfectly content to change his clothes and go to sleep. He was assigned to the Directional Applications Section for a month of project orientation, after which he'd receive a permanent job assignment. He was wondering what "directional applications" meant when he drifted off to sleep.

The nice thing about vans was that lots of people owned them, and the casual observer couldn't see who was inside, Jack thought as the white one pulled into his carport. The driver was CIA, of course, as was the security man in the right seat. He dismounted and surveyed the area for a moment before pulling the side door open. It revealed a familiar face.

"Hello, Marko," Ryan said.

"So, this is house of spy!" Captain First Rank Marko Aleksandrovich Ramius, Soviet Navy (retired), said boisterously. His English was better, but like many Russian émigrés he often forgot to use articles in his speech. "No, house of helmsman!"

Jack smiled and shook his head. "Marko, we can't talk about that."

"Your family does not know?"

"Nobody knows. But you can relax. My family's away."

"Understand." Marko Ramius followed Jack into the house. On his passport, Social Security card, and Virginia driver's license he was now known as Mark Ramsey. Yet another piece of CIA originality, though it made perfect sense; you wanted people to remember their names. He was, Jack saw, a little thinner now that he was eating a less starchy diet. And tan. When they'd first met, at the forward escape trunk of the missile submarine *Red October*, Marko—Mark!—had worn the pasty-white skin of a submarine officer. Now he looked like an ad for Club Med.

"You seem tired," "Mark Ramsey" observed.

"They fly me around a lot. How do you like the Bahamas?"

"You see my tan, yes? White sand, sun, warm every day. Like Cuba when I went there, but nicer people."

"AUTEC, right?" Jack asked.

"Yes, but I cannot discuss this," Marko replied. Both men shared a look. AUTEC—Atlantic Underwater Test and Evaluation Center—was the Navy's submarine test range, where men and ships engaged in exercises called miniwars. What happened there was classified, of course. The Navy was very protective of its submarine operations. So Marko was at work developing tactics for the Navy, doubtless playing the role of a Soviet commander in the war games, lecturing, teaching. Ramius had been known as "the Schoolmaster" in the Soviet Navy. The important things never change.

"How do you like it?"

"Tell this to nobody, but they let me be captain of American submarine for a week—the real Captain he let me do everything, yes? I kill carrier!

Yes! I kill *Forrestal*. They would be proud of me at Red Banner Northern Fleet, yes?"

Jack laughed. "How'd the Navy like that?"

"Captain of submarine and me get very drunk. *Forrestal* Captain angry, but—good sport, yes? He join us next week and we discuss exercise. He learn something, so good for all of us." Ramius paused. "Where is family?"

"Cathy's visiting her father. Joe and I don't get along very well."

"Because you are spy?" Mark/Marko asked.

"Personal reasons. Can I get you a drink?"

"Beer is good," he replied. Ramius looked around while Jack went into the kitchen. The house's cathedral ceiling towered fifteen feet—five meters, he thought—above the lush carpeting. Everything about the house testified to the money spent to make it so. He was frowning when Ryan returned.

"Ryan, I am not fool," he said sternly. "CIA does not pay so good as this."

"Do you know about the stock market?" Ryan asked with a chuckle.

"Yes, some of my money is invested there." All of the officers from *Red October* had enough money salted away that they'd never need to work again.

"Well, I made a lot of money there, and then I decided to quit and do something else."

That was a new thought for Captain Ramius. "You are not—what is word? Greed. You have no more greed?"

"How much money does one man need?" Ryan asked rhetorically. The Captain nodded thoughtfully. "So, I have some questions for you."

"Ah, business." Marko laughed. "This you have not forgotten!"

"In your debriefing, you mentioned that you ran an exercise in which you fired a missile, and then a missile was fired at you."

"Yes, years ago—was 1981 . . . April, yes, it was twenty April. I command Delta-class missile submarine, and we fire two rockets from White Sea, one into Okhotsk Sea, other at Sary Shagan. We test submarine rockets, of course, but also the missile defense radar and counterbattery system—they simulated firing a missile at my submarine."

"You said it failed."

Marko nodded. "Submarine rockets fly perfectly. The Sary Shagan radar work, but too slow to intercept—was computer problem, they say. They say get new computer, last thing I hear. Third part of test almost work."

"The counterfire part. That's the first we heard of it," Ryan noted. "How did they actually run the test?"

"They *not* fire land rocket, of course," Marko said. He held up a finger. "They do this, and you understand nature of test, yes? Soviets are not so stupid as you think. Of course you know that entire Soviet border covered with radar fence. These see rocket launch and compute where submarine is—very easy thing to do. Next they call Strategic Rocket Force Headquarters. Strategic Rocket Force have regiment of old rockets on alert for this. They were ready to shoot back three minutes after detecting my missile on radar." He stopped for a moment. "You not have this in America?"

"No, not that I know of. But our new missiles fire from much farther away."

"Is true, but still good thing for Soviets, you see."

"How reliable is the system?"

That drew a shrug. "Not very. Problem is how alert the people are. In time of—how you say?—time of crisis, yes? In time of crisis, everyone is alert, and system may work some of time. But every time system works, many, many bombs do not explode in Soviet Union. Even one could save hundred thousand citizens. This is important to Soviet leadership. Hundred thousand more slaves to have after war end," he added to show his distaste for the government of his former homeland. "You have nothing like this in America?"

"Not that I have ever heard about," Ryan said truthfully.

Ramius shook his head. "They tell us you do. When we fire our rockets, then we dive deep and race at flank speed, straight line in any direction."

"Right now I'm trying to figure out how interested the Soviet government is in copying our SDI research."

"Interested?" Ramius snorted. "Twenty million Russians died in Great Patriotic War. You think they want to have this happen again? I tell you, Soviets are more intelligent about this than Americans—we have harder lesson, and we learn better. Someday I tell you about my home city after war, destruction of everything. Yes, we have very good lesson in protect *Rodina.*"

That's the other thing to remember about the Russians, Jack reminded himself. It wasn't so much that they had abnormally long memories; they had things in their history that no one would forget. To expect the Soviets to forget their losses in the Second World War was as futile as asking Jews to forget the Holocaust, and just as unreasonable.

So, a little over three years ago, the Russians staged a major ABM exercise against submarine-launched ballistic missiles. The acquisition and tracking radar worked, but the system failed due to a computer problem. That was important. But—

"The reason the computer didn't work well enough—"

"That is all I know. All I can say is was honest test."

"What do you mean?" Jack asked.

"Our first . . . yes, our original orders were to fire from known location. But the orders were changed just as submarine left dock. Eyes-only to Captain, new orders signed by aide to Defense Minister. Was Red Army colonel, I think. Do not remember name. Orders from Minister, but Colonel sign them, yes? He wanted the test to be—how you say?"

"Spontaneous?"

"Yes! Not spontaneous. Real test should be surprise. So my orders sent me to different place and said to shoot at different time. We have general aboard from Voyska PVO, and when see new orders he is banana. Very, very angry, but what kind of test is it without no surprise? American missile submarines do not call on telephone and tell Russians day that they shoot. You either are ready or not ready," Ramius noted.

"We did not know that you were coming," General Pokryshkin noted dryly.

Colonel Bondarenko was careful to keep his face impassive. Despite having written orders from the Defense Minister, and despite belonging to a completely different uniformed service, he was dealing with a general officer with patrons of his own in the Central Committee. But the General, too, had to be wary. Bondarenko was wearing his newest and best-tailored uniform, complete with several rows of ribbons, including two awards for bravery in Afghanistan and the special badge worn by Defense Ministry staff officers.

"Comrade General, I regret whatever inconvenience I have caused you, but I do have my orders."

"Of course," Pokryshkin noted with a broadening smile. He gestured to a silver tray. "Tea?"

"Thank you."

The General poured two cups himself instead of summoning his orderly. "Is that a Red Banner I see? Afghanistan?"

"Yes, Comrade General, I spent some time there."

"And how did you earn it?"

"I was attached to a *Spetznaz* unit as a special observer. We were tracking a small band of bandits. Unfortunately, they were smarter than the unit commander believed, and he allowed us to follow them into an ambush. Half the team was killed or wounded, including the unit commander." *Who earned his death,* Bondarenko thought. "I assumed command and called in help. The bandits withdrew before we could bring major forces to bear, but they did leave eight bodies behind."

"How did a communications expert—"

"I volunteered. We were having difficulties with tactical communications, and I decided to take the situation in hand myself. I am not a real combat soldier, Comrade General, but there are some things you have to see for yourself. That is another concern I have with this post. We are perilously close to the Afghan border, and your security seems . . . not lax, but perhaps overly comfortable."

Pokryshkin nodded agreement. "The security force is KGB, as you have doubtless noted. They report to me, but are not strictly under my orders. For early warning of possible threats, I have an arrangement with Frontal Aviation. Their aerial-reconnaissance school uses the valleys around here as a training area. A classmate of mine at Frunze has arranged coverage of this entire area. If anyone approaches this installation from Afghanistan, it's a long walk, and we'll know about it long before they get here."

Bondarenko noted this with approval. Procurer for wizards or not, Pokryshkin hadn't forgotten everything, as too many general officers tended to do.

"So, Gennady Iosifovich, exactly what are you looking for?" the General asked. The atmosphere was somewhat milder now that both men had established their professionalism.

"The Minister wishes an appraisal of the effectiveness and reliability of your systems."

"Your knowledge of lasers?" Pokryshkin asked with a raised eyebrow.

"I am familiar with the applications side. I was on the team with Academician Goremykin that developed the new laser communications systems."

"Really? We have some of them here."

"I didn't know that," Bondarenko said.

"Yes. We use them in our guard towers, and to link our laboratory facilities with the shops. It's easier than stringing telephone lines, and is more secure. Your invention has proven very useful indeed, Gennady Iosifovich. Well. You know our mission here, of course."

"Yes, Comrade General. How close are you to your goal?"

"We have a major system test coming up in three days."

"Oh?" Bondarenko was very surprised by that.

"We received permission to run it only yesterday. Perhaps the Ministry hasn't been fully informed. Can you stay for it?"

"I wouldn't miss it."

"Excellent." General Pokryshkin rose. "Come, let's go to see my wizards."

The sky was clear and blue, the deeper blue that comes from being above most of the atmosphere. Bondarenko was surprised to see that the General did his own driving in a UAZ-469, the Soviet equivalent of a jeep.

"You do not have to ask, Colonel. I do my own driving because we do not have room up here for unnecessary personnel, and—well, I was a fighter pilot. Why should I trust my life to some beardless boy who barely knows how to shift gears? How do you like our roads?"

Not at all, Bondarenko didn't say as the General speeded down a slope. The road was barely five meters wide, with a precipitous drop on the passenger side of the car.

"You should try this when it's icy!" The General laughed. "We've been lucky on weather lately. Last autumn we had nothing but rain for two weeks. Most unusual here; the monsoon's supposed to drop all the water on India, but the winter has been agreeably dry and clear." He shifted gears as the road bottomed out. A truck was coming from the other direction, and Bondarenko did all he could not to cringe as the jeep's right-side tires spun through rocks at the road's uneven edge. Pokryshkin was having some fun with him, but that was to be expected. The truck swept past with perhaps a meter of clearance, and the General moved back to the center of the blacktopped road. He shifted gears again as they came to an upslope.

"We don't even have room for a proper office here—for me at any rate," Pokryshkin noted. "The academicians have priority."

Bondarenko had seen only one of the guard towers that morning as he ran around the residential facility, and as the jeep climbed the last few meters, the Bright Star test area became visible.

There were three security checkpoints. General Pokryshkin stopped his vehicle and showed his pass at each of them.

"The guard towers?" Bondarenko asked.

"All manned round the clock. It is hard on the *chekisti.* I had to install electric heaters in the towers." The General chuckled. "We have more electrical power here than we know how to use. We originally had guard dogs running between the fences, too, but we had to stop that. Two weeks ago several of them froze to death. I didn't think that would work. We still have a few, but they walk about with the guards. I'd just as soon get rid of them."

"But—"

"More mouths to feed," Pokryshkin explained. "As soon as it snows, we have to bring food in by helicopter. To keep guard dogs happy, they must eat meat. Do you know what it does for camp morale to have dogs on a meat diet when our scientists don't have enough? Dogs aren't worth the trouble. The KGB commander agrees. He's trying to get permission to dispense with them altogether. We have starlight-scopes in all the towers. We can see an intruder long before a dog would smell or hear one."

"How big is your guard force?"

"A reinforced rifle company. One hundred sixteen officers and men, commanded by a lieutenant colonel. There are at least twenty guards on duty round the clock. Half here, half on the other hill. Right here, two men in each of the towers at all times, plus four on roving patrol, and of course the people at the vehicle checkpoints. The area is secure, Colonel.

A full rifle company with heavy weapons on top of this mountain—to be sure, we had a *Spetznaz* team run an assault exercise last October. The umpires ruled them all dead before they got to within four hundred meters of our perimeter. One of them almost was, as a matter of fact. One pink-faced lieutenant damned near fell off the mountain." Pokryshkin turned. "Satisfied?"

"Yes, Comrade General. Please excuse my overly cautious nature."

"You didn't get those pretty ribbons from being a coward," the General observed lightly. "I am always open to new ideas. If you have something to say, my door is never locked."

Bondarenko decided that he was going to like General Pokryshkin. He was far enough from Moscow not to act like an officious ass, and unlike most generals, he evidently didn't see a halo in the mirror when he shaved. Perhaps there was hope for this installation after all. Filitov would be pleased.

"It is like being a mouse, with a hawk in the sky," Abdul observed.

"Then do what a mouse does," the Archer replied evenly. "Stay in the shadows."

He looked up to see the An-26. It was five thousand meters overhead, and the whine of its turbine engines barely reached them. Too far for a missile, which was unfortunate. Other *mudjaheddin* missileers had shot the Antonovs down, but not the Archer. You could kill as many as forty Russians that way. And the Soviets were learning to use the converted transports for ground surveillance. That made life harder on the guerrillas.

The two men were following a narrow path along the side of yet another mountain, and the sun hadn't reached them yet, though most of the valley was fully lit under the cloudless winter sky. The bombed-out ruins of a village lay next to a modest river. Perhaps two hundred people had lived there once, until the high-altitude bombers came. He could see the craters, laid out in uneven lines two or three kilometers in length. The bombs had marched through the valley, and those who had not been killed were gone— to Pakistan—leaving only emptiness behind. No food to be shared with the freedom fighters, no hospitality, not even a mosque in which to pray. Part of the Archer still wondered why war had to be so cruel. It was one thing for men to fight one another; there was honor in that, at times enough to be shared with a worthy enemy. But the Russians didn't fight that way. *And they call us savages . . .*

So much was gone. What he had once been, the hopes for the future he'd once held, all of his former life slipped further away with the passage of every day. It seemed that he only thought of them when asleep now— and when he awoke, the dreams of a peaceful, contented life wafted away from his grasp like the morning mist. But even those dreams were fading away. He could still see his wife's face, and his daughter's, and his son's, but they were like photographs now, flat, lifeless, cruel reminders of times that would not return. But at least they gave his life purpose. When he felt pity for his victims, when he wondered if Allah really approved of what he did—of the things that had sickened him at first—he could close his eyes for a moment and remind himself why the screams of dying Russians were as sweet to his ears as the passionate cries of his wife.

"Going away," Abdul noted.

The Archer turned to look. The sun glinted off the plane's vertical rudder as it passed beyond the far ridges. Even if he'd been atop that rocky edge, the An-26 would have been too high. The Russians weren't fools. They flew no lower than they had to. If he really wanted to get one of those, he'd have to get close to an airfield . . . or perhaps come up with a new tactic. That was a thought. The Archer started ordering the problem in his mind as he walked along the endless rocky path.

"Will it work?" Morozov asked.

"That is the purpose of the test, to see if it works," the senior engineer explained patiently. He remembered when he'd been young and impatient. Morozov had real potential. His documents from the university had shown that clearly enough. The son of a factory worker in Kiev, his intelligence and hard work had won him an appointment at the Soviet Union's most prestigious school, where he had won the highest honors—enough to be excused from military service, which was unusual enough for someone without political connections.

"And this is new optical coating . . ." Morozov looked at the mirror from a distance of only a few centimeters. Both men wore overalls, masks, and gloves so that they would not damage the reflecting surface of the number-four mirror.

"As you have guessed, that is one element of the test." The engineer turned. "Ready!"

"Get clear," a technician called.

They climbed down a ladder fixed to the side of the pillar, then across the gap to the concrete ring that surrounded the hole.

"Pretty deep," he observed.

"Yes, we have to determine how effective our vibration-isolation measures are." The senior man was worried about that. He heard a jeep motor and turned to see the base commander lead another man into the laser building. Another visitor from Moscow, he judged. *How do we ever get work done with all those Party hacks hanging over our shoulders?*

"Have you met General Pokryshkin?" he asked Morozov.

"No. What sort of man is he?"

"I've met worse. Like most people, he thinks the lasers are the important part. Lesson number one, Boris Filipovich: it's the mirrors that are the important part—that and the computers. The lasers are useless unless we can focus their energy on a specific point in space." This lesson told Morozov which part of the project came under this man's authority, but the newly certified engineer already knew the real lesson—the entire system had to work perfectly. One faulty segment would convert the most expensive piece of hardware in the Soviet Union into a collection of curious toys.

5. Eye of the Snake/Face of the Dragon

The converted Boeing 767 had two names. Originally known as the Airborne Optical Adjunct, it was now called Cobra Belle, which at least sounded better. The aircraft was little more than a platform for as large an infrared telescope as could be made to fit in the wide-bodied airliner.

The engineers had cheated somewhat, of course, giving the fuselage an ungainly humpback immediately aft of the flight deck that extended half its length, and the 767 did look rather like a snake that had just swallowed something large enough to choke on.

What was even more remarkable about the aircraft, however, was the lettering on its vertical tail: U.S. ARMY. This fact, which infuriated the Air Force, resulted from unusual prescience or obstinacy on the part of the Army, which even in the 1970s had never shut down its research into ballistic-missile defense, and whose "hobby shop" (as such places were known) had invented the infrared sensors on the AOA.

But it was now part of an Air Force program whose cover-all name was Cobra. It worked in coordination with the Cobra Dane radar at Shemya, and often flew in conjunction with an aircraft called Cobra Ball—a converted 707—because Cobra was the code name for a family of systems aimed at tracking Soviet missiles. The Army was smugly satisfied that the Air Force needed its help, though wary of ongoing attempts to steal its program.

The flight crew went through its checklist casually, since they had plenty of time. They were from Boeing. So far the Army had successfully resisted attempts by the Air Force to get its own people on the flight deck. The copilot, who was ex-Air Force, ran his finger down the paper list of things to do, calling them off in a voice neither excited nor bored while the pilot and flight engineer/navigator pushed the buttons, checked the gauges, and otherwise made their aircraft ready for a safe flight.

The worst part of the mission was the weather on the ground. Shemya, one of the western Aleutians, is a small island, roughly four miles long by two wide, whose highest point is a mere two hundred thirty-eight feet above the slate-gray sea. What passed for average weather in the Aleutians would close most reputable airports, and what they called bad weather here made the Boeing crew wish for Amtrak. It was widely believed on the base that the only reason the Russians sent their ICBM tests to the Sea of Okhotsk was to make life as miserable as possible for the Americans who monitored them. Today the weather was fairly decent. You could see almost to the far end of the runway, where the blue lights were surrounded by little globes of mist. Like most flyers, the pilot preferred daylight, but in winter that was the exception here. He counted his blessings: there was supposed to be a ceiling at about fifteen hundred feet, and it wasn't raining yet. The crosswinds were a problem, too, but the wind never blew where you wanted up here—or more correctly, the people who laid out the runway hadn't known or cared that wind was a factor in flying airplanes.

"Shemya Tower, this is Charlie Bravo, ready to taxi."

"Charlie Bravo, you are cleared to taxi. Winds are two-five-zero at fifteen." The tower didn't have to say that Cobra Belle was number one in line. At the moment, the 767 was the only aircraft on the base. Supposedly in California for equipment tests, it had been rushed here only twenty hours earlier.

"Roger. Charlie Bravo is rolling." Ten minutes later the Boeing started down the runway, to begin what was expected to be yet another routine mission.

Twenty minutes later the AOA reached its cruising altitude of 45,000 feet. The ride was the same smooth glide known by airline passengers, but instead of downing their first drinks and making their dinner selections, the people aboard this aircraft had already unbuckled and gone to work.

There were instruments to activate, computers to recycle, data links to set up, and voice links to check out. The aircraft was equipped with every communications system known to man, and would have had a psychic aboard if that Defense Department program—there was one—had progressed as well as originally hoped. The man commanding it was an artilleryman with a masters in astronomy, of all things, from the University of Texas. His last command had been of a Patriot missile battery in Germany. While most men looked at airplanes and wished to fly them, his interest had always been in shooting them out of the sky. He felt the same way about ballistic missiles, and had helped develop the modification that enabled the Patriot missile to kill other missiles in addition to Soviet aircraft. It also gave him an intimate familiarity with the instruments used to track missiles in flight.

The mission book in the Colonel's hands was a facsimile print-out from the Washington headquarters of the Defense Intelligence Agency (DIA) telling him that in four hours and sixteen minutes the Soviets would conduct a test firing of the SS-25 ICBM. The book didn't say how DIA had obtained that information, though the Colonel knew that it wasn't from reading an ad in *Izvestia*. Cobra Belle's mission was to monitor the firing, intercept all telemetry transmissions from the missile's test instruments, and, most important, to take pictures of the warheads in flight. The data collected would later be analyzed to determine the performance of the missile, and most particularly the accuracy of its warhead delivery, a matter of the greatest interest to Washington.

As mission commander, the Colonel didn't have a great deal to do. His control board was a panel of colored lights that showed the status of various onboard systems. Since the AOA was a fairly new item in the inventory, everything aboard worked reasonably well. Today the only thing currently "down" was a backup data link, and a technician was working to put that back on line while the Colonel sipped his coffee. It was something of an effort for him to look interested while he had nothing in particular to do, but if he started looking bored, it would set a bad example for his people. He reached in the zippered sleeve pocket of his flight suit for a butterscotch candy. These were healthier than the cigarettes he'd smoked as a lieutenant, though not so good for his teeth, the base dentist liked to point out. The Colonel sucked on the candy for five minutes before he decided that he had to do *something*. He unstrapped from his command chair and went to the flight deck forward.

" 'Morning, people." It was now 0004-Lima, or 12:04 A.M., local time.

"Good morning, Colonel," the pilot replied for his crew. "Everything working in back, sir?"

"So far. How's the weather in the patrol area?"

"Solid undercast at twelve-to-fifteen thousand," the navigator answered, holding up a satellite photograph. "Winds three-two-five at thirty knots. Our nav systems check out with the track from Shemya," she added. Ordinarily the 767 operates with a crew of two flight officers. Not this one. Since the Korean Air 007 flight had been shot down by the Soviets, every flight over the Western Pacific was especially careful with its navigation. This was doubly true of Cobra Belle; the Soviets hated all intelligence-gathering platforms. They never went within fifty miles of Soviet territory, nor into the Russian Air Defense Identification Zone, but twice the Soviets had sent fighters to let the AOA know they cared.

"Well, we aren't supposed to get very close," the Colonel observed. He

leaned between the pilot and copilot to look out the windows. Both turbofans were performing well. He would have preferred a four-engined
aircraft for extended over-water flight, but that hadn't been his decision.
The navigator raised an eyebrow at the Colonel's interest and got a pat
on the shoulder by way of apology. It was time to leave.

"Time to observation area?"

"Three hours, seventeen minutes, sir; three hours thirty-nine minutes
to orbit point."

"Guess I have time for a nap," the Colonel said on his way to the door.
He closed it and walked aft, past the telescope assembly to the main cabin.
Why was it that the crews doing the flying now were so damned young?
They probably think I *need* a nap instead of being bored to death.

Forward, the pilot and copilot shared a look. *Old fart doesn't trust us to
fly the goddamned airplane, does he?* They adjusted themselves in their
seats, letting their eyes scan for the blinking lights of other aircraft while
the autopilot controlled the aircraft.

Morozov was dressed like the other scientists in the control room, in a
white laboratory coat adorned with a security pass. He was still going
through orientation, and his assignment to the mirror-control team was
probably temporary, though he was beginning to appreciate just how important this part of the program was. In Moscow, he'd learned how lasers
work, and done some impressive lab work with experimental models, but
he'd never truly appreciated the fact that when the energy came out the
front of the instruments the task had only begun. Besides, Bright Star had
already made its breakthrough in laser power.

"Recycle," the senior engineer said into his headset.

They were testing the system calibration by tracking their mirrors on a
distant star. It didn't even matter which star. They picked one at random
for each test.

"Makes one hell of a telescope, doesn't it?" the engineer noted, looking
at his TV screen.

"You were concerned about the stability of the system. Why?"

"We require a very high degree of accuracy, as you might imagine. We've
never actually tested the complete system. We can track stars easily enough,
but . . ." He shrugged. "This is still a young program, my friend. Just like
you."

"Why don't you use radar to select a satellite and track on that?"

"That's a fine question!" The older man chuckled. "I've asked that
myself. It has to do with arms-control agreements or some such nonsense.
For the moment, they tell us, it is enough that they feed us coordinates of
our targets via landline. We do not have to acquire them ourselves. Rubbish!" he concluded.

Morozov leaned back in his chair to look around. On the other side of
the room, the laser-control team were shuffling about busily, with a flock
of uniformed soldiers behind them whispering to themselves. Next he
checked the clock—sixty-three minutes until the test began. One by one,
the technicians were drifting off to the rest room. He didn't feel the need,
nor did the section chief, who finally pronounced himself satisfied with his
systems, and placed everything on standby.

At 22,300 miles over the Indian Ocean, an American Defense Support
Program satellite hung in geosynchronous orbit over a fixed point on the

Indian Ocean. Its huge cassegrain-focus Schmidt telescope was permanently aimed at the Soviet Union, and its mission was to provide first warning that Russian missiles had been launched at the United States. Its data was downlinked via Alice Springs, Australia, to various installations in the United States. Viewing conditions were excellent at the moment. Almost the entire visible hemisphere of the earth was in darkness, and the cold, wintry ground easily showed the smallest heat source in precise definition.

The technicians who monitored the DSPS in Sunnyvale, California, routinely amused themselves by counting industrial facilities. There was the Lenin Steel Plant at Kazan, and there was the big refinery outside Moscow, and there—

"Heads up," a sergeant announced. "We have an energy bloom at Plesetsk. Looks like one bird lifting off from the ICBM test facility."

The Major who had the duty this night immediately got on the phone to "Crystal Palace," the headquarters of the North American Aerospace Defense Command—NORAD—under Cheyenne Mountain, Colorado, to make sure that they were copying the satellite data. They were, of course.

"That's the missile launch they told us about," he said to himself.

As they watched, the bright image of the missile rocket exhaust started turning to an easterly heading as the ICBM arced over into the ballistic flight path that gave the missile its name. The Major had the characteristics of all Soviet missiles memorized. If this were an SS-25, the first stage would separate right about . . . now.

The screen bloomed bright before their eyes as a fireball six hundred yards in diameter appeared. The orbiting camera did the mechanical equivalent of a blink, altering its sensitivity after its sensors were dazzled by the sudden burst of heat energy. Three seconds later it was able to track on a cloud of heated fragments, curving down to earth.

"Looks like that one blew," the sergeant observed unnecessarily. "Back to the drawing board, Ivan . . ."

"Still haven't licked the second-stage problem," the Major added. He wondered briefly what the problem was, but didn't care all that much. The Soviets had rushed the -25 into production and had already begun deploying them on railcars for mobility, but they were still having problems with the solid-fuel bird. The Major was glad for it. It didn't take a great degree of unreliability in missiles to make their use a very chancy thing. And that uncertainty was still the best guarantee of peace.

"Crystal Palace, we call that test a failure at fifty-seven seconds after launch. Is Cobra Belle up to monitor the test?"

"That's affirmative," the officer on the other end replied. "We'll call them off."

"Right. 'Night, Jeff."

Aboard Cobra Belle, ten minutes later, the mission commander acknowledged the message and cut off the radio channel. He checked his watch and sighed. He didn't feel like heading back to Shemya yet. The Captain in charge of the mission hardware suggested that they could always use the time to calibrate their instruments. The Colonel thought about that one and nodded approval. The aircraft and crew were new enough that everyone needed the practice. The camera system was put in the MTI-mode. A computer that registered all the energy sources the telescope found began to search only for targets that were moving. The technicians on the screens watched as the Moving-Target Indicator rapidly eliminated the stars and began to find a few low-altitude satellites and fragments of orbiting space junk. The camera system was sensitive enough to detect the heat of a human body at a range of one thousand miles, and soon they had their choice of targets. The camera locked on them one by one and made its photographic images in digital code on computer tape. Though mainly a practice drill, this data would automatically be forwarded to NORAD, where it would update the register of information of orbiting objects.

"The power-output breakthrough you've made is breathtaking," Colonel Bondarenko said quietly.

"Yes," General Pokryshkin agreed. "Amazing how that happens, isn't it? One of my wizards notices something and tells another, who tells another, and the third says something that works its way back to the first, and so on. We have the best minds in the country here, and still the discovery process seems about as scientific as stubbing your toe on a chair! That's the odd part. But that's what makes it so exciting. Gennady Iosifovich, this is the most exciting thing I've done since I won my wings! This place will change the world. After thirty years of work, we may have discovered the basis of a system to protect the *Rodina* against enemy missiles."

Bondarenko thought that was an overstatement, but the test would demonstrate just how much of an overstatement. Pokryshkin was the perfect man for this job, however. The former fighter pilot was a genius at directing the efforts of the scientists and engineers, many of whom had egos as large as a battle tank, though far more fragile. When he had to bully, he bullied. When he had to cajole, he cajoled. He was by turns the father, uncle, and brother to all of them. It took a man with a large Russian heart to do that. The Colonel guessed that commanding fighter pilots had been good training for this task, and Pokryshkin must have been a brilliant regimental commander. The balance between pressure and encouragement was so hard to strike, but this man managed it as easily as breathing. Bondarenko was watching how he did it very closely. There were lessons here that he could use in his own career.

The control room was separate from the laser building itself, and too small for the men and equipment it held. There were over a hundred engineers—sixty doctorates in physics—and even those called technicians could have taught the sciences at any university in the Soviet Union. They sat or hovered at their consoles. Most smoked, and the air-conditioning system needed to cool the computers struggled mightily to keep the air clear. Everywhere were digital counters. Most showed the time: Greenwich Mean Time, by which the satellites were tracked; local time; and, of course, Moscow Standard Time. Other counters showed the precise coordinates of the target satellite, Cosmos-1810, which bore the international satellite designator 1986-102A. It had been launched from the Cosmodrome at Tyuratam on December 26, 1986, and was still up because it had failed to deorbit with its film. Telemetry showed that its electrical systems were still functioning, though its orbit was slowly decaying, with a current perigee— the lowest point in its orbit—of one hundred eighty kilometers. It was now approaching perigee, directly over Bright Star.

"Powering up!" the chief engineer called over the intercom headsets. "Final system check."

"Tracking cameras on line," one technician reported. The wall speakers filled the room with his voice. "Cryogen flows nominal."

"Mirror tracking controls in automatic mode," reported the engineer sitting next to Morozov. The young engineer was on the edge of his swivel chair, eyes locked to a television screen that was as yet blank.

"Computer sequencing in automatic," a third said.

Bondarenko sipped at his tea, trying and failing to calm himself. He'd always wanted to be present for a space rocket launch, but never been able to arrange it. This was the same sort of thing. The excitement was overpowering. All around him machines and men were uniting into a single entity to make something happen as one after another announced the readiness of himself and his equipment. Finally:

"All laser systems are fully powered and on-line."

"We are ready to shoot," the chief engineer concluded the litany. All eyes turned to the right side of the building, where the team on the tracking cameras had their instruments trained on a section of the horizon to the northwest. A white dot appeared, coming upward into the black dome of the night sky . . .

"Target acquisition!"

Next to Morozov, the engineer lifted his hands from the control panel to ensure that he wouldn't inadvertently touch a button. The "automatic" light was blinking on and off.

Two hundred meters away, the six mirrors arrayed around the laser building twisted and turned together, coming almost vertical with the ground as they tracked after a target sitting above the jagged, mountainous horizon. On the next knoll over, the four mirrors of the imaging array did the same. Outside, alarm klaxons sounded, and rotating hazard lights warned everyone in the open to turn away from the laser building.

On the TV screen next to the chief engineer's console sat a photograph of Cosmos-1810. As the final assurance against mistakes, he and three others had to make positive visual identification of their target.

"That one's Cosmos-1810," the Captain was telling the Colonel aboard Cobra Belle. "Broken recon bird. Must have had a reentry-motor failure— it didn't come back down when they told it to. It's in degenerating orbit, should have about four more months left. The satellite's still sending routine telemetry data out. Nothing important, far as we can tell, just telling Ivan that it's still up there."

"The solar panels must still be working," the Colonel observed. The heat came from internal power.

"Yeah. I wonder why they didn't just turn it off . . . Anyway, the onboard temperature reads out at, oh, fifteen degrees Celsius or so. Nice cold background to read it against. In sunlight we might not have been able to pick out the difference between onboard and solar heating . . ."

The mirrors in the laser-transmitter array tracked slowly, but the movement was discernible on the six television screens that monitored them. A low-power laser reflected off one mirror, reaching out to find the target . . . In addition to aiming the whole system, it made a high-resolution image on the command console. The identity of the target was now confirmed. The chief engineer turned the key that "enabled" the entire system. Bright Star was now fully out of human hands, controlled wholly by the site's main computer complex.

"There's target lock," Morozov observed to his senior.

The engineer nodded agreement. His range readout was rapidly dropping as the satellite came toward them, circling its way to destruction at 18,000 miles per hour. The image they had was of a slightly oblong blob, white with internal heat against a sky devoid of warmth. It was exactly in the center of the targeting reticle, like a white oval in a gunsight.

They didn't hear anything, of course. The laser building was fully insulated against temperature and sound. Nor did they see anything on ground level. But, watching the television screens in the control building, a hundred men balled hands into fists at the same instant.

"What the hell!" the Captain exclaimed. The image of Cosmos-1810 suddenly went as bright as the sun. The computer instantly adjusted its sensitivity, but for several seconds failed to keep pace with the change in the target's temperature.

"What in hell hit . . . Sir, that can't be internal heat." The Captain punched up a command on his keyboard and got a digital readout of the satellite's apparent temperature. Infrared radiation is a fourth-power function. The heat given off by an object is the *square of the square* of its temperature. "Sir, the target temperature went from fifteen-C to . . . looks like eighteen hundred-C in under two seconds. Still climbing . . . wait, it's dropping—no, it's climbing again. Rate of rise is irregular, almost like . . . Now it's dropping. What in the hell was that?"

To his left, the Colonel started punching buttons on his communications console, activating an encrypted satellite link to Cheyenne Mountain. When he spoke, it was in the matter-of-fact tone that professional soldiers save for only the worst nightmares. The Colonel knew exactly what he'd just seen.

"Crystal Palace, this is Cobra Belle. Stand by to copy a Superflash message."

"Standing by."

"We have a high-energy event. I say again, we are tracking a high-energy event. Cobra Belle declares a Dropshot. Acknowledge." He turned to the Captain, and his face was pale.

At NORAD headquarters, the senior watch officer had quickly to check his memory to remember what a Dropshot was. Two seconds later, a "Jesus" was spoken into his headset. Then: "Cobra Belle, we acknowledge your last. We acknowledge your Dropshot. Stand by while we get moving here. Jesus," he said again, and turned to his deputy. "Transmit a Dropshot Alert to the NMCC and tell them to stand by for hard data. Find Colonel Welch and get him in code here." The watch officer next lifted a phone and punched the code for his ultimate boss, Commander in Chief of North American Aerospace Defense Command, CINC-NORAD.

"Yes," a gruff voice said over the phone.

"General, this is Colonel Henriksen. Cobra Belle has declared a Dropshot Alert. They say they have just seen a high-energy event."

"Have you informed NMCC?"

"Yes, sir, and we're calling Doug Welch in also."

"Do you have their data yet?"

"It'll be ready when you get here."

"Very well, Colonel. I'm on the way. Get a bird up to Shemya to fly that Army guy down."

*   *   *

The Colonel aboard Cobra Belle was now talking to his communications officer, ordering him to send everything they had via digital link to NORAD and Sunnyvale. This was accomplished in under five minutes. Next the mission commander told the flight crew to return to Shemya. They still had enough fuel for two more hours of patrolling, but he figured that nothing else would be happening tonight. What had taken place to this point was enough. The Colonel had just had the privilege of witnessing something that few men in human history ever saw. He had just seen the world change, and unlike most men, he understood the significance of it. It was an honor, he told himself, that he would just as soon have never seen.

"Captain, they got there first." *Dear God.*

Jack Ryan was just about to take the cloverleaf exit off I-495 when his car phone rang.

"Yes?"

"We need you back here."

"Right." The line clicked off. Jack took the exit and stayed in the curb lane, continuing to take another of the sweeping cloverleaf exits back onto the Washington Beltway, and back to CIA. It never failed. He'd taken the afternoon off to meet with the SEC people. It had turned out that the company officers had been cleared of any wrongdoing, and that cleared him, too—or would, if the SEC investigators ever closed their file. He'd hoped to call it a day and drive home. Ryan grumbled as he headed back toward Virginia, wondering what today's crisis was.

Major Gregory and three members of his software team were all standing by a blackboard, diagramming the flow of their mirror-control program package when a sergeant entered the room.

"Major, you're wanted on the phone."

"I'm busy; can it wait?"

"It's General Parks, sir."

"His master's voice," Al Gregory grumbled. He tossed the chalk to the nearest man and walked out of the room. He was on the phone in a minute.

"There's a helicopter on its way to pick you up," the General said without any pleasantries.

"Sir, we're trying to nail down—"

"There'll be a Lear waiting for you at Kirtland. Not enough time to get you here on a commercial bird. You won't need to pack. Get moving, Major!"

"Yessir."

"What went wrong?" Morozov asked. The engineer stared at his console, an angry frown on his face.

"Thermal blooming. Damn! I thought we'd put that one behind us."

Across the room, the low-powered laser system was making another image of the target. The monocolor image was like a close-up black-and-white photograph, though what would have been black was maroon instead. The television technicians made up a split-screen image to compare before and after.

"No holes," Pokryshkin noted sourly.

"So what?" Bondarenko said in surprise. "My God, man, you melted the thing! That looks like it was dipped in a ladle of molten steel." And indeed it did. What had been flat surfaces were now rippled from the intense heat that was still radiating away. The solar cells arrayed on the body of the satellite—which were designed to absorb light energy—appeared to be burned off entirely. On closer inspection, the entire satellite body was distorted from the energy that had blasted it.

Pokryshkin nodded, but his expression hadn't changed. "We were supposed to have chopped a hole right through it. If we can do that, it would look as though a piece of orbiting space junk had impacted the satellite. That's the kind of energy concentration we were looking for."

"But you can now destroy any American satellite you wish!"

"Bright Star wasn't built to destroy satellites, Colonel. We can already do that easily enough."

And Bondarenko got the message. Bright Star had, in fact, been built for that specific purpose, but the power breakthrough that had justified the funding for the installation exceeded expectations by a factor of four, and Pokryshkin wanted to make two leaps at once, to demonstrate an antisatellite capability *and* a system that could be adapted to ballistic-missile defense. This was an ambitious man, though not in the usual sense.

Bondarenko set that aside and thought about what he'd seen. What had gone wrong? It must have been thermal blooming. As the laser beams chopped through the air, they'd transferred a fractional amount of their power as heat in the atmosphere. This had roiled the air, disturbing the optical path, moving the beam on and off the target and also spreading the beam wider than its intended diameter.

But despite that, it had still been powerful enough to melt metal one hundred eighty kilometers away! the Colonel told himself. This was no failure. It was a giant leap toward a wholly new technology.

"Any damage to the system?" the General asked the project director.

"None, otherwise we'd not have gotten the follow-up image. It would appear that our atmospheric-compensation measures are sufficient for the imaging beam but not for the high-power transmission. Half a success, Comrade General."

"Yes." Pokryshkin rubbed his eyes for a moment and spoke more firmly. "Comrades, we have demonstrated great progress tonight, but there is still more work to be done."

"And that's my job," Morozov's neighbor said. "We'll solve this son of a bitch!"

"Do you need another man for your team?"

"It's part mirrors and part computers. How much do you know about those?"

"That is for you to decide. When do we begin?"

"Tomorrow. It'll take twelve hours for the telemetry people to organize their data. I'm going to catch the next bus back to my flat and have a drink. My family is away for another week. Care to join me?"

"What do you think that was?" Abdul asked.

They had just gotten to the top of a ridge when the meteor had appeared. At least, it had looked like a meteor's fiery track across the sky at first. But the thin golden line had hung there, and actually marched upward—very quickly, but it had been discernible.

A thin golden line, the Archer thought. The air itself had glowed. What made the air do that? He forgot where and who he now was for a moment, thinking back to his university days. *Heat* made air do that. Only heat.

When a meteor came down, the friction of its passage . . . but this line could not have been a meteor. Even if the upward stroke had been an illusion—and he wasn't sure of that; eyes could play tricks—the golden line had lasted for nearly five seconds. Perhaps longer, the Archer reflected. Your mind couldn't measure time either. Hmph. He sat down abruptly and pulled out his note pad. The CIA man had given him that and told him to keep a diary of events. A useful thing to do; it hadn't ever occurred to him. He wrote down the time, date, place, and approximate direction. In a few more days he'd be heading back to Pakistan, and perhaps the CIA man would find this interesting.

6. One if by Land

It was dark when he arrived. Gregory's driver came off the George Washington Parkway toward the Pentagon's Mall entrance. The guard raised the gate, allowing the nondescript government Ford—the Pentagon was buying Fords this year—to proceed up the ramp, loop around the handful of parked cars, and drop him off at the steps right behind a shuttle bus. Gregory knew the routine well enough: show the guard the pass, walk through the metal detector, then down the corridor filled with state flags, past the cafeteria, and down the ramp to the shopping arcade lit and decorated in the style of a 12th-century dungeon. In fact, Gregory had played Dungeons and Dragons in high school, and his first trip to the dreary polygon of a building had convinced him that the authors' inspiration had come from this very place.

The Strategic Defense Initiative Office was beneath the Pentagon's shopping concourse (its entrance, in fact, directly under the pastry shop), a space about a thousand feet long that had previously been the bus and taxi stand—before the advent of car bombs had persuaded the nation's defense community that automobiles were not all that fine a thing to have under the E-ring. This portion of the building, therefore, was the newest and most secure office—for the nation's newest and least secure military program. Here Gregory took out his other pass. He showed it to the four people at the security desk, then held it against the wall panel that interrogated its electromagnetic coding and decided that the Major could enter. This took him through a waiting room to double glass doors. He smiled at the receptionist as he went through, then at General Parks's secretary. She nodded back, but was annoyed to be staying so late and was not in a smiling mood.

Neither was Lieutenant General Bill Parks. His spacious office included a desk, a low table for coffee and intimate talks, and a larger conference table. The walls were covered with framed photographs of various space activities, along with numerous models of real and imagined space vehicles . . . and weapons. Parks was usually a genial man. A former test pilot, he'd marched through a career so accomplished that one would expect a bluff-hearty handshaker to have done it. Instead, Parks was an almost monkish person, with a smile that was at once engagingly shy and quietly intense. His many ribbons did not adorn his short-sleeved shirt, only a miniature of his command-pilot's wings. He didn't have to impress people with what he'd done. He could do so with what he was. Parks was one of the brightest people in government, certainly in the top ten, perhaps in the top one. Gregory saw that the General had company tonight.

"We meet again, Major," Ryan said, turning. In his hands was a ring binder of perhaps two hundred pages that he was halfway through.

Gregory came to attention—for Parks—and reported-as-ordered, sir.

"How was the flight?"

"Super. Sir, is the soda machine in the same place? I'm a little dried out."

Parks grinned for half a second. "Go ahead, we're not in that much of a hurry.

"You have to love the kid," the General said after the door closed behind him.

"I wonder if his mom knows what he's doing after school." Ryan chuckled, then turned serious. "He hasn't seen any of this yet, right?"

"No, we didn't have time, and the Colonel from the Cobra Belle won't be here for another five hours."

Jack nodded. That was why the only CIA people here were himself and Art Graham from the satellite unit. Everyone else would get a decent night's sleep while they prepared the full briefing for tomorrow morning. Parks could have skipped it himself and left the work to his senior scientists, but he wasn't that sort of man. The more Ryan saw of Parks, the more he liked him. Parks fulfilled the first definition of a leader. He was a man with a vision—and it was a vision with which Ryan agreed. Here was a senior man in uniform who hated nuclear weapons. That wasn't terribly unusual—people in uniform tend to be rather tidy, and nuclear weapons make for a very untidy world. Quite a few soldiers, sailors, and airmen had swallowed their opinions and built careers around weapons that they hoped would never be used. Parks had spent the last ten years of his career trying to find a way to eliminate them. Jack liked people who tried to swim against the tide. Moral courage was more rare a commodity than the physical kind, a fact as true of the military profession as any other.

Gregory reappeared with a can of Coca-Cola from a machine near the door. Gregory didn't like coffee. It was time for work.

"What gives, sir?"

"We have a videotape from Cobra Belle. They were up to monitor a Soviet ICBM test. Their bird—it was an SS-25—blew, but the mission commander decided to stay up and play with his toys. This is what he saw." The General lifted the remote-control for the VCR and thumbed the Play button.

"That's Cosmos-1810," Art Graham said, handing over a photograph. "It's a recon bird that went bad on them."

"Infrared picture on the TV, right?" Gregory asked, sipping at his Coke. "God!"

What had been a single dot of light blossomed like an exploding star in a science-fiction movie. But this wasn't science fiction. The picture changed as the computerized imaging system fought to keep up with the energy burst. At the bottom of the screen a digital display appeared, showing the apparent temperature of the glowing satellite. In a few seconds the image faded, and again the computer had had to adjust to keep track on the Cosmos.

There was a second or two of static on the screen, then a new image began to form.

"This is ninety minutes old. The satellite went over Hawaii a few orbits later," Graham said. "We have cameras there to eyeball the Russian satellites. Look at the shot I gave you."

" 'Before' and 'After,' right?" Gregory's eyes flicked from one image to another. "Solar panels are gone . . . wow. What's the body of the satellite made of?"

"Aluminum, for the most part," Graham said. "The Russians go in for ruggeder construction than we do. The internal frames may be made of steel, but more likely titanium or magnesium."

"That gives us a top-end figure for the energy transfer," Gregory said. "They killed the bird. They got it hot enough to fry the solar cells right off, and probably enough to disrupt the electrical circuitry inside. What height was it at?"

"One hundred eighty kilometers."

"Sary Shagan or that new place Mr. Ryan showed me?"

"Dushanbe," Jack said. "The new one."

"But the new power lines aren't finished yet."

"Yeah," Graham observed. "They can at least double the power we just saw demonstrated. Or at least they think they can." His voice was that of a man who had just discovered a fatal disease at work on a family member.

"Can I see the first sequence again?" Gregory said. It was almost an order. Jack noted that General Parks carried it out at once.

This continued for another fifteen minutes, with Gregory standing a bare three feet from the television monitor, drinking his Coke and staring at the screen. The last three times, the picture was advanced frame by frame while the young Major took notes at every one. Finally he'd had enough.

"I can have you a power figure in half an hour, but for the moment, I think they've got some problems."

"Blooming," General Parks said.

"And aiming difficulty, sir. At least, it looks like that, too. I need some time to work, and a good calculator. I left mine at work," he admitted sheepishly. There was an empty pouch on his belt, next to his beeper. Graham tossed one over, an expensive Hewlett-Packard programmable.

"What about the power?" Ryan asked.

"I need some time to give you a good number," Gregory said as though to a backward child. "Right now, at least eight times anything we can do. I need a quiet place to work. Can I use the snack room?" he asked Parks. The General nodded, and he left.

"*Eight* times . . ." Art Graham observed. "Christ, they might be able to smoke the DSPS birds. It's for damned sure they can wreck any communications satellite they want. Well, there are ways to protect them . . ."

Ryan felt a little left out. His education was in history and economics, and he hadn't quite learned the language of the physical sciences yet.

"Three years," General Parks breathed as he poured some coffee. "At least three years ahead of us."

"Only in power throughput," Graham said.

Jack looked from one to another, knowing the significance of what they were worried about, but not its substance. Gregory came back in twenty minutes.

"I make their peak power output something between twenty-five and thirty million watts," he announced. "If we assume six lasers in the transmission assembly, that's—well, that's enough, isn't it? It's just a matter of racking enough of them together and directing them at a single target.

"That's the bad news. The good news is, they definitely had blooming problems. They only delivered peak power on target for the first few thousandths of a second. Then it started blooming out on them. Their average power delivery was between seven and nine megawatts. And it looks like they had an aiming problem on top of the blooming. Either the mounts aren't shock-mounted properly or they can't correct for the earth's rotational jitter. Or maybe both. Whatever the actual reason, they have trouble aiming more accurately than three seconds of arc. That means they're only going to accurate plus or minus two hundred forty meters for a geostationary satellite—of course, those targets are pretty stationary, and the movement factor could count either way."

"How's that?" Ryan asked.

"Well, on one hand, if you're hitting a moving target—and low-earth-orbit birds move across the sky pretty fast; something like eight thousand meters per second—there are fourteen hundred meters per degree of arc; so we're tracking a target that's moving about five degrees per second. Okay so far? Thermal blooming means that the laser is giving up a lot of its energy to the atmosphere. If you're tracking across the sky rapidly, you keep having to drill a new hole in the air. But it takes time for the bloom to get real bad—and that helps you. On the other hand, if you've got vibration problems, every time you change your aiming point, you add a new variable into your targeting geometry, and that makes things a lot worse. Shooting at a fairly stationary target, like a communications satellite, you simplify your aiming problem, but you keep shooting up the same thermal bloom until you lose almost all your energy into the air. See what I mean?"

Ryan grunted agreement, though his mind had again reached beyond its limit. He barely understood the language the kid was speaking, and the information Gregory was trying to communicate was in a field that he simply didn't understand. Graham jumped in.

"Are you telling me we don't have to worry about this?"

"No, sir! If you got the power, you can always figure out how to deliver it. Hell, we've already done that. That's the easy part."

"As I told you," the engineer told Morozov, "the problem isn't getting the lasers to put the power out—that's the easy part. The hard part is delivering the energy to the target."

"Your computer cannot correct for—what?"

"It must be a combination of things. We'll be going over that data today. The main thing? Probably the atmospheric-compensation programming. We'd thought that we could adjust the aiming process to eliminate blooming—well, we didn't. Three years of theoretical work went into yesterday's test. My project. And it didn't work." He stared off at the horizon and frowned. The operation on his sick child hadn't quite been successful but, the doctors said, there was still hope.

"So the increase in laser output came from this?" Bondarenko asked.

"Yes. Two of our younger people—he's only thirty-two and she's twenty-eight—came up with a way to increase the diameter of the lasing cavity. What we still need to do, however, is come up with better control of the wiggler magnets," Pokryshkin said.

The Colonel nodded. The whole point of the free-electron laser that both sides were working on was that one could "tune" it much like a radio, choosing the light frequency that one wished to transmit—or that was the theory. As a practical matter, the highest power output was always in about the same frequency range—and it was the wrong one. If they'd been able to put out a slightly different frequency the day before—one that penetrated the atmosphere more efficiently—the thermal blooming might have been reduced by fifty percent or so. But that meant controlling the superconducting magnets better. They were called wigglers because they induced an oscillating magnetic field through the charged electrons in the lasing cavity. Unfortunately, the breakthrough that made the lasing cavity larger had also had an unexpected effect on their ability to control magnetic-field flux. There was no theoretical explanation for this as yet, and the thinking of the senior scientists was that there was a minor, though undiscovered, engineering problem in the magnet design. The senior engineers, of course, said that there was something wrong in the theorists' explanation for what was happening, because *they* knew the magnets worked properly. The arguments that had already rocked the conference rooms were spirited but cordial. A number of very bright people were struggling together to find Truth—the scientific kind that did not depend on human opinion.

Bondarenko's mind reeled at the details even as he scribbled down his notes. He'd thought himself knowledgeable on lasers—he had, after all, helped to design a wholly new application for them—but looking at the work that had been done here, he thought himself a toddling child wandering through a university laboratory and wondering at the pretty lights. The principal breakthrough, he wrote, was in the lasing-cavity design. It allowed the enormous increase in power output, and had been made over a table in the canteen when an engineer and a physicist had jointly stumbled across a piece of Truth. The Colonel smiled to himself. *Pravda* was actually the word they used. "Truth" was the exact translation, and the two young academicians had spoken it so artlessly. Indeed, that was a word that had gained currency at Bright Star, and Bondarenko wondered how much of that was an inside joke of some sort or another. "But is it *pravilno*," they would ask of a fact. "Is it truthful?"

Well, he told himself, one thing was truthful enough. Those two people who'd met to discuss their love life—Bondarenko had already heard the story in greater detail—over a canteen table had combined to make a colossal leap forward in laser power. The rest would come in good time, Bondarenko told himself. It always did.

"So it appears that your main problem is computer control, both of your magnetic flux field and the mirror array."

"Correct, Colonel." Pokryshkin nodded agreement. "And we need some additional funding and support to correct these difficulties. You must tell them in Moscow that the most important work has already been done, and proven to work."

"Comrade General, you have won me over."

"No, Comrade Colonel. You merely have the intelligence to perceive the *truth!*" Both men had a good laugh as they shook hands. Bondarenko couldn't wait for the flight back to Moscow. The time had long passed when a Soviet officer needed to fear at the delivery of bad news, but the delivery of good news was always good for one's career.

"Well, they can't be using adaptive optics," General Parks said. "What I want to know is where their optical coatings came from."

"That's the second time I heard about that one." Ryan stood and walked around the table to get his circulation going. "What's the big deal about the mirror? It's a glass mirror, isn't it?"

"Not glass—can't handle the energy. Right now we're using copper or molybdenum," Gregory said. "A glass mirror has its reflecting surface at the back. This kind of mirror, the reflecting surface is on the front. There's a cooling system on the back."

"Huh?" *You should have taken more science courses at BC, Jack.*

"Light doesn't reflect off the bare metal," Graham said. It seemed to Ryan that he was the only dummy in the room. And he, of course, was the one tapped to write the Special National Intelligence Estimate. "It reflects off an optical coating. For really precise applications—an astronomical telescope, for example—what's on the face of the mirror looks like a skim of gasoline on a puddle."

"Then why use metal at all?" Jack objected. The Major answered.

"You use metal to keep the reflecting surface as cool as possible. We're trying to get away from it, as a matter of fact. Project ADAMANT: Accelerated Development of Advanced Materials and New Technologies Group. We're hoping the next mirror will be made out of diamond."

"*What?*"

"Artificial diamond made from pure Carbon-12—that's an isotopic form of regular carbon, and it's perfect for us. The problem is energy absorption," Gregory went on. "If the surface retains much of the light, the heat energy can blast the coating right off the glass, then the mirror blows apart. I watched a half-meter mirror let go once. Sounded like God snapping His fingers. With C-12 diamond you have a material that's almost a superconductor of heat. It permits increased power density, and a smaller mirror. General Electric just learned how to make gemstone-quality diamond out of Carbon-12. Candi's already working to see how we can make a mirror out of it."

Ryan looked through his thirty pages of notes, then rubbed his eyes.

"Major, with the General's permission, you're coming up to Langley with me. I want you to brief our Science and Technology people, and I want you to see everything we've got on the Soviet project. Okay with you, sir?" Jack asked Parks. The General nodded.

Ryan and Gregory left together. It turned out that you needed a pass to get out of here, too. The guards had changed shifts, but looked at everyone just as seriously. On reaching the parking lot, the Major thought Jack's XJS was "boss." *Do they still say that?* Jack asked himself.

"How does a Marine get to work for the Agency?" Gregory asked as he admired the interior leather. *And where does he get the coin to afford this?*

"They invited me. Before that, I taught history at Annapolis." *Nothing like being the famous Sir John Ryan. Well, I don't suppose they have me listed in any laser textbooks . . .*

"Where'd you go to school?"

"Bachelor's at Boston College, and I got my doctorate right across the river there, at Georgetown."

"You didn't say you were a doctor," the Major observed.

Ryan laughed at that. "Different field, pal. I have a lot of trouble understanding what the hell you're up to, but they stuck me with the job of explaining what it all means to—well, to the people who do the arms negotiations. I've been working with them on the intelligence side for the last six months." This drew a grunt.

"That bunch wants to put me out of business. They want to trade it all away."

"They have their job, too," Jack allowed. "I need your help to persuade them that what you do is important."

"The Russians think it's important."

"Yeah, well, we just saw that, didn't we?"

Bondarenko got off the plane and was agreeably surprised to find an official car waiting for him. It was a Voyska PVO car. General Pokryshkin had called ahead. The working day was over, and the Colonel instructed the driver to take him home. He'd write up his report tomorrow and present it to Colonel Filitov and later, perhaps, brief the Minister himself. He asked himself over a glass of vodka whether Pokryshkin had handled—he didn't know the Western expression "stroked"—him enough to create a false impression. Not enough, he told himself. The General had done quite a job of selling both his program and himself, but this was not mere *pokazhuka*. They hadn't faked the test, and they'd been honest in detailing their problems. All they were asking for was what was really needed. No, Pokryshkin was a man with a mission, willing to put his career—well, if not behind it, then at least alongside it; and that was all anyone could reasonably ask. If he was building his own empire, it was an empire worth building.

The pickup was made in a way that was both unique and routine. The shopping mall was quite ordinary, a roofed-over promenade of ninety-three shops, plus a cluster of five small-screen theaters. There were six shoe stores, and three for jewelry. In keeping with the western location of the place, there was a sporting-goods store that catered to sportsmen, and had a wall full of Winchester Model 70 hunting rifles, something one does not often see in the East. Three up-scale men's clothing establishments dotted the concourse, along with seven for women. One of the latter adjoined the gunshop.

That suited the owner of Eve's Leaves, since the gunshop had an elaborate burglar-alarm system; this, combined with the mall's own security staff, allowed her to maintain a sizable stock of exclusive women's fashions without an overly expensive insurance package. The shop had started shakily enough—the fashions of Paris, Rome, and New York do not translate well west of the Mississippi River, except perhaps along the Pacific Coast—but much of the academic community came from both coasts, and clung to their ways. It didn't take much exposure at the country clubs for Anne Klein II to become a hot item even in the Rocky Mountains.

Ann strolled into the shop. She was a very easy customer to fit, the owner knew. A perfect six, she put the clothing on only to see how it looked. She never needed any alterations, which made life easy on everyone and allowed the owner to discount what she bought by five percent. In addition to being easy to fit, she also spent a lot of her money here, never less than $200 per visit. She was a regular, coming in every six weeks or so. The owner didn't know what she did, though she looked and acted like a doctor. So precise, so careful about everything. Oddly, she paid cash, the other reason for the discount she got, since credit card companies got a percentage of the sales figure in return for a guarantee of payment. This returned the five percent to the owner, and then some. It was a pity, she thought, that all of her customers couldn't be like this. Ann had brown bedroom eyes and hair, the latter shoulder-length and slightly wavy. Willowy, with a petite figure. The other odd thing was that she didn't ever seem to use perfume of any kind; that's what made the owner think she was a doctor. That and the hours she came in—never when it was crowded, as though she were entirely her own boss. That had to be true, and the "doctor" dressed the part. This appealed to the owner. Every time she moved about, you could see the purpose in her stride.

She picked up the skirt and blouse combination, leaving for the dressing rooms in the back. Though the store owner didn't know it, Ann always used the same dressing cubicle. While in there, she unzipped her skirt, unbuttoned her blouse, but before she put the new set on, she reached under the plain wooden shelf that you could sit on and removed a cassette of microfilm that had been taped there the evening before. This went into her purse. Next she dressed and paraded outside to the mirrors.

How can American women wear this garbage? Tania Bisyarina asked her smiling image in the mirror. A captain in Directorate S of the First Chief (also known as the "Foreign") Directorate of the KGB, she reported to Directorate T, which oversees scientific espionage and works in cooperation with the State Committee for Science and Technology. Like Edward Foley, she "ran" a single agent. That agent's code name was Livia.

The cost of the outfit was two hundred seventy-three dollars, and Captain Bisyarina paid in cash. She told herself that she'd have to remember to wear this outfit the next time she came back, even if it did look like rubbish.

"See you soon, Ann," the shop owner called to her. That was the only name by which she was known in Santa Fe. The Captain turned and waved back. The owner was a pleasant-enough woman, for all her stupidity. Like any good intelligence officer, the Captain looked and acted quite ordinary. In the context of this area, that meant dressing in what passed for a moderately fashionable way, driving a decent but not flashy car, and living in a style that denoted comfort short of actual wealth. In this sense, America was an easy target. If you had the right lifestyle, nobody questioned where it came from. Getting across the border had been almost a comic exercise. All the time she'd spent getting her documents and background "legend" exactly right, and all the Border Patrol had done was to have a dog sniff the car for drugs—she'd come in over the Mexican border at El Paso— and wave her through with a smile. *And for that*—she smiled to herself eight months later now—*I actually got excited.*

It took forty minutes for her to drive home, checking as always to be sure that she didn't have anyone following her, and once there she developed the film and made her copies; not quite the same way Foley did, but close enough not to matter. In this case she had photographs of actual government documents. She placed the developed film in a small projector and focused the frame on the white paint of her bedroom wall. Bisyarina had a technical education, one of the reasons for her current assignment, and knew a little about how to evaluate what she'd just received. She was sure it would make her seniors happy.

The next morning she made her drop, and the photographs traveled across the border into Mexico on a tractor-trailer rig belonging to a long-haul concern based in Austin. It was delivering oil-drilling machinery. By the end of the day the photos would be in the Soviet Embassy in Mexico City. The day after that, in Cuba, where they would be placed on an Aeroflot flight direct to Moscow.

7. Catalysts

"So, Colonel, what is your assessment?" Filitov asked.

"Comrade, Bright Star may be the most important program in the Soviet Union," Bondarenko said with conviction. He handed over forty handwritten pages. "Here is the first draft of my report. I did that on the airplane. I'll have a proper copy typed today, but I thought that you'd—"

"You thought correctly. I understand that they ran a test . . ."

"Thirty-six hours ago. I saw the test, and I was allowed to inspect much of the equipment both before and after. I was profoundly impressed with the installation and the people who run it. If I may be permitted, General Pokryshkin is an outstanding officer, and the perfect man for that post. He is decidedly not a careerist, but rather a progressive officer of the finest type. To manage the academics on that hilltop is no easy task—"

Misha grunted agreement. "I know about academicians. Are you telling me he has them organized like a military unit?"

"No, Comrade Colonel, but Pokryshkin has learned how to keep them relatively happy and productive at the same time. There is a sense of . . . a sense of mission at Bright Star that one rarely encounters even in the officer corps. I do not say this lightly, Mikhail Semyonovich. I was most impressed by all aspects of the operation. Perhaps it is the same at the space facilities. I have heard such, but having never been there, I cannot draw the comparison."

"And the systems themselves?"

"Bright Star is not yet a weapon. There are still technical difficulties. Pokryshkin identified and explained them at length to me. For the moment, this is still nothing more than an experimental program, but the most important breakthroughs have been made. In several years, it will be a weapon of enormous potential."

"What of its cost?" Misha asked. That drew a shrug.

"Impossible to estimate. It will be costly, but the expensive part of the program, the research and development phase, is largely completed. The actual production and engineering costs should be less than one might expect—for the weapon itself, that is. I cannot evaluate the costs of the support equipment, the radars, and surveillance satellites. That was not part of my brief in any case." Besides, like soldiers all over the world, he thought in terms of mission, not cost.

"And the system reliability?"

"That will be a problem, but a manageable one. The individual lasers are complex and difficult to maintain. On the other hand, by building more than the site actually needs, we could easily cycle them through a regular maintenance program, and always have the necessary number on-line. In fact, this is the method proposed by the chief project engineer."

"So they've solved the power-output problem, then?"

"My draft report describes that in rough terms. My final paper will be more specific."

Misha allowed himself a smile. "So that even I can understand it?"

"Comrade Colonel," Bondarenko replied seriously, "I know that you have a better understanding of technical matters than you care to admit. The important aspects of the power breakthrough are actually quite simple—in theory, that is. The precise engineering details are rather complex, but can easily be deduced from the redesign of the lasing cavity. As with the first atomic bomb, once the theory is described, the engineering can be worked out."

"Excellent. You can finish your report by tomorrow?"

"Yes, Comrade Colonel."

Misha stood. Bondarenko did the same. "I will read over your preliminary report this afternoon. Get me the complete report tomorrow and I will digest it over the weekend. Next week we will brief the Minister."

Allah's ways were surely mysterious, the Archer thought. As much as he'd wanted to kill a Soviet transport aircraft, all he had to do was return to his home, the river town of Ghazni. It had been only a week since he'd left Pakistan. A local storm had grounded Russian aircraft for the past several days, allowing him to make good time. He arrived with his fresh supplies of missiles and found his chieftain planning an attack on the town's outlying airport. The winter weather was hard on everyone, and the infidels left the outer security posts to Afghan soldiers in the service of the traitorous government in Kabul. What they did not know, however, was that the Major commanding the battalion on perimeter duty worked for the local *mudjaheddin*. The perimeter would be open when the time came, allowing three hundred guerrillas to attack straight into the Soviet camp.

It would be a major assault. The freedom fighters were organized into three companies of one hundred men each. All three were committed to the attack; the chieftain understood the utility of a tactical reserve, but had too much front to cover with too few men. It was a risk, but he and his men had been running risks since 1980. What did one more matter? As usual, the chieftain would be in the place of greatest danger, and the Archer would be nearby. They were heading for the airfield and its hated aircraft from windward. The Soviets would try to fly their craft off at the first sign of trouble, both to get them out of the way and allow them to provide defensive support. The Archer inspected four Mi-24 helicopters through his binoculars, and all had ordnance hanging on their stubby wings. The *mudjaheddin* had but a single mortar with which to damage them on the ground, and because of this the Archer would be slightly behind the assault wave to provide support. There was no time to set up his usual trap, but at night this was not likely to matter.

A hundred yards ahead, the chieftain met at the appointed place with the Major of the Afghan Army. They embraced and praised Allah's name. The prodigal son had returned to the Islamic fold. The Major reported that two of his company commanders were ready to act as planned, but the commander of Three Company remained loyal to the Soviets. A trusted sergeant would kill this officer in a few minutes, allowing that sector to be used for the withdrawal. All around them, men waited in the bone-chilling wind. When the sergeant had accomplished his mission, he'd fire off a flare.

The Soviet Captain and the Afghan Lieutenant were friends, which in reflective moments surprised them both. It helped that the Soviet officer had made a real effort to be respectful of the ways of the local people, and that his Afghan counterpart believed Marxism-Leninism was the way of the future. Anything had to be better than the tribal rivalries and vendettas that had characterized this unhappy country for all of remembered history. Spotted early on as a promising candidate for ideological conversion, he'd been flown to the Soviet Union and shown how good things were there—compared to Afghanistan—especially the public health services. The Lieutenant's father had died fifteen years before of infection from a broken arm, and because he had never found favor with the tribal chief, his only son had not led an idyllic youth.

Together the two men were looking at a map and deciding on patrol activities for the coming week. They had to keep patrolling the area to keep the *mudjaheddin* bandits away. Today the patrols were being handled by Two Company.

A sergeant entered the command bunker with a message form. His face didn't show the surprise he felt at finding two officers there instead of one. He handed the envelope over to the Afghan Lieutenant with his left hand. In his right palm was the hilt of a knife, now held vertically up the baggy sleeve of his Russian-style tunic. He tried to be impassive as the Russian Captain stared at him, and merely watched the officer whose death was his responsibility. Finally the Russian turned away to look out of the bunker's weapon slit. Almost on cue, the Afghan officer tossed the message on the map table and framed his reply.

The Russian turned back abruptly. Something had alerted him, and he knew that something was wrong before he'd had time to wonder why. He watched the sergeant's arm come up in a rapid underhand movement toward his friend's throat. The Soviet Captain dove for his rifle as the Lieutenant threw himself backward to avoid the first lunge. He succeeded only because the sergeant's knife caught in the overly long sleeve of his tunic. Cursing, he freed it and lunged forward, slashing his target across the abdomen. The Lieutenant screamed, but managed to grab the sergeant's wrist before the knife reached his vital organs. The faces of the two men were close enough that each could smell the other's breath. One face was too shocked to be afraid, the other too angry. In the end, the Lieutenant's life was saved by the cloth of an ill-fitting tunic sleeve, as the Soviet flipped the safety off his rifle and fired ten rounds into the assassin's side. The sergeant fell without a sound. The Lieutenant held a bloody hand to his eyes. The Captain shouted the alarm.

The distinctive metallic chatter of the Kalashnikov rifle carried the four hundred meters to where the *mudjaheddin* waited. The same thought rippled through everyone's mind: the plan had been blown. Unfortunately, there was no planned alternative. To their left, the positions of Three Company were suddenly alight with the flashes of gunfire. They were firing at nothing—there were no guerrillas there—but the noise could not help but alert the Russian positions three hundred meters ahead. The chieftain ordered his men forward anyway, supported by nearly two hundred Afghan Army troops for whom the change of side had come as a relief. The additional men did not make as much of a difference as one might expect. These new *mudjaheddin* had no heavy weapons other than a few crew-served machine guns, and the chieftain's single mortar was slow setting up.

The Archer cursed as he watched lights go off at the airfield, three kilometers away. They were replaced with the wiggling dots of flashlights as flight crews raced to their aircraft. A moment later parachute flares began turning night to day. The harsh southeast wind blew them rapidly away, but more kept appearing. There was nothing he could do but activate his launcher. He could see the helicopters . . . and the single An-26 transport. With his left hand the Archer lifted his binoculars and saw the twin-engine, high-wing aircraft sitting there like a sleeping bird in an unprotected nest. A number of people were running to it as well. He turned his glasses back to the helicopter area.

An Mi-24 helicopter lifted off first, struggling with the thin air and howling wind to gain altitude, as mortar rounds began to drop within the airfield perimeter. A phosphorus round fell within a few meters of another Hind, its searing white flash igniting the Mi-24's fuel, and the crew leaped out, one of them aflame. They'd barely gotten clear when the aircraft exploded, taking a second Hind with it. The last one lifted off a moment later, rocking backward and disappearing into the black night, its flying lights off. They'd both be back—the Archer was sure of that—but they'd gotten two on the ground, and that was better than he'd expected.

Everything else, he saw, was going badly. Mortar rounds were falling in front of the assault troops. He saw flashes of guns and explosives. Above the noises came the other sound of the battlefield: the battle cries of warriors and the screams of the wounded. At this distance it was hard to distinguish Russian from Afghan. But that was not his concern.

The Archer didn't need to tell Abdul to scan the sky for the helicopters. He tried using the missile launcher to search for the invisible heat of their engines. He found nothing, and returned his eyes to the one aircraft he could still see. There were mortar rounds falling near the An-26 now, but the flight crew already had the engines turning. In a moment he saw some lateral movement. The Archer gauged the wind and decided that the aircraft would try coming into the wind, then flare left over the safest portion of the perimeter. It would not be easy to climb in this thin air, and when the pilot turned, he'd rob his wings of lift in the quest for speed. The Archer tapped Abdul on the shoulder and began running to the left. He made it a hundred meters when he stopped and looked again for the Soviet transport. It was moving now, through the black showers of dirt, bouncing across the frozen, uneven ground as it accelerated.

The Archer stood to give the missile a better look at the target, and immediately the seeker chirped on finding the hot engines against the cold, moonless night.

"V-One," the copilot shouted over the noise of battle and engines. His eyes were locked on the instruments while the pilot fought to hold the aircraft straight. "V-R—*rotate!*"

The pilot eased back on the yoke. The nose came up, and the An-26 took a final bounce off the hard dirt strip. The copilot instantly retracted the landing gear to reduce drag, allowing the plane to speed up that much quicker. The pilot brought the aircraft into a gentle right turn to avoid what seemed to be the heaviest concentration of ground fire. Once clear, he'd come back to the north for Kabul and safety. Behind him, the navigator wasn't looking at his charts. Rather, he was deploying parachute flares every five seconds. These were not to help the troops on the ground, though they did have that effect. They were to fool ground-launched missiles. The manual said to deploy one every five seconds.

The Archer timed the flares carefully. He could hear the change in the seeker's tone when they fell clear of the aircraft's cargo hatch and ignited. He needed to lock on to the plane's left-side engine and to time his shot carefully if he wanted to hit his target. In his mind he had already measured the point of closest approach—about nine hundred meters—and just before reaching it, the aircraft ejected another flare. A second later, the seeker returned to its normal acquisition tone, and he squeezed the trigger.

As always, it was almost a sexual release when the launcher tube bucked in his hands. The sounds of battle around him vanished as he concentrated on the speeding dot of yellow flame.

The navigator had just released another flare when the Stinger impacted on the left-side engine. His first thought was one of outrage—the manual was wrong! The flight engineer had no such thoughts. Automatically, he punched the "emergency-kill" switch to the number-one turbine. That shut down the fuel flow, cut off all electrical power, feathered the propeller, and activated the fire extinguisher. The pilot pushed the rudder pedal to compensate for left yaw induced by the loss of portside power and pushed the nose down. That was a dangerous call, but he had to measure speed against altitude, and he decided that he needed speed most of all. The engineer reported that the left-side fuel tank was punctured, but it was only a hundred kilometers to Kabul. What came next was worse:

"Fire warning light on number one!"

"Pull the bottle!"

"Already done! Everything's off."

The pilot resisted the temptation to look around. He was only a hundred meters above the ground now, and couldn't allow anything to interfere with his concentration. His peripheral vision caught a flash of yellow-orange flame, but he shut it out. His eyes went from the horizon to his airspeed and altimeter and back again.

"Losing altitude," the copilot reported.

"Ten degrees more flaps," the pilot ordered. He reckoned that he had enough speed now to risk it. The copilot reached down to deploy them ten degrees farther, and so doomed the aircraft and its passengers.

The missile explosion had damaged the hydraulic lines to the left-side flaps. The increased pressure needed to change the setting ruptured both the lines, and the flaps on the left wing retracted without warning. The loss of left-lift nearly snap-rolled the aircraft, but the pilot caught it and leveled out. Too many things were going wrong at once. The aircraft started sinking, and the pilot screamed for more power, knowing that the right-side engine was already firewalled. He prayed that getting into the ground effect might save his bird, but just holding her straight was nearly impossible, and he realized that they were sinking too fast in the thin air. He had to put her down. At the last moment the pilot switched on his landing lights to find a flat spot. He saw only a field of rocks, and used his last vestige of control to aim his falling bird between the two biggest. A second before the aircraft hit the ground he snarled a curse, not a cry of despair, but one of rage.

For a moment the Archer thought that the aircraft might escape. The flash of the missile was unmistakable, but for several seconds there was nothing. Then came the trailing tongue of flame that told him that his target was fatally injured. Thirty seconds after that, there was an explosion on the ground, perhaps ten kilometers away, not far from the planned escape route. He'd be able to see what he'd done before dawn. But he turned back now, hearing the sputtering whine of a helicopter overhead. Abdul had already discarded the old launch tube and attached the acquisition/

guidance package to a new tube with a speed that would have done a trained soldier proud. He handed the unit over, and the Archer searched the skies for yet another target.

Though he didn't know it, the attack on Ghazni was falling apart. The Soviet commander had reacted instantly to the sound of gunfire—the Afghan Army Three Company was still shooting at nothing at all, and the Soviet officer there couldn't get things going right—and gotten his men into their positions in a matter of two hectic minutes. The Afghans now faced a fully alerted battalion of regular troops, supported by heavy weapons and hidden in protective bunkers. Withering machine-gun fire halted the attack wave two hundred meters from the Soviet positions. The chieftain and the defecting Major tried to get things going again by personal example. A ferocious war cry echoed down the line, but the chieftain stood directly into a line of tracers that transfixed him for nearly a second before he was thrown aside like a child's toy. As generally happens with primitive troops, the loss of their leader broke the heart of the attack. Word spread throughout the line almost before the radio call was received by the unit leaders. At once, the *mudjaheddin* disengaged, firing their weapons wildly as they pulled back. The Soviet commander recognized this for what it was, but did not pursue. He had helicopters for that.

The Archer knew something was wrong when the Russian mortars started deploying flares in a different place. Already a helicopter was firing rockets and machine guns at the guerrillas, but he couldn't lock on to it. Next he heard the shouts of his comrades. Not the reckless howls of the advance, they were the warning cries of men in retreat. He settled down and concentrated on his weapon. His services would really be needed now. The Archer ordered Abdul to attach his spare seeker unit to another missile tube. The teenager had it done in under a minute.

"There!" Abdul said. "To the right."

"I see it." A series of linear flashes appeared in the sky. A Hind was firing its rocket pods. He trained his launcher on the spot and was rewarded with the acquisition sound. He didn't know the range—one cannot judge distances at night—but he'd have to risk it. The Archer waited until the sound was completely steady and fired off his second Stinger of the night.

The pilot of the Hind saw this one. He'd been hovering a hundred meters above the burning parachute flares, and pushed his collective control all the way down to dive among them. It worked. The missile lost lock and ran straight at one, missing the helicopter by a bare thirty meters. The pilot immediately pivoted his aircraft and ordered his gunner to salvo ten rockets back down the missile's flight path.

The Archer fell to the ground behind the boulder he'd selected for his perch. The rockets all fell within a hundred meters of his position. So it was man against man this time . . . and this pilot was a clever one. He reached for the second launcher. The Archer regularly prayed for this situation.

But the helicopter was gone now. Where would he be?

The pilot swept to leeward, using the wind, as he'd been taught, to mask his rotor noise. He called in for flares on this side of the perimeter and got a response almost instantly. The Soviets wanted every missile-shooter they could get. While the other airborne helicopter pounded the retreating *mudjaheddin*, this one would track down their SAM support. Despite the danger involved, it was a mission for which the pilot lusted. The missileers were his personal enemy. He kept clear of the known range of the Stinger and waited for the flares to light the ground.

The Archer was again using his seeker to search for the helicopter. It was an inefficient way to search, but the Mi-24 would be somewhere in an arc that his knowledge of Soviet tactics could easily predict. Twice he got chirps and lost them as the helicopter danced left and right, altering altitude in a conscious effort to make the Archer's job impossible. This was truly a skilled enemy, the guerrilla told himself. His death would be all the more satisfying. Flares were dotting the sky above him, but he knew that the flickering light made for poor viewing conditions as long as he kept still.

"I see movement," the Hind's gunner reported. "Ten o'clock."

"Wrong place," the pilot said. He brought his cyclic control to the right and slid horizontally as his eyes searched the ground. The Soviets had captured several of the American Stingers, and had tested them exhaustively to determine their speed, range, and sensitivity. He figured himself to be at least three hundred meters beyond its range, and if fired upon, he'd use the missile's track to fix his target, then rush in to get the missileer before he could shoot again.

"Get a smoke rocket," the Archer said.

Abdul had only one of those. It was a small, finned plastic device, little more than a toy. It had been developed for the training of U.S. Air Force pilots, to simulate the feel—the terror—of having missiles shot at them. At a cost of six dollars, all it could do was fly in a fairly straight line for a few seconds while leaving a trail of smoke. They'd been given to the *mudjaheddin* merely as a means to scare Soviet flyers when their SAMs had run out, but the Archer had found a real use for them. Abdul ran a hundred meters and set it up on the simple steel-wire launcher. He came back to his master's side, trailing the launching wire behind him.

"Now, Russian, where are you?" the Archer asked the night.

"Something to our front, something moved, I am sure of it," the gunner said.

"Let's see." The pilot activated his own controls and fired two rockets. They hit the ground two kilometers away, well to the Archer's right.

"Now!" the Archer shouted. He'd seen where the Russian had launched from, and had his seeker on the spot. The infrared receiver began chirping.

The pilot cringed as he saw the moving flame of a rocket, but before he could maneuver, it was clear that the missile would miss him. It had been launched close to where he'd fired before.

"I have you now!" he shouted. The gunner started pouring machine-gun fire at the spot.

The Archer saw the tracers and heard the bullets sprinkling the ground to his right. This one was good. His aim was nearly perfect, but in firing his own guns, he gave the Archer a perfect point of aim. And the third Stinger was launched.

"Two of them!" the gunner shouted over the intercom.

The pilot was already diving and veering, but he had no flares around him this time. The Stinger exploded against a rotor blade and the helicopter fell like a stone. The pilot managed to slow his descent, but still hit the ground hard. Miraculously there was no fire. A moment later armed men appeared at his window. One, the pilot saw, was a Russian captain.

"Are you all right, Comrade?"

"My back," the pilot gasped.

The Archer was already moving. He had tested Allah's favor enough for one night. The two-man missile team left the empty launcher tubes behind and ran to catch up with the retreating guerrillas. If the Soviet troops had pursued, they might have caught them. As it was, their commander kept them in place, and the sole surviving helicopter was content to circle the encampment. Half an hour later he learned that his chieftain was dead. The morning would bring Soviet aircraft to catch them in the open, and the guerrillas had to reach the rockfields quickly. But there was one more thing to do. The Archer took Abdul and three men to find the transport that he'd killed. The price of the Stinger missiles was the inspection of every downed aircraft for items in which the CIA might have interest.

Colonel Filitov finished the diary entry. As Bondarenko had pointed out, his knowledge of technical material was far better than one might suspect from his academic credentials. After over forty years in the higher echelons of the Defense Ministry, Misha was self-taught in a number of technical fields ranging from gas-protection suits to communications-encryption equipment to . . . lasers. Which was to say that while he didn't always comprehend the theory as well as he might have wished, he could describe the working equipment as well as the engineers who assembled it. It had taken four hours to transcribe it all into his diary. This data had to go out. The implications were too frightening.

The problem with a strategic-defense system was simply that no weapon had ever been "offensive" or "defensive" in and of itself. The nature of any weapon, like the beauty of any woman, lay in the eye of the beholder— or the direction in which it was pointed—and throughout history, success in warfare was determined by the proper balance of offensive and defensive elements.

Soviet nuclear strategy, Misha thought to himself, made far more sense than that of the West. Russian strategists did not consider nuclear war unthinkable. They were taught to be pragmatic: The problem, while complex, did have a solution—while not a perfect one, unlike many Western thinkers they acknowledged that they lived in an imperfect world. Soviet strategy since the Cuban Missile Crisis of 1962—the event had killed Filitov's recruiter, Colonel Oleg Penkovskiy—was based on a simple phrase: "Damage Limitation." The problem wasn't destroying one's enemy with nuclear weapons. With nuclear weapons, it was more a question of *not* destroying so much that there would be nothing left with which to negotiate the "war-termination" phase. The problem that occupied Soviet minds was preventing enemy nuclear weapons from destroying the Soviet Union. With twenty million dead in *each* of two world wars, the Russians had tasted enough destruction, and craved no more.

This task was not viewed as an easy one, but the reason for its necessity was as much political as technical. Marxism-Leninism casts history as a process: not a mere collection of past events, but a scientific expression of man's social evolution that will—must—culminate in mankind's collective recognition that Marxism-Leninism is the ideal form for all human society. A committed Marxist, therefore, believed in the ultimate ascendancy of his creed as surely as Christian, Jew, and Muslim believed in an afterlife. And just as religious communities throughout history have shown a willingness to spread their good news with fire and sword, so it was the duty of the Marxist to make his vision a reality as quickly as possible.

The difficulty here, of course, was that not everyone in the world had the Marxist-Leninist view of history. Communist doctrine explained this away as the reactionary forces of imperialism, capitalism, the bourgeoisie, and the rest of their pantheon of enemies, whose resistance was predictable—but whose *tactics* were not. As a gambler who has rigged his gaming table, the communists "knew" that they would win, but like a gambler, in their darker moments they reluctantly admitted that luck—or more scientifically, random chance—could alter their equation. In lacking the proper scientific outlook, the Western democracies also lacked a common ethos, and that made them unpredictable.

More than any other reason, that was why the East feared the West. Ever since Lenin had assumed control of—and renamed—the Soviet Union, the communist government had invested billions in spying on the West. As with all intelligence functions, its prime purpose was to predict what the West would and could do.

But despite countless tactical successes, the fundamental problem remained: Time and again the Soviet government had gravely misread Western actions and intentions; and in a nuclear age unpredictability could mean that an unbalanced American leader—and, to a lesser extent, English or French—could even spell the end of the Soviet Union and the postponement of World Socialism for generations. (To a Russian, the former was more grave, since no ethnic Russian wanted to see the world brought to Socialism under Chinese leadership.) The Western nuclear arsenal was the greatest threat to Marxism-Leninism; countering that arsenal was the prime task of the Soviet military. But unlike the West, the Soviets did not see the prevention of its use as simply the prevention of war. Since the Soviets viewed the West as politically unpredictable, they felt that they could not depend on deterring it. They needed to be able to eliminate, or at least degrade, the Western nuclear arsenal if a crisis threatened to go beyond the point of mere words.

Their nuclear arsenal was designed with precisely this task in mind. Killing cities and their millions of inhabitants would always be a simple exercise. Killing the missiles that their countries owned was not. To kill the American missiles had meant developing several generations of highly accurate—and hugely expensive—rockets like the SS-18, whose sole mission was to reduce America's Minuteman missile squadrons to glowing dust, along with the submarine and bomber bases. All but the last were to be found well distant from population centers; consequently, a strike aimed at disarming the West might be carried off without necessarily resulting in world holocaust. At the same time, the Americans did not have enough really accurate warheads to make the same threat against the Soviet missile force. The Russians, then, had an advantage in a potential "counterforce" attack—the sort aimed at weapons rather than people.

The shortcoming was naval. More than half of the American warheads were deployed on nuclear submarines. The U.S. Navy thought that its missile submarines had never been tracked by their Soviet counterparts. That was incorrect. They had been tracked exactly three times in twenty-seven years, and then never more than four hours. Despite a generation of work by the Soviet Navy, no one predicted that this mission would ever be accomplished. The Americans admitted that *they* couldn't track their own "boomers," as the missile submarines were known. On the other hand, the Americans *could* track Soviet missile submarines, and for this reason the Soviets had never placed more than a fraction of their warheads at sea, and until recently neither side could base accurate counterforce weapons in submarines.

But the game was changing yet again. The Americans had fabricated another technical miracle. Their submarine-launched weapons would soon be Trident D-5 missiles with a hard-target-kill capability. This threatened Soviet strategy with a mirror-image of its own potential, though a crucial element of the system was the Global Positioning Satellites, without which the American submarines would be unable to determine their own locations accurately enough for their weapons to kill hardened targets. The twisted logic of the nuclear balance was again turning on itself—as it had to do at least once per generation.

It had been recognized early on that missiles were offensive weapons with a defensive mission, that the ability to destroy the opponent was the classical formula both to prevent war and achieve one's goals in peace. The fact that such power, accrued to both sides, had transformed the historically proven formula of unilateral intimidation into bilateral deterrence, however, made that solution unpalatable.

Nuclear Deterrence: preventing war by the threat of mutual holocaust. Both sides told the other in substance, *If you kill our helpless civilians, we will kill yours.* Defense was no longer protection of one's own society, but the threat of senseless violence against another. Misha grimaced. No tribe of savages had ever formulated such an idea—even the most uncivilized barbarians were too advanced for such a thing, but that was precisely what the world's most advanced peoples had decided—or stumbled—upon. Although deterrence could be said to work, it meant that the Soviet Union—and the West—lived under a threat with more than one trigger. No one thought that situation satisfactory, but the Soviets had made what they considered the best of a bad bargain by designing a strategic arsenal that could largely disarm the other side if a world crisis demanded it. In achieving the ability to eliminate much of the American arsenal, they had the advantage of dictating how a nuclear war would be fought; in classical terms that was the first step toward victory, and in the Soviet view, Western denial that "victory" was a possibility in a nuclear war was the first step toward Western defeat. Theorists on both sides had always recognized the unsatisfactory nature of the entire nuclear issue, however, and quietly worked to deal with it in other ways.

As early as the 1950s, both America and the Soviet Union had begun research in ballistic-missile defense, the latter at Sary Shagan in southwestern Siberia. A workable Soviet system had almost been deployed in the late 1960s, but the advent of MIRVs had utterly invalidated the work of fifteen years—perversely, for both sides. The struggle for ascendancy between offensive and defensive systems always tended to the former.

But no longer. Laser weapons and other high-energy-projection systems, mated to the power of computers, were a quantum jump into a new strategic realm. A workable defense, Bondarenko's report told Colonel Filitov, was now a real possibility. And what did that mean?

It meant that the nuclear equation was destined to return to the classic balance of offense *and* defense, that both elements could now be made part of a single strategy. The professional soldiers found this a more satisfying system in the abstract—what man wishes to think of himself as the greatest murderer in history?—but now tactical possibilities were raising their ugly heads. Advantage and disadvantage; move and countermove. An *American* strategic-defense system could negate all of Soviet nuclear posture. If the Americans could prevent the SS-18s from taking out their land-based missiles, then the disarming first strike that the Soviets depended upon to limit damage to the *Rodina* was no longer possible. And that meant that all of the billions that had been sunk into ballistic-missile production were now as surely wasted as though the money had been dumped into the sea.

But there was more. Just as the *scutum* of the Roman legionnaire was seen by his barbarian opponent as a weapon that enabled him to stab with impunity, so today SDI could be seen as a shield from behind which an enemy could first launch his own disarming first strike, then use his defenses to reduce or even eliminate the effect of the resulting retaliatory strike.

This view, of course, was simplistic. No system would ever be foolproof—and even if the system worked, Misha knew, the political leaders would find a way to use it to its greatest *dis*advantage; you could always depend on politicians for that. A workable strategic defense scheme would have the effect of adding a new element of uncertainty to the equation. It was unlikely that any country could eliminate all incoming warheads, and the death of as "few" as twenty million citizens was too ghastly a thing to contemplate, even for the Soviet leadership. But even a rudimentary SDI system might kill enough warheads to invalidate the whole idea of counterforce.

If the Soviets had such a system first, the meager American counterforce arsenal could be countered more easily than the Soviet one, and the strategic situation for which the Soviets had worked thirty years would remain in place. The Soviet government would have the best of both worlds, a far larger force of accurate missiles with which to eliminate American warheads, and a shield to kill most of the retaliatory strike against their reserve missile fields—and the American sea-based systems could be neutralized by elimination of their GPS navigation satellites, without which they could still kill cities, but the ability to attack missile silos would be irretrievably gone.

The scenario Colonel Mikhail Semyonovich Filitov envisaged was the standard Soviet case study. Some crisis erupted (the Middle East was the favorite, since nobody could predict what would happen there), and while Moscow moved to stabilize matters, the West interfered—clumsily and stupidly, of course—and started talking openly in the press about a nuclear confrontation. The intelligence organs would flash word to Moscow that a nuclear strike was a real possibility. Strategic Rocket Force's SS-18 regiments would secretly go to full alert, as would the new ground-based laser weapons. While the Foreign Ministry airheads—no military force is enamored of its diplomatic colleagues—struggled to settle things down, the West would posture and threaten, perhaps attacking a Soviet naval force to show its resolve, certainly mobilizing the NATO armies to threaten invasion of Eastern Europe. Worldwide panic would begin in earnest. When the tone of Western rhetoric reached its culmination, the launch orders would be issued to the missile force, and 300 SS-18s would launch, allocating three warheads to each of the American Minuteman silos. Smaller weapons would go after the submarine and bomber bases to limit collateral casualties as much as possible—the Soviets had no wish to exacerbate the situation more than necessary. Simultaneously, the lasers would disable as many American reconnaissance and navigation satellites as possible but leave the communications satellites intact—a gamble calculated to show "good" intent. The Americans would not be able to respond to the attack before the Soviet warheads struck. (Misha worried about this, but information from KGB and GRU said that there were serious flaws in the American command-and-control system, plus the psychological factors involved.) Probably the Americans would keep their submarine weapons in reserve and launch their surviving Minutemen at Soviet missile silos, but it was expected that no more than two to three hundred warheads would survive the first strike; many of those would be aimed at empty holes anyway, and the defense system would kill most of the incoming weapons.

At the end of the first hour, the Americans would realize that the usefulness of their submarine missiles was greatly degraded. Constant, carefully prepared messages would be sent via the Moscow-Washington Hot Line: WE CANNOT LET THIS GO ANY FURTHER. And, probably, the Americans would stop and think. That was the important part—to make people stop and think. A man might attack cities on impulse or in a state of rage, but not after sober reflection.

Filitov was not concerned that either side would see its defense systems as a rationale for an offensive strike. In a crisis, however, their existence could mitigate the fear that prevented its launch—if the other side had no defenses. Both sides, therefore, had to have them. That would make a first strike far less likely, and *that* would make the world a safer place. Defensive systems could not be stopped now. One might as easily try to stop the tide. It pleased this old soldier that intercontinental rockets, so destructive to the ethic of the warrior, might finally be neutralized, that death in war would be returned to armed men on the field of battle, where it belonged . . .

Well, he thought, *you're tired, and it's too late for that sort of deep thinking.* He'd finish up this report with the data from Bondarenko's final draft, photograph it, and get the film to his cutout.

8. Document Transfer

It was almost dawn when the Archer found the wreckage of the airplane. He had ten men with him, plus Abdul. They'd have to move fast. As soon as the sun rose over the mountains the Russians would come. He surveyed the wreck from a knoll. Both wings had been sheared off at the initial impact, and the fuselage had rocketed forward, up a gentle slope, tumbling and breaking apart until only the tail was recognizable. He had no way of knowing that it had taken a brilliant pilot to accomplish this much, that getting the airplane down under any kind of control was a near miracle. He gestured to his men, and moved quickly toward the main body of wreckage. He told them to look for weapons, then any kind of documents. The Archer and Abdul went to what was left of the tail.

As usual, the scene of the crash was a contradiction. Some of the bodies were torn apart, while others were superficially intact, their deaths caused by internal trauma. These bodies looked strangely at peace, stiff but not yet frozen by the low temperature. He counted six who'd been in the after section of the aircraft. All, he saw, were Russians, all in uniform. One wore the uniform of a KGB captain and was still strapped in his seat. There was a pink froth around his lips. He must have lived a little after the crash and coughed up blood, the Archer thought. He kicked the body over and saw that handcuffed to the man's left hand was a briefcase. That was promising. The Archer bent down to see if the handcuff could be taken off easily, but he wasn't that lucky. Shrugging, he took out his knife. He'd just have to cut it off the body's wrist. He twisted the hand around and started—

—when the arm jerked and a high-pitched scream made the Archer leap to his feet. Was this one alive? He bent down to the man's face and was rewarded by a coughing spray of blood. The blue eyes were now open, wide with shock and pain. The mouth worked, but nothing intelligible came out.

"Check to see if any more are still living," the Archer ordered his assistant. He turned back to the KGB officer and spoke in Pashtu: "Hello, Russian." He waved his knife within a few centimeters of the man's eyes.

The Captain started coughing again. The man was fully awake now, and in considerable pain. The Archer searched him for weapons. As his hands moved, the body writhed in agony. Broken ribs at the least, though his limbs seemed intact. He spoke a few tortured words. The Archer knew some Russian but had trouble making them out. It should not have been hard—the message the officer was trying to convey was the obvious one, though it took the Archer nearly half a minute to recognize it.

"Don't kill me . . ."

Once the Archer understood it, he continued his search. He removed the Captain's wallet and flipped through its contents. It was the photographs that stopped him. The man had a wife. She was short, with dark hair and a round face. She was not beautiful, except for the smile. It was the smile a woman saved for the man she loved, and it lit up her face in a way that the Archer himself had once known. But what got his attention were the next two. The man had a son. The first photo had been taken at age two perhaps, a young boy with tousled hair and an impish smile. You could not hate a child, even the Russian child of a KGB officer. The next picture of him was so different that it was difficult to connect the two. His hair was gone, his skin tightly drawn across the face . . . and transparent like the pages of an old Koran. The child was dying. Three now, maybe four? he wondered. A dying child whose face wore a smile of courage and pain and love. *Why must Allah visit his anger on the little ones?* He turned the photo to the officer's face.

"Your son?" he asked in Russian.

"Dead. Cancer," the man explained, then saw that this bandit didn't understand. "Sickness. Long sickness." For the briefest moment his face cleared of pain and showed only grief. That saved his life. He was amazed to see the bandit sheathe his knife, but too deeply in pain to react in a visible way.

No. I will not visit another death upon this woman. The decision also amazed the Archer. It was as though the voice of Allah Himself reminded him that mercy is second only to faith in the human virtues. That was not enough by itself—his fellow guerrillas would not be persuaded by a verse of scripture—but next the Archer found a key ring in the man's pants pocket. He used one key to unlock the handcuffs and the other to open the briefcase. It was full of document folders, each of which was bordered in multicolored tape and stamped with some version of SECRET. That was one Russian word he knew.

"My friend," the Archer said in Pashtu, "you are going to visit a friend of mine. If you live long enough," he added.

"How serious is this?" the President asked.

"Potentially very serious," Judge Moore answered. "I want to bring some people over to brief you."

"Don't you have Ryan doing the evaluation?"

"He'll be one of them. Another's this Major Gregory you've heard about."

The President flipped open his desk calendar. "I can give you forty-five minutes. Be here at eleven."

"We'll be there, sir." Moore hung up the phone. He buzzed his secretary next. "Send Dr. Ryan in here."

Jack came through the door a minute later. He didn't even have time to sit down.

"We're going in to see The Man at eleven. How ready is your material?"

"I'm the wrong guy to talk about the physics, but I guess Gregory can handle that end. He's talking to the Admiral and Mr. Ritter right now. General Parks coming, too?" Jack asked.

"Yeah."

"Okay. How much imagery do you want me to get together?"

Judge Moore thought that one over for a moment. "We don't want to razzle-dazzle him. A couple of background shots and a good diagram. You really think it's important, too?"

"It's not any immediate threat to us by any stretch of the imagination, but it's a development we could have done without. The effect on the arms-control talks is hard to gauge. I don't think there's a direct connec—"

"There isn't, we're certain of that." The DCI paused for a grimace. "Well, we think we're certain."

"Judge, there is data on this issue floating around here that I haven't seen yet."

Moore smiled benignly. "And how do you know that, son?"

"I spent most of last Friday going over old files on the Soviet missile-defense program. Back in '81 they ran a major test out of the Sary Shagan site. We knew an awful lot about it—for example, we knew that the mission parameters had been changed from within the Defense Ministry. Those orders were sealed in Moscow and hand-delivered to the skipper of the missile sub that fired the birds—Marko Ramius. He told me the other side of the story. With that and a few other pieces I've come across, it makes me think that we have a man inside that place, and pretty high up."

"What other pieces?" the Judge wanted to know.

Jack hesitated for a moment, but decided to go ahead with his guesses. "When *Red October* defected, you showed me a report that had to come from deep inside, also from the Defense Ministry; the code name on the file was WILLOW, as I recall. I've only seen one other file with that name, on a different subject entirely, but also defense-related. That makes me think there's a source with a rapidly changing code-name cycle. You'd only do that with a very sensitive source, and if it's something I'm not cleared for, well, I can only conclude that it's something closely held. Just two weeks ago you told me that Gregory's assessment of the Dushanbe site was confirmed through 'other assets,' sir." Jack smiled. "You pay me to see connections, Judge. I don't mind being cut out of things I don't need to know, but I'm starting to think that there's something going on that's part of what I'm trying to do. If you want me to brief the President, sir, I should go in with the right information."

"Sit down, Dr. Ryan." Moore didn't bother asking if Jack had discussed this with anyone. Was it time to add a new member to the Δ fraternity? After a moment he delivered his own sly smile.

"You've met him." The Judge went on for a couple of minutes.

Jack leaned back in his chair and closed his eyes. After a moment's thought, he could see the face again. "God. And he's getting us the information . . . But will we be able to use it?"

"He's gotten us technical data before. Most of it we've put to use."

"Do we tell the President this?" Jack asked.

"No. That's his idea, not ours. He told us some time ago that he didn't want the details of covert operations, just the results. He's like most politicians—he talks too much. At least he's smart enough to know that. We've had agents lost because presidents talked too much. Not to mention the odd member of Congress."

"So when do we expect this report to come in?"

"Soon. Maybe this week, maybe as long as three—"

"And if it works, we can take what they know and add it to what we know . . ." Ryan looked out the window at the bare limbs of trees. "Ever since I've been here, Judge, I've asked myself at least once a day—what's most remarkable about this place, the things we know or the things we don't?"

Moore nodded agreement. "The game's like that, Dr. Ryan. Get your briefing notes together. No reference to our friend, though. I'll handle that if I have to."

Jack walked back to his office, shaking his head. He'd suspected a few times that he was cleared for things the President never saw. Now he was sure. He asked himself if this was a good idea and admitted that he didn't know. What filled his mind was the importance of this agent and his information. There were precedents. The brilliant agent Richard Sorge in Japan in 1941, whose warnings to Stalin were not believed. Oleg Penkovskiy, who'd given the West information on the Soviet military that might have prevented nuclear war during the Cuban Missile Crisis. And now another. He didn't reflect on the fact that alone in CIA, he knew the agent's face but not his name or code name. It never occurred to him that Judge Moore didn't know CARDINAL's face, had for years avoided looking at the photograph for reasons that he could never have explained even to his deputy directors.

The phone rang, and a hand reached out from under a blanket to grab it. "H'lo."

" 'Morning, Candi," Al Gregory said in Langley.

Two thousand miles away, Dr. Candace Long twisted around in her bed and stared at the clock. "You at the airport?"

"Still in Washington, honey. If I'm lucky, I'll fly back later today." He sounded tired.

"What's happening anyway?" she asked.

"Oh, somebody ran a test, and I have to explain what it means to some people."

"Okay. Let me know when you're coming in, Al. I'll come out to get you." Candi Long was too groggy to realize that her fiancé had bent a rule of security to answer her question.

"Sure. Love ya."

"Love you, too, honey." She replaced the phone and rechecked the clock. There was time for another hour's sleep. She made a mental note to ride into work with a friend. Al had left his car at the lab before flying east, and she'd ride that one out to pick him up.

Ryan got to drive Major Gregory again. Moore took General Parks in his Agency limo.

"I asked you before: what are the chances that we'll find out what Ivan is doing at Dushanbe?"

Jack hesitated before answering, then realized that Gregory would hear it all in the Oval Office. "We have assets that are working to find out what they did to increase their power output."

"I'd love to know how you do that," the young Major observed.

"No, you don't. Trust me." Ryan looked away from the traffic for a moment. "If you know stuff like that, and you make a slip, you could kill people. It's happened before. The Russians come down pretty hard on spies. There's still a story floating around that they cremated one—I mean they slid him into a crematorium alive."

"Aw, come on! Nobody's that—"

"Major, one of these days you ought to get out of your lab and find out just how nasty the world can really be. Five years ago, I had people try to kill my wife and kid. They had to fly three thousand miles to do it, but they came anyway."

"Oh, right! You're the guy—"

"Ancient history, Major." Jack was tired of telling the story.

"What's it like, sir? I mean, you've actually been in combat, the real thing, I mean—"

"It's not fun." Ryan almost laughed at himself for putting it that way. "You just have to perform, that's all. You either do it right or you lose it. If you're lucky, you don't panic until it's all over."

"You said out at the lab that you used to be a Marine . . ."

"That helped some. At least somebody bothered to teach me a little about it, once upon a time." *Back when you were in high school or so*, Jack didn't say. Enough of that. "Ever meet the President?"

"No, sir."

"The name's Jack, okay? He's a pretty good guy, pays attention and asks good questions. Don't let the sleepy look fool you. I think he does that to fool politicians."

"They fool easy?" Gregory wondered.

That got a laugh. "Some of them. The head arms-control guy'll be there, too. Uncle Ernie. Ernest Allen, old-time career diplomat, Dartmouth and Yale; he's smart."

"He thinks we ought to bargain my work away. Why does the President keep him?"

"Ernie knows how to deal with the Russians, and he's a pro. He doesn't let personal opinions interfere with his job. I honestly don't know what he thinks about the issues. It's like with a doc. A surgeon doesn't have to like you personally. He just has to fix whatever's wrong. With Mr. Allen, well, he knows how to sit through all the crap that the negotiations entail. You've never learned anything about that, have you?" Jack shook his head and smiled at the traffic. "Everybody thinks it's dramatic, but it's not. I've never seen anything more boring. Both sides say exactly the same thing for hours—they repeat themselves about every fifteen or twenty minutes, all day, every day. Then after a week or so, one side or the other makes a small change, and keeps repeating that for hours. The other side checks with its capital, and makes a small change of its own, and keeps repeating that. It goes on and on that way for weeks, months, sometimes years. But Uncle Ernie is good at it. He finds it exciting. Personally, after about a week, I'd be willing to start a war just to put an end to the negotiation process"—another laugh—"don't quote me on that. It's about as exciting as watching paint dry, tedious as hell, but it's important and it takes a special kind of mind to do it. Ernie's a dry, crusty old bastard, but he knows how to get the job done."

"General Parks says that he wants to shut us down."

"Hell, Major, you can ask the man. I wouldn't mind finding out myself." Jack turned off Pennsylvania Avenue, following the CIA limousine. Five minutes later, he and Gregory were sitting in the west wing's reception room under a copy of the famous painting of Washington crossing the Delaware while the Judge was talking to the President's national security advisor, Jeffrey Pelt. The President was finishing up a session with the Secretary of Commerce. Finally, a Secret Service agent called to them and led the way through the corridors.

As with TV studio sets, the Oval Office is smaller than most people expect. Ryan and Gregory were directed to a small sofa along the north wall. Neither man sat down yet; the President was standing by his desk. Ryan noted that Gregory appeared a little pale now, and remembered his own first time here. Even White House insiders would occasionally admit to being intimidated by this room and the power it contained.

"Hello again, Jack!" The President strode over to take his hand. "And you must be the famous Major Gregory."

"Yes, sir." Gregory nearly strangled on that, and had to clear his throat. "I mean, yes, Mr. President."

"Relax, sit down. You want some coffee?" He waved to a tray on the corner of his desk. Gregory's eyes nearly bugged out when the President got him a cup. Ryan did his best to suppress a smile. The man who'd made the presidency "imperial" again—whatever that meant—was a genius for putting people at ease. Or appearing to, Jack corrected himself. The coffee routine often made them even more uneasy, and maybe that was no accident. "Major, I've heard some great things about you and your work. The General says you're his brightest star." Parks shifted in his chair at that. The President sat down next to Jeff Pelt. "Okay, let's get started."

Ryan opened his portfolio and set a photograph on the low table. Next came a diagram. "Mr. President, this is a satellite shot of what we call sites Bach and Mozart. They're on a mountain southeast of the city of Dushanbe in the Tadzhik Soviet Socialist Republic, about seventy miles from the Afghan border. The mountain is about seventy-six hundred feet high. We've had it under surveillance for the past two years. This one"—another photo went down—"is Sary Shagan. The Russians have had ballistic-missile-defense work going on here for the past thirty years. This site right here is believed to be a laser test range. We believe that the Russians made a major breakthrough in laser power here two years ago. They then changed the activity at Bach to accommodate it. Last week they ran what was probably a full-power test.

"This array here at Bach is a laser transmitter."

"And they blasted a satellite with it?" Jeff Pelt asked.

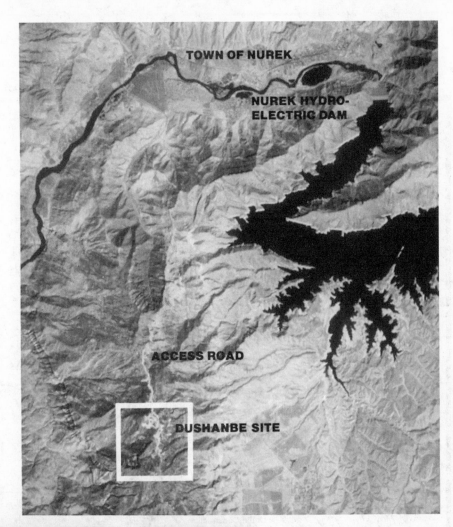

TOWN OF NUREK

NUREK HYDRO-
ELECTRIC DAM

ACCESS ROAD

DUSHANBE SITE

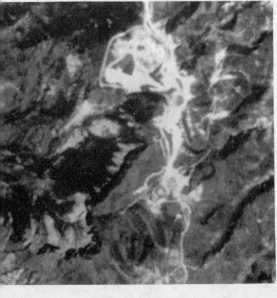

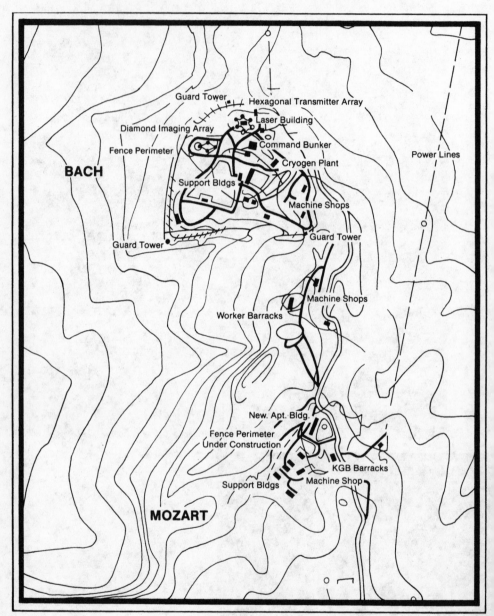

Guard Tower
Hexagonal Transmitter Array
Diamond Imaging Array
Laser Building
Fence Perimeter
Command Bunker
Power Lines
BACH
Cryogen Plant
Support Bldgs
Machine Shops
Guard Tower
Guard Tower
Machine Shops
Worker Barracks
New. Apt. Bldg.
Fence Perimeter
Under Construction
KGB Barracks
Support Bldgs
Machine Shop
MOZART

Detail of Dushanbe site.

"Yes, sir," Major Gregory answered. "They 'slagged it down,' as we say at the lab. They pumped enough energy into it to, well, to melt some of the metal and destroy the solar power cells entirely."

"We can't do that yet?" the President asked Gregory.

"No, sir. We can't put that much power out the front end."

"How is it that they got ahead of us? We're putting a lot of money into lasers, aren't we, General?"

Parks was uncomfortable with the recent developments, but his voice was dispassionate. "So are the Russians, Mr. President. They've made quite a few leaps because of their efforts in fusion. They've been investing in high-energy physics research for years as part of an effort to get fusion-power reactors. About fifteen years ago that effort was mated with their missile-defense program. If you put that much time and effort into basic research, you can expect a return, and they've gotten plenty. They invented the RFQ—the radio-frequency quadrapole—that we use in our neutral-particle beam experiments. They invented the Tokamak magnetic-containment device that we copied up at Princeton, and they invented the Gyrotron. Those are three major breakthroughs in high-energy physics that we know about. We've used some of them in our own SDI research, and it's for sure that they've figured out the same applications."

"Okay, what do we know about this test they ran?"

It was Gregory's turn again. "Sir, we know that it came from Dushanbe because the only other high-energy laser sites, at Sary Shagan and Semipalatinsk, were under the visible horizon—I mean, they couldn't see the satellite from there. We know that it wasn't an infrared laser, because the beam would have been seen by the sensors on the Cobra Belle aircraft. If I had to guess, sir, I'd say that the system uses the free-electron laser—"

"It does," Judge Moore noted. "We just confirmed that."

"That's the one we're working on at Tea Clipper. It seems to offer the best potential for weapons applications."

"Can I ask why, Major?" the President asked.

"Power efficiency, sir. The actual lasing occurs in a stream of free electrons—that means they're not attached to atoms like they usually are, sir—in a vacuum. You use a linear accelerator to produce a stream of the electrons and shoot them into the cavity, which has a low-energy laser shining along its axis. The idea is that you can use electromagnets to oscillate the electrons crosswise to their path. What you get is a beam of light coincident with the oscillation frequency of the wiggler magnets—that means you can tune it, sir, like a radio. By altering the energy of the beam, you can select the exact light frequency you generate. Then you can recycle the electrons back into the linear accelerator and shoot them back into the lasing cavity again. Since the electrons are already in a high-energy state, you gain a lot of power efficiency right there. The bottom line, sir, is that you can theoretically pump out forty percent of the energy you pump in. If you can achieve that reliably, you can kill anything you can see—when we talk about high energy levels, sir, we're speaking in relative terms. Compared to the electrical power that this country uses to cook food, the amount needed for a laser defense system is negligible. The trick is making it really work. We haven't done that yet."

"Why not?" The President was interested now, leaning forward slightly in his chair.

"We're still learning how to make the laser work, sir. The fundamental problem is in the lasing cavity—that's where the energy comes off the electrons and turns into a beam of light. We haven't been able yet to make a very wide one. If the cavity is too narrow, then you have such a high power density that you fry the optical coatings both in the cavity itself and on the mirrors that you use to aim the beam."

"But they've beaten the problem. How do you think they did it?"

"I know what we're trying to do. As you draw energy into the laser beam, the electrons become less energetic, okay? That means you have to taper the magnetic field that contains them—and remember that at the same time you have to continue the wiggling action of the field, too. We haven't figured that out yet. Probably they have, and that probably came from their research into fusion power. All the ideas for getting energy out of controlled fusion are concerned with using a magnetic field to contain a mass of high-energy plasma—in principle the same thing we're trying to do with the free electrons. Most of the basic research in that field comes from Russia, sir. They're ahead of us because they've spent more time and money in the most important place."

"Okay, thank you, Major." The President turned to Judge Moore. "Arthur, what does CIA think?"

"Well, we're not going to disagree with Major Gregory—he just spent a day briefing our Science and Technology people. We have confirmed that the Soviets do have six free-electron lasers at this place. They have made a breakthrough in power output and we're trying to find out exactly what the breakthrough was."

"Can you do that?" General Parks asked.

"I said we're trying, General. If we're very lucky, we'll have an answer by the end of the month."

"Okay, we know they can build a very powerful laser," the President said. "Next question: is it a weapon?"

"Probably not, Mr. President," General Parks said. "At least not yet. They still have a problem with thermal blooming because they haven't learned how to copy our adaptive optics. They've gotten a lot of technology from the West, but so far they don't have that. Until they do, they can't use the ground-based laser as we have, that is, relaying the beam by orbiting mirror to a distant target. But what they have now can probably do great damage to a satellite in low-earth orbit. There are ways to protect satellites against that, of course, but it's the old battle between heavier armor and heavier warheads. The warhead usually wins in the end."

"Which is why we should negotiate the weapons out of existence." Ernie Allen spoke for the first time. General Parks looked over to him with unconcealed irritation. "Mr. President, we are now getting a taste—just a taste—of how dangerous and destabilizing these weapons might be. If we merely consider this Dushanbe place to be an antisatellite weapon, look at the implications it has for verification of arms-treaty compliance, and for intelligence-gathering in general. If we don't try to stop these things now, all we'll get is chaos."

"You can't stop progress," Parks observed.

Allen snorted. "Progress? Hell, we have a draft treaty on the table now to reduce weapons by half. *That's* progress, General. In the test you just ran over the South Atlantic, you missed with half your shots—I can take out as many missiles as you can."

Ryan thought the General might come off his chair at that one, but instead he adopted his intellectual guise. "Mr. Allen, that was the first test of an experimental system, and half of its shots did hit. In fact, *all* of the targets were eliminated in under a second. Major Gregory here will have that targeting problem beaten by summer—won't you, son?"

"Yes, sir!" Gregory piped up. "All we have to do is rework the code some."

"Okay. If Judge Moore's people can tell us what the Russians have done to increase their laser power, we have most of the rest of the system architecture already tested and validated. In two or three years, we'll have it all—and then we can start thinking seriously about deployment."

"And if the Soviets start shooting your mirrors out of space?" Allen asked dryly. "You could have the best laser system ever made on the ground, but it won't do much more than defend New Mexico."

"They'll have to find 'em first, and that's a much harder problem than you think. We can put 'em pretty high up, between three hundred and a thousand miles. We can use stealth technology to make them hard to locate on radar—you can't do that with most satellites, but we can do it with these. The mirrors will be relatively small, and light. That means we can deploy a lot of them. Do you know how big space is, and how many *thousands* of pieces of junk are orbiting up there? They'd never get them all," Parks concluded with confidence.

"Jack, you've been looking at the Russians. What do you think?" the President asked Ryan.

"Mr. President, the main force we're going against here is the Soviet fixation on defending their country—and I mean actually *defending* it against attack. They've invested thirty years of work and quite a pile of money in this field because they think it's something worth doing. Back in the Johnson administration, Kosygin said, 'Defense is moral, offense is immoral.' That's a Russian talking, sir, not just a communist. To be honest, I find that a hard argument to disagree with. If we do enter a new phase of competition, at least it would be defensive instead of offensive. Kind of hard to kill a million civilians with a laser," Jack noted.

"But it will change the whole balance of power," Ernest Allen objected.

"The current balance of power may be fairly stable, but it's still fundamentally crazy," Ryan said.

"It works. It keeps the peace."

"Mr. Allen, the peace we have is one continuous crisis. You say we can reduce inventories by half—again, so what? You could cut Soviet inventories by two thirds and still leave them with enough warheads to turn America into a crematorium. The same thing is true of our inventory. As I said coming back from Moscow, the reduction agreement now on the table is cosmetic only. It does not provide any degree of additional safety. It is a symbol—maybe an important one, but only a symbol with very little substance."

"Oh, I don't know," General Parks observed. "If you reduce my target load by half, I wouldn't mind all that much." That earned him a nasty look from Allen.

"If we can find out what the Russians are doing different, where does that leave us?" the President asked.

"If the CIA gives us data that we can use? Major?" Parks turned his head.

"Then we'll have a weapons system that we can demonstrate in three years, and deploy over the five to ten years after that," Gregory said.

"You're sure," the President said.

"As sure as I can be, sir. Like with the Apollo Program, sir, it's not so much a question of inventing a new science as learning how to engineer technology we already have. It's just working out the nuts and bolts."

"You're a very confident young man, Major," Allen said professorially.

"Yes, sir, I am. I think we can do it. Mr. Allen, our objective isn't all that different from yours. You want to get rid of the nukes, and so do we. Maybe we can help you, sir."

Zing! Ryan thought with a hastily concealed smile. A discreet knock came at the door. The President checked his watch.

"I have to cut this one short. I have to go over some antidrug programs over lunch with the Attorney General. Thank you for your time." He took one last look at the Dushanbe photo and stood. Everyone else did the same. They filed out by the side door, the one concealed in the white plaster walls.

"Nice going, kid," Ryan observed quietly to Gregory.

Candi Long caught the car outside her house. It was driven by a friend from Columbia, Dr. Beatrice Taussig, another optical physicist. Their friendship went back to undergraduate days. She was flashier than Candi. Taussig drove a Nissan 300Z sports car, and had the traffic citations to prove it. The car fitted well with her clothes, however, and the Clairoled hairstyle, and the brash personality that turned men off like a light switch.

" 'Morning, Bea." Candi Long slipped into the car and buckled the seat belt before she closed the door. Driving with Bea, you always buckled up—though she never seemed to bother.

"Tough night, Candi?" This morning it was a severe, not quite mannish wool suit, topped by a silk scarf at the neck. Long could never see the point. When you spent your day covered in a cheap white lab coat, who gave a damn what was under it—except Al, of course, but he was interested in what was under what was under, she thought to herself, smiling.

"I sleep better when he's here."

"Where'd he go?" Taussig asked.

"Washington." She yawned. The rising sun cast shadows on the road ahead.

"How come?" Bea downshifted as she accelerated the car up the freeway on-ramp. Candi felt herself pressed sideways against the seat belt. Why did her friend have to drive this way? This wasn't the Grand Prix of Monaco.

"He said that somebody ran a test, and he has to explain it to somebody or other."

"Hmph." Beatrice looked at her mirror and left the car in third as she selected a slot in the rush-hour traffic. She matched velocities expertly and slid into a space only ten feet longer than her Z-car. That earned her an angry beep from the car behind. She just smiled. The nondriving part of her psyche took note of the fact that whatever test Al was explaining hadn't been American. And there weren't too many people doing tests that this particular little geek had to explain. Bea didn't understand what Candi saw in Al Gregory. Love, she told herself, is blind, not to mention deaf and dumb—especially dumb. Poor, plain Candi Long, she could have done so much better. If only she'd been able to room with Candi at school . . . if only there were a way to let her know . . . "When's Al going to be back?"

"Maybe tonight. He's going to call. I'll take his car. He left it at the lab."

"Put a towel over the seat before you sit in it." She chuckled. Gregory drove a Chevy Citation. The perfect car for a geek, Bea Taussig thought. It was filled with the cellophane wrappers from Hostess Twinkies, and he washed it once a year whether the car needed it or not. She wondered what he was like in bed, but stifled the thought. Not in the morning, not after you just woke up. The thought of her friend . . . involved with *that* made her skin crawl. Candi was just so naive, so innocent—so *dumb!* about some things. Well, maybe she'd come around. There was still hope. "How's the work on your diamond mirror coming?"

"ADAMANT? Give us another year and we'll know. I wish you were still working with my team," Dr. Long said.

"I can see more on the administrative side," Bea answered with remarkable honesty. "Besides, I know I'm not as smart as you."

"Just prettier," Candi noted wistfully.

Bea turned to look at her friend. Yes, there was still hope.

Misha had the finished report by four. It was delayed, Bondarenko explained, because all the most-secret-cleared secretaries were busy with other material. It was forty-one pages long, including the diagrams. The young Colonel was as good as his word, Filitov saw. He'd translated all of the engineering gobbledygook into plain, clear language. Misha had spent the previous week reading everything he could find in the files on lasers. While he didn't really understand the principles of their operation all that clearly, he had the engineering details committed to his trained memory. It made him feel like a parrot. He could repeat the words without comprehending their significance. Well, that was enough.

He read slowly, memorizing as he went. For all his peasant voice and gruff words, his mind was an even sharper razor than Colonel Bondarenko believed. And as things turned out, it didn't have to be. The important part of the breakthrough appeared simple enough, not a matter of increasing the size of the lasing cavity, but of adapting its shape to the magnetic field. With the proper shape, size could be increased almost at will . . . and the new limiting factor became a part of the superconducting magnetic-pulse-control assembly. Misha sighed. The West had done it yet again. The Soviet Union did not have the proper materials. So, as usual, the KGB had secured them in the West, this time shipped through Czechoslovakia via Sweden. Wouldn't they ever learn?

The report concluded that the other remaining problem was in the optical and computer systems. *I'll have to see what our intelligence organs are doing about that*, Filitov told himself. Finally, he spent twenty minutes going over the diagram of the new laser. When he got to the point at which he could close his eyes and recall every single detail, he put the report back in its folder. He checked his watch and punched the button for his secretary. The warrant officer appeared at the door in a few seconds.

"Yes, Comrade Colonel?"

"Take this down to Central Files—Section 5, maximum security. Oh, and where's today's burn-bag?"

"I have it, Comrade."

"Get it for me." The man went back to the anteroom and returned a moment later with the canvas bag that went daily to the document-destruction room. Misha took it and started putting papers into it. "Dismissed. I'll drop this off on the way out."

"Thank you, Comrade Colonel."

"You work hard enough, Yuri Il'ych. Good night." When the door closed behind his secretary, Misha produced some additional pages, documents that had not originated at the Ministry. Every week or so he took care of the burn-bag himself. The warrant officer who handled Filitov's clerical work assumed that it was because of his Colonel's kindness, and perhaps also because there were some especially sensitive papers to be destroyed. In any case, it was a habit that long predated his own service to the Colonel, and the security services viewed it as routine. Three minutes later, on the way to his car, Misha walked into the destruct room. A young sergeant greeted the Colonel as he might have greeted his grandfather, and held open the chute to the incinerator. He watched as the Hero of Stalingrad set down his briefcase and used his crippled arm to open the bag as the good arm elevated it, dumping perhaps a kilogram of classified documents into the gas-fed fire in the Ministry's basement.

He could not have known that he was helping a man destroy evidence of high treason. The Colonel signed off in the log for having destroyed the documents from his section. With a friendly nod, Misha left the burn-bag on its hook and walked out the door to his waiting staff car.

Tonight the ghosts would come again, Misha knew, and tomorrow he'd take steam again, and another package of information would go to the West. On the way to his apartment, the driver stopped off at a special grocery store that was open only to the elite. Here the lines were short. Misha bought some sausage and black bread, and a half-liter bottle of Stolichnaya vodka. In a gesture of comradeliness, he even got one for his driver. For a young soldier, vodka was better than money.

In his apartment fifteen minutes later, Misha extracted his diary from its drawer, and first of all reproduced the diagram appended to Bondarenko's report. Every few minutes he'd spend a second or two looking at the framed photograph of his wife. For the most part, the formal report had tracked with the handwritten one; he had to write only ten new pages, carefully inserting the critical formulae as he went. CARDINAL reports were always models of brevity and clarity, something that came from a lifetime of writing operational directives. When he was finished, he put on a pair of gloves and walked into the kitchen. Magnetically attached to the back side of the steel panel at the bottom of his West German–made refrigerator was a small camera. Misha operated the camera with ease, despite the inconvenience of the gloves. It took only a minute for him to photograph the new diary pages, after which he rewound the film and extracted the film cassette. He pocketed this and replaced the camera in its hiding place before removing the gloves. Next he adjusted the window shades. Misha was nothing if not careful. Close examination of his apartment's door would show scratches on the lock, indicating that it had been picked open by an expert. In fact, anyone could make the scratches. When it was confirmed that his report had reached Washington—tire scuff marks on a predetermined section of curb—he'd tear the pages out of the diary, take them to the Ministry in his pocket, put them in the burn-bag, and dump them down the chute himself. Misha had supervised the installation of the document-destruction system twenty years before.

When the task was complete, Colonel Mikhail Semyonovich Filitov looked again at Elena's picture and asked if he'd done the right thing. But Elena merely smiled as she had always done. *All these years*, he thought, *and it still troubles my conscience.* He shook his head. The final part of the ritual followed. He ate sausage and bread while his long-dead comrades of the Great Patriotic War came to visit, but he couldn't bring himself to ask those who had died for their country if he was justified in betraying it. He thought they would understand even better than his Elena, but was afraid to find out. The half-liter of vodka didn't provide the answer either. At least it drugged his brain to insensibility, and he staggered off to bed just after ten, leaving the lights on behind him.

Just after eleven, a car drove by the wide boulevard that fronted the apartment block, and a pair of blue eyes checked the Colonel's windows. It was Ed Foley this time. He noted the shades. On the way to his own flat, another covert message was passed. A Moscow sanitation worker set up a collection of signals. They were innocuous things, a chalk mark on a lamp post, for example, each of which would tell a part of the cutout team to be at their assigned posts. Another member of the CIA Moscow Station staff would check the cues at dawn, and if anything was amiss, Foley himself could abort everything.

As tense as his job was, Ed Foley found many aspects of it amusing. For one thing, the Russians themselves had made it easier by giving CARDINAL an apartment on a heavily traveled street. For another, in making such a hash of the new embassy building, they prevented him and his family from living in the new compound, and that forced Foley or his wife to drive down this boulevard every night. And they were so glad to have his son on their hockey team. That was one thing he'd miss on leaving this place, Foley told himself as he got out of the car. He now liked junior-league hockey better than baseball. Well, there was always soccer. He didn't want his son to play football. Too many kids got hurt, and he'd never be big enough. But that was in the future, and he still had the present to worry about.

He had to be careful saying things aloud in his own apartment. Every room in every flat occupied by Americans was assumed to be more heavily bugged than an ant farm, but over the years, Ed and Mary Pat had made a joke of that, too. After he came in and hung up his coat, he kissed his wife, then tickled her ear at the same time. She giggled in recognition, though both were thoroughly tired of the stress that came with this post. Just a few more months.

"So how was the reception?" she asked for the benefit of the wall microphones.

"The usual crap," was the recorded answer.

9. Opportunities

Beatrice Taussig didn't make up a report, though she considered the slip Candi had made significant. Cleared for nearly everything that happened at Los Alamos National Laboratory, she hadn't been told about an unscheduled test, and while some SDI work was being done in Europe and Japan, none of it required Al Gregory as an interpreter. That made it Russian, and if they'd flown the little geek to Washington—and, she remembered, he'd left his car at the lab; so they'd sent him a helicopter, too—it had to have been something big. She didn't like Gregory, but she had no reason to doubt the quality of his brain. She wondered what the test was, but she wasn't cleared for what the Russians were up to, and her curiosity was disciplined. It had to be. What she was doing was dangerous. But that was part of the fun, wasn't it? She smiled to herself.

"That leaves three unaccounted for." Behind the Afghans, the Russians were sifting through the wreckage of the An-26. The man talking was a KGB major. He'd never seen an air crash before, and only the cold air on his face had kept him from losing his breakfast.

"Your man?" The infantry Captain of the Soviet Army—until very recently a battalion advisor to the puppet Afghan Army—looked around to make sure his troops were manning the perimeter properly. His stomach was as settled as it could be. Watching his friend nearly gutted before his eyes had been the greatest shock of his life, and he was wondering if his Afghan comrade would survive emergency surgery.

"Still missing, I think." The aircraft's fuselage had broken into several pieces. Those passengers in the forward section had been bathed in fuel when the plane had hit the ground, and were burned beyond recognition. Still, the troops had assembled the pieces for nearly all the bodies. All but three, that is, and the forensic experts would have to determine who was surely dead and who was still missing. They were not normally so solicitous for the victims of an airline crash—the An-26 had technically been part of Aeroflot rather than the Soviet Air Force—but a full effort was being made in this case. The missing Captain was part of the KGB's Ninth "Guards" Directorate, an administrative officer who'd been making a tour of the region, checking up on personnel and security activities at certain sensitive areas. His travel documents included some highly sensitive papers, but, more important, he had intimate knowledge of numerous KGB personnel and activities. The papers could have been destroyed—the remains of several briefcases had been found, burned to ashes, but until the death of the Captain could be confirmed there would be some very unhappy people at Moscow Center.

"He left a family—well, a widow. His son died last month, they tell me. Some kind of cancer," the KGB Major noted quietly.

"I hope you will take proper care of his wife," the Captain replied.

"Yes, we have a department to manage that. Might they have dragged him off?"

"Well, we know they were here. They always loot crash sites, looking for weapons. Documents?" The Captain shrugged. "We're fighting ignorant savages, Comrade Major. I doubt that they have much interest in documents of any kind. They might have recognized his uniform as that of a KGB officer, then dragged him off to mutilate the body. You wouldn't believe what they do to captives."

"Barbarians," the KGB man muttered. "Shooting down an unarmed airliner." He looked around. "Loyal" Afghan troops—that was an optimistic adjective for them, he grumbled—were putting the bodies, and the pieces, into rubber bags to be helicoptered back to Ghazni, then flown to Moscow for identification. "And if they dragged my man's body off?"

"We'll never find it. Oh, there's some chance, but not a good one. Every circling vulture we see, we'll send a helicopter out, but . . ." The Captain shook his head. "The odds are that you already have the body, Comrade Major. It will just require some time to confirm the fact."

"Poor bastard—desk man. Wasn't even his territory, but the man assigned here is in the hospital with gallbladder problems, and he took this job in addition to his own."

"What's his usual territory?"

"The Tadzhik SSR. I suppose he wanted the extra work to get his mind off his troubles."

"How are you feeling, Russian?" the Archer asked his prisoner. They couldn't provide much in the way of medical attention. The nearest medical team, made up of French doctors and nurses, was in a cave near Hasan Khél. Their own walking casualties were heading there now. Those more seriously hurt . . . well, what could they do? They had a goodly supply of painkillers, morphine ampuls manufactured in Switzerland, and injected the dying to ease their pain. In some cases the morphine helped them along, but anyone who showed hope of recovery was placed on a litter and carried southeast toward the Pakistani border. Those who survived the sixty-mile journey would receive care in something that passed for a real hospital, near the closed airfield at Miram Shah. The Archer led this party. He'd successfully argued with his comrades that the Russian was worth more alive than dead, that the *Americastani* would give them much for a member of the Russian political police and his documents. Only the tribal headman could have defeated this argument, and he was dead. They'd given the body as hasty a burial as their faith permitted, but he was now in Paradise. That left the Archer now as the most senior and trusted warrior of the band.

Who could have told from his flint-hard eyes and cold words that for the first time in three years there was pity in his heart? Even he was bemused by it. Why had those thoughts entered his head? Was it the will of Allah? *It had to be*, he thought. *Who else could stop me from killing a Russian?*

"Hurt," the Russian answered finally. But the Archer's pity didn't stretch that far. The morphine the *mudjaheddin* carried was only for their own. After looking to be sure that no one saw, he passed the Russian the photographs of his family. For the briefest instant his eyes softened. The KGB officer looked at him in surprise that overcame the pain. His good hand took the photographs, cupping them to his chest. There was gratitude on his face, gratitude and puzzlement. The man thought of his dead son, and contemplated his own fate. The worst thing that could happen, he decided within the cloud of pain, was that he'd rejoin his child, wherever he was. The Afghans could not hurt him worse than he already was in body and soul. The Captain was already to the point that the pain had become like a drug, so familiar that the agony had become tolerable, almost comfortable. He'd heard that this was possible, but not believed it until now.

His mental processes were still not fully functional. In his twilight state he wondered why he hadn't been killed. He'd heard enough stories in Moscow about how the Afghans treated captives . . . *and was that why you volunteered to handle this tour in addition to your own . . . ?* He wondered now at his fate, and how he'd brought it about.

You cannot die, Valeriy Mikhailovich, you must live. You have a wife, and she has suffered enough, he told himself. *Already she is going through . . .* The thought stopped of its own accord. The Captain slid the photo into a breast pocket and surrendered himself to the beckoning unconsciousness as his body labored to heal itself. He didn't wake as he was bound to a board and placed aboard a travois. The Archer led his party off.

*   *   *

Misha woke with the sounds of battle reverberating through his head. It was still dark outside—the sun would not rise for some time—and his first considered action was to go into the bathroom, where he splashed cold water on his face and washed down three aspirin. Some dry heaves followed, over the toilet, but all that came out was yellow bile, and he rose to look in the mirror to see what treason had done to a Hero of the Soviet Union. He could not—would not—stop, of course, but . . . *but look what it is doing to you, Misha.* The once clear-blue eyes were bloodshot and lifeless, the ruddy complexion gray like a corpse. His skin sagged, and the gray stubble on his cheeks blurred a face that had once been called handsome. He stretched his right arm, and as usual the scar tissue was stiff, looking like plastic. Well. He washed out his mouth and trudged off to the kitchen to make some coffee.

At least he had some of that, also bought in a store that catered to the members of the *nomenklatura*, and a Western-made machine with which to brew it. He debated over eating something, but decided to stick with coffee alone. He could always have some bread at his desk. The coffee was ready in three minutes. He drank a cup straight down, ignoring the damaging heat of the liquid, then lifted his phone to order his staff car. He wanted to be picked up early, and though he didn't say that he wanted to visit the baths this morning, the sergeant who answered the phone at the motor pool knew what the reason was.

Twenty minutes later Misha emerged from the front of his building. His eyes were already watering, and he squinted painfully into the cold northwest wind that tried to sweep him back through the doors. The sergeant thought to reach out and steady his Colonel, but Filitov shifted his weight slightly to fight against the invisible hand of nature that held him back and got into the car as he always did, as though he were boarding his old T-34 for combat.

"The baths, Comrade Colonel?" the driver asked after getting back in front.

"Did you sell the vodka I gave you?"

"Why, yes, Comrade Colonel," the youngster answered.

"Good for you, that's healthier than drinking it. The baths. Quickly," the Colonel said with mock gravity, "and I might yet live."

"If the Germans couldn't kill you, my Colonel, I doubt that a few drops of good Russian vodka can," the boy said cheerfully.

Misha allowed himself a laugh, accepting the flash in his head with good humor. The driver even looked like his Corporal Romanov. "How would you like to be an officer someday?"

"Thank you, Comrade Colonel, but I wish to return to the university to study. My father is a chemical engineer and I plan to follow him."

"He is a lucky man, then, Sergeant. Let's get moving."

The car pulled up to the proper building in ten minutes. The sergeant let his Colonel out, then parked in the reserved spaces from which he could see the doors. He lit a cigarette and opened a book. This was very good duty, better than tromping around in the mud with a motor-rifle company. He checked his watch. Old Misha wouldn't be back for nearly an hour. Poor old bastard, he thought, to be so lonely. What miserable luck that a hero should come to this.

Inside, the routine was so fixed that Misha could have done it asleep. After undressing, he got his towels, and slippers, and birch branches, and moved off to the steam room. He was earlier than usual. Most of the regulars hadn't shown up yet. So much the better. He increased the flow of water onto the firebricks and sat down to allow his pounding head to clear. Three others were scattered about the room. He recognized two of them, but they weren't acquaintances, and none seemed in the mood to talk. That was fine with Misha. The mere act of moving his jaw hurt, and the aspirin were slow today.

Fifteen minutes later the sweat poured off the white body. He looked up to see the attendant, heard the usual cant about a drink—nobody wanted one just yet—plus the line about the swimming pool. It seemed the likely thing for a man in this job to say, but what the precise wording meant was: *All secure. I am ready for the transfer.* By way of reply, Misha wiped the sweat off his brow in an exaggerated gesture common to elderly men. *Ready.* The attendant left. Slowly, Misha began counting to three hundred. When he got to two hundred and fifty-seven, one of his fellow alcoholics stood and walked out. Misha took note of this, but didn't worry about it. He had far too much practice. When he got to three hundred he rose with a jerking movement of his knees and left the room without a word.

The air was much cooler in the robing room, but he saw that the other man hadn't left yet. He was talking to the attendant about something or other. Misha waited patiently for the attendant to notice him, which he did. The young man came over, and the Colonel took a few steps to meet him. Misha stumbled on a loose tile and nearly fell. His good arm went forward. The attendant caught him, or nearly did. The birch sticks fell to the floor.

The young man swept them up in an instant and helped Misha to his feet. In another few seconds he'd given him a fresh towel for his shower and sent him on his way.

"Are you all right, Comrade?" the other man asked from the far end of the room.

"Yes, thank you. My old knees, and these old floors. They should pay more attention to the floor."

"Indeed they should. Come, we can shower together," the man said. He was about forty, and nondescript except for his bloodshot eyes. Another drinker, Misha observed at once. "You were in the war, then?"

"Tanker. The last German gun got me—but I got him, too, at the Kursk Bulge."

"My father was there. He served in the Seventh Guards Army under Konev."

"I was on the other side: Second Tanks, under Konstantin Rokossovskiy. My last campaign."

"I can see why, Comrade . . ."

"Filitov, Mikhail Semyonovich, Colonel of Tank Troops."

"I am Klementi Vladimirovich Vatutin, but I am no one's hero. It is a pleasure to meet you, Comrade."

"It is good for an old man to be shown respect."

Vatutin's father had served in the Kursk Campaign, but as a political officer. He'd retired a colonel in the NKVD, and his son had followed in his footsteps, in the agency later redesignated KGB.

Twenty minutes later, the Colonel was off to his office, and the bath attendant had slipped out the rear door again and entered that of the dry-cleaners. The store manager had to be called from the machine room, where he'd been oiling a pump. As a matter of simple security, the man who took the cassette from his hand was supposed to know neither the man's name nor where he worked. He pocketed the cassette, passed over three half-liter bottles of liquor, and returned to finish oiling the pump, his heart rate up as it always was on these days. He was quietly amused that his cover assignment as a CIA "agent"—a Soviet national working for the American intelligence agency—worked very much to his personal fiscal benefit. The under-the-counter marketing of alcohol paid him in "certificate" rubles that could be used to buy Western goods and premium foodstuffs at the hard-currency stores. He balanced that against the tension of his assignment as he washed the machine oil off his hands. He'd been part of this line of cutouts for six months, and though he didn't know it, his work along this line would soon be ended. He'd still be used to pass along information, but not for CARDINAL. Soon thereafter the man at the baths would seek another job, and this link of nameless agents would be dissolved—and untraceable even to the relentless counterintelligence officers of the KGB's Second Chief Directorate.

Fifteen minutes later, a regular customer appeared with one of her English coats. It was an Aquascutum with the zippered-in liner removed. As always, she said something about taking special care to use the gentlest process on the coat, and as always he nodded and protested that this was the best cleaning shop in all of the Soviet Union. But it didn't have pre-printed check forms, and he wrote out three by hand on carbon-sets. The first was attached to the coat with a straight pin, the second went into a small box, and the third—but first he checked the pockets.

"Comrade, you've left some change. I thank you, but we do not need the extra money." He handed this, and the receipt, over. Plus something else. It was so easy. Nobody ever checked the pockets, just as in the West.

"Ah, truly you are an honorable man," the lady said with an odd formalism common in the Soviet Union. "Good day, Comrade."

"And to you," the man replied. "Next!"

The lady—her name was Svetlana—walked off to the Metro station as usual. Her schedule allowed for a leisurely walk in case of problems at either end of her exchange. The streets of Moscow were invariably crowded with bustling, unsmiling people, many of whom looked at her coat with brief glances of envy. She had a wide selection of English clothing, having traveled to the West many times as part of her job at GOSPLAN, the Soviet economics planning ministry. It was in England that she'd been recruited by the British Secret Intelligence Service. She was used in the CARDINAL chain because the CIA didn't have all that many agents in Russia who could be used, and she was carefully given jobs only in the center of the chain, never at either end. The data she herself gave the West was low-level economic information, and her occasional services as a courier were actually more useful than the information of which she was so proud. Her case officers never told her this, of course; every spy deems him- or herself to possess the most vital intelligence ever to make its way out. It made the game all the more interesting, and for all their ideological (or other) motivations, spies view their craft as the grandest of all games, since they must invariably outsmart the most formidable resources of their own countries. Svetlana actually enjoyed living on the jagged edge of life and death, though she did not know why. She also believed that her highly placed father—a senior Central Committee member—could protect her from anything. After all, his influence enabled her to travel to Western Europe two or three times a year, didn't it? A pompous man, her father, but Svetlana was his only child, the mother of his only grandchild, and the center of his universe.

She entered the Kuznetskiy Most station in time to see one train leave. Timing was always the tricky part. In rush hour, the Moscow Metro trains run a mere thirty seconds apart. Svetlana checked her watch, and again she had timed her arrival perfectly. Her contact would be on the next one. She walked along the platform to the exact spot for the forward door on the second car of that train, ensuring that she'd be the first one aboard. Her clothing helped. She was often mistaken for a foreigner, and Moscovites treated foreigners with deference ordinarily reserved for royalty— or the gravely ill. She didn't have to wait long. Soon she heard the rumble of an approaching train. Heads turned, as they always did, to see the lights of the lead car, and the sound of brakes filled the vaulted station with high-pitched noise. The door opened, and a rush of people emerged. Then Svetlana stepped in and took a few steps toward the back of the car. She grabbed the overhead bar—all the seats were filled, and no man offered his—and faced forward before the train lurched forward again. Her un-gloved left hand was in her coat pocket.

She'd never seen the face of her contact on this train, but she knew that he'd seen hers. Whoever he was, he appreciated her slim figure. She knew that from his signal. In the crush of the crowded train, a hand hidden by a copy of *Izvestia* ran along her left buttock and stopped to squeeze gently. That was new, and she fought off the impulse to see his face. Might he be a good lover? She could use another one. Her former husband was such a . . . but, no. It was better this way, more poetic, more Russian, that a man whose face she'd never know found her beautiful and desirable. She clasped the film cassette between her thumb and forefinger, waiting the next two minutes for the train to stop at Pushkinskaya. Her eyes were closed, and a millimeter of smile formed on her lips as she contemplated the identity and attributes of the cutout whose hand caressed her. It would have horrified her case officer, but she gave no other outward sign of anything.

The train slowed. People rose from their seats, and those standing shuf-fled about in preparation to leave. Svetlana took her hand out of the pocket. The cassette was slippery, whether from water or some oily substance from the cleaners she didn't know. The hand left her hip—a last, lingering trail of gentle pressure—and came upward to receive the small metal cylinder as her face turned to the right.

Immediately behind her, an elderly woman tripped on her own feet and bumped into the cutout. His hand knocked the cassette from Svetlana's. She didn't realize it for a moment, but the instant the train stopped, the man was on all fours grabbing for it. She looked down more in surprise than horror to see the back of his head. He was going bald, and the shroud of hair about his ears was gray—he was an old man! He had the cassette in a moment and sprang back to his feet. Old, but spry, she thought, catching the shape of his jaw. A strong profile—yes, he'd be a good lover, and perhaps a patient one, the best kind of all. He scurried off the train, and she cleared her mind. Svetlana didn't notice that a man sitting on the left side of the car was up and moving, exiting the car against traffic a second before the doors closed again.

His name was Boris, and he was a night-watch officer at KGB head-quarters now on his way home to sleep. Ordinarily he read the sports newspaper—known originally as *Sovietskiy Sport*—but today he'd forgotten to get one at the kiosk in the headquarters building, and he'd accidentally happened to see on the dirty black floor of the subway car what could only be a film cassette, and one too small to come from an ordinary camera. He hadn't seen the attempted pass, and didn't know who'd dropped it. He assumed that the fiftyish man had, and noted the skill with which the man had retrieved it. Once off the car, he realized that a pass must have taken place, but he'd been too surprised to respond properly, too surprised and too tired after a long night's duty.

He was a former case officer who'd operated in Spain before being invalided home after a heart attack and set on the night desk in his section. His rank was major. He felt he deserved a colonelcy for the work he'd done, but this thought, too, was not in his mind at the moment. His eyes searched the platform for the gray-haired man in the brown coat. *There!* He moved off, feeling a small twinge in his left chest as he walked after the man. He ignored that. He'd quit smoking a few years before, and the KGB doctor said that he was doing well. He got within five meters of the man, and closed no more. This was the time for patience. He followed him through the crossover to the Gor'kovskaya Station and onto the platform. Here things got tricky. The platform was crowded with people heading to their offices, and he lost visual contact with his quarry. The KGB officer was a short man and had trouble in crowds. Could he dare to close further? It would mean pushing through the crowd . . . and calling attention to himself. That was dangerous.

He'd been trained in this, of course, but that was over twenty years behind him, and he frantically searched his mind for procedures. He knew fieldcraft, knew how to identify and shake a tail, but he was a First Directorate man, and the shadowing skills used by the ferrets of the Second Directorate were not part of his repertoire. *What do I do now?* he raged at himself. Such a chance this was! The First Directorate men naturally hated their counterparts in the Second, and to catch one of them at—but what if there might be a "Two" man here? Might he be observing a training exercise? Might he now be the subject of curses from a "Two" man who had a case running on this courier? Could he be disgraced by this? *What do I do now?* He looked around, hoping to identify the counterintelligence men who might be working this courier. He couldn't hope to discern which face it was, but he might get a wave-off signal. He thought he remembered those. Nothing. *What do I do now?* He was sweating in the cold subway station, and the pain in his chest increased to add another factor to his dilemma. There was a system of covert telephone lines built into every segment of the Moscow subway system. Every KGB officer knew how to use them, but he knew he didn't have time to find and activate the system.

He had to follow the man. He had to run the risk. If it turned out to be the wrong decision, well, he was an experienced field officer in his own right, and he *had* looked for the wave-off. The "Two" people might tongue-lash him, but he knew he could depend on his First Directorate supervisors to protect him. The decision now made, the chest pain subsided. But there was still the problem of seeing him. The KGB officer wormed his way through the crowd, enduring grumbles as he did so, but finally finding his way blocked by a gang of laborers who were talking about something or other. He craned his neck to get a look at his quarry—*yes! still standing there, looking to the right* . . . The sound of the subway train came as a relief.

He stood there, trying not to look too often at his target. He heard the subway doors open with a hiss, heard the sudden change in noise as the people got off, then the rasping shuffle of feet as people crowded forward toward the doors.

The car was full! His man was inside, but the doors overflowed with bodies. The KGB officer raced to the rear door and fought his way in a moment before it shut. He realized with a chill that he might have been too obvious, but there was nothing he could do about that. As the train began moving, he worked his way forward. The people seated and standing noticed this untoward movement. As he watched, a hand adjusted a hat. Three or four newspapers rattled—any of these signals could be a warning to the courier.

One of them was. Ed Foley was looking away after adjusting his glasses with a right hand that wore one glove and held another. The courier turned back forward and went over his escape procedures. Foley went over his own. The courier would dispose of the film, first exposing it by pulling it out of the metal cylinder, then dumping it in the nearest trash receptacle. That had happened twice before that he knew of, and in both cases the cutout had gotten away cleanly. *They're trained how*, Foley told himself. *They know how*. CARDINAL would be warned, and another film would be made, and . . . but this had never happened on Foley's watch, and it took all of his discipline to keep his face impassive. The courier didn't move at all. He got off at the next stop anyway. He'd done nothing unusual, nothing that didn't appear normal. He would say that he'd found this funny little thing with the—*was it film, Comrade?*—stuff pulled out on the floor of the train, and thought it merely trash to be disposed of. In his pocket, the man was trying to pull the film out of the cassette. Whoever took it always left a few millimeters out so that you could yank all of it—or so they'd told him. But the cassette was slippery and he couldn't quite get a grip on the exposed end. The train stopped again and the courier moved out. He didn't know who was trailing him. He knew nothing other than that he'd gotten his wave-off signal, and that signal also told him to destroy what he had in the prescribed way—but he'd never had to do it before. He tried not to look around, and moved out of the station as quickly as anyone else in the crowd. For his part, Foley didn't even look out of the train's windows. It was nearly inhuman but he managed it, fearing above all that he might endanger his cutout.

The courier stood alone on a moving step of the escalator. Just a few more seconds and he'd be on the street. He'd find an alley to expose the film, and a sewer to dump it in, along with the cigarette he'd just lit. One smooth motion of the hand, and even if he were picked up, there would be no evidence, and his story, drilled into his head and practiced there every day, was good enough to make the KGB wonder. His career as a spy was now over. He knew that, and was surprised at the wave of relief that enveloped him like a warm, comfortable bath.

The air was a cold reminder of reality, but the sun was rising, and the sky was beautifully clear. He turned right and walked off. There was an alley half a block away, and a sewer grate that he could use. His cigarette would be finished just as he got there, yet another thing that he'd practiced. Now, if only he could get the film out of the cassette and exposed to sunlight . . . Damn. He slipped off his other glove and rubbed his hands together. The courier used his fingernails to get the film. Yes! He crumpled the film and put the cassette back into his pocket, and—

"Comrade." The voice was strong for a man of his age, the courier thought. The brown eyes sparkled with alertness, and the hand at his pocket was a strong one. The other, he saw, was in the man's pocket. "I wish to see what is in your hand."

"Who are you?" the courier blustered. "What is this?"

The right hand jerked in the pocket. "I am the man who will kill you, here on the street, unless I see what is in your hand. I am Major Boris Churbanov." Churbanov knew that this would soon be false. From the look on the man's face, he knew that he had his colonelcy.

Foley was in his office ten minutes later. He sent one of his men—actually a woman—out on the street to look for the signal that the dump had been made successfully, and his hope was that he'd simply goofed, that he'd overreacted to a commuter who was trying too hard to get to work. But . . . but there was something about that face that had said *professional.* Foley didn't know what, but it had been there. He had his hands flat on the desk and stared at them for several minutes.

What did I do wrong? he asked himself. He'd been trained to do that, too, to analyze his actions step by step, looking for flaws, for mistakes, for . . . Had he been followed? He frequently was, of course, like all Americans on the embassy staff. His personal tail was a man he thought of as "George." But George wasn't there very often. The Russians didn't know who Foley was. He was sure of that. That thought caught in his throat. Being certain about anything in the intelligence business was the surest route to disaster. That was why he'd never broken craft, why he never deviated from the training that had been drilled into him at Camp Peary, on the York River in Virginia, then practiced all over the world.

Well. The next thing he had to do was predetermined. He walked to the communications room and sent a telex to Foggy Bottom. This one, however, went to a box number whose traffic was never routine. Within a minute of its receipt, a night-watch officer from Langley drove to State to retrieve it. The wording of the message was innocuous, but its meaning was not: TROUBLE ON THE CARDINAL LINE. FULL DATA TO FOLLOW.

They didn't take him to Dzerzhinskiy Square. KGB headquarters, so long used as a prison—a dungeon for all that happened there—was now exclusively an office building since, in obedience to Parkinson's Law, the agency had expanded to absorb all its available space. Now the interrogations were done at Lefortovo Prison, a block from the Sputnik Cinema. There was plenty of room here.

He sat alone in a room with a table and three chairs. It had never occurred to the courier to resist, and even now he didn't realize that if he'd run away or fought the man who'd arrested him, he might still be free. It wasn't the idea that Major Churbanov had had a gun—he hadn't—but simply that Russians, in lacking freedom, often lack the concepts needed for active resistance. He'd seen his life end. He accepted that. The courier was a fearful man, but he feared only what had to be. You cannot fight against destiny, he told himself.

"So, Churbanov, what do we have?" The questioner was a Captain of the Second Chief Directorate, about thirty years old.

"Have someone develop this." He handed over the cassette. "I think this man is a cutout." Churbanov described what he'd seen and what he'd done. He didn't say that he'd rewound the film into the cassette. "Pure chance that I spotted him," he concluded.

"I didn't think you 'One' people knew how, Comrade Major. Well done!"

"I was afraid that I'd blundered into one of your operations and—"

"You would have known by now. It is necessary for you to make a full report. If you will accompany the sergeant here, he'll take you to a stenographer. Also, I will summon a full debriefing team. This will take some hours. You may wish to call your wife."

"The film," Churbanov persisted.

"Yes. I will walk that down to the lab myself. If you'll go with the sergeant, I'll rejoin you in ten minutes."

The laboratory was in the opposite wing of the prison. The Second Directorate had a small facility here, since much of its work centered on Lefortovo. The Captain caught the lab technician between jobs, and the developing process was started at once. While he waited, he called his Colonel. There was as yet no way to measure what this "One" man had uncovered, but it was almost certainly an espionage case, and those were all treated as matters of the utmost importance. The Captain shook his head. That old war-horse of a field officer, just stumbling into something like that.

"Finished." The technician came back. He'd developed the film and printed one blow-up, still damp from the process. He handed back the film cassette, too, in a small manila envelope. "The film has been exposed and rewound. I managed to save part of one frame. It's interesting, but I have no idea what it actually is."

"What about the rest?"

"Nothing can be done. Once film is exposed to sunlight, the data is utterly destroyed."

The Captain scanned the blow-up as the technician said something else. It was mainly a diagram, with some caption printed in block letters. The words at the top of the diagram read: BRIGHT STAR COMPLEX #1, and one of the other captions was LASER ARRAY. The Captain swore and left the room at a run.

Major Churbanov was having tea with the debrief team when the Captain returned. The scene was comradely. It would get more so.

"Comrade Major, you may have discovered something of the highest importance," the Captain said.

"I serve the Soviet Union," Churbanov replied evenly. It was the perfect reply—the one recommended by the Party. Perhaps he might leap over the rank of lieutenant colonel and become a full colonel . . .

"Let me see," the chief debriefer said. He was a full colonel, and examined the photographic print carefully. "This is all?"

"The rest was destroyed."

The Colonel grunted. That would create a problem, but not all that much of one. The diagram would suffice to identify the site, whatever it was. The printing looked to be the work of a young person, probably a woman because of its neatness. The Colonel paused and looked out the window for a few seconds. "This has to go to the top, and quickly. What is described in here is—well, I have never heard of it, but it must be a matter of the greatest secrecy. You comrades begin the debrief. I'm going to make a few calls. You, Captain, take the cassette to the lab for fingerprints and—"

"Comrade, I touched it with my bare hands," Churbanov said ashamedly.

638 • TOM CLANCY

"You have nothing to apologize for, Comrade Major, your vigilance was more than exemplary," the Colonel said generously. "Check for prints anyway."

"The spy?" the Captain asked. "What about interrogating him?"

"We need an experienced man. I know just the one." The Colonel rose. "I'll call him, too."

Several pairs of eyes watched him, measuring him, his face, his determination, his intelligence. The courier was still alone in the interrogation room. The laces had been taken from his shoes, of course, and his belt, and his cigarettes, and anything else that might be used as a weapon against himself, or to settle him down. There was no way for him to measure time, and the lack of nicotine made him fidgety and even more nervous than he might have been. He looked about the room and saw a mirror, which was two-way, but he didn't know that. The room was completely soundproofed to deny him even the measure of time from footsteps in the outside corridor. His stomach growled a few times, but otherwise he made no sound. Finally the door opened.

The man who entered was about forty and well dressed in civilian clothes. He carried a few sheets of paper. The man walked around to the far side of the table and didn't look at the courier until he sat down. When he did look at him, his eyes were disinterested, like a man at the zoo examining a creature from a distant land. The courier tried to meet his gaze impassively, but failed. Already the interrogator knew that this one would be easy. After fifteen years, he could always tell.

"You have a choice," he said after another minute or so. His voice was not hard, but matter-of-fact. "It can go easily for you or it can go very hard. You have committed treason against the Motherland. I do not need to tell you what happens to traitors. If you wish to live, you will tell me now, today, everything you know. If you do not do this, we will find out anyway, and you will die. If you tell us today, you will be allowed to live."

"You will kill me anyway," the courier observed.

"This is not true. If you cooperate, today, you will at worst be sentenced to a lengthy term in a labor camp of strict regime. It is even possible that we can use you to uncover more spies. If so, you will be sent to a camp of moderate regime, for a lesser term. But for that to happen, you must cooperate, today. I will explain. If you return to your normal life at once, the people for whom you work may not know that we have arrested you. They will, therefore, continue to make use of you, and this will enable us to use you to catch them in the act of spying against the Soviet Union. You would testify in the trial against them, and this will allow the State to show mercy. To show such mercy in public is also useful to the State. But for all this to happen, to save your life, and to atone for your crimes, you must cooperate, today." The voice paused for a beat, and softened further.

"Comrade, I take no pleasure in bringing pain to people, but if my job requires it, I will give the order without hesitation. You cannot resist what we will do to you. No one can. No matter how brave you may be, your body has its limits. So does mine. So does anyone's. It is only a matter of time. Time is important to us only for the next few hours, you see. After that, we can take all the time we wish. A man with a hammer can break the hardest stone. Save yourself the pain, Comrade. Save your life," the voice concluded, and the eyes, which were oddly sad and determined at the same time, stared into the courier's.

The interrogator saw that he'd won. You could always tell from the eyes. The defiant ones, the hard ones, didn't shift their eyes. They might stare straight into yours, or more often at a fixed point of the wall behind you, but the hard ones would fix to a single place and draw their strength from it. Not this one. His eyes flickered around the room, searching for strength and finding none. Well, he'd expected this one to be easy. Perhaps one more gesture . . .

"Would you like a smoke?" The interrogator fished out a pack and shook one loose on the table.

The courier picked it up, and the white paper of the cigarette was his flag of surrender.

10. Damage Assessment

"What do we know?" Judge Moore asked.

It was a little after six in the morning at Langley, before dawn, and the view outside the windows matched the gloom that the Director and his two principal subordinates felt.

"Somebody was trailing cutout number four," Ritter said. The Deputy Director for Operations riffled through the papers in his hand. "He spotted the tail just before the pass was made and waved the guy off. The tail probably didn't see his face, and took off after the cutout. Foley said he looked clumsy—that's pretty strange, but he went with his instincts, and Ed's pretty good at that. He put an officer on the street to catch the shake-off signal from our agent, but it wasn't put up. We have to assume that he's been burned, and we have to assume that the film is in their hands, too, until we can prove otherwise. Foley has broken the chain. CARDINAL will be notified never to use his pickup man again. I'm going to tell Ed to use the routine data-lost signal, not the emergency one."

"Why?" Admiral Greer asked. Judge Moore answered.

"The information he had en route is pretty important, James. If we give him the scramble signal, he may—hell, we've told him that if that happens he's to destroy everything that might be incriminating. What if he can't re-create the information? We need it."

"Besides, Ivan has to do a lot to get back to him," Ritter went on. "I want Foley to get the data restored and out, and then—then I want to bust CARDINAL out once and for all. He's paid his dues. After we get the data, then we'll give him the emergency signal, and if we're lucky it'll scare him enough that we can get him to come out."

"How do you want to do it?" Moore asked.

"The wet way, up north," the DDO answered.

"Opinions, James?" Moore asked the DDI.

"Makes sense. Take a little time to set up. Ten to fourteen days."

"Then let's do that today. You call the Pentagon and make the request. Make sure they give us a good one."

"Right." Greer nodded, then smiled. "I know which one to ask for."

"As soon as we know which, I'll send our man to her. We'll use Mr.

Clark," Ritter said. Heads nodded. Clark was a minor legend in the Operations Directorate. If anybody could do it, he could.

"Okay, get the message off to Foley," the Judge said. "I'll have to brief the President on this." He wasn't looking forward to that.

"Nobody lasts forever. CARDINAL's beat the odds three times over," Ritter said. "Make sure you tell him that, too."

"Yeah. Okay, gentlemen, let's get to it."

Admiral Greer went immediately to his office. It was just before seven, and he called the Pentagon, OP-02, the office of the Assistant Chief of Naval Operations (Undersea Warfare). After identifying himself, he asked his first question: "What's *Dallas* up to?"

Captain Mancuso was already at work, too. His last deployment on USS *Dallas* would begin in five hours. She'd sail on the tide. Aft, the engineers were already bringing the nuclear reactor on line. While his executive officer was running things, the Captain was going over the mission orders again. He was heading "up north" one last time. In the U.S. and Royal navies, up north meant the Barents Sea, the Soviet Navy's backyard. Once there, he'd conduct what the Navy officially termed *oceanographic research*, which in the case of USS *Dallas* meant that she'd spend all the time possible trailing Soviet missile submarines. It wasn't easy work, but Mancuso was an expert at it, and he had, in fact, once gotten a closer look at a Russian "boomer" than any other American sub skipper. He couldn't discuss that with anyone, of course, not even a fellow skipper. His second Distinguished Service Medal, awarded for that mission, was classified and he couldn't wear it; though its existence did show in the confidential section of his personnel file, the actual citation was missing. But that was behind him, and Mancuso was a man who always looked forward. If he had to make one final deployment, it might as well be up north. His phone rang.

"Captain speaking," he answered.

"Bart, Mike Williamson," said the Submarine Group Two commander. "I need you here, right now."

"On the way, sir." Mancuso hung up in surprise. Within a minute he was up the ladder, off the boat, and walking along the blacktopped quay in the Thames, where the Admiral's car was waiting. He was in the Group Two office four minutes after that.

"Change in orders," Rear Admiral Williamson announced as soon as the door was closed.

"What's up?"

"You're making a high-speed run for Faslane. Some people will be meeting you there. That's all I know, but the orders originated at OP-02 and came through SUBLANT in about thirty seconds." Williamson didn't have to say anything else. Something very hot was up. Hot ones came to *Dallas* quite often. Actually, they came to Mancuso, but then, he was *Dallas*.

"My sonar department's still a little thin," the Captain said. "I've got some good young ones, but my new chief's in the hospital. If this is going to be especially hairy . . ."

"What do you need?" Admiral Williamson asked, and got his answer.

"Okay, I'll get to work on that. You have five days to Scotland, and I can work something out on this end. Drive her hard, Bart."

"Aye aye, sir." He'd find out what was happening when he got to Faslane.

*   *   *

"How are you, Russian?" the Archer asked.

He was better. The previous two days, he'd been sure that he'd die. Now he wasn't so sure. False hope or not, it was something he hadn't had before. Churkin wondered now if there might really be a future in his life, and if it were something he might have to fear. Fear. He'd forgotten that. He'd faced death twice in a small expanse of time. Once in a falling, burning airplane, hitting the ground and seeing the instant when his life ended; then waking up from death to find an Afghan bandit over him with a knife, and seeing death yet again, only to have it stop and leave. Why? This bandit, the one with the strange eyes, both hard and soft, pitiless and compassionate, wanted him to live. Why? Churkin had the time and energy to ask the question now, but they didn't give him an answer.

He was riding in something. Churkin realized that he was lying on a steel deck. A truck? No, there was a flat surface overhead, and that, too, was steel. Where am I? It had to be dark outside. No light came through the gunports in the side of—he was in an armored personnel carrier! Where did the bandits get one of those? Where were they—

They were taking him to Pakistan! They would turn him over to . . . Americans? And hope changed yet again to despair. He coughed again, and fresh blood erupted from his mouth.

For his part, the Archer felt lucky. His group had met up with another, taking two Soviet BTR-60 infantry carriers out to Pakistan, and they were only too happy to carry the wounded of his band out with them. The Archer was famous, and it could not hurt to have a SAM-shooter protect them if Russian helicopters showed up. But there was little danger of that. The nights were long, the weather had turned foul, and they averaged almost fifteen kilometers per hour on the flat places, and no less than five on the rocky ones. They'd be to the border in an hour, and this segment was held by the *mudjaheddin*. The guerrillas were starting to relax. Soon they'd have a week of relative peace, and the Americans always paid handsomely for Soviet hardware. This one had night-vision devices that the driver was using to pick his way up the mountain road. For that they could expect rockets, mortar shells, a few machine guns, and medical supplies.

Things were going well for the *mudjaheddin*. There was talk that the Russians might actually withdraw. Their troops no longer craved close combat with the Afghans. Mainly the Russians used their infantry to achieve contact, then called in artillery and air support. Aside from a few vicious bands of paratroopers and the hated *Spetznaz* forces, the Afghans felt that they had achieved moral ascendancy on the battlefield—due, of course, to their holy cause. Some of their leaders actually talked about winning, and the talk had gotten to the individual fighters. They, too, now had hope of something other than continued holy war.

The two infantry carriers reached the border at midnight. From there the going was easier. The road down into Pakistan was now guarded by their own forces. The APC drivers were able to speed up and actually enjoy what they were doing. They reached Miram Shah three hours later. The Archer got out first, taking with him the Russian prisoner and his wounded.

He found Emilio Ortiz waiting for him with a can of apple juice. The man's eyes nearly bugged out when he realized that the man the Archer was carrying was a Russian.

"My friend, what have you brought me?"

"He is badly hurt, but here is what he is." The Archer handed over one of the man's shoulder boards, then a briefcase. "And this is what he was carrying."

"Son of a bitch!" Ortiz blurted in English. He saw the crusted blood around the man's mouth and realized that his medical condition was not promising, but . . . what a catch this was! It took another minute of following the wounded to the field hospital before the next question came to the case officer: *What the hell do we do with him?*

The medical team here, too, was composed mainly of Frenchmen, with a leavening of Italians and a few Swedes. Ortiz knew most of them, and suspected that many of them reported to the DGSE, the French foreign intelligence agency. What mattered, however, was that there were some pretty good doctors and nurses here. The Afghans knew that, too, and protected them as they might have protected the person of Allah. The surgeon who had triage duty put the Russian third on the operating schedule. A nurse medicated him, and the Archer left Abdul to keep an eye on things. He hadn't brought the Russian this far to have him killed. He and Ortiz went off to talk.

"I heard what happened at Ghazni," the CIA officer said.

"God's will. This Russian, he lost a son. I could not—perhaps I had killed enough for one day." The Archer let out a long breath. "Will he be useful?"

"These are." Ortiz was already riffling through the documents. "My friend, you do not know what you have done. Well, shall we talk about the last two weeks?"

The debrief took until dawn. The Archer took out his diary and went over everything he'd done, pausing only while Ortiz changed tapes in his recorder.

"That light you saw in the sky."

"Yes . . . it seemed very strange," the Archer said, rubbing his eyes.

"The man you brought out was going there. Here is the base diagram."

"Where is it, exactly—and what is it?"

"I don't know, but it's only about a hundred kilometers from the Afghan border. I can show you on the map. How long will you be staying on this side?"

"Perhaps a week," the Archer answered.

"I must report this to my superiors. They may want to see you. My friend, you will be greatly rewarded. Make a list of what you need. A long list."

"And the Russian?"

"We will talk to him, too. If he lives."

The courier walked down Lazovskiy Pereulok, waiting for his contact. His own hopes were both high and low. He actually believed his interrogator, and by late afternoon he'd taken the chalk that he used and made the proper mark in the proper place. He knew that he'd done so five hours later than he was supposed to, but hoped that his controller would put that off to the evasion process. He hadn't made the false mark, the one that would warn the CIA officer that he'd been turned. No, he was playing too dangerous a game now. So he walked along the dreary sidewalk, waiting for his handler to show up for the clandestine meet.

What he didn't know was that his handler was sitting in his office at the

American Embassy, and would not travel to this part of Moscow for several weeks. There were no plans to contact the courier for at least that long. The CARDINAL line was gone. So far as CIA was concerned, it might never have existed.

"I think we're wasting our time," the interrogator said. He and another senior officer of the Second Directorate sat by the window of an apartment. At the next window was another "Two" man with a camera. He and the other senior officer had learned this morning what Bright Star was, and the General who commanded the Second Chief Directorate had given this case the highest possible priority. A leak of colossal proportions had been uncovered by that broken-down war-horse from "One."

"You think he lied to you?"

"No. This one was easy to break—and, no, it was not too easy. He broke," the interrogator said confidently. "I think we failed to get him back on the street quickly enough. I think they know, and I think they've broken off the line."

"But what went wrong—I mean from their point of view, it might have been routine."

"*Da.*" The interrogator nodded agreement. "But we know that the information is highly sensitive. So, too, must be its source. They have therefore taken extraordinary measures to protect it. We cannot do things the easy way now."

"Bring him in, then?"

"Yes." A car drove up to the man. They watched him get in before they walked to their own vehicle.

Within thirty minutes they were all back in Lefortovo Prison. The interrogator's face was sad.

"Tell me, why is it I think that you have lied to me?" the man asked.

"But I have not! I did everything I was supposed to do. Perhaps I was late, but I told you that."

"And the signal you left, was it the one to tell them that we had you?"

"*No!*" The courier nearly panicked. "I explained all of that, too."

"The problem, you see, is that we cannot tell the difference between one chalk mark and another. If you are being clever, you may have deceived us." The interrogator leaned forward. "Comrade, you *can* deceive us. Anyone can—for a time. But not a very long time." He paused to let that thought hover in the air for a minute. It was so easy, interrogating the weak ones. Give hope, then take it away; restore it, and remove it yet again. Take their spirits up and down until they no longer knew which was which—and, lacking a measure of their own feelings, those feelings became yours to use.

"We begin again. The woman you meet on the train—who is she?"

"I do not know her name. She is over thirty, but young for her age. Fair hair, slim and pretty. She is always dressed well, like a foreigner, but she is not a foreigner."

"Dressed like a foreigner—how?"

"Her coat is usually Western. You can tell from the cut and the cloth. She is pretty, as I have said, and she—"

"Go on," the interrogator said.

"The signal is that I put my hand on her rump. She likes it, I think. Often she presses back against my hand."

The interrogator hadn't heard that detail before, but he immediately deemed it the truth. Details like that one were never made up, and it fitted the profile. The female contact was an adventuress. She was not a true professional, not if she reacted like that. And that probably—almost certainly—made her a Russian.

"How many times have you met her like this?"

"Only five. Never the same day of the week, and not on a regular schedule, but always on the second car of the same train."

"And the man you pass it to?"

"I never see his face, not all of it, I mean. He is always standing with his hand on the bar, and he moves his face to keep his arm between it and me. I have seen some of it, but not all. He is foreign, I think, but I don't know what nationality."

"Five times, and you have never seen his face!" the voice boomed, and a fist slammed down on the table. "Do you take me for a fool!"

The courier cringed, then spoke rapidly. "He wears glasses; they are Western, I am sure of it. He usually wears a hat. Also, he has a paper folded, *Izvestia*, always *Izvestia*. Between that and his arm, you cannot see more than a quarter of his face. His go-ahead signal is to turn the paper slightly, as though to follow a story, then he turns away to shield his face."

"How is the pass made, again!"

"As the train stops, he comes forward, as though to get ready to leave at the next station. I have the thing in my hand, and he takes it from behind as I start to leave."

"So, you know her face, but she does not know yours. He knows your face, but you do not know his . . ." *The same method that this one uses to make his pickup. That's a nice piece of fieldcraft, but why do they use the same technique twice on the same line?* The KGB used this one too, of course, but it was harder than other methods, doubly so on the Metro's crowded, frantic rush-hour schedule. He was beginning to think that the most common means of transferring information, the dead-drop, wasn't part of this line. That, too, was very curious. There should have been at least one dead-drop, else the KGB could roll up the line—maybe . . .

They were already trying to identify the source of the leak, of course, but they had to be careful. There was always the possibility that the spy was himself (or herself?) a security officer. That was, indeed, the ideal post for an intelligence agent, since with the job came access to everything, plus foreknowledge of any counterintelligence operations under way. It had happened before—the investigation of a leak had itself alerted the spy, a fact not discovered until some years after the investigation had been terminated. The other really odd thing was that the one photographic frame they had was not of a real diagram, but rather of a hand-drawn one . . .

Handwriting—was that the reason that there were no dead-drops? The spy could be identified that way, couldn't he? What a foolish way to—

But there was nothing foolish here, was there? No, and there wasn't anything accidental either. If the techniques on this line were odd, they were also professional. There was another level to this, something that the interrogator didn't have yet.

"I think that tomorrow, you and I will ride the Metro."

Colonel Filitov woke up without a pounding in his head, which was pleasure enough. His "normal" morning routine was not terribly different from the other sort, but without the pain and the trip to the baths. He checked the diary tucked away in the desk drawer after he dressed, hoping that he'd be able to destroy it, as per his usual procedure. He already had a new blank diary that he'd begin with when this one was destroyed. There had been hints of a new development on the laser business the previous day, plus a paper on missile systems that he'd be seeing the following week.

On entering the car, he settled back, more alert than usual, and looked out the window during the drive into work. There were a number of trucks on the street, early as it was, and one of them blocked his view of a certain piece of curb. That was his "data-lost" signal. He was slightly annoyed that he couldn't see where it was, but his reports were rarely lost, and it didn't trouble him greatly. The "transfer successful" signal was in a different place, and was always easy to see. Colonel Filitov settled back in his seat, gazing out the window as he approached the spot . . . there. His head turned to track on the spot, looking for the mark . . . but it wasn't there. Odd. Had the other marker been set? He'd have to check that on the trip home tonight. In his years of work for CIA, several of his reports had been lost one way or another, and the danger signal hadn't been set, nor had he gotten the telephone call asking for Sergey that would tell him to leave his apartment at once. So there was probably no danger. Just an annoying inconvenience. Well. The Colonel relaxed and contemplated his day at the Ministry. ·

This time the Metro was fully manned. Fully a hundred Second Directorate men were in this one district, most dressed like ordinary Moscovites, some like workmen. These latter were operating the "black" phone lines installed along with electrical service panels throughout the system. The interrogator and his prisoner were riding trains back and forth on the "purple" and "green" lines, looking for a well-dressed woman in a Western coat. Millions of people traveled the Metro every day, but the counterintelligence officers were confident. They had time working for them, and their profile of the target—an adventuress. She was probably not disciplined enough to separate her daily routine from her covert activities. Such things had happened before. As a matter of faith—shared with their counterparts throughout the world—the security officers held that people who spied on their homeland were defective in some fundamental way. For all their cunning, such traitors would sooner or later connive at their own destruction.

And they were right, at least in this case. Svetlana came onto the station platform holding a bundle wrapped in brown paper. The courier recognized her hair first of all. The style was ordinary, but there was something about the way she held her head, something intangible that made him point, only to have his hand yanked down. She turned and the KGB Colonel got a look at her face. The interrogator saw that she was relaxed, more so than the other commuters who displayed the grim apathy of the Moscovite. His first impression was of someone who enjoyed life. That would change.

He spoke into a small radio, and when the woman got on the next train, she had company. The "Two" man who got on with her had a radio earpiece, almost like a hearing aid. Behind them at the station, the men working the phone circuit alerted agents at every station on the line. When she got off, a full shadow team was ready. They followed her up the long escalator onto the street. Already a car was here, and more officers began the surveillance routine. At least two men always had visual contact with the subject, and the close-in duty rotated rapidly among the group as more and more men joined in the chase. They followed her all the way to the GOSPLAN Building on Marksa Prospekt, opposite the Hotel Moscow. She never knew that she was being followed, and never even attempted to look for evidence of it. Within half an hour, twenty photographs were developed and were shown to the prisoner, who identified her positively.

The procedure after that was more cautious. A building guard gave her name to a KGB officer who admonished him not to discuss the inquiry with anyone. With her name, a full identity was established by lunchtime, and the interrogator, who was now running all aspects of the case, was appalled to learn that Svetlana Vaneyeva was the child of a senior Central Committee member. That would be a complication. Quickly, the Colonel assembled another collection of photographs and reexamined his prisoner, but yet again he selected the right woman from a collection of six. The family member of a Central Committee man was not someone to—but they had identification, and they had a major case. Vatutin went to confer with the head of his directorate.

What happened next was tricky. Though deemed all-powerful by the West, the KGB has always been subservient to the Party apparatus; even the KGB needed permission to trifle with a family member of so powerful an official. The head of the Second Directorate went upstairs to the KGB Chairman. He returned thirty minutes later.

"You may pick her up."

"The Secretary of the Central Committee—"

"Has not been informed," the General said.

"But—"

"Here are your orders." Vatutin took the handwritten sheet, personally signed by the Chairman.

"Comrade Vaneyeva?"

She looked up to see a man in civilian clothes—GOSPLAN was a civilian agency, of course—who stared at her oddly. "Can I help you?"

"I am Captain Klementi Vladimirovich Vatutin of the Moscow Militia. I would like you to come with me." The interrogator watched closely for a reaction, but got nothing.

"Whatever for?" she asked.

"It is possible that you can help us in the identification of someone. I cannot elaborate further here," the man said apologetically.

"Will it take long?"

"Probably a few hours. We can have someone drive you home afterward."

"Very well. I have nothing critical on my desk at the moment." She rose without another word. Her look at Vatutin betrayed a certain sense of superiority. The Moscow Militia was not an organization that was lavished with respect by local citizens, and the mere rank of captain for a man of his age told her much of his career. Within a minute she had her coat on and the bundle under her arm, and they headed out of the building. At least the Captain was *kulturny*, she saw, holding the door open for her. Svetlana assumed from this that Captain Vatutin knew who she was—more precisely, who her father was.

A car was waiting and drove off at once. She was surprised at the route, but it wasn't until they drove past Khokhlovskaya Square that she was sure.

"We're not going to the Ministry of Justice?" she asked.

"No, we're going to Lefortovo," Vatutin replied offhandedly.

"But—"

"I didn't want to alarm you in the office, you see. I am actually *Colonel*

Vatutin of the Second Chief Directorate." There was a reaction to that, but Vaneyeva recovered her composure in an instant.

"And what is it that I am to help you with, then?"

She was good, Vatutin saw. This one would be a challenge. The Colonel was loyal to the Party, but not necessarily to its officials. He was a man who hated corruption almost as much as treason. "A small matter—you'll doubtless be home for dinner."

"My daughter—"

"One of my people will pick her up. If things run a little late, your father will not be upset to see her, will he?"

She actually smiled at that. "No, Father loves to spoil her."

"It probably won't take that long anyway," Vatutin said, looking out the window. The car pulled through the gates into the prison. He helped her out of the car, and a sergeant held the door open for both of them. *Give them hope, then take it away.* He took her gently by the arm. "My office is this way. You travel to the West often, I understand."

"It is part of my work." She was on guard now, but no more than anyone would be here.

"Yes, I know. Your desk deals with textiles." Vatutin opened his door and waved her in.

"That's her!" a voice called. Svetlana Vaneyeva stopped dead, as though frozen in time. Vatutin took her arm again and directed her to a chair.

"Please sit down."

"What is this!" she said, finally in alarm.

"This man here was caught carrying copies of secret State documents. He has told us that you gave them to him," Vatutin said as he sat behind his desk.

Vaneyeva turned and stared at the courier. "I have never seen that face in my life! Never!"

"Yes," Vatutin said dryly. "I know that."

"What—" She searched for words. "But this makes no sense."

"You've been very well trained. Our friend here says that his signal to pass on the information is that he runs his hand across your rump."

She turned to face her accuser. "*Govnoed!* This *thing* said that! This"— she sputtered for another moment—"worthless person. Rubbish!"

"So you deny the charge?" Vatutin inquired. Breaking this one would really be a pleasure.

"Of course! I am a loyal Soviet citizen. I am a Party member. My father—"

"Yes, I know about your father."

"He will hear of this, *Colonel* Vatutin, and if you threaten me—"

"We do not threaten you, Comrade Vaneyeva, we ask for information. Why were you on the Metro yesterday? I know that you have your own car."

"I often ride the Metro. It is simpler than driving, and I had to make a stop." She picked her package up off the floor. "Here. I dropped off the coat for cleaning. It is inconvenient to park the car, go in, and then drive on. So I took the underground. Same thing today, when I picked it up. You can check at the cleaners."

"And you did not pass this to our friend here?" Vatutin held up the film cassette.

"I don't even know what that is."

"Of course." Colonel Vatutin shook his head. "Well, there we are." He pressed a button on his intercom set. The office's side door opened a moment later. Three people came in. Vatutin waved to Svetlana. "Prepare her."

Her reaction was not so much panic as disbelief. Svetlana Vaneyeva tried to bolt from the chair, but a pair of men grabbed her by the shoulders and held her in place. The third rolled up the sleeve on her dress and stuck a needle in her arm before she had the presence of mind to shout. "You can't," she said, "you can't . . ."

Vatutin sighed. "Ah, but we can. How long?"

"That'll keep her under for at least two hours," the doctor replied. He and his two orderlies picked her out of the chair. Vatutin came around and got the parcel. "She'll be ready for you as soon as I do the medical check, but I anticipate no problems. Her medical file is clean enough."

"Excellent. I'll be down after I have something to eat." He gestured to the other prisoner. "You can take him away. I think we're done with him."

"Comrade, I—" the courier began, only to be cut off.

"Do not dare to use that word again." The reprimand was all the harsher for its soft delivery.

Colonel Bondarenko now ran the Ministry's laser-weapons desk. It was by the decision of Defense Minister Yazov, of course, as recommended by Colonel Filitov.

"So, Colonel, what news do you bring us?" Yazov asked.

"Our colleagues at KGB have delivered to us partial plans for the American adaptive-optics mirror." He handed over two separate copies of the diagrams.

"And we cannot do this ourselves?" Filitov asked.

"The design is actually quite ingenious, and, the report says, an even more advanced model is in the design stages right now. The good news is that it requires fewer actuators—"

"What is that?" Yazov asked.

"The actuators are the mechanisms which alter the contours of the mirror. By lowering the number of them you also reduce the requirements of the computer system that operates the mirror assembly. The existing mirror—this one here—requires the services of an extremely powerful supercomputer, which we cannot yet duplicate in the Soviet Union. The new mirror is projected to require only a fourth as much computer power. This allows both a smaller computer to operate the mirror and also a simpler control program." Bondarenko leaned forward. "Comrade Minister, as my first report indicated, one of the principal difficulties with Bright Star is the computer system. Even if we were able to manufacture a mirror like this one, we do not as yet have the computer hardware and software to operate it at maximum efficiency. I believe we could do so if we had this new mirror."

"But we don't have the new mirror plans yet?" Yazov asked.

"Correct. The KGB is working on that."

"We can't even replicate these 'actuators' yet," Filitov groused. "We've had the specifications and diagrams for several months and still no factory manager has delivered—"

"Time and funds, Comrade Colonel," Bondarenko chided. Already he was learning to speak with confidence in this rarest of atmospheres.

"Funding," Yazov grunted. "Always funding. We can build an invulnerable tank—with enough funds. We can catch up with Western submarine technology—with enough funding. Every pet project of every academician in the Union will deliver the ultimate weapon—if only we can provide enough funding. Unfortunately there is not enough for all of them." *There's one way in which we've caught up with the West!*

"Comrade Minister," Bondarenko said, "I have been a professional soldier for twenty years. I have served on battalion and divisional staffs, and I have seen close combat. Always I have served the Red Army, only the Red Army. Bright Star belongs to another service branch. Despite this, I tell you that if necessary we should deny funds for tanks, and ships, and airplanes in order to bring Bright Star to completion. We have enough conventional weapons to stop any NATO attack, but we have nothing to stop Western missiles from laying waste to our country." He drew back. "Please forgive me for stating my opinion so forcefully."

"We pay you to think," Filitov observed. "Comrade Minister, I find myself in agreement with this young man."

"Mikhail Semyonovich, why is it that I sense a palace coup on the part of my colonels?" Yazov ventured a rare smile, and turned to the younger man. "Bondarenko, within these walls I expect you to tell me what you think. And if you can persuade this old cavalryman that your science-fiction project is worthwhile, then I must give it serious thought. You say that we should give this program crash status?"

"Comrade Minister, we should consider it. Some basic research remains, and I feel that its funding priority should be increased dramatically." Bondarenko stopped just short of what Yazov suggested. That was a political decision, one into which a mere colonel ought not stick his neck. It occurred to the CARDINAL that he had actually underestimated this bright young colonel.

"Heart rate's coming up," the doctor said almost three hours later. "Time zero, patient conscious." A reel-to-reel tape recorder took down his words.

She didn't know the point at which sleep ended and consciousness began. The line is a fuzzy one for most people, particularly so in the absence of an alarm or the first beam of sunlight. She was given no signals. Svetlana Vaneyeva's first conscious emotion was puzzlement. *Where am I?* she asked herself after about fifteen minutes. The lingering aftereffects of the barbiturates eased away, but nothing replaced the comfortable relaxation of dreamless sleep. She was . . . floating?

She tried to move, but . . . couldn't? She was totally at rest, every square centimeter of her body was evenly supported so that no muscle was stretched or strained. Never had she known such wonderful relaxation. *Where am I?*

She could see nothing, but that wasn't right, either. It was not black, but . . . gray . . . like a night cloud reflecting the city lights of Moscow, featureless, but somehow textured.

She could hear nothing, not the rumble of traffic, not the mechanical sounds of running water or slamming doors . . .

She turned her head, but the view remained the same, a gray blankness, like the inside of a cloud, or a ball of cotton, or—

She breathed. The air had no smell, no taste, neither moist nor dry, not even a temperature that she could discern. She spoke . . . but incredibly she heard nothing. *Where am I!*

Svetlana began to examine the world more carefully. It took about half an hour of careful experimentation. Svetlana kept control of her emotions, told herself forcefully to be calm, to relax. It had to be a dream. Nothing untoward could really be happening, not to her. Real fear had not yet begun, but already she could feel its approach. She mustered her determination and fought to hold it off. *Explore the environment.* Her eyes swept left and right. There was only enough light to deny her blackness. Her arms were there, but seemed to be away from her sides, and she could not move them inward, though she tried for what seemed like hours. The same was true of her legs. She tried to ball her right hand into a fist . . . but she couldn't even make her fingers touch one another.

Her breathing was more rapid now. It was all she had. She could feel the air come in and out, could feel the movement of her chest, but nothing else. Closing her eyes gave her the choice of a black nothing over a gray one, but that was all. *Where am I!*

Movement, she told herself, more movement. She rolled around, searching for resistance, searching for any tactile feeling outside her own body. She was rewarded with nothing at all, just the same slow, fluid resistance—and whichever way she turned, the sensation of floating was the same. It mattered not—she could tell not—whether gravity had her up or down, left side or right. It was all the same. She screamed as loudly as she could, just to hear something real and close, just to be sure that she at least had herself for company. All she heard was the distant, fading echo of a stranger.

The panic started in earnest.

"Time twelve minutes . . . fifteen seconds," the doctor said into the tape recorder. The control booth was five meters above the tank. "Heart rate rising, now one forty, respiration forty-two, acute anxiety reaction onset." He looked over to Vatutin. "Sooner than usual. The more intelligent the subject . . ."

"The greater the need for sensory input, yes," Vatutin said gruffly. He'd read the briefing material on this procedure, but was skeptical. This was brand-new, and required a kind of expert assistance that he'd never needed in his career.

"Heart rate appears to have peaked at one seventy-seven, no gross irregularities."

"How do you mute her own speech?" Vatutin asked the doctor.

"It's new. We use an electronic device to duplicate her voice and repeat it back exactly out of phase. That neutralizes her sound almost completely, and it's as though she were screaming in a vacuum. It took two years to perfect." He smiled. Like Vatutin he enjoyed his work, and he had here a chance to validate years of effort, to overturn institutional policy with something new and better, that had his name on it.

Svetlana hovered on the edge of hyperventilation, but the doctor altered the gas mixture going into her. He had to keep a very close watch on her vital signs. This interrogation technique left no marks on the body, no scars, no evidence of torture—it was, in fact, not a form of torture at all. At least, not physically. The one drawback to sensory deprivation, however, was that the terror it induced could drive people into tachycardia—and that could kill the subject.

"That's better," he said, looking at the EKG readout. "Heart rate stabilized at one thirty-eight, a normal but accelerated sinus rhythm. Subject is agitated but stable."

*　　*　　*

Panic didn't help. Though her mind was still frantic, Svetlana's body drew back from damaging itself. She fought to assert control and again felt herself become strangely calm.

Am I alive or dead? She searched all her memories, all her experiences, and found nothing . . . but . . .

There *was* a sound.

What is it?

Lub-dub, lub-dub . . . what was it . . . ?

It was a heart! Yes!

Her eyes were still open, searching the blankness for the source of the sound. There was something out there, if only she could find it. Her mind searched for a way. *I have to get to it. I must grab hold of it.*

But she was trapped inside something that she couldn't even describe. She started moving again. Again she found nothing to grab, nothing to touch.

She was only beginning to understand how alone she was. Her senses cried out for data, for input, for *something!* The sensory centers of her brain were seeking sustenance and finding only a vacuum.

What if I am dead? she asked herself.

Is this what happens when you're dead . . . Nothingness . . . ? Then a more troubling thought:

Is this hell?

But there was something. There was that sound. She concentrated on it, only to find that the harder she tried to listen, the harder it was to hear. It was like trying to grab for a cloud of smoke, it was only there when she didn't try to—but she had to grab it!

And so she tried. Svetlana screwed her eyes shut and concentrated all of her will on the repeating sound of a human heart. All she accomplished was to blank the sound out of her own senses. It faded away, until it was only her imagination that heard it and then that, too, became bored.

She moaned, or thought she did. She heard almost nothing. How could she speak and not hear it?

Am I dead? The question had an urgency that demanded an answer, but the answer might be too dreadful to contemplate. There had to be something . . . but did she dare? Yes!

Svetlana Vaneyeva bit her tongue as hard as she could. She was rewarded with the salty taste of blood.

I am alive! she told herself. She reveled in this knowledge for what seemed a very long time. But even long times had to end:

But where am I? Am I buried . . . alive? BURIED ALIVE!

"Heart rate increasing again. Looks like the onset of the secondary anxiety period," the doctor observed for the recording. It really was too bad, he thought. He'd assisted in preparing the body. A very attractive woman, her smooth belly marred only by a mother's stretchmarks. Then they'd oiled her skin and dressed her in the specially made wetsuit, one made of the best-quality Nomex rubber, so smooth that you could barely feel it when dry—and when filled with water, it hardly seemed there at all. Even the water in the tank was specially formulated, heavy in salt content so that she was neutrally buoyant. Her gyrations around the tank had twisted her upside down and she hadn't known. The only real problem was that she might tangle the air lines, but a pair of divers in the tank prevented this, always careful not to touch her or to allow the hose to do so. Actually, the divers had the hardest job in the unit.

The doctor gave Colonel Vatutin a smug look. Years of work had gone into this most secret part of Lefortovo's interrogation wing. The pool, ten meters wide and five deep, the specially salted water, the custom-designed suits, the several man-years of experimentation to back up the theoretical work—all these went to devise a means of interrogation that was in all ways better than the antiquated methods KGB had used since the revolution. Except for the one subject that had died of an anxiety-induced heart attack . . . The vital signs changed again.

"There we go. Looks like we're into the second stage. Time one hour, six minutes." He turned to Vatutin. "This is usually the long phase. It will be interesting to see how long it lasts with this subject."

It seemed to Vatutin that the doctor was a child playing an elaborate, cruel game; as much as he wanted what this subject knew, part of him was horrified by what he watched. He wondered if it came from fear that one day it might be tried on him . . .

Svetlana was limp. Tremors from the extended hours of terrors had exhausted her limbs. Her breaths now came in shallow pants, like a woman holding off the urge to deliver her child. Even her body had deserted her now, and her mind sought to escape its confines and explore on its own. It seemed to her consciousness that she separated from the useless sack of flesh, that her spirit, soul, whatever it was, was alone now, alone and free. But the freedom was no less a curse than what had gone before.

She could move freely now, she could see the space around her, but it was all empty. She moved as though swimming or flying in a three-dimensional space whose limits she could not discern. She felt her arms and legs moving effortlessly, but when she looked to see her limbs, she found that they were out of her field of view. She could feel them move, but . . . they weren't there. The part of her mind that was still rational told her that this was all an illusion, that she was swimming toward her own destruction—but even that was preferable to being alone, wasn't it?

This effort lasted for an eternity. The most gratifying part was the lack of fatigue in her invisible limbs. Svetlana shut out her misgivings and reveled in the freedom, in being able to see the space around her. Her pace speeded up. She imagined that the space ahead of her was brighter than that behind her. If there were a light she would find it, and a light would make all the difference. Part of her remembered the joy of swimming as a child, something she hadn't done in . . . fifteen years, wasn't it? She was the school champion at swimming underwater, could hold her breath far longer than all the others. The memories made her young again, young and spry and prettier and better-dressed than all the others. Her face took on an angelic smile and ignored the warnings from the remaining shreds of her intellect.

She swam for days, it seemed, for weeks, always toward the brighter space ahead. It took a few more days to realize that the space never got any brighter, but she ignored this last warning of her consciousness. She swam harder, and felt fatigue for the first time. Svetlana Vaneyeva ignored that, too. She had to use her freedom to advantage. She had to find where she was, or better yet find a way out of this place. This horrible place.

Her mind moved yet again, traveling away from her body, and when it had reached a sufficient height, it looked back down at the distant, swimming figure. Even from its great height it could not see the edges of this wide, amorphous world, but she could see the tiny figure below her, swimming alone in the void, moving its spectral limbs in futile rhythm . . . going nowhere.

The scream from the wall speaker almost made Vatutin bolt from his chair. Perhaps Germans had heard that once, the scream of the victims of their death camps when the doors were shut and the gas crystals had sprinkled down. But this was worse. He'd seen executions. He'd seen torture. He had heard cries of pain and rage and despair, but he had never heard the scream of a soul condemned to something worse than hell.

"There . . . that ought to be the beginning of the third stage."

"What?"

"You see," the doctor explained, "the human animal is a *social* animal. Our beings and our senses are designed to gather data that allow us to react both to our environment and our fellow human beings. Take away the human company, take away all sensory input, and the mind is totally alone with itself. There is ample data to demonstrate what happens. Those Western idiots who sail around the world alone, for example. A surprising number go insane, and many disappear; probably suicides. Even those who survive, those who use their radios on a daily basis—they often need physicians to monitor them and warn them against the psychological hazards of such solitude. And they can *see* the water around. They can see their boats. They can feel the motion of the waves. Take all that away . . ." The doctor shook his head. "They'd last perhaps three days. We take everything away, as you see."

"And the longest they've lasted in here?"

"Eighteen hours—he was a volunteer, a young field officer from the First Directorate. The only problem is that the subject cannot know what is happening to him. That alters the effect. They still break, of course, but not as thoroughly."

Vatutin took a breath. That was the first good news that he'd heard here. "And this one, how much longer?"

The doctor merely looked at his watch and smiled. Vatutin wanted to hate him, but recognized that this physician, this healer, was merely doing what he'd been doing for years, more quickly, and with no visible damage that might embarrass the State at the public trials that the KGB now had to endure. Then, there was the added benefit that even the doctor hadn't expected when he'd begun the program . . .

"So . . . what is this third stage?"

Svetlana saw them swimming around her form. She tried to warn it, but that would mean getting back inside, and she didn't dare. It was not so much something she could see, but there *were* shapes, predatory shapes plying the space around her body. One of them closed in, but turned away. Then it turned back again. And so did she. She tried to fight against it, but something drew her back into the body that was soon to be extinguished. She got there just in time. As she told her limbs to swim faster, it came up from behind. The jaws opened and enveloped her entire body, then closed slowly around her. The last thing she saw was the light toward which she'd been swimming—the light, she finally knew, that was never there. She knew her protest was a vain one, but it exploded from her lips.

"*No!*" She didn't hear it, of course.

She returned now, condemned to go back to her useless real body, back to the gray mass before her eyes and the limbs that could move only without purpose. She somehow understood that her imagination had tried to protect her, to get her free—and had failed utterly. But she couldn't turn her imagination off, and now its efforts turned destructive. She wept without sound. The fear she felt now was worse than mere panic. At least panic was an escape, a denial of what she faced, a retreat into herself. But there was no longer a self that she could find. She'd watched that die, had been there when it happened. Svetlana was without a present, certainly without a future. All she had now was a past, and her imagination selected only the worst parts of that . . .

"Yes, we're in the final stage now," the doctor said. He lifted the phone and ordered a pot of tea. "This was easier than I expected. She fits the profile better than I realized."

"But she hasn't told us anything yet," Vatutin objected.

"She will."

She watched all the sins of her life. That helped her to understand what was happening. This was the hell whose existence the State denied, and she was being punished. That had to be it. And she helped. She had to. She had to see it all again and understand what she'd done. She had to participate in the trial within her own mind. Her weeping never stopped. Her tears ran for days as she watched herself doing things that she ought never to have done. Every transgression of her life played out before her eyes in fullest detail. Especially those of the past two years . . . Somehow she knew that those were the ones that had brought her here. Svetlana watched every time she had betrayed her Motherland. The first coy flirtations in London, the clandestine meetings with serious men, the warnings not to be frivolous, and then the times she had used her importance to breeze through customs control, playing the game and enjoying herself as she committed her most heinous crimes. Her moans took on a recognizable timbre. Over and over she said it without knowing.

"I'm sorry . . ."

"Now comes the tricky part." The doctor put on his headset. He had to make some adjustments on his control board. "Svetlana . . ." he whispered into the microphone.

She didn't hear it at first, and it was some time before her senses were able to tell her that there was *something* crying out to be noticed.

Svetlana . . . the voice called to her. Or was it her imagination . . . ?

Her head twisted around, looking for whatever it was.

Svetlana . . . it whispered again. She held her breath as long as she could, commanded her body to be still, but it betrayed her yet again. Her heart raced, and the pounding blood in her ears blanked out the sound, if it was a sound. She let out a despairing moan, wondering if she had imagined the voice, wondering if it was only getting worse . . . or might there be some hope . . . ?

Svetlana . . . Slightly more than a whisper, enough to detect emotional content. The voice was so sad, so disappointed. *Svetlana, what have you done?*

"I didn't, I didn't—" she sputtered, and still could not hear her own voice as she called out from the grave. She was rewarded with renewed silence. After what seemed an hour she screamed: "Please, *please* come back to me!"

Svetlana, the voice repeated finally, *what have you done . . . ?*

"I'm sorry . . ." she repeated in a voice choked with tears.

"What have you done?" it asked again. "What about the film . . . ?"

"Yes!" she answered, and in moments she told all.

"Time eleven hours, forty-one minutes. The exercise is concluded." The doctor switched off the tape recorder. Next he flicked the lights in the pool room on and off a few times. One of the divers in the tank waved acknowledgment and jabbed a needle into Subject Vaneyeva's arm. As soon as her body went completely limp, she was taken out. The doctor left the control room and went down to see her.

She was lying on a gurney when he got there, the wetsuit already taken off. He sat beside the unconscious form and held her hand as the technician jabbed her with a mild stimulant. She was a pretty one, the doctor thought as her breathing picked up. He waved the technician out of the room, leaving the two of them alone.

"Hello, Svetlana," he said in his gentlest voice. The blue eyes opened, saw the lights on the ceiling, and the walls. Then her head turned toward him.

He knew he was indulging himself, but he'd worked long into the night and the next day on this case, and this was probably the most important application of his program to date. The naked woman leaped off the table into his arms and nearly strangled him with a hug. It wasn't because he was particularly good-looking, the doctor knew, just that he was a human being, and she wanted to touch one. Her body was still slick with oil as her tears fell on his white laboratory coat. She would never commit another crime against the State, not after this. It was too bad that she'd have to go to a labor camp. Such a waste, he thought as he examined her. Perhaps he could do something about that. After ten minutes she was sedated again, and he left her asleep.

"I gave her a drug called Versed. It's a new Western one, an amnesiac."

"Why one of those?" Vatutin asked.

"I give you another option, Comrade Colonel. When she wakes up later this morning, she will remember very little. Versed acts like scopolamine, but is more effective. She will remember no firm details, and very little else that happened to her. It will all seem to be a fearful dream. Versed is also an hypnotic. For example, I can go back to her now and make a suggestion that she will not remember anything, but that she may never betray the State again. There is roughly an eighty-percent probability that both suggestions will never be violated."

"You're joking!"

"Comrade, one effect of this technique is that she has condemned herself more forcefully than the State ever could. She feels more remorse now for her actions than she would before a firing squad. Surely you have read *1984*? It might have been a dream when Orwell wrote it, but with modern technology, we can do it. The trick is not breaking the person from without, but doing it from within."

"You mean we can use her now . . . ?"

11. Procedures

"He's not going to make it." Ortiz had gotten the embassy doctor, an Army surgeon whose real job was to assist in the treatment of wounded Afghans. Churkin's lungs were too badly damaged to fight off the pneumonia that had developed during his transit. "He probably won't last out the day. Sorry, just too much damage. A day sooner and maybe we might have saved him, but . . ." The doctor shook his head. "I'd like to get a preacher to him, but that's probably a waste of time."

"Can he talk?"

"Not much. You can try. It won't hurt him any more than he already is. He'll be conscious for a few more hours, then he's just going to fade out."

"Thanks for the try, doc," Ortiz said. He almost sighed with relief, but the shame of such a gesture stopped him cold. What would they have done with a live one? Give him back? Keep him? Trade him? he asked himself. He wondered why the Archer had brought him out at all. "Well," he said to himself, and entered the room.

Two hours later he emerged. Then Ortiz drove down to the embassy, where the canteen served beer. He made his report to Langley, then over the next five hours, sitting alone at a corner table he left only for refills, he got himself thoroughly and morosely drunk.

Ed Foley could not allow himself that luxury. One of his couriers had disappeared three days earlier. Another had left her desk at GOSPLAN and returned two days later. Then, only this morning, his man in the dry-cleaners had called in sick. He'd sent a warning to the kid at the baths, but didn't know if it had gotten to him or not. This was not mere trouble in his CARDINAL network, it was a disaster. The whole point of using Svetlana Vaneyeva was her supposed immunity from KGB's more forceful measures, and he'd depended on several days' resistance from her to get his people moved. Warning orders for the CARDINAL breakout had arrived but were still awaiting delivery. There was no sense in spooking the man before things were fully ready. After that, it should be a simple matter for Colonel Filitov to come up with an excuse to visit the Leningrad Military District headquarters—something he did every six months or so—and get him out.

If that works, Foley reminded himself. It had been done only twice that he knew of, and as well as it had gone before . . . there were no certainties, were there? *Not hardly.* It was time to leave. He and his wife needed time off, time away from all this. Their next post was supposed to be on the training staff at "the Farm" on the York River. But these thoughts didn't help him with his current problem.

He wondered if he should alert CARDINAL anyway, warn him to be more careful—but then he might destroy the data that Langley was screaming for, and the data was paramount. That was the rule, a rule that Filitov knew and understood, supposedly as well as Foley did. But spies were more than objects that provided information, weren't they?

Field officers like Foley and his wife were supposed to regard them as valuable but expendable assets, to distance themselves from their agents, to treat them kindly when possible but ruthlessly when necessary. To treat them like children, really, with a mixture of indulgence and discipline. But they weren't children. CARDINAL was older than his own father, had been an agent when Foley was in second grade! Could he *not* show loyalty to Filitov? Of course not. He had to protect him.

But how?

Counterespionage operations were often nothing more than police work, and as a result of this, Colonel Vatutin knew as much about the business of investigation as the best men in the Moscow Militia. Svetlana had given him the manager of the dry-cleaning shop, and after two perfunctory days of surveillance, he'd decided to bring the man in for interrogation. They didn't use the tank on him. The Colonel still did not trust the technique, and besides, there was no need to go easy on him. It annoyed Vatutin that Vaneyeva now had a chance to remain free—free, after working for enemies of the State! Somebody wanted to use her as a bargaining chip for something or other with the Central Committee, but that was not the Colonel's concern. Now the dry-cleaner had given him a description of another member of this endless chain.

And the annoying part was that Vatutin thought he knew the boy! The dry-cleaner had soon told him of his suspicion that he worked at the baths, and the description matched the attendant whom he himself had talked to! Unprofessional as it was, it enraged Vatutin that he'd met a traitor that morning last week and not recognized him for what . . .

What was that colonel's name? he asked himself suddenly. The one who'd tripped? Filitov—Misha Filitov? Personal aide to Defense Minister Yazov?

I must have really been hung over not to make the connection! Filitov of Stalingrad, the tanker who'd killed Germans while he burned within a knocked-out tank. Mikhail Filitov, three times Hero of the Soviet Union . . . It had to be the same one. Could he be the—

Impossible, he told himself.

But nothing was impossible. If he knew anything, Vatutin knew that. He cleared out his mind and considered the possibilities coldly. The good news here was that everyone of consequence in the Soviet Union had a file at 2 Dzerzhinskiy Square. It was a simple thing to get Filitov's.

The file was a thick one, he saw fifteen minutes later. Vatutin realized that he actually knew little about the man. As with most war heroes, exploits performed in a brief span of minutes had expanded to cover a whole life. But no life was ever that simple. Vatutin started reading the file.

Little of it had to do with his war record, though that was covered in full, including the citations for all of his medals. As personal aide to three successive defense ministers, Misha had been through rigorous security screenings, some of which Filitov knew about, some of which not. These papers were also in order, of course. He turned to the next bundle.

Vatutin was surprised to see that Filitov had been involved in the infamous Penkovskiy case. Oleg Penkovskiy had been a senior officer in the GRU, the Soviet military intelligence command; recruited by the British, then "run" jointly by the SIS and CIA, he'd betrayed his country as thoroughly as any man could. His penultimate treason had been to leak to the West the state of preparedness—or lack thereof—of the Strategic Rocket Forces during the Cuban Missile Crisis; this information had enabled American President Kennedy to force Khrushchev to withdraw the missiles that he'd so recklessly placed on that wretched island. But Penkovskiy's twisted loyalty to foreigners had forced him to take too many risks in delivering that data, and a spy could take only so many risks. He'd already been under suspicion. You could usually tell when the other side was getting just a little too clever, but . . . Filitov had been the one who provided the first real accusation . . .

Filitov was the one who'd denounced Penkovskiy? Vatutin was astounded. The investigation had been fairly advanced at that point. Continuous surveillance had shown Penkovskiy to be doing some unusual things, including at least one possible dead-drop, but—Vatutin shook his head. *The coincidences you encounter in this business.* Old Misha had gone to the senior security officer and reported a curious conversation with his GRU acquaintance, one that might have been innocent, he'd said, but it made his antennae twitch in an odd way, and so he felt constrained to report it. On instructions from KGB, he'd followed it up, and the next conversation hadn't been quite so innocent. By this time the case against Penkovskiy had been firmed up, and the additional proof hadn't really been needed, though it had made everyone involved feel a little better . . .

It was an odd coincidence, Vatutin thought, but hardly one to cast suspicion on the man. The personal section of the file showed that he was a widower. A photo of his wife was there, and Vatutin took his time admiring it. There was also a wedding picture, and the Second Chief Directorate man smiled when he saw that the old war-horse had indeed been young once, and a raffishly handsome bastard at that! On the next page was information on two sons—both dead. That got his attention. One born immediately before the war, the other soon after it began. But they hadn't died as a result of the war . . . What, then? He flipped through the pages.

The elder had died in Hungary, Vatutin saw. Because of his political reliability he'd been taken from his military academy, along with a number of cadets, and sent to help suppress the 1956 counterrevolution. A crewman in a tank—following in his father's footsteps, he'd died when his vehicle had been destroyed. Well, soldiers took their chances. Certainly his father had. The second—also a tanker, Vatutin noted—died when the breech on the gun in his T-55 had exploded. Poor quality-control at the factory, the bane of Soviet industry, had killed the whole crew . . . and when had his wife died? The following July. Broken heart, probably, whatever the medical explanation had been. The file showed both sons had been models of young Soviet manhood. All the hopes and dreams that just have died with them, Vatutin thought, and then to lose your wife, too.

Too bad, Misha. I guess you used up all your family's good luck against the Germans, and the other three had to pay the bill . . . So sad that a man who has done so much should be . . .

Should be given a reason to betray the Rodina? Vatutin looked up, and out the window of his office. He could see the square outside, the cars curving around the statue of Feliks Dzerzhinskiy. "Iron Feliks," founder of the *Cheka.* By birth a Pole and a Jew, with his odd little beard and ruthless intellect, Dzerzhinskiy had repelled the earliest efforts by the West to penetrate and subvert the Soviet Union. His back was to the building, and wags said that Feliks was condemned to perpetual isolation out there, as Svetlana Vaneyeva had been isolated . . .

Ah, Feliks, what would you advise me right now? Vatutin knew that answer easily enough. Feliks would have had Misha Filitov arrested and interrogated ruthlessly. The merest possibility of suspicion had been enough back then, and who knew how many innocent men and women had been broken or killed for no reason? Things were different now. Now even the KGB had rules to follow. You couldn't just snatch people off the street and torture whatever you wanted out of them. And that was better, Vatutin thought. KGB was a professional organization. They had to work harder now to do their job, and that made for well-trained officers, and better performance . . . His phone rang.

"Colonel Vatutin."

"Come up here. We're going to brief the Chairman in ten minutes." The line clicked off.

KGB headquarters is an old building, built around the turn of the century to be the home office of the Rossiya Insurance Company. The exterior walls were of rust-colored granite, and the inside was a reflection of the age in which it had been built, with high ceilings and oversized doors. The long, carpeted corridors of the building, however, were not terribly well lit, since one was not supposed to take too great an interest in the faces of the people who walked them. There were many uniforms in evidence. These officers were members of the Third Directorate, which kept an eye on the armed services. One thing that set the building apart was its silence. Those walking about did so with serious faces and closed mouths, lest they inadvertently let loose one of the million secrets that the building held.

The Chairman's office also faced the square, though with a far better view than Colonel Vatutin's. A male secretary rose from his desk and took the two visitors past the pair of security guards who always stood in the corners of the reception room. Vatutin took a deep breath as he walked through the opened door.

Nikolay Gerasimov was in his fourth year as Chairman of the Committee for State Security. He was not a spy by profession, but rather a Party man who'd spent fifteen years within the CPSU bureaucracy before being appointed to a middle-level post in the KGB's Fifth Chief Directorate, whose mission was the suppression of internal dissent. His delicate handling of this mission had earned him steady promotion and finally appointment as First Deputy Chairman ten years earlier. There he had learned the business of foreign intelligence from the administrative side, and performed well enough to gain the respect of professional field officers for his instincts. First and foremost, however, he was a Party man, and that explained his chairmanship. At fifty-three he was fairly young for his job, and looked younger still. His youthful face had never been lined by contemplation of failure, and his confident gaze looked forward to further promotion. For a man who already had a seat both on the Politburo and the Defense Council, further promotion meant that he considered himself in the running for the top post of all: General Secretary of the Communist Party of the Soviet Union. As the man who wielded the "sword and shield" of the Party (that was indeed the official motto of the KGB), he knew all there was to know about the other men in the running. His ambition, though never openly expressed, was whispered about the building, and any number of bright young KGB officers worked every day to tie their own fortunes to this rising star. A charmer, Vatutin saw. Even now he rose from his desk and waved his visitors to chairs opposite the massive oak desk. Vatutin was a man who controlled his thoughts and emotions; he was also too honest a man to be impressed by charmers.

Gerasimov held up a file. "Colonel Vatutin, I have read the report of your ongoing investigation. Excellent work. Can you bring me up to date?"

"Yes, Comrade Chairman. We are currently looking for one Eduard

Vassilyevich Altunin. He is an attendant in the Sandunovski Baths. Interrogation of the dry-cleaner revealed to us that he is the next step in the courier chain. Unfortunately he disappeared thirty-six hours ago, but we should have him by the end of the week."

"I've gone to the baths myself," Gerasimov noted with irony. Vatutin added his own.

"I still do, Comrade Chairman. I have myself seen this young man. I recognized the photograph in the file we're putting together. He was a corporal in an ordnance company in Afghanistan. His Army file shows that he objected to certain weapons being used there—the ones we use to discourage the civilians from helping the bandits." Vatutin referred to the bombs that were disguised as toys and designed to be picked up by children. "His unit political officer wrote up a report, but the first verbal warning shut him up, and he finished his tour of duty without further incident. The report was enough to deny him a factory job, and he's floated from one menial assignment to another. Co-workers describe him as ordinary but fairly quiet. Exactly what a spy should be, of course. He has never once referred to his 'troubles' in Afghanistan, even when drinking. His flat is under surveillance, as are all of his family members and friends. If we don't have him very quickly, we'll know he's a spy. But we'll get him, and I will talk to him myself."

Gerasimov nodded thoughtfully. "I see you used the new interrogation technique on this Vaneyeva woman. What do you think of it?"

"Interesting. Certainly it worked in this case, but I must say that I have misgivings about placing her back on the street."

"That was my decision, in case no one told you," Gerasimov said offhandedly. "Given the sensitivity of this case, and the doctor's recommendation, I think that the gamble is one worth taking for the moment. Do you agree that we shouldn't call too much attention to the case? Charges against her remain open."

Oh, and you can use it against her father, can't you? Her disgrace is his also, and what father would want to see his only child in the GULAG? Nothing like a little blackmail, is there, Comrade Chairman? "The case is certainly sensitive, and is likely to get more so," Vatutin replied carefully.

"Go on."

"The one time I saw this Altunin fellow, he was standing beside Colonel Mikhail Semyonovich Filitov."

"Misha Filitov, Yazov's aide?"

"The same, Comrade Chairman. I reviewed his file this morning."

"And?" This question came from Vatutin's boss.

"Nothing at all that I can point to. I hadn't known of his involvement in the Penkovskiy case . . ." Vatutin stopped, and for once his face showed something.

"Something is troubling you, Colonel," Gerasimov observed. "What is it?"

"Filitov's involvement in the Penkovskiy matter came soon after the death of his second son and his wife." Vatutin shrugged after a moment. "An odd coincidence."

"Wasn't Filitov the first witness against him?" asked the head of the Second Directorate. He'd actually worked on the fringes of the case.

Vatutin nodded. "That's right, but it was after we already had the spy under surveillance." He stopped for another moment. "As I said, an odd coincidence. We are *now* after a suspected courier who was running defense data. I saw him standing next to a senior Defense Ministry official, who was involved in another similar case almost thirty years ago. On the other hand, Filitov was the man who first reported Penkovskiy, and he is a distinguished war hero . . . who lost his family under unfortunate circumstances . . ." It was the first time he had strung all his thoughts together.

"Has there ever been a hint of suspicion against Filitov?" the Chairman asked.

"No. His career could scarcely be more impressive. Filitov was the only aide who stayed with the late Minister Ustinov throughout his career, and he's hung on there ever since. He functions as a personal inspector-general for the Minister."

"I know," Gerasimov said. "I have here a request over Yazov's signature for our file on American SDI efforts. When I called about it, the Minister told me that colonels Filitov and Bondarenko are assembling data for a full report to the Politburo. The code word on that photographic frame you recovered was Bright Star, was it not?"

"Yes, Comrade Chairman."

"Vatutin, we now have three coincidences," Gerasimov observed. "Your recommendation?"

That was simple enough: "We should place Filitov under surveillance. Probably this Bondarenko fellow also."

"Very carefully, but with the utmost thoroughness." Gerasimov closed the file. "This is a fine report, and it would seem that your investigative instincts are as sharp as ever, Colonel. You will keep me posted on this case. I expect to see you three times a week from now until its conclusion. General," he said to the head of "Two," "this man will get all the support he needs. You may requisition resources from any part of the Committee. If you run into objections, please refer them to me. We may be certain that there is a leak at the highest level of the Defense Ministry. Next: this case is classified to my eyes and yours. No one—I repeat, *no one* will know of this. Who can say where the Americans have managed to place their agents? Vatutin, run this one to earth and you will have general's stars by summer. But"—he held up a finger—"I think you should cease drinking until you are finished with this one. We need your head clear."

"Yes, Comrade Chairman."

The corridor was nearly empty outside the Chairman's office when Vatutin and his boss left. "What about Vaneyeva?" the Colonel asked *sotto voce*.

"It's her father, of course. General Secretary Narmonov will announce his election to the Politburo next week," the General replied in a neutral, quiet voice.

And it won't hurt to have another friend of the KGB at court, Vatutin thought to himself. *Might Gerasimov be making some sort of move?*

"Remember what he said about drinking," the General said next. "I've heard that you're hitting the bottle very hard of late. That's one area of agreement between the Chairman and the General Secretary, in case no one ever told you."

"Yes, Comrade General," Vatutin replied. *Of course, it's probably the only area of agreement.* Like any good Russian, Vatutin thought that vodka was as much a part of life as air. It occurred to him to note that his hangover had encouraged him to take steam that morning and notice the crucial coincidence, but he refrained from pointing out the irony involved. Back at his desk a few minutes later, Vatutin took out a pad and began planning the surveillance on two colonels of the Soviet Army.

Gregory took usual commercial flights home, changing planes at Kansas City after a two-hour layover. He slept through most of the transit and walked straight into the terminal without having to chase after any baggage. His fiancée was waiting for him.

"How was Washington?" she asked after the usual welcome-home kiss.

"Never changes. They ran me all over the place. I guess they figure scientific types don't ever sleep." He took her hand for the walk out to the car.

"So what happened?" she asked when they were outside.

"The Russians ran a big test." He stopped to look around. This was a technical violation of security—but Candi was part of the team, wasn't she? "They slagged down a satellite with the ground-based lasers at Dushanbe. What's left looks like a plastic model that got put in the oven."

"That's bad," Dr. Long observed.

"Sure is," Dr. Gregory agreed. "But they have optical problems. Blooming and jitter both. It's for sure they don't have anybody like you over there to build mirrors. They must have some good folks on the laser end, though."

"How good?"

"Good enough that they're doing something we haven't figured out yet," Al grumped as they reached his Chevy. "You drive, I'm still a little dopey."

"Will we figure it out?" Candi asked as she unlocked the door.

"Sooner or later." He couldn't go any further than that, fiancée or not.

Candi got in and reached to unlock the right-side door. As soon as Al was seated and strapped in, he opened the glove compartment and extracted a Twinkie. He always had a stash. It was a little stale, but he didn't mind. Sometimes Candi wondered if his love for her resulted from the fact that her nickname reminded him of junk food.

"How's work on the new mirror going?" he asked after snapping down half of the Twinkie.

"Marv has a new idea that we're modeling out. He thinks we should thin out the coating instead of thickening it. We're going to try it next week."

"Marv's pretty original for an old guy," Al observed. Dr. Marv Greene was forty-two.

Candi laughed. "His secretary thinks he's pretty original, too."

"He should know better than to fool around with somebody at work," Gregory said seriously. He winced a moment later.

"Yeah, honey." She turned to look at him, and they both laughed. "How tired are you?"

"I slept on the flight."

"Good."

Just before reaching around her, Gregory crumpled the Twinkie wrapper and tossed it on the floor, where it joined about thirty others. He flew around quite a bit, but Candi had a sure cure for jet lag.

"Well, Jack?" Admiral Greer asked.

"I'm worried," Ryan admitted. "It was pure dumb luck that we saw the test. The timing was cute. All of our recon birds were well below the optical horizon. We weren't supposed to notice—which is hardly surprising, since it's a technical violation of the ABM treaty. Well, probably." Jack shrugged. "Depends on how you read the treaty. Now you get into the 'strict' or 'loose' interpretation argument. If we pulled something like this, the Senate would go nuts."

"They wouldn't like the test that you saw." Very few people knew how far along Tea Clipper was. The program was "black." More classified than top secret, "black" programs simply did not exist.

"Maybe. But we were testing the aiming system, not an actual weapon."

"And the Soviets were testing a system to see if it was—" Greer chuckled and shook his head. "It's like talking metaphysics, isn't it? How many lasers can dance on the head of a pin?"

"I'm sure Ernie Allen could give us an opinion on that." Jack smiled. He didn't agree with Allen, but he had to like the man. "I hope our friend in Moscow can deliver."

12. Success and Failure

One of the problems with surveillance of any individual is that one must determine how he or she spends an ordinary day before one can establish what resources are needed for the operation. The more solitary the person or the activity, the harder it generally is to keep a covert eye on him. Already, for example, the KGB officers trailing Colonel Bondarenko hated him thoroughly. His daily jogging routine was an ideal activity for a spy, they all thought. He ran about entirely alone on city streets that were largely vacant—vacant enough that everyone out at that time was undoubtedly known to him by sight, and vacant enough that he would immediately notice anything out of the ordinary. As he ran around the residential blocks in this part of Moscow, the three agents assigned to keep an eye on him lost visual contact with him no less than five times. The sparse trees they might hide behind were bare of leaves, and the apartment buildings stood like tombstones on flat, open land. In any of those five times, Bondarenko might have stopped to retrieve something from a dead-drop or could have made one himself. It was more than frustrating, and added to this was the fact that this Soviet Army Colonel had a service record that was as immaculate as a field of freshly fallen snow: exactly the cover that any spy would contrive to acquire for himself, of course.

They spotted him again turning the corner for home, his legs pumping vigorously, his breath marked in the air behind him as small clouds of vapor. The man in charge of this part of the case decided that half a dozen "Two" officers would be needed just to shadow the subject for his morning runs. And they'd have to be here an hour earlier than he was expected to run, enduring the dry, bitter cold of the Moscow dawn. People from the Second Chief Directorate never considered themselves fully appreciated for the hardships of their job.

Several kilometers away, another team of three was quite satisfied with their subject. In this case, an eighth-floor apartment in the building opposite the subject's was obtained—the diplomat who lived there was abroad. A pair of telephoto lenses was focused on Misha's windows, and he was not a man who troubled to lower his shades or even to adjust them properly. They watched him go through the morning routine of a man who'd had too much to drink the night before, and that was familiar enough to the "Two" men who watched in heated comfort from across the street.

Misha was also sufficiently senior at the Defense Ministry that he rated a car and driver. It was an easy thing to reassign the sergeant and to substitute a shiny young face fresh from the KGB's counterintelligence school. A tap on his phone recorded his request for an early pickup.

Ed Foley left his apartment earlier than usual. His wife drove him over today, with the kids in the back of the car. The Soviet file on Foley noted with amusement that she kept the car on most days to run the kids around and generally socialize with the wives of other Western diplomats. A Soviet husband would keep the car for his own use. At least she wasn't making him take the Metro today, they observed; decent of her. The militiaman at the entrance to the diplomatic compound—he was really KGB, as everyone knew—noted the time of departure and the occupancy of the car. It was slightly out of the ordinary, and the gate guard looked around to see if Foley's KGB shadow was here today. He wasn't. The "important" Americans got much more regular surveillance.

Ed Foley had a Russian-style fur hat, and his overcoat was sufficiently old and worn that it didn't look terribly foreign. A wool scarf clashed slightly with it, protecting his neck and hiding his striped tie. The Russian security officers who knew him by sight noted that, as with most foreigners, local weather was the great equalizer. If you lived through a Russian winter, you soon started dressing and acting like a Russian, even to the point of looking slightly downward when you walked.

First the kids were dropped off at school. Mary Pat Foley drove normally, her eyes flicking back and forth to the mirror every three or four seconds. Driving here wasn't all that bad, compared to American cities. Although Russian drivers could do the most extraordinary things, the streets weren't terribly crowded, and having learned to drive in New York City, she could handle nearly anything. As with commuters all over the world, she had a route composed of indirect shortcuts that avoided the handful of traffic bottlenecks and saved a few minutes each day at the cost of an extra liter or two of *benzin*.

Immediately after turning a corner, she moved expertly to the curb and her husband hopped out. The car was already moving as he slammed the door shut and moved off, not too quickly, toward the side entrance of the apartment block. For once Ed Foley's heart was beating fast. He'd done this only once before and didn't like it at all. Once inside, he avoided the elevators and bounded up the eight flights of stairs, looking at his watch.

He didn't know how his wife did it. It pained his male ego to admit that she drove so much more precisely than he did, and could place her car at any spot she wished with an accuracy of five seconds, plus or minus. He had two minutes to get to the eighth floor. Foley accomplished it with seconds to spare. He opened the fire door, and anxious eyes scanned the corridor. Wonderful things, corridors. Especially the straight, bare ones in high-rise apartment buildings. Nowhere for people to lurk with their cameras, with a bank of elevators in the middle, and fire stairs at both ends. He walked briskly past the elevators, heading toward the far end. He could measure the time with his heartbeats now. Twenty yards ahead, a door opened, and a man in uniform came out. He turned to set the lock on his apartment door, then picked up the briefcase and headed toward Foley. A passerby, if there had been one, might have thought it odd that neither man moved to avoid the other.

It was over in an instant. Foley's hand brushed against CARDINAL's, taking the film cassette and passing back a tiny rolled slip of paper. He thought he noted a look of irritation in the agent's eyes, but nothing more than that, not even a "Please excuse me, Comrade," as the officer continued toward the elevators. Foley walked straight into the fire stairs. He took his time going down.

Colonel Filitov emerged from the building at the appointed time. The sergeant holding the door of his car noted that his mouth was working on something, perhaps a crumb of bread caught between his teeth.

"Good morning, Comrade Colonel."

"Where's Zhdanov?" Filitov asked as he got in.

"He took ill. An appendix, they think." This drew a grunt.

"Well, move off. I want to take steam this morning."

Foley came out of the building's back entrance a minute later and walked past two other apartment blocks as he made his way to the next street over. He was just reaching the curb when his wife pulled over, picked him up almost without stopping. Both took a few deep breaths as she headed toward the embassy.

"What are you doing today?" she asked, her eyes still checking the mirror.

"The usual," was the resigned reply.

Misha was already in the steam room. He noted the absence of the attendant and the presence of a few unfamiliar faces. That explained the special pickup this morning. His face gave nothing away as he traded a few friendly words with the regulars. It was a pity that he'd run out of film in his camera. Then there was the warning from Foley. If he were under surveillance again—well, every few years some security officer or other would get a bug up his ass and recheck everyone at the Ministry. CIA had noticed and broken up the courier chain. It was amusing, he thought, to see the look on that young man's face in the corridor. So few people were left who knew what combat was like. People were so easy to frighten. Combat taught a man what to fear and what to ignore, Filitov told himself.

Outside the steam room, a "Two" man was riffling through Filitov's clothing. In the car, his briefcase was being searched. In each case, the job was done quickly and thoroughly.

Vatutin himself supervised the search of Filitov's apartment. It was a job for experts whose hands were in surgical gloves, and they spent much of their time looking for "telltales." It could be the odd scrap of paper, a crumb, even a single human hair placed in a specific spot whose removal would tell the man who lived in the flat that somebody had been here. Numerous photographs were taken and rushed off for developing, and then the searchers went to work. The diary was found almost at once. Vatutin leaned down to look at the simple book that sat openly in the desk drawer to be sure that its placement wasn't secretly marked. After a minute or two, he picked it up and started reading.

Colonel Vatutin was irritable. He hadn't slept well the previous night. Like most heavy drinkers, he needed a few drinks to sleep, and the excitement of the case added to the lack of a proper sedative had given him a fitful night of tossing and turning; it showed enough on his face to warn his team to keep their mouths shut.

"Camera," he said curtly. A man came over and started photographing the pages of the diary as Vatutin turned them.

"Somebody's tried to pick the door lock," a major reported. "Scratches around the keyhole. If we dismantle the lock, I think we'll see scratches on the tumblers also. Somebody's probably been in here."

"I have what they were after," Vatutin said crossly. Heads turned throughout the apartment. The man checking the refrigerator popped off the front panel, looked underneath the appliance, then put the panel back in place after the interruption. "This man keeps a fucking diary! Doesn't anybody read security manuals anymore?"

He could see it now. Colonel Filitov used personal diaries to sketch out official reports. Somehow, someone had learned this, and got into his flat to make copies of . . .

But how likely is that? Vatutin asked himself. *About as likely as a man who writes out his memories of official documents when he could just as easily copy them at his desk in the Defense Ministry.*

The search took two hours, and the team left in ones and twos, after replacing everything exactly the way they'd found it.

Back at his office, Vatutin read the photographed diary in full. At the apartment he'd merely skimmed it. The fragment from the captured film exactly matched a page at the beginning of Filitov's journal. He spent an hour going through the photographs of the pages. The data itself was impressive enough. Filitov was describing Project Bright Star in considerable detail. In fact, the old Colonel's explanation was better than the brief he'd been given as part of the investigation directive. Tossed in were details of Colonel Bondarenko's observations about site security and a few complaints on the way priorities were assigned at the Ministry. It was evident that both colonels were very enthusiastic about Bright Star, and Vatutin already agreed with them. But Minister Yazov, he read, was not yet sure. Complaining about funding problems—well, that was an old story, wasn't it?

It was clear that Filitov had violated security rules by having records of top-secret documents in his home. That was itself a matter sufficiently serious that any junior or middle-level bureaucrat would lose his job for it, but Filitov was as senior as the Minister himself, and Vatutin knew all too well that senior people regarded security rules as inconveniences to be ignored in the Interest of the State, of which they viewed themselves as the ultimate arbiters. He wondered if the same were true elsewhere. Of one thing he was sure: before he or anyone else at KGB could accuse Filitov of anything, he needed something more serious than this. Even if Misha were a foreign agent—*Why am I looking for ways to deny that?* Vatutin asked himself in some surprise. He took himself back to the man's flat, and remembered the photographs on the walls. There must have been a hundred of them: Misha standing atop the turret of his T-34, binoculars to his eyes; Misha with his men in the snows outside Stalingrad; Misha and his tank crew pointing to holes in the side armor of a German tank . . . and Misha in a hospital bed, with Stalin himself pinning his third Hero of the Soviet Union medal to his pillow, his lovely wife and both children at his side. These were the memorabilia of a patriot and a hero.

In the old days that wouldn't have mattered, Vatutin reminded himself. *In the old days we suspected everyone.*

Anyone could have scratched the door lock. He'd leaped to the assumption that it was the missing bath attendant. A former ordnance technician, he probably knew how. *What if that is a coincidence?*

But if Misha were a spy, why not photograph the official documents himself? In his capacity as aide to the Defense Minister, he could order up any documents he wanted, and smuggling a spy camera into the Ministry was a trivial exercise.

If we'd gotten the film with a frame from such a document, Misha would already be in Lefortovo Prison . . .

What if he's being clever? What if he wants us to think that someone else is stealing material from his diary? I can take what I have to the Ministry right now, but we can accuse him of nothing more than violating in-house security rules, and if he answers that he was working at home, and admits to breaking the rule, and the Minister defends his aide—would the Minister defend Filitov?

Yes. Vatutin was sure of that. For one thing, Misha was a trusted aide and a distinguished professional soldier. For another, the Army would always close ranks to defend one of its own against the KGB. *The bastards hate us worse than they hate the West.* The Soviet Army had never forgotten the late 1930s, when Stalin had used the security agency to kill nearly every senior uniformed officer, and then as a direct result nearly lost Moscow to the German Army. No, if we go to them with no more than this, they'll reject all our evidence and launch their own investigation with the GRU.

Just how many irregularities are going to show up in this case? Colonel Vatutin wondered.

Foley was wondering much the same thing in his cubbyhole a few miles away. He had had the film developed and was reading it over. He noted with irritation that CARDINAL had run out of film and hadn't been able to reproduce the entire document. The part he had before him, however, showed that the KGB had an agent inside an American project that was called Tea Clipper. Evidently Filitov deemed this of more immediate interest to the Americans than what his own people were up to, and on reading the data, Foley was tempted to agree. Well. He'd get CARDINAL some more film cassettes, get the full document out, and then let him know that it was time to retire. The breakout wasn't scheduled for another ten days or so. Plenty of time, he told himself despite a crawly feel at the back of his neck that was telling him something else.

For my next trick, how do we get the new film to CARDINAL? With the usual courier chain destroyed, it would take several weeks to establish a new one, and he didn't want to risk a direct contact again.

It had to happen eventually, he knew. Sure, everything had gone smoothly the whole time he'd run this agent, but sooner or later something happened. Random chance, he told himself. Eventually the dice would come up the wrong way. When he'd first been assigned here and learned the operational history of CARDINAL, he'd marveled that the man had lasted so long, that he'd rejected at least three offers for breakout. How far could one man push his luck? The old bastard must have thought he was invincible. *Those whom the gods would destroy, they first make proud,* Foley thought.

He put it aside and continued with the task of the day. By evening, the courier was heading west with a new CARDINAL report.

"It's on the way," Ritter told the Director of Central Intelligence.

"Thank God." Judge Moore smiled. "Now let's concentrate on getting him the hell out of there."

"Clark's being briefed. He flies over to England tomorrow, and he meets the submarine the day after that."

"That's another one who's pushed his luck," the Judge observed.

"The best we got," Ritter replied.

"It's not enough to move with," Vatutin told the Chairman after outlining the results of his surveillance and search. "I'm assigning more people to the operation. We've also placed listening devices in Filitov's apartment—"

"And this other colonel?"

"Bondarenko? We were unable to get in there. His wife does not work and stays home all day. We learned today that the man runs a few kilometers every morning, and some additional men have been assigned to this case also. The only information we have at present is a clean record—indeed, an exemplary one—and a goodly portion of ambition. He is now the official Ministry representative to Bright Star, and as you see from the diary pages, an enthusiastic supporter of the project."

"Your feeling for the man?" The Chairman's questions were delivered in a curt but not menacing voice. He was a busy man who guarded his time.

"So far, nothing that would lead us to suspect anything. He was decorated for service in Afghanistan; he took command of a *Spetznaz* group that was ambushed and fought off a determined bandit attack. While at this Bright Star place, he upbraided the KGB guard force for laxness, but his formal report to the Ministry explained why, and it is hard to fault his reasons."

"Is anything being done about it?" Gerasimov asked.

"The officer who was sent out to discuss the matter was killed in a plane crash in Afghanistan. Another officer will be sent out shortly, they tell me."

"The bath attendant?"

"We are still looking for him. No results as yet. Everything is covered: airports, train stations, everything. If anything breaks, I'll report to you immediately."

"Very well. Dismissed, Colonel." Gerasimov went back to the papers on his desk.

The Chairman of the Committee for State Security allowed himself a smile after Vatutin left. He was amazed at how well things were going. The masterstroke was the Vaneyeva matter. It wasn't often that you uncovered a spy ring in Moscow, and when you did so, the congratulations were always mixed with the question: *Why did it take you so long?* That wouldn't happen this time. No, not with Vaneyeva's father about to be appointed to the Politburo. And Secretary Narmonov thought that he'd be loyal to the man who'd arranged the promotion. Narmonov, with all his dreams of reducing arms, of loosening the grip of the Party on the life of the nation, of "liberalizing" what had been bequeathed to the Party . . . Gerasimov was going to change all that.

It wouldn't be easy, of course. Gerasimov had only three firm allies on the Politburo, but among them was Alexandrov, the ideologue whom the Secretary had been unable to retire after he'd changed allegiance. And now he had another, one quite unknown to the Comrade General Secretary. On the other hand, Narmonov had the Army behind him.

That was a legacy of Mathias Rust, the German teenager who'd landed his rented Cessna in Red Square. Narmonov was a shrewd operator. Rust had flown into the Soviet Union on Border Guards Day, a coincidence that he could not explain—and Narmonov had denied KGB the opportunity to interrogate the hooligan properly! Gerasimov still growled about that. The young man had staged his flight on the only day in the year when one could be sure that the KGB's vast force of border guards would be gloriously drunk. That had got him across the Gulf of Finland undetected. Then the air defense command, Voyska PVO, had failed to detect him, and the child had landed right in front of St. Basil's!

General Secretary Narmonov had acted quickly after that: firing the chief of Voyska PVO and Defense Minister Sokolov after a stormy Politburo session where Gerasimov had been unable to raise any objections, lest he endanger his own position. The new Defense Minister, D. T. Yazov, was the Secretary's man, a nobody from far down the numerical list of senior officers; a man who, having failed to earn his post, depended on the Secretary to stay there. That had covered Narmonov's most vulnerable flank. The complication it added now was that Yazov was still learning his job, and he obviously depended on old hands like Filitov to teach it to him.

And Vatutin thinks that this is merely a counterespionage case, Gerasimov grunted to himself.

The security procedures that revolved around CARDINAL data precluded Foley from sending any information in the normal way. Even one-time-pad ciphers, which were theoretically unbreakable, were denied him. So the cover sheet on the latest report would warn the Δ fraternity that the data being dispatched wasn't quite what was expected.

That realization lifted Bob Ritter right off his chair. He made his photocopies and destroyed the originals before walking to Judge Moore's office. Greer and Ryan were already there.

"He ran out of film," the DDO said as soon as the door was closed.

"What?" Moore asked.

"Something new came in. It seems that our KGB colleagues have an agent inside Tea Clipper who just gave them most of the design work on this new gollywog mirror gadget, and CARDINAL decided that that was more important. He didn't have enough film left for everything, so he prioritized on what the KGB is up to. We only have half of what their laser system looks like."

"Half might be enough," Ryan observed. That drew a scowl. Ritter was not the least bit happy that Ryan was now Δ-cleared.

"He discusses the effects of the design change, but there's nothing about the change itself."

"Can we identify the source of the leak on our side?" Admiral Greer asked.

"Maybe. It's somebody who really understands mirrors. Parks has to see this right quick. Ryan, you've actually been there. What do you think?"

"The test I watched validated the performance of the mirror and the computer software that runs it. If the Russians can duplicate it—well, we know they have the laser part down pat, don't we?" He stopped for a moment. "Gentlemen, this is scary. If the Russians get there first, it blows away all the arms-control criteria, and it faces us with a deteriorating strategic situation. I mean, it would take several years before the problem manifests itself, but . . ."

"Well, if our man can get another goddamned film cassette," the Deputy Director for Operations said, "we can get to work on it ourselves. The good news is that this Bondarenko guy that Misha selected to run the laser desk at the Ministry will report to our man regularly on what's happening. The bad news—"

"Well, we don't have to go into that now," Judge Moore said. Ryan didn't need to know any of that, his eyes told Ritter, who nodded instant agreement. "Jack, you said you had something else?"

"There's going to be a new appointment to the Politburo Monday—Ilya Arkadyevich Vaneyev. Age sixty-three, widower. One daughter, Svetlana, who works at GOSPLAN; she's divorced, with one child. Vaneyev is a pretty straight guy, honest by their standards, not much in the way of dirty laundry that we know about. He's moving up from a Central Committee slot. He's the guy who took over the agricultural post that Narmonov held and did fairly well at it. The thinking is that he's going to be Narmonov's man. That gives him four full voting members of the Politburo who belong to him, one more than the Alexandrov faction, and—" He stopped when he saw the pained looks on the other three faces in the office. "Something wrong?"

"That daughter of his. She's on Sir Basil's payroll," Judge Moore told him.

"Terminate the contract," Ryan said. "It would be nice to have that kind of source, but that kind of scandal now would endanger Narmonov. Put her into retirement. Reactivate her in a few years, maybe, but right now shut her the hell off."

"Might not be that easy," Ritter said, and let it go at that. "How's the evaluation coming?"

"Finished it yesterday."

"It's for the President's eyes plus a few others, but this one's going to be tightly held."

"Fair enough. I can have it printed up this afternoon. If that's all . . . ?" It was. Ryan left the room. Moore watched the door close before speaking.

"I haven't told anyone yet, but the President is concerned about Narmonov's political position again. Ernie Allen is worried that the latest change in the Soviet position indicates a weakening in Narmonov's support at home, and he's convinced the boss that this is a bad time to push on a few issues. The implication of that is, if we bring CARDINAL out, well, it might have an undesired political effect."

"If Misha gets caught, we get the same political effect," Ritter pointed out. "Not to mention the slightly deleterious effect it'll have on our man. Arthur, they are after him. They may have gotten to Vaneyev's daughter already—"

"She's back at work in GOSPLAN," the DCI said.

"Yeah, and the man at the cleaners has disappeared. They got to her and broke her," the DDO insisted. "We have to break him out once and for all. We can't leave him flapping in the breeze, Arthur. We *owe* this man."

"I cannot authorize the extraction without presidential approval."

Ritter came close to exploding. "Then get it! Screw the politics—in this

THE CARDINAL OF THE KREMLIN • 671

case, screw the politics. There is a practical side to this, Arthur. If we let a man like this go down, and we don't lift a finger to protect him, the word will get out—hell, the Russians'll make a TV miniseries out of it! It will cost us more in the long term than this temporary political garbage."

"Hold it for a minute," Greer said. "If they broke this Party guy's daughter, how come she's back to work?"

"Politics?" Moore mused. "You suppose the KGB's unable to hurt this guy's family?"

"Right!" the DDO snorted. "Gerasimov's in the opposing faction, and he'd pass the opportunity to deny a Politburo seat to Narmonov's man? It smells like politics, all right, but not that kind. More likely our friend Alexandrov has the new boy in his back pocket and Narmonov doesn't know about it."

"So, you think they've broken her, but let her go and are using her as leverage on the old man?" Moore asked. "It does make sense. But there's no evidence."

"Alexandrov's too old to go after the post himself, and anyway the ideologue never seems to get the top spot—more fun to play kingmaker. Gerasimov's his fair-haired boy, though, and we know that he's got enough ambition to have himself crowned Nicholas the Third."

"Bob, you've just come up with another reason not to rock the boat right now." Greer sipped at his coffee for a moment. "I don't like the idea of leaving Filitov in place either. What are the chances that he can just lay low? I mean, the way things are set up, he might just talk his way out of anything they can bring against him."

"No, James." Ritter shook his head emphatically. "We can't have him lay low, because we need the rest of this report, don't we? If he runs the risk of getting it out despite the attention he's getting, we can't then leave him to fate. It's not right. Remember what this man's done for us over the years." Ritter argued on for several minutes, demonstrating the ferocious loyalty to his people that he'd learned as a young case officer. Though agents often had to be treated like children, encouraged, supported, and often disciplined, they became like your own children, and danger to them was something to be fought.

Judge Moore ended the discussion. "Your points are well taken, Bob, but I still have to go to the President. This isn't just a field operation anymore."

Ritter stood his ground. "We put all the assets in place."

"Agreed, but it won't be carried out until we get approval."

The weather at Faslane was miserable, but at this time of year it usually was. A thirty-knot wind was lashing the Scottish coast with snow and sleet when *Dallas* surfaced. Mancuso took his station atop the sail and surveyed the rocky hills on the horizon. He'd just completed a speed run, zipping across the Atlantic at an average of thirty-one knots, about as hard as he cared to push his boat for any extended period of time, not to mention his running submerged far closer to the coast than he would have preferred. Well, he was paid to follow orders, not to love them.

The seas were rolling about fifteen feet, and his submarine rolled with them, wallowing her way forward at twelve knots. The seas came right over the spherical bow and splashed high on meeting the blunt face of the sail. Even the foul-weather gear didn't help much. Within a few minutes he was soaked and shivering. A Royal Navy tug approached and took station off *Dallas'* port bow, leading her in to the loch while Mancuso came to terms with the rolling. One of his best-kept professional secrets was an occasional touch of seasickness. Being on the sail helped, but those inside the submarine's cylindrical hull were now regretting the heavy lunch served a few hours earlier.

Within an hour they were in sheltered waters, taking the S-turns into the base that supported British and American nuclear submarines. Once there, the wind helped, easing the slate-gray bulk of the submarine up to the pier. People were already waiting there, sheltered in a few cars as the lines were passed and secured by the submarine's deck crew. As soon as the brow was passed, Mancuso went below to his cabin.

His first visitor was a commander. He'd expected a submarine officer, but this one had no service badges at all. That made him an intelligence type.

"How was the crossing, Captain?" the man asked.

"Quiet." *Well, get on with it!*

"You sail in three hours. Here are your mission orders." He handed over a manila envelope with wax seals, and a note on the front that told Mancuso when he could open it. Though often a feature in movies, it was the first time this had happened to him as a CO. You were supposed to be able to discuss your mission with the people who gave it to you. But not this time. Mancuso signed for them, locked them in his safe under the watchful eyes of the spook, and sent him back on his way.

"Shit," the Captain observed to himself. Now his guests could come aboard.

There were two of them, both in civilian clothes. The first came down the torpedo-loading hatch with the aplomb of a real sailor. Mancuso soon saw why.

"Howdy, skipper!"

"Jonesy, what the hell are you doing here?"

"Admiral Williamson gave me a choice: either be recalled to temporary active duty or come aboard as a civilian tech-rep. I'd rather be a tech-rep. Pay's better." Jones lowered his voice. "This here's Mr. Clark. He doesn't talk much."

And he didn't. Mancuso assigned him to the spare bunk in the engineer's stateroom. After his gear came down the hatch, Mr. Clark walked into the room, closed the door behind him, and that was that.

"Where do you want me to stash my stuff?" Jones asked.

"There's a spare bunk in the goat locker," Mancuso replied.

"Fine. The chiefs eat better anyway."

"How's school?"

"One more semester till my masters. I'm already getting nibbles from some contractors. And I'm engaged." Jones pulled out his wallet and showed the Captain a photo. "Her name's Kim, and she works in the library."

"Congratulations, Mr. Jones."

"Thanks, skipper. The Admiral said you really needed me. Kim understands. Her dad's Army. So, what's up? Some kind of spec-op, and you couldn't make it without me, right?" "Special Operations" was a euphemism that covered all sorts of things, most of which were dangerous.

"I don't know. They haven't told me yet."

"Well, one more trip 'up north' wouldn't be too bad," Jones observed. "To be honest, I kind of missed it."

Mancuso didn't think they were going there, but refrained from saying so. Jones went aft to get settled. Mancuso went into the engineer's stateroom.

"Mr. Clark?"

"Yes, sir." He'd hung up his jacket, revealing that he wore a short-sleeved shirt. The man was a little over forty, Mancuso judged. On first inspection, he didn't look all that special, perhaps six-one, and slim, but then Mancuso noted that the man didn't have the normal middle-age roll at the waist, and his shoulders were broader than they looked on the tall frame. It was the second glance at an arm that added a piece to the jigsaw. Half hidden under the black hair on his forearm was a tattoo, a red seal, it seemed to be, with a wide, impudent grin.

"I knew a guy with a tattoo like that. Officer—he's with Team-Six now."

"Once upon a time, Captain. I'm not supposed to talk about that, sir."

"What's this all about?"

"Sir, your mission orders will—"

"Humor me." Mancuso smiled out the order. "They just took in the brow."

"It involves making a pickup."

My God. Mancuso nodded impassively. "Will you need any additional support?"

"No, sir. Solo shot. Just me and my gear."

"Okay. We can go over it in detail after we sail. You'll eat in the wardroom. Right down the ladder outside, then a few feet aft, on the starboard side. One other thing: is time a problem?"

"Shouldn't be, unless you mind waiting. Part of this is still up in the air—and that's all I can say for now, Captain. Sorry, but I have my orders, too."

"Fair enough. You take the top bunk. Get some sleep if you need it."

"Thank you, sir." Clark watched the Captain leave, but didn't smile until the door closed. He'd never been on a Los Angeles–class submarine before. Most intelligence missions were conducted by the smaller, more maneuverable Sturgeons. He always slept in the same place, always in the upper bunk in the engineer's stateroom, the only spare bed on the ship. There was the usual problem stowing his gear, but "Clark" had done it enough to know all the tricks. When he'd finished that, he climbed up into the bunk. He was tired from the flight and needed a few hours to relax. The bunk was always the same, hard against the curved hull of the submarine. It was like being in a coffin with the lid half-open.

"One must admire the Americans for their cleverness," Morozov said. It had been a busy several weeks at Dushanbe. Immediately after the test—more precisely, immediately after their visitor from Moscow had left—two of the six lasers had been defrosted and disassembled for service, and it was found that their optics had been badly scorched. So there was still a problem with the optical coating, after all. More likely quality-control, his section chief had observed, dismissing the problem to another team of engineers. What they had now was far more exciting. Here was the American mirror design that they'd heard about for years.

"The idea came from an astronomer. He wanted a way to make stellar photographs that didn't suffer from 'twinkling.' Nobody bothered to tell him that it was impossible, so he went ahead and did it. I knew the rough idea, but not the details. You are right, young man. This is very clever.

Too clever for us," the man growled briefly as he flipped to the page on computer specifications. "We don't have anything that can duplicate this performance. Just building the actuators—I don't know if we can even do that."

"The Americans are building the telescope—"

"Yes, at Hawaii. I know. But the one at Hawaii is far behind this one, technically speaking. The Americans have made a breakthrough that has not yet found its way into the general scientific community. Note the date on the diagram. They may actually have this one operating now." He shook his head. "They're ahead of us."

"You have to leave."

"Yes. Thank you for protecting me this long." Eduard Vassilyevich Altunin's gratitude was genuine. He'd had a floor on which to sleep, and several warm meals to sustain him while he made his plans.

Or attempted to. He couldn't even appreciate the disadvantages under which he labored. In the West he could easily have obtained new clothing, a wig to disguise his hair, even a theatrical makeup kit that came with instructions on how to alter his features. In the West he could hide in the back seat of a car, and be driven two hundred miles in under four hours. In Moscow he had none of those options. The KGB would have searched his flat by now, and determined what clothing he wore. They'd know his face and hair color. The only thing they evidently did not know was his small circle of friends from military service in Afghanistan. He'd never talked to anyone about them.

They offered him a different sort of coat, but it didn't fit, and he had no wish to endanger these people further. He already had his cover story down: he'd hidden out with a criminal group a few blocks away. One fact about Moscow little known in the West was its crime situation, which was bad and getting worse. Though Moscow had not yet caught up with American cities of comparable size, there were districts where the prudent did not walk alone at night. But since foreigners didn't often visit such areas, and since the street criminals rarely troubled foreigners—doing so guaranteed a vigorous response from the Moscow Militia—the story was slow getting out.

He walked out onto Trofimovo, a dingy thoroughfare near the river. Altunin marveled at his stupidity. He'd always told himself that if he needed to escape from the city, he'd do so on a cargo barge. His father had worked on them all his life, and Eduard knew hiding places that no one could find—but the river was frozen, and barge traffic was at a stop, and he hadn't thought of it! Altunin raged at himself.

There was no sense worrying about that now, he told himself. There had to be another way. He knew that the Moskvich auto plant was only a kilometer away, and the trains ran year round. He'd try to catch one going south, perhaps hide in a freight car filled with auto parts. With luck he'd make it to Soviet Georgia, where no one would inspect his new papers all that closely. People could disappear in the Soviet Union. After all, it was a country of 280,000,000, he told himself. People were always losing or damaging their papers. He wondered how many of these thoughts were realistic and how many were simply an attempt to cheer himself up.

But he couldn't stop now. It had started in Afghanistan and he wondered if it would ever stop.

He'd been able to shut it out at first. A corporal in an ordnance company, he worked with what the Soviet military euphemistically referred to as "counterterrorist devices." These were distributed by air, or most often by Soviet soldiers completing a sweep through a village. Some were the prototypical Russian *matryoshka* dolls, a bandanaed figure with a roly-poly bottom; or a truck; or a fountain pen. Adults learned fast, but children were cursed both with curiosity and the inability to learn from the mistakes of others. Soon it was learned that children would pick up anything, and the number of doll-bombs distributed was reduced. But one thing remained constant: when picked up, a hundred grams of explosive would go off. His job had been assembling the bombs and teaching the soldiers how to use them properly.

Altunin hadn't thought about it much at first. It had been his job, the orders for which came from on high; Russians are neither inclined by temperament nor conditioned by education to question orders from on high. Besides, it had been a safe, easy job. He hadn't had to carry a rifle and go walking in the bandit country. The only dangers to him had been in the bazaars of Kabul, and he'd always been careful to walk about in groups of five or more. But on one such trip he'd seen a young child— boy or girl, he didn't know—whose right hand was now a claw, and whose mother stared at him and his comrades in a way he would never forget. He'd known the stories, how the Afghan bandits took particular delight in flaying captured Soviet pilots alive, how their women often handled the matter entirely. He'd thought it clear evidence of the barbarism of these primitive people—but a child wasn't primitive. Marxism said that. Take any child, give it proper schooling and leadership, and you'd have a communist for life. Not that child. He remembered it, that cold November day two years ago. The wound was fully healed, and the child had actually been smiling, too young to understand that its disfigurement would last forever. But the mother knew, and knew how and why her child had been punished for being . . . born. And after that, the safe, easy job hadn't been quite the same. Every time he screwed the explosives section onto the mechanism, he saw a small, pudgy child's hand. He started seeing them in his sleep. Drink, and even an experiment with hashish hadn't driven the images away. Speaking with his fellow technicians hadn't helped—though it had earned him the wrathful attention of his company *zampolit*. It was a hard thing he had to do, the political officer had explained, but necessary to prevent greater loss of life, you see. Complaining about it would not change matters, unless Corporal Altunin wanted transfer to a rifle company, where he might see for himself why such harsh measures were necessary.

He knew now that he should have taken that offer, and hated himself for the cowardice that had prevented the impulse. Service in a line company might have restored his self-image, might have—might have done a lot of things, Altunin told himself, but he hadn't made the choice and it hadn't made the difference. In the end, all he'd earned for himself was a letter from the *zampolit* that would travel with him for the rest of his life.

So now he tried to expiate that wrong. He told himself that perhaps he already had—and now, if he were very lucky, he could disappear, and perhaps he could forget the toys that he'd prepared for their evil mission. That was the only positive thought that his mind had room for, this cold, cloudy night.

He walked north, keeping off the dirt sidewalks, staying in shadows, away from the streetlamps. Shift workers coming home from the Moskvich plant made the streets agreeably crowded, but when he arrived at the railyard outside the plant, all the commuting was over. Snow started to fall heavily, reducing visibility to a hundred meters or so, with small globes of flakes around each of the lights over the stationary freight cars. A train seemed to be forming up, probably heading south, he told himself. Switching locomotives were moving back and forth, shunting boxcars from one siding to another. He spent a few minutes huddled by a car to make sure that he knew what was happening. The wind picked up as he watched, and Altunin looked for a better vantage point. There were some boxcars fifty or so meters away, from which he could observe better. One of them had an opened door, and he'd need to inspect the locking mechanism if he wanted to break inside one. He walked over with his head down to shield his face from the wind. The only thing he could hear, other than the crunch of snow under his boots, was the signal whistles of the switch engines. It was a friendly sound, he told himself, the sound that would change his life, perhaps lead the way to something like freedom.

He was surprised to see that there were people in the boxcar. Three of them. Two held cartons of auto parts. The third's hands were empty, until he reached into his pocket and came out with a knife.

Altunin started to say something. He didn't care if they were stealing parts for sale on the black market. He wasn't concerned at all, but before he could speak, the third one leaped down on him. Altunin was stunned when his head struck a steel rail. He was conscious, but couldn't move for a second, too surprised even to be afraid. The third one turned and said something. Altunin couldn't make out the reply, but knew it was sharp and quick. He was still trying to understand what was happening when his assailant turned back and slashed his throat. There wasn't even any pain. He wanted to explain that he wasn't . . . concerned . . . didn't care . . . just wanted to . . . one of them stood over him, two cartons in his arms, and clearly he was afraid, and Altunin thought this very odd, since he was the one who was dying . . .

Two hours later, a switch engine couldn't stop in time when its engineer noted an odd, snow-covered shape on the rails. On seeing what he'd run over, he called for the yardmaster.

13. Councils

"Beautiful job," Vatutin commented. "The bastards." *They've broken the rule,* he said to himself. The rule was unwritten but nevertheless very real: CIA does not kill Soviets in the Soviet Union; KGB does not kill Americans, or even Soviet defectors, in the United States. So far as Vatutin knew, the rule had never been broken by either side—at least not obviously so. The rule made sense: the job of intelligence agencies was to gather intelligence; if KGB and CIA officers spent their time killing people—with the inevitable retaliation and counterretaliation—the primary job would not get done. And so the business of intelligence was a civilized, *predictable* business. In third-world countries, different rules applied, of course, but in America and the Soviet Union, the rules were assiduously followed.

Until now, that is—unless I'm supposed to believe that this poor, sad bastard was murdered by auto-parts thieves! Vatutin wondered if CIA might have contracted the job out to a criminal gang—he suspected that the Americans used Soviet criminals for some things too sensitive for their own lily-white hands. *That would not be a* technical *violation of the rules, would it?* He wondered if the First Directorate men ever used a similar dodge . . .

All he knew right now was that the next step in the courier chain was dead at his feet, and with it his only hope of linking the microfilm to the American spy in the Defense Ministry. Vatutin corrected himself: He also knew that he'd have to report this to the Chairman in about six hours. He needed a drink. Vatutin shook his head and looked down at what was left of his suspect. The snow was falling so rapidly that you couldn't see the blood anymore.

"You know, if they'd only been a little bit more clever putting his body on the tracks, we might have written it off to an accident," another KGB officer observed. Despite the horrendous work done to the body by the wheels of the locomotive, it was clear that Altunin's throat had been expertly sliced by a narrow-bladed knife. Death, the responding physician reported, could not have taken longer than a minute. There were no signs of a struggle. The victim's—the traitor's!—hands were not bruised or cut. He hadn't fought back against whoever had killed him. Conclusion: His killer was probably known to him. Might it have been an American?

"First thing," Vatutin said. "I want to know if any Americans were away from their flats between eighteen and twenty-three hours." He turned. "Doctor!"

"Yes, Colonel?"

"Time of death again?"

"Judging by the temperature of the larger pieces, between twenty-one and midnight. Earlier rather than later, I think, but the cold and snow cover complicate matters." *Not to mention the state of the remains,* he didn't add.

Vatutin turned back to his principal assistant. "Any who were away from quarters, I want to know who, where, when, and why."

"Step up surveillance of all the foreigners?" the man wondered aloud.

"I'll have to go to the Chairman for that, but I'm thinking about it. I want you to speak to the chief Militia investigator. This is to be classified most-secret. We don't need a mob of fumbling policemen messing this affair up."

"Understood, Comrade Colonel. They'd only be interested in recovering the auto parts anyway," the man noted sourly. *This* perestroika *business is turning everyone into a capitalist!*

Vatutin walked over to the locomotive driver. "It's cold, isn't it?"

The message was received. "Yes, Comrade. Perhaps you'd like something to take away the chill?"

"That would be very kind of you, Comrade Engineer."

"My pleasure, Comrade Colonel." The engine driver produced a small bottle. As soon as he'd seen that the man was a colonel of the KGB, he'd thought himself doomed. But the man seemed decent enough. His colleagues were businesslike, their questions had been reasonable ones, and the man was almost at ease—until he realized that he could be punished for having a bottle on the job. He watched the man take a long pull, then hand the bottle back.

"Spasibo," the KGB man said, and walked off into the snow.

*   *   *

Vatutin was waiting in the Chairman's anteroom when he arrived. He'd heard that Gerasimov was a serious worker, always at his desk by seven-thirty. The stories were right. He came through the door at seven twenty-five and waved for the "Two" man to follow him into his office.

"Well?"

"Altunin was killed late last night in the railyards outside the Moskvich Auto Factory. His throat was cut and his body left on the tracks, where a switch engine ran over it."

"You're sure it's him?" Gerasimov asked with a frown.

"Yes, he was positively identified. I recognized the face myself. He was found next to a railcar that had ostensibly been broken into, and some auto parts were missing."

"Oh, so he stumbled upon a gang of black marketeers and they conveniently killed him?"

"So it is meant to appear, Comrade Chairman." Colonel Vatutin nodded. "I find the coincidence unconvincing, but there is no physical evidence to contradict it. Our investigations are continuing. We are now checking to see if any of Altunin's comrades from his military service live in the area, but I am not hopeful along these lines."

Gerasimov rang for tea. His secretary appeared in an instant, and Vatutin realized that this had to be part of the regular morning routine. The Chairman was taking things more easily than the Colonel had feared. Party man or not, he acted like a professional:

"So, to this point, we have three confessed document couriers, and one more positively identified, but unfortunately dead. The dead one was seen in close physical proximity to the senior aide of the Defense Minister, and one of the live ones has identified his contact as a foreigner, but cannot positively identify his face. In short, we have the middle of this line, but neither end."

"That is correct, Comrade Chairman. Surveillance of the two Ministry colonels continues. I propose that we step up surveillance of the American Embassy community."

Gerasimov nodded. "Approved. It's time for my morning brief. Keep pushing for a break in the case. You look better now that you've cut back on your drinking, Vatutin."

"I feel better, Comrade Chairman," he admitted.

"Good." Gerasimov rose, and his visitor did the same. "Do you really think that our CIA colleagues killed their own man?"

"Altunin's death was most convenient for them. I realize that this would be a violation of our—our agreement along these lines, but—"

"But we are probably dealing with a highly placed spy, and they are undoubtedly most interested in protecting him. Yes, I understand that. Keep pushing, Vatutin," Gerasimov said again.

Foley was already at his office also. On his desk were three film cassettes for CARDINAL. The next problem was delivering the damned things. The business of espionage was a mass of interlocking contradictions. Some parts of it were devilishly hard. Some carried the sort of danger that made him wish he'd stayed with the *New York Times*. But others were so simple that he could have had one of his kids handle it. That very thought had occurred to him several times—not that he'd ever entertain it seriously, but in moments when his mind was affected by a few stiff drinks, he'd muse that Eddie could take a piece of chalk and make a certain mark in a certain place. From time to time, embassy personnel would walk about Moscow doing things that were just slightly out of the ordinary. In summer, they'd wear flowers in buttonholes, and remove them for no apparent reason—and the KGB officers watching them would anxiously scan the sidewalks for the person at whom the "signal" was aimed. Year round, some would wander about, taking photographs of ordinary street scenes. In fact, they scarcely needed to be told. Some of the embassy people merely had to act like their eccentric American selves to drive the Russians nuts. To a counterespionage officer, *anything* could be a secret sign: a turned-down sun visor in a parked car, a package left on its front seat, the way the wheels were pointed. The net effect of all these measures, some deliberate, some merely random, had "Two" men scurrying all over the city running down things that simply didn't exist. It was something Americans did better than Russians, who were too regimented to act in a truly random fashion, and it was something that made life thoroughly miserable for the counterspies of the Second Chief Directorate.

But there were thousands of them, and only seven hundred Americans (counting dependents) assigned to the embassy.

And Foley still had the film to deliver. He wondered why it was that CARDINAL had always refused to use dead-drops. It was the perfect expedient for this. A dead-drop was typically an object that looked like an ordinary stone, or anything else common and harmless, hollowed out to hold the thing to be transferred. Bricks were especially favored in Moscow, as the city was mainly one of brick, many of which were loose due to the uniformly poor workmanship found here, but the variety of such devices was endless.

On the other hand, the variety of ways to make a brush-pass was limited, and depended upon the sort of timing to be found in a wishbone backfield. Well, the Agency hadn't given him this job because it was easy. He couldn't risk it again himself. Perhaps his wife could make the transfer . . .

"So, where's the leak?" Parks asked his security chief.

"It could be any one of a hundred or so people," the man answered.

"That's good news," Pete Wexton observed dryly. He was an inspector in the FBI's counterintelligence office. "Only a hundred."

"Could be one of the scientific people, or somebody's secretary, or someone in the budget department—that's just in the program itself. There are another twenty or so here in the D.C. area who're into Tea Clipper deep enough to have seen this stuff, but they're all very senior folks." SDIO's security chief was a Navy captain who customarily wore civilian clothes. "More likely, the person we're looking for is out West."

"And they're mostly scientific types, mostly under forty." Wexton closed his eyes. *Who live inside computers and think the world's just one big videogame.* The problem with scientists, especially the young ones, was simply that they lived in a world very different from that understood and appreciated by the security community. To them, progress depended on the free transfer of information and ideas. They were people who got excited about new things, and talked about them among themselves, unconsciously seeking the synergism that made ideas sprout like weeds in the disordered garden of the laboratory. To a security officer the ideal world was one where nobody talked to anyone else. The problem with that, of course, was that such a world rarely did anything worth securing in the first place. The balance was almost impossible to strike, and the security people were always caught exactly in the middle, hated by everyone.

"What about internal security on the project documents?" Wexton asked.

"You mean canary traps?"

"What the hell is that?" General Parks asked.

"All these papers are done on word processors. You use the machine to make subtle alterations in each copy of the important papers. That way you can track every one, and identify the precise one that's being leaked to the other side," the Captain explained. "We haven't done much of that. It's too time-intensive."

"CIA has a computer subroutine that does it automatically. They call it Spookscribe, or something like that. It's closely held, but you should be able to get it if you ask."

"Nice of 'em to tell us about it," Parks groused. "Would it matter in this case?"

"Not at the moment, but you play all the cards you got," the Captain observed to his boss. "I've heard about the program. It can't be used on scientific documents. The way they use language is too precise. Anything more than inserting a comma—well, it can screw up what they're trying to say."

"Assuming anyone can understand it in the first place," Wexton said with a rueful shake of the head. "Well, it's for damned sure that the Russians can." He was already thinking about the resources that this case would require—possibly hundreds of agents. They'd be conspicuous. The community in question might be too small to absorb a large influx of people without someone's notice.

The other obvious thing to do was restrict access to information on the mirror experiments, but then you ran the risk of alerting the spy. Wexton wondered why he hadn't stuck to simple things like kidnappings and Mafia racketeering. But he'd gotten his brief on Tea Clipper from Parks himself. It was an important job, and he was the best man for it. Wexton was sure of this: Director Jacobs had said so himself.

Bondarenko noticed it first. He'd had an odd feeling a few days previously while doing his morning run. It was something he'd always had, but those three months in Afghanistan had taken a latent sixth sense and made it blossom fully. There were eyes on him. *Whose?* he wondered.

They were good. He was sure of that. He also suspected that there were five or more of them. That made them Russian . . . probably. Not certainly. Colonel Bondarenko was one kilometer into his run, and decided to perform a small experiment. He altered his route, taking a right where he normally took a left. That would take him past a new apartment block whose first-floor windows were still polished. He grinned to himself, but his right hand unconsciously slapped down on his hip, searching for his service automatic. The grin ended when he realized what his hand had done, and felt the gnawing disappointment that he did not have the where-withal to defend himself with anything other than bare hands. Bondarenko knew how to do that quite well, but a pistol has longer reach than a hand or foot. It wasn't fear, not even close to it, but Bondarenko was a soldier, accustomed to knowing the limits and rules of his own world.

His head swiveled, looking at the reflection of the windows. There was a man a hundred meters behind him, holding a hand to his face, as though speaking on a small radio. Interesting. Bondarenko turned and ran backward for a few meters, but by the time his head had come around, the man's hand was at his side, and he was walking normally, seemingly uninterested in the jogging officer. Colonel Bondarenko turned and resumed his normal pace. His smile was now thin and tight. He'd confirmed it. But what had he confirmed? Bondarenko promised himself that he'd know that an hour after getting to his office.

Thirty minutes later, home, showered, and dressed, he read his morning paper—for him it was *Krasnaya Zvesda,* "Red Star," the Soviet military daily—while he drank a mug of tea. The radio was playing while his wife prepared the children for school. Bondarenko didn't hear either, and his eyes merely scanned the paper while his mind churned. *Who are they? Why are they watching me? Am I under suspicion? If so, suspicion of what?*

"Good morning, Gennady Iosifovich," Misha said on entering his office.

"Good morning, Comrade Colonel," Bondarenko answered.

Filitov smiled. "Call me Misha. The way you're going, you will soon outrank this old carcass. What is it?"

"I'm being watched. I had people following me this morning when I did my run."

"Oh?" Misha turned. "Are you sure?"

"You know how it is when you know you're being watched—I'm certain *you* know, Misha!" the young Colonel observed.

But he was wrong. Filitov had noticed nothing unusual, nothing to arouse his instincts until this moment. Then it hit him that the bath attendant wasn't back yet. What if the signal was about something more than a routine security check? Filitov's face changed for an instant before he got it back under control.

"You've noticed something, too, then?" Bondarenko asked.

"Ah!" A wave of the hand, and an ironic look. "Let them look; they will find this old man more boring than Alexandrov's sex life." The reference to the Politburo's chief ideologue was becoming a popular one in the Defense Ministry. A sign, Misha wondered, that General Secretary Narmonov was planning to ease him out?

They ate in the Afghan way, everyone taking food barehanded from a common plate. Ortiz had a virtual banquet laid out for lunch. The Archer had the place of honor, with Ortiz at his right hand to act as translator. Four very senior CIA people were there, too. He thought they were overdoing things, but then, the place that put the light in the sky must have been important. Ortiz opened the talking with the usual ceremonial phrases.

"You do me too much honor," the Archer replied.

"Not so," the senior CIA visitor said through Ortiz. "Your skill and courage are well known to us, and even among our soldiers. We are ashamed that we can give you no more than the poor help that our government allows."

"It is our land to win back," the Archer said with dignity. "With Allah's help it will be ours again. It is well that Believers should strive together against the godless ones, but the task is that of my people, not yours."

He doesn't know, Ortiz thought. *He doesn't know that he's being used.*

"So," the Archer went on. "Why have you traveled around the world to speak with this humble warrior?"

"We wish to talk with you about the light you saw in the sky."

The Archer's face changed. He was surprised at that. He'd expected to be asked about how well his missiles worked.

"It was a light—a strange light, yes. Like a meteor, but it seemed to go up instead of down." He described what he had seen in detail, giving the time, where he'd been, the direction of the light, and the way it had sliced across the sky.

"Did you see what it hit? Did you see anything else in the sky?"

"Hit? I don't understand. It was a light."

Another of the visitors spoke. "I am told that you were a teacher of mathematics. Do you know what a laser is?"

His face changed at the new thought. "Yes, I read of them when I was in university. I—" The Archer sipped at a glass of juice. "I know little of lasers. They project a beam of light, and are used mainly for measuring and surveying. I have never seen one, only read of them."

"What you saw was a test of a laser weapon."

"What is its purpose?"

"We do not know. The test you saw used the laser system to destroy a satellite in orbit. That means—"

"I know of satellites. A laser can be used for this purpose?"

"Our country is working on similar things, but it would seem that the Russians are ahead of us."

The Archer was surprised by that. Was not America the world's leader in technical things? Was not the Stinger proof of that? Why had these men flown twelve thousand miles—merely because he'd seen a light in the sky?

"You are fearful of this laser?"

"We have great interest," the senior man replied. "Some of the documents you found gave us information about the site which we did not have, and for this we are doubly in your debt."

"I, too, have interest now. Do you have the documents?"

"Emilio?" The senior visitor gestured at Ortiz, who produced a map and a diagram.

"This site has been under construction since 1983. We were surprised that the Russians would build so important a facility so near to the borders of Afghanistan."

"In 1983, they still thought they would win," the Archer observed darkly. The idea that they'd felt that way was taken as an insult. He noted the position on the map, the mountaintop nearly surrounded by a sweeping loop of the Vakhsh River. He saw immediately why it was there. The power dam at Nurek was only a few kilometers away. The Archer knew more than he let on. He knew what lasers were, and a little of how they operated. He knew that their light was dangerous, that it could blind . . .

It destroyed a satellite? Hundreds of kilometers up in space, higher than airplanes could fly . . . what could it do to people on the ground . . . perhaps they'd built so close to his country for another reason . . .

"So you merely saw the light? You have heard no stories about such a place, no stories of strange lights in the sky?"

The Archer shook his head. "No, only the one time." He saw the visitors exchange looks of disappointment.

"Well, that does not matter. I am permitted to offer you the thanks of my government. Three truckloads of weapons are coming to your band. If there is anything else you need, we will try to get it for you."

The Archer nodded soberly. He'd expected a great reward for the delivery of the Soviet officer, then been disappointed at his death. But these men had not visited him about that. It was all about the documents and the light—was this place so important that the death of the Russian was considered trivial? Were the Americans actually afraid of it?

And if they were fearful, how should he feel?

"No, Arthur, I don't like it," the President said tentatively. Judge Moore pressed the attack.

"Mr. President, we are aware of Narmonov's political difficulties. The disappearance of our agent will not have any more of an effect than his arrest by the KGB, possibly less. After all, the KGB can't very well raise too much of a ruckus if they let him slip away," the DCI pointed out.

"It's still too great a risk," Jeffrey Pelt said. "We have a historic opportunity with Narmonov. He really wants to make fundamental changes in their system—hell, your people are the ones who made the assessment."

We had this chance before and blew it, during the Kennedy Administration, Moore thought. *But Khrushchev fell, and we had twenty years of Party hacks. Now there may be another chance. You're afraid we might never get another opportunity as good as this one. Well, that's one way to look at it,* he admitted to himself.

"Jeff, his position will not be affected any more by extracting our man than by his capture—"

"If they're on to him, why haven't they grabbed him already?" Pelt demanded. "What if you're overreacting?"

"This man has been working for us over thirty years—thirty years! Do you know the risks he's run for us, the information we've gotten from him? Can you appreciate the frustration he's felt the times we ignored his advice? Can you imagine what it's like to live with a death sentence for thirty years? If we abandon the man, what's this country all about?" Moore said with quiet determination. The President was a man who could always be swayed by arguments based on principle.

"And if we topple Narmonov in the process?" Pelt demanded. "What if Alexandrov's clique does take over, and it's back to the bad old days all over again—more tension, more arms races? How do we explain to the American people that we sacrificed this opportunity for the life of one man?"

"For one thing, they'd never know unless somebody leaked it," the DCI replied coldly. "The Russians wouldn't make it all public, and you know that. For another, how would we explain throwing this man away like a used Kleenex?"

"They wouldn't know that either, unless somebody leaked it," Pelt answered in an equally cold voice.

The President stirred. His first instinct had been to put the extraction operation on hold. How could he explain any of this? Either by an act of commission or omission, they were discussing the best way to prevent something unfavorable from happening to America's principal enemy. *But you can't even say that in public,* the President reflected. *If you said out loud that the Russians are our enemy, the papers would throw a fit. The Soviets have thousands of nuclear warheads aimed at us, but we can't risk offending their sensibilities . . .*

He remembered his two face-to-face meetings with the man, Andrey Il'ych Narmonov, General Secretary of the Communist Party of the Soviet Union. Younger than he was, the President reflected. Their initial conversations had been cautious, each man feeling out the other, looking both for weaknesses and common ground, for advantage and compromise. A man with a mission, a man who probably did wish to change things, the President thought—

But is that a good thing? What if he did decentralize their economy, introduce market forces, give them a little freedom—not much, of course, but enough to get things moving? Quite a few people were warning him about that possibility: Imagine a country with the Soviets' political will, backed up by an economy that could deliver quality goods both in the civilian and military sectors. Would it make the Russian people believe again in their system; would it revive the sense of mission that they'd had in the 1930s? *We might be faced with a more dangerous enemy than ever before.*

On the other side, he was told that there is no such thing as a little freedom—one could ask Duvalier of Haiti, Marcos of the Philippines, or the ghost of Shah Mohammed Reza Pahlavi. The momentum of events could bring the Soviet Union out of the dark ages and into the 20th-century era of political thought. It might take a generation, perhaps two, but what if the country did start to evolve into something approaching a liberal state? There was another lesson of history: Liberal democracies don't make war on one another.

Some choice I have, the President thought. *I can be remembered as the regressive idiot who reinstated the Cold War in all its grim majesty—or the Pollyanna who expected the leopard to change its spots, only to find that it had grown bigger, sharper fangs. Jesus,* he told himself as he stared at his two interlocutors, *I'm not thinking about success at all, only the consequences of failure.*

That's one area in which America and Russia have paralleled their history—our postwar governments have never lived up to the expectations of our people, have they? I'm the President, *I'm supposed to* know *what the Right Thing is. That's why the people elected me. That's what they're paying me for. God, if they only knew what frauds we all are. We're not talking about how to succeed. We're talking about who'll leak the reason for the failure of policy. Right here in the Oval Office, we're discussing who'll get the blame if something we haven't yet decided upon doesn't work.*

"Who knows about this?"

Judge Moore held his hands out. "Admiral Greer, Bob Ritter, and me at CIA. A few field personnel know about the proposed operation—we had to send out the heads-up signal—but they do not know the political issues, and never will. They don't need to know. Aside from that, only we three at the Agency have the entire picture. Add you, sir, and Dr. Pelt, and that makes five."

"And already we're talking about leaks! Goddamn it!" the President swore with surprising passion. "How did we ever get so screwed up as this!"

Everyone sobered up. There was nothing like a presidential curse to settle people down. He looked at Moore and Pelt, his chief intelligence advisor, and his national-security advisor. One was pleading for the life of a man who had served America faithfully and well, at peril of his life; the other took the long, cold look at the *realpolitik* and saw a historic opportunity more important than any single human life.

"Arthur, you're saying that this agent—and I don't even want to know his name—has been giving us critically important data for thirty years, up to and including this laser project that the Russians have operating; you say that he is probably in danger, and it's time to run the risk of getting him out of there, that we have a moral obligation to do so."

"Yes, Mr. President."

"And you, Jeff, you say that the timing's bad, that the revelation of a leak so high up in their government could endanger Narmonov politically, could topple him from his leadership position and replace him with a government less attractive to us."

"Yes, Mr. President."

"And if this man dies because we haven't helped him?"

"We would lose important information," Moore said. "And it might have no tangible difference in its effect on Narmonov. And we'd be betraying a trust to a man who has served us faithfully and well for thirty years."

"Jeff, can you live with that?" the President asked his national-security advisor.

"Yes, sir, I can live with that. I don't like it but I can live with it. With Narmonov we have already gotten an agreement on intermediate nuclear arms, and we have a chance at one on strategic forces."

It's like being a judge. Here I have two advocates who believe fully in their positions. I wonder if their principles would be quite so firm if they were in my chair, if they had to make the decision?

But they didn't run for President.

This agent's been serving the United States since I was a junior prosecutor handling whores in night court.

Narmonov may be the best chance we've had for world peace since God knows when.

The President stood and walked to the windows behind his desk. They were very thick, to protect him from people with guns. They could not protect him against the duties of his office. He looked at the south lawn, but found no answers. He turned back.

"I don't know. Arthur, you can get your assets in place, but I want your word that nothing will happen without my authorization. No mistakes, no initiative, no action at all without my say-so. I'm going to need time on this one. We have time, don't we?"

"Yes, sir. It will take several more days before we have the pieces in place."

"I'll let you know when I make my decision." He shook hands with both men and watched them leave. The President had five more minutes before his next appointment, and used the time to visit the bathroom that adjoins the office. He wondered if there were any underlying symbolism in the act of washing his hands, or did he just want the excuse to look at himself in the mirror? *And you're supposed to be the man with all the fucking answers!* the image told him. *You don't even know why you went to the bathroom!* The President smiled at that. It was funny, funny in a way that few other men would ever understand.

"So what the hell do I tell Foley?" Ritter snapped twenty minutes later.

"Back off, Bob," Moore warned. "He's thinking about it. We don't need an immediate decision, and a 'maybe' beats hell out of a 'no.' "

"Sorry, Arthur. It's just that—damn it, I've tried to get him to come out before. We can't let this man go down."

"I'm sure he won't make a final decision until I've had a chance to talk with him again. For the moment, tell Foley to continue the mission. And I want a fresh look at Narmonov's political vulnerability. I get the impression that Alexandrov may be on the way out—he's too old to take over from the current man; the Politburo wouldn't stand for replacing a relatively young man with an old one, not after the death parade they had a few years back. Who does that leave?"

"Gerasimov," Ritter said at once. "Two others may be in the running, but he's the ambitious one. Ruthless, but very, very smooth. The Party bureaucracy likes him because he did such a nice job on the dissidents. And if he wants to make a move, it'll have to be pretty soon. If the arms agreement goes through, Narmonov gains a lot of prestige, and the political clout that goes with it. If Alexandrov isn't careful, he'll miss the boat entirely, get moved out himself, and Narmonov will have his seat nice and safe for years."

"That'll take at least five years to accomplish," Admiral Greer noted, speaking for the first time. "He may not have five years. We do have those indications that Alexandrov may be on the way out. If that's more than a rumor, it might force his hand."

Judge Moore looked up at the ceiling. "It sure would be easier to deal with the bastards if they had a predictable way of running things." *Of course, we have it, and they can't predict us.*

"Cheer up, Arthur," Greer said. "If the world made sense, we'd all have to find honest work."

14. Changes

Passage through the Kattegat is a tricky affair for a submarine, doubly so when it is necessary to be covert. The water is shallow there, too shallow to run submerged. The channels can be tricky in daylight. They are worse at night, and worse still without a pilot. Since *Dallas'* passage was supposedly a secret one, a pilot was out of the question.

Mancuso rode the bridge. Below, his navigator sweated at the chart table while a chief quartermaster manned the periscope and called out bearings to various landmarks. They couldn't even use radar to help with navigation, but the periscope had a low-light amplifier, which didn't quite turn night to day, but at least made the starless darkness look like twilight. The weather was a gift, with low clouds and sleet that restricted visibility just enough that the low, dark shape of the 688-class submarine would be difficult to spot from land. The Danish Navy knew of the submarine's transit, and had a few small craft out to ward off any possible snoopers—there were none—but aside from that, *Dallas* was on her own.

"Ship on the port bow," a lookout called.

"I got him," Mancuso answered at once. He held a pistol-like light-amplifying scope and saw the medium-sized container ship. The odds, he thought, made it an East Bloc vessel. Within a minute, the course and speed of the inbound ship were plotted, with a CPA—Closest Point of Approach—of seven hundred yards. The Captain swore and gave his orders.

Dallas had her running lights on—the Danes had insisted on it. The rotating amber one above the masthead light marked her positively as a submarine. Aft, a seaman struck down the American flag and replaced it with a Danish one.

"Everybody look Scandinavian," Mancuso noted wryly.

"Ja-ja, Kept'n," a junior officer chuckled in the darkness. It would be hard for him. He was black. "Slow bearing change on our friend. He isn't altering course that I can tell, sir. Look—"

"Yeah, I see 'em." Two of the Danish craft were racing forward to interpose themselves between the container ship and *Dallas*. Mancuso thought that would help. All cats are gray at night, and a submarine on the surface looks like . . . a submarine on the surface, a black shape with a vertical sail.

"I think she's Polish," the Lieutenant observed. "Yeah, I got the funnel now. Maersk Line."

The two ships closed at a rate of a half a mile per minute. Mancuso turned to watch, keeping his scope on the ship's bridge. He saw no special activity. Well, it was three in the morning. The bridge crew had a tough navigating job to do, and probably their interest in his submarine was the same as his main interest in their merchantman—*please don't hit me, you idiot.* It was over surprisingly fast, and then he was staring at her stern light. It occurred to Mancuso that having the lights on was probably a good idea. If they'd been blacked out and then spotted, greater notice might have been taken.

They were in the Baltic Sea proper an hour later, on a course of zero-six-five, using the deepest water they could find as *Dallas* picked her way east. Mancuso took the navigator into his stateroom and together they plotted the best approach to, and the safest place on, the Soviet coast. When they'd selected it, Mr. Clark joined them, and together the three discussed the delicate part of the mission.

In an ideal world, Vatutin thought wryly, they would take their worries to the Defense Minister, and he would cooperate fully with the KGB investigation. But the world was not ideal. In addition to the expected institutional rivalries, Yazov was in the pocket of the General Secretary and knew of the differences of opinion between Gerasimov and Narmonov. No, the Defense Minister would either take over the entire investigation through his own security arm, or use his political power to close the case entirely, lest KGB disgrace Yazov himself for having a traitor for an aide, and so endanger Narmonov.

If Narmonov fell, at best the Defense Minister would go back to being the Soviet Army's chief of personnel; more likely, he'd be retired in quiet humiliation after the removal of his patron. Even if the General Secretary managed to survive the crisis, Yazov would be the sacrificial goat, just as Sokolov had been so recently. What choice did Yazov have?

The Defense Minister was also a man with a mission. Under the cover of the "restructuring" initiative of the General Secretary, Yazov hoped to use his knowledge of the officer corps to remake the Soviet Army—in the hope, supposedly, of professionalizing the entire military community. Narmonov said that he wanted to save the Soviet economy, but no less an authority than Alexandrov, the high priest of Marxism-Leninism, said that he was destroying the purity of the Party itself. Yazov wanted to rebuild the military from the ground up. It would also have the effect, Vatutin thought, of making the Army personally loyal to Narmonov.

That worried Vatutin. Historically, the Party had used the KGB to keep the military under control. After all, the military had all the guns, and if it ever awoke to its power and felt the loosening of Party control . . . it was too painful a concept on which to dwell. An army loyal exclusively to the General Secretary rather than the Party itself was even more painful to Vatutin, since it would change the relationship the KGB had to Soviet society as a whole. There could then be no check on the General Secretary. With the military behind him, he could break KGB to his will and use it to "restructure" the entire Party. He would have the power of another Stalin.

How did I ever start along this line? Vatutin asked himself. *I'm a counterintelligence officer, not a Party theorist.* For all his life, Colonel Vatutin had never dwelt on the Big Issues of his country. He'd trusted his superiors to handle the major decisions and allow him to handle the small details. No longer. By being taken into Chairman Gerasimov's confidence he was now inextricably allied with the man. It had happened so easily! Virtually overnight—*you have to be noticed to get general's stars,* he thought with a sardonic smile. *You always wanted to get noticed. So, Klementi Vladimirovich, you got yourself noticed all right. Now look where you are!*

Right in the middle of a power play between the KGB Chairman and the General Secretary himself.

It was actually quite funny, he told himself. He knew it would be less so if Gerasimov miscalculated—but the crowning irony of all was that if the KGB Chairman fell, then the liberal influences already put in place by Narmonov would protect Vatutin, who was, after all, merely doing the job assigned him by his duly appointed superiors. He didn't think that he'd be imprisoned, much less shot, as had once been the case. His advancement would be at an end. He'd find himself demoted, running the KGB regional office at Omsk, or the least pleasant opening they could find, never again to return to Moscow Center.

That wouldn't be so bad, he thought. On the other hand, if Gerasimov succeeded . . . head of "Two" perhaps? And that wouldn't be very bad at all.

And you actually believed that you could advance your career without becoming "political." But that was no longer an option. If he tried to get out, he'd be disgraced. Vatutin was trapped, and knew it. The only way out was to do his job to the best of his ability.

The revery ended as he turned back to his reports. Colonel Bondarenko was totally clean, he thought. His record had been examined and reexamined, and there was nothing to indicate that he was anything less than a patriot and an above-average officer. Filitov is the one, Vatutin thought. As insane as it seemed on the surface, this decorated hero was a traitor.

But how the hell do we prove that? How do we even investigate it properly without the cooperation of the Defense Minister? That was the other rub. If he failed in his investigation, then Gerasimov would not look kindly upon his career; but the investigation was hindered by political constraints imposed by the Chairman. Vatutin remembered the time he'd almost been passed over for promotion to major and realized how unlucky he'd been when the promotion board had changed its mind.

Oddly, it did not occur to him that all his problems resulted from having a KGB Chairman with political ambition. Vatutin summoned his senior officers. They arrived in a few minutes.

"Progress on Filitov?" he asked.

"Our best people are shadowing him," a middle-level officer answered. "Six of them round the clock. We're rotating schedules so that he doesn't see the same faces very often, if at all. We now have continuous television surveillance all around his apartment block, and half a dozen people check the tapes every night. We've stepped up coverage of suspected American and British spies, and of their diplomatic communities in general. We're straining our manpower and risking counterdetection, but there's no avoiding that. About the only new thing I have to report is that Filitov talks in his sleep occasionally—he's talking to somebody named Romanov, it sounds like. The words are too distorted to understand, but I have a speech pathologist working on it, and we may get something. In any case, Filitov can't fart without our knowing it. The only thing we can't do is maintain continuous visual contact without getting our people in too close. Every day, turning a corner or entering a shop, he's out of sight for five to fifteen seconds—long enough to make a brush-pass or a dead-drop. Nothing I can do about that unless you want us to risk alerting him."

Vatutin nodded. Even the best surveillance had its limitations.

"Oh, there is one odd thing," the Major said. "Just learned about it yesterday. About once a week or so, Filitov takes the burn-bag down to the incinerator chute himself. It's so routine there that the man in the destruct room forgot to tell us until last evening. He's a youngster, and came in himself to report it—after hours, and in civilian clothes. Bright boy. It turns out that Filitov looked after the installation of the system, years back. I checked the plans myself, nothing out of the way. Completely normal installation, just like what we have here. And that's all. For all practical purposes the only unusual thing about the subject is that he ought to be retired by now."

"What of the Altunin investigation?" Vatutin asked next.

Another officer opened his notebook. "We've no idea where he was before being killed. Perhaps he was hiding out alone somewhere, perhaps he was protected by friends whom we have been unable to identify. We've established no correlation between his death and the movement of foreigners. He was carrying nothing incriminating except some false papers that looked amateurishly done, but probably good enough for the outlying republics. If he was murdered by CIA, it was a remarkably complete job. No loose ends. None."

"Your opinions?"

"The Altunin case is a dead end," the Major answered. "There are still a half-dozen things that we have to check out, but none has the least promise of an important break." He paused for a moment. "Comrade . . ."

"Go on."

"I believe this was a coincidence. I think Altunin was the victim of a simple murder, that he tried to get aboard the wrong railcar at the wrong time. I have no evidence to point to, but that is how it feels to me."

Vatutin considered that. It took no small amount of moral courage for an officer of the Second Chief Directorate to say that he was *not* on a counterespionage case.

"How sure are you?"

"We'll never be sure, Comrade Colonel, but if CIA had done the murder, would they not have disposed of the body—or, if they were trying to use his death to protect a highly placed spy, why not leave evidence to implicate him as a totally separate case? There were no false flags left behind, even though this would seem the place to do so."

"Yes, we would have done that. A good point. Run down all your leads anyway."

"Of course, Comrade Colonel. Four to six days, I think."

"Anything else?" Vatutin asked. Heads shook negatively. "Very well, return to your sections, Comrades."

She'd do it at the hockey game, Mary Pat Foley thought. CARDINAL would be there, alerted by a wrong-number telephone call from a pay phone. She'd make the pass herself. She had three film cassettes in her purse, and a simple handshake would do it. Her son played on this junior-league team, as did Filitov's grand-nephew, and she went to every game. It would be unusual if she didn't go, and the Russians depended on people to stick to their routines. She was being followed. She knew it. Evidently the Russians had stepped up surveillance, but the shadow she rated wasn't all that good—or at least they were using the same one on her, and Mary Pat knew when she saw a face more than once in a day.

Mary Patricia Kaminskiy Foley had typically muddled American ancestry, though some aspects of it had been left off her passport documents. Her grandfather had been an equerry to the House of Romanov, had taught the Crown Prince Aleksey to ride—no small feat since the youngster was tragically stricken with hemophilia, and the utmost caution had needed to be exercised. That had been the crowning achievement of an otherwise undistinguished life. He'd been a failure as an Army officer, though friends at court had ensured his advancement to colonel. All that had accomplished was the utter destruction of his regiment in the Tannenberg Forests, and his capture by the Germans—and his survival past 1920. Upon learning that his wife had died in the revolutionary turmoil that followed the First World War, he'd never returned to Russia—he always called it *Russia*— and eventually drifted to the United States, where he'd settled in the suburbs of New York and remarried after establishing a small business. He'd lived to the ripe old age of ninety-seven, outliving even a second wife twenty years his junior, and Mary Pat never forgot his rambling stories. On entering college and majoring in history, she learned better, of course. She learned that the Romanovs were hopelessly inept, their court irredeemably corrupt. But one thing she'd never forget was the way her grandfather wept when he got to the part about how Aleksey, a brave, determined young man, and his entire family had been shot like dogs by the Bolsheviks. That one story, repeated to her a hundred times, gave Mary Pat a view of the Soviet Union which no amount of time or academic instruction or political realism could ever erase. Her feelings for the government which ruled her grandfather's land were completely framed by the murder of Nicholas II, his wife, and his five children. Intellect, she told herself in reflective moments, had very little to do with the way people feel.

Working in Moscow, working against that same government, was the greatest thrill of her life. She liked it even more than her husband, whom she'd met while a student at Columbia. Ed had joined CIA because *she* had decided very early in life to join CIA. Her husband was good at it, Mary Pat knew, with brilliant instincts and administrative skills—but he lacked the passion she gave to the job. He also lacked the genes. She had learned the Russian language at her grandfather's knee—the richer, more elegant Russian that the Soviets had debased into the current patois—but more importantly she understood the people in a way that no number of books could relate. She understood the racial sadness that permeates the Russian character, and the oxymoronic private openness, the total exposure of self and soul displayed only to the closest friends and denied by a Moscovite's public demeanor. As a result of this talent, Mary Pat had recruited five well-placed agents, only one shy of the all-time record. In the CIA's Directorate of Operations, she was occasionally known as Supergirl, a term she didn't care for. After all, Mary Pat was the mother of two, with the stretchmarks to prove it. She smiled at herself in the mirror. *You've done it all, kid.* Her grandfather would be proud.

And the best part of all: nobody had the least suspicion of what she really was. She made a final adjustment in her clothing. Western women in Moscow were supposed to be more conscious of their dress than Western men. Hers were always just a touch overdone. The image she projected to the public was carefully conceived and exquisitely executed. Educated but shallow, pretty but superficial, a good mother but little more, quick with her Western display of emotions but not to be taken very seriously. Scurrying about as she did, substitute-teaching occasionally at the kids' school, attending various social functions, and endlessly wandering about like a perpetual tourist, she fitted perfectly the preconceived Soviet notion of an American female bubblehead. One more smile in the mirror: *If the bastards only knew.*

Eddie was already waiting impatiently, his hockey stick jerking up and down at the drab carpet in the living room. Ed had the TV on. He kissed his wife goodbye, and told Eddie to kick ass—the senior Foley had been a Rangers fan before he learned to read.

It was a little sad, Mary Pat thought on the elevator. Eddie had made some real friends here, but it was a mistake to get too friendly with people in Moscow. You might forget that they were the enemy. She worried that Eddie was getting the same sort of indoctrination that she'd gotten, but from the wrong direction. Well, that was easily remedied, she told herself. In storage at home she had a photograph of the Czarevich Aleksey, autographed to his favorite teacher. All she really had to do was explain how he'd died.

The drive to the arena was the routine one, with Eddie getting ever more hyper as game time approached. He was tied as the league's third leading scorer, only six points behind the lead center for the team they were playing tonight, and Eddie wanted to show Ivan Whoeverhewas that Americans could beat Russians at their own game.

It was surprising how crowded the parking lot was, but then it wasn't a very large parking lot and ice hockey is the closest thing to religion permitted in the Soviet Union. This game would decide the playoff standings for the league championship, and quite a few people had come to see it. That was fine with Mary Pat. She'd barely set the parking brake when Eddie tore open the door, lifted his dufflebag, and waited impatiently for his mother to lock the car. He managed to walk slowly enough for his mother to keep up, then raced into the locker room as she went up to the rink.

Her place was predetermined, of course. Though reluctant to be overly close to foreigners in public, at a hockey game the rules were different. A few parents greeted her, and she waved back, her smile just a little too broad. She checked her watch.

692   •   TOM CLANCY

*   *   *

"I haven't seen a junior-league game in two years," Yazov said as they got out of the staff car.

"I don't go much either, but my sister-in-law said that this one is important, and little Misha demanded my presence." Filitov grinned. "They think I am good luck—perhaps you will be too, Comrade Marshal."

"It is good to do something a little different," Yazov conceded with mock gravity. "The damned office will still be there tomorrow. I played this game as a boy, you know."

"No, I didn't. Were you any good?"

"I was a defenseman, and the other children complained that I checked too hard." The Defense Minister chuckled, then waved for his security people to go ahead.

"We never had a rink out where I grew up—and the truth is I was too clumsy as a child. Tanks were perfect for me—you're expected to destroy things with them." Misha laughed.

"So how good is this team?"

"I like the junior league better than the real ones," Colonel Filitov answered. "More—more exuberant. I suppose I just like to see children having a good time."

"Indeed."

There weren't many seats around the rink—and besides, what real hockey fan wanted to sit? Colonel Filitov and Marshal Yazov found a convenient place near some of the parents. Their Soviet Army greatcoats and glistening shoulder boards guaranteed them both a good view and breathing space. The four security people hovered about, trying not to look too obviously at the game. They were not terribly concerned, since the trip to the game had been a spur-of-the-moment decision on the Minister's part.

The game was an exciting one from the first moment. The center for the other team's first line moved like a weasel, handling the puck with skillful passes and adroit skating. The home team—the one with the American and Misha's grand-nephew—was pressed back into its own zone for most of the first period, but little Misha was an aggressive defenseman, and the American boy stole a pass, taking it the length of the rink only to be foiled by a dazzling save that evoked cheers of admiration from supporters of both sides. Though as contentious a people as any on earth, the Russians have always been imbued with generous sportsmanship. The first period ended zero-zero.

"Too bad," Misha observed while people hustled off to the rest rooms.

"That was a beautiful breakaway, but the save was marvelous," Yazov said. "I'll have to get them this child's name for Central Army. Misha, thanks for inviting me to this. I'd forgotten how exciting a school game could be."

"What do you suppose they're talking about?" the senior KGB officer asked. He and two other men were up in the rafters, hidden by the lights that illuminated the rink.

"Maybe they're just hockey fans," the man with the camera replied. "Shit, it sounds like quite a game we're missing. Look at those security guards—fucking idiots are watching the ice. If I wanted to kill Yazov . . ."

"Not a terribly bad idea, I hear," observed the third man. "The Chairman—"

"That is not our concern," the senior man snapped, ending the conversation.

"Come on, Eddieeee!" Mary Pat screamed as the second period began. Her son looked up in embarrassment. His mom always got too excited at these things, he thought.

"Who was that?" Misha asked, five meters away.

"Over there, the skinny one—we met her, remember?" Yazov said.

"Well, she's a fan," Filitov noted as he watched the action swing to the other end. *Please, Comrade Minister, you do it . . .* He got his wish.

"Let's go over and say hello." The crowd parted before them, and Yazov sidled up on her left.

"Mrs. Foley, I believe?"

He got a quick turn and a quicker smile before she turned back to the action. "Hello, General—"

"Actually, my rank is Marshal. Your son is number twelve?"

"Yes, and did you see how the goalie robbed him!"

"It was a fine save," Yazov said.

"Then let him do it to somebody else!" she said as the other team started moving into Eddie's end.

"Are all American fans like you?" Misha asked.

She turned again, and her voice showed a little embarrassment. "It's terrible, isn't it? Parents are supposed to act—"

"Like parents?" Yazov laughed.

"I'm turning into a little-league mom," Mary Pat admitted. Then she had to explain what that was.

"It is enough that we've taught your son to be a proper hockey wingman."

"Yes, perhaps he'll be on the Olympic team in a few years," she replied with a wicked, though playful smile. Yazov laughed. That surprised her. Yazov was supposed to be a tight, serious son of a bitch.

"Who's the woman?"

"American. Her husband's the press attaché. Her son's on this team. We have a file on both of them. Nothing special."

"Pretty enough. I didn't know Yazov was a lady's man."

"Do you suppose he wants to recruit her?" the photographer suggested, snapping away.

"I wouldn't mind."

The game had unexpectedly settled down into a defense struggle that hovered around center ice. The children lacked the finesse necessary for the precise passing that marked Soviet hockey, and both teams were coached not to play an overly physical game. Even with their protective equipment, they were still children whose growing bones didn't need abuse. That was a lesson the Russians could teach Americans, Mary Pat thought. Russians had always been highly protective of their young. Life for adults was difficult enough that they always tried to shield their children from it.

Finally, in the third period, things broke loose. A shot on goal was stopped, and the puck rebounded out from the goalie. The center took it and turned, racing directly for the opposite goal, with Eddie twenty feet to his right. The center passed an instant before being poke-checked, and

Eddie swept around to the corner, unable to take a shot at the goal and blocked from approaching it himself by a charging defenseman.

"*Center it!*" his mother screamed. He didn't hear her, but didn't need to. The center was now in place, and Eddie fired the puck to him. The youthful center stopped it with his skate, stepped back, and sent a blazing shot between the legs of the opposing goalie. The light behind the cage flashed, and sticks went soaring into the air.

"Fine centering pass," Yazov noted with genuine admiration. He continued on in a chiding tone. "You realize that your son now possesses State secrets, and we cannot allow him to leave the country."

Mary Pat's eyes widened in momentary alarm, persuading Yazov that she was indeed a typical bubbleheaded Western female, though she was probably quite a handful in bed. *Too bad that I'll never find out.*

"You're joking?" she asked quietly. Both the soldiers broke out into laughter.

"The Comrade Minister is most certainly joking," Misha said after a moment.

"I thought so!" she said rather unconvincingly before she turned back to the game. "*Okay, let's get another one!*"

Heads turned briefly, mainly in amusement. Having this American at the game was always good for a laugh. Russians find the exuberance of Americans immensely entertaining.

"Well, if she's a spy, I'll eat this camera."

"Think on what you just said, Comrade," the officer in charge whispered. The amusement in his voice died in an instant. *Think on what he just said,* the man told himself. *Her husband, Edward Foley, is regarded by the American press as a dolt, not smart enough to be a proper reporter, certainly not good enough to be on the staff of the* New York Times. The problem was, while that was the sort of cover that every real intelligence officer dreamed of, it was one naturally shared by all the government-service dolts serving every nation in the world. He himself knew that his cousin was a cretin, and *he* worked for the Foreign Ministry.

"Are you sure you have enough film?"

Eddie got his chance with forty seconds left. A defenseman fanned on a shot from the point, and the puck skittered back to center ice. The center flipped it to the right as the flow of the game changed. The other team had been on the verge of pulling its goalie, and the youngster was out of position when Eddie took the pass and streaked in from his left. Edward Foley II turned sharply and fired behind the goalie's back. The puck *clang*ed on the post, but fell right on the goal line and dribbled across.

"*Score!*" Mary Pat howled, jumping up and down like a cheerleader. She threw her arms around Yazov, much to the consternation of his security guards. The Defense Minister's amusement was tempered by the realization that he'd have to write up a contact report on this tomorrow. Well, he had Misha as a witness that they'd discussed nothing untoward. She grabbed Filitov next.

"I *told* you you were good luck!"

"My God, are all American hockey fans like this?" Misha asked, disengaging himself. Her hand had touched his for a half-imaginary fraction of a second, and the three film cassettes were inside the glove. He felt them there and was amazed that it had been done so skillfully. Was she a professional magician?

"Why are you Russians so grim all the time—don't you know how to have a good time?"

"Maybe we should have more Americans around," Yazov conceded. *Hell, I wish my wife were as lively as this one!* "You have a fine son, and if he plays against us in the Olympics, I will forgive him." He was rewarded with a beaming smile.

"That's such a nice thing to say." *I hope he kicks your commie asses all the way back to Moskva.* If there was anything she couldn't stand, it was being patronized. "Eddie got two more points tonight, and that Ivan Somebody didn't get any!"

"Are you really that competitive, even with children's games?" Yazov asked.

Mary Pat slipped, just a little, so fast that her brain couldn't keep up with the automatic reply: "Show me a good loser, and I'll show you a loser." She paused, then covered the mistake. "Vince Lombardi, a famous American coach, said that. Excuse me, you must think me *nekulturny*. You're right, this is just a game for children." She smiled broadly. *In your face!*

"Did you see anything?"

"A foolish woman who gets overly excited," the photographer replied.

"How quickly will you have the film developed?"

"Two hours."

"Get moving," the senior man said.

"Did *you* see anything?" the remaining officer asked his boss.

"No, I don't think so. We've watched her for nearly two hours, and she acts like a typical American parent who gets too worked up at an athletic match, but just happens to attract the attention of the Defense Minister and the main suspect of a treason case. I think that's enough, Comrade, don't you?" *What a grand game this is . . .*

Two hours later, over a thousand black-and-white photographs were laid on the officer's desk. The camera was a Japanese one that put a time reference on the lower edge, and the KGB photographer was as good as any newspaper professional. He'd shot almost continuously, stopping only long enough to replace the oversized film magazines on the autodriven camera. At first he'd wished to use a portable TV camera, but the photographer had talked him out of it. The resolution wasn't as good, nor was the speed. A still camera was still the best for catching something quick and small, though you couldn't read lips from its record as you could with a videotape.

Each frame required a few seconds as the officer used a magnifying glass to examine the subjects of his interest. When Mrs. Foley entered the sequence of photos, he needed a few more seconds. He examined her clothing and jewelry at some length, and her face. Her smile was particularly mindless, like something in a Western television commercial, and he remembered hearing her screams over the crowd. Why were Americans so damned noisy?

Good dresser, though, he admitted to himself. *Like most American women in a Moscow scene, she stood out like a pheasant in a barnyard—*

he snorted annoyance at the thought. So what that the Americans spend more money on clothing? What did clothing matter to anyone? *Through my binoculars, she looked like she had the brains of a bird . . . but not in these photos—why?*

It was the eyes, he thought. In the still photos her eyes sparkled with something different from what he'd watched in person. Why was that?

In the photographs, her eyes—they were blue, he remembered—were always focused on something. The face, he noticed, had vaguely Slavic cheekbones. He knew that Foley was an Irish name, and assumed that her ancestry was Irish, too. That America was a country of immigrants, and that immigrants cross ethnic lines in marriage, were foreign concepts to the Russians. Add a few kilograms, change her hair and clothing, and she could be any face encountered on a street in Moscow . . . or Leningrad. The latter was more likely, he thought. She looked more like a Leningrader. Her face proclaimed the slight arrogance affected by people from that city. *I wonder what her ancestry really is.*

He kept flipping through the photos, and remembered that the Foleys had never been given this sort of scrutiny. The file on both was a relatively thin one. They were regarded by "Two" as nonentities. Something told him that this was a mistake, but the voice in the back of his head wasn't yet loud enough. He approached the last of the photographs, checking his watch. Three in the damned morning! he grumbled to himself and reached for another cup of tea.

Well, that must have been the second score. She was jumping like a gazelle. Nice legs, he saw for the first time. As his colleagues had noted up in the rafters, she was probably very entertaining in bed. Only a few more frames till the end of the game and . . . yes, there she was, embracing Yazov—that randy old goat!—then hugging Colonel Filitov—

He stopped dead. The photograph caught something that he hadn't seen through the binoculars. While giving Filitov a hug, her eyes were locked on one of the four security guards, the only one not watching the game. Her hand, her left hand, was not wrapped around Filitov at all, but rather down by his right one, hidden from view. He flipped back a few frames. Right before the embraces her hand had been in her coat pocket. Around the Defense Minister, it was balled into a fist. After Filitov, it was open again, and still her eyes were on the security guard, a smile on her face that was very Russian indeed, one that stopped at the lips—but in the next frame, she was back to her normal, flighty self. In that moment he was sure.

"Son of a bitch," he whispered to himself.

How long have the Foleys been here? He searched his weary memory but couldn't dredge it up. *Over two years at least—and we didn't know, we didn't even suspect . . . what if it's only her?* That was a thought—what if she were a spy and her husband were not? He rejected the idea out of hand, and was correct, but for the wrong reason. He reached for the phone and called Vatutin's home.

"Yes," the voice answered after only half a ring.

"I have something of interest," the officer said simply.

"Send a car."

Vatutin was there twenty-five minutes later, unshaven and irritable. The Major merely set out the crucial series of photographs.

"We never suspected her," he said while the Colonel examined the pictures through a magnifying glass.

"A fine disguise," Vatutin observed sourly. He'd been asleep only for an hour when the phone rang. He was still learning how to sleep without a few stiff drinks beforehand—trying to learn, he corrected himself. The Colonel looked up.

"Can you believe it? Right in front of the Defense Minister and four security guards! The *balls* of this woman! Who's her regular shadow?"

The Major merely handed over the file. Vatutin leafed through it and found the proper sheet.

"That old fart! He couldn't follow a child to school without being arrested as a pervert. Look at this—a lieutenant for twenty-three years!"

"There are seven hundred Americans attached to the embassy, Comrade Colonel," the Major observed. "We have only so many really good officers—"

"All watching the wrong people." Vatutin walked to the window. "No more! Her husband, too," he added.

"That will be my recommendation, Comrade Colonel. It would seem likely that they both work for CIA."

"She passed something to him."

"Probably—a message, perhaps something else."

Vatutin sat down and rubbed his eyes. "Good work, Comrade Major."

It was already dawn at the Pakistan-Afghanistan border. The Archer was preparing to return to his war. His men had packed their new weapons while their leader—now that was a new thought, the Archer told himself—reviewed his plans for the coming weeks. Among the things he'd received from Ortiz was a complete set of tactical maps. These were made from satellite photographs, and were updated to show current Soviet strongpoints and areas of heavy patrol activity. He had a long-range radio now on which he could tune to weather forecasts—including Russian ones. Their journey wouldn't start until nightfall.

He looked around. Some of his men had sent their families to this place of safety. The refugee camp was crowded and noisy, but a far happier place than the deserted villages and towns bombed flat by the Russians. There were children here, the Archer saw, and children were happy anywhere they had their parents, and food, and friends. The boys were already playing with toy guns—and with the older ones, they were not toys. He accepted that with a degree of regret that diminished on every trip. The losses among the *mudjaheddin* demanded replacements, and the youngest were the bravest. If freedom required their deaths—well, their deaths came in a holy cause and Allah was beneficent to those who died for Him. The world was indeed a sad place, but at least here a man could find a time for amusement and rest. He watched one of his riflemen helping his firstborn son to walk. The baby could not do it alone, but with each tottering step he looked up at the smiling, bearded face of a father he'd seen only twice since birth. The new chief of the band remembered doing the same for his son . . . now being taught to walk a very different path . . .

The Archer returned to his own work. He couldn't be a missileer anymore, but he'd trained Abdul well. Now the Archer would lead his men. It was a right that he'd earned, and, better still, his men thought him lucky. It would be good for morale. Though he had never in his life read books on military theory, the Archer felt that he knew their lessons well enough.

There was no warning—none at all. The Archer's head snapped around as he heard the crackling sound of exploding cannon shells, then he saw the dart-shapes of the Fencers, barely a hundred meters high. He hadn't yet reached for his rifle when he watched the bombs falling free of the ejector racks. The black shapes wobbled slightly before the fins stabilized them, their noses tipping down in slow motion. The engine noise of the Soviet Su-24 attack-bombers came next, and he turned to follow them as his rifle came up to his shoulder, but they were too fast. There was nothing left to do but dive to the ground, and it seemed that everything was happening very, very slowly. He was almost hovering in the air, the earth reluctant to come to meet him. His back was turned to the bombs, but he knew they were there, heading down. His eyes snapped up to see people running, his rifleman trying to cover the infant son with his body. The Archer turned to look up and was horrified to see that one bomb seemed to come straight at him, a black circle against the clear morning sky. There was no time even to say Allah's name as it passed over his head, and the earth shook.

He was stunned and deafened by the blast, and felt wobbly when he stood. It seemed strange to see and feel noise, but not to hear it. Instinct alone flipped the safety off his rifle as he looked around for the next plane. There it was! The rifle came up and fired of its own accord, but made no difference. The next Fencer dropped its load a hundred meters farther on and raced away before a trail of black smoke. There were no more.

The sounds came back slowly, and seemed distant, like the noises of a dream. But this was no dream. The place where his man and the baby had been was now a hole in the ground. There was no trace of the freedom fighter or his son, and even the certainty that both now stood righteously before their God could not mask the blood-chilling rage that coursed through his body. He remembered showing mercy to the Russian, feeling some regret at his death. No more. He'd never show mercy to an infidel again. His hands were chalk-white around the rifle.

Too late, a Pakistani F-16 fighter streaked across the sky, but the Russians were already across the border, and a minute later, the F-16 circled over the camp twice before heading back to its base.

"Are you all right?" It was Ortiz. His face had been cut by something or other, and his voice was far away.

There was no verbal answer. The Archer gestured with his rifle as he watched a newly made widow scream for her family. Together the two men looked for wounded who might be saved. Luckily, the medical section of the camp was unhurt. The Archer and the CIA officer carried a half-dozen people there, to see a French doctor cursing with the fluency of a man accustomed to such things, his hands already bloody from his work.

They found Abdul on their next trip. The young man had a Stinger up and armed. He wept as he confessed that he'd been asleep. The Archer patted his shoulder and said it wasn't his fault. There was supposed to be an agreement between the Soviets and the Pakistanis that prohibited cross-border raids. So much for agreements. A television news crew—French—appeared, and Ortiz took the Archer to a place where neither could be seen.

"Six," the Archer said. He didn't mention the noncombatant casualties.

"It is a sign of weakness that they do this, my friend," Ortiz replied.

"To attack a place of women and children is an abomination before God!"

"Have you lost any supplies?" To the Russians this was a guerrilla camp, of course, but Ortiz didn't bother voicing their view of things. He'd been here too long to be objective about such matters.

"Only a few rifles. The rest is outside the camp already."

Ortiz had no more to say. He'd run out of comforting observations. His nightmare was that his operation to support the Afghans was having the same effect as earlier attempts to aid the Hmong people of Laos. They'd fought bravely against their Vietnamese enemies, only to be virtually exterminated despite all their Western assistance. The CIA officer told himself that this situation was different, and, objectively, he thought that this was true. But it tore at what was left of his soul to watch these people leave the camp, armed to the teeth, and then to count the number that returned. Was America really helping the Afghans to redeem their own land, or were we merely encouraging them to kill as many Russians as possible before they, too, were wiped out?

What is the right policy? he asked himself. Ortiz admitted that he didn't know.

Nor did he know that the Archer had just made a policy decision of his own. The old-young face turned west, then north, and told himself that Allah's will was no more restricted by borders than was the will of His enemies.

15. Culmination

"All we need to do now is spring the trap," Vatutin told his Chairman. His voice was matter-of-fact, his face impassive as he gestured to the evidence laid out on Gerasimov's desk.

"Excellent work, Colonel!" The Chairman of the KGB allowed himself a smile. Vatutin saw that there was more in it than the satisfaction of closing a difficult and sensitive case. "Your next move?"

"Given the unusual status of the subject, I believe we should attempt to compromise him at the time of document transfer. It would seem that the CIA knows that we have broken the courier chain from Filitov to them. They took the unusual step of using one of their own officers to make this transfer—and make no mistake, this was an act of desperation despite the skill with which it was done. I would like to expose the Foleys at the same time. They must be a proud pair for having deceived us this long. To catch them in the act will destroy that pride and be a major psychological blow to CIA as a whole."

"Approved." Gerasimov nodded. "It is your case to run, Colonel. Take all the time you want." Both men knew that he meant less than a week.

"Thank you, Comrade Chairman." Vatutin returned at once to his office, where he briefed his section chiefs.

The microphones were very sensitive. Like most sleepers, Filitov tossed and turned quite a bit in his sleep, except when dreaming, and the reel-to-reel tape recorders kept a record of the rustle of linen and the barely intelligible murmurs. Finally a new sound came through and the man with the headphones gestured to his comrades. It sounded like a sail filling with wind, and it meant that the subject was tossing the covers off the bed.

Next came the coughing. The old man had lung problems, his medical file said. He was particularly vulnerable to colds and respiratory infections. Evidently he was coming down with something. Next he blew his nose, and the KGB men smiled at one another. It sounded like a locomotive whistle.

"Got him," the man on the TV camera said. "Heading toward the bathroom." The next set of sounds was predictable. There were two television cameras whose powerful lenses were framed on the apartment's two windows. Special settings allowed them to see into the apartment despite the glare of morning light.

"You know, doing this to someone is enough," a technician observed. "If you showed anyone a tape of one of us right after waking, we'd die of simple embarrassment."

"This one's death will be of another cause," the senior officer noted coldly. That was one problem with these investigations. You started identifying too closely with the subject, and had to remind yourself periodically just how loathsome traitors were. *Where did you go wrong?* the Major wondered. *A man with your war record!* He was already wondering how the case would be handled. A public trial? Could they dare to go public with so famous a war hero? That, he told himself, was a political question.

The door opened and closed, indicating that Filitov had gotten the copy of *Red Star* dropped off daily by a Defense Ministry messenger. They heard the gurgling of his coffee machine, and shared a look—this bastard traitor drinks good coffee every morning!

He was visible now, sitting at the small kitchen table and reading his paper. He was a note-taker, they saw, scratching on a pad or marking the paper itself. When the coffee was ready he rose to get milk from the small refrigerator. He sniffed at it before adding it to the cup to be sure it hadn't gone bad. He had enough butter to spread it lavishly on his black bread, which they knew was his usual breakfast.

"Still eats like a soldier," the cameraman said.

"He was a good one once," another officer observed. "You foolish old man, how could you do it?"

Breakfast was over soon thereafter, and they watched Filitov walk toward the bathroom, where he washed and shaved. He returned to view to dress. On the videoscreen, they saw him take out a brush to polish his boots. He always wore his boots, they knew, which was unusual for Ministry officers. But so were the three gold stars on his uniform blouse. He stood before the bureau mirror, inspecting himself. The paper went into his briefcase, and Filitov walked out the door. The last noise they heard was the key setting the lock on the apartment door. The Major got on the phone.

"Subject is moving. Nothing unusual this morning. Shadow team is in place."

"Very well," Vatutin replied and hung up.

One of the cameramen adjusted his instrument to record Filitov's emergence from the building. He took the salute from the driver, got into the car, and disappeared down the street. A completely unremarkable morning, they all agreed. They could afford to be patient now.

The mountains to the west were sheathed in clouds, and a fine drizzle was falling. The Archer hadn't left yet. There were prayers to be said, people to console. Ortiz was off having his face attended to by one of the French doctors, while his friend was riffling through the CIA officer's papers.

It made him feel guilty, but the Archer told himself that he was merely looking for records that he himself had delivered to the CIA officer. Ortiz was a compulsive note-taker, and, the Archer knew, a map fancier. The map he wanted to see was in its expected place, and clipped to it were several diagrams. These he copied by hand, quickly and accurately, before replacing all as it had been.

"You guys are so square," Bea Taussig laughed.

"It would be a shame to spoil the image," Al replied, a smile masking his distaste for their guest. He never understood why Candi liked this . . . whatever the hell she was. Gregory didn't know why she rang bells in the back of his head. It wasn't the fact that she didn't like him— Al didn't give a damn one way or the other about that. His family and his fiancée loved him, and all his co-workers respected him. That was enough. If he didn't fit into somebody's notion of what an Army officer was supposed to be, screw 'em. But there was *something* about Bea that—

"Okay, we'll talk business," their guest said with amusement. "I have people from Washington asking me how soon—"

"Somebody ought to tell those bureaucrats that you don't just turn things like this on and off," Candi growled.

"Six weeks, tops." Al grinned. "Maybe less."

"When?" Candi asked.

"Soon. We haven't had a chance to run it on the simulator yet, but it feels right. It was Bob's idea. He was about due, and it streamlined the software package even better than what I was trying. We don't have to use as much AI as I thought."

"Oh?" The use of AI—artificial intelligence—was supposed to be crucial to mirror performance and target discrimination.

"Yeah, we were overengineering the problem, trying to use reason instead of instinct. We don't have to tell the computer how to think everything out. We can reduce the command load twenty percent by putting pre-set options in the program. It turns out to be quicker and easier than making the computer make most judgments off a menu."

"What about the anomalies?" Taussig asked.

"That's the whole point. The AI routines were actually slowing things down more than we thought. We were trying to make the thing so flexible that it had trouble doing anything. The expected laser performance is good enough that it can take the fire-option faster than the AI program can decide whether to aim it—so why not take the shot? If it doesn't fit the profile, we pop it anyway."

"Your laser specs have changed," Bea observed.

"Well, I can't talk about that."

Another grin from the little geek. Taussig managed to smile back. *I know something you don't know!*, is it? Just looking at him made her skin crawl, but what was worse was the way Candi looked at him, like he was Paul Newman or something! Sallow complexion, even zits, and she loved this thing. Bea didn't know whether to laugh or cry . . .

"Even us admin pukes have to be able to plan ahead," Taussig said.

"Sorry, Bea. You know the security rules."

"Makes you wonder how we get anything done." Candi shook her head.

"If it gets any worse, Al and I won't be able to talk to each other between . . ." She smiled lecherously at her lover.

Al laughed. "I have a headache."

"Bea, do you believe this guy?" Candi asked.

Taussig leaned back. "I never have."

"When are you going to let Dr. Rabb take you out? You know he's been mooning over you for six months."

"The only mooning I expect out of him is from a car. God, that's a ghastly thought." Her look at Candi masked her feelings exquisitely well. She also realized that the programming information that she'd gotten out was now invalid. Damn the little geek for changing it!

"That's something. Question is, what?" Jones keyed his microphone. "Conn, Sonar, we have a contact bearing zero-nine-eight. Designate this contact Sierra-Four."

"You sure it's a contact?" the young petty officer asked.

"See this?" Jones ran his finger along the screen. The "waterfall display" was cluttered with ambient noise. "Remember that you're looking for nonrandom data. This line ain't random." He typed in a command to alter the display. The computer began processing a series of discrete frequency bands. Within a minute the picture was clear. At least Mr. Jones thought so, the young sonarman noted. The stroke of light on the screen was irregularly shaped, bowing out and narrowing down, covering about five degrees of bearing. The "tech-rep" stared at the screen for several more seconds, then spoke again.

"Conn, Sonar, classify target Sierra-Four as a Krivak-class frigate, bearing zero-nine-six. Looks like he's doing turns for fifteen or so knots." Jones turned to the youngster. He remembered his own first cruise. This nineteen-year-old didn't even have his dolphins yet. "See this? That's the high-frequency signature from his turbine engines, it's a dead giveaway and you can hear it a good ways off, usually, 'cause the Krivak doesn't have good sound-isolation."

Mancuso came into the compartment. *Dallas* was a "first-flight" 688, and didn't have direct access from the control room to sonar as the later ones did. Instead, you had to come forward and step around a hole in the deck that led below. Probably the overhaul would change that. The Captain waved his coffee mug at the screen.

"Where's the Krivak?"

"Right here, bearing still constant. We have good water around us. He's probably a good ways off."

The skipper smiled. Jones was always trying to guess range. The hell of it was that in the two years that Mancuso had had him aboard as a member of the crew he'd been right more often than not. Aft in the control room, the fire-control tracking party was plotting the position of the target against *Dallas'* known track to determine range and course of the Soviet frigate.

There wasn't much activity on the surface. The other three sonar contacts plotted were all single-screw merchantmen. Though the weather was decent today, the Baltic Sea—an oversized lake to Mancuso's way of thinking—was rarely a nice place in the winter. Intelligence reports said that most of the opposition's ships were tied alongside for repairs. That was good news. Better still, there wasn't much in the way of ice. A really cold season could freeze things solid, and that would put a crimp in their mission, the Captain thought.

Thus far only their other visitor, Clark, knew what that mission was.

"Captain, we have a posit on Sierra-Four," a lieutenant called from control.

Jones folded a slip of paper and handed it to Mancuso.

"I'm waiting."

"Range thirty-six thousand, course roughly two-nine-zero."

Mancuso unfolded the note and laughed. "Jones, you're still a fucking witch!" He handed it back, then went aft to alter the submarine's course to avoid the Krivak.

The sonarman at Jones's side grabbed the note and read it aloud. "How did you know? You aren't supposed to be able to do that."

"Practice, m'boy, practice," Jones replied in his best W. C. Fields accent. He noted the submarine's course change. It wasn't like the Mancuso he remembered. In the old days, the skipper would close to get photos through the periscope, run a few torpedo solutions, and generally treat the Soviet ship like a real target in a real war. This time they were opening the range to the Russian frigate, creeping away. Jones didn't think Mancuso had changed all that much, and started wondering what the hell this new mission was all about.

He hadn't seen much of Mr. Clark. He spent a lot of time aft in the engine room, where the ship's fitness center was—a treadmill jammed between two machine tools. The crew was already murmuring that he didn't talk very much. He just smiled and nodded and went on his way. One of the chiefs noted the tattoo on Clark's forearm and was whispering some stuff about the meaning of the red seal, specifically that it stood for the real SEALs. *Dallas* had never had one of those aboard, though other boats had, and the stories, told quietly except for the occasional "no shit!" interruptions, had circulated throughout the submarine community but nowhere else. If there was anything submariners knew how to do, it was keeping secrets.

Jones stood and walked aft. He figured he'd taught enough lessons for one day, and his status as a civilian technical representative allowed him to wander about at will. He noted that *Dallas* was taking her own sweet time, heading east at nine knots. A look at the chart told him where they were, and the way the navigator was tapping his pencil on it told him how much farther they'd be going. Jones started to do some serious thinking as he went below for a Coke. He'd come back for a really tense one after all.

"Yes, Mr. President?" Judge Moore answered the phone with his own tense look. *Decision time?*

"That thing we talked about in here the other day . . ."

"Yes, sir." Moore looked at the phone. Aside from the handset that he held, the "secure" phone system was a three-foot cube, cunningly hidden in his desk. It took words, broke them into digital bits, scrambled them beyond recognition, and sent them out to another similar box which put them back together. One interesting sidelight of this was that it made for very clear conversations, since the encoding system eliminated all the random noise on the line.

"You may go ahead. We can't—well, I decided last night that we can't just leave him." This had to be his first call of the morning, and the emotional content came through, too. Moore wondered if he'd lost sleep over the life of the faceless agent. Probably he had. The President was that sort of man. He was also the sort, Moore knew, to stick with a decision once made. Pelt would try to change it all day, but the President was getting it out at eight in the morning and would have to stick with it.

"Thank you, Mr. President. I'll set things in motion." Moore had Bob Ritter in his office two minutes later:

"The CARDINAL extraction is a 'go'!"

"Makes me glad I voted for the man," Ritter said as he smacked one hand into the other. "Ten days from now we'll have him in a nice safe house. Jesus, the debrief'll take *years!*" Then came the sober pause. "It's a shame to lose his services, but we owe it to him. Besides, Mary Pat has recruited a couple of real live ones for us. She made the film pass last night. No details, but I gather that it was a hairy one."

"She always was a little too—"

"More than a little, Arthur, but all field officers have some cowboy in them." The two Texas natives shared a look. "Even the ones from New York."

"Some team. With those genes, you gotta wonder what their kids'll be like," Moore observed with a chuckle. "Bob, you got your wish. Run with it."

"Yes, sir." Ritter went off to send his message, then informed Admiral Greer.

The telex went via satellite and arrived in Moscow only fifteen minutes later: TRAVEL ORDERS APPROVED. KEEP ALL RECEIPTS FOR ROUTINE REIMBURSEMENT.

Ed Foley took the decrypted message into his office. *So, whatever desk-sitter got cold feet on us found his socks after all,* he thought. *Thank God.*

Only one more transfer to go! We'll pass the message at the same time, and Misha'll catch a flight to Leningrad, then just follow the plan. One good thing about CARDINAL was that he'd practiced his escape routine at least once a year. His old tank outfit was now assigned to the Leningrad Military District, and the Russians understood that kind of sentiment. Misha had also seen to it over the years that his regiment was the first to get new equipment and to train in new tactics. After his death, it would be designated the Filitov Guards—or at least that's what the Soviet Army was planning to do. It was too bad, Foley thought, that they'd have to change that plan. On the other hand, maybe CIA would make some other sort of memorial to the man . . .

But there was still that one more transfer to make, and it would not be an easy one. One step at a time, he told himself. First we have to alert him.

Half an hour later, a nondescript embassy staffer left the building. At a certain time he'd be standing at a certain place. The "signal" was picked up by someone else who was not likely to be shadowed by "Two." This person did something else. He didn't know the reason, only where and how the mark was to be made. He found that very frustrating. Spy work was supposed to be exciting, wasn't it?

"There's our friend." Vatutin was riding in the car, wanting to see for himself that things were going properly. Filitov entered his car, and the driver took him off. Vatutin's car followed for half a kilometer, then turned off as a second car took over, racing over to a parallel street to keep pace.

He kept track of events by radio. The transmissions were crisp and businesslike as the six cars rotated on and off surveillance, generally with one ahead of the target vehicle and one behind. Filitov's car stopped at a grocery store that catered to senior Defense Ministry officials. Vatutin had a man inside—Filitov was known to stop there two or three times per week—to see what he bought and whom he talked to.

He could tell that things were going perfectly, as was not unexpected once he'd explained to everybody on the case that the Chairman had personal interest in this one. Vatutin's driver raced ahead of their quarry, depositing the Colonel across the street from Filitov's apartment building. Vatutin walked inside and went up to the apartment that they had taken over.

"Good timing," the senior officer said as Vatutin came in the door.

The "Two" man looked discreetly out the window and saw Filitov's car come to a halt. The trailing car motored past without a pause as the Army Colonel walked into the building.

"Subject just entered the building," a communications specialist said. Inside, a woman with a string-bag full of apples would get on the elevator with Filitov. Up on Filitov's floor, two people who looked young enough to be teenagers would stroll past the elevator as he got out, continuing down the corridor with overly loud whispers of undying love. The surveillance mikes caught the end of that as Filitov opened the door.

"Got him," the cameraman said.

"Let's keep away from the windows," Vatutin said unnecessarily. The men with binoculars stood well back from them, and so long as the lights in the apartment were left off—the bulbs had been removed from the fixtures—no one could tell that the rooms were occupied.

One thing they liked about the man was his aversion to pulling down the shades. They followed him into the bedroom, where they watched him change into casual clothes and slippers. He returned to the kitchen and fixed himself a simple meal. They watched him tear the foil top off a half-liter bottle of vodka. The man was sitting and staring out the window.

"An old, lonely man," one officer observed. "Do you suppose that's what did it?"

"One way or another, we'll find out."

Why is it that the State can betray us? Misha asked Corporal Romanov two hours later.

Because we are soldiers, I suppose. Misha noted that the corporal was avoiding the question, and the issue. Did he know what his Captain was trying to ask?

But if we betray the State . . . ?

Then we die, Comrade Captain. That is simple enough. We earn the hatred and contempt of the peasants and workers, and we die. Romanov stared across time into his officer's eyes. The corporal now had his own question. He lacked the will to ask it, but his eyes seemed to proclaim: *What have you done, my Captain?*

Across the street, the man on the recording equipment noted sobbing, and wondered what caused it.

"What're you doing, honey?" Ed Foley asked, and the microphones heard.

"Starting to make lists for when we leave. So many things to remember, I'd better start now."

Foley bent over her shoulder. She had a pad and a pencil, but she was writing on a plastic sheet with a marker pen. It was the sort of arrangement that hung on many refrigerators, and could be wiped clean with a swipe of a damp cloth.

I'LL DO IT, she'd written. I HAVE A PERFECT DODGE. Mary Pat smiled and held up a team photo of Eddie's hockey squad. Each player had signed it, and at the top in scrawling Russian, Eddie had put, with his mother's coaching: "To the man who brings us luck. Thanks, Eddie Foley."

Her husband frowned. It was typical of his wife to use the bold approach, and he knew that she'd used her cover with consummate skill. But . . . he shook his head. But what? The only man in the CARDINAL chain who could identify him had never seen his face. Ed may have lacked her *panache*, but he was more circumspect. He felt that he was better than his wife at countersurveillance. He acknowledged Mary Pat's passion for the work, and her acting skill, but—damn it, she was just too bold sometimes. *Fine—why don't you tell her?* he asked himself.

He knew what would happen—she'd go practical on him. There wasn't time to establish another series of cutouts. They both knew that her cover was a solid one, that she hadn't even come close to suspicion yet.

But—Goddamn it, this business is one continuous series of fucking BUTs! OK BUT COVER YOUR CUTE LITTLE ASS!!!! he wrote on the plastic pad. Her eyes sparkled as she wiped it clean. Then she wrote her own message: LET'S GIVE THE MICROPHONES A HARD-ON!

Ed nearly strangled trying not to laugh. *Every time before a job,* he thought. It wasn't that he minded. He did find it a little odd, though.

Ten minutes later, in a room in the basement of the apartment building, a pair of Russian wiretap technicians listened with rapt attention to the sounds generated in the Foley bedroom.

Mary Pat Foley woke up at her customary six-fifteen. It was still dark outside, and she wondered how much of her grandfather's character had been formed by the cold and the dark of the Russian winters . . . and how much of hers. Like most Americans assigned to Moscow, she thoroughly hated the idea of listening devices in her walls. She occasionally took perverse pleasure in them, as she had the previous night, but then there was also the thought that the Soviets had placed them in the bathroom, too. That seemed like something they'd do, she thought, looking at herself in the mirror. The first order of business was to take her temperature. They both wanted another child, and had been working on it for a few months—which beat watching Russian TV. Professionally, of course, pregnancy made one hell of a cover. After three minutes she noted the temperature on a card she kept in the medicine cabinet. *Probably not yet,* she thought. *Maybe in a few more days.* She dropped the remains of an Early Pregnancy Test kit in the waste can anyway.

Next, there were the children to rouse. She got breakfast going, and shook everyone loose. Living in an apartment with but a single bathroom imposed a rigid schedule on them. There came the usual grumbles from Ed, and the customary whines and groans from the kids.

God, it'll be nice to get home, she told herself. As much as she loved the challenge of working in the mouth of the dragon, living here wasn't exactly fun for the kids. Eddie loved his hockey, but he was missing a normal childhood in this cold, barren place. Well, that would change soon enough. They'd load everyone aboard the Pan Am clipper and wing home, leaving Moscow behind—if not forever, at least for five years. Life in Virginia's tidewater country. Sailing on the Chesapeake Bay. *Mild winters!*

You had to bundle kids up here like Nanook of the fucking North, she thought. *I'm always fighting off colds.*

She got breakfast on the table just as Ed vacated the bathroom, allowing her to wash and dress. The routine was that he managed breakfast, then dressed while his wife got the kids going.

In the bathroom, she heard the TV go on, and laughed into the mirror. Eddie loved the morning exercise show—the woman who appeared on it looked like a longshoreman, and he called her Workerwom*mannn!* Her son yearned for mornings of the Transformers—"More than meets the eye!" he still remembered the opening song. Eddie would miss his Russian friends some, she thought, but the kid was an American and nothing would ever change that. By seven-fifteen everyone was dressed and ready to go. Mary Pat tucked a wrapped parcel under her arm.

"Cleaning day, isn't it?" Ed asked his wife.

"I'll be back in time to let her in," Mary Pat assured him.

"Okay." Ed opened the door and led the procession to the elevator. As usual, his family was the first one to get moving in the morning. Eddie raced forward and punched the elevator button. It arrived just as the rest of the family reached the door. Eddie jumped onto it, enjoying the usual springiness of Soviet elevator cables. To his mother, it always seemed as though the damned thing was going to fall all the way to the basement, but her son thought it entertaining when the car dropped a few inches. Three minutes later they got into the car. Ed took the wheel this morning. On the drive out, the kids waved at the militiaman, who was really KGB, and who waved back with a smile. As soon as the car had turned onto the street, he lifted the phone in his booth.

Ed kept his eye on the rearview mirror, and his wife had already adjusted the outside one so that she could see aft also. The kids got into a dispute in the back, which both parents ignored.

"Looks like a nice day," he said quietly. *Nothing following us.*

"Uh huh." *Agreed.* They had to be careful what they said around the kids, of course. Eddie could repeat anything they said as easily as the opening ditty of the Transformers cartoon. There was always the chance of a radio bug in the car, too.

Ed drove to the school first, allowing his wife to take the kids in. Eddie and Katie looked like teddy bears in their cold-weather clothing. His wife looked unhappy when she came out.

"Nikki Wagner called in sick. They want me to take over her class this afternoon," she told him on reentering the car. Her husband grunted. Actually, it was perfect. He dropped the Volkswagen into gear and pulled back onto Leninskiy Prospekt. *Game time.*

Now their checks of the mirrors were serious.

Vatutin hoped that they'd never thought of this before. Moscow streets are always full of dumptrucks, scurrying from one construction site to another. The high cabs of the vehicles made for excellent visibility, and the meanderings of the look-alike vehicles appeared far less sinister than would those of unmarked sedans. He had nine of them working for him today, and the officers driving them communicated via encrypted military radios.

Colonel Vatutin himself was in the apartment next door to Filitov's. The family who lived there had moved into the Hotel Moscow two days before. He'd watched the videotapes of his subject, drinking himself to insensibility, and used the opportunity to get three other "Two" officers in. They had their own spike-microphones driven into the party wall between the two flats, and listened intently to the Colonel's staggering through his morning routine. Something told him that this was the day.

It's the drinking, he told himself while he sipped tea. That drew an amused grimace. Perhaps it takes one drinker to understand another. He was sure that Filitov had been working himself up to something, and he also remembered that the time he'd seen the Colonel with the traitorous bath attendant, he'd come into the steam room with a hangover . . . *just as I had.* It fitted, he decided. Filitov was a hero who'd gone bad—but a hero still. It could not have been easy for him to commit treason, and he probably needed the drink to sleep in the face of a troubled conscience. It pleased Vatutin that people felt that way, that treason was still a hard thing to do.

"They're heading this way," a communications man reported over the radio.

"Right here," Vatutin told his subordinates. "It will happen within a hundred meters of where we stand."

Mary Pat ran over what she had to do. Handing over the wrapped photo would allow her to recover the film that she would slip inside her glove. Then there was the signal. She'd rub the back of her gloved hand across her forehead as though wiping off sweat, then scratch her eyebrow. That was the danger-breakout signal. She hoped he'd pay attention. Though she'd never done the signal herself, Ed had once offered a breakout, only to be rejected. It was something she understood better than her husband had—after all, her work with CIA was based more on passion than reason—but enough was enough. This man had been sending data West when she'd learned to play with dolls.

There was the building. Ed headed for the curb, jostling over the potholes as her hand gripped the parcel. As she grabbed the door handle, her husband patted her on the leg. *Good luck, kid.*

"Foleyeva just got out of the car and is headed to the side entrance," the radio squawked. Vatutin smiled at the Russification of the foreign name. He debated drawing the service automatic in his belt, but decided against it. Better to have his hands free, and a gun might go off accidentally. This was no time for accidents.

"Any ideas?" he asked.

"If it was me, I'd try a brush-pass," one of his men offered.

Vatutin nodded agreement. It worried him that they'd been unable to establish camera surveillance of the corridor itself, but technical factors had militated against it. That was the problem with the really sensitive cases. The smart ones were the wary ones. You couldn't risk alerting them, and he was sure that the Americans were alerted already. Alerted enough, he thought, to have killed one of their own agents in that railyard.

Fortunately, most Moscow apartments had peepholes installed in them now. Vatutin found himself grateful for the increase in burglaries, because his technicians had been able to replace the regular lens with one that allowed them to see most of the corridor. He took this post himself.

We should have put microphones on the stairwells, he told himself. *Make a note of that for the next time. Not all enemy spies use elevators.*

* * *

Mary Pat was not quite the athlete her husband was. She paused on the landing, looking up and down the stairwell and listening for any sound at all as her heart rate slowed somewhat. She checked her digital watch. Time.

She opened the firedoor and walked straight down the middle of the corridor.

Okay, Misha. I hope you remembered to set your watch last night.

Last time, Colonel. Will you for Christ's sake take the breakout signal this time, and maybe they'll do the debrief on the Farm, and my son can meet a real Russian hero . . . ?

God, I wish my grandfather could see me now . . .

She'd never been here before, never done a pass in this building. But she knew it by heart, having spent twenty minutes going over the diagram. The CARDINAL's door was . . . that one!

Time! Her heart skipped a beat as she saw the door open, thirty feet away.

What a pro! But what came next was as cold as a dagger made of ice.

Vatutin's eyes widened in horror at the noise. The deadbolt on the apartment door had been installed with typical Russian workmanship, about half a millimeter out of line. As he slipped it in preparation to leap from the room, it made an audible *click.*

Mary Pat Foley scarcely broke stride. Her training took over her body like a computer program. There was a peephole on the door that went from dark to light:

—there was somebody there

—that somebody just moved

—that somebody just slipped the door lock.

She took half a step to her right and rubbed the back of her gloved hand across her forehead. She wasn't pretending to wipe sweat away.

Misha saw the signal and stopped cold, a curious look on his face that began to change to amusement until he heard the door wrenched open. He knew in an instant that the man who emerged was not his neighbor.

"You are under arrest!" Vatutin shouted, then saw that the American woman and the Russian man were standing a meter apart, and both had their hands at their sides. It was just as well that the "Two" officers behind him couldn't see the look on his face.

"Excuse me?" the woman said in excellent Russian.

"*What!*" Filitov thundered with the rage only possible to a hung-over professional soldier.

"You"—he pointed to Mrs. Foley—"up against the wall."

"I'm an American citizen, and you can't—"

"You're an American spy," a captain said, pushing her against the wall.

"What?" Her voice contained panic and alarm, not the least amount of professionalism here, the Captain thought, but then his mind nearly choked on the observation. "What are you talking about? What is this? Who are you?" Next she started screaming: "*Police—somebody call the police. I'm being attacked! Somebody help me, please!*"

Vatutin ignored her. He had already grabbed Filitov's hand, and as another officer pushed the Colonel against the wall, he took a film cassette.

For a flicker of time that seemed to stretch into hours, he'd been struck with the horrible thought that he'd blown it, that she really wasn't CIA. With the film in his hand, he swallowed and looked into Filitov's eyes.

"You are under arrest for treason, *Comrade Colonel*." His voice hissed out the end of the statement. "Take him away."

He turned to look at the woman. Her eyes were wide with fear and outrage. Four people now had their heads out of doors, staring into the hall.

"I am Colonel Vatutin of the Committee for State Security. We have just made an arrest. Close your doors and go about your business." He noted that compliance with his order took under five seconds. Russia was still Russia.

"Good morning, Mrs. Foley," he said next. He saw her struggle to gain control of herself.

"Who are you—and what is this all about?"

"The Soviet Union does not look kindly upon its guests stealing State secrets. Surely they told you that in Washington—excuse me, Langley."

Her voice trembled as she spoke. "My husband is an accredited member of the U.S. diplomatic mission to your country. I wish to be put in contact with my embassy at once. I don't know what you're jabbering about, but I do know that if you make the pregnant wife of a diplomat lose her baby, you'll have a diplomatic incident big enough to make the TV news! I didn't talk to that man. I didn't touch him, and he didn't touch me—and you know it, mister. What they warned me about in Washington is that you clowns love to embarrass Americans with your damned-fool little spy games."

Vatutin took all of the speech impassively, though the word "pregnant" did get his attention. He knew from the reports of the maid who cleaned their apartment twice a week that Foleyeva had been testing herself. And if—there would be a larger incident over this than he wanted. Again the political dragon raised its head. Chairman Gerasimov would have to rule on this.

"My husband is waiting for me."

"We'll tell him that you are being detained. You will be asked to answer some questions. You will not be mistreated."

Mary Pat already knew that. Her horror at what had just happened was muted by her pride. She'd performed beautifully and knew it. As part of the diplomatic community, she was fundamentally safe. They might hold on to her for a day, even two, but any serious mistreatment would result in having a half-dozen Russians shipped home from Washington. Besides, she wasn't really pregnant.

All that was beside the point. She didn't shed any tears, showed no emotion other than what was expected, what she'd been briefed and trained to show. What mattered was that her most important agent was blown, and with him, information of the highest importance. She wanted to cry, needed to cry, but she wouldn't give the fuckers the satisfaction. The crying would come on the plane ride home.

16. Damage Assessment

"It says a lot about the man that the first thing he did was to get to the embassy and send the telex," Ritter said at last. "The Ambassador delivered his protest note to their Foreign Ministry before they went public on the arrest 'for conduct incompatible with diplomatic status.' "

"Some consolation," Greer noted gloomily.

"We ought to have her back in a day or less," Ritter went on. "They're already PNG'd, and they're going on the next Pan Am flight out."

Ryan squirmed in his chair. *What about CARDINAL?* he wondered. *Jesus, they tell me about this superagent, and a week later . . . They sure as hell don't have a Supreme Court over there that makes it hard to execute people.*

"Any chance we can do a trade for him?" Jack asked.

"You are kidding, boy." Ritter rose and walked to the window. At three in the morning, the CIA parking lot was nearly empty, only a loose handful of cars sitting among the piles of plowed snow. "We don't even have anybody big enough to trade for a mitigation of sentence. No way in hell they'll let him out, even for a chief of station, which we don't have."

"So he's dead and the data is lost with him."

"That's what the man's saying," Judge Moore agreed.

"Help from the allies?" Ryan asked. "Sir Basil might have something hopping that can help us."

"Ryan, there is nothing we can do to save the man." Ritter turned to take out his anger on the nearest target of opportunity. "He's dead—sure, he's still breathing, but he's dead all the same. A month, or two, or three from now, the announcement will be made, and we'll confirm it through other assets, and then we'll pry open a bottle and have a few to his memory."

"What about *Dallas?*" Greer asked.

"Huh?" Ryan turned.

"You don't need to know about that," Ritter said, now grateful to have a target. "Give her back to the Navy."

"Okay." Greer nodded. "This is likely to have some serious consequences." That earned the Admiral a baleful look from Judge Moore. He now had to go to the President.

"What about it, Ryan?"

"On the arms-control talks?" Jack shrugged. "Depends on how they handle it. They have a wide range of options, and anybody who tells you he can predict which one they'll choose is a liar."

"Nothing like an expert opinion," Ritter observed.

"Sir Basil thinks Gerasimov wants to make a move on the top spot. He could conceivably use this toward that end," Ryan said coolly, "but I think Narmonov has too much political clout now that he has that fourth man on the Politburo. He can, therefore, choose to go forward toward the agreement and show the Party how strong he is by moving forward for peace, or if he senses more political vulnerability than I see in the picture, he can consolidate his hold on the Party by trashing us as the incorrigible enemies of Socialism. If there's a way to put a probability assessment on that choice that's anything more than a wild-ass guess, I haven't seen it yet."

"Get to work on it," Judge Moore ordered. "The President'll want something hard enough to grab hold of before Ernie Allen starts talking about putting SDI on the table again."

"Yes, sir." Jack stood. "Judge, do we expect the Sovs to go public on CARDINAL's arrest?"

"There's a question," Ritter said.

Ryan headed for the door and stopped again. "Wait a minute."

"What is it?" Ritter asked.

"You said that the Ambassador delivered his protest before their Foreign Ministry said anything, right?"

"Yeah, Foley worked real fast to beat them to the punch."

"With all due respect to Mr. Foley, nobody's that fast," Ryan said. "They should have had their press release already printed before they made the pickup."

"So?" Admiral Greer asked.

Jack walked back toward the other three. "So the Foreign Minister is Narmonov's man, isn't he? So's Yazov at the Defense Ministry. They didn't know," Ryan said. "They were as surprised as we were."

"No chance," Ritter snorted. "They don't do things like that."

"Assumption on your part, sir." Jack stood his ground. "What evidence backs up that statement?"

Greer smiled. "None that we know of right now."

"Damn it, James, I know he's—"

"Keep going, Dr. Ryan," Judge Moore said.

"If those two ministers didn't know what was going down, it puts a different spin on this case, doesn't it?" Jack sat on the back of a chair. "Okay, I can see cutting Yazov out—CARDINAL was his senior aide— but why cut out the Foreign Minister? This sort of thing, you want to move fast, catch the newsies with the breaking story—for damned sure you don't want the other side to get the word out first."

"Bob?" the DCI asked.

The Deputy Director for Operations never had liked Ryan very much— he thought that he'd come too far too fast—but, for all that, Bob Ritter was an honest man. The DDO sat back down and sipped at his coffee for a moment. "Boy may have a point. We'll have to confirm a few details, but if they check out . . . then it's as much a political operation as a simple 'Two' case."

"James?"

The Deputy Director for Intelligence nodded agreement. "Scary."

"We may not be talking about just losing a good source," Ryan went on, speculating as he spoke. "KGB might be using this for political ends. What I don't see is his power base. The Alexandrov faction has three solid members. Narmonov now has four, counting the new guy, Vaneyev—"

"Shit!" This was Ritter. "We assumed that when his daughter was picked up and let go that they either didn't break her—hell, they say she looks okay—or her father was too important for them to—"

"Blackmail." Now it was Judge Moore's turn. "You were right, Bob. And Narmonov doesn't know. You have to hand it to Gerasimov, the bastard has some beautiful moves . . . If all this is true, Narmonov is out-numbered and doesn't know it." He paused for a frown. "We're speculating like a bunch of amateurs."

"Well, it makes for one hell of a scenario." Ryan almost smiled until he reached the logical conclusion. "We may have brought down the first Soviet government in thirty years that wanted to liberalize their own country." *What will the papers make of that?* Jack asked himself. *And you know that it'll get out. Something like this is too juicy to stay secret long . . .*

"We know what you've been doing, and we know how long you've been doing it. Here is the evidence." He tossed the photographs onto the table.

"Nice pictures," Mary Pat said. "Where's the man from my embassy?"

"We don't have to let anyone talk with you. We can keep you here as long as we wish. Years, if necessary," he added ominously.

"Look, mister, I'm an American, okay? My husband is a diplomat. He has diplomatic immunity and so do I. Just because you think I'm a dumb American housewife, you think you can push me around and scare me into signing that damned-fool confession that I'm some kind of idiot spy. Well, I'm not, and I won't, and my government will protect me. So as far as I'm concerned you can take that confession and spread mustard on it and eat it. God knows the food over here is so bad you could use the fiber in your diet," she observed. "And you're saying that that nice old man I was taking the picture to was arrested too, eh? Well, I think you're just crazy."

"We know that you have met him many times."

"Twice. I saw him at a game last year, too—no, excuse me, I met him at a diplomatic reception a few weeks ago. That's three times, but only the hockey matters. That's why I brought the picture. The boys on the team think he's good luck for them—ask them, they all signed the picture, didn't they? Both times he came, we won big games and my son scored a couple of goals. And you think he's a spy just because he went to a junior-league hockey game? My God, you guys must think American spies are under every bed."

She was actually enjoying herself. They treated her carefully. Nothing like a threatened pregnancy, Mary Pat told herself, as she broke yet another time-honored rule in the spy business: *Don't say anything.* She jabbered on, as would any outraged private citizen—with the shield of diplomatic immunity, of course—at the rank stupidity of the Russians. She watched her interrogator closely for a reaction. If there was anything Russians hated, it was to be looked down on, and most of all by the Americans, to whom they had a terminal inferiority complex.

"I used to think the security people at the embassy were a pain," she huffed after a moment. "Don't do this, don't do that, be careful taking pictures of things. I wasn't taking a picture, I was *giving* him a picture! And the kids in it are Russian kids—except for Eddie." She turned away, looking into the mirror. Mary Pat wondered if the Russians had thought that touch up themselves or if they had gotten the idea from American cop shows.

"Whoever trained that one knew his business," Vatutin observed, looking through the mirror from the next room. "She knows we're here but doesn't let on. When are we turning her loose?"

"Late this afternoon," the head of the Second Chief Directorate answered. "Holding her isn't worth the effort. Her husband is already packing up the apartment. You should have waited a few more seconds," the General added.

"I know." There was no point in explaining the faulty door lock. The KGB didn't accept excuses, even from colonels. That was beside the point in any case, Vatutin and his boss knew. They'd caught Filitov—not quite in the act, but he was still caught. That was the objective of the case, at least so far as they were concerned. Both men knew the other parts of it, but treated them as though they didn't exist. It was the smartest course for both.

"Where is my man!" Yazov demanded.

"He is in Lefortovo Prison, of course," Gerasimov answered.

"I want to see him. At once." The Defense Minister hadn't even paused to take off his cap, standing there in his calf-length greatcoat, his cheeks still pink from the chilly February air—or perhaps with anger, Gerasimov thought. Maybe even with fear . . .

"This is not a place to make demands, Dmitri Timofeyevich. I, too, am a Politburo member. I, too, sit on the Defense Council. And it may be that you are implicated in this investigation." Gerasimov's fingers played with a file on the desktop.

That changed Yazov's complexion. He went pale, definitely not from fear. Gerasimov was surprised that the soldier didn't lose control, but the Marshal made a supreme effort and spoke as though to a new draftee:

"Show me your evidence here and now if you have the balls for it!"

"Very well." The KGB Chairman flipped open the folder and removed a series of photographs, handing them over.

"You had *me* under surveillance?"

"No, we've been watching Filitov. You just happened to be there."

Yazov tossed the prints back with contempt. "So what? Misha was invited to a hockey game. I accompanied him. It was a good game. There is an American boy on the team—I met the mother at some reception or other— oh, yes, it was in George Hall when the American negotiators were last over. She was at this game, and we said hello. She is an amusing woman, in an empty-headed sort of way. The next morning I filled out a contact report. So did Misha."

"If she is so empty-headed, why did you bother?" Gerasimov inquired.

"Because she is an American, and her husband is a diplomat of some kind or other, and I was foolish enough to allow her to touch me, as you see. The contact report is on file. I will send you a copy of mine, and Colonel Filitov's." Yazov was speaking with more confidence now. Gerasimov had miscalculated somewhat.

"She is an agent of the American CIA."

"Then I am confident that Socialism will prevail, Nikolay Borissovich. I didn't think that you employed such fools—not until today, that is."

Defense Minister Yazov allowed himself to calm down. Though new to the Moscow scene—until very recently he'd been commander of the Far East Military District, where Narmonov had spotted him—he knew what the real struggle here was all about. He did not, could not believe that Filitov was a traitor—did not believe because of the man's record; could not believe because the scandal would destroy one of the most carefully planned careers in the Soviet Army. His.

"If you have real evidence against my man, I want my own security people to review it. You, Nikolay Borissovich, are playing a political game with my Ministry. I will not have KGB interference in the way I run my

Army. Someone from GRU will be here this afternoon. You will cooperate with him or I will take this to the Politburo myself."

Gerasimov showed no reaction at all as the Defense Minister left the room, but realized that he'd made an error of his own. He'd overplayed his hand—no, he told himself, you played it a day too soon. You expected Yazov to collapse, to bend to the pressure, to accept a proposal not yet made.

And all because that fool Vatutin hadn't gotten positive evidence. Why couldn't he have waited one more second!

Well, the only thing to do is to get a full confession from Filitov.

Colin McClintock's official job was in the commercial office at Her Britannic Majesty's Embassy, just across the Moscow River from the Kremlin, a location that predated the revolution and had annoyed the Soviet leadership since Stalin's time. But he, too, was a player in the Great Game. He was, in fact, the case officer who "ran" Svetlana Vaneyeva and had seconded her to the CIA for a purpose which had never been explained, but the orders for which had come direct from London's Century House, the headquarters of the SIS. At the moment, he was taking a group of British businessmen through GOSPLAN, introducing them to some of the bureaucrats with whom they'd have to negotiate the contracts for whatever they hoped to sell to the local barbarians, McClintock thought. An "Islander" from Whalsay off the Scottish coast, he regarded anyone from south of Aberdeen as a barbarian, but worked for the Secret Intelligence Service anyway. When he spoke in English, he used a lilting accent laced with words spoken only in Northern Scotland, and his Russian was barely comprehensible, but he was a man who could turn accents on and off as though with a switch. And his ears had no accent at all. People invariably think that a person who has trouble speaking a language also has trouble hearing it. It was an impression that McClintock assiduously cultivated.

He'd met Svetlana this way, had reported her to London as a possible target for recruitment, and a senior SIS officer had done just that in the second-floor dining room of Langan's Brasserie on Stratton Street. Since then McClintock had seen her only on business, only with other British subjects and Russians around. Other SIS officers in Moscow handled her dead-drops, though he was actually responsible for her operations. The data that she'd gotten out was disappointing but occasionally useful in a commercial sense. With intelligence agents you tended to take what you got, and she did forward insider gossip that she picked up from her father.

But something had gone wrong with Svetlana Vaneyeva. She'd disappeared from her desk, then returned, probably after interrogation at Lefortovo, the CIA had said. That made little sense to McClintock. Once they got you into Lefortovo, they had you for more than a day or two. Something very strange had happened, and he'd waited for a week to figure a way to find out exactly what it might have been. Her drops were untouched now, of course. Nobody from SIS would ever go near them except to see if they'd been disturbed, from a discreet distance.

Now, however, he had his chance, taking his trade delegation across the room that held the textile section of the planning agency. She looked up and saw the foreigners walking by. McClintock gave the routine interrogation signal. He didn't know which reply he'd get, nor what the reply would really mean. He had to assume that she'd been broken, totally compromised, but she had to react some way. He gave the signal, a brush of his hands against his hair as natural as breathing, as all such signals were. Her reply was to open a desk drawer and extract either a pencil or a pen. The former was the "all clear" signal, the latter a warning. She did neither, and merely returned to the document she was reading. It almost surprised the young intelligence officer enough to stare, but he remembered who and where he was, and turned away, scanning other faces in the room as his hands fluttered nervously about, doing various things that could have meant anything to whoever was watching.

What stuck in his mind was the look on her face. What had once been animated was now blank. What had once been lively was now as emotionless as any face on a Moscow street. The person who'd once been the privileged daughter of a very senior Party man was different now. It wasn't an act. He was sure of it; she didn't have the skill for that.

They got to her, McClintock told himself. *They got to her and let her go.* He didn't have a clue why they'd let her go, but that wasn't his concern. An hour later he drove the businessmen back to their hotel and returned to his office. The report he dashed off to London was only three pages long. He had no idea of the firestorm it would ignite. Nor did he know that another SIS officer had sent another report the same day, in the same pouch.

"Hello, Arthur," the voice on the phone said.

" 'Morning—excuse me, good afternoon, Basil. How's the weather in London?"

"Cold, wet, and miserable. Thought I might come over to your side of the pond and get some sun."

"Be sure to stop over to the shop."

"I planned to do that. First thing in the morning?"

"I always have room on the calendar for you."

"See you tomorrow, then."

"Great. See ya." Judge Moore hung up.

That was some day, the Director of Central Intelligence thought. *First we lose CARDINAL, now Sir Basil Charleston wants to come over here with something he can't talk about over the most secure phone system NSA and GCHQ ever came up with!* It was still before noon and he'd already been in his office for nine hours. *What the hell else is going wrong?*

"You call this evidence?" General Yevgeniy Ignat'yev was in charge of the counterespionage office of the GRU, the Soviet military's own intelligence arm. "To these tired old eyes it looks as though your people have jumped onto thin ice looking for a fish."

Vatutin was amazed—and furious—that the KGB Chairman had sent this man into *his* office to review *his* case.

"If you can find a plausible explanation for the film, the camera, and the diary, perhaps you would be so kind as to share it with me, Comrade."

"You say you took it from his hand, not the woman's." A statement, not a question.

"A mistake on my part for which I make no excuses," Vatutin said with dignity, which struck both men as slightly odd.

"And the camera?"

"It was found attached magnetically to the inside of the service panel on his refrigerator."

"You didn't find it the first time you searched the apartment, I see. And it had no fingerprints on it. And your visual record of Filitov does not show him using it. So if he tells me that you planted both the film and the camera on him, how am I supposed to convince the Minister that he's the one doing the lying?"

Vatutin was surprised by the tone of the question. "You believe that he is a spy after all?"

"What I believe is of no importance. I find the existence of the diary troubling, but you would not believe the breaches of security I have to deal with, especially at the higher levels. The more important people become, the less important they think the rules are. You know who Filitov is. He's more than just a hero, Comrade. He is famous throughout the Soviet Union—Old Misha, the Hero of Stalingrad. He fought at Minsk, at Vyasma, outside Moscow when we stopped the fascists, the Kharkov disaster, then the fighting retreat to Stalingrad, then the counterattack—"

"I have read his file," Vatutin said neutrally.

"He is a symbol to the entire Army. You cannot execute a symbol on evidence as equivocal as this, Vatutin. All you have are these photographic frames, with no objective evidence that he shot them."

"We have not yet interrogated him."

"And you think that will be easy?" Ignat'yev rolled his eyes. His laugh was a harsh bark. "Do you know how tough this man is? This man killed Germans while he was on fire! This man looked at death a thousand times and pissed on it!"

"I can get what I want out of him," Vatutin insisted quietly.

"Torture, is it? Are you mad? Keep in mind that the Taman Guards Motor-Rifle Division is based a few kilometers from here. You think the Red Army will sit still while you torture one of its heroes? Stalin is dead, Comrade Colonel, and so is Beriya."

"We can extract the information without doing physical harm," Vatutin said. That was one of KGB's most closely guarded secrets.

"Rubbish!"

"In that case, General, what do you recommend?" Vatutin asked, knowing the answer.

"Let me take over the case. We'll see to it that he never betrays the *Rodina* again, you can be sure of that," Ignat'yev promised.

"And save the Army the embarrassment, of course."

"We would save embarrassment for everyone, not the least you, Comrade Colonel, for fucking up this so-called investigation."

Well, that's about what I expected. A little bluster and a few threats, mixed with a little sympathy and comradeliness. Vatutin saw that he had a way out, but that the safety it promised also promised to end his advancement. The handwritten message from the Chairman had made that clear enough. He was trapped between two enemies, and though he could still win the approval of one, the largest goal involved the largest risk. He could retreat from the true objective of the investigation, and stay a colonel the rest of his life, or he could do what he'd hoped to do when he began—without any political motives, Vatutin remembered bleakly—and risk disgrace. The decision was paradoxically an easy one. Vatutin was a "Two" man—

"It is my case. The Chairman has given it to me to run, and I will run it in my way. Thank you for your advice, Comrade General."

Ignat'yev appraised the man and the statement. It wasn't often that he encountered integrity, and it saddened him in a vague, distant way that he could not congratulate the man who demonstrated this rarest of qualities. But loyalty to the Soviet Army came first.

"As you wish. I expect to be kept informed of all your activities." Ignat'yev left without another word.

Vatutin sat at his desk for a few minutes, appraising his own position. Then he called for his car. Twenty minutes later he was at Lefortovo.

"Impossible," the doctor told him before he had even asked the question.

"What?"

"You want to put this man into the sensory-deprivation tank, don't you?"

"Of course."

"It would probably kill him. I don't think you want to do that, and I am sure that I will not risk my project on something like this."

"It's my case, and I'll run it—"

"Comrade Colonel, the man in question is over seventy years old. I have his medical file here. He has all the symptoms of moderate cardiovascular disease—normal at this age, of course—and a history of respiratory problems. The onset of the first anxiety period would explode his heart like a balloon. I can almost guarantee it."

"What do you mean—explode his heart—"

"Excuse me—it's difficult to explain medical terms to the layman. His coronary arteries are coated with moderate amounts of plaque. It happens to all of us; it comes from the food we eat. His arteries are more blocked than yours or mine because of his age, and also, because of his age, the arteries are less flexible than those of a younger person. If his heart rate goes too high, the plaque deposits will dislodge and cause a blockage. That's what a heart attack is, Colonel, a blockage of a coronary artery. Part of the heart muscle dies, the heart stops entirely or becomes arrhythmic; in either case it ceases to pump blood, and the whole patient dies. Is that clear? Use of the tank will almost certainly induce a heart attack in the subject, and that attack will almost certainly be fatal. If not a heart attack, there is the somewhat lesser probability of a massive stroke—or both could happen. No, Comrade Colonel, we cannot use the tank for this man. I do not think that you wish to kill him before you get your information."

"What about other physical measures?" Vatutin asked quietly. *My God, what if I can't . . . ?*

"If you're certain that he's guilty, you can shoot him at once and be done with it," the physician observed. "But any gross physical abuse is likely to kill the patient."

And all because of a goddamned door lock, Colonel Vatutin told himself.

It was an ugly rocket, the sort of thing that a child might draw or a fireworks company might build, though either would know better than to put it on top of an airplane instead of its proper place, underneath. But it was atop the airplane, as the runway's perimeter lights showed in the darkness.

The airplane was the famous SR-71 Blackbird, Lockheed's Mach-three reconnaissance aircraft. This one had been flown in from Kadena Air Force Base on the western rim of the Pacific two days before. It rolled down the runway at Nellis Air Force Base, Nevada, before the twin flames of its afterburning engines. Fuel that leaked from the SR-71's tanks—the Blackbird leaked a lot—was ignited by the heat, much to the entertainment of the tower crew. The pilot pulled back on the stick at the appropriate time, and the Blackbird's nose came up. He held the stick back for longer than usual, pointing the bird into a steep forty-five-degree climb on full burner, and in a moment all that was left on the ground was a thundering memory. The last view the people had was of the twin angry dots of the engines, and soon these disappeared through the clouds that wafted by at ten thousand feet.

The Blackbird kept going up. The air-traffic controllers at Las Vegas noted the blip on their screens, saw that it was barely moving laterally, though its altitude readout was changing as rapidly as the wheels of the slot machines on the airport concourse. They shared a look—another Air Force hot dog—then they went back to work.

The Blackbird was now passing through sixty thousand feet, and leveled off to head southeast toward the White Sands Missile Range. The pilot checked his fuel—there was plenty—and relaxed after the exhilarating climb. The engineers had been right. The missile sitting on the aircraft's back hadn't mattered at all. By the time he'd gotten to fly the Blackbird, the purpose of the back mount had been overtaken by events. Designed to hold a single-engine photoreconnaissance drone, the fittings had been removed from nearly all the SR-71s, but not this one, for reasons that were not clear from the aircraft's maintenance book. The drone had originally been designed to go places the Blackbird could not, but it had become redundant on discovery of the fact that there was nowhere the SR-71 could not go in safety, as the pilot regularly proved on flights from Kadena. The only limit on the aircraft was fuel, and that didn't play today.

"Juliet Whiskey, this is Control. Do you read, over," the sergeant said into the headset.

"Control, this is Juliet Whiskey. All systems go. We are nominal to profile."

"Roger. Commence launch sequence on my mark. Five, four, three, two, one: *mark!*"

A hundred miles away, the pilot punched burners again and hauled back on the stick. The Blackbird performed as beautifully as always, standing on her tail and rocketing into the sky before nearly a hundred thousand pounds of thrust. The pilot's eyes were locked on his instruments as the altimeter spun around like a maddened clock. His speed was now thirteen hundred miles per hour and increasing, while the SR-71 showed her contempt for gravity.

"Separation in twenty seconds," the systems operator in the back seat told the pilot. The Blackbird was now passing through a hundred thousand feet. The target was one-twenty. The controls were already mushy. There wasn't enough air up here to control the aircraft properly, and the pilot was being even more careful than usual. He watched his speed hit nineteen hundred several seconds early, then:

"Standby for separation . . . breakaway, breakaway!" the man in back called. The pilot dropped the nose and started a gentle turn to the left that would take him right across New Mexico before heading back to Nellis. This was much easier than flying along the Soviet border—and, occasionally, across it. . . . The pilot wondered if he could drive down to Vegas to catch a show after he landed.

The target kept going up for a few more seconds, but surprisingly did not ignite its rocket motor. It was now a ballistic object, traveling in obedience to the laws of physics. Its oversized fins provided enough aerodynamic drag to keep it pointed in the proper direction as gravity began to reclaim the object for its own. The rocket tipped over at one hundred thirty thousand feet, reluctantly pointing its nose at the earth.

Then its motor fired. The solid-fuel engine burned for only four seconds, but that was enough to accelerate its conical nose to a speed that would have terrified the Blackbird's pilot.

"Okay," an Army officer said. The point-defense radar went from standby to active. It immediately saw the inbound. The target rocket was pushing itself down through the atmosphere at roughly the same speed as an ICBM warhead. He didn't have to give a command. The system was fully automated. Two hundred yards away a fiberglass cover exploded off a concrete hole drilled in the gypsum flats, and a FLAGE erupted skyward. The Flexible Lightweight Agile Guided Experiment looked more like a lance than a rocket, and was nearly that simple. Millimeter-wave radar tracked the inbound, and the data was processed through an onboard microcomputer. The remarkable part of this was that all the parts had been taken off the shelf from existing high-tech weaponry.

Outside, men watched from behind a protective earthen berm. They saw the upward streak of yellow light and heard the roar of the solid rocket motor, then nothing for several seconds.

The FLAGE homed in on its target, maneuvering a few fractions of degrees with tiny attitude-control rockets. The nosecap blew off, and what unfolded would have looked to an outsider like a collapsing umbrella's framework, perhaps ten yards across . . .

It looked just like a Fourth of July rocket, but without the noise. A few people cheered. Though both the target and the FLAGE "warhead" were totally inert, the energy of the collision converted metal and ceramic to incandescent vapor.

"Four for four," Gregory said. He tried not to yawn. He'd seen fireworks before.

"You're not going to get all the boosters, Major," General Parks chided the younger man. "We still need the midcourse systems, and the terminal-defense ones."

"Yes, sir, but you don't need me here. It works."

For the first three tests, the target rocket had been fired from a Phantom fighter, and people in Washington had claimed that the test series had underestimated the difficulty of intercepting the inbound warheads. Using the SR-71 as the launch platform had been Parks's idea. Launching the drone from higher altitude, and with a higher initial speed, had made for a much faster reentry target. This test had actually made things slightly harder than was expected, and the FLAGE hadn't cared a bit. Parks had been a little worried about the missile-guidance software, but, as Gregory had noted, it worked.

"Al," Parks said, "I'm starting to think that this whole program is going to work."

"Sure. Why not?" *If those Agency pukes can get us the plans for the Russian laser . . .*

CARDINAL sat alone in a bare cell, one and a half meters wide, two and a half meters long. There was a bare light bulb overhead, a wooden cot with a bucket underneath, but not a window except the spy hole in the rusted iron door. The walls were solid concrete, and there was no sound at all. He couldn't hear the pacing of the corridor guard, nor even the rumble of traffic on the street outside the prison. They'd taken his uniform blouse, and belt, and his polished boots, replacing the last with cheap slippers. The cell was in the basement. That was all he knew, and he could tell from the damp air. It was cold.

But not so cold as his heart. The enormity of his crime came to him as it never had. Colonel Mikhail Semyonovich Filitov, three times Hero of the Soviet Union, was alone with his treason. He thought of the magnificent, broad land in which he lived, whose distant horizons and endless vistas were peopled with his fellow Russians. He'd served them all his life with pride and honor, and with his own blood, as the scars on his body proclaimed. He remembered the men with whom he'd served, so many of whom had died under his command. And how they had died, defiantly cursing the German tanks and guns as they burned alive in T-34s, retreating only when forced to, preferring to attack even when they knew it to be doomed. He remembered leading his troops in a hundred engagements, the frantic exhilaration that accompanied the roar of the diesel engines, the reeking clouds of smoke, the determination even unto the death that he had cheated so many times.

And he'd betrayed it all.

What would my men say of me now? He stared at the blank concrete wall opposite his cot.

What would Romanov say?

I think we both need a drink, my Captain, the voice chimed in. Only Romanov could be both serious and amused at the same time. *Such thoughts are more easily considered with vodka or Samogan.*

Do you know why? Misha asked.

You've never told us why, my Captain. And so Misha did. It took but a brief flicker of time.

Both your sons, and your wife. Tell me, Comrade Captain, for what did we die?

Misha didn't know that. Even during the shooting he hadn't known. He'd been a soldier, and when a soldier's country is invaded, the soldier fights to repel the enemy. So much the easier when the enemy is as brutal as the Germans were . . .

We fought for the Soviet Union, Corporal.

Did we, now? I seem to remember fighting for Mother Russia, but mainly I remember fighting for you, Comrade Captain.

But—

A soldier fights for his comrades, my Captain. I fought for my family. You and our troop, they were my only family. I suppose you also fought for your family, the big one and the little one. I always envied you that, my Captain, and I was proud that you made me part of both in the way that you did.

But I killed you. I shouldn't have—

We all have our destiny, Comrade Captain. Mine was to die young at Vyasma without a wife, without children, but even so I did not die without a family.

I avenged you, Romanov. I got the Mark-IV that killed you.

I know. You avenged all the dead of your family. Why do you think we loved you? Why do you think we died for you?

You understand? Misha asked in surprise.

The workers and peasants may not, but your men will. We understand destiny now, as you cannot.

But what shall I do?

Captains do not ask such questions of corporals. Romanov laughed. *You had all the answers to our questions.*

Filitov's head jerked up as the latch slipped on the door of his cell.

Vatutin expected to find a broken man. The isolation of the cell, the prisoner stripped of identity and alone with his fears and his crimes, always had the proper effect. But while he looked at a tired, crippled old man, he saw the eyes and mouth change.

Thank you, Romanov.

"Good morning, Sir Basil," Ryan said as he reached for the man's bags.

"Hello, Jack! I didn't know they were using you as a gofer."

"Depends on who I'm going-fer, as they say. The car's over this way." He waved. It was parked fifty yards away.

"Constance sends her love. How is the family?" Sir Basil Charleston asked.

"Fine, thanks. How's London?"

"Surely you haven't forgotten our winters already."

"No." Jack laughed as he wrenched open the door. "I remember the beer, too." A moment later both doors were closed and locked.

"They sweep the wheels every week," Jack said. "How bad is it?"

"How bad? That's what I came over here to find out. Something very odd is happening. Your chaps had an op go wrong, didn't you?"

"I can say yes to that, but the rest'll have to come from the Judge. Sorry, but I was just cleared for part of it."

"Recently, I'll wager."

"Yep." Ryan shifted up as he took the turn off the airport road.

"Then let's see if you can still put two and two together, Sir John."

Jack smiled as he changed lanes to pass a truck. "I was doing the intelligence estimate on the arms talks when I broke into it. Now I'm supposed to be looking at Narmonov's political vulnerability. Unless I'm wrong, that's why you've flown over."

"And unless I'm very far off the mark, your op has triggered something very serious indeed."

"Vaneyev?"

"Correct."

"Jesus." Ryan turned briefly. "I hope you have some ideas, 'cause we sure as hell don't." He took the car to seventy-five. Fifteen minutes later he pulled into Langley. They parked in the underground garage and took the VIP elevator to the seventh floor.

"Hello, Arthur. It's not often I have a knight chauffeur me about, even in London." The head of SIS took a chair while Ryan summoned Moore's department chiefs.

"Hi, Bas'," Greer said on entering. Ritter just waved. It was his operation that had triggered this crisis. Ryan took the least comfortable chair available.

"I'd like to know exactly what went wrong," Charleston said simply, not even waiting for the coffee to be passed around.

"An agent got arrested. A very well-placed agent."

"Is that why the Foleys are flying out today?" Charleston smiled. "I didn't know who they were, but when two people get ejected from that delightful country, we generally assume—"

"We don't know what went wrong yet," Ritter said. "They should be landing at Frankfurt right about now, then ten more hours till we have them here for the debrief. They were working an agent who—"

"Who was an aide to Yazov—Colonel M. S. Filitov. We've deduced that much. How long have you had him?"

"It was one of your folks who recruited him for us," Moore replied. "He was a colonel, too."

"You don't mean . . . Oleg Penkovskiy . . . ? Bloody hell!" Charleston was amazed for once, Ryan saw. It didn't happen often. "*That* long?"

"That long," Ritter said. "But the numbers caught up with us."

"And the Vaneyeva woman we seconded to you for courier service was part of that—"

"Correct. She never came close to either end of the chain, by the way. We know that she was probably picked up, but she's back at work. We haven't checked her out yet, but—"

"We have, Bob. Our chap reported that she'd—changed somehow. He said it was hard to describe but impossible to miss. Like the hoary tales of brainwashing, Orwell and all that. He noted that she was free—or what passes for it over there—and related that to her father. Then we learned of something big in the Defense Ministry—that a senior aide to Yazov had been arrested." Charleston paused to stir his coffee. "We have a source inside the Kremlin that we guard rather closely. We have learned that Chairman Gerasimov spent several hours with Alexandrov last week and under fairly unusual circumstances. This same source has warned us that Alexandrov has a considerable urge to sidetrack this *perestroika* business.

"Well, it's clear, isn't it?" Charleston asked rhetorically. It was quite clear to everyone. "Gerasimov has suborned a Politburo member thought to be loyal to Narmonov, at the very least compromised the support of the Defense Minister, *and* been spending a good deal of time with the man who wants Narmonov out. I'm afraid that your operation may have triggered something with the most unpleasant consequences."

"There's more," the DCI said. "Our agent was getting us material on Soviet SDI research. Ivan may have made a breakthrough."

"Marvelous," Charleston observed. "A return to the bad old days, but this time the new version of the 'missile gap' is potentially quite real, I take it? I am awfully old to change my politics. Too bad. You know, of course, that there is a leak in your program?"

"Oh?" Moore asked with a poker face.

"Gerasimov told Alexandrov that. No details, unfortunately, except that KGB think it highly important."

"We've had some warnings. It's being looked at," Moore said.

"Well, the technical matters can sort themselves out. They generally do. The political question, on the other hand, has created a bit of a bother with the PM. There's trouble enough when we bring down a government that we wish to bring down, but to do so by accident . . ."

"We don't like the consequences any more than you do, Basil," Greer noted. "But there's not a hell of a lot we can do about it from this end."

"You can accept their treaty terms," Charleston suggested. "Then our friend Narmonov would have his position sufficiently strengthened that he might be able to tell Alexandrov to bugger off. That, in any case, is the unofficial position of Her Majesty's government."

And that's the real purpose of your visit to us, Sir Basil, Ryan thought. It was time to say something:

"That means putting unreasonable restrictions on our SDI research and reducing our warhead inventory in the knowledge that the Russians are racing forward with their own program. I don't think that's a very good deal."

"And a Soviet government headed by Gerasimov is?"

"And what if we end up with that anyway?" Ryan asked. "My estimate is already written. I recommend against additional concessions."

"One can always change a written document," Charleston pointed out.

"Sir, I have a rule. If something goes out with my name on the front, it says what I think, not what somebody else tells me to think," Ryan said.

"Do remember, gentlemen, that I am a friend. What is likely to happen to the Soviet government would be a greater setback to the West than a temporary restriction on one of your defense programs."

"The President won't spring for it," Greer said.

"He might have to," Moore replied.

"There has to be another way," Ryan observed.

"Not unless you can bring Gerasimov down." It was Ritter this time. "We can't offer any direct help to Narmonov. Even if we assume that he'd take a warning from us, which he probably wouldn't, we'd be running an even greater risk by involving ourselves in their internal politics. If the rest of the Politburo got one whiff of that . . . I suppose it might start a little war."

"But what if we can?" Ryan asked.

"What if we can *what?*" Ritter demanded.

17. Conspiracy

"Ann" came back to Eve's Leaves earlier than expected, the owner noted. With her usual smile, she selected a dress off the rack and took it to the dressing room. She was out by the full-length mirrors only a minute later, and accepted the customary compliments on how it looked rather more perfunctorily than usual. Again she paid cash, leaving with yet another engaging smile.

Out in the parking lot, things were a little different. Captain Bisyarina broke tradecraft by opening the capsule and reading the contents. That evoked a brief but nasty curse. The message was but a single sheet of notepaper. Bisyarina lit a cigarette with a butane lighter, then burned the paper in her car's ashtray.

All that work wasted! And it was already in Moscow, was already being analyzed. She felt like a fool. It was doubly annoying that her agent had been completely honest, had forwarded what she'd thought was highly classified material, and on learning that it had been rendered invalid, had gotten that word out quickly. She would not even have the satisfaction of forwarding a small portion of the reprimand that she would surely get for wasting Moscow Center's time.

Well, they warned me about this. It may be the first time, but it will not be the last. She drove home and dashed off her message.

The Ryans weren't known for their attendance on the Washington cocktail circuit, but there were a few that they couldn't avoid. The reception was intended to raise money for D.C. Children's Hospital, and Jack's wife was a friend of the chief of surgery. The evening's entertainment was the big draw. A prominent jazz musician owed his granddaughter's life to the hospital, and he was paying off that debt with a major benefit performance at the Kennedy Center. The reception was intended to give the D.C. elite a chance to meet him "up close and personal" and hear his sax in greater privacy. Actually, as with most "power" parties, it was really for the elite to see and be seen by one another, confirming their importance. As was true in most parts of the world, the elite felt the need to pay for the privilege. Jack understood the phenomenon, but felt that it made little sense. By eleven o'clock the elite of Washington had proved that they could talk just as inanely about just as little, and get just as drunk, as anyone else in the world. Cathy had held herself to one glass of white wine, however; Jack had won the toss tonight: he could drink and she had to drive. He'd indulged himself tonight, despite a few warning looks from his wife, and was basking in a mellow, philosophical glow that made him think he'd overdone the act a little bit—but then it wasn't supposed to look like an act. He just hoped to God everything went as planned tonight.

The amusing part was the way in which Ryan was treated. His position at the Agency had always been a sketchy one. The opening comments went something like, "How are things at Langley?" usually in an affected conspiratorial tone, and Jack's reply that CIA was just another government bureaucracy, a large building that contained lots of moving paper, surprised most questioners. The CIA was thought to have thousands of active field spooks. The actual figure was classified, of course, but far lower.

"We work normal business hours," Jack explained to a well-dressed woman whose eyes were slightly dilated. "I even have tomorrow off."

"Really?"

"Yes, I killed a Chinese agent on Tuesday and you always get a day off with pay for that sort of thing," he said seriously, then grinned.

"You're kidding!"

"That's right, I'm kidding. Please forget that I ever said it." *Who is this overaged bimbo?* he wondered.

"What about the reports that you're under investigation?" another person asked.

Jack turned in surprise. "And who might you be?"

"Scott Browning, *Chicago Tribune*." He didn't offer to shake hands. The game had just begun. The reporter didn't know that he was a player, but Ryan did.

"Could you run that one by me again?" Jack said politely.

"My sources tell me that you're being investigated for illegal stock transactions."

"It's news to me," Jack replied.

"I know that you've met with investigators from the SEC," the reporter announced.

"If you know that, then you also know that I gave them the information they wanted, and they left happy."

"You're sure of that?"

"Of course I am. I didn't do anything wrong and I have the records to prove it," Ryan insisted, perhaps a little too forcefully, the reporter thought. He loved it when people drank too much. *In vino veritas*.

"That's not what my sources tell me," Browning persisted.

"Well, I can't help that!" Ryan said. There was emotion in his voice now, and a few heads turned.

"Maybe if it wasn't for people like you, we might have an intelligence agency that worked," observed a newcomer.

"And who the fuck are you!" Ryan said before he turned. *Act I, Scene 2.*

"Congressman Trent," the reporter said. Trent was on the House Select Committee.

"I think an apology is owed," Trent said. He looked drunk.

"What for?" Ryan asked.

"How about for all the screw-ups across the river?"

"As opposed to the ones on this side?" Jack inquired. People were drifting over. Entertainment is where you find it.

"I know what you people just tried to pull off, and you fell right on your ass. You didn't let us know, as the law requires. You went ahead anyway, and I'm telling you, you're going to pay, you're going to pay big."

"If we have to pay your bar bill, we'll have to pay big." Ryan turned, dismissing the man.

"Big man," Trent said behind his back. "You're heading for a fall, too."

Perhaps twenty people were watching and listening now. They saw Jack take a glass of wine off a passing tray. They saw a look that could kill, and a few people remembered that Jack Ryan was a man who had killed. It was a fact and a reputation that gave him a sort of mystery. He took a measured sip of the chablis before turning back around.

"What sort of fall might that be, Mr. Trent?"

"You might be surprised."

"Nothing you do would surprise me, pal."

"That may be, but you've surprised us, Dr. Ryan. We didn't think you were a crook, and we didn't think you were dumb enough to be involved in that disaster. I guess we were wrong."

"You're wrong about a lot of things," Jack hissed.

"You know something, Ryan? For the life of me I can't figure just what the hell kind of a man you are."

"That's no surprise."

"So, what kind of man are you, Ryan?" Trent inquired.

"You know, Congressman, this is a unique experience for me," Jack observed lightheartedly.

"How's that?"

Ryan's manner changed abruptly. His voice boomed across the room. "I've never had my manhood questioned by a *queer* before!" *Sorry, pal . . .*

The room went very quiet. Trent made no secret of his orientation, had gone public six years before. That didn't prevent him from turning pale. The glass in his hand shook enough to spill some of its contents onto the marble floor, but the Congressman regained his control and spoke almost gently.

"I'll break you for that."

"Take your best shot, sweetie." Ryan turned and walked out of the room, the eyes heavy on his back. He kept going until he stared at the traffic on Massachusetts Avenue. He knew that he'd drunk too much, but the cold air started to clear his head.

"Jack?" His wife's voice.

"Yeah, babe?"

"What was that all about?"

"Can't say."

"I think it's time for you to go home."

"I think you're right. I'll get the coats." Ryan walked back inside and handed over the claim check. He heard the silence happen when he returned. He could feel the looks at his back. Jack shrugged into his overcoat and slung his wife's fur over his arm, before turning to see the eyes on him. Only one pair held any interest for him. They were there.

Misha was not an easy man to surprise, but the KGB succeeded. He'd steeled himself for torture, for the worst sort of abuse, only to be . . . disappointed? he asked himself. That certainly wasn't the right word.

He was kept in the same cell, and so far as he could determine he was alone on this cellblock. That was probably wrong, he thought, but there was no evidence that anyone else was near him, no sounds at all, not even taps on the concrete walls. Perhaps they were too thick for that. The only "company" he had was the occasional metallic rasp of the spy hole in his cell's door. He thought that the solitude was supposed to do something to him. Filitov smiled at that. *They think I'm alone. They don't know about my comrades.*

There was only one possible answer: this Vatutin fellow was afraid that he might actually be innocent—but that *wasn't* possible, Misha told himself. That *chekist* bastard had taken the film from his hand.

He was still trying to figure that one out, staring at the blank concrete wall. None of it made any sense.

But if they expected him to be afraid, they would have to live with their disappointment. Filitov had cheated death too many times. Part of him even yearned for it. Perhaps he would be reunited with his comrades. He talked to them, didn't he? Might they still be . . . well, not exactly alive, but not exactly gone either? What *was* death? He'd reached the point in life where the question was an intellectual one. Sooner or later he'd find out, of course. The answer to that question had brushed past him many times, but his grasp—and its—had never quite been firm enough . . .

The key rattled in the door, and the hinges creaked.

"You should oil that. Machinery lasts longer if you maintain it properly," he said as he stood.

The jailer didn't reply, merely waving him out of the cell. Two young guards stood with the turnkey, beardless boys of twenty or so, Misha thought, their heads tilted up with the arrogance common to the KGB. Forty years earlier and he might have done something about that, Filitov told himself. They were unarmed, after all, and he was a combat soldier for whom the taking of life was as natural as breathing. They were not effective soldiers. One look confirmed it. It was fine to be proud, but a soldier should also be wary . . .

Was that it? he thought suddenly. *Vatutin treats me with wariness despite the fact that he knows . . .*

But why?

"What does this mean?" Mancuso asked.

"Kinda hard for me to tell," Clark answered. "Probably some candyass in D.C. can't make up his mind. Happens all the time."

The two signals had arrived within twelve hours of one another. The first had aborted the mission and ordered the submarine back to open waters, but the second told *Dallas* to remain in the western Baltic and await further orders.

"I don't like being put on hold."

"Nobody does, Captain."

"How does it affect you?" Mancuso asked.

Clark shrugged eloquently. "A lot of this is mental. Like you work up to play a ball game. Don't sweat it, Cap'n. I teach this sort of thing—when I'm not actually doing it."

"How many?"

"Can't say, but most of them went pretty well."

"Most—not all? But when they don't—"

"It gets real exciting for everybody." Clark smiled. "Especially me. I have some great stories, but I can't tell 'em. Well, I expect you do, too."

"One or two. Does take some of the fun out of life, doesn't it?" The two men traded an insider's look.

Ryan was shopping alone. His wife's birthday was coming up—it would happen during his next Moscow trip—and he had to get everything out of the way early. The jewelry stores were always a good place to start. Cathy still wore the heavy gold necklace he'd given her a few years before, and he was looking for earrings that would go with it. The problem was that he had trouble remembering the exact pattern . . . His hangover didn't help, nor did his nervousness. What if they didn't bite?

"Hello, Dr. Ryan," a familiar voice said. Jack turned with some surprise.

"I didn't know they let you guys come out this far." *Act II, Scene 1.* Jack didn't let his relief show. In that respect the hangover helped.

"The travel radius cuts right through Garfinckels, if you examine the map carefully," Sergey Platonov pointed out. "Shopping for your wife?"

"I'm sure my file gave you all the necessary clues."

"Yes, her birthday." He looked down at the display case. "A pity that I cannot afford such things for mine . . ."

"If you were to make the appropriate overtures, the Agency could probably arrange something, Sergey Nikolay'ch."

"But the *Rodina* might not understand," Platonov said. "A problem with which you are becoming familiar, are you not?"

"You're remarkably well informed," Jack muttered.

"That is my function. I am also hungry. Perhaps you might use some of your fortune to buy me a sandwich?"

Ryan looked up and down the mall with professional interest.

"Not today." Platonov chuckled. "A few of my fellow . . . a few of my comrades are busy today, more than usual, and I fear your FBI is undermanned for its surveillance task."

"A problem the KGB does not have," Jack observed as they moved away from the store.

"You might be surprised. Why do Americans assume that our intelligence organs are any different from yours?"

"If by that you mean screwed up, I suppose it's a comforting thought. How does a hot dog grab you?"

"If it's kosher," Platonov answered, then explained. "I'm not Jewish, as you know, but I prefer the taste."

"You've been here too long," Jack said with a grin.

"But the Washington area is such a nice place."

Jack walked into a fast-food shop that specialized in bagels and corned beef, but also served other fare. Service was quick, and the men took a white plastic table that sat by itself in the center of the mall's corridor. Cleverly done, Jack thought. People could walk past and not hear more than a few random words. But he knew Platonov was a pro.

"I have heard that you face some rather unfortunate legal difficulties." With every word, Platonov smiled. It was supposed to appear that they were discussing ordinary pleasantries, Jack supposed, with the added dimension that his Russian colleague was enjoying himself.

"Do you believe that little prick last night? You know, one thing I actually admire about Russia is the way you handle—"

"Antisocial behavior? Yes—five years in a camp of strict regime. Our new openness does not extend to condoning sexual perversion. Your friend Trent made an acquaintance on his last trip to the Soviet Union. The young . . . *man* in question is now in such a camp." Platonov didn't say that he had refused to cooperate with the KGB, and so earned his sentence. Why confuse the issue? he thought.

"You can have him with my blessings. We have enough of them over here," Jack growled. He felt thoroughly awful; his eyes were pounding to escape from his head as a result of all the wine and insufficient sleep.

"So I have noticed. And may we have the SEC also?" Platonov asked.

"You know, I didn't do anything wrong. Not a damned thing! I got a tip from a friend and I followed up on it. I didn't go looking for it, it just happened. So I made a few bucks—so what? I write intelligence briefs for the President! I'm good at it—and they're coming after *me!* After all the—" Ryan stopped and stared painfully into Platonov's eyes. "So what the hell do you care?"

"Ever since we first met at Georgetown some years ago, frankly I have admired you. That business with the terrorists. I do not agree with your political views, as you plainly do not agree with mine. But as one man to another, you took some vermin off the street. You may choose to believe this or not, but I have argued against State support for such animals. True Marxists who want to free their peoples—yes, we should support them in any way we can—but bandits are murderers, they are mere scum who view us as a source of arms, nothing more. My country gains nothing by it. Politics aside, you are a man of courage and honor. Of course I respect that. It is a pity that your country does not. America only places its best men on pedestals so that lesser ones can use them as targets."

Ryan's wary look was replaced briefly with one of measurement. "You have that one right."

"So, my friend—what will they do to you?"

Jack let out a long breath as he focused his eyes down the corridor. "I have to get a lawyer this week. I suppose he'll know. I'd hoped to avoid that. I thought I could talk my way out of it, but—but this new bastard in SEC, a pansy that Trent—" Another breath. "Trent used his influence to get the job for him. How much you want to bet that the two of them . . . I find myself in agreement with you. If one must have enemies, they should at least be enemies you can respect."

"And CIA cannot help you?"

"I don't have many friends there—well, you know that. Moved up too fast, richest kid on the block, Greer's fair-haired boy, my connections with the Brits. You make enemies that way, too. Sometimes I wonder if one of them might have . . . I can't prove it, but you wouldn't believe the computer network we have at Langley, and all my stock transactions are stored in computer systems . . . and you know what? Computer records can be changed by someone who knows how . . . But try to prove that one, pal." Jack took two aspirins from a small tin and swallowed them.

"Ritter doesn't like me at all, never has. I made him look bad on something a few years back, and he isn't the sort of man to forget that sort of thing. Maybe one of his people . . . he has some good ones. The Admiral wants to help, but he's old. The Judge is on his way out, supposed to have left a year ago, but he's hanging on somehow—he couldn't help me if he wanted to."

"The President likes your work. We know that."

"The President's a lawyer, a prosecutor. He gets even a whiff that you might have bent a law, and—it's amazing how quick you can get lonely. There's a bunch in the State Department who're after my ass, too. I don't see things quite their way. This is a bitch of a town to be honest in."

It's correct, then, Platonov thought. They'd gotten the report first from Peter Henderson, code-named Cassius, who'd been feeding data to the KGB for over ten years, first as special assistant to the retired Senator Donaldson of the Senate's intelligence committee, now an intelligence analyst for the General Accounting Office. KGB knew Ryan to be the bright, rising star of the CIA's Intelligence Directorate. His evaluation at Moscow Center had at first called him a wealthy dilettante. That had changed a few years ago. He'd done something to earn him presidential attention, and now wrote nearly half of the special intelligence briefing papers that went to the White House. It was known from Henderson that he had assembled a massive report on the strategic-arms situation, one that had raised hackles at Foggy Bottom. Platonov had long since formed his own impression. A good judge of character, from their first meeting at Georgetown's Galleria he'd deemed Ryan a bright opponent, and a brave one—but a man too accustomed to privilege, too easily outraged at personal attack. Sophisticated, but strangely naive. What he saw over lunch confirmed it. Fundamentally, Ryan was too American. He saw things in blacks and whites, goods and bads. But what mattered today was that Ryan had felt himself invincible, and was only now learning that this was not the case. Because of that, Ryan was an angry man.

"All that work wasted," Jack said after a few seconds. "They're going to trash my recommendations."

"What do you mean?"

"I mean that Ernest *Fucking* Allen has talked the President into putting SDI on the table." It required all of Platonov's professionalism not to react visibly to that statement. Ryan went on: "It's all been for nothing. They've discredited my analysis because of this idiot stock thing. The Agency isn't backing me up like they should. They're throwing me to the fucking dogs. Not a damned thing I can do about it, either." Jack finished off the hot dog.

"One can always take action," Platonov suggested.

"Revenge? I've thought of that. I could go to the papers, but the *Post* is going to run a story about the SEC thing. Somebody on the Hill is orchestrating the hanging party. Trent, I suppose. I bet he put that reporter on me last night, too, the bastard. If I try to get the real word out, well, who'll listen? Christ, I'm putting my tight little ass on the line just sitting here with you, Sergey."

"Why do you say that?"

"Why don't you guess?" Ryan allowed himself a smile that ended abruptly. "I'm not going to go to jail. I'd rather die than have to disgrace myself like that. God damn it, I've risked my life—I've put it all on the line. Some things you know about, and one that you don't. I have risked my life for this country, and they want to send me to prison!"

"Perhaps we can help." The offer finally came across.

"Defect? You have to be joking. You don't really expect me to live in your workers' paradise, do you?"

"No, but for the proper incentive, perhaps we could change your situation. There will be witnesses against you. They could have accidents . . ."

"Don't give me that shit!" Jack leaned forward. "You don't do jobs like that in our country and we don't do them in yours."

"Everything has a price. Surely you understand that better than I." Platonov smiled. "For example, the 'disaster' Mr. Trent referred to last night. What might that have been?"

"And how do I know who you're really working for?" Jack asked.

"What?" That surprised him. Ryan saw past the pain in his sinuses.

"You want an incentive? Sergey, I am about to put my life on the line. Just because I've done it before, don't you think that it's easy. We have somebody inside Moscow Center. Somebody big. You tell me now what that name would buy me."

"Your freedom," Platonov said at once. "If he's as high as you say, we would do very much indeed." Ryan didn't say a word for over a minute. The two men stared at each other as though over cards, as though they were gambling for everything each man owned—and as though Ryan knew that he held the lesser hand. Platonov matched the power of the American's stare, and was gratified to see that it was his power that prevailed.

"I'm flying to Moscow the end of the week, unless the story breaks before then, in which case I'm fucked. What I just told you, pal, it doesn't go through channels. The only person I'm sure it *isn't* is Gerasimov. It goes to the Chairman himself, direct to him, no intermediaries, or you risk losing the name."

"And why am I supposed to believe you know it?" The Russian pressed his advantage, but carefully.

It was Jack's turn to smile. His hole card had turned out to be a good one. "I don't know the *name,* but I know the data. With the four things that I know came from CONDUCTOR—that's the code name—your troops can handle the rest. If your letter goes through channels, probably I don't get on the airplane. That's how far up the chain he is—if it's a he, but it probably is. How do I know you'll keep your word?"

"In the intelligence business one must keep one's promises," Platonov assured him.

"Then tell your Chairman that I want to meet him if he can arrange it. Man to man. No bullshit."

"The Chairman? The Chairman doesn't—"

"Then I'll make my own legal arrangements and take my chances. I'm not going to jail for treason either, if I can help it. That's the deal, Comrade Platonov," Jack concluded. "Have a nice drive home."

Jack rose and walked away. Platonov did not follow. He looked around and found his own security man, who signaled that they had not been observed.

And he had his own decision to make. Was Ryan genuine? Cassius said so.

He had run Agent Cassius for three years. Peter Henderson's data had always checked out. They'd used him to track down and arrest a colonel in Strategic Rocket Forces who'd been working for CIA, had gotten priceless strategic and political intelligence, and even inside American analysis of that *Red October* business of the previous—no, it was two years now, wasn't it, right before Senator Donaldson had retired—and now that he worked in the GAO, he had the best of all possible worlds: direct access to classified defense data and all his political contacts on the Hill. Cassius had told them some time before that Ryan was under investigation. At the time it had been merely a tidbit, no one had taken it seriously. The Americans were always investigating one another. It was their national sport. Then a second time he'd heard the same story, then the scene with Trent. Was it really possible . . . ?

A leak high up in KGB, Platonov thought. There was a protocol, of course, for getting important data directly to the Chairman. The KGB allowed for any possibility. Once that message was sent, it would have to be followed up. Just the hint that CIA had an agent high in the KGB hierarchy . . .

But that was only one consideration.

Once we set the hook, we will own Dr. Ryan. Perhaps he is foolish enough to think that a one-time exchange of information for services is possible, that he will never again . . . more likely that he is so desperate that he does not care at the moment. What kind of information might we get from him?

Special assistant to the Deputy Director for Intelligence! Ryan must see nearly everything! To recruit so valuable an agent—that hadn't been done since Philby, and *that* was over fifty years ago!

But is it important enough to break the rules? Platonov asked himself as he finished off his drink. Not in living memory had the KGB committed an act of violence in the United States—there *was* a gentlemen's agreement on that. But what were rules against this sort of advantage? Perhaps an American or two might have an auto accident, or an unexpected heart attack. That would also have to be approved by the Chairman. Platonov would give his recommendation. It would be followed. He was sure of that.

The diplomat was a fastidious man. He wiped his face with the paper napkin, put all the trash in the paper drink cup, and deposited it in the nearest receptacle. He left nothing behind to suggest that he'd ever been there.

The Archer was sure that they were winning. On announcing his mission to his subordinates, the reaction could not have been better. Grim, amused smiles, sideways looks, nods. The most enthusiastic of all had been their new member, the former Major of the Afghan Army. In their tent, twenty kilometers inside Afghanistan, the plans had been put together in five tense hours.

The Archer looked down at phase one, already complete. Six trucks and three BTR-60 infantry carriers were in their hands. Some were damaged, but that was not unexpected. The dead soldiers of the puppet army were being stripped of their uniforms. Eleven survivors were being questioned. They would not join in this mission, of course, but if they proved to be reliable, they would be allowed to join allied guerrilla bands. For the others . . .

The former Army officer recovered maps and radio codes. He knew all the procedures that the Russians had so assiduously taught to their Afghan "brothers."

There was a battalion base camp ten kilometers away, due north on the Shékábád road. The former Major contacted it on the radio, indicating that "Sunflower" had repulsed the ambush with moderate losses and was heading in. This was approved by the battalion commander.

They loaded a few of the bodies aboard, still in their bloody uniforms. Trained former members of the Afghan Army manned the heavy machine guns on the BTR carriers as the column moved out, keeping proper tactical formation on the gravel road. The base camp was just on the far side of the river. Twenty minutes later they could see it. The bridge had long since been wrecked, but Russian engineers had dumped enough gravel to make a ford. The column halted at the guard post on the east side.

This was the tense part. The Major made the proper signal, and the guard post waved them through. One by one the vehicles moved across the river. The surface was frozen and the drivers had to follow a line of sticks across to keep from becoming trapped in the deep water that lay under the crackling ice. Another five hundred meters.

The base camp was on a small rise. It was surrounded by low-lying bunkers made of sandbags and logs. None were fully manned. The camp was well sited, with wide fields of fire in all directions, but they'd only man their weapons pits fully at night. Only a single company of troops was actually in the post, while the remainder were out patrolling the hills around the camp. Besides, the column was coming in at mealtime. The battalion motor pool was in sight.

The Archer was in the front of the lead truck. He wondered to himself why he trusted the defected Major so fully, but decided that this was not a good time for that particular worry.

The battalion commander came out of his bunker, his mouth working on some food as he watched the soldiers jump out of the trucks. He was waiting for the unit commander, and showed some annoyance as the side door on the BMP opened slowly, and a man in an officer's uniform appeared.

"Who the devil are you?"

"*Allahu akhbar!*" the Major screamed. His rifle cut down the questioner. The heavy machine guns on the infantry carriers ripped into the mass of men eating their noon meal while the Archer's men raced to the half-manned bunkers. It took ten minutes before all resistance ceased, but there was never a chance for the defenders, not with nearly a hundred armed men inside the camp. Twenty prisoners were taken. The only Russians in the post—two lieutenants and a communications sergeant—were killed out of hand and the rest were placed under guard as the Major's men ran to the motor pool.

They got two more BTRs there and four trucks. That would have to be enough. The rest they burned. They burned everything they couldn't carry. They took four mortars, half a dozen machine guns, and every spare uniform they could find. The rest of the camp was totally destroyed—especially the radios, which were first smashed with rifle butts, then burned. A small guard force was left behind with the prisoners, who would also be given the chance to join the *mudjaheddin*—or die for their loyalty to the infidel.

It was fifty kilometers to Kabul. The new, larger vehicle column ran north. More of the Archer's men linked up with it, hopping aboard the vehicles. His force now numbered two hundred men, dressed and equipped like regular soldiers of the Afghan Army, rolling north in Russian-built army vehicles.

Time was their most dangerous enemy. They reached the outskirts of Kabul ninety minutes later, and encountered the first of several checkpoints.

The Archer's skin crawled to be near so many Russian soldiers. When dusk came, the Russians returned to their laagers and bunkers, he knew, leaving the streets to the Afghans, but even the setting sun did not make him feel secure. The checks were more perfunctory than he expected, and the Major talked his way through all of them, using travel documents and code words from the base camp so recently extinguished. More to the point, their route of travel kept them away from the most secure parts of the city. In less than two hours the city was behind them, and they rolled forward under the friendly darkness.

They went until they began to run out of fuel. At this point the vehicles were rolled off the roads. A Westerner would have been surprised that the *mudjaheddin* were happy to leave their vehicles behind, even though it meant carrying weapons on their backs. Well rested, the guerrillas moved at once into the hills, heading north.

The day had held nothing but bad news, Gerasimov noted, as he stared at Colonel Vatutin. "What do you mean, you cannot break him?"

"Comrade Chairman, our medical people advise me that both the sensory-deprivation procedure, or any form of physical abuse"—*torture* was no longer a word used at KGB headquarters—"might kill the man. In view of your insistence on a confession, we must use . . . primitive interrogation methods. The subject is a difficult man. Mentally, he is far tougher than any of us expected," Vatutin said as evenly as he could. He would have killed for a drink at the moment.

"All because you bungled the arrest!" Gerasimov observed coldly. "I had high hopes for you, *Colonel.* I thought you were a man with a future. I thought you were ready for advancement. Was I mistaken, Comrade Colonel?" he inquired.

"My concern with this case is limited to exposing a traitor to the Motherland." It required all of Vatutin's discipline not to flinch. "I feel that I have already done this. We know that he has committed treason. We have the evidence—"

"Yazov will not accept it."

"Counterintelligence is a KGB matter, not one for the Defense Ministry."

"Perhaps you would be so kind as to explain that to the Party General Secretary," Gerasimov said, letting his anger out a bit too far. "Colonel Vatutin, I must have this confession."

Gerasimov had hoped to score another intelligence coup today, but the FLASH report from America had invalidated it—worse still, Gerasimov had delivered the information a day before he'd learned that it was valueless. Agent Livia was apologetic, the report said, but the computer-program data so recently transmitted through Lieutenant Bisyarina was, unfortunately, obsolete. Something that might have helped to smooth the water between KGB and the Defense Ministry's darling new project was now gone.

He had to have a confession, and it had to be a confession that was not extracted by torture. Everyone knew that torture could yield anything that the questioners wanted, that most subjects would have enough incentive in their pain to say whatever was required of them. He needed something good enough to take to the Politburo itself, and the Politburo members no longer held KGB in so much fear that they would take Gerasimov's words at face value.

"Vatutin, I need it, and I need it soon. When can you deliver?"

"Using the methods to which we are now limited, no more than two weeks. We can deprive him of sleep. That takes time, more so since the elderly need less sleep than the young. He will gradually become disoriented and crack. Given what we have learned of this man, he will fight us with all of his courage—this is a brave man. But he is only a man. Two weeks," Vatutin said, knowing that ten more days ought to be sufficient. Better to deliver early.

"Very well." Gerasimov paused. It was time for encouragement. "Comrade Colonel, objectively speaking you have handled the investigation well, despite the disappointment at the final phase. It is unreasonable to expect perfection in all things, and the political complications are not of your making. If you provide what is required, you will be properly rewarded. Carry on."

"Thank you, Comrade Chairman." Gerasimov watched him leave, then called for his car.

The Chairman of the KGB did not travel alone. His personal Zil—a handmade limousine that looked like an oversized American car of thirty years before—was followed by an even uglier Volga, full of bodyguards selected for their combat skills and absolute loyalty to the office of chairman. Gerasimov sat alone in the back, watching the buildings of Moscow flash by as the car was routed down the center lane of the wide avenues. Soon he was out of the city, heading into the forests where the Germans had been stopped in 1941.

Many of those captured—those who had survived typhus and poor food—had built the dachas. As much as the Russians still hated the Germans, the *nomenklatura*—the ruling class of this classless society—was addicted to German workmanship. Siemens electronics and Blaupunkt appliances were as much a part of their homes as the copies of *Pravda* and the uncensored "White TASS" news. The frame dwellings in the pine forests west of Moscow were as well built as anything left behind by the czars. Gerasimov often wondered what had happened to the German soldiers who had labored to make them. Not that it mattered.

The official dacha of Academician Mikhail Petrovich Alexandrov was no different from the rest, two stories, its wood siding painted cream, and a steeply pitched roof that might have been equally at home in the Black Forest. The driveway was a twisty gravel path through the trees. Only one car was parked there. Alexandrov was a widower, and past the age when he might crave young female company. Gerasimov opened his own door, checking briefly to see that his security entourage was dispersing as usual into the trees. They paused only to pull cold-weather gear from the trunk of their car, thickly insulated white anoraks and heavy boots to keep their feet warm in the snow.

"Nikolay Borissovich!" Alexandrov got the door himself. The dacha had a couple who did the cooking and cleaning, but they knew when to stay out of the way. This was such a time. The academician took Gerasimov's coat and draped it on a peg by the door.

"Thank you, Mikhail Petrovich."

"Tea?" Alexandrov gestured toward the table in the sitting room.

"It is cold out there," Gerasimov admitted.

The two men sat on opposite sides of the table in old overstuffed chairs. Alexandrov enjoyed being a host—at least to his associates. He poured the tea, then dished out a small amount of white-cherry preserves. They drank their tea in the traditional way, first putting some of the sweetened cherries into their mouths, then letting the tea wash around them. It made conversation awkward, but it was Russian. More to the point, Alexandrov liked the old ways. As much as he was married to the ideals of Marxism, the Politburo's chief ideologue kept to the ways of his youth in the small things.

"What news?"

Gerasimov gestured annoyance. "The spy Filitov is a tough old bird. It will take another week or two to get the confession."

"You should shoot that Colonel of yours who—"

The KGB Chairman shook his head. "No, no. One must be objective. Colonel Vatutin has done very well. He ought to have left the actual arrest to a younger man, but I told him that it was his case, and he doubtless took my instructions too literally. His handling of the rest of the case was nearly perfect."

"You grow generous too soon, Kolya," Alexandrov observed. "How hard is it to surprise a seventy-year-old man?"

"Not him. The American spy was a good one—as one might expect. Good field officers have sharp instincts. If they were not so skilled, World Socialism would have been realized by now," he added offhandedly. Alexandrov lived within his academic world, the Chairman knew, and had little understanding of how things worked in the real one. It was hard to respect a man like that, but not so hard to fear him.

The older man grunted. "I suppose we can wait a week or two. It troubles me to do this while the American delegation is here—"

"It will be after they leave. If agreement is reached, we lose nothing."

"It is madness to reduce our arms!" Alexandrov insisted. Mikhail Petrovich still thought nuclear weapons were like tanks and guns: the more, the better. Like most political theorists, he didn't bother learning facts.

"We will retain the newest and the best of our rockets," Gerasimov explained patiently. "More importantly, our Project Bright Star is progressing well. With what our own scientists have already accomplished, and what we are learning about the American program, in less than ten years we will have the ability to protect the *Rodina* against foreign attack."

"You have good sources within the American effort?"

"Too good," Gerasimov said, setting down his tea. "It seems that some data we just received was sent out too soon. Part of the American computer instructions were sent to us before they were certified, and turned out to be faulty. An embarrassment, but if one must be embarrassed, better that it should result from being too effective than not effective enough."

Alexandrov dismissed the subject with a wave of the hand. "I spoke to Vaneyev last night."

"And?"

"He is ours. He cannot bear the thought of that darling slut of a daughter in a labor camp—or worse. I explained what is required of him. It was very easy. Once you have the confession from the Filitov bastard, we will do everything at the same time. Better to accomplish everything at once."

The academician nodded to reinforce his words. He was the expert on political maneuvering.

"I am troubled by possible reactions from the West . . ." Gerasimov noted cautiously.

The old fox smiled into his tea. "Narmonov will have a heart attack. He is of the proper age. Not a fatal one, of course, but enough to make him step aside. We will assure the West that his policies will continue—I can even live with the arms agreement if you insist." Alexandrov paused. "It does make sense to avoid alarming them unduly. All that concerns me is the primacy of the Party."

"Naturally." Gerasimov knew what was to follow, and leaned back to hear it yet again.

"If we don't stop Narmonov, the Party is doomed! The fool, casting away all we have worked for. Without the leadership of the Party, a *German* would be living in this house! Without Stalin to put steel in the people's backbone, where would we be, and Narmonov condemns our greatest hero—after Lenin," the academician added quickly. "This country needs a strong hand, *one* strong hand, not a thousand little ones! Our people understand that. Our people *want* that."

Gerasimov nodded agreement, wondering why this doddering old fool always had to say the same thing. The Party didn't want one strong hand, much as Alexandrov denied the fact. The Party itself was composed of a thousand little, grabbing, grasping hands: the Central Committee members, the local *apparatchiki* who had paid their dues, mouthed their slogans, attended the weekly meetings until they were sick to death of everything the Party said, but still stayed on because that was the path to advancement, and advancement meant privilege. Advancement meant a car, and trips to Sochi . . . and Blaupunkt appliances.

All men had their blind spots, Gerasimov knew. Alexandrov's was that so few people really believed in the Party anymore. Gerasimov did not. The Party was what ran the country, however. The Party was what nurtured ambitions. Power had its own justification, and for him, the Party was the path to power. He'd spent all of his working life protecting the Party from those who wished to change the power equation. Now, as Chairman of the Party's own "sword and shield," he was in the best possible position to take the Party's reins. Alexandrov would have been surprised, scandalized to learn that his young student saw power as his only goal, and had no plan other than *status quo ante*. The Soviet Union would plod along as before, secure behind its borders, seeking to spread its own form of government into whatever country offered the opportunity. There would be progress, partly from internal changes, partly from what could be obtained from the West, but not enough to raise expectations too much, or too rapidly, as Narmonov threatened to do. But best of all, Gerasimov would be the man with the reins. With the power of the KGB behind him, he need not fear for his security—certainly not after breaking the Defense Ministry. So he listened to Alexandrov's ranting about Party theory, nodding when appropriate. To an outsider it would look like the thousands of old pictures—nearly all of them fakes—of Stalin listening with rapt attention to the words of Lenin, and like Stalin, he would use the words to his own advantage. Gerasimov believed in Gerasimov.

18. Advantages

"But I just finished eating!" Misha said.

"Rubbish," the jailer responded. He held out his watch. "Look at the time, you foolish old man. Eat up, it'll be time for your interrogation soon." The man bent forward. "Why don't you tell them what they want to hear, Comrade?"

"I am not traitor! I'm not!"

"As you wish. Eat hearty." The cell door hit its frame with a metallic rattle.

"I am not a traitor," Filitov said after the door closed. "I'm not," the microphone heard. "I'm not."

"We're getting there," Vatutin said.

What was happening to Filitov was little different in net effect from what the doctor was trying to achieve in the sensory-deprivation tank. The prisoner was losing touch with reality, though much more slowly than the Vaneyeva woman had. His cell was in the interior of the building, denying the prisoner the march of day and night. The single bare light bulb never went off. After a few days Filitov lost all track of what time was. Next his bodily functions began to show some irregularity. Then they started altering the interval between meals. His body knew that something was wrong, but it sensed that so many things were wrong, and was so unsuccessful in dealing with the disorientation, that what happened to the prisoner was actually akin to mental illness. It was a classic technique, and it was a rare individual indeed who could withstand it for more than two weeks, and then it was generally discovered that the successful resister had depended on some outside register unknown to his interrogators, such as traffic or plumbing sounds, sounds that followed regular patterns. Gradually "Two" had learned to isolate out all of these. The new block of special cells was sound-isolated from the rest of the world. Cooking was done on a floor above to eliminate smells. This part of Lefortovo reflected generations of clinical experience in the business of breaking the human spirit.

It was better than torture, Vatutin thought. Torture invariably affected the interrogators, too. That was the problem. Once a man—and in rare cases, a woman—became too good at it, that person's mind changed. The torturer would gradually go mad, resulting in unreliable interrogation results and a useless KGB officer who would then have to be replaced, and, occasionally, hospitalized. In the 1930s such officers had often been shot when their political masters realized what they had created, only to be replaced with new ones until interrogators looked for more creative, more intelligent methods. Better for everyone, Colonel Vatutin knew. The new techniques, even the abusive ones, inflicted no permanent physical harm. Now it almost seemed that they were treating the mental illnesses that they inflicted, and the physicians who managed the affair for the KGB could now confidently observe that treason against the Motherland was itself a symptom of a grave personality disorder, something that demanded decisive treatment. It made everyone feel better about the job. While one could feel guilty inflicting pain on a brave enemy, one need only feel good about helping to cure a sick mind.

This one is sicker than most, Vatutin thought wryly. He was a touch too cynical to believe all the folderol that the new crop of "Two" people got today in Training-and-Orientation. He remembered the nostalgic stories of the men who'd trained him almost thirty years before—the good old days under Beriya . . . Though his skin had crawled to hear those madmen speak, at least they were honest about what they did. Though he was grateful that he had not become like them, he didn't delude himself by believing that Filitov was mentally ill. He was, in fact, a courageous man who had chosen of his own free will to betray his country. An evil man, to be sure, because he had violated the rules of his parent society, he was a worthy adversary for all that. Vatutin looked into the fiber-optic tube that ran into the ceiling of Filitov's cell, watching him as he listened to the sound pickup from the microphone.

How long have you been working for the Americans? Since your family died? That long? Nearly thirty years . . . is it possible? the Colonel of the Second Chief Directorate wondered. It was an awesome amount of time. Kim Philby hadn't lasted nearly so long. Richard Sorge's career, though brilliant, had been a brief one.

But it made sense. There was also homage to pay to Oleg Penkovskiy, the treasonous GRU Colonel whose capture was one of Two's greatest cases—but now poisoned by the thought that Penkovskiy had used his own death to elevate the career of an even greater spy . . . whom he himself had probably recruited. That was courage, Vatutin told himself. *Why must such virtue be invested in treason!* he raged at himself. *Why can they not love their Motherland as I do?* The Colonel shook his head. Marxism demanded objectivity of its adherents, but this was too much. There was always the danger of identifying too closely with one's subject. He rarely had the problem, but then he had never handled a case like this one. Three times Hero of the Soviet Union! A genuine national icon whose face had been on the covers of magazines and books. Could we ever let it be known what he had done? How would the Soviet people react to the knowledge that Old Misha, Hero of Stalingrad, one of the most courageous warriors of the Red Army . . . had turned traitor to the *Rodina?* The effect on national morale was something to be considered.

Not my problem, he told himself. He watched the old man through the hi-tech peephole. Filitov was trying to eat his food, not quite believing that it was time to eat, but not knowing that his breakfast—all meals were the same, for obvious reasons—had been only ninety minutes before.

Vatutin stood and stretched to ease the ache in his back. A side effect of this technique was the way it disrupted the lives of the interrogators themselves. His own schedule was wrecked. It was just past midnight, and he'd gotten a bare seven hours of sleep in the past thirty-six. But at least he knew the time, and the day, and the season. Filitov, he was sure, did not. He bent back down to see his subject finishing off his bowl of kasha.

"Get him," Colonel Klementi Vladimirovich Vatutin ordered. He walked into the washroom to splash some cold water on his face. He peered into the mirror and decided that he didn't need to shave. Next he made sure that his uniform was perfectly turned out. The one constant factor in the prisoner's disrupted world had to be the face and image of his interrogator. Vatutin even practiced his look in the mirror: proud, arrogant, but also compassionate. He was not ashamed of what he saw. *That is a professional,* he told himself of the reflection in the mirror. *Not a barbarian, not a degenerate, but only a skilled man doing a difficult, necessary job.*

Vatutin was seated in the interrogation room, as always, when the prisoner came in. He invariably appeared to be doing something when the door opened, and his head always had to come up in semisurprise as though to say, *Oh, is it time for you again?* He closed the folder before him and placed it in his briefcase as Filitov sat in the chair opposite his. That was good, Vatutin noted without looking. *The subject doesn't have to be told what he must do.* His mind was fixing upon the only reality he had: Vatutin.

"I hope you slept well," he told Filitov.

"Well enough," was the answer. The old man's eyes were clouded. The blue no longer had the luster that Vatutin had admired in their first session.

"You are being properly fed, I trust?"

"I have eaten better." A weary smile, still some defiance and pride behind it, but not as much as its wearer thought. "But I have also eaten worse."

Vatutin dispassionately gauged the strength in his prisoner; it had diminished. *You know,* the Colonel thought, *you know that you must lose. You know that it is only a matter of time. I can see it,* he said with his eyes, looking for and finding weakness under his stare. Filitov was trying not to wilt under the strain, but the edges were frayed, and something else was coming loose as Vatutin watched. *You know you're losing, Filitov.*

What is the point, Misha? part of him asked. *He has time—he controls time. He'll use all he needs to break you. He's winning. You know that,* despair told him.

Tell me, Comrade Captain, why do you ask yourself such foolish things? Why do you need to explain to yourself why you are a man? asked a familiar voice. *All the way from Brest-Litovsk to Vyasma we knew we were losing, but I never quit, and neither did you. If you can defy the German Army, certainly you can defy this city-soft slug of a chekist!*

Thank you, Romanov.

How did you ever get on without me, my Captain? the voice chuckled. *For all your intelligence, you can be a most foolish man.*

Vatutin saw that something had changed. The eyes blinked clear, and the weary old back straightened.

What is sustaining you? Hate? Do you so detest the State for what happened to your family . . . or is it something else entirely . . . ?

"Tell me," Vatutin said. "Tell me why you hate the Motherland."

"I do not," Filitov replied. "I have killed for the Motherland. I have bled for the Motherland. I have *burned* for the Motherland. But I did not do these things for the likes of you." For all his weakness, the defiance blazed in his eyes like a flame. Vatutin was unmoved.

I was close, but something changed. If I can find what that is, Filitov, I will have you! Something told Vatutin that he already had what he needed. The trick was to identify it.

The interrogation continued. Though Filitov would successfully resist this time, and the next time, and even the time after that, Vatutin was drawing down on the man's physical and emotional energy. Both knew it. It was just a matter of time. But on one issue both men were wrong. Both thought that Vatutin controlled time, even though time is man's final master.

Gerasimov was surprised by the new FLASH dispatch from America, this one from Platonov. It arrived by cable, alerting him to an Eyes-Only-

Chairman message en route in the diplomatic pouch. That was truly unusual. The KGB, more than other foreign-intelligence agencies, still depended on one-time-pad cipher systems. These were unbreakable, even in a theoretical sense, unless the code sequence itself were compromised. It was slow, but it was sure, and the KGB wanted "sure." Beyond that level of transmission, however, was another protocol. For each major station, there was a special cipher. It didn't even have a name, but ran directly from the *rezident* to the Chairman. Platonov was more important than even CIA suspected. He was the *rezident* for Washington, the chief of station.

When the dispatch arrived, it was brought directly to Gerasimov's office. His personal code clerk, a captain with impeccable credentials, was not called. The Chairman deciphered the first sentence himself, to learn that this was a mole warning. The KGB did not have a stock term for a traitor within its own ranks, but the higher ranks knew the Western word.

The dispatch was a lengthy one and took Gerasimov fully an hour to decode, cursing all the while at his clumsiness as he deciphered the random transpositions in the thirty-three-letter Russian alphabet.

An agent-in-place inside KGB? Gerasimov wondered. *How high?* He summoned his personal secretary and ordered the files on Agent Cassius, and Ryan, I.P., of CIA. As with all such orders, it didn't take long. He set Cassius aside for the moment and opened the file on Ryan.

There was a six-page biographical sketch, updated only six months previously, plus original newspaper clippings and translations. He didn't need the latter. Gerasimov spoke acceptable though accented English. Age thirty-five, he saw, with credentials in the business world, academia, and the intelligence community. He'd advanced rapidly within CIA. Special liaison officer to London. His first short-form evaluation at Dzerzhinskiy Square had been colored by some analyst's political views, Gerasimov saw. A rich, soft dilettante. No, that was not right. He'd advanced too rapidly for that, unless he had political influence that appeared absent from the profile. Probably a bright man—an author, Gerasimov saw, noting that there were copies of two of his books in Moscow. Certainly a proud one, accustomed to comfort and privilege.

So you broke American money-exchange laws, did you? The thought came easily to the KGB Chairman. Corruption was the way to wealth and power in any society. Ryan had his flaw, as did all men. Gerasimov knew that his own flaw was a lust for power, but he deemed the desire for anything less the mark of a fool. He turned back to Platonov's dispatch.

"Evaluation," the message concluded. "The subject is motivated neither by ideological nor by monetary considerations, but by anger and ego. He has a genuine fear of prison, but more of the personal disgrace. I. P. Ryan probably has the information which he claims. If CIA does have a highly placed mole in Moscow Center, it is likely that Ryan has seen data from him, though not the name or face. The data should be sufficient to identify the leak.

"Recommendation: The offer should be accepted for two reasons. First, to identify the American spy. Second, to make use of Ryan in the future. The unique opportunity offered has two faces. If we eliminate witnesses against the subject, he is in our debt. If this action is discovered, it can be blamed on CIA, and the resulting inquiries will damage the American intelligence service severely."

"Hmm," Gerasimov murmured to himself as he set the file aside.

Agent Cassius's file was far thicker. He was on his way to becoming one of KGB's best sources in Washington. Gerasimov had already read this one several times, and merely skimmed until he reached the most recent information. Two months earlier, Ryan had been investigated, details unknown—Cassius had reported it as unsubstantiated gossip. That was a point in its favor, the Chairman thought. It also disconnected Ryan's overtures from anything else that had developed recently . . .

Filitov?

What if the highly placed agent whom Ryan could identify was the one we just arrested? Gerasimov wondered.

No. Ryan was himself sufficiently high in CIA that he would not confuse one ministry with another. The only bad news was that a leak high in KGB wasn't something Gerasimov needed at the moment. Bad enough that it existed at all, but to let the word get outside the building . . . That could be a disaster. *If we launched a real investigation, word will get out. If we don't find the spy in our own midst . . . and if he's placed as highly as this Ryan says . . . what if CIA discovered what Alexandrov and I . . . ?*

What would they do?

What if this . . . ?

Gerasimov smiled and looked out the window. He'd miss this place. He'd miss the game. Every fact had at least three sides, and every thought had six. No, if he were to believe that, then he had to believe that Cassius was under CIA control, and that this had all been planned before Filitov had been arrested. That was plainly impossible.

The Chairman of the Committee for State Security checked his calendar to see when the Americans were coming over. There would be more social affairs this time. If the Americans had really decided to put their Star Wars systems on the table—it would make General Secretary Narmonov look good, but how many Politburo votes would that sway? *Not many, so long as I can keep Alexandrov's obstinacy in control. And if I can show that I've recruited an agent of our own that high in CIA . . . if I can predict that the Americans will trade away their defense programs, then I can steal a march on Narmonov's peace initiative myself . . .*

The decision was made.

But Gerasimov was not an impulsive man. He sent a signal to Platonov to verify some details through Agent Cassius. This signal he could send via satellite.

That signal arrived in Washington an hour later. It was duly copied from the Soviet Raduga-19 communications bird both by the Soviet Embassy and by the American National Security Agency, which put it on a computer tape along with thousands of other Russian signals that the Agency worked round the clock to decipher.

It was easier for the Soviets. The signal was taken to a secure section of the embassy, where a KGB lieutenant converted the scrambled letters into clear text. Then it was locked up in a guarded safe until Platonov arrived in the morning.

That happened at 6:30. The usual newspapers were on his desk. The American press was very useful to the KGB, he thought. The idea of a free press was so alien to him that he never even considered its true function. But other things came first. The night-watch officer came in at 6:45 and briefed him on the events of the previous night, and also delivered messages from Moscow, where it was already after lunch. At the top of the message list was a notice of an eyes-only-*rezident*. Platonov knew what that had to be, and walked to the safe at once. The young KGB officer who guarded this part of the embassy checked Platonov's ID scrupulously—his predecessor had lost his job by being so bold as to assume that he knew Platonov by sight after a mere nine months. The message, properly labeled in a sealed envelope, was in its proper cubbyhole, and Platonov tucked it in his pocket before closing and locking the door.

The KGB's Washington station was larger than that of CIA in Moscow, though not large enough to suit Platonov, since the number of people in the mission had been reduced to numerical equivalence with the American Embassy staff in the Soviet Union, something the Americans had taken years to do. He usually summoned his section chiefs at 7:30 for their morning conference, but today he called one of his officers early.

"Good morning, Comrade Colonel," the man said correctly. The KGB is not known for its pleasantries.

"I need you to get some information from Cassius on this Ryan business. It is imperative that we confirm his current legal difficulties as quickly as possible. That means today if you can manage it."

"Today?" the man asked in some discomfort as he took the written instructions. "There is risk in moving so rapidly."

"The Chairman is aware of that," Platonov observed dryly.

"Today," the man nodded.

The *resident* smiled inwardly as his man left. That was as much emotion as he'd shown in a month. This one had a real future.

"There's Butch," an FBI agent observed as the man came out of the embassy compound. They knew his real name, of course, but the first agent who'd shadowed him had noted that he looked like a Butch, and the name had stuck. His normal morning routine was ostensibly to unlock a few embassy offices, then to run errands before the senior diplomatic personnel appeared at nine. That involved catching breakfast at a nearby coffee shop, buying several newspapers and magazines . . . and frequently leaving a mark or two in one of several places. As with most counterintelligence operations, the really hard part was getting the first break. After that it was straight police work. They'd gotten the first break on Butch eighteen months before.

He walked the four blocks to the shop, well dressed for the cold—he probably found Washington winters pretty mild, they all agreed—and turned into the place right on schedule. As with most coffee shops, this one had a regular trade. Three of them were FBI agents. One was dressed like a businesswoman, always reading her *Wall Street Journal* by herself in a corner booth. Two wore the toolbelts of carpenters, and swaggered to the counter either before or after Butch entered. Today they were waiting for him. They were not always there, of course. The woman, Special Agent Hazel Loomis, coordinated her schedule with a real business, careful to miss work holidays. It was a risk, but a close surveillance, no matter how carefully planned, could not be too regular. Similarly, they appeared at the café on days when they knew Butch was away, never altering their routine to show that their interest was in their subject.

Agent Loomis noted his arrival time on the margin of an article—she was always scribbling on the paper—and the carpenters watched him in the mirrored wall behind the counter as they savaged their way through their hash-browns and traded a few boisterous jokes. As usual, Butch had gotten four different papers from a newsstand right outside the coffee shop.

The magazines he got all hit the stands on Tuesdays. The waitress poured his coffee without being asked. Butch lit his customary cigarette—an American Marlboro, the favorite of the Russians—and drank his first cup of coffee as he scanned the first page of the *Washington Post,* which was *his* usual paper.

Refills were free here, and his arrived on schedule. He took a scant six minutes, which was about right, everyone noted. Finished, he picked up his papers and left some money on the table. When he moved away from the plate, they could all see that he'd crumpled his paper napkin to a ball and set it in the saucer next to the empty coffee cup.

Business, Loomis noted at once. Butch took his bill to the register at the end of the counter, paid it, and left. He was good, Loomis noted yet again. She knew where and how he made the drop, but still she rarely caught him planting it.

Another regular came in. He was a cabdriver who usually got a cup of coffee before beginning his day, and sat alone at the end of the counter. He opened his paper to the sports page, looking around the café as he usually did. He could see the napkin on the saucer. He wasn't quite as good as Butch. Setting the paper in his lap, he reached under the counter and retrieved the message, tucking it in the Style section.

After that, it was pretty easy. Loomis paid her bill and left, hopping into her Ford Escort and driving to the Watergate apartments. She had a key to Henderson's apartment.

"You're getting a message today from Butch," she told Agent Cassius.

"Okay." Henderson looked up from his breakfast. He didn't at all enjoy having this girl "running" him as a double agent. He especially didn't like the fact that she was on the case because of her looks, that the "cover" for their association was a supposed affair which, of course, was pure fiction. For all her sweetness, her syrupy Southern accent—and her stunning good looks! he grumped—Henderson knew all too well that Loomis viewed him as half a step above a microbe. "Just remember," she'd told him once, "there's a room waiting for you." She was referring to the United States Penitentiary—not "correctional facility"—at Marion, Illinois, the one that had replaced Alcatraz as the home of the worst offenders. No place for a Harvard man. But she'd only done that once, and otherwise treated him politely, even occasionally grabbing his arm in public. That only made it worse.

"You want some good news?" Loomis asked.

"Sure."

"If this one goes through the way we hope, you might be clear. All the way out." She'd never said that before.

"What gives?" Agent Cassius asked with interest.

"There's a CIA officer named Ryan—"

"Yeah, I heard the SEC's checking him out—well, they did, a few months back. You let me tell the Russians about that . . ."

"He's dirty. Broke the rules, made half a million dollars on insider information, and there's a grand jury meeting in two weeks that's going to burn his ass, big-time." Her profanity was all the more vivid from the sweet, Southern-Belle smile. "The Agency's going to hang him out to dry. No help from anybody. Ritter hates his guts. You don't know why, but you heard it from Senator Fredenburg's aide. You get the impression that he's a sacrificial goat for something that went wrong, but you don't know what. Something a few months back in Central Europe, maybe, but that's all you heard. Some of it you tell right off. Some you make them wait till this afternoon. One more thing—you've heard a rumor that SDI may actually be on the table. You think it's bad information, but you heard a senator say something about it. Got it?"

"Yeah." Henderson nodded.

"Okay." Loomis walked off to the bathroom. Butch's favorite coffee shop was too greasy for her system.

Henderson went to his bedroom and selected a tie. *Out?* he wondered as he knotted it partway, then changed his mind. If that were true—he had to admit that she'd never lied to him. *Treated me like scum, but never lied to me,* he thought. *Then I can get out . . . ?* Then what? he asked himself. *Does it matter?*

It mattered, but it mattered more that he'd get out.

"I like the red one better," Loomis observed from the door. She smiled sweetly. "A 'power' tie for today, I think."

Henderson dutifully reached for the red one. It never occurred to him to object. "Can you tell me . . . ?"

"I don't know—and you know better. But they wouldn't let me say this unless everybody figured that you paid some back, Mr. Henderson."

"Can't you call me Peter, just once?" he asked.

"My father was the twenty-ninth pilot shot down over North Vietnam. They got him alive—there were pictures of him, alive—but he never came out."

"I didn't know."

She spoke as evenly as though discussing the weather. "You didn't know a lot of things, Mr. Henderson. They won't let me fly airplanes like Daddy did, but in the Bureau I make life as hard on the bastards as I can. They let me do that. I just hope that it hurts 'em like they've hurt me." She smiled again. "That's not very professional, is it?"

"I'm sorry. I'm afraid I don't know what else to say."

"Sure you do. You'll tell your contact what I told you to say." She tossed him a miniature tape recorder. It had a special computerized timer and an antitamper device. While in the taxicab, he'd be under intermittent surveillance. If he tried to warn his contact in any way, there was a chance—how great or small he did not know—that he'd be detected. They didn't like him and they didn't trust him. He knew that he'd never earn affection or trust, but Henderson would settle for getting out.

He left his apartment a few minutes later and walked downstairs. There was the usual number of cabs circulating about. He didn't gesture, but waited for one to come to him. They didn't start talking until it pulled into the traffic on Virginia Avenue.

The cab took him to the General Accounting Office headquarters on G Street, Northwest. Inside the building, he handed the tape recorder over to another FBI agent. Henderson suspected that it was a radio as well, though actually it was not. The recorder went to the Hoover Building. Loomis was waiting when it got there. The tape was rewound and played.

"CIA got it right for once," she observed to her supervisor. Someone even more senior was here. This was more important than she'd thought, Loomis knew at once.

"It figures. A source like Ryan doesn't come along real often. Henderson got his lines down pretty good."

"I told him that this may be his ticket out." Her voice said more than that.

"You don't approve?" the Assistant Director asked. He ran all of the FBI's counterintel operations.

"He hasn't paid enough, not for what he did."

"Miss Loomis, after this is all over, I'll explain to you why you're wrong. Put that aside, okay? You've done a beautiful job handling this case. Don't blow it now."

"What'll happen to him?" she asked.

"The usual, into the witness-protection program. He may end up running the Wendy's in Billings, Montana, for all I know." The AD shrugged. "You're getting promoted and sent to the New York Field Office. We have another one we think you're ready for. There's a diplomat attached to the UN who needs a good handler."

"Okay." The smile this time was not forced.

"They bit. They bit hard," Ritter told Ryan. "I just hope you're up to it, sonny boy."

"No danger involved." Jack spread his hands. "This ought to be real civilized."

Only the parts you know about. "Ryan, you are still an amateur so far as field ops are concerned. Remember that."

"I have to be for this to work," Jack pointed out.

"Those whom the gods would destroy, they first make proud," the DDO said.

"That's not the way Sophocles said it." Jack grinned.

"My way's better. I even had a sign put up at the Farm that quotes me."

Ryan's idea for the mission had been a simple one—too simple, and Ritter's people had refined it over a period of ten hours into a real operation. Simple in concept, it would have its complications. They all did, but Ritter didn't like that fact.

Bart Mancuso had long since gotten used to the idea that sleeping wasn't included in the list of things that submarine skippers were expected to do, but what he especially hated was a knock on the door fifteen minutes after he *was* able to lie down.

"Come!" *And die!* he didn't say.

"FLASH traffic, eyes-only-captain," the Lieutenant said apologetically.

"It better be good!" Mancuso snarled, snapping the covers off the bunk. He walked aft in his skivvies to the communications room, to port and just aft of the attack center. Ten minutes later he emerged and handed a slip of paper to the navigator.

"I want to be there in ten hours."

"No sweat, Cap'n."

"The next person who bothers me, it better be a grave national emergency!" He walked forward, barefoot on the tile deck.

"Message delivered," Henderson told Loomis over dinner.

"Anything else?" *Candlelight and all,* she thought.

"Just wanted to confirm. They didn't want new info, just to back up what they already had from some different sources. At least, that's the way I read it. I have another delivery for them."

"Which one's that?"

"The new battlefield air-defense report. I never could understand why they bother. They can read it in *Aviation Week* before the end of the month anyway."

"Let's not blow the routine now, Mr. Henderson."

This time the message could be handled as routine intelligence traffic. It would be flagged to the Chairman's attention because it was "personal" information on a senior enemy intelligence official. Gerasimov was known in the higher echelons of KGB to be a man interested as much in Western gossip as Russian.

It was waiting when he arrived the next morning. The KGB Chairman hated the eight-hour time differential between Moscow and Washington—it made things so damned inconvenient! For Moscow Center to order any immediate action automatically risked having his field officers cue the Americans as to who they were. As a result, few real "immediate-action" signals were ever sent out, and it offended the KGB Chairman that his personal power could be undone by something as prosaic as longitudinal lines.

"Subject P," the dispatch began, the English "R" being a "P" in the Cyrillic alphabet, "is now the target of a secret criminal investigation as part of a nonintelligence matter. It is suspected, however, that interest in P is politically based, probably an effort on the part of progressive congressional elements to damage CIA because of an unknown operational failure—possibly involving Central Europe, but this is not RPT not confirmed. P's criminal disgrace will be damaging to higher CIA officials due to his placement. This station grades the intelligence reliability of the case as A. Three independent sources now confirm the allegations dispatched in my 88(B)531-C/EOC. Full details to follow via pouch. Station recommends pursuing. *Rezident* Washington. Ends."

Gerasimov tucked the report away in his desk.

"Well," the Chairman murmured to himself. He checked his watch. He had to be at the regular Thursday-morning Politburo meeting in two hours. How would it go? One thing he knew: it would be an interesting one. He planned to introduce a new variant on his game—the Power Game.

His daily operational briefing was always a little longer on Thursdays. It never hurt to drop a few harmless tidbits at the meetings. His fellow Politburo members were all men to whom conspiracy came as easily as breathing, and there hadn't been a government anywhere in the last century whose senior members did not enjoy hearing about covert operations. Gerasimov made a few notes, careful to choose only things that he could discuss without compromising important cases. His car came around at the appointed time, as always accompanied by a lead car of bodyguards, and sped off to the Kremlin.

Gerasimov was never the first to arrive, and never the last. This time he walked in just behind the Defense Minister.

"Good morning, Dmitri Timofeyevich," the Chairman said without a smile, but cordially enough for all that.

"And to you, Comrade Chairman," Yazov said warily. Both men took their seats. Yazov had more than one reason to be wary. In addition to the fact that Filitov was hanging over his head like a sword out of myth, he was not a full voting member of the supreme Soviet council. Gerasimov was. That gave KGB more political power than Defense, but the only times in recent history that the Defense Minister had had a vote in this room, he'd been a Party man first—like Ustinov had been. Yazov was a soldier first. A loyal Party member for all that, his uniform was not the costume it had been for Ustinov. Yazov would never have a vote at this table.

Andrey Il'ych Narmonov came into the room with his usual vigor. Of all the Politburo members, only the KGB Chairman was younger than he, and Narmonov felt the need to show bustling energy whenever he appeared before the older men who were arrayed around "his" conference table. The strain and stress of his job were telling on him. Everyone could see it. The black bush of hair was beginning to gray rapidly, and it also seemed that his hairline was receding. But that was hardly unusual for a man in his fifties. He gestured for everyone to sit.

"Good morning, Comrades," Narmonov said in a businesslike voice. "The initial discussion will concern the arrival of the American arms-negotiations team."

"I have good news to report," Gerasimov said at once.

"Indeed?" Alexandrov asked before the General Secretary could, staking out his own position.

"We have information that suggests that the Americans are willing in principle to place their strategic-defense program on the table," the KGB Chairman reported. "We do not know what concessions they will demand for this, nor the extent of the concessions in their program that they are willing to make, but this is nevertheless a change in the American posture."

"I find that difficult to believe," Yazov spoke up. "Their program is well along—as you yourself told me last week, Nikolay Borissovich."

"There are some political dissenters within the American government, and possibly a power struggle under way within CIA itself at the moment, we have just learned. In any case, that is our information, and we regard it to be fairly reliable."

"That is quite a surprise." Heads turned to where the Foreign Minister was sitting. He looked skeptical. "The Americans have been totally adamant on this point. You say 'fairly reliable,' but not totally so?"

"The source is highly placed, but the information has not been adequately confirmed as yet. We will know more by the weekend."

Heads nodded around the table. The American delegation would arrive noon Saturday, and negotiations would not begin until Monday. The Americans would be given thirty-six hours to overcome their jet lag, during which there would be a welcoming dinner at the Academy of Sciences Hotel, and little else.

"Such information is obviously a matter of great interest to my negotiating team, but I find it most surprising, particularly in view of the briefings we've been given here on our Bright Star Program, and their counterpart to it."

"There is reason to believe that the Americans have learned of Bright Star," Gerasimov replied smoothly. "Perhaps they have found our progress sobering."

"Bright Star penetrated?" another member asked. "How?"

"We're not sure. We're working on it," Gerasimov replied, careful not to look in Yazov's direction. *Your move, Comrade Defense Minister.*

"So the Americans might really be more interested in shutting our program down than in curtailing theirs," Alexandrov observed.

"And they think that our efforts have been the reverse of that." The Foreign Minister grunted. "It would be nice for me to be able to tell my people what the real issues are!"

"Marshal Yazov?" Narmonov said. He didn't know that he was putting his own man on the spot.

Until now, Gerasimov hadn't been sure about Yazov, about whether he might not feel safe taking his political vulnerability over the Filitov matter to his master. This would give him the answer. *Yazov was afraid of the possibility—CERTAINTY,* he corrected himself, *Yazov has to know that by now—that we can disgrace him. He's also afraid that Narmonov won't risk his own position to save him. So have I co-opted both Yazov and Vaneyev? If so, I wonder if it might be worth keeping Yazov on after I replace the General Secretary . . . Your decision, Yazov . . .*

"We have overcome the problem of laser power output. The remaining problem is in computer control. Here we are far behind American techniques due to the superiority of their computer industry. Only last week, Comrade Gerasimov furnished us with some of the American control program, but we had not even begun to examine it when we learned that the program was itself overtaken by events.

"I do not mean this to be criticism of the KGB, of course—"

Yes! In that moment Gerasimov was sure. *He's making his own overture to me. And the best part—no other man in the room, not even Alexandrov, understands what just happened.*

"—actually, it illustrates the technical problem rather clearly. But it is only a technical problem, Comrades. This one, too, can be overcome. My opinion is that we are ahead of the Americans. If they know this, they will be fearful of it. Our negotiating position to this point has been to object to space-based programs only, never ground-based, since we have known all along that our ground-based systems have greater promise than their American counterparts. Possibly the change in the American position confirms this. If so, I would recommend against trading Bright Star for anything."

"That is a defensible opinion," Gerasimov commented after a moment. "Dmitri Timofeyevich has raised a thoughtful issue here." Heads nodded around the table—knowingly, they all thought, but more wrongly than any would dare guess—as the Chairman of the Committee for State Security and the Minister of Defense consummated their bargain with nothing more than a glance and a raised eyebrow.

Gerasimov turned back to the head of the table as the discussion went on around him. General Secretary Narmonov watched the debate with interest, making a few notes, not noticing the gaze of his KGB Chairman.

I wonder if that chair is more comfortable than mine.

19. Travelers

Even the 89th Military Airlift Wing worried about security, Ryan was glad to see. The sentries who guarded the "President's Wing" at Andrews Air Force Base carried loaded rifles and wore serious looks to impress the "Distinguished Visitors"—the U.S. Air Force eschews the term Very Important Persons. The combination of armed troops and the usual airport rigamarole made it certain that no one would hijack the airplane and take it to . . . Moscow. They had a flight crew to accomplish that.

Ryan always had the same thought before flying. As he waited to pass through the doorway-shaped magnetometer, he imagined that someone had engraved on the lintel: ABANDON ALL HOPE YE WHO ENTER HERE. He'd just about overcome his terror of flying; his anxiety now was of something else entirely, he told himself. It didn't work. Fears are additive, not parallel, he discovered as he walked out of the building.

They were taking the same plane as the last time. The tail number was 86971. It was a 707 that had rolled out of Boeing's Seattle plant in 1958 and had been converted to the VC-137 configuration. More comfortable than the VC-135, it also had windows. If there was anything Ryan hated, it was being aboard a windowless aircraft. There was no level jetway to traverse into the bird. Everyone climbed up an old-fashioned wheeled stairway. Once inside, the plane was a curious mix of the commonplace and the unique. The forward washroom was in the usual place, just across from the front door, but aft of that was the communications console that gave the plane instantaneous, secure satellite-radio links with anyplace in the world. Next came the relatively comfortable crew accommodations, and then the galley. Food aboard the airplane was pretty good. Ryan's seat was in the almost-DV area, on one of two couches set on either side of the fuselage, just forward of the six-seat space for the really important folks. Aft of that was the five-across seating for reporters, Secret Service, and other people considered less distinguished by whoever made such decisions. It was mainly empty for this trip, though some junior members of the delegation would be back there, able to stretch out a bit for a change.

The only really bad thing about the VC-137 was its limited range. It couldn't one-hop all the way to Moscow, and usually stopped off for refueling at Shannon before making the final leg. The President's aircraft—actually there were *two* Air Force Ones—were based on the longer-range 707-320, and would soon be replaced with ultramodern 747s. The Air Force was looking forward to having a presidential aircraft that was younger than most of its flight crew. So was Ryan. This one had rolled out of the factory door when he'd been in second grade, and it struck him as odd that it should be so. But what should have happened? he wondered. Should his father have taken him to Seattle, pointed to the airplane and said, *See, you'll fly to Russia on that one someday . . . ?*

I wonder how you predict fate? I wonder how you predict the future . . . At first playful, in a moment the thought chilled him.

Your business is predicting the future, but what makes you think that you can really do it? What have you guessed wrong on this time, Jack?

Goddamn it! he raged at himself. *Every time I get on a fucking airplane . . .* He strapped himself in, facing across the airplane some State Department technical expert who loved to fly.

The engines started a minute later, and presently the airplane started to roll. The announcements over the intercom weren't very different from that on an airliner, just enough to let you know that the ownership of the plane was not corporate. Jack had already deduced that. The stewardess had a mustache. It was something to chuckle about as the aircraft taxied to the end of runway One-Left.

The winds were northerly, and the VC-137 took off into them, turning right a minute after it lifted off. Jack turned, too, looking down at U.S. Route 50. It was the road that led to his home in Annapolis. He lost sight of it as the aircraft entered the clouds. The impersonal white veil had often seemed a beautiful curtain, but now . . . but now it just meant that he couldn't see the way home. Well, there wasn't much he could do about that. Ryan had the couch to himself, and decided to take advantage of the fact. He kicked off his shoes and stretched out for a nap. One thing he'd need would be rest. He was sure of that.

Dallas had surfaced at the appointed time and place, then been told of a hitch in the plans. Now she surfaced again. Mancuso was the first one up the ladder to the control station atop the sail, followed by a junior officer and a pair of lookouts. Already the periscope was up, scanning the surface for traffic, of course. The night was calm and clear, the sort of sky you get only at sea, ablaze with stars, like gemstones on a velvet sheet.

"Bridge, conn."

Mancuso pressed the button. "Bridge, aye."

"ESM reports an airborne radar transmitter bearing one-four-zero, bearing appears steady."

"Very well." The Captain turned. "You can flip on the running lights."

"All clear starboard," one lookout said.

"All clear port," echoed the other.

"ESM reports contact is still steady on one-four-zero. Signal strength is increasing."

"Possible aircraft fine on the port bow!" a lookout called.

Mancuso raised his binoculars to his eyes and started searching the blackness. If it was here already, it didn't have his running lights on . . . but then he saw a handful of stars disappear, occulted by something . . .

"I got him. Good eye, Everly! Oh, there go his flying lights."

"Bridge, conn, we have a radio message coming in."

"Patch it," Mancuso replied at once.

"Done, sir."

"Echo-Golf-Nine, this is Alfa-Whiskey-Five, over."

"Alfa-Whiskey-Five, this is Echo-Golf-Nine. I read you loud and clear. Authenticate, over."

"Bravo-Delta-Hotel, over."

"Roger, thank you. We are standing by. Wind is calm. Sea is flat." Mancuso reached down and flipped on the lights for the control station instruments. Not actually needed at the moment—the Attack Center still had the conn—they'd give the approaching helicopter a target.

They heard it a moment later, first the flutter of the rotor blades, then the whine of the turboshaft engines. Less than a minute later they could feel the downdraft as the helicopter circled twice overhead for the pilot to orient himself. Mancuso wondered if he'd turn on his landing lights . . . or hot-dog it.

He hot-dogged it, or more properly, he treated it as what it was, a covert personnel transfer: a "combat" mission. The pilot fixed on the submarine's cockpit lights and brought the aircraft to a hover fifty yards to port. Next he reduced altitude and sideslipped the helo toward the submarine. Aft, they saw the cargo door slide open. A hand reached out and grabbed the hook-end of the winch cable.

"Stand by, everybody," Mancuso told his people. "We've done it before. Check your safety lines. Everybody just be careful."

The prop wash from the helicopter threatened to blow them all down the ladder into the Attack Center as it hovered almost directly overhead. As Mancuso watched, a man-shape emerged from the cargo door and was lowered straight down. The thirty feet seemed to last forever as the shape came down, twirling slightly from the torsion of the steel winch cable. One of his seamen reached and grabbed a foot, pulling the man toward them. The Captain got his hand and both men pulled him inboard.

"Okay, we got ya," Mancuso said. The man slipped from the collar and turned as the cable went back up.

"Mancuso!"

"Son of a bitch!" the Captain exclaimed.

"Is this any way to greet a comrade?"

"Damn!" But business came first. Mancuso looked up. The helicopter was already two hundred feet overhead. He reached down and blinked the sub's running lights on and off three times: TRANSFER COMPLETE. The helicopter immediately dropped its nose and headed back toward the German coast.

"Get on below." Bart laughed. "Lookouts below. Clear the bridge. Son of a bitch," he said to himself. The Captain watched his men go down the ladder, switched off the cockpit lights, and made a final safety check before heading down behind them. A minute later he was in the Attack Center.

"Now do I request permission to come aboard?" Marko Ramius asked.

" 'Gator?"

"All systems aligned and checked for dive. We are rigged for dive," the navigator reported. Mancuso turned automatically to check the status boards.

"Very well. Dive. Make your depth one hundred feet, course zero-seven-one, one-third." He turned. "Welcome aboard, Captain."

"Thank you, Captain." Ramius wrapped Mancuso in a ferocious bear-hug and kissed him on the cheek. Next he slipped off the backpack he was wearing. "Can we talk?"

"Come on forward."

"First time I come aboard your submarine," Ramius observed. A moment later a head poked out of the sonar room.

"Captain Ramius! I thought I recognized your voice!" Jones looked at Mancuso. "Beg pardon, sir. We just got a contact, bearing zero-eight-one. Sounds like a merchant. Single screw, slow-speed diesels driving it. Probably a ways off. Being reported to the ODD now, sir."

"Thanks, Jonesy." Mancuso took Ramius into his stateroom and closed the door.

"What the hell was that?" a young sonarman asked Jones a moment later.

"We just got some company."

"Didn't he have an accent, sort of?"

"Something like that." Jones pointed to the sonar display. "That contact has an accent, too. Let's see how fast you can decide what kinda merchie he is."

It was dangerous, but all life was dangerous, the Archer thought. The Soviet-Afghan border here was a snow-fed river that snaked through gorges it had carved through the mountains. The border was also heavily guarded. It helped that his men were all dressed in Soviet-style uniforms. The Russians have long put their soldiers in simple but warm winter gear. Those they had on were mainly white to suit the snowy background, with just enough stripes and spots to break up their outline. Here they had to be patient. The Archer lay athwart a ridge, using Russian-issue binoculars to sweep the terrain while his men rested a few meters behind and below him. He might have gotten a local guerrilla band to provide help, but he'd come too far to risk that. Some of the northern tribes had been co-opted by the Russians, or at least that was what he'd been told. True or not, he was running enough risks.

There was a Russian guard post atop the mountain to his left, six kilometers away. A large one, perhaps a full platoon lived there, and those KGB soldiers were responsible for patrolling this sector. The border itself was covered with a fence and minefields. The Russians loved their minefields . . . but the ground was frozen solid, and Soviet mines often didn't work well in frozen ground, although occasionally they'd set themselves off when the frost heaved around them.

He'd chosen the spot with care. The border here looked virtually impassable—on a map. Smugglers had used it for centuries, however. Once across the river, there was a snaky path formed by centuries of snowmelt. Steep, and slippery, it was also a mini-canyon hidden from any view except direct overhead. If Russians guarded it, of course, it would be a deathtrap. That would be Allah's will, he told himself, and consigned himself to destiny. It was time.

He saw the flashes first. Ten men with a heavy machine gun and one of his precious mortars. A few yellow tracer streaks cut across the border into the Russian base camp. As he watched, a few of the bullets caromed off the rocks, tracing erratic paths in the velvet sky. Then the Russians started returning fire. The sound reached them soon after that. He hoped that his men would get away as he turned and waved his group forward.

They ran down the forward slope of the mountain, heedless of safety. The only good news was that winds had swept the snow off the rocks, making for decent footing. The Archer led them down toward the river. Amazingly enough, it was not frozen, its path too steep for the water to stop, even in subzero temperatures. There was the wire!

A young man with a two-handed pair of cutters made a path, and again the Archer led them through. His eyes were accustomed to the darkness, and he went more slowly now, looking at the ground for the telltale humps that indicated mines in the frozen ground. He didn't need to tell those behind him to stay in single file and walk on rocks wherever possible. Off to the left flares now decorated the sky, but the firing had died down somewhat.

It took over an hour, but he got all of his men across and into the smugglers' trail. Two men would stay behind, each on a hilltop overlooking the wire. They watched the amateur sapper who'd cut the wire make repairs to conceal their entry. Then he, too, faded into the darkness.

The Archer didn't stop until dawn. They were on schedule as they all paused a few hours for rest and food. All had gone well, his officers told him, better than they had hoped.

The stopover in Shannon was a brief one, just long enough to refuel and take aboard a Soviet pilot whose job it was to talk them through the Russian air-traffic-control system. Jack awoke on landing and thought about stretching his legs, but decided that the duty-free shops could wait until the return leg. The Russian took his place in the cockpit jump seat, and 86971 started rolling again.

It was night now. The pilot was in a loquacious mood tonight, announcing their next landfall at Wallasey. All of Europe, he said, was enjoying clear, cold weather, and Jack watched the orange-yellow city lights of England slide beneath them. Tension on the aircraft increased—or perhaps anticipation was a better word, he thought, as he listened to the pitch of the voices around him increase somewhat, though their volume dropped. You couldn't fly toward the Soviet Union without becoming a little conspiratorial. Soon all the conversations were in raspy whispers. Jack smiled thinly at the plastic windows, and his reflection asked what was so damned funny. Water appeared below them again as they flew across the North Sea toward Denmark.

The Baltic came next. You could tell where East and West met. To the south, the West German cities were all gaily lit, each surrounded by a warm glow of light. Not so on the eastern side of the wire-minefield barrier. Everyone aboard noticed the difference, and conversations grew quieter still.

The aircraft was following air route G-24; the navigator in front had the Jeppesen chart partially unfolded on his table. Another difference between East and West was the dearth of flight routes in the former. Well, he told himself, not many Pipers and Cessnas here—of course, there was that *one* Cessna . . .

"Coming up on a turn. We'll be coming to new heading zero-seven-eight, and entering Soviet control."

"Right," the pilot—"aircraft commander"—responded after a moment. He was tired. It had been a long day's flying. They were already at Flight Level 381—38,100 feet, or 11,600 meters as the Soviets preferred to call it. The pilot didn't like meters, even though his instruments were calibrated both ways. After executing the turn, they flew for another sixty miles before crossing the Soviet border at Ventspils.

"We're heeere," somebody said a few feet from Ryan. From the air, at night, Soviet territory made East Germany look like New Orleans at Mardi Gras. He remembered night satellite shots. It was so easy to pick out the camps of the GULAG. They were the only lighted squares in the whole country . . . what a dreary place that only the prisons are well lighted . . .

The pilot marked the entry only as another benchmark. Eighty-five more minutes, given the wind conditions. The Soviet air-traffic-control system along this routing—called G-3 now—was the only one in the country that spoke English. They didn't really need the Soviet officer to complete the mission—he was an air-force intelligence officer, of course—but if something went wrong, things might be different. The Russians liked the idea of positive control. The orders he got now for course and altitude were far more exact than those given in American air space, as though he didn't know what to do unless some jerk-off on the ground told him. Of course there was an element of humor to it. The pilot was Colonel Paul von Eich. His family had come to America from Prussia a hundred years before, but none of them had been able to part with the "von" that had once been so important to family status. Some of his ancestors had fought down there, he reflected, on the flat, snow-covered Russian ground. Certainly a few more recent relatives had. Probably a few lay buried there while he whizzed overhead at six hundred miles per hour. He wondered vaguely what they'd think of his job while his pale blue eyes scanned the sky for the lights of other aircraft.

Like most passengers, Ryan judged his height above the ground by what he could see, but the dark Soviet countryside denied him that. He knew they were close when the aircraft commenced a wide turn to the left. He heard the mechanical whine as the flaps went down and noted the reduced engine noise. Soon he could just pick out individual trees, racing by. The pilot's voice came on, telling smokers to put them out, and that it was time for seat belts again. Five minutes later they returned to ground level again at Sheremetyevo Airport. Despite the fact that airports all over the world look exactly alike, Ryan could be sure of this one—the taxiways were the bumpiest anywhere.

The cabin talk was more lively now. The excitement was beginning as the airplane's crew started moving about. What followed went in a blur. Ernie Allen was met by a welcoming committee of the appropriate level and whisked off in an embassy limousine. Everyone else was relegated to a bus. Ryan sat by himself, still watching the countryside outside the German-made vehicle.

Will Gerasimov bite—really bite?

What if he doesn't?

What if he does? Ryan asked himself with a smile.

It had all seemed pretty straightforward in Washington, but here, five thousand miles away . . . well. First he'd get some sleep, aided by a single government-issue red capsule. Then he'd talk to a few people at the embassy. The rest would have to take care of itself.

20. The Key of Destiny

It was bitterly cold when Ryan awoke to the beeping sound of his watch alarm. There was frost on the windows even at ten in the morning, and he realized that he hadn't made sure the heat in his room was operating. His first considered action of the day was to pull on some socks. His seventh-floor room—it was called an "efficiency apartment"—overlooked the compound. Clouds had moved in, and the day was leaden gray with the threat of snow.

"Perfect," Jack observed to himself on the way to the bathroom. He knew that it could have been worse. The only reason he had this room was that the officer who ordinarily lived here was on honeymoon leave. At least the plumbing worked, but he found a note taped to the medicine cabinet mirror admonishing him not to mess the place up the way the last transient had. Next he checked the small refrigerator. Nothing: *Welcome to Moscow.* Back in the bathroom, he washed and shaved. One other oddity of the embassy was that to get down from the seventh floor, you first had to take an elevator up to the ninth floor and another one down from there to the lobby. Jack was still shaking his head over that one when he got into the canteen.

"Don't you just love jet lag?" a member of the delegation greeted him. "Coffee's over there."

"I call it travel shock." Ryan got himself a mug and came back. "Well, the coffee's decent. Where's everybody else?"

"Probably still sacked out, even Uncle Ernie. I caught a few hours on the flight, and thank God for the pill they gave us."

Ryan laughed. "Yeah, me too. Might even feel human in time for dinner tonight."

"Feel like exploring? I'd like to take a walk, but—"

"Travel in pairs." Ryan nodded. The rule applied only to the arms negotiators. This phase of negotiations would be sensitive, and the rules for the team were much tighter than usual. "Maybe later. I have some work to do."

"Today and tomorrow's our only chance," the diplomat pointed out.

"I know," Ryan assured him. He checked his watch and decided that he'd wait to eat until lunchtime. His sleep cycle was almost in synch with Moscow, but his stomach wasn't quite sure yet. Jack walked back to the chancery.

The corridors were mainly empty. Marines patrolled them, looking very serious indeed after the problems that had occurred earlier, but there was little evidence of activity on this Saturday morning. Jack walked to the proper door and knocked. He knew it was locked.

"You're Ryan?"

"That's right." The door opened to admit him, then was closed and relocked.

"Grab a seat." His name was Tony Candela. "What gives?"

"We have an op laid on."

"News to me—you're not operations, you're intelligence," Candela objected.

"Yeah, well, Ivan knows that, too. This one's going to be a little strange." Ryan explained for five minutes.

" 'A little strange,' you say?" Candela rolled his eyes.

"I need a keeper for part of it. I need some phone numbers I can call, and I may need wheels that'll be there when required."

"This could cost me some assets."

"We know that."

"Of course, if it works . . ."

"Right. We can put some real muscle on this one."

"The Foleys know about this?"

" 'Fraid not."

"Too bad, Mary Pat would have loved it. She's the cowboy. Ed's more the button-down-collar type. So, you expect him to bite Monday or Tuesday night?"

"That's the plan."

"Let me tell you something about plans," Candela said.

They were letting him sleep. The doctors had warned him again, Vatutin growled. How was he supposed to accomplish anything when they kept—

"There's that name again," the man with the headphones said tiredly. "Romanov. If he must talk in his sleep, why can't he confess . . . ?"

"Perhaps he's talking with the Czar's ghost," another officer joked. Vatutin's head came up.

"Or perhaps someone else's." The Colonel shook his head. He'd been at the point of dozing himself. Romanov, though the name of the defunct royal family of the Russian Empire, was not an uncommon one—even a Politburo member had had it. "Where's his file?"

"Here." The joker pulled open a drawer and handed it over. The file weighed six kilograms, and came in several different sections. Vatutin had committed most of it to memory, but had concentrated on the last two parts. This time he opened the first section.

"Romanov," he breathed to himself. "Where have I seen that . . . ?"

It took him fifteen minutes, flipping through the frayed pages as speedily as he dared.

"I have it!" It was a citation, scrawled in pencil. "Corporal A. I. Romanov, killed in action 6 October 1941, '. . . defiantly placed his tank between the enemy and his disabled troop commander's, allowing the commander to withdraw his wounded crew . . .' Yes! This one's in a book I read as a child. Misha got his crew on the back deck of a different tank, jumped inside, and personally killed the tank that got Romanov's. He'd saved Misha's life and was posthumously awarded the Red Banner—" Vatutin stopped. He was calling the subject *Misha,* he realized.

"Almost fifty years ago?"

"They were comrades. This Romanov fellow had been part of Filitov's own tank crew through the first few months. Well, he was a hero. He died for the Motherland, saving the life of his officer," Vatutin observed. *And Misha still talks to him . . .*

I have you now, Filitov.

"Shall we wake him up and—"

"Where's the doctor?" Vatutin asked.

It turned out that he was about to leave for home and was not overly pleased to be recalled. But he didn't have the rank to play power games with Colonel Vatutin.

"How should we handle it?" Vatutin asked after outlining his thoughts.

"He should be weary but wide awake. That is easily done."

"So we should wake him up now and—"

"No." The doctor shook his head. "Not in REM sleep—"

"What?"

"Rapid Eye Movement sleep—that's what it's called when the patient is dreaming. You can always tell if the subject is in a dream by the eye movement, whether he talks or not."

"But we can't see that from here," another officer objected.

"Yes, perhaps we should redesign the observation system," the doctor mused. "But that doesn't matter too much. During REM sleep the body is effectively paralyzed. You'll notice that he's not moving now, correct? The mind does that to prevent injury to the body. When he starts moving again, the dream is over."

"How long?" Vatutin asked. "We don't want him to get too rested."

"Depends on the subject, but I would not be overly concerned. Have the turnkey get a breakfast ready for him, and as soon as he starts moving, wake him up and feed him."

"Of course." Vatutin smiled.

"Then we just keep him awake . . . oh, eight hours or so more. Yes, that should do it. Is it enough time for you?"

"Easily," Vatutin said with more confidence than he should have. He stood and checked his watch. The Colonel of "Two" called the Center and gave a few orders. His system, too, cried out for sleep. But for him there was a comfortable bed. He wanted to have all of his cleverness when the time came. The Colonel undressed fastidiously, calling for an orderly to polish his boots and press his uniform while he slept. He was tired enough that he didn't even feel the need for a drink. "I have you now," he murmured as he faded into sleep.

"G'night, Bea," Candi called from the door as her friend opened up her car. Taussig turned one last time and waved before getting in. Candi and the Geek couldn't have seen the way she stabbed the key into the ignition. She drove only half a block, turning a corner before pulling to the curb and staring at the night.

They're doing it already, she thought. *All the way through dinner, the way he looked at her—the way she looked at him! Already those wimpy little hands are fumbling with the buttons on her blouse . . .*

She lit a cigarette and leaned back, picturing it while her stomach tightened into a rigid, acid-filled ball. Zit-face and Candi. She'd endured three hours of it. Candi's usual beautifully prepared dinner. For twenty minutes while the finishing touches had been under way, she'd been stuck in the living room with *him,* listening to his idiot jokes, having to smile back at him. It was clear enough that Alan didn't like her either, but because she was Candi's friend he'd felt obligated to be nice to her, nice to poor Bea, who was heading toward old-maidhood, or whatever they called it now— she'd seen it in his stupid eyes. To be patronized by him was bad enough, but to be pitied . . .

And now he was touching her, kissing her, listening to her murmurs, whispering his stupid, disgusting endearments—and Candi liked it! How was that *possible?*

Candace was more than just pretty, Taussig knew. She was a free spirit. She had a discoverer's mind mated to a warm, sensitive soul. She had real feelings. She was so wonderfully feminine, with the kind of beauty that begins at the heart and radiates out through a perfect smile.

But now she's giving herself to that thing! He's probably doing it already. That geek doesn't have the first idea of taking his time and showing real love and sensitivity. I bet he just does it, drooling and giggling like some punk fifteen-year-old football jock. How can she!

"Oh, Candace." Bea's voice broke. She was swept with nausea, and had to fight to control herself. She succeeded, and sat alone in her car for twenty minutes of silent tears before she managed to drive on.

"What do you make of that?"

"I think she's a lesbian," Agent Jennings said after a moment.

"Nothing like that in her file, Peggy," Will Perkins observed.

"The way she looks at Dr. Long, the way she acts around Gregory . . . that's my gut feeling."

"But—"

"Yeah, but what the hell can we do about that?" Margaret Jennings noted as she drove away. She toyed briefly with the idea of going after Taussig, but the day had been long enough already. "No evidence, and if we got it, and acted on it, there'd be hell to pay."

"You suppose the three of them . . . ?"

"Will, you've been reading those magazines again." Jennings laughed, breaking the spell for a moment. Perkins was a Mormon, and had never been seen to touch pornographic material. "Those two are so much in love they don't have the first idea of what's going on around them—except work. I bet their pillow talk is classified. What's happening, Will, is that Taussig is being cut out of her friend's life and she's unhappy about it. Tough."

"So how do we write this one up?"

"Zip. A whole lot of nothing." Their assignment for the evening had been to follow up a report that strange cars were occasionally seen at the Gregory-Long residence. It had probably originated, Agent Jennings thought, from a local prude who didn't like the idea of the two young people living together without the appropriate paperwork. She was a little old-fashioned about that herself, but it didn't make either one of them a security risk. On the other hand—

"I think we ought to check out Taussig next."

"She lives alone."

"I'm sure." It would take time to look at every senior staffer at Tea Clipper, but you couldn't rush this kind of investigation.

"You shouldn't have come here," Tania observed at once. Bisyarina's face didn't show her rage. She took Taussig's hand and brought her inside.

"Ann, it's just so awful!"

"Come sit down. Were you followed?" *Idiot! Pervert!* She'd just gotten out of the shower, and was dressed in a bathrobe, with a towel over her hair.

"No, I watched all the way."

Sure, Bisyarina thought. She would have been surprised to learn that it was true. Despite the lax security at Tea Clipper—it allowed someone like this inside!—her agent had broken every rule there was in coming here.

"You cannot stay long."

"I know." She blew her nose. "They've about finished the first draft of the new program. The Geek has cut it down by eighty thousand lines of code—taking out all that AI stuff really made a difference. You know, I think he has the new stuff memorized—I know, I know, that's impossible, even for *that.*"

"When will you be able—"

"I don't know." Taussig smiled for a second. "You ought to have him working for you. I think he's the only one who really understands the whole program—I mean, the whole project."

Unfortunately all we have is you, Bisyarina didn't say. What she did was very hard. She reached out and took Taussig's hand.

The tears started again. Beatrice nearly leaped into Tania's arms. The Russian officer held her close, trying to feel sympathy for her agent. There had been many lessons at the KGB school, all of them intended to help her in handling agents. You had to have a mixture of sympathy and discipline. You had to treat them like spoiled children, mixing favors and scoldings to make them perform. And Agent Livia was more important than most.

It was still hard to turn her face toward the head on her shoulder and kiss the cheek that was salty with tears both old and new. Bisyarina breathed easier at the realization that she needed go no further than this. She'd never yet needed to go further, but lived in fear that "Livia" would one day demand it of her—certainly it would happen if she ever realized that her intended lover had not the slightest interest in her advances. Bisyarina marveled at that. Beatrice Taussig was brilliant in her way, certainly brighter than the KGB officer who "ran" her, but she knew so little about people. The crowning irony was that she was very much like that Alan Gregory man she so detested. Prettier, more sophisticated though Taussig was, she lacked the capacity to reach out when she needed to. Gregory had probably done it only once in his life, and that was the difference between him and her. He had gotten there first because Beatrice had lacked the courage. It was just as well, Bisyarina knew. The rejection would have destroyed her.

Bisyarina wondered what Gregory was really like. Probably another academic—what was it the English called them? Boffins. A brilliant boffin—well, everyone attached to Tea Clipper was brilliant in one way or another. That frightened her. In her way, Beatrice was proud of the program, though she deemed it a threat to world peace, a point on which Bisyarina agreed. Gregory was a boffin who wanted to change the world. Bisyarina understood the motivation. She wanted to change it, too. Just in a different way. Gregory and Tea Clipper were a threat to that. She didn't hate the man. If anything, she thought, she'd probably like him. But personal likes and dislikes had absolutely nothing to do with the business of intelligence.

"Feel better?" she asked when the tears stopped.

"I have to leave."

"Are you sure you're all right?"

"Yes. I don't know when I'll be able to—"

"I understand." Tania walked her to the door. At least she'd had the good sense to park her car on a different block, "Ann" noticed. She waited, holding the door cracked open, to hear the distinctive sound of the sports car. After closing the door, she looked at her hands and went back to the bathroom to wash them.

Night came early in Moscow, the sun hidden by clouds that were starting to shed their load of snow. The delegation assembled in the embassy's foyer and filed off into their assigned cars for the arrival dinner. Ryan was in car number three—a slight promotion from the last trip, he noted wryly. Once the procession started moving, he remembered a driver's remark from the last time, that Moscow had street names mainly to identify the pothole collections. The car jolted its way east through the city's largely empty streets. They crossed the river right at the Kremlin, and motored past Gorkiy Park. He could see that the place was gaily lit, with people ice-skating in the falling snow. It was nice to see real people having real fun. Even Moscow was a city, he reminded himself, full of ordinary people living fairly ordinary lives. It was a fact too easy to forget when your job forced you to concentrate on a narrow group of enemies.

The car turned off October Square, and after an intricate maneuver, pulled up to the Academy of Sciences Hotel. It was a quasi-modern building that in America might have been taken for an office block. A forlorn string of birch trees sat between the gray concrete wall and the street, their bare, lifeless branches reaching into the speckled sky. Ryan shook his head. Given a few hours of snowfall, and it might actually be a beautiful scene. The temperature was zero or so—Ryan thought in Fahrenheit, not Celsius—and the wind almost calm. Perfect conditions for snow. He could feel the air heavy and cold around him as he walked into the hotel's main entrance.

Like most Russian buildings, it was overheated. Jack removed his overcoat and handed it over to an attendant. The Soviet delegation was already lined up to greet their American counterparts, and the Americans shuffled down the rank of Soviets, ending at a table of drinks of which everyone partook. There would be ninety minutes of drinking and socializing before the actual dinner. Welcome to Moscow. Ryan approved of the plan. Enough alcohol could make any meal seem a feast, and he'd yet to experience a Russian meal that rose above the ordinary. The room was barely lit, allowing everyone to watch the falling snow through the large plate-glass windows.

"Hello again, Dr. Ryan," a familiar voice said.

"Sergey Nikolayevich, I hope you are not driving tonight," Jack said, gesturing with his wineglass to Golovko's vodka. His cheeks were already florid, his blue eyes sparkling with alcoholic mirth.

"Did you enjoy the flight in last night?" the GRU Colonel asked. He laughed merrily before Ryan could reply. "You still fear flying?"

"No, it's hitting the ground that worries me." Jack grinned. He had always been able to laugh at his own pet fear.

"Ah, yes, your back injury from the helicopter crash. One can sympathize."

Ryan waved at the window. "How much snow are we supposed to get tonight?"

"Perhaps half a meter, perhaps more. Not a very large storm, but to-morrow the air will be fresh and clear, and the city will sparkle with a clean blanket of white." Golovko was almost poetic in his description.

Already he's drunk, Ryan told himself. Well, tonight was supposed to be a social occasion, nothing more, and the Russians could be hospitable as hell when they wanted to be. Though one man was experiencing something very different, Jack reminded himself.

"Your family is well?" Golovko asked within earshot of another American delegate.

"Yes, thank you. Yours?"

Golovko gestured for Ryan to follow him over to the drink table. The waiters hadn't come out yet. The intelligence officer selected another glass of clear liquor. "Yes, they are all well." He smiled broadly. Sergey was the very image of Russian good fellowship. His face didn't change a whit as he spoke his next sentence: "I understand that you want to meet Chairman Gerasimov."

Jesus! Jack's expression froze in place; his heart skipped a beat or two. "Really? How did you ever get that idea?"

"I'm not GRU, Ryan, not really. My original assignment was in Third Directorate, but I have since moved on to other things," he explained before laughing again. This laugh was genuine. He'd just invalidated CIA's file on himself—and, he could see, Ryan's own observation. His hand reached out to pat Ryan on the upper arm. "I will leave you now. In five minutes you will walk through the door behind you and to the left as though looking for the men's room. After that, you will follow instructions. Understood?" He patted Ryan's arm again.

"Yes."

"I will not see you again tonight." They shook hands and Golovko moved off.

"Oh, shit," Ryan whispered to himself. A troupe of violins came into the reception room. There must have been ten or fifteen of them, playing gypsy airs as they circulated about. They must have practiced hard, Jack thought, to play in perfect synchronization despite the dark room and their own random meanderings. Their movement and the relative darkness would make it hard to pick out individuals during the reception. It was a clever, professional touch aimed at making it easier for Jack to slip away.

"Hello, Dr. Ryan," another voice said. He was a young Soviet diplomat, a gofer who kept notes and ran errands for the senior people. Now Jack knew that he was also KGB. Gerasimov was not content with a single surprise for the evening, he realized. He wanted to dazzle Ryan with KGB's prowess. *We'll see about that,* Jack thought, but the bravado seemed hollow even to himself. Too soon. Too soon.

"Good evening—we've never met." Jack reached into his pants pocket and felt for his keychain. He hadn't forgotten it.

"My name is Vitaliy. Your absence will not be noticed. The men's room is that way." He pointed. Jack handed over his glass and walked toward the door. He nearly stopped dead on leaving the room. No one inside could have known it, but the corridor had been cleared. Except for one man at the far end, who gestured once. Ryan walked toward him.

Oh, shit. Here we go . . .

He was a youngish man, on the short side of thirty. He looked like the physical type. Though his build was concealed by an overcoat, he moved in the brisk, efficient way of an athlete. His facial expression and penetrating eyes made him a bodyguard. The best thought that came to Ryan was that he was supposed to appear nervous. It didn't require much in the way of talent to do so. The man took him around the corner and handed him a Russian-made overcoat and fur hat, then spoke a single word:

"Come."

He led Ryan down a service corridor and out into the cold air of an alley. Another man was waiting outside, watching. He nodded curtly to Ryan's escort, who turned once and waved for Jack to hurry. The alley ended on Shabolovka Street, and both men turned right. This part of town was old, Jack saw at once. The buildings were mostly pre-revolution. The center of the street had trolley tracks embedded in cobblestones, and overhead were the catenary wires that supplied power to the streetcars. He watched as one rumbled past—actually it was two trams linked together, the colors white over red. Both men sprinted across the slippery street toward a red brick building with what looked like a metal roof. Ryan wasn't sure what it was until they turned the corner.

The car barn, he realized, remembering similar places from his boyhood in Baltimore. The tracks curved in here, then diverged to the various bays in the barn. He paused for a moment, but his escort waved him forward urgently, moving to the left-most service bay. Inside it, of course, were streetcars, lined up like sleeping cattle in the darkness. It was totally still in there, he realized with surprise. There should have been people working, the sound of hammers and machine tools, but there was none of that. Ryan's heart pounded as he walked past two motionless trams. His escort stopped at the third. Its doors were open, and a third bodyguard-type stepped down and looked at Ryan. He immediately patted Jack down, seeking weapons but finding none in a quick but thorough search. A jerk of the thumb directed him up and into the tram.

It had evidently just come in, and there was snow on the first step. Ryan slipped and would have fallen had not one of the KGB men caught his arm. He gave Jack a look that in the West would have been accompanied by a smile, but the Russians are not a smiling people except when they want to be. He went up again, his hands firm on the safety rails. *All you have to do . . .*

"Good evening," a voice called. Not very loudly, but it didn't have to be. Ryan squinted in the darkness and saw the glowing orange light of a cigarette. He took a deep breath and walked toward it.

"Chairman Gerasimov, I presume?"

"You do not recognize me?" A trace of amusement. The man flicked his Western-made butane lighter to illuminate his face. It was Nikolay Borissovich Gerasimov. The flame gave his face exactly the right sort of look. The Prince of Darkness himself . . .

"I do now," Jack said, struggling to control his voice.

"I understand that you wish to speak with me. How may I be of service?" he asked in a courtly voice that belied the setting.

Jack turned and gestured to the two bodyguards who were standing at the front of the car. He turned back but didn't have to say anything. Gerasimov spoke a single word in Russian, and both men left.

"Please excuse them, but their duty is to protect the Chairman, and my people take their duties seriously." He waved to the seat opposite his. Ryan took it.

"I didn't know your English was so good."

"Thank you." A courteous nod followed by a businesslike observation: "I caution you that time is short. You have information for me?"

"Yes, I do." Jack reached inside his coat. Gerasimov tensed for a moment, then relaxed. Only a madman would try to kill the chief of the KGB, and he knew from Ryan's dossier that he was not mad. "I have something for you," said Ryan.

"Oh?" Impatience. Gerasimov was not a man who liked to be kept waiting. He watched Ryan's hands fumble with something, and was puzzled to hear the rasp of metal scraping against metal. Jack's clumsiness disappeared when the key came off the ring, and when he spoke, he was a man claiming another's pot.

"Here." Ryan handed it over.

"What is this?" Suspicion now. Something was very badly wrong, wrong enough that his voice betrayed him.

Jack didn't make him wait. He spoke in a voice he'd been rehearsing for a week. Without knowing it, he spoke faster than he'd planned. "That, Chairman Gerasimov, is the warhead-control key from the Soviet ballistic-missile submarine *Krasny Oktyabr*. It was given to me by Captain Marko Aleksandrovich Ramius when he defected. You will be pleased to know that he likes his new life in America, as do all of his officers."

"The submarine was—"

Ryan cut him off. There was scarcely enough light to see the outline of his face, but that was enough to see the change in the man's expression.

"Destroyed by her own scuttling charges? No. The spook aboard whose cover was ship's cook, Sudets, I think his name was—well, no sense in hiding it. I killed him. I'm not especially proud of that, but it was either him or me. For what it's worth, he was a very courageous young man," Jack said, remembering the ten horrible minutes in the submarine's missile room. "Your file on me doesn't say anything about operations, does it?"

"But—"

Jack cut him off again. It was not yet the time for finesse. They had to jolt him, had to jolt him hard.

"Mr. Gerasimov, there are some things we want from you."

"Rubbish. Our conversation is ended." But Gerasimov didn't rise, and this time Ryan made him wait for a few beats.

"We want Colonel Filitov back. Your official report to the Politburo on *Red October* stated that the submarine was positively destroyed, and that a defection had probably never been planned, but rather that GRU security had been penetrated and that the submarine had been issued bogus orders after her engines had been sabotaged. That information came to you through Agent Cassius. He works for us," Jack explained. "You used it to disgrace Admiral Gorshkov and to reinforce your control over the military's internal security. They're still angry about that, aren't they? So, if we do not get Colonel Filitov back, this coming week in Washington a story will be leaked to the press for the Sunday editions. It will have some of the details of the operation, and a photograph of the submarine sitting in a covered drydock in Norfolk, Virginia. After that we will produce Captain Ramius. He'll say that the ship's political officer—one of your Department Three men, I believe—was part of the conspiracy. Unfortunately, Putin died after arriving, of a heart attack. That's a lie, but try proving it."

"You cannot blackmail me, Ryan!" There was no emotion at all now.

"One more thing. SDI is not on the bargaining table. Did you tell the Politburo that it was?" Jack asked. "You're finished, Mr. Gerasimov. We have the ability to disgrace you, and you're just too good a target to pass up. If we don't get Filitov back, we can leak all sorts of things. Some will be confirmed, but the really good ones will be denied, of course, while the FBI launches an urgent investigation to identify the leakers."

"You did not do all this for Filitov," Gerasimov said, his voice measured now.

"Not exactly." Again he made him wait for it: "We want you to come out, too."

Jack walked out of the tram five minutes later. His escort walked him back to the hotel. The attention to detail was impressive. Before rejoining the reception, Jack's shoes were wiped dry. On reentering the room he walked at once to the drink table, but found it empty. He spotted a waiter with a tray, and took the first thing he could reach. It turned out to be vodka, but Ryan gunned it down in a single gulp before reaching for another. When he finished that one, he started wondering where the men's room really was. It turned out to be exactly where he'd been told. Jack got there just in time.

It was as worked up as anyone had ever been with a computer simulation. They'd never run one quite this way before, of course, and that was the purpose of the test. The ground-control computer didn't know what it was doing, nor did any of the others. One machine was programmed to report a series of distant radar contacts. All it did was to receive a collection of signals like those generated by an orbiting Flying Cloud satellite, cued in turn by one of the DSPS birds at geosynchronous height. The computer relayed this information to the ground-control computer, which examined its criteria for weapons-free authority and decided that they had been met. It took a few seconds for the lasers to power up, but they reported being ready a few seconds later. The fact that the lasers in question did not exist was not pertinent to the test. The ground mirror did, and it responded to instructions from the computer, sending the imaginary laser beam to the relay mirror eight hundred kilometers overhead. This mirror, so recently carried by the space shuttle and actually in California, received its own instructions and altered its configuration accordingly, relaying the laser beam to the battle mirror. This mirror was at the Lockheed factory rather than in orbit, and received its instructions via landline. At all three mirrors a precise record was kept of the ever-changing focal-length and azimuth settings. This information was sent to the score-keeping computer at Tea Clipper Control.

There had been several purposes to the test that Ryan had observed a few weeks before. In validating the system architecture, they had also received priceless empirical data on the actual functioning characteristics of the hardware. As a result they could simulate real exercises on the ground with near-absolute confidence in the theoretical results.

Gregory was rolling a ballpoint pen between his hands as the data came up on the video-display terminal. He'd just stopped chewing on it for fear of getting a mouth full of ink.

"Okay, there's the last shot," an engineer observed. "Here comes the score . . ."

"Wow!" Gregory exclaimed. "Ninety-six out of a hundred! What's the cycle time?"

"Point zero-one-six," a software expert replied. "That's point zero-zero-four *under* nominal—we can double-check every aim-command while the laser cycles—"

"And that increases the Pk thirty percent all by itself," Gregory said. "We can even try doing shoot-look-shoot instead of shoot-shoot-look and still save time on the back end. *People!*"—he jumped to his feet—"*we have done it! The software is in the fuckin' can!" Four months sooner than promised!*

The room erupted with cheering that no one outside the team of thirty people could possibly have understood.

"Okay, you laser pukes!" someone called. "Get your act together and build us a death ray! The gunsight is *finished!*"

"Be nice to the laser pukes." Gregory laughed. "I work with them too."

Outside the room, Beatrice Taussig was merely walking past the door on her way to an admin meeting when she heard the cheering. She couldn't enter the lab—it had a cipher lock, and she didn't have the combination—but didn't have to. The experiment that they'd hinted at over dinner the night before had just been run. The result was obvious enough. Candi was in there, probably standing right next to the Geek, Bea thought. She kept walking.

"Thank God there's not much ice," Mancuso observed, looking through the periscope. "Call it two feet, maybe three."

"There will be a clear channel here. The icebreakers keep all the coastal ports open," Ramius said.

"Down 'scope," the Captain said next. He walked over to the chart table. "I want you to move us two thousand yards south, then bottom us out. That'll put us under a hard roof and ought to keep the Grishas and Mirkas away."

"Aye, Captain," the XO replied.

"Let's go get some coffee," Mancuso said to Ramius and Clark. He led them down one deck and to starboard into the wardroom. For all the times he'd done things like this in the past four years, Mancuso was nervous. They were in less than two hundred feet of water, within sight of the Soviet coast. If detected and then localized by a Soviet ship, they would be attacked. It had happened before. Though no Western submarine had ever suffered actual damage, there was a first time for everything, especially if you started taking things for granted, the Captain of USS *Dallas* told himself. Two feet of ice was too much for the thin-hulled Grisha-class patrol boats to plow through, and their main antisubmarine weapon, a multiple rocket launcher called an RBU-6000, was useless over ice, but a Grisha could call in a submarine. There were Russian subs about. They'd heard two the previous day.

"Coffee, sir?" the wardroom attendant asked. He got a nod and brought out a pot and cups.

"You sure this is close enough?" Mancuso asked Clark.

"Yeah, I can get in and out."

"It won't be much fun," the Captain observed.

Clark smirked. "That's why they pay me so much. I—"

Conversation stopped for a moment. The submarine's hull creaked as it settled on the bottom, and the boat took on a slight list. Mancuso looked at the coffee in his cup and figured it for six or seven degrees. Submariner machismo prevented him from showing any reaction, but he'd never done this, at least not with *Dallas*. A handful of submarines in the U.S. Navy were specially designed for these missions. Insiders could identify them at a glance from the arrangement of a few hull fittings, but *Dallas* wasn't one of them.

"I wonder how long this is going to take?" Mancuso asked the overhead.

"May not happen at all," Clark observed. "Almost half of them don't. The longest I've ever had to sit like this was . . . twelve days, I think. Seemed like an awfully long time. That one didn't come off."

"Can you say how many?" Ramius asked.

"Sorry, sir." Clark shook his head.

Ramius spoke wistfully. "You know, when I was a boy, I fished here— right here many times. We never knew that you Americans came here to fish also."

"It's a crazy world," Clark agreed. "How's the fishing?"

"In the summer, very good. Old Sasha took me out on his boat. This is where I learned the sea, where I learned to be a sailor."

"What about the local patrols?" Mancuso asked, getting everyone back to business.

"There will be a low state of readiness. You have diplomats in Moscow, so the chance of war is slight. The surface patrol ships are mainly KGB. They guard against smugglers—and spies." He pointed to Clark. "Not so good against submarines, but this was changing when I left. They were increasing their ASW practice in Northern Fleet, and, I hear, in Baltic Fleet also. But this is bad place for submarine detection. There is much fresh water from the rivers, and the ice overhead—all makes for difficult sonar conditions."

That's good to hear, Mancuso thought. His ship was in an increased state of readiness. The sonar equipment was fully manned and would remain so indefinitely. He could get *Dallas* moving in a matter of two minutes, and that should be ample, he thought.

Gerasimov was thinking, too. He was alone in his office. A man who controlled his emotions even more than most Russians, his face displayed nothing out of the way, even though there was no one else in the room to notice. In most people that would have been remarkable, for few can contemplate their own destruction with objectivity.

The Chairman of the Committee for State Security assessed his position as thoroughly and dispassionately as he examined any aspect of his official duties. *Red October.* It all flowed out from that. He had used the *Red October* incident to his advantage, first suborning Gorshkov, then disposing of him; he'd also used it to strengthen the position of his Third Directorate arm. The military had begun to manage its own internal security—but Gerasimov had seized upon his report from Agent Cassius to convince the Politburo that the KGB alone could ensure the loyalty and security of the Soviet military. That had earned him resentment. He'd reported, again via Cassius, that *Red October* had been destroyed. Cassius had told KGB that Ryan was under criminal suspicion, and—

And we—I!—walked into the trap.

How could he explain that to the Politburo? One of his best agents had been doubled—but when? They'd ask that, and he didn't know the answer; therefore all the reports received from Cassius would become suspect. Despite the fact that much good data had come from the agent, knowledge that he'd been doubled at an unknown time tainted all of it. And that wrecked his vaunted insights into Western political thought.

He'd wrongly reported that the submarine hadn't defected, and not discovered the error. The Americans had gotten an intelligence windfall, but KGB didn't know of it. Neither did GRU, but that was little comfort.

And he'd reported that the Americans had made a major change in their arms-negotiation strategy, and that, too, was wrong.

Could he survive all three disclosures at once? Gerasimov asked himself. Probably not.

In another age he would have faced death, and that would have made the decision all the easier. No man chooses death, at least not a sane one, and Gerasimov was coldly sane in everything he did. But that sort of thing didn't happen now. He'd end up with a subministerial job somewhere or other, shuffling papers. His KGB contacts would be useless to him beyond such meaningless favors as access to decent groceries. People would watch him walking on the street—no longer afraid to look him in the face, no longer fearful of his power, they'd point and laugh behind his back. People in his office would gradually lose their deference, and talk back, even shout at him once they knew that his power was well and truly gone. No, he said to himself, I will not endure that.

To defect, then? To go from being one of the world's most powerful men to becoming a hireling, a mendicant who traded what he knew for money and a comfortable life? Gerasimov accepted the fact that his life would become more comfortable in physical terms—but to lose his *power!*

That was the issue, after all. Whether he left or stayed, to become just another man . . . *that would be like death, wouldn't it?*

Well, what do you do now?

He had to change his position, had to change the rules of the game, had to do something so dramatic . . . but what?

The choice was between disgrace and defection? To lose everything he'd worked for—within sight of his goal—and face a choice like this?

The Soviet Union is not a nation of gamblers. Its national strategy has always been more reflective of the Russians' national passion for chess, a series of careful, pre-planned moves, never risking much, always protecting its position by seeking small, progressive advantages wherever possible. The Politburo had almost always moved in that way. The Politburo itself was largely composed of similar men. More than half were *apparatchiks* who had spoken the appropriate words, filled the necessary quotas, taking what advantages they could, and who had won advancement through a stolidness whose perfection they could display around the table in the Kremlin. But the function of those men was to provide a moderating influence on those who aspired to rule, and these men were the gamblers. Narmonov was a gambler. So was Gerasimov. He'd play his own game, allying himself with Alexandrov to establish his ideological constituency, blackmailing Vaneyev and Yazov to betray their master.

And it was too fine a game to quit so easily. He had to change the rules again, but the game did not really have any rules—except for the one: Win.

If he won—the disgraces would not matter, would they?

Gerasimov took the key from his pocket and examined it for the first time in the light of his desk lamp. It looked ordinary enough. Used in the designed manner, it would make possible the deaths of—fifty million? A hundred? More? The Directorate Three men on the submarines and in the land-based rocket regiments held that power—the *zampolit,* the political officer alone had the authority to activate the warheads without which the rockets were mere fireworks. Turn this key in the proper way at the proper time, he knew, and the rockets were transformed into the most frightening instruments of death yet devised by the mind of man. Once launched, nothing could stop them . . .

But that rule was going to be changed, too, wasn't it?

What was it worth to be the man who could do that?

"Ah." Gerasimov smiled. It was worth more than all the other rules combined, and he remembered that the Americans had broken a rule, too, in killing their courier in the Moskvich railyard. He lifted his phone and called for a communications officer. For once the longitudinal lines worked in his favor.

Dr. Taussig was surprised when she saw the signal. One thing about "Ann" was that she never altered her routine. Despite the fact that she'd impulsively visited her contact, heading to the shopping center was her normal Saturday routine. She parked her Datsun fairly far out, lest some klutz in a Chevy Malibu smash his door against hers. On the way in, she saw Ann's Volvo, and the driver's side visor was down. Taussig checked her watch and increased her pace to the entrance. On going in, she turned left.

Peggy Jennings was working alone today. They were spread too thin to get the job done as fast as Washington wanted, but that wasn't exactly a new story, was it? The setting was both good and bad. Following her subject to the shopping mall was fairly easy, but once inside it was damned near impossible to trail a subject properly, unless you had a real team of agents operating. She got to the door only a minute behind Taussig, already knowing that she'd lost her. Well, this was only a preliminary look at her. Routine, Jennings told herself on opening the door.

Jennings looked up and down the mall and failed to see her subject. Frowning for a moment, she commenced a leisurely stroll from shop to shop, gazing in the windows and wondering if Taussig had gone to a movie.

"Hello, Ann!"

"Bea!" Bisyarina said inside Eve's Leaves. "How are you?"

"Keeping busy," Dr. Taussig replied. "That looks wonderful on you."

"She's so easy to fit," the shop owner observed.

"Easier than me," Taussig agreed glumly. She lifted a suit from the nearest rack and walked to a mirror. Severely cut, it suited her present mood. "Can I try this one on?"

"Surely," the owner said at once. It was a three-hundred-dollar outfit. "Need a hand?" "Ann" asked.

"Sure—you can tell me what you're up to." Both women walked back to the dressing rooms.

Within the booth, both women chatted away, discussing the everyday things that differ little between women and men. Bisyarina handed over a slip of paper, which Taussig read. The latter's conversation stuttered for a moment before she nodded agreement. Her face switched from shock to acceptance, then switched again to something that Bisyarina did not like at all—but the KGB didn't pay her to like her job.

The suit fitted rather nicely, the owner saw when they came out. Taussig paid the way most people did, with a credit card. Ann waved and left, turning to walk past the gun shop on her way out the mall.

Jennings saw her subject come out of the shop a few minutes later, carrying a clear plastic garment bag. *Well, that's what it was,* she told herself. *Whatever was bothering her the other night, she went shopping to make herself feel better and got another one of those suits.* Jennings followed her for another hour before breaking off the surveillance. Nothing there.

"He's one cool dude," Ryan told Candela. "I didn't expect him to jump into my lap and thank me for the offer, but I expected *some* reaction!"

"Well, if he bites, he'll get word to you easy enough."

"Yeah."

21. Knave's Gambit

The Archer tried to tell himself that the weather was no man's ally, but surely this was not true. The skies were clear, the winds cold and from the northeast, sweeping down from the frigid center of Siberia. He wanted clouds. They could move only in darkness now. That made progress slow, and the longer they were here in Soviet territory, the greater the chance that someone would notice them, and if they were noticed . . .

There was little need to speculate about that. All he had to do was raise his head to watch the armored vehicles motoring along the Dangara road. There was at least a battalion stationed around here, possibly a whole regiment of motor-rifle troops who constantly patrolled the roads and tracks. His force was large and formidable by *mudjaheddin* standards, but against Russians in regimental force on their own land, only Allah Himself could save them. *And perhaps not even Him?* the Archer wondered, then chastised himself for the unspoken blasphemy.

His son was not far away, probably less than the distance they'd traveled to be here—but where? A place he would never find. The Archer was certain of that. He'd given up hope long ago. His son would be raised in the alien, infidel ways of the Russians, and all he could do was pray that Allah would come to his son before it was too late. To steal children, surely that was the most heinous of all crimes. To rob them of their parents and their faith . . . well, there was no need to dwell on that.

Every one of his men had reason enough to hate the Russians. Families killed or scattered, homes bombed. His men did not know that this was the usual business of modern war. As "primitives," they felt that battles were affairs for warriors alone. Their leader knew that this had stopped being true long before any of them was born. He didn't understand why the "civilized" nations of the world had changed this sensible rule, but he only needed to know that it was. With this knowledge had come the awareness that his destiny was not the one he'd selected for himself. The Archer wondered if any man truly chose his fate, or was it not all in greater hands than those which held book or rifle? But that was another complex, useless thought, since for the Archer and his men, the world had distilled itself to a few simple truths and a few deep hates. Perhaps that would someday change, but for the *mudjaheddin* the world was limited to what they could see and feel now. To search further was to lose sight of what mattered, and that meant death. The only great thought held by his men was their faith, and for the moment that was enough.

The last vehicle in the column disappeared around the bend in the road. The Archer shook his head. He'd had enough of thinking for the present. The Russians he'd just watched had all been inside their tracked BMP infantry carriers, inside where they could be kept warm by the fighting vehicle's heater; inside where they could not see out very well. That was what mattered. He raised his head to see his men, well camouflaged by their Russian-issue clothing and hidden behind rocks, lying in crevices, paired off, which allowed one to sleep while the other, like their leader, watched and kept guard.

The Archer looked up to see the sun now in decline. Soon it would slide behind the mountain ridge, and his men could resume their march north. He saw the sun glint off the aluminum skin of an aircraft as it turned in the air high overhead.

Colonel Bondarenko had a window seat and was staring down at the forbidding mountains. He remembered his brief tour of duty in Afghanistan, the endless, leg-killing mountains where one could travel in a perfect circle and seem to go uphill all the way. Bondarenko shook his head. That, at least, was behind him. He'd served his time, tasted combat, and now he could go back to applied engineering science which was, after all, his first love. Combat operations were a young man's game, and Gennady Iosifovich was over forty now. Having once proven that he could climb the rocks with the young bucks, he was resolved never to do so again. Besides, there was something else on his mind.

What's happening with Misha? he asked himself. When the man had disappeared from the Ministry, he'd naturally assumed that the older man was ill. When the absence had lasted several days, he took it to be serious and asked the Minister if Colonel Filitov had been hospitalized. The reply at the time had been reassuring—but now he wondered. Minister Yazov had been a little too glib—then Bondarenko had gotten orders to return to Bright Star for an extended evaluation of the site. The Colonel felt that he was being shuffled out of the way—but why? Something about the way Yazov had reacted to his innocent inquiry? Then there was the matter of the surveillance he'd spotted. Could the two things be connected? The connection was so obvious that Bondarenko ignored it without conscious consideration. It was simply impossible that Misha could have been the target of a security investigation, and even less possible that the investi-

THE CARDINAL OF THE KREMLIN • 771

gation should develop substantive evidence of misdeeds. The most likely thing, he concluded, was that Misha was off on a top-secret job for Yazov. Surely he did a lot of that. Bondarenko looked down at the massive earth-work of the Nurek power dam. The second string of power lines was almost done, he noted, as the airliner dropped flaps and wheels for a landing at Dushanbe-East. He was the first man to leave the aircraft after landing.

"Gennady Iosifovich!"

"Good morning, Comrade General," Bondarenko said in some surprise.

"Come with me," Pokryshkin said, after returning the Colonel's salute. "You don't want to ride that damned bus." He waved to his sergeant, who wrested away Bondarenko's bag.

"You didn't need to come yourself."

"Rubbish." Pokryshkin led the parade to his personal helicopter, whose rotor was already turning. "One day I must read that report you drafted. I just had three *ministers* here yesterday. Now everyone understands how important we are. Our funding is being increased twenty-five percent—I wish *I* could write that kind of report!"

"But I—"

"Colonel, I don't want to hear it. You have seen the truth and com-municated it to others. You are now part of the Bright Star family. I want you to think about coming to us full time after your Moscow tour is finished. According to your file, you have excellent engineering and administrative credentials, and I need a good second-in-command." He turned with a conspiratorial look. "I don't suppose I could talk you into an air-force uniform?"

"Comrade General, I—"

"I know, once a soldier of the Red Army, always a soldier of the Red Army. We will not hold it against you. Besides, you can help me with those KGB boneheads on perimeter guard. They can bluster their expertise at a broken-down fighter pilot, but not against a man with the Red Banner for close combat." The General waved for the pilot to take off. Bondarenko was surprised that the commander wasn't flying the aircraft himself. "I tell you, Gennady, in a few years this will be a whole new service branch. 'Cosmic Defense Troops,' perhaps. There will be room for you to create a whole new career, and plenty of room for advancement. I want you to give that some serious thought. You will probably be a general in three or four years anyway, but I can guarantee you more stars than the Army can."

"For the moment, however . . . ?" He'd think about that, but not in a helicopter.

"We're looking at the mirror and computer plans the Americans are using. The chief of our mirror group thinks he can adapt their designs to our hardware. It will take about a year to come up with the plans, he says, but he doesn't know about the actual engineering. Meanwhile we're as-sembling some reserve lasers and trying to simplify the design to make maintenance easier."

"That's another two years' work," Bondarenko observed.

"At least," General Pokryshkin agreed. "This program will not come to fruition before I leave. That's inevitable. If we have one more major test success, I will be recalled to Moscow to head the Ministry office, and at best the system will not be deployed before I retire." He shook his head sadly. "It's a hard thing to accept, how long these projects take now. That's why I want you here. I need a young man who will carry this project all the way through. I've looked at a score of officers. You're the best of them, Gennady Iosifovich. I want you here to take over from me when the time comes."

Bondarenko was stunned. Pokryshkin had selected him, doubtless in preference to men from his own service branch. "But you hardly know me—"

"I did not get to be a general officer by being ignorant of people. You have the qualities that I look for, and you are at just the right part of your career—ready for an independent command. Your uniform is less important than the type of man you are. I've already telexed the Minister to this effect."

Well. Bondarenko was still too surprised to be pleased. *And all because Old Misha decided that I was the best man to make an inspection tour. I hope he's not too ill.*

"He's been going over nine hours now," one of the officers said almost accusingly to Vatutin. The Colonel bent to look in the fiber-optic tube and watched the man for several minutes. He was lying down at first, tossing and turning fitfully as he tried willing himself to sleep, but that effort was doomed to failure. After that came the nausea and diarrhea from the caffeine that denied him sleep. Next he rose and resumed the pacing he'd been doing for hours, trying to tire himself into the sleep that part of his body demanded while the remainder objected.

"Get him up here in twenty minutes." The KGB Colonel looked at his subordinate with amusement. He'd slept only seven hours and spent the last two making sure that the orders he'd given before turning in had been carried out in full. Then he'd showered and shaved. A messenger had fetched a fresh uniform from his apartment while an orderly had polished his boots to a mirrorlike luster. Vatutin finished off his own breakfast and treated himself to an extra cup of coffee brought down from the senior-officers' mess. He ignored the looks he was getting from the other members of his interrogation team, not even giving them a cryptic smile to indicate that he knew what he was doing. If they didn't know that by now, then the hell with them. Finished, he wiped his mouth with the napkin and walked to the interrogation room.

Like most such rooms, the bare table it held was more than it appeared to be. Under the lip where the tabletop overlapped the supporting frame were several buttons that he could press without anyone's noticing. Several microphones were set in the apparently blank walls, and the single adornment on them, a mirror, was actually two-way, so that the subject could be observed and photographed from the next room.

Vatutin sat down and got out the folder that he'd be putting away when Filitov arrived. His mind went over what he'd do. He already had it fully planned, of course, including the wording of his verbal report to Chairman Gerasimov. He checked his watch, nodded to the mirror, and spent the next several minutes composing himself for what was to come. Filitov arrived right on time.

He looked strong, Vatutin saw. Strong but haggard. That was the caffeine with which his last meal had been laced. The façade he projected was hard, but brittle and thin. Filitov showed irritation now. Before, he'd shown only resolve.

"Good morning, Filitov," Vatutin said, hardly looking up.

"*Colonel* Filitov to you. Tell me, when will this charade be over?"

He probably believes that, too, Vatutin told himself. The subject had so often repeated the story of how Vatutin had placed the film cassette in his hand that he might have halfway believed it now. That was not unusual. He took his chair without asking permission, and Vatutin waved the turnkey out of the room.

"When did you decide to betray the Motherland?" Vatutin asked.

"When did you decide to stop buggering little boys?" the old man replied angrily.

"Filitov—excuse me, *Colonel* Filitov—you know that you were arrested with a microfilm cassette in your hand, only two meters from an American intelligence officer. On that microfilm cassette was information about a highly secret State defense-research installation, which information you have been giving for years to the Americans. There is no question of this, in case you have forgotten," Vatutin explained patiently. "What I am asking is, how long have you been doing this?"

"Go bugger yourself," Misha suggested. Vatutin noticed a slight tremor in his hands. "I am three times Hero of the Soviet Union. I was killing the enemies of this country while you were an ache in your father's crotch, and you have the balls to call me traitor?"

"You know, when I was in grammar school, I read books about you. Misha, driving the *fascisti* back from the gates of Moscow. Misha, the demon tankist. Misha, the Hero of Stalingrad. Misha, killer of Germans. Misha, leading the counterattack at the Kursk Bulge. Misha," Vatutin said finally, "traitor to the Motherland."

Misha waved his hand, looking in annoyance at the way it shook. "I have never had much respect for the *chekisti*. When I was leading my men, they were there—behind us. They were very efficient at shooting prisoners—prisoners that real soldiers had taken. They were also rather good at murdering people who'd been forced to retreat. I even remember one case where a *chekist* lieutenant took command of a tank troop and led it into a fucking swamp. At least the Germans I killed were men, fighting men. I hated them, but I could respect them for the soldiers they were. Your kind, on the other hand . . . perhaps we simple soldiers never really understood who the enemy was. Sometimes I wonder who has killed more Russians, the Germans—or people like you?"

Vatutin was unmoved. "The traitor Penkovskiy recruited you, didn't he?"

"Rubbish! I reported Penkovskiy myself." Filitov shrugged. He was surprised at the way he felt, but was unable to control it. "I suppose your kind does have its use. Oleg Penkovskiy was a sad, confused man who paid the price that such men have to pay."

"As will you," Vatutin said.

"I cannot prevent you from killing me, but I have seen death too many times. Death has taken my wife and my sons. Death has taken so many of my comrades—and death has tried to take me often enough. Sooner or later death will win, whether from you or someone else. I have forgotten how to fear that."

"Tell me, what do you fear?"

"Not you." This was delivered not with a smile, but with a cold, challenging glare.

"But all men fear something," Vatutin observed. "Did you fear combat?" *Ah, Misha, you're talking too much now. Do you even know that?*

"Yes, at first. The first time a shell hit my T-34, I wet my pants. But only that first time. After that I knew that the armor would stop most hits. A man can get accustomed to physical danger, and as an officer you are often too busy to realize that you're supposed to be afraid. You fear for the men under your command. You fear failure in a combat assignment, because others depend on you. You always fear pain—not death, but pain." Filitov surprised himself by talking this much, but he'd had enough of this KGB slug. It was almost like the frenetic excitement of combat, sitting here and dueling with this man.

"I have read that all men fear combat, but that what sustains them is their self-image. They know that they cannot let their comrades perceive them to be less than what they are supposed to be. Men, therefore, fear cowardice more than danger. They fear betraying their manhood, and their fellow soldiers." Misha nodded slightly. Vatutin pressed one of the buttons under the table. "Filitov, you have betrayed your men. Can't you see that? Don't you understand that in giving defense secrets to the enemy, you have betrayed all the men who served with you?"

"It will take more than your words to—"

The door opened quietly. The young man who entered wore dirty, greasy coveralls, and wore the ribbed helmet of a tank crewman. All the details were right: there was a trailing wire for the tank's interphones, and the powerful smell of powder came into the room with the young man. The coverall was torn and singed. His face and hands were bandaged. Blood dripped down from the covered eye, clearing a trail through the grime. And he was the living image of Aleksey Il'ych Romanov, Corporal of the Red Army, or as close to it as the KGB could manage in one frantic night's effort.

Filitov didn't hear him enter, but turned as soon as he noticed the smell. His mouth dropped open in shock.

"Tell me, Filitov," Vatutin said. "How do you think your men would react if they learned what you have done?"

The young man—he was in fact a corporal who worked for a minor functionary in the Third Directorate—did not say a word. The chemical irritant in his right eye was making it water, and while the youngster struggled not to grimace at the pain it caused him, the tears ran down his cheeks. Filitov didn't know that his meal had been drugged—so disoriented was he by his stay in Lefortovo that he no longer had the ability to register the things that were being done to him. The caffeine had induced the exact opposite of a drunken state. His mind was as wide awake as it had been in combat, all his senses sought input, noticed everything that was happening around him—but all through the night there had been nothing to report. Without data to pass on, his senses had begun making things up, and Filitov had been hallucinating when the guards had come to fetch him. In Vatutin he had a target on which to fix his psyche. But Misha was also tired, exhausted by the routine to which he had been subjected, and the combination of wakefulness and bone-crushing fatigue had placed him in a dreamlike state where he no longer had the ability to distinguish the real from the imaginary.

"Turn *around*, Filitov!" Vatutin boomed. "Look at me when I address you! I asked you a question: *What of all the men who served you?*"

"Who—"

"Who? The men you led, you old fool!"

"But—" He turned again, and the figure was gone.

"I've been looking through your file, all those citations you wrote for your men—more than most commanders. Ivanenko here, and Pukhov, and this Corporal Romanov. All the men who died for you, what would they think now?"

"They would understand!" Misha insisted as the anger took over completely.

"What would they understand? Tell me now, what is it that they would understand?"

"Men like you killed them—not I, not the Germans, but men like you!"

"And your sons, too, eh?"

"Yes! My two handsome sons, my two strong, brave boys, they went to follow in my footsteps and—"

"Your wife, too?"

"That above all!" Filitov snarled back. He leaned forward across the table. "You have taken everything from me, you *chekist* bastard—and you wonder that I needed to fight back at you? No man has served the State better than I, and look at my reward, look at the gratitude of the Party. All that was my world you have taken away, and you say that I have betrayed the *Rodina*, do you? *You* have betrayed her, and you have betrayed me!"

"And because of that, Penkovskiy approached you, and because of that you have been feeding information to the West—you've fooled us all these years!"

"It is no great thing to fool the likes of you!" He pounded his fist on the table. "Thirty years, Vatutin, thirty years I have—I have—" He stopped, a curious look on his face, wondering what he had just said.

Vatutin took his time before speaking, and when he did so, his voice was gentle. "Thank you, Comrade Colonel. That is quite enough for now. Later we will talk about exactly what you have given the West. I despise you for what you have done, Misha. I cannot forgive or understand treason, but you're the bravest man I have ever met. I hope that you can face what remains of your life with equal bravery. It is important now that you face yourself and your crimes as courageously as you faced the *fascisti,* so that your life can end as honorably as you lived it." Vatutin pressed a button and the door opened. The guards took Filitov away, still looking back at the interrogator, more surprised than anything else. Surprised that he'd been tricked. He'd never understand how it had been done, but then they rarely did, the Colonel of the Second Chief Directorate told himself. He rose, too, after a minute, collecting his files in a businesslike way before he walked out of the room and upstairs.

"You would have been a fine psychiatrist," the doctor observed first of all.

"I hope the tape machines got all of that," Vatutin said to his technicians.

"All three, plus the television record."

"That was the hardest one I've ever come across," a major said.

"Yes, he was a hard one. A brave one. Not an adventurer, not a dissident. That one was a patriot—or that's what the poor bastard thought he was. He wanted to save the country from the Party." Vatutin shook his head in wonderment. "Where do they get such ideas?"

Your Chairman, he reminded himself, *wants to do much the same thing— or more accurately to save the country* for *Party.* Vatutin leaned against the wall for a moment while he tried to decide how similar or how different the motivation was. He concluded quickly that this was not a proper thought for a simple counterintelligence officer. At least not yet. *Filitov got his ideas from the clumsy way the Party treated his family. Well, even though the Party says it never makes mistakes, we all know differently. What a pity that Misha couldn't make that allowance. After all, the Party is all we have.*

"Doctor, make sure he gets some rest," he said on the way out. There was a car waiting for him.

Vatutin was surprised to see that it was morning. He'd allowed himself to focus too fully these last two days, and he'd thought that it would be nighttime. So much the better, though: he could see the Chairman right now. The really amazing part was that he was actually on a fairly normal schedule. He could go home tonight and get a normal night's sleep, reacquaint himself with wife and family, watch some television. Vatutin smiled to himself. He could also look forward to a promotion, he told himself. After all, he'd broken the man earlier than promised. That ought to make the Chairman happy.

Vatutin caught him between meetings. He found Gerasimov in a pensive mood, staring out his window at the traffic on Dzerzhinskiy Square.

"Comrade Chairman, I have the confession," Vatutin announced. Gerasimov turned.

"Filitov?"

"Why, yes, Comrade Chairman." Vatutin allowed his surprise to show.

Gerasimov smiled after a moment. "Excuse me, Colonel. There is an operational matter on my mind at the moment. You do have his confession?"

"Nothing detailed yet, of course, but he did admit that he was sending secrets to the West, and that he has been doing so for thirty years."

"Thirty years—and all that time we didn't detect it . . ." Gerasimov noted quietly.

"That is correct," Vatutin admitted. "But we have caught him, and we will spend weeks learning all that he has compromised. I think we will find that his placement and operational methods made detection difficult, but we will learn from this, as we have learned from all such cases. In any event, you required the confession and now we have it," the Colonel pointed out.

"Excellent," the Chairman replied. "When will your written report be ready?"

"Tomorrow?" Vatutin asked without thinking. He nearly cringed awaiting the reply. He expected to have his head snapped off, but Gerasimov thought for an infinity of seconds before nodding.

"That is sufficient. Thank you, Comrade Colonel. That will be all."

Vatutin drew himself to attention and saluted before leaving.

Tomorrow? he asked himself in the corridor. *After all that, he's willing to wait until tomorrow?*

What the hell? It didn't make any sense. But Vatutin had no immediate explanation, either, and he did have a report to file. The Colonel walked to his office, pulled out a lined pad, and started drafting his interrogation report.

"So that's the place?" Ryan asked.

"That's it. Used to be they had a toy store right across from it, over there. Called Children's World, would you believe? I suppose somebody finally noticed how crazy that was, and they just moved it. The statue in the middle is Feliks Dzerzhinskiy. That was a cold bloody piece of work— next to him Heinrich Himmler was a boy scout."

"Himmler wasn't as smart," Jack observed.

"True enough. Feliks broke at least three attempts to bring Lenin down, and one of them was pretty serious. The full story on that never has gotten out, but you can bet the records are right in there," the driver said. He was an Australian, part of the company contracted to handle perimeter security for the embassy, and a former commando of the Aussie SAS. He never performed any actual espionage activities—at least not for America—but he often played the part, doing strange things. He'd learned to spot and shake tails along the way, and that made the Russians certain that he was CIA or some sort of spook. He made an excellent tour guide, too.

He checked the mirror. "Our friends are still there. You don't expect anything, do you?"

"We'll see." Jack turned. They weren't being very subtle, but he hadn't expected that they would. "Where's Frunze?"

"South of the embassy, mate. You should have told me that you wanted to go there, we'd have hit it first." He made a legal U-turn while Ryan kept looking back. Sure enough, the Zhiguli—it looked like an old Fiat—did the same, following them like a faithful dog. They went past the American compound again on the way, past the former Greek Orthodox church known to embassy wags as Our Lady of the Microchips for all the surveillance devices it surely contained.

"What exactly are we doing?" the driver asked.

"We're just driving around. The last time I was here, all I saw was the way to and from the Foreign Ministry and the inside of a palace."

"And if our friends get any closer?"

"Well, if they want to talk with me, I suppose I might oblige," Ryan answered.

"Are you serious?" He knew Ryan was CIA.

"You bet." Jack chuckled.

"You know I have to do a written report on things like that?"

"You have your job. I have mine." They drove around for another hour, but nothing happened. That was to Ryan's disappointment, and the driver's relief.

They arrived the usual way. Though the crossing points were shuffled at random, the car—it was a Plymouth Reliant, about four years old, with Oklahoma tags—stopped at the Border Patrol control booth. There were three men inside, one of whom appeared to be asleep and had to be roused.

"Good evening," the Border Patrolman said. "Could I see some identification, please?" All three men handed over driver's licenses, and the photographs matched. "Anything to declare?"

"Some booze. Two quarts—I mean liters—for each of us." He watched with interest as a dog sniffed around the car. "You want us to pull over and pop the trunk?"

"Why were you in Mexico?"

"We represent Cummings-Oklahoma Tool and Die. Pipeline and refinery equipment," the driver explained. "Mainly large-diameter control valves and like that. We're trying to sell some to Pemex. The sales stuff is in the trunk, too."

"Any luck?" the Border Patrolman asked.

"First try. It'll take a few more. They usually do."

The dog handler shook his head negatively. His Labrador wasn't interested in the car. No smell of drugs. No smell of nitrates. The men in the car didn't fit the profile. They looked fairly clean-cut, but not overly so, and had not chosen a busy time to make the crossing.

"Welcome back," the patrolman said. "Safe trip home."

"Thank you, sir." The driver nodded and dropped the car into drive. "See ya."

"I don't believe it," the man in the back said, once they were a hundred meters away from the control point. He spoke in English. "They don't have the first idea of security."

"My brother's a major in the Border Guards. I think he'd have a heart attack if he saw how easy that was," the driver observed. He didn't laugh. The hard part would be getting out, and as of now they were in enemy territory. He drove right at the posted speed limit while local drivers whizzed by him. He liked the American car. Though it lacked power, he'd never driven a car with more than four cylinders and didn't really know the difference. He'd been in the United States four times before, but never for a job like this, and never with so little preparation.

All three spoke perfect American English, with a prairie twang to co-incide with their identification papers—that's how they all thought of their driver's licenses and Social Security cards, even though they could hardly be called proper "papers." The odd thing was that he liked America, especially the easy availability of inexpensive, wholesome food. He'd stop at a fast-food place on the way to Santa Fe, preferably a Burger King, where he'd indulge his love for a charcoal-cooked hamburger served with lettuce, tomatoes, and mayonnaise. That was one of the things Soviets found most amazing about America, the way anyone could get food without standing in a block-long line. And it was usually good food. How could Americans be so good at difficult tasks like food production and distri-bution, he wondered, and be so stupid about simple things like proper security? They just didn't make any sense at all, but it was wrong—dan-gerous—to be contemptuous of them. He understood that. The Americans played by a set of rules so different as to be incomprehensible . . . and there was so much *randomness* here. That frightened the KGB officer in a fundamental way. You couldn't tell which way they'd jump any more than you could predict the behavior of a driver on a highway. More than anything else, it was that unpredictability that reminded him that he was on the enemy's ground. He and his men had to be careful, had to keep to their training. Being at ease in an alien environment was the surest route to disaster—that lesson had been pounded home all the way through the academy. There were just too many things that training could not do. The KGB could scarcely predict what the American government would do. There was no way they could be prepared for the individual actions of two hundred-plus million people who bounced from decision to decision.

That was it, he thought. They have to make so many *decisions* every day. Which food to buy, which road to take, which car to drive. He won-dered how his countrymen would handle such a huge load of decisions, forced upon you every day. Chaos, he knew. It would result in anarchy, and that was historically the greatest fear of Russians.

"I wish we had roads like this at home," the man next to him said. The one in the back was asleep, for real this time. For both of them it was the first time in America. The operation had been laid on too fast. Oleg had done several jobs in South America, always covered as an American busi-nessman. A Moscovite, he remembered that there, once you were twenty kilometers beyond the outer ring road, all the roads were gravel, or simply dirt. The Soviet Union did not have a single paved road that led from one border to another.

The driver—his name was Leonid—thought about that. "Where would the money come from?"

"True," Oleg agreed tiredly. They'd been driving for ten hours. "But you'd think we could have roads as good as Mexico."

"Hmph." *But then people would have to choose where they wanted to go, and no one had ever bothered to train them how.* He looked at the clock on the dashboard. Six more hours, maybe seven.

Captain Tania Bisyarina came to much the same conclusion as she checked the dashboard clock in her Volvo. The safe house in this case wasn't a house at all, but an old house-trailer that looked more like the sort used as mobile offices by contractors and engineers. It had started life as the former, but ended as the latter when an engineering firm had abandoned it a few years before, after half-completing their project in the hills south of Santa Fe. The drainage lines and sewers they'd been installing for a new housing development had never been finished. The developer had lost his financing, and the property was still tied up in court battles. The location was perfect, close to the interstate, close to the city, but hidden away behind a ridge and marked only by a dirt access road that even the local teenagers hadn't discovered yet for their post-dance parking. The visibility question was both good and bad news. Scrub pines hid the trailer from view, but also allowed clandestine approach. They'd have to post an outside guard. Well, you couldn't have everything. She'd driven in without lights, having carefully timed her arrival for a time when the nearest road was effectively deserted. From the back of her Volvo, she unloaded two bags of groceries. The trailer had no electricity, and all the food had to be nonperishable. That meant the meat was plastic-wrapped sausage, and she had a dozen cans of sardines. Russians love them. Once the groceries were in, she got a small suitcase from her car and set it next to the two jerricans of water in the nonfunctional bathroom.

She would have preferred curtains on the windows, but it was not a good idea to alter the appearance of the trailer too much. Nor was it a very good idea to have a car there. After the team arrived, they'd find a heavily wooded spot a hundred meters up the dirt road to leave it. That was also a minor annoyance, but one for which they had to prepare. Setting up safe houses was never as easy as people thought, certainly not the covert kind, even in places as open as America. It would have been somewhat easier if she'd had decent warning, but this operation had been laid on virtually overnight, and the only place she had was the rough-and-ready spot she'd picked out soon after arriving. It wasn't intended for anything other than a place for her to hole up, or perhaps safeguard her agent should it ever become necessary. It had never been intended for the mission at hand, but there wasn't time to make any other arrangements. The only other alternative was her own home, and that was definitely out. Bisyarina wondered if she'd be disciplined for not having scouted out a better location, but knew that she'd followed her instructions to the letter in all of her field activities.

The furniture was functional, though dirty. With nothing better to do, she wiped it off. The team leader coming in was a senior officer. She didn't know his name or face, but he had to have more rank than she did for this kind of job. When the trailer's single couch was reasonably presentable, she stretched out for a nap, having first set a small alarm clock to wake her in several hours. It seemed that she'd just lain down when the bell startled her off the vinyl cushions.

They arrived an hour before dawn. The road signs made it easy, and Leonid had the route completely memorized. Five miles—he had to think in miles now—off the interstate, he turned right onto a side road. Just past a road sign advertising a cigarette, he saw the dirt road that seemingly led nowhere. He switched off the car's lights and coasted up to it, careful to keep his foot off the brake lest his taillights betray him in the trees. Over the first small ridge, the road dropped and curved to the right. There was the Volvo. Next to it was a figure.

This was always the tense part. He was making contact with a fellow KGB officer, but he knew of cases where things hadn't gone quite right. He set the parking brake and got out.

"Lost?" the woman's voice asked.

"I'm looking for Mountain View," he replied.

"That's on the other side of town," she said.

"Oh, I must have taken the wrong exit." He could see her relax when he completed the sequence.

"Tania Bisyarina. Call me Ann."

"I'm Bob," Leonid said. "In the car are Bill and Lenny."

"Tired?"

"We've been driving since dawn yesterday," Leonid/Bob answered.

"You can sleep inside. There's food and drink. No electricity, no running water. There are two flashlights and a gasoline lantern—you can use that to boil water for coffee."

"When?"

"Tonight. Get your people inside and I'll show you where to move the car."

"How about getting out?"

"I don't know yet. What we have to do later today is complex enough." That launched her into a description of the operation. What surprised her, though it shouldn't have, was the professionalism of the three. Each of them had to be wondering what Moscow Center had in its head when it ordered this operation. What they were doing was insane enough, much less the timing. But none of them allowed their personal feelings to interfere with business. The operation was ordered by Moscow Center, and Moscow knew what it was doing. The manuals all said so, and the field officers believed it, even when they knew they shouldn't.

Beatrice Taussig awoke an hour later. The days were getting longer, and now the sun didn't shine in her face when she drove to work. Instead it stared right through her bedroom window like an accusing eye. Today, she told herself, the dawn marked what was supposed to be a really new day, and she prepared herself to meet it. She started off with a shower and blow-dried her hair. Her coffee machine had already switched on, and she drank her first cup while she decided what she'd wear today. She told herself that it was an important decision, and found that it required more of a breakfast than a cup of coffee and a muffin. Such things require energy, she told herself gravely, and fixed eggs to go along with the rest. She'd have to remind herself to go light on lunch as a result. Taussig had kept to a constant weight for the past four years, and was very careful of her figure.

Something frilly, she decided. She didn't have many outfits like that, but maybe the blue one . . . She switched on the TV as she ate her breakfast, catching the CNN Headline News blurb about the arms negotiations in Moscow. Maybe the world would become a safer place. It was good to think that she was working for something. A fastidious person, she put all her dishes in the dishwasher rack before returning to her bedroom. The blue outfit with the frills was a year out of date, but few at the project would notice—the secretaries would, but who cared about them? She added a paisley scarf around her neck to show that Bea was still Bea.

Taussig pulled into her reserved parking place at the normal time. Her security pass came out of her purse and went around her neck, suspended by a gold chain, and she breezed in the door, past the security checkpoints.

" 'Mornin', doc," said one of the guards. It had to be the outfit, Bea thought. She gave him a smile anyway, which made it an unusual morning for both of them, but didn't say anything, not to some high-school dropout.

She was the first one in her office, as usual. That meant that she fixed the coffee machine the way she liked, very strong. While it was perking, she opened her secure file cabinet and took out the package that she'd been working on the previous day.

Surprisingly, the morning went much more quickly than she had expected. The work helped. She had to deliver a cost-projection analysis by the end of the month, and to do that she had to shuffle through reams of documents, most of which she'd already photographed and forwarded to Ann. It was so convenient to have a private office with a door, and a secretary who always knocked before entering. Her secretary didn't like her, but Taussig didn't much care for her, either, a born-again jerk whose idea of a good time was practicing hymns. Well, a lot of things would change, she told herself. This *was* the day. She'd seen the Volvo on the drive in, parked in the appropriate place.

"Eight-point-one on the dyke-meter," Peggy Jennings said. "You ought to see the clothes she buys."

"So she's eccentric," Will Perkins observed tolerantly. "You see something I don't, Peg. Besides, I saw her coming in this morning, and she looked fairly decent, except for the scarf."

"Anything unusual?" Jennings asked. She put her personal feelings aside.

"No. She gets up awfully early, but maybe she takes time to get untracked in the morning. I don't see any special reason to extend the surveillance." The list was long, and manpower was short. "I know you don't like gays, Peg, but you haven't even got a confirmation on that yet. Maybe you just don't like the gal," he suggested.

"The subject is flamboyant in mannerisms but conservative in dress. Outspoken on most things, but she doesn't talk at all about work. She's a collection of contradictions." *And that fits the profile*, she didn't have to add.

"So maybe she doesn't talk about work because she's not supposed to, like the security weenies tell them. She drives like an Easterner, always in a hurry, but she dresses in conservative clothes—maybe she likes the way she looks in clothes like that? Peg, you can't be suspicious about everything."

"I thought that was our job," Jennings snorted. "Explain what we watched the other night."

"I can't explain it, but you're putting your own spin on it. There's no evidence, Peg, not even enough to intensify the surveillance. Look, after we get through the people on the list, we'll take another look at her."

"This is crazy, Will. We have a supposed leak in a top-security project, and we have to pussyfoot around like we're afraid we might offend somebody." Agent Jennings stood and walked over to her desk for a moment. It wasn't much of a walk. The local FBI office was crowded with arrivals from the Bureau's counterintel office, and the headquarters people had usurped the lunchroom. Their "desks" were actually lunch tables.

"Tell you what—we can take the people who have access to the leaked material and put 'em all on the box." *On the box* meant subjecting everyone to a lie-detector test. The last time that had been done here, it had nearly started a revolution at Tea Clipper. The scientists and engineers were not intelligence types who understood that such things were necessary, but academics who considered the whole process an insult to their patriotism. Or a game: one of the software engineers had even tried using biofeedback techniques to screw up the test results. The main result from this effort, eighteen months before, had been to show that the scientific staff had a great deal of hostility to the security weenies, which was not much of a surprise. What had finally stopped the testing was a wrathful paper from a senior scientist who'd shown that a few deliberate lies he'd told went undetected. That, and the disruption it had caused within the various sections, had ended things before the program had been completed.

"Taussig didn't go on the box the last time," Jennings noted. She'd checked. "None of the admin people did. The revolt stopped things before they got that far. She was one of the people who—"

"Because the software bunch brought their protests to her. She's admin, remember, she's *supposed* to keep all the scientific people happy." Perkins had checked, too. "Look, if you feel this strongly about it, we can come back to her later. I don't see anything myself, but I'll trust your instincts— *but* for now, we have all these others to check out."

Margaret Jennings nodded her surrender. Perkins was right, after all. They had nothing solid to point to. It was just her—*what?* Jennings wondered. She thought Taussig was gay, but that wasn't such a big thing anymore—the courts had said so in enough cases—and there was no proof to support her suspicion anyway. That's what it was, she knew. Three years earlier, right before she'd joined the counterintelligence office, she'd handled a kidnapping involving a couple of . . .

She also knew that Perkins was being more professional about it. Even though a Mormon, and straighter than most arrows, he didn't let his personal feelings interfere with business. What she couldn't shake was the gut feeling that despite everything logic and experience told her, she was still right. Right or wrong, she and Will had six reports to fill out before they went back into the field. You couldn't spend more than half your time in the field anymore. The rest was always stuck at a desk—or a converted lunch table—explaining to people what it was that you did when you weren't stuck at a desk.

"Al, this is Bea. Could you come over to my office?"

"Sure. Be over in five minutes."

"Great. Thanks." Taussig hung up. Even Bea admired Gregory for his punctuality. He came through the door exactly on time.

"I didn't interrupt anything, did I?"

"No. They're running another target-geometry simulation, but they don't need me for that. What's up?" Major Gregory asked, then said, "I like the outfit, Bea."

"Thanks, Al. I need you to help me with something."

"What?"

"It's a birthday present for Candi. I'm picking it up this afternoon and I need somebody to help me with it."

"Eek, you're right. It is in three weeks, isn't it?"

Taussig smiled at Al. He even made geeky noises. "You're going to have to start remembering those things."

"So what are you getting her?" He grinned like a little boy.

"It's a *surprise,* Al." She paused. "It's something Candi needs. You'll see. Candi drove herself in today, didn't she?"

"Yeah, she has to see the dentist after work."

"And don't tell her anything, please? It's a big surprise," Bea explained.

He could see that it was all she could do to keep her face straight. It must be some surprise, he smiled. "Okay, Bea. I'll see you at five."

They woke after noon. "Bob" trudged to the bathroom first before he remembered that there was no running water. He checked the windows for signs of activity before he went outside. By the time he was back, the others had water boiling. They only had instant coffee, but Bisyarina had gotten them a decent brand, and the breakfast food was all typically American, loaded with sugar. They knew that they'd need it. When each had finished his "morning" routine, they got out their maps and their tools and went over the operation's details. Over a period of three hours, they walked through them mentally until each man knew exactly what had to happen.

And there it was, the Archer told himself. Mountains made for long views. In this case, the objective was still two nights' march away, despite the fact that they could see it now. While his subordinates tucked their men into hiding places, he rested his binoculars on a rock and examined the site, still . . . twenty-five kilometers away? he wondered, then checked his map. Yes. He'd have to take his men downhill, cross a small stream, then up the slopes on a man-killing climb, and they would make their last camp . . . there. He concentrated his viewing on that spot. Five kilometers from the objective itself, shielded from view by the mountain's contours . . . the final climb would be a hard one. But what choice was there? He might give his people an hour's rest before the actual assault. That would help, and he'd also be able to brief his men on their individual missions, and give them all time to pray. His eyes went back to the objective.

Clearly, construction was still under way, but on this sort of place, they'd never stop building. It was well that they were here now. In a few more years it would be impregnable. As it was . . .

His eyes strained to make out the details. Even with binoculars he couldn't make out anything smaller than the guard towers. In the first light of dawn he could see the individual bumps that marked buildings. He'd have to be closer to make out items on which the last-minute details of his plan would depend, but for the moment his interest was in the lay of the land. How best to approach the place? How to use the mountain to their advantage? If this place were guarded by KGB troops, as the CIA documents he'd inspected had said, he knew that they were as lazy as they were cruel.

Guard towers, three, north side. There will be a fence there. Mines? he wondered. Mines or not, those guard towers would have to go fast. They'd hold heavy machine guns, and the view from them commanded the terrain. How to do that?

"So that is the place?" The former Army Major came down beside him. "The men?"

"All hidden," the Major answered. He spent a minute examining the place in silence. "Remember the stories about the Assassins' stronghold in Syria?"

"Oh." The Archer turned sharply. That's what it reminded him of! "And how was that fortress taken?"

The Major smiled, keeping his eyes to the objective. "With more resources than we have, my friend . . . if they ever fortify the whole hilltop, it would take a regiment with helicopter support even to get inside the perimeter. So how do you plan to do it?"

"Two groups."

"Agreed." The Major didn't agree with any of this. His training—all of it supplied by the Russians—told him that this mission was madness for so small a force, but before he could contradict a man like the Archer he would have to show his combat skills. That meant running mad risks. In the meantime, the Major would try to nudge his tactics in the right direction.

"The machines are on the slopes to the north. The people are on the knoll to the south." As they watched, the headlights of buses were moving from one place to the other. It was shift-change. The Archer considered that, but he had to make his attack in darkness and leave in darkness, else they'd never get away.

"If we can get in close without being detected . . . may I make a suggestion?" the Major asked quietly.

"Go on."

"Take everything in together to the high ground in the center, then attack downhill against both places."

"It's dangerous," the Archer noted at once. "There is much open ground to be covered on both sides."

"It's also easier to reach the jump-off point unobserved. An approach by one group is less likely to be spotted than one by two groups. Place our heavy weapons there, and they can observe and support both assault teams . . ."

Here was the difference between an instinctive warrior and a trained soldier, the Archer admitted to himself. The Major knew better than he how to measure hazards one against the other. "I don't know about the guard towers, though. What do you think?"

"I'm not sure. I—" The Major pushed his commander's head down. A moment later an airplane streaked down the valley.

"That was a MiG-21, reconnaissance version. We are not dealing with fools." He looked to make sure that all his men were under cover. "We may just have had our pictures taken."

"Did they—"

"I don't know. We'll have to trust in God for that, my friend. He has not let us come this far to fail," the Major said, wondering if that were true or not.

"So where are we going?" Gregory asked in the parking lot.

"Meet me at the mall, south side of the lot, okay? I just hope it'll fit in the car."

"See you there." Gregory walked to his car and drove off.

Bea waited a few minutes before following. There was no sense in having anyone notice that they left at the same time. She was excited now. To combat this, she tried driving slowly, but it was so out of character that it merely fed her excitement, and as though by its own accord the Datsun seemed to work its way up through the gears and change lanes. She arrived in the mall parking lot twenty minutes later.

Al was waiting. He'd parked his car two spaces away from a station wagon, well out from the nearest store. He'd even picked more or less the right place, Bea Taussig noticed as she pulled in alongside his car and got out.

"What kept you?" he asked.

"No real hurry."

"So now what?"

Bea didn't really know. She knew what was to happen, but not how they planned to do it—in fact, she didn't even know for sure that it was a *they* doing it. Perhaps Ann was going to handle the thing all by herself. She laughed to cover her nervousness.

"Come on," she said, waving for him to follow.

"This must be some birthday present," Gregory noted. Off to his right, he noted a car backing out of its place.

Bea noted that the lot was crowded with cars but not people. The afternoon shoppers had gone home for dinner, the new arrivals were just beginning their activity, and the movie crowd wouldn't come for another hour or so. Even so, she was tense as her eyes scanned left and right. She was to be one lane over from the movie entrance. The time was right. If anything went wrong, she almost giggled to herself, she'd have to pick out a large, bulky present. But she didn't have to. Ann was walking toward her. She carried nothing but a large purse.

"Hi, Ann!" Taussig called.

"Hello, Bea—oh, it's Major Gregory."

"Hi," Al said, while he tried to remember if he knew this woman or not. Al didn't have much of a memory for faces, so occupied was his brain with numbers.

"We met last summer," Ann said, confusing him all the more.

"What are you doing here?" Taussig asked her controller.

"Just some quick shopping. I have a date tonight, and I needed—well, I'll show you."

She reached into her purse and pulled out what to Gregory looked like a perfume dispenser—or whatever they called those little spray gadgets, he thought while he waited. He was glad Candi wasn't like this. Ann seemed to spray some of the stuff on her wrist and held it up to Bea's nose as a car came down the lane.

"Candi would love it—what do you think, Al?" Bea asked as the dispenser came up toward his face.

"Huh?" At that moment he got a face full of chemical Mace.

Ann had timed it perfectly, spraying Gregory just as he was taking a breath, and aimed it to get under the glasses into his eyes. It seemed that his face had been set afire, and the searing pain went down into his lungs. In a moment he was on his knees, hands to his face. He couldn't make a sound, and couldn't see the car stop right beside him. The door opened, and the driver only had to take half a step before chopping him on the side of the neck.

Bea watched him go limp—so perfect, she thought. The car's rear door opened and hands came out to grab his shoulders. Bea and Ann helped with the legs as the driver got back in. Just as the rear door closed, Gregory's car keys flew out the window to them, and the Plymouth rolled away, having hardly stopped at all.

Instantly, Ann looked around. No one had seen them. She was sure of it as she and Bea walked back away from the stores to where the cars were.

"What are you going to do with him?" Bea asked.

"What do you care?" Bisyarina replied quickly.

"You're not going—"

"No, we're not going to kill him." Ann wondered if that were true or not. She didn't know, but suspected that a murder was not in the cards. They'd broken one inviolable rule. That was enough for one day.

22. Active Measures

Leonid, whose current cover required him to say, "Call me Bob," headed for the far end of the parking lot. For an operation with virtually no planning, its most dangerous phase had gone smoothly enough. Lenny, in back, had the job of controlling the American officer they'd just kidnapped. A physical type, he'd once been part of the Soviet "special-purpose" forces, known by the abbreviation *Spetznaz*. Bill, next to him, had been assigned to the mission because he was a scientific intelligence specialist; the fact that his area of expertise was chemical engineering hadn't mattered to Moscow. The case called for a scientific specialist, and he was the closest.

In the back, Major Gregory started to moan and move. The chop on his neck had been enough to stun, but not enough to produce any injury more serious than a blinding headache. They hadn't gone to all this trouble to kill the man by accident, something that had happened before. For the same reason, he hadn't been drugged. An exercise much more dangerous than most people might think, it had once accidentally killed a Soviet defector whose mind, as a result, had never been picked by the people of the Second Chief Directorate. To Lenny he seemed much like an infant coming out of a long sleep. The smell of chemical Mace was thick enough in the car that all of the windows were down a few inches to keep it from overpowering the KGB officers. They wanted to use physical restraints on their prisoner, but those might be troublesome if spotted. Lenny was able to control the American, of course. It was just that caution, the distillation of experience, taught them to take nothing for granted. For all they knew, Gregory's hobby might have been unarmed combat—stranger things had happened. When he became vaguely conscious, the first thing he saw was an automatic pistol's silencer pressed against his nose.

"Major *Gregoriy*," Lenny said, using the Russian pronunciation for a purpose, "we know that you are a bright young man, and perhaps a courageous one also. If you resist, you will be killed," he lied. "I am very skilled in this. You will say nothing at all, and you will be still. If you do these things, no harm will come to you. Do you understand—just nod if you do."

Gregory was fully conscious. He'd never quite been out, merely stunned by the blow that still made his head as taut as a swollen balloon. His eyes were shedding tears as though from a leaky faucet, and every breath seemed to light a fire in his chest. He'd commanded himself to move as they pulled him into the car, but his limbs had ignored his frantic wishes while his mind raged at them. It had come to him in an instant: *That's why I hate Bea!* It wasn't her snotty manner and her weird way of dressing at all. But he set that one far aside. There were more important things to worry about, and his mind was racing as it had never raced before. He nodded.

"Very good," the voice said, and strong arms lifted him off the floor and onto the rear seat. The metallic prod of the pistol was against his chest, hidden under the other man's left arm.

"The effect of the chemical irritant will pass in about an hour," Bill told him. "There will be no permanent effect."

"Who are you?" Al asked. His voice was a mere whisper, as raspy as sandpaper.

"Lenny told you to be still," the driver replied. "Besides, someone as bright as you must already know who we are. Am I correct?" Bob looked in the mirror and was rewarded with a nod.

Russians! Al told himself in a combination of amazement and certainty. *Russians here, doing this . . . why do they want me? Will they kill me?* He knew that he could not believe a thing they said. They'd say anything to keep him under control. He felt like a fool. He was supposed to be a man, an officer, and he was as helpless as a four-year-old girl—and crying like one, he realized, hating every tear that dripped from his eyes. Never in his life had Gregory felt such a killing rage. He looked to his right and realized that he didn't have the smallest chance. The man with the gun was almost twice his weight, and besides, he did have the gun pressed right against his chest. Gregory's eyes were blinking now almost like the windshield wipers of a car. He couldn't see well, but he could tell that the man with the gun was watching him with clinical interest, no emotion at all in his eyes. The man was a professional in the application of violence. *Spetznaz*, Gregory thought at once. Al took a deep breath, or tried to. He nearly exploded in a convulsion of coughs.

"You don't want to do that," the man in the right-front seat cautioned. "Take shallow breaths. The effect will pass in time." Wonderful stuff, this chemical Mace, Bill thought. And anyone could buy it in America. Amazing.

Bob was now out of the enormous parking lot and driving back to the safe house. He had the route memorized, of course, though he was not entirely at ease. He hadn't had the chance to drive it beforehand, to practice travel times and plot out alternative routes, but he had spent enough time in America that he knew how to drive lawfully and carefully. Driving habits here were better than in the Northeast—except on the interstates, where every Westerner felt the God-given right to race like a maniac. But he wasn't on the interstate, and on this four-lane highway the late rush-hour traffic moved placidly from light to light. He realized that his time estimate had been overly optimistic, but that didn't matter. Lenny would have no problem controlling their guest. It was quite dark, there were few street-lights, and theirs was just one more car driving home from work.

Bisyarina was already five miles away, heading in the opposite direction. The inside of the car was worse than she'd expected. A neat person, she was appalled to see that the young man had virtually covered the floor with plastic wrappers of some sort, and she wondered why the Chevy wasn't full of ants. The very thought made her skin crawl. She checked her mirror to make sure that Taussig was there. Ten minutes later she pulled into a working-class neighborhood. All of the houses had driveways, but even here most families had more than one car, and the extra ones were parked on the street. She found a vacant spot by a corner and pulled over to it. Taussig's Datsun appeared beside the Chevy, and she left it there, just another car parked at the curb. When Taussig halted at the next stop sign, Bisyarina rolled down her window and tossed Gregory's keys into a sewer. With that ended what was the most dangerous part of the mission for her. Without being told, Taussig drove back toward the shopping mall, where Bisyarina would retrieve her Volvo.

"You're sure you won't kill him," Bea said again after another minute.

"Quite positive, Bea," Ann replied. She wondered why Taussig had suddenly acquired a conscience. "If I guess correctly, he might even be given the chance to continue his work . . . elsewhere. If he cooperates, then he will be treated very well."

"You'll even assign him a girlfriend, won't you?"

"It's one way of keeping men happy," Bisyarina admitted. "Happy people work better."

"Good," Taussig said, surprising her controller quite a bit. Taussig explained after a moment: "I don't want him hurt. What he knows will help both sides make the world safer." *And I just want him out of my way!* she didn't say.

"He's too valuable to hurt," Ann observed. *Unless things go wrong, in which case other orders might apply . . . ?*

Bob was surprised when the traffic backed up. He was right behind a mini-van. Like many American drivers, he hated the things because he couldn't see around them. He opened the ashtray and pushed in the cigarette lighter while he frowned in frustration. Bill, next to him, fished out a smoke also. If nothing else, it helped to mask the acrid stink of the Mace which still permeated the cloth upholstery of the car. Bob decided that he'd leave all the windows open when he parked tonight, just to get rid of the smell. His own eyes were watering, now that there was no blowing air to carry the chemical vapors out of the car. It almost made him feel sorry about the straight dose they'd given their prisoner, but at least it was preferable to a drug that might kill, or a blow that could break his scrawny little neck. At least he was behaving himself. If all went according to plan, by the end of the week he'd be in Moscow. They'd wait a day or so before heading into Mexico. A different crossing point would be used, and a diversion, not yet set up, would probably be used to ensure their speedy crossing into that convenient country, where one could catch a plane to Cuba, and from there a direct flight to Moscow. After that, this team of the First Chief Directorate would have a month's rest. It would be good, Bob told himself, to see his family again. It was always lonely abroad. So lonely that once or twice he'd been unfaithful to his wife, which was also a violation of standing orders. Though not a violation that many officers took seriously, it was something of which he wasn't proud. Perhaps he could get a new posting at the KGB Academy. He had the seniority now, and with a mission like this under his belt . . .

Traffic started moving again. He was surprised to see the mini-van's blinkers go on. Two minutes later he was horrified to see why. A jackknifed tractor-trailer blocked the entire road, with the remains of a small car crushed beneath its front wheels. What looked like a score of rotating ambulance lights illuminated the efforts of police officers and firemen to extricate whatever fool had been driving the small import. Bob couldn't even tell what sort of car it had been, but like the majority of the other drivers, he stared at the wreckage with fascination for a few seconds, until he reminded himself who and where he was. A black-clad police officer was replacing flares on the pavement and waving all southbound traffic onto a side road. Bob reverted to intelligence officer in a moment. He waited until there was a clear path around the cop, and shot past. That earned him an angry look, but nothing more. Most important, the policeman hadn't gotten much of a look at the car. Bob raced up a hill before he realized that another effect of his hesitation was that he couldn't see where the detoured traffic was heading.

I didn't bring the map, he thought next. He'd destroyed it because of all the markings on it. In fact, the car held no maps at all. Maps were dangerous things to have, and besides, he knew how to memorize all the information he needed for his missions. But he hadn't been here long enough to learn the area, and knew only one route back to the safe house.

Goddamn these "immediate-priority" operations!

He took a left at the first crossroads, onto a curving street into a residential development. It took several minutes for him to realize that the land here was so hilly that all the roads curved back and forth upon themselves to the point where he didn't know which direction he was heading. For the first time, he began to lose his composure, but only for an instant. One mental curse in his native language reminded him that he couldn't even think in Russian. Bob lit another cigarette and drove slowly as he tried to orient himself. The tears in his eyes didn't help.

He's lost, Gregory realized after a moment. He'd read enough spy novels to know that they were taking him to a safe house—or a clandestine airfield?—or another vehicle that would carry him . . . where?—but as soon as he recognized the same car that they'd passed a few minutes before, he had to stop himself from smiling. They'd actually done something wrong. The next turn they took went downhill, and Gregory confirmed his suspicion when he again saw the rotating lights at the car wreck. He noted the curses as the driver pulled into a driveway and had to back up before they could climb the hill again.

Everything Russians hated about America flooded back into Bob's consciousness. Too many roads, too many cars—some damned fool of an American had run a stop sign and—*I hope he's dead!* the driver raged at the parked cars on the residential street. *I hope he died screaming in agony.* It felt better to get that thought out from the back of his mind.

Now what?

He continued on a different route, taking the road over the crest of the hill, where he was able to look down and see another highway. Perhaps if he went south on this one, it might connect with the road he'd been on . . . It was worth a try, he thought. To his right, Bill gave him a questioning look, but Lenny in the back was too busy with the prisoner to know that anything was badly wrong. As they picked up speed, at least the air through the windows allowed his eyes to clear. There was a traffic light at the bottom of the hill—but there was also a sign that said NO LEFT TURN.

Govno! Bob thought to himself as he turned right. This four-lane road was divided by a concrete barrier.

You should have spent more time studying the map. You should have taken a few hours to drive around the area. But it was too late for that now, and he knew that he hadn't had the time. That left them heading back north. Bob checked his watch, forgetting that there was a clock on the dashboard. He'd already lost fifteen minutes. He was out in the open and vulnerable, on enemy ground. What if someone had seen them in the parking lot? What if the policeman at the wreck had taken down their number?

Bob didn't panic. He was too well trained for that. He commanded himself to take a deep breath and mentally examined all the maps he'd seen of the area. He was west of the interstate highway. If he could find that, he still remembered the exit he'd used earlier in the day—was it still the same day?—and get to the safe house blindfolded. If he were west of the interstate, all he had to do was find a road that went east. Which way was east—right. Another deep breath. He'd head north until he saw what looked like a major east-west road, and he'd turn right. Okay.

It took nearly five minutes, but he found an east-west highway—he didn't bother to look for the name. Five minutes after that he was grateful to see the red, white, and blue shield that informed him the interstate was half a mile ahead. Now he breathed easier.

"What's the trouble?' Lenny finally asked from the back. Bob replied in Russian.

"Had to change routes," he said in a tone far more relaxed than he'd felt only a few minutes earlier. In turning to reply, he missed a sign.

There was the overpass. The green signs announced that he could go north or south. He wanted to go south, and the exit ramp would be—

In the wrong place. He was in the right lane, but the exit went to the left, and was only fifty meters ahead. He swerved across the highway without looking. Immediately behind him, an Audi driver stood on his brakes and jammed his hand on the horn. Bob ignored the irrelevancy as he took the left turn onto the ramp. He was on the upward, sweeping curve and was looking at the traffic on the interstate when he saw lights flashing in the grille of the black car behind him. The headlights blinked at him, and he knew what would come next.

Don't panic, he told himself. He didn't have to say anything to his comrades. Bob didn't even consider making a run for it. They'd been briefed on this, too. American police are courteous and professional. They didn't demand payment on the spot, as the Moscow traffic police did. He also knew that American cops were armed with Magnum revolvers.

Bob pulled his Plymouth over just beyond the overpass and waited. As he watched his mirror, the police car stopped behind his, slightly more to the left. He could see the officer getting out, carrying a clipboard in his left hand. That left the right one free, Bob knew, and that was the gun hand. In the back, Lenny told the prisoner what would happen if he made a noise.

"Good evening, sir," the police officer said. "I don't know what the rules are in Oklahoma, but here we prefer that you don't change lanes like that. Could I have your driver's license and registration, please?" His black uniform and silver trim made Leonid think of the SS, but this wasn't the time for such thoughts. *Just be polite,* he told himself calmly, *take the ticket and move on.* He handed over the proper cards and waited as the police officer started filling out the ticket blank. Perhaps an apology was due now . . . ?

"Sorry, officer, I thought the exit was on the right side, and—"

"That's why we spend all that money on signs, Mr. Taylor. Is this your correct address?"

"Yes, sir. Like I said, I'm sorry. If you have to give me a ticket, I guess I deserve it."

"I wish everybody was that cooperative," the officer observed. Not everyone was, and he decided to see what this polite fellow looked like. He looked at the photograph on the license and bent down to make sure it was the right person. He shined the light in Bob's face. It was the same face, but . . . "What the hell is that smell?"

Mace, the officer knew an instant later. The light swiveled. The people in the car looked normal enough, two in the front, two in the back, and . . . one of the people in the back was wearing what looked like a uniform jacket . . .

Gregory wondered if his life was really on the line. He decided that he'd find out, and prayed the policeman was alert.

In back, the one on the left side—the one in the jacket—mouthed a single word: *Help.* That merely made the policeman more curious, but the one in the right-front seat saw him do it and stirred. The cop's instincts all lit off at once. His right hand slid down to his service revolver, flipping the safety strap off the hammer.

"Out of the car, one at a time, and *right now!*"

He was horrified to see a gun. It appeared as though by magic from the guy in the right-rear, and before he could get his own revolver out—

Gregory's right hand didn't get there in time, but his elbow did, spoiling Lenny's aim.

The officer was surprised that he didn't hear anything except a shout in a language he couldn't understand, but by the time that occurred to him, his jaw had already exploded in a puff of white more heard than felt. He fell backward, his gun out now and shooting of its own accord.

Bob cringed and dropped the car into gear. The front wheels spun on the loose gravel, but caught, hauling the Plymouth all too slowly away from the noise of the gun. In the back, Lenny, who'd gotten off the one shot, slammed the butt of his automatic on Gregory's head. His perfectly aimed shot should have gone straight through the policeman's heart, but he'd gotten the face instead, and he didn't know how good the shot had been. He shouted something that Bob didn't bother listening to.

Three minutes later the Plymouth went off the interstate. Below the accident that still blocked the highway, the road was nearly clear. Bob took the dirt road off it, lights out, and was at the trailer before the prisoner regained consciousness.

Behind them, a passing motorist saw the policeman on the shoulder and pulled over to assist him. The man was in agony, with a bloody wound to his face and nine missing teeth. The motorist ran to the police car and put out a radio call. It took a minute before the dispatcher got things straight, but three minutes after that a second radio car was there, then five more in as many minutes. The wounded officer was unable to speak, but handed up his clipboard, which had the car's description and tag number written down. He also still had "Bob Taylor's" driver's license. That was message enough for the other officers. An immediate call was put out over all local police frequencies. Someone had shot a police officer. The actual crime that had been committed was far more serious than that, but the police did not know, nor would they have cared.

Candi was surprised to see that Al wasn't home. Her jaw was still numb from the Xylocaine shots, and she decided on soup. *But where's Al? Maybe he had to stay late for something.* She knew that she could call, but it wasn't that big a deal, and with the way her mouth felt, there wasn't much in the way of talking she could have done anyway.

At police headquarters on Cerrillos Road, the computers were already humming. A telex was dispatched at once to Oklahoma, where brother police officers took immediate note of the magnitude of the crime and punched up their own computer records. They learned at once that there was no license for Robert J. Taylor of 1353 N.W. 108th Street, Oklahoma City, OK 73210, nor was there a Plymouth Reliant with tag number XSW-498. The tag number, in fact, did not exist. The sergeant who ran the computer section was more than surprised. To be told that there was no record of a tag wasn't all that unusual, but to get a no-hit on a tag and a license, *and* in a case with an officer-involved shooting was pushing the laws of probability too hard. He lifted the phone for the senior watch officer.

"Captain, we have something really crazy here on the Mendez shooting."

The state of New Mexico is filled with areas belonging to the federal government, and has a long history of highly sensitive activities. The Captain didn't know what had happened, but he knew at once that this wasn't a traffic incident. One minute after that, he was on the phone to the local FBI office.

Jennings and Perkins were there before Officer Mendez came out of surgery. The waiting room was so crowded with policemen that it was fortunate the hospital had no other surgical patients at the moment. The Captain running the investigation was there, as were the state police chaplain and half a dozen other officers who worked the same watch as Mendez, plus Mrs. Mendez, who was seven months pregnant. Presently the doctor came out and announced that he'd be fine. The only major blood vessel damaged had been easily repaired. The officer's jaw and teeth had taken most of the damage, and a maxillary surgeon would start repairing that damage in a day or two. The officer's wife cried a bit, then was taken to see her husband before two of his fellows drove her home. Then it was time for everyone to get to work.

"He must have had the gun in the poor bastard's back," Mendez said slowly, his words distorted by the wires holding his jaw together. He'd already refused a pain medication. He wanted to get the information out quickly, and was willing to suffer a little to do it. The state police officer was a very angry man. "Only way he coulda got it out so fast."

"The photo on the license, is it accurate?" Agent Jennings asked.

"Yes, ma'am." Pete Mendez was a young officer, and managed to make Jennings feel her age with that remark. He next got out rough descriptions of the other two. Then came the victim: "Maybe thirty, skinny, glasses. He was wearing a jacket—like a uniform jacket. I didn't see any insignia, but I didn't get much of a look. He had his hair cut like he was in the service, too. Don't know the eye color, either, but there was something funny . . . his eyes were shiny, like—oh, the Mace smell. Maybe that was it. Maybe they Maced him. He didn't say anything, but, like, he mouthed the words, you know? I thought that was funny, but the guy in the right-front reacted real strong to that. I was slow. I shoulda reacted faster. Too damned slow."

"You said that one of them said something?" Perkins asked.

"The bastard who shot me. I don't know what it was. Not English, not Spanish. I just remember the last word . . . *maht*, something like that."

"*Yob' tvoyu mat'!*" Jennings said at once.

"Yeah, that's it." Mendez nodded. "What's it mean?"

"It means 'fuck your mother.' Excuse me," Perkins said, his Mormon face fairly glowing scarlet. Mendez went rigid on his bed. One doesn't say such things to an angry man with a Hispanic name.

"What?" the state police Captain asked.

"It's Russian, one of their favorite curses." Perkins looked at Jennings.

"Oh, boy," she breathed, scarcely able to believe it. "We're calling Washington right now."

"We have to identify the—wait a minute!—Gregory?" Perkins said. "God almighty. You call Washington. I'll call the project office."

It turned out that the state police could move the fastest. Candi answered a knock on the door and was surprised to see a policeman standing there. He asked politely if he could see Major Al Gregory, and was told that he wasn't home by a young woman whose numbed jaw was coming back to normal as the world around her began to shatter. She'd scarcely gotten the news when Tea Clipper's security chief pulled up. She was a mere spectator as a radio call was sent out to look for Al's car, too shocked even to cry.

The license photo of "Bob Taylor" was already in Washington, being examined by members of the FBI's counterintelligence branch, but it wasn't in their file of identified Soviet officers. The Assistant Director who ran counterintel ops was called in from his Alexandria home by the senior watch officer. The AD in turn called FBI Director Emil Jacobs, who arrived at the Hoover Building at two in the morning. They could scarcely believe it, but the wounded police officer positively identified the photograph of Major Alan T. Gregory. The Soviets had never committed a violent crime in the United States. This rule was so well established that the most senior Soviet defectors, if they wished, were able to live openly and without protection. But this was even worse than the elimination of a person who was, under Soviet law, a condemned traitor. An American citizen had been kidnapped; to the FBI, kidnapping is a crime hardly different from murder.

There was, of course, a plan. Even though it had never happened, the operations experts whose job it was to think about unthinkable happenings had a pre-set protocol of things that had to be done. Before dawn thirty senior agents were taking off from Andrews Air Force Base, among them members of the elite Hostage Rescue Team. Agents from field offices throughout the Southwest briefed Border Patrol officers on the case.

*   *   *

Bob/Leonid sat by himself, drinking tepid coffee. *Why didn't I just keep going and make a U-turn down the street?* he asked himself. *Why was I in a hurry? Why was I excited when I didn't have to be?*

It was time to be excited now. His car had three bullet holes in it, two on the left side and one in the trunk lid. His driver's license was in the hands of the police, and that carried his photograph.

You won't get a teaching post at the academy this way, Tovarishch. He smiled to himself grimly.

He was in a safe house. He had that much consolation. It might even be safe for a day or two. This was clearly Captain Bisyarina's bolt-hole, never intended to be any more than a place where the officer could hide out if forced to run. Because of that, it had no telephone, and he had no way of communicating with the local resident officer. *What if she doesn't come back?* That was clear enough. He'd have to risk driving a car with known license tags—and bullet holes!—far enough to steal another. He had visions of thousands of police officers patrolling the roads with a single thought: find the maniacs who shot their comrade. How could he have let things go so bad, so fast!

He heard a car approach. Lenny was still guarding their prisoner. Bob and Bill picked up their pistols and peered around the edge of the single window that faced on the dirt road to the trailer. Both breathed easier when they saw it was Bisyarina's Volvo. She got out and made the proper all-clear gesture, then came toward the trailer, holding a large bag.

"Congratulations: you've made the television news," she said on entering. *Idiot.* That part didn't need to be said. It hung in the air like a thundercloud.

"It's a long story," he said, knowing it to be a lie.

"I'm sure." She set the bag on the table. "Tomorrow I'll rent you a new car. It's too dangerous to move yours. Where did you—"

"Two hundred meters up the road, in the thickest trees we could squeeze it into, covered with branches. It will be hard to spot, even from the air."

"Yes, keep that in mind. The police here have some helicopters. Here." She tossed Bob a black wig. Next came some glasses, one pair set with clear lenses, and the other, a pair of mirror-type sunglasses. "Are you allergic to makeup?"

"What?"

"*Makeup,* you fool—"

"Captain . . ." Bob began with some heat. Bisyarina cut him off with a look.

"Your skin is pale. In case you haven't noticed, a large number of the people in this area are Spanish. This is my territory and you will now do exactly as I say." She paused for a beat. "I'll get you out of here."

"The American woman, she knows you by sight—"

"Obviously. I suppose you want her eliminated? After all, we've broken one rule, why not another? What fucking *madman* ordered this operation?"

"The orders came from very high," Leonid replied.

"*How* high?" she demanded, and got only a raised eyebrow that spoke volumes. "You're joking."

"The nature of the order, the 'immediate action' prefix—what do you think?"

"I think all of our careers are ruined, and that assumes that we—well, we will. But I will not agree to the murder of my agent. We have as yet not killed anyone, and I do not think that our orders contemplated—"

"That is correct," Bob said aloud, while his head shook emphatically from side to side. Bisyarina's mouth dropped open.

"This could start a war," she said quietly, in Russian. She didn't mean a real war, but rather something almost as bad, open conflict between KGB and CIA officers, something that almost never happened, even in third-world countries, where it usually involved surrogates killing other surrogates, and for the most part never knowing why—and even that was rare enough. The business of intelligence services was to gather information. Violence, both sides tacitly agreed, got in the way of the real mission. But if both sides began killing the strategic assets of their opponents . . .

"You should have refused the order," she said after a moment.

"Certainly," Bob observed. "I understand that the Kolyma camps are lovely this time of year, all glistening white with their blanket of snow." The odd thing—at least it would seem so to a Westerner—was that neither officer bothered considering surrendering with a request of political asylum. Though it would have ended their personal dangers, it would mean betraying their country.

"What you do here is your account, but I will not kill my agent," "Ann" said, ending discussion of the issue. "I'll get you out."

"How?"

"I don't know yet. By car, I think, but I will have to come up with something new. Perhaps not a car. Perhaps a truck," she mused. There were lots of trucks out here, and it was not the least unusual for a woman to drive one. Take a van across the border, perhaps? A van with boxes in it . . . Gregory in a box, drugged or gagged . . . perhaps all of them . . . what are customs procedures like for such things? She'd never had to worry about that before. With a week's warning, as she would have had for a proper operation, she'd have had time to answer a lot of questions.

Take your time, she told herself. *We've had enough of hurrying, haven't we?*

"Two days, perhaps three."

"That's a long time," Leonid observed.

"I may need that long to evaluate the countermeasures that we are likely to face. For the moment, don't bother shaving."

Bob nodded after a moment. "It is your territory."

"When you get back, you can write this up as a case study in why operations need proper preparation," Bisyarina said. "Anything else you need?"

"No."

"Very well. I will see you again tomorrow afternoon."

"No," Beatrice Taussig told the agents. "I saw Al this afternoon. I"—she glanced uneasily at Candi—"I wanted him to help me with—well, with picking up a birthday present for Candace tomorrow. I saw him in the parking lot, too, but that was it. You really think—I mean, the Russians . . . ?"

"That's what it looks like," Jennings said.

"My God."

"Does Major Gregory know enough that—" Jennings was surprised that Taussig answered instead of Dr. Long.

"Yes, he does. He's the only one who really understands the whole project. Al's a very bright guy. And a friend," she added. That earned her a warm smile from Candi. There were real tears in Bea's eyes now. It hurt her to see her friend in pain, even though she knew that it was all for the best.

"Ryan, you're going to love this." Jack had just gotten back from the latest round of negotiations at the Foreign Ministry building, twenty stories of Stalinesque wedding cake on Smolenskiy Bul'var. Candela handed over the dispatch.

"That son of a bitch," Ryan breathed.

"You didn't expect him to cooperate, did you?" the officer asked sardonically, then changed his mind. "I beg your pardon, doc. I wouldn't have expected this either."

"I know this kid. I've driven him around Washington myself, when he came east to brief us . . ." *It's your fault, Jack. It was your move that caused this to happen . . . wasn't it?* He asked a few questions.

"Yeah, that's a virtual certainty," Candela said. "They screwed things up, looks like. That sounds like an overnighter. Hey, the KGB officers aren't supermen either, pal, but they follow their orders, just like we do."

"You have some ideas?"

"Not much we can do from this end but hope the local cops can straighten things out."

"But if it goes public—"

"Show me some evidence. You don't accuse a foreign government of something like this without evidence. Hell, there's half a dozen engineers in Europe who've been murdered by left-wing terrorist gangs in the last two years, all working on the fringes of the SDI program, not to mention a few 'suicides.' We haven't made a public issue of that, either."

"But this breaks the *rules,* damn it!"

"When you get down to it, there's only one rule, doc: Win."

"Does USIA still have that global TV operation going?"

"Worldnet, you mean? Sure. It's a hell of a program."

"If we don't get him back, I will personally break the *Red October* story world-wide, and fuck the consequences!" Ryan swore. "If it costs my career, I'll do it."

"*Red October*?" Candela had no idea what he was talking about.

"Trust me, it's a good one."

"Tell your KGB friends—hell, it might even work."

"Even if it doesn't," Ryan said, more in control now. *It's your fault, Jack,* he told himself again. Candela agreed; Jack could see it.

The funny part, the state police thought, was that the press wasn't given the real meat of the case. As soon as the FBI team arrived, the rules were established. For the moment, this was a simple case of a police shooting. The federal involvement was to be kept secret, and if it broke, the word would be that an international drug-trafficker was on the loose and that federal assistance had been requested. The Oklahoma authorities were told to tell any inquiring journalist that they'd merely provided identification help to a fellow police force. Meanwhile, the FBI took over the case, and federal assets began to flood the area. Citizens were told that nearby military bases were conducting routine exercises—special search-and-rescue drills—which explained the abnormal helicopter activity. People at Project Tea Clipper were briefed on what had happened and told to keep this secret as close as all of the others.

Gregory's car was located in a matter of hours. No fingerprints were found—Bisyarina had worn gloves, of course—nor was any other useful evidence, though the placement of his car and the location of the shooting merely confirmed the professionalism of the event.

Gregory had been the Washington guest of men more important than Ryan. The President's first appointment of the morning was with General Bill Parks, FBI Director Emil Jacobs, and Judge Moore.

"Well?" the President asked Jacobs.

"These things take time. I've got some of our best investigative minds out there, Mr. President, but looking over their shoulder only slows things down."

"Bill," the President asked next, "how important is the boy?"

"He's priceless," Parks answered simply. "He's one of my top three men, sir. People like that cannot be replaced very easily."

The President took this information seriously. Next he turned to Judge Moore. "We caused this, didn't we?"

"Yes, Mr. President, in a manner of speaking. Obviously, we hit Gerasimov in a very tender spot. My estimate agrees with the general's. They want what Gregory knows. Gerasimov probably thinks that if he can get information of this magnitude, he can overcome the political consequences of the *Red October* disclosure. That's a hard call to make from this side of the ocean, but certainly there's a good chance that his evaluation is correct."

"I knew we shouldn't have done this . . ." the President said quietly, then shook his head. "Well, that's my responsibility. I authorized it. If the press . . ."

"Sir, if the press gets wind of this, it sure as hell won't be from CIA. Second, we can always say that this was a desperate—I'd prefer to say 'vigorous'—attempt to save the life of our agent. It doesn't have to go any further than that, and such action is expected of intelligence services. They go to great lengths to protect their agents. So do we. That's one of the rules of the game."

"Where does Gregory fit into the rules?" Parks asked. "What if they think we might have a chance of rescuing him?"

"I don't know," Moore admitted. "If Gerasimov succeeds in saving himself, he'll probably get word to us that we forced him into it, he's sorry, and it won't happen again. He'd expect us to retaliate once or twice, but it would probably stop at that, because neither KGB nor CIA wants to start a war. To answer your question directly, General, my opinion is that they may have orders to eliminate the asset entirely."

"You mean murder him?" the President asked.

"That is a possibility. Gerasimov must have ordered this mission very quickly. Desperate men make for desperate orders. It would be incautious of us to assume otherwise."

The President considered that for a minute. He leaned back in his chair and sipped at his coffee. "Emil, if we can find where he is . . . ?"

"The Hostage Rescue Team is standing by. I have the men in place. Their vehicles are being flown out by the Air Force, but for the moment all they can do is sit and wait."

"If they move in, what are the chances that they'll save him?"

"Pretty good, Mr. President," Jacobs replied.

" 'Pretty good' doesn't cut it," Parks said. "If the Russians have orders to take him out—"

"My people are as well trained as anyone in the world," the FBI Director said.

"What are their rules of engagement?" Parks demanded.

"They are trained to use deadly force in the protection of themselves or any innocent person. If any subject appears to be threatening a hostage, he's a dead man."

"That's not good enough," Parks said next.

"What do you mean?" the President asked.

"How long does it take to turn around and blow somebody's head off? What if they're willing to die to accomplish their mission? We expect our people to be, don't we?"

"Arthur?" Heads turned to Judge Moore.

The DCI shrugged. "I can't predict the dedication of Soviets. Is it possible? Yes, I suppose it is. Is it certain? I don't know that. Nobody does."

"I used to drive fighter planes for a living. I know what human reaction times are," Parks said. "If a guy does decide to turn and shoot, even if your man has a gun on him, he might not be fast enough to keep Al alive."

"What do you want me to do, tell my people just to kill everybody in sight?" Jacobs asked quietly. "We don't do that. We *can't* do that."

Parks turned to the President next. "Sir, even if the Russians don't get Gregory, if we lose him, they win. It might be years before we can replace him. I submit, sir, that Mr. Jacobs' people are trained to deal with criminals, not folks like this, and not for this situation. Mr. President, I recommend that you call in the Delta Force from Fort Bragg."

"They don't have jurisdiction," Jacobs noted at once.

"They have the right kind of training," the General said.

The President was quiet for another minute. "Emil, how good are your people at following orders?"

"They will do what you say, sir. But it will have to be your order, in writing."

"Can you get me in touch with them?"

"Yes, Mr. President." Jacobs picked up the phone and routed a call through his own office in the Hoover Building. Along the way it was scrambled.

"Agent Werner, please . . . Agent Werner, this is Director Jacobs. I have a special message for you. Stand by." He handed the phone over. "This is Gus Werner. He's been the team leader for five years. Gus passed on a promotion to stay with the HRT."

"Mr. Werner, this is the President. Do you recognize my voice? Good. Please listen closely. In the event that you are able to attempt the rescue of Major Gregory, your only mission is to get him out. All other considerations are secondary to that objective. The arrest of the criminals in question is not, I repeat, not a matter of concern. Is that clear? Yes, even the possibility of a threat to the hostage is sufficient grounds for the use of deadly force. Major Gregory is an irreplaceable national asset. His survival is your only mission. I will put that in writing and hand it to the Director. Thank you. Good luck." The President replaced the phone. "He says that they've considered this possibility."

"He would." Jacobs nodded. "Gus has a good imagination. Now the note, sir."

The President took a small sheet of writing paper from his desk and made the order official. It wasn't until he was finished that he realized what he'd done. This was not an intellectual exercise. He'd just handwritten a death warrant. It turned out to be a depressingly easy thing to do.

"General, are you satisfied?"

"I hope these people are as good as the Director says," was all Parks was willing to say.

"Judge, any repercussions from the other side?"

"No, Mr. President. Our Soviet colleagues understand this sort of thing."

"Then that's it." *And may God have mercy on my soul.*

No one had slept. Candi hadn't gone to work, of course. With the arrival of the investigative team from Washington, Jennings and Perkins were baby-sitting her. There was the remote possibility that Gregory would escape, and in this event, it was deemed that he'd call here first. There was another reason, of course, but that wasn't official yet.

Bea Taussig was a veritable tornado of energy. She'd spent the night straightening the house and brewing coffee for everyone. Odd as it seemed, it gave her something to do besides sitting with her friend. She did a lot of that, too, which no one thought especially odd. It was one of the things friends do.

Jennings took several hours to note that she was wearing an outfit that actually looked feminine. She had, in fact, gone to the trouble the previous day to make herself look rather nice. Most of that was wreckage now. Once or twice she'd shed tears herself when she and Candi cried together, and what had been a properly decorated face now showed streaks. Her clothes were wrinkled and the paisley scarf was in the closet, wrapped around the same hanger that held her coat. But the most interesting thing about Taussig, Jennings thought from her chair, was her mental state. There was tenseness there. The bustling activity of the long night had alleviated it to some degree, but . . . there was more to it than just being helpful, the agent thought. She didn't say this to Perkins.

Taussig didn't notice or care about what the agent thought. She looked out the window, expecting to see the sun rising for the second time since she'd last slept, and wondered where all her energy was coming from. Maybe the coffee, she thought to herself with an inward smile. It was always funny when you lied to yourself. She wondered at the danger that she herself might face, but put that worry aside. She trusted Ann's professionalism. One of the first things she'd been told on starting her second career was that she would be protected, even to the death. Such promises had to be real, Ann had said, because they had a practical dimension. It was a business, Bea thought, and she felt confident that those in it knew how to handle themselves. The worst thing that could happen was that the police and FBI would rescue Al, but they were probably already gone, she told herself. Or maybe they'd kill him, despite what Ann had told her the previous night. That would be too bad. She wanted him out of the way. Not dead, just out of the way. She remembered the table talk at the project about how some German, Italian, and British people working in SDI-related projects had died mysteriously. So there was a precedent, wasn't there? If Al got back alive . . . well, that was that, wasn't it? She had to trust her controller to run things. Too late now. She turned her attention to her friend.

Candi was staring blankly at the far wall. There was a picture there, a laser-print of the space shuttle lifting off from Cape Canaveral. Not a proper picture, but something Al had picked up for free from one contractor or another and decided to hang on the wall. Bea's thoughts returned to Candace. Her eyes were puffy from all the tears.

"You have to get some rest," Bea told her. Candace didn't even turn her head, hardly reacted at all, but Bea put her arm around her friend's shoulder and lifted her from the couch. "Come on."

Candi rose as though in a dream, and Bea guided her out of the living room and up the steps toward the bedroom. Once inside, she closed the door.

"Why, Bea? Why did they do it?" Candi sat on the bed, and her stare was merely at a different wall.

"I don't know," Bea said, more honestly than she knew. She really didn't know, but then, she really didn't care.

The tears started again, and the gasping breaths, and the running nose as she watched her friend contemplate a world that someone else had torn apart. She felt momentary guilt that she was one of those who'd done it, but knew that she would make it whole again. A timid person despite all her flamboyance, Bea had found unexpected courage in herself by working for a foreign government, and more courage still in doing something that she had never expected them to ask. One more thing remained. She sat down next to her friend and held her close, bringing her head down on the offered shoulder. It was so hard for Bea. Her previous experiences had been passing college affairs. She'd tried to find in herself something different, but the men she'd dated had not satisfied. Her first sexual experience at the clumsy hands of a teenage football player had been so awful . . . but she wasn't one to psychoanalyze herself. With strangers or mere acquaintances it was one thing, but now she had to face herself, to face her own image in the eyes of a friend. A friend in pain. A friend who needed. A friend, she reminded herself coldly, whom she'd betrayed. It wasn't that she hated Gregory any the less, but she could not ignore the fact that he meant something to her friend, and in that sense he was still between them even here, alone in the bedroom. That worthless little caricature of a man who had on this very bed . . .

Will you ever replace him? she asked herself.

Will you even try?

If you were willing to remove him, and hurt her, and then not even take the risk . . . what does that make you?

She wrapped her arms tight around her friend, and was rewarded with a returning grasp. Candi was merely trying to hold on to part of her shattering world, but Bea didn't know that. She kissed her friend on the cheek, and Candi's grip grew stronger still.

She needs you.

It took all of Bea's courage. Already her heart was beating fast, and she ridiculed herself as she had for years. Bea the Confident. Bea the Tough, who snarled back at whomever she wished, who drove her kind of car, and wore her kind of clothes, and to hell with what anyone thought. Bea the Coward, who even after she had risked everything lacked the courage to reach out to the one person in all the world who mattered. One more hesitant step. She kissed her friend again, tasting the salt of her tears and feeling the desperate need in the arms that wrapped around her chest. Taussig took a deep breath and moved one hand down to her friend's breast.

* * *

Jennings and Perkins came through the door less than five seconds after hearing the scream. They saw the horror on Long's face, and something both similar and very different on Taussig's.

23. Best-Laid Plans

"It is the position of the United States government," Ernest Allen said from his side of the table, "that systems designed to defend innocent civilians from weapons of mass destruction are neither threatening nor destabilizing, and that restrictions on the development of such systems serve no useful purpose. This position has been consistently stated for the past eight years, and we have absolutely no reason to change it. We welcome the initiative of the government of the Union of Soviet Socialist Republics to reduce offensive weapons by as much as fifty percent, and we will examine the details of this proposal with interest, but a reduction of offensive weapons is not relevant to defensive weapons, which are not an issue for negotiation beyond their applicability to existing agreements between our two countries.

"On the question of on-site inspections, we are disappointed to note that the remarkable progress made only so recently should be . . ."

You had to admire the man, Ryan thought. He didn't agree with what he was saying, but it was the position of his country, and Ernie Allen was never one to let personal feelings out of whatever secret compartment he locked up before beginning these sessions.

The meeting officially adjourned when Allen finished his discourse, which had just been delivered for the third time today. The usual courtesies were exchanged. Ryan shook hands with his Soviet counterpart. In doing so, he passed over a note, as he'd been taught to do at Langley. Golovko gave no reaction at all, which earned him a friendly nod at the conclusion of the handshake. Jack had no particular choice. He had to continue with the plan. He knew that he'd learn in the next few days just how much of a high-roller Gerasimov was. For him to run the risk of the CIA disclosures, especially with the threat of a few even more spectacular than Jack had promised . . . But Ryan could not admire the man. His view was that Gerasimov was the chief thug in the main thug agency of a country that allowed itself to be controlled by thugs. He knew that it was a simplistic, dangerous way to think, but he was not a field officer, though he was now acting like one, and hadn't yet learned that the world which he ordinarily viewed from the air-conditioned safety of his desk on CIA's seventh floor was not so well defined as his reports about it. He'd expected that Gerasimov would cave in to his demand—after taking time to evaluate his position, of course, but still cave in. It hit him that he'd thought like a chess master because that's how he'd expected the KGB Chairman to think, only to be confronted with a man who was willing to throw the dice—as Americans were wont to do. The irony should have been entertaining, Jack told himself in the marble lobby of the Foreign Ministry. But it wasn't.

*   *   *

Jennings had never seen anyone so thoroughly destroyed as Beatrice Taussig had been. Beneath the brittle, confident exterior had beaten what was after all a lonely human heart, consumed by solitary rage at a world that hadn't treated her in the way that she desired, but was unable to make happen. She almost felt sorry for the woman in handcuffs, but sympathy did not extend to treason, and certainly not to kidnapping, the highest—or lowest—crime in the FBI's institutional pantheon.

Her collapse was agreeably complete, however, and that's what mattered right now, that and the fact that she and Will Perkins had gotten the information out of her. It was still dark when they took her outside to a waiting FBI car. They left her Datsun in the driveway to suggest that she was still there, but fifteen minutes later she came in the back door of the Santa Fe FBI office and gave her information to the newly arrived investigators. It wasn't all that much, really, just a name, an address, and a type of car, but it was the beginning the agents needed. A Bureau car drove by the house soon thereafter and noted that the Volvo was in place. Next, a crisscross telephone directory enabled them to call the family directly across the street, giving them one minute's warning that two FBI agents were about to knock on their back door. The two agents set up surveillance in the family's living room, which was both frightening and exciting to the young couple who owned the tract house. They told the agents that "Ann," as she was known, was a quiet lady whose profession was unknown to the family, but who had caused no trouble in the neighborhood, though she did occasionally keep eccentric hours, like quite a few single people. Last night, for example, she hadn't gotten home until rather late, the husband noted, about twenty minutes before the Carson show ended. A heavy date, he thought. Odd that they'd never seen her bring anyone home, though . . .

"She's up. There go some lights." One agent picked up binoculars, hardly needed to see across the street. The other one had a long-lens camera and high-speed film. Neither man could see anything more than a moving shadow through the drawn curtains. Outside, they watched a man in a tubular bicycle helmet ride past her car on his ten-speed, getting his morning exercise. From their vantage point they could see him place the radio beeper on the inside surface of the Volvo's rear bumper, but only because they knew what to look for.

"Who teaches them to do that," the man with the camera asked, "David Copperfield?"

"Stan something—works at Quantico. I played cards with him once," the other chuckled. "He gave the money back and showed me how it's done. I haven't played poker for money since."

"Can you tell us what this is all about?" the homeowner asked.

"Sorry. You'll find out, but no time for it now. Bingo!"

"Got it." The camera started clicking and winding.

"We timed that one close!" The man with the binoculars lifted his radio. "Subject is moving, getting in the car."

"We're ready," the radio replied.

"There she goes, heading south, about to lose visual contact. That's it. She's yours now."

"Right. We got her. Out."

No fewer than eleven cars and trucks were assigned to the surveillance, but more important were the helicopters orbiting four thousand feet above the ground. One more helicopter was on the ground at Kirtland Air Force Base. A UH-1N, the two-engine variant of the venerable Huey of Vietnam fame, it had been borrowed from the Air Force and was now being fitted with rappelling ropes.

Ann drove her Volvo in what appeared to be a grossly ordinary fashion, but behind her sunglasses her eyes returned to her mirrors every few seconds. She needed all her skills now, all her training, and despite a mere five hours of sleep she kept to her professional standards. Next to her on the seat was a thermos of coffee. She'd already had two cups for herself, and would give the rest to her three colleagues.

Bob was moving too. Dressed in work clothes and boots, he was jogging cross-country through the woods, pausing only to look at a compass on a two-mile path through the pines. He'd given himself forty minutes to make the trip, and realized that he needed all of it. The high altitude and thin air had him gasping for breath even before he had to deal with the slopes here. He had put all the recriminations behind. All that mattered now was the mission. Things had gone wrong for field operations before, though not any of his, and the mark of a real field officer was the ability to deal with adversity and fulfill his task. At ten minutes after seven he could see the road, and on the near side of it was the convenience store. He stopped twenty yards inside the woodline and waited.

Ann's path was a random one, or seemingly so. Her driving took her on and off the main road twice before she settled down to the final part of the trip. At seven-fifteen she pulled into the parking lot of the small store and went inside.

The FBI was down to two cars now, so skillful had the subject been at evading the surveillance. Every random turn she made had forced a car off her tail—it was assumed that she could identify any car seen more than once—and a frantic call had been sent out for additional vehicles. She'd even chosen the convenience store with care. It could not be watched from anyplace on the road itself; traffic flow would not permit it. Car number ten went into the same parking lot. One of its two occupants went inside, while the other stayed with the vehicle.

The inside man got the Bureau's first real look at Ann, while she bought some donuts and decided to get some more coffee in large Styrofoam cups, plus some soft drinks, all of them high in caffeine content, though the agent didn't take note of that. He checked out right behind her with a paper and two large coffees. He watched her go out the door, and saw that a man joined her, getting into the car as naturally as the fiancé of a woman who liked to drive her own car. He hustled out of the door to his car, but still they almost lost her.

"Here." Ann handed over a paper. Bob's picture was on the front page. It had even been done in color, though the picture quality from the tiny license frame was not exciting. "I'm glad you remembered to wear the wig," she observed.

"What is the plan?" Leonid asked.

"First I will rent you a new car to get you back to the safe house. Next I will purchase some makeup so that all of you can alter your complexions. After that, I think we will get a small truck for the border crossing. We'll also need some packing crates. I don't know about those yet, but I will by the end of the day."

"And the crossing?"

"Tomorrow. We'll leave before noon and make the crossing about dinnertime."

"So fast?" Bob asked.

"*Da*. The more I think about it—they will flood the area with assets if we linger too much." They drove the rest of the way in silence. She went back into the city and parked her car in a public lot, leaving Leonid there as she crossed the street and walked half a block to a rental car agency right across the street from a large hotel. There she went through the proper procedures in less than fifteen minutes, and soon thereafter parked a Ford beside her Volvo. She tossed the keys to Bob and told him to follow her to the interstate, after which he'd be on his own.

By the time they got to the freeway, the FBI was nearly out of cars. A decision had to be made, and the agent in charge of the surveillance guessed right. An unmarked state police vehicle took up the coverage on the Volvo while the last FBI car followed the Ford onto the highway. Meanwhile five cars from the early part of the morning's surveillance of "Ann" raced to catch up with "Bob" and his Ford. Three of them took the same exit, then followed him along the secondary road leading to the safe house. As he matched his driving to the posted speed limit, two of the cars were forced to pass him, but the third was able to lay back—until the Ford pulled to the shoulder and stopped. This section of the road was as straight as an arrow for over a mile, and he'd stopped right in the middle of it.

"I got him, I got him," a helicopter observer reported, watching the car from three miles away through a pair of stabilized binoculars. He saw the minuscule figure of a man open the hood, then bend down and wait for several minutes before closing it and driving on. "This boy is a pro," the observer told the pilot.

Not pro enough, the pilot thought, his own eyes locked on the distant white dot of a car's roof. He could see the Ford turn off the road onto a dirt track that disappeared in the trees.

"Bingo!"

It had been expected that the safe house would be isolated. The geography of the area easily lent itself to that. As soon as the site was identified, an RF-4C Phantom of the 67th Tactical Reconnaissance Wing lifted off from Bergstrom Air Force Base in Texas. The two-man crew of the aircraft thought it was all something of a joke, but they didn't mind the trip, which took less than an hour. As a mission, it was simple enough that anyone could have done it. The Phantom made a total of four high-altitude passes over the area, and after shooting several hundred feet of film through its multiple camera systems, the Phantom landed at Kirtland Air Force Base, just outside Albuquerque. A cargo plane had brought additional ground crew and equipment a few hours earlier. While the pilot shut down his engines, two groundcrewmen removed the film canister and drove it to the trailer that served as an air-portable photolab. Automatic processing equipment delivered the damp frames to the photointerpreters half an hour after the plane had stopped moving.

"There you go," the pilot said when the right frame came up. "Good conditions for it: clear, cold, low humidity, good sun angle. We didn't even leave any contrails."

"Thank you, Major," the sergeant said as she examined the film from the KA-91 panoramic camera. "Looks like we have a dirt road coming off this highway here, snakes over the little ridge . . . and looks like a house trailer, car parked about fifty yards—another one, covered up some. Two cars, then. Okay, what else . . . ?"

"Wait a minute—I don't see the second car," an FBI agent said.

"Here, sir. The sun's reflecting off something, and it's too big to be a Coke bottle. Car windshield, probably. Maybe a back window, but I think it's the front end."

"Why?" the agent asked. He just had to know.

She didn't look up. "Well, sir, if it was me, and I was hiding a car, like, I'd back it in so's I could get out quick, y'know?"

It was all the man could do not to laugh. "That's all right, Sarge."

She cranked to a new frame. "There we go—here's a flash off the bumper, and that's probably the grille, too. See how they covered it up? Look by the trailer. That might be a man there in the shadows . . ." She went to the next frame. "Yep, that's a person." The man was about six feet, athletic, with dark hair and a shadow on his face suggesting that he'd neglected to shave today. No gun was visible.

There were thirty usable frames of the site, eight of which were blown up to poster size. These went to the hangar with the UH-1N. Gus Werner was there. He didn't like rush jobs any more than the people in that trailer did, but his choices were as limited as theirs had been.

"So, Colonel Filitov, we now have you to 1976."

"Dmitri Fedorovich brought me with him when he became Defense Minister. It simplified things, of course."

"And increased your opportunities," Vatutin observed.

"Yes, it did."

There were no recriminations now, no accusations, no comments on the nature of the crime that Misha had committed. They were past that for the moment. The admission had come first as it always did, and that was always hard, but after that, once they'd been broken or tricked into confessing, then came the easy part. It could last for weeks, and Vatutin had no idea where this one would end. The initial phase was aimed at outlining what he'd done. The detailed examination of each episode would follow, but the two-phase nature of the interrogation was crucial to establishing a cross-referencing index, lest the subject later try to change or deny particular things. Even this phase, glossing over the details as they went, horrified Vatutin and his men. Specifications for every tank and gun in the Soviet Army, including the variations never sent to the Arabs—which was as good as giving them to the Israelis, therefore as good as giving them to the Americans—or even the other Warsaw Pact countries, had gone out to the West even before the design prototypes had entered full production. Aircraft specifications. Performance on both conventional and nuclear warheads of every description. Reliability figures for strategic missiles. Inside squabbling in the Defense Ministry, and now, entering the time when Ustinov had become a full voting member of the Politburo, political disputes at the highest level. Most damaging of all, Filitov had given the West everything he knew of Soviet strategy—and he knew all there was to know. As sounding board and confidant for Dmitri Ustinov, and in his capacity as a legendary combat soldier, he'd been the bureaucrat's eyepiece onto the world of actual war-fighting.

And so, Misha, what do you think of this . . . ? Ustinov must have asked that same question a thousand times, Vatutin realized, but he'd never suspected . . .

"What sort of man was Ustinov?" the Colonel of "Two" asked.

"Brilliant," Filitov said at once. "His administrative talents were unparalleled. His instincts for manufacturing processes, for example, were like nothing I've seen before or since. He could smell a factory and tell if it was doing proper work or not. He could see five years in the future and determine which weapons would be needed and which would not. His only weakness was in understanding how they were actually used in combat, and as a result we fought occasionally when I tried to change things to make them easier to use. I mean, he looked for easier manufacturing methods to speed production while I looked at the ease with which the end product could be used on the battlefield. Usually I won him over, but sometimes not."

Amazing, Vatutin thought as he made a few notes. *Misha never stopped fighting to make the weapons better even though he was giving everything to the West . . . why?* But he couldn't ask that now, nor for a very long time. He couldn't let Misha see himself as a patriot again until all of his treason was fully documented. The details of this confession, he knew now, would take months.

"What time is it in Washington?" Ryan asked Candela.

"Coming up on ten in the morning. You had a short session today."

"Yeah. The other side wanted an early recess for something or other. Any word from D.C. on the Gregory matter?"

"Nothing," Candela replied gloomily.

"You told us they would put their defense systems on the table," Narmonov said to his KGB chief. The Foreign Minister had just reported otherwise. They'd actually learned that the day before, but now they were totally sure that it wasn't mere gamesmanship. The Soviets had hinted at reneging on the verification section of the proposal that had already been settled in principle, hoping this would shake the Americans loose, even a little, on the SDI question. That gambit had met a stone wall.

"It would seem that our source was incorrect," Gerasimov admitted. "Or perhaps the expected concession will take more time."

"They have not changed their position, nor will they change it. You've been misinformed, Nikolay Borissovich," the Foreign Minister said, defining his position to be in firm alliance with the Party's General Secretary.

"Is this possible?" Alexandrov inquired.

"One of the problems gathering intelligence on the Americans is that they themselves often do not know what their position is. Our information came from a well-placed source, and this report coincided with that from another agent. Perhaps Allen wished to do this, but was forbidden to."

"That is possible," the Foreign Minister allowed, unwilling to push Gerasimov too hard. "I've long felt that he has his own thoughts on the issue. But that does not matter now. We will have to change our approach somewhat. Might this signal that the Americans have made another technical breakthrough?"

"Possibly. We're working on that right now. I have a team trying to bring out some rather sensitive material." Gerasimov didn't dare to go further. His operation to snatch the American Major was more desperate than Ryan himself guessed. If it became public, he'd stand accused within the Politburo of trying to destroy important negotiations—and to have done so without first consulting his peers. Even Politburo members were supposed to discuss what they did, but he couldn't do that. His ally Alexandrov would want to know why, and Gerasimov could not risk revealing his entrapment to anyone. On the other hand, he was certain that the Americans would not do anything to reveal the kidnapping. For them to do so would run an almost identical risk—political elements in Washington would try to accuse conservatives of using the incident to scuttle the talks for reasons of their own. The game was as grand as it had ever been, and the risks Gerasimov was running, though grave, merely added spice to the contest. It was too late to be careful. He was beyond that, and even though his own life was on the line, the scope of the contest was worthy of its goal.

"We don't know that he's there, do we?" Paulson asked. He was the senior rifleman on the Hostage Rescue Team. A member of the Bureau's "Quarter-Inch Club," he could place three aimed shots within a circle less than half an inch in diameter at two hundred yards—and of that half-inch, .308 inches was the diameter of the bullet itself.

"No, but it's the best we got," Gus Werner admitted. "There's three of them. We know for sure that two of them are there. They wouldn't leave one man guarding the hostage while they were someplace else—that's unprofessional."

"It all makes sense, Gus," Paulson agreed. "But we don't *know*. We go with this, then." That part wasn't a question.

"Yeah, and fast."

"Okay." Paulson turned and looked at the wall. They were using a pilot's ready room. The cork on the walls, put there for sound-absorption, was also perfect for hanging maps and photos. The trailer, they all saw, was a cheap-o. Only a few windows, and of the two original doors, one had been boarded over. They assumed that the room near the remaining door was occupied by the "bad guys" while the other held the hostage. The one good thing about the case was that their opponents were professionals, and therefore somewhat predictable. They'd do the sensible thing in most cases, unlike common criminals, who only did things that occurred to them at the time.

Paulson switched his gaze to a different photo, then to the topographical map, and started picking his approach route. The high-resolution photographs were a godsend. They showed one man outside, and he was watching the road, the most likely route of approach. He'd walk around some, Paulson thought, but mostly he'd watch the road. So, the observer/sniper team would approach overland from the other side.

"You think they're city folks?" he asked Werner.

"Probably."

"I'll come in this way. Marty and I can approach to within four hundred yards or so behind this ridge, then come down along here parallel to the trailer."

"Where's your spot?"

"There." Paulson tapped the best of the photos. "I'd say we should bring the machine gun in with us." He explained why, and everyone nodded.

"One more change," Werner announced. "We have new Rules of Engagement. If anybody even thinks that the hostage might be in danger, the bad guys go down. Paulson, if there's one near him when we make the move, you take him down with the first shot, whether he's got a weapon out or not."

"Hold it, Gus," Paulson objected. "There's sure as hell going to be—"

"The hostage is important, and there is reason to suspect that any attempt to rescue him will result in his death—"

"Somebody's been watching too many movies," another team member observed.

"Who?" Paulson asked both quietly and pointedly.

"The President. Director Jacobs was on the phone, too. He's got it in writing."

"I don't like it," the rifleman said. "They will have somebody in there baby-sitting him, and you want me to blow him away whether he is threatening the hostage or not."

"That's exactly right," Werner agreed. "If you can't do it, tell me now."

"I have to know why, Gus."

"The President called him a priceless national asset. He's the key man in a project important enough that he briefed the President himself. That's why they kidnapped him, and the thinking is that if they see that they can't have him, they won't want us to have him either. Look at what they've done already," the team leader concluded.

Paulson weighed this for a moment and nodded agreement. He turned to his backup man, Marty, who did the same.

"Okay. We have to go through a window. It's a two-rifle job."

Werner moved to a blackboard and sketched out the assault plan in as much detail as he could. The interior arrangement of the trailer was unknown, and much would depend on last-minute intelligence to be gathered on the scene by Paulson's ten-power gunsight. The details of the plan were no different from a military assault. First of all, Werner established the chain of command—everyone knew it, but it was precisely defined anyway. Next came the composition of the assault teams and their parts of the mission. Doctors and ambulances would be standing by, as would an evidence team. They spent an hour, and still the plan was not as complete as any of them would like, but their training allowed for this. Once committed, the operation would depend on the expertise and judgment of the individual team members, but in the final analysis, such things always did. When they were finished, everyone started moving.

She decided on a small U-Haul van, the same-size vehicle as that used for mini-buses or small business deliveries. A larger truck, she thought, would take too long to fill with the proper boxes. These she picked up an hour later from a business called the Box Barn. It was something she'd never had to do before—all of her information transfers had been done with film cassettes that fitted easily into one's pocket—but all she'd needed to do was look through the Yellow Pages and make a few calls. She purchased ten shipping crates made with wood edges and plastic-covered cardboard sides, all neatly broken down for easy assembly. The same place sold her labels to indicate what was inside, and polystyrene shipping filler to protect her shipment. The salesperson insisted on the latter. Tania watched as two men loaded her truck, and drove off.

"What do you suppose that is all about?" an agent asked.

"I suppose she wants to take something someplace." The driver followed

THE CARDINAL OF THE KREMLIN • 809

her from several hundred yards back while his partner called in agents to talk to the shipping company. The U-Haul van was far easier to track than a Volvo.

Paulson and three other men stepped out of the Chevy Suburban at the far end of a housing development about two thousand yards from the trailer. A child in the front yard stared at the men—two carrying rifles, a third carrying an M-60 machine gun as they walked into the woods. Two police cars stayed there after the Suburban drove off, and officers knocked on doors to tell people not to discuss what they had—or in most cases, hadn't—seen.

One nice thing about pine trees, Paulson thought one hundred yards into the treeline, was that they dropped needles, not the noisy leaves that coated the western Virginia hills which he trudged every autumn looking for deer. He hadn't gotten one this year. He'd had two good opportunities, but the bucks he'd seen were smaller than what he preferred to bring home, and he'd decided to leave them for next year while waiting for another chance that had never presented itself.

Paulson was a woodsman, born in Tennessee, who was never happier than when in the back country, making his way quietly through ground decorated with trees and carpeted with the fallen vegetation that covered the untended ground. He led the other three, slowly and carefully, making as little noise as possible—like the revenuers who'd finally convinced his grandfather to discontinue the production of mountain-brewed White Lightning, he thought without smiling. Paulson had never killed anyone in his fifteen years of service. The Hostage Rescue Team had the best-trained snipers in the world, but they'd never actually applied their craft. He himself had come close half a dozen times, but always before, he'd had a reason not to shoot. It would be different today. He was almost certain of that, and that made his mood different. It was one thing to go into a job knowing that a shooting was possible. In the Bureau that chance was always there. You planned for it, always hoping that it would not be necessary—he knew all too well what happened when a cop killed some-one, the nightmares, the depression that rarely seemed to appear on TV cop shows. The doc was already flying out, he thought. The Bureau kept a psychiatrist on retainer to help agents through the time after a shooting, because even when you knew that there'd been no choice at all, the human psyche quails before the reality of unnecessary death and punishes the survivor for being alive when his victim is not. That was one price of progress, Paulson thought. It hadn't always been so, and with criminals in most cases it still wasn't. That was the difference between one community and the other. But what community did his target belong to? Criminal? No, they'd be trained professionals, patriots after the fashion of their society. People doing a job. *Just like me.*

He heard a sound. His left hand went up, and all four men dropped behind cover. Something was moving . . . over to the left. It kept going left, away from their path. Maybe a kid, he thought, a kid playing in the woods. He waited to be sure it was heading away, then started moving again. The shooter team wore standard military camouflage clothing over their protective gear, the woodland pattern's blend of greens and browns. After half an hour, Paulson checked his map.

"Checkpoint One," he said into his radio.

"Roger," Werner answered from three miles away. "Any problems?"

"Negative. Ready to move over the first ridge. Should have the objective in sight in fifteen minutes."

"Roger. Move in."

"Okay. Out." Paulson and his team formed line abreast to get to the first ridge. It was a small one, with the second two hundred yards beyond it. From there they'd be able to see the trailer, and now things went very slowly. Paulson handed his rifle to the fourth man. The agent moved forward alone, looking ahead to pick out the path that promised the quietest passage. It was mainly a question of looking where you walked rather than how, after all, something lost on city people who thought a forest floor was an invariably noisy place. Here there were plenty of rocky outcroppings, and he snaked his way among them and reached the second ridge in five minutes of nearly silent travel. Paulson snuggled up next to a tree and pulled out his binoculars—even these were coated with green plastic.

" 'Afternoon, folks," he said to himself. He couldn't see anyone yet, but the trailer blocked his view of where he expected the outside man to be, and there were also plenty of trees in the way. Paulson searched his immediate surroundings for movement. He took several minutes to watch and listen before waving for his fellow agents to come forward. They took ten minutes. Paulson checked his watch. They'd been in the woods for ninety minutes, and were slightly ahead of schedule.

"Seen anyone?" the other rifleman asked when he came down at Paulson's side.

"Not yet."

"Christ, I hope they haven't moved," Marty said. "Now what?"

"We'll move over to the left, then down the gully over there. That's our spot." He pointed.

"Just like on the pictures."

"Everybody ready?" Paulson asked. He decided to wait a minute before setting off, allowing everyone a drink of water. The air was thin and dry here, and throats were getting raspy. They didn't want anyone to cough. *Cough drops,* the lead sniper thought. *We ought to include those in the gear . . .*

It took another half hour to get to their perches. Paulson selected a damp spot next to a granite boulder that had been deposited by the last glacier to visit the area. He was about twenty feet above the level of the trailer, about what he wanted for the job, and not quite at a ninety-degree angle to it. He had a direct view of the large window on its back end. If Gregory were there, this was where they expected him to be kept. It was time to find out. Paulson unfolded the bipod legs on his rifle, flipped off the scope covers, and went to work. He grabbed for his radio again, fitting the earpiece. He spoke in a whisper lower than that of the wind in the pine branches over his head.

"This is Paulson. We're in place, looking now. Will advise."

"Acknowledged," the radio replied.

"Jeez," Marty said first. "There he is. Right side."

Al Gregory was sitting in an armchair. He had little choice in the matter. His wrists were cuffed in his lap—that concession had been made to his comfort—but his upper arms and lower legs were roped in place. His glasses had been taken away, and every object in the room had a fuzzy edge. That included the one who called himself Bill. They were taking turns guarding him. Bill sat at the far end of the room, just beyond the window. There was an automatic pistol tucked in his belt, but Gregory couldn't tell the type, merely the unmistakable angular shape.

"What—"

"—will we do with you?" Bill completed the question. "Damned if I know, Major. Some people are interested in what you do for a living, I suppose."

"I won't—"

"I'm sure," Bill said with a smile. "Now, we told you to be quiet or I'll have to put the gag back. Just relax, kid."

"What did she say the crates were for?" the agent asked.

"She said that her company was shipping a couple of statues. Some local artist, she said—a show in San Francisco, I think."

There's a Soviet consulate in San Francisco, the agent thought at once. *But they can't be doing that . . . could they?*

"Man-sized crates, you said?"

"You could put two people in the big ones, easy, and a bunch of little ones."

"How long?"

"You don't need special tools. Half an hour, tops."

Half an hour . . . ? One of the agents left the room to make a phone call. The information was relayed by radio to Werner.

"Heads up," the radio earpiece announced. "We got a U-Haul truck— make that a small van—coming in off the main road."

"We can't see it from here," Paulson groused quietly to Marty at his left. One problem with their location was that they couldn't see all of the trailer, and could only catch glimpses of the road that led to it. The trees were too thick for that. To get a better view meant moving forward, but that meant a risk that they were unwilling to run. The laser rangefinder placed them six hundred and eleven feet from the trailer. The rifles were optimized for two-hundred-yard range, and their camouflage clothing made them invisible, so long as they didn't move. Even with binoculars, the trees so cluttered the view that there were simply too many things for the human eye to focus on.

He heard the van. Bad muffler, he thought. Then he heard a metal door slam and the squeak of another opening. Voices came next, but though he could tell that people were talking, he couldn't make out a single word.

"This should be big enough," Captain Bisyarina told Leonid. "I have two of these and three of the smaller ones. We'll use these to stack on top."

"What are we shipping?"

"Statuary. There's an art show three days from now, and we're even going to make the crossing at the point nearest to it. If we leave in two hours, we'll hit the border at about the right time."

"You're sure—"

"They search parcels coming north, not going south," Bisyarina assured him.

"Very well. We'll assemble the boxes inside. Tell Oleg to come out."

Bisyarina went inside. Lenny was stationed outside since he knew more about working in the wilderness than the other two officers. While Oleg and Leonid carried the crates inside, she went into the back of the trailer to check on Gregory.

"Hello, Major. Comfortable?"

"I got another one," Paulson said the moment she came into view. "Female, that's the one from the photos—the Volvo one," he said into the radio. "She's talking to the hostage."

"Three men now visible," the radio said next. Another agent had a perch on the far side of the trailer. "They're carrying crates inside the trailer. Say again, three male subjects. Female subject inside and out of sight."

"That should be all of the subjects. Tell me about the crates." Werner stood by the helicopter in a field several miles away, holding a diagram of the trailer.

"They're broken down, not assembled. I guess they're going to put 'em together."

"Four's all we know about," Werner said to his men. "And the hostage is there . . ."

"That ought to tie up two of them, assembling the crates," one of the assault team said. "One outside, one with the hostage . . . sounds good to me, Gus."

"Attention, this is Werner. We're moving. Everybody stand by." He gestured to the helicopter pilot, who began the engine-start sequence. The HRT leader made his own mental check while his men boarded the helicopter. If the Russians tried to drive him away, his men could try to take them on the move, but that kind of van had windows only for the driver and passenger . . . that meant that two or three of them would be out of sight . . . and perhaps able to kill the hostage before his men could prevent it. His first instinct was right: They had to go now. The team's Chevy Suburban with four men pulled onto the main road leading to the site.

Paulson flipped the safety off his rifle, and Marty did the same. They agreed on what would happen next. Ten feet from them, the machine-gunner and his loader readied their weapon slowly, to mute the metallic sounds of the gun's action.

"Never goes according to plan," the number-two rifleman noted quietly.

"That's why they train us so much." Paulson had his crosshairs on the target. It wasn't easy because the glass window reflected much light from the surrounding woods. He could barely make out her head, but it was a woman, and it was someone positively identified as a target. He estimated the wind to be about ten knots from his right. Applied over two hundred yards, that would move his bullet about two inches to the left, and he'd have to allow for that. Even with a ten-power scope, a human head is not a large target at two hundred yards, and Paulson swiveled the rifle slightly to keep her head transfixed on the crosshairs of his sight as she walked about. He wasn't so much watching his target as the crosshair reticle of the sight itself, keeping it aligned with the target rather than the other way around. The drill he followed was automatic. He controlled his breathing, positioned himself on his elbows, and snugged the rifle in tight.

*   *   *

"Who are you?" Gregory asked.

"Tania Bisyarina." She walked about to work the stiffness out of her legs.

"Are your orders to kill me?" Tania admired the way he'd asked that. Gregory wasn't exactly the image of a soldier, but the important part was always hidden from view.

"No, Major. You will be taking a little trip."

"There's the truck," Werner said. *Sixty seconds from the road to the trailer.* He lifted his radio. "Go go go!" The doors on the helicopter slid back and coiled ropes were readied. Werner crashed his fist down on the pilot's shoulder hard enough to hurt, but the flyer was too busy to notice. He pushed down on the collective and dove the helicopter toward the trailer, now less than a mile away.

They heard it before they saw it, the distinctive *whop-whop-whop* of the twin-bladed rotor. There was enough helicopter traffic over the area that the danger it brought was not immediately obvious. The one outside came to the edge of the trailer and looked through the treetops, then turned when he thought he heard the sound of an approaching vehicle. Inside, Leonid and Oleg looked up from their half-assembled crate in irritation rather than concern, but that changed in an instant when the sound of the helicopter became a roar as the chopper came into a hover directly overhead. In the back of the trailer, Bisyarina went to the window and saw it first. It was the last thing she would ever see.

"On target," Paulson said.

"On target," the other rifleman agreed.

"Shoot!"

They fired at nearly the same moment, but Paulson knew the other shot had gone first. That one broke the thick window, and the bullet went wild, deflected by the breaking glass. The second hollow-point match bullet was a split-second behind it, and struck the Soviet agent in the face. Paulson saw it, but it was the instant of firing that was locked in his mind, the crosshairs on the target. To their left, the machine-gunner was already firing when Paulson called his shot: "Center-head."

"Target is down," the second rifleman said into the radio. "Female target is down. Hostage in view." Both reloaded their rifles and searched for new targets.

Weighted ropes dropped from the helicopter, and four men rappelled down. Werner was in front, and swung his way through the broken window, his MP-5 submachine gun in hand. Gregory was there, shouting something. Werner was joined by another team member, who threw the chair on its side and knelt between it and the rest of the structure. Then a third man came through, and all three trained their weapons the other way.

Outside, the Chevy Suburban arrived in time to see one of the KGB men firing a pistol at an agent who'd landed atop the trailer and was caught on something, unable to bring his weapon around. Two agents leaped from the vehicle and fired three rounds each, dropping the man in his tracks. The agent atop the trailer freed himself and waved.

Inside, Leonid and Oleg were reaching for their weapons. One looked back to see a constant stream of machine-gun bullets chewing through the metal sides of the trailer, clearly to keep them from approaching Gregory. But those were their orders.

"Hostage is safe, hostage is safe. Female target is down," Werner called over the radio.

"Outside target is down," another agent called. From the outside. He watched another team member put a small explosive charge on the door. The man backed up and nodded. "Ready!"

"Machine-gunner, cease fire, cease fire," Werner ordered.

The two KGB officers inside heard it stop and went toward the back. The front door of the trailer was blown off its hinges as they did so. The blast was supposed to be sufficient to disorient, but both men were too alert for that. Oleg turned, bringing his weapon up in two hands to cover Leonid. He fired at the first figure through the door, hitting the man in the arm. That agent fell, trying to bring his weapon around. He fired and missed, but drew Oleg's attention to himself. The second man in the door had his MP-5 cradled in his arm. His gun fired two rounds. Oleg's last impression was one of surprise: he hadn't heard them shoot. He understood when he saw the canlike silencers.

"Agent wounded and bad guy down. Another bad guy heading back. Lost him turning the corner." The agent ran after him, but tripped on a packing case.

They let him come through the door. One agent, his torso protected with a bullet-resistant vest, was between the door and the hostage. They could take the chance now. It was the one who'd gotten the rent-a-car, Werner knew at once, and his weapon wasn't pointed at anybody yet. The man saw three HRT members dressed in black Nomex jump suits and obviously protected with body armor. His face showed the beginnings of hesitation.

"Drop the gun!" Werner screamed. "Don't—"

Leonid saw where Gregory was and remembered his orders. The pistol started coming around.

Werner did what he'd always told his people not to do, but would never remember why. He loosed half a dozen rounds at the man's arm, going for the gun—and miraculously enough, it worked. The gun hand jerked like a puppet's and the pistol fell free in a cloud of spraying blood. Werner leaped forward, knocking the subject down and placing the muzzle of his silenced gun right on his forehead.

"Number three is down! Hostage safe! Team: check in!"

"Outside, number one down and dead."

"Trailer, number two down and dead! One agent hit in the arm, not serious."

"Female down and dead," Werner called. "One subject wounded and in custody. Secure the area! Ambulances, now!" From the time of the sniper shots, it had taken a total of twenty-nine seconds.

Three agents appeared at the window through which Werner and the other two had arrived. One of the agents inside pulled out his combat knife and cut through the ropes that held Gregory, then practically threw him out the window, where he was caught and carried off like a rag doll. Al was put in the back of the HRT truck and rushed off. On the highway, an Air Force helicopter landed. As soon as Gregory was tossed inside, it lifted off.

All HRT members have medical training, and two on the assault team had trained with firemen-paramedics. One of them was wounded in the arm, and directed the bandaging done by the man who'd shot Oleg. The other trained paramedic came back and started working on Leonid.

"He'll make it. The arm's gonna need some surgery, though. Radius, ulna, and humerus all fractured, boss."

"You should have dropped the gun," Werner told him. "You didn't have much of a chance."

"Jesus." It was Paulson. He stood at the window and looked to see what his single bullet had done. An agent was searching the body, looking for a weapon. He stood up, shaking his head. That told the rifleman something he would have preferred not to know. In that moment, he knew that he'd never hunt again. The bullet had entered just below the left eye. Most of the rest of her head was on the wall opposite the window. Paulson told himself that he should never have looked. The rifleman turned away after five long seconds and unloaded his weapon.

The helicopter took Gregory directly to the project. Six armed security people were waiting when it landed, and hustled him inside. He was surprised when someone snapped some pictures. Someone else tossed Al a can of Coke, and he anointed himself with carbonated spray when he worked the pop-top. After taking a drink, he spoke: "What the hell was all that?"

"We're not even sure ourselves," the chief of project security replied. It took a few more seconds for Gregory's mind to catch up with what had happened. That's when he started shaking.

Werner and his people were outside the trailer while the evidence team took over. A dozen New Mexico State Police officers were there also. The wounded agent and the wounded KGB officer were loaded into the same ambulance, though the latter was handcuffed to his stretcher and doing his best not to scream with the pain of three shattered bones in his arm.

"Where you taking him?" a state police captain asked.

"The base hospital at Kirtland—both of them," Werner replied.

"Long ways."

"Orders are to keep this one under wraps. For what it's worth, the guy who popped your officer is that one over there—from the description he gave us, it's him anyway."

"I'm surprised you took one alive." That earned the Captain a curious look. "I mean, they were all armed, right?"

"Yeah," Werner agreed. He smiled in an odd sort of way. "I'm surprised, too."

24. The Rules of the Game

The amazing thing was that it didn't make the news. Only a handful of unmuffled shots had been fired, and gunfire is not all that unusual a thing in the American West. An inquiry to the New Mexico State Police had gotten the reply that the investigation into the shooting of Officer Mendez was still continuing, with a break expected at any time, but that the helicopter activity was merely part of a routine search-and-rescue exercise conducted jointly by the state police and Air Force personnel. It wasn't all that good a story, but good enough to keep reporters off everyone's back for a day or two.

The evidence team sifted through the trailer and not surprisingly found little of note. A police photographer took the requisite pictures of all the victims—he called himself a professional ghoul—and handed over the film to the senior FBI agent on the scene. The bodies were bagged and driven to Kirtland, from which they were flown to Dover Air Force Base, where there was a special receiving center staffed by forensic pathologists. The developed photos of the dead KGB officers were sent electronically to Washington. The local police and FBI began talking about how the case against the surviving KGB agent would be handled. It was determined that he'd broken at least a dozen statutes, evenly divided between federal and state jurisdiction, and various attorneys would have to sort that mess out, even though they knew that the real decision would be made in Washington. They were wrong in that assessment, however. Part of it would be decided elsewhere.

It was four in the morning when Ryan felt a hand on his shoulder. He rolled over and looked in time to see Candela flip on the bedstand light.

"What?" Ryan asked as coherently as he could manage.

"The Bureau pulled it off. They have Gregory and he's fine," Candela said. He handed over some photos. Ryan's eyes blinked a few times before going very wide.

"That's a hell of a thing to wake up to," Jack said, even before seeing what had happened to Tania Bisyarina. "Holy shit!" He dropped the photos on the bed and walked into the bathroom. Candela heard the sound of running water, then Ryan emerged and walked to the refrigerator. He pulled out a can of soda and popped it open.

"Excuse me. You want one?" Jack gestured at the refrigerator.

"It's a little early for me. You made the pass to Golovko yesterday?"

"Yeah. The session starts this afternoon. I want to see our friend about eight. I was planning to get up about five-thirty."

"I thought you'd want to see these right away," Candela said. That elicited a grunt.

"Sure. It beats the morning paper . . . We got his ass," Ryan noted, staring at the carpet. "Unless . . ."

"Unless he wants to die real bad," the CIA officer agreed.

"What about his wife and daughter?" Jack asked. "If you got opinions, I sure as hell want to hear them."

"The meet's where I suggested?"

"Yep."

"Push him as hard as you can." Candela lifted the pictures off the bed and tucked them in an envelope. "Make sure you show him these. I don't think it'll trouble his conscience much, but it'll damned well show him we're serious. If you want an opinion, I thought you were crazy before. Now"—he grinned—"I think you're just about crazy enough. I'll be back when you're all woke up."

Ryan nodded and watched him leave before heading into the shower. The water was hot, and Jack took his time, in the process filling the small room with steam that he had to wipe off the mirror. When he shaved, he made a conscious effort to stare at his beard rather than his eyes. It wasn't a time for self-doubt.

It was dark outside his windows. Moscow was not lit the same way as an American city. Perhaps it was the near-total absence of cars at this hour. Washington always had people moving about. There was always the unconscious certainty that somewhere people were up and about their business, whatever that might be. The concept didn't translate here. Just as the words of one language never exactly, never quite correspond to those of another, so Moscow was to Ryan just similar enough to other major cities he'd visited to seem all the more alien in its differences. People didn't go about *their* business here. For the most part they went about the business assigned to them by someone else. The irony was that he would soon be one of the people giving orders, to a person who'd forgotten how to take them.

Morning came slowly to Moscow. The traffic sounds of trolley cars and the deeper rumble of truck diesels were muted by the snow cover, and Ryan's window didn't face in the proper direction to catch the first light of dawn. What had been gray began to acquire color, as though a child were playing with the controls on a color television. Jack finished his third cup of coffee, and set down the book he'd been reading at seven-thirty. Timing was everything on occasions like this, Candela told him. He made a final trip to the bathroom before dressing for his morning walk.

The sidewalks had been swept clean of the Sunday-night snowstorm, though there were still piles at the curbs. Ryan nodded to the security guards, Australian, American, and Russian, before turning north on Chay-kovskogo. The bitter northerly wind made his eyes water, and he adjusted the scarf around his neck slightly as he walked toward Vosstaniya Square. This was Moscow's embassy district. The previous morning he'd turned right at the far side of the square and seen half a dozen legations mixed together randomly, but this morning he turned left on Kudrinskiy Pereu-lok—the Russians had at least nine ways of saying "street," but the nuances were lost on Jack—then right, then left again on Barrikadnaya.

"Barricade" seemed an odd name for both a street and a movie theater. It looked odder still in Cyrillic lettering. The B was recognizable, though the Cyrillic "B" is actually a V, and the Rs in the word looked like Roman Ps. Jack altered his course somewhat, walking as close to the buildings as possible as he approached. Just as expected, a door opened and he turned into it. Again he was patted down. The security man found the sealed envelope in the coat pocket, but didn't open it, to Ryan's relief.

"Come." The same thing he'd said the first time, Jack noted. Perhaps he had a limited vocabulary.

Gerasimov was sitting on an aisle seat, his back confidently to Ryan as Jack walked down the slope to see the man.

"Good morning," he said to the back of the man's head.

"How do you like our weather?" Gerasimov asked, waving the security man away. He stood and led Jack down toward the screen.

"Wasn't this cold where I grew up."

"You should wear a hat. Most Americans prefer not to, but here it is a necessity."

"It's cold in New Mexico, too," Ryan said.

"So I'm told. Did you think I would do nothing?" the KGB Chairman asked. He did so without emotion, like a teacher to a slow student. Ryan decided to let him enjoy the feeling for a moment.

"Am I supposed to negotiate with you for Major Gregory's freedom?"

Jack asked neutrally—or tried to. The extra morning coffee had put an edge on his emotions.

"If you wish," Gerasimov replied.

"I think you will find this to be of interest." Jack handed over the envelope.

The KGB Chairman opened it and took out the photographs. He didn't display any reaction as he flipped through the three frames, but when he turned to look at Ryan his eyes made the morning's wind seem like the breath of spring.

"One's alive," Jack reported. "He's hurt, but he'll recover. I don't have his picture. Somebody screwed up on that end. We have Gregory back, unhurt."

"I see."

"You should also see that your options are now those which we intended. I need to know which choice you will make."

"It is obvious, is it not?"

"One of the things I have learned in studying your country is that nothing is as obvious as we would like." That drew something that was almost a smile.

"How will I be treated?"

"Quite well." *A hell of a lot better than you deserve.*

"My family?"

"Them also."

"And how do you propose to get the three of us out?"

"I believe your wife is Latvian by birth, and that she often travels to her home. Have them there Friday night," Ryan said, continuing with some details.

"Exactly what—"

"You do not need that information, Mr. Gerasimov."

"Ryan, you cannot—"

"Yes, sir, I can," Jack cut him off, wondering why he'd said "sir."

"And for me?" the Chairman asked. Ryan told him what he'd have to do. Gerasimov agreed. "I have one question."

"Yes?"

"How did you fool Platonov? He's a very clever man."

"There really was a minor flap with the SEC, but that wasn't the important part." Ryan got ready to leave. "We couldn't have done it without you. We had to stage a really good scene, something that you don't fake. Congressman Trent was over here six months ago, and he met a fellow named Valeriy. They got to be very close friends. He found out later that you gave Valeriy five years for 'antisocial activity.' Anyway, he wanted to get even. We asked for his help and he jumped at it. So I suppose you could say that we used your own prejudices against you."

"What would you have us do with such people, Ryan?" the Chairman demanded. "Do you—"

"I don't make laws, Mr. Gerasimov." Ryan walked out. It was nice, he thought on the return to the embassy compound, to have the wind at his back for a change.

"Good morning, Comrade General Secretary."

"You need not be so formal, Ilya Arkadyevich. There are Politburo members more senior to you who do not have the vote, and we have been comrades too . . . long. What is troubling you?" Narmonov asked cautiously. The pain in his colleague's eyes was evident. They were scheduled to talk about the winter wheat crop, but—

"Andrey Il'ych, I do not know how to begin." Vaneyev nearly choked on the words, and tears began to stream from his eyes. "It is my daughter . . ." He went on for ten fitful minutes.

"And?" Narmonov asked, when it seemed that he'd finally stopped— but as was obvious, there had to be more. There was.

"Alexandrov and Gerasimov, then." Narmonov leaned back in his chair and stared at the wall. "It took great courage indeed for you to come to me with this, my friend."

"I cannot let them—even if it means my career, Andrey, I cannot let them stop you now. You have too many things to do, we—you have too many things to change. I must leave. I know that. But you must stay, Andrey. The people need you here if we are to accomplish anything."

It was noteworthy that he'd said *people* rather than *Party*, Narmonov thought. The times really were changing. No. He shook his head. It wasn't that, not yet. All he had accomplished was to create the atmosphere within which the times might have the possibility of change. Vaneyev was one who understood that the problem was not so much goals as process. Every Politburo member knew—had known for years—the things that needed to be changed. It was the method of change that no one could agree on. It was like turning a ship to a new course, he thought, but knowing that the rudder might break if you did so. Continuing in the same path would allow the ship to plow on into . . . what? Where was the Soviet Union heading? They didn't even know that. But to change course meant risk, and if the rudder broke—if the Party lost its ascendancy—then there would be only chaos. That was a choice that no rational man would wish to face, but it was a choice whose necessity no rational man could deny.

We don't even know what our country is doing, Narmonov thought to himself. For at least the past eight years all figures on economic performance had been false in one way or another, each compounding itself on the next until the economic forecasts generated by the GOSPLAN bureaucracy were as fictitious as the list of Stalin's virtues. The ship he commanded was running deeper and deeper into an enveloping fog of lies told by functionaries whose careers would be destroyed by the truth. That was how he spoke of it at the weekly Politburo meetings. Forty years of rosy goals and predictions had merely plotted a course on a meaningless chart. Even the Politburo itself didn't know the state of the Soviet Union— something the West hardly suspected.

The alternative? That was the rub, wasn't it? In his darker moments, Narmonov wondered if he or anyone else could really change things. The goal of his entire political life had been to achieve the power that he now held, and only now did he fully understand how circumscribed that power was. All the way up the ladder of his career he'd noted things that had to change, never fully appreciating how difficult that would be. The power he wielded wasn't the same as Stalin's had been. His more immediate predecessors had seen to that. Now the Soviet Union wasn't so much a ship to be guided, as a huge bureaucratic spring that absorbed and dissipated energy and vibrated only to its own inefficient frequency. Unless that changed . . . the West was racing into a new industrial age while the Soviet Union still could not feed itself. China was adopting the economic lessons of Japan, and in two generations might become the world's third economy: *a billion people with a strong, driving economy, right on our* border, hungry for land, and with a racial hatred of all Russians that could make Hitler's fascist legions seem like a flock of football hooligans. That was a strategic threat to his country that made the nuclear weapons of America and NATO shrivel to insignificance—and still the Party bureaucracy didn't see that it had to change or risk being the agent of its own doom!

Someone has to try, and that someone is me.

But in order to try, he first had to survive himself, survive long enough to communicate his vision of national goals, first to the Party, then to the people—or perhaps the other way around? Neither would be easy. The Party had its ways, resistant to change, and the people, the *narod,* no longer gave a moment's thought to what the Party and its leader said to them. That was the amusing part. The West—the enemies of his nation—held him in higher esteem than his own countrymen.

And what does that mean? he asked himself. *If they are enemies, does their favor mean that I am proceeding on the right path—right for whom?* Narmonov wondered if the American President were as lonely as he. But before facing that impossible task, he still had the day-to-day tactical problem of personal survival. Even now, even at the hands of a trusted colleague. Narmonov sighed. It was a very Russian sound.

"So, Ilya, what will you do?" he asked a man who could not commit an act of treason more heinous than his daughter's.

"I will support you if it means my disgrace. My Svetlana will have to face the consequences of her action." Vaneyev sat upright and wiped his eyes. He looked like a man about to face a firing squad, assembling his manhood for one last act of defiance.

"I may have to denounce you myself," Narmonov said.

"I will understand, Andrushka," Vaneyev replied, his voice laden with dignity.

"I would prefer not to do this. I need you, Ilya. I need your counsel. If I can save your place, I will."

"I can ask for no more than that."

It was time to build the man back up. Narmonov stood and walked around his desk to take his friend's hand. "Whatever they tell you, agree to it without reservation. When the time comes, you will show them what kind of *man* you are."

"As will you, Andrey."

Narmonov walked him to the door. He had another five minutes till his next scheduled appointment. His day was full of economic matters, decisions that came to him because of indecision in men with ministerial rank, seeking him for his blessing as though from the village priest . . . *As though I don't have troubles enough,* the General Secretary of the Communist Party of the Soviet Union told himself. He spent his five minutes counting votes. It should have been easier for him than for his American counterpart—in the Soviet Union only full Politburo members had the right to vote, and there were only thirteen of them—but each man represented a collection of interests, and Narmonov was asking each of them to do things never before contemplated. In the final analysis, power still counted for more than anything else, he told himself, and he could still count on Defense Minister Yazov.

"I think you will like it here," General Pokryshkin said as they walked the perimeter fence. The KGB guards saluted as they passed, and both men returned the halfhearted gestures. The dogs were gone now, and Gennady thought that a mistake, food problems or no.

"My wife will not," Bondarenko replied. "She's followed me from one camp to another for almost twenty years, and finally to Moscow. She likes it there." He turned to look outside the fence and smiled. *Could a man ever tire of this view? But what will my wife say when I tell her this?* But it was not often that a Soviet soldier had the chance to make this sort of choice, and she would understand that, wouldn't she?

"Perhaps general's stars will change her mind—and we are working to make the place more hospitable. Do you have any idea how hard I had to fight for that? Finally I told them that my engineers were like dancers, and that they had to be happy to perform. I think that Central Committeeman is a devotee of the Bolshoy, and that finally made him understand. That's when the theater was authorized, and that's when we started getting decent food trucked in. By next summer the school will be finished, and all the children will be here. Of course"—he laughed—"we'll have to put up another block of apartments, and the next Bright Star commander will also have to be a schoolmaster."

"In five years we may not have room for the lasers. Well, you left the highest point for them, I see."

"Yes, that argument lasted nine months. Just to convince them that we might eventually want to build something more powerful than the one we already have."

"The real Bright Star," Bondarenko noted.

"You will build it, Gennady Iosifovich."

"Yes, Comrade General, I will build it. I will accept the appointment if you still want me." He turned to survey the terrain again. *Someday this will all be mine . . .*

"Allah's will," the Major said with a shrug.

He was getting tired of hearing that. The Archer's patience and even his faith were being tested by the forced change in plans. The Soviets had been running troops along the valley road on and off for the last thirty-six hours. He'd gotten half his force across when it had begun, then suffered while his men had been divided, each side watching the rolling trucks and personnel carriers and wondering if the Russians would halt and hop out, and climb the hills to find their visitors. There would be a bloody fight if they tried that, and many Russians would die—but he wasn't here merely to kill Russians. He was here to hurt them in a way that the simple loss of soldiers could never do.

But there was a mountain to climb, and he was now grossly behind schedule, and all the consolation anyone could offer was Allah's will. *Where was Allah when the bombs fell on my wife and daughter? Where was Allah when they took my son away? Where was Allah when the Russians bombed our refugee camp . . . ? Why must life be so cruel?*

"It is hard to wait, isn't it?" the Major observed. "Waiting is the hardest thing. The mind has nothing to occupy it, and the questions come."

"And your questions?"

"When will the war end? There is talk . . . but there has been talk for years. I am tired of this war."

"You spent much of it on the other—"

The Major's head snapped around. "Do not say that. I have been giving your band information for years! Didn't your leader tell you this?"

"No. We knew that he was getting something, but—"

"Yes, he was a good man, and he knew that he had to protect me. Do you know how many times I sent my troops on useless patrols so that they'd miss you, how many times I was shot at by my own people—knowing that they wanted to kill me, knowing how they cursed my name?" The sudden flood of emotion amazed both men. "Finally I could bear it no more. Those of my troops who wanted to work for the Russians—well, it was not hard to send them into your ambushes, but I couldn't merely send those, could I? Do you know, my friend, how many of my troops—my good men—I consigned to death at your hands? Those I had left were loyal to me, and loyal to Allah, and it was time to join the freedom fighters once and for all. May God forgive me for all those who did not live long enough for this." Each man had his tale to tell, the Archer reflected, and the only consistent thread made but a single sentence:

"Life is hard."

"It will be harder still for those atop this mountain." The Major looked around. "The weather is changing. The wind blows from the south now. The clouds will bring moisture with them. Perhaps Allah has not deserted us after all. Perhaps He will let us continue this mission. Perhaps we are His instrument, and He will show them through us that they should leave our country lest we come to visit them."

The Archer grunted and looked up the mountain. He could no longer see the objective, but that didn't matter because, unlike the Major, he couldn't see the end to the war either.

"We'll bring the rest across tonight."

"Yes. They will all be well rested, my friend."

"Mr. Clark?" He'd been on the treadmill for nearly an hour. Mancuso could tell from the sweat when he flipped the off switch.

"Yes, Captain?" Clark took off the headphones.

"What sort of music?"

"That sonar kid, Jones, lent me his machine. All he has is Bach, but it does keep the brain occupied."

"Message for you." Mancuso handed it over. The slip of paper merely had six words. They were code words, had to be, since they didn't actually mean anything.

"It's a go."

"When?"

"It doesn't say that. That'll be the next message."

"I think it's time you tell me how this thing goes," the Captain observed.

"Not here," Clark said quietly.

"My stateroom is this way." Mancuso waved. They went forward past the submarine turbine engines, then through the reactor compartment with its annoyingly noisy door, and finally through the Attack Center and into Mancuso's cabin. It was about as far as anyone could walk on a submarine. The Captain tossed Clark a towel to wipe the sweat from his face.

"I hope you didn't wear yourself out," he said.

"It's the boredom. All your people have jobs to do. Me, I just sit around and wait. Waiting is a bitch. Where's Captain Ramius?"

"Asleep. He doesn't have to be in on the thing this soon, does he?"

"No," Clark agreed.

"What exactly is the job? Can you tell me now?"

"I'm bringing two people out," Clark replied simply.

"Two Russians? You're not picking up a *thing?* Two *people?*"

"That's right."

"And you're going to say that you do it all the time?" Mancuso asked.

"Not exactly *all* the time," Clark admitted. "I did one three years ago, another one a year before that. Two others never came off, and I never found out why. 'Need-to-know,' you know."

"I've heard the phrase before."

"It's funny," Clark mused. "I bet the people who make those decisions have never had their ass hanging out in the breeze . . ."

"The people you're picking up—do they know?"

"Nope. They know to be at a certain place at a certain time. My worry is that they're going to be surrounded by the KGB version of a SWAT team." Clark lifted a radio. "Your end is real easy. I don't say the right thing in the right way, on the right schedule, you and your boat get the hell out of here."

"Leave you behind." It wasn't a question.

"Unless you'd prefer to join me at Lefortovo Prison. Along with the rest of the crew, of course. It might look bad in the papers, Captain."

"You struck me as a sensible man, too."

Clark laughed. "It's a real long story."

"Colonel Eich?"

"Von Eich," the pilot corrected Jack. "My ancestors were Prussians. You're Dr. Ryan, right? What can I do for you?" Jack took a seat. They were sitting in the Defense Attaché's office. The attaché, an Air Force general, was letting them use it.

"You know who I work for?"

"I seem to recall you're one of the intel guys, but I'm just your driver, remember? I leave the important stuff to the folks in soft clothes," the Colonel said.

"Not anymore. I have a job for you."

"What do you mean, a job?"

"You'll love it." Jack was wrong. He didn't.

It was hard to keep his mind on his official job. Part of that was the mind-numbing boredom of the negotiating process, but the largest part was the heady wine of his unofficial job, and his mind was locked on that while he fiddled with his earpiece to get all of the simultaneous translation of the Soviet negotiator's second rendition of his current speech. The hint of the previous day, that on-site inspections would be more limited than previously agreed, was gone now. Instead they were asking for broader authority to inspect American sites. That would make the Pentagon happy, Jack thought with a concealed smile. Russian intelligence officers climbing over factories and descending into silos to get looks at American missiles, all under the watchful eyes of American counterintel officers and Strategic Air Command guards—who'd be fingering their new Beretta pistols all the while. And the submarine boys, who often regarded the rest of their *own* Navy as potential enemies, what would they think of having Russians aboard? It sounded as though they wouldn't get any further than standing on the deck while the technicians inside opened the tube doors under the watchful eyes of the boats' crews and the Marines who guarded the boomer bases. The same would happen on the Soviet side. Every officer sent to be on the inspection teams would be a spook, perhaps with the odd line-officer thrown in to take note of things that only an operator would notice. It was amazing. After thirty years of U.S. demands, the Soviets had finally accepted the idea that both sides should allow officially recognized spying. When that happened, during the previous round of talks on intermediate weapons, the American reaction had been stunned suspicion—*Why were the Russians agreeing to our terms? Why did they say yes? What are they really trying to do?*

But it was progress, once you got used to the idea. Both sides would have a way of knowing what the other did and what the other had. Neither side would trust the other. Both intelligence communities would see to that. Spies would still be prowling about, looking for indications that the other side was cheating, assembling missiles at a secret location, hiding them in odd places for a surprise attack. They'd find such indications, write interim warning reports, and try to run the information down. Institutional paranoia would last longer than the weapons themselves. Treaties wouldn't change that, despite all the euphoria in the papers. Jack shifted his eyes to the Soviet who was doing the talking.

Why? Why did you guys change your mind? Do you know what I said in my National Intelligence Estimate? It hasn't made the papers yet, but you might have seen it. I said that you finally realized (1) how much the god-damned things cost, (2) that ten thousand warheads was enough to fry all of America eight times over when three or four times was probably enough, and (3) that you'd save money by eliminating all your old missiles, the ones that you can't maintain very well anymore. It's just business, I told them, not a change in your outlook. Oh, yes: (4) it's very good public relations, and you still love to play PR games, even though you screw it up every time.

Not that we mind, of course.

Once the agreement went through—and Jack thought it would—both sides would save about three percent of their defense outlays; maybe as much as five percent for the Russians because of their more diverse missile systems, but it was hard to be sure. A small fraction of total defense outlays, it would be enough for the Russians to finance a few new factories, or maybe build some roads, which was what they really needed. How would they reallocate their savings? For that matter, how would America? Jack was supposed to make an assessment of that, too, another Special National Intelligence Estimate. Rather a high-sounding title for what was, after all, nothing more than an official guess, and at the moment, Ryan didn't have a clue.

The Russian speech concluded, and it was time for a coffee break. Ryan closed his leather-bound folder and trooped out of the room with everyone else. He selected a cup of tea, just to be different, and decorated his saucer with finger food.

"So, Ryan, what do you think?" It was Golovko.

"Is this business or socializing?" Jack asked.

"The latter, if you wish."

Jack walked to the nearest window and looked out. *One of these days,* he promised himself, *I will see something of Moscow. They must have something here that's worth snapping a few pictures. Maybe peace will break out someday and I'll be able to bring the family over . . .* He turned. *But not today, not this year, nor the year after that. Too bad.*

"Sergey Nikolayevich, if the world made sense, people like you and me would sit down and hammer all this crap out in two or three days. Hell, you and I know that both sides want to cut inventories by half. The issue we've been fighting over all week is how many hours of notice there'll be before the surprise-inspection team arrives, *but* because neither side can get its act together on the answer, we're talking about stuff that we've *already* come to terms on instead of getting on with it. If it was just between you and me, I'd say one hour, and you'd say eight, and we'd eventually talk down to three or four—"

"Four or five." Golovko laughed.

"Four, then." Jack did, too. "You see? We'd *settle* the son of a bitch, wouldn't we?"

"But we are not diplomats," Golovko pointed out. "We know how to strike bargains, but not in the accepted way. We are too direct, you and I, too practical. Ah, Ivan Emmetovich, we will make a Russian of you yet." He'd just Russianized Jack's name. Ivan Emmetovich. John, son of Emmet.

Business time again, Ryan thought. He changed gears and decided to yank the other man's chain in turn. "No, I don't think so. It gets a little too cool here. Tell you what, you go to your chief talker, and I'll go to Uncle Ernie, and we'll tell them what we decided on inspection-warning time—four hours. Right now. How 'bout it?"

That rattled him, Jack saw. For the briefest fraction of a second, Golovko thought that he was serious. The GRU/KGB officer recovered his composure in a moment, and even Jack barely noticed the lapse. The smile was hardly interrupted, but while the expression remained fixed around the mouth, it faded momentarily about the man's eyes, then returned. Jack didn't know the gravity of the mistake he had just made.

You should be very nervous, Ivan Emmetovich, but you are not. Why? You were before. You were so tense at the reception the other night that I thought you would explode. And yesterday when you passed the note, I could feel the sweat on your palm. But today, you make jokes. You try to unnerve me with your banter. Why the difference, Ryan? You are not a field officer. Your earlier nervousness proved that, but now you are acting like one. Why? he asked himself as everyone filed back into the conference room. Everyone sat for the next round of monologues, and Golovko kept an eye on his American counterpart.

Ryan wasn't fidgeting now, he noted with some surprise. On Monday and Tuesday he had been. He merely looked bored, no more uncomfortable than that. *You should be uncomfortable, Ryan,* Golovko thought.

Why did you need to meet with Gerasimov? Why twice? Why were you nervous before and after the first . . . and before but not after the second?

It didn't make much sense. Golovko listened to the droning words in his earpiece—it was the American's turn to ramble on about things that had already been decided—but his mind was elsewhere. His mind was in Ryan's KGB file. Ryan, John Patrick. Son of Emmet William Ryan and Catherine Burke Ryan, both deceased. Married, two children. Degrees in economics and history. Wealthy. Brief service in U.S. Marine Corps. Former stockbroker and history teacher. Joined CIA on a part-time basis four years before, after a consulting job the year before that. Soon thereafter became a full-time officer-analyst. Never trained at the CIA's field school at Camp Peary, Virginia. Ryan had been involved in two violent incidents, and in both cases deported himself well—the Marine training, Golovko supposed, plus his innate qualities as a man, which the Russian respected. Very bright, brave when he had to be: a dangerous enemy. Ryan worked directly for the DDI, and was known to have prepared numerous special intelligence evaluations . . . but a special intelligence mission . . . ? He had no training for that. He was probably the wrong sort of personality. Too open, Golovko thought; there was little guile in the man. When he was hiding something, you would never know what, but you would know that he was hiding something . . .

You were hiding something before, but not now, are you?

And what does that mean, Ivan Emmetovich? What the hell kind of name is Emmet? Golovko wondered irrelevantly.

Jack saw the man looking at him and saw the question in his eyes. The man was no dummy, Jack told himself, as Ernest Allen spoke on about some technical issue or other. We thought he was GRU, and he really turned out to be KGB—or so it would seem, Jack corrected himself. Is there something else about him that we don't know?

At parking position number nine at Sheremetyevo Airport, Colonel von Eich was standing at the aft passenger door of his aircraft. In front of him, a sergeant was fiddling with the door seal, an impressive array of tools spread out before him. Like most airliner doors, it opened outward only after opening inward, allowing the airtight seal to unseat itself and slide out of the way so that it would not be damaged. Faulty door seals had killed aircraft before, the most spectacular being the DC-10 crash outside Paris a decade before. Below them, a uniformed KGB guard stood with loaded rifle outside the aircraft. His own flight crew had to pass security checks. All Russians took security very seriously indeed, and the KGB were outright fanatics on the subject.

"I don't know why you're getting the warning light, Colonel," the sergeant said after twenty minutes. "The seal's perfect, the switch that goes to the light seems to be in good shape—anyway, the door is fine, sir. I'll check the panel up front next."

You get that? Paul von Eich wanted to ask the KGB guard fifteen feet below, but couldn't.

His crew was already readying the plane for its return trip. They'd had a couple of days to see the sights. This time it had been an old monastery about forty miles outside the city—the last ten miles of which had been over roads that were probably dirt in summertime but were a mixture of mud and snow now. They'd had their guided, guarded tour of Moscow, and now the airmen were ready to go home. He hadn't briefed his men on what Ryan had told him yet. The time for that would come tomorrow evening. He wondered how they would react.

The session ended on schedule, with a hint from the Soviets that they'd be willing to talk over inspection times tomorrow. They'd have to talk fast, Ryan thought, because the delegation would be leaving tomorrow night, and they had to have something to take back home from this round of talks. After all, the summit meeting was already scheduled informally. This one would be in Moscow. Moscow in the spring, Jack thought. I wonder if they'll bring me along for the signing ceremony? I wonder if there'll be a treaty to sign? There had better be, Ryan concluded.

Golovko watched the Americans leave, then waved for his own car, which took him to KGB headquarters. He walked directly to the Chairman's office.

"So what did our diplomats give away today?" Gerasimov asked without preamble.

"I think tomorrow we'll make our amended proposal for inspection timing." He paused before going on. "I spoke with Ryan today. He seems to have changed somewhat and I thought I should report it."

"Go on," the Chairman said.

"Comrade Chairman, I do not know what the two of you discussed, but the change in his demeanor is such that I thought you should know of it." Golovko went on to explain what he'd seen.

"Ah, yes. I cannot discuss our conversations because you are not cleared for that compartment, but I would not be concerned, Colonel. I am handling this matter personally. Your observation is noted. Ryan will have to learn to control his emotions better. Perhaps he is not Russian enough." Gerasimov was not a man who made jokes, but this was an exception. "Anything else on the negotiations?"

"My notes will be written up and on your desk tomorrow morning."

"Good. Dismissed." Gerasimov watched the man leave. His face didn't change until the door clicked shut. Bad enough to lose, he thought, and to lose to a nonprofessional . . . But he had lost, and, he reminded himself, he wasn't a professional either, merely the Party man who gave them orders. That decision was behind him. It was too bad about his officers in—wherever the place was—but they had failed, and earned their fates. He lifted his phone and ordered his private secretary to arrange for his wife and daughter to fly the following morning to Talinn, the capital of the Estonian Soviet Socialist Republic. Yes, they would need a car and a driver also. No, just one. The driver would double as their security guard. Not many people knew who his wife was, and the trip was unscheduled, just to see old friends. Very good. Gerasimov hung up his phone and looked around his office. He'd miss it. Not so much the office itself: the power. But he knew that he'd miss his life more.

"And this Colonel Bondarenko?" Vatutin asked.

"A fine young officer. Very bright. He'll make a good general when the time comes."

Vatutin wondered how his final report would handle that issue. There was no suspicion about that man, except for his association with Filitov. But there had been no suspicion about Filitov, despite his connection with Oleg Penkovskiy. Colonel Vatutin shook his head in amazement. That fact would be talked about in security classes for a generation. Why didn't they see? the young officer-trainees would demand. How could anyone be so stupid? Because only the most trusted people can be spies—you don't give classified information to someone you cannot trust. The lesson was as it had always been: Trust no one. Coming back to Bondarenko, he wondered what would happen to him. If he were the loyal and exceptional officer he seemed to be, then he should not be tainted by this affair. But—there was always a *but*, wasn't there?—there were also some additional questions to ask, and Vatutin went to the bottom of his list. His initial interrogation report was due on Gerasimov's desk the following day.

The climb took all night in total darkness. The clouds that had swept in from the south covered both moon and stars, and the only illumination was from the perimeter lights of their objective, reflected off the clouds. Now they were within easy sight of it. Still a sizable march, they were close enough that the individual units could be briefed on their tasks, and could see what they had to do. The Archer picked for himself a high spot and rested his binoculars on a rock to steady them as he surveyed the site. There seemed to be three encampments. Only two of them were fenced, though at the third he could make out piles of posts and fencing material near an orange-white light atop the sort of pole used in cities to illuminate the streets. The extent of the construction surprised him. To do all this— on the top of a mountain! How important could such a place be to deserve all the effort, all the expense? Something that sent a laser beam into the sky . . . to what end? The Americans had asked him if he'd seen what the light-beam had hit. They knew it had hit something, then? Something in the sky. Whatever it was, it had frightened the Americans, had frightened the same people who made the missiles with which he had killed so many Russian pilots . . . What could frighten people so clever as that? The Archer could see the place, but did not see anything more frightening than the guard towers that held machine guns. One of those buildings held armed soldiers who would have heavy weapons. That was something to be frightened about. Which building? He had to know that, because that building had to be attacked first. His mortars would put their shells on that one first of all. But which one was it?

After that . . . ? He'd deploy his men into two sections of almost a hundred each. The Major would take one and go left. He'd take the other and go right. The Archer had selected his objective as soon as he saw the mountaintop. That building, he told himself, was where the people were. That was where the Russians lived. Not the soldiers, but those the soldiers guarded. Some of the windows were lighted. An apartment building built atop a mountain, he thought. What sort of people would they be that the Russians would put up a building of the sort found only in cities? People who needed comfort. People who had to be guarded. People who worked on something the Americans were afraid of. People he would kill without mercy, the Archer told himself.

The Major came down to lie at his side.

"All the men are well hidden," the man said. He trained his own binoculars on the objective. It was so dark that the Archer barely saw the man's outline, only the contours of his face and the vague shadow of his bristling mustache. "We misjudged the ground from the other hilltop. It will take three hours to close in."

"Closer to four, I think."

"I don't like those guard towers," the Major noted. Both men shivered with the cold. The wind had picked up, and they no longer were sheltered from it by the bulk of the mountain. It would be a difficult night for all of the men. "One or two machine guns in each of them. They can sweep us off the mountainside as we make the final assault."

"No searchlights," the Archer noted.

"Then they'll be using night-vision devices. I've used them myself."

"How good?"

"Their range is limited because of the way they work. They can see large things, like trucks, out to this distance. A man on a broken background like this one . . . perhaps three thousand meters. Far enough for their purposes, my friend. The towers must go first. Use the mortars on them."

"No." The Archer shook his head. "We have less than a hundred shells. They must go on the guard barracks. If we can kill all of the sleeping soldiers, so much the easier for us when we get inside."

"If the machine-gunners in those towers see us coming, half of our men will be dead before the guards wake up," the Major pointed out.

The Archer grunted. His comrade was right. Two of the towers were sited in a way that would allow the men in them to sweep the steep slope that they'd have to climb before getting to the mountain's flat summit. He could counter that with his own machine guns . . . but duels of that sort were usually won by the defender. The wind gusted at them, and both men knew that they'd have to find shelter soon or risk frostbite.

"Damn this cold!" the Major swore.

"Do you think the towers are cold also?" the Archer asked after a moment.

"Even worse. They are more exposed than we."

"How will the Russian soldiers be dressed?"

The Major chuckled. "The same as we—after all, we're all wearing their clothing, are we not?"

The Archer nodded, searching for the thought that hovered at the edge of his consciousness. It came to him through his cold-numbed brain, and he left his perch, telling the Major to remain. He came back carrying a Stinger missile launcher. The metal tube was cold to the touch as he assembled it. The acquisition units were all carried inside his men's clothing, to protect the batteries from the cold. He expertly assembled and activated the weapon, then rested his cheek on the metal conductance bar and trained it on the nearest guard tower . . .

"Listen," he said, and handed the weapon over. The officer took it and did as he was directed.

"Ah." His teeth formed a Cheshire-cat grin in the black night.

Clark was busy, too. Obviously a careful man, Mancuso noted as he watched, he was laying out and checking all of his equipment. The man's clothing looked ordinary, though shabby and not well made.

"Bought in Kiev," Clark explained. "You can't exactly wear Hart, Schaffner, and Marx and expect to look like a local." He also had a coverall to put over it, with camouflage stripes. There was a complete set of identity papers—in Russian, which Mancuso couldn't read—and a pistol. It was a small one, barely larger than the silencer that sat next to it.

"Never seen one of these before," the Captain said.

"Well, that's a Qual-A-Tec baffle-type silencer with no wipes and a slide-lock internal to the can," Clark said.

"What—"

Mr. Clark chuckled. "You guys have been hitting me with subspeak ever since I got aboard, skipper. Now it's my turn."

Mancuso lifted the pistol. "This is only a twenty-two."

"It's damned near impossible to silence a big round unless you want a silencer as long as your forearm, like the FBI guys have on their toys. I have to have something that'll fit in a pocket. This is the best Mickey can do, and he's the best around."

"Who?"

"Mickey Finn. That's his real name. He does the design work for Qual-A-Tec, and I wouldn't use anybody else's silencer. It isn't like TV, Cap'n. For a silencer to work right, it has to be a small caliber, you have to use a subsonic round, and you have to have a sealed breech. And it helps if you're out in the open. In here, you'd hear it 'cause of the steel walls. Outside, you'd hear something out to thirty feet or so, but you wouldn't know what it was. The silencer goes on the pistol like this, and you twist it"—he demonstrated—"and now the gun's a single shot. The silencer locks the action. To get off another round, you have to twist it back and cycle the action manually."

"You mean you're going in there with a twenty-two single-shot?"

"That's how it's done, Captain."

"Have you ever—"

"You really don't want to know. Besides, I can't talk about it." Clark grinned. "I'm not cleared for that myself. If it makes you feel any better, yeah, I'm scared, too, but this is what they pay me for."

"But if—"

"You get the hell out of here. I have the authority to give you that order, Captain, remember? It hasn't happened yet. Don't worry about it. I do enough worrying for the both of us."

25. Convergence

Maria and Katryn Gerasimov always got the sort of VIP treatment that they deserved as the immediate family of a Politburo member. A KGB car took them from their guarded eight-room apartment on Kutuzovskiy Prospekt to Vnukovo Airport, which was used mainly for domestic flights, where they waited in the lounge reserved for the *vlasti*. It was staffed by more people than ever seemed to use the facility at any one time, and this morning the only others present kept to themselves. An attendant took their hats and coats while another walked them to a couch, where a third asked if they wanted anything to eat or drink. Both ordered coffee and nothing more. The lounge staff eyed their clothing with envy. The cloakroom attendant ran her hands over the silky texture of their furs, and it struck her that her ancestors might have looked upon the czarist nobility with the same degree of envy that she felt toward these two. They sat in regal isolation, with only the distant company of their bodyguards as they sipped at their coffee and gazed out the plate-glass windows at the parked airliners.

Maria Ivanovna Gerasimova was not actually an Estonian, though she'd been born there fifty years before. Her family was composed entirely of ethnic Russians, since the small Baltic state had been part of the Russian Empire under the czars, only to experience a brief "liberation"—as the trouble-makers called it—between the world wars, during which the Estonian nationalists had not made life overly easy for ethnic Russians. Her earliest childhood memories of Talinn were not all that pleasant, but like all children she had made friends who would be friends forever. They'd even survived her marriage to a young Party man who had, to everyone's surprise—most especially hers—risen to command the most hated organ of the Soviet government. Worse, he'd made his career on repressing dissident elements. That her childhood friendships had withstood this fact was testimony to her intelligence. Half a dozen people had been spared sentences in labor camps, or been transferred from one of strict regime to a milder place due to her intercession. The children of her friends had attended universities because of her influence. Those who had taunted her Russian name as a child did less well, though she'd helped one of them a little, enough to appear merciful. Such behavior was enough to keep her part of the small Talinn suburb despite her long-past move to Moscow. It also helped that her husband had only once accompanied her to her childhood home. She was not an evil person, merely one who used her vicarious power as a princess of an earlier age might have done, arbitrarily but seldom maliciously. Her face had the sort of regal composure that fitted the image. A beautiful catch twenty-five years ago, she was still a handsome woman, if somewhat more serious now. As an ancillary part of her husband's official identity, she had to play her part in the game—not as much as the wife of a Western politician, of course, but her behavior had to be proper. The practice stood her in good stead now. Those who watched her could never have guessed her thoughts.

She wondered what was wrong, knowing only that it was gravely serious. Her husband had told her to be at a specific place at a specific time, to ask no questions of him, only to promise that she would do exactly as she was told, regardless of consequences. The order, delivered in a quiet, emotionless monotone while the water was running in their kitchen, was the most frightening thing she had heard since the German tanks had rumbled into Talinn in 1941. But one legacy of the German occupation was that she knew just how important survival was.

Her daughter knew nothing of what they were doing. Her reactions could not be trusted. Katryn had never known danger in her life as her mother had, only the rare inconvenience. Their only child was in her first year at Moscow State University, where she majored in economics and traveled with a crowd of similarly important children of similarly important people, all of ministerial rank at least. Already a Party member—eighteen is the earliest age permitted—she played her role, too. The previous fall she'd traveled with some of her classmates and helped harvest wheat, mainly for a photograph that had been displayed on the second page of *Komsomolskaya Pravda*, the paper of the Young Communist League. Not that she'd liked it, but the new rules in Moscow "encouraged" the children of the powerful at least to appear to be doing their fair share. It could have been worse. She'd returned from the ordeal with a new boyfriend, and her mother wondered if they'd been intimate, or had the young man been frightened off by the bodyguards and the knowledge of who her father was? Or did he see her as a chance to enter the KGB? Or was he one of the new generation that simply didn't care? Her daughter was one of these. The Party was something you joined to secure your position, and her father's post put her on the inside track for a comfortable job. She sat beside her mother in silence, reading a West German fashion magazine that was now sold in the Soviet Union and deciding what new Western fashions she would like to wear to classes. She would have to learn, her mother thought, remembering that at eighteen the world is a place with horizons both near and far, depending on one's mood.

About the time they finished their coffee, the flight was called. They waited. The plane wouldn't leave without them. Finally, when the last call came, the attendant brought their coats and hats, and another led them and their guards down the stairs to their car. The other passengers had already ridden out to the aircraft on a bus—the Russians haven't quite discovered jetways yet—and when their car arrived, they were able to walk right up the stairs. The stewardess guided them solicitously to their first-class seats in the forward cabin. They weren't called first class, of course, but they were wider, they had greater leg room, and they were reserved. The airliner lifted off at ten o'clock, Moscow time, stopped first at Leningrad, then proceeded to Talinn, where it landed just after one.

"So, Colonel, you have your summary of the subject's activity?" Gerasimov asked casually. He seemed preoccupied, Vatutin noted at once. He should have been more interested, particularly with a Politburo meeting only an hour away.

"Books will be written about this one, Comrade Chairman. Filitov had access to virtually all of our defense secrets. He even helped make defense policy. I needed thirty pages merely to summarize what he's done. The full interrogation will require several months."

"Speed is less important than thoroughness," Gerasimov said offhandedly.

Vatutin did not react. "As you wish, Comrade Chairman."

"If you will excuse me, the Politburo is meeting this morning."

Colonel Vatutin came to attention, pivoted on his heels, and left. He found Golovko in the anteroom. The two knew each other casually. They'd been a year apart at the KGB Academy, and their careers had advanced at roughly the same rate.

"Colonel Golovko," the Chairman's secretary said. "The Chairman must leave now, and suggests that you return tomorrow morning at ten."

"But—"

"He's leaving now," the secretary said.

"Very well," Golovko replied and stood. He and Vatutin left the room together.

"The Chairman is busy," Vatutin observed on the way out.

"Aren't we all?" the other man replied after the door closed. "I thought he wanted this. I arrived here at four to write this goddamned report! Well, I think I'll have some breakfast. How go things in 'Two,' Klementi Vladimirovich?"

"Also busy—the people do not pay us to sit on our backsides." He'd also arrived early to complete his paperwork, and his stomach was growling audibly.

"You must be hungry, too. Care to join me?"

Vatutin nodded, and both men made for the canteen. Senior officers—colonel and above—had a separate dining room and were served by white-coated waiters. The room was never empty. The KGB worked round the clock, and odd schedules made for irregular meals. Besides, the food was good, especially for senior officers. The room was a quiet place. When people talked here, even if they were discussing sports, they did so almost in whispers.

"Aren't you attached to the arms negotiations now?" Vatutin asked as he sipped his tea.

"Yes—nursemaiding diplomats. You know, the Americans think I'm GRU." Golovko arched his eyebrows, partly in amusement at the Americans, partly to show his not-quite classmate how important his cover was.

"Really?" Vatutin was surprised. "I would have thought that they were better informed—at least . . . well . . . ." He shrugged to indicate that he couldn't go any further. *I, too, have things that I cannot discuss, Sergey Nikolayevich.*

"I suppose the Chairman is preoccupied by the Politburo meeting. The rumors—"

"He's not ready yet," Vatutin said with the quiet confidence of an insider.

"You're sure?"

"Quite sure."

"Where do you stand?" Golovko asked.

"Where do *you* stand?" Vatutin replied. Both traded a look of amusement, but then Golovko turned serious.

"Narmonov needs a chance. The arms agreement—if the diplomats ever get their thumbs out and execute it—will be a good thing for us."

"You really think so?" Vatutin didn't know one way or the other.

"Yes, I do. I've had to become an expert on the arms of both camps. I know what we have, and I know what they have. Enough is enough. Once a man is dead, you do not need to shoot him again and again. There are better ways to spend the money. There are things that need changing."

"You should be careful saying that," Vatutin cautioned. Golovko had traveled too much. He had seen the West, and many KGB officers came back with tales of wonder—if only the Soviet Union could do this, or that, or the other thing . . . Vatutin sensed the truth of that, but was inherently a more cautious man. He was a "Two" man, who looked for dangers, while Golovko, of the First Chief Directorate, looked for opportunities.

"Are we not the guardians? If we cannot speak, who can?" Golovko said, then backed off. "Carefully, of course, with the guidance of the Party at all times—but even the Party sees the need for change." They had to agree on that. Every Soviet newspaper proclaimed the need for a new approach, and every such article had to be approved by someone important, and of political purity. The Party was never wrong, both men knew, but it certainly did change its *kollektiv* mind a lot.

"A pity that the Party does not see the importance of rest for its guardians. Tired men make mistakes, Sergey Nikolayevich."

Golovko contemplated his eggs for a moment, then lowered his voice even further. "Klementi . . . let us assume for a moment I know that a senior KGB officer is meeting with a senior CIA officer."

"How senior?"

"Higher than directorate head," Golovko replied, telling Vatutin exactly who it was without using a name or a title. "Let us assume that I arrange the meetings, and that he tells me I do not need to know what the meetings are about. Finally, let us assume that this senior officer is acting . . . strangely. What am I to do?" he asked, and was rewarded with an answer right from the book:

"You should write up a report for the Second Directorate, of course."

Golovko nearly choked on his breakfast. "A fine idea. Immediately afterward I can slash my throat with a razor and save everyone the time and trouble of an interrogation. Some people are above suspicion—or have enough power that no one dares to suspect them."

"Sergey, if there is anything I have learned in the past few weeks, it is that there is no such thing as 'above suspicion.' We've been working a case so high in the Defense Ministry . . . you would not believe it. I scarcely do." Vatutin waved for a waiter to bring a fresh pot of tea. The pause gave the other man a chance to think. Golovko had intimate knowledge of that ministry because of his work on strategic arms. Who could it be? There were not many men whom the KGB was unable to suspect—that was hardly a condition the agency encouraged—and fewer still high in the Ministry of Defense, which the KGB is supposed to regard with the utmost suspicion. But . . .

"Filitov?"

Vatutin blanched, and made a mistake: "Who told you?"

"My God, he briefed *me* last year on intermediate arms. I heard he was sick. You're not joking, are you?"

"There is nothing the least bit amusing about this. I cannot say much, and it may not go beyond this table, but—yes, Filitov was working for . . . for someone outside our borders. He's confessed, and the first phase of the interrogation is complete."

"But he knows everything! The arms-negotiation team should know of this. It alters the whole basis for the talks," Golovko said.

Vatutin hadn't considered that, but it wasn't his place to make policy decisions. He was, after all, nothing more than a policeman with a very special beat. Golovko might have been right in his assessment, but rules were rules.

"The information is being closely held for the moment, Sergey Niko-layevich. Remember that."

"Compartmentalization of information can work both for and against us, Klementi," Golovko warned, wondering if he should warn the negotiators.

"That's true enough," Vatutin agreed.

"When did you arrest your subject?" Golovko asked, and got his reply. *The timing* . . . He took a breath, and forgot about the negotiations. "The Chairman has met at least twice with a senior CIA officer—"

"Who, and when?"

"Sunday night and yesterday morning. His name is Ryan. He's my counterpart on the American team, but he's an intelligence type, not a field officer as I once was. What do you make of that?"

"You're sure he's not an operations man?"

"Positive. I can even tell you the room he works in. This is not a matter of uncertainty. He's an analyst, a senior one, but only a desk man. Special assistant to their Deputy Director for Intelligence, before that he was part of a high-level liaison team in London. He's never been in the field."

Vatutin finished his tea and poured another cup. Next he buttered a piece of bread. He took his time thinking about this. There was ample opportunity to delay a response, but—

"All we have here is unusual activity. Perhaps the Chairman has something going that is so sensitive—"

"Yes—or perhaps that is how it's supposed to appear," Golovko observed.

"For a 'One' man, you seem to have our way of thinking, Sergey. Very well. What we would do ordinarily—not that a case like this is ordinary, but you know what I mean—is that we assemble information and take it to the Director of the Second Chief Directorate. The Chairman has bodyguards. They would be taken aside and questioned. But such a thing would have to be handled very, very carefully. My chief would have to go to—who?" Vatutin asked rhetorically. "A Politburo member, I suppose, or perhaps the Secretary of the Central Committee, but . . . the Filitov matter is being handled very quietly. I believe the Chairman may wish to use it as political leverage against both the Defense Minister and Vaneyev . . ."

"*What?*"

"Vaneyev's daughter was acting as a spy for the West—well, a courier to be precise. We broke her, and—"

"Why has this not become public knowledge?"

"The woman is back at her job, by order of the Chairman," Vatutin replied.

"Klementi, do you have any idea what the hell is going on here?"

"No, not now. I assumed that the Chairman was seeking to strengthen his political position, but the meetings with a CIA man . . . you're *sure* of this?"

"I arranged the meetings myself," Golovko repeated. "The first must have been agreed upon before the Americans arrived, and I merely handled the details. Ryan requested the second. He passed a note to me—about as well as a trainee-officer on his first job. They met at the Barricade Theater yesterday, as I told you. Klementi, something very strange is happening."

"It would seem so. But we have nothing—"

"What do you mean—"

"Sergey, investigation is *my* job. We have nothing but disparate bits of information that might easily be explained. Nothing queers an investigation like moving too rapidly. Before we can act, we must assemble and analyze what we have. Then we can go to see my chief, and *he* can authorize further action. Do you think two colonels can act on this without clearing it with higher authority? You have to write up everything you know and bring it to me. How soon can you do that?"

"I have to be at the negotiating session in"—he checked his watch—"two hours. That will last until sixteen hours, followed by a reception. The Americans leave at twenty-two hours."

"Can you skip the reception?"

"It will be awkward, but yes."

"Be in my office at sixteen-thirty," Vatutin said formally. Golovko, who was the senior officer by a year, smiled for the first time.

"By your order, Comrade Colonel."

"Marshal Yazov, what is the position of the Ministry?" Narmonov asked.

"No less than six hours," the Defense Minister said. "In that time we should be able to conceal most of the highly sensitive items. As you know, we would prefer not to have our sites inspected at all, though examining American facilities does offer some intelligence advantages."

The Foreign Minister nodded. "The Americans will ask for less, but I think we can settle on that number."

"I disagree." Heads of the Politburo members turned to Alexandrov's chair. The ideologue's florid complexion was displaying itself again. "It is bad enough to reduce our arsenals at all, but to have Americans examine the factories, to get all our secrets, this is madness."

"Mikhail Petrovich, we have been through this," General Secretary Narmonov said patiently. "Further discussion?" He looked around the table. Heads nodded. The General Secretary checked off the item on his note pad. He waved to the Foreign Minister.

"Six hours, nothing less."

The Foreign Minister whispered instruction to an aide, who left the room at once to call the chief negotiator. Next he leaned forward. "That leaves only the question of which arms will be eliminated—the hardest question of all, of course. That will require another session—a long one."

"We are scheduled to have our summit in three months . . ." Narmonov observed.

"Yes. It should be decided by then. Preliminary excursions into this question have not met any serious obstacles."

"And the American defensive systems?" Alexandrov asked. "What of them?" Heads turned again, now to the KGB Chairman.

"Our efforts to penetrate the American Tea Clipper program continue. As you know, it corresponds very closely to our Project Bright Star, though it would seem that we are further along in the most important areas," Gerasimov said, without looking up from his scratch pad.

"We cut our missile force in half while the Americans learn to shoot our missiles down," Alexandrov groused.

"And they will cut their force in half while we work to the same end," Narmonov went on. "Mikhail Petrovich, we've been working along these lines for over thirty years, and much harder than they have."

"We are also further along in testing," Yazov pointed out. "And—"

"They know of it," Gerasimov said. He referred to the test the Americans had observed from the Cobra Belle aircraft, but Yazov didn't know about that, and even the KGB hadn't discovered how the test had been observed, merely that the Americans knew of it. "They have intelligence services too, remember."

"But they haven't said anything about it," Narmonov observed.

"The Americans have occasionally been reticent to discuss such things. They complain about some technical aspects of our defense activity, but not all of them, for fear of compromising their intelligence-gathering methods," Gerasimov explained casually. "Possibly they have conducted similar tests, though we have not learned of it. The Americans, too, are able to maintain secrecy when they wish." Taussig had never gotten that information out either. Gerasimov leaned back to let others speak.

"In other words, both sides will continue as before," Narmonov concluded.

"Unless we are able to win a concession," the Foreign Minister said. "Which is unlikely to happen. Is there anyone at this table who thinks we should restrict our missile-defense programs?" There wasn't. "Then why should we realistically expect the Americans to feel any differently?"

"But what if they get ahead of us!" Alexandrov demanded.

"An excellent point, Mikhail Petrovich," Narmonov seized the opportunity. "Why do the Americans always seem to get ahead of us?" he asked the assembled chieftains of his country.

"They do so not because they are magicians, but because we allow them to—because we cannot make our economy perform as it should. That denies Marshal Yazov the tools our men in uniform need, denies our people the good things of life that they are coming to expect, and denies us the ability to face the West as equals."

"Our weapons make us equals!" Alexandrov objected.

"But what advantage do they give us when the West has weapons, too? Is there anyone around this table who is content to be equal to the West? Our rockets do that for us," Narmonov said, "but there is more to national greatness than the ability to kill. If we are to defeat the West, it cannot be with nuclear bombs—unless you want the Chinese to inherit our world." Narmonov paused. "Comrades, if we are to prevail we have to get our economy moving!"

"It is moving," Alexandrov said.

"Where? Do any of us know that?" Vaneyev asked, igniting the room's atmosphere.

The discussion turned boisterous for several minutes before settling down to the collegial sort of discussion normal to the Politburo. Narmonov used it to measure the strength of his opposition. He deemed his faction more than equal to that of Alexandrov's. Vaneyev hadn't tipped his hand—Alexandrov expected him to *pretend* to be on the Secretary's side, didn't he? And the General Secretary still had Yazov. Narmonov had also used the session to defuse the political dimension of his country's economic problems by couching the need for reforms as a means of improving the country's military power—which was true, of course, but was also an issue difficult for Alexandrov and his clique to deny. By taking the initiative, Narmonov judged, he'd been able to evaluate the other side's strength yet again, and by putting the argument in the open, he'd put them on the psychological defensive at least temporarily. It was all he could hope for at the moment. He'd lived to fight another day, Narmonov told himself. Once the arms-control treaty went through, his power at this table would increase another notch. The *people* would like that—and for the first time in Soviet history, the feelings of the people were beginning to matter. Once it had been decided which arms would be eliminated, and over what sort of schedule, they'd know how much additional money there would be to spend. Narmonov could control that discussion from his seat, using the funds to barter for additional power in the Politburo as members vied for it in pursuit of their own pet projects. Alexandrov could not interfere with that, since his power base was ideological rather than economic. It occurred to Narmonov that he would probably win out. With Defense at his back, and with Vaneyev in his pocket, he would win the confrontation, break KGB to his will, and put Alexandrov out to pasture. It was only a matter of deciding when to force the issue. There had to be agreement on the treaty, and he would gladly trade away small advantages on that score in order to secure his position at home. The West would be surprised by that, but someday it would be more surprised to see what a viable economy would do for its principal rival. Narmonov's immediate concern was his political survival. After that came the task of bringing life back into his country's economy. There was a further objective, one that hadn't changed in three generations, though the West was always discovering new ways to ignore it. Narmonov's eyes weren't fixed on it, but it was still there.

Last session, Ryan told himself. *Thank God.* The nervousness was back. There was no reason that everything shouldn't go well—the odd part was that Ryan had no idea what would happen with Gerasimov's family. "Need-to-know" had again raised its wearisome head on that score, but the part about getting Gerasimov and CARDINAL out was so breathtakingly simple that he would never have come up with it. That part was Ritter's doing, and the crusty old bastard did have a flair.

The Russians spoke first this time, and five minutes into the speech, they proposed a warning time for surprise on-site inspections. Jack would have preferred zero-time, but that was unreasonable. It wasn't necessary to see what the insides of the birds looked like, desirable as that would be. It was enough to count the launchers and the warheads, and anything under ten hours was probably enough for that—especially if the snap visits were coordinated with satellite passes to catch any attempt at sleight-of-hand. The Russians offered ten hours. Ernest Allen, in his reply, demanded three. Two hours later the respective figures were seven and five. Two hours after that, much to everyone's surprise, the Americans said *six,* and the chief

Russian delegate nodded consent. Both men rose and leaned across the table to shake hands. Jack was glad it was all over, but would have held out for five. After all, he and Golovko had agreed on four, hadn't they?

Four and a half hours to settle on one damned number, Jack thought. *And that may be an all-time record.* There was even some applause when everyone stood, and Jack joined the line for the nearest men's room. A few minutes later he returned. Golovko was there.

"Your people let us off easy," the KGB officer said.

"I guess you're lucky it wasn't my job," Jack agreed. "This is a hell of a lot of work for two or three little things."

"You think them little?"

"In the Great Scheme of Things . . . well, they're significant, but not overly so. Mainly what this means is that we can fly home," Jack observed, and some unease crept into his voice. *It isn't over yet.*

"You look forward to this?" Golovko asked.

"Not exactly, but there you are." *It isn't the flight that makes me nervous this time, sport.*

The flight crew had stayed at the Hotel Ukrania, just on the Moscow River, doubling up in the huge rooms, shopping in the "friendship store" for souvenirs, and generally seeing what they could while maintaining a guard team on the aircraft. Now they checked out together and boarded a fifty-passenger tourist bus that crossed over the river and headed east on Kalinina Prospekt on its way to the airport, a half-hour drive in the light traffic.

When Colonel von Eich arrived, the British Airways ground crew that provided maintenance support was finishing up the fueling under the watchful eyes of his crew chief—the chief master sergeant who "owned" the aircraft—and the Captain who'd serve as copilot in the VC-137's right seat. The members of the crew checked through the KGB control point, whose officers were assiduously thorough in verifying everyone's identity. Finished, the crew filed aboard, stowed its gear, and began getting the converted 707 ready for its flight back to Andrews Air Force Base. The pilot gathered five of his people together in the cockpit, and under the covering noise of somebody's boomer-box, informed them of what they'd be doing tonight that was "a little different."

"Christ, sir," the crew chief noted, "that's different all right."

"What's life without a little excitement?" von Eich asked. "Everybody clear on your duties?" He got nods. "Then let's get to work, people." The pilot and copilot picked up their checklists and went outside with the crew chief to pre-flight the aircraft. It would be good to get back home, they all agreed—assuming that they could unstick the tires from the pavement. It was, the crew chief observed, as cold as a witch's tit. Their hands gloved, and dressed now in Air Force–issue parkas, they took their time as they walked around the aircraft. The 89th Military Airlift Wing had a spotless safety record ferrying "DVs" all over the world, and the way they maintained that was through uncompromising attention to every detail. Von Eich wondered if their 700,000 hours of accident-free flying would be undone tonight.

Ryan was already packed. They'd be leaving right from the reception to the airport. He decided to shave and brush his teeth again before putting his shaving kit in one of the pockets of his two-suiter. He was wearing one of his English suits. It was almost warm enough for the local climate, but Jack promised himself that if he ever again came to Moscow in the winter, he'd remember to bring long johns. It was almost time when a knock came at the door. It was Tony Candela.

"Enjoy the flight home," he said.

"Yeah." Ryan chuckled.

"Thought I'd give you a hand." He hefted the two-suiter, and Jack merely had to grab his briefcase. Together they walked to the elevator, which took them from the seventh floor up to the ninth, where they waited for another elevator to take them down to the lobby.

"Do you know who designed this building?"

"Obviously someone with a sense of humor," Candela replied. "They hired the same fellow to handle construction of the new embassy." Both men laughed. That story was worthy of a Hollywood disaster epic. There were enough electronic devices in that building to cobble up a mainframe computer. The elevator came a minute later, taking both men to the lobby. Candela handed Ryan his suitcase.

"Break a leg," he said before walking away.

Jack walked out to where the cars were waiting and dropped his case in the open trunk. The night was clear. There were stars in the sky, and the hint of the aurora borealis on the northern horizon. He'd heard that this natural phenomenon was occasionally seen from Moscow, but it was something that he'd never witnessed.

The motorcade left ten minutes later and made its way south to the Foreign Ministry, repeating the route that nearly encapsulated Ryan's slim knowledge of this city of eight million souls. One by one the cars curved onto the small traffic circle and their occupants were guided into the building. This reception was not nearly as elaborate as the last one in the Kremlin had been, but this session had not accomplished quite as much. The next one would be a bear, as the summit deadline approached, but the next session was scheduled to be in Washington. The reporters were already waiting, mainly print, with a few TV cameras present. Someone approached Jack as soon as he handed off his topcoat.

"Dr. Ryan?"

"Yeah?" He turned.

"Mike Paster, *Washington Post*. There's a report in Washington that your SEC problems have been settled."

Jack laughed. "God, it's nice not to talk about the arms business for a change! As I said earlier, I didn't do anything wrong. I guess those—jerks, but don't quote me on that—folks finally figured it out. Good. I didn't want to have to hire a lawyer."

"There's talk that CIA had a hand in—" Ryan cut him off.

"Tell you what. Tell your Washington bureau that if they give me a couple days to unwind from this business, I'll show them everything I did. I do all my transactions by computer, and I keep hard copies of everything. Fair enough?"

"Sure—but why didn't—"

"You tell me," Jack said, reaching for a glass of wine as a waiter went past. He had to have one, but tonight it would be one only. "Maybe some people in D.C. have a hard-on for the Agency. For Christ's sake don't quote me on that, either."

"So how'd the talks go?" the reporter asked next.

"You can get the details from Ernie, but off the record, pretty good. Not as good as last time, and there's a lot left to handle, but we settled a couple of tough ones, and that's about all we expected for this trip."

"Will the agreement go through in time for the summit?" Paster inquired next.

"Off the record," Jack said immediately. The reporter nodded. "I'd call the chances better than two out of three."

"How's the Agency feel about it?"

"We're not supposed to be political, remember? From a technical point of view, the fifty-percent reduction is something I think we can live with. It doesn't really change anything, does it? But it is 'nice.' I grant you that."

"How do you want me to quote this?" Paster asked.

"Call me a Very Junior Administration Official." Jack grinned. "Fair enough? Uncle Ernie can speak on the record, but I'm not allowed to."

"What about the effect this will have on Narmonov's remaining in power?"

"Not my turf," Ryan lied smoothly. "My opinions on that are private, not professional."

"So . . ."

"So ask somebody else about that," Jack suggested. "Ask me the really important things, like who the 'Skins ought to draft in the first round."

"Olson, the quarterback at Baylor," the reporter said at once.

"I like that defensive end at Penn State myself, but he'll probably go too early."

"Good trip," the reporter said as he closed his note pad.

"Yeah, you enjoy the rest of the winter, pal." The reporter made to go away, then paused. "Can you say anything, completely off the record, about the Foley couple that the Russians sent home last—"

"Who? Oh, the ones they accused of spying? Off the record, and you never heard this from me, it's bullshit. Any other way, no comment."

"Right." The reporter walked off with a smile.

Jack was left standing alone. He looked around for Golovko, but couldn't find him. He was disappointed. Enemy or not, they could always talk, and Ryan had come to enjoy their conversations. The Foreign Minister showed up, then Narmonov. All the other fixtures were there: the violins, the tables laden with snacks, the circulating waiters with silver trays of wine, vodka, and champagne. The State Department people were knotted in conversation with their Soviet colleagues. Ernie Allen was laughing with his Soviet counterpart. Only Jack was standing alone, and that wouldn't do. He walked over to the nearest group and hung on the periphery, scarcely noticed as he checked his watch from time to time and took tiny sips of the wine.

"Time," Clark said.

Getting to this point had been difficult enough. Clark's equipment was already set in the watertight trunk that ran from the Attack Center to the top of the sail. It had hatches at both ends and was completely watertight, unlike the rest of the sail, which was free-flooding. One more sailor had volunteered to go in with him, and then the bottom hatch was closed and dogged down tight. Mancuso lifted a phone.

"Communications check."

"Loud and clear, sir," Clark replied. "Ready whenever you are."

"Don't touch the hatch until I say so."

"Aye aye, Cap'n."

The Captain turned around. "I have the conn," he announced.

"Captain has the conn," the officer of the deck agreed.

"Diving Officer, pump out three thousand pounds. We're taking her off the bottom. Engine room, stand by to answer bells."

"Aye." The diving officer, who was also Chief of the Boat, gave the necessary orders. Electric trim pumps ejected a ton and a half of saltwater, and *Dallas* slowly righted herself. Mancuso looked around. The submarine was at battle stations. The fire-control tracking party stood ready. Ramius was with the navigator. The weapons-control panels were manned. Below in the torpedo room, all four tubes were loaded, and one was already flooded.

"Sonar, conn. Anything to report?" Mancuso asked next.

"Negative, conn. Nothing at all, sir."

"Very well. Diving Officer, make your depth nine-zero feet."

"Nine-zero feet, aye."

They had to get off the bottom before giving the submarine any forward movement. Mancuso watched the depth gauge change slowly as the Chief of the Boat, also known as the Cob, slowly and skillfully adjusted the submarine's trim.

"Depth nine-zero feet, sir. It'll be very hard to hold."

"Maneuvering, give me turns for five knots. Helm, right fifteen degrees rudder, come to new heading zero-three-eight."

"Right fifteen degrees rudder, aye, coming to new heading zero-three-eight," the helmsman acknowledged. "Sir, my rudder is right fifteen degrees."

"Very well." Mancuso watched the gyrocompass click around to the northeasterly course. It took five minutes to get out from under the ice. The Captain ordered periscope depth. Another minute.

"Up 'scope!" Mancuso said next. A quartermaster twisted the control wheel, and the Captain met the rising instrument as the eyepiece cleared the deck. "Hold!"

The periscope stopped a foot below the surface. Mancuso looked for shadows and possible ice, but saw nothing. "Up two feet." He was on his knees now. "Two more and hold."

He used the slender attack periscope, not the larger search one. The search periscope had better light-gathering capacity, but he didn't want to risk the larger radar cross-section, and the submarine for the past twelve hours had been using red internal lights only. It made the food look odd, but it also gave everyone better night vision. He made a slow sweep of the horizon. There was nothing to be seen but drifting ice on the surface.

"Clear," he announced. "All clear. Raise the ESM." There was the hiss of hydraulics as the electronic-sensor mast went up. The thin reed of fiberglass was only half an inch wide, and nearly invisible on radar. "Down 'scope."

"I got that one surface-surveillance radar, bearing zero-three-eight," the ESM technician announced, giving frequency and pulse characteristics. "Signal is weak."

"Here we go, people." Mancuso lifted a phone to the bridge tube. "You ready?"

"Yes, sir," Clark replied.

"Stand by. Good luck." The Captain replaced the phone and turned. "Put her on the roof and stand by to take her down fast."

It took a total of four minutes. The top of *Dallas'* black sail broached the surface, pointing directly at the nearest Soviet radar to minimize its radar cross-section. It was more than tricky to hold depth.

"Clark, go!"

"Right."

With all the drifting ice on the water, the screen for that radar should be heavily cluttered, Mancuso thought. He watched the indicator light for the hatch change from a dash, meaning closed, to a circle, meaning open.

The bridge trunk ended on a platform a few feet below the bridge itself. Clark wrenched open the hatch and climbed up. Next he hauled out his raft with the help of the seaman below on the ladder. Alone now in the submarine's tiny bridge—the control station atop the sail—he set the thing athwart the top of the sail and pulled the rope that inflated it. The high-pitched rasp of the rushing air seemed to scream into the night, and Clark winced to hear it. As soon as the rubberized fabric became taut, he called to the sailor to close the trunk hatch, then grabbed the bridge phone.

"All ready here. The hatch is closed. See you in a couple of hours."

"Right. Good luck," Mancuso said again.

Aloft, Clark climbed smoothly into the raft as the submarine sank beneath him, and started the electric motor. Below, the bottom hatch of the bridge tube was opened only long enough for the sailor to leap down, then he and the Captain levered it shut.

"Straight board shut, we are rigged for dive," the Cob reported when the last indicator light changed back to a dash.

"That's it," Mancuso noted. "Mr. Goodman, you have the conn, and you know what to do."

"I have the conn," the OOD replied as the Captain went forward to the sonar room. Lieutenant Goodman immediately dived the boat, heading her for the bottom.

It was like old times, Mancuso thought, with Jones as lead sonarman. The submarine came right, pointing her bow-mounted sonar array at the path that Clark was taking. Ramius arrived a minute later to observe.

"How come you didn't want to use the 'scope?" Mancuso asked.

"A hard thing to see one's home and know that one cannot—"

"There he goes." Jones tapped his finger on the video display. "Doing turns for eighteen knots. Pretty quiet for an outboard. Electric, eh?"

"Right."

"I sure hope he's got good batteries, skipper."

"Rotating-anode lithium. I asked."

"Cute." Jones grunted. He tapped a cigarette out of his pack and offered one to the Captain, who forgot for the moment that he'd quit, again. Jones lit it and took on a contemplative expression.

"You know, sir, now I remember why I retired . . ." His voice trailed off as Jonesy watched the sonar trail stretch off in the distance. Aft, the fire-control party updated the range, just to have something to do. Jones craned his neck and listened. *Dallas* was about as quiet as she ever got, and the tension filled the air far more thickly than cigarette smoke ever could.

Clark lay nearly flat in the boat. Made of rubberized nylon, its color scheme was green and gray stripes, not very different from the sea. They'd thought of some white patches because of the ice to be found in the area in winter, but then it was realized that the channel here was always tended by an icebreaker, and a rapidly moving white spot on a dark surface might not be a terribly good idea. Mainly Clark was concerned about radar. The submarine's sail might not have been picked up through all the clutter, but if the Russian radar sets had a moving-target-indicator setting, the simple computer that monitored the returning signals might well lock in on something traveling at twenty miles per hour. The boat itself was only a foot out of the water, the motor a foot higher than that and coated with radar-absorbing material. Clark kept his head level with the motor and wondered again if the half-dozen metal fragments that decorated his anatomy were large enough to be seen. He knew that this was irrational—they didn't even set off an airport metal-detector—but lonely men in dangerous places tended to develop unusually active minds. It was better, really, to be stupid, he told himself. Intelligence only allowed you to realize how dangerous things like this were. After such missions were over, after the shakes went away, after the hot shower, you could bask in the glow of how brave and clever you were, but not now. Now it just seemed dangerous, not to say crazy, to be doing something like this.

The coastline was clearly visible, a clean series of dots that covered the visible horizon. It seemed ordinary enough, but it was enemy territory. That knowledge was far more chilling than the clean night air.

At least the seas were calm, he told himself. Actually a few feet of chop would have made for more favorable radar conditions, but the smooth, oily surface made for speed, and speed always made him feel better. He looked aft. The boat didn't make much of a wake, and he'd reduce it further by slowing when he got close to the harbor.

Patience, he told himself uselessly. He hated the idea of patience. Who likes to wait for anything? Clark asked himself. *If it has to happen, let it happen and be done with it.* That wasn't the safe way, rushing into things, but at least when you were up and moving, you were doing something. But when he taught people how to do this sort of thing, which was his normal occupation, he always told them to be patient. *You friggin' hypocrite!* he observed silently.

The harbor buoys told him the distance from the coast. He cut his speed to ten knots, then to five, and finally to three. The electric motor made a barely audible hum. Clark turned the handle and steered the boat to a ramshackle pier. It had to have been an old one; its piles had been splintered and abraded by the harbor ice of many winters. Ever so slowly, he pulled out a low-light 'scope and examined the area. There was no movement he could see. He could hear things now, mainly traffic sounds that carried across the water to him, along with some music. It was Friday night, after all, and even in the Soviet Union there were parties going on at restaurants. People were dancing. In fact his plan depended on the presence of nightlife here—Estonia is livelier than most of the country—but the pier was derelict, as his briefers said it would be. He moved in, tying the boat off to a piling with considerable care—if it drifted away, he'd have real problems. Next to the pile was a ladder. Clark slipped out of his coverall and climbed up, pistol in hand. For the first time he noted the harbor smell. It was little different from its American equivalent, heavy with bilge oil and decorated with rotting wood from the piers. To the north, a dozen or so fishing boats were tied to another pier. To the south was yet another, that one piled up with lumber. So the harbor was being rebuilt. That explained the condition of this one, Clark thought. He checked his watch—it was a battered Russian "Pilot"—and looked around for a place to wait. Forty minutes until he had to move. He'd allowed for choppier seas for his trip in, and all the calm had really done for him was to give him the additional time to meditate on how much a lunatic he was for taking on another of these extraction jobs.

Boris Filipovich Morozov walked outside the barracks where he still lived, staring upward. The lights at Bright Star made the sky into a feathery dome of descending flakes. He loved moments like this.

"Who's there?" a voice asked. It had authority in it.

"Morozov," the young engineer answered as the figure came into the light. He saw the wide-brimmed hat of a senior Army officer.

"Good evening, Comrade Engineer. You're on the mirror-control team, aren't you?" Bondarenko asked.

"Have we met?"

"No." The Colonel shook his head. "Do you know who I am?"

"Yes, Comrade Colonel."

Bondarenko gestured at the sky. "Beautiful, isn't it? I suppose that's one consolation for being at the far end of nothing."

"No, Comrade Colonel, we are at the leading edge of something very important," Morozov pointed out.

"That is good for me to hear! Do all of your team feel that way?"

"Yes, Comrade Colonel. I asked to come here."

"Oh? And how did you know of this place?" the Colonel wondered.

"I was here last fall with the Komsomol. We assisted the civil engineers in the blasting, and siting the mirror-pillars. I was a graduate student in lasers, and I guessed what Bright Star was. I did not tell anyone, of course," Morozov added. "But I knew this was the place for me."

Bondarenko regarded the youngster with visible approval. "How goes the work?"

"I had hoped to join the laser team, but my section chief press-ganged me into joining his group." Morozov laughed.

"You are unhappy with this?"

"No—no, please excuse me. You misunderstand. I didn't know how important the mirror group was. I've learned. Now we're trying to adapt the mirror systems to more precise computer control—I may soon be an assistant section leader," Morozov said proudly. "I am also familiar with computer systems, you see."

"Who's your section chief—Govorov, isn't it?"

"Correct. A brilliant field engineer, if I may say so. May I ask a question?"

"Certainly."

"It is said that you—you're the new Army colonel they've been talking about, correct? They say that you may be the new deputy project officer."

"There may be some substance to those rumors," Bondarenko allowed.

"Then may I make a suggestion, Comrade?" Morozov asked.

"Certainly."

"There are many single men here . . ."

"And not enough single women?"

"There *is* a need for laboratory assistants."

"Your observation is noted, Comrade Engineer," Bondarenko replied with a chuckle. "We also plan a new apartment block to relieve the crowding. How are the barracks?"

"The atmosphere is comradely. The astronomy and chess clubs are very active."

"Ah. It has been time since I played chess seriously. How tough is the competition?" the Colonel asked.

The younger man laughed. "Murderous—even savage."

Five thousand meters away, the Archer blessed his God's name. Snow was falling, and the flakes gave the air the magical quality so beloved by poets . . . and soldiers. You could hear—you could *feel* the hushed silence as the snow absorbed all sound. All around them, as far up and down as they could see, was the curtain of white that cut visibility to under two hundred meters. He assembled his subunit commanders and began organizing the assault. They moved out in a few minutes. They were in tactical formation. The Archer was with the lead section of the first company, while his second-in-command stayed with the other.

The footing was surprisingly good. The Russians had dumped the spoil from their blasting all over the area, and even though coated with snow, the rock chips were not slippery. This was well, since their path took them perilously close to a sheer wall at least a hundred meters high. Navigating was difficult. The Archer was going from memory, but he'd spent hours examining the objective and knew every curve of the mountain—or so he'd thought. The doubts came now, as they always did, and it took all his concentration to keep his mind on the mission. He had mapped out a dozen checkpoints in his memory before setting out. A boulder here, a dip there, this the place where the path turned to the left, and that one where it went to the right. At first progress seemed maddeningly slow, but the closer they came to the objective, the more rapid became the pace. They were guided at all times by the glow of the lights. How confident the Russians were, to have lights here, he thought. There was even a moving vehicle, a bus, by the sound of it, with its headlights lit. The small, moving points of light shone through the enveloping white cloud. Within the larger bubble of light, those on guard duty would be at a disadvantage now. Ordinarily the outwardly aimed spotlights would serve to dazzle and blind an intruder, but now the reverse was true. Little of their glow penetrated the snow, and much was reflected back, ruining the night vision of the armed troops. Finally the lead party reached the last checkpoint. The Archer deployed his men and waited for the rest to catch up. It took half an hour. His men were grouped in knots of three or four, and the *mud-jaheddin* took the time to drink some water and commit their souls to Allah, preparing both for the battle and for its possible aftermath. Theirs was the warrior's creed. Their enemy was also the enemy of their God. Whatever they did to the people who had offended Allah would be forgiven them, and every one of the Archer's men reminded himself of friends and family who had died at Russian hands.

"This is amazing," the Major whispered as he arrived.

"Allah is with us, my friend," the Archer replied.

"He must be." They were now only five hundred meters from the site, and still unseen. *We might actually survive* . . .

"How much closer can we—"

"One hundred meters. The low-light equipment they have will penetrate snow to about four hundred. The nearest tower is six hundred meters that way." He pointed unnecessarily. The Archer knew exactly where it was, and the next one, two hundred meters farther down.

The Major checked his watch and thought for a moment.

"The guard will change in another hour if they follow the same pattern here as in Kabul. Those on duty will be tired and cold, and the relief troops aren't yet awake. This is the time."

"Good luck," the Archer said simply. Both men embraced.

" ' "Why should we refuse to fight for the cause of Allah, when we and our children have been driven from our dwellings?" ' "

" 'When they met Goliath and his warriors they cried: "Lord fill our hearts with steadfastness. Make us firm of foot and help us against the unbelievers." ' "

The quote was from the Koran, and neither man thought it strange that the passage actually referred to the Israelites' battle against the Philistines. David and Saul were known to the Muslims, too, as was their cause. The Major smiled one last time before running off to join his men.

The Archer turned and waved to his missile team. Two of them shouldered their Stingers and followed the leader as he continued his way across the mountain. One more knoll and they were looking down at the guard towers. He was surprised that he could actually see three of them from here, and a third missile was brought out. The Archer gave his instructions and left them to rejoin the main body. On the knoll, the target-acquisition units sang their deadly song to each missileer. The guard towers were heated—and the Stinger searches only for heat.

Next the Archer ordered his mortar team in close—closer than he would have preferred, but the miserable visibility was not entirely on the side of the *mudjaheddin.* He watched the Major's company slide down to the left, disappearing into the snow. They would assault the laser test facility itself, while he and his eighty men went for the place where most of the people lived. Now it was their turn. The Archer led them forward as far as he dared, just to the edge of where the floodlights penetrated the snow. He was rewarded with the sight of a sentry, bundled up for the cold, his breath left behind in a series of small white clouds that drifted in the wind. Ten more minutes. The Archer pulled out his radio. They had only four of them, and hadn't dared to use them until now for fear of being detected by the Russians.

We should never have gotten rid of the dogs, Bondarenko told himself. *First thing I do when I get settled here, get the dogs back.* He was walking around the camp, enjoying the cold and the snow and using the quiet atmosphere to order his thoughts. There were things that needed changing here. They needed a real soldier. General Pokryshkin was too confident in the security scheme, and the KGB troops were too lazy. For example, they did not have night patrols out. Too dangerous on this terrain, their commander said, our day patrols will detect anyone who tries to get close, the guard towers have low-light scanners, and the rest of the site is floodlit. But low-light devices had their effectiveness cut eighty percent by this sort of weather. What if there was a group of Afghans out there right now? he wondered. *First thing,* Bondarenko told himself, *I'll call Colonel Nikolayev at* Spetznaz *headquarters, and* I'll *lead a practice assault on this place to show those KGB idiots how vulnerable they are.* He looked up the hill. There was a KGB sentry, flapping his arms to keep warm, rifle slung over his shoulder—it would take him four seconds to get it unslung, aimed, and taken off safety. *Four seconds, for the last three of which he'd be dead if there were anyone competent out there right now* . . . Well, he told himself, the assistant commander of any post is supposed to be a ruthless son of a bitch, and if those *chekisti* want to play at soldiers they'll damned well have to act like soldiers. The Colonel turned to walk back to the apartment block.

Gerasimov's car pulled up to Lefortovo Prison's administrative entrance. His driver stayed with the car while the bodyguard followed him in. The KGB Chairman showed his ID card to the guard and walked by without breaking stride. The KGB was careful with security, but all its members knew the face of the Chairman and knew even better the power that it represented. Gerasimov turned left and headed for the administration offices. The prison superintendent wasn't there, of course, but one of his deputies was. Gerasimov found him filling out some forms.

"Good evening." The man's eyes were saved from bugging out by the glasses he wore.

"Comrade Chairman! I was not—"

"You weren't supposed to be."

"How may I—"

"The prisoner Filitov. I need him immediately," Gerasimov said gruffly. "Immediately," he repeated for effect.

"At once!" The second deputy prison superintendent leaped to his feet and ran to another room. He was back in under a minute. "It will take five minutes."

"He must be properly dressed," Gerasimov said.

"His uniform?" the man asked.

"Not that, you idiot!" the Chairman snarled. "Civilian clothes. He must be presentable. You have all his personal effects here, don't you?"

"Yes, Comrade Chairman, but—"

"I do not have all night," he said quietly. There was nothing more dangerous than a quiet KGB Chairman. The second deputy superintendent fairly flew from the room. Gerasimov turned to his bodyguard, who smiled in amusement. Nobody liked jailers. "How long do you think?"

"Less than ten minutes, Comrade Chairman, even though they have to find his clothes. After all, that pipsqueak knows what a wonderful place this is to live in. I know him."

"Oh?"

"He was originally a 'One' man, but he performed poorly on his first assignment and has been a jailer ever since." The bodyguard checked his watch.

It took eight minutes. Filitov appeared with his suit most of the way on, though his shirt was not buttoned, and his tie merely draped around his neck. The second deputy superintendent was holding a threadbare topcoat. Filitov never had been one to buy a lot of civilian clothes. He was a Colonel of the Red Army, and was never comfortable out of his uniform. The old man's eyes were confused at first, then he saw Gerasimov.

"What is this?" he asked.

"You are coming with me, Filitov. Button your shirt. At least try to look like a man!"

Misha nearly said something, but bit it off. The look he gave the Chairman was enough to make the bodyguard move his hand a centimeter. He buttoned his shirt and tied his tie. It ended up crooked in his collar because he didn't have a mirror.

"Now, Comrade Chairman, if you will sign this—"

"You give me custody of a criminal like this?"

"What—"

"Handcuffs, man!" Gerasimov boomed.

Unsurprisingly, the second deputy superintendent had a pair in his desk. He got them, put them on Filitov, and nearly pocketed the key before he saw Gerasimov's outstretched hand.

"Very good. I'll have him back to you tomorrow night."

"But I need you to sign—" The second deputy superintendent found that he was talking to a receding back.

"Well, with all the people under me," Gerasimov observed to his bodyguard, "there have to be a few . . ."

"Indeed, Comrade Chairman." The bodyguard was an immensely fit man of forty-two, a former field officer who was an expert in all forms of armed and unarmed combat. His firm grip on the prisoner told Misha all of these things.

"Filitov," the Chairman observed over his shoulder, "we are taking a brief trip, a flight that is. You will not be harmed. If you behave yourself, we might even allow you a decent meal or two. If you do not behave, Vasiliy here will make you wish you did. Is that clear?"

"Clear, Comrade *Chekist.*"

The guard snapped to attention, then pushed open the door. The outside guards saluted and were rewarded with nods. The driver held open the back door. Gerasimov stopped and turned.

"Put him in back with me, Vasiliy. You should be able to cover things from the front seat."

"As you wish, Comrade."

"Sheremetyevo," Gerasimov told the driver. "The cargo terminal on the south side."

There was the airport, Ryan thought. He stifled a belch that tasted of wine and sardines. The motorcade entered the airport grounds, then curved to the right, bypassing the regular entrance to the terminal and heading out onto the aircraft parking area. Security, he noted, was *tight*. You could always depend on the Russians for that. Everywhere he looked were rifle-toting soldiers in KGB uniforms. The car drove right past the main terminal, then past a recent addition. It was unused, but looked like the alien spaceship in Spielberg's *Close Encounters*. He'd meant to ask somebody why it had been built, but wasn't yet in use. Maybe next time, Ryan thought.

The formal goodbyes had been made at the Foreign Ministry. A few junior officials stood at the bottom of the stairs to shake hands, and nobody was in a hurry to leave the heated comfort of the limousines. Progress was correspondingly slow. His car lurched forward and stopped, and the man to Ryan's right opened the door as the driver popped the trunk open. He didn't want to go outside either. It had taken most of the drive to get the car warm. Jack got his bag and his briefcase and headed for the stairs.

"I hope you enjoyed your visit," the Soviet official said.

"I would like to come back and see the city sometime," Jack replied as he shook the man's hand.

"We would be delighted."

Sure you would, Jack thought as he went up the stairs. Once in the aircraft, he looked forward. A Russian officer was in the cockpit jump seat to assist with traffic control. His eyes were on the curtained-off communications console. Ryan nodded at the pilot through the door and got a wink.

"The political dimension scares the hell out of me," Vatutin said. At 2 Dzerzhinskiy Square, he and Golovko were comparing their written notes.

"This isn't the old days. They can't shoot us for following our training and procedures."

"Really? What if Filitov was being run with the knowledge of the Chairman?"

"Ridiculous," Golovko observed.

"Oh? What if his early work on the dissidents put him in contact with the West? We know that he personally intervened in some cases—mainly from the Baltic region, but some others, too."

"You're really thinking like a 'Two' man now!"

"Think for a minute. We arrest Filitov and immediately thereafter the Chairman meets personally with a CIA man. Has that ever happened before?"

"I've heard stories about Philby, but—no, that was only after he came over."

"It's one hell of a coincidence," Vatutin said as he rubbed his eyes. "They do not train us to believe in coincidences, and—"

"*Tvoyu mat'!*" Golovko said. Vatutin looked up in annoyance to see the other man roll his eyes. "The last time the Americans were over—how could I forget this! Ryan spoke with Filitov—they collided as though by accident, and—"

Vatutin lifted his phone and dialed. "Give me the night superintendent . . . This is Colonel Vatutin. Wake up the prisoner Filitov. I want to see him within the hour . . . What was that? Who? Very well. Thank you." The Colonel of the Second Chief Directorate stood. "Chairman Gerasimov just took Filitov out of Lefortovo fifteen minutes ago. He said that they were taking a special trip."

"Where's your car?"

"I can order—"

"No," Golovko said. "Your personal car."

26. Black Operations

There was no hurry, yet. While the cabin crew got everybody settled in, Colonel von Eich ran down the pre-flight checklist. The VC-137 was taking electrical power from a generator truck that would also allow them to start their engines more easily than internal systems allowed. He checked his watch and hoped everything would go as planned.

Aft, Ryan walked past his normal place, just forward of Ernie Allen's midships cabin, and took a seat in the back row of the after part of the aircraft. It looked much like part of a real airliner, though the seating was five-across, and this space handled the overflow from the "distinguished visitor" areas forward. Jack picked one on the left side, where the seats were in pairs, while ten or so others entered the cabin and kept as far forward as possible for the smoother ride, as advised by another crew member. The aircraft's crew chief would be across the aisle to his right instead of in the crew quarters forward. Ryan wished for another man to help, but they couldn't be too obvious. They had a Soviet officer aboard. That was part of the regular routine, and diverging from it would attract attention. The whole point of this was that everyone would be comfortably secure in the knowledge that everything was exactly as it should be.

Forward, the pilot got to the end of the checklist page.

"Everybody aboard?"

"Yes, sir. Ready to close the doors."

"Keep an eye on the indicator light for the crew door. It's been acting funny," von Eich told the flight engineer.

"A problem?" the Soviet pilot asked from the jump seat. Sudden depressurization is something every flyer takes seriously.

"Every time we check the door it looks fine. Probably a bad relay in the panel, but we haven't found the sucker yet. I've checked the goddamned door-seal myself," he assured the Russian. "It has to be an electrical fault."

"Ready to start," the flight engineer told him next.

"Okay." The pilot looked to make sure the stairs were away while the flight crew donned their headsets. "All clear left."

"All clear right," the copilot said.

"Turning one." Buttons were pushed, switches were toggled, and the left-outboard engine began to rotate its turbine blades. The needles on several indicator dials started moving and were soon in normal idling range. The generator truck withdrew now that the plane could supply its own electric power.

"Turning four," the pilot said next. He toggled his microphone to the cabin setting. "Ladies and gentlemen, this is Colonel von Eich. We're getting the engines started, and we should be moving in about five minutes. Please buckle your seat belts. Those of you who smoke, try to hang in there another few minutes."

At his seat in the back row, Ryan would have killed for a smoke. The crew chief glanced over to him and smiled. He certainly seemed tough enough to handle it, Jack thought. The chief master sergeant looked to be pushing fifty, but he also looked like a man who could teach manners to an NFL linebacker. He was wearing leather work gloves with the adjustment straps pulled in tight.

"All ready?" Jack asked. There was no danger of being heard. The engine noise was hideous back here.

"Whenever you say, sir."

"You'll know when."

"Hmph," Gerasimov noted. "Not here yet." The cargo terminal was closed, and dark except for the security floodlights.

"Should I make a call?" the driver asked.

"No hurry. What—" A uniformed guard waved for them to stop. They'd already come through one checkpoint. "Oh, that's right. The Americans are getting ready to leave. That must be screwing things up."

The guard came to the driver's window and asked for passes. The driver just waved to the back.

"Good evening, Corporal," Gerasimov said. He held up his identification card. The youngster snapped to attention. "A plane will be here in a few minutes for me. The Americans must be holding things up. Is the security force out?"

"Yes, Comrade Chairman! A full company."

"While we're here, why don't we do a fast inspection? Who is your commander?"

"Major Zarudin, Com—"

"What the hell is—" A lieutenant came over. He got as far as the corporal before he saw who was in the car.

"Lieutenant, where is Major Zarudin?"

"In the control tower, Comrade Chairman. That is the best place to—"

"I'm sure. Get him on your radio and tell him that I am going to inspect the guard perimeter, then I will come to see him and tell him what I think. Drive on," he told the driver. "Go right."

"Sheremetyevo Tower, this is niner-seven-one requesting permission to taxi to runway two-five-right," von Eich said into his microphone.

"Nine-seven-one, permission granted. Turn left onto main taxiway one. Wind is two-eight-one at forty kilometers."

"Roger, out," the pilot said. "Okay, let's get this bird moving." The copilot advanced the throttles and the aircraft started to roll. On the ground in front of them, a man with two lighted wands gave them unneeded directions to the taxiway—but the Russians always assumed that everyone needed to be told what to do. Von Eich left the parking pad and headed south on taxiway nine, then turned left. The small wheel that controlled the steerable nose-gear was stiff, as always, and the aircraft came around slowly, pushed by the outboard engine. He always took things easy here. The taxiways were so rough that there was always the worry of damaging something. He didn't want that to happen tonight. It was the best part of a mile to the end of the number-one main taxiway, and the bumps and rolls were enough to make one motion-sick. He finally turned right onto taxiway five.

"The men seem alert," Vasiliy observed as they crossed runway twenty-five-left. The driver had his lights off and kept to the edge. There was an airplane coming, and both driver and bodyguard were keeping their eyes on that hazard. They didn't see Gerasimov take the key from his pocket and unlock the handcuffs of an amazed prisoner Filitov. Next the Chairman pulled an automatic pistol from inside his coat.

"Shit—there's a car there," Colonel von Eich said. "What the hell is a car doing here?"

"We'll clear it easy," the copilot said. "He's way over on the edge."

"Great." The pilot turned right again to the end of the runway. "Fucking Sunday drivers."

"You're not going to like this either, Colonel," the flight engineer said. "I got a light on the rear door again."

"God damn it!" von Eich swore over the intercom. He flipped his mike to the cabin setting again, but had to adjust his voice before speaking. "Crew chief, check the rear door."

"Here we go," the sergeant said. Ryan flipped off his seat belt and moved a few feet as he watched the sergeant work the door handle.

"We got a short in here someplace," the flight engineer said on the flight deck, forward. "Just lost the aft cabin lights. The breaker just popped and I can't get it to reset."

"Maybe it's a bad breaker?" Colonel von Eich asked.

"I can try a spare," the engineer said.

"Go ahead. I'll tell the folks in back why the lights just went out." It was a lie, but a good enough one, and with everyone buckled in, it wasn't all that easy to turn around and see the back of the cabin.

"Where's the Chairman?" Vatutin asked the Lieutenant.

"He's conducting an inspection—who are you?"

"Colonel Vatutin—this is Colonel Golovko. Where's the fucking Chairman, you young idiot!"

The Lieutenant sputtered for a few seconds, then pointed.

"Vasiliy," the Chairman said. It was too bad really. His bodyguard turned to see the muzzle of a pistol. "Your gun, please."

"But—"

"No time for talking." He took the gun and pocketed it. Next he handed over the cuffs. "Both of you, and put your hands through the steering wheel."

The driver was aghast, but both men did as they were told. Vasiliy snapped one ring on his left wrist and reached through the steering wheel to attach the other to the driver. While they did so, Gerasimov detached the receiver from his car's radiophone and pocketed that.

"The keys?" Gerasimov asked. The driver handed them over with his free left hand. The nearest uniformed guard was a hundred meters away. The airplane was a mere twenty. The Chairman of the Committee for State Security opened the car door himself. He hadn't done that in months. "Colonel Filitov, will you come with me, please?"

Misha was as surprised as everyone else, but did as he was told. In full view of everyone at the airport—at least, those few who were bothering to watch the routine departure—Gerasimov and Filitov walked toward the VC-137's red, white, and blue tail. As though on command, the after door opened.

"Let's hustle, people." Ryan tossed out a rope ladder.

Filitov's legs betrayed him. The wind and blast from the jet engines made the ladder flutter like a flag in the breeze, and he couldn't get both feet on it despite help from Gerasimov.

"My God, look!" Golovko pointed. "Move!"

Vatutin didn't say anything. He floored his car and flipped on the high-beam lights.

"Trouble," the crew chief said when he saw the car. There was a man with a rifle running this way, too. "Come on, pop!" he urged the Cardinal of the Kremlin.

"Shit!" Ryan pushed the sergeant aside and jumped down. It was too far, and he landed badly, twisting his right ankle and ripping his pants at his left knee. Jack ignored the pain and leaped to his feet. He took one of Filitov's shoulders while Gerasimov took the other, and together they got him up the ladder far enough that the sergeant at the door was able to haul him aboard. Gerasimov went next, with Ryan's help. Then it was Jack's turn—but he had the same problem Filitov had. His left knee was already stiff, and when he tried to climb up on his sprained ankle, his right leg simply refused to work. He swore loudly enough to be heard over the sound of the engines and tried to do it hand over hand, but he lost his grip and fell to the pavement.

"*Stoi, stoi!*" somebody with a gun shouted from ten feet away. Jack looked up at the aircraft door.

"*Go!*" he screamed. "Close the fucking door and go!"

The crew chief did exactly that without a moment's hesitation. He reached around to pull the door shut, and Jack watched it seat itself in a matter of seconds. Inside, the sergeant lifted the interphone and told the pilot that the door was properly sealed.

"Tower, this is niner-seven-one, rolling now. Out." The pilot advanced the throttles to takeoff power.

The force of the engine blast hurled all four men—the rifleman had just arrived at the scene, too—right off the end of the icy runway. Jack watched from flat on his belly as the blinking red light atop the aircraft's tall rudder diminished in the distance, then rose. His last view of it was the glow of the infrared jammers that protected the VC-137 against surface-to-air missiles. He almost started laughing, when he was rolled over and saw a pistol against his face.

"Hello, Sergey," Ryan said to Colonel Golovko.

"Ready," the radio told the Archer. He raised a flare pistol and fired a single star-shell round that burst directly over one of the shops.

Everything happened at once. To his left, three Stinger missiles were launched after a long and boring wait. Each streaked toward a guard tower—or more precisely, to the electric heaters inside them. The paired sentries in each had time enough only to see and be surprised by the signal round over the central region of the installation, and only one of the six saw an inbound streak of yellow, too fast to permit a reaction. All three of the missiles hit—they could hardly miss a stationary target—and in each case the six-pound warhead functioned as designed. Less than five seconds after the first round had been fired, the towers were eliminated, and with them also the machine guns that protected the laser facility.

The sentry to the Archer's front died next. He hadn't a chance. Forty rifles fired on him at once, with half of the bursts connecting. Next the mortars fired ranging rounds, and the Archer used his radio to adjust the fire onto what he thought was the guards' barracks.

The sound of automatic-weapons fire cannot be mistaken for anything else. Colonel Bondarenko had just decided that he'd spent enough time communing with a cold though beautiful nature and was walking back to his quarters when the sound stopped him in his tracks. His first thought was that one of the KGB guards had accidentally discharged his weapon, but that impression lasted less than a second. He heard a *crack!* overhead and looked up to see the star shell, then heard the explosions from the laser site, and as though a switch had been thrown, he changed from a startled man to a professional soldier under attack. The KGB barracks were two hundred meters to his right, and he ran there as fast as he could.

Mortar rounds were falling, he saw. They were falling on the big new machine shop just beyond the barracks. Men were stumbling out the door of the latter when he arrived, and he had to stop and hold up his arms to avoid being shot.

"I am Colonel Bondarenko! Where is your officer?"

"Here!" A lieutenant came out. "What—" Someone had just learned of his mistake. The next mortar round hit the back of the barracks.

"Follow me!" Bondarenko screamed, leading them away from the most obvious target in sight. All around them was the deadly chatter of rifles—Soviet rifles; the Colonel noted at once that he couldn't use sound to identify who was who. *Wonderful!* "Form up!"

"What is—"

"We're under attack, Lieutenant! How many men do you have?"

He turned and counted. Bondarenko did it faster still. There were forty-one, all with rifles, but there were no heavy weapons, and no radios. The machine guns he could do without, but radios were vital.

The dogs, he told himself stupidly, *they should have kept the dogs . . .*

The tactical situation was appallingly bad, and he knew that it would only get worse. A series of explosions sundered the night.

"The lasers, we must—" the Lieutenant said, but the Colonel grabbed his shoulder.

"We can rebuild the machines," Bondarenko said urgently, "but we cannot rebuild the scientists. We're going to get to the apartment building and hold that until relieved. Send a good sergeant to the bachelor quarters and get them to the apartments."

"No, Comrade Colonel! My orders are to protect the lasers, and I must—"

"I am ordering you to get your men—"

"*No!*" the Lieutenant screamed back at him.

Bondarenko knocked him down, took his rifle, flipped off the safety, and fired two rounds into his chest. He turned. "Who's the best sergeant?"

"I am, Colonel," a young man said shakily.

"I am Colonel Bondarenko, and I am in command!" the officer announced as forcefully as a command from God. "You take four men, get to the bachelor barracks, and bring everyone up the hill to the apartment building. Fast as you can!" The sergeant pointed to four others and ran off. "The rest of you, follow me!" He led them into the falling snow. There wasn't time for him or them to wonder what awaited. Before they'd gone ten meters, every light in the camp went out.

At the gate of the laser site a GAZ jeep sat, with a heavy machine gun aboard. General Pokryshkin ran from the control building when he heard the explosions, and was stunned to see that only blazing stumps remained of his three guard towers. The commander of the KGB detachment raced down to him on his vehicle.

"We're under attack," the officer said unnecessarily.

"Get your men together—right here." Pokryshkin looked up to see running men. They were dressed in Soviet uniforms, but somehow he knew that they were not Russians. The General climbed into the back of the jeep and brought the machine gun around over the head of the astonished KGB officer. The first time he pressed the trigger nothing happened, and he had to ratchet a round into the chamber. The second time, Pokryshkin had the satisfaction of watching three men fall. The guard force commander needed no further encouragement. He barked rapid orders into his radio. The battle under way degenerated at once into confusion, as it had to—both sides were wearing identical uniforms and using identical weapons. But there were more Afghans than Russians.

*   *   *

Morozov and several of his unmarried friends had stepped outside when they heard the noise. Most of them had military experience, though he did not. It didn't matter—nobody had the first idea what they should do. Five men came running out of the darkness. They were wearing uniforms and carrying rifles.

"Come! All of you come, follow us!" More weapons started firing close by, and two of the KGB troops went down, one dead, one wounded. He fired back, emptying his rifle in one long burst. There was a scream in the darkness, followed by shouts. Morozov ran inside and called for people to make for the door. The engineers needed little prompting.

"Up the hill," the sergeant said. "To the apartment block. Fast as you can!" The four KGB troops waved them along, looking for targets, but seeing only flashes. Bullets were flying everywhere now. Another of the troops went down screaming out his last breath, but the sergeant got the one who killed him. When the last engineer left the room, he and a private grabbed the spare rifles and helped their comrade back up the hill.

It was too big a mission for eighty men, the Archer realized too late. Too much ground to cover, too many buildings, but there were many unbelievers running around, and that was why he'd brought his men here. He watched one of them explode a bus with an RPG-7 antitank round. It burst into flames and slid off the road, rolling down the side of the mountain while those inside screamed. Teams of men with explosives went into the buildings. They found machine tools bathed in oil and set their charges quickly, running out before the explosions could begin the fires. The Archer had realized a minute too late which building was the guard barracks, and now that was ablaze as he led his section in to mop up the men who'd been kept there. He was too late, but didn't know it yet. A stray mortar round had cut the power line that handled all of the site's lighting, and all of his men were robbed of their night vision by the flashes of their own weapons.

"Well done, Sergeant!" Bondarenko told the boy. He'd already ordered the engineers upstairs. "We'll set our perimeter around the building. They may force us back. If so, we'll make our stand on the first floor. The walls are concrete. RPGs can hurt us, but the roof and walls will stop bullets. Pick one man to go inside and find men with military experience. Give them those two rifles. Whenever a man goes down, retrieve his weapon and get it to someone who knows how to use it. I'm going inside for a moment to see if I can get a telephone to work—"

"There's a radiotelephone in the first-floor office," the sergeant said. "All the buildings have them."

"Good! Hold the perimeter, Sergeant. I'll be back to you in two minutes." Bondarenko ran inside. The radiotelephone was hanging on a wall hook, and he was relieved to see it was a military type, powered by its own battery. The Colonel shouldered it and ran back outside.

The attackers—who were they? he wondered—had planned their attack poorly. First they had failed to identify the KGB barracks before launching their assault; second, they hadn't hit the residential area as quickly as they should have. They were moving in now, but they found a line of Border Guards lying in the snow. They were only KGB troops, Bondarenko knew, but they did have basic training, and most of all they knew that there was no place to run. That young sergeant was a good one, he saw. He moved from point to point along the perimeter, not using his weapon but encouraging the men and telling them what to do. The Colonel activated the radio.

"This is Colonel G. I. Bondarenko at Project Bright Star. We are under attack. I repeat, Bright Star is under attack. Any unit on this net respond at once, over."

"Gennady, this is Pokryshkin at the laser site. We're in the control building. What is your situation?"

"I'm at the apartments. I have all the civilians we could find inside. I have forty men, and we're going to try to hold this place. What about help?"

"I'm trying. Gennady, we cannot get you any help from here. Can you hold?"

"Ask me in twenty minutes."

"Protect my people, Colonel. Protect my people!" Pokryshkin shouted into the microphone.

"To the death, Comrade General. Out." Bondarenko kept the radio on his back and hefted his rifle. "Sergeant!"

"Here, Colonel!" The young man appeared. "They're probing now, not really attacking yet—"

"Looking for weaknesses." Bondarenko got back down to his knees. The air seemed alive with gunfire, but it was not yet concentrated. Above and behind the two, windows were shattering. Bullets pounded into the pre-cast concrete sections that formed the building wall, spraying everyone outside with chips. "Position yourself at the corner opposite this one. You'll command the north and east walls. I'll handle these two. Tell your men to fire only when they have targets—"

"Already done, Comrade."

"Good!" Bondarenko punched the young man on the shoulder. "Don't fall back until you have to, but tell me if you do. The people in this building are priceless assets. They must survive. Go!" The Colonel watched the sergeant run off. Perhaps the KGB did train some of its people. He ran to this corner of the building.

He now had twenty—no, he counted eighteen men. Their camouflage clothing made them hard to spot. He ran from man to man, his back bowed by the weight of the radio, spacing them out, telling them to husband their rounds. He was just finishing the line on the west side when there came a chorus of human voices from the darkness.

"Here they come!" a private screamed.

"Hold your fire!" the Colonel bellowed.

The running figures appeared as though by magic. One moment the scene was empty of anything but falling snow—the next, there was a line of men firing Kalashnikov rifles from the hip. He let them get to within fifty meters.

"Fire!" He saw ten of them go down in an instant. The rest wavered and stopped, then fell back, leaving two more bodies behind. There was more firing from the opposite side of the building. Bondarenko wondered if the sergeant had held, but that was not in his hands. Some nearby screams told him that his men had taken casualties, too. On checking the line he found that one had made no noise at all. He was down to fifteen men.

* * *

The climb-out was routine enough, Colonel von Eich thought. A few feet behind him, the Russian in the jump seat was giving the electrical panel an occasional look.

"How's the electricity doing?" the pilot asked in some irritation.

"No problem with engine and hydraulic power. Seems to be in the lighting system," the engineer replied, quietly turning off the tail and wingtip anticollision lights.

"Well . . ." The cockpit instrument lights were all on, of course, and there was no additional illumination for the flight crew. "We'll fix it when we get to Shannon."

"Colonel." It was the voice of the crew chief in the pilot's headset.

"Go ahead," the engineer said, making sure that the Russian's headset was not on that channel.

"Go ahead, Sarge."

"We have our two . . . our two new passengers, sir, but Mr. Ryan—he got left behind, Colonel."

"Repeat that?" von Eich said.

"He said to move out, sir. Two guys with guns, sir, they—he said to move out, sir," the crew chief said again.

Von Eich let out a breath. "Okay. How are things back there?"

"I got them in the back row, sir. I don't think anybody noticed, even, what with the engine noise and all."

"Keep it that way."

"Yes, sir. I have Freddie keeping the rest of the passengers forward. The aft can is broke, sir."

"Pity," the pilot observed. "Tell 'em to go forward if they gotta go."

"Right, Colonel."

"Seventy-five minutes," the navigator advised.

Christ, Ryan, the pilot thought. *I hope you like it there . . .*

"I should kill you here and now!" Golovko said.

They were in the Chairman's car. Ryan found himself facing four very irate KGB officers. The maddest seemed to be the guy in the right-front seat. Gerasimov's bodyguard, Jack thought, the one who worked close in. He looked like the physical type, and Ryan was glad that there was a seatback separating them. He had a more immediate problem. He looked at Golovko and thought it might be a good idea to calm him down.

"Sergey, that would set off an international incident like you would not believe," Jack said calmly. The next conversations he heard were in Russian. He couldn't understand what they were saying, but the emotional content was clear enough. They didn't know what to do. That suited Ryan just fine.

Clark was walking along a street three blocks from the waterfront when he saw them. It was eleven forty-five. They were right on time, thank God. This part of the city had restaurants and, though he scarcely believed it, some discos. They were walking out of one when he spotted them. Two women, dressed as he'd been told to expect, with a male companion. The bodyguard. Only one, also as per orders. It was an agreeable surprise that so far everything had gone according to plan. Clark counted another dozen or so other people on the sidewalk, some in loud groups, some in quiet couples, many of them weaving from too much drink. But it was a Friday night, and that's what people all over the world did on Friday night. He maintained visual contact with the three people who concerned him, and closed in.

The bodyguard was a pro. He stayed on their right, keeping his gun hand free. He was ahead of them, but that didn't keep his head from scanning in all directions. Clark adjusted the scarf on his neck, then reached in his pocket. The pistol was there as he increased his pace to catch up. It wasn't hard. The two women seemed to be in no hurry as they approached the corner. The older one seemed to be looking around at the city. The buildings looked old, but weren't. The Second World War had swept through Talinn in two explosive waves, leaving behind nothing but scorched stones. But whoever made such decisions had opted to rebuild the city much as it had been, and the town had a feel very different from the Russian cities Clark had visited before. It made him think of Germany somehow, though he couldn't imagine why. That was his last frivolous thought of the night. He was now thirty feet behind them, just another man walking home on a cold February night, his face lowered to avoid the wind and a fur hat pulled down over his head. He could hear their voices now, and they were speaking Russian. Time.

"*Russkiy,*" Clark said with a Moscow accent. "You mean not everyone in this city is an arrogant Balt?"

"This is an old and lovely city, Comrade," the older woman answered. "Show some respect."

Here we go . . . Clark told himself. He walked forward with the curving steps of a man in his cups.

"Your pardon, lovely lady. Have a good evening," he said as he passed. He moved around the women and bumped into the bodyguard. "Excuse me, Comrade—" The man found that there was a pistol aimed at his face. "Turn left and go into the alley. Hands out where I can see them, Comrade."

The shock on the poor bastard's face was amusing as hell, Clark thought, reminding himself that this was a skilled man with a gun in *his* pocket. He grabbed the back of the man's collar and kept him out at arm's length, with his gun held in tight.

"Mother . . ." Katryn said in quiet alarm.

"Hush and do as I say. Do as this man says."

"But—"

"Against the wall," Clark told the man. He kept the gun aimed at the center of the bodyguard's head while he switched hands, then he chopped hard on the side of his neck with his right hand. The man fell stunned, and Clark put handcuffs on his wrists. Next he gagged him, tied up his ankles, and dragged him to the darkest spot he could find.

"Ladies, if you will come with me, please?"

"What is this?" Katryn asked.

"I don't know," her mother admitted. "Your father told me to—"

"Miss, your father has decided that he wants to visit America, and he wants you and your mother to join him," Clark said in flawless Russian.

Katryn did not reply. The lighting in the alley was very poor, but he could see her face lose all of the color it had. Her mother looked little better.

"But," the young girl said finally. "But that's treason . . . I don't believe it."

"He told me . . . he told me to do whatever this man says," Maria said. "Katryn—we must."

"But—"

"Katryn," her mother said. "What will happen to your life if your father defects and you remain behind? What will happen to your friends? What will happen to you? They will use you to get him back, anything they have to do, Katusha . . ."

"Time to leave, folks." Clark took both women by the arm.

"But—" Katryn gestured at the bodyguard.

"He'll be fine. We don't kill people. It's bad for business." Clark led them back to the street, turning left toward the harbor.

The Major had divided his men into two groups. The smaller one was setting explosive charges on everything they could find. A light pole or a laser, it didn't matter to them. The large group had cut down most of the KGB troops who'd tried to come here, and was arrayed around the control bunker. It wasn't actually a bunker, but whoever had made the construction plans for the place had evidently thought that the control room should have the same sort of protection as those at the Leninsk Cosmodrome, or maybe he'd thought that the mountain might someday be subjected to a nuclear airburst attack. Most likely was that someone had decided the manual prescribed this sort of structure for this sort of place. What had resulted was a building with reinforced-concrete walls fully a meter thick. His men had killed the KGB commander and taken his vehicle, with the heavy machine gun, and were pouring fire into the vision slits cut in the structure. In fact, no one used them for looking, and their rounds had long since pounded through the thick glass and were chewing into the room's computers and control gear.

Inside, General Pokryshkin had taken command by default. He had thirty or so KGB troops, armed only with light weapons and what little ammunition they'd been carrying when the attack had begun. A lieutenant was handling the defense as best he could, while the General was trying to get help by radio.

"It will take an hour," a regimental commander was saying. "My men are moving out right now!"

"Fast as you can!" Pokryshkin said. "People are dying here." He'd already thought of helicopters, but in this weather they'd accomplish nothing at all. A helicopter assault would not even have been a gamble, just suicide. He set down the radio and picked up his service automatic. He could hear the noise from the outside. All the site's equipment was being blown up. He could live with that now. As great a catastrophe as that was, the people mattered more. Nearly a third of his engineers were in the bunker. They'd been finishing up a lengthy conference when the attack began. Had that not been the case, fewer would be here, but those would have been out working on the equipment. At least here they had a chance.

On the other side of the bunker's concrete walls, the Major was still trying to figure this one out. He'd hardly expected to find this sort of structure. His RPG antitank rounds merely chipped the wall, and aiming them at the narrow slits was difficult in the darkness. His machine-gun rounds could be guided to them with tracers, but that wasn't good enough.

Find the weak points, he told himself. *Take your time and think it out.* He ordered his men to maintain a steady rate of fire and started moving around the building. Whoever was inside had his weapons equally dispersed, but buildings like this one always had at least one blind spot . . . The Major merely had to find it.

"What is happening?" his radio squawked.

"We have killed perhaps fifty. The rest are in a bunker and we're trying to get them, too. What of your target?"

"The apartment building," the Archer replied. "They're all in there, and—" The radio transmitted the sound of gunfire. "We will have them soon."

"Thirty minutes and we must leave, my friend," the Major said.

"Yes!" The radio went silent.

The Archer was a good man, and a brave one, the Major thought as he examined the bunker's north face, but with just a week's formal training he'd be so much more effective . . . just a week to codify the things that he was learning on his own . . . and to pass on the lessons that others had shed blood for . . .

There was the place. There was a blind spot.

The last mortar rounds were targeted on the roof of the apartment block. Bondarenko smiled as he watched. Finally the other side had done something really foolish. The 82-millimeter shells didn't have a chance of breaking through the concrete roof slabs, but if they'd spread them around the building's periphery he'd have lost many of his men. He was down to ten, two of them wounded. The rifles of the fallen were inside the building now, being fired from the second floor. He counted twenty bodies outside his perimeter, and the attackers—they were Afghans, he was sure of that now—were milling about beyond his vision, trying to decide what to do. For the first time Bondarenko felt that they just might survive after all. The General had radioed to say that a motorized regiment was on the way down the road from Nurek, and though he shuddered to think what it would be like driving BTR infantry carriers over snow-covered mountain roads, the loss of a few infantry squads was as nothing compared to the corporate expertise that he was trying to protect now.

The incoming rifle fire was sporadic now, just harassment fire while they decided what to do next. With more people he'd try a counterattack, just to throw them off balance, but the Colonel was tied to his post. He couldn't risk it, not with a mere squad left to cover two sides of the building.

Do I pull back now? The longer I can keep them away from the building, the better, but should I do my withdrawal now? His thoughts wavered at that decision. Inside the building his troops would have far better protection, but he'd lose the ability to control them when each man was separated from the next by the interior walls. If they pulled inside and withdrew to the upper floors, they'd allow the Afghan sappers to drop the building with explosive charges—no, that was the counsel of despair. Bondarenko listened to the scattered rifle shots that punctuated the sounds of wounded and dying men and couldn't make up his mind.

Two hundred meters away, the Archer was about to do that for him. Mistaking the casualties he'd taken here to mean that this part of the building was the most heavily defended, he was leading what was left of his men to the other side. It required five minutes to do so, while those he left behind kept up a steady drumbeat of fire into the Russian perimeter. Out of mortar rounds, out of RPG projectiles, the only thing left to him besides rifles were a few grenades and six satchel charges. All around him fires blazed into the night, separate orange-red flames reaching upward to melt the falling snow. He heard the cries of his own wounded as he formed up the fifty men he had left. They'd attack as one mass, behind the leader who'd brought them here. The Archer flipped the safety off his AK-47, and remembered the first three men he'd killed with it.

Bondarenko's head snapped around when he heard the screams from the other side of the building. He turned back and saw that nothing was happening. It was time to do something, and he hoped that it was the right thing:
"Everyone back to the building. Move!" Two of his remaining ten were wounded, and each had to be helped. It took over a minute as the night shattered yet again with volleys of rifle fire. Bondarenko took five and ran down the building's main first-floor corridor and out the other side.
He couldn't tell if there'd been a breakthrough, or if the men here were also falling back—again he had to hold fire because both sides were identically uniformed. Then one of those running toward the building fired, and the Colonel went to one knee and dropped him with a five-round burst. More appeared, and he nearly fired until he heard their shouts.
"*Nashi, nashi!*" He counted eight. The last of them was the sergeant, wounded in both legs.
"Too many, we couldn't—"
"Get inside," Bondarenko told him. "Can you still fight?"
"Fuck, yes!" Both men looked around. They couldn't fight from the individual rooms. They'd have to make their stand in the corridors and stairwells.
"Help is on the way. A regiment is coming down from Nurek if we can hold on!" Bondarenko told his men. He didn't tell them how long it was supposed to take. It was the first good news in over half an hour. Two civilians came downstairs. Both carried rifles.
"You need help?" Morozov asked. He'd avoided military service, but he had just learned that a rifle wasn't all that hard to use.
"How are things up there?" Bondarenko asked.
"My section chief is dead. I took this from him. Many people are hurt, and the rest are as terrified as I am."
"Stay with the sergeant," the Colonel told him. "Keep your head, Comrade Engineer, and we may yet live through this. Help's on the way."
"I hope the bastards hurry." Morozov helped the sergeant—who was even younger than the engineer—go to the far end of the corridor.
Bondarenko put half of his men at the stairwell and the other half by the elevators. It was quiet again. They could hear the jabbering of voices outside, but the shooting had died down for the moment.

"Down the ladder. Carefully," Clark said. "There's a cross-member at the bottom. You can stand on that."
Maria looked with disgust at the slimy wood, doing as she was told like a person in a dream. Her daughter followed. Clark went last, stepped around them, and got into the boat. He untied the ropes and moved the boat by hand underneath where the women were standing. It was a three-foot drop.
"One at a time. You first, Katryn. Step down slowly and I'll catch you." She did so, her knees wobbling with doubt and fear. Clark grabbed her ankle and pulled it toward him. She fell into the boat as elegantly as a sack of beans. Maria came next. He gave the same instructions, and she

followed them, but Katryn tried to help, and in doing so moved the boat. Maria lost her grip and fell into the water with a scream.

"What is that?" someone called from the landside end of the pier.

Clark ignored it, grabbing the woman's splashing hands and pulling her aboard. She was gasping from the cold, but there wasn't much Clark could do about that. He heard the sound of running feet along the pier as he turned on the boat's electric motor and headed straight out.

"*Stoi!*" a voice called. It was a cop, Clark realized, it would have to be a damned cop. He turned to see the glimmer of a flashlight. It couldn't reach the boat, but it was fixed on the wake he'd left behind. Clark lifted his radio.

"Uncle Joe, this is Willy. On the way. The sun is out!"

"They may have been spotted," the communications officer told Mancuso.

"Great." The Captain went forward. "Goodman, come right to zero-eight-five. Move her in toward the coast at ten knots."

"Conn, sonar, contact bearing two-nine-six. Diesel engine," Jones's voice announced. "Twin screws."

"Will be KGB patrol frigate—Grisha, probably," Ramius said. "Routine patrol."

Mancuso didn't say anything, but he pointed to the fire-control tracking party. They'd work up a position on the seaward target while *Dallas* moved into the coast at periscope depth, keeping her radio antenna up.

"Nine-seven-one, this is Velikiye Luki Center. Turn right to new course one-zero-four," the Russian voice told Colonel von Eich. The pilot squeezed the microphone trigger on his wheel.

"Say again, Luki. Over."

"Nine-seven-one, you are ordered to turn right to new heading one-zero-four and return to Moscow. Over."

"Ah, thank you, Luki, negative, we are proceeding on a heading of two-eight-six as per our flight plan. Over."

"Nine-seven-one, you are ordered to return to Moscow!" the controller insisted.

"Roger. Thank you. Out." Von Eich looked down to see that his autopilot was on the proper heading, then resumed his outside scanning for other aircraft.

"But you are not turning back," the Russian said over the intercom.

"No." Von Eich turned to look at the man. "We didn't leave anything behind that I know of." *Well* . . .

"But they ordered you—"

"Son, I am in command of this aircraft, and my orders are to fly to Shannon," the pilot explained.

"But—" The Russian unsnapped his straps and started to stand up.

"Sit down!" the pilot ordered. "Nobody leaves my flight deck without my permission, mister! You are a guest on my airplane, and you'll goddamned well do what I say!" *Damn, it was supposed to be easier than this!* He gestured to the engineer, who toggled off another switch. That shut off all the cabin lights in the aircraft. The VC-137 was now totally blacked out. Von Eich keyed his radio again. "Luki, this is niner-seven-one. We have some electrical problems aboard. I don't want to make any radical course changes until we have them figured out. Do you copy? Over."

"What is your problem?" the controller asked. The pilot wondered what he'd been told as he gave out the next set of lies.

"Luki, we don't know just yet. We're losing electrical power. All our lights have gone bad. The bird is blacked out at the moment, say again we are running without lights. I'm a little worried, and I don't need any distractions right now." That bought him two minutes of silence, and twenty miles of westward progress.

"Nine-seven-one, I have notified Moscow of your problems. They advise that you return at once. They will clear you for an emergency approach," the controller offered.

"Roger, thank you, Luki, but I don't want to risk a course change right now, if you know what I mean. We're working to fix the problem. Please stand by. Will advise. Out." Colonel von Eich checked the clock in his instrument panel. Thirty more minutes to the coast.

"What?" Major Zarudin asked. "Who got on the airplane?"

"Chairman Gerasimov and an arrested enemy spy," Vatutin said.

"On an American airplane? You tell me that the *Chairman* is defecting on an American airplane!" The officer commanding the airport security detail had taken charge of the situation, as his orders allowed him to do. He found that he had two colonels, a lieutenant colonel, a driver, and an American in the office he used here—along with the craziest damned story he'd ever heard. "I must call for instructions."

"I am senior to you!" Golovko said.

"You are not senior to my commander!" Zarudin pointed out as he reached for the phone. He'd been able to have the air traffic controllers try to recall the American plane, but it had not come as a surprise to his visitors that it had decided not to turn.

Ryan sat perfectly still, barely breathing, not even moving his head. He told himself that as long as they didn't get too excited he would be completely safe. Golovko was too smart to do anything crazy. He knew who Jack was, and he knew what would happen if an accredited member of a diplomatic mission to his country was so much as scratched. Ryan had been scratched, of course. His ankle hurt like hell, and his knee was oozing blood, but he'd done that to himself. Golovko glared at him from five feet away. Ryan didn't return the look. He swallowed his fear and tried to look exactly as harmless as he was right now.

"Where's his family?" Vatutin asked.

"They flew to Talinn yesterday," Vasiliy answered lamely. "She wanted to see some friends . . ."

Time was running out for everyone. Bondarenko's men were down to less than half a magazine each. Two more were dead from grenades that had been tossed in. The Colonel had watched a private leap on one, ripped to shreds to save his comrades. The boy's blood covered the tile floor like paint. Six Afghans were piled up at the door. It had been like this at Stalingrad, the Colonel told himself. No one excelled the Russian soldier at house-to-house fighting. How far away was that motorized regiment? An hour was such a short period of time. Half a movie, a television show, a pleasant night's stroll . . . such a short time, unless people were shooting at you. Then every second stretched before your eyes, and the hands of your watch seemed frozen, and the only thing that went fast was your heart. It was only his second experience with close combat. He'd been decorated after the first, and he wondered if he'd be buried after the second. But he couldn't let that happen. On the floors above him were several hundred people, engineers and scientists, their wives and their children, all of whose lives rested on his ability to hold the Afghan invaders off for less than an hour.

Go away, he wished at them. *Do you think that we* wanted *to come and be shot at in that miserable rockpile you call a country? If you want to kill those who are responsible, why don't you go to Moscow?* But that wasn't the way things were in war, was it? The politicians never seemed to come close enough to see what they had wrought. They never really knew what they did, and now the bastards had nuclear-tipped missiles. They had the power to kill millions, but they didn't even have the courage to see the horror on a simple, old-fashioned battlefield.

The nonsense you think at times like this! he raged at himself.

He'd failed. His men had trusted him with command, and he'd failed them, the Archer told himself. He looked around at the bodies in the snow and each seemed to accuse him. He could kill individuals, could pluck aircraft from the sky, but he'd never learned how to lead a large body of men. Was this Allah's curse on him for torturing the Russian flyers? No! There were still enemies to kill. He gestured to his men to enter the building through several broken, ground-floor windows.

The Major was leading from the front, as the *mudjaheddin* expected. He had gotten ten of them right up to the side of the bunker, then led them along the wall toward the main door, covered by fire from the rest of his company. It was going well, he thought. He'd lost five men, but that was not very many for a mission like this . . . *Thank you for all the training you gave me, my Russian friends . . .*

The main door was steel. He personally set a pair of satchel charges at both lower corners and set the fuses before crawling back around the corner. Russian rifles blazed over his head, but those inside the building didn't know where he was. That would change. He set the charges, pulled the fuse cords, and dashed back around the corner.

Pokryshkin cringed as he heard it happen. He turned to see the heavy steel door flying across the room and smashing into a control console. The KGB Lieutenant was killed instantly by the blast, and as Pokryshkin's men raced to cover the breach in the wall, three more explosive packs flew in. There was nowhere to run. The Border Guards kept firing, killing one of the attackers at the door, but then the charges went off.

It was a strangely hollow sound, the Major thought. The force of the explosions was contained by the stout concrete walls. He led his men in a second later. Electrical circuits were sparking, and fires would soon begin in earnest, but everyone he could see inside was down. His men moved swiftly from one to another, seizing weapons and killing those merely unconscious. The Major saw a Russian officer with general's stars. The man was bleeding from his nose and ears, trying to bring up his pistol when the Major cut him down. In another minute they were all dead. The building was rapidly filling with thick, acrid smoke. He ordered his men out.

"We're finished here," he said into his radio. There was no answer. "Are you there?"

The Archer was against a wall next to a half-open door. His radio was switched off. Just outside his room was a soldier, facing down the corridor. It was time. The freedom fighter threw the door aside with the barrel of his rifle and shot the Russian before the man had had a chance to turn. He screamed a command, and five other men emerged from their rooms, but two were killed before they got a chance to shoot. He looked up and down the corridor and saw nothing but gun flashes and half-hidden silhouettes.

Fifty meters away, Bondarenko reacted to the new threat. He shouted an order for his men to stay under cover, and then with murderous precision, the Colonel identified and engaged the targets moving in the open, identified by the emergency lighting in the corridor. The corridor was exactly like a shooting gallery, and he got two men with as many bursts. Another ran toward him, screaming something unintelligible and firing his weapon in a single extended burst. Bondarenko's shots missed, to his amazement, but someone else got him. There was more shooting, and the sound of it reverberating off the concrete walls completely deafened everyone. Then, he saw, there was only one man left. The Colonel watched two more of his men fall, and the last Afghan chipped concrete only centimeters from his face. Bondarenko's eyes stung from it, and the right side of his face recoiled at the sudden pain. The Colonel pulled back from the line of fire, flipped his weapon to full automatic, took a deep breath, and jumped into the corridor. The man was less than ten meters away.

The moment stretched into eternity as both men brought their weapons to bear. He saw the man's eyes. It was a young face there, immediately below the emergency light, but the eyes . . . the rage there, the hatred, nearly stopped the Colonel's heart. But Bondarenko was a soldier before all things. The Afghan's first shot missed. His did not.

The Archer felt shock, but not pain in his chest as he fell. His brain sent a message to his hands to bring the weapon to the left, but they ignored the command and dropped it. He fell in stages, first to his knees, then on his back, and at last he was staring up at a ceiling. It was finally over. Then the man stood by his side. It was not a cruel face, the Archer thought. It was the enemy, and it was an infidel, but he was a man, too, wasn't he? There was curiosity there. He wants to know who I am, the Archer told him with his last breath.

"*Allahu akhbar!*" God is great.

Yes, I suppose He is, Bondarenko told the corpse. He knew the phrase well enough. *Is that why you came?* He saw that the man had a radio. It started to make noise, and the Colonel bent down to grab it.

"Are you there?" the radio asked a moment later. The question was in Pashtu, but the answer was delivered in Russian.

"It is all finished here," Bondarenko said.

The Major looked at his radio for a moment, then blew his whistle to assemble what was left of his men. The Archer's company knew the way to the assembly point, but all that mattered now was getting home. He counted his men. He'd lost eleven and had six wounded. With luck he'd get to the border before the snow stopped. Five minutes later his men were heading off the mountain.

*   *   *

"Secure the area!" Bondarenko told his remaining six men. "Collect weapons and get them handed out." It was probably over, he thought, but "over" would not truly come until that motor-rifle regiment got here.

"Morozov!" he called next. The engineer appeared a moment later.

"Yes, Colonel?"

"Is there a physician upstairs?"

"Yes, several—I'll get one."

The Colonel found that he was sweating. The building still held some warmth. He dropped the field radio off his back and was stunned to see that two bullets had hit it—and even more surprised to see blood on one of the straps. He'd been hit and hadn't known it. The sergeant came over and looked at it.

"Just a scratch, Comrade, like those on my legs."

"Help me off with this coat, will you?" Bondarenko shrugged out of the knee-length greatcoat, exposing his uniform blouse. With his right hand he reached inside, while his left removed the ribbon that designated the Red Banner. This he pinned to the young man's collar. "You deserve better, Sergeant, but this is all I can do for the present."

"Up 'scope!" Mancuso used the search periscope now, with its light-amplifying equipment. "Still nothing . . ." He turned to look west. "Uh-oh, I got a masthead light at two-seven-zero—"

"That's our sonar contact," Lieutenant Goodman noted unnecessarily.

"Sonar, conn, do you have an ident on the contact?" Mancuso asked.

"Negative," Jones replied. "We're getting reverbs from the ice, sir. Acoustic conditions are pretty bad. It's twin screw and diesel, but no ident."

Mancuso turned on the 'scope television camera. Ramius needed only one look at the picture. "Grisha."

Mancuso looked at the tracking party. "Solution?"

"Yes, but it's a little shaky," the weapons officer replied. "The ice isn't going to help," he added. What he meant was that the Mark 48 torpedo in surface-attack mode could be confused by floating ice. He paused for a moment. "Sir, if that's a Grisha, how come no radar?"

"New contact! Conn, sonar, new contact bearing zero-eight-six—sounds like our friend, sir," Jones called. "Something else near that bearing, high-speed screw . . . definitely something new there, sir, call it zero-eight-three."

"Up two feet," Mancuso told the quartermaster. The periscope came up. "I see him, just on the horizon . . . call it three miles. There's a light behind them!" He slapped the handles up and the 'scope went down at once. "Let's get there fast. All ahead two-thirds."

"All ahead two-thirds, aye." The helmsman dialed up the engine order.

The navigator plotted the position of the inbound boat and ticked off the yards.

Clark was looking back toward the shore. There was a light sweeping left and right across the water. Who was it? He didn't know if the local cops had boats, but there had to be a detachment of KGB Border Guards: they had their own little navy, *and* their own little air force. But how alert were they on a Friday night? Probably better than they were when that German kid decided to fly into Moscow . . . right through this sector, Clark remembered. *This area's probably pretty alert . . . where are you,* Dallas? He lifted his radio.

"Uncle Joe, this is Willy. The sun is rising, and we're far from home."

"He says he's close, sir," communications reported.

" 'Gator?" Mancuso asked.

The navigator looked up from his table. "I gave him fifteen knots. We should be within five hundred yards now."

"All ahead one-third," the Captain ordered. "Up 'scope!" The oiled steel tube hissed up again—all the way up.

"Captain, I got a radar emitter astern, bearing two-six-eight. It's a Don-2," the ESM technician said.

"Conn, sonar, both the hostile contacts have increased speed. Blade count looks like twenty knots and coming up on the Grisha, sir," Jones said. "Confirm target ident is Grisha-class. Easterly contact still unknown, one screw, probably a gas engine, doing turns for twenty or so."

"Range about six thousand yards," the fire-control party said next.

"This is the fun part," Mancuso observed. "I have them. Bearing— *mark!*"

"Zero-nine-one."

"Range." Mancuso squeezed the trigger for the 'scope's laser-range-finder. *"Mark!"*

"Six hundred yards."

"Nice call, 'Gator. Solution on the Grisha?" he asked fire control.

"Set for tubes two and four. Outer doors are still closed, sir."

"Keep 'em that way." Mancuso went to the bridge trunk's lower hatch. "XO, you have the conn. I'm going to do the recovery myself. Let's get it done."

"All stop," the executive officer said. Mancuso opened the hatch and went up the ladder to the bridge. The lower hatch was closed behind him. He heard the water rushing around him in the sail, then the splashes of surface waves. The intercom told him he could open the bridge hatch. Mancuso spun the locking wheel and heaved against the heavy steel cover. He was rewarded with a faceful of cold, oily saltwater, but ignored it and got to the bridge.

He looked aft first. There was the Grisha, its masthead light low on the horizon. Next he looked forward and pulled the flashlight from his hip pocket. He aimed directly at the raft and tapped out the Morse letter D.

"A light, a light!" Maria said. Clark turned back forward, saw it, and steered for it. Then he saw something else.

The patrol boat behind Clark was a good two miles off, its searchlight look-ing in the wrong place. The Captain turned west to see the other contact. Mancuso knew in a distant sort of way that Grishas carried searchlights, but had allowed himself to disregard the fact. After all, why should search-lights concern a submarine? *When she's on the surface,* the Captain told himself. The ship was still too far away to see him, light or not, but that would change in a hurry. He watched it sweep the surface aft of his sub-marine, and realized too late that they probably had *Dallas* on radar now.

"Over here, Clark, move your ass!" he screamed across the water, swing-ing the light left and right. The next thirty seconds seemed to last into the following month. Then it was there.

"Help the ladies," the man said. He held the raft against the submarine's sail with his motor. *Dallas* was still moving, had to be to maintain this precarious depth, not quite surfaced, not quite dived. The first one felt and moved like a young girl, the skipper thought as he brought her aboard. The second one was wet and shivering. Clark waited a moment, setting a small box atop the motor. Mancuso wondered how it stayed balanced there until he realized that it was either magnetic or glued somehow.

"Down the ladder," Mancuso told the ladies.

Clark scrambled aboard and said something—probably the same thing—in Russian. To Mancuso he spoke in English. "Five minutes before it blows."

The women were already halfway down. Clark went behind them, and finally Mancuso, with a last look at the raft. The last thing he saw was the harbor patrol boat, now heading directly toward him. He dropped down and pulled the hatch behind himself. Then he punched the intercom button. "Take her down and move the boat!"

The bottom hatch opened underneath them all, and he heard the executive officer. "Make your depth ninety feet, all ahead two-thirds, left full rudder!"

A petty officer met the ladies at the bottom of the bridge tube. The astonishment on his face would have been funny at any other time. Clark took them by the arm and led them forward to his stateroom. Mancuso went aft.

"I have the conn," he announced.

"Captain has the conn," the XO agreed. "ESM says they got some VHF radio traffic, close in, probably the Grisha talking to the other one."

"Helm, come to new course three-five-zero. Let's get her under the ice. They probably know we're here—well, they know something's here. 'Gator, how's the chart look?"

"We'll have to turn soon," the navigator warned. "Shoal water in eight thousand yards. Recommend come to new course two-nine-one." Mancuso ordered the change at once.

"Depth now eight-five feet, leveling out," the diving officer said. "Speed eighteen knots." A small bark of sound announced the destruction of the raft and its motor.

"Okay, people, now all we have to do is leave," Mancuso told his Attack Center crew. A high-pitched snap of sound told them that this would not be easy.

"Conn, sonar, we're being pinged. That's a Grisha death-ray," Jones said, using the slang term for the Russian set. "Might have us."

"Under the ice now," the navigator said.

"Range to target?"

"Just under four thousand yards," the weapons officer replied. "Set for tubes two and four."

The problem was, they couldn't shoot. *Dallas* was inside Russian territorial waters, and even if the Grisha shot at them, shooting back wasn't self-defense, but an act of war. Mancuso looked at the chart. He had thirty feet of water under his keel, and a bare twenty over his sail—minus the thickness of the ice . . .

"Marko?" the Captain asked.

"They will request instructions first," Ramius judged. "The more time they have, the better chance they will shoot."

"Okay. All ahead full," Mancuso ordered. At thirty knots he'd be in international waters in ten minutes.

"Grisha is passing abeam on the portside," Jones said. Mancuso went forward to the sonar room.

"What's happening?" the Captain asked.

"The high-frequency stuff works pretty good in the ice. He's searchlighting back and forth. He knows something's here, but not exactly where yet."

Mancuso lifted a phone. "Five-inch room, launch two noisemakers."

A pair of bubble-making decoys was ejected from the portside of the submarine.

"Good, Mancuso," Ramius observed. "His sonar will fix on those. He cannot maneuver well with the ice."

"We'll know for sure in the next minute." Just as he said it, the submarine was rocked by explosions aft. A very feminine scream echoed through the forward portion of the submarine.

"All ahead flank!" the Captain called aft.

"The decoys," Ramius said. "Surprising that he fired so quickly . . ."

"Losing sonar performance, skipper," Jones said as the screen went blank with flow noise. Mancuso and Ramius went aft. The navigator had their course track marked on the chart.

"Uh-oh, we have to transit this place right here where the ice stops. How much you want to bet he knows it?" Mancuso looked up. They were still being pinged, and he still couldn't shoot back. And that Grisha might get lucky.

"Radio—Mancuso, let me speak on radio!" Ramius said.

"We don't do things that way—" Mancuso said. American doctrine was to evade, never to let them be sure there was a submarine there at all.

"I know that. But we are not American submarine, Captain Mancuso, we are Soviet submarine," Ramius suggested. Bart Mancuso nodded. He'd never played this card before.

"Take her to antenna depth!"

A radio technician dialed in the Soviet guard frequency, and the slender VHF antenna was raised as soon as the submarine cleared the ice. The periscope went up, too.

"There he is. Angle on the bow, zero. Down 'scope!"

"Radar contact bearing two-eight-one," the speaker proclaimed.

The Captain of the Grisha was coming off a week's patrolling on the Baltic Sea, six hours late, and had been looking forward to four days off. Then first came a radio transmission from the Talinn harbor police about a strange craft seen leaving the docks, followed by something from the KGB, then a small explosion near the harbor police boat, next several sonar contacts. The twenty-nine-year-old senior lieutenant with all of three months in command had made his estimate of the situation and fired at what his sonar operator called a positive submarine contact. Now he was wondering if he'd made a mistake, and how ghastly it might be. All he knew was that he had not the smallest idea what was happening, but if he were chasing a submarine, it would be heading west.

And now he had a radar contact forward. The speaker for the guard radio frequency started chattering.

"Cease fire, you idiot!" a metallic voice screamed at him three times.

"Identify!" the Grisha's commander replied.

"This is *Novosibiirsk Komsomolets*! What the hell do you think you're doing firing live ammunition in a practice exercise! *You* identify!"

The young officer stared at his microphone and swore. *Novosibiirsk Komsomolets* was a special-ops boat based at Kronshtadt, always playing *Spetznaz* games . . .

"This is *Krepkiy*."

"Thank you. We will discuss this episode the day after tomorrow. Out!"

The Captain looked around at the bridge crew. "What exercise . . . ?"

"Too bad," Marko said as he replaced the microphone. "He reacted well. Now he will take several minutes to call his base, and . . ."

"And that's all we need. And they still don't know what happened." Mancuso turned. " 'Gator, shortest way out?"

"Recommend two-seven-five, distance is eleven thousand yards."

At thirty-four knots, the remaining distance was covered quickly. Ten minutes later the submarine was back in international waters. The anticlimax was remarkable for all those in the control room. Mancuso changed course for deeper water and ordered speed reduced to one-third, then went back to sonar.

"That should be that," he announced.

"Sir, what was this all about?" Jones asked.

"Well, I don't know that I can tell you."

"What's her name?" From his seat Jones could see into the passageway.

"I don't even know that myself. But I'll find out." Mancuso went across the passageway and knocked on the door of Clark's stateroom.

"Who is it?"

"Guess," Mancuso said. Clark opened the door. The Captain saw a young woman in presentable clothes, but wet feet. Then an older woman appeared from the head. She was dressed in the khaki shirt and pants of *Dallas'* chief engineer, though she carried her own things, which were wet. These she handed to Mancuso with a phrase of Russian.

"She wants you to have them cleaned, skipper," Clark translated, and started laughing. "These are our new guests. Mrs. Gerasimov, and her daughter, Katryn."

"What's so special about them?" Mancuso asked.

"My father is head of KGB!" Katryn said.

The Captain managed not to drop the clothes.

"We got company," the copilot said. They were coming in from the right side, the strobe lights of what had to be a pair of fighter planes. "Closing fast."

"Twenty minutes to the coast," the navigator reported. The pilot had long since spotted it.

"Shit!" the pilot snapped. The fighters missed his aircraft by less than two hundred yards of vertical separation, little more in horizontal. A moment later, the VC-137 bounced through their wake turbulence.

"Engure Control, this is U.S. Air Force flight niner-seven-one. We just had a near miss. What the hell is going on down there?"

"Let me speak to the Soviet officer!" the voice answered. It didn't sound like a controller.

"I speak for this aircraft," Colonel von Eich replied. "We are cruising on a heading of two-eight-six, flight level eleven thousand six hundred meters. We are on a correctly filed flight plan, in a designated air corridor, and we have electrical problems. We don't need to have some hardrock fighter jocks playing tag with us—this is an American aircraft with a diplomatic mission aboard. You want to start World War Three or something? Over!"

"Nine-seven-one, you are ordered to turn back!"

"Negative! We have electrical problems and cannot repeat cannot comply. This airplane is flying without lights, and those crazy MiG drivers damned near rammed us! Are you trying to kill us, over!"

"You have kidnapped a Soviet citizen and you must return to Moscow!"

"Repeat that last," von Eich requested.

But the Captain couldn't. A fighter ground-intercept officer, he'd been rushed to Engure, the last air-traffic-control point within Soviet borders, quickly briefed by a local KGB officer, and told to force the American aircraft to turn back. He should not have said what he had just said in the clear.

"You must stop the aircraft!" the KGB General shouted.

"Simple, then. I order my MiGs to shoot it down!" the Captain replied in kind. "Do you give me the order, Comrade General?"

"I do not have the authority. You have to make it stop."

"It cannot be done. We can shoot it down, but we cannot make it *stop*."

"Do you wish to be shot?" the General asked.

"Where the hell is it now?" the Foxbat pilot asked his wingman. They'd only seen it once, and that for a single ghastly instant. They could track the intruder—except that it was leaving, and wasn't really an intruder, they both knew—on radar, and kill it with radar-guided missiles, but to close on the target in darkness . . . Even in the relatively clear night, the target was running without lights, and trying to find it meant running the risk of what American fighter pilots jokingly called a Fox-Four: midair collision, a quick and spectacular death for all involved.

"Hammer Lead, this is Toolbox. You are ordered to close on the target and force it to turn," the controller said. "Target is now at your twelve o'clock and level, range three thousand meters."

"I know that," the pilot said to himself. He had the airliner on radar, but he did not have it visually, and his radar could not track precisely enough to warn him of an imminent collision. He also had to worry about the other MiG on his wing.

"Stay back," he ordered his wingman. "I'll handle this alone." He advanced his throttles slightly and moved the stick a hair to the right. The MiG-25 was heavy and sluggish, not a very maneuverable fighter. He had a pair of air-to-air missiles hanging from each wing, and all he had to do to stop this aircraft was . . . But instead of ordering him to do something he was trained to do, some jackass of a KGB officer was—

There. He didn't so much see the aircraft, but saw something ahead disappear. *Ah!* He pulled back on the stick to gain a few hundred meters of altitude and . . . yes! He could pick the Boeing out against the sea. Slowly and carefully, he moved forward until he was abeam of the target and two hundred meters higher.

"I got lights on the right side," the copilot said. "Fighter, but I don't know what kind."

"If you were him, what would you do?" von Eich asked.

"Defect!" *Or shoot us down . . .*

Behind them in the jump seat, the Russian pilot, whose only job was to talk Russian in case of an emergency, was strapped down in his seat and had not the first idea what to do. He'd been cut out of the radio conversations and had only intercom now. Moscow wanted them to turn the aircraft back. He didn't know why, but—but what? he asked himself.

"Here he comes, sliding over toward us."

As carefully as he could, the MiG pilot maneuvered his fighter to the left. He wanted to get over the Boeing's cockpit, from which position he could gently reduce altitude and force it downward. To do this required as much skill as he could muster, and the pilot could only pray that the American was equally adept. He positioned himself so that he could see . . . but—

The MiG-25 was designed as an interceptor, and the cockpit gave the pilot very restricted visibility. He could no longer see the airplane with which he was flying formation. He looked ahead. The shore was only a few kilometers away. Even if he were able to make the American reduce altitude, he'd be over the Baltic before it would matter to anyone. The pilot pulled back on his stick and climbed off to the right. Once clear, he reversed course.

"Toolbox, this is Hammer Lead," he reported. "The American will not change course. I tried, but I will not collide with his airplane without orders."

The controller had watched the two radar blips merge on his scope, and was now amazed that his heart hadn't stopped. What the hell was going on? This was an American plane. They couldn't force it to stop, and if there were an accident, who would be blamed for it? He made his decision.

"Return to base. Out."

"You will pay for this!" the KGB General promised the ground-intercept officer. He was wrong.

"Thank God," von Eich said as they passed over the coastline. He called up the chief cabin steward next. "How are the folks in back?"

"Mainly asleep. They must have had a big party tonight. When are we getting the electricity back?"

"Flight engineer," the pilot said, "they want to know about the electrical problems."

"Looks like it was a bad breaker, sir. I think . . . Yeah, I fixed it."

The pilot looked out his window. The wingtip lights were back on, as were the cabin lights, except in back. Passing Ventspils, they turned left to a new heading two-five-nine. He let out a long breath. Two and a half hours to Shannon. "Some coffee would be nice," he thought aloud.

Golovko hung up the phone and spat out a few words that Jack didn't understand exactly, though their message seemed rather clear.

"Sergey, could I clean my knee up?"

"What exactly have you done, Ryan?" the KGB officer asked.

"I fell out of the airplane and the bastards left without me. I want to be taken to my embassy, but first, my knee hurts."

Golovko and Vatutin stared at each other and both wondered several things. What had actually happened? What would happen to them? What to do with Ryan?

"Who do we even call?" Golovko asked.

27. Under Wraps

Vatutin decided to call his directorate chief, who called the KGB's First Deputy Chairman, who called someone else, and then called back to the airport office where they were all waiting. Vatutin noted the instructions, took everyone to Gerasimov's car, and gave directions that Jack didn't understand. The car headed straight through Moscow's empty early-morning streets—it was just after midnight, and those who had been out to the movies or the opera or the ballet were now at home. Jack was nestled between the two KGB colonels, and hoped that they'd be taking him to the embassy, but they kept going, crossing the city at a high rate of speed, then up into the Lenin Hills and beyond to the forests that surround the city. Now he was frightened. Diplomatic immunity seemed a surer thing at the airport than it did in the woods.

The car slowed after an hour, turning off the paved main road onto a gravel path that meandered through trees. There were uniforms about, he saw through the windows. Men with rifles. That sight made him forget the pain from his ankle and knee. Exactly where was he? Why was he being brought here? Why the people with guns . . . ? The phrase that came to him was a simple, ominous one: Take him for a ride . . .

No! They can't be doing that, reason told him. *I have a diplomatic passport. I was seen alive by too many people. Probably the Ambassador is already—* But he wouldn't be. He wasn't cleared for what had happened, and unless they got word off the plane . . . Regardless, they couldn't possibly . . . But in the Soviet Union, the saying went, things happened that simply *didn't* happen. The car's door flew open. Golovko got out and pulled Ryan with him. The only thing Jack was sure of now was that there was no point in resistance.

It was a house, a quite ordinary frame house in the woods. The windows glowed yellow from lights behind the curtains. Ryan saw a dozen or so people standing around, all with uniforms, all with rifles, all staring at him with the same degree of interest given a paper target. One, an officer, came over and frisked Ryan with considerable thoroughness, eliciting a grunt of pain when he got to the bloody knee and torn trousers. He surprised Ryan with what might have been a perfunctory apology. The officer nodded to Golovko and Vatutin, who handed over their automatics and led Ryan into the house.

Inside the door, a man took their coats. Two more men in civilian clothes were obvious police or KGB types. They wore unzipped jackets, and they had to be packing pistols from the way they stood, Jack knew. He nodded politely to them, and got no response other than another frisking from one while the other watched from a safe shooting distance. Ryan was astonished when the two KGB officers were frisked as well. When this was complete, the other one motioned them through a doorway.

General Secretary of the Communist Party of the Soviet Union Andrey Il'ych Narmonov was sitting in an overstuffed chair in front of a newly built fire. He rose when the four men entered the room, and gestured for them to sit on the sofa opposite his place. The bodyguard took position standing behind the head of the Soviet government. Narmonov spoke in Russian. Golovko translated.

"You are?"

"John Ryan, sir," Jack said. The General Secretary pointed him to a chair opposite his own, and noted that Ryan favored his leg.

"Anatoliy," he said to the bodyguard, who took Ryan's arm and walked him to a first-floor bathroom. The man dampened a washcloth with warm water and handed it over. Back in the sitting room, he could hear people talking, but Ryan's knowledge of Russian was too thin to catch any of it. It was good to wash off the leg, but it looked as though the pants were finished, and the nearest change of clothes—he checked his watch—was probably near Denmark by now. Anatoliy watched him the whole time. The bodyguard pulled a gauze bandage from the medicine cabinet and helped Jack tape it in place, then walked him back as gracefully as Ryan's aches and pains allowed.

Golovko was still there, though Vatutin had left, and the empty chair was still waiting. Anatoliy took his former place behind Narmonov.

"The fire feels good," Jack said. "Thank you for letting me wash the knee off."

"Golovko tells me that we did not do that to you. Is this correct?"

It seemed an odd question to Jack, since Golovko was handling the translating. *So Andrey Ily'ch speaks a little English, does he?*

"No, sir, I did it to myself. I have not been mistreated in any way." *Just had the piss scared out of me,* Ryan thought to himself. *But that's my own damned fault.* Narmonov looked at him with silent interest for perhaps a minute before speaking again.

"I did not need your help."

"I do not know what you mean, sir," Ryan lied.

"Did you really think that Gerasimov could remove me?"

"Sir, I don't know what you are talking about. My mission was to save the life of one of our agents. To do this meant compromising Chairman Gerasimov. It was just a matter of fishing with the proper bait."

"And fishing for the proper fish," Narmonov commented. The amusement in his voice did not show on his face. "And your agent was Colonel Filitov?"

"Yes, sir. You know that."

"I just learned it."

Then you know that Yazov was compromised also. Just how close might they have come, Comrade General Secretary? Ryan did not say. Probably Narmonov didn't know either.

"Do you know why he turned traitor?"

"No, I don't. I was briefed only on what I needed to know."

"And therefore you do not know about the attack on our Project Bright Star?"

"What?" Jack was very surprised, and showed it.

"Don't insult me, Ryan. You do know the name."

"It's southeast of Dushanbe. I know it. Attacked?" he asked.

"As I thought. You know that was an act of war," Narmonov observed.

"Sir, KGB officers kidnapped an American SDI scientist several days ago. That was ordered by Gerasimov himself. His name is Alan Gregory. He's a major in the U.S. Army, and he was rescued."

"I don't believe it," Golovko said before translating. Narmonov was annoyed by the interruption, but shocked by the substance of Ryan's statement.

"One of your officers was captured. He's alive. It is true, sir," Jack assured him.

Narmonov shook his head and rose to toss another log on the fire. He maneuvered it into place with a poker. "It's madness, you know," he said at the hearth. "We have a perfectly satisfactory situation now."

"Excuse me? I don't understand," Ryan asked.

"The world is stable, is it not? Yet your country wishes to change this, and forces us to pursue the same goal." That the ABM test site at Sary Shagan had been operating for over thirty years was, for the moment, beside the point.

"Mr. Secretary, if you think the ability to turn every city, every home in my country into a fire like the one you have right there—"

"My country, too, Ryan," Narmonov said.

"Yes, sir, your country, too, and a bunch of others. You can kill most every civilian in my country, and we can murder almost every person in your country, in sixty minutes or less from the time you pick up the phone— or my President does. And what do we call that? We call it *'stability.'* "

"It is stability, Ryan," Narmonov said.

"No, sir, the technical name we use is MAD: Mutual Assured Destruction, which isn't even good grammar, but it's accurate enough. The situation we have now is mad, all right, and the fact that supposedly intelligent people have thought it up doesn't make it any more sensible."

"It works, doesn't it?"

"Sir, why is it stabilizing to have several hundred million people less than an hour away from death? Why do we view weapons that might protect those people to be dangerous? Isn't that backwards?"

"But if we never use them . . . Do you think that I could live with such a crime on my conscience?"

"No, I don't think that any man could, but someone might screw up. He'd probably blow his brains out a week after the fact, but that might be a little late for the rest of us. The damned things are just too easy to use. You push a button, and they go, and they'll work, probably, because there's nothing to stop them. Unless something stands in their way, there's no reason to think that they won't work. And as long as somebody thinks they might work, it's too easy to use them."

"Be realistic, Ryan. Do you think that we'll ever rid ourselves of atomic arms?" Narmonov asked.

"No, we'll never get rid of all the weapons. I know that. We'll both always have the ability to hurt each other badly, but we can make that process more complicated than it is now. We can give everybody one more reason not to push the button. That's not destabilizing, sir. That's just good sense. That's just something more to protect your conscience."

"You sound like your President." This was delivered with a smile.

"He's right." Ryan returned it.

"It is bad enough that I must argue with one American. I will not do so with another. What will you do with Gerasimov?" the General Secretary asked.

"It will be handled very quietly, for the obvious reason," Jack said, hoping that he was right.

"It would be very damaging to my government if his defection became public. I suggest that he died in a plane crash . . ."

"I will convey that to my government if I am permitted to do so. We can also keep Filitov's name out of the news. We have nothing to gain by publicity. That would just complicate things for your country and mine. We both want the arms treaty to go forward—all that money to save, for both of us."

"Not so much," Narmonov said. "A few percentage points of the defense budgets on both sides."

"There is a saying in our government, sir. A billion here and a billion there, pretty soon you're talking about some real money." That earned Jack a laugh. "May I ask a question, sir?"

"Go on."

"What will you do with the money on your side? I'm supposed to figure that one out."

"Then perhaps you can offer me suggestions. What makes you think that I know?" Narmonov asked. He rose, and Ryan did the same. "Back to your embassy. Tell your people that it is better for both sides if this never becomes public."

Half an hour later Ryan was dropped off at the front door of the embassy. The first one to see him was a Marine sergeant. The second was Candela.

The VC-137 landed at Shannon ten minutes late, due to headwinds over the North Sea. The crew chief and another sergeant herded the passengers out the front way, and when all had left the aircraft, came back to open the rear door. While cameras flashed in the main terminal, steps were rolled to the Boeing's tail and four men left wearing the uniform parkas of U.S. Air Force sergeants. They entered a car and were driven to a far end of the terminal, where they boarded another plane of the 89th Military Airlift Wing, a VC-20A, the military version of the Gulfstream-III executive jet.

"Hello, Misha." Mary Pat Foley met him at the door and took him forward. She hadn't kissed him before. She made up for it now. "We have food and drink, and another plane ride home. Come, Misha." She took his arm and led him to his seat.

A few feet away, Robert Ritter greeted Gerasimov.

"My family?" the latter asked.

"Safe. We'll have them in Washington in two days. At this moment they are aboard a U.S. Navy ship in international waters."

"I am supposed to thank you?"

"We expect you to cooperate."

"You were very lucky," Gerasimov observed.

"Yes," Ritter agreed. "We were."

The embassy car drove Ryan to Sheremetyevo the following day to catch the regular Pan Am 727 flight to Frankfurt. The ticket they provided him was tourist, but Ryan upgraded it to first class. Three hours later he connected with a 747 for Dulles, also Pan Am. He slept most of the way.

Bondarenko surveyed the carnage. The Afghans had left forty-seven bodies behind, with evidence of plenty more. Only two of the site's laser assemblies had survived. All of the machine shops were wrecked, along with the theater and bachelor quarters. The hospital was largely intact, and full of wounded people. The good news was that he'd saved three-quarters of the scientific and engineering personnel and nearly all of their dependents. Four general officers were there already to tell him what a hero he was, promising medals and promotion, but he'd already gotten the only reward that mattered. As soon as the relief force had arrived, he'd seen that the people were safe. Now, he just looked from the roof of the apartment block.

"There is much work to do," a voice noted. The Colonel, soon to be a General, turned.

"Morozov. We still have two of the lasers. We can rebuild the shops and laboratories. A year, perhaps eighteen months."

"That's about right," the young engineer said. "The new mirrors and their computer control equipment will take at least that long. Comrade Colonel, the people have asked me to—"

"That is my job, Comrade Engineer, and I had my own ass to save, remember? This will never happen again. We'll have a battalion of motorized infantry here from now on, from a guards regiment. I've already seen to that. By summer this installation will be as safe as any place in the Soviet Union."

"Safe? What does that mean, Colonel?"

"That is my new job. And yours," Bondarenko said. "Remember?"

Epilogue: Common Ground

It didn't surprise Ortiz when the Major came in alone. The report of the battle took an hour, and again the CIA officer was given a few rucksacks of equipment. The Archer's band had fought its way out, and of the nearly two hundred who had left the refugee camp, fewer than fifty returned on this first day of spring. The Major went immediately to work making contact with other bands, and the prestige of the mission which his group had carried out enabled him to deal with older and more powerful chieftains as a near equal. Within a week he had made good his losses with eager new warriors, and the arrangement the Archer had made with Ortiz remained in force.

"You're going back already?" the CIA officer asked the new leader.

"Of course. We're winning now," the Major said with a degree of confidence that even he did not understand.

Ortiz watched them leave at nightfall, a single file of small, ferocious warriors, led now by a trained soldier. He hoped it would make a difference.

Gerasimov and Filitov never saw each other again. The debriefings lasted for weeks, and were conducted at separate locations. Filitov was taken to Camp Peary, Virginia, where he met a spectacled U.S. Army major and told what he remembered of the Russian breakthrough in laser power. It seemed curious to the old man that this boy could be so excited about things that he'd memorized but never fully understood.

After that came the routine explanations of the second career that had joined and paralleled his first. A whole generation of field officers visited him for meals and walks, and drinking sessions that worried the doctors but which no one could deny the Cardinal. His living quarters were closely guarded, and even bugged. Those who listened to him were surprised that he occasionally spoke in his sleep.

One CIA officer who was six months from his retirement paused from reading the local paper when it happened again. He smiled at the noise in his headphones and set down the article he was reading about the President's visit to Moscow. *That sad, lonely old man,* he thought as he listened. *Most of his friends dead, and he only sees them in his sleep. Was that why he went to work for us?* The murmuring stopped, and in the quarters next door, the Cardinal's baby-sitter went back to his paper.

"Comrade Captain," Romanov said.

"Yes, Corporal?" It seemed more real than most of his dreams, Misha noted. A moment later he knew why.

They were spending their honeymoon under the protection of security officers, all four days of it—which was as long as Al and Candi were willing to stay away from work. Major Gregory got the phone when it rang.

"Yeah—I mean, yes, sir," Candi heard him say. A sigh. A shake of the head in the darkness. "Not even anyplace to send flowers, is there? Can Candi and I— Oh . . . I understand. Thanks for calling, General." She heard him replace the phone and let out another breath.

"Candi, you awake?"

"Yeah."

"Our first kid, his name's going to be Mike."

Major General Grigoriy Dalmatov's post of Defense Attaché at the Soviet Embassy in Washington carried a number of ceremonial duties that conflicted with his primary mission, intelligence gathering. He was slightly annoyed when the telephone call from the Pentagon had come, asking him to drive over to the American military headquarters—and to his great surprise, to do so in full uniform. His car dropped him off at the River entrance, and a young paratroop captain had escorted him inside, then to the office of General Ben Crofter, Chief of Staff, United States Army.

"May I ask what is going on?"

"Something that we thought you should see, Grigoriy," Crofter answered cryptically. They walked across the building to the Pentagon's own helicopter pad, where to Dalmatov's astonishment they boarded a Marine helicopter of the Presidential Fleet. The Sikorsky lifted off at once, heading northwest into the Maryland hills. Twenty minutes later they were descending. Dalmatov's mind registered yet another surprise. The helicopter was landing at Camp David. A member of the Marine guard force in dress blues saluted at the foot of the stairs as they left the aircraft and escorted them into the trees. Several minutes later they came to a clearing. Dalmatov hadn't known there were birch trees here, perhaps half an acre of them, and the clearing was near a hilltop that offered a fine view of the surrounding country.

And there was a rectangular hole in the ground, exactly six feet deep. It seemed strange that there was no headstone, and that the sod had been carefully cut and set aside for replacement.

Around the scene, Dalmatov could make out more Marines in the treeline. These wore camouflage fatigues and pistol belts. Well, it was no particular surprise that there was heavy security here, and the General found it rather comforting that in the past hour one unsurprising thing had taken place.

A jeep appeared first. Two Marines—in dress blues again—got out and erected a prefabricated stand around the hole. They must have practiced, the General thought, since it took them only three minutes by his watch. Then a three-quarter-ton truck came through the trees, followed by some more jeeps. Cradled in the back of the truck was a polished oak coffin. The truck pulled to within a few meters of the hole and stopped. An honor guard assembled.

"May I ask why I am here?" Dalmatov asked when he couldn't stand it any longer.

"You came up in tanks, right?"

"Yes, General Crofter, as did you."

"That's why."

The six men of the honor guard set the coffin on the stand. The gunnery sergeant in command of the detail removed the lid. Crofter walked toward it. Dalmatov gasped when he saw who was inside.

"Misha."

"I thought you knew him," a new voice said. Dalmatov spun around.

"You are Ryan." Others were there, Ritter of CIA, General Parks, and a young couple, in their thirties, Dalmatov thought. The wife seemed to be pregnant, though rather early along. She was weeping silently in the gentle spring breeze.

"Yes, sir."

The Russian gestured to the coffin. "Where—how did you—"

"I just flew back from Moscow. The General Secretary was kind enough to give me the Colonel's uniform and decorations. He said that—he said that in the case of this man, he prefers to remember the reason he got those three gold stars. We hope that you will tell your people that Colonel Mikhail Semyonovich Filitov, three times Hero of the Soviet Union, died peacefully in his sleep."

Dalmatov went red. "He was a traitor to his country—I will not stand here and—"

"General," Ryan said harshly, "it should be clear that your General Secretary does not agree with that sentiment. That man may be a greater hero than you know, for your country and for mine. Tell me, General, how many battles have you fought? How many wounds have you received for your country? Can you really look at that man and call him traitor? In any case . . ." Ryan gestured to the sergeant, who closed the coffin. When he'd finished, another Marine draped a Soviet flag over it. A team of riflemen appeared and formed at the head of the grave. Ryan took a paper from his pocket and read off Misha's citations for bravery. The riflemen brought up their weapons and fired off their volleys. A trumpeter played Taps.

Dalmatov came to rigid attention and saluted. It seemed a pity to Ryan that the ceremony had to be secret, but its simplicity made for dignity, and that at least was fitting enough.

"Why here?" Dalmatov asked when it was finished.

"I would have preferred Arlington, but then someone might notice. Right over those hills is the Antietam battlefield. On the bloodiest day in our Civil War, the Union forces repelled Lee's first invasion of the North after a desperate battle. It just seemed like the right place," Ryan said.

"If a hero must have an unmarked grave, it should at least be close to where his comrades fell."

"Comrades?"

"One way or another we all fight for the things we believe in. Doesn't that give us some common ground?" Jack asked. He walked off to his car, leaving Dalmatov with the thought.